REFERENCE ONLY

This book must not be removed from the library

£8-40

THERMODYNAMIC CONSTANTS OF INORGANIC AND ORGANIC COMPOUNDS

M.Kh. Karapet'yants and M. L. Karapet'yants

THERMODYNAMIC CONSTANTS OF INORGANIC AND ORGANIC COMPOUNDS

Translated by J. SCHMORAK
Israel Program for Scientific Translations

ANN ARBOR – HUMPHREY SCIENCE PUBLISHERS
ANN ARBOR · LONDON · 1970

ANN ARBOR–HUMPHREY SCIENCE PUBLISHERS, INC.
Drawer No. 1425, 600 S. Wagner Road, Ann Arbor, Michigan 48106

ANN ARBOR–HUMPHREY SCIENCE PUBLISHERS, LTD.
5 Great Russell Street London W.C. 1

©1970 Ann Arbor–Humphrey Science Publishers, Inc.

Library of Congress Catalog Card Number 72–122509
SBN 250 86419 3

This book is a translation of

OSNOVNYE TERMODINAMICHESKIE KONSTANTY
NEORGANICHESKIKH I ORGANICHESKIKH VESHCHESTV

Izdatel'stvo "Khimiya"
Moskva 1968

FOREWORD

This book contains the values of some principal thermodynamic properties of different substances, most of them determined during the past 15 years. It may therefore be regarded as supplementing the standard works of Britske, Kapustinskii, Veselovskii, Shamovskii, Chentsova and Anvaer [61] and of Rossini, Wagman, Evans, Levine and Jaffe [2245] which appeared in 1949 and 1952 respectively. It includes not only new data, but also results obtained by repeating former determinations.

It was not the purpose of the authors to present a consistent system of thermodynamic magnitudes. The reason for it was not only that such a task would be highly difficult if not altogether impossible, but also that in their view the value of any required magnitude ought to be chosen by the worker himself from the original sources. If this is considered unnecessary, the values which are recommended in appropriate reviews may be adopted; such reviews have been extensively employed in compiling the tables here presented.

Another difference between our tables and those found in most handbooks [61, 2245] is the inclusion of magnitudes found by approximate calculations. Their inclusion permits at least an approximate solution of many problems of practical importance which cannot be solved with the experimental data or theoretical calculations at present at our disposal.

The handbook includes about 15,000 data for more than 4,000 compounds; the list of references comprises about 2,800 items; the literature has been covered up to January 1966.

The authors wish to express their gratitude to V.A. Medvedev for his valuable comments in reviewing the manuscript.

The Authors

18 July 1966

TABLE OF CONTENTS

INTRODUCTION

The tables contain the values of four principal thermodynamic properties of compounds at 25°C: standard heat (enthalpy) of formation ΔH°_{298}, standard free energy of formation ΔG°_{298}, standard entropy S°_{298} and standard heat capacity C°_{p298}. In addition, the values of the hypothetical heat (enthalpy) of formation ΔH°_0 at 0°K are given for a number of compounds.

The first part of the book includes the inorganic compounds, while the second comprises organic compounds, element-organic* compounds and salts of organic acids. The elements and their compounds are arranged in alphabetical order. The organic compounds are arranged in the order of increasing number of carbon atoms (the first number indicates the number of carbon atoms in the molecule, while the second indicates the number of the other atomic species); carbon is followed by hydrogen, which is in turn followed by the other elements in alphabetical order. Some carbon compounds appear both in the first and in the second part.

An asterisk indicates that the value has been obtained by approximate calculation; two asterisks indicate the values of ΔG°_{298} calculated from the equation $\Delta G^\circ_{298} = \Delta H^\circ_{298} - 298, 2\Delta S^\circ_{298}$, using values of ΔS°_{298} given in recent publications. Values in parentheses have been determined anew, the former values having been included in [61] and [2245]. The following abbreviations are employed: g – gas, l – liquid, c – crystalline, v – vitreous, a – amorphous, d – in dilute solution. Thermodynamic data for individual ions are given for the aqueous solutions and are referred to the H^+ ion, for which they are assumed to be zero in the standard state. Each value of ΔH°_{298}, ΔH°_0, ΔG°_{298}, S°_{298} and C°_{p298} is accompanied by a literature reference. The list of references will be found at the end of the book.

Three points must be borne in mind when using the tables: 1. The fact that a value is given, in accordance with the original source to within, say, two decimal places, does not by any means indicate that the accuracy is to within 0.01; almost invariably, the true accuracy is at least one order lower. 2. If identical values of a given magnitude are found in two or more sources, the reader must check, by reference to the original papers, whether these values are in fact based on independent experimental determinations or are simply the same result quoted in different reviews. 3. The standard states employed by different workers may not be the same (e.g., for sulfur and phosphorus); some of the values refer to 1 gram-atom; values given for solutions do not invariably correspond to infinite dilution.

* [Organic compounds containing elements other than C, H, O, N, P and S.]

INORGANIC COMPOUNDS

Compound	Phase	ΔH°_{298}, $\frac{kcal}{mole}$		ΔG°_{298}, $\frac{kcal}{mole}$		S°_{298}, $\frac{cal}{mole\cdot°C}$		C_{p298}, $\frac{cal}{mole\cdot°C}$	
1	2	3		4		5		6	
Ac	g	94.0*	[402]						
	c					15.00	[1685, 2479]	6.50	[2479]
$AcCl_3$	c	–271*	[1069]						
AcF_3	c	–477*	[1069]						
AcFO	c	–265*	[1069]						
Ac_2O_3	c	–490*	[1480]	–468*	[1480]	32.0	[2662]		
		–444*	[887]	–425*	[1045]				
Ag	g	(68.400)	[2479]	(15.129)	[2479]				
		(68.10)[1]	[1589]	(58.82)	[1589]	(41.32)	[1589, 1685]		
		(68.45)	[2156]			(29.09)	[2156]		
		(67.7)	[396]			(28.61)	[2156]		
		(68.14)	[2090]			(23.38)	[2156]		
	c					(10.20)	[1685, 2358]	(6.10)	[1685, 2358]
						(8.99)	[577]		
Ag^+	g					39.95	[66]		
	d	(25.234)	[2358]	(18.433)	[2358[	(17.40)	[2358]		
						(17.54)	[1685]		
Ag^{2+}	d			64.1	[323]				
AgAt		–10.8*	[418]			31.8*	[418]	13.3*	[418]
$Ag_{0.7441}Au_{0.2559}$	c							5.96[2]	[1589]
$AgAuF_4$	c	–149.4	[2706]						
AgBr	g					61.2	[1685]	8.72	[1685]
	c	–2399	[2358]	(–23.16)	[2358]	(25.6)	[2358]		
				(–22.77)	[176]	(25.0*)	[176]		
				(–22.68*)	[250]				
$AgBrO_2$	c	–38*	[232]			37.3*	[245]		
						33.6*	[249]		
$AgBrO_3$	c			23.55*	[177]				
				17.6*	[323]				
AgCN	c			(38.73*)	[177]	(21.7*)	[177]		
$Ag(CN)_2^-$	g					73.6	[728]		
AgCNO	c			–14.7*	[323]				

1. $\Delta H^\circ_0 = (67.99)$ [1589]. 2. $T = 273\,°K$.

1	2	3		4		5		6	
AgCNS	c			26.00*	[250]				
				23.3*	[323]				
$Ag_{0.5}Cd_{0.5}$, ρ	c	−2.17[1]	[1589]						
$Ag_{0.5}Cd_{0.5}$, ξ	c	−1.84[1]	[1589]						
AgCd	c	2.6	[2625]			23.5	[1775]		
$AgCd_2$	c	4.1	[2625]						
AgCl	c	−30.37	[2358]	(−26.244)	[2358]	(23.0)	[2358]		
				(−26.24)	[176]	(23.0*)	[176]		
AgCl·KCl	c			−123.2*	[229]				
$AgClO_3$	c			16*	[323]	37.7*	[323]		
				13.5*	[229]	34.8*[2]	[245]		
$AgClO_4$	c			21*	[323]	38.8*	[323]		
				15.9*	[229]				
$AgCrO_4$	c			−147.48*	[177]				
AgD	g					50.3	[1685]	7.1	[1685]
AgF	g					56.0	[1685]		
	c			(−44.6*)	[250]	(19.8)*	[225]	11.5*	[225]
						(18.5)	[1685]		
$AgF·H_2O$	c			−101.8*	[323]	27.4*	[323]		
$AgF·2H_2O$	c	(−191*)	[230]						
$AgF·4H_2O$	c			−268.6*	[323]	45.9*	[323]		
AgF_2	c	(−83.0)	[890]			63.0	[1685]	8.79	[1685]
AgHS	c			−37.5	[371a]				
AgI	g								
	c	−14.78	[2358]	(−15.82)	[2358]	27.6	[1680, 1685, 2358]	(13.58)	[1685, 2358]
				(−15.83*)	[176]	(27.3*)	[176]		
				(−15.54*)	[250]				
$AgIO_2$	c					34.2*	[249]		
$AgIO_3$	c	−41.7*	[323]	−24.08*	[323]				
		−39.8*	[232]	−25.19*	[177]				
		−41.6	[2457]						
$Ag_{0.935}Mn_{0.065}$	c							6.18[3]	[1589]
$AgMnO_4$	c	−118*	[232]	−97.51*	[177]				
AgN_3	c	(74.17)	[1356]	90.46	[1356]	23.70	[1356]		
				87.2*	[232]				
				90*	[323]				

$Ag(NH_3)_2^+$	d			–4.16*	[323]	57.8*	[323]		
						57.8	[1685]		
$AgNO_2$	c	(–8.5*)	[232]	(5.69*)	[177]	(30.64)	[1685]	(19.17)	[1685]
								(22.5*)	[1620]
AgO	g					57.0	[1685]	8.24	[1685]
	c	(–2.769)	[768]	(3.463)	[768]	(13.81)	[768]		
				(2.6*)	[323]				
AgO^+	d			53.9*	[323]				
AgO^-	d			–5.49*	[323]				
AgO_2	c	–7.18	[80a]	–2.625	[80a]	43.96[4]	[80a]		
AgOH	c			(–29.83*)	[176]				
$[Ag(OH)_2]^-$	d			–62.38*	[6]				
AgP_2	c	(–10.7)	[1772]			21.0*	[1772]		
AgP_3	c	(–16.5)	[1772]			25.2*	[1772]		
$Ag_{1.29}S$	c					34.278	[2612]	18.20	[2612]
$Ag(SO_3)_2^{3-}$	d			–225.4*	[323]				
$AgSO_4$	d					33	[2724]		
$Ag(S_2O_3)_2^{3-}$	d			–247.6*	[323]				
$Ag_{1.09}Se$	c					35.890	[2612]	19.47	[2612]
$Ag_{1.83}Te$	c					35.512	[2612]	19.98	[2612]
Ag_2CO_3	c			(–104.65*)	[177]	(40.6*)	[177]		
Ag_2CrO_4	c	(–176.2)*	[323]	(–154.7*)	[323]	(51.8*)	[323]		
		(–172.37)	[1769]	(–150.78)	[1769]	(52.1)	[1769]		
		(–168.7*)	[232]	(–147.48*)	[177]	(52.0)	[1685]	34.00	[1685]
$Ag_2Cr_2O_7$	c			–278.78*	[177]				
Ag_2MoO_4	c	–216.6	[1769]	–197.7	[1769]	61.9	[1769]		
		–200.4	[1995]	–196.4	[323]				
Ag		–230.7	[1354]						
$Ag_2N_2O_2$	c			29.4*	[323]	42*	[323]		
Ag_2O	c	(–7.42)	[2358]	(–2.68)	[2358]	(29.0)	[2358]		
				(–2.63*)	[176]	(29.2*)	[176]		
						(29.1)	[1685]	(15.75)	[1685]
Ag_2O, macroporous	c			–2.691	[1390]	28.91	[1389]	15.70[5]	[1302]
Ag_2O_2	c			–8.8*	[229]	6.6*	[1045]		
Ag_2O_3	c			20.8*	[323]				
				6.6*	[1045]				
Ag_2ReCl_6	c	–231.5*	[203]						

1. $T = 304$ °K; supercooled alloy. 2. Recalculated [234] from the erroneous (37.5) to the correct value (S°_{298}) $AgIO_3 = 35.7$ [2245]. 3. $T = 400$ °K. Calculated [234] from the values $\Delta S = 15.25$ [80a] and (S°_{298}) for Ag (c) and O_2(g) [2245]. 5. $T = 294.66$ °K.

1	2	3		4		5		6	
Ag_2S	c			(−9.67*)	[176]	(35.1*)	[176]		
						(35.0)	[1680]		
						(33.5)	[1685]		
Ag_2SO_3	c	−114.4	[614]						
		−110.1	[1172]						
Ag_2SO_4	c	(−172.6*)	[1460]	(−147.20*)	[177]	(47.9*)	[177]		
		(−171.22)	[1675]			(47.9)	[1675, 1685]		
Ag_2Se	c	(5.0)	[2625]	−2.9*	[229]	39.0	[1773]	19.7*	[2065]
				−7.56	[790a]				
Ag_2SeO_3	c	(−83.22)	[511]	(−73.64)	[511]	(74.36)	[511]		
Ag_2SeO_4	c	−105.05	[503]	−80.78	[503]	44.0*	[498]	30.3*	[2709]
		−143.3*	[232]	−70.0	[229]	46.91	[503]		
Ag_2SiO_3	c					42.4	[1685]	30.36	[1685]
Ag_2Te	c	7.0	[1772]	−8.3	[4]	40.7	[1772]		
Ag_2WO_4	c	−228.1	[1769]	−198.5	[1769]	27.4	[1769]		
		−230.7	[1350]	−206.0*	[323]				
Ag_3AsO_4	c			−122.63*	[177]				
Ag_3N	c	61.0	[1469]						
Ag_3PO_4	c	−236.1	[232]	−214.01*[1]	[177]				
Ag_3Sb	c	5.5	[1773]			41.0	[1773]		
$Ag_4Fe(CN)_6$	c			−188.4*	[323]				
$HAg(OH)_2$	c			−86.48	[5]				
Al	g	(77.42)[2]	[1830]			(39.8038)	[1830]	(5.1125)	[1830]
		(76.06)[3]	[570]			(39.304)	[570, 1618a]	(5.112)	[1618a]
		(77.50)	[1582]	(67.80)	[1582]	(39.30)	[1589, 1685]	(5.11)	[1589, 1685[
		(77.40)[4]	[1589]	(66.77)	[1589]				
		(78.0)[5]	[1618a]	(68.30)	[1618a]				
		(74.72)[6]	[456]						
		(78)	[1631]						
		(77.5)	[2174]						
		(77.4)	[896]						
		(77.5)	[1540]						
	l	2.40	[1618a]	1.724	[1618a]	9.035	[1618a]	7.000	[1618a]
	c					(6.77)	[570, 1589, 1685]	(5.82)	[570, 1589, 1618a, 1685]
	d					(6.775)	[1830]	(5.818)	[1830]
Al^+	g	(215.411)[7]	[570]			35.8135	[570]		

Al^{3+}	g					35.82	[66]		
	d							−20.[10]	[1089]
Al_2	g	106.017[8]	[570]			54.890	[570]		
		116.8998[9]	[1830]			53.2735	[1830]	8.7508	[1830]
AlAs	c	−35.4	[1531]						
$Al(BH_4)_3$	l	−72.1	[2256]						
AlBr	g	(4.77)[11]	[528]			57.303	[716]	8.572	[716]
		(3.6*)[12]	[1618a]	−6.026*	[1618a]	57.246	[1618a]	8.509	[1618a]
						57.2	[1685]	8.48	[1685]
$AlBr_3$	g	−98.3[13]	[1618a]	−104.188	[1618a]	81.094	[1618a]	17.596	[1618a]
	l	−121.03	[1618a]	−116.245	[1618a]	45.297	[1618a]	29.500	[1618a]
	c	(−123.4)	[1618a]	(−116.738)	[1618a]	(49.0*)	[890]		
						(39.0)	[1618a]	(24.3)	[1618a]
AlC	g	164.8[14]	[1618a]	151.308	[1618a]	53.39	[1618a]	7.71	[1618a]
$Al_{0.67}Ca_{0.33}$	c	−17.50[15]	[1589]						
$Al_{0.80}Ca_{0.20}$	c	−10.30[16]	[1589]						
$Al_{0.25}Ce_{0.75}$	c	−5.5*[17]	[1589]						
$Al_{0.80}Ce_{0.20}$	c	−7.8*[18]	[1589]						
AlCl	g	(−11.58)[19]	[1830]			54.4744	[1830]	8.2870	[1830]
		(−10.963)[20]	[570]			54.461	[570]		
		(−13.3)	[1260]			77*	[1260]		
		(−11.6)	[1412]	−10.8*	[227]	54.462	[716]	8.284	[716]
		(−11.2)[21]	[1618a]	−17.479	[1618a]	54.474	[1618a]	8.287	[1618a[
		(−16.0)	[529]			56.94[22]	[1340]	8.56[22]	[1340]
		(−10.7)	[2257]			54.5	[1685]	8.26	[1685]
	c	17.0	[2628a]			54.0	[2628a]		
AlClF	g	−120*[23]	[1618a]	−122.907*	[1618a]	67.388	[1618a]	11.586	[1618a]
$AlClF_2$	g	−237.60[24]	[1618a]	−234.434	[1618a]	71.242	[1618a]	15.663	[1618a]
AlClO	g	−83.2*[25]	[1618a]	−83.664*	[1618a]	59.471	[1618a]	11.967	[1618a]
		−92.07227[26]	[1830]			61.013	[1830]	12.3149	[1830]
		−84	[1373]						
	c	−189.60	[1618a]	−176.208	[1618a]	13.00	[1618a]	13.60	[1618a]
		−190	[2297]			13	[2297]		

1. $t = 20\,°C$. 2. $\Delta H_0^\circ = (\underline{76}.8576)$ [1830]. 3. $\Delta H_0^\circ = (75.5)$ [570]. $\Delta H_0^\circ = (76.84)$ [1589]. 5. $\Delta H_0^\circ = (77.440)$ [1618a]. 6. ΔH_0°. 7. $\Delta H_0^\circ = (213.543)$ [570]. 8. $\Delta H_0^\circ = 106^*$ [570]. 9. $\Delta H_0^\circ = 116.7152$ [1830]. 10. C_{p298}. 11. Calculated [234] from the ΔH values of the reaction $Al(c) + \frac{1}{2}Br_2(g) = AlBr(g)$ [528] and $(\Delta H_{vap})Br_2$ [224]. 12. $\Delta H_0^\circ = 5.337^*$ [1618a]. 13. $\Delta H_0^\circ = -92.492$ [1618a]. 14. $\Delta H_0^\circ = 164.012$ [1618a]. 15. $T = 296\,°K$; phase Al_2Ca. 16. $T = 296\,°K$; phase Al_4Ca. 17. Phase α-Al_4Ce. 18. Phase α-$AlCe_3$. 19. $\Delta H_0^\circ = -11.6208$ [1830]. 20. $\Delta H_0^\circ = -11$ [570]. 21. $\Delta H_0^\circ = -11.238$ [1618a]. 22. $T = 400\,°K$. 23. $\Delta H_0^\circ = -119.624^*$ [1618a]. 24. $\Delta H_0^\circ = -236.83^*$ [1618a]. 25. $\Delta H_0^\circ = -82.698^*$ [1618a]. 26. $\Delta H_0^\circ = -91.7751$ [1830].

1	2	3		4		5		6	
$AlCl_2$	g	−76[1]	[570]			69.660	[570]		
		−75*[2]	[1618a]	−77.611*	[1618a]	68.815	[1618a]	12.341	[1618a]
$AlCl_2F$	g	−188.6*[3]	[1618a]	−185.641*	[1618a]	74.356	[1618a]	16.410	[1618a]
$AlCl_3$	g	−142.593[4]	[570]			75.564	[570]		
		−140.42[5]	[1830]			74.8849	[1830]	17.1405	[1830]
		−139.70[6]	[1618a]	−136.098	[1618a]	74.621	[1618a]		
						74.5	[1685]	17.22	[1685]
	l	−160.56	[1618a]	−147.665	[1618a]	43.451	[1618a]	24.580	[1618a]
	c	(−168.57)[7]	[570, 1049]			(26.0)	[570]	(21.60)	[570]
		(−166.8)	[2245, 2375]			(26.58)	[1685]	(22.48)	[1685]
						(26.3)	[2687]		
		(−168.58)[8]	[1618a]	(−150, 616)	[1618a]	(26.450)	[1618a]	(21.951)	[1618a]
$AlCl_3 \cdot 6H_2O$	c	(−643.60)	[1049]						
$AlCl_3 \cdot 3KCl$	c			−260.7*	[323]	48.8*	[323]		
$2AlCl_3 \cdot 3KCl$	c			−622*	[323]	114.3*	[323]		
$AlCl_4^-$	g					81.1	[728]		
$Al_{0.50}Co_{0.50}$, β	c	−13.2	[1589]						
$Al_{0.677}Co_{0.333}$	c	−10.6[9]	[1589]						
$Al_{0.714}Co_{0.286}$	c	(−10.0)[10]	[1589]						
$Al_{0.80}Co_{0.20}$	c	(−7.7)[11]	[1589]						
Al + Cu	c							0.0995*[12]	[424]
								0.1025*[13]	[424]
								0.1075*[14]	[424]
								0.095[15]	[424]
$Al_{0.10}Cu_{0.90}$, α	c	−1.7	[1589]						
$Al_{0.17}Cu_{0.83}$, α	c	−2.9	[1589]						
$Al_{0.32}Cu_{0.68}$, γ_2	c	−5.5	[1589]						
$Al_{0.35}Cu_{0.65}$, γ_2	c	−5.45	[1589]						
$Al_{0.37}Cu_{0.63}$, γ_2	c	(−5.4)	[1589]						
$Al_{0.40}Cu_{0.60}$, δ	c	(−5.25)	[1589]						
$Al_{0.50}Cu_{0.50}$, η_2	c	(−4.9)	[1589]						
		(−4.75)	[2625]						
$Al_{0.67}Cu_{0.33}$, θ	c	(−3.25)	[1589]						
$AlCu_2$	c	(−16.0)	[2625]						
AlD	g					46.27	[1685]	7.17	[1685]

AlF	g	(−61.4)[16]	[1830]	−44.4*	[227]	51.3990	[1618a, 1830]	7.632	[716, 1618a, 1830]
		(−60.65)	[1538]			51.93	[1538]		
		(−62.4)	[787]			51.42	[787[		
		(−61.025)[17]	[570]			51.399	[570, 716]		
		(−60.9)	[1520]			51.6	[1685]	7.61	[1685]
		(−59.2)	[1415]						
		(−61.0)	[2697]						
		(−62.5)[18]	[1618a]	−68.584	[1618a]				
		(−61.18)	[365]						
AlFO	g	−140.20[19]	[1618a]	−140.347	[1618a]	55.986	[1618a]	10.692	[1618a]
AlF_2	g	−173.43[20]	[570]						
		−149.2[21]	[1164]			63.457	[570]		
		−165*	[1618a]	−167.434*	[1618a]	63.381	[1618a]	10.949	[1618a]
AlF_3	g	−280.0[22]	[2697]						
		−287.5[23]	[164]						
		−285.513[24]	[570]			65.451	[570]		
		−283.6[25]	[1830]			65.7697	[1830]	14.6027	[1830]
		−286.5[26]	[1618a]	−282.543	[1618a]	66.167	[1618a]	14.966	[1618a]
	c	(−357)[27]	[570]			(15.89)	[570, 1721]	17.95	[570, 1685, 1721, 1830]
		(−356.3)[28]	[1830]			(15.6523)	[1830]		
		(−355.7)	[1415]					18.0	[189, 1721]
		(−358.0)[29]	[1618a]	(−339.05)	[1618a]	(15.881)	[1618a]	17.951	[1618a]
$AlF_3 \cdot H_2O$	c	−525*	[234]						
AlF_6^{3-}	d			−539.6*	[323]	−40*	[323]		
$AlF_2H_2PO_4$	c	−599.1	[439]						
AlFO	g	−139.2[30]	[1198, 1830]			55.99	[1198]	10.69	[1189]
						57.8335	[1830]	11.512	[2713]
$Al_{0.10}Fe_{0.90}$	c	−1.15[31]	[1589]						
$Al_{0.20}Fe_{0.80}$	c	−2.50[31]	[1589]						

1. $\Delta H_0^\circ = -75.786$* [570]. 2. $\Delta H_0^\circ = -74.724$* [1618a]. 3. $\Delta H_0^\circ = -187.991$ [1618a]. 4. $\Delta H_0^\circ = -142.185$ [570]. 5. $\Delta H_0^\circ = -139.9543$ [1830]. 6. $\Delta H_0^\circ = -139.19$ [1618a]. 7. $\Delta H_0^\circ = -168.185$ [570]. 8. $\Delta H_0^\circ = -168.299$ [1618a]. 9. Phase $CoAl_2$. 10. Phase Co_2Al_5. 11. Phase $CoAl_4$. 12. 5% Al; after preliminary annealing (*cal/g*·°C); $t = 200$ °C. 13. 10% Al (cf.note 12). 14. 15.9%Al (cf.note 12). 15. 15.9%Al; after preliminary hardening at 700°C (*cal/g*·°C); $t = 200$ °C. 16. $\Delta H_0^\circ = (-61.379)$ [1830]. 17. $\Delta H_0^\circ = (-61)$ [570]. 18. $\Delta H_0^\circ = (-62.476)$ [1618a]. 19. $\Delta H_0^\circ = -139.461$ [1618a]. 20. $\Delta H_0^\circ = -173$ [570]. 21. $\Delta H_0^\circ = -164.575$ [1618a]. 22. Calculated [234] from $(\Delta H_0^\circ)_{subl} = 72.2$ [251] and $(\Delta H_{298}^\circ)\,AlF_3(c) = -355.7$ [1415]. 23. Calculated [234] from $(\Delta H_0^\circ)_{subl} = 73.46$ [164] and $(\Delta H_0^\circ)\,AlF_3(c) = -355.7$ [1415]. 24. $\Delta H_0^\circ = -284.577$ [570]. 25. $\Delta H_0^\circ = -282.6165$ [1830]. 26. $\Delta H_0^\circ = -285.612$ [1618a]. 27. $\Delta H_0^\circ = -355.517$ [570]. 28. $\Delta H_0^\circ = -354.8264$ [1830]. 29. $\Delta H_0^\circ = -356.519$ [1618a]. 30. $\Delta H_0^\circ = -138.7509$ [1830]. 31. $T = 293$ °K.

1	2	3		4		5		6	
$Al_{0.30}Fe_{0.70}$	c	−3.86[1]	[1589]						
$Al_{0.40}Fe_{0.60}$	c	−5.09[1]	[1589]						
$Al_{0.51}Fe_{0.49}$, α	c	(−6.07)[1]	[1589]						
$Al_{0.667}Fe_{0.333}$, δ	c	−6.25[1]	[1589]						
$Al_{0.71}Fe_{0.29}$, η	c	−6.85[1]	[1589]						
$Al_{0.75}Fe_{0.25}$	c	(−6.65)[1]	[1589]						
$Al_{0.78}Fe_{0.22}$, θ	c	−6.25[1]	[1589]						
AlFe	c	−12.2	[2625]						
AlH	g	(60.10)[2]	[570]	52.7	[227]	44.871	[570]		
		(61.5547)[3]	[1830]			44.8745	[1830]	7.0197	[1830]
		(62.00)[4]	[1618a]	55.291	[1618a]	44.875	[1618a]	7.020	[1618a]
						44.83	[1685]	7.00	[1685]
AlH^-	g					49.3	[728]		
AlHO[5]	g	8*[6]	[1618a]	6.632*	[1618a]	51.464	[1618a]	8.262	[1618a]
$AlHO_2$[8]	g	−63*[9]	[1618a]	−59.838*	[1618a]	60.722	[1618a]		
AlI	g	14.3[7]	[1618a]	2.793	[1618a]	59.1	[1685]	8.60	[1685]
						59.243	[1618a]	8.634	[1618a]
AlI_3	c					46.0	[1685]		
		(−74.1)	[2245, 2665]	(−74.4)	[1032]				
		(−73.9)	[1618a]	(−72.974)	[1618a]	(45.3)	[1618a]	23.64	[1618a]
$AlK(SO_4)_2 \cdot H_2O$	c			−604.4*	[229]				
$AlK(SO_4)_2 \cdot 2H_2O$	c			−663.8*	[229]				
$AlK(SO_4)_2 \cdot 3H_2O$	c			−720.8	[229]				
$AlKSiO_4$, kaliophilite	c					31.8	[1687]	28.63	[1687]
$AlKSi_2O_6$, leucite	c	−46.2[10]	[1681]	−48.1[10]	[1681]	44.0	[1681]	39.23	[1687]
$AlKSi_3O_8$, adular	c			−820*	[224]	51.4	[2548]		
						52.5	[1687]		
$AlKSi_3O_8$, orthoclase	c	−51.0[10]	[1681]	−52.7[10]	[1681]			48.28[11]	[1687]
								48.62	[1687]
$Al_{0.67}La_{0.33}$	c	−12.0[12]	[1589]						
$Al_{0.8}La_{0.2}$	c	−8.4[13]	[1589]						
AlLi	c	−12.0	[1773]						
		−13	[535]						
AlN	g	117.998[14]	[570]			54.139	[570]		
		104*[15]	[1618a]	97.762*	[1618a]	50.575	[1618a]	7.445	[1618a]

	c	(−76)[16]	[570]			(4.80)	[570]	(7.19)	[570]
		(−76.0)[17]	[1618a]	(−68.595)	[1618a]	(4.816)	[1618a]	(7.201)	[1618a]
		(−76.47)	[2046]						
AlNa	c	(−57.6)	[31]						
		(−76.1)	[1123, 1510, 1511]						
		(−63*)	[2307]						
$AlNa(SO_4)_2$	c	−571.18	[2064]						
$AlNa(SO_4)_2 \cdot 2H_2O$	c	−719.713	[2064]						
$AlNa(SO_4)_2 \cdot 5H_2O$	c	−936.907	[2064]						
$AlNa(SO_4)_2 \cdot 6H_2O$	c	−1008.265	[2064]						
$AlNa(SO_4)_2 \cdot 12H_2O$	c	−1430.716	[3108]						
$Al_{0.05}Ni_{0.95}$, α	c	−1.95	[1589]						
$Al_{0.08}Ni_{0.902}$, α	c	−3.80	[1589]						
$Al_{0.220}Ni_{0.780}$, α'	c	−7.50	[1589]						
$Al_{0.282}Ni_{0.718}$, α'	c	−10.05	[1589]						
$Al_{0.412}Ni_{0.588}$, β'	c	−12.26	[1589]						
$Al_{0.50}Ni_{0.50}$, β'	c	(−14.05)	[1589]						
		(−14.15)	[1773]						
$Al_{0.55}Ni_{0.45}$, β'	c	−14.07	[1589]						
$Al_{0.594}Ni_{0.406}$, δ	c	−13.85	[1589]						
$Al_{0.638}Ni_{0.362}$, δ	c	(−12.40)	[1589]						
$Al_{0.75}Ni_{0.25}$, ϵ	c	(−9.00)	[1589]						
$AlNi_3$	c	(−36.6)	[1773]						
AlO	g	(20.8160)[18]	[1830]			52.1709	[1830]	7.3815	[1830]
		(19.457)[19]	[570]	15.167	[1618a]	52.170	[570, 1618a]	7.381	[1618a]
		(21.398)[20]	[1618a]						
		(10.0*)	[896]	4.0*	[896]	54.40[21]	[1340]	7.77[21]	[1340]
						5216	[1685]	7.37	[1685]
						48.967	[427]		
	c	20.8	[1128]						
AlOH	g	−8*[22]	[1618a]	−10.652*	[1618a]	55.770	[1618a]	8.474	[1618a]

1. $T=293^\circ$K. 2. $\Delta H_0^\circ=(60.132)$ [570]. 3. $\Delta H_0^\circ=(61.5860)$ [1830]. 4. $\Delta H_0^\circ=(62.034)$ [1618a]. 5. Oxyhydride. 6. $\Delta H_0^\circ=8.988$* [1618a]. 7. $\Delta H_0^\circ=14.641$ [1618a]. 8. Oxyhydroxide. 9. $\Delta H_0^\circ=-61.621$* [1618a]. 10. From K_2O, Al_2O_3, α and SiO_2, α. 11. $T=296.47$ °K; orthoclase includes Fe^{2+} and Fe^{3+}. 12. Phase Al_2La. 13. Phase Al_4La. 14. $\Delta H_0^\circ=118.036$* [570]. 15. $\Delta H_0^\circ=104.024$* [1618a]. 16. $\Delta H_0^\circ=-74.794$ [570]. 17. $\Delta H_0^\circ=-74.795$ [1618a]. 18. $\Delta H_0^\circ=(20.8441)$ [1830]. 19. $\Delta H_0^\circ=(19.487)$ [570]. 20. $\Delta H_0^\circ=(21.429)$ [1618a]. 21. Calculated [234] from $(\Delta H_{298}^\circ)_{subl}=72.7$ [251] and $(\Delta H_{298}^\circ)_{AlF_3(c)}=-355.7$ [1415]. 22. $\Delta H_0^\circ=-7.257$* [1618a].

1	2	3		4		5		6	
$Al(OH)_3$	c	(−307.7*)	[815]	−274.8*	[815]	20.4*		(22.26*)	[815]
		(−189*)	[2683]	−272.40*	[176]	20.4*	[176]		
	v			−271.9*	[323]	17*	[323]		
				−272.4*	[229]				
$Al(OH)_4^-$	d			−309.39*	[6]				
				−303.90	[7]				
AlO_2^-	d			−204.7*	[323]	25*	[323]		
AlOOH	c	(−234.9*)	[815]	(−217.1*)	[815]			(15.11*)	[815]
AlP	c	−39.5[1]	[1669]						
		−40	[535]						
$AlPO_4$	c	−412.1	[1662]			21.70	[1151]	22.27	[1151]
$AlPO_4 \cdot 2H_2O$	c	−461.3	[439]			40.5	[1151]		
$Al_{0.80}Pr_{0.20}$	c	−10.40[2]	[1589]						
Al + Pu[3]	c					17.52	[2268]	7.74	[2268]
$AlRb(SO_4)_2$	c	−516.3*	[229]						
$AlRb(SO_4)_2 \cdot H_2O$	c	−566.2*	[229]						
$AlRb(SO_4)_2 \cdot 2H_2O$	c	−626.1*	[229]						
$AlRb(SO_4)_2 \cdot 3H_2O$	c	−727.1*	[229]						
$AlRb(SO_4)_2 \cdot 12H_2O$	c	−1202*	[229]						
AlS	g	48*[4]	[1618a]	35.868*	[1618a]	55.136[5]	[2104]	7.978[5]	[2104]
						55.090	[1618a]	7.982	[1618a]
AlSb	c	−23	[1773]			16.5	[1773]		
						7.68[6]	[2146]	5.460[6]	[2146]
								5.535[7]	[2146]
$Al_{0.095}Ti_{0.905}$, α_1	c	−2.50	[1589]						
$Al_{0.195}Ti_{0.805}$, α_2	c	−4.70	[1589]						
$Al_{0.250}Ti_{0.750}$, α_2	c	−5.95	[1589]						
$Al_{0.290}Ti_{0.710}$, ϵ	c	−6.90	[1589]						
$Al_{0.370}Ti_{0.630}$, α_2	c	−7.60	[1589]						
$Al_{0.495}Ti_{0.505}$, γ	c	−9.50	[1589]						
$Al_{0.545}Ti_{0.455}$, γ	c	−9.65	[1589]						
$Al_{0.595}Ti_{0.405}$, γ	c	−9.80	[1589]						
$Al_{0.750}Ti_{0.250}$, δ	c	−8.80	[1589]						
AlTi	c	−19.3	[1772]						
$AlTi_3$	c	−24.0	[1772]						

Al_2Br_6	g	−226.6*[8]	[1618a]	−226.516*	[1618a]	122.409	[1618a]	40.084	[1618a]
Al_2C_2	g					65.9	[1685]	14.52	[1685]
Al_2Ce	c	−39.0	[2625]						
Al_2Ce_3	c	−42.0	[2625]						
Al_2Cl_6	g	(−309.2)[9]	[1618a, 2297]	−291.42	[1618a]	119.5	[2297]		
						113.769	[1618a]	37.912	[1618a]
		(−304.6)	[1773]						
	l			−274.9	[229]				
Al_2Cu	c	(−9.5)	[2625]						
Al_2Fe	c	(−19.5)	[2625]						
Al_2I_6	g	−121.0[10]	[1618a]	−133.76	[1618a]	139.608	[1618a]	40.892	[1618a]
$Al_2K(OH)(PO_4)\cdot 2H_2O$	c					70.43	[1160]	76.53	[1160]
$Al_2X(OH)_2(Si_3O_8)$, muscovite	c	−1421.2	[774]	−1330.1	[774]	305.4[12]	[774]		
Al_2O	g	−32.6738[11]	[1830]			61.6645	[1830]	10.2927	[1830]
		−32.426[13]	[570]			63.225	[570]		
		−31.44[14]	[1618a]	−38.503	[1618a]	61.73	[1618a]	10.293	[1618a]
		−33.5*	[896]	−42.5*	[896]	61.933	[1669]	10.911	[1669]
		−40.9*	[2174]			59.75	[427]		
		−40*	[1286]						
Al_2O_2	g	−94.64[15]	[1830]			63.6550	[1830]	12.4959	[1830]
		−95.397[16]	[1618a]	−96.149	[1618a]	65.065	[1618a]	12.496	[1618a]
Al_2O_3	l	−373.356	[1618a]	−354.478	[1618a]	23.728	[1618a]	18.889	[1618a]
Al_2O_3, *a*	c	(−400.4)[17]	[1830, 1618a, 1892]	(−378.078)	[1618a]	(12.175)	[570, 1830]	(18.884)	[1830]
						(12.174)	[1618a]	(18.889)	[1618a]
		(−402)	[2311]			(12.7)	[1268]	(18.88)	[570, 1685]
						(12.18)	[1685]	(18.95)	[480]
						(12.17)	[589]	(18.99)	[598]
								(19.01)	[144]
								(18.6079)	[421]
$Al_2O_3\cdot a$, corundum	c	(−399.6)	[1335]	−365.0*	[229]				
		(−400.4)	[570]						
Al_2O_3, synthetic sapphire	c	−400.29	[1335]	−380.4*	[229]	12.16	[1699]	19.09	[1699]
$Al_2O_3\cdot BaO$	c	−556.5	[2139]	−530.0*	[229]				
		−550.34	[178a]	−559.37	[178a]	30.3	[178a]		
		−561.2	[147]						
$Al_2O_3\cdot BaO\cdot H_2O$	c	−633.8	[2139]	−587.3*	[229]				

1. From yellow phosphorus. 2. $T=292°K$. 3. Melt (stable δ-phase). 4. $\Delta H_0^\circ=47.975$* [1618a]. 5. $T=300°K$. 6. $T=273°K$. 7. $T=298°K$. 8. $\Delta H_0^\circ=-216.002$* [1618a]. 9. $\Delta H_0^\circ=-308.594$ [1618a]. 10. $\Delta H_0^\circ=-119.029$ [1618a]. 11. $\Delta H_0^\circ=-32.0983$ [1830]. 12. ΔS_{298}°. 13. $\Delta H_0^\circ=-32.013$ [570]. 14. $\Delta H_0^\circ=-30.859$ [1618a]. 15. $\Delta H_0^\circ=-93.3118$ [1830]. 16. $\Delta H_0^\circ=-94.063$ [1618a]. 17. $\Delta H_0^\circ=-397.50$ [1830]; −397.494 [1618a].

1	2	3		4		5		6	
$Al_2O_3 \cdot BaO \cdot 2H_2O$	c	−705.5	[2139]	−620.4*	[229]				
$Al_2O_3 \cdot BaO \cdot 4H_2O$	c	−851.1	[2139]						
$Al_2O_3 \cdot BaO \cdot 7H_2O$	c	−1062.0	[2139]	−926.6*	[229]				
$Al_2O_3 \cdot 2BaO \cdot 5H_2O$	c	−1086.6	[2139]	−977.4*	[229]				
$Al_2O_3 \cdot 3BaO$	c	−844.2	[2139]	−804.5*	[229]				
$Al_2O_3 \cdot BeO$	c					66.291	[2528]	105.38	[2528]
0.5 $Al_2O_3 \cdot CaO \cdot 0.5Ga_2O_3 \cdot 2SiO_2$	v	−18.0[1]	[1681]	−20.2[1]	[1681]				
$Al_2O_3 \cdot CaO$	c	(−554.8)	[1046]	−526.8	[1046]				
		(−548)	[147]	−517.8**	[232]	27.3	[1719]		
				−518.5*	[232]				
	v			−518.5*	[229]				
$Al_2O_3 \cdot CaO \cdot 2SiO_2$	c	−994.5	[771]	−904.8	[771]	45.8	[771]		
		−998.1	[127]	−932.7	[127]				
$Al_2O_3 \cdot CaO \cdot 2SiO_2$	v	−4.4[2]	[1681]	−8.4[2]	[1681]				
$Al_2O_3 \cdot CaO \cdot 2SiO_2$, anorthite, hexagonal	c	−16.9[2]	[771]	−18.5[2]	[771]				
		−989.6	[[771]	−935.1	[771]				
$Al_2O_3 \cdot CaO \cdot 2SiO_2 \cdot 2H_2O$	c	−21.83[2]	[771]	−23.85[2]	[771]				
lawsonite		−1146.5	[771]	−1062.1	[771]	56.8	[771]		
$Al_2O_3 \cdot CaO \cdot 6SiO_2$	c	−1722*	[229]						
$Al_2O_3 \cdot 2CaO \cdot SiO_2$, helenite	c	−952.8	[773]			47.4	[2630]	49.10	[3173]
		−22.8[3]	[1681]	−24.6[3]	[1681]				
$Al_2O_3 \cdot 2CaO \cdot SiO_2$, talcum	c	−1415.5	[773]						
$Al_2O_3 \cdot 2CaO \cdot SiO_2$	v	−10.4[3]	[1681[	−14.4[3]	[1681]				
$Al_2O_3 \cdot 3CaO$	c	(−850.0)	[1046]	−821.3*	[229]	49.1	[1719]		
		(−867.2)	[178a]	−880.1	[178a]	43.28	[178a]		
		(0.43)[4]	[1940]	−821.8**	[232[				
	v			−808.3*	[229]				
				−807.9	[1046]				
$Al_2O_3 \cdot 3CaO \cdot 30H_2O$	c	−16228[5]	[832]						
$Al_2O_3 \cdot 3CaO \cdot CaCO_3 \cdot 10.68H_2O$	c	−1956	[833]						
		−1957	[834]						
$Al_2O_3 \cdot 3CaO \cdot CaSO_4 \cdot 12H_2O$	c	−2100	[834]						
$Al_2O_3 \cdot 3CaO \cdot CaSO_4 \cdot 31H_2O$	c	−4123	[834]						
$Al_2O_3 \cdot 3CaO \cdot CaSO_4 \cdot 32H_2O$	c	−4194	[834]						
$Al_2O_3 \cdot 3CaO \cdot 2SiO_2$	c			−1237*	[229]				
$Al_2O_3 \cdot 4CaO$	c			−979.7*	[229]				
$Al_2O_3 \cdot 4CaO \cdot Fe_2O_3$	c			−1145*	[229]				

$Al_2O_3 \cdot 3H_2O$, gibbsite	c	(−630.2)	[2325]	(−547.0)	[775]				
$Al_2O_3 \cdot 2KF \cdot MgF_2$ $5MgO \cdot 6SiO_2$, fluophlogopite	c	-82.8^{6}	[1684]						
$Al_2O_3 \cdot MgO$	c					(19.26)	[1719]		
$Al_2O_3 \cdot SiO_2$, andalusite	c			(−607.0*)	[232]	(22.3)	[1680]	(29.34)	[1685, 2545]
				(−608.7*)	[232]	(22.28)	[1685]	29.10	[1685, 2545]
$Al_2O_3 \cdot SiO_2$, disthene	c			(−616.3*)	[232]	20.02	[1685, 2545]	34.6^{7}	[336a]
				(−614.0**)	[232]	20.0	[1680]		
$Al_2O_3 \cdot SiO_2$, sillimanite	c	(−620.40)	[1618a]	(−585.351)	[1618a]	(22.97)	[1685, 2545]	(29.31)	[1618a, 1685, 2545]
						(22.991)	[1618a]		
						(23.0)	[1680]		
$Al_2O_3 \cdot 2SiO_2$, *m*-kaolinite	c	−804.2	[85]	−757.1*	[85]	35.2	[85]		
$Al_2O_3 \cdot 2SiO_2 \cdot 2H_2O$, halloysite	c	−960.23	[775]	−883.6	[775]	48.6	[1688]		
$Al_2O_3 \cdot 2SiO_2 \cdot 2H_2O$, dickite	c	−964.40	[775]	−887.4	[775]	47.1	[1688]		
$Al_2O_3 \cdot 2SiO_2 \cdot 2H_2O$, kaolinite	c	−964.7	[775]	−888.1	[775]	48.5	[1688]		
		−954	[85]			48.4	[1685]		
$Al_2O_3 \cdot SrO$	c	−541.87	[178a]	−549.51	[178a]	25.6	[178a]		
$2Al_2O_3 \cdot CaO$	c					42.5	[1719]		
$2Al_2O_3 \cdot 2CaO \cdot 8SiO_2 \cdot 7H_2O$, leonardite	c	−3338.4	[771]	−3087.7	[771]				
$2Al_2O_3 \cdot 6CaO \cdot Fe_2O_3$	c	−1924.4	[2053]						
$2Al_2O_3 \cdot 2MgO \cdot 5SiO_2$, cordierite	c					97.3	[2630]	108.1	[2630]
$3Al_2O_3 \cdot 3CaO \cdot CaF_2$, kalfidin	c	−1845.3	[1541]						
$3Al_2O_3 \cdot 2SiO_2$, mullite	c			−1580*	[224]	60.8	[2096]	77.94	[2096]
$6Al_2O_3 \cdot 7BaO \cdot 3H_2O$	c	−6062.5	[2139]	−5343*	[229]				
$7Al_2O_3 \cdot 12CaO$	c	(−4630.5)	[1046]	−4392.2	[1046]	249.7	[1719]		
Al_2S_3	c	(−172.9)	[204]						
$Al_2(SO_4)_3$	c	(−665.7*)	[1172]						
$Al_2(SO_4)_3 \cdot 18H_2O$	c			−1777.6*	[229]				
Al_2Se	g	25*	[1294]						
Al_2Se_3	c	−135	[204]						
		−129.7	[2311]						
		−129.0	[204, 2311]						
Al_2Te_3	c	−78	[204]						
Al_2TiO_5	c					26.2	[1685, 1716]	32.6	[1685, 1716]
Al_2U	c	−22.3	[188]			25.5	[2207]		
Al_2Zr	c			−40.8	[2313]				

1. From CaO(c); $Al_2O_3(a)$; $Ga_2O_3(c)$ and $SiO_2(a)$. 2. From CaO(c); $Al_2O_3(a)$ and $SiO_2(a)$. 3. From CaO(c); $Al_2O_3(a)$ and $SiO_2(a)$. 4. From Al_2O_3 and CaO. 5. In *kjoules/mole*.
6. From KF, MgF_2, MgO, $Al_2O_3(a)$ and $SiO_2(a)$. 7. $t = 100°C$.

1	2	3		4		5		6	
Al_3Ca	c	(−54.0*)	[1774]						
Al_3Fe	c	−26.8	[2625]						
Al_3Mg_2	c	−10	[535]						
Al_3Ni	c	−36.0	[1773]						
Al_3Pu	c	−43.2	[43]						
Al_3Ti	c	−35.3	[1771]						
Al_3U	c	−25.2	[188]						
Al_3Zr_2	c			−64.0	[2313]				
Al_3Zr_4	c			−72.1	[2313]				
Al_4C_3	c	(−51*)	[1953]	(34.2*)	[2226]			(31.4)	[1649]
		(−46.7*)	[1773]			(31.3)	[1773]		
		(−53.4)	[1904]			(21.264)	[1269, 1618a]	(27.909)	[1269]
		(−49.7)	[1520]						
		(−49*)[1]	[1618a]	(−46.052*)	[1618a]			(27.912)	[1618a]
Al_4Pu	c	−43.2	[43]						
Al_4U	c	−31.2	[188]						
$Al_5K_3H_6(PO_4)_8 \cdot 18H_2O$	c	−4523	[1159]			335.6	[1159]	354.3	[1159]
$HAl(OH)_4$	c			−329.05*	[5]				
$H_2AlO_3^-$	d			−255.2*	[323]				
$H_3Al(OH)_6$	c			−442.35*	[5]				
Am	c					15.0*	[323]		
						17.2	[2662]		
Am^{3+}	d	−163.2	[1434]	−160.5	[323]	−38.0*	[323]		
		−162.4	[1263]						
Am^{4+}	d	−122.3*	[323]	−110.2*	[323]	−89*	[323]		
		−116	[1434]			−77*	[1434]		
		−115.9	[1189]						
$AmCl_3$	c	−251.3	[1810]	−233.7	[229]				
		−248*	[2655]						
		−249.2	[1263]						
AmClO	c	−243.6	[1810]						
		−227.6	[1263]						
AmF_2^+	d					−11.9	[1231]		
AmF_3	d					17.6	[1231]		
AmO_2	c	−240*	[1045]	−227.5*	[1045]				
		−240.3	[1810]	−231*	[323]	20*	[323]		
		−239.9	[1189]	−226.7*	[229]	20.0	[2078]		
AmO_2^+	d	−207.7	[1434]	−194.5*	[323]	−2*	[1434]		

AmO_2^{2+}	d	−170.8	[1434]	−156.7*	[323]	18*	[1434]		
$Am(OH)_3$	c			−300.0*	[323]				
$Am(OH)_4$	c			−347.0*	[323]				
Am_2O_2	c	−420*	[887]	−401*	[1045]	37.8	[2662]		
Ar	g					(36.9831)	[570]		
						(36.982)	[568]		
						(36.9822)	[2358]		
	d	−2.86	[568]						
		−2.9	[2358]	3.9	[2358]	14.2	[2358]		
Ar^+	g	(364.907)[2]	[568]	362.596	[568]	39.745	[568]	5.003	[568]
		(364.90)[3]	[2358]						
Ar^{2+}	g	(1000.5)[4]	[568]						
		(1003.5)[5]	[2358]						
Ar^{3+}	g	(1944)[4]	[568]						
		(1948.3)[6]	[2358]						
Ar^{4+}	g	(3323)[4]	[568]						
		(3329)[7]	[2358]						
Ar^{5+}	g	(5053)[4]	[568]						
		(5060)[8]	[2358]						
Ar^{6+}	g	(7159)[4]	[568]						
		(7168)[9]	[2358]						
Ar^{7+}	g	(10017)[4]	[568]						
		(10029)[10]	[2358]						
Ar^{8+}	g	(13326)[4]	[568]						
		(13340)[11]	[2358]						
Ar·HCl	g	−23.0[12]	[568]						
$Ar\cdot 6H_2O$, cubic	c	−424.8	[568]						
As	g	(69.00)	[2479]	(59.10)	[2479]				
		(79)	[1540]						
		72.3[13]	[2358]	(62.4)	[2358]	41.61	[1685, 2358]	4.968	[2358]
As, α, gray	c	3.24	[812]			(8.40)	[2479]	(5.90)	[2479]
As, γ, yellow		3.5	[2358]			(8.4)	[1685, 2358]	(5.89)	[1685, 2358]
As, β	v	1.0	[2358]						
As^+	g	300.12[14]	[2358]						
As^{2+}	g	767.64[15]	[2358]						

1. $\Delta H_0^\circ = -47.804$*[1618a]. 2. $\Delta H_0^\circ = (363.424)$ [568]. 3. $\Delta H_0^\circ = (363.42)$ [2538]. 4. ΔH_0°. 5. $\Delta H_0^\circ = (1000.5)$ [2358]. 6. $\Delta H_0^\circ = (1943.9)$ [2358]. 7. $\Delta H_0^\circ = (3323)$ [2358]. 8. $\Delta H_0^\circ = (5053)$ [2358]. 9. $\Delta H_0^\circ = (7159)$ [2358]. 10. $\Delta H_0^\circ = (10019)$ [2358]. 11. $\Delta H_0^\circ = (13328)$ [2358]. 12. $T = 240°K$. 13. $\Delta H_0^\circ = 72.04$ [2358]. 14. $\Delta H_0^\circ = 298.38$ [2358]. 15. $\Delta H_0^\circ = 764.42$ [2358].

1	2	3		4		5		6	
As^{3+}	g	1422.14[1]	[2358]			38.8	[66]		
As^{4+}	g	2579.76[2]	[2358]						
As^{5+}	g	4025.48[3]	[2358]			38.87	[66]		
As^{6+}	g	6968.42[4]	[2358]						
As_2	g	(48.00)	[2479]	(35.96)	[2479]	(51.19)	[2479]	(8.36)	[2479]
		(53.1)[5]	[2358]	(41.1)	[2358]	(57.2)	[1685, 2358]	(8.366)	[2358]
								(8.37)	[1685]
As_4	g	(34.50)	[2479]	(22.15)	[2479]	(75.00)	[2479]	18.48	[2479]
		(35.5)	[1540]						
		(34.4)	[2358]	(22.1)	[2358]	(75)	[2358]		
$AsBr_3$	g	–31[6]	[2358]	–28	[2358]	86.94	[2358]	18.92	[2358]
		–43.57	[812]			87.72	[2484]	19.12	[2484]
	c	–47.2	[2358]	–38.3*	[323]	38.5*	[323]		
				–42.5*	[227]				
$AsCl_2$	g	16[7]	[2358]						
$AsCl_3$	g	–61.80[8]	[2358]	– 58,77	[2358]	78.17	[2358]	18.10	[1685, 2358]
						77.97	[2484]	18.04	[2484]
						78.3	[1685]		
	l	–72.9	[2358]	–61.37	[2358]	49.6	[2358]		
						55.9	[1685]		
	c	(–92*)	[358]						
$AsCl_5$	c	–211*	[358]						
$AsDT_2$	g					59.45	[2537]	11.20	[2537]
						59.48	[27]	11.28	[27]
AsD_2T						58.84	[2537]	10.84	[2537]
						58.89	[27]	10.97	[27]
						56.08	[588]	10.67	[588, 1685]
AsD_3	g					55.99	[2489]	10.55	[2489]
						55.96	[1685]		
AsF_3	g	–220.04[9]	[2358]	–216.46	[2358]	(69.07)	[2358]	15.68	[1685, 2358]
						(69.08)	[1685, 2484]	15.69	[2489]
	l	–228.55	[2358]	–217.29	[2358]	(43.31)	[2358]	30.25	[1685, 2358]
						(43.3)	[1685]		
						(43.1)	[1680]		
AsF_5	g	–255.6	[2068a]	–280.2	[2068a]	78.00	[709a]	21.27[10]	[709a]
						84.46	[1296]	25.31	[1296]
$AsHD_2$	g					57.45	[27]	10.19	[27]
						57.32	[2537]	9.48	[2537]

	g					57.37	[589]	10.09	[589]
AsHDT	g					58.14	[27]	10.49	[27]
$AsHT_2$	g					58.64	[2537]	10.59	[2537]
						58.78	[27]	10.79	[27]
AsH_2D	g					56.52	[27]	9.70	[27]
						56.43	[2537]	9.51	[2537]
						56.44	[589]	9.61	[589]
AsH_2T	g					57.16	[2537]	9.76	[2537]
AsH_2T	g					57.27	[27]	10.01	[27]
AsH_3	g	(15.88)[11]	[2358]	16.47	[2358]				
		(15.87)	[1442]	16.10	[1442]	53.18	[1442]		
		(18.0)	[36]	42.0*	[323]	52*	[323]		
		(5.09)[12]	[2367]	32.8*	[229]	53.15	[2637]	9.21	[1442, 1685, 2367]
		(17.9*)	[157]	22.4*	[232]	53.29	[588]	9.22	[588]
				18.6**	[232]	53.22	[1685, 2358, 2489]	9.10	[2358, 2489]
AsI_3	g	8.81[13]	[1064a]			108.67	[1064a]		
						92.7	[1685]	19.28	[1685]
						92.79	[2358]	19.27	[2358]
	c	−13.9[14]	[2358]	−14.2	[2358]	50.92	[2358]	25.28	[2358]
				−10.64*	[323]	49*	[323]		
				−15.2*	[227]	66.3	[1064a]		
AsN	g	46.91[15]	[2358]	40.15	[2358]	53.9	[1685, 2358]	7.27	[1685, 2358]
AsO	g	16.72[16]	[2358]	−1.6*	[227]	55.6	[1685]	7.72	[1685]
AsO^+	d			−39.15	[2358]				
AsO_2^-	d	−102.54	[2358]	−83.66	[2358]	9.9	[2358]		
AsO_3F^{2-}	d			−245.59	[2358]				
AsO_4^{3-}	d	−212.27	[2358]	−155.00	[2358]	−38.9	[2358]		
						−34.6	[1685]		
AsS	c					15.18	[2632]	11.24	[2632]
AsT_3	g					57.85	[2488]	11.58	[2488]
As_2H_4	g	35.2	[2260]						
As_2O_3, arsenolite	c					27.89	[145]	24.44	[145]
As_2O_3, claudenite	c	−156.15	[1743]			29.33	[1756]		
As_2O_3, monoclinic	c	−152.9	[1045]	−136.0	[1045]				
As_2O_3, octahedral	c	−160.3	[812]						
As_2O_3, orthorhombic	c	−157.0	[1045]	−137.7	[1045]	25.89	[1743]		

1. $\Delta H_0^\circ = 1417.44$ [2358]. 2. $\Delta H_0^\circ = 2573.58$ [2358]. 3. $\Delta H_0^\circ = 4017.82$ [2358]. 4. $\Delta H_0^\circ = 6959.28$ [2358]. 5. $\Delta H_0^\circ = 53.30$ [2358]. 6. $\Delta H_0^\circ = 25.55$ [2358]. 7. $\Delta H_0^\circ = 16$ [2358]. 8. $\Delta H_0^\circ = 61.42$ [2358]. 9. $\Delta H_0^\circ = -218.68$ [2358]. 10. C_ν. 11. $\Delta H_0^\circ = 17.70$ [2358]. 12. $(\Delta H_0^\circ)_{subl}$. 13. Calculated [234] from $(\Delta H_{298}^\circ)_{subl} = 22.71$ [1064a] and $(\Delta H_{298}^\circ) AsI_3(c) = -13.9$ [2358]. 14. $\Delta H_0^\circ = -13.91$ [2358]. 15. $\Delta H_0^\circ = 47$ [2358]. 16. $\Delta H_0^\circ = 16.88$ [2358].

1	2	3		4		5		6	
As_2O_3	v					30.49	[145]	25.40	[145]
$As_2O_3 \cdot SO_3$	c	−285.45	[2358]						
As_2O_4	c	−175.5	[1045]	−149	[1045]				
		−190.4	[1815]						
		−189.72	[2358]						
As_2O_5	c	−221.05	[2358]	−187.0	[2358]	25.2	[1685, 2358]	27.85	[1685, 2358]
		−221.14	[812]						
	d	−227.4	[2358]						
$As_2O_5 \cdot 4H_2O$	c	−503.0	[2358]	−411.1*	[323]	62.6*	[323]		
$3As_2O_5 \cdot 5H_2O$	c	−1015.4	[2358]						
As_2S_2	c	−34.1	[2358]	−32.15	[323]	32.9	[323]		
				−31.2	[229]				
As_2S_3	c	(−30.0)	[2625]	−32.46*	[323]	26.8	[323]		
		(−40.4)	[2358]	−40.3	[2358]	39.1	[480, 2358]	27.8	[2358]
				−34.1*	[229]			27.65	[480]
As_2S_5	c	−35.0	[2625]						
As_2Se_3	c			−133.6*	[229]				
As_4O_6	g	−289.0	[2358]	−262.4	[2358]	91	[2358]		
						101	[1685]		
As_4O_6	c	(−273.1*)	[229]						
As_4O_6, monoclinic	c	−313.0	[2358]	−275.82	[2358]	56	[2358]		
As_4O_6, octahedral	c	−314.04	[2358]	−275.46	[2358]	51.2	[2358]	45.72	[2358]
As_4O_6	d	−299.6	[2358]						
$HAsO_2$	d	−109.1	[2358]	−96.25	[2358]	30.1	[2358]		
						30.3	[1685]		
$HAsO_3F^-$	d			−253.60	[2358]				
$HAsO_4^{2-}$	d	−216.62	[2358]	−170.82	[2358]	−0.4	[2358]		
						0.9	[1685]		
$H_2AsO_3^-$	d	−170.84	[2358]	−140.35	[2358]	26.4	[2358]		
				−140.4*	[323]				
$H_2AsO_4^-$	d	−217.39	[2358]	−180.04	[2358]	28	[1685, 2358]		
H_3AsO_3	d	−177.4	[2358]	−152.94	[2358]	46.6	[2358]		
						47.0	[1685]		
H_3AsO_4	c	−216.6	[2358]	−179.3*	[229]				
H_3AsO_4	d	−215.7	[2358]	−183.11	[2358]	44	[2358]		
						49.3	[1685]		
At	g	22.0	[2479]	13.00	[2479]	44.68	[2479]		
		23.240[1]	[568]	14.239	[568]	44.69	[568]		

At^+	g	235[2]	[568]			45.13	[568]		
At^{2+}	g	498[2]	[568]						
At^-	g	−42.7[3]	[568]	−48.391	[568]	41.93	[568]		
At_2	g	20[4]	[568]	9.595	[568]	63.9	[568]	8.86	[568]
		21.60	[2479]	10.57	[2479]	66.00	[2479]	8.90	[2479]
	c					29.00	[2479]	14.00	[2479]
						29.0	[568, 1685]	13.0	[568]
At_2^+	g	212[5]	[568]						
Au	g	(84.700)	[2479]	(75.219)	[2479]				
		(87.30)[6]	[1589]	(77.82)	[1589]	43.12	[1589, 1685]		
		(86.8)	[396]						
		(88.3)	[1509]						
Au^+	g					41.75	[66]		
	d			39.0	[323]				
Au^{3+}	d			103.6*	[323]				
AuBr	c	(−8.0)[7]	[656]	−3.7*	[323]	27*	[323]		
				−3.2*	[227]	27.0*	[1773]		
						13[7,8]	[588]		
$AuBr_3$	c	(−26.5)[7]	[656]	−5.9*	[323]	24*	[323]		
				−9.5*	[227]	−6[7,9]	[656]		
$Au(CN_2)^-$	g					73.5	[728]		
$Au(CN_2)^-$	d			64.4*	[323]	29.5*	[323]		
$Au(CNS)_2^-$	d			57.7	[323]				
$Au(CNS)_4^-$	d			130.1	[323]				
$Au_{0.5}Cd_{0.5}$	c	−4.64	[1589]	−4.66	[1589]				
AuCl	g					60.4	[1685]	8.47	[1685]
	c	(−8.3)	[658, 2245]	−4.2*	[323]	24*	[323]		
		(−8.9)[10]	[658]	−3.9*	[227]	22.2	[658]		
$AuCl_3$	c	(−27.5)	[658, 2245]	−11.6*	[323]	35*	[323]		
		(−27)[10]	[658]	−14.8*	[227]	35.4	[658]		
$AuCl_3 \cdot 2H_2O$	c			−123.3*	[323]	54*	[323]		
				−125.4*	[229]				
AuCu	c	−3.62	[1772]			20.6	[1772]		
$AuCu_3$	c	−6.5	[1772]			35.9	[1772]		
		−1.71	[1589]	−1.74	[1589]				
AuD	g					51.80	[1685]	7.01	[1685]

1. $\Delta H_0^\circ = 23.359$ [568]. 2. ΔH_0°. 3. $\Delta H_0^\circ = -41.1$ [568]. 4. $\Delta H_0^\circ = 20.717$ [568]. 5. ΔH_0°. 6. $\Delta H_0^\circ = 87.25$ [1589]. 7. $T = 350$–$450°K$; from gaseous bromine. 8. Calculated [234] from $\Delta S^\circ_{350-450} = -17$ [656]; from gaseous bromine. 9. Calculated [234] from $\Delta S^\circ 350$–$450 = -60$ [656]; from gaseous bromine. 10. $T = 420$–$520°K$.

1	2	3		4		5		6	
AuF	g	−18*	[230]	−14*	[229]	20.8*	[2602]		
AuF_3	c	−83.3	[2706]	−71.1*	[234]	27.3*	[1773]		
AuH	g					50.41	[1685]	6.96	[1685]
AuI	c	0.2	[323]	−0.76	[323]	28.5*	[323, 1773]		
				−0.4*	[227]	24.15[1]	[79]		
				−7.6	[250]				
AuI_3	c	28*	[2683]						
$Au_{0.517}Ni_{0.483}$	c							6.29	[1589]
$AuPb_2$	c	−1.5	[1772]			41.9	[1772]		
$AuSb_2$	c	(−4.65)	[1772]			28.5	[1772]		
$Au_{0.5}Sn_{0.5}$	c	−3.64	[1589]	3.57	[1589]	2		6.03	[1589]
AuSn	c	−6.4	[1772]			23.6	[1772]		
$AuSn_2$	c	−5.7	[1772]						
Au_2O_3	c	(−0.8)	[1045]	(18.55)	[1045]				
				(18.08*)	[176]				
Au_2P_3	c	−23.3*	[1772]			36.0	[1772]		
Au_2S_2	c	64*	[2683]						
B	g	(135.0)[2]	[2233]	(130.3)	[2566]	(36.65)	[1685]		
		(131.219)[3]	[570]			(36.6492)	[570]		
		(141,000)	[2479]	(130.490)	[2479]	(36.649)	[2686]		
		(138.0)[4]	[2233]						
		(127.3)	[2587]						
		(128.1)[5]	[2587]						
		(131.6)[5]	[5]						
		(101)[5]	[457]						
		(129.4)[5]	[975]						
		(133)[5]	[2533]						
		(134)[5]	[1156]						
		(135.22)	[1187]						
		(139*)	[2352]						
		(136.9)	[2127]						
		(135.7)	[1512]						
		(135)[6]	[1830]						
		(132.8)[7]	[1618a]						
	l	5.26	[1618a]	4.625	[1618a]	3.533	[1618a]		
	c					(1.403)	[570, 1618a, 1648, 1685]	(2.650)	[1648, 1618a, 2693]

						(1.402)	[2693]	(2.63)	[1656]
								(2.67)	[1857]
								(2.65)	[570, 1648, 1685]
	v	(0.376)[8]	[1187]			(1.564)[9]	[1648]	(2.858)	[1648, 2693]
		(0.4)[10]	[1830]			(1.564)	[2693]		
		(0.8)	[1433]			(1.81)	[1685]	(2.85)	[1685]
B^{3+}	g					33.10	[66]		
B_2	g			107.5*	[229]	48.240	[2686]	7.304	[2686]
		(199.209)[11]	[570]			48.230	[570]		
		(205.0716)[12]	[1830]			48.2261	[1830]	7.3005	[1830]
		(195.0)[13]	[1618a]	181.457	[1618a]	48.228	[1618a]	7.301	[1618a]
						48.2	[1685]	7.30	[1685]
BBr	g			(49.7)	[1773]	53.785	[716]	7.846	[716]
						53.9	[1685]	7.84	[1685]
		(56.0)[14]	[1618a]	45.817	[1618a]	53.75	[1618a]	7.837	[1618a]
BBrCl	g	−2.5*[15]	[1618a]	−9.303*	[1618a]	69.056	[1618a]	11.197	[1618a]
$BBrCl_2$	g	−80.5[16]	[1618a]	−80.881	[1618a]	74.163	[1618a]	15.392	[1618a]
	l	76.7	[361]						
$^{10}BBrCl_2$	g					73.70	[2018]	15.28	[2018]
$^{11}BBrCl_2$	g					73.79	[2018]	15.42	[2464]
BBrClI	l	42.8*	[361]						
BBrF	g	−57.5*[17]	[1618a]	−64.08*	[1618a]	65.887	[1618a]	10.408	[1618a]
$BBrF_2$	g	−196.0*[18]	[1618a]	−196.114*	[1618a]	68.424	[1618a]	13.492	[1618a]
$^{10}BBrF_2$	g					67.83	[2018]	13.41	[2018]
$^{11}BBrF_2$	g					67.94	[2018]	13.51	[2018]
BBrO	g	−60*[19]	[1618a]	−64.581*	[1618a]	59.463	[1618a]	11.188	[1618a]
BBr_2	g	15*[20]	[1618a]	5.276*	[1618a]	70.402	[1618a]	11.486	[1618a]
$BBrI_2$	l	8.8*	[361]						
BBr_2Cl	g	65*[21]	[1618a]	−68.72*	[1618a]	76.909	[1618a]	15.781	[1618a]
	l	59.7	[361]						
$^{10}BBr_2Cl$	g					76.38	[2018]	15.64	[2018]
$^{11}BBr_2Cl$	g					76.61	[2018]	15.81	[2018]
BBr_2F	g	−123*[22]	[1618a]	−126.524*	[1618a]	74.066	[1618a]	14.894	[1618a]
$^{10}BBr_2F$	g					73.76	[2018]	14.78	[2018]
$^{11}BBr_2F$	g					73.87	[2018]	14.92	[2018]

1. Calculated [234] from $\Delta S^\circ_{298} = 1.2$ [79] and S°_{298} for Au(c) [2245]. 2. $\Delta H^\circ_0 = (133.8)$ [2233]. 3. $\Delta H^\circ_0 = (130)$ [570]. 4. $\Delta H^\circ_0 = (136.8)$ [2233]; (135.7) [1512]. 5. ΔH°_0. 6. $\Delta H^\circ_0 = (133.7807)$ [1830]. 7. $\Delta H^\circ_0 = (131.581)$ [1618a]. 8. ΔH°_0. 9. $S^\circ_{298} - S^\circ_0$. 10. $\Delta H^\circ_0 = 0.3783$ [1830]. 11. $\Delta H^\circ_0 = (197.7^*)$ [570]. 12. $\Delta H^\circ_0 = (203.5615)$ [1830]. 13. $\Delta H^\circ_0 = (193.49)$ [1618a]. 14. $\Delta H^\circ_0 = 57.071$ [1618a]. 15. $\Delta H^\circ_0 = -1.023^*$ [1618a]. 16. $\Delta H^\circ_0 = -78.561$ [1618a]. 17. $\Delta H^\circ_0 = -55.902^*$ [1618a]. 18. $\Delta H^\circ_0 = -193.723^*$ [1618a]. 19. $\Delta H^\circ_0 = -58.361^*$ [1618a]. 20. $\Delta H^\circ_0 = -18.233^*$ [1618a]. 21. $\Delta H^\circ_0 = -61.359^*$ [1618a]. 22. $\Delta H^\circ_0 = -119.181^*$ [1618a].

1	2	3		4		5		6	
BBr_2I	l	−25.8*	[361]						
BBr_3	g					(77.50)	[1685]	(16.30)	[1685]
$^{10}BBr_3$	g	(−48.8)[1]	[1618a]	(−55.213)	[1618a]	(77.487)	[1618a]	(16.198)	[1618a]
	g					77.38	[1614]	16.08	[1614]
						78.633	[2017]	15.83	[2017]
$^{11}BBr_3$	g					77.53	[1614]	16.23	[1614]
						79.007	[2017]	16.239	[2017]
BBr_3	l	(−57.9)	[2392]						
		(−57.0)	[1618a]	(−56.619)	[1618a]	(54.7)	[1618a]	30.6	[1618a]
BC	g	198*[2]	[1618a]	183.966*	[1618a]	49.822	[1618a]	7.099	[1618a]
BC_2	g	171*[3]	[368]						
BCO	g	171	[1512]			59.48	[1277]	13.86	[1277]
BCl	g	(45.0587)[4]	[1830]	18.5*	[227]	50.9403	[1830]	(7.5663)	[1830]
		(41.279)[5]	[570]			50.943	[570]		
		(33.8)[6]	[1618a]	26.974	[1618a]	50.942	[1618a]	(7.567)	[1618a]
						50.967	[716]	(7.574)	[716]
BClF	g	−77.2596[7]	[1830]			63.5691	[1830]	10.6908	[1830]
		−75.0[8]	[1618a]	−78.267	[1618a]	63.229	[1618a]	10.169	[1618a]
BClO	g	−88.0291[9]	[1830]			56.368	[1830]	10.5555	[1830]
		−75.6*[10]	[1618a]	−76.843*	[1618a]	56.720	[1618a]	10.765	[1618a]
		−74.8	[860]			57.8	[860]		
$BClF_2$	g	−211.5	[1443]			65.67	[1443]		
		−211.6[11]	[1618a]	−208.37	[1618a]	65.662	[1618a]	13.018	[1618a]
	l	25.8	[361]						
$^{10}BClF_2$	g					65.13	[2018]	12.94	[2018]
$^{11}BClF_2$	g					65.23	[2018]	13.03	[2018]
BCl_2	g	−26.691[12]	[570]			65.231	[570]		
		−20*[13]	[1618a]	−23.06*	[1618a]	64.956	[1618a]	10.919	[1618a]
		−19.5413[14]	[1830]			65.4200	[1830]	11.4680	[1830]
BCl_2F	g	−153.9	[1443]			68.72	[1443]		
		−154[15]	[1618a]	−150.964	[1618a]	68.732	[1618a]	14.117	[1618a]
$^{10}BCl_2F$	g					66.895	[2018]	14.01	[2018]
$^{11}BCl_2F$	g					68.47	[2018]	14.15	[2018]
BCl_2H	g	−60.37	[1827]	−56.68	[1827]	64.088	[1827]	11.879	[1827]
BCl_2I	l	59.7*	[361]						
BCl_3	g	(−97.11)[16]	[1830]			(69.3115)	[1830]	(14.9949)	[1830]
		(−97.3)	[2390]			(69.3)	[1685]	(14.99)	[1685]
		(−108)	[210]			(69.32)	[1443]		

		(−97.0)	[114]						
		(−97.0)[17]	[570]			(69.298)	[570]		
		(−96.89)[18]	[1640]						
		(−97.1)[19]	[1187]						
		(−97.51)[20]	[1640]						
		(−97.11)	[1640]						
		(−96.0)	[115]						
$^{10}BCl_3$	g	(−96.9)	[210]						
		(−96.31)[21]	[1618a]	(−92.73)	[1618a]	(69.328)	[1618a]	(14.912)	[1618a]
						69.17	[2026]	14.87	[1614, 2026]
						69.23	[1614]		
						69.31	[2026]	15.01	[1614, 2026]
						69.36	[1614]		
$^{11}BCl_3$	g	(−102.3)	[1433]	(−102.9)	[210]				
		(−102.4)[22]	[1794]						
		(−103.0)	[2390]						
		(−102.9)	[114]						
		(−102.7)	[1640]						
		(−101.04)	[1202]						
BCl_3	c	(−103.11)[23]	[1640]	99.2*	[229]				
BD	g					42.46	[1685]	6.99	[1685]
BF	g	(−43.1327)[24]	[1830]			44.8896	[1830]	7.0724	[1830]
		(−35.771)[25]	[570]			47.879	[570]		
		(−29)	[861]			47.6	[861]		
		(−27.5)	[1517]			47.91	[716]	7.076	[716]
						47.9	[1685]	7.07	[1685]
		(−27.7)[26]	[1618a]	−34.338	[1618a]	47.89	[1618a]	7.073	[1618a]
BFO	g	−144[27]	[1195, 1522, 1618a]	−142	[1195]	53	[1195]		
				−145.066	[1618a]	53.705	[1618a]	9.798	[1618a]
				−144[28]	[1830]	53.5635	[1830]	8.3596	[1830]
		−172.413[29]	[570]			54.207	[570]		
				−144	[62]	53	[62]		
				−142	[887]				

1. $\Delta H_0^\circ = -43.475$ [1618a]. 2. $\Delta H_0^\circ = 196.464$* [1618a]. 3. ΔH_0°. 4. $\Delta H_0^\circ = (44.3291)$ [1830]. 5. $\Delta H_0^\circ = (40.55*)$ [570]. 6. $\Delta H_0^\circ = (33.071)$ [1618a]. 7. $\Delta H_0^\circ = -77.5159$ [1830]. 8. $\Delta H_0^\circ = -75.187$* [1618a]. 9. $\Delta H_0^\circ = -88.0843$ [1830]. 10. $\Delta H_0^\circ = -75.709$* [1618a]. 11. $\Delta H_0^\circ = -211.046$ [1618a]. 12. $\Delta H_0^\circ = -30$* [570]. 13. $\Delta H_0^\circ = -20.289$* [1618a]. 14. $\Delta H_0^\circ = -19.9225$ [1830]. 15. $\Delta H_0^\circ = -153.63$ [1618a]. 16. $\Delta H_0^\circ = -96.8899$ [1830]. 17. $\Delta H_0^\circ = -96.776$ [570]. 18. ΔH_0°. 19. $\Delta H_0^\circ = -96.88$ [1187]. 20. From amorphous boron. 21. $\Delta H_0^\circ = -96.078$ [1618a]. 22. Calculated [1185] from the data of [1794]. 23. From amorphous boron. 24. $\Delta H_0^\circ = (-43.8643)$ [1830]. 25. $\Delta H_0^\circ = (-35.5*)$ [570]. 26. $\Delta H_0^\circ = (-28.43)$ [1618a]. 27. $\Delta H_0^\circ = -143.99$ [1618a] [1618a]. 28. $\Delta H_0^\circ = -143.9660$ [1830]. 29. $\Delta H_0^\circ = -172.513$* [570].

1	2	3		4		5		6	
BF_2	g	−134.9516[1]	[1830]			55.0563	[1830]	9.8434	[1830]
		−152.838[2]	[570]			59.253	[570]		
		−130[3]	[1618a, 1920]	−132.727	[1618a]	58.996	[1618a]	9.618	[1618a]
BF_2HO	g	−259[4]	[1618a]	−251.354	[1618a]	64.31	[1618a]	12.424	[1618a]
BF_3	g	(−270.0)[5]	[1187]			(60.72)	[1187]	(12.06)	[1187]
		(−268)[6]	[570]			(60.715)	[570]		
		(−270.1)[7]	[1618a]						
		(−270.1)[8]	[1830]			(60.7135)	[1830]	(12.0569)	[1830]
		(−269.88)	[2696]	−269.89	[2696]	(60.7)	[1680, 1685]		
		(−271.6)	[1419]			(60.71)	[1443]		
		(−270.8)	[1419]						
$^{10}BF_3$	g					60.64	[1614]	11.99	[1614]
						61.05	[2026]	11.98	[2026]
$^{11}BF_3$	g					60.73	[1614]	12.08	[1614]
						61.13	[2026]	12.07	[2026]
BF_3	c	(−268)	[2606]						
BF_3OH	d	−363.1	[2277]						
BF_4^-	g	−395*	[725]			64.28	[206]	16.33	[206]
	d	(−342*)	[725]	(−352*)	[487]				
BH	g	(116.9702)[9]	[1830]			(41.0471)	[1830]	(6.9743)	[1830]
		(113.396)[10]	[570]			(41.050)	[570]		
						(41.047)	[2686]	(6.974)	[2686]
						(40.99)	[1685]	(6.96)	[1685]
		105.8[11]	[1618a]	98.632	[1618a]	41.047	[1618a]	6.975	[1618a]
BHO	g	−20*[12]	[1618a]	−22.109*	[1618a]	48.584	[1618a]	8.635	[1618a]
BHO_2	g	−134.0[13]	[1618a]	−131.395	[1618a]	57.273	[1618a]	10.094	[1618a]
	c	−191.87	[1618a]	−175.677	[1618a]	11.70	[1618a]	13.00	[1618a]
BH_2	g	48[14]	[1618a]	44.889*	[1618a]	43.045	[1618a]	8.133	[1618a]
BH_2O	g	−114*[15]	[1618a]	−106.994*	[1618a]	58.116	[1618a]	12.432	[1618a]
BH_3	g	18[16]	[1830]			44.8806	[1830]	8.6573	[1830]
		18.01	[1438]			44.9	[794]		
		18	[1438]						
		25.5*[17]	[1618a]	26.494*	[1618a]	44.880	[1618a]	8.657	[1618a]
BH_4^-	g	−23*	[724]			45.23	[724]	9.08	[724]
	d					26.7	[1685]		
BI	g	73*[18]	[1618a]	60.978*	[1618a]	55.604	[1618a]	8.021	[1618a]
BI_2	g	58*[19]	[1618a]	44.642*	[1618a]	73.964	[1618a]	11.731	[1618a]
BI_3	g	6.30	[1219]	−5.74	[1219]	83.431	[946]	16.846	[946]

		10.08	[2537a]			83.431	[1216]		
		17*[20]	[1618a]	4.99*	[1618a]	83.322	[1618a]	16.919	[1618a]
$^{10}BI_3$	g					83.393	[2017]	16.786	[2017]
						83.21	[1614]	16.79	[1614]
						83.668	[1216, 1219]	17.005	[946, 1219]
$^{11}BI_3$	g					83.543	[2017]	16.943	[2017]
						83.36	[1614]	16.95	[1614]
BI_3		9.24	[1219]						
BN	g	151.284*	[570]			50.729	[570]		
		154.8084[21]	[1830]			50.7093	[1830]	7.0369	[1830]
						50.69	[1685]	7.03	[1685]
		152[22]	[1618a]	144.724*	[1618a]	48.681	[1618a]	10.237	[1618a]
	c	(−60.29)[23]	[1830]	(−53.4*)	[232]	(3.673)	[570, 1139]	(4,783)	[1139]
		(−59.51)[24]	[1618a]	(−53.326)	[1618a]	(3.536)	[1618a]		
		(−60.7)	[113, 1139]	(−54.5**)	[232]	(3.537)	[2647]	(4.713)	[1618a, 2647]
		(−26.7)	[31]					(4.69)	[39, 1048]
		(−60)	[1532, 2307]			(3.67)	[1685]	(4,78)	[570, 1685]
		(−59.8)	[1510, 1511]						
BO	g	(5.7441)	[1830]			(48.6044)	[1830]	(6.9782)	[1830]
		(5.744)[25]	[570]			(48.607	[570, 1618a]		
		(≥5.3*)[26]	[2418]			(48.61)	[2686]	(6.978)	[1618a, 2686]
		(10.744*)[27]	[1618a]	3.975*	[1618a]				
		(5.75)[28]	[1187]			(48.60)	[1685]	(6.98)	[1685]
BO_2	g	−69[29]	[485]						
		−68[30]	[486]						
		−64.812[31]	[570]			54.850	[570]		
		−84.6[32]	[1830]			54.9672	[1830]		
		−75.27[33]	[1618a]	−76.63	[1618a]	54.967	[1618a]	10.059	[1618a]
BO_2^-	d		—	−169.6*	[323]	−20*	[323]	10.0595	[1830]
BP	c	99.6*[34]	[368]						
		73.2	[2013]						
BS	g	82.4240[35]	[1830]			51.7457	[1830]	7.1825	[1830]
		80*[36]	[1618a]	67.296*	[1618a]	51.645	[1618a]	7.182	[1618a]
						51.24	[1685]	7.18	[1685]

1. $\Delta H_0^\circ = -135.1093$ [1830]. 2. $\Delta H_0^\circ = -153^*$ [570]. 3. $\Delta H_0^\circ = -130.141^*$ [1618a]. 4. $\Delta H_0^\circ = -257.351$ [1618a]. 5. $\Delta H_0^\circ = -269.33$ [1187]. 6. $\Delta H_0^\circ = -267.326$ [570]. 7. $\Delta H_0^\circ = -269.427$ [1618a]. 8. $\Delta H_0^\circ = -269.4277$ [1830]. 9. $\Delta H_0^\circ = (116.209)$ [1830]. 10. $\Delta H_0^\circ = (112.632)$ [570]. 11. $\Delta H_0^\circ = 105.039$ [1618a]. 12. $\Delta H_0^\circ = -19.873^*$ [1718a]. 13. $\Delta H_0^\circ = -133.175$ [1618a]. 14. $\Delta H_0^\circ = 48.163^*$ [1618a]. 15. $\Delta H_0^\circ = -112.423^*$ [1618a]. 16. $\Delta H_0^\circ = 18.9065$ [1830]. 17. $\Delta H_0^\circ = 26.407^*$ [1618a]. 18. $\Delta H_0^\circ = 72.791^*$ [1618a]. 19. $\Delta H_0^\circ = 58.453^*$ [1618a]. 20. $\Delta H_0^\circ = 17.998^*$ [1618a]. 21. $\Delta H_0^\circ = (154.0602)$ [1830]. 22. $\Delta H_0^\circ = 150.912^*$ [1618a]. 23. $\Delta H_0^\circ = (-59.6031)$ [1830]. 24. $\Delta H_0^\circ = -58.81$ [1618a]. 25. $\Delta H_0^\circ = (5^*)$ [570]. 26. ΔH_0°. 27. $\Delta H_0^\circ = 10.0^*$ [1618a]. 28. $\Delta H_0^\circ = (5^*)$ [1187]. 29. ΔH_0°. 30. $\Delta H_0^\circ = -0.3$ [486]. 31. $\Delta H_0^\circ = -65$ [570]. 32. $\Delta H_0^\circ = -84.6478$ [1830]. 33. $\Delta H_0^\circ = -75.317$ [1618a]. 34. ΔH_{1473}°. 35. $\Delta H_0^\circ = 81.6842$ [1830]. 36. $\Delta H_0^\circ = 79.26$ [1618a].

1	2	3		4		5		6	
BTi	c	–41*	[1618a]	–40.546	[1618a]	7.20	[1618a]	7.40	[1618a]
B_2Br_4	g	–50*	[1219]						
$B_2ClH_2O_3$	g	–314.5	[2172]						
$B_2Cl_2HO_3$	g	–342.2	[2172]						
B_2BI_4	g	–118.2	[1441]						
		–116.9	[1618a]	–109.859	[1618a]	85.767	[1618a]	22.667	[1618a]
	l	–126.2	[1441]			62.7	[1685]	32.94	[1685]
B_2D_6	g	3.04	[1439]						
		–585.29[1]	[1439]			59.06	[2485]	16.77	[2485]
B_2F_4	g	–342.0[2]	[1437]						
		–342.2	[1618a]	–335.162	[1618a]	76.093	[1618a]	18.378	[1618a]
B_2H_6	g	(7.53)[3]	[1187]			(55.34)	[1187]	(13.30)	[1187, 1685]
		(6.73)	[2187]			(55.45)	[2485]	(13.33)	[2485]
		(9.8)[4]	[1618a]	21.941	[1618a]	(55.709)	[1618a]	(13.886)	[1618a]
		(8.6)	[1433]			(55.7)	[1685]		
		(5.0)	[1437a]						
		(9.4)[2]	[157]						
		(7.5)	[1438]						
B_2I_4	g	20*	[1219]						
B_2O_2	g	–111.3981[5]	[1830]			(57.935)	[1830]	(13.6873)	[1830]
		–108.608[6]	[570]			(58.410)	[570]		
		–110.9[2]	[2418]			(59.42)	[2686]	(14.418)	[2686]
		–105*[2]	[1185]			(59.40)	[1685]	(14.42)	[1685]
		–111.7[2]	[2222]						
		–107*	[2352]						
		–109.0[7]	[1618a]	–110.833	[1618a]	(57.958)	[1618a]	(13.695)	[1618a]
B_2O_3	g	–205*[8]	[1187]			65.71	[1187]	(14.28)	[1187]
		–207.62[9]	[1187]						
		–207.003[10]	[570]			65.162	[570]		
		–202[11]	[1830]			67.0021	[1830]	(15.8476)	[1830]
		–214[8]	[2418]						
		–212.68[12]	[398]						
		–203.1*[13]	[1952]						
		–207.5*[14]	[2676]						
		–212.9[15]	[2352]						
		–212.6[16]	[2419]						
		–199.14[17]	[1618a]	–196.602	[1618a]	67.798	[1618a]	(15.979)	[1618a]
$^{10}B_2O_3$	g					66.243	[2034]	13.979	[2034]

$^{11}B_2O_3$	g					66.755	[2034]	14.228	[2034]
	l	−299.28	[1618a]	−282.115	[1618a]	18.739	[1618a]	15.05	[1618a]
B_2O_3	c	(−305.76)[18]	[570]			(12.87)	[570, 1618a, 1698, 1830]	(14.83)	[570]
		(−305.34)[19]	[1830]					(15.05)	[1698, 1618a, 1830]
		(−305.34)[20]	[1187]			(12.91)	[1187, 1685]	(15.04)	[1187]
		(−302.0)[21]	[1648]	(−283.1)	[1648]			(14.98)	[1685]
		(−341)	[210]	(−322)	[210]				
		(−300.98)	[2188]						
		(−306.16)[22]	[2188]						
		(−305.50)	[1436]						
		(−288.6)[23]	[678]						
		(−305.3)	[1640]						
		(−306.3)	[2386]						
		(−303.63)	[1203]						
		(−303.64)[24]	[1618a]	(−284.725)	[1618a]				
	v	(−300.9)	[1045]	(−283.7)	[1045]	(18.58)	[1045]		
		(−300.98)	[1830]			(18.64)	[1830]	(14.25)	[1830]
						(16.09)[25]	[2642]	(14.96)	[2642]
		(−301.7)	[887]			(18.55)	[1187]	(14.8)	[1187]
		(−304.6)	[1142]			(18.6)	[1685]		
		(−301.1)[26]	[114]						
		(−300.98)	[2188]						
		(−301.78)[27]	[2188]						
		(−301.0)	[113]						
		(−301.6)	[115]						
		(−298.7)	[112]						
		(−299.30)	[1203]						
$B_2O_3Cl_3$	g	−378.8	[2172]						
$B_2O_3FH_2$	g	−392	[2175]						
$B_2O_3F_2H$	g	−479	[2175]						

1. From B(g) and D(g). 2. ΔH_0°. 3. $\Delta H_0^\circ = 11.35$ [1187]. 4. $\Delta H_0^\circ = 13.552$ [1618a]. 5. $\Delta H_0^\circ = -111.7$ [1830]. 6. $\Delta H_0^\circ = -109$ [570]. 7. $\Delta H_0^\circ = -109.304$ [1618a]. 8. ΔH_0°. 9. $\Delta H_0^\circ = -207$ [1187]. 10. $\Delta H_0^\circ = -206.282$ [570]. 11. $\Delta H_0^\circ = -201.6479$ [1830]. 12. Calculated [234] from $(\Delta H_0^\circ)_{subl} = 89.32$ [398] and $(\Delta H_0^\circ)B_2O_3(c) = -302.0$ [2228]. 13. Calculated [234] from $(\Delta H_0^\circ)_{subl} = 99$ [1952] and $(\Delta H_{298}^\circ)B_2O_3(c) = -302.0$ [2228]. 14. Calculated [234] from $(\Delta H_0^\circ)_{subl} = 94.5$ [2676] and $(\Delta H_{298}^\circ)B_2O_3(c) = -302.0$ [2228]. 15. Calculated [234] from $(\Delta H_0^\circ)_{subl} = 99$ [1952] and $(\Delta H_{298}^\circ)B_2O_3(c) = -302.0$ [2228]. 16. Calculated [234] from $(\Delta H_0^\circ)_{subl} = 94.5$ [2676] and $(\Delta H_{298}^\circ)B_2O_3(c) = -302.0$ [2228]. 17. $\Delta H_0^\circ = -198.87$ [1618a]. 18. $\Delta H_0^\circ = -304.282$ [570]. 19. $\Delta H_0^\circ = -303.8628$ [1830]. 20. $\Delta H_0^\circ = -303.87$ [1187]. 21. $\Delta H_0^\circ = -300.5$ [6148]. 22. Calculated [234] from $(\Delta H_0^\circ)_{subl} = 94.5$ [2676] and $(\Delta H_{298}^\circ)B_2O_3(c) = -302.0$ [2228]. 23. Average of −287.8 and −289.47 [678]. 24. $\Delta H_0^\circ = -302.162$ [1618a]. 25. $S_{298}^\circ - S_0^\circ$. 26. Average of −298.7; 301.8; −301.6 [114]. 27. From amorphous boron.

1	2	3		4		5		6	
$B_2O_3H_3$, boroxine	g	−307	[2175]						
		−302	[2373]						
$B_2O_3H_2OH$, hydro-boroxine	g	−393	[2373]						
$B_2(OH)_4$ hypoboric acid	c	−335.1	[1219]						
$^{10}B_2S_3$	g					77.382	[2034]	19.054	[3043]
$^{11}B_2S_3$	g					77.960	[2034]	19.243	[3043]
B_2S_3	c			−53.3*	[323]	13.7	[323]		
				−55.9	[229]				
$B_3Cl_3H_3N_3$	c	−252	[2577]						
$B_3Cl_3O_3$	g	−396.7[1]	[858, 1830]			87.5307	[1830]	28.8075	[1830]
		−390.0[2]	[1618a]	−370.238	[1618a]	91.367	[1618a]	31.436	[1618a]
						92.5	[858]		
$B_3FH_2O_3$	g	−382[3]	[1618a]	−364.731	[1618a]	75.225	[1618a]	22.764	[1618a]
$B_3F_2HO_3$	g	−475[4]	[1618a]	−456.169	[1618a]	78.608	[1618a]	24.744	[1618a]
$B_3F_3O_3$	g	−566.8	[1522]			85.3	[1889]		
		−567.8[5]	[1193, 1830]			88.7	[1193]		
		−565.3[6]	[1618a]	−544.859	[1618a]	81.825	[1618a]	27.489	[1618a]
						82.628	[1830]	27.143	[1830]
	c	−585	[1889]			63*	[1889]		
		−586.5	[1618a]	−557.166	[1618a]	52	[1618a]	30.0	[1618a]
$B_3H_3N_3$, borazole	g	−124.1	[1703]			(69.0)	[1685]	(23.18)	[1618a]
	l	−131.1	[1703]						
$B_3H_6N_3$	g	−121.9[7]	[1618a]	−92.829	[1618a]	68.983	[1618a]	23.166	[1618a]
$B_3H_3O_8$	g	−291*[8]	[1618a]	−274.666*	[1618a]	69.744	[1618a]	20.992	[1618a]
	c	−307	[2175]						
		−301.7*	[1618a]	−276.498*	[1618a]	40*	[1618a]	23.5	[1618a]
B_4C	g					(6.47)	[1685]	(12.56)	[1685]
	l	14.684	[1618a]	11.802	[1618a]	16.592	[1618a]	12.545	[1618a]
	c	−13.8	[2403]	−13.6	[2403]			(12.7)[9]	[1711]
				−14.5*	[232]				
		−12.7[10]	[1618a]	−12.567	[1618a]	6.482	[1618a]	(12.545)	[1618a]
B_4H_4	g	8.3*	[792]			61.5*	[792]		
B_4H_{10}		13.9*	[792]			63−70*	[792]		
		13.8	[1438]						
		2.8[11]	[1187]						
	c	(−15.8)[12]	[1187, 1638]						
		(−14.0)	[116]						
	v	−19.8	[1638]						

B_5H_3	g	(15.02)[13]	[1187]			(65.85)	[1187]	(22.4)	[1187]
		(12.99)	[2187]			(66.0)	[1685]	(23.52)	[1685]
		(15.0)	[1438]						
		(15.01)	[66]						
		(17.5)[15]	[1618a]	41.843	[1618a]	(65.803)	[1618a]	(22.423)	[1618a]
	l	(7.74)[16]	[1187]			(44.03)	[1187]	(36.12)	[1187, 1618a, 1685]
		(10.24)	[1618a]	41.067	[1618a]	(44.056)	[1618a]		
		(5.69)[14]	[2187]			(44.0)	[1685]		
B_5H_{11}	g	16.5*	[792]			67–71	[792]		
		22.2	[1438]						
B_6H_{10}	g	17.2*	[792]			69.60*	[792]		
		19.6	[1438]						
B_8H_{14}	g	23.5*	[792]			77.30*	[792]		
						85.1	[1685]	40.0	[1685]
$B_{10}H_{14}$	g	11.3[17]	[1618a]	55.527	[1618a]	84.147	[1618a]	42.92	[1618a]
	l	–1.7	[1618a]	50.83	[1618a]	56.299	[1618a]	52.87	[1618a]
	c	2.8	[1438]			42.2	[1685]	52.09	[1685]
						42.48	[1697]	52.42	[1697]
						41.27	[1272]	50.02	[1272]
		–6.9[18]	[1618a]	49.834	[1618a]	42.20	[1618a]	52.092	[1618a]
$B_{12}H_{13}$	g	24.7*	[792]			88.80*	[792]	42.92	[792]
						84.34	[1187]		
HBO	g	–19.504[19]	[570]			45.538	[570]		
HBO_2	g	–135.7240[20]	[1830]			57.2738	[1830]	10.0939	[1830]
		–135[21]	[570]			57.409	[570]		
		–134.9	[2208]			57.66	[1187]	10.46	[1187]
		–140.78[22]	[1185]						
HBO_2, I	c	–192.56	[1705]						
		–192.77	[1706]						
		–189.0	[555]						
HBO_2, II	c	–190.3	[555]						
HBO_2, monoclinic	c	(–190.6)	[1185]						
HBO_2, orthorhombic	c	(–189.0)	[1185]						
		(–189.13)	[1706]						
$HB(OH)_2$	g	–153.8	[2173]						

1. $\Delta H_0^\circ = -394.9672$ [1830]. 2. $\Delta H_0^\circ = -388.778$ [1618a]. 3. $\Delta H_0^\circ = -379.205$ [1618a]. 4. $\Delta H_0^\circ = -472.461$ [1618a]. 5. $\Delta H_0^\circ = -565.8927$ [1830]. 6. $\Delta H_0^\circ = -563.331$ [1618a]. 7. $\Delta H_0^\circ = -115.8$ [1618a]. 8. $\Delta H_0^\circ = -288.002$* [1618a]. 9. Extrapolated [234] from the equation recommended in [1711] to $T = 300$ °K. 10. $\Delta H_0^\circ = -12.628$ [1618a]. 11. $\Delta H_0^\circ = -4.45$ [1187]. 12. $\Delta H_0^\circ = -5.492$ [1187]. 13. $\Delta H_0^\circ = -21.98$ [1187]. 14. From amorphous boron. 15. $\Delta H_0^\circ = 24.444$ [1618a]. 16. $\Delta H_0^\circ = 11.187$ [1187]. 17. $\Delta H_0^\circ = 22.451$ [1618a]. 18. $\Delta H_0^\circ = 3.462$ [1618a]. 19. $\Delta H_0^\circ = -19.381$* [570]. 20. $\Delta H_0^\circ = -134.9$ [1830]. 21. $\Delta H_0^\circ = -134.175$ [570]. 22. $\Delta H_0^\circ = -140.5$ [1185].

1	2	3		4		5		6	
H_2BOH	g	–70	[2173]						
$H_2B_2O_3$[1]	g	–200.4	[790]						
$H_2B_4O_7$	c			–624.7	[229]				
H_3BO_2	g	–238.4[2]	[1830]			66.1901	[1830]	16.9017	[1830]
		–247[3]	[570]			72.520	[570]		
		–238.6[4]	[1185]			75.46[5]	[1187]	15.65[4]	[1187]
						72.99[6]	[1187]	18.60[6]	[1187]
						66.12	[2485]	16.99	[2485]
		–237.16[7]	[1618a]	–221.9	[1618a]	70.539	[1618a]	15.616	[1618a]
	c	–260.23[8]	[1648]	(–230.3)	[1648]	(21.32)[9]	[1648]		
		(–262.6)[10]	[1185]	(–228.7*)	[229]	(21.21)	[1618a, 1650]	(19.44)	[1618a, 1650]
		(–262.3)	[2390]						
		(–261.7)	[1433]						
		(–261.6)	[2401]						
		(–255.0)	[2401]						
		(–261.47)[11]	[1618a]	(–231.503)	[1618a]				
H_3BO_3[12]	d	(–257.40)	[1436]						
$H_3BO_3 \cdot 504H_2O$	d	–256.02	[1203]						
$H_3B_2O_3$	g	–291	[2172]						
	c	–301.7	[2172]						
$H_3B_3O_6$	g	–545.8	[859]						
		–542.1945[13]	[1830]			83.0481	[1830]	32.8080	[1830]
		–537.5	[2208]						
		–543.0[14]	[1618a]	–508.717	[1618a]	83.047	[1618a]	32.807	[1618a]
Ba	g	(41.74)	[2479]	(34.23)	[2479]	(40.6637)	[2479]		
		(46.641)[15]	[570]			(40.6650)	[570]		
		(41.7)	[1932]			(40.664)	[1589]		
						(40.67)	[1685]		
	c			(32.52*)	[1589]	(16.0*)	[1589]		
						(14.5)	[570]	(6.76)	[570]
						(16.0)	[1685]		
						(16.2*)	[244]		
						(15.50)	[2479]		
Ba^+	g	(168.304)[16]	[570]			42.0424	[570]		
Ba^{2+}	g					40.67	[66]		
	d					(2.3)	[1685]		
$Ba(BF_4)_2$		27.6[17]	[2100]						

BaBi	c	–40.2	[648]						
BaBr	g					64.9	[1685]	8.80	[1685]
	c	–57.7	[1170]						
BaBrH	c	–116.2	[1166]						
$BaBr_2$	g					78.56*	[297]	14.661*	[297]
	c	(–180.8)	[1166]	–174.4*	[323]	35.5*	[323]		
				–175*	[227]	36.2*	[698]		
						34*	[2243]		
$BaBr_2 \cdot 4H_2O$	c	–467*	[230]						
$BaBr_2 \cdot 6H_2O$	c	–611*	[230]						
$Ba(BrO_3)_2$	c	–148.6*	[232]	–118.31*	[177]	(60.5*)	[699]		
$Ba(BrO_3)_2 \cdot H_2O$	c			–192.9*	[323]	68.8	[1685]	52.90	[1685]
$BaCO_3$	c	–295*	[358]			26.8	[1685]	20.40	[1685]
				(–271.55*)	[177]	(24.6*)	[177]		
						(26.1*)	[699]		
BaC_2	c	12.1*	[1529]						
$Ba(CN)_2$	c			–46.7*	[323]	25.7	[323]		
$Ba(CNS)_2$	c	–99*	[693]						
		–93*	[2683]						
$BaCS_3$	c	(–130.1)	[1789a]			11.2^{18}	[1789a]		
BaCl	g			17.5	[227]	62.2	[1685]	8.67	[1685]
		–63.6	[1170]						
	c			–105.3*	[323]	23.4*	[323]		
BaClH		–128.1	[1166]						
$BaCl_2$	g					72.76*	[297]	14.349*	[297]
	c	(–205.2)	[1166]			(30.5*)	[698]		
		(–219.3)	[2375]			(28)	[2243]		
$BaCl_2 \cdot BaF_2$	c	–507.6	[2243]	–49.6*	[229]				
		–508.4	[96]						
$BaCl_2 \cdot 2H_2O$	c			(–309.68)	[190]				
$BaCl_2 \cdot 4H_2O$	c	–487*	[230]						
$BaCl_2 \cdot 6H_2O$	c	–629*	[230]						
$BaCl_2 \cdot K_2Cl_2$	c	$–1.42^{13}$	[685]						

1. HB(–O–)(–O–O–)BH (ring). 2. $\Delta H_0^\circ = -235.4733$. [1830]. 3. $\Delta H_0^\circ = -244.47$ [570]. 4. $\Delta H_0^\circ = -238.22$ (free rotation), –238.34 (impeded rotation) [1187]. 5. Free rotation of OH-groups. 6. Internal rotation barrier of OH-groups of 2,000 *cal/mole*. 7. $\Delta H_0^\circ = -231.294$ [1618a]. 8. $\Delta H_0^\circ = -233.87$ [1648]. 9. Calculated [234] from $\Delta S_{298}^\circ = -110.56$. 10. $\Delta H_0^\circ = -258.93$ [1187]. 11. $\Delta H_0^\circ = -258.231$ [1618a]. 12. $H_3BO_3 \cdot 1000H_2O$; from B(v). 13. $\Delta H_0^\circ = -537.5$ [1830]. 14. $\Delta H_0^\circ = -538.303$ [1618a]. 15. $\Delta H_0^\circ = 46.8$ [570]. 16. $\Delta H_0^\circ = 166.982$ [570]. 17. $T \simeq 550°K$. 18. ΔS_{298}°. 19. From $BaCl_2$ and KCl.

1	2	3		4		5		6	
$Ba(ClO_2)_2$	c			−136.8*	[323]	47.7*	[323]		
				−135.4*	[229]				
$Ba(ClO_3)_2$	c			−133.1*	[323]	53.7*	[323]		
						56.8*	[699]		
$Ba(ClO_4)_2$	c	−205.3	[90]	−127.9*	[323]	57.7*	[323]		
						61.5*	[699]		
$BaCrO_4$	c	(−327)	[481]	−315.95*	[177]	34.7*	[177]		
				−324.0*	[323]	36.7*	[323]		
						37.6*	[699]		
$Ba(CrO_2)_2$	c					36.2*	[251]		
BaF	g			−14.8*	[227]	59.6	[1685]	8.28	[1685]
		−85.2	[1170]						
BaF_2	g	−92.3	[1370]			66.42*	[297]	13.767	[297]
	c	(−286.0)	[890]	(−274.04*)	[176]	(21.5*)	[176]		
				(−272.5*)	[323]	(23.1*)	[323]		
						(23.6*)	[698]		
						(23.03)	[1685]		
$BaGeO_3$. pseudo-wollastonite form	c	−300.0	[149]						
BaH	g			(37.18)	[77]	(52.318)	[77]		
						(52.28)	[1685]	(7.20)	[1685]
$Ba(HCO_3)_2$	c	−472*	[693]						
		−471*	[2683]						
BaHI	c	−98.3	[1166]						
$BaHPO_4$	c			−435.8*	[229]				
$Ba(HS)_2$	c	−126*	[693]						
		−127*	[2683]						
$Ba(HSO_4)_2$	c	−553*	[2683]						
BaH_2	c	(−42.7)	[1166]	−31.6*	[323]				
				−30.9*	[229]				
$BaHfO_3$	c	−429.7	[353]						
BaI	g	−39.4	[1170]						
BaI_2	g					81.98	[297]	14.732	[297]
	c	(−144.7)	[1166]	−143.1*	[323]	40.9*	[323]		
				−148*	[227]	40.0	[1794]		
						40.5*	[698]		
						38	[2243]		

$Ba(IO_3)_2$	c	−249.5	[2457]	−210.94*	[177]				
		−250.7	[617]						
$Ba(IO_3)_2 \cdot H_2O$	c			−211.1*	[323]				
$BaMnO_4$	c			−257*	[323]	36.8*	[323]		
				−236.2*	[177]				
$Ba(MnO_4)_2$	c	−373*	[693]			70.9*	[699]		
$BaMoO_3$	c	−308.7	[171]	−285.0*	[171]				
$BaMoO_4$	c	−375*	[172]	−350*	[172]				
		−373.4*	[170, 172]	−349.6*	[170, 172]	24.2	[319]		
				−349.3	[323]	38.7*	[323]		
$Ba(NO_2)_2$	c			(−126.0*)	[323]	(43.7*)	[323]		
$Ba(NO_3)_2$	c			(−190.06)	[190]	51.2*	[699]	(36.18)	[1685]
BaN_2	c	−43.6[1]	[38]						
$Ba(N_3)_2$	c	(−5.32)	[1356]	30.50	[1356]	29.8	[1356]		
				23.5	[323]	47.7*	[323]		
				23.0	[232]				
BaO	g	−32.6[2]	[366]	129.1	[77]	(56.251)	[77]		
		−31.737[3]	[570]			(56.252)	[570]		
		−29.7[4]	[1015]			(56.2)	[1685]	(7.93)	[1685]
	c	(−139.1)	[1900]	(−132.0)	[1900]	(16.8)	[570, 1685]	(10.82)	[570]
		(−135*)	[358]						
		(−128.8)	[576]						
		(−131.3)	[575]						
		(−133.4)[5]	[570]						
		(−139.06)	[1902]						
$BaO \cdot Fe_2O_3$	c	−306.6	[1939]						
$2BaO \cdot Fe_2O_3$	c	−421.6	[1939]						
$7BaO \cdot 2Fe_2O_3$	c	−1324.5	[1939]						
BaO_2	c	(−153*)	[1045]	−140.5*	[1045]				
		(−151.89)	[76]	−135.8*	[323]	15.7*	[323]		
		(−152.5)	[887]	−133.6*	[229]				
		(−151.1)	[1766]						
$BaO_2 \cdot H_2O$	c			−195*	[323]	25.1*	[323]		
$Ba(OH)_2$	l	−965.06[6]	[280]	−848.66[6]	[280]				
	c	(−949.98)[7]	[280]	−886.14[7]	[280]	124.35[8]	[280]		
		(−258*)	[358]	−204.3*	[249]	24.0*	[249]		
				−204.7*	[323]	22.7*	[323]		
				−199.7*	[229]	24.8*	[699]		

1. $T = 291\ ^\circ K$. 2. $\Delta H_0^\circ = -32.1$ [366]. 3. $\Delta H_0^\circ = -31.213$ [570]. 4. ΔH_0°. 5. $\Delta H_0^\circ = -133.103$ [570]. 6. In *joules/kg-mole*$\cdot 10^6$. 7. In *joules/kg-mole*$\cdot 10^6$. 8. In *joules/(kg-mole*$\cdot ^\circ C) \cdot 10^3$.

1	2	3		4		5		6	
$Ba(OH)_2 \cdot H_2O$	c	−1253.5[1]	[280]	−1333.9[1]	[280]	171.24[2]	[280]		
$Ba(OH)_2 \cdot 3H_2O$	c	−1862.7[1]	[280]	−1616[1]	[280]	211.01[2]	[280]		
$Ba(OH)_2 \cdot 8H_2O$	c			−666.8*	[323]				
		−3363.7[1]	[280]	−2816[1]	[280]	366.76[2]	[280]		
$Ba(ReO_4)_2$	c	−513*	[2683]						
BaS	g	12.0*	[1015]						
	c	(−108)	[1015]	−104.5	[323, 1734]	18.7*	[323]		
		(−110.4)	[1015]	−104.8	[229]	20.8*	[247]		
		(−112.4)	[1068]	−110.4	[1068]	16.3	[1068]		
				−111.1*	[232]	22.0	[1794]		
						18.7	[1685, 1734]	11.80	[1685, 1734]
						21.5	[1789a]		
						20.1*	[698]		
$BaSO_3$	c			−262.4*	[323]	28.6*	[323]		
				−264.5*	[229]				
$BaSO_4$	c			(−324.94*)	[177]	(36.9*)	[177]		
				(−323.5*)[3]	[250]	(31.3*)	[699]		
				(−324.64)	[77]				
BaSe	c			−73.3*	[229]	23.0*	[228]		
						23.7*	[698]		
$BaSeO_3$	c	−249.31	[345. 507]	−232.3	[339]	42.5	[339]		
$BaSeO_4$	c	(−279.2)	[505]	−249.1	[505]	23.06	[505]		
				−253.8*	[323]	36.1*	[323]		
				−248.65	[504]	25.8	[504]		
				−253.7*	[229]	23.1*	[498]	24.12	[498]
$BaSiO_3$	c	(−38.05)[4]	[1681]	−38.2[4]	[1681]	27.2	[246]		
		(−378*)	[2683]	−338.7*	[323]	24.2*	[323]		
		(−381.7)	[776]	−339.1*	[227]	27.2*	[246]		
						26.8	[1773]		
$BaSi_2O_5$	c	−41.3[4]	[1681]	−41.4[4]	[1681]				
				−595.2	[776]				
$Ba_{0.543}Sr_{0.457}TiO_3$	c					27.4	[1685[	23.98	[1685]
$BaSrTiO_4$	c					45.8	[1685]	34.95	[1685]
BaTe	c	−63.5*	[1773]			26;2*	[698]		
$BaTiO_3$	c	−394.6	[431]						
		−394.8	[575]						
$BaTiO_3$, II	c	−397.6	[2243]	−376.4	[2243]	25.82	[2554]	24.49	[1685, 2554]
						25.8	[1685]		

$BaWO_4$	c	(−403.0*)	[170, 172]	−377.9*	[179, 172]				
				−373.6*	[323]	41*	[323]		
$BaZrO_3$	c	−421.1	[350]	−400.5	[350]	29.8	[1685, 1733]	24.31	[1685, 1733]
Ba_2GeO_4,	c	−457.2	[149]						
Ba_2N	c	−53.4	[39]						
Ba_2O	c			−140.4*	[229]				
Ba_2O_2	g	148.6[5]	[1015]						
Ba_2Pb	c	−70.0	[1774]						
Ba_2S_2	g	89.9[5]	[1015]						
Ba_2SiO_4	c	(−64.5)[6]	[1681]	−64.6[2]	[1681]	42.6*	[251]		
		(−541.5)[7]	[776]	−470.6*	[323]	46.4*	[323]		
				−471.0*	[229]	43.5	[1773]		
$Ba_2Si_3O_8$	c	−82.4[4]	[1681]	−82.7[4]	[1681]				
		−980.0	[776]	−925*	[234]				
Ba_2Sn	c	(−90.0)	[1774]						
Ba_2TiO_4	c	−538.0	[2243]	−511.1	[2243]	47.0	[1685, 2555]	36.48	[1685, 2555]
$Ba_3(AsO_4)_2$	c			−768.4*	[229]				
Ba_3Bi_2	c	(−128.1)	[648]						
		(−160.0)	[1774]						
Ba_3GeO_3,									
	c	−607.4	[149]						
Ba_3N_2	c			−75.7*	[229]	36.4	[1678]		
Ba_3P_2	c	−118.0*	[1773]						
$Ba_3(PO_4)_2$	c			−944.4*	[323]	85.1*	[323]		
		−946.5*	[229]						
Ba_3Sb_2	c	(−175)	[1774]						
Ba_3SiO_5	c	−695*	[148]						
Ba_4SiO_6	c	−836*	[148]						
Be	g	(77.90)	[2479]	(68.87)	[2479]				
		(78.255)[8]	[1618a]	(69.231)	[1618a]	(32.545)	[1618a]		
		(78.04)[9]	[1589]	(69.02)	[1589]	(32.55)	[1685]		
		(78.013)[10]	[570]			(32.5452)	[570]		
		(77.9)[11]	[1830]			(32.5451)	[1830]		
	l	2.881	[1618a]	2.381	[1618a]	3.954	[1618a]	3.805	[1618a]
	c					(2.297)	[1830]	(3.932)	[1830]
								(3.93)[12]	[1447a]

1. In *joules/kg-mole*$\cdot 10^6$. 2. In *joules/(kg-mole*$\cdot$°C)$\cdot 10^3$. 3. Recalculated [234] from $(H^\circ_{298})_{diss} = 138.5$ [250] to 145.84 [2245], with the aid of G°_{298} values for SO_3(g) and BaO(c) [2245]. 4. From BaO(c) and $SiO_2(a)$. 5. ΔH°_0. 6. From BaO(c) and $SiO_2(a)$. 7. Calculated [234] from $(H^\circ_{298})_{form}$ from the oxides [776]. 8. $\Delta H^\circ_0 = 77.241$ [1618a]. 9. $\Delta H^\circ_0 = 77.03$ [1589]. 10. $t = 50$°C. 11. $\Delta H^\circ_0 = 76.8874$ [1830]. 12. C_v; $T = 300$ °K.

1	2	3		4		5		6	
Be	c					(2.28)	[570, 1618a, 1685]	(3.93)	[570, 1524, 1589, 1685]
						(2.30)	[1524]	4.19[1]	[370]
Be^{2+}	g					32.56	[66]		
	d			−85.2*	[323]	−55*	[323]		
				−90.7	[801]				
$BeAl_2O_4$	c	−545*[2]	[1618a]	−515.786*	[1618a]	15.843	[1618a]	25.177	[1618a]
BeBr	g	8.8*[3]	[1618a]	−1.447*	[1618a]	54.839	[1618a]	7.719	[1618a]
$BeBr_2$	g					63.83*	[297]	12.134*	[297]
		−57.3[4]	[1618a]	−65.569	[1618a]	66.4	[1618a]	13.036	[1618a]
	l	−85.88	[1618a]	−82.721	[1618a]	28.07	[1618a]	16.50	[1618a]
	c	(−79.4*)	[890]	−84.7*	[227]	29*	[890]		
				−84.6*	[323]	26.1*	[323]		
		(−88.4)	[1618a]	−84.445	[1618a]	25.4	[1618a]	16.50	[1618a]
BeC_2	g					52.405	[2035]	9.869	[2035]
		135[5]	[1618a]	120.917	[1618a]	52.232	[1618a]	9.867	[1618a]
						52.3	[1685]	9.90	[1685]
$Be(CN)_2$	c	7*	[2683]						
$Be(CNS)_2$	c	−10*	[2683]						
$BeCO_3$	c	−241	[481]	−225.8*	[229]				
		−249*	[2683]						
		−234.6	[217]						
BeCl	g	−7[6]	[1830]			51.9099	[1830]	7.5655	[1830]
		−3.898*[7]	[570]			51.892	[570]		
		3.7	[1372]			53.0	[1372]		
		3.0[8]	[1618a]	−3.876	[1618a]	51.986	[1618a]	7.563	[1618a]
BeClF	g	−134.15[9]	[1830]			56.3959	[1830]	10.2088	[1830]
		−124*[10]	[1618a]	−124.832*	[1618a]	55.938	[1618a]	9.667	[1618a]
$BeCl_2$	g	−84[11]	[1830]			57.8878	[1830]	11.3383	[1830]
		−84.9[12]	[1378]			43.2[13]	[1378]		
		−84[14]	[488]			57.10	[297]	11.262*	[297]
		−86.3[15]	[1618a]	−86.999	[1618a]	57.912	[1618a]	11.328	[1618a]
		−85.351[16]	[570]			57.762	[570]		
	l	−115.384	[1618a]	−104.888	[1618a]	20.339	[1618a]	11.48	[1618a]
	c	(−118.03)[17]	[570]	−111.7*	[227]	15.0	[570]	17.0	[570]
		(−109.2)	[2375]	−111.8*	[323]	20.5*	[323]		
		(−118.0)	[1633]			21.5	[1773]		
		(−118.25)	[2532]			23*	[890]		

						19.76[18]	[1853]	15.50[18]	[1853]
						18.12[19]	[1853]	14.92[19]	[1853]
		(−117.8)	[1618a]	−106.131	[1618a]	16.43	[1618a]	11.331	[1618a]
$BeCl_2 \cdot H_2O$	c	−203*	[230]						
$BeCl_2 \cdot 2H_2O$	c	−281*	[230]						
$BeCl_2 \cdot 4H_2O$	c			−376*	[323]	58.1*	[323]		
				−371.0*	[229]				
$BeCl_2 \cdot 6H_2O$	c	−587*	[230]						
$Be(ClO_3)_2$	c	−92*	[2683]						
$Be(ClO_4)_2$	c	−105*	[2683]						
$BeCrO_4$	c	−280	[481]						
$Be(CrO_2)_2$	c					22.8*	[251]		
BeF	g	−49.6[20]	[1830]			45.1523	[1830]	7.1397	[1830]
		−52.6	[1375]			49.13	[1680, 1685]	7.13	[1685]
		−48.3	[1375]			51.1	[1375]		
		−63.942*[21]	[570]			49.151	[570]		
		−45[22]	[1377]						
		−49.678[23]	[1618a]	−56.431	[1618a]	49.152	[1618a]	7.140	[1618a]
BeF_2	g	−186.063[24]	[570]			52.329	[570]		
		−191.2	[1371]			52.4	[1371]		
		−191.3	[1371]			52.38	[297]	10.170*	[297]
		−187.5[25]	[1618a]	−188.681	[1618a]	54.689	[1618a]	11.18	[1618a]
BeF_2	g	−191.2[26]	[1830]			52.3617	[1830]	9.1338	[1830]
		−176.7	[1520]			47.8[27]	[862]		
	l	−240.926	[1618a]	−230.134	[1618a]	14.529	[1618a]	9.857	[1618a]
	c	−241.2[28]	[570]	−225*	[227]	10.80	[570]	12.0	[570]
		−235*	[230]			10.7*	[225]	14.7	[228]
		−242*	[583]			13.7*	[1794]		
		−241.2[29]	[275]			17*	[890]		
		−227.0*	[890]						
		−180*[30]	[584]						
		−177*[31]	[584]						
		−187.0	[1521]						

1. $t = 50\ ^\circ C$. 2. $\Delta H_0^\circ = -541.322^*$ [1618a]. 3. $\Delta H_0^\circ = 10.062^*$ [1618a]. 4. $\Delta H_0^\circ = -54.173$ [1618a]. 5. $\Delta H_0^\circ = 133.535$ [1618a]. 6 $\Delta H_0^\circ = -7.5524$ [1830]. 7. $\Delta H_0^\circ = -4.45^*$ [570]. 8. $\Delta H_0^\circ = 2.447$ [1618a]. 9. $\Delta H_0^\circ = -133.7733$ [1830]. 10. $\Delta H_0^\circ = -123.682^*$ [1618a]. 11. $\Delta H_0^\circ = -83.9380$ [1830]. 12. Calculated [245] from $(\Delta H_{298}^\circ)_{subl} = 31.1$ [1378] and $(\Delta H_{298}^\circ)BeCl_2(c) = -118.0$ [570]. 13. $(\Delta S_{298}^\circ)_{subl}$. 14. Calculated [234] from $(\Delta H_{298}^\circ)_{subl} = 34$ [488]. 15. $\Delta H_0^\circ = -86.235$ [1618a]. 16. $\Delta H_0^\circ = -85.268$ [570]. 17. $\Delta H_0^\circ = -118.268$ [570]. 18. α'-phase. 19. β-phase. 20. $\Delta H_0^\circ = -50.1568$ [1830]. 21. $\Delta H_0^\circ = -64.5^*$ [570]. 22. Temperature not stated. 23. $\Delta H_0^\circ = -50.237$ [1618a]. 24. $\Delta H_0^\circ = -185.721$ [570]. 25. $\Delta H_0^2 = -187.573$ [1618a]. 26. $\Delta H_0^\circ = -190.8666$ [1830]. 27. $(\Delta S_{298}^\circ)_{subl}$. 28. $\Delta H_0^\circ = -240.521$ [570]. 29. β-Cristoballite. 30. Calculated [234] from $(\Delta H_0^\circ)_{subl} = 55.2$ [584] and $(\Delta H_{298}^\circ)BeF_2(c)$ [230]. 31. Calculated from (ΔH_0°) subl $= 58.0$ [584] and $(\Delta H_{298}^\circ)BeF_2(c)$[230].

1	2	3		4		5		6	
BeF_2	c	58.1[1]	[1862]						
		−242.3[2]	[1618a]	−230.978	[1618a]	12.752	[1618a]	12.375	[1618a]
$BeFe_2O_4$	c	−325*	[464]						
		−229	[481]						
BeH	g	(76.222)[3]	[570]			(42.235)	[570]		
		(78.1020)[4]	[1830]			(42.2358)	[1830]	(6.9841)	[1830]
						(42.19)	[1685]	(6.97)	[1685]
		(76.768)[5]	[1618a]	69.507	[1618a]	(42.236)	[1618a]	(6.985)	[1618a]
BeHO	g	−25*[6]	[1618a]	−28.25*	[1618a]	53.285	[1618a]	8.229	[1618a]
BeH_2	c	30[7]	[1618a]	27.656	[1618a]	41.35	[1618a]	7.259	[1618a]
	c	0.4*	[2683]						
BeH_2O_2	c	−216.6	[1618a]	−195.762	[1618a]	12.6	[1618a]	15.35	[1618a]
$Be(HCO_3)_2$	c	−413*	[2683]						
$Be(HS)_2$	c	−49*	[2683]						
$Be(HSO_4)_2$	c	−478*	[2683]						
BeI	g	24.7[8]	[1618a]	12.612	[1618a]	56.703	[1618a]	7.886	[1618a]
BeI_2	g	−20.3[5]	[1618a]	−32.346	[1618a]	67.49*	[297]	12.569*	[297]
						70.441	[1618a]	13.364	[1618a]
	l	−47.446	[1618a]	−48.149	[1618a]	32.397	[1618a]	17.0	[1618a]
	c	(−39.4*)	[890]	−50.8*	[227]	31*	[890]		
				−51*	[323]	31.5*	[323]		
		(−50.6)	[1618a]	−50.231	[1618a]	28.8	[1618a]	17.0	[1618a]
$BeMoO_4$	c	(−316.3*)	[170, 172]	−293.6*	[170, 172]				
				−306*	[323]	26*	[323]		
BeN	g	150.109*[10]	[570]			48.419	[570]		
		101.981[11]	[1618a]	94.615	[1618a]	49.872	[1618a]	7.192	[1618a]
$Be(NH_2)_2$	c	−55*	[2683]						
$Be(NO_2)_2$	c	−122*	[2683]						
$Be(NO_3)_2$	c	−162*	[2683]						
BeO	g	(11)*[12]	[54]						
		(30.4445)[13]	[1830]			(47.2088)	[1830]	(7.0465)	[1830]
		(30.158)[14]	[570]			(47.206)	[570]		
		(30.2)[15]	[366]			(47.20)	[1685]	(7.04)	[1685]
		(31.0)[16]	[1618a]	24.91	[1618a]	(47.208)	[1618a]	(7.046)	[1618a]
	l	−129.562	[1618a]	−123.975	[1618a]	8.042	[1618a]	6.10	[1618a]
	c	(−143.1)[17]	[1830]	(−136.1)	[1045]	(3.4926)	[1830]	(6.090)	[1830]
		(−143.1)[18]	[570]			(3.37)	[142, 570, 1781]	(6.11)	[570]

		(−140.93)	[545]					(6.102)	[2595]
		(−143.1)[19]	[1041, 1618a]	(−136.122)	[1618a]	(3.378)	[1618a]	(6.10)	[1618a]
BeOBe(OH)$_2$, precipitated	c			−338*	[323]	16.7*	[323]		
BeOH	g	−23	[718]						
BeO$_2$	c	−142	[2683]						
BeO_2^{2-}	d			−155.3	[323]	−27*	[323]		
Be(OH)$_2$	g	−158	[718]						
		−156.7[20]	[1830]			53.2425	[1830]	10.2849	[1830]
	c	158.5[21]	[1618a]	−151.188	[1618a]	57.969	[1618a]	12.312	[1618a]
	c	−161	[718]			11.2	[799]		
Be(OH)$_2$, α	c	(−215.75)	[801]	−195.15	[801]	13.4	[801]	15.35	[801]
				−196.2*	[323]	13.3*	[323]		
Be(OH)$_2$, β	c	(−216.5)	[801]	−195.65	[801]	12.6	[801, 1618a]	15.35	[801, 1618a]
		(216.6)	[1618a]	−195.762	[1618a]				
				−195.8[22]	[249]	11.9*[23]	[249]		
				−194.8*	[229]				
Be(OH)$_2$, γ	c			−195.5*	[229]				
Be(OH)$_2$, precipitated	c	−213.1	[801]	−194.3	[801]	20	[801]		
Be(OH)$_3$	d	−229.4	[801]						
$Be(OH)_4^{2-}$	d	−266.7	[801]						
Be(ReO$_4$)$_2$	c	−429*	[2683]						
BeS	c			−55.9*	[323]	9.3*	[323]		
				−55.2*	[229]	7.4*	[247]		
						8.4*	[1953]		
BeSO$_3$	c	−219*	[2683]						
		−234.9*	[1172]						
BeSO$_4$	c	(−286.41)	[1675]	−260.2*	[323]	21.5*	[323]		
				−259.6*	[229]	20.0*	[228]		
				−260.4[24]	[234]	18.62	[2517]	(20.48)	[2517]
BeSO$_4$·H$_2$O	c			−322.1*	[229]				
BeSO$_4$·2H$_2$O	c			−379.3*	[229]				
BeSO$_4$·4H$_2$O	c			−492.4*	[229]				
				−490.54	[190]				
BeSe	c					9.5*	[228]		

1. $(\Delta H^\circ_{298})_{subl}$. 2. $\Delta H^\circ_0 = -241.746$ [1618a]. 3. $\Delta H^\circ_0 = 75.632$ [570]. 4. $\Delta H^\circ_0 = 77.5158$ [1830]. 5. $\Delta H^\circ_0 = 76.181$ [1618a]. 6. $\Delta H^\circ_0 = -24.866$* [1618a]. 7. $\Delta H^\circ_0 = 30.409$ [1618a]. 8. $\Delta H^\circ_0 = 24.588$ [1618a]. 9. $\Delta H^\circ_0 = -20.018$ [1618a]. 10. $\Delta H^\circ_0 = 149.536$* [570]. 11. $\Delta H^\circ_0 = 101.4$ [1618a]. 12. Calculated [234] from $(\Delta H^\circ_0)_{subl} = 154.6$ [54] and (ΔH°_{298})BeO(c) [2245]. 13. $\Delta H^\circ_0 = 29.8740$ [570]. 14. $\Delta H^\circ_0 = 29.587$ [570]. 15. $\Delta H^\circ_0 = 30.2$ [366]. 16. $\Delta H^\circ_0 = 30.429$ [1618a]. 17. $\Delta H^\circ_0 = -142.2847$ [1830]. 18. $\Delta H^\circ_0 = -142.281$ [570]. 19. 19. $\Delta H^\circ_0 = -142.282$ [1618a]. 20. $\Delta H^\circ_0 = -154.5048$ [1830]. 21. $\Delta H^\circ_0 = -156.683$ [1618a]. 22. Recalculated [234] from $\Delta H^\circ_{298} = -206.8$ [249] to -216.8 [2245]. 23. Modification not stated. 24. Calculated with the aid of values recommended in [250] and [2245].

1	2	3		4		5		6	
BeSe	c					9.5	[228]		
$BeSeO_4$	c	−213.24	[525]						
$BeSeO_4 \cdot 2H_2O$	c	−360.82	[525]						
$BeSeO_4 \cdot 4H_2O$	c	−505.54	[525]						
$BeSiO_3$	c	−339*	[2683]			12.9*	[228]		
$BeWO_4$	c	−342.9*	[170, 172]	−318.9*	[170, 172]	27.6	[1618a]	23.27	[1618a]
Be_2C	l	−3.798	[1618a]	−5.416	[1618a]	11.345	[1618a]	10.337	[1618a]
	c	−21.8*	[2163]	−21.2*	[2163]				
		−32.8	[386]			4.36	[386]		
		−21.7	[1618a]	−21.098	[1618a]	3.90	[1618a]	10.377	[1618a]
Be_2Cl_4	g	44[1]	[488]						
	g	−185.0[2]	[1618a]	−171.519*	[1618a]	65.923	[1618a]	17.301	[1618a]
Be_2O	g	−8*	[2528]						
		−15*[3]		−22.064*	[1618a]	52.754	[1618a]	9.788	[1618a]
Be_2O^{2+}	d			−218*	[323]				
Be_2O_2	g	−104.5[4]	[1830]			59.9879	[1830]	12.3009	[1830]
		−98*[5]	[1618a]	−99.667*	[1618a]	59.156	[1618a]	11.792	[1618a]
$Be_2O_3^{2-}$	d			−298*	[323]				
Be_2SiO_4	c			−208.7*	[229]	(15.37)	[1685]		
Be_2TiO_4	c					17.8*	[228]		
Be_3N_2	l	−113.536	[1618a]	−104.562	[1618a]	22.51	[1618a]	15.405	[1618a]
	c	(−135.0)	[31]	−122.5*	[229]				
		(−134.7*)	[2628]						
		(−140.3)	[2720]						
		(−140.6)	[1618a]	−128.492	[1618a]	12.0	[1618a]	15.405	[1618a]
Be_3O_3	g	−255.3[6]	[1830]			64.2520	[1830]	15.3690	[1830]
		−252*[7]	[1618a]	−247.515*	[1618a]	65.304	[1618a]	15.167	[1618a]
Be_4O_4	g	−380.4[8]	[1830]			70.8054	[1830]	21.1897	[1830]
		−380*[9]	[1618a]	−369.614*	[1618a]	72.292	[1618a]	21.364	[1618a]
Be_5O_5	g	−505*[10]	[1618a]	−488.104*	[1618a]	77.24	[1618a]	26.773	[1618a]
Be_6O_6	g	−636*[11]	[1618a]	−612.538*	[1618a]	82.00	[1618a]	31.459	[1618a]
$Be_{13}Pu$	c			35.7	[42]				
$Be_{13}U$	c	−39.3	[187]			41.5	[2207]		
$H_2Be(OH)_4$	c			−292.57*	[6]				
Bi	g	(47.500)	[2479]	(38.231)	[2479]				
		(49.5)[12]	[2358]	(40.2)	[2358]	44.669	[2358]	4.968	[2358]
		(49.56)	[1589]						
	c					(13.58)	[2479]	(6.11)	[2479]
						(13.56)	[1100, 2358]	(6.10)	[2358]

						(13.51)	[1589]	(6.20)	[1589, 1685]
						(13.5)	[1685]	(6.151)[13]	[1251]
Bi^+	g	(219.13)[14]	[2358]						
Bi^{2+}	g	(605.4)[15]	[2358]						
Bi^{3+}	g	(1196.4)[16]	[2358]			41.93	[66]		
	d			19.8	[2358]				
Bi^{4+}	g	(2242.9)[17]	[2358]						
Bi^{5+}	g	(3535.9)[18]	[2358]						
Bi^{6+}	g	(5574)[19]	[2358]						
Bi_2	g	(55.300)	[2479]	(43.899)	[2479]				
		(53.12)[20]	[1589]						
		(52.72)	[713]						
		(52.5)	[2358]						
$BiAsO_4$	c			−148	[2358]				
BiBr	g					(63.6)	[1685]	8.78	[1685]
$BiBr^{2+}$	d			−8.1	[2358]				
$BiBr_2^+$	d			−35.9	[2358]				
$BiBr_3$	c	−65*	[2385]					26	[2358]
		−60*	[230]						
		−58*	[583]						
		−59.0*	[1773]						
		−63	[1063]						
	d			−63.3	[2358]				
$BiBr_4^-$	d			−90.2	[2358]				
BiCl	g	(7*)	[1062]			(60.9)	[1685]	8.62	[1685]
	c	−30.4	[1078]	−24.0	[1078]	22	[1078]		
		−31.2	[2358]	−25.9	[2358]	22.6	[2358]		
$BiCl^{2+}$	d			−14.64	[2358]				
$BiCl_2^+$	d			−49.1	[2358]				
$BiCl_3$	g	(−63.5)[21]	[2358]	(−61.2)	[2358]	(85.74)	[2358]	(19.04)	[2358]
						(85.4)	[1685]	(19.02)	[1685, 2484]
						(85.24)	[2484]		
	c	(−90.6)	[2358]	(−75.3)	[2358]	(42.3)	[2358]	25	[2358]
				(−73.6)	[1078]	(36.4)	[1078]		
						(36.3)	[1685]		

1. $(\Delta H^\circ_{298})_{subl}$. 2. $\Delta H^\circ_0 = -182.956$ [1618a]. 3. $\Delta H^\circ_0 = -15.399$* [1618a]. 4. $\Delta H^\circ_0 = -104.3538$ [1830]. 5. $\Delta H^\circ_0 = -97.716$ [1618a]. 6. $\Delta H^\circ_0 = -253.8171$ [1830]. 7. $\Delta H^\circ_0 = -250.668$* [1618a]. 8. $\Delta H^\circ_0 = -378.1601$ [1830]. 9. $\Delta H^\circ_0 = -377.929$* [1618a]. 10. $\Delta H^\circ_0 = -502.035$* [1618a]. 11. $\Delta H^\circ_0 = -632.101$* [1618a]. 12. $\Delta H^\circ_0 = 49.56$ [2358]. 13. $T = 273$ °K. 14. $\Delta H^\circ_0 = 217.65$ [2358]. 15. $\Delta H^\circ_0 = 602.5$ [2358]. 16. $\Delta H^\circ_0 = 1192.0$ [2358]. 17. $\Delta H^\circ_0 = 2237.0$ [2358]. 18. $\Delta H^\circ_0 = 3528.5$ [2358]. 19. $\Delta H^\circ_0 = 5565$ [2358]. 20. ΔH°_0. 21. $\Delta H^\circ_0 = -63.32$ [2358].

1	2	3		4		5		6	
$BiCl_4^-$	melt			−6.56	[409]				
	d			−115.1	[2358]				
				−114.2*	[323]				
BiD	g					52.68	[1685]	7.18	[1685]
BiF	g			−0.9*	[227]	58.2	[1685]	8.19	[1685]
BiF_3	c	−216*	[583]						
		−212*	[1624]						
		−183*	[2358]						
BiH	g			37.0*	[227]	51.27	[1685]	7.00	[1685]
BiH_3	g	66.4	[2259]						
BiI	g					(65.4)	[1685]	8.84	[1685]
BiI^{2+}	d			3.8	[2358]				
BiI_3	g					99.77	[1065]	19.65	[1065]
	c	−26*	[2358]	−41.9	[2358]	55.9	[1065]		
		−24.0*	[890]						
BiI_4^-	d			−49.9	[2358]				
$Bi_{0.25}K_{0.75}$	c	−13.25	[1589]						
$Bi_{0.25}Li_{0.75}$	c	−13.4[1]	[1589]						
$Bi_{0.50}Li_{0.50}$	c	−9.2*[2]	[1589]						
$BiLi_3$	c	(−39.5)	[648]						
		(−55.5)	[2625]						
$Bi_{0,7}Mn_{0,6}$	c	−7.35[3]	[1589]						
BiMn	c	−4.7	[653]						
$Bi(NO_3)_3 \cdot 5H_2O$	c	−478.7	[24]						
$Bi_{0,25}Na_{0.75}$	c	−11.4[4]	[1589]						
$Bi_{0.50}Na_{0.50}$	c	−7.7[5]	[1589]						
$BiNa_3$	c	(−45.5)	[2625]						
		(−48.2)	[377]						
BiO	g			−11.1*	[229]	58.9	[1685]	7.80	[1685]
	c			−43.5*	[323]	17*	[323]		
				−43.2*	[229]				
BiO^+	d			(−35.0)	[2358]				
BiOBr	c			−71.0	[2358]				
BiOCl	c	(−87.7)	[2358]	(−77.0)	[2358]	(28.8)	[2358]		
$BiOH^{2+}$	d			−35.0	[2358]				
$BiONO_3$	c			−67.0	[2358]				

BiOOH	c			−88.4*	[323]				
				−88.0	[2358]				
$Bi(OH)_2Cl$	c			−128.71	[2358]				
$Bi(OH)_3$	c	(−170.0)	[2358]	−137*	[323]	24.6*	[323]		
				−138.55*	[176]	29.8*	[176]		
				−138.6*	[229]				
$Bi_{0.547}Pb_{0.453}$	l							7.45^{6}	[1589]
BiS	g	43	[2358]	29	[2358]	68	[2358]		
BiS^{+}	g	229	[2358]						
$Bi_{0.50}Sb_{0.50}$	c	0*	[1589]						
BiSe	g	42.0	[2358]						
BiTe	g	42.8	[2358]						
$Bi_{0.6}Tl_{0.4}$	c							6.5	[1589]
$BiTl_4$	c	−4.0	[2625]			79.2	[1775]		
Bi_2Mg_3	c	(−40.5)	[1779, 2625]						
$Bi_2O_2SeO_3$	c	−229.7	[24]						
Bi_2O_3	c	(−137.16)	[2358]	(−118.0)	[2358]	(36.2)	[1685, 2358]	(27.13)	[1685. 2358]
		(−138.1)	[1292]						
Bi_2O_4	c			−109*	[323]				
Bi_2O_5	c					35.7*	[1480]		
Bi_2S_3	c	(−34.2)	[2358]	(−33.6)	[2358]	(47.9)	[480, 2358]	29.2	[2358]
		(−42.2*)	[2625]			(37.2*)	[2625]	29.15	[2625]
		(−36.4)	[25]			(37.1*)	[869]		
$Bi_2(SO_4)_3$	c	(−608.1)	[2358]	−617.5*	[229]				
		(−438.1*)	[1172]						
Bi_2Se_3	c	−41.1	[180]						
		−31.0*	[4]	−25.4*	[4]	38.6	[4]		
		−13.9	[1292]						
Bi_2Te_3	c	−18.5	[2358]	−18.4	[2358]	62.36	[2358]	28.8	[3121]
		−26.4	[4]	−21.2	[4]	45.6*	[4]	37.1	[869]
		−8*	[1292]			73.2	[180]		
		-4.88^{7}	[686]	-3.76^{7}	[686]	-1.67^{7}	[686]	$3.0 \cdot 10^{-2} + 2.0 \cdot 10^{-5} T^{7}$	[869]
Bi_3Tl_2	c	−3.0	[2625]			77.0	[1775]		
Bi_4U_3	c	−98.1	[2207]			58.5	[2207]		
$Bi_6O_6^{6+}$	d			−220.6	[2358]				
$Bi_6O_6(OH)_3^{3+}$	d			−379.6	[2358]				
$Bi_6(OH)_{12}^{6+}$	d			−561.9	[2358]				

1. $BiLi_3$ phase. 2. BiLi phase. 3. In *cal/g-atom*. 4. $BiNa_3$ phase. 5. BiNa phase. 6. $T = 400$ °K. 7. $t = 400$ °C; 0.4 Bi (l) + 0.6 Te(c) = $Bi_{0.4}Te_{0.6}$(c).

1	2	3		4		5		6	
$Bi_9(OH)_{20}^{7+}$	d			−951.5	[2358]				
$Bi_9(OH)_{21}^{6+}$	d			−1003.8	[2358]				
$Bi_9(OH)_{22}^{5+}$	d			−1056.9	[2358]				
$HBi(OH)_4$	d			−195.20*	[6]				
$H_3Bi(OH)_6$	d			−308.50*	[6]				
BkO_2, cubic	c			20.6	[2078]				
				21.2	[2662]				
Br	g	(23.049)[1]	[1186]	(19.327)	[1186]	(41.8052)	[1186]		
		(26.760)	[2479]	(19.699)	[2479]	(41.8052)	[570]		
		(26.730)[2]	[568]	(19.690)	[568]	(41 803)	[568, 1618a]		
		(26.741)[3]	[2358]	(19.700)	[2358, 1618a]	(41.805)	[2358]		
		(26.740)	[1618a]			(41.8)	[1685]		
Br^+	g	(301.183)[4]	[568]	292.523	[568]	42.247	[568]		
		(301.41)	[570]						
Br^-	g	(−52.310)[5]	[568]	−57.042	[568]	(39.049)	[568]	19.7	[1685]
		(−55.91)	[570]			(39.0504)	[570]		
						(39.06)	[66]		
	d	(−29.05)	[570]	(−24.85)	[570]	(19.7)	[570]	(−33.9)	[570]
		(−28.4)	[91]						
		(−28.40)	[568]						
Br^{2+}	g	(804.0)[6]	[568]						
		(800.7)	[570]						
Br^{3+}	g	(1631.8)[6]	[568]						
		(1630.0)	[570]						
Br^{4+}	g	(2723)[6]	[568]						
		(2789)	[570]						
Br^{5+}	g	(4100)[6]	[568]						
Br^{6+}		6143[6]	[568]						
Br^{7+}	g	8519[6]	[568]						
Br^{8+}	g	12964[6]	[568]						
Br_2	g	(7.387)[7]	[568, 1618a]	(0.749)	[568, 1618a]	(58.645)	[568]	(8.617)	[568]
		(7.7)	[1896]			(58.63)	[1896]	(8.616)	[1618a]
		(7.45)	[2479]	(0.773)	[2479]	(58.647)	[1186, 1618a]	(8.62)	[1186, 1685]
		(7.434)	[1255]			(58.65)	[1685]	(8.50)	[2243]
						(58.648)	[570]		
						(58.62)	[1514]		

	l					(36.384)	[1514]	18.089	[1514]
						(36.25)	[2479]	17.00	[2479]
						(36.7)	[1680]	18.09	[568, 1685]
						(36.496)	[1618a]	18.077	[1618a]
	d	(−0.62)	[2358]	0.94	[2358]	31.2	[2358]		
		(−1.1*)	[323]	0.977*	[323]				
		(−0.20)	[2713]	1.38	[2713]	31.1	[2713]		
		(−0.2)	[568]						
Br_2	g	256.4*[6]	[568]			(36.38)	[568]		
		253.5	[2358]						
Br_2^{2+}	g	706*[6]	[568]			(36.4)	[1685]		
$Br_2 \cdot 10H_2O$	l	(−700.0)	[568]						
Br_3	g	−3.8[8]	[1074]						
	d	(−31.17)	[2358]	(−25.59)	[2358]	51.5	[2358]		
		(−30.1)	[568]	−25.27*	[323]				
Br_5^-	d	(−34.0)	[2358]	−24.8	[2358]	75.7	[2358]		
		(−33.7)	[568]						
BrCN	g					(59.367)	[2037]	11.228	[2037]
BrCl	g	(−3.55)[9]	[568]	(−0.178)	[568]	(57.34)	[568, 1685]	8.36	[568, 1186]
		(−0.212)[10]	[1186]	(−0.620)	[1186]	(57.338)	[1186]	8.38	[1685]
		(−3.518)[11]	[570]	(−0.187)	[1184]	(57.342)	[570]		
		(3.50)	[2358]			(57.339)	[1008]	8.384	[1008]
		(3.53)	[1943]			(57.325)	[1943]	8.362	[1943]
		(3.48)[12]	[1618a]	(−0.247)	[1618a]	(57.337)	[1618a]	8.363	[1618a]
$BrCl^+$	g	261[6]	[568]						
		261.0	[2358]						
$BrCl^-$	d			−35.0	[2358]				
BrD	g	−8.352[13]	[568]	−12.331	[568]	48.846	[568]	6.983	[568]
		−8.929[14]	[570]			48.848	[570]		
BrF	g	−18.361[15]	[1186]	−18.705	[1186]	54.700	[1186, 1618a]	7.88	[568, 1186]
		−10.131[16]	[568]	−13.794	[568]	54.70	[568, 1685]	7.87	[1685]
		−17.7	[1850]	−18.0	[1850]	54.703	[1008]	7.869	[1008]
		−14.007[17]	[1618a]	−17.669	[1618a]	54.702	[570]	7.877	[1618a]
BrF^+	g	263.8[6]	[568]						
BrF_3	g	−61.1[18]	[568]	−54.849	[568]	69.9	[568, 1685]	15.9	[568]
		−61.09[19]	[2358]			69.89	[2358]	15.92	[2358]

1. $\Delta H_0^\circ = 22.73$ [1186]. 2. $\Delta H_0^\circ = 28.178$ [568]. 3. $\Delta H_0^\circ = -28.188$ [2358]. 4. $\Delta H_0^\circ = 301.15$ [568]. 5. $\Delta H_0^\circ = -49.38$ [568]. 6. ΔH_0°. 7. $\Delta H_0^\circ = 10.921$ [568]; 10.922 [1618a]. 8. $Br_2 + Br^- = Br_3^-$. 9. $\Delta H_0^\circ = -5.330$ [568]. 10. $\Delta H_0^\circ = -0.20$ [1186]. 11. $\Delta H_0^\circ = -5.297$ [2342]. 12. $\Delta H_0^\circ = 5.259$ [1618a]. 13. $\Delta H_0^\circ = -6.47$ [568]. 14. $\Delta H_0^\circ = -7.043$ [570]. 15. $\Delta H_0^\circ = -18.3$ [1186]; −19.983 ($^{79}Br^{19}F$); −19.528 ($^{81}Br^{19}F$) [1008]. 16. $\Delta H_0^\circ = -8.302$ [2342]. 17. $\Delta H_0^\circ = -12.178$ [1618a]. 18. $\Delta H_0^\circ = -58.424$ [568]. 19. $\Delta H_0^\circ = -58.41$ [2358].

1	2	3		4		5		6	
BrF_3		−82*	[837]			69.905	[977]	15.943	[977]
						71.57	[2074]	15.94	[1685]
		−61.099[1]	[1618a]	−54.831	[1618a]	69.872	[1618a]	15.893	[1618a]
	l	−72.45	[568]	−58.051	[568]	42.57	[568]	29.78	[568, 1685]
		−71.9	[2358]	−57.5	[2358]	42.6	[1685. 2358]		
		−64.8	[1850]	−55.2	[1850]	42.57	[2074]	29.8*	[2074]
		−75	[2461]	−57	[2451]				
BrF_3, rhombic	c	−73.797[2]	[568]						
BrF_5	g	−124.0[3]	[1186]	−101.9	[1186]	76.44	[1186]	23.93	[1186]
		−102.5[4]	[568]	−83.712	[568]	76.3	[568]	23.8	[568]
		−102.5[5]	[2358]	−83.8	[2358]	76.50	[2358]	23.81	[2358]
		−106.2	[1074]	−84.1	[1074]	77.96[6]	[2454]	24.49[6]	[2454]
				−103.8*	[232]	76.4	[1685]	23.70	[2454]
						77.84[6]	[1860]	24.38[6]	[1860]
		−102.467[7]	[1618a]	−83.72	[1618a]	76.435	[1618a]	23.93	[1618a]
	l	−109.6	[2358]	−84.1	[2358]	(53.8)	[2358]		
		−110.1	[568]			(36.384)	[1514]	18.089	[1514]
BrI	g					61.752	[1008]	8.721	[1008]
		9.740[8]	[1618a]	0.866	[1618a]	61.834	[1618a]	8.723	[1618a]
BrI_2^-	d	−30.6	[2358]	−26.3	[2358]	47.2	[2358]		
BrN	g	71.883[9]	[1618a]	67.357	[1618a]	56.256	[1618a]	7.819	[1618a]
BrO	g	30.026[10]	[528]	25.847	[528]	56.71	[528]	7.68	[528]
		30.06[11]	[2358]			56.75	[2358]	7.67	[2358]
						55.7	[1685]	7.75	[1685]
						56.713	[570]		
	d	−23.05	[1850]	−8.2	[1850]	8.5[12]	[1850]		
		−22.5	[2358]	−8;0	[2358]	10	[2358]		
		−22.6	[2713]	−7.8	[2713]	8.8	[2713]		
		−23,6	[568]	−8.0*	[323]				
BrO_2	l			0.7*	[229]				
	c	12.5	[2144]						
		12.5	[568]						
		11.6	[2358]						
BrO_3^-	d	(−20.0)	[2358]	(0.4)	[2358]	(39.0)	[2358]		
		(−18.3)	[1950]	(2.1)	[1950]	(38.5)	[1685]		
		(−17.6)	[568]	(5.0*)	[323]	(38.5*)	[323]		
BrT	g	−8.424[13]	[568]	−12.349	[568]	49.665	[568]	7.027	[568]
		−8.999[14]	[570]			49.667	[570]		

Br_2Cl	d	–40.7	[2358]	–30.7	[2358]	29.5	[2358]		
Br_2Cl^-	g	–1.7[15]	[1075]						
HBr	g	(–8.16)	[568]	(–12.238)	[568]	(47.464)	[568]	(6.965)	[568]
		(–8.70)[16]	[2358]	(–12.77)	[2358]	(47.463)	[2358]		
		(–12.5)[17]	[1686]	(–13.08)	[2243]				
		(–8.71)[18]	[1784]	(–13.25)	[1686]				
		(–8.74)[19]	[570]			(47.468)	[570]		
		(–8.66)[20]	[1618a]	(–12.727)	[1618a]	(47.437)	[1618a]	(6.964)	[1618a]
	d	(–29.05)	[2358]	(–24.85)	[2358]	(19.7)	[2358]	(–33.9)	[2358]
		(–28.40)	[568]						
$HBr \cdot 3000H_2O$	d	(–29.05)	[2498]						
HBr^+	g	261	[1214]						
		261.7	[568]						
		260.7	[2358]						
$HBrI_2$	d	–30.6	[2385]	–26.3	[2358]	47.2	[2358]		
HBrO	g	–19	[568]						
	d	–27.0	[2358]	–19.7	[2358]	34	[2358]		
		–29.4	[2713]	–19.5	[2713]	25.4	[2713]		
		–30.4	[568]	–19.9*	[323]				
$HBrO_3$	c					27.7*	[251]		
	d	(–20.0)	[2358]	0.4	[2358]	39.0	[2358]		
				5.0	[323]				
C	g	(171.291)[21]	[2358]	(160.040)	[2074]	(37.7597)	[2358]	(4.9805)	[2358]
		(170.913)[22]	[570]			(37.7613)	[155, 570]		
		(170.890)	[2479]			(37.76)	[1685]		
		(171.3009)[23]	[1830]			(37.7612)	[1830]	(4.9807)	[1830]
		(170.9)	[1879]						
		(170.886)[24]	[1618a]	(160.033)	[1618a]	(37.761)	[1618a]	(4.981)	[1618a]
C, diamond	c	(0.4533)[25]	[2358]	(0.6930)	[2358]	(0.568)	[1096, 2358]	(1.4615)	[2358]
		(0.453)[26]	[570]			(0.585)	[1685]	(1.45)	[1685]
C, amorphous	a	3.95	[266]			(0.5664)	[2593]	(1.462)	[2593]
C, graphite	c					1.3718	[1830]	2.038	[1618a, 1830, 2358]
						1.36	[1685]	2.05	[1685]
						1.372	[2358]		

1. $\Delta H_0^\circ = -58.406$ [1618a]. 2. ΔH_0°. 3. $\Delta H_0^\circ = -122$ [1186]. 4. $\Delta H_0^\circ = -98.736$ [568]. 5. $\Delta H_0^\circ = -98.75$ [2358]. 6. $T = 313.7$ °K. 7. $\Delta H_0^\circ = -98.736$ [1618a]. 8. $\Delta H_0^\circ = 11.877$ [1618a]. 9. $\Delta H_0^\circ = 73.7$ [1618a]. 10. $\Delta H_0^\circ = 31.863$ [568]. 11. $\Delta H_0^\circ = 31.9$ [2358]. 12. S_{298}. 13. $\Delta H_0^\circ = -6.54$ [568]. 14. $\Delta H_0^\circ = -7.115$ [570]. 15. $Br_2 + Cl^- = Br_2Cl^-$. 16. $\Delta H_0^\circ = -6.825$ [3121]. 17. From gaseous bromine. 18. $\Delta H_0^\circ = -6.73$ [1186]. 19. $\Delta H_0^\circ = -6.868$ [570]. 20. $\Delta H_0^\circ = -6.785$ [1618a]. 21. $\Delta H_0^\circ = (169.98)$ [2358]. 22. $\Delta H_0^\circ = (169.585)$ [570]. 23. $\Delta H_0^\circ = (169.9898)$ [1830]. 24. $\Delta H_0^\circ = 169.576$ [1618a]. 25. $\Delta H_0^\circ = (0.5797)$ [2358]. 26. $\Delta H_0^\circ = (0.562)$ [570].

1	2	3		4		5		6	
C, graphite	c					1.290	[570]	2.05[1]	[2186]
						1.359	[1618a]		
	g	(432.267)[2]	[570]						
		(432.420)[3]	[2358]						
C^{2+}	g	(996.173)[4]	[2358]						
C^{3+}	g	(2101.73)[5]	[2358]						
C^{4+}	g	(3590.46)[6]	[2358]						
C^{5+}	g	(12633.8)[7]	[2358]						
C^{6+}	g	(23934)[8]	[2358]						
C^-	g	94	[1214]						
C_2	g	(200.00)	[2479]	186.532	[2479]	47.91	[2479]	7.00	[2479, 1830]
		(200.0258)[9]	[1830]			47.6302	[1830]	10.313	[1830]
		(198.061)[10]	[570]			47.6331	[570]		
		(190)	[976]			47.628	[717, 1618a]	10.311	[717]
		(215*)	[1001]			49.27	[1685]		
		(199.026)[11]	[1618a]	185.636	[1618a]			10.317	[1618a]
C_2^+	g	487	[1104]						
C_3	g	200.00	[2479]	184.772	[2479]	55.18	[2479]	10.41	[2479]
		189.664[12]	[570]			50.931	[570]		
		189.6653[13]	[1830]			50.688	[1830]	9.3883	[1830]
		189.67	[1618a]	175.777	[1618a]	50.688	[1618a]	9.388	[1618a]
C_3^+	g	493	[1104]						
C_4	g	242.321[14]	[1618a]	226.629	[1618a]	58.083	[1618a]	12.803	[1618a]
C_4^+	g	523	[1104]						
C_5	g	242.374[15]	[1618a]	226.634	[1618a]	59.608	[1618a]	16.218	[1618a]
C_5^+	g	530	[1104]						
CBN	c	33.58	[2358]						
CBrN	g	56.1	[1817]	38.3	[1817]	(59.07)	[321, 1817]		
		44.5[16]	[2358]	39.5	[2358]	(59.32)	[2358]	11.22	[2358]
CN	g	70	[679]			45.2	[1797]		
CN_4	g			−73.4*	[229]				
CNI	g	(38.3)	[1817]	(45.5)	[1718]	61.33	[1817]		
		(53.9)[17]	[2358]	(47.0)	[2358]	61.35	[2358]	11.54	[2358]
	c	39.71	[2358]	44.22	[2358]	23.0	[2358]		
CNO^-	d	(−34.9)	[2358]	(−23.3)	[2358]	(25.5)	[2358]		
CNS^-	d	(18.27)	[2358]	22.15	[2358]	34.5	[2358]	−9.6	[2358]
				21.2*	[323]	36*	[323]		

CO	g	(−26.416)	[2358]	(−32.781)	[2358]	(47.219)	[2358]	(6.959)	[2358]
		(−26.416)[18]	[570]			(47.2178)	[1830]	(6.9652)	[1830]
						(47.30)	[1685]	(6.96)	[1685]
		(−26.417)[19]	[1618a]	(−32.783)	[1618a]	(47.214)	[1618a]	(6.965)	[1618a]
	d	−28.91	[2358]	(−28.66)	[2358]	−25.0	[2358]		
CO^+	g	(298.243)[20]	[570]			48.5480	[570]		
		(298.16)[21]	[2358]			48.5480	[155]		
CO^{2+}	g	945.5[22]	[2358]						
$CO(NH_2)_2$, urea	c	−79.56	[2358]	−47.04	[2358]	25.00	[2358]	22.26	[2358]
	d	−76.117	[2358]						
COS	g					(55.35)[23]	[2103]	(9.93)[23]	[2103]
CO_2		(−94.05)[24]	[2358]	(−94.258)	[2358]	(51.06)	[2358]	(8.87)	[2358]
	g	(−94.0518)[25]	[1830]			(51.0701)	[1830]	(8.8740)	[1830]
		(−94.054)[26]	[570, 1618a]			(51.071)	[570]	(8.89)[27]	[1245]
						(51.08)	[1685]	(8.88)	[1685]
				(−94.265)	[1618a]	(51.072)	[1618a]	(8.874)	[1618a]
	d	(−98.90)	[2358]	(−92.26)	[2358]	(28.1)	[2358]		
CO_2^+	g	(225.23)[28]							
CO_3^{2-}	d	(−161.84)	[2358]	(−126.17)	[2358]	(−13.6)	[2358]		
						(−13.0)	[1685]		
CP	g	86.5204[29]	[1830]			(51.6627)	[1830]	(7.1492)	[1830]
		107.541[30]	[570]			(51.661)	[570, 1618a]		
						(51.65)	[1685]	(7.14)	[1685]
		111.7	[1618a]	98.327	[1618a]			(7.149)	[1618a]
CS	g	55*	[1879]			(50.29)	[1685]	(7.12)	[1685]
		60*	[2295]	80*	[229]				
$CS(NH_2)_2$, thiourea	c	−21.1	[2358]						
$CS(NH_2)_2 \cdot HNO_3$	c	−73.1	[2358]						
CSSe	g					61.24[4]	[2103]	11.42	[2103]
CSTe	c					62.71	[2103]	11.71	[2103]
CS_2	g	26.1	[1214]			(56.84)[4]	[2103]	(10.88)	[2103]
		(27.7)	[1428]			(56.85)	[1685]	(10.91)	[1685]
	l					(36.2)	[1685]	(18.06)	[1685]
CS_2^+	g	261	[1214]						

1. $T = 300$ °K. 2. $\Delta H_0^\circ = (429.430)$ [570]. 3. $\Delta H_0^\circ = (429.628)$ [2358]. 4. $\Delta H_0^\circ = (991.900)$ [2358]. 5. $\Delta H_0^\circ = (2095.98)$ [2358]. 6. $\Delta H_0^\circ = (3583.23)$ [2358]. 7. $\Delta H_0^\circ = (12625.1)$ [2358]. 8. $\Delta H_0^\circ = (23924)$ [2358]. 9. $\Delta H_0^\circ = (198)$ [1830]. 10. $\Delta H_0^\circ = (196.00)$ [570]. 11. $\Delta H_0^\circ = 197.0$ [1618a]. 12. $\Delta H_0^\circ = 188.00$ [570]. 13. $\Delta H_0^\circ = 188.1$ [1830]. 14. $\Delta H_0^\circ = 240.5$ [1618a]. 15. $\Delta H_0^\circ = 240.298$ [1618a]. 16. $\Delta H_0^\circ = 46.07$ [2358]. 17. $\Delta H_0^\circ = 54.04$ [2358]. 18. $\Delta H_0^\circ = (-27.218)$ [570]. 19. $\Delta H_0^\circ = -27.20$ [1618a]. 20. $\Delta H_0^\circ = (295.961)$ [570]. 21. $\Delta H_0^\circ = 295.9$ [2358]. 22. $\Delta H_0^\circ = 942$ [2358]. 23. $t = 26.1$ °C. 24. $\Delta H_0^\circ = (-93.964)$ [2358]. 25. $\Delta H_0^\circ = (-93.9641)$ [1830]. 26. $\Delta H_0^\circ = (-93.984)$ [570]; (−93.965) [1618a]. 27. $t = 26.1$ °C. 28. $\Delta H_0^\circ = (223.8)$ [2358]. 29. $\Delta H_0^\circ = 85.9708$ [1830]. 30. $\Delta H_0^\circ = 106.956$ [570].

1	2	3		4		5		6	
CSe	g					53.2	[1685]	7.30	[1685]
CSe_2	g					62.93[1]	[2103]	11.96[1]	[2103]
						62.9	[1685]		
	l	(39.4)	[2358]						
CT_4	g					10.72	[1654]	55.17[2]	[1654]
C_3O_2	g	−8.00[3]	[570]			61.573	[570]		
						58.0	[1685]	13.89	[1685]
DCNS	g	−26.4157[4]	[1830]			61.14	[1885]	12.45	[1185]
HCN	g	(32.3)[5]	[2358]	(29.8)	[2358]	(48.20)	[2358]	(8.57)	[2358]
	l	(26.02)	[2358]	(29.86)	[2358]	(26.97)	[2358]	(16.88)	[2358]
	d	36.0	[2358]	41.2	[2358]	22.5	[2358]		
HCN, nonionized	d	(25.6)	[2358]	(28.6)	[2358]	(29.8)	[2358]		
HCNO, isocyanic acid	g					56.85	[2358]	10.72	[2358]
HCNO, ionized	d	−34.9	[2358]	−23.3	[2358]	25.5	[2358]		
HCNO, nonionized	d	(−36.90)	[2358]	(−28.0)	[2358]	(33.9)	[2358]		
HCNS, isothiocyanic acid	g	30.5	[2358]	27.0	[2358]	59.2	[2358]	11.2	[2358]
						58.47	[1885]	10.90	[1885]
HCNS, ionized	d	(18.27)	[2358]	22.15	[2358]	34.5	[2358]	9.6	[2358]
HCNS, nonionized	d			23.31	[2358]				
HCO_3^-	d					(22.2)	[1685]		
H_2CO_3	d	(−167.22)	[2358]	(−148.94)	[2358]	(44.8)	[2358]		
						(45.1)	[1685]		
Ca	g	(42.200)	[2479]	(34.138)	[2479]	(36.9923)	[77]		
		(42.204)[6]	[570]			(36.9933)	[570]		
		(42.37)[7]	[1589]	(34.31)	[1589]	(36.99)	[1685]		
		(42.3)	[1932]						
		(42.81)	[2405]						
		(42.3)[8]	[385]						
	c							(6.26)	[1574]
						(9.97)	[570]	(6.30)	[570, 2479]
Ca^+	g	(184.660)[9]	[570]			38.3707	[570]		
Ca^{2+}	g					37.00	[1346]		
	d					(−11.4)	[1685]		
$Ca(BF_4)_2$	g	34.1	[2101]						
		46.6[10]	[2100]						
CaBr	c	−54.0[11]	[1170]			60.9	[1685]	8.66	[1685]
$CaBr_2$	g					72.91*	[297]	14.252*	[297]

	c	(–163*)	[230]			(32.0*)	[1773]		
		(–163.6)	[1166]			(32.2)	[1685]		
						(30.1*)	[698]		
$CaBr_2 \cdot H_2O$	c	–239*	[230]						
$CaBr_2 \cdot 2H_2O$	c	–311*	[230]						
$CaBr_2 \cdot 4H_2O$	c	–453*	[230]						
$CaBr_2 \cdot 6H_2O$	c			–506.42	[190]	72.83	[190]		
$Ca(BrO_3)_2$	c	–154.4	[618]			54.4*	[699]		
CaC_2	c	(–14.1)	[2226]					19.94	[1685]
$Ca(CN)_2$	c			–33.1*	[323]	21.3*	[323]		
$Ca(CNO)_2$	c	–203*	[693]						
		–200	[481]						
$Ca(CNS)_2$	c	–80*	[693, 2683]						
		–93	[481]						
$CaCO_3$	c	–42.62[12]	[1947]	(–269.75*)	[177]	(22.1*)	[177]		
						(20.2*)	[699]		
$CaCO_3 \cdot MgCO_3$				–520.0*	[229]	37.09	[2467]	37.65	[2467]
$CaCd_2$	c	–30	[2625]						
$CaCd_3$	c	–29.5	[1589]						
CaCl	g			0.6*	[227]	58.2	[1685]	8.50	[1685]
						58.0	[1680]		
		–60.7[13]	[1170]						
$CaCl_2$	g	–116.7	[1518]			67.17*	[297]	13.842	[297]
	c	(–187.8)	[2375]			(24.4*)[14]	[698]	(17.35)	[1685]
		(–191.1)	[1166]						
		75.9[15]	[800]						
$CaCl_2 \cdot 3Ca_3(PO_4)_2$	c	–3172	[1346]						
$CaCl_2 \cdot H_2O$	c			–241.6*	[229]				
$CaCl_2 \cdot 2H_2O$	c	(–338*)	[230]	–197.9*	[229]				
$CaCl_2 \cdot 4H_2O$	c			–410.04	[190]	50.81	[190]		
				–414.4*	[229]				
$CaCl_2 \cdot 6H_2O$	c			–525.22	[190]	68.10	[190]		
				–529.2*	[229]				
$CaCl_2O$	c			–162.0*	[229]				
$Ca(ClO_3)_2$	c	–166*	[693, 2683]			50.8*	[699]		
		–181	[481]						

1. $t = 26.1\ ^\circ C$. 2. Including nuclear spin. 3. $\Delta H_0^\circ = -8.505$ [570]. 4. $\Delta H_0^\circ \doteq -27.1997$ [1830]. 5. $\Delta H_0^\circ = 32.39$ [2358]. 6. $\Delta H_0^\circ = 42.204$ [570]. 7. $\Delta H_0^\circ = 42.26$ [1589]. 8. ΔH_0°. 9. $\Delta H_0^\circ = (183.075)$ [570]. 10. $T = 550\ ^\circ K$. 11. $\Delta H_0^\circ = -57.5$ [1170]. 12. From oxides; $t = 35^\circ$. 13. $\Delta H_0^\circ = -57.5$ [1170]. 14. The value of 27.2 recommended in [227] was stated to be inaccurate [698]. See also [692]. 15. $(\Delta H_{298}^\circ)_{subl}$.

1	2	3		4		5		6	
$Ca(ClO_4)_2$	c	–173.94	[90]			55.7*	[699]		
		–164*	[693]						
		–179*	[2683]						
$CaCrO_4$	c			(–303.22*)[1]	[177]	(25.2*)[1]	[177]		
				(–312.8*)	[323]	(32*)	[323]		
$Ca(CrO_2)_2$	c	–494.4	[415]	–462.8	[415]	28.9	[251]		
CaD	g					49.61	[1685]	7.30	[1685]
CaF	g	–86.4[2]	[1170]	–15.1*	[227]	54.9	[1685]	8.03	[1685]
						54.8	[1680]		
CaF_2	g	–188.0	[1517]			62.14*	[297]	13.235*	[297]
		–181[3]	[2319]						
	c	–177[4]	[865]						
	c			(–278.57*)	[176]	(19.2*)	[176]		
				(–278*)	[371]	(17.3*)	[698]		
$CaF_2 \cdot 3Ca_3(PO_4)_2$	c	–3262	[1346]						
$CaFe_2O_4$	c	(–365.9)	[465]	–340.2	[465]	34.7	[1685, 1715]	36.72	[1685, 1715]
CaH	g			35.25	[77]	48.209	[77]		
						48.18	[1685]	7.12	[1685]
CaH_2	c	(–41.65)	[1070]	(–32.61)	[1070]	–30.4[5]	[1070]		
						(9.9)	[1685]		
CaHBr	c	–106.6	[1166]						
$Ca(HCO_3)_2$	c	(–463.7*)	[693]						
		(–466*)	[2683]						
CaHCl	c	–120.5	[1166]						
CaHI	c	–88.2	[1166]						
$CaHPO_4$	c			(–400.91*)	[177]	(19.2*)	[177]		
						(26.62)	[1153]	(26.30)	[1153]
$CaHPO_4 \cdot 2H_2O$	c			(45.28)	[2620]	(47.10)	[2620]		
$Ca(H_2PO_4)_2$	c	(–746.04)	[1156]	–672*[6]	[323]	45.3*[6]	[323]		
						45.63	[1685]	62.1	[1685]
$Ca(H_2PO_4)_2 \cdot H_2O$	c	(–816.82)	[1156]	–739.7**	[232]	62.10	[1156]		
				–734*	[232]				
$Ca(HS)_2$	c	–107*	[693]						
		–115*	[2683]						
$Ca(HSO_4)_2$	c	–542*	[2683]						
$CaHfO_3$	c	–425.4	[353]						
CaI	c	–43.5[7]	[1170]			62.6	[1685]	8.73	[1685]
						75.98*	[297]	14.435	[297]

CaI_2	c	-128.1	[1166]			(34.1*)	[698]		
						(35.0)	[1685]		
$Ca(IO_3)_2$	c			-204.77*	[177]				
$CaMg_2$	c	(-4.4)	[2405]						
		(-8.3)	[2407]			24.4[8]	[2407]		
$Ca(MnO_4)_2$	c	-343*	[694]			65.1*	[699]		
$CaMoO_4$	c	-369.5	[772]	-344.0	[772]	29.3	[2633]	27.33	[2633]
		-369.9	[170]	-345.8*	[170]				
		-369.9*	[172]	-345.8*	[172]				
		-367.3	[1997]	-347	[1349]				
		-372.3	[332]			28.6	[332]		
$Ca(NO_2)_2$	c			-144.2*	[323]	39.3*	[323]		
				-147.6*	[229]	45.1*	[699]		
$Ca(NO_3)_2$	c							35.70	[1685]
$Ca(NO_3)_2 \cdot 4H_2O$	c			(-407.48)	[190]	(83.16)	[190]		
$Ca(N_3)_2$	c	(11.03)	[1356]						
CaO	g	-14.188[9]	[570]			52.489	[570]		
		-14.2[10]	[366]	108.88	[77]	52.488	[77]		
		-17.6[11]	[1015]			52.6	[1685]	7.91	[1685]
		-5*[12]	[757]						
	c	(-151.79)[13]	[570, 1577]			(9.5)	[570, 1685]	10.24	[570]
		(-150.65)	[1045]	(-143.25)	[1045]	(9.7*)	[698]	10.23	[1685]
		(-151.93)	[1030]						
$CaO \cdot 2B_2O_3$	v			-739.9*	[229]				
$CaO \cdot FeO \cdot Fe_2O_3$	c	-433.33*	[599]			44.4*	[599]		
$CaO \cdot 3FeO \cdot Fe_2O_3$	c	-567.17*	[599]			73.0*	[599]		
$CaO \cdot MgO \cdot SiO_2$, monticellite	c	-528.7	[2049]						
		-27.55[14]	[1681]	-27.5[14]	[1681]				
$CaO \cdot MgO \cdot 2SiO_2$, diopside	c	-35.25[14]	[1681]	-34.7[14]	[1681]	34.2	[1685, 1723]	39.80	[1685]
$CaO \cdot SiO_2$, wollastonite	c	-21.25[15]	[1681]	-21.25[15]	[1681]				
$CaO \cdot SiO_2$, pseudowollastonite	c	-19.6[15]	[1681]	-20.0[15]	[1681]				
$CaO \cdot 2SiO_2 \cdot 2H_2O$, okenite	c	-725.64*	[387]	-661.70*	[387]				
$CaO \cdot SiO_2 \cdot TiO_2$	c	-26.85[16]	[1681]	-26.65[16]	[1681]				
		-613.95	[1686]	-580.15	[1686]	30.9	[1685, 1731]	33.21	[1685, 1731]
		-26.86[16]	[2552]						
		-612.9	[2552]	-579.1	[2552]				

1. $t = 18\ ^\circ C$. 2. $\Delta H_0^\circ = -83.6$ [1170]. 3. Calculated [234] from (ΔH_{298}°) subl $= 101.3$ [2319] and $(\Delta H_{298}^\circ)_{CaF_2(c)} = -290.3$ [2245]. 4. Calculated [234] from (ΔH_{298}°) subl $= 103.3$ [865] and $(\Delta H_{298}^\circ) CaF_2(c) = 290.3$ [2245]. 5. ΔS_{298}°. 6. Precipitated. 7. $\Delta H_0^\circ = -41.2$ [1170]. 8. Calculated [234] from the value of $\Delta S_{298}^\circ = -1.1$ [2407] for the formation of $CaMg_2$. 9. $\Delta H_0^\circ = -13.913$ [570]. 10. $\Delta H_0^\circ = -13.9$ [336]. 11. ΔH_0°. 12. Calculated [245] from $(\Delta H_{298}^\circ)_{subl} = 147^*$ [757] and $(\Delta H_{298}^\circ)_{CaO(c)} = -152$. 13. $\Delta H_0^\circ = -151.046$ [570]. 14. From CaO(c), MgO(c) and $SiO_2(\alpha)$. 15. From CaO(c) and $SiO_2(\alpha)$. 16. From CaO(c), TiO_2(c) and $SiO_2(\alpha)$.

1	2	3		4		5		6	
$CaO \cdot SiO_2 \cdot TiO_2$	c	−54.2[1]	[60]						
$2CaO \cdot Al_2O_3$	c			−670.9*	[229]				
$2CaO \cdot Al_2O_3$	v			−661.9*	[229]				
$2CaO \cdot Al_2O_3 \cdot 8SiO_2$, leonhardite	c	−50.0[2]	[60]						
		−389	[135]	−370	[135]	22.4	[135, 1685]	23.34	[1685]
		−397.4	[428]			22.04	[1735]		
$2CaO \cdot 3B_2O_3$	c			−1207*	[229]				
$2CaO \cdot Fe_2O_3$	c	−507.7	[2053]						
$2CaO \cdot MgO \cdot 2SiO$, akermanite	c	−43.85[3]	[1681]	−43.7[3]	[1681]	50.0	[2630]	50.67	[2630]
$2CaO \cdot MgO \cdot 2SiO_2$	v	−36.1[3]	[1681]	−37.1[3]	[1681]				
$2CaO \cdot SiO_2$, β	c	(−539.5)	[1712]	−512.0	[2543]	30.5	[1685]	30.74	[1685]
		(−30.2)[4]	[1681]	−30.65[4]	[1681]				
				−512.7	[323]	37.6	[323]		
$2CaO \cdot SiO_2$, γ	c			−510**	[232]	30.5	[2543]	30.74	[2543]
				−513.7*	[323]	37.6*	[323]		
				−511.7*	[232]	28.8	[1685, 1723]	30.31	[1685]
		−32.7[4]	[1681]	−32.65[4]	[1681]	28.0*	[251]		
$2CaO \cdot SiO_2 \cdot 1.17H_2O$, hillebrandite	c	−624.8*	[387]	−580.55*	[387]				
$2CaO \cdot 3SiO_2 \cdot 2.5H_2O$, gyrolite	c	−1138.82*	[387]	−1048.62*	[387]				
$3CaO \cdot CaF_2 \cdot 2SiO_2$, cuspidine	c	−1219.9	[1541]						
$3CaO \cdot MgO \cdot 2SiO_2$, merwinite	c	−57.0[3]	[1681]	−56.8[3]	[1681]	60.5	[2630]	60.29	[2630]
$3CaO \cdot MgO \cdot 2SiO_2$	c	−1067	[2048]						
$3CaO \cdot SiO_2$	c	−27[5]	[1681]	−27.5[5]	[1681]	40.3	[1685, 2543]	41.08	[1685, 2543]
		(687.8)	[907]	−651.0**, −655.3*	[323]				
		(−688.1)	[1712]	−653.3	[2543]				
$3CaO \cdot 2SiO_2$	c	−945*	[148]			50.4	[1685, 1723]	51.24	[1685]
$3CaO \cdot 2SiO_2$, rankinite	c	−54.8[5]	[1681]	−55.3[5]	[1681]				
$3CaO \cdot 2SiO_2 \cdot 3H_2O$, afwillite	c	−1118.45*	[387]	−1028.25*	[387]				
$4CaO \cdot 3SiO \cdot 1.5H_2O$, foshagite	c	−1402,85*	[387]	−1310.85*	[387]				
$5CaO \cdot 6SiO_2 \cdot 3H_2O$, riversideite	c	−2300.90*	[387]	−2140.9*	[387]				

$5CaO \cdot 6SiO_2 \cdot 5.5H_2O$, tobermorite	c	−2482.15*	[387]	−2287.35*	[387]				
$5CaO \cdot 6SiO_2 \cdot 10H_2O$, plombierite	c	−2837.15*	[387]	−2573.20*	[387]				
$6CaO \cdot 6SiO_2 \cdot H_2O$, xonotlite	c	−2334.11*	[387]	−2196.61*	[387]				
$23CaO \cdot K_2O \cdot 12SiO_2$	c	−6420	[2051]						
CaO_2	c	(−156.5)	[1045]	−143*	[323]	10.3*	[323]		
		(−155.77)	[76]	−139.4*	[229]				
$Ca(OH)^+$	d					−4.4	[1541]		
$Ca(OH)_2$	c	(−235.71)	[1490]	(−214.77)	[1490]	(19.93)	[1685]	(20.91)	[1490, 1685]
				(−214.33*)	[176]	(18.2*)	[176]		
						(18.6*)	[699]		
	d	(−239.09)	[1384]	(−207.52)	[1384]	(−15.8)	[1384]		
$Ca(OH)_2 \cdot Ca_3(PO_4)_2$	c	−3231	[1346]			(19.93)	[1490]		
						(17.4)	[1680]		
$Ca(PO_3)_2$	c					35.12	[1148]	34.693	[1148]
						35.0	[1685]	34.68	[1685]
	v	-78.2^{6}	[1917]						
CaPb	c	(−28.6)	[2625]						
$Ca(ReO_4)_2$	c	−500*	[2683]						
CaS	g	33.5^{7}	[1015]						
	c	(−114.5*); (−114.8)	[1015]	(−114.1)	[1734]	(14.3*)	[698]		
$CaSO_3$	c	−276.3*	[1172]						
$CaSO_4$	c			$(-315.3^*)^{8}$	[230]				
				(−315.25*)	[177]	(24.4*)	[177]		
		−343.69	[1675]			(26.0)	[1675]		
						(25.7*)	[699]		
$CaSO_4$, insoluble anhydrite	c					(25.5)	[1685]	(23.82)	[1685]
$CaSO_4$, soluble, α	c					(25.9)	[1685]	(23.95)	[1685]
$CaSO_4$, soluble, β	c					(25.9)	[1685]	(23.67)	[1685]
$CaSO_4 \cdot 0.5H_2O$, α	c					(31.2)	[1685]	(28.54)	[1685]
$CaSO_4 \cdot 0.5H_2O$, β	c					(32.1)	[1685]	(29.69)	[1685]
$CaSO_4 \cdot 2H_2O$	c					(46.4)	[1685]	(46.46)	[1685]
$CaSO_4 \cdot 6H_2O$	c	−715.3*	[229]	(−529.2*)	[229]				
$CaSO_4 \cdot K_2SO_4 \cdot 6H_2O$	c			−702.1*	[229]				
$5CaSO_4 \cdot K_2SO_4 \cdot H_2O$	c			−1969*	[229]				
$CaSO_4 \cdot Na_2SO_4$	c			−620.6*	[229]				
$CaSO_4 \cdot 2Na_2SO_4$	c			−1028*	[229]				
CaSe	c			18.0*	[698]	(15.7*)	[247]		
$CaSeO_3 \cdot 2H_2O$	c	−385.6	[341]	−342.3	[341]	59.57	[341]		
$CaSeO_4$	c	−270.11	[524]			15.1*	[498]	20.76*	[498]
$CaSeO_4 \cdot 2H_2O$	c	−412.77	[523, 524]	−335.18	[523, 524]	31.5	[523, 524]	31.5*	[498]

1. From CaO(c), $SiO_2(\alpha)$ and TiO_2. 2. From CaO(c), Al_2O_3(c) and $SiO_2(\alpha)$. 3. From CaO(c) MgO(c) and $SiO_2(\alpha)$. 4. From CaO(c) and SiO_2(c). 5. From CaO(c) and $SiO_2(\alpha)$. 6. From oxides; $t = 35$ °C. 7. ΔH°_0. 8. Recalculated [234] from $(\Delta H^\circ_{298})_{diss} = 122.61$ [250] to 119.56 [2245] using the ΔG°_{298} values for SO_3 and CaO [2245].

1	2	3	4	5	6
$CaSn_3$	c	(−43.0) [2625]			
CaTe	c	−65.0* [1773]	20.6 [698]	(19.3*) [247]	
$CaTiO_3$, monotitanate	c	−470 [192]			
$CaTiO_3$, perovskite	c	−395.5 [2243]	−375.1 [2243]		
		−396.9 [1686]	−376.5 [1686]		
		−395.5 [2552]	−375.2 [2552]		
CaTl	c	(−39.0) [1774, 2625]			
$CaUO_4$	c	−470 [192]			
$CaWO_4$	c	(−402.4) [772]	−376.9 [772]		26.81 [684]
			−368.7* [323]	36.1* [323]	
			−368.2* [229]		
		(−242.9)[1] [468]	−221.7[1] [468]		
$Ca_{0.091}Zn_{0.909}$	c	−4.36[2] [1589]			
$Ca_{0.20}Zn_{0.80}$	c	−5.90[3] [1589]			
$Ca_{0.40}Zn_{0.60}$	c	−8.00[4] [1589]			
$Ca_{0.80}Zn_{0.20}$	c	(−6.49)[5] [1589]			
$CaZrO_3$	c	−10.4[6] [60]		24*[6] [60]	
$Ca_{1.5}Li_3P_4O_{13}$	v	−2.82[7] [1947]			
$Ca_{1.5}Zn_{1.5}P_4O_{13}$	v	−2.72[7] [1947]			
Ca_2C	c	$\leqslant$ 7* [651]			
$Ca_2Fe_2O_5$	c			45.1 [1685, 1715]	46.10 [1685, 1715]
Ca_2Ge	c	> 90* [651]			
$Ca_2Mg_5Si_8O_{22}(OH)_2$, tremolite	c			131.2 [2231]	156.7 [2231]
$Ca_2P_2O_7$, β	c			45.25 [1149]	44.87 [1149]
				45.2 [1685]	44.89 [1685]
$Ca_2P_2O_7$	c	−136.5[8] [1947]			
Ca_2Pb	c	(−97) [651]			
		(−51.5) [2625]			
Ca_2Si	c	(−116) [651]			
Ca_2Sn	c	(−93) [651]			
Ca_2TiO_4	c			31.0* [228]	
Ca_3As_2	c	−138.6 [650]			
$Ca_3(AsO_4)_2$	c		−747.3 [229]		
Ca_3Bi_2	c	(−115*) [2625]			
		(−75) [650]			
Ca_3Mg_4	c	−0.04 [2243]			

Ca_3N_2	c	(-105.0*)	[2625]						
Ca_3P_2	c	(-120.0*)	[2625]						
		(-125)	[650]						
$Ca_3(PO_4)_2$	c	(-984.5)	[1947]	(-920.84)	[177]				
$Ca_3(PO_4)_2$, α	c	(-978)	[548]						
$Ca_3(PO_4)_2$, β	c	(-983)	[548]						
$3Ca_3(PO_4)_2 \cdot CaCl_2$	c	-3172	[1609]						
$3Ca_3(PO_4)_2 \cdot CaF_2$	c	-3296	[394]						
$3Ca_3(PO_4)_2 \cdot CaF_2$, fluorapatite	c	-3629	[548]			185.5	[1155]		
						185.4	[1685]	179.7	[1685]
$3Ca_3(PO_4)_2 \cdot Ca(OH)_2$	c	-3229	[1609]						
		-3231	[1129]						
$3Ca_3(PO_4)_2 \cdot Ca(OH)_2$, hydroxyapatite	c	-3212	[548]			186.6	[1154, 1685]	184.0	[1685]
$Ca_3P_4O_{13}$	v	-203.0[9]	[1947]						
$Ca_3Ti_2O_7$	c	-944.1	[1686]	-896.4	[1686]	56.1	[1685, 1716]	57.20	[1685, 1716]
		-940.3	[2552]	-892.6	[2552]				
Cd	g	(26.75)[10]	[2479]	(18.491)	[2479]	(40.07)	[1685]		
		(26.77)[11]	[1589]	(18.51)	[1589]				
		(26.48)[10]	[1914]						
		(26.55)[10]	[393]						
		(26.90)[10]	[711]						
		(26.64)	[712]						
		(26.54)	[1370a]						
Cd, α	c					(12.37)	[1059, 1589, 1685, 2479]	(6.22)	[1059, 2479]
								(6.21)	[1589, 1685]
Cd^{2+}	g					40.08	[66]		
	d					(-15.6)	[1685]		
Cd_2	g			40.4*	[229]				
$CdAs_2$	c	-1.5[12]	[1829]						
CdBr	g					(63.1)	[1685]	8.75	[1685]
$CdBr_2$	g			(-69.5*)	[227]	(32.0)	[1680]		
						(33.18)	[195]	18.32	[195]
						(34.9)	[1685]		
$CdBr_2 \cdot 4H_2O$	c			(-297.48)	[190]	(74.23)	[190]		

1. From CaO, W and $\frac{3}{2}O_2$. 2. $T = 293\ ^\circ K$. 3. $T = 293\ ^\circ K$; phases $CaZn_2 + CaZn_5$. 4. $T = 293\ ^\circ K$; phases $CaZn + CaZn_2$. 5. $T = 293\ ^\circ K$; phases $Ca + Ca_5Zn_2$. 6. From oxides; 7. From oxides; $t = 35\ ^\circ C$. 8. From oxides; $t = 35\ ^\circ C$. 9. From oxides. 10. ΔH_0°. 11. $\Delta H_0^\circ = (26.78)$ [1589]. 12. Calculated [234] from $\Delta H_{298}^\circ = 11$ [1829] for the reaction $CdAs_2(c) = \frac{1}{3} Cd_3As_2(c) + \frac{1}{3} As_2(g)$, using the values of ΔH_0° of dissociation of Cd_3As (c) [1817] and ΔH_0° of formation of Cd (g) [2245] and As_4 (g) [2245].

1	2	3		4		5		6	
$Cd(CN)_2$	c			49.7*	[323]	24.9*	[323]		
$Cd(CNS)_2$	c	−14.3	[690]	−6*	[229]				
		−15*	[696]						
$CdCO_3$	c	(−179.027)	[2263]	(−159.925)	[2263]	(23.1)	[2263]		
				(−163.35*)	[177]	(24.0)	[1773]		
				(−160.8*)	[232]	(23.3)	[1685]		
				(−161.17)	[1279]				
	v			−159.3*	[229]				
$CdCl$	g					(60.4)	[1685]	8.57	[1685]
$CdCl^+$	d			−51.8*	[323]	5.6*	[323]		
$CdCl_2$	g	43.3	[1694]			69.1	[1694]		
	c					(27.55)	[194]	17.84	[194]
						(31.2)	[1680]		
						(29.3)	[1685]		
$CdCl_2 \cdot {}^5/_2H_2O$	c			(−225.34)	(190)				
$Cd(ClO_3)_2$	c	−56*	[2683]						
$Cd(ClO_4)_2$	c	−64*	[2683]						
$Cd(ClO_4)_2 \cdot 6H_2O$	c	−490.4	[23]						
$CdCl_3^-$	d			−115.9*	[323]	50.7*	[323]		
CdD	g					52.11	[1685]	7.26	[1685]
CdF	g					57.7	[1685]	8.13	[1685]
CdF_2	c	(−167.39)	[2251]	(−155.2)	[2251]				
		(−166.5)	[890]			(22.5*)	[890]		
		(72.6)[1]	[839]			(19.9)	[1685]		
$CdFe_2O_4$	c	−265*	[464]						
CdH	g					(50.72)	[1685]	7.09	[1685]
CdH_2	c	−27*	[2683]						
$Cd(HCO_3)_2$	c	−358*	[2683]						
$Cd(HS)_2$	c	−12*	[2683]						
$Cd(HSO_4)_2$	c	−432*	[2683]						
$Cd(H_2O)_2NO_3^+$	d	−5.24	[65]	−0.42	[65]	−16.2[2]	[65]		
$Cd_{0.23}Hg_{0.77}$, β	c	−0.55[3]	[1589]	−0.65	[1589]				
$Cd_{0.30}Hg_{0.70}$	c	−0.66	[1589]	−0.79	[1589]				
$Cd_{0.40}Hg_{0.60}$	c	−0.78	[1589]	−0.91	[1589]				
$Cd_{0.50}Hg_{0.50}$	c	−0.80	[1589]	−0.96	[1589]				
$Cd_{0.60}Hg_{0.40}$	c	−0.70	[1589]	−0.91	[1589]				
$Cd_{0.66}Hg_{0.34}$, β[2]	c	−0.55	[1589]	−0.84	[1589]				

$Cd_{0.79}Hg_{0.21}$, a[2]	c	–0.355	[1589]	–0.66	[1589]				
$Cd_{0.90}Hg_{0.10}$, a	c	–0.165	[1589]						
CdI	g					(65.0)	[1685]	8.83	[1685]
CdI_2	c			(–47.7)*	[232]	(38.50)	[1140]	19.11	[1140]
				(–47.5**)	[232]	(37.67)	[194]	18.53	[194]
						(39.5)	[1685]	19.07	[1685]
CdLi	c	(–10.2)	[1773]						
$Cd_{0.25}Mg_{0.75}$	c	–1.34	[1589]	–1.295	[1589]				
$Cd_{0.75}Mg_{0.25}$	c	–1.14	[1589]	–1.19	[1589]				
CdMg	c	–3.3*	[1589]	–3.48	[1589]			6.17	[1589]
$CdMg_3$	c							5.96	[1589]
$CdMoO_4$	c	–261.1*	[170, 172]	–238.3*	[170, 172]				
$Cd(NO_2)_2$	c	–72*	[2683]						
$Cd(NO_3)_2$	c	(–107.6)	[690]	–61*	[323]	47.3*	[323]		
				–63.1*	[227]				
$Cd(NO_3)_2 \cdot 2H_2O$	c			–179.0*	[229]				
$Cd(NO_3)_2 \cdot 4H_2O$	c			–290.9*	[229]				
CdO	g					55.05*	[249]		
						56.3	[1685]		
	c	(–61.2)	[1891]	(–54.1)	[1891]				
		(–62.2)	[1045]	(–55.1)	[1045]				
		(–61.1)	[887, 1891]	(–54.2*)	[232]				
CdO_2	c	–60*	[2683]						
$CdOH^+$	d			–64.48	[556]				
CdOHBr	c			–95.08;					
				–95.01	[556]				
$Cd(OH)_{1.1}Br_{0.9}$	c			–97.25;					
				–95.01	[556]				
$Cd(OH)_2$	c			(–112.75*)	[176]	(23.7*)	[176]		
				(–113.36)	[2304]	(21.5)	[1685]	7.26	[1685]
				(–112.99)	[556]				
$Cd(OH)_2$	c			–105.64	[556]				
$[Cd(OH)_3]^-$	d			–142.80	[556]				
$[Cd(OH)_4]^{2-}$	d			–180.45	[556]				
$[Cd(OH)_5]^{3-}$	d			–217.17	[556]				
$[Cd(OH)_6]^{4-}$	d			–253.56	[556]				
$Cd(ReO_4)_2$	c	–413*	[2683]						

1. $(\Delta H^\circ_{298})_{subl}$. 2. ΔS°_{298}. 3. Phase boundary.

1	2	3		4		5		6	
CdS	c	(−35.7)	[704]	(−34.8)	[704]	(17)	[1680]	10.2[1]	[1324]
						(16.8)	[1685]		
$CdSO_3$	c	−152*	[2683]						
		−163.9	[616]						
		−164.4	[1172]						
$CdSO_4$	c			(−194.7*)[2]	[250]	(29.4)	[1685, 2098]	23.81	[1685, 2098]
				(−195.0*)	[232]				
				(−195.6**)	[232]				
$CdSO_4 \cdot H_2O$	c			(−256.8*)	[232]	(36.82)	[1685, 2098]	32.16	[1685, 2098]
				(−253.6**)	[232]				
$CdSO_4 \cdot \frac{8}{3} H_2O$	c			−349.50	[190]	(54.89)	[1685, 2098]	50.97	[1685, 2098]
$CdSO_4 \cdot Cd(OH)_2$	c	−491.0*	[229]	−427.69	[587]				
$CdSO_4 \cdot (NH_4)_2SO_4$	c					116.09	[2450]	94.09[3]	[1005]
$2CdSO_4 \cdot Cd(OH)_2$	c	−576.5*	[229]	−512.07	[587]				
CdSb	c	(−1.72)	[1589]	−1.555	[1589]	22.0	[1680]		
						22.6	[1685]		
CdSe	c	(−37.5)	[2711]			(18.6)	[2711]		
		(−25.0)	[2625]			(19.2*)	[247]		
		(−48*)	[282]						
$CdSeO_3$	c	−138.0	[507]						
$CdSeO_4$	c	−137.04	[514]			25.0*	[498]		
		−138.33	[342]						
		−155.45	[516]						
		−157*	[2683]						
	v	−138.00	[340]	−120.09	[340]				
$CdSeO_4 \cdot H_2O$	c	−229.41	[516]						
$CdSiO_3$	c	−276.3	[770]	−256.3	[770]	(23.3)[4]	[1727]	21.17	[1685, 1727]
		−276*	[2683]			(23.3)	[1685]		
		−4.8[5]	[1681]	−4.84[5]	[1681]	(25.6*)	[246]		
CdTe	c	−43.46[6]	[281]			(22.2)	[1680, 1685]		
$CdWO_4$	c	−282*	[172]	−258*	[172]				
		−282.3*	[170, 172]	−258.5*	[170, 172]				
$Cd_2Fe(CN)_6$	c	−109.5	[2234]						
Cd_2Mg_3	c	−3.6	[908]						
Cd_3As_2	c	−14.5	[2639]						
		−14.0*	[1773]						

		−10.0	[646]						
		-7.2^{7}	[1829]						
Cd_3Cu_2	c	(−3.0)	[2625]						
Cd_3Mg	c							7.06	[1589]
Cd_3N_2	c			−29.3	[229]				
Cd_3P_2	c	−24.4	[646]						
Cd_3Sb_2	c	(−13.9)	[646]			(80.0)	[1685]		
$Cd_{11}U$	c	−12.0	[2207]			137.3	[2207]		
$[HCd(OH)_4]^-$	d			−198.17**	[6]				
$H_2Cd(OH)_4$	c			−226.05*	[6]				
$H_4Cd(OH)_6$	c			−339.35*	[6]				
Ce	g	$(111.60)^{8}$	[1456]	91.85*	[1589]				
				75.5*	[229]				
	c					(16.6)	[1685, 2109]	(7.02)	[1685]
						(16.64)	[2479]	(6.89)	[2479]
						$(18.12)^{9}$	[2423]	(6.44)	[1589, 2423]
						(13.8)	[2424]		
						(16.78)	[2396]		
						(13.7*)	[323]		
						(15.3)	[1589]		
Ce^{3+}	g					44.29	[66]		
	d	(−167.43)	[2424]	(−161.54)	[2424]	(−52.8)	[2424]		
				(−162*)	[1976]	(−47)	[1976]		
				(−171.75*)	[323]				
Ce^{4+}	d	(−122*)	[1976]	−111*	[1976]	−84	[1976]		
		(−134.2)	[1183]						
$CeBr_3$	c	−218*	[230]			49.5	[1685]		
		−212*	[2683]						
$CeBr_4$	c	−226*	[2683]						
CeClO		−241.3	[46]			(21.5*)	[46]		
						(20.68*)	[242]		
$CeCl_2$	c	−131*	[442]						
$CeCl_2$	c	(−252.84)	[2424]	−235.16	[2424]	34.5*	[323, 2424]		
		$(83.0)^{10}$	[441]	−242.4*	[323]	41.0	[1685]		
				−239.7**	[232]				

1. C_p. 2. Recalculated [234] from $(\Delta H^\circ_{298})_{diss} = 86.1$ [1099] to 89.54 [2245], using the values of ΔG°_{298} for SO_3 and CdO [2245]. 3. $t = 300$ °C. 4. $T = 292.18$ °K. 5. From CdO(c) and $SiO_2(a)$. 6. $t = 450$ 650 °C. 7. Calculated [234] from $\Delta H^\circ_{298} = 11$ [1829] for the reaction $Cd_3As_2(c) = 3\ Cd(g) + \frac{1}{2}\ As_4(g)$, using the values of ΔH°_{298} of formation of Cd(g) [2245] and As_4(g) [2245]. 8. $\Delta H^\circ_0 = 111.76$ [1456]. 9. $S^\circ_{298} - S^\circ_0$. 10. $(\Delta H^\circ_0)_{vap}$.

1	2	3		4		5		6	
$CeCl_3$	c			−243.3*	[227]				
				−242.7*[1]	[232]				
				211.26	[1162]				
				234*	[1976]				
$CeCl_3 \cdot 7H_2O$	c	−758.46	[2424]	−644.26	[2424]	101	[2424]		
				−644*	[1976]				
$CeCl_3 \cdot 3KCl$	c	6.34[2]	[45]			−1.0[2]	[45]		
$2CeCl_3 \cdot 3KCl$	c	12.60[2]	[45]			16.4	[45]		
$3CeCl_3 \cdot KCl$	c	8.10[2]	[45]			10.0	[45]		
$CeCl_4$	c	−270*	[2683]						
CeF_3	c	−410.0*	[1773]			27.54	[2314, 2647]	22.34	[2314, 2647]
						27.6	[1685]	22.16	[1685]
								27.6	[1729]
$CeF_3 \cdot ½H_2O$	c	−425.3	[1778]	−412*	[1976]				
CeF_4	c	−442*	[229]	−419*	[229]				
CeH_2	c	−33.9	[1999]			13.33	[2434]	9.78	[2434]
CeI_3	c	(−156.3)	[1533, 2424]	−163.1*	[227, 323]	51.3*	[323]		
		(−163.4)	[1533]	156*	[1976]				
CeI_4	c	−168*	[2683]						
CeN	c			−71.3*	[229]				
$Ce(NO_3)_4 \cdot 5H_2O$	c	−684.9	[44]						
$Ce(NO_3)_3 \cdot (OH) \cdot 3H_2O$	c	−548.5	[44]						
CeO	g	−28	[2613]						
$CeO_{1.5}$, hexagonal	c	−217.46	[2662]	−207.0	[2662]				
$CeO_{1.67}$, body-centered	c	−233	[2662]	−221	[2662]	17.2	[2662]		
$CeO_{1.72}$, rhombic	c	−238	[2662]	−255	[2662]	16.5	[2662]		
$CeO_{1.78}$, rhombic	c	−244	[2662]	−231	[2662]	16.2	[2662]		
$CeO_{1.81}$, rhombic	c	−247	[2662]	−234	[2662]	16.2	[2662]		
CeO_2, body-centered	c			−245.0	[2662]	14.7	[2662]		
CeO_2	c	(−260.1)	[310]	−245.1	[310]	14.9	[310]		
		(−260.18)	[1574, 1812]	−219*	[323]	15.8*	[323]		
		(−245)	[887]	−245*	[1976]	17.7*	[1773]	(15.1)[4]	[1976]
				−246.9*	[229]	14.89	[2647, 2648]	(14.73)	[2647, 2648]
				−230*	[1045]	14.88	[2673]		
CeO_3	c	240*	[1976]	−218*	[1976]				
$Cc(OH)_{2.33}Cl_{0.67}$	c			−285.57	[12]				

$Ce(OH)_3$	c			−313.18	[12]				
				−311.6*	[323]				
CeS	c	(−118.0)	[1181]	−107.5*	[1976]	18.7	[1685]	11.94	[1685]
				−118.0*	[323]				
CeS_2	c			−151.5*	[323]	18.8*	[323]		
				−152*	[229]				
				−142.4*	[1976]				
$Ce(SO_3)_2$	c	−443.8*	[1172]						
$Ce(SO_4)_2$	c			−507.4*	[323]	48.2*	[323]		
				−507.3*	[229]				
Ce_2O_3	c	−425.0	[310]	−412.3	[310]	30.8	[310]	27.8*	[242]
		−436*	[1976]	−412*	[1976]	36.4	[2662]		
		−435*	[887]	−411.5*	[1045]	36.0	[2633]		
		−434.93	[311]			34.86*	[242]		
Ce_2S_3	c	(−300.5)	[1184]	−293.1*	[323]	31.5*	[323]		
				−295.2*	[229]	43.1	[1685]	30.77	[1685]
				−276.6*	[1976]				
$Ce_2(SO_4)_3 \cdot 5H_2O$	c			−1157*	[323]	115.7*	[323]		
				−1159.6*	[229]				
$Ce_2(SO_4)_3 \cdot 8H_2O$	c	−1541*	[229]						
$Ce_2(SO_4)_3 \cdot 9H_2O$	c	−1605*	[229]						
Ce_3H_8	c			−130.0*	[229]				
Ce_3S_4	c	−421.5	[1181]	−416.7*	[234]				
				−415.2*	[1976]				
Cl	g	(28.942)[5]	[1186]	(25.122)	[1186]	(39.4569)	[570, 1186]	(5.2203)	[1186]
		(28.9506)[6]	[1830]			(39.4563)	[1830]	(5.2194)	[1830]
		(28.993)[7]	[568]	(25.174)	[568]	(39.455)	[568, 2178]	(5.220)	[568, 2179]
		(28.952)[8]	[570]			(39.46)	[1685]	(5.22)	[1685]
		(28.922)[9]	[1618a]	(25.102)	[1618a]	(39.456)	[1618a]	(5.219)	[1618a]
Cl^+	g	(330.710)[10]	[568]	325.236	[568]	40.019	[568]	5.487	[568]
		(330.74)[11]	[2358]						
Cl^{2+}	g	(877.7)[12]	[568]						
		(881.17)[13]	[2358]						
Cl^{3+}	g	(1798.2)[12]	[568]						
		(1803.10)[14]	[2358]						
Cl^{4+}	g	(3031.2)[12]	[568]						
		(3037.3)[15]	[2358]						

1. $t = 400\ ^\circ C$. 2. From $CeCl_3$(c) and KCl(c). 3. ΔS°_{298}; from $CeCl_3$(c) and KCl(c). 4. Average of the values for 273 and 373 °K. 5. ΔH°_0 =(28.54) [1186]. 6. ΔH°_0 = (28.5484) [1830]. 7. ΔH°_0 = = (28.591) [568]. 8. ΔH°_0 = (28.850) [570]. 9. ΔH°_0 = 28.52 [1618a]. 10. ΔH°_0 = (328.8) [568]. 11. ΔH°_0 = (328.86) [2358]. 12. ΔH°_0. 13. ΔH°_0 = (877.81) [2358]. 14. ΔH°_0 = (1798.26) [2358]. 15. ΔH°_0 = (3031.0) [2358].

1	2	3		4		5		6	
Cl^{5+}	g	(4595)[1]	[568]						
		(4602,7)[2]	[2358]						
Cl^{8+}	g	(6823)[1]	[568]						
		(6835)[2]	[2358]						
Cl^{8+}	g	(9459)[2]	[568]						
		(9472)[4]	[2358]						
Cl^{8+}	g	(17493)[1]	[568]						
		(17508)[5]	[2358]						
Cl^{2+}	g	(26737)[1]	[568]						
		(26753)[6]	[2358]						
Cl^{19+}	g	(37239)[1]	[568]						
		(37257)[7]	[2358]						
Cl^-	g	(−55.837)[2]	[568]	−57.326	[568]	36.627	[568]		
		(−59.547)[2]	[570]			36.6280	[570]		
		(−58.9)[10]	[2358]			36.64	[66]		
	d	(−39.952)	[2358]	(−31.372)	[2358]	(13.5)	[1685, 2358]	−32.6	[2358]
		(−39.86)	[91, 568]	(−31.5)	[574]				
Cl_2	g					(51.882)	[1186]	(7.88)	[1186]
						(53.289)	[1618a, 2179]	(8.111)	[1618a, 2179]
						(52.293)	[568]	(8.112)	[568]
						(53.2905)	[1830]	(8.1116)	[1830]
						(53.288)	[2358]	(8.104)	[2358]
						(53.29)	[1685]	(8.11)	[1685]
						(53.31)	[1896]		
						(53.290)	[2366]		
						(53.295)	[1106]		
	d	(−6.16)	[1027]	1.659	[1027]	27.1	[1027]		
		(−5.6)	[2358]	1.65	[2358]	29	[2358]		
		(−6.4)	[568]	1.65*	[323]				
Cl_2^+	g	261	[1214]						
		264.8	[568]						
		266.3[21]	[2358]						
Cl_2^{2+}	g	750	[568]						
		755[12]	[2358]						
$Cl_2 \cdot 6H_2O$	l	−426.8	[568]						
Cl_2	g	(25.7)	[568]						
Cl_3^-	d			−20	[2358]				

ClF	g	(–13.423)[13]	[1186]	(–13.779)	[1186]	(52.062)	[1186, 1618a, 2081]	(7.67)	[1186, 1685]
		(–13.4524)[14]	[1830]			(52.0639)	[1830]	(7.6682)	[1830]
		(–11.974)[15]	[570]			(52.065)	[570]	(7.668)	[2081, 1618a]
		(–11.923)[16]	[568]	(–12.278)	[568]	(52.06)	[568, 1685]	(7.669)	[568, 1008]
		(–11.6)	[2681]			(52.080)	[1008]		
		(–11.92)[17]	[2358]	(–12.28)	[2358]	(52.05)	[2177, 2358]	(7.66)	[2358]
		(–13.510)	[1618]						
		(–13.501)[18]	[1618a]	(–13.857)	[1618a]				
ClF^+	g	281.1[19]	[568]						
$ClFO_3$	g	–5.12[20]	[1618a, 2044]			67.0	[1655]	17.0	[1685]
		–5.7[21]	[2358]			66.65	[2358]	15.52	[2358]
		–5.5	[568]	12.09	[1618a]	66.653	[1618a]	15.517	[1618a]
$ClFO_3^+$	g	310[1]	[568]						
ClF_3	g	(–38.79)[22]	[1186]	(–29.46)	[1186]	(68.04)	[1186]	(15.55)	[1186]
		(–37.702)[23]	[568]	(–28.149)	[568]	(67.28)	[568]	(15.26)	[568, 1685]
		(–38.7380)[24]	[1830]			(67.2833)	[1830]	(15.2597)	[1830]
		(–38.0)[25]	[2358]	(–28.4)	[2358]	(67.58)	[2299]	(15.38)	[2299]
		(–38.869)[24]	[1618, 1618a]			(67.282)	[977]	(15.260)	[977]
		(–28.4)	[2618]			(67.4)	[1685]		
						(66.87)[27]	[1403]		
				(–29.542)	[1618a]	(68.034)	[1618a]	(15.549)	[1618a]
	l	–31.317	[568]	–15.106	[568]	44.95	[568]	28.45	[568]
		–44.3	[2358]			45.0	[1685]	28.50	[1685]
						43.66[27]	[1403]		
ClF_3, I, rhombic	c	–46.985[1]	[568]						
ClF_3^+	g	–263[1]	[568]						
		263.5[28]	[2358]						
$ClF_2 \cdot HF$	g	–107.5	[2358]	–90.8	[2358]	83	[2358]		
ClO	g	(24.34)[29]	[2358]	23.46	[2358]	54.14	[2358]	7.52	[2358]
		(24.218)[30]	[568]	23.326	[568]	54.14	[568]	7.54	[568, 1618a]
		(24.2065)[31]	[1830]	31.8*	[229]	54.1485	[1830]	7.5432	[1830]
		(24.192)[32]	[1618a]	23.298	[1618a]	54.145	[1618a]		

1. ΔH_0°. 2. $\Delta H_0^\circ=(4594.9)$ [2358]. 3. $\Delta H_0^\circ=(6825)$ [2358]. 4. $\Delta H_0^\circ=(9461)$ [2358]. 5. $\Delta H_0^\circ=(17495)$ [2358]. 6. $\Delta H_0^\circ=(26739)$ [2358]. 7. $\Delta H_0^\circ=(37241)$ [2358]. 8. $\Delta H_0^\circ=$ $=(-54.74)$ [568]. 9. $\Delta H_0^\circ=(-58.450)$ [570]. 10. $\Delta H_0^\circ=(-57.9)$ [2358]. 11. $\Delta H_0^\circ=264.8$ [2358]. 12. $\Delta H_0^\circ=752$ [2358]. 13. $\Delta H_0^\circ=-13.4$ [1186]; -12.637 (${}_{35}Cl_{19}F$); -13.995 (${}_{37}Cl_{19}F$) [1008]. 14. $\Delta H_0^\circ=-13.430$ [1830]. 15. $\Delta H_0^\circ=-11.95$ [570]. 16. $\Delta H_0^\circ=-11.899$ [568]. 17. $\Delta H_0^\circ=-11.9$ [2358]. 18. $\Delta H_0^\circ=-13.478$ [1618a]. 19. ΔH_0°. 20. $\Delta H_0^\circ=-3.034$ [1618a]. 21. $\Delta H_0^\circ=$ $=-3.6$ [2358]. 22. $\Delta H_0^\circ=-37.9$ [1186]. 23. $\Delta H_0^\circ=-36.7$ [568]. 24. $\Delta H_0^\circ=-37.7388$ [1830]. 25. $\Delta H_0^\circ=-37.0$ [2358]. 26. $\Delta H_0^\circ=-37.978$ [1618a]. 27. $T=284.91$ °K. 28. $\Delta H_0^\circ=$ $=262.8$ [2358]. 29. $\Delta H_0^\circ=24.36$ [2358]. 30. $\Delta H_0^\circ=24.236$ [568]. 31. $\Delta H_0^\circ=2249$ [1830]. 32. $\Delta H_0^\circ=24.211$ [1618a].

1	2	3		4		5		6	
ClO	g	(24.179)[1]	[570]	33.0*	[1045]	54.139	[570]		
ClO^-	g	264[2]	[568]						
	d	−25.76	[436]	−9.06	[436]	(10.75)	[436]		
		−25.73	[582]	−9.21	[[582]	(11.36)	[582]		
		−25.94	[1027]	−8.858	[1027]	(9.5)	[1027]		
		−25.6	[2358]	−8.8	[2358]	(10)	[2358]		
		−26.2	[1852]	−8.59	[1852]	(8.6)	[1852]		
		−26.4	[89, 568]	−8.9*	[323]	(10.0*)	[323]		
						(10.0)	[1685]		
ClO_2	g	(25.0)[3]	[1186, 1618a]	(29.6)	[1186]	(60.055)	[1186]	10.00	[1186, 1685]
		(24.5)[4]	[2358]	(28.8)	[2358]	(61.36)	[2358]	10.03	[568, 2358]
		(25)[5]	[568, 1830]	(29.24)	[568]	(61.43)	[568, 570]		
						(61.3706)	[1830]	10.0341	[1830]
				(29.232)	[1618a]	(61.453)	[1618a]	10.037	[1618a]
		(22.69)	[581]	(28.44)	[581]	(56.3)	[581]		
						(61.4)	[1685]		
						(59.991)	[2033]	9.969	[2033]
	d	(17.9)	[2358]	(28.1)	[2358]	(41.4)	[2358]		
		(18.4)	[568]						
		(16.09)	[581]	(26.50)	[581]	(44.2)	[581]		
ClO_2^+	g	282[2]	[568]						
ClO_2^-	d	(−16.9)	[89, 568]						
		(−15.9)	[2358]	(4.1)	[2358]	24.2	[2358]		
		(−17.18*)	[323]	(2.74*)	[323]	(24.1*)	[323]		
		(−17.54)	[580, 581]	(4.04)	[580]	(18.9)	[580]		
				(4.96)	[581]	(15.8)	[581]		
						(24.1)	[1685]		
ClO_3	g	37	[568, 2358]	45.9*	[229]				
				48.5*	[1045]				
ClO_3^+	g	307[2]	[568]						
ClO_3^-	d	(−23.7)	[2358]	(−0.8)	[2358]	(38.8)	[2041, 2358]		
		(−22,76)	[89, 93, 568]			(39.4)	[1685]		
ClO_4^-	g	−92.0	[1034]			43.6	[1685]		
	d	(−30.87)	[850]	(−2.14)	[850]	(43.9)	[850]		
		(−30.91)	[2358]	(−2.06)	[2358]	(43.5)	[2358]		
		(−29.46)	[89, 568]						
Cl_2F_6	g	−78.7	[568]						
		−79.9	[2358]						

Cl_2O	g	(18.15)[6]	[1186]	(21.64)	[1186]	(61.78)	[1186]	10.3	[1186]
		(18.10)	[1618a]	(22.316)	[1618a]	(63.654)	[1618a]	10.849	[1618a]
		(18.1)[7]	[568, 1830]	(22.323)	[568]	(63.63)	[568 1823]	10.85	[568, 1823, 2358]
						(63.6307)	[1830]	10.8491	[1830]
		(19.2)[8]	[2358]	(23.4)	[2358]	(63.60)	[1685, 2358]	10.90	[1685]
						(63.629)	[570]		
Cl_2O_7	g	(68.58)	[568]	95.4*	[229]				
		(65.0)	[2358]	97.5*	[1045]				
	l	76.7	[568]						
		56.9	[2358]						
DCl	g	−22.241[9]	[568]	−22.862	[568]	46.039	[568]	6.970	[568]
		−22.365[10]	[570]			46.041	[570]		
HCl	g	(−21.94)	[568]	(−22.656)	[568]	(44.644)	[568, 570, 2179]	(6.963)	[568, 2179]
		(−22.062)[11]	[2358]			(44.646)	[2358]	(6.96)	[2358]
		(−22.05)	[1896]	(−22.08)	[1896]	(44.645)	[1618a, 2366]	(6.964)	[1618a]
		(−22.063)[12]	[570, 1618a, 1830]	(−22.778)	[1618a]	(44.6457	[1830]	(6.9639)	[1830]
	d	(−39.952)	[2358]	(−31.372)	[2358]	(13.5)	[2358]	(−32.6)	[2358]
		(−39.86)	[568]						
HCl^+	g	274	[1214]						
		271.9[2]	[568]						
HCl^{2+}	g	802*[2]	[568]						
$(HCl)_2$	g	−46.0[13]	[568]						
HClO	g	−20[14]	[568]	−16.948	[568]	56.51	[568]	8.88	[568, 2358]
		−21.535[15]	[570]			56.516	[570]		
						56.14	[1823]	8.89	[1823]
						56.54	[2358]		
		−22.0[16]	[1618a]	−18.958	[1618a]	56.546	[1618a]	8.884	[1618a]
	d	−31.37	[582]	−19.17	[582]	25.54	[582]		
		−29.39	[1027]	−19.040	[1027]	32.0	[1027]		
		−31.47	[580]	19.02	[580]	25.25	[580]		
		−28.9	[2358]	−19.1	[2358]	35	[2358]		
		−31.40	[436]	−19.0	[436]	31*	[323]		
$HClO_2$	d	2.9[17]	[574]	2.65[17]	[574]				

1. $\Delta H_0^\circ = 24.17$ [570]. 2. ΔH_0°. 3. $\Delta H_0^\circ = (25.59)$ [1186, 1618a]. 4. $\Delta H_0^\circ = 25.09$ [2358]. 5. $\Delta H_0^\circ = 25.592$ [568]; 25.5910 [1830]. 6. $\Delta H_0^\circ = 18.61$ [1186]. 7. $\Delta H_0^\circ = 18.614$ [568]; 18.6127 [1830]. 8. $\Delta H_0^\circ = 19.71$ [2358]. 9. $\Delta H_0^\circ = -22.19$ [568]. 10. $\Delta H_0^\circ = -22.309$ [570]. 11. $\Delta H_0^\circ = (-22.020)$ [2358]. 12. $\Delta H_0^\circ = (-22.022)$ [570]; (−22.0193) [1830]; (−22.019) [1618a]. 13. $T = 240\ ^\circ K$. 14. $\Delta H_0^\circ = -19.296$ [568]. 15. $\Delta H_0^\circ = -20.831*$ [570]. 16. $\Delta H_0^\circ = -21.294$ [1618a]. 17. For the dissociation $HClO_2(d) \rightleftarrows H^+(d) + ClO_2^-(d)$.

1	2	3		4		5		6	
$HClO_2$	d	(−13.68*)	[323]	0.07*	[323]	42*	[323]		
		(−12.8)	[568]						
$HClO_2$, nondissociated	d	(−12.4)	[2358]	6.8	[2358]	45.0	[2358]		
$HClO_2$, dissociated	d	(−20.44)	[581]	2.31	[581]	14.5	[581]		
$HClO_3$	c					26.2*	[251]		
	d	(−23.7)	[2358]	−0.8	[2358]	38.8	[2358]		
		(−22.76)	[568]						
$HClO_4$	g	1.25[1]	[568]	21.958	[568]	70.8	[568]	17.5	[568]
		−0.4	[1600]			68.2	[2563]		
	l	(−8.25)	[568]	20.150	[568]	45.0	[568]	28.80	[568, 2563]
		(−9.70)	[2358]			45.02	[2563]		
		(−8.62)	[90]						
	d	(−30.91)	[2358]	−2.06	[2358]	43.5	[2358]		
		(−29.460)	[568]						
$HClO_4 \cdot H_2O$, I, rhombic	c	(−89.90)	[568]						
		(−91.35)	[2358]						
$HClO_4 \cdot 2H_2O$	l	(−160.60)	[568]						
		(−162.04)	[2358]						
TCl	g	−22.374[2]	[568]	−22.944	[568]]	46.868	[568]	6.995	[568]
		−22.485[3]	[570]			46.870	[570]		
CfO_2, cubic	c					20.3	[2078]		
						20.9	[2662]		
CmF_2^+	d					−12.1	[1231]		
CmF_3	c					18.9	[1231]		
$CmO_{1.5}$, cubic	c					19.2	[2662]		
CmO_2	c					20.9	[2662]		
						20.3	[2078]		
Co	g	(101.5)[4]	[1589]	(90.86)	[1589]	(42.88)	[1685]	(5.50)	[1685]
		(101.600)	[2479]	(90.995)	[2479]				
		(101.6)	[1540]						
								24.9[5]	[882]
	c					(7.18)	[1589, 1685, 2479]	(5.93)	[1589]
								(5.95)	[1685]
								(5.89)	[2479]
								(5.86)	[998]

Co^{2+}	g					42.73	[66]		
	d	(−14.2*)	[323]	(−12.8*)	[323]	(−27*)	[323]		
						(−26.6)	[1749]		
Co^{3+}	g					42.52	[66]		
	d			(28.9*)	[323]	(−26.7)	[51]		
CoAs	c	−13.6	[295]			15.4	[295]		
$CoAs_2$	c	−22.0	[295]			22.2	[295]		
$CoBr_2$	c	(−53.5*)	[323]	−50.3*	[323]	32.4*	[323]	19.04	[2718]
		(−51.0*)	[890]	−50.0*	[229]				
$CoBr_2 \cdot 2H_2O$	c	−200*	[232]						
$CoBr_2 \cdot 4H_2O$	c	−343*	[232]						
$CoBr_3$	c			−52.4*	[227]				
$Co(CN)_2$	c	50*	[2683]						
$Co(CN)_6^{3-}$	d							55.7	[1500]
$Co(CNS)_2$	c	30*	[2683]						
$CoCO_3$	c			−154.89*	[177]	21.9*	[177]		
				−154.7*	[227]	88.5[5]	[292]		
				−155.57*	[323]				
$CoCO_3 \cdot K_2CO_3$	c			−412.7*	[227]				
$CoCl_2$	c	(−76.064)	[1756]	(−65.501)	[1756]	(24.66)	[1756]		
		(−75.8*)	[323]	(−65.5*)	[323]	(25.4)	[1685]	(18.76)	[973, 1685]
						(26.09)	[973]		
$CoCl_2 \cdot 2H_2O$	c			−185.3*	[229]				
$CoCl_2 \cdot 4H_2O$	c			−301.4*	[229]				
$CoCl_2 \cdot 6H_2O$	c			−414.9*	[229]				
$Co(ClO_3)_2$	c	−39*	[2683]						
$Co(ClO_4)_2$	c	−48*	[2683]						
$Co(ClO_4)_2 \cdot 6H_2O$	c	−490.4	[23]						
$CoCr_2O_4$	c	−351.0	[330]	−32.0	[330]	27*	[330]		
CoF_2	c	(−157*)	[323]	−146.5*	[323]	20*	[323]		
$CoF_2 \cdot 4H_2O$	c	−455*	[229]						
CoF_3	c	(−185*)	[323]	−168*	[323]	22.6*	[323]		
				−170.3*	[229]				
$CoFe_2O_4$	c	−260*	[464]			32.2[6]	[1685, 1720]	36.53	[1685, 1720]
CoH	c			0.7*	[229]				
CoH_2	c			−0.7*	[229]				
$Co(HCO_3)_2$	c	−347*	[2683]						
$Co(HS)_2$	c	4*	[2683]						
$Co(HSO_4)_2$	c	−418*	[2683]						

1. $\Delta H_0^\circ = 3.997$ [568]. 2. $\Delta H_0^\circ = -22.32$ [568]. 3. $\Delta H_0^\circ = -22.431$ [570]. 4. $\Delta H_0^\circ = 101.12$ [1589]. 5. In *joules/mole* $\cdot$°C. 6. $S_{298}^\circ - S_0^\circ$.

1	2	3		4		5		6	
CoI_2	c	(−22.2*)	[323]	−23.3*	[323]	37.8*	[323]		
		(−21.0*)	[890]	−25.1*	[227]				
$C(IO_3)_2$	c			−85.0*	[229]				
$CoMoO_4$	c	−246.6*	[170, 172]	−224.0*	[170, 172]				
$Co(NH_2)_2$	c	−5*	[2683]						
$[Co(NH_3)_3(N_3)_3]$	c	95.7	[1107]						
trans-$[Co(NH_3)_4(N_3)_2]$ (N_3)	c	90.4	[1107]						
cis-$[Co(NH_3)_4(N_3)_2](N_3)$	c	90.9	[1107]						
$[Co(NH_3)_5Cl]Cl_2$	c			−144.90	[1981]				
$[Co(NH_3)_5N_3](N_3)_2$	c	50.4	[1107]						
$Co(NH_3)_6^{2+}$	d			(−57.7*)	[323]				
$Co(NH_3)_6^{3+}$	d			(−55.2*)	[323]				
$[Co(NH_3)_6]Br_2$	c			−136.12	[1982]				
$[Co(NH_3)_6]Cl_3$	c			−154.55	[1982]				
$[Co(NH_3)_6](ClO_4)_3$	c			−71.40	[1982]				
$[Co(NH_3)_6](N_3)_3$	c	30.7	[1107]						
$[Co(NH_3)_6](NO_3)_3$	c			−141.68	[1982]				
$Co(NO_2)_2$	c	−60*	[2683]						
$Co(NO_3)_2$	c	(−100.9*)	[323]	−55.1*	[323]	46*	[323]		
				−58.1*	[227]				
$Co(NO_3)_2 \cdot 6H_2O$	c			−395.7*	[229]				
CoO	c	(−57.1)	[878]	(−50.4)	[1878]	(12.66)	[1685, 1722]	13.20	[1685]
		(−55.2*)	[323]	(−49.0*)	[323]				
				(−51.6)	[1045]	(13.63)	[1045]		
				(−50.5*)	[232]				
$Co(OH)_2$	c	(−129.3*)	[323]	−109.0*	[323]	19.6*	[323]		
				−108.89*	[176]				
				−110.5*	[229]				
$Co(OH)_3$	c	(−174.6*)	[323]	−142.6*	[323]	20*	[323]		
				−141.27*	[176]				
				−145.6*	[229]				
CoP	c	(−38.0*)	[2245, 2628]						
CoP_3	c	(−69.0*)	[2245, 2628]						
$Co(ReO_4)_2$	c	−394*	[2683]						
$CoS_{0.89}$	c	20.4	[1772, 2239]			13,6	[1772, 2239]		
CoS	c	(−19.3*)[1]	[323]	(−19.8*)[1]	[229]	(16.1*)[1]	[323]		
		(−18.6)	[264]	(−22.99*)	[176]	(14.7*)	[176]		
		(−22.77)	[2481]	(−22.96*)	[2481]				

				(−22.4*)	[232]				
CoS_2	c	−33.5	[1772, 2239]						
$CoSO_3$	c	−142*	[2683]						
		−155.1*	[1172]						
$CoSO_4$	c	(−205.5*)	[323]	(−180.1*)	[323]				
		(−215*)	[358]	(−182.5*)[2]	[250]				
$CoSO_4 \cdot 6H_2O$	c			−530.8*	[229]	87.863	[2209]	84.458	[2909]
$CoSO_4 \cdot 7H_2O$	c			−586.4*	[229]	97.048	[2209]	(93.332)	[2209]
$Co_{0.25}Sb_{0.75}$	c	−3.9*[3]	[1589]						
$Co_{0.33}Sb_{0.67}$	c	−4.4*[4]	[1589]						
$Co_{0.5}Sb_{0.5}$	c	−5.0*[5]	[1589]						
CoSe	c			−9.7*	[229]				
$CoSeO_3 \cdot 2H_2O$	c	−268.50	[513]	−224.65	[513]	54.6	[513]		
		−287.1	[357]						
		−268.41	[974]						
$CoSeO_3 \cdot 6H_2O$	c	−569.8	[357]						
$CoSeO_4$	c	−135.0*	[499]						
		−146*	[2683]						
$CoSeO_4 \cdot H_2O$	c	−574.0*	[499]						
$CoSeO_4 \cdot 7H_2O$	c	−644.0*	[499]						
CoSi	c	(−92.9)[6]	[200]			44.35[7]	[200]		
$CoSiO_3$	c	−268	[2683]						
$Co_{0.333}Sn_{0.667}$	c	−2.3*[8]	[1589]						
$Co_{0.585}Sn_{0.415}$	c	−2.9*[9]	[1589]						
CoSn	c	−7.1	[2625]						
CoTe	c			−8.7*	[229]				
$CoTe_{1.2}$	c	−20.15	[33]						
$CoTe_{1.38}$	c					24.0*	[180]		
$CoTe_{1.5}$	c	−25.18	[33]						
$CoTe_{2.0}$	c	−32.27	[33]						
$CoTiO_3$	c	−288.1	[137]	−269.0	[137]	23.8	[137]		
$CoWO_4$		−289.8	[416]	−270.4	[416]	22.8	[416]		
$CoWo_4$	c	(−263*)	[172]	−239*, −245.5*	[172]			27.95	[684]
		(−269.3*)	[96, 172]	−245.5*	[170, 172]				
Co_2As	c	−13.5	[295]			23.0	[295]		
Co_2As_2	c	−34.4	[295]			39.2	[295]		

1. Precipitated, *a*. 2. Recalculated [234] from $(\Delta H^\circ_{298})_{diss}$ = 79.75 [250] to 79.3 [2245], using the values of ΔG°_{298} for SO_3 and CaO [2245]. 3. $CoSb_3$ phase. 4. $CoSb_2$ phase. 5. CoSb phase. 6. In *kjoules/mole*. 7. In *joules/mole*. 8. $CoSn_2$ phase. 9. γ or γ' phase.

1	2	3		4		5		6	
Co_2C	c	4.0	[2226]	3.3*	[323]	17.8	[2226]		
Co_2Nb	c	−13.7	[160]	−13.3	[160]	21.6	[160]		
Co_2S_3	c	(−47*)	[323]	−50.0	[229]				
		(−40.1)	[425]						
Co_2SiO_4	c	−8.0[1]	[326]	−6.6[1]	[326]	37.9	[1685]	32.10	[1685]
		−330.7	[325]	−304.8	[325]				
Co_3Nb	c	−14.1	[160]	−13.8	[160]	29.1	[160]		
Co_3O_4	c	(−204*)	[323]	−179.4*	[323]	35.8*	[323]		
		(−207)	[1045]	−182	1045]	35.77	[1045]		
		(−216.3)	[1773]	−183.6*	[229]	24.5	[1685, 1772]	29.50	[1685]
Co_3S_4	c	(−75.0)	[1772, 2239]						
Co_3W	c	−10.0	[473]	−8.0	[473]				
Co_5As_2	c	−26.6	[295]			53.3	[295]		
Co_7W_6	c							79.3[1]	[460]
Co_9S_8	c	(−197.0)	[2239]			110.0*	[1773]		
$HCo(OH)_4$	c			−197.92*	[6]				
$H_2Co(OH)_4$	c			−222.60*	[6]				
$H_3Co(OH)_4$	c			−311.22*	[6]				
Cr	g	(95.000)	[2479]	(84.284)	[2479]	(41.64)	[1685]	11.22[2]	[304]
		(92.952)	[392]						
		(94.85)[3]	[1589]	(84.13)	[1589]				
		(94.9)	[1932]						
		(94.8)[4]	[1105]						
	c					(5.70)	[2479]	(5.56)	[2479]
						(5.64)	[992, 993]	(5.463)[5]	[992, 993]
								(24.3)[6]	[1755]
Cr^{2+}	g					37.78	[66]		
	d			−42.1*	[323]				
Cr^{3+}	g					40.54	[66]		
	d	−55.5	[1183]						
Cr^{6+}	g					37.78	[66]		
CrB	c					8.4*	[1959]	8.57	[1959]
CrB_2	c	30*	[307]	30.1*	[307]	9.3	[307]	12.3	[307]
								10.65*	[305]
								12.36[1]	[492]
						6.6*	[1959]	12.80	[1959]
CrBr	c	9.3	[2143]	12.8*	[2143]	23.2*	[2143]		

$CrBr_2$	c	–77*	[230]						
		–86*	[583]						
		–76.0*	[1773]						
$CrBr_2$	c	–96*	[230]						
$Cr(CO)_6$	g	–240.4	[1042]	–227.2	[1042]	116.53	[1495]	50.97	[1495]
	c	–257.08	[603]	–234.7*	[229]			55.77[7]	[604]
		–257.5	[1042]	–232.2	[1042]			56.74	[604]
		–256.2	[693, 1042]						
$CrCl$	c	–1.2	[2143]	2.4	[2143]	20.2*	[2143]		
$CrClO$	c	–139	[2293]			16.3	[2293]		
$CrCl_2$	c	(–94.52)	[2466]			(27.56)	[2466]	17.01	[2466]
		(–95.2)	[1391]			(27.8)	[1680]		
		(–97.0)	[890]			(27.7)	[1685]		
$CrCl_2 \cdot 2H_2O$	c			–199.4*	[229]				
$CrCl_2 \cdot 3H_2O$	c			–257.3*	[229]				
$CrCl_2 \cdot 4H_2O$	c			–318.7*	[229]				
$CrCl_2O_2$	l	(–143.1*)	[323]	–125.4*	[323]	50*	[323]		
$CrCl_3$	c	(–132.0)	[890]			(29.38)	[1474]	(21.94)	[1474, 1685]
						(29.4)	[1685]		
						(30.0)	[1680]		
$CrCl_4$	g	–79.3	[410]	–103.4*	[229]	–23.1[8]	[410]		
	c	–98	[410]			–54[8]	[410]		
CrF	c	–52.7	[2143]	–48.5	[2143]	15.7	[2143]		
CrF_2	c	(–182.0*)	[890]	–170.3*	[227]	20.0*	[890]		
				–170.7*	[323]	19.6*	[323]		
CrF_3	c	(–266.0*)	[890]	–249.3*	[227]	22.44	[1474, 1685]	18.82	[1474, 1685]
				–248.3*	[323]	22.2*	[323]		
CrF_4	c	(–286.5)	[2617]						
$Cr_{0.094}Fe_{0.906}$, *a*	c							5.80	[1589]
$Cr_{0.20}Fe_{0.80}$	c							6.2	[1589]
$Cr_{0.30}Fe_{0.70}$	c							6.1	[1589]
$Cr_{0.40}Fe_{0.60}$	c							6.2	[1589]
$Cr_{0.50}Fe_{0.50}$	c							6.0[9]	[2318]
								6.3	[1589]
$Cr_{0.60}Fe_{0.40}$	c							6.4	[1589]
$Cr_{0.65}Fe_{0.35}$	c							6.2	[1589]
$Cr_{0.70}Fe_{0.30}$	c							6.2	[1589]

1. $t = 300\ ^\circ C$. 2. *cal/g*·°C. 3. $\Delta H_0^\circ = 94.34$ [1589]. 4. ΔH_0°. 5. $t = 0\ ^\circ C$. 6. $T = 320\ ^\circ K$; *joules/g-atom*·°C. 7. $t = 20.6 ^\circ C$. 8. ΔS_{298}°. 9. 60%Fe.

1	2	3		4		5		6	
$Cr_{0.72}Fe_{0.28}$	c							6.2	[1589]
$Cr_{0.75}Fe_{0.25}$	c							6.2	[1589]
$Cr_{0.76}Fe_{0.234}$	c							5.9	[1589]
$Cr_{0.782}Fe_{0.218}$	c							5.8	[1589]
$Cr_{0.784}Fe_{0.216}$	c							5.86	[1589]
$Cr_{0.799}Fe_{0.201}$	c							6.2	[1589]
$Cr_{0.825}Fe_{0.175}$	c							6.0	[1589]
$Cr_{0.841}Fe_{0.159}$	c							5.9	[1589]
CrI	c	24.9	[2143]	28.7*	[2143]	24.8*	[2143]		
CrI_2		(−37.8)	[1391, 2245]	−55.3*	[323]	37.4*	[323]		
	c			−54.3*	[227]	36.9*	[714]		
CrI_3	c	(−47.8)	[1391]	−48.4*	[229]				
$CrK(SO_4)_2$				−510*	[323]	57.4*	[323]		
	c			−509.3*	[229]				
$CrK(SO_4)_2 \cdot H_2O$	c			−597.5*	[229]				
$CrK(SO_4)_2 \cdot 2H_2O$	c			−660.4*	[229]				
$CrK(SO_4)_2 \cdot 6H_2O$	c			−840.6*	[229]				
$CrK(SO_4)_2 \cdot 12H_2O$				−1164*	[323]	169.2*	[323]		
	c			−1174*	[229]				
CrN	c	(−28.2)	[1772]	−24.7*	[229]	8.0	[1773]		
$Cr_{0.259}Ni_{0.741}$	g							5.91	[1589]
CrO				57.8*	[227]	53.0	[1685]	7.47	[1685]
	g					50*	[323]		
CrO_2	c					61.872	[2029]	12.499	[2029]
		−139.4[1]	[40]	−126.2*	[229]				
	d	−142.5	[887]	−130*	[1045]				
CrO_2^-	g			−125	[323]				
CrO_3	c					63.622	[2029]	13.513	[2029]
		(−140.0)	[1045]	−121.0	[1045]	17.2*	[1480]		
		(−142.1)	[2045]	−118.5*	[229]				
		(−138.5)	[887]						
	c	(−145.8*)	[323]						
$CrO_3 \cdot K_2Cr_2O_7$	d	−637*	[611]						
CrO_4^{2-}		(−213.7*)	[323]	(−176.1*)	[323]	(10.5)	[1685]		
		(−208.6)	[1499]	(−171.1)	[1499]				
		(−208.0)	[1996]						

$Cr(OH)_2$	c	−162*	[232]	−140.5*	[323]				
				−141.45*	[176]				
$Cr(OH)_3$	c	(−239*)	[2683]	−215.3*	[323]	19.2*	[323]		
				−215.7*	[229]				
				−202.92*	[176]				
CrS_3	c	66*	[1480]						
$CrSi$	c	−19*	[142]					9.25	[142]
		−19	[355]					9.5	[2143]
$CrSi_2$	c	−29*	[142]					12.8	[142]
		−29	[355]					12.9	[2143]
Cr_2N	c	(−25.5)	[1772]	−17.7*	[229]			18.0*	[1773]
Cr_2O_3	c	(−272.7)	[1891]	(−253.2)	[1891]				
		(−268.5)	[2205]	(−252.8*)	[232]				
		(−270.0)	[1773]						
		(−271)	[142, 355]						
$Cr_2O_7^{2-}$	d	(−364.0*)	[323]	(−315.4*)	[323]				
		(−352.2)	[1499]	(−305.9)	[1499]				
Cr_2S_3	c	−75*	[2683]						
$Cr_2(SO_4)_3$	c	−723*	[2683]						
Cr_2Ta	c					25.85	[1213]		
Cr_2Te_3	c					49.865[2]	[1410]	30.81	[1410]
Cr_3C_2	c	(−24.62)[3]	[1266]			(20.42)	[1098, 1685]	(23.53)	[1098, 1685]
Cr_3Si	c	−33*	[142]					24.7	[142]
		−33	[355]					24.5	[2143]
Cr_3Te_4	c					70.056[2]	[1410]	77.369	[1410]
								74.5	[2143]
Cr_5Si_3	c	−78	[142, 355]					35.2	[142]
Cr_5Te_6	c					112.508[2]	[1410]	76.56	[1410]
Cr_7H_2	c			5.8*	[229]				
$Cr_{23}C_6$	c					145.8	[1685]	149.2	[1685]
$HCrO_4^-$	d	(−220.2*)	[323]	(−184.9*)	[323]				
		(−207.9)	[1499]	(−180.0)	[1499]				
$HCr(OH)_4$	c			−259.57*	[6]				
$H_3Cr(OH)_6$	c			−372.87*	[6]				
Cs	g	(18.670)	[2479]	(12.176)	[2479]	(41.94)	[1685]		
		(18.67)[4]	[570]			(41.9442)	[570]		
		(18.7)	[1540]						

1. $CrO_{1.98}$. 2. $S^\circ_{298}-S^\circ_0$. 3. $\Delta H^\circ_0 = -23.41$ [1266]. 4. $\Delta H^\circ_0 = 19.048$ [570].

1	2	3		4		5		6	
Cs	g	(19.05)[1]	[1589]						
	c					(20.16)	[570, 1589, 2479]	(7.50)	[570, 2479]
						(20.1)	[1685]	(7.65)	[1589, 1685]
						(21.2)	[1079]	(7.24)	[2243]
								(7.70)	[1215]
Cs^+	g	(109.951)[2]	[570]			40.5668	[570]		
						40.58	[66]		
	d	(–62.6)	[1257]	(–70.8)	[1257]	(32.0)	[1685]		
		(–59.91)	[554]						
Cs_2	g	(26.00)[3]	[1185]	18.34[4]	[1185]	67.855	[1185]	9.112	[1185]
		(26.630)	[2479]	18.417	[2479]	67.8	[1685]	9.11	[1685]
		(26.6)	[1540]	18.4*	[229]	66.6	[1680]	8.94	[1679]
		(27.0)	[2243]						
		(27.7)	[1589]						
$CsAlH_4$	c	–39.46	[2409]	–23.5	[2409]	36.0*	[2409]		
$CsAl(SO_4)_2$	c			–517.2*	[229]				
$CsAl(SO_4)_2 \cdot H_2O$	c			–568.1*	[229]				
$CsAl(SO_4)_2 \cdot 2H_2O$	c			–629.1*	[229]				
$CsAl(SO_4)_2 \cdot 3H_2O$	c			–687.0*	[229]				
$CsAl(SO_4)_2 \cdot 12H_2O$	c					(163*)	[1685]		
CsAt	c					32.14*[6]	[304a]	11.88*[7]	[304a]
$CsBH_4$	c	–63*	[724]						
$CsBO_3$	c	–89.51	[875]	–68.00	[875]	38.8	[875]		
CsBr	g	–48*	[2243]			63.5	[2243]		
		49[5]	[2300]			64.0	[1685]	8.87	[1685]
	c	(–98.0)	[2300]	(–90.5*)[8]	[250]	(24)	[2300]		
						(27.1)	[2063]		
						(27.9*)	[698]]		
$CsBrO_3$	c	–89.51	[875]	–68.00	[875]	38.8	[875]		
						40.3*	[699]		
$CsBrO_4$	c					43.4*	[249]		
CsCN	c	–27*	[693]						
		–26*	[2182]						
		–21*	[2683]						
CsCNO	c	–96*	[693]						
CsCNS	c	–50*	[693]						
		–51*	[2683]						

CsCl	g	–56	[2243]			61.3	[2243]		
		–54.0[9]	[395]			61.1	[1685]	8.78	[1685]
		49.4[10]	[2300]						
	c	–103.5	[2300]	–96.8[11]	[250]	21.5	[2300]	12.6	[2243]
				–96.6*	[227, 323]	23.3*	[323]		
				–97.5*	[224]	24*	[224]		
						24.18	[2516]	12.54	[2516]
						25.1*	[698]		
						23.5	[890]		
						38.4*	[699]		
$CsClO_3$	c	–92.3	[481]						
		–94.6	[84]						
		–97*	[2683]						
$CsClO_4$	c	(–478)	[192]			(41.9)	[1685]	(25.93)	[1685]
		(–104*)	[2683]			(40.9*)	[699]		
CsF	g	–81	[2243]			58.8	[1685]	8.76	[1685]
		49[12]	[2300]						
	c	–126.9	[2300]			19	[2300]	11.45[13]	[1668]
				–119.5*	[323]	19.1*	[323]	12.1	[2243]
				–120.8*	[227]	19.8	[1773]		
				–120.17*[14]	[250]	21.6*	[698]		
						22*	[890]		
CsF·HF	c					32.31	[2243]	20.86	[913]
CsH	g					(51.36)	[1685]	(7.53)	[1685]
	c	–11.92	[2409]	–7.0	[2409]	19.3*	[2409]		
		–13.48	[1501]	–7.3*	[323]				
		–11*	[2683]	–8.6*	[229]				
$CsHCO_3$	c			–198.8*	[323]	31*	[323]		
$CsHSO_3$	c	–156*	[693]						
$Cs_{0.002}Hg_{0.998}$	l	–0.063[15]	[1589]	–0.059[15]	[1589]				
$Cs_{0.005}Hg_{0.995}$	l	–0.156[15]	[1589]	–0.143[15]	[1589]				
$Cs_{0.01}Hg_{0.99}$	l	–0.365[15]	[1589]	–0.279[15]	[1589]				
$Cs_{0.02}Hg_{0.98}$	l	–0.584[15]	[1589]	–0.534[15]	[1589]				
Cs(Hg)	l	–31.2	[1257]						
CsI	g	–33	[2243]			65.2	[2243]		

1. ΔH_0°. 2. $\Delta H_0^\circ = 108.848$ [570]. 3. Calculated [234] from $\Delta H_{298}^\circ = 10.38$ for the reaction $Cs_2(g) = 2\,Cs(g)$ [1183]. 4. Calculated [234] from $\Delta G_{298}^\circ = 5.89$ for the reaction $Cs_2(g) = 2Cs(g)$ [1183]. 5. $(\Delta H_{298}^\circ)_{subl}$. 6. $T = 300°K$. 7. C_p; $T = 300$ °K. 8. Recalculated [234] from $\Delta H_{298}^\circ = -97.65$ [842] to −94.3 [2245]. 9. Calculated [234] from $(\Delta H_0^\circ)_{subl} = 49.54$ [395] $(\Delta H_{298}^\circ)_{CsCl(c)} = -103.5$ [2245]. 10. $(\Delta H_{298}^\circ)_{subl}$. 11. Recalculated [234] from the value $\Delta H_{298}^\circ = -106.32$ [842] to −103.5 [2245]. 12. $(\Delta H_{298}^\circ)_{subl}$. 13. $T = 300°K$. 14. Recalculated [234] from $\Delta H_{298}^\circ = -131.68$ [842] to −126.9 [2245]. 15. From Cs(l).

1	2	3		4		5		6	
CsI	g	48.5[1]	[2300]			65.5	[1685]	8.87	[1685]
	c			(78.9*)[2]	[250]	(30.0*)	[1773]		
						(28)	[2243]		
						(30.1*)	[698]		
						(29.41)	[2516]	12.62	[2516]
$CsIO_3$	c	−125.8	[617]						
$CsIO_4$	c					44.0*	[249]		
CsK	g					64.5	[1680]		
CsLi	g					58.2	[1680]	8.84	[1679]
$CsMnO_4$	c					47.0*	[249]		
$CsNO_2$	c	−85*	[693]						
		−87*	[2683]						
$CsNO_3$	c	(−140*)	[358]	−94*	[323]	35.3*	[323]		
				−94.4*	[227]	35.6*	[699]		
CsN_3	c	−2.37	[1356]						
CsNa	g					62.1	[1680]	8.93	[1679]
$CsNbCl_6$	c	−24.4[1]	[547]						
CsO_2	c	−76.0*	[887]	−50.5*	[1045]				
		−69.2	[1109]						
CsOH	c			−84.9*	[323]	18.6*	[323]		
				−86.6*	[229]	22.3*	[699]		
$Cs(PtNH_3Cl_3)$	c	−185	[423]						
CsRb	g							8.94	[1679]
$CsTaCl_6$	c	−28.0[3]	[547]						
$CsTiBr_3$	c	−222.6	[629]						
Cs_2CO_3	c			−243.6*	[323]	42.4*	[323]		
				−248.3*	[227]	45.1*	[699]		
	d			−261.0*	[323]				
Cs_2CrO_4	c					56.8*	[699]		
Cs_2MnO_4	c					45.6*	[699]		
Cs_2MoO_4	c	−358*	[2683]						
Cs_2O	c			−65.6*	[323]	29.6*	[323]		
				−69.3*	[229]				
				−65*	[1045]				
Cs_2O_2	c			−78.2*	[323]	28.2*	[323]		
				−79.3*	[229]				
				−79.5*	[1045]				
Cs_2O_3	c	(−135.0*)	[887]	−86.1*	[323]	28.7*	[323]		

				−86.5*	[229]				
				−88.5*	[1045]				
Cs_2O_4	c			−92.5*	[323]	31.2*	[323]		
				−91.7	[229]				
$Cs_2[PtCl_4]$	c	−257.2	[423]						
Cs_2ReCl_6	c	−409.1*	[203]						
Cs_2S	c	(−87*)	[1480]	−77.6*	[323]	35.4*	[323]		
Cs_2SO_3	c	−262.0*	[1172]						
		−270*	[2683]						
		−263.6	[618]						
Cs_2SO_4	c			−310.7*	[323]	49.2*	[323]		
						51.1*	[699]		
$Cs_2S_2O_5$	c	−363.5	[618]						
Cs_2Se	c	−66*	[693]						
Cs_2SeO_4	c	−272.3	[519]			45.8*	[498]		
		−272*	[2683]						
Cs_2SiF_6	c			−629.6*	[323]	63.5*	[323]		
Cs_2SiO_3	c	−365.6	[364]						
		−353*	[2683]						
$Cs_2Si_2O_5$	c	−586.7*	[374]						
$Cs_2Si_4O_9$	c	−1031*	[364]						
Cs_2TiBr_6	c	−392.8	[629]						
Cs_2UO_4	c	−478	[364]						
Cs_2WO_4	c	−392*	[2683]						
Cs_3TiBr_6	c	−463.1	[629]						
$Cs_3Ti_2Br_9$	c	−623.0	[629]						
$Cs_{23}C_6$	c			−101*	[2226]				
Cu	g	(81.100)	[2479]	(71.628)	[2479]	(39.74)	[1685]		
		$(80.86)^4$	[1589]	(71.39)	[1589]				
		$(80.807)^5$	[1833]						
		$(80.9)^5$	[396]						
		$(80.3)^5$	[1887]						
		(76.5)	[756]						
	c					(7.92)	[1952]	(5.84)	[960a, 1952]
						(7.97)	[1588, 1589, 1685]	(5.86)	[1589, 1685]
Cu^+	g					38.38	[66]		
	d	(17.1)	[2603]	(12.0)	[2603]	(9.4)	[1685, 2603]		
						(8.3)	[1588]		

1. $(\Delta H^\circ_{298})_{subl}$. 2. Recalculated [234] from $\Delta H^\circ_{298} = -83.90$ [842] to −80.5 [2245]. 3. From chlorides. 4. $\Delta H^\circ_0 = (80.58)$ [1589]. 5. ΔH°_0.

1	2	3		4		5		6	
Cu^{2+}	g					42.96[1]	[66]		
						42.75[2];			
						41.94	[66]		
	d					(−26.5)	[1588, 1685]		
						(−24.1)	[1550]		
						(−20.4)	[1749]		
CuBr	g					59.2	[1685]		
	c	(−24.9)	[1549]	(−23.81)	[1549]	(23.0)	[1549]	13.08	[1549, 1685]
				(−23.86)	[176]	(22.0*)	[176]		
				(−24.2)[3]	[250]	(22.6)	[1685]		
				(−23.702)[4]	[655]				
$CuBr_2$	c	(−31.08*)	[655]	−24.961*[4]	[655]				
		(−30)	[230]	−30.3*	[323]	22.6*	[323]		
				−24.3*	[232]	34.02	[780]		
				−24.4[5]	[655]				
$CuBr_2 \cdot 4H_2O$	c			−258.4*	[323]	70.2*	[323]		
$Cu(CN)_2$	c	69*	[2683]						
$Cu(CN)_2^-$	d			69.3*	[323]				
$Cu(CNS)_2$	c	51*	[2683]						
$CuCo_3$	c			(−123.82*)	[177]	(21.2*)	[177]		
						(22.0)	[1685]		
$CuCo_3 \cdot K_2CO_3$	c			−384.5*	[229]				
$CuCo_3 \cdot Na_2CO_3$	c			−377.4*	[229]				
CuCl	g							8.39	[1685]
	c	(−31.9)	[655]	(−27.732)	[655]	(21.8)	[655]		
				(−28.55*)	[176]	(22.4*)	[176]		
				(−28.1*)[6]	[250]	(20*)	[224]		
				(−27.1*)	[232]	(20.8)	[1680, 1685]		
$CuCl_2$	c	(−41.2)	[655]	−31.400	[655]	28.4	[655]		
				−42*	[323]	26.8*	[323]		
				−31.8*	[232]	27.0*	[890, 2617]		
				−39.7*	[227]	25.83	[2466]	17.18	[2466]
$CuCl_2 \cdot CuO$	c			−70.0*	[229]				
$CuCl_2 \cdot H_2O$	c	−123*	[230]						
$CuCl_2 \cdot 2H_2O$	c			−155.4*	[229]				
$CuCl_2 \cdot 4H_2O$	c	−334*	[230]						
$CuCl_2 \cdot 6H_2O$	c	−473*	[230]						
$Cu(ClO_3)_2$	c	(−13*)	[2683]						

$CuClO_4$	d	−47.4	[2603]						
$Cu(ClO_4)_2$	c	(−20*)	[2683]						
CuD	g					48.30	[1685]	7.08	[1685]
CuF	g			37.1*	[227]	54.1	[1685]	7.95	[1685]
	c	(−50*)	[230]	−45.5	[227]	15.5	[1685]		
		(−60.0*)	[2617]	−55*	[229]	16.3*	[2602]		
				−83.01	[1356]				
CuF_2	c	(−128.0*)	[890, 2617]	−116*	[323]	20.2*	[323]		
				−114.3*	[227]	22.0*	[890]		
$CuFeO_2$	c	−126.8	[777]	−114.2	[777]	21.2	[777]	19.13	[777]
$Cu_{0.75}Fe_{2.25}O_4$	c					36.2	[1685]	36.13	[1685]
$CuFe_2O_4$	c	−235.7	[464]	−209.0	[464]	33.7	[777, 1685]	35.52	[777, 1685]
		−230.3	[777]	−204.85	[777]				
$CuFeS_2$	c	−40.94*	[134]	−51.49*	[134]	35.4	[134]		
CuH	g					46.90	[1685]		
$Cu(HCO_3)_2$	c	−322*	[2683]						
$Cu(HS)_2$	c	28*	[2683]						
$Cu(HSO_4)_2$	c	−392*	[2683]						
CuH_2	c	−6	[2683]						
CuI	g					61.1	[1685]		
	c			(−16.66*)	[176]	(23.5*)	[176]		
				(−17.0*)[7]	[250]				
CuI_2	c			−5.7*	[323]	(38*)	[323]		
				−2.8*	[227]	(39)	[655]		
CuI_2^-	d			−24.6*	[323]				
$Cu(IO_3)_2$	c			−58.62*	[177]				
				−58.4*	[323]				
$Cu(IO_3)_2 \cdot H_2O$	c					39.4	[2203]		
$CuMg_2$	c	−4.0	[2406]			30.3	[2406]		
$Cu_{0.769}Mn_{0.231}$	c							6.05	[1589]
$CuMoO_4$	c	(−225.7*)	[170, 172]	−202.7*	[170, 172]	33.8*	[323]		
				−204.6*	[229]				
CuN_3	c	(60.23)	[2503]	71.219	[2503]	39.68	[2503]		
		(67.23)	[1356]	73.75*	[232]	25.53	[1356]		
$Cu(NH_2)_2$	c	10*	[2683]						
$Cu(NH_3)^+$	d			(−2.8*)	[323]				
$Cu(NH_3)_2^+$	d					63*	[323]		

1. The electronic configuration of the ion is (Ar) $3d^8 4s$. 2. The electronic configuraion of the ion is (Ar)$3d^9$. 3. Recalculated [234] from $\Delta H^\circ_{298} = -25.7$ [842] to 25.1 [2245]. 4. In the original the values of ΔG°_{298} are given for the reaction with gaseous bromine. 5. From gaseous bromine. 6. Recalculated [234] from $\Delta H^\circ_{298} = -34.3$ [842] to −32.2 [2245]. 7. Recalculated [234] from $\Delta H^\circ_{298} = = -17.8$ [842] to −16.2 [2245].

1	2	3		4		5		6	
$Cu(NO_2)_2$	c	–36*	[2683]						
$Cu(NO_3)_2$	c			–27.3*	[323]	46.2*	[323]		
				–29.2*	[227]				
$Cu_{0.1}Ni_{0.9}$	c							6.3	[1589]
$Cu_{0.2}Ni_{0.8}$	c							6.4	[1589]
$Cu_{0.33}Ni_{0.67}$	c							6.18	[1589]
$Cu_{0.40}Ni_{0.60}$	c							5.76	[1589]
$Cu_{0.50}Ni_{0.50}$	c							5.57	[1589]
$Cu_{0.80}Ni_{0.20}$	c	0.75[1]	[1589]					5.58	[1589]
$Cu_{0.90}Ni_{0.10}$	c	0.60[1]	[1589]					5.69	[1589]
Cu + Ni	c							6.2*[2]	[424]
								6.7*[3]	[424]
CuO	g	(27*)	[863]	28.2*	[227]	55.3	[1685]	7.94	[1685]
	c	(–34.271)	[968]	(–31.0)	[1045]	(10.4)	[968]	(10.109)	[1550]
		(–37.5)	[763]			(10.19)	[1550, 1685]	(10.11)	[1685]
$CuO \cdot CuSO_4$	c	–220.01	[1675]			40.95	[1675]		
						34.1	[1685]		
$Cu(OH)_2$	c			–85.90*	[176]	16.7*	[176]		
				–85.3*	[323]	19*	[323]		
				–86.6*	[229]				
$Cu(OH)_2 \cdot H_2O$	c			–25.6	[117]				
CuO_2	c	–37*	[2683]						
CuP_2	c	(–23.5)	[2464]						
CuPt	c	–3.2	[2625]						
$Cu(ReO_4)_2$	c	–374*	[2683]						
CuS	c	(–12.1)	[1773]	(–15.58*)	[176]	(29.1*)	[176]		
$CuSO_3$	c	–128.8*	[1172]						
$CuSO_4$	c	(–182.31)	[1675]	(–157.7*)[4]	[250]	(29.24)	[1675]		
		(–114*)	[2683]			(25.3)	[1680, 1685]		
$CuSO_4 \cdot 2Cu(OH)_2$	c	–401.1*	[587]	–339.21	[587]				
				–67.5	[117]				
$CuSO_4 \cdot H_2O$	c					(33.0)	[1685]		
$CuSO_4 \cdot 3H_2O$	c					(52.4)	[1685]		
$CuSO_4 \cdot 5H_2O$	c					(70.2)	[1685]		
$CuSO_4 \cdot K_2SO_4 \cdot 2H_2O$	c			–617.6*	[229]				
$CuSO_4 \cdot K_2SO_4 \cdot 6H_2O$	c			–843.5*	[229]				

$CuSO_4 \cdot 3NH_3$	c	(−285.3)	[737]						
CuSe	c	(−9.45)	[1293]	−7.9*	[323]	22.2*	[323]		
				−14.9*	[229]				
				7.8	[790a]				
$CuSe_2$	c	−10.3	[1293]						
$CuSeO_3$	c	−93.6	[344]						
$CuSeO_3 \cdot 2H_2O$	c	−239.8	[344]	−197.8	[344]	61.8	[344]		
$CuSeO_4$	c	(−118.5)	[522]			16.6*	[498]		
		(−119*)	[2683]						
$CuSeO_4 \cdot 5H_2O$	c	(−475.6)	[522]						
$CuSiO_3$	c	−245*	[2683]						
$CuWO_4$	c	−247.3*	[170, 172]	−223.1*	[170, 172]	35.8*	[323]		
				−227.7*	[229]				
$Cu_{0.525}Zn_{0.475}$	c							5.89	[1589]
Cu + Zn	c							0.0965*[5]	[424]
$Cu_2K_2[Fe(CN)_6]$	c	23.1	[2234]						
Cu_2Mg	c	−1.85	[1589]	−2.12	[1589]			5.88	[1589]
		−5.4	[2406]			26.5	[2406]		
		−4.0	[2405]						
Cu_2O	c	(−39.84)	[968]	(−34.2*)	[232]	(23.0)	[968]	(15.21)	[1548, 1685]
		(−40.8)	[763]	(−35.18*)	[176]	(24.8*)	[176]		
		(−34.309*)	[968]			(22.44)	[1548]		
		(−40.4)	[1045]			(24.1)	[969]		
		(−40.0)	[1773]			(22.4)	[1685]		
Cu_2S	c	(−19.97)	[906]	(−21.198)	[906]	(27.6)	[906]		
		(−16.134)	[1702]	(−19.13)	[1702]	(33.59)	[1702]		
		(−19.94)	[2481]	(−21.29)	[2481]	(33.6)	[2481]		
		(−19.6)	[1773]	(−19.6*)	[232]	(28.5)	[1773]		
		(−18.50)	[290]	(−22.24*)	[176]	(34.6)	[176]		
				(−22.607)[6]	[2608]				
Cu_2SO_4	c			(−156*)	[323]	43.6*	[323]		
				(−153.9*)	[229]				
Cu_2SO_4, β	c	(−181.4)	[2697]						
Cu_2SO_4	d	(−181.4)	[2603]						
$Cu_{1.8}Se$	c	−13.23	[1293]						
Cu_2Se, α	c	−14.17	[1293]	−15.8*	[4]	30.1*	[4]		
				−16.3	[790a]	35.4*	[579]		
						37.2*	[180]		

1. $T = 273$ °K. 2. 5%Ni. 3. 10%Ni. 4. Recalculated [234] from $(\Delta H^\circ_{298})_{diss} = 75.3$ [250] to 75.9 [2245] using the values of ΔG°_{298} for SO_3 and CuO [2245]. 5. 5% Zn (*cal/g·°C*); $t = 200$ °C (alloy was previously annealed). 6. $T = 300$ °K.

1	2	3		4		5		6	
Cu_2Se, β	c	(−13.01)	[1293]	−5.3*	[229]				
Cu_2SeO_4	c	−108.5*	[499]			34.4*	[4]		
						38.3	[180]		
						39.8	[579]		
						38.6*	[774]		
Cu_2Te	c			−74*	[4]				
Cu_3As	c	−25.6	[2625]						
Cu_3N	c			−13.2*	[229]				
Cu_3P	c	(−36.0)	[1772]						
		(−36.4)	[1482a]						
Cu_3Pt	c	−4.2	[2625]						
Cu_3Sb	c	(−2.5)	[2525]						
Cu_3Se_2	c	−23.64	[1293]						
Cu_3Sn	c	(−7.2)	[2625]						
$HCuO_2^-$	d			(−61.42*)	[323]				
$HCu(OH)_3$	c			−142.55*	[6]				
$H_2Cu(OH)_4$	c			−199.20*	[6]				
Dy	g	(71.3)[1]	[2697]	77.4*	[229]				
		(70.91)[2]	[1456]	61.09*	[1589]				
		(61.6)	[2678]						
	c					(17.87)	[1399]	6.73	[1399, 1685]
						(17.9)	[1589, 1685]	6.51	[2479]
						(17.80)	[2396]		
Dy^{3+}	d			(−162.8*)	[323]	−43.3*	[323]		
DyB_6	c	−120.0	[455]						
$DyBr_3$	c	−197*	[230, 2683]						
$DyCl_{0.25}(OH)_{1.5}$	c			−286.6	[15]				
$DyCl_{0.5}(OH)_{2.5}$	c			−300.1	[15]				
DyClO	c	−233*	[46]						
$DyCl(OH)_2$	c			−292.3	[15]				
$DyCl_2$	c	−148*	[442]						
$DyCl_3$, β	c	−233*	[442]	−219.9*	[323]	35.0*	[323]		
		(76.4)[3]	[441]	−217.2*	[227]				
$DyCo_5$	c					55.61	[2666]	38.54	[2666]
DyI_3, β	c	(−144)	[1533]	−143.2*	[323]	51.9*	[323]		
				−143.5*	[227]				
$DyO_{1.5}$, body-centered	c			−212.7	[2662]				

$Dy(OH)_3$	c	−355.7*	[229]	(−305.4*)	[323]				
				(−309.3)	[15]				
		−445.84	[1562, 2666]	−424.06	[2666]	35.8	[2662, 2666]		
				−422*	[1976]	38.1	[2662]		
				−356.0*	[234]				
Dy_2S_3	c	−251*	[2683]						
$Dy_2(SO_4)_3$	c	(−950*)	[2683]						
$Dy_2(SO_4)_3 \cdot 8H_2O$	c	−1515*	[229]			155.9*	[323]		
Er	g	66.4	[2678]						
		81.79[4]	[1456]						
	c					17.5	[1685]	6.72	[1685, 2479]
						17.59	[2396]		
						17.48	[2397]		
						17.46	[1589]		
						14.3*	[323]		
Er^{3+}	d	(−158.79)	[2422]	(−158.86*)	[323]	−44*	[323]		
				(−152*)	[1976]	−51*	[1976]		
ErB_6	c	−126.0	[455]						
$ErBr_3$	c	−191*	[230]						
		−190*	[2683]						
$ErCl_{0.5}(OH)_{2.5}$	c			−298.4	[16]				
				−298.64	[8]				
ErClO	c	−231*	[46]						
$ErCl(OH)_2$	c			−290.4	[16]				
$ErCl_2$	c	−150*	[442, 445]						
$ErCl_3$	c	−229*	[46]						
$ErCl_3$, γ	c	(−229.07)	[2422]	−211.4	[2422]	35.1	[2422]		
		(76.0)[3]	[441]	−214*	[323]	35.1*	[323]		
				−215.2*	[227]				
				−211.4*	[232]				
				−210*	[1976]				
$ErCl_3 \cdot 6H_2O$	c	−677.19	[2422]	−578.6	[2422]	91.5	[2422]		
				−576*	[1976]				
				−578.5*	[232]				
ErI_3, β	c			−138.8*	[323]	52*	[323]		
				−139.2*	[227]				
				−135*	[1976]				
$ErO_{1.5}$, body-centered	c	−226.80	[2662]	−216.2	[2662]				

1. Average of data reported in [2697] (71.2; 71.4). 2. $\Delta H_0^\circ = 71.23$ [1456]. 3. $(\Delta H_0^\circ)_{vap}$. 4. $\Delta H_0^\circ = 81.98$ [1456].

1	2	3		4		5		6	
$Er(OH)_3$	c			−308.5*	[229]				
				−302.8*	[323]				
				−307.86	[8]				
Er_2O_3	c	−453.60	[2666]	−432.6	[2666]	36.6	[1456, 2666]	(12.4*)[1]	[1976]
		−453.59	[1563]	−430*	[1976]	37.6	[1456]	(25.26)	[2095]
Er_2S_3	c	−267*	[2683]						
$Er_2(SO_4)_3$	c	−910*	[2683]						
$Er_2(SO_4)_3 \cdot 8H_2O$	c	−1504*	[229]						
Eu	g	(43.200)	[2479]	34.821	[2479]				
		(41.92)[2]	[1456]	33.90*	[1589]				
	c					17.00	[1685, 2479]	6.40	[1685, 2479]
						14.0*	[323]		
Eu^{2+}	d	−150	[1976]	(−149*)	[1976]	−18*	[1976]		
		−120.9	[2474]						
Eu^{3+}	d			(−158*)	[1976]	−50*	[1976]		
				(−166.5*)	[323]	−42.3*	[323]		
EuB_6	c	−112.2	[455]						
$EuBr_3$	c	(−205*)	[230]						
$EuCl_{0.5}(OH)_{2.5}$				−306.24	[10]				
EuClO	c	−234*	[46]						
$EuCl(OH)_2$	c			−298.12	[10]				
$EuCl_2$	c	−217	[455, 446]			32	[446]		
		−200	[442]						
		−195.8	[2474]						
$EuCl_3$	c	(−239*)	[691]	−229.2*	[323]	34.8*	[323]		
		(−241]	[442, 446]	−230.3*	[227]	34*	[446]		
		(−192.8)	[2474]						
		(79.1)[3]	[441]						
EuI_3	c	−152*	[230]						
EuO	c					16.3*	[2662]		
$EuO_{1.5}$, monoclinic	c	−217.0	[2662]	−206*	[2662]				
$Eu(OH)_3$	c			−308.6	[323]				
				−315.46	[10]				
Eu_2O_3	c	−432	[46]						
		−435.6	[455]			35	[455]		
Eu_2O_3, C-type	c	−389.6	[1561]					75	[592]
Eu_2O_3, monoclinic	c	−393.9	[1561]						

$Eu_2(SO_4)_3 \cdot 8H_2O$	c	–1523.4*	[323]			156*	[323]		
		–1524*	[229]			160.6	[1685]	(146.0)	[1685]
F	g	(18.903)[4]	[1186]	(14.82)	[1186]	(37.9173)	[1186]	(5.4365)	[1186]
		(18.8582)[5]	[1830]	(15.4*)	[232]	(37.9170)	[1618a, 1830]	(5.4367)	[1830]
		(19.003)[6]	[568]	(14.921)	[568]	(37.916)	[568]	(5.436)	[568, 1009]
		(18.5)	[1773]			(37.92)	[1685]	(5.44)	[1685]
		(20.6)[7]	[1968]			(37.9163)	[2178]	(5.4364)	[2178]
		(18.86)[8]	[1618a, 2438]			(37.933)	[1009]	(5.437)	[1618a]
		(18.8*)	[783]			(37.9172)	[570]		
F^+	g	(422.31)[9]	[568]						
		(422.14)[10]	[2358]						
F^{2+}	g	(1227.1)[7]	[568]						
		(1230.44)[11]	[2358]						
F^{3+}	g	(2672.1)[7]	[568]						
		(2676.9)[12]	[2358]						
F^{4+}	g	(4682)[7]	[568]						
		(4690.6)[13]	[2358]						
F^{5+}	g	(7317)[7]	[568]						
		(7326.6)[14]	[2358]						
F^{6+}	g	(10941)[7]	[568]						
		(10952.3)[15]	[2358]						
F^{7+}	g	(15212)[7]	[568]						
		(15224.2)[16]	[2358]						
F^{8+}	g	(37209)[7]	[568]						
		(37222)[17]	[2358]						
F^-	g	(–62.066)[18]	[568]	–63.722	[568]	34.767	[568]		
		(–74.9)	[481]	–76.7	[481]	34.78	[66]		
		(–64.656)[19]	[570]			34.7683	[570]		
		(–64.7)[20]	[2358]						
	d	(–79.50)	[2358]	(–66.64)	[2358]	(–3.3)	[2358]	(–25.5)	[2358]
		(–79.23)	[568]			(2.3)	[1685]		
		(–79.13)	[91]						
F_2	g					(48.484)	[2009]	(7.466)	[2009]
						(48.506)	[1009]	(7.4870)	[1009]
						(48.589)	[64]	(7.569)	[64]
						(48.445)	[2178]	(7.485)	[2178]

1. Average value of 273 and 373 °K. 2. $\Delta H_0^\circ = 42.04$ [1456]. 3. $(\Delta H_0^\circ)_{vap}$. 4. $\Delta H_0^\circ = (18.4)$ [1186]. 5. $\Delta H_0^\circ = 18.355$[1830]. 6. $\Delta H_0^\circ = 18.5$ [568]. 7. ΔH_0°. 8. $\Delta H_0^\circ = (18.36)$ [2438]; (18.357) [1618a]. 9. $\Delta H_0^\circ = (420.28)$ [568]. 10. $\Delta H_0^\circ = (420.16)$ [2358]. 11. $\Delta H_0^\circ = (1226.98)$ [2358]. 12. $\Delta H_0^\circ = (2672.0)$ [2358]. 13. $\Delta H_0^\circ = (4684.2)$ [2358]. 14. $\Delta H_0^\circ = (7318.7)$ [2358]. 15. $\Delta H_0^\circ = (10942.9)$ [2358]. 16. $\Delta H_0^\circ = (15213.4)$ [2358]. 17. $\Delta H_0^\circ = (37209)$ [2358]. 18. $\Delta H_0^\circ = (-61.01)$ [568]. 19. $\Delta H_0^\circ = (-63.600)$ [570]. 20. $\Delta H_0^\circ = (-63.7)$ [2358].

1	2	3		4		5		6	
F_2	g					(48.447)	[570, 1186, 1618a]	(7.49)	[568, 1186, 1618a, 1685]
						(48.49)	[1685]		
						(48.5)	[1680, 2008]		
						(48.4460)	[1830]	(7.4869)	[1830]
						(48.44)	[2358]	(7.48)	[2358]
						(48.56)	[1896]		
						(48.45)	[568]		
F_2^+	g	(362.3)[1]	[568]						
		(366.6)[2]	[2358]						
FCN	g	3.8	[2358]			53.639	[2037]	9.982	[2037]
$FClO_4$	c	−18.5	[884]						
FO	g	33.502*[3]	[570]			52.071	[570]		
		32.5[4]	[568]	31.503	[568]	52.07	[568]	7.45	[568]
		32.4*[5]	[1618a]	31.803	[1618a]	50.73	[1618a]	7.355	[1618a]
		41[6]	[2358]						
FO^+	g	332.5[1]	[568]						
F_2DN	g					60.8337[7]	[745]	10.8614[7]	[745]
F_2HN	g					60.4512[7]	[745]	10.3913	[2937]
F_2O	g	(−4.40)	[854]			58.965	[2022]	10.345	[2022]
		(7.6)[8]	[1186]	(11.8)	[1186]	(58.99)	[1186]	10.35	[568, 1186, 1685, 2358]
		(−4.39)[9]	[1618a]	(−0.267)	[1618a]	(59.12)	[1618a]	10.349	[1618a]
		(−5.2)[10]	[2358]	(12.2*)	[232]	(59.11)	[2358]		
		(7.997)[11]	[570]			(59.145)	[570]		
		(6.0)[12]	[568]			(59.03)	[568]		
		(5.5*)	[323]	(9.7*)	[323]	(58.9*)	[2177]		
						(59.0)	[1685]		
F_2O^+	g	322.5	[568]						
		311.[13]	[2358]						
F_2O_2	g	4.73	[568, 1742]						
		4.3	[2358]						
F_2O_3	g	6.24	[568, 1742]						
DF	g	−64.905[14]	[570]			42.924	[570]		
		−65.415[15]	[568]			42.923	[2178]	6.964	[2178]
$(DF)_4$	g	−285	[568]						
$(DF)_6$	g	−432	[568]						
HF	g	(−64.7)[16]	[568]	−65.203	[568]	(41.51)	[568]	(6.964)	[568, 2178]

		(−64.8)[17]	[367, 1830, 2358]			(41.5092)	[1830]	(6.9645)	[1830]
						(41.508)	[2358]	(6.963)	[2358]
		(−64.2)	[1896]			(41.509)	[2178]		
		(−64.4)	[739]	−64.7	[1896]	(41.526)	[1009]	(6.960)	[1009]
		(−64.2)[18]	[570]			(41.510)	[570]		
		(−64.6)	[91]			(42.79)	[1551]		
		(−64.92)	[1204]						
	l	−71.65	[2358]			18.02	[2358]	12.35	[2358]
								12.18[19]	[1790]
		−71.8	[1507]			21.2	[2358]	12.09[20]	[1551]
HF, undissociated	d	(−76.50)	[2358]	(−70.95)	[2358]				
		(−79.23)	[568]	(−70.41*)	[323]				
		(−80.45)	[1057]						
HF, ionized	d	−79.50	[2358]	−66.64	[2358]	−3.3	[2358]	−25.5	[2358]
HF^+	g	314[21]	[1214]						
$(HF)_2$	g	−135.4	[568]						
$(HF)_3$	g	−210	[568]						
$(HF)_4$	g	−277.8	[568]						
$(HF)_5$	g	−356	[568]						
$(HF)_6$	g	(−428)	[568]						
$HF\cdot 650H_2O$	d	−77.04	[1057]						
HFO	g	−26.10[22]	[1618a]	−23.029	[1618a]	54.034	[1618a]	8.648	[1618a]
HF_2	d					1[23]	[1057]		
HF_2^-	g	−185	[568]			50.8	[728]		
	d	(−155.34)	[2358]	−138.18	[2358]	22.1	[2358]		
		(−153.4)	[568]	−137.5*	[323]	0.5*	[323]		
TF	g	−65.717[24]	[568]	−66.085	[568]	43.768	[568]	6.966	[568]
		−65.195[25]	[570]			46.768	[570]		
Fe	g	(99.830)	[2479]	(88.912)	[2479]			6.14	[1685]
		(99.55)[26]	[1589]	(88.64)	[1589]				
		(99.50)[27]	[1618a]	(88.593)	[1618a]	43.112	[1618a]	6.137	[1618a]
		(91.8; 99.1)[1]	[397]						
	l	3.138	[1618]	2.641	[1618a]	8.195	[1618a]	5.985	[1618a]
Fe α	c					(5.84)	[2693]	(5.99)	[2479]
						(6.52)	[1589]	(6.00)	[1589]
								(5.97)	[1685]

1. ΔH_0°. 2. $\Delta H_0^\circ = 365.1$ [2358]. 3. $\Delta H_0^\circ = 33.487$* [570]. 4. $\Delta H_0^\circ = 32.485$ [568]. 5. $\Delta H_0^\circ = 32.395$ [1618a]. 6. $\Delta H_0^\circ = 41$ [2358]. 7. $T = 300$ °K. 8. $\Delta H_0^\circ = 8.14$ [1186]. 9. $\Delta H_0^\circ = -3.847$ [1618a]. 10. $\Delta H_0^\circ = -5.7$ [2358]. 11. $\Delta H_0^\circ = (8.541)$ [570]. 12. $\Delta H_0^\circ = 6.545$ [568]. 13. $\Delta H_0^\circ = 310$ [2358]. 14. $\Delta H_0^\circ = -64.886$ [570]. 15. $\Delta H_0^\circ = -65.4$ [568]. 16. $\Delta H_0^\circ = -64.69$ [568]. 17. $\Delta H_0^\circ = (-64.7886)$ [1830]; (−64.788) [2358]. 18. $\Delta H_0^\circ = -64.19$ [570]. 19. $t = 19.0$ °C. 20. $T = 289.09$ °K. 21. $\Delta H_0^\circ = 299.0$ [568]. 22. $\Delta H_0^\circ = -25.413$ [1618a]. 23. $\bar{S}^\circ_{298}$. 24. $\Delta H_0^\circ = -65.7$ [568]. 25. $\Delta H_0^\circ = 65.178$ [570]. 26. $\Delta H_0^\circ = 98.99$ [1589]. 27. $\Delta H_0^\circ = 98.938$ [1618a].

1	2	3		4		5		6	
Fe, *α*	c					(6.529)	[1618a]	(5.989)	[1618a]
Fe^{2+}	g					42.36	[66]		
	d					(–26.2)	[1749]		
						(–25.9)	[1685]		
Fe^{3+}	g					41.55	[66]		
	d					(–61*)	[1685]		
$FeAl_2O_4$	c	–477.5	[333]	–445.7	[333]	25.4[1]	[1685, 1720]	29.53	[1685, 1720]
		–474	[472]	–446.8	[472]				
				9.6[2]	[329a]	22.4	[329a]		
$FeBr^{2+}$	d					(–28.19)	[2641]		
$FeBr_2$	c	(–66.0)[3]	[1392]	–56.1[3]	[1392]	33.62	[1392]		
		(–58.7)	[1805]	–56.8*	[227, 323]	32.2*	[323]		
		(–59.1)	[1773]			34.2	[1680, 1685]	20.07	[1685]
$FeBr_3$	g	–39.7[3]	[1392]	–38.7[3]	[1392]	91.1	[1392 1685]		
	c	–74.0	[1886]	–58.9	[1886]	43.9	[1685, 1886]		
		–62.8	[1805]	–58.4*	[229]				
		–64*	[1393]						
$FeBrCl_2$	c	–82.9	[1805]	–73.8*	[229]				
$Fe(CN)_2$	c	47*	[2683]						
$Fe(CN)_6^{3-}$	d	151.8	[2451]	192.1	[2451]	64	[2451]	(63.4)	[1500]
		150.6	[919]	176.6	[919]	64.8[4]	[919]		
$Fe(CN)_6^{4-}$	d	(126.7)	[2451]	183.9	[2451]	22	[2451]		
		(130.2)	[919]	168.4	[919]	24.0[4]	[919]		
$Fe(CNS)_2$	c	25*	[2683]						
$FeCO_3$	c	(–180*)	[166]			96.1[5]	[292]		
		(–179*)	[2683]	(–161.09*)	[177]	(22.3*)	[177]		
$Fe(CO)_5$	g	–178.7[6]	[1730]	–168.3	[1730]	106.2	[1730]	41.6	[1730]
						106.4	[1797]		
						105.2	[2068]		
						105.1	[2074]		
						102.6	[1969]		
						104.9	[1143]		
						105.0	[2240]	40.7	[2240]
	l	(–182.6)	[1043]					5.56	[2636]
FeClO	c	–99.0	[2296]			19.3	[2296]		
						17.7*	[2536]		
$FeCl_2$	g	–152.6	[2689]	–135.9	[2689]				
	c	(–81.5)	[1392, 1805]	(–72.1)	[1392]	(28.7)	[1680, 1685]	(18.24)	[1685]

		(−81.86)	[1752]			(32.2)	[2550]	(22.69)	[2550]
						(28.19)	[2641]		
$FeCl_2 \cdot 2H_2O$	c			−190.6*	[229]				
$FeCl_2 \cdot 4H_2O$	c			−304.9*	[229]				
$FeCl_2 \cdot 6H_2O$	c	(−513*)	[230]	−433.3*	[229]				
$FeCl_3$	g	−58.1	[1392]	−58.3	[1392]	86.9	[1392, 1685]		
	c	(−94.7)	[2689]	−81.3*	[227]	34.8	[2689]		
		(−93.4*)	[1805]	−78.6	[1392]	36.9	[1392]		
		(−95.70)	[1752]	−80.4*	[323]	31.1*	[323]		
		(−95.7)	[1773]			32.2	[1685, 2550]	22.69	[1685, 2550]
$FeCl_3 \cdot 2H_2O$	c	−244*	[230]						
$FeCl_3 \cdot 4H_2O$	c	−388*	[230]						
$Fe(ClO_3)_2$	c	−80*	[2683]						
$Fe(ClO_4)_2$	c	−56*	[2683]						
$Fe(ClO_4)_2 \cdot 6H_2O$	c	−495	[23]						
$FeCo_2O_4$	c					30.0[7]	[1685, 1720]	34.27	[1685, 1720]
						32.2	[1722]		
$FeCr_2O_4$	c	−349.1	[470]	−325.0	[470]	34.9	[1680, 1685]	31.94	[1680, 1685]
		−347.60	[415]	−322.67	[415]				
		−11.25[2]	[374]	−11.68[2]	[374]				
FeF_2	c	−160*	[230]	−150*	[227]	20.8	[2465]	16.28	[948]
		−168.0*	[890]	−158*	[229]	20.79	[1685]	16.26	[1685]
FeF_3	c	−235.0*	[890]						
FeH_2	c	−0.2*	[2683]						
$Fe(HCO_3)_2$	c	−354*	[2683]						
$Fe(HS)_2$	c	−3*	[2683]						
$Fe(HSO_4)_2$	c	−425*	[2683]						
FeI_2	c			−30.9*	[323]	37.6*	[323]	20.0	[2072]
				−30.6*	[227]	36.8	[1685]	20.12	[1685]
FeI_3	c	−14*	[2683]						
$Fe_{0.50}Mn_{0.50}$	c							6.50*	[1589]
$Fe_{0.70}Mn_{0.30}$	c							6.58*	[1589]
$Fe_{0.806}Mn_{0.194}$	c							6.90*	[1589]
$FeMoO_4$	c			−234.8*	[323]	33.4*	[323]		
				−235.1*	[229]				
		(−258.1*)	[170, 172]	−235.3*	[170, 172]				
$Fe(NH_2)_2$	c	−36*	[2683]						

1. $S^\circ_{298} - S^\circ_0$. 2. From oxides. 3. From gaseous bromine. 4. $\bar{S}^\circ_{298}$. 5. In *joules/mole*·°C. 6. $\Delta H^\circ_0 = -177.3$ [1730]. 7. $S^\circ_{298} - S^\circ_0$.

1	2	3		4		5		6	
$FeNO^{2+}$	d			1.5*	[323]	−10.6*	[323]		
$Fe(NO_2)_2$	c	−67*	[2683]						
$Fe(NO_3)_2$	c	−106*	[694]						
		−107*	[2683]						
		−109	[481]						
$Fe(NO_3)_2 \cdot 9H_2O$	c			−583.4*	[229]				
FeO	c	(−63.8)	[1595]	(−58.66)**	[232]	(13.74)	[1595]		
		(−63.2)	[1772]	(−57.2*)	[232]	(14.05)	[2309]		
				(−58.75)	[1045]	(14.2)	[2549]	11.50	[2549]
						(13.74)[1]	[1685]		
$Fe(OH)_2$	c	(−136*)	[2683]	(−115.64*)	[176]	(19.1*)	[176]		
						(22.7*)	[249]		
$Fe(OH)_3$	c			−166*	[323]	23*	[323]		
				−165.9*	[229]				
				−166.3*	[176]	28.8*	[176]		
FeP	c	(−29.0)	[1772]						
FeP_2	c	(−43.2)	[1772]						
$FePO_4$	c			−272*	[323]	22.4	[323]		
				−276.6*	[229]				
$FePO_4 \cdot 2H_2O$	c	−451.5	[1158]			40.93	[1185]	43.15	[1185]
$FePO_4 \cdot 2H_2O$	v	−444.1	[1158]			45.07	[1158]	45.27	[1158]
$Fe(ReO_4)_2$	c	−398*	[2683]			14.52	[1685]		
$Fe_{0.877}S$	c					14.529	[1411]	11.92	[1411, 1684]
FeS	c	(−23.8)	[704]	(−23.9)	[704]	(14.41)	[1685]	(12.07)	[1685]
		(−23.0)	[205]	(−23.67*)	[232]				
		(−22.8)	[2239, 2625]	(−23.6)**	[232]	(14.415)	[1411]	(12.08)	[1411]
		(−23.2)	[2313]	(−25.43*)	[176]	(16.1)	[1680]		
FeS, β	c			−21.0*	[229]				
FeS_2, marcasite	c	(−42.4)	[2227, 2625]	−36.2*	[229]			14.84	[1685]
FeS_2, native pyrite	c					12.65	[1409]	14.86	[1409]
FeS_2, synthetic pyrite						20.75	[1409]	17.42	[1409]
$FeSO_3$	c	−151*	[2683]						
		−164.3*	[1172]						
$FeSO_4$	c			−198.3*	[323]	27.6*	[323]		
				−194.8*	[229]	25.7	[1680, 1685]	24.04	[1685]
				−196.17*	[250]				
$FeSO_4 \cdot 2Fe(OH)_3$	c	−497.9	[229]	−434.57	[587]				

$FeSO_4 \cdot H_2O$	c	(−296.80)	[703]	−257.5	[703]				
				−258.7*	[229]				
$FeSO_4 \cdot 4H_2O$	c			−425.0*	[229]				
$FeSO_4 \cdot 7H_2O$	c	−719.98	[703]	−599.44	[703]	97.8	[1685]	94.28	[1685]
				−597*	[323]	93.4*	[323]		
				−591.2*	[229]				
$Fe_{0.33}Sb_{0.67}$, δ	c	−1.2	[1589]						
$Fe_{0.55}Sb_{0.45}$, ε	c	−1.10	[1589]						
$Fe_{0.4286}Se_{0.5714}$	c					9.554[2]	[1407]	7.515	[1407]
$Fe_{0.4667}Se_{0.5333}$	c					9.780[2]	[1407]	7.045	[1407]
$Fe_{0.5163}Se_{0.4897}$	c					8.437[2]	[1407]	6.655	[1407]
FeSe	c	(−18.0)	[205]	−13.9*[3]	[323]	16.5*[3]	[323]		
				−13.9*	[4]	17.3*	[4]		
				−17.7*	[229]				
$FeSeO_4$	c	−149.5*	[499]						
$FeSeO_4 \cdot H_2O$	c	−225.5*	[499]						
$FeSeO_4 \cdot 4H_2O$	c	−437.0*	[499]						
$FeSeO_4 \cdot 7H_2O$	c	−649.5*	[499]						
FeSi	c			−19.5	[224]	12.0*	[1773]		
FeSi, α	c	−17.6	[79]			−2.6[4]	[79]		
						11.0	[300, 301, 302]	11.4	[302]
FeSi, ε	c	−17.6	[78]			−2.6[4]	[78]		
$FeSiO_3$	c			−257*	[323]	20.9*	[323]		
				−255.2*	[246]	23.0*	[246]		
				−256.1	[227]				
$FeSi_2$, ferrosilicine , α	c					16.58	[303]	17.55	[303]
$FeSi_2$, ferrosilicine, β	c	−19.4	[79]			−3.3[4]	[79]		
						13.26	[300, 301, 303]	15.77	[303]
$FeSi_{2.33}$, ferrosilicine, α	c	−14.4	[79]			16.58	[300]		
		−15.7*	[78]						
$Fe_{0.333}Te_{0.667}$, ε	c							5.87	[1589]
$Fe_{0.536}Te_{0.474}$, β	c							6.23	[1589]
$Fe_{1.1}Te$, β	c					21.272[2]	[2651]	13.15	[1685, 2651]
						21.27	[1685]		

1. $Fe_{0.947}O$. 2. $S^\circ_{298} - S^\circ_0$. 3. Precipitated. 4. ΔS°_{298}.

1	2	3		4		5		6	
$FeTe_2$, *e*	c					23.94[1]	[1685, 2651]	17.60	[1685, 2651]
FeTi	c	−9.7	[1772a]						
$FeTiO_3$, ilmenite	c	(−299.7)	[334]	(−280.4)	[334]	(34.1)	[334]		
		(−295.3)	[2243]	(−276.8)	[2243]	(25.3)	[1680, 1685]	23.78	[1685]
		(−295.55)	[1686]	(−277.05)	[1685]				
$FeWO_4$	c	−276*	[172]	−252*	[172]				
		−281.5	[170, 172]	−250.4*	[323]	35.4*	[323]		
				−251.5*	[229]				
				−255.9*	[170]				
Fe_2Br_6	g	−113.5[2]	[1392]	−101.8*[2]	[1392]	149.2	[1392, 1685]		
Fe_2C_6	c			4.2*	[2226]				
Fe_2Cl_6	g	−148.45	[1686]	−136.6	[1686]	133.10	[1686]		
		−149.0	[1392]	−139.9	[1392]	142.2	[1392 1685]		
		−150.2*	[2689]			135.9	[2689]		
	c	−168.8	[1686]	−154.45	[1686]				
Fe_2CoO_4	c					32.2	[1720]		
Fe_2N	c	(3.0)	[911]						
Fe_2O_3, *α*, hematite	c	(−196.3)	[1772]			(21.5)	[1772]		
						(20.889)	[1408]	(24.80)	[1408]
						(20.90)	[1685]	(24.81)	[1685]
Fe_2P	c	(−38.1)	[1772]						
		(−36.0)	[1482a]						
Fe_2P_4	c	−6.5	[2449]						
Fe_2S_3	c			−59*	[323]				
$Fe_2(SO_4)_3$	c	−622.22	[1675]			62.54	[1675]		
$Fe_2(SO_4)_2 \cdot Fe(OH)_3$	c	−820*	[229]	−722.64	[173]				
$5Fe(SO_4)_3 \cdot 2Fe(OH)_3$	c	−3480*	[229]	−3093.37	[173]				
Fe_2SiO_4	c	(−339.8)[3]	[1727]	(−315.5*)	[232]	(34.7)	[1680, 1685]	31.78	[1685]
		(−346.0)	[1713]	(−322.0)	[1713]				
		(−348.41)	[214]	(−315.8**)	[232]				
		(−343.7)	[324, 325]	(−319.8)	[324, 325]				
Fe_2SiO_4, fayalite	c	−8.2[4]	[1681]	−7.2[4]	[1681]				
		−4.3[4]	[2265]						
Fe_2TiO_4	c					40.4	[1685]	34.01	[1685]
						39.0	[2553]	34.0	[2553]
								37.4	[2553]
Fe_2TiO_5	c					37.4	[1685, 2553]	39.26	[1685, 2553]
Fe_2ZnO_4	c					33.26	[1720]		

Fe_3C, β	c	(5.96)	[1589]	(4.76)	[1589]	(25.0)	[1589]	(25.2)	[1589]
						(24.2)	[1680, 1685]	(25.33)	[1685]
$Fe_3KH_8(PO_4)_6 \cdot 6H_2O$	c	(5.4)	[1773]	(4.5*)	[224]	222.17	[1152]	208.2	[1152]
Fe_3O_4. β	c	(−267.8)	[1045]	(−242.3)	[1045]				
		(−266.9)	[1772]			(36.2)	[1772]	34.28	[1685]
Fe_3P	c	(−39.0)	[1772]						
		(−40.0)	[1482a]						
Fe_3Si, α′	c	(18.3)[5]	[299]			24.76	[299, 300, 301]		
		(−22.4)	[78, 79]			−1.2[6]	[78, 79]		
Fe_4N	c	(3.7)[7]	[910]			37.4	[1685]		
		(4.5)	[911]						
Fe_5Si_2, η	c					50.1	[302]	47.7	[302]
						49.87	[300, 301]		
Fe_7W_6	c					77.8[8]	[460]		
$HFe(OH)_4$	c			−228.94*	[7]				
$H_3Fe(OH)_6$	c			−336.25*	[7]				
Fr	g	17.400	[2479]	11.145	[2479]	43.48	[2479]		
		16.5*	[402]			43.49	[1685]		
	c					22.50	[1685, 2479]	7.60	[1685, 2479]
Fr_2	g	24.0*	[402]						
FrAt	c					35.11*[9]	[304a]	11.89*[10]	[304a]
FrBr	g	44.4	[296]			65.59	[296]		
	c	−95*	[230, 418]			29.9*	[698]		
						30.94*[9]	[304a]	11.84*[10]	[304a]
						29.6*	[418]		
$FrBrO_3$	c					42.2*	[418, 698]		
FrCl	g	55.8	[296]			62.81	[296]		
	c	−104*	[229]			27.0*	[698]		
						25.73*[9]	[304a]	11.80*[10]	[304a]
		−105*	[418]			26.7*	[418]		
$FrClO_3$	c					40.2*	[418]		
						40.4*	[699]		
FrF	g	82.6	[296]			59.85	[296]		
	c	−125*	[418]			23.6	[418]		
						20.47*[9]	[304a]	11.61*[10]	[304a]
		−122*	[230]			23.5*	[698]		
FrI	g	33.9	[296]			67.37	[296]		
	c	−83*	[418]			32.8*	[418]		

1. $S^\circ_{298} - S^\circ_0$. 2. From gaseous bromine. 3. Precipitated. 4. For the reaction $2Fe_{0.947}O + 0.106Fe + SiO_2$, α-$Fe_2SiO_4$. 5. $t = 20$ °C. 6. ΔS°_{298}. 7. $t = 350–480$ °C. 8. $t = 300$ °C. 9. $T = 300$ °K. 10. $T = 300$ °K; C_p.

1	2	3		4		5		6	
FrI	c					34.19*[1]	[304a]	11.88*[2]	[304a]
		−82*	[230]			32.2*	[698]		
$FrMnO_4$	c					47.5*	[699]		
						47.4*	[418]		
$FrNO_3$	c					35.7*	[699]		
						37.4*	[418]		
FrOH	c					24.3*	[418, 699]		
Fr_2CO_3	c					49.0*	[699]		
						49.3*	[418]		
Fr_2CrO_3	c					60.6*	[699]		
						61.0*	[418]		
Fr_2O	c	−81*	[1480]	−71.5*	[1480]	37.5*	[1480]		
Fr_2SO_4	c					54.0*	[699]		
						55.3*	[1480]		
Ga	g	(65.000)	[2479]	(55.888)	[2479]			(6.06)	[1685]
		(65.30)[3]	[1589]					(6.058)	[1589]
		(68.96)	[327]						
		(65.4)	[2003]						
		(59.0*)	[1130]						
	l	(59.0)[12]	[153]					6.44	[294]
	c					(9.77)	[1589, 1685]	(6.18)	[1589, 1685]
						(9.82)	[153, 706]	(6.23)	[2479]
Ga^{2+}	d			−21.0*	[323]				
Ga^{3+}	g	−20.96	[535a]	−18.18	[535a]	38.63	[66]		
GaAs	c					7.67	[2146]	5.481	[2146]
GaBr	g					60.2	[1685]	8.70	[1685]
$GaBr_3$	c			−84.5*	[323]	38.2*	[323]		
				−87.5*	[227]	42.6	[1685]		
GaCl	g			2.8*	[227]	57.4	[1685]	8.50	[1685]
$GaCl_3$	c	(−125.0)	[890]	−117.8*	[323]	31.9*	[323]		
		(−131*)	[385]	−110.4*	[227]	40.5*	[1773]		
						34.2	[1685]		
$GaCl_3 \cdot PCl_3$	c	−203.2	[1388]						
GaF	g					54.5	[1685]		
GaF_3	c			−225*	[227]	20.0	[1685]		
GaI	g					62.0	[1685]	8.77	[1685]

GaI_3	c	(−51.0)	[890]	−52.0*	[227]	48.7*	[323]		
						51.4*	[327]		
						46.8	[1685]		
GaN	c			−18.6*	[323]	8.4*	[323]		
				−20.1*	[229]	11.0*	[1773]		
GaO	g			58.8*	[227]	55.5	[1685]	7.69	[1685]
						53.86	[2217]	7.66	[2217]
$Ga(OH)_3$	c	−242.5	[229]	(−198.88*)	[176]	20.3*	[323]		
$Ga(OH)_6^{3-}$	d			−342.02	[6]				
GaP	c	−20.9	[2316]						
		−29.1	[169a]						
GaS	c	−46.4	[1459]						
GaSb	c	−9.94	[2317]	−9.12	[2317]	19.32[4]	[2317]		
		−10.6	[123]	−9.8	[123]	−2.6[5]	[123]	11.321	[294]
		−9.79	[535a]	−9.39	[535a]				
		−9.4	[3]	−9.0	[3]	18.18	[2146]	11.511	[2146]
	c	−10.7	[601]			19.34	[3]		
GaSe	c	−35.0	[1459]						
GaTe	c	−30	[2]	−26.5	[2]	11.49	[2]	15.8	[2]
		−28.6	[1459]					22.78	[359]
Ga_2C_2	g					71.4	[1685]	16.40	[1685]
$Ga_2(COO)_2 \cdot 2H_2O$	c	−660.4*6	[234]						
$Ga_2(COO)_2 \cdot 4H_2O$	c	−805*[7]	[234]						
Ga_2O_2	g	−20.7[8]	[1262]			57.3[9]	[1262]		
		−17.4	[327]			69.54	[1262]		
	c			−75.2*	[323]	22*	[32]		
				−75.4*	[229]				
				−75.0*	[1045]				
Ga_2O_3	g	−121*	[662]			−15*[10]	[662]	28*	[662]
		137[8]	[662]						
	c	(−257.5)	[887]	−237.2*	[323]	24*	[323]		
		(−261.05)[11]	[1897]	−293.4[11]	[1897]	20.23	[705]	(21.95)	[705]
		(−258.6)	[103]	−236.5	[1045]	20.31	[1685, 1724]	(22.02)	[1685, 1724]
				−238.1*	[229]				
$Ga(OH)_3$	c	−231*	[2683]						
Ga_2S_3	g	−78*	[2683]					15.5*	[103]
	c	−136.8	[1459]						

1. $T = 300\ ^\circ K$. 2. $T = 300\ ^\circ K$; C_p. 3. $\Delta H_0^\circ = 65.07$ [1589]. 4. Calculated [234] from the value $\Delta S_{298}^\circ = -1.4$ [2317]. 5. ΔS_{298}°. 6. An apparently erroneous value (−689) is quoted in [2245]. 7. An apparently erroneous value (−847) is quoted in [2245]. 8. $(\Delta H_{298}^\circ)_{subl}$. 9. $(\Delta S_{298}^\circ)_{subl}$. 10. ΔS_{298}°. 11. Ga_2O_3, β. ΔH_0°.

1	2	3		4		5		6	
$Ga_2(SO_4)_3$	c	−711*	[2683]						
Ga_2Se_3	c	−105.0	[1459]						
		−110	[103]						
Ga_2Te_3	g	−82	[2]	−72	[2]	31[1]	[2]	38.8	[103]
	c	−65	[1459]						
$HGa(OH)_4$	c			−255.53*	[6]				
$H_3Ga(OH)_6$	c			−368.83*	[6]				
Gd	g	(82.500)	[2479]	(73.361)	[2479]	(46.42)	[1685]	(6.59)	[1685]
		(83.6)	[2678]			(36.0)	[2523]		
		(84.1)[2]	[2679]						
		(95.75)[3]	[1456]						
		(108.5)[4]	[2261]						
	c					(15.77)	[2479]	8.72	[2479]
						(16.36)	[1589]	8.86	[1589]
						(16.2)	[1685]	8.80	[1685]
						(15.74)	[2396]	8.96	[1398, 1399]
Gd^{3+}	d	(−163.01)	[2422]	(−165.7*)	[323]	(−43*)	[323]		
				(−157*)	[1976]	(−50*)	[1976]		
						(−32.5)	[1685]		
GdB_6	c	−114.7	[455]						
$GdBr_3$	c	−203*	[230]						
		−200*	[2683]						
GdC_2	g	143[5]	[1606]						
$GdCl_{0.5}(OH)_{2.5}$	c	−305.77	[9]						
$GdCl(OH)_2$	c	−295.41	[9]						
$GdClO$	c			−221.9*	[1976]				
$GdCl_2$	c	−117*	[442]						
$GdCl_3$	c	(−240.09)	[2422]	−222.5	[2422]	34.9	[2422]	25[6]	[1623]
				−227.6*	[323]	34.9*	[323]		
		78.5[5]	[441]	−222*	[1976]				
				−224.4*	[232]				
				−228.7*	[227]				
$GdCl_3 \cdot 6H_2O$	c	−684.37	[2422]	−583.7	[2422]	91.3	[2422]		
				−585.7*	[232]				
				−583*	[1976]				
GdI_3	c			−146.3*	[323]	51.8*	[323]		
				−146.6*	[227]				

				−140*	[1976]				
$GdO_{1.5}$, monoclinic	c	−216.97	[2662]	−206.7	[2662]				
$Gd(OH)_3$	c	−358.1*	[229]	(−308.0*)	[323]				
				(−314.03)	[9]				
Gd_2O_3	c	−433.94[7]	[2679]	−412*	[1976]	36.0	[2523, 2679]		
		−433.94	[1576, 1659]	−413.37	[1659]	28.24[8]	[1659]	25.22	[1659]
						36.3	[2662]		
						36.02	[1659]		
Gd_2S_3	c	−253*	[2683]						
$Gd_2(SO_4)_3$	c	(−952*)	[2683]						
$Gd_2(SO_4)_3 \cdot 8H_2O$	c			(−1317*)	[1976]				
Ge	g	(90.000)	[2470]	(80.259)	[2479]	(40.11)	[1685]	(7.35)	[1685]
		(89*)[9]	[1539]						
	c					(7.43)	[1329, 1685]	(5.58)	[1329, 2146]
								(5.59)	[1685]
						(7.46)[10]	[2146]	(5.518)[10]	[2146]
Ge_2	g	119*	[1540]						
		121.5*	[402]						
GeBr	g					61.5	[1685]	(8.87)	[1685]
$GeBrH_3$	g					65.71	[1402]	13.42	[1402]
$GeBr_2$	g			34.3*	[229]	79.0*	[1245a]	10*	[1245a]
$GeBr_3H$	g					87.042	[2020]	20.428	[2020]
$GeBr_4$	g	−83.3	[1187]	−90*	[229]	94.77	[1651]	24.34	[1651, 1685, 1776]
						94.67	[1776]		
						94.7	[1685]		
	l	−78.5	[1176]	−78.5*	[229]				
	c	−79.0	[1176]	−77.5*	[234]				
$GeCND_3$	g					69.1948[11]	[1765]	18.6216[12]	[2984]
$GeCNH_3$	g					66.6911[11]	[1765]	46.4619	[1765]
GeCl	g	(32.45*)	[323]			58.8	[1685]	(8.81)	[1685]
$GeClD_3$	g					65.6	[1685]	(15.3)	[1685]
$GeClH_3$	g					63.0	[1817a]	13.09	[1817a]
$GeCl_3H$	g					78.544	[2020]	19.521	[2020]
$GeCl_4$	g	(−122)	[1176]	−117.8	[229]	83.05	[1651]	22.97	[1651]
						82.94	[1776]	22.96	[1685, 1776]
						83.0	[1685]		

1. ΔS°_{298}. 2. ΔH°_0. 3. $\Delta H^\circ_0 = 96.10$ [1456]. 4. $t = 1120$–1310 °C. 5. $(\Delta H^\circ_{298})_{subl}$. 6. $t = 17.5$ °C. 7. $\Delta H^\circ_0 = -431.5$ [2679]. 8. $S^\circ_{298} - S^\circ_{10}$. 9. $T = 1150$ °K. 10. $T = 273$ °K. 11. $T = 300$ °K.

1	2	3		4		5		6	
$GeCl_4$	c	−171*	[358]						
	l	(−136*)	[323]	−119*	[323]	60*	[323]		
	c			−102.7*	[234]				
$GeDH_3$	g					55.64*	[29, 256]	11.36	[29]
						55.36	[257]	11.26	[257]
$GeDI_3$	g					97.07	[29]	21.96	[29]
$GeDHI_2$	g					88.50	[29]	18.43	[29]
$GeDH_2I$	g					74.96	[29]	14.89	[29]
$GeDT_3$	g					60.05	[1765]	14.31	[1765]
GeD_2HI	g					75.53	[29]	15.49	[29]
GeD_2H_2	g					57.36	[29]	11.96	[29]
						56.81	[257]	11.88	[257]
GeD_2I_2	g					87.48	[29]	19.03	[29]
GeD_2T_2	g					60.25	[256]	13.93	[256]
GeD_3H	g					57.39	[29]	12.55	[29]
						57.33	[257]	12.52	[257]
GeD_3I	g					73.93	[29]	16.09	[29]
GeD_3T	g					58.82	[256]	13.54	[256]
GeD_4	g					55.42	[257]	13.15	[257]
GeF	g					56.1	[1685]	8.32	[1685]
$GeFH_3$	g					60.08	[1402]	12.23	[1402]
GeF_2	g	113	[1163]						
GeF_4	g					72.07	[2596]	19.57	[1651, 1685, 2596]
						72.35	[1776]	19.56	[1776]
						72.51	[1651]	19.5*	[1412]
						72.5	[1685]		
						72.1	[1773]		
$GeHI_3$	g					96.72	[29]	21.37	[29]
$GeHT_3$	g					59.37	[256]	13.72	[256]
GeH_2I_2	g					86.75	[29]	17.83	[29]
GeH_2T_2	g					58.79	[256]	12.73	[256]
GeH_3I	g					72.12	[29]	14.30	[29]
GeH_3T	g					56.42	[256]	11.75	[256]
GeH_4	g	20.8	[2259]	28	[1192]	(51.90)	[257]	(10.76)	[257, 1776]
		21.6	[1437, 1437a]			(56.86)	[1776]		
		24.5[1]	[157]			(51.62)	[1685]	(10.59)	[1685]
GeI	g					63.3	[1685]		

GeI_2	c	–27*	[323]	–26*	[323]	36*	[323]		
GeI_4	g	–42.0	[1187]	–52	[229]	107.9	[1651]	25.1	[1651]
						102.45	[1776]	24.84	[1776]
						102.60	[133]	24.90	[133]
						102.5	[1685]	24.93	[1685]
	c	–42*	[323]	–41*	[323]	64*	[323]		
		–30.5	[1176]	–30.5*	[229]				
GeO	g	(–10.8)	[58, 1651]	(–29.5*)	[1045]	(53.5)	[1651]		
		(–10.756)[1]	[58]			(54.0)	[1685]	(7.36)	[1685]
		(–6)	[56]						
	c	–73*	[323]	–66*	[323]	12*	[323]		
		–61*	[887]	–55*	[1045]				
	v	–60.8*	[1127]						
		53.1[2]	[1127]						
GeO_2	g	–45*[3]	[56]						
		–31.24[1]	[58]						
	l							24.0*	[58]
	c	(–141*)[4]	[323]	–127*[5]	[323]	12*[5]	[323]		
		(–132.3)	[2561]	–119.7	[2561]	13.21[4]	[1724]	24.45[4]	[1724]
		(–129.2)	[1652]	–116.0*	[229]	13.21	[1685]	12.45	[1685]
		(–128.1)	[909]			10.8	[2368]	21.0*	[58]
		(–133)	[58]			12.5	[1773]		
		(–132.3)	[2722]	–119.7	[2722]	13*	[176]		
		(–129.08)	[1899]	–116.19	[1899]				
		(–132.3)	[846]						
	v	–125.8	[1899]	–113.57	[1899]				
				–115.1*	[229]				
				–115.9	[1045]				
GeP	c	–6.5	[2415]			14.6	[2415]		
		–6.0[1]	[2628]						
GeS	g	23.50*	[59]			56.3	[1685]		
		23.525	[59]						
	c	–17.00[1]	[59]						
		–16.975	[59]			15.77	[2632]	11.42	[2632]
		–21.4	[970]	–21.7	[970]	16.0	[970]		
		–25.8*	[785]						
GeS_2	c	–37.811[6]	[59]						
GeSe	g					59.2	[1685]	(8.42)	[1685]
	c	–19.7	[970]	–20.1	[970]	18.9	[970]		

1. ΔH_0°. 2. v→g. 3. Calculated [234] from $(\Delta H_0^\circ)_{subl} = 84$ [56] and $(\Delta H_{298}^\circ)GeO_2(c) = -129$ [1773]. 4. Soluble form. 5. Precipitated. 6. $\Delta H_0^\circ = -37.6$ [59].

1	2	3		4		5		6	
GeT_4	g					57.87	[1765]	14.70	[1765]
GeTe	g					61.1	[1685]	8.59	[1685]
						61.6	[885]		
	l	48.6	[954]			18.8	[954]		
	c	−8.0	[970]	−8.2	[970]	19.9	[970]		
		−6.0	[954]						
		−8.9	[1525]	8.1	[1525]				
Ge_2H_6	g	38.7	[1437a]						
		39.1	[2260]						
Ge_2Nb	c	−10.4[1]	[936]						
Ge_2O_2	c					75.1	[1127]		
Ge_2O_3	c					99.3	[1127]		
Ge_3H_8	g	54.2	[1440]						
		48.4	[2260]						
Ge_3N_4	c	(−15.6)	[2625]	1.3*	[229]	40.0*	[1773]		
$HGeO_3$	d	(−198*)	[323]	−170*	[323]	21*	[323]		
H_2GeO_3	d	(−203*)	[323]	−182*	[323]	43*	[323]		
H	g	(52.098)[2]	[568]	(48.582)	[568]	(27.391)	[568]		
		(52.095)[3]	[2358]	(48.580)	[2358]	(27.39)	[1685]		
		(52.0977)[4]	[1830]			(27.3924)	[1830]		
		(52.104)[5]	[570]			(27.3919)	[570]		
		(52.102)[6]	[1618a]	(48.587)	[1618a]	(27.392)	[1618a]		
H^+	g	(367.163)[7]	[568]	362.570	[568]	26.014	[568]		
		(367.185)[8]	[570]			26.015	[570]		
		(367.161)[9]	[2358]						
	d	37*	[695]	51.9*	[323]				
		48*	[695]						
H^-	g	33.391[10]	[568]	31.772	[568]	26.015	[568]		
		33.423[11]	[570]			26.0164	[570]		
		33.78[12]	[2358]						
		34.9*	[2182]						
H_2	g					(31.33)	[1685]	(6.89)	[1685]
						(31.1946)	[570]		
						(31.2079)	[1830]	(6.8918)	[1830]
						(31.195)	[568]	(6.891)	[568]
						(31.208)	[1618a, 2358]	(6.889)	[2358]
						(31.22)	[1896]	(6.892)	[1618a]

						(31.208)	[2366]		
	d	−1.0	[2358]	4.2	[2358]	13.8	[2358]		
		−0.9	[568]						
H_2^+	g	356	[1214]						
		355.76[13]	[568]						
		357.22[14]	[2358]						
HD	g	(0.075)[15]	[570]			(34.345)	[570]		
		(0.076)[16]	[2358]			(34.343)	[2358]	(6.978)	[2358]
						(34.34)	[1685]		
HD+	g	356.24[13]	[568]						
HDO	g	(−58.63)[17]	[570]			(47.71)[18]	[1256]	(8.08)[18]	[1256]
		(−58.63)[19]	[568]	(−55.722)	[568]	(47.659)	[568]	(8.082)	[568]
	l	(−69.30)	[568]			(47.661)	[570]		
		(−69.285)	[2358]	(−57.818)	[2358]				
HDO_2	g	−33.49	[1352]			57.86	[1311]	10.68	[1311]
		−33.479[20]	[568]	−26.319	[568]	57.9	[568]	10.7	[568]
		−33.459[21]	[570]			57.939	[570]		
HO_2	g	4.9	[1352]						
		3.933[22]	[570]			55.170	[570]		
	d			3.0*	[323]				
HO_2^+	g	271[23]	[2358]						
HO_2^-	d	(−38.20)	[372]	−15.61*	[323]	−20.1	[974]		
		(−38.32)	[2358]	−16.1	[2358]				
		(−38.16)	[490]						
HT	g	(0.175)[24]	[570]			35.428	[570]		
		(0.176)	[568]	(−0.277)	[568]	(35.428)	[568]	(6.978)	[568, 1655]
				(−0.28)	[1655]	(38.202)	[1655]		
						(35.45)	[1685]	(6.98)	[1685]
HTO	g	(−58.976)[25]	[570]			48.421	[570]		
						48.46[26]	[1256]	8.105[26]	[1256]
		(−58.98)[27]	[568]	−56.001	[568]	48.419	[568]	8.117	[568]
	l	−70.18	[568]			19.3	[454]		
H_2O	g	(−57.796)[28]	[568]	(−54.638)	[568]	(45.106)	[568, 1618a]	8.025	[568, 1618a]
		(−57.7979)[29]	[1830]	(−54.635)	[2358]				
						(45.1054)	[1830]	(8.0256)	[1830]
		(−57.798)[30]	[570]	(−54.636)	[1618a]	(45.15)[26]	[1256]	(8.027)[26]	[1256]

1. In *kcal/g-atom* Ge. 2. $\Delta H_0^\circ = (51.626)$ [568]. 3. $\Delta H_0^\circ = (51.626)$ [2358]. 4. $\Delta H_0^\circ = (51.6284)$ [1830]. 5. $\Delta H_0^\circ = (51.632)$ [570]. 6. $\Delta H_0^\circ = 51.632$ [1618a]. 7. $\Delta H_0^\circ = (362.21)$ [568]. 8. $\Delta H_0^\circ = (365.232)$ [570]. 9. $\Delta H_0^\circ = 365.211$ [2358]. 10. $\Delta H_0^\circ = 34.4$ [568]. 11. $\Delta H_0^\circ = 34.432$ [570]. 12. $\Delta H_0^\circ = 34.40$ [2358]. 13. ΔH_0°. 14. $\Delta H_0^\circ = 355.74$ [2358]. 15. $\Delta H_0^\circ = (0.079)$ [570]. 16. $\Delta H_0^\circ = (0.079)$ [2358]. 17. $\Delta H_0^\circ = (-57.927)$ [570]. 18. $T = 300$ °K. 19. $\Delta H_0^\circ = (-57.931)$ [568]. 20. $\Delta H_0^\circ = -32.03$ [568]. 21. $\Delta H_0^\circ = -32.007$ [570]. 22. $\Delta H_0^\circ = 4.606$ [570]. 23. $\Delta H_0^\circ = 272$ [2358]. 24. $\Delta H_0^\circ = 0.175$ [570]. 25. $\Delta H_0^\circ = (-58.276)$ [570]. 26. $T = 300$ °K. 27. $\Delta H_0^\circ = -58.28$ [568]. 28. $\Delta H_0^\circ = (-57.108)$ [568]. 29. $\Delta H_0^\circ = (-57.1035)$ [1830]. 30. $\Delta H_0^\circ = (-57.110)$ [570]; (−57.103) [1618a].

1	2	3		4		5		6	
H_2O	g					(45.108)	[570]		
						(45.13)	[1896]		
	l	(−68.3149)	[568]	(−56.703)	[568]	(16.75)	[568]	(17.997)	[568]
		(−68.315)[1]	[2358]	(−56.688)	[2358]	(16.71)	[2358]	(17.995)	[2358]
	c	−68.436	[568]			10.54*	[251]		
H_2O^+	g	233	[1214]						
		233.7[1]	[568]						
		234.2[2]	[2358]						
H_2O_2	g	(−32.53)[3]	[1311, 1618a]	−25.20	[1311]	55.66	[1311, 1618a]	10.31	[568, 1311]
		(−32.5)	[823]	−25.208	[1618a]				
		(−32.30)	[1310]	−24.55	[1310]	54.18	[1310]	10.22	[1310]
		(−32.54)[4]	[568]	(−25.223)	[568]	55.66	[568]	10.305	[1618a]
		(−32.58)[5]	[2358]	−25.25	[2358]	55.6	[2358]	10.3	[2358]
		(−32.45)	[2610]	−24.7	[2610]	55.661	[570]		
	l	(−44.88)	[568]	−28.771	[568]	26.17	[568]	21.35	[568]
				−28.78	[2358]	26.2	[2358]	21.3	[2358]
		(−44.79)	[1240]	−27.84*	[323]	22*	[323]		
				−28.1	[1045]	25.3	[1773]		
	c	−46.507[1]	[568]						
	d	(−45.69)	[2358]	−32.05	[2358]	34.4	[2358]		
	d	(−45.72)	[568]	−31.47*	[323]				
$H_2O_2^+$	g	247	[1214]						
		220.8[1]	[568]						
		220.7[6]	[2358]						
H_2O_3	g	−13.5*	[823]						
H_2O_4	g	5.5*	[823]						
		6.1	[568]						
	l	−5.9	[568]						
	c	−27.9[7]	[1061]						
H_3O	g					45.92	[986]	8.40	[986]
H_3O^+	g	139.2[1,7]	[568]						
	d	−68.3149	[568]						
D	g	(52.985)[8]	[568]	(49.364)	[568]	(29.455)	[568]		
		(52.990)[9]	[570]			(29.4559)	[570]		
		(52.981)[10]	[2358]						
D^+	g	(366.20)[1]	[568]						
	d			−0.08*	[323]				

D_2	g					(34.622)	[568]	(6.978)	[568, 2358]
						(34.63)	[1685]	(6.98)	[1685]
						(34.651)	[570]		
						(34.620)	[2358]		
D_2^+	g	(356.74)[1]	[568]						
DO	g	8.603[11]	[568]			45.308	[568]	7.156	[568]
		8.5	[1352]			45.307	[570]		
DO^+	g	312.8[1]	[568]						
DOT	g					49.51[13]	[1256]	8.259[13]	[1256]
		−59.935[12]	[568]	−56.759	[568]	49.470	[568]	8.264	[568]
		−59.919[14]	[570]			49.472	[570]		
DO_2	g	4.009[15]	[568]	0.728	[568]	55.31	[568]	8.60	[568]
		5*	[1352]						
DT	g	0.022	[568]	−0.395	[568]	37.018	[568, 570]	6.978	[568]
		0.017[16]	[570]			37.04	[1685]	6.98	[1685]
DT^+	g	356.95[1]	[568]						
D_2O	g	(−59.561)[17]	[568]	(−56.060)	[568]	(47.381)	[568]	(8.207)	[568]
						(47.43)[13]	[1256]	(8.19)[13]	[1256]
		(−59.563)[18]	[570]			(47.383)	[570]		
	l	(−70.411)	[568]	(−58.192)	[568]	(18.14)	[568]	(20.15)	[568]
	c	−70.791[1]	[568]					34.2353	[2202]
	d	−70.3789	[568]	(−58.196)	[2358]	(18.15)	[2358]	(20.16)	[2358]
D_2O_2	g	−34.45[19]	[1311]	−26.59	[1311]	57.28	[1311]	11.14	[568, 1311]
		−34.423[20]	[568]	−26.568	[568]	57.28	[568]		
		−34.510[21]	[570]			57.274	[570]		
	l	−46.933[22]	[568]						
$D_2O_2^4$	d	−47.74	[568]						
T	g	(53.390)[23]	[570]			(30.6595)	[579]		
		(52.981)	[570]			(30.66)	[1685]		
T_2	g					(36.63)	[1685]	6.98	[1685]
						(36.620)	[570]		
TO	g					46.160	[570]		
T_2O	g					(48.84)[24]	[1256]	(8.35)[24]	[1256]
		−60.308[25]	[570]			(48.790)	[570]		
	l					19.0	[454]		

1. ΔH_0°. 2. $\Delta H_0^\circ = 233.5$ [2358]. 3. $\Delta H_0^\circ = -31.04$ [1311]; −31.025 [1618a]. 4. $\Delta H_0^\circ = -31.04$ [568]. 5. $\Delta H_0^\circ = -31.07$ [2358]. 6. $t = 220.7$ [2358]. 7. $t = -196$ °C. 8. $\Delta H_0^\circ = (52.528)$ [568]. 9. $\Delta H_0^\circ = (52.537)$ [570]. 10. $\Delta H_0^\circ = (52.524)$ [2358]. 11. $\Delta H_0^\circ = 8.513$ [568]. 12. $\Delta H_0^\circ = -59.23$ [568]. 13. $T = 300$ °K. 14. $\Delta H_0^\circ = -59.210$ [570]. 15. $\Delta H_0^\circ = 4.7$ [568]. 16. $\Delta H_0^\circ = 0.021$ [570]. 17. $\Delta H_0^\circ = (-58.857)$ [568]. 18. $\Delta H_0^\circ = (-58.850)$ [570]. 19. $\Delta H_0^\circ = -33.05$ [1311]. 20. $\Delta H_0^\circ = -33.01$ [568]. 21. $\Delta H_0^\circ = -33.089$ [570]. 22. $D_2O_2 \cdot \infty D_2O$. 23. $\Delta H_0^\circ = (52.938)$ [570]. 24. $T = 300$ °K. 25. $\Delta H_0^\circ = -59.606$ [570].

1	2	3		4		5		6	
He	g					(30.1528)	[570]		
						(30.125)	[568]		
						(30.1258)	[1830]		
						(30.1244)	[2358]		
	d					13.3	[2358]		
He^+	g	(568.481)[1]	[568]	566.584	[[568]	31.501	[568]		
		(568.459)[2]	[2358]						
$^3He^+$	g	566.97[3]	[568]						
He^{2+}	g	(1821.90)[3]	[568]						
$^3He^{2+}$	g	1821.81[3]	[568]						
Hf	g	168.000	[2479]	157.943	[2479]	(44.64)	[1685]		
		155*	[1589]						
		145.5	[2092]						
		147.39	[1828]						
		146.59	[1828]						
	c					(10.91)	[1685, 2479]	(6.10)	[1685, 2479]
						(10.54)	[1828]	(6.15)	[1492]
Hf^{4+}	g					41.46	[66]		
HfB_2	c					11.2*	[1959]	14.23	[1959]
$HfBr_2$	c	–108*	[1826]						
$HfBr_3$	c	–157*	[1826]						
$HfBr_4$	g					102.0	[18]	24.89	[18]
						102.2	[1685]		
	c	–219*	[230]						
		–200*	[1826]			57.0	[1685]		
$HfC_{0.67}$	c	–51.7	[175]						
$HfC_{0.78}$	c	–52.7	[175]						
$HfC_{0.91}$	c	–53.7	[175]						
$HfC_{0.958}$	c	–50.08	[1905]						
$HfC_{0.96}$	c	–53.3	[175]						
$HfC_{0.99}$	c	–54.2	[175]						
HfC	g	361.3	[1828]			16.49	[1828]		
		375.1	[1828]						
	c	–54.2	[175]			–3.0[4]	[2709]		
		–51.9	[1905]			10.9	[1685]		
$HfC_{0.95}O_{0.05}$	c	–73.7	[174]	119.4	[174]	6.7*	[174]		

$HfCl_2$	c	−130*	[1826]						
		−150*	[483, 484]			31.0*	[483, 484]	18.2*	[483]
$HfCl_3$	c	−220*	[483, 484]			36.1*	[483, 484]	23.8*	[483]
$HfCl_4$	g					91.15	[18]	23.85	[18]
						89.8	[1685]		
	c	−255*	[483, 484]			48.0*	[483]		
		−250*	[1773]			45.6	[1685, 2547]	28.80	[2547]
		−237.5*	[2285]						
		−246	[1518]						
		−239.4*	[1826]						
		−236.7	[1413]						
		−236.97	[111]						
HfF_2	c	−219	[230]						
HfF_4	g					77.7	[1685]		
	c	−461.4	[1381]	−437.16	[1381]	31.5	[1685]		
HfI_2	c	−72*	[1826]						
HfI_3	c	−113*	[1826]						
HfI_4	g					110.7	[18]	25.33	[18]
						112.8	[1685]		
HfI_4	c	−140*	[1826]			64.5	[1685]		
$Hf(OH)_4$	c			−325.5*	[323]				
Hg	g	(14.650)	[2479]	(7.613)	[2479]	(41.79)	[2479]		
		(15.44)[3]	[1589]						
		(14.649)[5]	[570]			(41.794)	[570]		
		(14.658)[6]	[1505]						
		(14.652)[7]	[1618a]	7.609	[1618a]	41.794	[1618a]		
	l					(18.17)	[1505]	(6.69)	[1589, 1685, 2479]
						(18.19)	[924]		
						(18.171)	[1618a]	(6.687)	[1618a]
						(18.17)	[1589 1685, 2358]		
Hg^{2+}	g					41.80	[66]		
	d	41.59*	[323]			−5.4*	[323]		
Hg_2	g			18.5*	[229]	66.0	[1685]	8.94	[1685]
Hg_2^{2+}	d			36.35*	[323]	17.7	[1685]		
HgBr	g	24.9[8]	[1618a]	16.399*	[1618a]	64.875	[1618a]	8.894	[1618a]
						76.5	[1685]	14.40	[1685]

1. $\Delta H_0^\circ = (567.00)$ [568]. 2. $\Delta H_0^\circ = (566.978)$ [2358]. 3. ΔH_0°. 4. ΔS_{298}°. 5. $\Delta H_0^\circ = 15.40$ [570]. 6. $(\Delta H_{298}^\circ)_{vap}$. 7. $\Delta H_0^\circ = 15.404$ [1618a]. 8. $\Delta H_0^\circ = 27.612^*$ [1618a].

1	2	3		4		5		6	
$HgBr_2$	g	−20.424[1]	[1618a]	−26.97	[1618a]	76.511	[1618a]	14.407	[1618a]
	l	−37.158	[1618a]	−34.845	[1618a]	46.797	[1618a]	18.0	[1618a]
				−35.22*	[323]	37.2*	[323]	18.4*	[224]
	c	−40.5	[1618a]	−36.371	[1618a]	40.706	[1618a]	18.0	[1618a]
						38.9	[1680]		
						40.7	[1685]		
$HgBr_4^{2-}$	d			−88.0*	[323]				
HgBrCl	g					71.546	[2035]	14.159	[2035]
HgBrI	g					76.59	[2035]	19.537	[2035]
$Hg(CN)_2$	c			74.3*	[323]	27.4*	[323]		
				62.44*	[177]				
$Hg(CN)_4^{2-}$	d			141.3*	[323]				
$HgCO_3$	c	(−132.24)	[2263]	−112.00	[2263]	44.0	[2263]		
		(−118*)	[2683]	−144.7*	[232]				
HgCl	g					(62.1)	[1685]		
		18.75	[1618a]	13.595	[1618a]	(62.105)	[1618a]	8.705	[1618a]
$HgCl_2$	g					70.3	[1685]		
		−34.965[2]	[1618a]	−34.650	[1618a]	70.433	[1618a]	13.889	[1618a]
						19.4	[1163]		
	l	−51.404	[1618a]	−42.239	[1618a]	40.721	[1618a]	17.664	[1618a]
	c			−44.4*	[323]	34.5*	[323]		
				−45.0*	[227]	34.5	[1685]		
		−55.0	[1618a]	−43.991	[1618a]	34.535	[1618a]	17.664	[1618a]
$HgCl_4^{2-}$	d			−107.7*	[323]				
$Hg(ClO_3)_2$	c	−2*	[2683]						
$Hg(ClO_4)_2$	c	−4*	[2683]						
HgD	g					53.89	[1685]	7.46	[1685]
HgF	g	−7.164[3]	[570]			59.655	[570]		
						59.3	[1685]	8.24	[1685]
		0.7[4]	[1618a]	−4.352	[1618a]	59.338	[1618a]	8.282	[1618a]
	c	−46.0*	[887]			22.0*	[887]		
						18.5	[1685]		
HgF_2	g	−70.185[5]	[1618a]	−69.269	[1618a]	63.545	[1618a]	12.899	[1618a]
						65.0	[1685]		
	l	−96.772	[1618a]	−86.475	[1618a]	32.083	[1618a]	17.891	[1618a]
	c	−100*	[230]	−86*	[229]	28.0*	[887]		
		−95*	[890]	−94*	[227]	25.0	[1685]		
		−101*	[1618a]	−89.426*	[1618a]	27.8	[1618a]	17.891	[1618a]

HgH	g					(52.41)	[1685]	(7.15)	[1685]
		57.0^{6}	[1618a]	51.421	[1618a]	(52.486)	[1618a]	(7.181)	[1618a]
HgH_2	c	−72*	[2683]						
$Hg(HCO_3)_2$	c	−304*	[2683]						
$Hg(HS)_2$	c	36*	[2683]						
$Hg(HSO_4)_2$	c	−377*	[2683]						
$Hg_{0.970}In_{0.030}$	l			-0.137^{7}	[1589]				
$Hg_{0.980}In_{0.020}$	l			-0.097^{7}	[1589]				
$Hg_{0.990}In_{0.10}$	l			-0.053^{7}	[1589]				
$Hg_{0.995}In_{0.005}$	l			-0.029^{7}	[1589]				
HgI	g					67.1	[1685]	8.88	[1685]
		31.90^{8}	[1618a]	21.459	[1618a]	67.068	[1618a]	9.055	[1618a]
	c					28.3*	[249]		
						27.5	[1685]		
HgI_2	g	-3.855^{9}	[1618a]	−14.112	[1618a]	80.331	[1618a]	14.608	[1618a]
						80.3	[1685]	14.61	[1685]
	l	−20.862	[1618a]	−22.536	[1618a]	51.544	[1618a]	18.582	[1618a]
HgI_2, yellow	c			−23.1	[323]	42.6*	[323]		
				−24.7*	[227]				
		−25.20	[1618a]	−24.427	[1618a]	43.338	[1618a]	18.582	[1618a]
HgI_2, red	c			−24.07*	[323]	42.6*	[323]		
				−25.4*	[227]	40.8*	[1680]		
HgI_4^{2-}	d			−51.15*	[323]				
$Hg(IO_3)_2$	c			−41.2*	[323]				
$Hg_{0.500}K_{0.500}$	c	-6.40^{10}	[1589]						
$Hg_{0.667}K_{0.833}$	c	-6.20^{11}	[1589]						
$Hg_{0.800}K_{0.200}$ [12]	l	−4.55	[1589]						
$Hg_{0.980}K_{0.020}$	l	-0.481^{13}	[1589]						
$Hg_{0.989}K_{0.111}$ [14]	c	−3.30	[1589]						
$Hg_{0.990}K_{0.010}$	l			-0.247^{13}	[1589]				
$Hg_{0.995}K_{0.005}$	l			-0.126^{13}	[1589]				
$Hg_{0.999}K_{0.001}$	l			-0.026^{13}	[1589]				
$Hg_{0.9925}K_{0.0005}$	l			-0.013^{13}	[1589]				

1. $\Delta H_0^\circ = -16.074$ [1618a]. 2. $\Delta H_0^\circ = -34.014$ [1618a]. 3. $\Delta H_0^\circ = -6.1$ [579]. 4. $\Delta H_0^\circ = 1.762$ [1618a]. 5. $\Delta H_0^\circ = -68.994$ [1618a]. 6. $\Delta H_0^\circ = 58.161$[1618a]. 7. $T = 293$ °K; from In (l). 8. $\Delta H_0^\circ = 33.179$ [1618a]. 9. $\Delta H_0^\circ = -2.253$ [1618a]. 10. HgK phase. 11. Hg_2K phase. 12. Hg_4K phase. 13. From K(l). 14. Hg_8K phase.

1	2	3		4		5		6	
$Hg_{0.510}Li_{0.490}$, β	c	−10.00[1]	[1589]						
$Hg_{0.620}Li_{0.380}$, β	c	−9.35[1]	[1589]						
$Hg_{0.667}Li_{0.333}$[2]	c	−7.75[1]	[1589]						
$Hg_{0.750}Li_{0.250}$[3]	c	−6.32[1]	[1589]						
$Hg_{0.975}Li_{0.025}$	l			−0.564[4]	[1589]				
$Hg_{0.980}Li_{0.020}$	l			−0.454[4]	[1589]				
$Hg_{0.985}Li_{0.015}$	l			−0.344[4]	[1589]				
$Hg_{0.990}Li_{0.010}$	c			−0.232[4]	[1589]				
$Hg_{0.995}Li_{0.005}$	c			−0.118[4]	[1589]				
$Hg_{0.998}Li_{0.002}$	c			−0.048[4]	[1589]				
$Hg_{0.50}Mg_{0.50}$	c			−9.0[5]	[1589]				
$HgMoO_4$	c	−211*	[2683]						
HgN_3	c	64.1*	[229]	77.3	[2500]				
$Hg(NH_2)_2$	c	4*	[2683]						
$Hg(NO_3)_2$	c	−23*	[2683]						
$Hg(NO_3)_2$	c	(−54*)	[2683]						
$Hg(NO_3)_2 \cdot ½H_2O$	c			−44.0	[229]				
$Hg(NO_3)_2 \cdot 2H_2O$	c			−134.7	[229]				
$Hg_{0.25}Na_{0.75}$[6]	c	−0.275	[1589]						
$Hg_{0.286}Na_{0.714}$[7]	c	−0.314	[1589]						
$Hg_{0.40}Na_{0.60}$[8]	c	−0.421	[1589]						
$Hg_{0.50}Na_{0.50}$[9]	c	−0.495	[1589]						
$Hg_{0.532}Na_{0.468}$[10]	c	−0.515	[1589]						
$Hg_{0.667}Na_{0.333}$[11]	c	−0.550	[1589]						
$Hg_{0.80}Na_{0.20}$[12]	c	−0.366	[1589]						
$Hg_{0.947}Na_{0.053}$	l	1.04[13]	[1589]	−1.03[13]	[1589]				
$Hg_{0.950}Na_{0.050}$	l	−0.978[13]	[1589]	−0.975[13]	[1589]				
$Hg_{0.960}Na_{0.04}$	l	−0.785[13]	[1589]	−0.790[13]	[1589]				
$Hg_{0.970}Na_{0.030}$	l	−0.590[13]	[1589]	−0.601[13]	[1589]				
$Hg_{0.980}Na_{0.020}$	l	−0.394[13]	[1589]	−0.408[13]	[1589]				
$Hg_{0.990}Na_{0.010}$	l	−0.198[13]	[1589]	−0.209[13]	[1589]				
HgO	g					57.7	[1685]	8.25	[1685]

HgO						56.9*	[249]		
HgO, red	c	(−21.708)	[796]	(−13.965)	[796]	(16.77)	[796]		
				(−14.25*)	[176]	(18.1*)	[176]		
				(−15.1*)	[232]	(16.8)	[1680, 1685]	(10.53)	[1685]
						(17.4)	[1390]		
		(−21.699)[14]	[1618a]	(13.983)	[1618a]	(16.795)	[1618a]	(10.531)	[1618a]
HgO, red, orthorhombic	c	−0.3–0.072[15]	[754]						
HgO, yellow	c					(17.3)	[1685]		
	c	−82*	[2683]	−71.2*	[176]				
$Hg(OH)_2$	d			−65.70*	[323]				
HgO_2	c	−14*	[2683]						
$Hg_{0.984}Pb_{0.016}$	l			−0.021[16]	[1589]				
$Hg_{0.990}Pb_{0.010}$	l			−0.015[16]	[1589]				
$Hg_{0.995}Pb_{0.005}$	l			−0.010[16]	[1589]				
$Hg_{0.999}Fb_{0.001}$	l			−0.1003[16]	[1589]				
$Hg(ReO_4)_2$	c	−383*	[2683]						
HgS	c			(−13.59*)	[176]	(25.2*)	[176]		
						(19.5)	[1773]		
						(19.72)	[1736]		
						(21.0)	[1685]		
$HgSO_3$	c	−83*	[2683]						
		−114.7*	[1172]						
$HgSO_4$	c			−141.0*	[323]	32.6*	[323]		
				−143.1*	[229]	36.7*	[291]		
				−141.1*[17]	[250]				
HgS_2	c			11.6*	[323]				
HgSe	c			−5.0*	[229]				
$HgSeO_4$	c	−97.0*	[499]			24.0*	[498]		
		−98*	[2683]						
$HgSiO_3$	c	−225*	[2683]						
$Hg_{0.9875}Sn_{0.0125}$	l			−0.016[18]	[1589]				
$Hg_{0.999}Sn_{0.010}$	l			−0.014[18]	[1589]				
$Hg_{0.9995}Sn_{0.005}$	l			−0.009[18]	[1589]				
HgTe	c	−3.0	[1773]						
$Hg_{0.58}Tl_{0.42}$	l	−0.250[19]	[1589]	−0.610[19]	[1589]				
$Hg_{0.60}Tl_{0.40}$	l	−0.250[19]	[1589]	−0.605[19]	[1589]				

1. $T = 292$ °K. 2. Hg_2Li phase. 3. Hg_3Li phase. 4. From Li(l). 5. $T = 291$ °K. 6. $HgNa_3$ phase. 7. Hg_2Na_5 phase. 8. Hg_2Na_3 phase. 9. HgNa phase. 10. Hg_8Na_7 phase. 11. Hg_2Na phase. 12. Hg_4Na phase. 13. From Na(l). 14. $\Delta H_0^\circ = -20.605$ [1618a]. 15. From HgO, hexagonal. 16. From Pb (l). 17. Recalculated [234] from $(\Delta H_{298}^\circ)_{diss} = 74.5$ [250] to 75.8 [2245] using the values of ΔG_{298}° for HgO and SO_3 [2245]. 18. From Sn(l). 19. From Tl(l).

1	2	3		4		5		6	
$Hg_{0.70}Tl_{0.30}$	l	–0.240[1]	[1589]	–0.565[1]	[1589]				
$Hg_{0.80}Tl_{0.20}$	l	–0.210[1]	[1589]	–0.470[1]	[1589]				
$Hg_{0.90}Tl_{0.10}$	l	–0.140[1]	[1589]	–0.30[1]	[1589]				
$Hg_{0.93}Tl_{0.07}$	l			–0.231[1]	[1589]				
$Hg_{0.94}Tl_{0.06}$	l			–0.201[1]	[1589]				
$Hg_{0.95}Tl_{0.05}$	l			–0.175[1]	[1589]				
HgTl	g					71.7	[1685]	8.91	[1685]
HWO_4	c	–224*	[2683]						
$Hg_{0.97}Zn_{0.03}$	l			–0.057[2]	[1589]				
$Hg_{0.99}Zn_{0.01}$	l			–0.025	[1589]				
Hg_2Br_2	c	(–49.224)	[1449]	(–42.726)	[1449]	(51.98)	[1449]	21.2	[1449]
				(–42.76*)	[176]	(51.1*)	[176]		
				(–42.2*)	[250]	(52.4)	[1685]		
				(–43.278)	[2683]				
		(–48.80)	[1618a]	(42.705)	[1618a]	(52.283)	[1618a]	25.0	[1618a]
$Hg_2(CN)_2$	c	–54*	[232]	–62.2*	[205]				
		–58*	[2683]	–62.44*	[177]				
$Hg_2(CNS)_2$	c	40*	[2683]	50.8*	[323]				
Hg_2CO_3	c	–123*	[2683]	(–111.26*)	[177]	(41.5*)	[177]	24.7*	[224]
				(–105.8*)	[323]				
Hg_2Cl_2	c	(–63.59)	[1448]	(–50.332)	[1448]	(47.34)	[1448]	(28.3)	[1448]
		(–63.39)	[2683]	(–50.337)	[2683]	(46.0)	[1685]	(24.3)	[1685]
		(–63.319[3])	[1618a]	(–50.315)	[1618a]	(46.017)	[1618a, 2683]	(24.371)	[1618a]
				(–50.31*)	[176]	(46.7*)	[176]		
$Hg_2(ClO_3)_2$	c	–11*	[2683]						
$Hg_2(ClO_4)_2$	c	–12*	[2683]						
Hg_2CrO_4	c			–143.82*	[177]	52.2*	[247]		
				–155.75*	[323]				
Hg_2F_2	c	–105.2	[863]						
		–117.6*	[863]						
		–116.0	[1618a]	–102.169	[1618a]	38.40	[1618a]	24.0	[1618a]
Hg_2H_2	c	–74*	[2683]						
$Hg_2(HCO_3)_2$	c	–309*	[2683]						
$Hg_2(HS)_2$	c	28*	[2683]						
$Hg_2(HSO_4)_2$	c	–466*	[2683]						
Hg_2I_2	l	–23.021	[1618a]	–23.646	[1618a]	66.868	[1618a]	25.3	[1618a]

	c			(−26.61)*	[176]	(57.2*)	[176]		
		−28.462	[1618a]	(−26.545)	[1618a]	(57.67)	[1618a]	25.3	[1618a]
				(−25.4*)	[250]				
				(−26.53)	[2683]				
$Hg_2(IO_3)_2$	c	−84*	[232]	−46.8*	[323]				
				−54.58*	[177]				
Hg_2MoO_4	c	−216*	[2683]						
$Hg_2(N_3)_2$	c	$(141.7)^4$	[1356]	179.3	[1356]	48.56	[1356]		
$Hg_2(NO_2)_2$	c	−28*	[2683]						
$Hg_2(NO_3)_2$	c	(−61*)	[2683]						
Hg_2O	c			−12.73*	[176]	31.1*	[176]		
				−21.5*	[229]				
				−13.0*	[1045]				
Hg_2O_2	c	−15*	[2683]						
$Hg_2(OH)_2$	c	−90*	[232]	−69.85*	[176]				
		−83*	[2683]						
$Hg_2(ReO_4)_2$	c	−385*	[2683]						
Hg_2S	c	−7.5*	[232]	−7.23*	[176]	28.3*	[249]		
		−19*	[2683]	−1.6	[323]				
Hg_2SO_3	c	−90*	[2683]						
Hg_2SO_4	c	(−177.61)	[2683]	(−149.589)	[2683]	(47.96)	[2683]	(31.54)	[2683]
				(−149.11*)	[177]	(47.9)	[177]		
						(47.963)	[2099]	(31.542)	[2099]
Hg_2SeO_4	c	−106.5	[499]						
		−104*	[2683]						
Hg_2SiO_3	c	−229*	[2683]						
Hg_2WO_4	c	−229*	[2683]						
Ho	g	69.5	[2678]						
		80	[1094]						
		70.60^5	[1456]						
	c					17.77	[2479]	6.51	[2479]
						17.97	[1303]	6.49	[1303. 1589, 1685]
						14.24*	[323]		
						17.83*	[2396]		
						18.0	[1589, 1685]		
Ho^{3+}	d			(−160.4*)	[323]	−43.7*	[323]		
HoB_6	c	−123.0	[455]						
HoB_3	c	−193*	[2683]						

1. Liquid. 2. From Zn(l). 3. $\Delta H_0^\circ = -62.269$ [1618a]. 4. Average of 141.5 and 141.86 [1356]. 5. $\Delta H_0^\circ = 70.81$ [1456].

1	2	3		4		5		6	
HoClO	c	−231.6	[2626]			21.9*	[2626]		
$HoCl_{0.5}(OH)_{2.5}$	c			−300.25	[10]				
$HoCl(OH)_2$	c			−292.03	[10]				
$HoCl_2$	c	−145*	[442]						
$HoCl_3$, γ	c	(−232.8)	[2626]	−216.2*	[227]	35.2*	[2626]		
		(−231*)	[442]	−215.0*	[323]	35.1*	[323]		
HoI_3, β	c			−140.5*	[323]	52*	[323]		
				−140.8*	[229]				
Ho_2O_3	c	−449.55	[1565, 2666]	−428.2	[2662, 2666]	37.8	[2666]		
				−426*	[1976]	38.2*	[2662]		
						37.8	[2662]		
Ho_2S_3	c	−252*	[2683]						
$Ho_2(SO_4)_3$	c	(−933*)	[2683]						
$Ho_2(SO_4)_3 \cdot 8H_2O$	c	−1511*	[229]			156.1*	[323]		
I	g	(18.042)[1]	[1186]	(14.452)	[1186]	(43.1838)	[1186]		
		(25.516)[2]	[568]	(16.78)	[568]	(43.182)	[568]		
		(25.535)[3]	[2683]	(16.798)	[2683]	(43.184)	[1618a, 2683]		
		(25.483)[4]	[570]			(43.1839)	[570]		
		(25.482)[5]	[62]			(43.18)	[1685]		
		(25.537)[6]	[1618a]	(16.18)	[1618a]				
I^+	g	(268.005)[7]	[568]	256.252	[568]	43.625	[568]		
		(268.16)[8]	[2358]			43.81	[66]		
I^{2+}	g	(706.7)[9]	[568]						
		(710.19)[10]	[2358]						
I^{3+}	g	1467[9]	[568]						
I^-	g	(−46.607)[11]	[568]	−53.035	[568]	40.427	[568]		
		(−50.999)[12]	[570]			40.4290	[570]		
		(−47.0)[13]	[2358]			40.54	[66]		
	d	(−13.19)	[2358]	(−12.33)	[2358]	(26.6)	[2358]	(−34.0)	[2358]
		(−13.2)	[91, 568]			(23.5)	[1685]		
I_2	g	(14.922)[14]	[568]	(4.629)	[568]	(62.284)	[568]	(8.817)	[568]
		(14.923)[15]	[2358]	(4.627)	[2358]	(62.28)	[2358]		
		(14.922)[16]	[2372]			(54.18)	[2372]		
		(14.880)	[2479]			(62.28)	[1685]	(8.81)	[1186, 1685]
		(14.855)[17]	[62]			(62.284)	[1186]		
		(14.9)	[1896]			(62.25)	[1896]		
						(62.287)	[570]		

		(14.924)[18]	[1618a]	(4.631)	[1618a]	(62.281)	[1618a]	(8.814)	[1618a]
	l	3.232	[1618a]	0.794	[1618a]	35.936	[1618a]	19.281	[1618a]
I_2, rhombic	c					(27.76)	[1685, 2372]	(13.01)	[568, 1685, 2372]
						(27.758)	[1618a]	(13.28)	[62]
						(27.76)	[568]		
						(27.757)	[2358]	(13.011)	[1618a, 2358]
	d	(5.4)	[2358]	3.93*	[323]				
				3.92	[2358]	32.8	[2358]		
		(5.2)	[2713]	3.93	[2030]	32.3	[2030]		
I_2^+	g	229.7[19]	[568]						
		231.2[20]	[2358]						
I^3	g	35.1[21]	[568]	24.468	[568]	77.3	[568]	14.64	[568]
I_3^-	d	4.34[22]	[474]			1.47[22]	[474]		
	d	(−12.3)	[2358]	(−12.3)	[2358]	57.2	[2358]		
		(−12.2)	[568]						
		(−11.9)	[2713]	(−12.35)	[2030]				
		(−12.72)	[2462]			56.0	[2462]		
IBr	g	(−1.422)[23]	[1186]	(−1.830)	[1186]	(61.835)	[1186]	(8.72)	[1186, 1685]
		(9.76)[24]	[2358]	(0.89)	[2358]	(61.822)	[2358]	(8.71)	[2358]
		(9.42)	[2243]			(61.752)	[2243]		
		(9.702)[25]	[570]			(61.842)	[570]		
		(9.733)[26]	[568]	(0.86)	[568]	(61.83)	[568]	(8.72)	[568]
IBr, rhombic	c	−2.47	[568]						
IBr	c	−2.5	[2358]			33.0	[2243]		
	d			−0.90*	[323]				
				−1.0	[2358]				
IBr^+	g	241.3[27]	[2358]						
		242.1[28]	[568]						
IBr_2^-	d			−28.97*	[323]				
				−29.4	[2358]				
ICN	g					(59.12)	[1685]	(8.49)	[1685]
						(61.373)	[2037]	(11.584)	[2037]

1. $\Delta H_0^\circ = (17.77)$ [1186]. 2. $\Delta H_0^\circ = (25.612)$ [568]. 3. $\Delta H_0^\circ = (25.631)$ [2683]. 4. $\Delta H_0^\circ = (25.587)$ [570]. 5. $\Delta H_0^\circ = (25.587)$ [62]. 6. $\Delta H_0^\circ = (25.633)$ [1618a]. 7. $\Delta H_0^\circ = (266.62)$ [568]. 8. $\Delta H_0^\circ = (266.77)$ [2358]. 9. ΔH_0°. 10. $\Delta H_0^\circ = (707.22)$ [2358]. 11. $\Delta H_0^\circ = (-45.03)$ [568]. 12. $\Delta H_0^\circ = (-49.013)$ [570]. 13. $\Delta H_0^\circ = -45.4$ [2358]. 14. $\Delta H_0^\circ = (15.658)$ [568]. 15. $\Delta H_0^\circ = (15.659)$ [2358]. 16. $\Delta H_0^\circ = (15.686)$ [2372]. 17. $\Delta H_0^\circ = (15.608)$ [62]. 18. $\Delta H_0^\circ = 15.66$ [1618a]. 19. ΔH_0°. 20. $\Delta H_0^\circ = 230.5$ [2358]. 21. $\Delta H_0^\circ = 36.007$ [568]. 22. For the process $I_2 . P + I^- P = I_3^- , P$. 23. $\Delta H_0^\circ = -1.42$ [1186]. 24. $\Delta H_0^\circ = 11.90$ [2358]. 25. $\Delta H_0^\circ = 11.848$ [570]. 26. $\Delta H_0^\circ = 11.87$ [568]. 27. $\Delta H_0^\circ = 242$ [2358]. 28. ΔH_0°.

1	2	3		4		5		6	
ICl	g	(4.161)[1]	[568]	(−1.389)	[568]	(59.14)	[568]	(8.50)	[568, 1186]
						(59.146)	[570]		
		(3.352)[2]	[1186]	(−3.757)	[1186]	(59.146)	[1186]		
		(4.25)[3]	[2358]	(−1.30)	[2358]	(59.123)	[1008]	(8.492)	[1008]
		(4.10)[4]	[1618a]	(−1.452)	[1618a]	(59.145)	[1618a]	(8.497)	[1618a]
	l	−5.71	[2358]	−3.34	[931]				
		−6.277	[1618a]	−3.338	[1618a]	30.666	[1618a]	25.58	[1618a]
		−5.789	[568]	−3.25	[2358]	32.3	[2358]		
ICl, monoclinic	c	−8.449	[568]						
ICl α	c	−8.70[5]	[931]	−3.36	[931]	23.405	[931]	13.200	[931]
		−8.099	[1618a]	−3.351	[1618a]	24.60	[1618a]	13.44	[1618a]
		−8.4	[2358]						
ICl	d			−4.0*	[323]				
				−4.1	[2358]				
ICl^+	g	242.4[5]	[568]						
		243.5	[2258]						
ICl_2	c	−8.03*	[323]	−3.24*	[323]	24.5	[323]		
	d			−38.35*	[323]				
ICl_2^-	d			−38.5	[2358]				
IC_3	c	(−21.4)	[2358]	(−5.34)	[2358]	(40.0)	[2358]		
ICl_3, triclinic	c	(−21.1)	[568]						
IF	g	−22.547[6]	[568]	−28.008	[568]	56.42	[568]	8.00	[568]
		−22.58[7]	[570]			56.422	[570]		
		−30.089[8]	[1186]	−30.405	[1186]	56.426	[1186]	8.00	[1186, 1685]
						56.454	[1108]	7.996	[1008]
		−2.10[9]	[2358]			56.42	[2358]	7.99	[2358]
						56.4	[1685]		
		−13.856[10]	[1618a]	−19.327	[1618a]	56.451	[1618a]	8.021	[1618a]
IF^+	g	220[5]	[568]						
IF_5	g	−199.4[11]	[568]	−182.583	[568]	78.6	[568]	23.7	[568, 2358]
		−202.6[12]	[1186]	−180.6	[1186]	78.63	[1185]	23.70	[1186, 1685, 1618a, 2027]
		−196.58[13]	[2358]	−179.68	[2358]	78.3	[2358]		
						68.413	[437]	23.696	[437]
						78.7	[1686]		
						68.42	[2027]		
		−200.04[14]	[1618a]	−183.233	[1618a]	78.626	[1618a]		
	l	−209.4	[568]						

		−204.7	[2705]						
		−206.7	[2358]						
IF_5^+	g	116.20[15]	[2358]						
IF_7	g	−228.5[16]	[568]	−198.728	[568]	83.6	[568]	32.9	[568]
		−231.7[17]	[1186]	−196.6	[1186]	82.73	[1186]	32.3	[1186, 1685]
		−225.6[18]	[2358]	−195.6	[2358]	82.8	[1685, 2358]	32.6	[2358]
		−229.14[19]	[1618a]	−200.506	[1618a]	87.404	[1618a]	32.565	[1618a]
	l	−177*	[837]						
IO^-	g	40.136[20]	[568]	34.102	[568]	58.62	[568]	7.86	[568]
		40.104	[570]			58.624	[570]		
IO^-	d			−8.5*	[323]				
IO_3^-	d	(−52.9)	[2358]	(−30.6)	[2358]	(28.3)	[2358]		
		(−54.8)	[2462]	(−32.25*)	[323]	(28.0*)	[323]		
		(−53.7)	[2713]	(−31.5)	[2030]	(28.0)	[1685]		
		(−55.9)	[568]						
IO_4^-	d	−35.2	[2358]						
I_2Cl	d	−31.7	[2358]						
I_2O	d	−19.7	[2358]						
I_2OH^-	d			−55.0	[2358]				
I_2O_5	c	(−43.8)	[568]	−6.5*	[1045]				
		(−37.78)	[2358]	−11.5*	[229]				
$I_2O_5 \cdot HIO_3$	c	(−92.2)	[2358]						
$3I_2O_5 \cdot H_2O$, monoclinic	c	(−205.6)	[568]						
DI	g	6.293[21]	[568]	0.467	[568]	50.731	[568]	7.009	[568]
		6.232[22]	[570]			50.733	[570]		
HI	g	6.35[23]	[568]	(0.425)	[568]	(49.350)	[568, 570]	6,967	[568]
		(6.33)[24]	[2358]	(−2.02)	[2243]	(49.351)	[2358, 1618a]	6.969	[2358, 1618a]
		(−1.25)	[1686]						
		(6.286)[25]	[570]						
		(6.30)[26]	[1618a]	(0.376)	[1618a]				
	d	(−13.19)	[2358]	−12.33	[2358]	26.6	[2358]	(−34.0)	[2358]
		(−13.22)	[568]						
HI^+	g	246	[1214]						
		246.3[27]	[568]						
HIO	g	−21	[568]						
HIO, undissociated	d	(−33.0)	[2358]	−23.7	[2358]	22.8	[2358]		

1. $\Delta H_0^\circ = 4.551$ [568]. 2. $\Delta H_0^\circ = -3.33$ [1186]. 3. $\Delta H_0^\circ = 4.64$ [2358]. 4. $\Delta H_0^\circ = 4.49$ [1618a]. 5. ΔH_0°. 6. $\Delta H_0^\circ = -22.088$ [568]. 7. $\Delta H_0^\circ = -22.113$ [570]. 8. $\Delta H_0^\circ = -30.0$ [1186]; −30.70 [1008]. 9. $\Delta H_0^\circ = -1.64$ [2358]. 10. $\Delta H_0^\circ = 13.40$ [1618a]. 11. $\Delta H_0^\circ = -197.111$ [568]. 12. $\Delta H_0^\circ = -200.68$ [1186]. 13. $\Delta H_0^\circ = -194.29$ [2358]. 14. $\Delta H_0^\circ = -197.753$ [1618a]. 15. $\Delta H_0^\circ = 117.0$ [2358]. 16. $\Delta H_0^\circ = -225.243$ [568]. 17. $\Delta H_0^\circ = -228.69$ [1186]. 18. $\Delta H_0^\circ = -225.4$ [2358]. 19. $\Delta H_0^\circ = -225.93$ [1618a]. 20. $\Delta H_0^\circ = 40.597$ [568]. 21. $\Delta H_0^\circ = 6.82$ [568]. 22. $\Delta H_0^\circ = 6.772$ [570]. 23. $\Delta H_0^\circ = (6.868)$ [568]. 24. $\Delta H_0^\circ = (6.85)$ [2358]. 25. $\Delta H_0^\circ = (6.812)$ [570]. 26. $\Delta H_0^\circ = 6.82$ [1618a]. 27. ΔH_0°.

1	2	3		4		5		6	
HIO	d	(−36)	[568]	−23.5	[323]				
HIO_3	c	(−58.1)	[568]	−34.5*	[251]	28.2*	[251]		
		−55.0	[2358]						
	d	(55.9)	[568]						
TI		(−50.5)	[2358]						
	g	6.273[1]	[568]	0.498	[568]	51.558	[568]	7.091	[568]
H_2OI^+		6.222[2]	[570]			51.560	[570]		
$H_3IO_6^{2-}$	d			−25.5	[2358]				
$H_4IO_6^-$	d	(−181.1)	[568]	−31.7	[2358]	39.9	[2358]		
	d	(−180.9)	[568]						
H_5IO_6		(−180.4)	[2358]						
	c	(−182.0)	[568]						
	d	(−176.5)	[2456]	−128.5*	[323]				
		(−181.0)	[568]						
		(−180.4)	[2358]						
In	g	(57.000)	[2479]	(48.744)	[2479]				
		(58.0)[3]	[1589]	(49.74)	[1589]				
		(55.74)	[348]						
		(57.7)	[153]						
		(52.7)	[586]						
	c					(13.82)	[1589, 2479]	(6.39)	[1589, 1685, 2479]
						(13.9)	[1680 1685]		
						(13.88)	[999]		
						(12.3*)	[244]		
In^+	d	−12.5	[1665]						
In^{3+}	g					40.14	[66]		
	d	(−43.4)	[1665]						
InAs	c	−6.2[13]	[1]	−5.8[13]	[1]	9.8[13]	[1]		
		−15.8[4]	[2317]						
		−13.8	[602]			9.05[5,13]	[2146]	5.670[5,13]	[2146]
InBr	g	28.3[6]	[788]			(62.07)	[788]		
	c	(−41.5)	[2404]			27.6*	[788]		
$InBr_3$	c	(−100.0)	[887]	−88.5*	[323]	40*	[323]		
				−91.6*	[227]				
InCl	g					(59.1)	[1685]		
	c	(−48.0)	[887]	−39.2*	[323]	23*	[323]		
				−39.5*	[227]	23.0*	[1773]		

				−39.7*	[250]				
$InCl_2$	c	(−96.0)	[887]	−75.9*	[323]	29.2*	[323]		
				−76.8*	[227]				
$InCl_3$	c	(−126.0)	[887]	−110.7*	[323]	33*	[323]		
				−113.4*	[227]				
InF	g					56.3	[1685]		
InF_3	c	−246*	[230]	−230*	[227]				
		−250*	[890]	−234*	[229]				
		−229*	[2683]						
InI	g	29.6[6]	[788]			(64.07)	[788]		
						(64.8)	[1685]		
	c	−27.8	[2404]			31.6*	[788]		
InI_3	c	(−59.5)	[887]	−33.9*	[323]	50.5*	[323]		
		(22.8)[7]	[578]	−55.7*	[227]				
InH	g					49.56	[1685]	7.05	[1685]
InN	c	(−4.6)	[2625]	−2.7*	[323]	10.2*	[323]		
				0.8*	[229]				
InO	g			83.5*	[227]	57.3	[1685]	7.79	[1685]
$In(OH)_4^-$	d			−222.10	[7]				
InP	c	22.1	[2221]			7.14[5,13]	[2146]	5.32[5,13]	[2146]
		21.5	[169a]						
		26.0	[2628]						
InP, cubic	c	21.2	[600]						
InS	c	−33.6	[797, 914]	−39.3	[797]				
		−53.0	[932]						
$InS_{1.12}$	c	−58.8	[932]					5.828	[2011]
InSb	g					10.30[5,13]	[374]	5.867[5,13]	[374]
								5.800[13]	[2011]
	c	−3.47[4,13]	[2317]	−3.02[13]	[2317]	21.03[8]	[2317]	12.3*[9]	[2015]
		−3.67[10,13]	[403]	−3.07[10,13]	[403]	10.6[10,11,13]	[403]		
		−4.11[13]	[2526]	−3.37[13]	[2526]				
		−3.4[13]	[2312]						
		−3.89[13]	[102]						
		−3.91[12,13]	[1747]						
		−7.84	[535a]	−6.44	[535a]				
InSe	c	−28.2	[1459]						
InTe	c	−23.0	[1459]						

1. $\Delta H_0^\circ = 6.80$ [568]. 2. $\Delta H_0^\circ = 6.767$ [570]. 3. $\Delta H_0^\circ = 58.1$ [1589]. 4. $t = 0$ °C. 5. $T = 273$ °K. 6. $(\Delta H_{298}^\circ)_{subl}$. 7. ΔH_{vap}°; $t = 200–290$ °C. 8. Calculated [234] from $\Delta S = -1.99$ [2317]. 9. Average heat capacity between 20 and 90 °C. 10. From In (l). 11. Calculated [234] from $\Delta S_0^\circ = -2.01$ [403]. 12. $t = 450$ °C. 13. Per 1 *g-atom*.

1	2	3		4		5		6	
In_2O_3	c	(−216.8)	[2476]	−196.4	[2476]	30.1	[2476]		
		(−221.27)	[1536]	−200.5*	[323]	29*	[323]		
		(−221.5)	[887, 1536]	−198.8	[1045]	27.0	[1773]		
		$(118)^1$	[664]	−202.0*	[229]	42^2	[664]		
In_2S	g	6.5^{11}	[1746]						
		14.6*	[1961]						
In_2S_3	c	−101.6	[1459]	−101	[1459]				
		−97*	[2683]	−100.1*	[232]				
		147.4^3	[1961]						
$In_2(SO_4)_3$	c	(−525.3*)	[1172]	−613.4*	[323]	67.1*	[323]		
				−617.5*	[229]				
In_2Se_3	c	−82.2	[1459]						
In_2Te_3	c	−47.4	[1459]						
In_3S_4	c	−141*	[232]	−139	[1459]				
In_5S_6	c	−227.0*	[2531]	−218	[1459]				
Ir	g	(150.000)	[2479]	(138.807)	[2479]	(42.64)	[1685]		
		(159.9)	[1471]						
		(158.4)	[2093]						
		(160.9)	[2128]						
		$(160.0)^4$	[1589]	(148.74)	[1589]				
	c					(8.48)	[1589, 1685]	(6.10)	[1685]
						(8.50)	[996]	(6.00)	[1589, 2479]
Ir^{3+}	d			69.2*	[323]				
IrBr	c	−15.0	[887]			25.0	[887]		
$IrBr_2$	c	−27.0*	[887]			36.0	[887]		
		−23*	[230]						
$IrBr_3$	c	−40.0	[887]						
IrCl	c	(−16.0)	[887]	−17.6*	[227]	22.0*	[887]		
				−19.8*	[323]	26.9*	[323]		
$IrCl_2$	c	(−33.0)	[887]	−33.4*	[227]	31.0*	[887]		
				−33.7*	[323]	31.4*	[323]		
$IrCl_3$	c	(−50.0)	[887]	−47.5*	[227]	37.0*	[887]		
				−45.6*	[323]	35.9*	[323]		
$IrCl_6^{2-}$	d			−111.2*	[323]	53*	[323]		
$IrCl_6^{3-}$	d			−134.7*	[323]	43*	[323]		
IrF_6	g	(−65.5)	[1038]			82.76	[2483]	29.00	[2483]
						81.524	[2019]	28.956	[2019]

						84.5	[1685]	28.95	[1685]
IrI	c	−11.0	[887]			26.0	[887]		
IrI_2	c	−20.0	[887]			38.0	[887]		
		5*	[230]						
IrO_2	c	(−65.5)	[1038, 1039]	−28.0*	[323, 1045]	17.2*	[323]		
		(−67.1)	[1038]	−26.9*	[229]	17.3*	[1794]		
		(−64.0)	[1039]						
		(−54.42)	[2281]						
IrO_3	g	2.0	[2281]			70.0	[2281]		
IrS_2	c			−30.4*	[323]	25.2*	[323]		
		(−34.2)	[2650]	−31.5	[2650]	14.7	[2650]		
				−29.4*	[229]				
$IrSe_2$	c					22.5*	[2650]		
$IrTe_2$	c					29.5*	[2650]		
Ir_2O_3	c			−39.82*	[176]				
				−42.0*	[323]				
Ir_2S_3	c	(−57.7)	[2650]	−52.7*	[2650]	23.2	[2650]		
		(−42.0*)	[2625]	−49.8*	[323]	34.3*	[323]		
				−50.0*	[229]	34.2*	[1794]		
K	g	(21.491)[5]	[1185]	(14.623)	[1185]	(38.2970)	[570, 1185]		
		(21.31)[6]	[1618a]	(14.50)	[1618a]		[1618a]		
		(21.420)	[2479]	(14.589)	[2479]	(38.30)	[1685]		
		(21.629)[7]	[1589]						
		(21.747)[7]	[2534]						
		(21.376)[8]	[2342]						
		(21.415)	[1505]						
	l	0.546	[1618a]	0.063	[1618a]	17.078	[1618a]	7.816	[1618a]
	c					(15.262)	[1185]	(7.16)	[570, 1185]
						(15.46)	[570]	(6.976)[9]	[1215]
						(15.34)	[1685, 2358]	(7.07)	[1079, 1589, 1685, 2358]
						(15.457)	[1618a]	(7.05)	[1618a]
						(15.39)	[2479]		
						(15.48)	[1505, 1589]		
K^+	g	(122.959)[10]	[570]			36.9195	[570]		
		(123.07)	[564]			37.03	[66]		
		(122.896)	[1618a]	115.01	[1618a]	36.919	[1618a]		
K^+	d	(−60.32)	[2358]	(−67.70)	[2358]	(24.5)	[2358]	5.2	[2358]
		(−60.34)	[88]			(24.2)	[1685]		
		(−60.4)	[1700]						

1. (ΔH°_{subl}) ($t = 1290–1490$ °C). 2. (ΔS°_{subl}) ($t = 1290–1490$ °C). 3. $In_2S_3 = In_2S(g) + S_2(g)$. 4. $\Delta H^\circ_0 = 159.78$ [1589]. 5. $\Delta H^\circ_0 = 21.71$ [1185]. 6. $\Delta H^\circ_0 = 21.522$ [1618a]. 7. ΔH°_0. 8. $\Delta H^\circ_0 = 21.59$ [570]. 9. $T = 290$ °K. 10. $\Delta H^\circ_0 = (121.692)$ [570]. 11. Per 1 *g-atom*.

1	2	3		4		5		6	
K_2	g	(30.735)[1]	[1185]	(22.026)	[1185]	(59.667)	[1185]	9.057	[1618a, 1185]
		(30.580)	[2479]	(21.965)	[2479]	(59.67)	[1685]	9.06	[1685]
		(30.374)[2]	[1618a]	(21.802)	[1618a]	(59.666)	[1618a]		
$KAg(CN)_2$	c			8.6*	[323]	34.0*	[323]		
$KAlCl_4$	c	−286.0	[1618a]	−261.61	[1618a]	47.0	[1618a]	37.40	[1618a]
$KAlH_4$	c	−39.8	[2409]	−23.8	[2409]	30.8*	[2409]		
KAt	c					26.42*[3]	[304a]	10.81*[4]	[1304a]
KBF_4	g	−369.7[5]	[1618a]	−353.08	[1618a]	74.779	[1618a]	21.258	[1618a]
	c	−451.6[6]	[845]						
		−449.7	[1618a]	−425.325	[1618a]	12.000	[1618a]	26.80	[1618a]
		−424*	[725]						
KBH_4	c	−58*	[724]			25.404[7]	[1274]	22.958	[1274]
		−54.7	[1643]			25.48	[1116, 1618a]	23.081	[1618a]
		−54.23[8]	[1618a]	−38.191	[1618a]				
$KB_5O_8{\cdot}4H_2O$	c					364.41[9]	[1273]	330.48[9]	[1273]
KBr	g	−43	[2243]			59.9	[1685]	8.78	[1685]
		−42.58[10]	[1618a]	−50.408	[1618a]	59.904	[1618a]	8.837	[1618a]
								5.76[11]	[2200]
	l	−89.254	[1618a]	−86.939	[1618a]	25.887	[1618a]	16.00	[1618a]
	c			(−90.55*)	[250]	(23.2)	[1685]	(12.46)	[1685]
		−93.73[12]	[1618a]	(−90.528)	[1618a]	(22.908)	[1618a]	(12.446)	[1618a]
						(22.9*)	[228]	(11.71)[11]	[1668]
						(23.3*)	[698]		
$KBrO_3$	c	(−88.04)	[875]	(−66.91)	[875]	(35.66)	[875]		
						(35.7)	[570]		
						(35.6*)	[699]		
$KBrO_4$	c					37.5*	[249]		
KCN	g	−17.0[13]	[1618a]	10.692	[1618a]	60.859	[1618a]	12.249	[1618a]
	l	−24.414	[1618a]	−23.107	[1618a]	35.317	[1618a]	15.55	[1618a]
	c			−20*	[323]	16.4*	[323]		
		−26.9	[1618a]	−24.828	[1618a]	32.75	[1618a]	15.55	[1618a]
KCNO	c			−89.3	[2246]				
KCl	g	(−51.449)[14]	[570]			(57.102)	[570]		
						(57.106)	[1618a]	(8.721)	[1618a]
		(−51.175)[15]	[1618a]	−55.649	[1618a]	(57.3)	[1685]	(8.67)	[1685]
	l	−100.615	[1618a]	−94.238	[1618a]	20.714	[1618a]	17.59	[1618a]
	c	(−104.5)[16]	[570]	(−97.66*)	[250]	(19.70)	[570, 1685]	(12.10)	[593]
						(19.68)	[559]	(12.20)	[559, 1685]

						(20.4*)	[698]	(12.18)	[421]
								(12.209)	[551]
								(11.58)[18]	[1668a]
		(−104.175)[17]	[1618a]	(−97.506)	[1618a]	(19.733)	[1618a]	(12.258)	[1618a]
$KCl \cdot 3LaCl_3$	c	−6.66[19]	[45]			−7.4[20]	[45]		
$2KCl \cdot LaCl_3$	c	−5.77[19]	[45]			−4.2[20]	[45]		
$KCl \cdot MgCl_2$	c			−243.0*	[229]			31.17	[1679]
$KCl \cdot MgCl_2 \cdot 6H_2O$	c			−603.3*	[229]				
$3KCl \cdot NdCl_3$	c	−15.36[19]	[45]			1.2[20]	[45]		
$3KCl \cdot 2NdCl_3$	c	−7.67[19]	[45]			−20.2[20]	[45]		
$3KCl \cdot PrCl_3$	c	−7.40[19]	[45]			+1.6[20]	[45]		
$3KCl \cdot 2PrCl_3$	c	−14.08[19]	[45]			−17.5[20]	[45]		
$KClO_3$	c	(−92.96)	[93]			(33.8*)	[699]		
		(−95.23)	[1318]			(34.2)	[1685]		
$KClO_4$	c	(−103.22)	[850, 1634]	(−72.73*)	[177]	(36.3*)	[177, 699]		
		(−101.9)	[90, 539]						
		(−102.8)[21]	[1618a]	(−71.79)	[1618a]	(36.1)	[1618a]	26.865	[1618a]
KD	g					48.96	[1685]	7.80	[1685]
	c	−13.238	[1435]						
KF	g	−75	[2243]			55.4	[2243]		
		−78.242[22]	[570]			54.079	[570]		
		−77.90[23]	[1618a]	−82.208	[1618a]	54.128	[1618a]	8.413	[1618a]
						54.9	[1685]	8.45	[1685]
	l	−130.955	[1618a]	−124.522	[1618a]	18.104	[1618a]	16.00	[1618a]
	c	(−134.8)[24]	[570]			(15.91)	[570, 1685]	(11.64)	[570]
		(−135.6)[25]	[1618a]	−128.515	[1618a]	(15.917)	[1618a]	(11.787)	[1618a]
								(11.72)	[1685]
								(11.23)[26]	[1668]
$KF \cdot H_2O$	c	−206*	[234]						
$4KF \cdot 3NbF_3O$	c	−1641*	[22]			108.9*	[22]		
$5KF \cdot 3NbF_3O$	c	−1791*	[22]			123.1*	[22]		
$KF \cdot Nb_2O_5$	c	−603*	[22]			32.7*	[22]		
$3KF \cdot 2Nb_2O_3$	c	−1352*	[22]			78.9	[22]		
$4KF \cdot 3TaF_3O$	c	−1649*	[22]			113.1*	[22]		
$5KF \cdot 3TaF_3O$	c	−1799*	[22]			127.8*	[22]		

1. $\Delta H_0^\circ = 31.57$ [1185]. 2. $\Delta H_0^\circ = 31.194$ [1618a]. 3. $T = 300$ °K. 4. C_v; $T = 300$ °K. 5. $\Delta H_0^\circ = -367.701$ [1618a]. 6. $\Delta H_0^\circ = -473$ [845]. 7. $S_{298}^\circ - S_0^\circ$. 8. $\Delta H_0^\circ = -52.146$ [1618a]. 9. In *joules/mole*· °C. 10. $\Delta H_0^\circ = -40.38$ [1618a]. 11. C_v; $T = 200$ °K. 12. $\Delta H_0^\circ = -92.022$ [1618a]. 13. $\Delta H_0^\circ = -16.972$ [1618a]. 14. $\Delta H_0^\circ = (-51.018)$ [570]. 15. $\Delta H_0^\circ = -50.746$ [1618a]. 16. $\Delta H_0^\circ = -104.418$ [570]. 17. $\Delta H_0^\circ = -104.101$ [1618a]. 18. $T = 300$ °K. 19. From KCl(l) and $MeCl_3$(c). 20. ΔS_{298}°; from KCl(c) and $MeCl_3$(c). 21. $\Delta H_0^\circ = -100.896$ [1618a]. 22. $\Delta H_0^\circ = -77.741$ [570]. 23. $\Delta H_0^\circ = -77.41$ [1618a]. 24. $\Delta H_0^\circ = -134.441$ [570]. 25. $\Delta H_0^\circ = -135.245$ [1618a]. 26. $T = 300$ °K.

1	2	3		4		5		6	
$KF \cdot Ta_2O_5$	c	−634*	[22]			34.3*	[22]		
$3KF \cdot 2Ta_2O_5$	c	−1410*	[22]			83.0*	[22]		
KH	g					(47.26)	[1685]	7.38	[1685]
		(29.4)[1]	[1618a]	24.557	[1618a]	(47.304)	[1618a]	7.418	[1618a]
	c	(−15.16)	[1954]	−9.2*	[229]	(16.9*)	[698]		
		(−14.11)	[1501]						
		(−13.819)	[1435, 1618a]	−8.136	[1618a]	(12.0)	[1618a]	9.06	[1618a]
		(−15.0)	[1908]						
$KHCO_3$	c			−205.7*	[323]	26.6*	[323]		
				−207.3*	[229]	27.3*	[161]		
KHF_2	l	−218.243	[1618a]	−204.168	[1618a]	32.3	[1618a]	18.344	[1618a]
	c	(−218)	[1084]					18.40	[1685]
		(−221.905)[2]	[1618a]	−205.653	[1618a]	25.0	[1618a]	18.361	[1618a]
$KHSO_4$	c			−249.4*	[229]				
KH_2PO_4	c			−339.2*	[323]	34.3*	[323]		
						32.23	[1685]	27.86	[1685]
KHg	c	(−13.4)	[2625]						
KHg_2	c	(−18.5)	[2625]						
KHg_3	c	(−20.0)	[2625]						
KHg_4	c	(−21.5)	[2625]						
KHg_5	c	−25.0	[2625]						
KI	g	−30	[2248]	−8.9*	[323]	(61.7)	[1685]	8.79	[1685]
						(62.3*)	[249]		
		−31.04[3]	[1618a]	−40.734	[1618a]	(61.848)	[1618a]	8.893	[1618a]
	l	−73.986	[1618a]	−74.098	[1618a]	29.712	[1618a]	16.0	[1618a]
	c	−78.310[4]	[1618a]	−77.458	[1618a]	(26.48)	[1618a]	(12.603)	[1618a]
				(−76.5*)[5]	[250]	(24.9)	[1685]	(12.21)	[1685]
						(25.0*)	[228]	(11.76)[6]	[1668]
						(25.6*)	[698]		
KI_3	c			−73.5*	[323]	46.7*	[323]		
				−75.5*	[229]				
KIO_3	c	(−120.3)	[2713]	(−100.5)	[2713]				
KIO_4	c	−112.8	[615]	−94.51*	[249]	38.1*	[249]		
KLi	g					54.6	[1680]	8.78	[1679]
$KMnO_4$	c					(41.0)	[1685]	28.10	[1685]
						(41.0*)	[699]		
KNCO	c	−99.85	[2578]						
	d	−95.01	[2578]						

KNH_4CrO_4	c			-257.3*	[229]				
KNO_2	c			-67.3*	[323]	28*	[323]		
				-62.3*	[229]				
$KNO_2 \cdot KOH$	c	-192.7	[475]						
KNO_3	c					(31.72)	[553]	(23.59)[7]	[682]
						(30.9*)	[699]		
						(31.81)	[1685]		
$KNO_3 \cdot KOH$	c	-220.2	[475]						
KN_3	c	-0.33	[1356]	18.04	[1356]	20.55	[1356]		
$K_{0.1}Na_{0.9}$ [8]	c			-0.135[9]	[1589]				
$K_{0.2}Na_{0.8}$ [8]	c			-0.190[9]	[1589]				
$K_{0.3}Na_{0.7}$	c			-0.225[9]	[1589]				
$K_{0.33}Na_{0.667}$	c	-0.111[9]	[1589]	-0.230[9]	[1589]				
		-0.145[9,10]	[1589]	-0.100[9,10]	[1589]			7.91[9,10]	[1589]
$K_{0.40}Na_{0.60}$	c			-0.245[9]	[1589]				
$K_{0.50}Na_{0.50}$	c	-0.125[9]	[1589]	-0.260[9]	[1589]				
$K_{0.60}Na_{0.40}$	c			-0.245[9]	[1589]				
$K_{0.667}Na_{0.333}$	c			-0.230[9]	[1589]				
$K_{0.70}Na_{0.30}$	c			-0.225[9]	[1589]				
$K_{0.80}Na_{0.20}$	c			-0.190[9]	[1589]				
$K_{0.90}Na_{0.10}$	c			-0.135[9]	[1589]				
KNa	g					58.83[11]	[573]	8.88	[1679]
						58.6	[1680]		
$KNbCl_6$	c	-315*	[22]			76.9*	[22]		
		-6.7[12]	[[609]						
$KNbF_6$	c	-537*	[22]			45.8*	[22]		
KO	g	10.132[13]	[1618a]	5.268	[1618a]	56.272	[1618a]	8.302	[1618a]
KOH	g	-54.6[14]	[1618a]	-55.58	[1618a]	58.849	[1618a]	9.565	[1618a]
	l	-98.72	[1618a]	-89.145	[1618a]	23.447	[1618a]	19.86	[1618a]
	c	(-101.52)	[2358]	-89.5*	[323]	14.2*	[323]		
				-93.5*	[229]	17.6*	[699]		
						18.5*	[161]		
		(-101.780)[15]	[1618a]	-90.866	[1618a]	18.958	[1618a]	15.743	[1618a]
	d	(-115.29)	[2358]	(-105.30)	[2358]	(21.9)	[2358]	-30.3	[2358]
		(-115.21)	[1701]						

1. $\Delta H_0^\circ = 30.003$ [1618a]. 2. $\Delta H_0^\circ = -220.744$ [1618a]. 3. $\Delta H_0^\circ = -30.232$ [1618a]. 4. $\Delta H_0^\circ = -78.075$ [1618a]. 5. Recalculated [234] from $\Delta H_{298}^\circ = -78.87$ [842] to -78.31 [2245]. 6. $T = 300\ ^\circ K$. 7. $t = 50\ ^\circ C$. 8. Metastable phase. 9. For the reaction $(1-x)$ K (l) $+ x$ Na (l) $= K_{1-x}Na_x$(l). 10. $T = 280\ ^\circ K$. 11. $T = 300\ ^\circ K$. 12. From salts. 13. $\Delta H_0^\circ = 10.629$ [1618a]. 14. $\Delta H_0^\circ = -53.428$ [1618a]. 15. $\Delta H_0^\circ = -100.964$ [1618a].

1	2	3		4		5		6	
KOH	d	(−115.323)	[1436]						
		(−115.37)	[1954]						
KO_2	c	−67.9	[198]	−56.8	[1045]	27.9	[1685, 2546]	18.53	[1618a, 1685, 2546]
				−59.393	[1618a]	27.888	[1618a]		
		−67.6^{1}	[1314, 1618a]	−57.4	[887]				
		−68.0	[1109]						
KO_3	c	−62.1	[408]	−45.5*	[1045]				
KPF_6	c					53.54	[2442]	37.89^{2}	[2442]
KPO_3	c					25.83	[1151]	21.56	[1151]
$K[PtNH_3Cl_3]$	c	−184.1	[423]						
KRb	g					63.6	[1685]	8.68	[1685]
						62.7	[1680]		
$KReO_4$	c	(−263.0)	[874]	−238.5	[874, 1002]	40.12	[1002]	29.303	[1002]
				−240.5	[232]	40.1	[1685]	29.31	[1685]
$K_{0.75}Sb_{0.25}$	c	−17.85	[1589						
KSO_2F		−18.3^{3}	[2354]			−38.4^{4}	[2354]		
$KTaCl_6$	c	−333*	[22]			74.7*	[22]		
		−31.1^{5}	[667]						
$KTaF_6$	c	−552*	[22]			47.8*	[22]		
$KTeO_4$	c	−242.54	[2413]	−219.25	[2413]	42.5	[2413]		
				−197.4*	[229]				
KTe	c	−13.5*	[1773]						
KVO_4	c			−245.1	[229]				
$KWCl_6$	c	−11.3^{5}	[183]						
$KZn_{1.5}Fe(CN)_6$		21.4	[2234]						
$K_2B_4O_7$	l	−786.1	[1618a]	−740.991	[1618a]	56.7	[1618a]	40.75	[1618a]
	c	−796.9	[1618a]	−749.734	[1618a]	49.8	[1618a]	40.75	[1618a]
$K_2B_6O_{10}$	c	−1107.44	[1618a]	−1040.549	[1618a]	60.0	[1618a]	62.6	[1618a]
$K_2B_8O_{13}$	c	−1420.92	[1618a]	−1334.318	[1618a]	70.2	[1618a]	76.79	[1618a]
$K_2B_8O_{17}$	c	−1403.57	[1618a]	−1317.295	[1618a]	71.295	[1618a]	77.22	[1618a]
K_2Br_2	g	−126.16^{6}	[1618a]	−133.28	[1618a]	91.179	[1618a]	19.587	[1618a]
K_2CO_3	l	−269.91	[1618a]	−249.192	[1618a]	36.29	[1618a]	40.0	[1618a]
	c			−255.5*	[323]	33.6	[323]		
						35.7	[699]		
		−273.93^{7}	[1618a]	−253.531	[1618a]	37.361	[1618a]	27.652	[1618a]
	d			−261.2	[323]				

$K_2CO_3 \cdot \frac{1}{2}H_2O$	c	−310.43[8]	[234]						
$K_2CO_3 \cdot 1\frac{1}{2}H_2O$	c	−383.40[9]	[234]						
$K_2C_2N_2$	g	−5.4*[10]	[1618a]	−8.427	[1618a]	89.556	[1618a]	26.410	[1618a]
$K_2CdFe(CN)_6$		−6.4	[2234]						
K_2CrO_4	g	−147.85[11]	[1618a]	−147.882	[1618a]	84.312	[1618a]	19.328	[1618a]
K_2CrO_4	c	(−307.7)	[452]	−307.35	[452]	47.8	[452, 1685]	34.9	[452, 1685]
		(−331*)	[232]	−307.1*	[229]	46.2*	[248]		
		(−332.8)	[1499]	−310.5*	[323]	44.6*	[323]		
						47.6*	[699]		
$K_2Cr_2O_7$	c	(−485.3)	[232]	−445.6	[452]	69.6	[452, 1685]	52.50	[452, 1685]
		(−488,3)	[1499]	−446.2*	[229]				
K_2F_2	g	−205.4[12]	[1618a]	−204.715	[1618a]	77.065	[1618a]	18.769	[1618a]
K_2IrCl_6	c			−244*	[323]	82.6*	[323]		
K_2I_2	g	−101.06[13]	[1618a]	−112.25	[1618a]	96.203	[1618a]	19.721	[1618a]
K_2MnO_4	c	−283	[1523]						
K_2MoO_4	c	−357.3	[2041]						
K_2NbF_7	c	−694*	[22]			60.2*	[22]		
K_2NbF_5O	c	−646*	[22]			45.9*	[22]		
$K_2NbF_5O \cdot Nb_2O_3$	c	−1101*	[22]			68.3*	[22]		
$K_2NbF_3O_2$	c	−562*	[22]			42.1*	[22]		
$2K_2NbF_7 \cdot Nb_2O_5$	c	−1904*	[22]			138.4*	[22]		
$2K_2NbF_7 \cdot Ta_2O_5$	c	−1925*	[22]			140.2*	[22]		
K_2O	c	(−86.8)	[1618a]	−76.986	[1618a]	22.5	[1618a]	20.0	[1618a]
		(−77*)	[887]	−86.4	[887]	20.8*	[323]		
				−75.7*	[251]	26.5*	[251]		
				−79.8*	[229]	23.5*	[1773]		
				−76.3*	[1045]				
				−76.2[14]	[65a]				
$K_2O \cdot 2SiO_2$	c	−77.5[15]	[1681]	−77.9[15]	[1681]				
		−593.5*	[364]						
	v	−73.0[15]	[1681]	−74.1[15]	[1681]				
$K_2O \cdot 4SiO_2$	c	−73.9[15]	[1681]	−74.3[15]	[1681]				
		−1035*	[364]						
	v	−69.3[15]	[1681]	−70.8[15]	[1681]				
K_2O_2	c	(−117)	[199]	−100.1*	[323]	19.4*	[323]		
		(−118.5)	[1618a]	−102.723	[1618]	27.0	[1618a]	23.94	[1618a]
				−103.3*	[229]				
				−102.0*	[1045]				

1. $\Delta H_0^\circ = -67.176$ [1618a]. 2. $T = 300$ °K. 3. From KF and SO_2. 4. ΔS_{298}°; from KF and SO_2. 5. From salts. 6. $\Delta H_0^\circ = -122.011$ [1618a]. 7. $\Delta H_0^\circ = -272.63$ [1618a]. 8. In [2245] the erroneous value of −210.43 was given. 9. [2245] contains the erroneous value of −283.40. 10. $\Delta H_0^\circ = -5.415$ [1618a]. 11. $\Delta H_0^\circ = -147.082$ [1618a]. 12. $\Delta H_0^\circ = -204.285$ [1618a]. 13. $\Delta H_0^\circ = -99.80$ [1618a]. 14. Corrected value −46.2* [323]. 15. From K_2O and $SiO_2(a)$.

1	2	3		4		5		6	
$K_2(OH)_2$	g	−162.0[1]	[1618a]	−152.403	[1618a]	78.939	[1618a]	19.466	[1618a]
K_2O_3	c			−100*	[323]	19.9*	[323]		
				−100.0*	[229]				
				−102.5*	[1045]				
K_2O_4	c			−99.6*	[323]	22.4*	[323]		
				−101.3*	[229]				
K_2OsCl_6	c			−242.5*	[323]	82.5*	[323]		
K_2PdBr_4	c			−211.6*	[323]	79.1*	[323]		
K_2PdCl_4	c			−238.1*	[323]	67.1*	[323]		
K_2PdCl_6	c			−247.9*	[323]	77.7*	[323]		
K_2PtBr_4	c			−209.7*	[323]	81.6*	[323]		
K_2PtBr_6	c			−222.4*	[323]	77.2*	[323]		
K_2PtCl_4	c			−229.0*	[323]	67.6*	[323]	41.9*	[594]
								43.10	[421]
K_2PtCl_6	c			(−264.80*)	[177]	(78.8*)[2]	[177]		
						(79.8)	[1685]	49.26	[1685]
$K_2[Pt(NO_2)Cl_3]$	c							50.37	[422]
Cis-$K_2[Pt(NO_2)_2Cl_2]$	c							53.26	[422]
$K_2[Pt(NO_2)$ [illegible]l]	c							62.75	[422]
$K_2[Pt(NO_2)_4]$	c							64.87	[422]
K_2ReBr_6	c					108.74	[920]	54.24	[920]
K_2ReCl_6	c					88.843	[921]	51.31	[921]
K_2S	c	(−102.4)	[1773]	−96.6*	[323]	26.6*	[323]		
				−98.8*	[229]				
K_2SO_3	c			−249.1*	[229]				
				−244.8*	[323]	37.4	[323]		
K_2SO_4	c					41.8*	[699]		
$K_2SO_4 \cdot Li_2SO_4$	c	−697.1	[96]	−596.1*	[229]				
$K_2SO_4 \cdot MgSO_4$	c			−597.4*	[229]				
	v			−601.6*	[229]				
$K_2SO_4 \cdot MgSO_4 \cdot 2H_2O$	c			−737.4*	[229]				
$K_2SO_4 \cdot MgSO_4 \cdot 4H_2O$	c			−855.1*	[229]				
$K_2SO_4 \cdot MgSO_4 \cdot 5H_2O$	c			−906.2*	[229]				
$K_2SO_4 \cdot MgSO_4 \cdot 6H_2O$	c			−961.6*	[229]				
$K_2SO_4 \cdot 2MgSO_4$	c			−928.9*	[229]				
$K_2SO_4 \cdot MnSO_4$	c			−544.7*	[229]				
$K_2SO_4 \cdot PbSO_4$	c			−514.7*	[229]				
$K_2SO_4 \cdot SrSO_4$	c			−633.9*	[229]				

$K_2SO_4 \cdot ZnSO_4$	c			-527.5*	[229]				
$K_2SO_4 \cdot ZnSO_4 \cdot 2H_2O$	c			-646.8*	[229]				
$K_2SO_4 \cdot ZnSO_4 \cdot 6H_2O$	c			-873.9*	[229]				
$K_2S_2O_8$	d			(-404.68)	[2524]				
K_2S_4	c			-110.8*	[323]	38.4*	[323]		
				-111.2*	[229]				
K_2S_4	c	(-89.0)	[1173]	-79.4*	[229]				
K_2SeO_4	c	(-265.3)	[502]			36.4*	[498]		
		(-271.66)	[518]						
		(-271.76)	[489]						
		(-271*)	[2683]						
K_2SiF_6	c			-651*	[323]	54.7*	[323]		
K_2SiO_3	c	-62.5	[2228]			33.0*	[1773]		
		-372.5*	[364]						
		-359*	[2683]						
K_2SmCl_5		-10.9[3]	[2200]						
K_2SnBr_6	c					105.9	[1980]	58.85[4]	[1980]
K_2SnCl_6	c					87.6	[1980]	52.85[4]	[1980]
$K_2TaF_3O_2$	c	-572*	[22]			44.9*	[22]		
K_2TaF_5O	c	-648*	[22]			47.4*	[22]		
$K_2TaF_5O \cdot Ta_2O_5$	c	-1141*	[22]			76.5*	[22]		
				-327.2*	[323]	75.1*	[323]		
K_2TaF_7	c	-712*	[22]			62.3*	[22]		
$2K_2TaF_7 \cdot Nb_2O_3$	c	-1934*	[22]			142.4*	[22]		
$2K_2TaF_7 \cdot Ta_2O_5$	c	-1963*	[22]			144.2*	[22]		
K_2TiCl_6	c	-27*	[1165]			87.8	[1771]		
K_2TiF_6	c	-695.4*	[50]			73.7*	[50]		
K_2TiO_3	c	-384.6	[431]			56.7	[81a]	166	[81a]
K_2UO_4	c	-485	[192]						
$K_3Al_2F_6$	c	-795*	[1618a]	-756.097*	[1618a]	68.0	[1618a]	53.25	[1618a]
K_3AlCl_9	c	-683.6	[1618a]	-627.634	[1618a]	112.0	[1618a]	80.60	[1618a]
K_2WCl_7	c	-12.7	[183]						
K_2WO_4	c	-392*	[2683]						
K_3AlCl_6	c	-500.0	[1618a]	-463.325	[1618a]	90.9	[1618a]	59.49	[1618a]
K_3Bi	c	-54.1	[378]						
		-50.0	[1773]						
$K_3Co(CN)_6$	c	-125.1	[2451]	-90.9	[2451]	96.0	[2451]		
						95.8	[1685]	74.00	[1685]

1. $\Delta H_0^\circ = -158.93$ [1618a]. 2. $t = 18$ °C. 3. From KCl(c) and $SmCl_3$(c). 4. $T = 300$ °K.

1	2	3		4		5		6	
K_3CrCl_6	c	−446.1	[1273]						
$K_3Cr_2Cl_9$	c	−568.8	[1273]						
$K_3Fe(CN)_6$	c	(−41.4)	[2451]	−12.4	[2451]	100.4	[1685, 2451]	75.60	[1685]
				−3.3	[323]	77*	[323]		
				−12.6*	[232]				
		0.7	[919]	−27.9	[919]	101.8	[919]		
K_3IrCl_6	c			−330.4*	[323]	91.4*	[323]		
K_3NbClF_7	c	−811*	[22]			78.6*	[22]		
K_3NbF_6O	c	−788*	[22]			60.5*	[22]		
K_3NbF_8	c	−841*	[22]			74.8*	[22]		
K_3RhCl_6	c			−307.5	[323]	94.1*	[323]		
K_3Sb	c	−71.4	[378]						
		−45.0	[1773]						
K_3SmCl_6	c	−6.4[1]	[2200]			61.9*	[22]		
K_3TaClF_7	c	−835*	[22]			80.6*	[22]		
K_3TaF_6O	c	−793*	[22]						
K_3TaF_8	c	−865*	[22]			76.8*	[22]		
K_3VCl_6	c	−14.4	[93]						
$K_3V_2Cl_9$	c	−18.6	[93]						
$K_4Fe(CN)_6 \cdot 3H_2O$	c	(−337.5*)	[232]	−262.3	[2451]				
Kr	g					(39.1918)	[570]		
						(39.190)	[568]		
						(39.1905)	[2358]		
	d	−3.7	[2358]	3.6	[2358]	14.7	[2358]		
		−3.78	[568]						
Kr^+	g	(324.314)[2]	[568]	322.005	[568]	41.945	[568]		
		(324.32)[3]	[2358]						
Kr^{2+}	g	(884.8)[4]	[568]						
		(892.43)[5]	[2358]						
Kr^{3+}	g	(1725)[4]	[568]						
		(1746.0)[6]	[2358]						
$Kr \cdot 6D_2O$, cubic	c	−438.8	[568]						
$Kr \cdot 6H_2O$, cubic	c	−424.2	[568]						
La	g	(99.600)	[2309]	(90.667)	[2309]	(43.57)	[1685]	(5.44)	[1685]
		(87.6)	[2275]						
		(94.0*)	[402]						
		(100.18)[7]	[1589]	(91.25)	[1589]				
		(103.0)	[2679]						

		(103.02)	[1456]	(102.96)	[1456]				
La, III	c					(13.64)	[1768]	(6.51)	[1685]
						(13.60)	[2109, 1589, 1685]	(6.65)	[1589]
La^{3+}	g					40.71	[52]		
	d	(−168.77)	[2422]	(−174.5*)	[323]	(−39*)	[323]		
		(−167.0)	[1565]	(−165*)	[1976]	(−46*)	[1976]		
$LaBr_3$	c	−221*	[230]	−215*	[227]				
		−214*	[2683]						
LaC_2	g					60.460	[2035]	10.891	[2035]
						61.7	[1685]	10.89	[1685]
$LaCl_2$	c	−128*	[442]						
$LaCl_3$	g	−179.5[8]	[441]						
	c	(−255.91)	[2422]	−238.3*	[2422, 232]	34.5	[2422]		
		(−256.18)	[1975]	−246.5*	[227]				
				−245.9*	[323]	34.5*	[323]		
				−238*	[1976]				
$LaCl_3 \cdot 7H_2O$	c	−759.50	[2422]	−645.0	[2422]	100.3	[2422]		
				−645*	[1976]				
				−646.7*	[232]				
LaClO	c	−228.2	[158]	−230.4	[1976]				
		−242.1	[46]	−308.65	[13]	23.6	[46]		
$LaCl_{0.5}(OH)_{2.5}$	c			−308.65	[13]				
$LaCl(OH)_2$	c			−300.4	[13]				
LaF_3	c	−415*	[230]						
		−405	[440]						
LaH_2	c	−49.7	[1999]						
LaI_3	c	(−157.0)	[1533]	−166.1*	[227, 323]	51.3*	[323]		
				−159*	[1976]				
$La(IO_3)_2$	c	−282.4*	[232]	−250.28*[9]	[177]				
$La_{0.25}Mg_{0.75}$	c	−3.20[10]	[1589]						
$La_{0.50}Mg_{0.50}$	c	−2.85[11]	[1589]						
LaN	c	(−71.5)	[2625]	−65.3	[229]				
				66*	[1976]				
LaO	g	−29.8	[1328]			58.3	[1685]	7.60	[1685]
$La(OH)_3$	c	−345.0*	[323]	(−313.2*)	[323]	25*	[323]		

1. From KCl(c) and SmCl(c). 2. $\Delta H_0^\circ = (322.833)$ [568]. 3. $\Delta H_0^\circ = (322.84)$ [2358]. 4. ΔH_0°. 5. $\Delta H_0^\circ = (889.47)$ [2358]. 6. $\Delta H_0^\circ = (1741.6)$ [2358]. 7. $\Delta H_0^\circ = 100.24$ [1589]. 8. Calculated [234] from $(\Delta H_{298}^\circ)_{vap} = 84.1$ [441] and $(\Delta H_{298}^\circ)_{LaCl_3(c)} = -263.6$ [2245]. 9. $t = 18\ ^\circ C$. 10. $LaMg_3$ phase; $T = 292\ ^\circ K$. 11. LaMg phase; $T = 292\ ^\circ K$.

1	2	3		4		5		6	
$La(OH)_3$	c	−351.6[1]	[2619]	(−315.25)	[13]				
		−363.1*	[229]	(−312.96*)	[176]				
LaS	g	141.4[2]	[948a]			61.66	[948a]		
	c					17.50	[948a]		
LaS_2	c			−154.7*	[323]	18.8*	[323]		
				−154.8*	[229]				
				−146*	[1976]				
LaSi	c	30	[493]						
$LaSi_2$	c	44.4	[493]						
La_2O_3, hexagonal	c	(−428.97)	[1230]	−407.6	[1658]	30.43	[1658]	(26.00)	[1658]
		(−428.83)	[1230]			30.7	[1685]	(25.80)	[1685]
		(−428.57)[3]	[2679]			30.6	[2679]		
		(−428.55)	[1738]	−407.7	[1738]	30.7	[1738]	(25.80)	[1738]
		(−428.58)	[2662]	−407.6	[2662]	30.4	[2662]		
		(−428.57)	[1575]			30.43	[2662]		
		(−430.5)	[887, 1575]	−408	[1976]	29.2*	[1976]		
		(−446)	[2619]	−426.9*	[323]	29.1*	[323]		
				−406.9	[1045]	30.58	[572, 1326]	(26.79)	[1326]
						26.28*	[242]		
La_2S_3	c			−301.2*	[323]	31.5*	[323]		
				−303.2*	[232]				
				−286*	[1976]				
$La_2(SO_4)_3$	c	−939.8	[1975]	−860*	[1976]				
		−975	[481]						
$La_2(SO_4)_3 \cdot 8H_2O$	c	−1612*	[232]						
$La_2(SO_4)_3 \cdot 9H_2O$	c	−1587.1	[1975]	−1382	[1976]				
La_3H_8	c			−339	[232]				
$HLa(OH)_4$	c			−369.61*	[6]				
$H_3La(OH)_6$	c			−482.91*	[6]				
Li	g	(38.439)[4]	[1185]	(30.570)	[1185]	(33.144)	[1185]		
		(38.439)[5]	[570]			(33.1435)	[570]		
		(38.164)	[1589]			(33.14)	[1685]		
		(38.41)[6]	[1618a]	(30.602)	[1618a]	(33.143)	[1618a]		
		(38.4251)[7]	[1830]						
		(38.584)	[1505]			(6.753)	[1185]	(5.91)	[1185]
	l	0.569	[1618a]	0.223	[1618a]	8.113	[1618a]	7.481	[1618a]
	c					(6.78)	[1115]	(5.89)	[1115]
						(6.954)	[1618a]	(5.887)	[1618a]

						(6.95)	[1932]	(5.95)	[1932]
						(6.69)	[1589]	(5.94)[8]	[1930]
						(6.75)	[2479]	(5.78)	[1589]
						(6.753)	[570]	(5.91)	[570]
						(6.951)	[1830]	(5.941)	[1830]
						(6.69)	[1505]		
						(6.70)	[1685]	(5.65)	[1685]
Li^+	g	(164.261)[9]	[570]			31.7661	[570]		
		(164.236)	[1618a]	155.351	[1618a]	31.766	[1618a]		
						31.77	[66]		
	d	(−66.58)	[88]			(2.46)	[1645]		
						(3.0)	[2449]		
						(2.5)	[967]		
						(4.7)	[1685]		
						(3.0)	[967]		
Li_2	g	(50.467)[10]	[1185]	(40.467)	[1185]	(47.047)	[1185]	(8.620)	[1185]
		(50.4396)[11]	[1830]			(47.0521)	[1830]	(8.6234)	[1830]
		(50.73)[12]	[570]			(47.087)	[570]		
						(46.99)	[1685]	(8.54)	[1685]
						(46.98)	[2243]		
		(50.4)[13]	[1618a]	(40.519)	[1618a]	(47.05)	[1618a]	(8.622)	[1618a]
$LiAlF_4$	g	−438*[14]	[1618a]	−427.207*	[1618a]	74.416	[1618a]	21.828	[1618a]
$LiAlH_4$	c	(−28.4)	[2409]	−12.9	[2409]			(23.5)	[2409]
		(−28.0)	[1618a]	−11.56	[1618a]	21.0	[1618a]	(20.65)	[1618a]
		(−24.67)	[1201]						
$LiAlO_2$	l	−273.301	[1618a]	−260.323	[1618a]	19.2	[1618a]	21.00	[1618a]
	c	−284.33	[1047]	−264.49	[1047]	12.7	[1718]	16.20	[1718]
						12.75	[1685]		
		−284.329[15]	[1618a]	−269.429	[1618a]	12.751	[1618a]	16.208	[1618a]
$LiBH_4$	c	(−44.15*)	[323]			18.13	[1467]	(19.73)	[1467]
						19.73	[1685]	(18.13)	[1685]
		(−45.522)[16]	[1618a]	−29.824	[1618a]	18.12	[1618a]	(19.727)	[1618a]
$LiBO_2$	g	−160.382[17]	[1618a]	−161.688	[1618a]	61.742	[1618a]	10.666	[1618a]
	l	−238.819	[1618a]	−226.365	[1618a]	15.591	[1618a]	14.291	[1618a]
$LiBO_3$	c	−85.19	[875]						
$LiBeF_3$	g	−212[18]	[1618a]	−206.629	[1618a]	63.889	[1618a]	14.601	[1618a]

1. Calculated [234] from the value of ΔH_{form} from oxides [2619] and $(\Delta H^\circ_{298})_{H_2O}$ and $(\Delta H^\circ_{298})_{La_2O_3}$ [2245]. 2. $(\Delta H^\circ_{298})_{subl}$; $(\Delta H^\circ_0)_{subl} = 141.7$ [948a]. 3. $\Delta H^\circ_0 = -427.0$ [2679]. 4. $\Delta H^\circ_0 = (38.05)$ [1185]. 5. $\Delta H^\circ_0 = (38.05)$ [579]. 6. $\Delta H^\circ_0 = 38.034$ [1618a]. 7. $\Delta H^\circ_0 = (38.05)$ [1830]. 8. Li + 0.95 at. % Mg. 9. $\Delta H^\circ_0 = (162.391)$ [570]. 10. $\Delta H^\circ_0 = (50.34)$ [1185]. 11. $\Delta H^\circ_0 = (50.3400)$ [1830]. 12. $\Delta H^\circ_0 = (50.6)$ [570]. 13. $\Delta H^\circ_0 = 50.298$ [1618a]. 14. $\Delta H^\circ_0 = -435.808*$ [1618a]. 15. $\Delta H^\circ_0 = -282.779$ [1618a]. 16. $\Delta H^\circ_0 = -43.105$ [1618a]. 17. $\Delta H^\circ_0 = -159.543$ [1618a]. 18. $\Delta H^\circ_0 = -210.240$ [1618a].

1	2	3		4		5		6	
LiBr	g					(53.581)	[716]	(8.091)	[716]
		−34.439[1]	[1618a]	−42.921	[1618a]	(53.956)	[1618a]	(8.116)	[1618a]
						(53.55)	[1685]	(8.06)	[1685]
						(53.670)[2]	[2108]	(8.122)[2]	[2108]
	l	−80.973	[1618a]	−78.886	[1618a]	18.144	[1618a]	16.0	[1618a]
	c			−81.2*	[227, 323]	16.5*	[323]	(10.83)[3]	[1667]
		−83.72	[1618a]	−80.993	[1618a]	16.0	[1618a]	(12.40)	[1618a]
				−81.24*	[250]	17.0*	[887]		
						15.9*	[698]		
						16.0	[1685]		
						19.	[890]		
$LiBr{\cdot}2H_2O$	c	(−300.0*)	[191]	−197.3*	[191]	26.7*	[191]		
$LiBrO_3$	c	−85.19	[875]						
		−76.5	[618]						
LiCN	c	−24*	[2683]						
LiCNS	c	−42*	[2683]						
LiCl	g	(−47.8)[4]	[1830]			(50.8546)	[1830]	(7.9492)	[1830]
						(51.04)	[1685]	(7.86)	[1685]
		(−46.778)[5]	[1618a]	−51.926	[1618a]	(50.864)	[1618a]	(7.946)	[1618a]
		(−45.967)[6]	[570]			(50.804)	[570]		
		(−46.7)	[1513]			(51.061)	[716]	(7.888)	[716]
						(50.921)[7]	[2108]	(7.957)[4]	[2108]
	l	−93.394	[1618a]	−88.965	[1618a]	18.745	[1618a]	11.479	[1618a]
	c	(−97.6)[8]	[570]			14.17	[570]	(11.51)	[570]
						14.22	[1685]	(11.71)	[1685]
		(−97.7)[9]	[1830]			14.170	[1830]	(11.470)	[1830]
		(−94.80)	[2376]	−91.7*	[323]	13.2*	[323]		
		(−96.9)	[2245, 2376]	−91.9*	[227]	14.17	[2371]	(11.47)	[2371]
		(−97.578)[10]	[1618a]	−91.786	[1618a]	14.173	[1618a]	(11.479)	[1618a]
				−91.95*	[250]	12.9*	[698]	(10.55)[11]	[698]
						13*	[224]		
						13.9*	[1680]		
						11.5*	[161]		
$LiCl{\cdot}2H_2O$	c			−209.2*	[229]				
$LiCl{\cdot}3H_2O$	c			−266.5*	[229]				
LiClO	g	−3.4*[12]	[1618a]	−4.342*	[1618a]	61.264	[1618a]	10.268	[1618a]
$LiClO_3$	c	−93*	[2683]						
$LiClO_4$	l	−85.684	[1618a]	−58.146	[1618a]	39.245	[1618a]	38.50	[1618a]

	c	−91.70	[1926]						
		−91.11	[850]						
		−89.98	[2285]						
		−90.89	[1317]						
		−89.80	[539]						
		−90.06	[539]						
		−91.0	[1618a]	−60.706	[1618a]	30.0	[1618a]	25.1	[1618a]
LiD	g					42.32	[1685]	7.30	[1685]
	c	−21.784	[1435]						
LiF	g	−79.8[13]	[1513, 1830]			47.7996	[1830]	7.4839	[1830]
						47.5	[1685]	7.85	[1685]
		−85.6[14]	[178]			47.948	[716]	7.928	[716]
		−80.838[15]	[570]			47.841	[570]		
						47.875[16]	[1777, 2107]	7.499[16]	[1777, 2107]
		−79.50[17]	[1618a]	−84.469	[1618a]	47.842	[1618a]	7.478	[1618a]
						49.2	[1680]		
	l	−140.548	[1618a]	−135.339	[1618a]	13.708	[1618a]	9.993	[1618a]
	c	(−146.4)[18]	[570]			(8.53)	[97, 570]	(10.02)	[570, 1685]
		(−146.3)[19]	[1830]			(8.4713)	[1830]	(10.011)	[1830]
		(−146.2)	[277]	(−139.41*)	[176]	(7.9)	[176]	(9.95*)	[97]
				(−140.8*[4])	[250]	(8.52)	[1114, 1685]	(9.48)[20]	[1667]
						(8.5)	[995]		
						(9.0*)	[698]		
		(−146.5)[21]	[1618a]	(−139.746)	[1618a]	(8.523)	[1618a]	(9.994)	[1618a]
$LiFeO_2$	c	−174	[1047]			18.0	[1685, 1718]	19.81	[1685, 1718]
LiH	g	(33.641)[22]	[570]			(40.821)	[570]		
						(40.77)	[1685]	(7.08)	[1685]
		(32.10)[23]	[1618a]	26.654	[1618a]	(40.825)	[1618a]	(7.106)	[1618a]
		(33.6204)	[1830]			(40.8224)	[570]	(7.1057)	[1830]
	l	−15.096	[1618a]	−11.804	[1618a]	11.515	[1618a]	6.689	[1618a]
	c	(−21.34)[24]	[570, 1954]	−16.7*	[323]	(4.79)	[291, 570]	(6.69)	[570]
		(−21.666)[25]	[1435, 1618a]	−16.368	[1618a]	(4.788)	[291, 1618a]	(6.690)	[291]
								(6.689)	[1618a]
						(5.9)	[1685]	(8.28)	[1685]
$LiHCO_3$	c	234*	[2683]						

1. $\Delta H_0^\circ = -32.598$ [1618a]. 2. $T = 300$ °K. 3. C_p at $T = 300$ °K. 4. $\Delta H_0^\circ = (-47.7630)$ [1830]. 5. $\Delta H_0^\circ = -46.742$ [1618a]. 6. $\Delta H_0^\circ = (-45.935)$ [570]. 7. $T = 300$ °K. 8. $\Delta H_0^\circ = -97.635$ [570]. 9. $\Delta H_0^\circ = -97.7207$ [1830]. 10. $\Delta H_0^\circ = -97.6$ [1618a]. 11. C_p; $T = 300$ °K. 12. $\Delta H_0^\circ = -2.755$* [1618a]. 13. $\Delta H_0^\circ = -79.7483$ [1830]. 14. Calculated [234] from $(\Delta H_0^\circ)_{subl} = 60.7$ [164] and (ΔH_{298}°) [2245]. 15. $\Delta H_0^\circ = -80.801$ [570]. 16. $T = 300$ °K. 17. $\Delta H_0^\circ = -74.449$ [1618a]. 18. $\Delta H_0^\circ = -145.80$ [570]. 19. $\Delta H_0^\circ = -145.6833$ [1830]. 20. C_p; $T = 300$ °K. 21. $\Delta H_0^\circ = -145.887$ [1618a]. 22. $\Delta H_0^\circ = (33.667)$ [570, 1830]. 23. $\Delta H_0^\circ = 32.141$ [1618a]. 24. $\Delta H_0^\circ = -20.142$ [570]. 25. $\Delta H_0^\circ = 20.452$ [1618a].

1	2	3		4		5		6	
$LiHF_2$	c	−224.2	[2649]	−208.1	[2649]	16.97	[2649]	16.77	[2649]
		−216.8	[912]			16.96	[995]		
LiHS	c	−60.8	[1660]	−54.5*	[229]				
$LiHSO_4$	c	−273*	[2683]						
LiHg	c	(21.0)	[2625]						
$LiHg_2$	c	(−25.0)	[2625]						
$LiHg_3$	c	(−26.8)	[2625]						
LiI	g	−19.10[1]	[1618a]	−29.43	[1618a]	(55.481)	[1618a]	(8.264)	[1618a]
						(55.557)[2]	[2108]	(8.270)[2]	[2108]
						(55.5)	[1685]	8.22	[1685]
	l	−62.369	[1618a]	−62.099	[1618a]	19.927	[1618a]	16.0	[1618a]
	c			−64*	[323]	18.1*	[323]		
				−64.28*	[250]	18.3*	[698]	(11.06)[3]	[198]
				−64.2*	[227]	17.5	[1685]		
		−64.79	[1618a]	−63.796	[1618a]		[1618a]	(13.027)	[1618a]
$LiIO_3$	c	−122.3	[615]						
LiN	g	39.04	[1618a]	32.774	[1618a]	50.716	[1618a]	7.019	[1618a]
LiN_3	c	2.58	[1356]	18.50	[1356]	17.15	[1356]		
		3.1	[37a]						
				16.6*	[232]				
$LiNO_2$	c			−79.5*	[323]	21.3*	[323]		
				−81.2	[2379]	17*	[224]		
$LiNO_3$	c			−93.1*	[323]	25.2*	[323]		
				−91.7*	[227]	21*	[890]		
						23.4*	[699]		
$LiNO_3 \cdot 0.5H_2O$	c			−119.5*	[191]				
$LiNO_3 \cdot 3H_2O$	c	−328.8*	[191]	−262.4	[191]	47.5*	[191]		
LiNa	g					52.4	[1685]		
LiNaO		−25*[5]	[1618a]	−30.222*	[1618a]	61.27	[1618a]	10.296	[1618a]
^7LiO	g	16.0[6]	[2677]						
LiO	g	19.031[7]	[570]			49.357	[570]		
		20.10[8]	[1618a]	14.453	[1618a]	50.395	[1618a]	7.745	[1618a]
		13.9877[9]	[1830]			49.3017	[1830]	7.3149	[1830]
LiOF	g	10*[10]	[1618a]	−10.947*	[1618a]	58.86	[1618a]	9.836	[1618a]
LiO_2	c	−62*	[1109]						
LiO_3	c	−63*	[2704]	−45*	[2704]	20*	[2704]		
LiOH	g	−57.219[11]	[570]			56.672	[570]		
		−57.2[12]	[1830]			56.5982	[1830]	8.5190	[1830]

		−57.7[13]	[1618a]	−59.351	[1618a]	52.601	[1618a]	8.377	[1618a]
	l	−114.052	[1618a]	−103.459	[1618a]	11.535	[1618a]	20.74	[1618a]
	c	(−116.34)[14]	[570]			(10.23)	[570, 797, 1685, 1830]	11.90	[570]
		(−116.45)	[1830]	(−105.5*)	[232]			11.85	[797, 1685, 1830]
		(−116.59)	[1645]	(−105.68)	[1645]	(10.2)	[838]		
				(−105.8*)	[232]	(9.7*)	[699]		
		(−116.60)[15]	[1618a]	(−105.619)	[1618a]	(10.232)	[1618a]	11.869	[1618a]
	d	(−121.572)	[1435]						
		(−121.42)	[1954]						
$LiOH \cdot H_2O$	c	(−188.93)	[1645]	(−163.44)	[1645]	(17.073)	[797]	19.001	[797]
						(17.07)	[1685]	19.00	[1685]
$Li(OH)_2$	g					64.8540	[1830]	17.1186	[1830]
$LiPO_3$	c	−50.5[16]	[1947]						
	v	−46.7[16]	[1947]						
$Li_{0.50}Pb_{0.50}$	c	−7.3*[17]	[1589]						
$Li_{0.78}Pb_{0.22}$	c	−8.4*[18]	[1589]						
LiRb	g								
						56.4	[1680]	8.82	[1680]
$Li_{0.60}Sb_{0.40}$	c					57.2	[1685]		
$Li_{0.50}Sn_{0.50}$	c	−8.7*[19]	[1589]						
$Li_{0.78}Sn_{0.22}$	c	−8.4*[20]	[1589]						
$Li_{0.80}Sn_{0.20}$	c	−9.6*[21]	[1589]						
$Li_{0.50}Tl_{0.50}$	c	−9.4*[22]	[1589]						
$Li_{0.05}Zn_{0.90}Fe_{2.05}O_4$[24]	c	−6.4[23]	[1589]						
$Li_{0.05}Zn_{0.90}Fe_{2.05}O_4$[25]	c					36.0	[1685]	33.39	[1685]
$Li_2B_6O_{10}$	c					36.3	[1685]	34.06	[1685]
$Li_2B_8O_{13}$	c	−1113.74	[1618a]	−1047.448	[1618a]	45.0	[1618a]	70.08	[1618a]
Li_2Br_2	g	−1413.57	[1618a]	−1330.011	[1618a]	63.4	[1618a]	77.80	[1618a]
						73.48	[793]	16.91	[793]
		−117.892[26]	[1618a]	−124.807	[1618a]	73.485	[1618a]	16.873	[1618a]
Li_2C_2	c			−15.4*	[227]				
		−14.2	[1618a]	−13.415	[1618a]	14.0	[1618a]	17.1	[1618a]

1. $\Delta H_0^\circ = -18.64$ [1618a]. 2. $T = 300$ °K. 3. C_v; $T = 300$ °K. 4. $\Delta H_0^\circ = 39.065$ [1618a]. 5. $\Delta H_0^\circ = -23.938$* [1618a]. 6. ΔH_0°. 7. $\Delta H_0^\circ = 19.037$ [570]. 8. $\Delta H_0^\circ = 20.105$ [1618a]. 9. $\Delta H_0^\circ = 14.0365$ [1830]. 10. $\Delta H_0^\circ = -9.333$* [1618a]. 11. $\Delta H_0^\circ = -56.5$ [570]. 12. $\Delta H_0^\circ = -56.4466$ [1830]. 13. $\Delta H_0^\circ = -56.938$ [1618a]. 14. $\Delta H_0^\circ = -114.973$ [570]. 15. $\Delta H_0^\circ = -115.218$ [1618a]. 16. From oxides; $t = 35$°C. 17. LiPb phase. 18. Li_7Pb_2 phase. 19. Li_3Sb_2 phase. 20. LiSn phase. 21. Li_7Sn_2 phase. 22. Li_4Sn phase. 23. LiTl phase. 24. Tempered. 25. Quenched. 26. $\Delta H_0^\circ = -113.538$ [1618a].

1	2	3		4		5		6	
Li_2CO_3	c			(−270.45*)	[177]	(20.9*)	[177]		
						(21.0*)	[699]		
						(21.60)	[1685]	23.23	[1685]
Li_2ClF	g	−180.2[1]	[1618a]	−179.98	[1618a]	64.037	[1618a]	15.019	[1618a]
Li_2Cl_2	g	−143.056[2]	[1618a]	−143.591	[1618a]	68.993	[1618a]	17.255	[1618a]
	c	−144.8[3]	[1830]			66.9946	[1830]	17.2555	[1830]
		−143.4	[1513]			67.83	[793]	16.11	[793]
Li_2CrO_4	c	−334*	[2683]						
Li_2F_2	g	−220.9[4]	[1830]			62.7978	[1830]	16.0654	[1830]
		−221.6[5]	[1618a]	−221.959	[1618a]	63.558	[1618a]	16.065	[1618a]
		−221.0	[1513]						
Li_2HfO_3	c	−423.2	[354]						
Li_2I_2	g					77.51	[793]	17.43	[793]
		−81.78[6]	[1618a]	−92.53	[1618a]	77.722	[1618a]	17.479	[1618a]
Li_2MoO_4	c	−368*	[2683]						
Li_2O	g	−39.90[7]	[1618a]	−44.767	[1618a]	54.732	[1618a]	11.893	[1618a]
		−31.839	[570]			57.037	[570]		
		−35.5425[9]	[1830]			55.9744	[1830]	9.4923	[1830]
		−47.0[8]	[163]						
		−47.5[10]	[391]						
		−38.8[11]	[820]						
	l	−132.129	[1618a]	−124.601	[1618a]	13.16	[1618a]	12.927	[1618a]
	c	(−142.8)[12]	[570]			9.056	[570]	12.95	[570]
						8.97	[1685]	12.92	[1685]
		(−142.4)[13]	[1830]					12.927	[1618a, 1830]
		(−142.56)	[1645]	−133.96	[1645]	9.06	[1645]	12.93	[1645]
		(−143.1)[14]	[1618a]	−134.348	[1618a]	9.056	[1618a]		
		(−142.5)	[1645, 2245]	−133.8	[1045]	9*	[683]		
		(−142.8)	[278]						
$^7Li_2O$	g	−43.7[15]	[2677]						
Li_2O_2	g	27.5[15]	[2677]						
		−58.0[16]	[1618a]	−58.729	[1618a]	65.357	[1618a]	17.383	[1618a]
	c	(−152*)	[887]	−135*	[323]	8*	[323]		
				−136.5*	[1045]				
		(−151.2)	[1618a]	−136.468	[1618a]	13.5	[1618a]	16.88	[1618a]
$Li_2(OH)_2$	g	−177.5[17]	[1830]						
		−169.4[18]	[1618a]	−159.195	[1618a]	59.898	[1618a]	13.338	[1618a]
	c	−185	[831]						

Li_2S	c	−106.5	[1661]						
		−117.7	[1983]						
Li_2SO_3	c	−275*	[2683]						
		−278.3*	[1172]						
		−279.4	[616]						
Li_2SO_4	c			−316.6*	[323]	27*	[323]		
				−315.9*	[229]	29*	[1794]		
						27.3*	[699]		
$Li_2SO_4 \cdot H_2O$	c			−374.2*	[229]				
Li_2SeO_4	c	−274.3	[526]			16.6*	[498]		
		−273*	[2683]						
$Li_2SeO_4 \cdot H_2O$	c	−344.2	[526]						
	l	−390.524	[1618a]	−369.337	[1618a]	20.848	[1618a]	23.306	[1618a]
Li_2SiO_3	c	−390.0*	[364]	−368.7*	[364]	20.0	[1773]		
		−378*	[2683]						
		−395.0	[1618a]	−373.023	[1618a]	18.20	[1618a]	23.306	[1618a]
		−34.4[19]	[1681]	−34.1[19]	[1681]				
	v			−356.1*	[323]	23.8*	[323]		
				−352.6*	[229]				
$Li_2Si_2O_5$	c	−602.5*	[364]	−568.4*	[364]	30*	[364]		
		−34.6[19]	[1681]	−34.9[19]	[1681]				
	v	−23.2[19]	[1681]	−25.8[19]	[1681]				
Li_2TiO_3	l	−374.374	[1618a]	−356.667	[1618a]	35.355	[1618a]	26.256	[1618a]
	c	−399.2	[2552]	−377.1	[2552]	21.9	[1716]	26.5	[1716]
		−398.9	[605]			21.93	[1618a, 1685]	26.54	[1685]
		−399.3[20]	[1618a]	−377.591	[1618a]			26.256	[1618a]
Li_2UO_4	c	−467	[192]						
Li_2WO_4	c	−396*	[2683]						
Li_2ZrO_3	c	−417.2	[352]						
$Li_{2.5}Na_{2.5}P_3O_{10}$	v	−2.18[21]	[1947]						
Li_3AlF_6	c	−802*	[1618a]	−764.143*	[1618a]	46*	[1618a]	48.0	[1618a]
Li_3As	c	−81.3	[37]						
		−54.0	[1773]						
Li_3Cl_3	g	−240.134[22]	[1618a]	−234.0	[1618a]	80.223	[1618a]	24.380	[1618a]

1. $\Delta H_0^\circ = -179.046$ [1618a]. 2. $\Delta H_0^\circ = -142.353$ [1618a]. 3. $\Delta H_0^\circ = -144.0955$ [1830]. 4. $\Delta H_0^\circ = -219.9632$ [1830]. 5. $\Delta H_0^\circ = -220.665$ [1618a]. 6. $\Delta H_0^\circ = -80.341$ [1618a]. 7. $\Delta H_0^\circ = -39.636$ [1618a]. 8. Calculated [234] from $(\Delta H_0^\circ)_{subl} = 98.845$ [163] and $(\Delta H_{298}^\circ) Li_2O(c) = -142.8$ [278]. 9. $\Delta H_0^\circ = -34.7825$ [1830]. 10. Calculated [234] from $(\Delta H_0^\circ)_{subl} = 95.28$ [391] and $(\Delta H_{298}^\circ) Li_2O(c) = -142.8$ [278]. 11. Calculated [234] from $(\Delta H_0^\circ)_{subl} = 104$ [820] and $(\Delta H_{298}^\circ) Li_2O(c) = -142.8$ [278]. 12. $\Delta H_0^\circ = -141.311$ [570]. 13. $\Delta H_0^\circ = -140.8824$ [1830]. 14. $\Delta H_0^\circ = -141.585$ [1618a]. 15. ΔH_0°. 16. $\Delta H_0^\circ = 57.504$ [1618a]. 17. $\Delta H_0^\circ = -174.6321$ [1830]. 18. $\Delta H_0^\circ = -165.895$ [1618a]. 19. From Li_2O and $SiO_2(\alpha)$. 20. $\Delta H_0^\circ = -396.77$ [1618a]. 21. $Li_2O(c)$, $Na_2O(c)$ and $P_4O_{10}(c)$; $t = 35\ ^\circ C$. 22. $\Delta H_0^\circ = -238.4$ [1618a].

1	2	3		4		5		6	
Li_3F_3	g	–345.3[1]	[1830]			71.1130	[1830]	20.9917	[2713]
		–362.0[2]	[1618a]	–355.302	[1618a]	71.067	[1618a]	20.799	[1618a]
Li_3N	c	(–47.0)	[2625]	–41.4*	[229]				
		(–47.5)	[1618a]	–37.142	[1618a]	9.00	[1618a]	18.09	[1618a]
Li_3PO_4	c	–502.6	[1947]						
Li_3Sb	c	(–77.8)	[636]						
		(–43.0)	[2625]						
$Li_4P_2O_7$	c	–160.8[3]	[1947]						
Li_4SiO_4	c	–552.5*	[364]	–522.8*	[364]	30*	[364]		
$Li_5P_3O_{10}$	v	–198.8[3]	[1947]						
$Li_6P_4O_{13}$	v	–243.5[3]	[1947]						
Lu	g	(87.200)	[2479]	57.43	[2479]	(44.15)	[1685]	(4.99)	[1685]
		(94.7)	[2678]						
		(94.7)[4]	[2679]						
	c					11.75	[2479]	6.45	[1685, 2479]
						12.18	[1627]	6.42	[1627]
						11.8	[1685]		
						11.79	[2396]		
						14.5*	[323]		
Lu^{3+}	d			(–156.0*)	[323]	–45.7*	[323]		
LuB_6	c	–134.0	[455]						
$LuBr_3$	c			–188*	[230]				
$LuCl_2$	c	–133*	[442]						
$LuCl_3$	c	(–221*)	[442]	–210.1*	[323]	35.4*	[323]		
		(74.5)[5]		–211.4	[227]				
$LuClO$	c	–227*	[46]						
LuI_3	c			–131*	[323]	51.3*	[323]		
				–132.5*	[227]				
$Lu(OH)_3$	c	–332.5*	[232]	–301.0*	[323]				
				–303.24*	[176]				
Lu_2O_3	c	–448.9*	[1567]	–427.8	[2662]	26.0	[2662]		
		–448.9[6]	[2679]			30.6	[2679]		
$Lu_2(SO_4)_3 \cdot 8H_2O$	c	–1498*	[229]			156.8*	[323]		
Mg	g	(35.600)	[2479]	(27.341)	[2479]	(35.5032)	[77]		
		(35.30)[7]	[1589]	(27.04)	[1589]	(35.50)	[1685]		
		(35.6)[8]	[1830]						
		(35.281)[9]	[1618a]	(27.025)	[1618a]	(35.5041)	[570, 1830]		
						(35.504)	[1618a]		

		(35.291)[10]	[570]						
		(35.11)	[2405]						
		(34.29)	[1370a]						
	l	2.158	[1618a]	1.459	[1618a]	10.159	[1618a]	5.953	[1618a]
	c					(7.81)	[1589, 1685, 2479]	(5.96)	[2479]
						(7.814)	[1618a]	(5.953)	[1618a]
						(7.780)	[1830]	(5.929)	[1830]
						(7.78)	[570, 1059]	(5.95)	[570. 1083]
						(7.87)	[1915]	(5.93)	[1059]
								(5.92)	[1685]
Mg^{11}	c							(6.10)[12]	[1855]
Mg^+	g	(213.10)[13]	[570]			36.8816	[570]		
Mg^{2+}	g					35.51	[66]		
	d					(−32.7)	[1685]		
$MgAl_2O_4$	c	−551	[720]			19.26	[1685]	27.71	[1685]
		−567.1	[182]			19.25	[1719]		
		−552	[719]			20.1	[349]		
		−551.2[14]	[1618a]	−521.358	[1618a]	19.268	[1618a]	27.771	[1618a]
$0.1MgAl_2O_4 \cdot 0.9MgFe_2O_4$	c					28.1	[349]		
$0.3MgAl_2O_4 \cdot 0.7MgFe_2O_4$	c					26.1	[349]		
$0.6MgAl_2O_4 \cdot 0.7MgFe_2O_4$	c					24.3	[349]		
$MgAs_4$	c	−27*	[2148]						
MgB_2	c	−21.98[15]	[1618a]	−21.378	[1618a]	8.60	[1618a, 2507]	11.43	[1618a, 2507]
						8.62	[1685]	11.70	[1685]
MgB_4	c	−25.1	[1618a]	−24.797	[1618a]	12.41	[2507]	16.81	[1618a, 2507]
						12.5	[1618a, 1685]	16.80	[1685]
MgBr	g					58.3	[1685]		
	c	−49.9	[1170]			68.57*	[297]	13.834*	[297]
$MgBr_2$	g					57.8	[2243]		
	c			(−119.3*)	[323]	29.4*	[323]		
				(−119.4*)	[227]	30	[2243]		
						26.1*	[698]		
						28.0	[1685]		
$MgBr_2 \cdot H_2O$	c	−202*	[230]						
$MgBr_2 \cdot 2H_2O$	c	−276*	[230]						

1. $\Delta H_0^\circ = -342.9722$ [1830]. 2. $\Delta H_0^\circ = -359.61$ [1618a]. 3. From Li_2O(c) and P_4O_{10}(c). 4. ΔH_0°. 5. $(\Delta H_0^\circ)_{vap}$. 6. $\Delta H_0^\circ = -447.5$ [2679]. 7. $\Delta H_0^\circ = 35.01$ [1589]. 8. $\Delta H_0^\circ = 35.3090$ [1830]. 9. $\Delta H_0^\circ = 34.996$ [1618a]. 10. $\Delta H_0^\circ = 35.291$ [570]. 11. 8 wt.% Al + 0.55 wt.% Zn + 0.14 wt.% Mn. 12. $T = 400$ °K. 13. $\Delta H_0^\circ = 211.328$ [570]. 14. $\Delta H_0^\circ = -547.349$ [1618a]. 15. $\Delta H_0^\circ = -21.825$ [1618a].

1	2	3		4		5		6	
$MgBr_2 \cdot 4H_2O$	c	–425*	[230]						
$MgBr_2 \cdot 6H_2O$	c	(–575.2*)	[689]	(–468.80)	[190]	(82.17)	[190]		
$Mg(BrO_3)_2$	c					51.1*	[699]		
MgC_2	c	21.0*	[1602]	21*	[2226]	14.0	[1773]		
			[1618a]	20.27	[1618a]	13.0	[1618a]	13.44	[1618a]
$Mg(CN)_2$	c	–16*	[2683]						
$Mg(CNS)_2$	c	–41*	[2683]						
$MgCO_3$	c	(–262.0)	[2245, 2247]	(–242.03*)	[177]	(16.8*)	[699]		
		(–266.0)	[1618a]	(–246.023)	[1618a]	(15.7)	[1618a]	18.07	[1618a]
$MgCO_3 \cdot 2H_2O$	c			0.07[1]	[1466]	–7.0[2]	[1466]		
$MgCO_3 \cdot 3H_2O$	c	2.68[1]	[1466]	3.82[1]	[1466]	–1.0[2]	[1466]		
				3.5	[1465]				
$MgCO_3 \cdot 5H_2O$	c			3.95[1]	[1466]	–28.0[2]	[1466]		
MgCd	c	(–1.920)	[2458]	–1.857	[2458]	4.79[3]	[2458]	6.16	[2458]
		(–1.96)	[908]			19.6	[1685]	12.34	[1685]
		(–3.9)	[908]						
$MgCd_3$	c	–6.5	[908]			44.8	[1685]	28.32	[1685]
MgCl	g	(1.5079)[4]	[1830]	–4.1*	[227]	55.7526	[1830]	8.3245	[1830]
						55.6	[1685]	8.29	[1685]
						55.668	[570]		
		(1*)[5]	[1618a]	–5.337*	[1618a]	55.723	[1618a]	8.325	[1618a]
		(–26.503)[8]	[570]						
	c	(–53*)	[323]	–46.5*	[323]	17.3*	[323]		
		(–57.2)[6]	[1170]			59.5993	[1830]	12.1246	[1830]
MgClF	g	–139.45[7]	[1830]						
		–138.9[9]	[1618a]	–139.183	[1618a]	59.641	[1618a]	12.184	[1618a]
MgClOH	c					(18.5)	[1685]		
$MgCl_2$	g	–100.8[10]	[1830]			61.4968	[1830]	13.0335	[1830]
		–100.7[11]	[1618a]	–100.814	[1618a]	61.496	[1618a]	13.033	[1618a]
		–100.934[12]	[570]			61.441	[570]		
		–94.4	[354, 1513]			63.60*	[297]	13.415*	[297]
	l	–144.979	[1618a]	–135.111	[1618a]	28.014	[1618a]	22.100	[1618a]
	c	(–153.4)[13]	[570]					(17.01)	[570]
		(–155*)	[358]	–127.8[14]	[1162]	(20.5*)	[698]	(16.98)	[1685]
		(59)[15]	[354]						
		(–153.22)[16]	[1618a]	–141.404	[1618a]	(21.483)	[1618a]	(16.992)	[1618a]
$MgCl_2 \cdot H_2O$	c							(27.55)	[1685]
$MgCl_2 \cdot 2H_2O$	c							38.05	[1685]

$MgCl_2 \cdot 4H_2O$	c							57.66	[1685]
$MgCl_2 \cdot 6H_2O$	c	(−600*)	[230]	(−501.73)	[190]	(77.86)	[190]	75.30	[1685]
						(84*)	[228]		
$MgCl_2 \cdot MgO$	c			(−294.1*)	[229]				
$Mg(ClO_3)_2$	c	−125*	[2683]			47.5*	[699]		
$Mg(ClO_3)_2 \cdot 6H_2O$	c	−473.3*	[689]						
$Mg(ClO_4)_2$	c	(−134.07)	[2285]	−79.4*	[323]	51.6*	[323]		
				−103.3	[190]	131.99	[190]		
						50.7	[699]		
$Mg(ClO_4)_2 \cdot 6H_2O$	c	(−583.2)	[23]						
$MgCrO_4$	c	(−303)	[481]	−295.1*	[229]				
$Mg(CrO_2)_2$	c	−453.1*	[375, 415]	−424.8*	[375, 415]	(25.1)	[349]	(30.30)	[1685]
						(28.4)	[699]		
$0.2MgCr_2O_5 \cdot 0.8MgFe_2O_4$	c					28.1	[349]		
$0.6MgCr_2O_4 \cdot 0.4MgFe_2O_4$	c					27.9	[349]		
MgD	g					47.58	[1685]	7.29	[1685]
MgD_2	c	−17.35	[2439]	−8.24	[2439]	9.9*	[2439]		
MgF	g	−89.7[17]	[1170]						
		(−20.2374)[18]	[1830]			(52.8222)	[1830]	(7.7861)	[1830]
		(−66.603*)[19]	[570]			(52.801)	[570]		
		(−53.1)[20]	[1618a]	−59.288	[1618a]	(52.793)	[1618a]	(7.782)	[1618a]
						(52.8)	[1685]	(7.77)	[1685]
MgF_2	g	93[21]	[354]			58.25	[297]	12.602	[297]
		−175.7[22]	[1618a]	−176.373	[1618a]	58.52	[1618a]	12.405	[1618a]
		88.0[21]	[1470]						
		83.95[21]	[1376]						
		−172.4	[354, 1513]						
		−177.227[23]	[570]			55.197	[570]		
		−178.1[24]	[1830]			55.4766	[1830]	11.2354	[1830]
		−170.5[25]	[1370]						
	l	−259.557	[1618a]	−247.341	[1618a]	15.29	[1618a]	22.57	[1618a]
	c	(−266.0)	[1415, 2245]	(−252.40)	[176]	(19.1*)	[176]	(15.21)	[570]
		(−263.5)[26]	[570, 1830]			(13.9635)	[1830]	(14.9700)	[1830]
		(−268.7)[27]	[1618a, 2252]	(−256.0)	[2252]	(13.6*)	[698]		
				(−256.005)	[1618a]	(13.683)	[1618a]	(14.72)	[1618a]

1. Hydration; $t = 15\,^\circ C$. 2. ΔS of hydration; $t = 15\,^\circ C$. 3. $S^\circ_{298} - S^\circ_0$. 4. $\Delta H^\circ_0 = 1.5574$ [1830]. 5. $\Delta H^\circ_0 = 1.055^*$ [1618a]. 6. ΔH°_0. 7. $\Delta H^\circ_0 = -138.8116$ [1830]. 8. $\Delta H^\circ_0 = -26.45^*$ [570]. 9. $\Delta H^\circ_0 = -138.264$ [1618a]. 10. $\Delta H^\circ_0 = -100.3903$ [1830]. 11. $\Delta H^\circ_0 = -100.284$ [1618a]. 12. $\Delta H^\circ_0 = -100.516$ [570]. 13. $\Delta H^\circ_0 = -153.316$ [570]. 14. $T = 400\,^\circ K$. 15. $(\Delta H^\circ_{298})_{subl}$. 16. $\Delta H^\circ_0 = -153.123$ [1618a]. 17. ΔH°_0. 18. $\Delta H^\circ_0 = -20.1360$ [1830]. 19. $\Delta H^\circ_0 = -66.5^*$ [570]. 20. $\Delta H^\circ_0 = 59.992$ [1618a]. 21. $(\Delta H^\circ_{298})_{subl}$. 22. $\Delta H^\circ_0 = -175.349$ [1618a]. 23. $\Delta H^\circ_0 = -176.569$ [570]. 24. $\Delta H^\circ_0 = -177.3239$ [1830]. 25. Calculated [245] from $(\Delta H^\circ_{298})_{subl} = 93$ [1870] and $(\Delta H^\circ_{298}) = -263.5$ [570] for MgF_2(c). 26. $\Delta H^\circ_0 = -262.569$ [570]; −262.5721 [1830]. 27. $\Delta H^\circ_0 = -267.764$ [1618a].

1	2	3		4		5		6	
$MgFe_2O_4$	c	–349.9	[465]	–322.9	[465]	28.3	[349, 1715]	34.35	[1655, 1715]
						29.6	[1685]		
MgH	g	(40.7102)[1]	[1830]			(46.1532)	[1830]	7.0701	[1830]
		(35.507)[2]	[570]	(41.89)	[77]	(46.146)	[77, 570]		
				(34*)	[323]	(46.11)	[1685]		
						(47.61)	[323]		
		(40.7)[3]	[1618a]	(33.928)	[1618a]	(46.141)	[1618a]	7.059	[1618a]
MgH_2	c	–17.79	[2439]	–8.79	[2439]	8*	[2439]		
		–17.7	[1693]						
		–21.71	[437]						
	c	–18.2[4]	[1618a]	–8.781	[1618a]	7.431	[1618a]	8.45	[1618a]
$Mg(HCO_3)_2$	c	–436*	[2683]						
$Mg(HS)_2$	c	–78*	[2683]						
$Mg(HSO_4)_2$	g	506*	[2683]						
MgI						60.2	[1685]	8.61	[1685]
						59.9	[2243]		
		–39.5[5]	[1170]						
MgI_2	g					72.53*	[297]	14.028*	[297]
	c			(–86.0*)	[323]	34.8*	[323]		
				(–85.6*)	[227]	30.1*	[698]		
						33	[2239]		
						31	[1685]		
$MgI_2 \cdot 8H_2O$	c			–577.44	[190]				
$Mg(IO_3)_2$	c	–204*	[617]						
$Mg(MnO_4)_2$	c					62.1*	[699]		
$MgMoO_4$	c	–336.5*	[170, 172]	–314.3*	[170, 172]	28.4*	[2633]	26.57	[2633]
		–334.8	[772]	–309.7	[772]				
		–341.2	[471]	–315.1	[471]				
MgN	g	112.423[6]	[570]			52.053	[570]		
		69.0[7]	[1618a]	62.138	[1618a]	53.713	[1618a]	7.823	[1618a]
MgN_2		–0.88; –0.6	[2405]						
$Mg(NH_2)_2$	c	–69*	[2683]						
$MgNH_4PO_4$	c	–439*	[232]	–390*	[323]				
				–390.29*	[177]				
$Mg(NO_2)_2$	c	–145*	[2683]						
$Mg(NO_3)_2$	c					(41.0*)	[699]	33.92	[1685]
$Mg(NO_3)_2 \cdot 6H_2O$	c			–495.31	[190]	108.30	[190]		
				–490.3*	[227]				
$MgNi_2$	c	–17.0	[1773]			21.20	[2701]	17.5	[270]

		−13.3	[2406]			21.6	[2406]		
MgO	g	−7.1[8]	[366]	94.08	[77]	50.945	[77, 570]		
		4.1970[9]	[1830]			50.9586	[1830]	7.6676	[1830]
		4.19[10]	[1618a]	−1.361	[1618a]	50.946	[1618a]	7.664	[1618a]
		−6.112[11]	[570]						
		15.2*[12]	[719]					8.906	[2595]
	c	(−143.7)[13]	[1830]			(6.6459)	[1830]	(9.0360)	[1830]
		(−143.84)[14]	[570]			(6.43)	[570]	(9.03)	[570, 1685]
		(−143.70)[15]	[1618a, 1535]			(5.58)[16]	[781]	(6.44)	[781]
				−135.981	[1618a]	(6.439)	[1618a]	(8.906)	[1618a]
		(−143.92)	[94]			(6.55)	[1680 1685]		
						(6.1*)	[698]		
$3MgO \cdot 4SiO_2 \cdot H_2O$, talcum	c	−43.6[17]	[2231]			62.33	[2231]	76.89	[2231]
MgO_2	c			−130.9*	[229]				
				−135.7*	[1045]				
MgOH	g	−12.2185[18]	[1830]			57.7813	[1830]	2.1209	[1830]
		−12.2*[19]	[1618a]	−15.128*	[1618a]	57.752	[1618a]	8.926	[1618a]
$Mg(OH)_2$	c			(−199.53*)	[176]	(16.0*)	[176]	18.43	[1685]
						(14.2*)	[699]		
		−221.0[20]	[1618a]	(−199.251)	[1618a]	(15.097)	[1618a]	18.412	[1618a]
$3Mg(OH)_2 \cdot MgSO_4 \cdot 8H_2O$	c	−1537.9	[2052]						
$Mg_{0.667}Pb_{0.333}$, β	c	−4.20[21]	[1589]	−3.65[21]	[1589]				
$Mg_{0.50}Pr_{0.50}$	c	−4.10[22]	[1589]						
$Mg_{0.75}Pr_{0.25}$	c	−2.75[23]	[1589]						
$Mg(ReO_4)_2$	c	−461*	[2683]						
MgS	g	34.2774[24]	[1830]			53.8962	[1830]	8.1926	[1830]
		33.200[25]	[1618a]	20.698	[1618a]	57.387	[1618a]	8.226	[1618a]
	c			(−83.6*)	[323]	12.6*	[323]		
				(−81.0*)	[229]	10.6*	[247]		
				(−81.4)	[1734]	10.2	[1773]		
						11.1*	[698]		
						11.0	[1618a, 1685]		
	l	−83.00	[1618a]	(−81.672)	[1618a]			10.0	[1618a]

1. $\Delta H_0^\circ = 40.8374$ [1830]. 2. $\Delta H_0^\circ = 35.632$ [570]. 3. $\Delta H_0^\circ = 40.835$ [1618a]. 4. $\Delta H_0^\circ = -16.25$ [1618a]. 5. ΔH_0°. 6. $\Delta H_0^\circ = 112.536^*$ [570]. 7. $\Delta H_0^\circ = 69.084$ [1618a]. 8. $\Delta H_0^\circ = -7.0$ [366]. 9. $\Delta H_0^\circ = 4.2956$ [1830]. 10. $\Delta H_0^\circ = 4.295$ [1618a]. 11. $\Delta H_0^\circ = -6.013$ [570]. 12. Calculated [234] from $(\Delta H_0^\circ)_{subl} = 158^*$ [719]. 13. $\Delta H_0^\circ = -142.7391$ [1830]. 14. $\Delta H_0^\circ = -142.846$ [570]. 15. $\Delta H_0^\circ = -142.702$ [1618a]. 16. S_{270}°. 17. From MgO(c), SiO_2(c) and H_2O(l). 18. $\Delta H_0^\circ = -11.4360$ [1830]. 19. $\Delta H_0^\circ = -11.402^*$ [1618a]. 20. $\Delta H_0^\circ = -218.43$ [1618a]. 21. $T = 293$ °K. 22. $T = 292$ °K. MgPr phase. 23. $T = 292$ °K; Mg_3Pr phase. 24. $\Delta H_0^\circ = 34.3125$ [1830]. 25. $\Delta H_0^\circ = 33.243$ [1618a].

1	2	3		4		5		6	
$MgSO_3$	c	(−249.8*)	[1172]	(−221.2*)	[323]	22.5*	[323]		
				(−223.5*)	[229]	21.1*	[161]		
$MgSO_4$	l	−302.733	[1618a]	−276.943	[1618a]	26.978	[1618a]	6.866	[1618a]
	c	(−311.05)	[1675]	(−278.2*)[3]	[250]	(21.9)*	[699, 1655, 1675]	(23.06)	[1685]
		(−385.9)[1]	[55]	(−278.5*)	[224]	(22.8*)	[228]		
$MgSO_4 \cdot H_2O$	c	(−305.5)	[1618a]	(−278.196)	[1618a]	(21.9)	[1618a]	(23.02)	[1618a]
		(−383.5)[2]	[55]						
		(−382*)[4]	[234]			30.2	[1685]		
$MgSO_4 \cdot {}^5/_4H_2O$	c	−399.9[1]	[55]						
		−399.4[2]	[55]						
$MgSO_4 \cdot 1.5H_2O$	c	−419.1[5]	[55]						
		−417.9[2]	[55]						
$MgSO_4 \cdot 2H_2O$	c	(−467.0)[5]	[55]	−329.0*	[229]				
		(−464.6)[6]	[55]						
$MgSO_4 \cdot 3H_2O$	c	−528.3[5]	[55]						
		−526.0[6]	[55]						
$MgSO_4 \cdot 4H_2O$	c	(−604.9)[5]	[55]	−511.2*	[229]				
		(−602.3)[6]	[55]						
$MgSO_4 \cdot 6H_2O$	c	(−741.9)[5]	[55]	−622.3*	[232]	87.20	[1058, 1685]	83.20	[1058, 1685]
		(−737.2)[6]	[55]	−627.9**	[232]				
				−622.3*	[227]				
				−628.26	[190]	83.37	[190]		
$MgSO_4 \cdot 7H_2O$	c	(−807.0)[5]	[55]	−679.4*	[229]				
		(−804.7)[6]	[55]	−685.37	[190]				
$MgSO_4 \cdot Na_2SO_4$	c					(139.95)	[905]		
MgSe		−65.2	[1773]			12.7*	[228]		
						14.9*	[698]		
$MgSeO_4$	c	−234.94	[621]			10.0*	[498]		
	c	−235.02	[527]						
		−239*	[2683]						
$MgSeO_4 \cdot H_2O$	c	−313.68	[621]						
		−313.16	[527]						
$MgSeO_4 \cdot 4H_2O$	c	−526.88	[621]						
		−526.96	[527]						
$MgSeO_4 \cdot 6H_2O$	c	−677.68	[621]						
		−667.76	[527]						
$MgSiO_3$	l	−357.97	[1618a]	−339.077	[1618a]	22.45	[1618a]	19.55	[1618a]

						(16.22)	[1685]	(19.62)	[1685]
	c	−369.89[7]	[1618a]	−349.131	[1618a]	(16.192)	[1618a]	(19.549)	[1618a]
$Mg_{0.67}Sn_{0.33}$	c	−6.28[8]	[1589]						
MgTe	c			(−50*)	[323]	19*	[323]		
				(−49.3*)	[229]	17.5*	[698]		
$MgTiO_3$	c	−374.7	[429]						
		−375.5	[1618a]	−354.373	[1618a]	(17.80)	[1618a]	21.922	[1618a]
$MgTiO_3$, geikielite	c	−375.6	[2243, 2552]	−354.5	[2243, 2552]	(17.82)	[1685]		
		−375.9	[1686]	−354.8	[1686]				
$MgTi_2O_5$	l	−583.417[9]	[1618a]	−552.258	[1618a]	40.487	[1618a]	35.155	[1618a]
	c	−599.2[10]	[2243, 2552, 1618a]	−565.0	[2243]	30.4	[1685, 2544]	35.15	[1685, 2544]
				−566.45	[1686]	33.2	[1618a, 1686]		
				−565.9	[2552]				
				−565.869	[1618a]			35.155	[1618a]
MgTl	c	(−12.0)	[2625]						
$MgWO_4$	c	−229.8	[469]	−208.2	[469]	16	[469]	14	[469]
		−348.6[11]	[1618a]	−321.925	[1618a]	24.184	[1618a]	26.14	[1618a]
		−361.1*	[170, 172]	−337.7*	[170, 172]				
MgY	c	−2.6	[2405]						
$Mg_{0.33}Zn_{0.67}$	c	−4.28	[1589]					5.9	[1589]
MgZn	c	2.5[12]	[2313]						
$MgZn_2$	c	(3.6)[12]	[2313]						
$MgZnO_3$	c	−421.1	[351]	−400.5	[351]				
Mg_2C_3	c	19.0*; 18*	[1602, 1618a]	18*	[2226]				
				17.729	[1618a]	24.0	[1618a]	22.41	[1618a]
Mg_2F_4	g	−414.4[13]	[1618a]	−403.103	[1618a]	74.632	[1618a]	22.287	[1618a]
Mg_2Ge	c	−8.37[14]	[169]	−25100[14]	[169]	−1.17[14]	[169]		
Mg_2Ni	c	−16.0	[2406]			16.7	[2406]		
$Mg_2P_2O_7$	c					37.02	[2073]	42.53	[2073]
Mg_2Pb	c	(−12.5)	[1774, 2625]			24.5	[1089]		
Mg_2Si	l	−0.792	[1618a]	−3.619	[1618a]	29.651	[1618a]	22.5	[1618a]
	c	(−6.32)	[347]			−6.69[15]	[347]		
		(−10.2)	[1404]			2.22[15]	[1404]		
		(−18.6)	[1618a]	−18.428	[1618a]	19.5	[1618a]	16.22	[1618a]

1. In the calculation the heat of dehydration, calculated according to Nernst's approximation, has been used. 2. Heat of dehydration used in the calculation, was obtained from standard entropies. 3. Recalculated [234] from $(\Delta H^\circ_{298})_{diss} = 98.03$ [250] to 90.7 [2245], using the values of ΔG°_{298} for SO_3 and MgO [2245]. 4. This value is erroneously attributed to $MgSO_4 \cdot 2H_2O$ in [2245] 5. In the calculation the heat of dehydration, calculated according to Nernst's approximation, has been used. 6. Heat of dehydration used in the calculation, was obtained from standard entropies. 7. $\Delta H^\circ_0 = -367.708$ [1618a]. 8. $T = 273$ °K. 9. $\Delta H^\circ_0 = -580.074$ [1618a]. 10. $\Delta H^\circ_0 = -595.857$ [1618a]. 11. $\Delta H^\circ_0 = -346.189$ [1618a]. 12. In *kcal/g-atom.* 13. $\Delta H^\circ_0 = -411.978$ [1618a]. 14. In *kcal/g-atom*; temperature range 700–900 °K. 15. ΔS°_{298}.

1	2	3		4		5		6	
Mg_2Si	c	(−19.0)	[1774]					18.349[1]	[1916]
Mg_2SiO_4	l	(−504.6)	[1618a]	(−478.097)	[1618a]	29.24	[1618a]	28.21	[1618a]
	c	(−504.8)	[212]	(−466.2)[2]	[369]	(22.75)	[1685]	(28.18)	[1685]
		(−520.02)[3]	[1618a]	(−491.577)	[1618a]	(22.734)	[1618a]	(28.237)	[1618a]
Mg_2Sn	c	(−18.3)	[1774, 2625]						
Mg_2TiO_4	l	−503.469[4]	[1618a]	−477.293	[1618a]	33.19	[1618a]	30.756	[1618a]
	c	−517.45	[1686]	−489.6	[1686]	27.51	[1686]		
		−517.2	[2243, 2552]	−488.5	[2243]	24.8	[2544]	30.76	[1685, 2544]
				−489.3	[2552]	26.1	[1685]		
		−517.0	[1618a]	−483.133	[1618a]	27.52	[1618a]	30.756	[1618a]
Mg_2Zn_{11}	c	2.4[5]	[2313]						
Mg_3As_2	c	−96	[37]						
$Mg_3(AsO_4)_2$	c			−679.3*	[323]	53.8*	[323]		
				−683.5*	[229]				
Mg_3N_2	c	(−110.7)	[31]	−98.3*	[229]	21.0	[1618a, 1678]		
		(−110.2)	[1618a]	−95.82	[1618a]			24.98	[1618a]
						22.	[2419]		
Mg_3P_2	c	−128	[1773]						
$Mg_3(PO_4)_2$	l	−876.897	[1618a]	−824.544	[1618a]	54.764	[1618a]	50.85	[1618a]
	c	(−895.1)	[1618a, 2073]	−839.3	[2073]	45.22	[2073]	51.02	[2073]
				−839.836	[1618a]	45.0	[1618a]	50.85	[1618a]
				−904*	[323]	56.8*	[323]		
				−910.5*	[229]				
Mg_3Sb_2	c	(−55.5)	[168]	−80	[624]	−4.87[6]	[168]		
		(−79.0)	[1772a, 2625]						
Mg_5Y_2	c	−3.1; −2.9	[2405]						
$Mg_{17}Y_3$	c	−2.3; −2.6	[2405]						
Mn	g	(66.730)	[2479]	(56.640)	[2479]	(41.49)	[1685]		
		(67.06)[7]	[1589]	(56.97)	[1589]				
		(70.0)	[163]						
		(61.5*)	[402]						
		(69.3)	[2682]						
		(67.15)	[1896]	(57.05)	[1896]				
Mn, *α*	c					(7.65)	[1252, 1589, 2479]	(6.104)[8]	[1252]
						(7.59)	[1896]	(6.59)	[1896]
						(7.64)	[1685]	(6.28)	[1685]
Mn, *β*	c							(6.40)[9]	[930]

Mn, γ	c					(7.75)	[1589]	(6.59)	[1589, 1685]
						(7.98)	[1252]	$(6.513)^{2}$	[1252]
						(7.72)	[1686, 1896]		
Mn^{2+}	g					41.50	[66]		
	d	(−53.3*)	[323]	(−54.4*)	[323]	(−17.9)	[1685]		
						(−19.1)	[201]		
						(−21)	[1749]		
Mn^{3+}	g	−27	[1896]	−19.6	[1896]	37.94	[66]		
	d	(−27*)	[323]	−19.6*	[95]				
Mn^{4+}	g					40.70	[66]		
MnAs	c	−13.6	[653]						
MnBr	g					63.2	[1685]	8.65	[1685]
$MnBr_2$	c	(−97.2)	[1896]	−87.45	[1896]	33.5	[1896]	18.5	[1896]
		(−90.0)	[890, 2245]	−87.4*	[323]	32.1*	[323]		
				−86.8*	[227]	33.0*	[1773]		
						36.0	[1685]		
$MnBr_2 \cdot 4H_2O$	c	(−375*)	[697]	−308.9*	[323]	69.7*	[323]		
$MnBr_2 \cdot 6H_2O$	c	−520*	[697]						
MnC	c	−17.0	[118]						
$Mn(CN)_2$	c	13*	[696]						
		16*	[2683]						
$Mn(CNS)_2$	c	−8*	[696]						
		−7*	[2683]						
$MnCO_3$	c	(−207.8)	[694]	(−207*)	[694]	$(112.9)^{10}$	[292]		
				(−192.30*)	[177]				
$MnCO_3$, precipitated	c			−194.3*	[323]	23.8*	[323]		
				−193.9*	[229]				
$Mn(CO)_6$	g	−211.1	[604]						
$MnCl_2$	g	−62.8	[1896]	−65.8	[1896]	60.5	[1896]	8.46	[1896]
	c	(−115.2)	[1896]	(−105.4)	[1896]			(17.45)	[1896]
		(−115.19)	[1752]	(−103*)	[227]	(28.26)	[973]	(17.43)	[973]
		(−112.0)	[890]						
$MnCl_2 \cdot H_2O$	c			−164.5*	[323]	35.9*	[323]		
				−165.0*	[229]				
$MnCl_2 \cdot 2H_2O$	c			−239.1*	[229]				
$MnCl_2 \cdot 4H_2O$	c	(−398.7)	[697]	−341.1*	[229]				

1. $T = 300$ °K. 2. Calculated [234] from $\Delta G^\circ_{298} = 7.140$ [369] for the reaction $MgO(c) + MgSiO_3(c) = Mg_2SiO_4(c)$ using the values of ΔG°_{298} for MgO and $MgSiO_3$ [2245]. 3. $\Delta H^\circ_0 = -516.838$ [1618a]. 4. $\Delta H^\circ_0 = -500.255$ [1618a]. 5. In *kcal/g-atom*. 6. ΔS°_{298}. 7. $\Delta H^\circ_0 = (66.77)$ [1589]. 8. $T = 273$ °K. 9. $t = 300$ °C. 10. In *joules/mole*·°C.

1	2	3		4		5		6	
$Mn(ClO_3)_2$	c	−80*	[2683]						
$Mn(ClO_4)_2$	c	−90*	[2683]						
$Mn(ClO_4)_2 \cdot 6H_2O$	c	−526	[23]						
MnF	g					57.7	[1685]	7.96	[1685]
MnF_2	c	(−189.5)	[1896]	(−179.4)	[1896]	(22.25)	[1685, 1896]		
		(−190.0)	[890]						
MnF_3	c	(−238)	[35]			28.0	[890]		
$MnFe_2O_4$	c	−292.5	[464]	−266.3	[464]				
		−292	[464]						
MnH	g					51.00	[1685]	7.03	[1685]
MnH_2	c	−27	[2683]						
$Mn(HCO_3)_2$	c	−386*	[2683]						
$Mn(HS)_2$	c	−35*	[2683]						
$Mn(HSO_4)_2$	c	−456*	[2683]						
$Mn(H_2O)_4^{2+}$	g	(177*)	[697]						
MnI	g					65.1	[1685]	8.74	[1685]
MnI_2	c	(−73.1)	[1896]	−63.15	[1896]	36.5	[1896]	20.5	[1896]
		(−58.0)	[890, 2245]	−59.9*	[323]	37.5*	[323]		
				−59.4*	[227]	36.0	[1773]		
						38.0	[1685]		
$MnI_2 \cdot 2H_2O$	c	(−203*)[1]	[234]						
$MnI_2 \cdot 4H_2O$	c	(−340*)[2]	[697]						
$MnI_2 \cdot 6H_2O$	c	(−490*)[3]	[688a]						
$MnMoO_4$	c	−290.7*	[170, 172]	−267.5*	[170, 172]				
MnN	c	28*	[653]						
MnN (5.72% N)	c	−62.4[4]	[902]						
MnN (9.27% N)	c	−46.1[4]	[902]						
$Mn(N_3)_2$	c			(122.8*)	[323]	44.3*	[323]		
$Mn(NH_2)_2$	c	−36*	[2683]						
$Mn(NO_2)_2$	c	−99*	[2683]						
$Mn(NO_3)_2$	c	(−138.7)[5]	[694]	−118.6*	[323]	40.3*	[323]		
		(−140*)	[2683]	−120.3	[227]				
$Mn(NO_3)_2 \cdot 3H_2O$	c			−257.2*	[229]				
$Mn(NO_3)_2 \cdot 6H_2O$	c			−432.5*	[229]				
MnO	g			27.8*	[227]	56.5	[1685]	7.56	[1685]
				27.95	[1896]				
				(−86.75)	[1976]	(14.27)	[1685, 2549]	(10.54)	[1685, 2549]
MnO_2	c	(−124.4)	[1896]	(−111.3)	[1976]	(12.68)	[1685, 1896]		

		(−124.3)	[887]	(−111.1*)	[323]				
MnO_4^-	d	(−129.7*)	[323]	(−107.4*)	[323]	(45.7)	[2041]		
						(46.7)	[1685]		
MnO_4^{2-}	d			−120.4*	[323]				
$Mn(OH)_2$	c			−146.86*	[176]	24.3*	[176]		
				−143.9*	[249]	22.5*	[249]		
$Mn(OH)_3$	c			−181*	[323]	23.8*	[323]		
MnP	c	−23.0	[653]					11.2*	[298]
$Mn(ReO_4)_2$	c	−430*	[2683]						
MnS	g	137.2[6]	[572]						
MnS green	c	(−49.5)	[1896]	(−50.55)	[1896]				
		(−49.49)	[1622]						
MnS	c	(51.0)	[704]	(−52.0)	[701]				
MnS, red	c	(−49.0)	[1715, 2625]	−46.9*	[229]				
MnS, precipitated	c			(−53.3*)	[323]				
$MnSO_3$	c	−184*	[2683]						
		−198.2*	[1172]						
$MnSO_4$	c	(−254.2)	[1896]	(−228.45)	[1896]			(24.02)	[1685, 1896]
				(−227.5*)[7]	[250]				
$MnSO_4 \cdot H_2O$, I	c			−290.3*	[229]			34.2	[1896]
$MnSO_4 \cdot 2H_2O$, II	c			−284.3*	[229]				
$MnSO_4 \cdot 4H_2O$	c			(−456.1*)	[229]				
$MnSO_4 \cdot 5H_2O$	c			(−511.4*)	[229]				
$MnSO_4 \cdot 7H_2O$	c			−621.9*	[229]				
$MnSO_4 \cdot Na_2SO_4$	c			−516.3*	[229]				
MnS_2	c	−55.1	[1896]			19.6	[1896]	16.0	[1896]
		−49.5	[2625]						
MnS_2O_6	c					(45)	[1685]		
$MnS_2O_6 \cdot 2H_2O$	c					57.63	[1685]		
$MnS_2O_6 \cdot 6H_2O$	c					110	[1685]		
MnSb	c	−12	[653]						
MnSe	c	(−37.7)	[383]	(−29.25)	[1896]				
$MnSeO_4$	c	−183.5*	[499]			16.5*	[498]		
		−186*	[2683]						
$MnSeO_4 \cdot H_2O$	c	−259.5*	[499]						
MnSi	c	−59.6[8]	[338]	−58.3[8]	[338]	44.80[9]	[338]	45.96[9]	[338]

1. The value −194.5 [2245] seems to be erroneous. 2. The value $\Delta H^\circ_{298} = -327.5$ [2245] has been reported [697] to be erroneous. 3. The value $\Delta H^\circ_{298} = -451$ [2245] has been reported [688a] to be erroneous. 4. Per 1 *mole* of bound nitrogen. 5. The value $\Delta H^\circ_{298} = -166.32$ [2245] has been stated to be erroneous [694]. 6. MnS = Mn(g) + ½S_2(g). 7. Recalculated [234] from $(\Delta H^\circ_{298})_{diss} = 83.8$ [250] to 89.3 [210] using the values of ΔG°_{298} for SO_3 and MnO [2245]. 8. In *joules/mole.* 9. In *joules/mole*·°C.

1	2	3		4		5		6	
MnSi	c	-11.6^{1}	[141]			46.4^{2}	[338a]	46.06^{2}	[338a]
		−17.0	[126]						
$MnSi_{1.7}$	c	-3.1^{1}	[141]			46.2^{2}	[338a]	58.7^{2}	[338a]
$MnSiO_3$	c	(−308.2)	[1713, 1896]	(−289.0)	[1713, 1896]			20.66	[1685, 1896]
								23.3	[572]
$MnSiO_3$, rhodonite	c	(−303.4)	[1727]	(−283.4)	[234]				
		$(-5.9)^{3}$	[1681]	$(-5.05)^{3}$	[1681]				
$MnSiO_3$	v			−275.8*	[229]				
$MnSiO_4$	c							33.1	[572]
MnTe	c	−26.6	[383]					17.40	[1685, 1896]
		−22.5	[1768]						
$MnWO_4$	c	−312.5	[458]					26.37	[684]
$Mn_{0.62}Zn_{0.38}Fe_2O_4$	c							62.4^{4}	[2586]
$Mn_2(CO)_{10}$	c	−400.9	[1330]						
Mn_2O_3	c	(−229.2; −229.4)	[887]	−212.3	[323]	22.1	[323]		
		(−228.4)	[1896]	−209.85	[1896]	26.4	[1685, 1714, 1896]	(25.73)	[1685, 1714, 1896]
		(−228.7)	[2082]	−212.2*	[229]				
				−213.5**	[232]				
				−210.6	[1045]				
Mn_2O_7	c	−174.1	[1321]						
$Mn_2(SO_4)_3$	c			−580.9*	[323]	61.7*	[323]		
				−589.6*	[229]				
Mn_2Si	c					19.8	[1916]		
Mn_2SiO_4	c	−406.05	[1896]	−381.95	[1896]	36.9	[1896]	31.04	[1685, 1896]
		-401.2^{5}	[1622]			39.0	[1685]		
Mn_2SiO_4, tephroite		-11.75^{6}	[2683]	-11.9^{6}	[2683]				
$Mn_{2.5}N$	c	−27.6	[1772]						
Mn_3AlC	c							29*	[2506]
Mn_3C	c	(−3.6)	[2625]	(−3.75)	[1896]			(22.33)	[1685, 1896]
				(−3.4*)	[2226]				
Mn_3O_4, α	c	(−331.3)	[1896]	(−305.85)	[1896]	(36.8)	[2082]		
$Mn_3(PO_4)_2$	c	(−771)	[1896]	−719	[1896]				
				−683	[323]	71.6*	[323]		
Mn_3Si	c	-8.2^{1}	[141]			103.4^{2}	[338a]	100.1^{2}	[338a]
Mn_3ZnC	c							33*	[2506]
Mn_4N	c	−30.3	[1893]	−23.65	[1976]	31	[1976]		

		−31.2	[2625]						
Mn_5N_2	c	(−70.0*)	[229]	−47.7*	[229]				
		(−48.2)	[1893]						
Mn_5Si_3	c	−6.9	[141]			238.5[2]	[337]	195.46[2]	[337]
Mn_8N_2	c			−70.0*	[229]				
$HMnO_2^-$	d			−120.9*	[323]				
$HMn(OH)_4$	c			−246.65*	[6]				
$H_2Mn(OH)_4$	c			−256.30*	[6]				
$H_3Mn(OH)_6$	c			−359.95*	[6]				
Mo	g	(157.500)	[2479]	(144.578)	[2479]	(43.46)	[1685]		
		(158.70)[7]	[1589]	(147.78)	[1589]				
		(147.4)	[756]						
		(157.80)	[2599]						
	c					(6.83)	[991]	(5.62)[11]	[991]
						(6.82)	[1685]	(5.71)	[1685]
								(5.68)	[1589, 2479]
Mo^{3+}	d			−13.8*	[323]				
MoB	c					10.5*	[1959]	9.42	[1959]
MoB_2	c					8.7*	[1959]	14.45	[1959]
$MoBr_2$		−62.14[12]	[630]	−53[11]	[630]				
	c			−26.3*	[227, 323]	34.1*	[323]		
$MoBr_2O$	c	−148.6	[70]						
	d	−165.0	[70]						
$MoBr_3$	c			−34.4*	[323]	39.3*	[323]		
$MoBr_4$	c	−74.5	[628]	−36.9*	[323]	52.3*	[323]		
$MoBr_5$	c			−40.7*	[323]	63*	[323]		
MoC	c	−2.4	[1903]			0.0*[13]	[2709]		
		−4.22	[893]						
$Mo(CO)_6$	g	−218.5	[1042]	−205.4	[1042]	121.07	[1495]	52.34	[1495]
						118.0	[1974]		
	c	−234.8	[1042]	−211.3	[1042]	77.9	[1685]	57.90	[1685]
		−233.12	[603]	−211.1*	[229]	78.17	[41]	57.92	[41]
		−235.3	[603. 1042]	−203.3*	[232]			59.83	[604]
				−209.7**	[232]				
$MoCl_2$	c	(−69*)	[634, 654]	−34.6*	[227, 323]	28.5*	[323]		
$MoCl_2O$	g	−157	[671]			63	[671]		
	c	−173	[671]			27	[671]		

1. In *kcal/g-atom*. 2. In *joules/mole*·C. 3. From MnO(c) and $SiO_2(a)$. 4. $t = 20\ ^\circ C$. 5. Calculated [234] from the standard heat of formation from MnO and $SiO_2(a)$ −11.8 [1622]. 6. From MnO(c) and $SiO_2(a)$. 7. $\Delta H_0^\circ = 158.31$ [1589]. 11. $t = 0\ ^\circ C$. 12. From $Br_2(g)$. 13. ΔS_{298}°.

1	2	3		4		5		6	
$MoCl_2O(OH)_2$	c	−245.2	[1351]						
$MoCl_2O_2$	g	−157	[676]			63	[676]		
		−153	[635]						
	c	−173	[414]			27	[676]		
		−169.8	[1351]						
$MoCl_2O_2 \cdot H_2O$	c	−247.6	[635]						
		−178	[414]						
$MoCl_3$	c	(−60*)	[230]	−48.8*	[323]	33.0*	[323]		
		(−93*)	[634]			32.6*	[161]		
		(−94*)	[654]						
$MoCl_3O$	g	−130	[671, 676]			65*	[671, 676]		
	c	−160*	[671, 676]			30*	[671, 676]		
$MoCl_4$	g	(−89*)	[654]						
		(−90)	[563]						
	c	(−114)	[414, 654]	−58.5*	[323]	44.7*	[323]		
				−60.3*	[227]	48	[563]		
$MoCl_4O$	g	−141	[671, 676]			75*	[671, 676]		
	c	−151	[414]			50*	[671, 676]		
		−154*	[654, 671]						
$MoCl_5$	g	−104	[671, 676]			101	[671, 676]		
		−108*	[654]						
	c	(−126)	[414, 654, 671]	−64.6*	[323]	53*	[323]		
				−67.5*	[227]	65.0*	[890]		
						57	[671, 676]		
$MoCl_6$	g	−105	[410]			−48[1]	[410]		
	c	(−96*)	[2285]	−58*	[323]	61*	[323]		
		(−125)	[410]	−62.4*	[227]	−82[1]	[410]		
MoF_6	g	-372.3_5	[2362]	-350.8_3	[2362]	79.76	[2483]	28.35	[2483]
		−382.0	[2014]			80.2	[1685]	28.32	[1685]
						80.6	[881]		
						79.105	[2019]	28.284	[2019]
	l	−388.6	[2014]	−361.2	[2014]	60.6	[881]	39.61	[881]
		−405	[1773]			79.0*	[1773]		
						59.9	[1685]		
MoI_2	c			−13.4*	[323]	39.5*	[323]		
				−12.9*	[227]				
MoI_3	c			−15.4*	[323]	49.8*	[323]		

				−16.4*	[227]				
MoI_4	c			−18.5*	[323]	64.3*	[323]		
				−19.9*	[227]				
MoI_5	c			−18.7*	[323]	78*	[323]		
				−20.5*	[227]				
MoO_2	c	(−140.8)	[1687, 1737, 1892]	−127.45	[1737]	11.06	[1685, 1724, 1737]	13.38	[1685, 1724, 1737]
		(−140.4)	[159]	−127.13	[159]				
		(−140.9)	[2440]	−117.3	[323]	13.3*	[323]		
		(−139.5)	[1772]	−119.0*	[232]	13.6	[1772]		
		(−132.234)	[1325]	−121.050	[1325]				
		(−132.5)	[1045]	−116.8*	[229]				
MoO_3	c	(−178.1)	[1687, 1737, 1892]	(−159.7)	[1737]	(18.58)	[1685, 1737]	(17.92)	[1685, 1737]
		(−180.3)	[887]	(−161.92)	[2402a]	(18.580)	[2402a]	(17.93)	[2402a]
		(−178.0)	[2440]	(−159.1*)	[232]	(18.656)	[1040]	(17.60)	[1040]
				(−159.6**)	[232]]				
$MoO_3 \cdot H_2O$	c	(−249.9)	[1349]	−227*	[323]	36*	[323]		
				−225.1*	[229]				
MoO_4	d			−154*	[323]	40*	[323]		
MoO_4^{2-}	d	(−238.2)	[1349]	−201.8	[1349]				
				−218.8*	[323]	14*	[323]		
MoS_2	c	(−55.91)	[356]	(−53.70)	[356]	(15.2)	[1685]	(15.22)	[1685]
		(−91.34)	[2475]	(−78.42)	[2475]	(16.9*)	[2475]		
MoS_3	c			(−60.1*)	[229]	(18*)	[323]		
				(−57.6*)	[323]				
$MoSi_2$	c	−31.4	[2232]						
		−26.0*	[1085]						
Mo_2B	c					22.8*	[1959]	18.79	[1959]
Mo_2C	c	(−11.7)	[1320]	(−6.7*)	[2226]	(19.8)	[1665]		
		(−11.0)	[1903]			(1.5)[1]	[2709]		
		(−2.00)	[893]						
		(−4.2)	[1773]						
Mo_2N	c	−16.6	[1772]			21.0	[1772]		
Mo_2S_3	c	−102.0	[1852]			28.0	[1852]		
Mo_3Si	c	−23.4	[1085]			25.4	[1685, 1728]	22.33	[1685]
Mo_4O_{11}	c	−664	[857]			88.9	[857]		
		−674	[1773]						
		−671*	[887]						

1. ΔS°_{298}.

1	2	3		4		5		6	
Mo_5Si_3	c	−67.8*	[1085]						
Mo_8O_{23}	c	−1392*	[887]						
Mo_9O_{26}	c	−1573*	[887]						
N	g	(113.0246)[1]	[1830]			(36.6145)	[1830]		
		(113.000)	[2479]	(108.760)	[2479]	(36.62)	[1685]	(7.87)	[2272]
		(112.981)[2]	[570]			(36.6146)	[570]		
		(112.979)[3]	[2358]	(108.883)	[2358]	(36.622)	[2358]		
						(38.813)	[476]		
						(38.081)	[680]		
		(112.965)[4]	[1618a]	(108.87)	[1618a]	(36.614)	[1618a]		
N^+	g	(450.203)[5]	[570]			(38.1671)	[570]		
		(449.589)[6]	[2358]			(40.366)	[476]	5.0845	[476]
N^{2+}	g	(1133.96)[7]	[2358]						
N^{3+}	g	(2229.41)[8]	[2358]						
N^{4+}	g	(4017.41)[9]	[2358]						
N^{5+}	g	(6276.26)[10]	[2358]						
N^{6+}	g	(19008.9)[11]	[2358]						
N^{7+}	g	(34392)[12]	[2358]						
N_2	g					(50.149)	[476]	(6.9586)	[476]
						(45.7711)	[1830]	(6.9611)	[1830]
						(45.77)	[1618a, 1685, 2358]	(6.961)	[1618a, 2358]
								(6.96)	[1685]
$^{14}N_2$	g					45.71	[1000]		
$^{15}N_2$	g					46.06	[1000]		
N_2^+	g	(360.792)[13]	[570]			51.606	[476]	6.9617	[476]
						47.1044	[680]		
						47.2291	[570]		
N_3	g	116[14]	[1357]			59.213	[570]		
		105*	[1352a]						
		113	[2378a]						
N_3^+	g	390.2[15]	[2358]						
N_3^-	g	(43.2)[16]	[2358]			50.7	[728]		
		(34.8)	[1352a]						
	d	(60.3)*	[323]	77.7*	[323]	32*	[323]		
		(65.76)	[2358]	83.2	[2358]	25.8	[2358]		
		(65.53)	[1356]						

NCO^-	d	−34.97	[609]						
NCl_3	l	55	[2358]						
NDHT	g					50.72	[27]	9.04	[27]
NDH_2	g					49.20	[27, 2537]	8.69	[27]
								8.49	[2537]
NDT_2	g					52.02	[2537]	9.33	[2537]
						52.03	[27]	9.39	[27]
ND_2H	g					50.10	[27]	8.91	[27]
						50.00	[2537]	8.71	[2537]
ND_2T	g					51.48	[27]	9.25	[27]
						51.47	[2537]	9.13	[2537]
ND_3	g					48.73	[588]	9.12	[588, 1685]
						48.71	[1685]		
						48.61	[2489]	8.97	[2489]
NF	g	71.042*[17]	[570]			51.149	[570]		
		65.9439[18]	[1830]			51.1033	[1830]	7.3828	[1830]
		61.4	[1503]						
		58.6*[19]	[1618a]	58.068*	[1618a]	48.889	[1618a]	7.355	[1618a]
NFS	g					62.07	[2358]	10.55	[2358]
NF_2	g	10.3[20]	[2358]	13.9	[2358]	59.71	[2358]	9.80	[1475, 2358]
		9.8	[1503]			59.70	[1475]		
		9.6180[21]	[1830]			59.7154	[1830]	9.8043	[1830]
		9.50[22]	[2342]			59.794	[570]		
		10.1[23]	[1618a]	13.564	[1618a]	59.715	[1618a]	9.801	[1618a]
NF_2^+	g	284[24]	[2358]						
NF_2D	g					60.8337[25]	[27]	10.8614[25]	[27]
NF_2H	g					60.40	[2358]	10.37	[2358]
						60.4512[26]	[27]	10.3913[26]	[27]
NF_2NO	g	20.4[27]	[1630]						
NF_3	g	(−29.8)[28]	[2358]	−8.0*	[229]	62.29	[2358]	12.7	[2358]
		(−29.7)[29]	[1830]	−30.7; −29.4	[2489]	62.2758	[1830]	12.7322	[1830]
		(−29.7)[30]	[742]	−30.4	[1821]	62.17	[2690]	12.74	[1685, 2690]
						62.276	[570]		
						62.28	[1685, 2485]	12.75	[2485]
		(−30.4)[31]	[1618a]	−20.485]	[1618a]	62.302	[1618a]	12.756	[1618a]

1. $\Delta H_0^\circ = (112.5795)$ [1830]. 2. $\Delta H_0^\circ = (112.536)$ [570]. 3. $\Delta H_0^\circ = (112.534)$ [2358]. 4. $\Delta H_0^\circ = (112.52)$ [1618a]. 5. $\Delta H_0^\circ = (448.056)$ [570]. 6. $\Delta H_0^\circ = (447.663)$ [2358]. 7. $\Delta H_0^\circ = (1130.55)$ [2358]. 8. $\Delta H_0^\circ = (2224.55)$ [2358]. 9. $\Delta H_0^\circ = (4011.04)$ [2358]. 10. $\Delta H_0^\circ = (6268.41)$ [2358]. 11. $\Delta H_0^\circ = (18999.5)$ [2358]. 12. $\Delta H_0^\circ = (34381.1)$ [2358]. 13. $\Delta H_0^\circ = (359.311)$ [570]. 14. $\Delta H_0^\circ = 116.906$ [570]. 15. $\Delta H_0^\circ = 389$ [2358]. 16. $\Delta H_0^\circ = 45$ [2358]. 17. $\Delta H_0^\circ = 71.036*$ [570]. 18. $\Delta H_0^\circ = 65.9345$ [1830]. 19. $\Delta H_0^\circ = 56.593*$ [1618a]. 20. $\Delta H_0^\circ = 9.68$ [2358]. 21. ΔH_0°. 22. $\Delta H_0^\circ = 10.103$ [570]. 23. $\Delta H_0^\circ = 10.718$ [1618a]. 24. $\Delta H_0^\circ = 282$ [2358]. 25. $T = 300$ °K. 26. $T = 300$ °K. 27. $T = 295$ °K. 28. $\Delta H_0^\circ = -28.43$ [2358]. 29. $\Delta H_0^\circ = -28.3267$ [1830]. 30. $\Delta H_0^\circ = -28.325$ [570]. 31. $\Delta H_0^\circ = -29.031$ [1618a].

1	2	3		4		5		6	
NF_3S	g					68.48	[2358]	17.18	[2358]
NH	g	(78.9195)[1]	[1830]			43.2950	[1830]	(6.9662)	[1830]
		(80)[2]	[2358]			43.25	[1685]	(6.96)	[1685]
		(81.183)[3]	[2342]			43.296	[570, 681]		
		(79.20)[4]	[1618a]	77.765	[1618a]	43.297	[1618a]	(6.966)	[1618a]
NHS_7	c	−67.4	[2358]						
NHT_2	g					51.26	[2537]	8.98	[2537]
						51.31	[27]	9.17	[27]
NH_2	g	42.320[5]	[2342]			46.521	[570]		
		41	[2358]			46.531	[681]		
		40.3[7]	[1618a]	42.976	[1618a]	45.113	[1618a]	8.012	[1618a]
NH_2HSO_3[6]	c	−161.3	[2358]						
	d	−156.3	[2358]						
NH_2NO_2[8]	c	−48.2	[2358]						
NH_2OH	c	(−27.3)	[2358]						
	d	(−23.5)	[2358]	−5.60*	[323]	40*	[323]		
$NH_2OH \cdot H^+$	d	(−32.8)	[2358]	−13.54*	[323]	37*	[323]		
$NH_2OH \cdot HCl$	c	(−75.9)	[2358]					22.2	[2358]
	d	(−72.6)	[2358]						
$NH_2OH \cdot HNO_3$	c	(−87.6)	[2358]						
	d	(−82.4)	[2358]						
$(NH_2OH)_2 \cdot H_2SO_4$	d	−281.3	[2358]						
$NH_2O_2^-$	d	(−9.4*)	[323]	(18.2*)	[323]	(34.0*)	[323]		
NH_2T	g					49.86	[27]	8.83	[27]
						49.94	[2537]	8.60	[2537]
$(NH_2)_2SO_2$	c	−129.3	[2358]						
NH_3	g	(−11.02)[9]	[2358]	−3.94	[2358]	(45.97)	[2358]	(8.38)	[2358]
		(−11.04)[10]	[1830, 1618a]	−3.966	[1618a]	(46.0451)	[1830]	(8.4975)	[1830]
		(−11.039)[11]	[2342]			(46.02)	[588, 1685]	(8.48)	[588, 1685]
						(45.967)	[1618a]	(8.375)	[1618a]
						(45.94)	[2489]	(8.35)	[2489]
						(46.026)	[1479]	(8.514)	[1479]
						(46.045)	[570, 681]		
	d	(−19.19)	[2358]	−6.35	[2358]	(26.6)	[2358]		
				−6.36*	[323]				
NH_3^+	g	224.53[12]	[2358]						
$NH_3B_3H_7$	g					68.8[13]	[2667]		
	c					39.90[13]	[2667]	38.22[13]	[2667]

						39.8	[1685]	37.10	[1685]
$NH_3 \cdot H_2O$	l	60.66	[254]	88.0	[254]	34.5	[254]		
$NH_3 \cdot 2H_2O$	l					55.81[14]	[957]		
						55.66	[957]	53.87	[957]
$NH_3 \cdot NI_3$	c	36.9	[2358]						
$NH_3 \cdot SbF_3$	c	−243.5	[2358]						
$2NH_3 \cdot SbF_3$	c	−266.6	[2358]						
$3NH_3 \cdot SbF_3$	c	−286.9	[2358]						
$4NH_3 \cdot SbF_3$	c	−305.5	[2358]						
$6NH_3 \cdot SbF_3$	c	−342.5	[2358]						
NH_4^+	g	(154)	[723]			41.23	[723]	8.34	[723]
		(147.9*)	[693]						
	d	(−31.67)	[2358]	(−18.97)	[2358]	(27.1)	[2358]	19.1	[2358]
		(−32.6)	[539, 1036]			(26.4)	[1685]		
						(26.6)	[2447]		
NH_4AsO_2	d	−134.21	[2358]	−102.63	[2358]	37.0	[2358]		
$NH_4B_5O_8 \cdot 4H_2O$	c					388.98[15]	[1273]	357.06[15]	[1273]
NH_4BiBr_4	d			−109.2	[2358]				
NH_4BiCl_4	d			−134.1	[2358]				
$NH_4BiCl_6^{2-}$	d			−197.6	[2358]				
NH_4Br	c	(−64.73)	[2358]	−41.9	[2358]	27	[2358]	23	[2358]
		(−64.61)	[1618a]	−41.386	[1618a]	25.6	[1618a, 1685]	21.7	[1618a]
	d	(−60.72)	[2358]	−43.69	[2358]	46.8	[2358]	−14.8	[2358]
$NH_4Br \cdot 1.5NH_3$	c	−93.9	[2358]	−47.0	[2358]	51	[2358]		
NH_4BrClI	c			−52.0	[2358]				
	d			−54.0	[2358]				
NH_4BrI_2	d	−62.3	[2358]	−45.3	[2358]	74.3	[2358]		
NH_4BrO	d	−54.2	[2358]	−27.0	[2358]	37	[2358]		
NH_4BrO_3	c	−51*	[221]						
	d	−51.7	[2358]	−18.6	[2358]	66.1	[2358]		
NH_4Br_2Cl	d	−72.4	[2358]	−49.7	[2358]	56.6	[2358]		
NH_4Br_2I	c	−70.8	[2358]	−46.9	[2358]	55.4	[2358]		
	d			−48.4	[2358]				
NH_4Br_3	c	−67.5	[2358]	−45.1	[2358]	65	[2358]		
	d	−62.84	[2358]	−44.56	[2358]	78.6	[2358]		
NH_4Br_5	d	−65.7	[2358]	−43.8	[2358]	102.8	[2358]		

1. $\Delta H_0^\circ = (78.9079)$ [1830]. 2. $\Delta H_0^\circ = 79$ [2358]. 3. $\Delta H_0^\circ = (81.168)$ [2342]. 4. $\Delta H_0^\circ = 79.188$ [1618a]. 5. $\Delta H_0^\circ = 43.00$ [2342]. 6. Sulfamic acid. 7. $\Delta H_0^\circ = 40.987$ [1618a]. 8. Nitramide. 9. $\Delta H_0^\circ = (-9.34)$ [2358]. 10. $\Delta H_0^\circ = (-9.362)$ [1618a]; (−9.3667) [1830]. 11. $\Delta H_0^\circ = (-9.374)$ [2342]. 12. $\Delta H_0^\circ = 224.7$ [2358]. 13. $T = 300$ °K. 14. Boiling liquid. 15. In *joules/mole*·°C.

1	2	3		4		5		6	
NH_4CN	c	0.10	[2358]					32	[2358]
		3.0	[2683]						
	d	4.3	[2358]	22.2	[2358]	49.6	[2358]		
NH_4CNS	c	−20*	[2683]						
		−18.8	[2358]						
	d	−13.40	[2358]	3.18	[2358]	61.6	[2358]	9.5	[2358]
NH_4Cl	c	(−17.15)	[2358]	(−48.51)	[2358]	(22.6)	[2358]	(20.1)	[2358]
		(−75.29)	[2607]			(22.33)	[2607]	(20.35)	[2607]
						(23.6)	[1685]	(20.71)	[1685]
						(22.28)	[2266]	(19.80)	[2266]
		(−75.38)	[1618a]	(−48.743)	[1618a]	(22.60)	[1618a]	(21.33)	[1618a]
	d	(−71.62)	[2358]	−50.34	[2358]	40.6	[2358]	−13.5	[2358]
NH_4ClI_2	d			−50.7	[2358]				
NH_4ClO	d	−57.3	[2358]	−27.8	[2358]	37	[2358]		
NH_4ClO_2	d	−47.6	[2358]	−14.9	[2358]	51.3	[2358]		
NH_4ClO_3	c	−65*	[221]						
		−61.0	[481]						
	d	−55.4	[2358]	−19.8	[2358]	65.9	[2358]		
NH_4ClO_4	c	(−70.63)	[850]	−21.02	[850]	43.6	[850]		
		(−70.58)	[2358]	−21.25	[2358]	44.5	[2358]		
		(−78.1*)	[191]	−21.7*	[191]	20.8*	[191]		
		(−69.54)	[90]						
		(−70.74)	[1317]						
		(−69.56)	[1108]						
		(−70.69)[1]	[1618a]	−21.217	[1618a]	44.02	[1618a]	30.61	[1618a]
	d	(−62.58)	[2358]	−21.03	[2358]	70.6	[2358]		
NH_4Cl_2I	c			−55.5	[2358]				
	d			−57.5	[2358]				
NH_4Cl_3	d			−39	[2358]				
NH_4Cl_4I	c			−59.2	[2358]				
NH_4F	c	(−110.89)[2]	[2358]	−83.36	[2358]	17.20	[1685, 2358]	15.60	[1685, 2358]
		(−111.0)	[1506, 1507]	−83.4**	[232]	15.60	[818]	17.20	[818]
		(−107*)	[2683]	−81.9*	[232]				
				−81.8*	[229]				
	d	(−111.17)	[2358]	−85.61	[2358]	23.8	[2358]	−6.4	[2358]
$NH_4F{\cdot}H_2O$	c					34.92	[1782]	37.22	[1782]
						16.83[3]	[1783]	17.23[3]	[1783]
NH_4FSO_3	d	−224.7	[2358]						

NH_4H	c	0.5*	[2683]						
NH_4HCO_3	c	−203.0	[2358]	−159.2	[2358]	28.9	[1685, 2358]		
	d	−197.06	[2358]	−159.23	[2358]	48.9	[2358]		
						49.7	[1685]		
NH_4HF_2	c	−191.9[4]	[2358]	−155.6	[2358]	27.61	[2358]	25.50	[2358]
		−190.8	[2321]						
		−191.4	[1506, 1507]						
	d	−187.01	[2358]	−157.15	[2358]				
$NH_4HN_2O_2$	d	−44.1	[2358]						
NH_4HO_2	d	−69.99	[2358]	−35.1	[2358]	32.8	[2358]		
NH_4HPO_3F	d			−305.4	[2358]				
NH_4HS	c	(−37.5)	[2358]	−12.1	[2358]	23.5	[2358]		
		(−34*)	[2683]			27.1	[1685]		
	d	(−35.9)	[2358]	−16.09	[2358]	42.1	[2358]		
NH_4HSO_3	c	(−183.7)	[2358]	−138.9*	[229]			25.50	[912]
	d	(−181.34)	[2358]	−145.12	[2358]	60.5	[2358]		
NH_4HSO_4	c	(−245.45)	[2358]	−194.4*	[229]			(30.48)[5]	[562]
	d	−243.75	[2358]						
NH_4HSe	c	−31.8	[2358]	−5.6	[2358]	23.1	[2358]		
	d	(−27.9)	[2358]	−8.5	[2358]	46	[2358]		
NH_4HSeO_3	d	−154.65	[2358]	−117.33	[2358]	60.2	[2358]		
NH_4HSeO_4	d	−170.7	[2358]	−127.1	[2358]	62.8	[2358]		
NH_4HTe	c	10.0	[1960]	22.09	[1960]	42.16[6]	[1960]		
		0.3	[2358]						
$NH_4H_2AsO_3$	d	−202.51	[2358]	−159.32	[2358]	53.5	[2358]		
$NH_4H_2AsO_4$	c	−253.3	[2358]	−199.1	[2358]	41.12	[1685, 2358]	36.13	[1685, 2358]
	d	−249.06	[2358]	−199.01	[2358]	55.1	[2358]		
$NH_4H_2PO_2$	c	−180.0	[2358]						
	d	−178.4	[2358]						
$NH_4H_2PO_3$	d	−263.4	[2358]						
$NH_4H_2PO_4$	c	−345.94	[2358]	−289.89	[2358]	36.32	[1685, 2358]	34.00	[2358]
								34.01	[1685]
	d	−342.05	[2358]	−289.70	[2358]	48.7	[2358]		
$NH_4H_3F_4$	c	−337.4	[1507]						
		−336.8	[2358]						
$NH_4H_3P_2O_7$	d	−575.8	[2358]	−503.7	[2358]	81	[2358]		
$NH_4H_4IO_6$	d	−212.1	[2358]						
$NH_4H_5TeO_6$	d	−333.2	[2358]						

1. $\Delta H_0^\circ = -66.391$ [1618a]. 2. $\Delta H_0^\circ = -107.41$ [2358]. 3. Eutectic (19.39% NH_4F). 4. $\Delta H_0^\circ = -187.94$ [2358]. 5. $t = 14$ °C. 6. Calculated [234] from $\Delta S_{298}^\circ = -37.6$ [1960].

1	2	3		4		5		6	
NH_4I	c	(−48.14)	[2358]	−26.9	[2358]	28	[2358]		
		(−48.3)	[1618a]	−26.78	[1618a]			19.54	[1618a]
						27.0	[1618a, 1685]		
	d	(−44.86)	[2358]	−31.30	[2358]	53.7	[2358]	−14.9	[2358]
$NH_4I \cdot NH_3$	c	(−69.0)	[2358]	−31.5	[2358]	43.1	[2358]		
$NH_4I \cdot 2NH_3$	c	−89.6	[2358]	−35.0	[2358]	55.5	[2358]		
$NH_4I \cdot 3SO_2$	c	−289.2	[2358]	−238.9	[2358]	100.3	[2358]		
NH_4I_3	c	−49.7	[2358]	−28.6	[2358]	56.1	[2358]		
NH_4IO	d	−57.4	[2358]	−28.2	[2358]	25.8	[2358]		
NH_4IO_3	c	−94.0	[221]						
		−92.2	[2358]						
	d	−84.6	[2358]	−49.6	[2358]	55.4	[2358]		
NH_4IO_4	c	−81*	[221]						
	d	−66.9	[2358]						
NH_4I_2OH	d			−74.0	[2358]				
NH_4MnO_4	c	−166*	[221]						
NH_4NH_2	c	−10*	[2683]						
NH_4NO_2	c	(−61.3)	[2358]						
	d	(−57.7)	[2358]	−27.9	[2358]	60.6	[2358]	−4.2	[2358]
NH_4NO_3	c			−43.86	[2447]	36.11	[2358, 2447]		
				−43.7*	[229]	36.06	[1685]	(33.31)	[1685]
				−44.3*	[232]	35.00	[1316]	(30.12)	[1167]
		(−87.37)	[2358]	−43.98*	[2358]			(33.3)	[2358]
	d	(−81.23)	[2358]	−45.58	[2358]	62.1	[2358]	−1.6	[2358]
NH_4N_3	c	(27.6)	[2358]	65.5	[2358]	26.9	[2358]		
		(26.79)	[1356]	47.3*	[323]	31.3*	[323]		
	d	(34.1)	[2358]	64.3	[2358]	52.7	[2358]		
NH_4OH	l	−86.33	[2358]	−60.74	[2358]	39.57	[1685, 2358]	37.02	[1685, 2358]
	c	−78*	[2358]	−43.6**	[232]	39.57	[1508]	37.022	[1508]
NH_4OH, undissociated	d	(−87.505)	[2358]	−63.04	[2358]	43.3	[2358]		
				−63.05*	[323]	42.8	[1685]		
		−86.64	[2358]	−56.56	[2358]	24.5	[2358]	−16.4	[2358]
$NH_4ONO_2^{2-}$	d	−42.4	[2358]						
NH_4PF_6	c					60.49	[2358, 2442]	40.33	[2358]
								40.33[1]	[2442]
$NH_4PF_6 \cdot NH_3$	c					79.8	[2358]		
NH_4PO_3	d	−265.2	[2358]						
$NH_4(PtH_3Cl_3)$	c	−152.6	[595]					44.51	[421]

NH_4ReCl_6	d	(−330.4)	[203]						
NH_4ReO_4	c	−235.6*	[611]						
		−231*	[2683]						
	d	−218.4	[203]						
NH_4SbO_2	d			−100.29	[2358]				
$(NH_4)_2SeO_4$	c	−213*	[221]						
NH_4UF_5	c	−674.2	[105]						
NH_4VO_3	c			−306.9*	[323]	34*	[323]		
				−304.8*	[229]	33.6	[1685]	30.91	[1685]
$(NH_4)_2CO_3$	c	−222*	[2683]						
	d	−225.18	[2358]	−164.11	[2358]	40.6	[2358]		
						41.2	[1685]		
$(NH_4)_2CrO_4$	c	(−282.6*)	[323]	−238*	[323]	40.1*	[323]		
				−214*	[229]				
$(NH_4)_2Cr(SO_4)_2 \cdot 12H_2O$	c	(−440.8*)	[323]	−339.6*	[229]	171	[1649]		
		(−429.1)	[2045]						
$(NH_4)_2Cr_2O_7$	c	(−430)	[220]						
$(NH_4)_2Cr_3O_{10}$	c	−580	[220]						
$(NH_4)_2FPO_3$	d			−318.7	[2358]				
$(NH_4)_2Gd_2SO_4$	c					116.09	[2450]		
$(NH_4)_2HAsO_4$	c	−282.4	[2358]						
	d	−279.9	[2358]	−208.7	[2358]	53.8	[2358]		
$(NH_4)_2HPO_3$	d	−249.9	[2358]						
$(NH_4)_2HPO_4$	c	−347.50	[2358]	−300.3*	[229]			45	[2358]
	d	−372.71	[2358]	−298.85	[2358]	46.2	[2358]		
$(NH_4)_2H_2P_2O_7$	d	−607.9	[2358]	−519.5	[2358]	96	[2358]		
$(NH_4)_2H_3IO_6$	d	−242.9	[2358]						
$(NH_4)_2H_4TeO_6$	d	−355.4	[2358]						
$(NH_4)_2I_2O$	d			−57.6	[2358]				
$(NH_4)_2MoO_4$	c	−306*	[2358]						
$(NH_4)_2N_2O_2$	d	−67.4	[2358]						
$(NH_4)_2O$	l	−102.94	[2358]	−63.84	[2358]	63.94	[1685, 2358]	59.08	[2358]
								56.36	[1685]
	c					63.94	[1508]	56.35	[1508]
$(NH_4)_2PdCl_4$	c	−204.8*	[611]						
$(NH_4)_2PoO_6$	d	−176	[2358]						
$(NH_4)_2PtCl_4$	c							55.6*	[594]
								56.79	[421]

1. $t = 300\ ^{\circ}C$.

1	2	3		4		5		6	
$(NH_4)_2PtCl_6$	c	−242.8	[613]						
$(NH_4)_2S$	c	−40*	[2683]						
	d	(−55.4)	[2358]	−17.4	[2358]	50.7	[2358]		
$(NH_4)_2SO_3$	c	(−211.6)	[2358]	−147.9*	[229]				
	d	(−215.2)	[2358]	−154.2	[2358]	47.2	[2358]		
$(NH_4)_2SO_3 \cdot H_2O$	c	(−283.8)	[2358]						
$(NH_4)_2SO_4$	c	(−281.5*)	[191]	(−215.3*)	[191]	(54.3*)	[191]		
		(−282.23)	[2358]	(−215.56)	[2358]	(52.6)	[1685, 2358]		
	d	−280.66	[2358]	−215.77	[2358]	58.6	[2358]	−31.8	[2358]
$(NH_4)_2SO_4 \cdot 3NH_3$	c	−341.7	[2358]	−223.7	[2358]	89.5	[2358]		
$(NH_4)_2SO_4 \cdot PbSO_4$	c			−411.7*	[229]				
$(NH_4)_2SO_4 \cdot SrSO_4$	c			−628.8*	[229]				
$(NH_4)_2S_2$	d	−56.1	[2358]	−18.9	[2358]	61.0	[2358]		
$(NH_4)_2S_2O_3$	d	−219.2	[2358]						
$(NH_4)_2S_2O_4$	d	−243.4	[2358]	−181.4	[2358]	76	[2358]		
$(NH_4)_2S_2O_6$	d	−349.7	[2358]						
$(NH_4)_2S_2O_7$	d	−398.2	[2358]						
$(NH_4)_2S_2O_8$	c	(−392.5)	[2358]						
	d	(−383.3)	[2358]	−303.3	[2358]	113.5	[2358]		
$(NH_4)_2S_3$	d	−57.1	[2358]	−20.3	[2358]	70.0	[2358]		
$(NH_4)_2S_3O_6$	d	−350.0	[2358]						
$(NH_4)_2S_4$	c	(−65.2)	[2358]						
	d	(−57.8)	[2358]	−21.4	[2358]	78.9	[2358]		
$(NH_4)_2S_4O_6$	d	−355.92	[2358]						
$(NH_4)_2S_5$	c	(−65.6)	[2358]						
	d	(−58.2)	[2358]	−22.2	[2358]	87.8	[2358]		
$(NH_4)_2S_5O_6$	d	−358.8	[2358]						
$(NH_4)_2S_8$	c	−66.0	[2358]						
$(NH_4)_2Sb_2S_4$	d	−115.7	[2358]	−61.7	[2358]	41.7	[2358]		
$(NH_4)_2Se$	d			−7.0	[2358]				
$(NH_4)_2SeO_3$	d	−185.0	[2358]	−126.3	[2358]	57.3	[2358]		
$(NH_4)_2SeO_4$	c	−211.3	[611]						
		−214*	[2683]						
		−209.0	[2358]						
	d	−206.5	[2358]	−143.4	[2358]	67.1	[2358]		
$(NH_4)_2SiF_6$, hexagonal	c					66.98	[2452]	54.52	[2452]
$(NH_4)_2SiF_6$. cubic	c					67.99	[2452]	59.25	[2452]
$(NH_4)_2SiO_3$	c	−309*	[2683]						

$(NH_4)_2SnBr_6$	c					120.5[1]	[1980]	63.97[1]	[1980]
$(NH_4)_2SnCl_6$	c	−306.1	[611]			99.1[1]	[1980]	63.30[1]	[1980]
$(NH_4)_2TeO_3$	d	−205.9	[2358]						
$(NH_4)_2U_2O_7$	c	−393	[687, 1036]						
$(NH_4)_2WO_4$	c	−336*	[2683]						
$(NH_4)_3AlF_6$	c	−692.4	[611]						
$(NH_4)_3AsO_4$	c	−307.4	[2358]	−215.5*	[229]				
	d	−307.28	[2358]	−211.91	[2358]	42.4	[2358]		
$(NH_4)_3AsO_4\cdot 3H_2O$	c	−517.9	[2358]						
$(NH_4)_3As_5H_6(PO_4)_8\cdot 18H_2O$	c	−4432	[1159]			339.9	[1159]	380.5	[1159]
$(NH_4)_3BiCl_6$	d			−235.42	[2358]				
$(NH_4)_3HP_2O_7$	d	−638.7	[2358]	−529.4	[2358]	96	[2358]		
$(NH_4)_3PO_4$	c	−399.6	[2358]	−306.9*	[229]				
	d	−400.9	[2358]	−300.9	[2358]	28	[2358]		
$(NH_4)_3PO_4\cdot 3H_2O$	c	−610.8	[2358]						
$(NH_4)_4P_2O_7$	d	−669.5	[2358]	−535.7	[2358]	83	[2358]		
NO	g	(21.57)[2]	[2358]	(20.69)	[2358]	(50.347)	[1618a, 2358]		
		(21.60)[3]	[1830]			(50.3462)	[1830]	(7.1333)	[1830]
		(21.60)[4]	[570]			(50.335)	[570]		
		(21.556)	[1261]	(20.674)	[1261]	(50.34)	[1685]	(7.14)	[1685]
		(21.8)	[1754]						
		(21.58)[5]	[1618a]	(20.697)	[1618a]			(7.133)	[1618a]
NO^+	g	236.347[6]	[570]			47.3509	[570]		
		236.4[7]	[2358]			47.2332	[680]		
						46.1	[728]		
NOBr	g	(19.64)	[2358]	(19.70)	[2358]	(65.38)	[1618a, 2358]	10.87	[916, 1685, 2358]
		(19.56)[8]	[1618a, 1646]			(65.4)	[1685]		
						(55.99)	[916]		
				(19.619)	[1618a]			10.869	[1618a]
NOCl	g	(12.36)[9]	[2358]	(15.78)	[2358]	(62.52)	[2358]	10.68	[916, 2358]
		(12.57)	[1646]			(53.29)	[916]	10.5*	[826a]
						(62.4)	[1685]	10.64	[1685]
						(62.527)	[1618a, 1341]	10.688	[1341]
						(65.09)[10]	[2193]	12.62[10]	[2193]
		(12.62)[11]	[1618a]	(16.049)	[1618a]			10.681	[1618a]
	d			16.04	[2358]				

1. $T = 300\ ^\circ K$. 2. $\Delta H_0^\circ = (21.45)$ [2358]. 3. $\Delta H_0^\circ = (21.4765)$ [1830]. 4. $\Delta H_0^\circ = (21.480)$ [570]. 5. $\Delta H_0^\circ = (21.456)$ [1618a]. 6. $\Delta H_0^\circ = 234.867$ [570]. 7. $\Delta H_0^\circ = 234.8$[2358]. 8. $\Delta H_0^\circ = 21.778$ [1618a]. 9. $\Delta H_0^\circ = (12.82)$ [2358]. 10. $t = 293\ ^\circ C$. 11. $\Delta H_0^\circ = 13.078$ [1618a].

1	2	3		4		5		6	
$NOClO_4$	c	−36.9	[2358]						
NOF	g	−15.9[1]	[2358]	−12.2	[2358]	59.27	[2358]	9.88	[1685, 2358, 2453]
		−16.0[2]	[570]			50.274	[570]		
		−15.8	[1646]			59.3	[1685]		
						59.24	[2453]		
		−15.7[3]	[1618a]	−12.023	[1618a]	59.273	[1618a]	9.883	[1618a]
NOI	g					67.0	[1685]		
		24.0[4]	[1618a]	22.09	[1618a]	67.673	[1618a]	11.205	[1618a]
NO_2	g	(7.93)[5]	[2358]			(57.35)	[2358]	(8.89)	[2358]
		(8.0075)[6]	[1830]			(57.3509)	[1830]	(8.8749)	[1830]
		(8.00)[7]	[2342]			(57.43)	[376]	(8.88)	[376]
						(57.32)	[727]	(8.87)	[727, 1685]
						(57.404)	[570]		
						(57.36)	[1685]		
		(7.91)[8]	[1618a]	12.247	[1618a]	(57.343)	[1618a]	(8.837)	[1618a]
NO_2^+	g	277.4[9]	[2358]			51.6	[728]		
		244.5	[1034]						
NO_2^-	d	(−25.0)	[2358]	−8.9	[2358]	33.5	[2358]	−23.3	[2358]
				−8.25*	[323]	29.9*	[323]		
						29.9	[1685]		
NO_2Cl	g	3.0[10]	[2358]	13.0	[2358]	65.02	[2358]	12.71	[1685, 2358]
		3.12	[2214]			65.46	[2214]	12.70	[1299]
						65.01	[1793]	12.71	[1793]
						62.70	[2581]	12.74	[2581]
						64.68	[1299]		
						65.1	[1685]		
		6.31[11]	[1618a]	16.30	[1618a]	65.028	[1618a]	12.712	[1618a]
NO_2ClO_4	c	8.7	[2358]						
		8.89	[1316]						
		8.0	[1034]						
NO_2F	g	−19.0[12]	[1618a, 2567]	−8.9	[2567]	62.178	[2567]	11.919	[2567]
						62.2	[2358]	11.9	[2358]
						61.69	[2154]	11.92	[2154 2581]
						62.14	[2581]		
						62.07[13]	[2193]	11.82[13]	[2193]
				−8.882	[1618a]	62.175	[1618a]	11.918	[1618a]
NO_3	g	(16.95)	[612]	27.36	[612]	60.36	[612]	11.22	[612]

				31.6	[229]				
		(17.0)[14]	[1618a]	27.745	[1618a]	60.352	[1618a]	11.218	[1618a]
NO_3^-	g	−61	[1789]	−60	[1789]				
		−89.0	[1034]						
	d	−49.56	[2358]	(−26.61)	[2358]	(35.0)	[1685, 2358]	−20.7	[2358]
				(−26.43)	[323]	(35.0*)	[323]		
NO_3F	g	−4.2[15]	[565]						
		2.5[16]	[1618a]	17.594	[1618a]	69.988	[1618a]	15.589	[1618a]
NS	g	63.6392[17]	[1830]			53.0642	[1830]	7.5999	[1830]
		55.915*[18]	[570]			53.061	[570]	7.59	[570]
						53.1	[1685]		
		63.0*[19]	[1618a]	56.278*	[1618a]	53.055	[1618a]	7.599	[1618a]
NSe	c	42.3	[2358]						
NT_3	g					50.36	[2488]	9.52	[2488]
N_2F_2 difluorodiazine[20]	g	19.4[21]	[1830]			62.7530	[1830]	12.7792	[1830]
		16.4	[741]						
N_2F_2	g	25.3	[426]						
trans-N_2F_2	g	19.4	[740, 741]						
		19.6	[2358]						
cis-N_2F_2	g	16.4	[740]						
		16.6	[2358]						
N_2F_4	g	−1.7[22]	[2358]	19.4	[2358]	71.96	[2358]	18.9	[2358]
		−2.0[23]	[1618a]	19.08	[1618a]	71.962	[1618a]	18.922	[1618a]
N_2H_2	g	55.3	[2412]	62.7	[2412]				
		48.7	[1241]						
N_2H_4	g	22.80[24]	[2358]	38.07	[2358]	56.97	[1618a, 2348, 2358]	11.85	[2358]
		22.740[25]	[2342]	30.56	[323]	56.968	[570, 681]		
		22.75	[1618a]	28.017	[1618a]			12.6	[1618a]
	l	(12.10)	[2358]	35.67	[2358]	28.97	[2358]	23.63	[2358]
	d	8.20	[2358]	30.6	[2358]	33	[2358]		
				30.56	[323]	33*	[323]		
$N_2H_4 \cdot H^+$	d	(−1.8)	[2358]	19.7	[2358]	36	[2358]	16.8	[2358]
				21.0*	[323]	31*	[323]		
$N_2H_4 \cdot HBr$	c	−37.2	[2358]						
	d	−30.8	[2358]	−5.2	[2358]	55.7	[2358]	17.1	[2358]

1. $\Delta H_0^\circ = -15.33$ [2358]. 2. $\Delta H_0^\circ = -15.429$ [570]. 3. $\Delta H_0^\circ = 15.129$ [1618a]. 4. $\Delta H_0^\circ = 24.761$ [1618a]. 5. $\Delta H_0^\circ = (8.60)$ [2358]. 6. $\Delta H_0^\circ = (8.6812)$ [1830]. 7. $\Delta H_0^\circ = (8.667)$ [570]. 8. $\Delta H_0^\circ = 8.586$ [1618a]. 9. $\Delta H_0^\circ = 276.6$ [2358]. 10. $\Delta H_0^\circ = 4.29$ [2358]. 11. $\Delta H_0^\circ = 7.602$ [1618a]. 12. $\Delta H_0^\circ = -17.6$ [2567]; −17.589 [1618a]. 13. $t = 293$ °C. 14. $\Delta H_0^\circ = 18.529$ [1618a]. 15. $t = 21$ °C. 16. $\Delta H_0^\circ = 4.313$ [1618a]. 17. $\Delta H_0^\circ = 63.4829$ [1830]. 18. $\Delta H_0^\circ = 55.761$* [570]. 19. $\Delta H_0^\circ = 62.843$* [1618a]. 20. Active isomer. 21. $\Delta H_0^\circ = 20.6591$ [1830]. 22. $\Delta H_0^\circ = 0.88$ [2358]. 23. $\Delta H_0^\circ = 0.582$ [1618a]. 24. $\Delta H_0^\circ = 26.18$ [2358]. 25. $\Delta H_0^\circ = 26.114$ [570].

1	2	3		4		5		6	
N_2H_42HBr	c	−64.8	[2358]						
$N_2H_4 \cdot 2HBr \cdot 2H_2O$	c	−206.6	[2358]						
$N_2H_4 \cdot HCl$	c	(−47.0)	[2358]						
	d	(−41.8)	[2358]						
$N_2H_4 \cdot 2HCl$	c	(−87.8)	[2358]						
$N_2H_4 \cdot HClO_4$	c	−42.2	[2358]						
		−42.9	[619]						
	d	−32.7	[2358]	17.6	[2358]	79.7	[2358]		
$N_2H_4 \cdot HClO_3 \cdot ½H_2O$	c	−78.18	[2358]						
$N_2H_4 \cdot 2HClO_4$	c	−70.1	[942]						
$N_2H_4 \cdot HNO_3$	c	−60.13	[2358]						
	d	(−51.41)	[2358]	−6.91	[2358]	71	[2358]		
$N_2H_4H_2^{2+}$	d			22.50*	[323]	19*	[323]		
$(N_2H_4)_2 \cdot H_2SO_3$	c	−157.0	[612]						
$(N_2H_4)_2 \cdot H_2SO_4$	c	(−226.9)	[612]						
		(−229.2)	[2358]						
	d	−221.0	[2358]	−138.6	[2358]	77	[2358]	−36	[2358]
$(N_2H_4)_2 \cdot H_2SO_4 \cdot H_2O$	c	−291.3	[2358]						
N_2H_5OH	g	−49.0	[2358]	−18.9	[2358]	63	[2358]		
	l	−58.01	[2358]						
	d	−60.11	[2358]	−26.1	[2358]	49,7	[2358]	17.5	[2358]
N_2O	g	(19.61)[1]	[2358]	24.90	[2358]	(52.52)	[2358]	(9.19)	[2358]
		(19.49)[2]	[1850]			(52.5567)	[1830]	(9.2304)	[1830]
						(52.55)	[1685]	(9.23)	[1618a, 1685]
		(19.514)[3]	[570]			(52.555)	[570]		
		(19.61)	[1618a]	24.896	[1618a]	(52.546)	[1618a]		
	d	13.4	[2358]						
N_2O_2	g					65.9	[1685]	14.75	[1685]
$N_2O_2^{2-}$	d	(−4.1)	[2358]	35.4*	[749]	6.6	[1685]		
N_2O_3	g	(20.00)	[612]	(33.49)	[612]	73.92	[612]	15.68	[612, 2358]
		(20.01)[4]	[2358]	43.2*	[323]	74.61	[2358]		
		(17.5*)	[1045]	33.5*	[1045]	68.0*	[826a]		
		(19.80)[5]	[1618a]	33.324	[1618a]	73.915	[1618a]	15.683	[1618a]
	l	12.02	[2358]						
$N_2O_3(SO_3)_2$	c	−253	[2358]						
N_2O_4	g	(2.3488)[6]	[1830]			(72.7063)	[1830]	(18.4750)	[1830]
		(2.19)[7]	[2358]	(23.38)	[2358]	(72.70)	[1685, 2358]	(18.47)	[612, 2358]
		(2.17)[8]	[1618a]	(23.355)	[1618a]	(72.724)	[1618a]	(18.465)	[1618a]

		(2.54)	[612]	(23.66)	[612]	(72.73)	[612]	(18.46)	[1685]
	l	−4.676[9]	[1618a]	23.282	[1618a]	50.007	[1618a]	34.06	[1618a]
		−4.66	[2358]	23.29	[2358]	50.0	[2358]	34.1	[2358]
	c	−8.373[10]	[1618a]	23.785	[1618a]	35.92	[1618a]	29.183	[1618a]
N_2O_5	g	(2.7)[11]	[2358]	27.5	[2358]	85.0	[2358]	20.2	[2358]
		(3.35)	[612]	28.18	[612]	85.00	[612]	20.22	[612]
		(3.50*)	[1045]	29.5*	[1045]	82	[1685]	23.8*	[1685]
		(3.06)	[2213]						
		(2.70)	[1618a]	28.186	[1618a]	82.801	[1618a]	23.017	[1618a]
	c	(−10.3)	[2358]	27.2	[2358]	42.6	[2358]	34.2	[1685, 2358]
				29.0*	[1045]	36.6	[1685]		
				32*	[323]	27.1*	[323]		
				23.1*	[229]				
N_3D	g					58.67	[2582]	10.80	[2582]
N_3H	g	(70.3)[12]	[2358]	(78.4)	[2358]	(57.09)	[2358]	(10.44)	[2358]
		(71.66)	[1356]	(79.38)	[1356]	(56.74)	[1356]		
						(57.08)	[1122]	(10.84)	[1122]
		(70.0)	[1108]	(78.3)	[1108]	(57.08)	[1108]		
	l	63.1	[2358]	78.2	[2358]	33.6	[2358]		
		64.37	[1356]	79.14	[1356]	33.02	[1356]		
	d	62.16	[2358]	76.9	[2358]	34.9	[2358]		
		61.93	[1356]	77.34	[1356]	30.90	[1356]		
				71.3*	[323]	48*	[323]		
N_3H^+	g	309.0[13]	[2358]						
N_4S_4	c	(128.0)	[2358]						
DNO_3	g					64.36	[2088]	19.39	[2088]
HNCO	g					56.08	[2582]	10.73	[2582]
HNCS	g	25*	[2365]			59.12	[2582]	11.51	[2582]
HNO	g	24.305[14]	[2342]			52.809	[570]		
		23.80[15]	[1618a]	26.859	[1618a]	52.729	[1618a]	8.279	[1618a]
HNO_2	g	−19.0[16]	[2358]	−11.0[16]	[2358]	60.7[16]	[2358]	10.9[16]	[2358]
		−18.58	[748]	−10.81	[748]	61.46	[748]		
		−18.8	[223]	0.5[17]	[565]				
		−18.0*	[826a]						
trans-HNO_2	g	−19.15[18]	[2358]	−10.82	[2358]	59.54	[727, 2358]	11.01	[727, 2358]
		−18.84[19]	[1618a]	−10.508	[1618a]	59.546	[1618a]	11.00	[1618a]

1. $\Delta H_0^\circ = (20.435)$ [2358]. 2. $\Delta H_0^\circ = (20.3100)$ [1830]. 3. $\Delta H_0^\circ = (20.334)$ [2342]. 4. $\Delta H_0^\circ = 21.628$ [2358]. 5. $\Delta H_0^\circ = 20.591$ [1618a]. 6. $\Delta H_0^\circ = (4.6525)$ [1830]. 7. $\Delta H_0^\circ = 4.49$ [2358]. 8. $\Delta H_0^\circ = 4.473$ [1618a]. 9. $\Delta H_0^\circ = -4.488$ [1618a]. 10. $\Delta H_0^\circ = -7.263$ [1618a]. 11. $\Delta H_0^\circ = 5.7$ [2358]. 12. $\Delta H_0^\circ = 71.82$ [2358]. 13. $\Delta H_0^\circ = 309$ [2358]. 14. $\Delta H_0^\circ = 25.00$ [2342]. 15. $\Delta H_0^\circ = 24.498$ [1618a]. 16. Mixture of cis- and trans-isomers. 17. $t = -45.9$ °C. 18. $\Delta H_0^\circ = -17.68$ [2358]. 19. $\Delta H_0^\circ = -17.369$ [1618a].

1	2	3		4		5		6	
cis-HNO_2	g	−18.64[1]	[2358]	−10.27	[2358]	59.43	[2358]	10.70	[2358]
						59.57	[727]	10.84	[727, 1618a]
		−18.34[2]	[1618a]	−10.02	[1618a]	59.586	[1618a]		
	d	(−28.5)	[2358]	−13.3	[2358]	36.5	[2358]		
				−12.82*	[323]				
HNO_3	g	−32.28[3]	[2358]	−17.87	[2358]	(63.34)	[2358]	12.75	[2358]
						(63.68)	[2088]	12.80	[2088]
		−32.10[4]	[1618a]	−17.69	[1618a]	(63.663)	[1618a]	12.748	[1618a]
	l	(−41.61)	[2358]	(−19.31)	[2358]				
	c					24.4*	[251]		
	d	−49.56	[2358]	−26.61	[2358]	35.0	[2358]	20.7	[2358]
$HNO_3 \cdot H_2O$	l	(−113.16)	[2358]	(−78.61)	[2358]	(51.84)	[2358]	(43.61)	[2358]
	c					21.0*	[251]		
$HNO_3 \cdot 3H_2O$	l	(−252.40)	[2358]	(−193.91)	[2358]	(82.93)	[2358]	(77.71)	[2358]
						29.0*	[251]		
$HN_2O_2^-$	d	(−12.4)	[2358]	20.4*	[749]	34*	[749]		
$H_2N_2O_2$	d	(−15.4)	[2358]	11.0*	[749]	52*	[749]		
Na	g	(25.857)[5]	[1185]	(18.574)	[1185]	(36.7141)	[570, 1185]		
		(25.5969)[6]	[1830]			(36.7140)	[1830]		
		(25.919)[7]	[570]			(36.71)	[1685]		
		(25.9159)	[1505]						
		(25.900)	[2479]	(18.595)	[2479]	(35.35)	[66]		
		(25.735)[8]	[1618a]	(18.475)	[1618a]	(36.714)	[1618a]		
	l	0.575	[1618a]	0.119	[1618a]	13.827	[1618a]	7.817	[1618a]
	c					(12.289)	[1185]	(6.74)	[1185]
						(12.24)	[1931, 2358]	(6.77)	[1931]
						(12.14)	[1505, 1589]	(6.72)	[1079, 1589]
						(12.298)	[1618a]	(6.73)	[1618a]
						(12.21)	[570]	(6.74)	[570]
						(12.247)	[1830]	(6.747)	[1830]
								(6.75)	[1685, 2358]
Na^+	g	(145.915)[9]	[570]			35.3366	[570]		
		(145.755)	[1618a]	137.399	[1618a]	35.336	[1618a]		
	d	(−57.39)	[2358]	−62.593	[2358]	(14.1)	[2358]	11.1	[2358]
		(−57.50)	[88]			(14.0)	[1685]		
		(−57.7)	[1700]						
Na_2	g	(33.705)[10]	[1185]	(24.637)	[1185]	(54.993)	[1185]	8.962	[1185]
		(32.87)[11]	[1618a]	(23.807)	[1618a]	(54.994)	[1618a]	8.963	[1618a]

		(33.8763)[12]	[1830]			(54.9974)	[1830]	8.9662	[1830]
		(33.800)	[2479]	(24.685)	[2479]	(54.99)	[1685]	8.96	[1685]
$NaAlCl_4$	c	−273.0	[1618a]	−248.956	[1618a]	45.0	[1618a]	37.04	[1618a]
$NaAlH_4$	c	−27.0	[2409]	−11.6	[2409]	29.6	[2409]		
$NaAlO_2$	c	(−270.84)[13]	[1047, 1618a]	−255.60	[1047]	16.9	[1685, 1718]	17.52	[1685, 1718]
				−255.561	[1618a]	16.826	[1618a]	17.61	[1618a]
				−257.8**	[232]				
				−259.8*	[232]				
$NaAlSiO_4$, nepheline	c	−30.9[14]	[1681]	−39.2[14]	[1681]	29.1	[2548]	29.7	[1685]
		−975.4	[127]	−463.8	[127]	29.7	[1685, 1687]	28.23	[1687]
								28.39[15]	[1687]
$NaAlSi_2O_6$	c	−626.0	[771]	−656.3	[771]	41.9	[1735]		
$NaAlSi_2O_6$, dehydrated analcite	c	−25.6[14]	[1681]	−27.6[14]	[1681]				
$NaAlSi_2O_6$, jadeite	c	−36.5[14]	[1681]	−35.5[14]	[1681]	31.9	[1685, 1687]	38.23	[1685, 1687]
$NaAlSi_2O_6 \cdot H_2O$	c	−771.5	[771]	−719.4	[771]	56.0	[1685, 1717]	50.17	[1685, 1717]
$NaAlSi_3O_8$, albite	c	−1806.8	[127]	−850.0	[127]	50.2	[1685, 1687]	48.97	[1685, 1687]
		−35.9[16]	[1681]	−37.4[16]	[1681]				
$NaAlSi_3O_8$	v	−23.8[16]	[1681]	−27.5[14]	[1681]				
$NaAl_{2.27}O_{4.41}$	c			5.7[17]	[329a]	22.9	[329a]		
NaAt	c	−55*	[418]			24*	[418]	12.54*	[418]
						22.10*[18]	[304a]	11.69*[19]	[304a]
$NaBF_4$	c	−42.4	[725]						
$NaBH_4$	c	−43.83*	[323]			(24.26)[20]	[1647]	(20.73)	[1647]
						(24.21)	[1685]	(20.74)	[1685]
						(24.26)	[1116]		
		−45.85[21]	[1618a]	−30.38	[1618a]	(24.232)	[1618a]	(20.670)	[1618a]
$NaBO_2$	g	−157.0[22]	[1618a]	−157.665	[1618a]	64.937	[1618a]	11.504	[1618a]
	l	−229.339	[1618a]	−216.773	[1618a]	20.56	[1618a]	15.76	[1618a]
	c					17.57	[1394, 1685]	(15.76)	[1394, 1618a, 1685]
		−234.0[23]	[1618a]	−220.554	[1618a]	17.573	[1618a]		
$NaBO_3$	c	(−81.93)	[875]	−60.38	[875]	31.2	[875]		
$NaB_5O_8 \cdot 4H_2O$	c					380.10[24]	[1273]	373.55[24]	[1273]
NaBi	c	−15.6	[2625]						
NaBr	g					57.7	[1685, 2243]	8.65	[1685]

1. $\Delta H_0^\circ = -17.12$ [2358]. 2. $\Delta H_0^\circ = -16.852$ [1618a]. 3. $\Delta H_0^\circ = -29.94$ [2358]. 4. $\Delta H_0^\circ = -29.755$ [1618a]. 5. $\Delta H_0^\circ = 25.92$ [1185]; 25.90 [1589]. 6. $\Delta H_0^\circ = 25.6494$ [1830]. 7. $\Delta H_0^\circ = 25.97$ [570]. 8. $\Delta H_0^\circ = 25.815$ [1618a]. 9. $\Delta H_0^\circ = 144.485$ [570]. 10. $\Delta H_0^\circ = (34.31)$ [1185]. 11. $\Delta H_0^\circ = 33.467$ [1618a]. 12. $\Delta H_0^\circ = (34.4598)$ [1830]. 13. $\Delta H_0^\circ = -268.974$ [1618a]. 14. From Na_2O, $Al_2O_3(\alpha)$ and $SiO_2(\alpha)$. 15. Synthetic. 16. From Na_2O, $Al_2O_3(\alpha)$ and $SiO_2(\alpha)$. 17. From oxides. 18. $T = 300$ °K. 19. C_v; $T = 300$ °K. 20. $S_{298}^\circ - S_0^\circ$. 21. $\Delta H_0^\circ = -43.862$ [1618a]. 22. $\Delta H_0^\circ = -155.83$ [1618a]. 23. $\Delta H_0^\circ = -232.874$ [1618a]. 24. In *joules/mole* °C.

1	2	3		4		5		6	
NaBr	g	−34.4[1]	[1618a]	−42.491	[1618a]	57.628	[1618a]	8.681	[1618a]
								8.60	[2243]
	l	−81.105	[1618a]	−79.45	[1618a]	24.94	[1618a]	14.9	[1618a]
	c	(−86.45)	[1773]	−83.1*	[323]	20.5*	[323]		
		(−86.38)[2]	[1618a]	−83.476	[1618a]	20.75	[1618a]	(12.285)	[1618a]
				−83.14	[1282]	20.75	[1282]	(12.28)	[1282]
				−82.9*	[250]	20.5*	[698]	(11.53)	[698]
				−83.5*	[227]	19.9*	[249]		
						21.8*	[224]		
						20.2	[1685]		
						20.0	[1680]		
$NaBr \cdot 2H_2O$	c	(−227.5*)	[191]	−197.7*	[191]	41.9*	[191]		
NaBrO	d	(−79.1)	[1850]						
$NaBrO_3$	c	−81.93	[875]	−60.38	[875]	31.2	[875]		
		−76.8	[221]			31.7*	[245]		
						31.1	[2426, 2439]		
						31.8*	[699]		
NaCN, III	g	30.442	[1618a]	21.238	[1618a]	67.412	[1618a]	13.0	[1618a]
	l	−18.333	[1618a]	−17.056	[1618a]	32.259	[1618a]	21.0	[1618a]
NaCNO	c	(−21.4)	[1817]	−14.7*	[323]	21.8*	[323]		[1618a]
		(−21.46)	[1618a]	−19.462	[1618a]	29.84	[1618a]	16.44	[1618a]
NaCNS	c	(−98.1)	[1817]	−85.9[3]	[2246]	28.5	[2246]	20.7	[2246]
	c	(−41.7*)	[191]	−36.6*	[191]	26.8*	[191]		
NaCl	g	(−43.678)[4]	[570]	−78.0*	[227]	54.882	[570]	8.52	[1685]
		(−43.5)[5]	[1830]			54.8953	[1830]	8.5547	[1830]
		(−43.36)[6]	[1618a]	−48.117	[1618a]	54.897	[1618a]	8.553	[1618a]
						55.0	[1685, 2243]	8.47	[2243]
	l	−92.237	[1618a]	−87.40	[1618a]	22.719	[1618a]	12.072	[1618a]
	c	(−98.54)[7]	[570]	(−92.06*)	[250]	(17.35)	[570]	(12.14)	[570]
						(17.33)	[1685]	(11.85)	[1685]
						(17.4)	[1773]	(11.39)[8]	[1667]
		(−98.26)[9]	[1618a]	(−91.788)	[1618a]	(17.5*)	[698]		
						(17.236)	[1618a]	(12.072)	[1618a]
$NaCl \cdot NbOCl_3$	c	1.1[10]	[610]						
$NaClO_2$	c			−54.45*	[323]	26.7*	[323]		
				−57.5*	[229]				
$NaClO_3$	c	(−85.52)	[93]	−59.1*	[245]	30.2*	[245]	25.0*	[224]
		(−87.33)	[1318]	−65.7*	[229]	31.0*	[699]		

						31.6	[161]		
$NaClO_4$	c	(−90.68)	[90]	−61.4*	[323]	33.5*	[323, 699]	(26.0)	[1027]
		(−91.48)	[1317, 1618a]	−67.4*	[229]				
		(−91.464)	[2579]						
		(−90.48)	[539]	−60.785	[1618a]	34.0	[1618a]	(26.6)	[1618a]
$NaClO_4 \cdot 6H_2O$	c			−118.4*	[191]				
NaD	g					46.50	[1685]	7.57	[1685]
	c	(−13.339)	[1435]						
NaF	g	(−70.6)[11]	[1830]	−76.6*	[227]	51.8226	[1830]	8.1958	[1830]
		(−70.1)[12]	[1618a]	−74.71	[1618a]	51.983	[1618a]	8.175	[1618a]
		(−70.123)[13]	[570]			51.872	[570]		
						52.7	[1685]		
						53.1	[2243]		
	l	−129.885	[1618a]	−124.308	[1618a]	17.818	[1618a]	11.196	[1618a]
	c	(−136.6)[14]	[570]	(−129.93*)	[250]	(12.26)	[570, 1685, 1618a, 1721]	(11.19)	[570, 1685, 1721]
		(−136.3)	[1048]			(13.8*)	[698]	(10.75)[15]	[1667]
		(−136.17)	[95]						
		(−137.1)[16]		(−129.866)	[1618a]			(11.196)	[1618a]
NaF·HF	c	−218.0	[1507]						
		−216.6	[2243]	−193.0	[2649]	21.73	[912, 2649]	17.93	[2649]
NaF·2HF	c	−292.5	[1507]						
$NaFeCl_4$	g	−154	[1173, 2225]						
$NaFeO_2$	c	−180*	[464]			21.1	[1685, 1718]	20.20	[1685, 1718]
NaH	g	(29.9388)[17]	[1830]			(44.9997)	[1830]	(7.2394)	[1830]
						(44.95)	[1685]	(7.21)	[1685]
		(29.70)[18]	[1618a]	24.602	[1618a]	(45.0)	[1618a]	(7.241)	[1618a]
		(−13.60)	[1954]	−9.0*	[209]				
		(−13.94)	[1501]						
		(−13.487)	[1435]						
		(−13.49)[19]	[1618a]	−8.023	[1618a]	9.564	[1618a]	8.698	[1618a]
$NaHCO_3$	c			(−202.89*)	[323]	(37.1*)	[323]		
$NaHCO_3 \cdot Na_2CO_3 \cdot 2H_2O$	c	−639.4	[1280]						
$3NaHCO_3 \cdot Na_2CO_3$	c	−952.9	[1280]						
NaHS	c			−51.0*	[229]				

1. $\Delta H_0^\circ = -32.274$ [1618a]. 2. $\Delta H_0^\circ = -84.68$ [1618a]. 3. Recalculated [234] from $\Delta H_{298}^\circ = -86.73$ [842] to −86.03 [2245]. 4. $\Delta H_0^\circ = (-43.345)$ [570. 5. $\Delta H_0^\circ = (-43.1670)$ [1830]. 6. $\Delta H_0^\circ = -43.02$ [1618a]. 7. $\Delta H_0^\circ = (-98.445)$ [570]. 8. C_V at $T = 300$ °K. 9. $\Delta H_0^\circ = -98.158$ [1618a]. 10. From salts. 11. $\Delta H_0^\circ = (-70.2197)$ [1830]. 12. $\Delta H_0^\circ = -69.709$ [1618a]. 13. $\Delta H_0^\circ = (-69.74)$ [570]. 14. $\Delta H_0^\circ = -136.04$ [570]. 15. C_V at $T = 300$ °K. 16. $\Delta H_0^\circ = -136.532$ [1618a]. 17. $\Delta H_0^\circ = (29.9983)$ [1830]. 18. $\Delta H_0^\circ = 30.166$ [1618a]. 19. $\Delta H_0^\circ = -12.433$ [1618a].

1	2	3		4		5		6	
$NaHSO_4$	c			−241.9*	[229]				
NaHg	c					29.1	[1772]		
$NaHg_2$	c					43.7	[1772]		
$NaHg_4$	c					79.4	[1772]		
NaI	g					59.5	[1685, 2243]	8.71	[1685]
	l	−63.695	[1618a]	−64.496	[1618a]	28.862	[1618a]	12.482	[1618a]
	c			−68.07	[1282]	23.55	[1282]	(12.45)	[1282]
				−67.91*	[250]	24.0*	[224]	(11.63)[1]	[1667]
		−68.80[2]	[1618a]	−68.014	[1618a]	23.542	[1618a]	(12.482)	[1618a]
				−68.2*	[227]	21.4*	[249]		
				−67.62[3]	[65a]	22.1*	[323]		
						22.8*	[698]		
						21.8	[2243]		
						21.9	[1685]		
$NaI \cdot H_2O$	c	−142	[230]						
$NaI \cdot 2H_2O$	c	(−211.5*)	[191]	−178.7*	[191]	27.6*	[191]		
$NaI \cdot 3H_2O$	c	−280*	[230]						
$NaIO_3$	c	−117.2	[613]			32.3*	[245]	30.0	[873]
		−117.1	[2007]						
$NaIO_3 \cdot H_2O$	c	−188.2	[2007]						
$NaIO_3 \cdot 5H_2O$	c	−468.9	[2007]						
$NaMgF_3$	c	−402.1*	[554]			29.83*	[554]	29.60	[554]
		−166.0	[2243]			31.5	[554]	29.8*	[554]
$NaMnO_4$	c	−402.1*	[554]			38.3*	[699]		
$NaNH_2$	c			−14.1	[1050]	18.38	[1050]	(15.81)	[1050]
						18.4	[1685]	(15.80)	[1685]
$NaNO_2$	c			−67.8*	[323]	25.3*	[323]	0.23*[4]	[2066]
				−70.6*	[229]				
$NaNO_2 \cdot NaOH$	c	−189.6	[475]						
$NaNO_3$, II	c					(28.1*)	[699]		
						(27.85)	[1685]		
						(27.6)	[552]		
$NaNO_3 \cdot NaOH$	c	−214.8	[475]						
$NaNO_3 \cdot 2NaOH$	c	−316.8	[475]						
NaN_3	c	5.08	[1356]	23.76	[1356]	16.85	[1356]		
$NaNbCl_6$	g	1.9[5]	[609]						
NaO	g	13.20[6]	[1618a]	8.056	[1618a]	54.058	[1618a]	7.896	[1618a]

		13.2231[7]	[1830]			52.6800	[1830]	7.8956	[1830]
		−55.44[8]	[1618a]	−56.782	[1618a]	56.909	[1618a]	9.487	[1618a]
NaOH	g	−55.84[9]	[1830]			56.9564	[1830]	9.7739	[1830]
	l	−100.353	[1618a]	−89.981	[1618a]	17.62	[1618a]	21.03	[1618a]
	c	(−102.3)	[1773]	−91.4*	[232]	15.400	[2010]	(14.228)	[2010]
		(−101.72)	[2358]	−91.0**	[232]	15.34	[1618a, 1689]	(14.21)	[1689]
				−90.1*	[323]	12.5*	[323]		
						15.4	[1685]	(14.24)	[1685]
						14.9*	[699]		
		(−102.24)	[1618a]	−91.188	[1618a]			(14.26)	[1618a]
	d	(−112.36)	[2358]	(−100.189)	[2358]	(11.5)	[2358]	−24.4	[2358]
		(112.483)	[1435]						
		(−112.37)	[1701]						
		(−112.55)	[1954]						
$NaOH \cdot H_2O$	c					23.775	[2010]	21.544	[2010]
NaO_2	c	(−62.1)	[1314]	−51.8*	[232]	27.7	[1685, 1618a, 2546]	17.24	[1685, 2546]
		(−62.3)[10]	[1618a]	−52.282	[1618a]			17.242	[1618a]
		(−62.0*)	[887]	−51.9**	[232				
		(−62.5)	[1773]	−44.7	[229]				
				−46.5*	[323]				
				−52.0*	[1045]				
$NaPO_3$	c	(64.2)[11]	[1947]	−270.5*	[229]				
	v	61.9[11]	[1947]						
$Na_{0.30}Pb_{0.70}$, β	c	−3.30	[1589]	−3.45	[1589]				
$Na_{0.50}Pb_{0.50}$	c	−5.80[12]	[1589]	−5.80[12]	[1589]				
$Na_{0.692}Pb_{0.308}$	c	−5.20[13]	[1589]	−5.00[13]	[1589]				
$Na_{0.714}Pb_{0.286}$	c			−4.90[14]	[1589]				
$Na_{0.80}Pb_{0.20}$	c	−4.00[15]	[1589]	−3.80[15]	[1589]				
$NaPb_3$	c	−11.6	[2625]						
NaRb	g					61.2	[1685]	9.03	[1685]
						60.4	[1680]	8.89	[1679]
$NaReO_4$	c					31.95	[708]		
$NaSO_4^-$	d	1.12	[755]						
$Na_{0.50}Sb_{0.50}$	c	−7.9*[16]	[1589]						
$Na_{0.75}Sb_{0.25}$	c	−11.80[17]	[1589]						

1. C_p at $T = 300$ °K. 2. $\Delta H_0^\circ = 68.615$ [1618a]. 3. Corrected value −56.7* [323]. 4. $t = 50$ °C. 5. From salts. 6. $\Delta H_0^\circ = 13.62$ [1618a]. 7. $\Delta H_0^\circ = 13.6364$ [1830]. 8. $\Delta H_0^\circ = -63.07$ [1618a]. 9. $\Delta H_0^\circ = -54.8271$ [1830]. 10. $\Delta H_0^\circ = -54.399$ [1618a]. 11. From oxides at 35°C. 12. NaPb phase. 13. Na_9Pb_4 phase. 14. Na_5Pb_2 phase. 15. $Na_{15}Pb$ phase. 16. NaSb phase. 17. Na_3Sb phase.

1	2	3		4		5		6	
NaSb	c	−15.8	[2625]						
$NaTaCl_6$	c	−25.3[1]	[667]						
NaTe	c	−42.0	[2625]						
NaTl	c	−9.0	[2625]						
Na_2Br_2	g	−116.24[2]	[1618]	−122.92	[1618a]	83.384	[1618a]	19.15	[1618a]
$Na_2B_4O_7$	l	−778.36	[1618a]	−732.383	[1618a]	47.513	[1618a]	44.80	[1618a]
	c	(−786.4)	[2659]	−739.7	[2659]	45.30	[1685, 2659]	(44.64)	[1685, 1618a, 2659]
				−733.9	[229]				
		(−783.16)[3]	[1618a]	−736.52	[1618a]	45.289	[1618a]		
	v	−781.5	[2659]			44.39[4]	[2659]	44.42	[1685, 2659]
						48.3	[1685]		
$Na_2B_6O_{10}$	c	−1094.76	[1618a]	−1028.411	[1618a]	55.5	[1618a]	58.2	[1618a]
Na_2C_2	c			−2.1*	[227]				
				8*	[2226]				
Na_2CO_3	l	−265.32	[1618a]	−245.698	[1618a]	33.663	[1618a]	32.375	[1618a]
	c	(−271.02)	[795]	(−251.11)	[795]	(32.5)	[795, 1685]	26.41	[1685]
		(−269.85)	[2264]	(−249.96)	[2264]	(32.7)	[2264]		
		(−76.95)[5]	[1947]			(32.5*)	[323]		
		(−271.6)	[1773]			(29.6*)	[699]		
		(−270.3)	[1618a]	(−250.361)	[1618a]	(32.6)	[1618a]	26.11	[1618a]
	d			−251.4*	[323]				
$Na_2CO_3 \cdot H_2O$	c	(−342.72)	[795]	−308.64	[795]	(94.5)	[795]		
		(−341.469)	[2264]	−307.493	[2264]	(114.0)	[2264]		
				−308.5*	[232]				
$Na_2CO_3 \cdot 7H_2O$	c	(−763.084)	[2264]	−648.894	[2264]	383.1	[2264]		
		(−765.62)	[795]	−647.89	[795]				
				−649.3*	[232]				
$Na_2CO_3 \cdot 10H_2O$	c	(−974.129)	[2264]	−819.456	[2264]	518.9	[2264]		
		(−975.98	[795]	−818.43	[795]				
				−818.6*	[232]				
Na_2Cl_2	g	−136.6912[6]	[1830]			77.4708	[1830]	18.8309	[1830]
		−135.3[7]	[1618a]	−135.262	[1618a]	77.757	[1618a]	18.831	[1618a]
Na_2CrO_4	c	(−301.5)	[1615]	−293.45*	[248]	39.8*	[248]		
		(−318.6)	[2041]	−294.4*	[229]	41.7*	[699]		
$Na_2CrO_4 \cdot 4MaOH$	c	−728.5	[475]						
$Na_2Cr_2O_7$	c	(−468.8)	[2041]						
		(−469.0)	[613]						

Na_2F_2	g	−199.3992[8]	[1830]			71.6288	[1830]	18.2522	[1830]
		−196.5[9]	[1618a]	−196.215	[1618a]	72.086	[1618a]	18.252	[1618a]
$Na_2Fe_2O_4$	c	(180*)	[464]						
Na_2HPO_3	c			−314.5*	[229]				
Na_2HPO_4	c			−388.1*	[229]				
Na_2MoO_4	c	(−350.8)	[1753]	−323.6	[772]	38.1	[2633]	33.87	[2633]
		(−350.4)	[1349]						
$Na_2Mo_2O_7$	c	−536.4	[1191]						
Na_2O	l	−93.996	[1618a]	−84.691	[1618a]	17.889	[1618a]	27.0	[1618a]
	c	(−122.1)	[1309]	(−89.9*)	[251]	(17.3*)	[251]		
		(−99.4)	[1618a]	(−90.125)	[1618a]	(17.99)	[1618a]	17.436	[1618a]
		(−100.7)	[1773]			(17.0)	[1680]		
						(17.5*)	[2228]		
						(18.2)	[1685]		
$Na_2O\cdot 8CaO\cdot 3Al_2O_3$	c	−2576	[2050]						
$Na_2O\cdot CuO_2$	c			−148.1*	[229]				
$Na_2O\cdot 3SiO_2$	c	−790.94*	[363]	−174.3*	[363]	51.6*	[363]		
Na_2O_2	c	(−122.1)	[1314]	−107.0	[1045]	22.6	[1685, 2546]	21.35	[1685, 2546]
		(−123.0)	[1773]	−102.8*	[323]	16*	[323]		
				−104.7*	[232]				
				−105.5**	[232]				
				−106	[887]				
		(−122.0)[10]	[1618a]	−106.817	[1618a]	22.677	[1618a]	21.361	[1618a]
$Na_2(OH)_2$	g	−166.7872[11]	[1830]			73.9232	[1830]	19.9932	[1830]
Na_2PbO_2	c	−163.7*	[346]			34*	[346]		
Na_2PbO_3	c			−188.0*	[229]				
Na_2PdCl_4	c	−234.0*	[579]			66.1*	[579]		
Na_2PtCl_6	c			−236.4*	[251]	74.8*	[251]		
						92.3*	[579]		
Na_2S	l	−87.87	[1618a]	−85.458	[1618a]	24.136	[1618a]	17.618	[1618a]
	c	(−88.5)	[2573]	−84.8	[2573]	18.5	[2573]		
		(−92.4)	[1773]	−86.52	[322]	23.5	[1773]		
		(−88)	[232]	−86.6*	[323]	23.2*	[323]		
				−88.1*	[229]				
		(−89)	[1618a]	−86.368	[1618a]	23.4	[1618a]	18.99	[1618a]
Na_2SO_3	c							28.71	[1685]
$Na_2SO_3\cdot 7H_2O$	c			−638.8*	[191]				

1. From NaCl and $TaCl_5$. 2. $\Delta H_0^\circ = -111.932$ [1618a]. 3. $\Delta H_0^\circ = -778.909$ [1618a]. 4. $S_{298}^\circ - S_0^\circ$. 5. From oxides at 35 °C. 6. $\Delta H_0^\circ = -135.8379$ [1830]. 7. $\Delta H_0^\circ = -134.433$ [1618a]. 8. $\Delta H_0^\circ = -198.3218$ [1830]. 9. $\Delta H_0^\circ = -195.409$ [1618a]. 10. $\Delta H_0^\circ = -120.599$ [1618a]. 11. $\Delta H_0^\circ = -163.8329$ [1830].

1	2	3		4		5		6	
Na_2SO_4, II	c	(−300.92)	[2050]					30.42	[1685]
		(−333.5)	[1773]						
Na_2SO_4, III	c					37.4	[1685]	32.25[1]	[620]
Na_2SO_4	d					(36.0*)	[699]		
$Na_2SO_4 \cdot 10H_2O$	c	(−1033.64)	[905]	(−870.67)	[905]	(141.46)	[905]	(137.3*)	[905]
		(−1033.6*)	[191]	(−870.7*)	[191]	(140.8*)	[191]		
						(140.0)	[1685]	(137.3)	[1685]
Na_2S_2	c	−98.5	[1773]						
$Na_2S_2O_3$	c			−249.2*	[229]				
$Na_2S_2O_6$	c			−366.1*	[229]				
Na_2S_3	c			−28.0*	[229]				
Na_2S_4	c	(−101.4)	[1773]						
Na_2Se	c	(−82.0)	[1994, 2245]	−82.0*	[229]				
Na_2SeO_3	c	−230.3	[255]						
Na_2SeO_4	c	(−261.33)	[518]	−231.9*	[229]	28.0*	[498]		
		(−261.27)	[521]						
$Na_2SeO_4 \cdot 10H_2O$	c	−960.0	[517]						
		−963.27	[521]						
Na_2Se_2	c	−93.0	[1773]						
Na_2SiF_6	c	(−681.1)	[87]	−610.4*	[323]	51.3*	[323]		
Na_2SiO_3	c	(−55.2)[2]	[1681]	(−54.9)[2]	[1681]				
		(−364.57)	[2324]						
		(−359.7)	[1766]						
	v	(−46.7)[2]	[1681]	−47.4[2]	[1681]				
		(−353.5)	[2324]	−340.9	[229]				
$Na_2Si_2O_5$	c	(−55.3)[2]	[1681]	(−55.7)[2]	[1681]				
		(−574.97)[3]	[2324]						
		(−576.37)[4]	[2324]						
		(−570.3)[3]	[1766]						
		(−568.6)[4]	[1766]						
		(−573.170)	[2463]						
	v	−49.1[2]	[1681]	−50.8[2]	[1681]				
		−561.4	[1766]						
		−553.1	[2324]						
$Na_2Si_3O_7$	c	−820.5*	[364]	−777.3*	[364]	64.5*	[364]		
Na_2SnO_3	c			−258.0*	[229]				
Na_2Te	c	(−75.0)	[2625]	−82.6*	[323]	31.5*	[323]		
				−83.0*	[229]				

Na_2TeO_4	c					18.5	[1957]	33.18[5]	[1958]
Na_2Te_2	c			−100.4*	[229]				
Na_2TiO_3	c	−379.5	[431]						
Na_2UO_4	c	(−478)	[192]	−475*	[323]	47*	[323]		
Na_2WO_4	c	(−379.6)	[1350]						
		(−379.2)	[1753]						
$Na_2WO_4 \cdot 2H_2O$	c	−4.66[6]	[639]						
$Na_2W_2O_7$	c	−594.0	[1753]						
$Na_2W_4O_{13}$	c	−1030.3	[1753]						
$Na_2Zn(SO_4)_2$	c			−514.3*	[229]				
$Na_2Zn(SO_4)_2 \cdot 4H_2O$	c			−749.0*	[229]				
$Na_{2.5}Zn_{1.25}P_3O_{10}$	v	−9.67[7]	[1947]						
Na_2AlCl_6	c	−473.0	[1618a]	−437.064	[1618a]	83.0	[1618a]	58.35	[1618a]
Na_3AlF_6	c	(−784.8)	[1048]	−720.8*	[229]	57.0	[1618a, 1685, 1721]	(51.60)	[1685, 1721]
								(52.3)	[189]
		(−789.5)[8]	[1618a]	−750.143	[1618a]			(51.635)	[1618a]
Na_3As	c	−52.0*	[1773]						
Na_3AsO_4	c	52.0	[377]	−341.1*	[229]				
Na_3CrCl_6	c	−415.7	[69]						
Na_3Hg	c	(−11.8)	[2625]						
Na_3Hg_2	c	(−23.0)	[2625]			67.0	[1772]		
$Na_3Li_3P_4O_{13}$	v	−3.56[7]	[1947]						
Na_3P	c	−32.0	[377]						
		−30.0	[2039-B]						
Na_3PO_4	c	(−462.6)	[1947]	−430.6*	[323]	46.5*	[323]		
				−434.8*	[229]	53.7	[1772]		
Na_3Sb	c	(−50.8)	[377]						
Na_3VCl_6	c	−6.1[9]	[71]						
$Na_4P_2O_7$	c	(−210.6)[7]	[1947]	−717.3*	[229]				
Na_4Sn	c	(−14.0)	[2625]						
Na_5Hg	c	(−23.0)	[2625]						
$Na_6P_3O_{10}$	v	−267.6[10]	[1947]						
$Na_6P_4O_{13}$	v	−331.0[10]	[1947]						
$Na_6Si_2O_7$	c	−136.5	[1766]						
Nb	g	(177.500)	[2479]	(166.837)	[2479]				
		(172.50)[11]	[1589]	(161.83)	[1589]				
		(172.53)[11]	[2425]						

1. $t = 45.87°C$. 2. From Na_2O and $SiO_2(a)$. 3. α-Modification. 4. β-Modification. 5. $T = 300\ °K$. 6. $Na_2WO_4 + 2H_2O(l) = Na_2WO_4 \cdot 2H_2O$. 7. From oxides at 35 °C. 8. $\Delta H_0^\circ = -786.559$ [1618a]. 9. From NaCl(c) and VCl_3(c). 10. From Na_2O(c) and P_4O_{10}(c) at 35 °C. 11. $\Delta H_0^\circ = 171.80$ [2425]; 171.60 [1589].

1	2	3		4		5		6	
Nb	c					(8.73)	[2479]	5.95	[2479]
						(8.70)	[1589]	5.88	[1493, 1589]
						(9.0)	[1685]	5.98	[1685]
						(8.47)	[121]	5.79	[121]
						(8.58)	[994]	5.83[1]	[994]
						(8.713)	[253a]	5.877	[253a]
Nb^{3+}	d			−76*	[323]				
$NbB_{1.963}$	c					8.91	[2653]	11.42	[2653]
NbB_2	c					8.6	[1959]	11.81	[1959]
$NbBr_3$	c	−135.2	[666]						
$NbBr_5$	c	−132.85	[1421]						
		−150*	[20]			73.0*	[20]		
$NbC_{0.147}$	c	−8.5[2]	[317]						
$NbC_{0.342}$	c	−16.2[2]	[317]						
		−16.2	[314]						
NbC_x^3	c	$6.60-70.95x+30.75x^2$	[366]						
$NbC_{0.50}$	c	−22.71	[314]			8.74*	[121]	7.25[4]	[121]
$NbC_{0.53}$	c	−23.3	[314]						
		−23.3[2]	[317]						
$NbC_{0.60}$	c	−26.0	[314]						
		−26.0[2]	[317]						
$NbC_{0.71}$	c	−28.0	[2710]			−1.6[5]	[2710]		
$NbC_{0.749}$	c	−30.3	[314, 317]			8.86*	[121]	8.23[4]	[121]
								7.01[6]	[317]
$NbC_{0.847}$	c	−33.1	[314]			8.93*	[121]	8.62[4]	[121]
$NbC_{0.867}$	c							7.64[6]	[317]
$NbC_{0.877}$	c	−33.1[2]	[317]						
$NbC_{0.913}$	c	−31	[285]						
$NbC_{0.936}$	c	−34.0	[314]						
		−34.0[2]	[317]						
$NbC_{0.964}$	c							8.36[7]	[317]
$NbC_{0.99}$	c	−31.8	[2710]			−1.6[8]	[2710]		
NbC	c	−34.8	[314, 317]			9.0	[121, 1685]	8.92[9]	[121]
		−33.6	[1906]						
		−33.6[10]	[1572]						

		−34	[285]						
NbC, α	c	−33.6	[2097]	−33.1	[2097]	8.46	[2097]	8.81	[2097]
$NbC_{1.029}$	c	−34.3[2]	[317]						
$NbC_{1.422}$	c	−34.8[2]	[317]						
$NbCl_2$	c	−98*	[2285]			28*	[2285]	17.2*	[2285]
$NbCl_{2.67}$	c	−126*	[2285]			32.8*	[2285]	20.4*	[2285]
$NbCl_3$	c	−139*	[2285]			35.2	[2285]	22.3*	[2285]
$NbCl_{3.13}$	c	−144*	[2285]			36.2	[2285]	23.3*	[2285]
$NbCl_4$	g	−136.6	[2285]			85*	[2285]	23.6*	[2285]
	c	−166.0	[2285]			44*	[2285]	28.7*	[2285]
$NbCl_5$	g	−169.9	[2285]			93*	[2285]	27.5	[2285]
						90.29	[1295]	27.53	[1295]
						90.867	[2021]	27.505	[2021]
	c	−190.5	[2285]			54*	[2285]	34.7*	[2285]
		−190.6*	[20]			58.6*	[20]		
		−188*	[2283]						
		−193.7	[676]						
		−190.6	[1420]						
		−193.7	[660]						
NbF_5	c	−370*	[20]						
	c	−433.5	[1379]	−406.22	[1379]	38.3	[881, 1685]	31.5	[1685]
		−432	[2014]	−405	[2014]	38.8*	[20]	32.23	[881]
$1/0.67\,NbGe_{0.67}$	c	−22.9[11]	[936]						
$1/0.54\,NbGe_{0.54}$	c	−27.1[11]	[936]						
$NbH_{0.883}$						7.72[12]	[844]	7.10[12]	[844]
NbI_5	c	−102*	[20]			82.0*	[20]		
NbN	c	−56.8	[1907]	−50.0	[1907]	9.0	[1685]		
				−50.6*	[232]				
NbO	c	−98.4	[320]	−92.4	[320]	−20.19[13]	[323]		
		−97.7	[314, 317]			11.5	[1773]	13.84[14]	[317]
		−99.13	[160]	−92.7	[160]	12.01	[121]	9.87	[121]
		−108.8	[379]			11.6[15]	[379]		
		−97.5	[887]						
		−106*	[608]						
		−97	[2287]						
		173.5*[16]	[665]						

1. $t=0\,°C$. 2. $\Delta H_{NbC_x} = -56.04x + 21.24x^2$; $x = 0.147$–1.00. 3. $x = 0.489$–0.984. 4. Calculated [234] from $\Delta S^\circ_{298} = -21.57$ [379]. 5. ΔS. 6. $T = 300\,°K$. 7. $T = 300\,°K$. 8. ΔS°_{298}.
9. Calculated [234] from $\Delta S^\circ_{298} = -21.57$ [379]. 10. Extrapolated. 11. ΔH°_0. 12. $t = 0\,°C$. 13. ΔS°_{298}. 14. $T = 300\,°K$. 15. Calculated [234] from $\Delta S^\circ_{298} = -21.57$ [379]. 16. $(\Delta H^\circ_{298})_{subl}$.

1	2	3		4		5		6	
$NbOBr_3$	c	−179.3[1]	[666]						
		−191	[21]						
$NbOCl_3$	c	−185	[2287]						
	g	−184.1	[2286]			82*	[2286]	23.6	[2286]
		−179.3	[1323]			90	[1323]		
	l	−210.2	[2286]			38*	[2286]		
	c							28.7	[2286]
		−220*	[21]			25.3*	[21]		
		−212.2	[670]						
$NbOF_3$	c	−340*	[21]			24.5*	[21]		
$NbOI_3$	c	−159*	[21]						
$NbO_{1.273}$	c	−124.8	[317]						
NbO_2	g	141[2]	[622]						
	c	−193.3	[320, 379]	−179.7	[320]	−45.76[3]	[320]		
		−191.7	[314, 317]			13.03	[1685, 1724]	(13.74)	[315, 1685, 1724]
		−190.9	[1894]			13.79	[121]	(13.84)[4]	[121]
		−185.5	[887, 1424]			13.0	[1773]		
NbO_2Cl	c	−235*	[21]			21.2*	[21]		
NbO_2F	c	−266*	[21]			20.7*	[21]		
Nb_2C	c	−14.5	[317]			−1.0[3]	[2709]		
		−46.6	[1572]						
Nb_2N	c	−61.1	[1894]						
Nb_2O_4	c	(−380.8)	[1045]	−354.5	[1045]	29.7	[1045]		
				−362.4*	[323]	29.2*	[323]		
Nb_2O_5	c	(−456.9)	[320]	−424.9	[320]	−107.43[3]	[320]	(34.3)	[1045]
		(−458.6)	[317]	−432*	[323]	33*	[323]	(31.69)[4]	[121, 317]
		(−455.2)	[1593]	−422.1*	[232]	32.8	[1685, 1714]	(31.57)	[1685, 1714]
		(−472.6)	[379]			32.80	[121]		
		(−458.6)	[314]			32.5	[1480]		
		(−455.1)	[316]						
		(−473.2)	[382]						
		(−454)	[1572]						
Nb_2O_5, β	c	−435.5	[287]						
		−453.5	[284]						
Nb_2S_5	c	−220*	[1480]						
$Nb_4S_{7.04}$	c	−331	[1487]						
Nb_5S_3	c	<−25*	[2279]						

		−63*	[2350]						
Nb_6Ci_{14}	c	−681	[2378]						
Nd	g	(76.800)	[2479]	68.529	[2479]	45.24	[2479]	5.28	[1685, 2479]
		(75.8*)[5]	[2275]	68.87	[1589]	45.25	[1685]		
		(77.30)[6]	[350]			37.9; 36.92	[2662]		
		(76.3)	[2578]						
		(76.5)[2]	[2679]						
		(78.33)[7]	[1456]						
	c					17.50[8]	[2423]	(6.57)	[2423]
						16.95	[1589]	(6.55)	[1589]
						17.5	[1685, 2109]	31.69[4]	[121]
						13.9	[2424]		
						13.8*	[323]		
						17.54	[2396]		
Nd^{3+}	d	(−163.27)	[2424]	(−155.40)	[2424]	−59.3	[2424]		
				(−168.2*)	[323]	−41.6*	[323]		
				(−157*)	[1976]	−49*	[1976]		
NdB_6	c	−102.8	[455]						
$NdBr_3$	c	−212*	[230]						
		−208*	[2683]						
$NdCl_2$	c	−169	[412, 413]	−158	[412]	31*	[412]		
		−163.2	[442, 445]	−167	[413]				
		−161*	[442]						
$NdCl_3$	g	80.8[2]	[441]			90.29	[1295]	27.53	[1295]
	c	(−245.61)	[2424]	−227.93	[2424]	34.6	[2424]		
		(−246.5)	[442]	−236.4*	[323]	34.6*	[323]		
				−236.6*	[232]				
				−236.7**	[232]				
				−237.4*	[2507]				
				−227*	[1976]				
$NdCl_3 \cdot 6H_2O$	c	(−683.58)	[2424]	−583.3	[2424]	92	[2424]		
				−591.8*	[323]	93.0*	[323]		
				−593.6	[229]				
				−582*	[1976]				
$Nd(HSO_4)_2$	c			−675*	[1976]				
NdH_2	c	−44.8	[1999]						
NdI_3	c	(−150.2)	[1533, 2424]	−157.7*	[227, 323]	51.4*	[323]		

1. From gaseous bromine. 2. ΔH°_0. 3. ΔS°_{298}. 4. $T = 300\ ^\circ K$. 5. Average from the values 75.0 and 76.7 obtained by the authors. 6. $\Delta H^\circ_0 = 77.51$ [1589]. 7. $\Delta H^\circ_0 = 78.54$ [1456]. 8. $S^\circ_{298} - S^\circ_0$.

1	2	3		4		5		6	
NdI_3		(−158.3)	[1533]	−150*	[1976]				
NdO	g	−30.0[1]	[1328]						
		−27[1]	[2613]						
$NdO_{1.5}$, hexagonal	c	−216.08	[2662]	−205.6	[2662]				
NdOCl	c	−237.5	[46]	−223.6*	[1976]	19.1	[46]		
$Nd(OH)_3$	c	−359.7	[229]	(−309.3*)	[323]				
Nd_2O_3	c	(−432.15)	[1573]	−411.1	[1658]	35.05	[1685]	26.61	[1658]
		(−426.0)	[887]	−412.3	[229]	33.607	[1326]	26.59	[1326, 1685]
				−408.75	[1045]	36.9	[1685]		
						36.58	[242]	28.7*	[242]
		(−433.15)[2]	[2679]			37.9	[2679]		
				−408*	[1976]	29.2*	[1976]		
						38.0	[2662]		
				−420.6*	[323]	29.3*	[323]		
Nd_2O_4	c			−361.3*	[229]				
Nd_2O_5	c			−430.1*	[229]				
Nd_2S_3	c	(−265.0)	[2245, 2424]	−276.2*	[323]	31.6*	[323]		
				−278.5*	[229]				
				−268*	[1976]				
$Nd_2(SO_4)_3$	c	(−932.0)	[2245, 2424]	−866.1*	[323]	68.9*	[323]		
				−868,0*	[229]				
$Nd_2(SO_4)_3 \cdot 5H_2O$	c			−1169.9*	[229]				
				−1148*	[1976]				
$Nd_2(SO_4)_3 \cdot 8H_2O$	c			(−1312*)	[1976]				
Ne	g					(34.9482)	[1830]	(4.9681)	[1830]
						(34.95)	[1685]		
						(34.9483)	[570]		
						(34.947)	[568]		
	d	−1.1	[2358]	4.6	[2358]	15.8	[2358]		
Ne^+	g	(498.794)[3]	[568]			37.801	[568]	5.206	[568]
		(498.77)	[2358]						
Ne^{2+}	g	(1447.7)[1]	[568]						
		(1447.6)[4]	[2358]						
Ne^{3+}	g	(2909.2)[1]	[568]						
		(2919)[5]	[2358]						
Ne^{4+}	g	(5147.3)[1]	[568]						
		(5162)[6]	[2358]						

Ne^{5+}	g	(8059.8)[1]	[568]						
		(8079)[7]	[2358]						
Ne^{6+}	g	(11703)[1]	[568]						
Ni	g	(101.260)	[2479]	(90.413)	[2479]	(43.52)	[1685, 2479]	(5.58)	[1685, 2479]
		(102.67)[8]	[1589]	(91.82)	[1589]				
		(107.7)	[756]						
	c					(7.14)	[922, 1589, 1685]	(6.23)	[1589, 1685, 2479]
						(7.12)	[1652]	(6.46*)	[2469]
Ni^{2+}	g					42.51	[66]		
	d			(11.53*)	[323]	(−29.4)[9]	[52]		
						(−29.5)	[1749]		
						(−29.1)	[1685]		
Ni^{3+}	g					42.72	[66]		
$NiAl_2O_4$	c	−463.6	[335]	−434.6	[335]	21.6	[335]		
NiAs	c	13.0*	[1773]			15.3*	[1773]		
$NiBr_2$	c	(51.8)	[890, 2245]	−50.8*	[323]	32.8*	[323]		
				−48*	[227]	30.8	[1685]		
$Ni(CN)_2$	c	(52*)	[2683]			22.5*	[323]		
$Ni(CN)_4^{2-}$	d	(−43.2)	[974]	−41.1	[974]				
				117.1	[323]	33*	[323]		
$Ni(CNS)_2$	c	31*	[2683]						
$Ni(CO)_4$	g	−52.6[10]	[2427]	−135.6	[2427]	(95.4)	[2427]		
		−39.1[10]	[1226]	−140.0	[1226]	(97.1)	[1685]	34.73	[1685]
		−47.3[10]	[542]			(98.2)	[2240]	34.6	[2240]
		−36.5[10]	[2509]			(87.0)	[1680]		
		−37.2[11]	[243]			(96.2)[11]	[243]		
		−38.8[10]	[2508]			(100.2)[12]	[243]		
	l					(74.9)	[1685]	48.89	[1685]
								48.9	[2427]
$NiCO_3$						85.4[13]	[292]		
	c	−158.7*	[323]	(−147.0*)	[323]	21.9*	[323]		
		−164.7*	[229]	(−146.69*)	[177]	21.7*	[177]		
		−170*	[694]			21.6*	[224]		
		−170	[481]						
		−163.8	[1683]						
NiCl	g			8.7*	[227]				

1. ΔH_0°. 2. $\Delta H_0^\circ = -431.4$ [2679]. 3. $\Delta H_0^\circ = (497.29)$ [568]. 4. $\Delta H_0^\circ = 1444.7$ [2358]. 5. $\Delta H_0^\circ = 2915$ [2358]. 6. $\Delta H_0^\circ = 5156$ [2358]. 7. $\Delta H_0^\circ = 8072$ [2358]. 8. $\Delta H_0^\circ = (102.18)$ [1589]. 9. Average of −29.6 and −29.1. 10. For the reaction of formation from Ni and CO; $\Delta H_0^\circ = -34.1$ [2509]. 11. Most reliable for the reaction Ni + 4CO = $Ni(CO)_4$. 12. ΔS_{298}°; most reliable for the reaction Ni + 4CO = $Ni(CO)_4$. 13. In *joules/mole*·°C.

1	2	3		4		5		6	
$NiCl_2$	c	(−72.101)	[1756]	(−61.871)	[1756]	(26.10)	[1756]		
		(−73.0)[1]	[890, 925]	(−61.92)	[925]	(23.35)	[925, 1680]		
		(−70.5)	[672]			(23.334)	[923]	(17.13)	[923, 1685]
						(23.33)	[1685]		
$NiCl_2 \cdot 2H_2O$	c			−183.2*	[229]				
$NiCl_2 \cdot 4H_2O$	c			−298.9*	[229]				
$Ni(ClO_3)_2$	c	−38*	[2683]						
$Ni(ClO_4)_2$	c	−47*	[2683]						
$Ni(ClO_4) \cdot 6H_2O$	c	(−490)	[23]						
		(−473.3)	[689]						
$NiCr_2O_4$	c	−347.0	[331]	−321.5	[331]	30.9	[331]		
NiF_2	c	(−158.0)	[890]	−149.2*	[227]	17.59	[947, 1685]	15.31	[947, 1685]
				−148.8*	[323]	19.9*	[323]		
				−146.7**	[232]				
$NiFe_2O_4$	c	−258*	[449]	−236.6	[449, 451]	47.0*	[449]	40.0	[449]
		−257.0	[451]			47	[451]		
		−257.6	[181]			30.1[2]	[1720]	34.81	[1681, 1720]
		−258*	[464]			31.5	[1685]		
$NiH_{0.5}$	c	−2.10[3]	[769]	5.64[1]	[769]				
NiH	g			85.3*	[227]				
	c			2.0*	[229]				
NiH_2	c			3.3*	[229]				
$Ni(HCO_3)_2$	c	−346*	[2683]						
$Ni(HS)_2$	c	5*	[2683]						
$Ni(HSO_4)_2$	c	−417*	[2683]						
NiI_2	c	(−23.0)	[890]	−21.3	[323]	37.7*	[323]		
				−21.2*	[227]	33.6	[1685]		
$Ni(IO_3)_2$	c			−86.7*	[323]	54.5*	[323]		
$NiMoO_4$	c	−251.5*	[170, 172]	−226.5*	[170, 172]				
$Ni(NH)_3CS_3$	c			−53.8	[1285]	144.6	[1285]		
$Ni(NH_2)_2$	c	−3*	[2683]						
$Ni(NH_3)_4^{2+}$	d			(−46.9*)	[323]				
$Ni(NH_3)_6^{2+}$	d			(−60.1*)	[323]				
$Ni(NO_2)_2$	c	−59*	[2683]						
$Ni(NO_3)_2$	c			−56.4*	[323]	45.9*	[323]		
				−57.4*	[227]				
$Ni(NO_3)_2 \cdot 6H_2O$	c			−397.4*	[229]				
NiO	c	(−57.3)	[878]	(−50.6)	[878]	(9.08)	[1685, 1722]	(10.59)	[1685]

		(−57.5)	[1772]	(−50.7)	[232]			(10.57)[4]	[2559]
$Ni(OH)_2$	c			(−106.56*)	[176]	(13.5*)	[176]		
$Ni(OH)_3$	c	(−162.1)	[2267]	−129.5*	[323]	19.5*	[323]		
				−131.2*	[229]				
$Ni(OH)_4$	c			−329.8	[549]				
				−329.79	[549]				
NiO_2	c			−47.5*	[329]				
NiOOH, β	c	−164	[2267]						
NiP_2	c	−40.0	[1772]						
NiP_3	c	−48.0	[1772]						
$Ni(ReO_4)_2$	c	−392*	[2683]						
NiS	c					12.66	[2632]	11.26	[2632]
NiS, α	c	(−22.2)	[2239, 2625]	−17.7	[323]	16.1	[2239]		
				−19.08	[176]	16.5*	[176]		
				−18.2*	[229]				
NiS, γ	c			−27.3*	[323]				
NiS precipitated	c			−17.2*	[229]				
$NiSO_3$	c	(−157.2*)	[1172]						
$NiSO_4$	c	(−212.5)	[2245]	(−187.14*)[5]	[244]	(23.2)	[1678]		
$NiSO_4 \cdot 6H_2O$, green	c			(−532.6*)	[229]				
$NiSO_4 \cdot 7H_2O$	c			−585.5*	[229]				
NiS_2	c	−34.0	[2239, 2625]			24.74	[1409]	18.04	[1409]
NiSb, γ	c	(−15.8)	[2625]						
$NiSb_2$	c	−17.7	[2625]						
$Ni_{0.80}Se$	c					8.506[2]	[1405]	6.037	[1405]
$Ni_{0.875}Se$	c					8.606[2]	[1405]	6.133	[1405]
$Ni_{0.950}Se$	c					8.754[2]	[1405]	6.154	[1405]
NiSe	c			−9.7*	[229]				
$NiSeO_3 \cdot 2H_2O$	c	−275.00	[507]						
		−275.0	[510]						
	v	−267.92	[501, 512]	−221.65	[512]	47.0	[512]		
		−267.9	[510]						
$NiSeO_4$	c	−142.5	[499]						
$NiSeO_4 \cdot 6H_2O$ green	c	−574.0	[499]						
$NiSeO_4 \cdot 6H_2O$, blue	c	−572.0	[499]						

1. $\Delta H_0^\circ = -73.075$ [925]. 2. $S_{298}^\circ - S_0^\circ$. 3. Per *mole* H_2. 4. $T = 300\ ^\circ K$. 5. Recalculated [234] from $(\Delta H_{298}^\circ)_{diss} = 83.75$ [250] to 83.44 [2245] using the values given in [2245] for ΔG_{298}° for SO_3 and NiO.

1	2	3		4		5		6	
$Ni_{0.60}Sn_{0.40}$, γ	c	−7.50[1]	[1589]						
$Ni_{0.75}Sn_{0.25}$, β	c	−5.60[1]	[1589]						
$Ni_{0.3333}Te_{0.6667}$	c							6.18	[1589]
$Ni_{0.3999}Te_{0.6001}$	c							6.09	[1589]
$Ni_{0.4761}Te_{0.5239}$	c							6.05	[1589]
$Ni_{0.5}Te_{0.5}$	c	−9.67*[2]	[1589]						
NiTe	c	−12.8	[550]	−8.7*	[229]				
$NiTe_{1.1}$	c	−13.9	[550]			9.567[3]	[2652]	6.184	[2652]
						20.10	[1685]	12.99	[1685]
$NiTe_{1.18}$	c	−14.1	[550]						
$NiTe_{1.25}$	c	−15.3	[550]						
$NiTe_{1.30}$	c	−15.6	[550]						
$NiTe_{1.35}$	c	−15.7	[550]						
$NiTe_{1.40}$	c	−16.2	[550]						
$NiTe_{1.5}$	c	−17.3	[550]			9.597[3]	[2652]	6.091	[2652]
						24.00	[1685]	15.23	[1685]
$NiTe_2$	c					9.586[3]	[2652]	6.049	[2652]
						28.76	[1685]	18.15	[1685]
$Ni_{0.33}Ti_{0.67}$	c	−6.40[4]	[1589]						
$Ni_{0.50}Ti_{0.50}$	c	−8.1*[5]	[1589]						
$Ni_{0.75}Ti_{0.25}$	c	−8.30[6]	[1589]						
$Ni_{0.93}Ti_{0.07}$	c	−1.90	[1589]						
NiTi	c	−15.9	[1775]						
$NiTiO_3$	c	−288.8	[136]	−268.1	[136]	19.6	[136]		
		−287.6	[416]	−267.3	[416]	21.2	[416]		
$NiTi_2$	c	−20.0	[1775]						
$NiWO_4$	c	(−274.5*)	[170, 172]	−248.1*	[170, 172]				
		(−271.0)	[458]	−244.8*	[172]				
$Ni_{0.1}Zn_{0.9}Fe_2O_4$	c					36.8	[1685]	33.89	[1685]
$Ni_{0.2}Zn_{0.8}Fe_2O_4$	c					36.9	[1685]	34.72	[1685]
$Ni_{0.3}Zn_{0.7}Fe_2O_4$	c					36.6	[1685]	35.54	[1685]
$Ni_{0.4}Zn_{0.6}Fe_2O_4$	c					36.8	[1685]	35.90	[1685]
$Ni_{0.50}Zn_{0.50}Fe_2O_4$	c							43.5[7]	[2586]
Ni_2S_2	c			−42.6	[229]	32.0	[2632]		
Ni_2SiO_4	c	−329.4	[252, 2663]						

Ni_3C	c	(9.0)	[2226, 2625]	7.6*	[2226]	25.4	[2226]		
				9.6*	[227]				
Ni_3Cr	c	0.41[8]	[288]						
Ni_3Fe	c	1.9[8]	[288]						
Ni_3Mn	c	2.40[8]	[288]						
Ni_3N	c	0.2	[1461]						
Ni_3P	c	(−52.4)	[1772]						
		(−53.0)	[1482a]						
Ni_3S_2	c	(−47.5)	[2239]			36.6	[2239]	28.12	[2632]
						32.0	[2632]		
Ni_3Si	c	−35.5	[2625]						
Ni_3Sn	c	−22.8	[2625]						
Ni_3Ti	c	8.4[1]	[288]						
		−33.5	[1775]						
Ni_3V	c	3.60[8]	[288]						
Ni_4W	c							25.70	[459]
Ni_5P_2	c	(−103.5)	[1772]						
$H_2Ni(OH)_4$	c			−219.86*	[6]				
Ni + Mn (alloy)	c							5.80[9]	[81]
Np	c					12.1*	[323]	7.4[10]	[1182]
Np^{3+}	d[11]			−128.4*	[323]	−31*	[323]		
Np^{4+}	d[11]			−124.9*	[323]	−78*	[323]		
$NpBr_3$	c			−169*	[323]	49*	[323]		
				−167.7*	[227]				
$NpBr_4$	c			−175*	[323]	58*	[323]		
				−175.9*	[227]				
$NpBr_5$	c	−186*	[230]						
$NpCl_3$	c	(−216)	[2656]	−200*	[323]	38*	[323]		
				−199.6*	[227]				
$NpCl_4$	c	(−238.0)	[2656]	−216*	[323]	47.5*	[323]		
				−214.9*	[227]				
$NpCl_5$	c	(−246)	[1309]	−221*	[323]	62*	[323]		
				−219.1*	[227]				
NpF_3	c			−342*	[323]	26*	[323]		
				−340.9*	[227]				
NpF_4	c			−406*	[323]	36*	[323]		
				−403.2*	[229]				

1. $T = 293\ ^\circ K$. 2. $T = 295\ ^\circ K$. 3. $S^\circ_{298} - S^\circ_0$. 4. $NiTi_2$ phase. 5. γ phase. 6. Ni_3Ti phase. 7. $t = 22\ ^\circ C$. 8. Heat of dissociation, *kcal/g-atom* at high temperatures. 9. $T = 257\ ^\circ K$. 10. $t = 60\ ^\circ C$. 11. In $HCl \cdot 55H_2O$.

1	2	3		4		5		6	
NpF_6	g					88.75	[2483]	30.92	[2483]
						88.640	[2019]	30.871	[3019]
NpH_2	c	–28	[2001]						
NpI_3	c			–121*	[323]	56*	[323]		
				–119.5*	[227]				
NpI_4	c			–120*	[227]				
NpI_5	c	–131*	[230]						
NpO, cubic	c					16.6	[2662]		
$NpOCl_2$	c	–248*	[687]			34*	[687]		
NpO_2	c	–277	[1069]	–233.5*	[1045]	19.19	[2665]	15.82	[2665]
		–246*	[887]						
NpO_2, cubic	c					19.8	[2662]		
NpO_2^+	d[1]			–221.0*	[323]	12*	[323]		
NpO_2^{2+}	d[1]			–194.5*	[323]	–17*	[323]		
$NpO_{2.67}$, orthorhombic	c					23.9	[2662]		
Np_2O_5	c	–510*	[887]						
$Np_2(SO_4)_3$	c	–911*	[2683]						
Np_2S_3	c	–218*	[2683]						
O	g	(59.556)[2]	[568]	(55.393)	[568]	(38.467)	[568]	(5.237)	[568, 1618a]
		(59.550)	[2479]	(55.387)	[2479]	(38.47)	[1685, 2479]	(5.24)	[1685, 2479]
		(59.553)[3]	[2358]	(55.388)	[2358]	(38.486)[4]	[476]	(5.2327)[4]	[476]
		(59.5566)[5]	[1830]			(38.4686)	[1830]	(5.2373)	[1830]
		(59.558)[6]	[570]			(38.4687)	[154, 570]		
		(59.559)[7]	[1618a]	(55.395)	[1618a]	(38.468)	[1618a]		
	d	55*	[695]						
O^+	g	(374.947)[8]	[568]	369.731	[568]	37.009	[568]		
		(374.963)[9]	[570]			37.0109	[154, 570]		
		(375.070)[10]	[2358]			37.027[4]	[476]	4.9662[4]	[476]
O^{2+}	g	(1182.85)[11]	[569]						
		(1187.26)[12]	[2358]						
O^{3+}	g	(2448.89)[11]	[568]						
		(2455.88)[13]	[2358]						
O^{4+}	g	(4234.12)[11]	[568]						
		(4242.6)[14]	[2358]						
O^{5+}	g	(6860.8)[11]	[568]						
		(6870.8)[15]	[2358]						
O^{6+}	g	(10046)[11]	[568]						

		(10057)[16]	[2358]						
O^{7+}	g	(27095)[11]	[568]						
		(2710)[17]	[2358]						
O^{8+}	g	(47189)[11]	[568]						
		(47203)[18]	[2358]						
O^-	g	24.243[19]	[568]	21.798	[568]	37.69	[568]	5.18	[563]
		24.240[20]	[570]			37.6886	[570]		
		24.29[21]	[2358]						
	d	−12*	[695]						
O^{2-}	g	231	[693]			34.26	[66]		
O_2	g					(49.0070)	[1830]	(7.0215)	[1830]
						(49.005)	[568]	(7.015)	[568]
						(49.030)[4]	[476]	(7.0208)[4]	[476]
						(49.01)	[1685, 2479]	(7.02)	[1685, 1618a, 2479]
						(49.004)	[1618a]		
						(48.996)	[2358]	(7.016)	[2358]
						(49.0065)	[154, 830]		
		(−2.8)	[2358]	3.9	[2358]	26.5	[2358]		
	d	(−3.8)	[2182]	13.0*	[323]				
		(−2.90)	[568]						
O_2^+		(280.121)[22]	[568]	278.612	[568]	49.077	[568]	7.331	[568]
	g	(280.176)[23]	[570]			49.0785	[154, 570]		
		(281.48)[24]	[2358]			49.307[4]	[476]	6.9795[4]	[476]
O_2^-		−17	[695]			47.1	[728]		
	g	−13.3[11]	[568]						
		−3*	[695]						
O_2^{2-}	d	120*	[695]			46.4	[728]		
	g	11*	[695]						
O_3	d	(34.0)[25]	[568]	(38.898)	[568, 1618a]	(57.08)	[568]	(9.38)	[568]
	g	(34.1)[26]	[1618a, 2358]	(39.0)	[2358]	(57.07)	[982]	(9.37)	[982, 1685]
		(34.5)[27]	[297]			(57.09)	[1685]		
						(57.082)	[570]		
				(38.997)	[1618a]			(9.378)	[1618a]

1. In $HCl \cdot 55H_2O$. 2. $\Delta H_0^\circ = (58.985)$ [568]. 3. $\Delta H_0^\circ = (58.983)$ [2358]. 4. $T = 300$ °K. 5. $\Delta H_0^\circ = (58.9865)$ [1830]. 6. $\Delta H_0^\circ = (58.597)$ [570]. 7. $\Delta H_0^\circ = (58.989)$ [1618a]. 8. $\Delta H_0^\circ = (373.022)$ [568]. 9. $\Delta H_0^\circ = (373.039)$ [570]. 10. $\Delta H_0^\circ = (373.019)$ [2358]. 11. ΔH_0°. 12. $\Delta H_0^\circ = (1183.73)$ [2358]. 13. $\Delta H_0^\circ = (2450.87)$ [2358]. 14. $\Delta H_0^\circ = (4236.1)$ [2358]. 15. $\Delta H_0^\circ = (6862.8)$ [2358]. 16. $\Delta H_0^\circ = (10048)$ [2358]. 17. $\Delta H_0^\circ = (27097)$ [2358]. 18. $\Delta H_0^\circ = 47191$ [2358]. 19. $\Delta H_0^\circ = 25.19$ [568]. 20. $\Delta H_0^\circ = 25.187$ [570]. 21. $\Delta H_0^\circ = 25.20$ [2358]. 22. $\Delta H_0^\circ = (278.49)$ [568]. 23. $\Delta H_0^\circ = (278.545)$ [570]. 24. $\Delta H_0^\circ = (280.0)$ [2358]. 25. $\Delta H_0^\circ = 34.637$ [568]. 26. $\Delta H_0^\circ = 34.74$ [1618a, 2358]. 27. $\Delta H_0^\circ = 35.132$ [570].

1	2	3		4		5		6	
O_3	d	(32.2)	[568]						
		(30.1)	[2358]						
O_3^+	g	329.8[1]	[568]						
O_3^-	g	−11	[2704]						
O_4	g	−0.13[1]	[568]						
OCN^-	g					53.0	[1797]		
OD	g	(8.81)[2]	[2358]	7.76	[2358]	(45.321)	[2358]	(7.140)	[2358]
		(8.824)[3]	[570]			(44.32)[4]	[1455]	(7.153)[5]	[1455]
		(8.5)	[1352]						
OH	g	(9.311)[6]	[568]	(8.181)	[568]	(43.890)	[568, 2358]	(7.143)	[568, 2358]
		(9.31)[7]	[2358]	(8.18)	[2358]	(49.92)[5]	[2104]	(7.136)	[1618a, 2104]
		(9.3125)[8]	[1830]			(43.8927)	[1830]	(7.1439]	[1830]
		(9.319)[9]	[570]			(43.8917)	[570]		
		(8.9)	[1352]			(43.93)[5]	[1455]	(7.14)[5]	[1455]
		(9.33)[10]	[1618a]	(8.194)	[1618a]	(43.918)	[1618a]		
OH^+	d	0*	[695]						
	g	314.809[11]	[568]	312.261	[568]	43.657	[568]	6.961	[568]
		314.768[12]	[570]			43.6592	[570]		
		327*	[2230]						
		317.5[13]	[2358]						
	d	143*	[695]						
OH^-	g	(−32.154)[14]	[568]	−30.926	[568]	40.97	[568]	6.96	[568]
		(−32.195)[15]	[570]			40.975	[570]		
		(−36)	[693]			38.4	[728]		
		(−33.67)[16]	[2358]						
	d	(−54.97)	[2358]	(−37.594)	[2358]	(−2.57)	[2358]	−35.5	[2358]
		(−54.98)	[88, 568]						
OT	g	8.628[17]	[570]			46.20[18]	[1455]	7.161[19]	[1455]
O_2H	g	4.907[20]	[568]	7.961	[568]	54.36	[568]	8.34	[568]
		5[21]	[2358]						
		−1*	[695]						
		5.0[22]	[1618a]	8.049	[1618a]	54.383	[1618a]	8.338	[1618a]
O_2H^+	g	271[23]	[2358]						
		280*	[2230]						
	d	110*	[695]						
O_2H^-	g	−42*	[695]						
	d	−38.32	[2358]	−16.1	[2358]				
		−38.0	[568]						

Os	g	(160.000)	[2479]	(148.610)	[2479]	(45.8*)	[244]		
		(186.4)	[2091]			(46.002)	[1589]		
		(189.0)	[937]			(46.00)	[1685]		
$OsCl_4$	c	−60.9	[262]			37.0	[262]		
$OsCl_6^{2-}$	d			−119*	[323]				
$OsCl_6^{3-}$	d			−139*	[323]				
OsF_6	g					85.556	[2627]	28.880	[2627]
OsO_2	g	46*	[405]	44*	[405]				
	c	−62*	[887]	−50*	[323]				
OsO_3	g	−35.1*	[2650]	−32.1*	[2650]	13.1*	[2650]		
		−25*	[407]	−21	[407]				
	c	−45.5	[263]			31.2	[263]		
OsO_4	g	(−80.5*)	[1045]	(−68.5*)	[1045]	(70.1)	[1685]	17.73	[1685]
OsO_4, white	c	(−92.5*)	[1045]	(−71.5*	[1045]	(39.2)	[1685]		
OsO_4, yellow	c	(−94.0*)	[1045]	(−71.5*)	[1045]	(32.2)	[1685]		
OsS_2	c	(−24.0)	[2625]	−34.4*	[323]	20.1*	[323]		
				−34.3*	[229]				
$OsSe_2$	c					19.5*	[2650]		
$OsTe_2$	c					24.0*	[2650]		
P	g	(79.800)	[2479]	(69.805)	[2479]	(38.97)	[1685]		
		(75.18)[24]	[1830]			(38.9800)	[1618a, 1830]	(4.9681)	[1830]
		(79.795)[25]	[1618a]	(69.798)	[1618a]				
		(75.588)[26]	[570]			(38.9799)	[570]		
						(38.978)	[2358]		
	l	4.322	[1618a]	2.891	[1618a]	10.249	[1618a]	6.292	[1618a]
P, white, cubic	c	4.180	[2479]	2.888	[2479]	(9.80)	[1685, 2479]	(5.63)	[1685, 2479]
		−4.173[27]	[1618a]	−2.871	[1618a]	(9.818)	[1618a]		
						(9.82)	[2358]	(5.698)	[1618a, 2358]
P, IV	c					9.981	[1830]	5.694	[1830]
P, red, triclinic	c	(−4.2)[28]	[2358]	−2.9	[2358]	5.45	[1618a, 2358]	5.07	[2358]
								5.069	[1618a]
						5.46	[1685, 2479]	4.98	[1685, 2479]
						7.0*	[323]		
P, red	v	−1.8	[2358]						
P, black	c	(−9.4)	[2358]			5.457	[435]	5.158	[435]

1. ΔH_0°. 2. $\Delta H_0^\circ = (8.72)$ [2358]. 3. $\Delta H_0^\circ = (8.739)$ [570]. 4. In $HCl \cdot 55H_2O$. 5. $T = 300\ ^\circ K$. 6. $\Delta H_0^\circ = (9.251)$ [568]. 7. $\Delta H_0^\circ = (9.25)$ [2358]. 8. $\Delta H_0^\circ = (9.2549)$ [1830]. 9. $\Delta H_0^\circ = (9.259)$ [570]. 10. $\Delta H_0^\circ = (9.723)$ [1618a]. 11. $\Delta H_0^\circ = 313.3$ [568]. 12. $\Delta H_0^\circ = 313.259$ [570]. 13. $\Delta H_0^\circ = 316$ [2358]. 14. $\Delta H_0^\circ = (-30.7)$ [568]. 15. $\Delta H_0^\circ = (-30.741)$ [570]. 16. $\Delta H_0^\circ = (-32.3)$ [2358]. 17. $\Delta H_0^\circ = 8.525$ [570]. 18. In $HCl \cdot 55H_2O$. 19. $T = 300\ ^\circ K$. 20. $\Delta H_0^\circ = 5.6$ [568]. 21. $\Delta H_0^\circ = 6$ [2358]. 22. $\Delta H_0^\circ = 5.697$ [1618a]. 23. $\Delta H_0^\circ = 272$ [2358]. 24. $\Delta H_0^\circ = 74.9810$ [1830]. 25. $\Delta H_0^\circ = 79.176$ [1618a]. 26. $\Delta H_0^\circ = 75.371$ [570]. 27. $\Delta H_0^\circ = 3.754$ [1618a]. 28. $\Delta H_0^\circ = -3.78$ [2358].

1	2	3		4		5		6	
P, black	c					5.3	[1685]		
P, violet	c					7.4	[1685]		
P_2	g	(42.725)	[2479]	(30.442)	[2479]	(52.11)	[1618a, 2479]	(7.65)	[1685, 2479]
		(34.5)	[2358]	(24.8)	[2358]	(52.108)	[2358]		
		(33.4457)[1]	[1830]			(52.1076)	[1830]	(7.6561)	[1830]
		(34.285)[2]	[570]			(52.092)	[570]		
		(42.68)[3]	[1618a]	(30.393)	[1618a]			(7.657)	[1618a]
						(52.10)	[1685]		
P_4	g	(14.08)[4]	[2358]	(5.85)	[2358]	(66.89)	[2358]	(16.05)	[2358]
		(14.04)[5]	[1830]			(66.8954)	[1830]	(16.0516)	[1830]
		(14.073)[6]	[570]			(66.890)	[570]		
		(13.2)	[2464]	(5.7)	[2464]	(64.08)	[2536]	(11.72)	[2536]
		(14.0)	[1073, 2479]			(66.72)	[1073]		
		(30.820)[7]	[2479]	(17.397)	[2479]	(66.85)	[2479]	(16.05)	[2358, 2479]
		(30.6)[8]	[2237]						
		(38.7)[9]	[2237]						
		(30.771)[10]	[1618a]	(17.327)	[1618a]	(66.893)	[1618a]	(16.051)	[1618a]
P_4, red, IV	c	−12.5	[1537]						
P_4, red	v	−7.0	[1537]						
PBr	g	43[11]	[1618a]	32.298	[1618a]	59.537	[1618a]	8.460	[1618a]
$PBrCl_2$	g					79.90	[27]		
$PBrF_2$	g					79.50	[27]		
PBr_2Cl	g					82.94	[27]		
PBr_2F	g					79.95	[27]		
PBr_3	g	(−33.3)	[2358]	(−38.9)	[2358]	(83.17)	[2358]	18.16	[2358]
		(−34.9)	[964]	(−43.8*)	[229]	(83.3)	[1685]	18.20	[1685]
		(−28.9)	[1482a]						
		(−30.7)[12]	[1618a]	(−37.611)	[1618a]	(83.206)	[1618a]	18.173	[1618a]
	l	(−44.1)	[2358]	−42.0	[2358]	57.4	[2358]		
		(−46.5)	[964]						
		(−40.5)	[1482a]						
	c	−54.6	[1220]						
PBr_5	c	−64.5	[2358]						
PCl	g	35.757*[13]	[570]			56.643	[570]		
		35.0[14]	[1618a]	27.625	[1618a]	56.829	[1618a]	8.298	[1618a]
$PClF_2$	g					70.08	[27]		
PCl_2F	g					73.63	[27]		
PCl_3	g	(−68.6)[15]	[2358]	(−64.0)	[2358]	(74.49)	[2358]	17.17	[1685, 2358]

		(−71.6)	[964]	(−65.30)	[2464, 2725[	(74.4)	[1818]	17.2	[1818]
		(−71.62)[16]	[1830]			(74.5039)	[1830]	17.1673	[1830]
		(−66.20)[17]	[570]			(74.505)	[570]		
		(−65.5)	[2039a]			(74.5)	[1685]		
		(−66.7)	[1773]						
		(−66.62)	[2039]						
		(−61.029)[18]	[1618a]	(−57.761)	[1618a]	(74.422)	[1618a]	17.215	[1618a]
	l	(−76.4)	[2358]	−65.1	[2358]	51.9	[2358]		
		(−74.4)	[370]	−68.6*	[323]	52.1	[1680]		
		(−79.4)	[964]	−69.7*	[229]	52.0	[1685]		
		(−79.6)	[2039]						
		(73.3)	[2039a]						
PCl_3^+	g	181[19]	[2358]						
PCl_5	g	(−89.6)[20]	[2358]	(−73.0)	[2358]	(87.11)	[2358]	26.96	[2358]
		(−88.287)[21]	[570]	(−74.80)	[2664, 2725]	(87.040)	[570]		
		(−84*)	[358]			(86.7)	[1685]	26.75	[1685]
		(−81.913)[22]	[1618a]	(−66.519)	[1618a]	(87.043)	[1618a]	26.743	[1618a]
	l			−92.0*	[229]				
	c	(−106.0)	[2358]			39.8	[1685]		
PD	g					48.3	[1685]	7.10	[1685]
PDHT	g					55.03	[27]	10.97	[27]
PDH_2	g					53.38	[589]	9.20	[589]
						53.44	[27]	9.29	[27]
						53.37	[2537]	9.06	[2537]
PDT_2	g					56.33	[2537]	10.60	[2537]
						55.36	[27]	10.65	[27]
PD_2H	g					54.30	[589]	9.61	[589]
						54.35	[27]	9.70	[27]
						54.25	[2537]	9.45	[2537]
PD_2T	g					55.72	[2537]	10.28	[2537]
						55.77	[27]	10.39	[27]
PD_3	g					52.94	[2489]	10.00	[2489]
						52.97	[588]	10.12	[588, 1685]
						52.9	[1685]		
PF	g	−11.331*[23]	[2342]			53.762	[1685]		
		−14.0[24]	[1618a]	−21.177	[1618a]	53.744	[1618a]	7.557	[1618a]

1. $\Delta H_0^\circ = 33.8821$ [1830]. 2. $\Delta H_0^\circ = 34.685$ [570]. 3. $\Delta H_0^\circ = 42.276$ [1618a]. 4. $\Delta H_0^\circ = 15.83$ [2358]. 5. $\Delta H_0^\circ = 15.7913$ [1830]. 6. $\Delta H_0^\circ = 15.751$ [570]. 7. From colorless modification. 8. From red modification. 9. From black modification. 10. $\Delta H_0^\circ = 30.841$ [1618a]. 11. $\Delta H_0^\circ = 44.519$ [1618a]. 12. $\Delta H_0^\circ = -25.293$ [1618a]. 13. $\Delta H_0^\circ = 35.921$* [570]. 14. $\Delta H_0^\circ = 34.727$ [1618a]. 15. $\Delta H_0^\circ = -67.85$ [2358]. 16. $\Delta H_0^\circ = -70.8642$ [1830]. 17. $\Delta H_0^\circ = -65.462$ [570]. 18. $\Delta H_0^\circ = 60.694$ [1618a]. 19. $\Delta H_0^\circ = 180$ [2358]. 20. $\Delta H_0^\circ = -88.33$ [2358]. 21. $\Delta H_0^\circ = -87.00$ [570]. 22. $\Delta H_0^\circ = -81.027$ [1618a]. 23. $\Delta H_0^\circ = -11.129$* [570]. 24. $\Delta H_0^\circ = -14.2$ [1618a].

1	2	3		4		5		6	
PF_2	g	−103.377*[1]	[2342]			62.330	[570]		
		−105*[2]	[1618a]	−107.478	[1618a]	62.207	[1618a]	10.677	[1618a]
PF_3	g	−226.03	[1137]	−242.36	[1217]	(65.15)	[1217]	14.03	[1217, 2358]
		−215.00*[3]	[570]			(65.152)	[570]		
		−222.3084[4]	[1830]			(65.1539)	[1830]	14.0278	[1830]
		−219.6[5]	[2358]			(65.28)	[2358]		
		−226.03	[1482]	−214.5	[2358]	(65.3)	[1685]	14.04	[1685]
		−212*[6]	[1618a]	−208.133	[1618a]	(65.151)	[1618a]	14.028	[1618a]
PF_5	g	−381.4	[2358]			(65.19)	[2690]	14.03	[2690]
		−315.00*[7]	[570]			(68.949)	[570]		
		−377.2[8]	[1618a]	−360.553	[1618a]	(70.735)	[1618a]	20.066	[1618a]
PH	g	56.757*	[570]	46.869	[570]				
		50.2825[9]	[1830]	40.8687	[1830]			6.9687	[1830]
		59.17[10]	[1618a]	51.467	[1618a]	46.891	[1618a]	6.969	[1618a]
PHT_2	g					55.67	[27]	10.24	[27]
						55.53	[2537]	10.00	[2537]
PH_2	g	30.1*[11]	[1618a]	25.884	[1618a]	50.8	[1618a]	8.312	[1618a]
PH_2T	g					54.18	[27]	9.56	[27]
						54.10	[2537]	9.27	[2537]
PH_3	g	(1.3)[12]	[1482a, 2358]	(3.2)	[2358]	(50.22)	[2358]	8.87	[588, 726, 1685, 2358]
		(4.1)	[2464]	(3.14)	[2464, 2725]	(50.23)	[726]		
		(1.75)[13]	[1830]	(1.3)	[1437]	(50.2243)	[1830]	8.8678	[1830]
		(3.1)[14]	[157]			(50.20)	[2489]	8.76	[2489]
		(2.3)	[2259]			(50.24)	[588]		
						(50.29)	[1685]		
		(5.47)[15]	[1618a]	(6.073)	[1618a]	(50.238)	[1618a]	8.868	[1618a]
	d	−2.16	[2358]	0.35	[2358]	48.2	[2358]		
PH_3^+	g	242.6[16]	[2358]						
PH_4^+	g	159	[1482a]			48.82	[726]	10.01	[726]
	d			16.2	[2358]				
PH_4Br	c	(−30.5)	[2358]	−11.4	[2358]	26.3	[2358]		
		(−29.5)	[2636a]	−5.6*	[229]				
PH_4Cl	c	(−34.7)	[2358]	−16.9*	[229]				
		(−42.5)	[2636a]						
PH_4I	c	(−16.7)	[2358]	0.2	[2358]	29.4	[2358]	(26.2)	[2358]
		(−15.8)	[2636a]	7.9	[229]	32.1	[1685]	(26.16)	[1685]
PH_4OH	d	−70.48	[2358]	−56.34	[2358]	65	[2358]		

PI_3	g					89.45	[2358]	18.73	[2358]
						89.5	[1685]	18.74	[1685]
	c	(−10.7)	[1221]	−8.99*	[323]	46*	[323]		
		(−10.9)	[2358]	−10.7*	[229]				
PN	g	(23.686)[17]	[570]			(50.434)	[570]		
		(23.322)[18]	[1830]			(50.4374)	[1830]	(7.0965)	[1830]
						(50.43)	[1685]	(7.10)	[1685]
						(50.437)	[2358]		
		(25.043)[19]	[1618a]	18.453	[1618a]	(50.437)	[1618a]	(7.096)	[1618a]
$\frac{1}{n}(PN)_n$	c	(−15)	[2358]						
$(PNCl_2)_3$	g	−175.9	[1483]						
	c	−194.1	[1483]						
$(PNCl_2)_4$	g	−236.1	[1483]						
	c	−259.2	[1483]						
PO	g	(−6.1067)[20]	[1830]	−15.9*	[227]	53.2245	[1830]	7.5874	[1830]
		(−7.20)[21]	[2342]	−15.0*	[1045]	53.14	[1685]	7.59	[1685]
		(−1.455)[22]	[1618a]	−8.391	[1618a]	53.213	[1618a]	7.587	[1618a]
						53.222	[570]		
						53.221	[2358]		
						59.3	[2585]	9.44	[2585]
PO_2	g	−71.0[23]	[1618a]	−72.834	[1618a]	60.607	[1618a]	9.897	[1618a]
$POBr_3$	g	−94	[964]			86.0	[1685]	21.15	[1685]
						85.97	[2358]	21.48	[2358]
						85.987	[2024]	21.480	[2024]
		−93[24]	[1618a]	−93.432	[1618a]	85.978	[1618a]	21.478	[1618a]
	c	(−110.1)	[964]	−102.9*	[229]				
		(−109.6)	[2358]						
$POClF_2$	g	−228.0[25]	[1618a]	−218.172	[1618a]	72.081	[1618a]	16.453	[1618a]
$POCl_2F$	g	−179.0[26]	[1618a]	−169.782	[1618a]	76.548	[1618a]	18.958	[1618a]
$POCl_3$	g	(−133.48)	[2358]	(−122.60)	[2358]	(77.76)	[2081, 2358]	20.30	[1685, 2081, 2358]
		(−134.3)	[964]	(−123.0*)	[229]	(77.37)	[2730]	20.16	[2730]
		(−134.60)[27]	[570]	(−127.30)	[2464, 2725]	(77.368)	[570]		
		(−134.0)	[2081]			(77.8)	[1685]		
						(77.213)	[2024]	20.160	[2024]

1. $\Delta H_0^\circ = -102.629^*$ [570]. 2. $\Delta H_0^\circ = -104.696^*$ [1618a]. 3. $\Delta H_0^\circ = -213.662^*$ [570]. 4. $\Delta H_0^\circ = -220.9539$ [1830]. 5. $\Delta H_0^\circ = -218.25$ [2358]. 6. $\Delta H_0^\circ = -211.065^*$ [1618a]. 7. $\Delta H_0^\circ = -312.009^*$ [570]. 8. $\Delta H_0^\circ = -374.88$ [1618a]. 9. $\Delta H_0^\circ = 50.5094$ [1830]. 10. $\Delta H_0^\circ = 58.977$ [1618a]. 11. $\Delta H_0^\circ = 30.594$ [1618a]. 12. $\Delta H_0^\circ = 3.2$ [2358]. 13. $\Delta H_0^\circ = 3.6452$ [570]. 14. From white phosphorus. 15. $\Delta H_0^\circ = 6.945$ [1618a]. 16. $\Delta H_0^\circ = 243$ [2358]. 17. $\Delta H_0^\circ = 23.907$ [570]. 18. $\Delta H_0^\circ = 23.5606$ [1830]. 19. $\Delta H_0^\circ = 24.861$ [1618a]. 20. $\Delta H_0^\circ = -6.0324$ [1830]. 21. $\Delta H_0^\circ = -7.142$ [570]. 22. $\Delta H_0^\circ = 1.801$ [1618a]. 23. $\Delta H_0^\circ = -70.611$ [1618a]. 24. $\Delta H_0^\circ = -87.056$ [1618a]. 25. $\Delta H_0^\circ = -226.287$ [1618a]. 26. $\Delta H_0^\circ = -177.779$ [1618a]. 27. $\Delta H_0^\circ = -133.226$ [570].

1	2	3		4		5		6	
$POCl_3$	g	(−129.631)[1]	[1618a]	(−120.055)	[1618a]	(77.767)	[1618a]	20.296	[1618a]
	l	(−142.7)	[2358]	−124.5	[2358]	53.17	[2081, 2358]	33.17	[2081, 2358]
		(−143.8)	[964]						
		(−144.4)	[2039]						
		(−143.2)	[2039a]						
	c	−146.4	[2081]						
		−145.81[2]	[2358]						
POF_3	g	−289.5[3]	[2358]	−277.9	[2358]	68.11	[2358]	16.41	[2358]
		−286*[4]	[570]			68.099	[570]		
						68.2	[1685]	16.43	[1685]
						68.25	[2730]	16.50	[2730]
		−282*[5]	[1618a]	−271.774*	[1618a]	68.222	[1618a]	16.506	[1618a]
POI_3	g					93.0	[1685]		
PO_3F^{2-}	d			−280.8	[2358]				
PS	g	10.8465[6]	[1830]			55.9688	[1830]	8.42	[1830]
		40.169*[7]	[570]			56.152	[570]		
		22.50[8]	[1618a]	9.694	[1618a]	56.033	[1618a]	8.423	[1618a]
$PSBr_3$	g					89.003	[2024]	22.696	[2024]
						89.07	[2358]	22.69	[1618a, 2358]
						88.8	[1685]		
		−63.0	[1618a]	−69.389	[1618a]	89.084	[1618a]		
	c					55.2	[2358]		
$PSCl_3$	g					(80.47)	[2358]	21.39	[2358]
						(79.241)	[2024]	20.991	[2024]
						(80.55)	[2730]	21.47	[1685, 2730]
						(80.6)	[1685]		
		−86.8[9]	[1618a]	−83.1	[1618a]	(80.604)	[1618a]	21.474	[1618a]
	l	−79.2	[1507]						
PSF	g	−37*[10]	[1618a]	−45.66*	[1618a]	66.35	[1618a]	10.621	[1618a]
PSF_3	g					71.3	[1685]	17.98	[1685]
						70.875	[2024]	17.971	[2024]
		−250[11]	[1618a]	−245.716	[1618a]	71.382	[1618a]	18.037	[1618a]
PSI_3	g					96.0	[1685]		
P_2H_4	g	5.0	[1437, 1437a]						
	l	−1.2	[2358]						
P_2I_4	g	10*	[1482a]						
	c			−19.8*	[323]	44.2*	[323]		
P_2O_3	c	−270	[1754]	−250.1*	[229]				

P_2O_5	c	-370	[887]			32.5*	[1773]		
						29.7*	[1501]		
$P_2O_7^{4-}$	d	(−542.8)	[2358]	-459.8	[2358]	-25	[2358]		
P_2S_3	c	−19.2	[2358]						
P_2S_5	c	60*	[1480]						
P_3N_5	c	(−71.53)	[1618a]	-45.658	[1618a]	44.0	[1618a]	35.602	[1618a]
		(−71.4)	[2358]					(36)	[2358]
P_4H_2	c	6.9*	[323]	16.0*	[323]	40*	[323]		
P_4H_4	c	9.9	[2260]						
P_4O_6	g	-530	[964]			82.87	[1035]	34.80	[1035]
		-504.0[12]	[570]			82.935	[570]		
		-512.54[13]	[1618a]	-486.831	[1618a]	82.584	[1618a]	34.402	[1618a]
	c	-392	[1482]						
		-375[14]	[1482a]						
P_4O_8	g	-569.948*[15]	[570]			92.242	[570]		
P_4O_{10}	g	-687.00[16]	[2342]			95.46	[1035]	46.27	[1035]
		-688	[1482a]			94.326	[570]		
		-675.1[17]	[1618a]	-623.109	[1618a]	92.441	[1618a]	42.482	[1618a]
P_4O_{10}, hexagonal	c	(−713.2)[18]	[1537]	-644.8	[734, 2358]	54.70	[2358]	50.60	[734, 2358]
				-653.8*	[229]	54.68	[734]		
				-654.5*	[1045]	67.0*	[2228]		
		(−696.51)[19]	[1618a]	-633.543	[1618a]	55.627	[1618a]	52.067	[1618a]
	v	-727	[2358]	-667.8*	[229]				
P_2S_3	g	-19.408	[1618a]	-28.826	[1618a]	76.28	[1618a]	37.0	[1618a]
	l	-36.077	[1618a]	-37.513	[1618a]	49.51	[1618a]	44.0	[1618a]
P_4S_3, II	c					48.60	[983]	38.87	[983]
		-37.0	[1618a]	-37.986	[1618a]	48.0	[1618a]	35.0	[1618a]
P_4S_{10}	c					91.24	[983]	70.74	[983]
P_4Se_3	c					57.26	[983]	39.72	[983]
HPO_3	c	(−233.5)	[2358]						
	d	(−234.8*)	[323]	-215.8*	[323]	36*	[323]		
HPO_3^{2-}	d	(−231.6)	[2358]	-194.0*	[323]				
HPO_3F^-	d			-286.4	[2358]				
HPO_4^{2-}	d	(−309.37)	[2358]	(−260.91)	[2358]	(−8.0)	[2358]		

1. $\Delta H_0^\circ = -128.714$ [1618a]. 2. ΔH_0°. 3. $\Delta H_0^\circ = -287.39$ [2358]. 4. $\Delta H_0^\circ = -283.902$* [570]. 5. $\Delta H_0^\circ = -280.327$* [1618a]. 6. $\Delta H_0^\circ = 10.8845$ [1830]. 7. $\Delta H_0^\circ = 40.058$ [570]. 8. $\Delta H_0^\circ = 22.117$ [1618a]. 9. $\Delta H_0^\circ = -86.135$ [1618a]. 10. $\Delta H_0^\circ = -36.684$* [1618a]. 11. $\Delta H_0^\circ = -248.596$ [1618a]. 12. $\Delta H_0^\circ = -498.325$* [570]. 13. $\Delta H_0^\circ = -508.401$ [1618a]. 14. Calculated [234] from $\Delta H_{298}^\circ = -392$ [1482] and $\Delta H_{subl} = 17$ [1482a]. 15. $\Delta H_0^\circ = -563$* [570]. 16. $\Delta H_0^\circ = 678.779$ [570]. 17. $\Delta H_0^\circ = -668.069$ [1618a]. 18. $\Delta H_0^\circ = -705.82$ [2358]. 19. $\Delta H_0^\circ = -690.945$ [1618a].

1	2	3		4		5		6	
$HP_2O_7^{3-}$	d	(−543.7)	[2358]	−472.5	[2358]	15	[2358]		
$H_2PO_2^-$	d	−146.7	[2358]	−122.4*	[323]				
$H_2PO_3^-$	d	(−231.7)	[2358]	−202.35*	[323]	19*	[323]		
H_2PO_3F	d			−287.5	[2358]				
$H_2PO_4^-$	d	(−310.38)	[2358]	(−270.73)	[2358]	(21.6)	[2358]		
$H_2P_2O_7^{2-}$	d	(−544.6)	[2358]	−481.6	[2358]	42	[2358]		
H_3PO_2	c	(−144.5)	[2358]	−120*	[229]				
	d			−125.1*	[323]	38*	[323]		
H_3PO_3	c	(−230.5)	[2358]	−200.7*	[229]				
	d	(−230.6)	[2358]	−204.8*	[323]	40*	[323]		
		(−227.1)	[964, 2039]						
		(−226.0)	[1482a]						
$H_3PO_3^-$	d			−202.35*	[323]	19*	[323]		
H_3PO_4	g	−142.3	[2358]						
	l	−302.6	[1150]						
		−302.1	[1537]						
		−302.8	[2358]						
		−298.81	[1618a]	−264.44	[1618a]	34.993	[1618a]	48.00	[1618a]
	c	(−305.7)[1]	[1537, 2358]	−267.5	[2358]	26.41	[1150, 2358]	25.35	[1150, 2358]
		(−301.53)[2]	[1618a]	−264.604	[1618a]	26.421	[1618a]	25.384	[1618a]
				−269.0*	[229]				
	d			−274.2*	[323]				
		−307.92	[2358]	−273.10	[2358]	−37.8	[2358]		
		−308.3	[1537a]						
		−309.44	[1147a]						
$H_3PO_4.HClO_4$	c	−325.3	[2358]						
$H_3PO_4 \cdot 0.5H_2O$	c	(−342.1)[3]	[2358]	−296.9	[2358]	30.87	[2358]	30.12	[2358]
$H_3PO_4 \cdot H_2O$	c	−374.96	[2358]						
$H_3P_2O_7^-$	d	(−544.1)	[2358]	−484.7	[2358]	54	[2358]		
$H_4P_2O_5$	d	(−393.6)	[2358]						
$H_4P_2O_6$	d			−392*	[323]				
$H_4P_2O_7$, supercooled	l	−533.4	[2358]						
$H_4P_2O_7$	c	(−535.6)	[2358]	−478.8	[229]				
	d	(−542.2)	[2358]	−486.8	[2358]	68	[2358]		
$H_4P_2O_7 \cdot {}^3/_2H_2O$	l	(−637.3)	[2358]						
	c	(−640.9)	[2358]						
Pa	c					12.40	[1685, 2479]	6.79	[2479]
Pa^{5+}	d					5	[1069]		

$PaCl_4$	c	−267*				47*	[687]		
$PaCl_2O$	c	−277*	[687]			32*	[949]		
PaF_4	c	−477	[1069]						
PaO, cubic	c					15.8	[2662]		
PaO_2, cubic	c	−275*	[687]			18.4	[2662]		
$PaO_{2.3}$, cubic	c					17.8	[1685, 2078]		
						19.5	[2662]		
$PaO_{2.5}$, orthorhombic	c					21.0	[2662]		
Pa_2O_5	c	−530*	[887]						
Pb	g	(46.800)	[2479]	(38.929)	[2479]				
		(46.60)[4]	[1482a]	(38.73)	[1482a]				
		(46.837)[5]	[570]			41.8905	[570]		
		(46.747)[6]	[1618]	(38.874)	[1618a]	41.89	[1618a]		
	l	1.025	[1618a]	0.531	[1618a]	17.141	[1618a]	6.414	[1618a]
	c					(15.49)	[570, 1113, 1482a, 1685]	(6.32)	[570, 1482a, 2479]
								(6.39)	[1685]
						(15.484)	[1618a]	(6.414)	[1618a]
Pb^{2+}	g					41.90	[66]		
	d					(3.9)	[1685]		
Pb^{4+}	g					41.90	[66]		
	d			72.3	[323]				
Pb_2	g	(70*)	[1598]	50.3*	[323]	65.0	[1685]	8.72	[1685]
		(71.0*)	[402]						
		(79.5)[7]	[1618a]	68.693	[1618a]	67.216	[1618a]	8.825	[1618a]
PbB_2O_4	c	−372.0	[1618a]	−346.628	[1618a]	31.2	[1618a]	25.6	[1618a]
PbB_4O_7	c	−683.0	[1618a]	−637.47	[1618a]	39.9	[1618a]	40.2	[1618a]
PbB_6O_{10}	c	−1003	[1618a]	−937.311	[1618a]	48.6	[1618a]	55.2	[1618a]
						65.0	[1685]	8.79	[1685]
PbBr	g	13.3*[8]	[1618a]	3.98*	[1618a]	64.936	[1618a]	8.825	[1618a]
$PbBr_2$	g	−24.176	[1618a]	−33.287	[1618a]	82.426	[1618a]	13.682	[1618a]
	l	−63.001	[1618a]	−60.267	[1618a]	42.699	[1618a]	19.246	[1618a]
	c	−66.073[9]	[1618a]	(−62.134)	[1618a]	38.658	[1618a]	19.246	[1618a]
				(−62.105*)	[176]	(38.10*)	[176]		
$PbBr_4$	g	−44.0[10]	[1618a]	−48.024	[1618a]	101.75	[1618a]	25.008	[1618a]
$Pb(BrO_3)_2$	c	−32*	[232]	10.81*	[177]				
$Pb(CN)_2$	c	47*	[696, 2683]						

1. $\Delta H_0^\circ = -301.29$ [2358]. 2. $\Delta H_0^\circ = -297.541$ [1618a]. 3. $\Delta H_0^\circ = -336.899$ [2358]. 4. $\Delta H_0^\circ = 46.76$ [1482a]. 5. $\Delta H_0^\circ = 47.0$ [570]. 6. $\Delta H_0^\circ = 46.910$ [1618a]. 7. $\Delta H_0^\circ = 80.397$ [1618a]. 8. $\Delta H_0^\circ = 15.449$ [1618a]. 9. $\Delta H_0^\circ = -63.199$ [1618a]. 10. $\Delta H_0^\circ = -36.827$ [1618a].

1	2	3		4		5		6	
$PbCO_3$	c	(−167.313)	[2263]	(−150.00)	[2263]	(32.4)	[2263]	(20.89)	[1685]
				(−149.52*)	[177]	(30.7*)	[177]		
PbCl	g					62.3	[1685]	8.63	[1685]
		3.5[1]	[1618a]	−2.506	[1618a]	62.272	[1618a]	8.658	[1618a]
PbClF	c	−126*	[232]	−114.91*	[177]				
$PbCl_2$	g	−40.610[2]	[1618a]	−42.953	[1618a]	76.63	[1618a]	13.37	[1618a]
	l	−81.488	[1618a]	−72.413	[1618a]	38.336	[1618a]	17.485	[1618a]
	c			(−75.01*)	[176]	(32.4*)	[176]		
		−86.20[3]	[1618a]	(−75.386)	[1618a]			17.483	[1618a]
						(32.5)	[1618a, 1685]	18.35	[1685]
$PbCl_2 \cdot PbO$	c			−128.4*	[229]				
$PbCl_2 \cdot 2PbO$	c			−177.6*	[229]				
$PbCl_2 \cdot 3PbO$	c			−225.8*	[229]				
$PbCl_4$	g					89.4	[1685]	22.14	[1685]
		−75.0[4]	[1618a]	−66.013	[1618a]	91.919	[1618a]	24.125	[1618a]
	l	−78.85	[312]	−62*	[229]				
$Pb(ClO_3)_2$	c	−47*	[2683]						
$Pb(ClO_4)_2$	c	−56*	[2683]						
$PbCrO_4$	g	(−225.2*)	[323]						
	c	−215*	[232]	−203.6*	[323]	36.5*	[323]		
				−195.9*	[229]				
				−193.37*	[177]				
PbF	g	−8.986[5]	[570]			59.691	[570]		
						59.6	[1685]	8.20	[1685]
		−9.0*[6]	[1618a]	−14.939*	[1618a]	59.627	[1618a]	8.224	[1618a]
PbF_2	g	−106.43[7]	[570]			69.508	[570]		
	l	−156.4	[1618a]	−145.716	[1618a]	28.097	[1618a]	21.5	[1618a]
	c	(−158.3)	[1415]	(−148.10*)	[176]	(29.2*)	[176]	17.4*	[228]
		(−160.4)[8]	[570]			(27.0)	[570]	17.7	[570]
						(27.0*)	[890]		
						(23.0)	[1685]		
		(−159.6)	[1618a]	(−147.993)	[1618a]	(25.0)	[1618a]	21.5	[1618a]
PbF_4	g	−186[9]	[1618a]	−176.26	[1618a]	79.709	[1618a]	21.735	[1618a]
	c			−178.1*	[323]	35.5*	[323]		
				−203.7*	[227]				
PbH	g					52.70	[1685]	7.03	[1685]
		56.450[10]	[1618a]	49.995	[1618a]	52.737	[1618a]	7.045	[1618a]
$Pb(HCO_3)_2$	c	−348*	[2683]						

$PbHPO_3$	c			−208.3*	[323]	31.9*	[323]		
$PbHPO_4$	c	−311*	[232]	−282.86*	[177]				
$Pb(HS)_2$	c	−2*	[2683]						
$Pb(HSO_4)_2$	c	−423*	[2683]						
PbH_2	c	−10*	[2683]						
PbH_4	c	59.7	[2259]						
PbI	g					66.8	[1685]	8.85	[1685]
		25.70*[11]	[1618a]	14.522*	[1618a]	66.855	[1618a]	8.87	[1618a]
PbI_2	g	0.156[12]	[1618a]	−12.878	[1618a]	85.911	[1618a]	13.771	[1618a]
	l	−40.637	[1618a]	(−40.501)	[1628a]	42.786	[1618a]	18.92	[1618a]
	c			(−41.50*)	[176]	(42.2*)	[176]		
		−41.855[13]	[1618a]	(−41.446)	[1618a]	(41.86)	[1618a]	18.918	[1618a]
						(42.2)	[1685]		
PbI_4	g	0.40[14]	[1618a]	−12.45	[1618a]	111.416	[1618a]	25.41	[1618a]
$Pb(IO_3)_2$	c	−118*	[232]	−88.17*	[177]				
		−123.0	[615]						
		−120.8	[2457]						
$PbMoO_4$	c	(−249.7)	[1997]	−225.7	[2631]	39.7	[2631]	28.61	[2631]
		(−257.2*)	[170, 172]	−236.4*	[170, 172]				
				−231.7*	[323]	38.5*	[323]		
				−239.6*	[229]				
$Pb(NH_2)_2$	c	−1*	[2683]						
$Pb(NO_2)_2$	c	−62*	[2683]						
$Pb(NO_3)_2$	c			−60.3*	[323]	50.9*	[323]		
				−59.5*	[227]				
$Pb(N_3)_2$	c	(115.5)	[1356]	149.89	[1356]				
				135.1*	[323]	49.5*	[323]		
				126.3	[2500]	35.76	[2500]		
$PbO_{0.33}$	c	−49.17[15]	[965]						
$PbO_{0.57}$	c	−50.47[15]	[965]						
PbO	g	10.1	[1045]	5.0	[1045]	(57.34)	[1685]	7.76	[1685]
		11.565[16]	[570]			(57.344)	[570]		
		7*	[863]						
		11.477[17]	[1618a]	6.301	[1618a]	(57.346)	[1618a]	7.769	[1618a]
		4.5[18]	[1543]						
		11.2[19]	[398]						

1. $\Delta H_0^\circ = 3.901$ [1618a]. 2. $\Delta H_0^\circ = -40.218$ [1618a]. 3. $\Delta H_0^\circ = -86.412$ [1618a]. 4. $\Delta H_0^\circ = -74.631$ [1618a]. 5. $\Delta H_0^\circ = -8.5$ [570]. 6. $\Delta H_0^\circ = -8.516$* [1618a]. 7. $\Delta H_0^\circ = -105.645$ [570]. 8. $\Delta H_0^\circ = -160.445$ [570]. 9. $\Delta H_0^\circ = -184.859$ [1618a]. 10. $\Delta H_0^\circ = 57.032$ [1618a]. 11. $\Delta H_0^\circ = 26.451$* [1618a]. 12. $\Delta H_0^\circ = 0.881$ [1618a]. 13. $\Delta H_0^\circ = -41.745$ [1618a]. 14. $\Delta H_0^\circ = 0.949$ [1618a]. 15. Per *g-atom* Pb. 16. $\Delta H_0^\circ = 12.104$ [570]. 17. $\Delta H_0^\circ = 12.017$ [1618a]. 18. ΔH_0°; calculated [234] from $(\Delta H_0^\circ)_{subl} = 56.58$ [1543] and $(\Delta H_{298}^\circ)_{PbO(c)} = -52.07$ [2245]. 19. Calculated [234] from $(\Delta H_0^\circ)_{subl} = 63.984$ [400] and $(\Delta H_0^\circ)_{PbO(c)} = 52.07$ [2245].

1	2	3		4		5		6	
PbO	g	11.34[1]	[400]						
	l	−46.712	[1618a]	−40.916	[1618a]	20.546	[1618a]	10.95	[1618a]
PbO, yellow	c	(−52.0)	[570]	(−45.12*)	[176]	(15.6*)	[176]		
						(16.1)	[1685, 1725]	(10.95)	[1685, 1725]
		(−52.066)[2]	[1618a]	(−44.949)	[1618a]	(16.114)	[1618a]	(10.958)	[1618a]
						(16.42)	[293]	(10.94)	[293]
PbO	c	−52.1	[970]	−44.9	[970]	(16.1)	[293]		
PbO, red	c	(−52.4)[3]	[570]			(15.8)	[570]	10.95	[570, 1685]
		(−52.407)[4]	[1618a]	−45.134	[1618a]	(15.592)	[1618a]	10.943	[1618a]
						(15.6)	[1685, 1725]		
PbO_2	c	−64.547[5]	[1618a]	−50.769	[1618a]	18.277	[1618a]	14.871	[1618a]
$Pb(OH)_2$	c			(−102.2*)	[176]	(26.0*)	[176]		
$Pb(OH)_4^{2-}$	d			178.91	[7]				
$PbOHNO_3$	c			−72.6*	[323]	37.7*	[323]		
				−76.5*	[229]				
$PbO_{1.40}$	c			−49.76	[966]				
$PbO_{1.55}$	c			−50.40	[966]				
PbO_2	c	(−51*)	[2683]	(−51.00*)	[176]	(13.8*)	[176]	(15.45)	[1685]
$Pb(ReO_4)_2$	c	−402*	[2683]						
PbS	g	55.7[6]	[1012]			60.24	[1685]	8.37	[1685]
	c	(−22.5)	[970]	(−22.1)	[970]	(21.8)	[970, 1685]	21.8	[1685]
				(−24.22*)	[176]	(28.9*)	[176]		
$PbSO_3$	c	−143*	[2683]						
		−157.6*	[1172]						
		−157.0	[614]						
$PbSO_4$	c	(−219.3)	[614]	(−192.9*)[7]	[250]	(33.51)	[1278]	(24.67)	[1278]
		(−219.26)	[614]	(−193.96*)	[177]	(35.5*)	[177]	(24.39)	[1685]
$PbSO_4 \cdot PbO$	c			−258.9*	[323]	48.7*	[323]		
						48	[1685]		
$PbSO_4 \cdot 2PbO$	c					63	[1685]		
$PbSO_4 \cdot 3PbO$	c					78	[1685]		
PbS_2O_3	c			−134.0*	[323]	35.4*	[323]		
				−141.7*	[229]				
PbS_3O_6	c			−213.8*	[323]	55.4*	[323]		
PbSe	g					63.0	[1685]	8.67	[1685]
	c	(−18.0)	[970]	−17.7	[970]	24.5	[970, 1685]	12.00	[1685]
				−15.4*	[323]	26.9*	[323]		
				−17.6*	[229]	23.4*	[247]		

				-20.6*	[4]				
$PbSeO_3$	c	-127.40	[507, 508]	-110.85	[508]	43.47	[508]		
$PbSeO_4$	c	(-148.7)	[505]	-120.5	[505]	28.81	[505]		
				-123.0*	[229]	28.9*	[498]	26*	[498]
				-122*	[323]	37*	[323]		
				-119.0	[215]	24.7	[215]		
$PbSiO_3$	c	-266.4	[770]	(-246.3)	[770]	(26.2)	[1685, 1727]	21.52	[1685, 1726]
		(-3.75)[8]	[1681]	(-3.95)[8]	[1681]	(32.0*)	[246]		
						(28.7)	[1680]		
	v			-239.2*	[229]	30.2	[1685]	22.43	[1685]
$PbSiO_4$	v			-285.9*	[229]				
Pb + Sn (50% Pb)	c							0.04272[9]	[2727]
PbTe	g					64.9	[1685]	8.78	[1685]
	c	(-16.6)	[970]	-16.3	[970]	26.3	[970, 1685]	12.08	[1685]
		(-16.0)	[2625]	-18.1*	[323]	27.6*	[323]		
				-17.1*	[229]	26.4	[1680]		
				-16.4*	[4]				
$PbWO_4$	c	-280.6*	[172]	-256.6*	[172]	40.2	[2631]	28.63	[2631]
		-273*	[2683]			36.3	[1725]	25.74	[1725]
		-277.0	[178]	-250.0	[178]	32.03	[178]		
$Pb_2B_{10}O_{17}$	c	-1694	[1618a]	-1581.528	[1618a]	84.3	[1618a]	97.2	[1618a]
$Pb_2Fe(CN)_6$	c	-134.2	[2234]						
Pb_2O_3	g					36.3	[1685]	25.74	[1685]
Pb_2S_2	g	66.6[10]	[1012]						
Pb_2SiO_4	c					(44.6)	[1685, 1726]	32.78	[1685]
Pb_3O_4	c	-175.311[11]	[1618a]	-147.265	[1618a]	50.394	[1618a]	35.136	[1618a]
$Pb_3(OH)_2(CO_3)_2$	c			-409.1*	[323]				
$Pb_3(PO_4)_2$	c					(84.5)	[1685]	(61.25)	[1685]
$Pb_3(VO_4)_2$	c	-39.37	[2721]						
		-39.80	[1682]						
$HPb(OH)_3$	c			-158.85*	[6]				
$HPbO_2^-$	d			-81.0*	[323]				
$H_2Pb(OH)_4$	c			-215.50*	[6]				
$H_4Pb(OH)_4$	c			-328.80*	[6]				
Pd	g	(94.000)	[2479]	(84.802)	[2479]	(39.90)	[1685]		
		(84.33)[12]	[1589]	(75.13)	[1589]				

1. Calculated [234] from $(\Delta H_0^\circ)_{subl} = 63.414$ [401] and $(\Delta H_{298}^\circ)_{PbO(c)} = -52.07$ [2245]. 2. $\Delta H_0^\circ = -51.594$ [1618a]. 3. $\Delta H_0^\circ = -51.896$ [570]. 4. $\Delta H_0^\circ = -51.504$ [1618a]. 5. $\Delta H_0^\circ = -63.59$ [1618a]. 6. $(\Delta H_{298}^\circ)_{subl}$. 7. Recalculated [234] from $(\Delta H_{298}^\circ)_{diss} = 95.5$ [614] to 96.5 [2245] using the values given in [2245] for the ΔG_{298}° for SO_3 and PbO. 8. From red PbO and SiO_2 (*a*). 9. $T = 300$ °K (*cal/g·°C*). 10. $2PbS(c) = Pb_2S_2(g)$. 11. $\Delta H_0^\circ = -173.373$ [1618a]. 12. $\Delta H_0^\circ = 84.16$ [1589].

1	2	3		4		5		6	
Pd	g	(91.0)	[1124]						
		(92.0)	[756]						
		(89.2)	[1472]						
		(89.8)	[2724]						
	c					(9.06)	[1589, 1685]	(6.21)	[1589, 1685]
						(9.05)	[2479]	(6.26)	[2479]
								(6.133)	[1970]
Pd^{2+}	d			45.5*	[323]				
$PdBr_2$	c	(−24.7)	[890]	−21.8*	[323]	34.5*	[323]		
				−22.3*	[227]				
$PdBr_4^{2-}$	d			−70.7*	[323]	44*	[323]		
$Pd(CN)_2$	c	(−83*)	[2683]						
$Pd(CNS)_2$	c	−61*	[2683]						
$PdCO_3$	c	−135*	[2683]						
$PdCl_2$	c	(−43.0)	[890]	−36.0*	[227]				
		(−40*)	[358]						
$PdCl_6^{2-}$	d			−99.6*	[323]	52*	[323]		
PdF_2	c	−112.0	[890]						
		−116*	[2683]						
$Pd(HCO_3)_2$	c	−312*	[2683]						
$Pd(HSO_4)_2$	c	−385*	[2683]						
PdHg	c	−22.6	[1619]						
PdI_2	c	−14	[674]			38	[674]		
		−10	[890]						
$PdI_2 \cdot H_2O$	c			−74.4*	[323]	49.3*	[323]		
PdI_3	c	−12*	[230]						
		−10	[890]						
$PdMoO_4$	c	−216*	[2683]						
$[Pd(NH_3)_4]Cl_2$	c							49.66[1]	[605]
$[Pd(NH_3)_4]Cl_2 \cdot 0.851H_2O$	c							59.03[2]	[606]
$[Pd(NH_3)_4]Cl_2 \cdot 0.863H_2O$	c							62.21[3]	[606]
$Pd(NO_2)_2$	c	−26*	[2683]						
$Pd(NO_3)_2$	c	−66*	[2683]						
$Pd(OH)_2$	c			−69.63*	[176]	17.7*	[176]		
				−72*	[323]	21.7*	[323]		
				−71.6*	[229]	20.7*	[161]		
$Pd(OH)_4$	c			−126.2*	[323]	24.7*	[323]		
				−128.5*	[229]				

$Pd(ReO_4)_2$	c	-363*	[2683]						
PdS	c					13.5*	[1406]		
$PdSO_3$	c	-107	[2683]						
$PdSO_4$	c	-180	[2683]						
PdSe	c	-14.0*	[579]			22.8*	[579]		
PdTe	c	-11.0*	[579]			24.1*	[579]		
						21.42^4	[1406]	12.13	[1406]
						20.6	[1406]		
$PdTe_2$	c					30.25	[2650]	18.31	[2650]
$PdWO_4$	c	-237*	[1976]						
Pd_2H	c			-4.1*	[229]	21.9	[1685]		
Pd_2Hg_5	c	-55.8	[1619]						
Pd_9Se_3	c					150.3*	[1406]		
$H_2Pd(OH)_4$	c			-182.93*	[7]				
$H_4Pd(OH)_6$	c			-296.23	[7]				
Pm	c					17.21	[2479]	6.50	[2479]
						17.25	[2396]		
						13.9*	[323]		
						17.2	[1685]		
Pm^{3+}	d			-167.6*	[323]	-41.2*	[323]		
PmB_6	c	-105.7	[455]						
$PmBr_3$	c	-210*	[230]						
$PmCl_2$	c	-178*	[442]						
$PmCl_3$	c	(-246*)	[442]	-234*	[323]	34.6*	[323]		
				-235.0*	[227]				
PmI_3	c	-157*	[230]						
PmOCl	c	-237*	[46]						
$Pm(OH)_3$	c			-309.0*	[227]				
Pm_2O_3	c	-428.0	[455]						
		-433*	[2662]	-206	[2662]				
Po	g	34.450	[2479]	25.467	[2479]	45.13*	[2479]		
		35.131^5	[569]	26.149	[569]	45.127	[569]		
						41.9*	[323]		
						45.13	[1685]		
	c					15.0	[569, 1685, 2479]	6.3	[569]
						15.5*	[323]	6.30	[1685, 2479]

1. $T = 287.43$ °K. 2. $T = 292.33$ °K. 3. $T = 298.42$ °K. 4. $t = 55$ °C. 5. $\Delta H_0^\circ = 35.25$ [569].

1	2	3		4		5		6	
Po^{+}	g	230.5[1]	[569]			44.683	[569]		
Po^{2+}	g	677[1]	[569]			41.929	[569]		
	d	17.1*	[323]	(17)	[2358]	4*	[323]		
Po^{3+}	g	13.10[1]	[569]						
Po^{4+}	d			70	[2358]				
Po_2	g	34.777[2]	[569]	23.484	[569]	67.88	[569]	8.90	[569]
		32.900	[2479]	22.226	[2479]	65.80	[1685, 2479]	8.84	[1685, 2479]
$PoBr_2$	c					37	[569]	18.9	[569]
$PoBr_4$, cubic	c					55	[569]	28.3	[569]
$PoCl_2$, rhombic	c					31	[569]	18.1	[569]
$PoCl_4$	c					47	[569]	28.7	[569]
$PoCl_6^{2-}$	d			−138	[2358]				
$Po(OH)_2^{4+}$	d			−113	[2358]				
$Po(OH)_4$	c			−130	[2358]				
PoO_2	c	−60.5*	[323]	(−46.6*)	[323]	18.3*	[323]		
		−60	[569]			17	[569]	14.7	[569]
		−58.7*	[229]						
PoO_3	c			−33*	[323]				
PoO_3^{2-}	d			−101*	[323]				
PoS	c			52	[2358]				
Pr	g	(85.2)[3]	[2275]	77.4*	[229]				
		(77.9)	[1569]	73.16*	[1589]				
		(89.09)[4]	[1456]						
	c					17.46	[2396]	(6.45)	[2479]
						13.7*	[323]		
						17.4	[2163]		
						17.5	[2109]		
						17.7	[1589]		
						17.6	[1685]		
Pr^{3+}	d	(−167.69)	[2422]	(−170.3*)	[323]	−41.1*	[323]		
		(−165.3)	[1810]	(−162*)	[1976]	−48*	[1976]		
Pr^{4+}	d	−108*	[1976]	−96*	[1976]	−86*	[1976]		
		−108.9	[1189]						
PrB_6	c	−99.6	[455]						
$PrBr_3$	c	−218*	[2683]						
		−215*	[230]						
PrClO	c	−242.6	[46]	−229.2*	[1976]	19.7	[46]		
		−228.8	[158]						

$PrCl_2$	c	−158	[2571]	−156	[2571, 2576]		
		−167	[2576]			31*	[2576]
		−156*	[442]				
		−163*	[444]				
		−173*	[411]				
		−163	[445]				
$PrCl_3$	g	82.1[1]	[441]				
$PrCl_3$, a	c	(−252.09)	[2422]	−234.5	[2422]	34.5	[2422]
		(−258*)	[411]	−239.9*	[323]	34.5*	[323]
				−240.7*	[227]		
				−233*	[1976]		
$PrCl_3 \cdot H_2O$	c			−302.6*	[229]		
				−292*	[1976]		
$PrCl_3 \cdot 6H_2O$	c	−687.80	[2422]	−588.2	[2422]	90.9	[2422]
				−589.1*	[232]		
				−586*	[1976]		
$PrCl_3 \cdot 7H_2O$	c	(−758.76)	[2422]	−645.4	[2422]	100.3	[2422]
				−646.0*	[232]		
				−651.7	[229]		
				−643*	[1976]		
PrF_3	c	−402*	[2140]	−383*	[229]	23*	[2140]
				−401	[440]		
PrF_4	c	−478*	[2140]	−454*	[2140]	32*	[2140]
				−454.3*	[232]		
$Pr(HSO_4)_3$	c			−676*	[1976]		
PrH_2	g	−47.8	[1999]				
PrI_3	c	(−152.5)	[1773]	−160.7*	[323]	51.3*	[323]
		(−161.5)	[1533]	−160.8*	[227]		
				−155*	[1976]		
$Pr(NO_3)_2$	d	−315.7	[1189]				
PrO	g	−38[1]	[2613]				
$Pr(OH)_3$	c	−360.9*	[229]	(−309.7*)	[323]	22.8*	[323]
$PrO_{1.5}$, hexagonal	c			−207.4	[2662]		
$PrO_{1.5}$, body-centered	c			−207.8	[2662]		
$PrO_{1.70}$, hexagonal	c	−225	[2662]	−218.8	[2662]		
$PrO_{1.70}$, body-centered	c					19.1	[2662]
$PrO_{1.703}$, body-centered	c	−223.5	[2472]	−210*	[1976]		
$PrO_{1.717}$, rhombohedric	c	−224.0	[2472]	−211*	[1976]		
$PrO_{1.74}$	c					19.2	[2662]

1. ΔH_0°. 2. $\Delta H_0^\circ = 35.15$ [569]. 3. Average of 85.1 and 85.3 [2275]. 4. $\Delta H_0^\circ = 89.36$ [1456].

1	2	3		4		5		6	
$PrO_{1.8}$ body-centered	c			−214.9	[2662]				
$PrO_{1.804}$, face-centered, cubic	c	−226.5	[2472]	−213*	[1976]				
$PrO_{1.83}$	c					19.1	[2662]		
$PrO_{1.833}$, face-centered, cubic	c	−227.6	[2472]						
PrO_2	c	(−232.9)	[1189]	−220.0*	[323]	15.8*	[323]		
		(−230.5)	[1045]	−217.5*	[1045]	19.1	[2662]		
		(−240.0)	[1773]	−220.8*	[229]				
				−215*	[1976]				
Pr_2O_3	c					37.9	[2662]		
		(−435.8)	[2472]	−423.1*	[323]	21.4*	[323]		
		(−440.0*)	[1045]	−420.5*	[1045]				
		(−436.8)	[1189]	−412.6	[2678]	31.0	[2678]	27.50	[2678]
				−424.6*	[229]	36.48*	[242]	27.9*	[242]
				−412*[1]	[1976]				
				−414*[2]	[1976]				
$Pr_2(SO_4)_3$	c			(−853*)	[1976]				
$Pr_2(SO_4)_3 \cdot 8H_2O$	c	−1536*	[323]			153*	[323]		
		−1530*	[229]						
Pr_2S_3	c	−270*	[2683]						
Pr_6O_{11}	c	(−1365.6)*	[1976]	−1284*	[1976]	92.4*	[1976]		
		(−1374*)	[1045]	−1302*	[1045]				
				−1282	[2678]	116.7	[2678]		
				−1318	[229]				
Pt	g	(134.800)	[2479]	(124.078)	[2479]			(6.10)	[1685]
		(134.97)[3]	[1589]	(124.23)	[1589]				
		(135.2)	[1124]						
		(134.9)	[1471]						
	c					(9.95)	[1589, 1685]	(6.19)	[2479]
								(6.18)	[1691]
Pt^{2+}	d			54.8*	[323]				
PtBr	c	−10.75*[4]	[673]						
$PtBr_2$	c	−22.6*[4]	[673]	−20.0	[234]	37.0*	[1773]		
		−19.2	[673, 890]						
$PtBr_3$	c	−33.6*[4]	[673]	−29.7	[234]	43.0*	[1773]		
		−30.5	[673, 890]						
$PtBr_4$	c	(−44.0)[4]	[673]	−33.1	[323]	55.2*	[323]		
		(−33.6)	[673, 890]	−36.2*	[227]	60.0*	[1773]		

$PtBr_4^{2-}$	d			-71.5*	[323]	49*	[323]		
PtCl	c	(-11.7*)[5]	[659]	-14.1*	[323]	24.9	[323]		
				-13.1*	[229]				
$PtCl_2$	c	(-33.4*)[5]	[659]	-26.3*	[323]	31.4*	[323]		
		(-28.2)	[659, 890]	-26.2	[227]	31.0*	[1773]		
						35.1*	[579]		
$PtCl_3$	c	(-48.1*)[5]	[659]	-33.6*	[323]	35.9*	[323]		
		(-45.2)	[659, 890]	-36.0*	[227]	35.5*	[1773]		
$PtCl_4$	c	(-62.7*)[5]	[659]	-42.3*	[323]	47.6*	[323]		
		(-54.0)	[659, 890]	-44.4*	[227]	50.0*	[1773]		
						57.7*	[579]		
$PtCl_4 \cdot 5H_2O$	c			-336.4*	[323]	94.6*	[323]		
				-336.5*	[229]				
$PtCl_4^{2-}$	d	(-122.4)	[558]						
PtF_6	g					83.165	[2627]	29.355	[2627]
PtI_2	c	-4.0	[890]			38.0*	[890]		
PtI_4	c	(-10.0)	[890]	-23.4*	[227]	64.0*	[890]		
				-22.0*	[323]	67.2*	[323]		
$PtNH_3Cl^-$	d	-114.0	[558]						
trans-$[Pt(NH_3)_2Cl_2]$	c							35.47	[421]
								34.8*	[593]
								35.4*	[596]
cis-$[Pt(NH_3)_2Cl_2]$	c							35.47	[421]
								34.5*	[593]
								35.4*	[596]
$[Pt(NH_3)_3Cl]^+$	d	-98.1	[558]						
$[Pt(NH_3)_3Cl] \cdot [PtNH_3Cl]$	c	-230	[595]						
$[Pt(NH_3)_3Cl]_2 \cdot [PtCl_4]$	c	-351	[595]						
$[Pt(NH_3)_3Cl]Br^+$	d	-137	[558]						
$[Pt(NH_3)_3Cl]Cl$	c					62.0	[2291]	42.5*	[594]
								43.78	[421]
$[Pt(NH_3)_3Cl_2]Cl$	c	-147.5	[594]						
trans-$[Pt(NH_3)_3Cl_3]$	c	-118.0	[595]						
cis-$[Pt(NH_3)_3Cl_3]$	c	-115.0	[595]						
$[Pt(NH_3)_4]^{2+}$	d	-90.4	[558]						
$[Pt(NH_3)_4]$ $[PtCl_4]$, green	c							0.1195[6]	[421]
$[Pt(NH_3)_4]$ $[PtCl_4]$, pink	c							0.1118[6]	[421]
$[Pt(NH_3)_4]$ $[PtNH_3Cl_3]_2$	c	-348	[595]					104.55	[421]

1. Hexagonal. 2. Cubic. 3. $\Delta H_0^\circ = 134.77$ [1589]. 4. From gaseous bromine. 5. $T = 300-500\,^\circ K$. 6. In $cal/g \cdot {}^\circ C$.

1	2	3		4		5		6	
$[Pt(NH_3)_4Cl_2]$	c	−177.1	[594]					52.1*	[594]
		−178.7	[692]					53.45	[421]
$[Pt(NH_3)_4I_2]$	c	−131.8	[558]						
PtO	g	41.30	[2291]						
	c	−17*	[887]	−11*	[887]				
PtO_2	c	−32*	[887]	−20*	[887]				
$Pt(OH)_2$	c			(−67.56*)	[176]	(28.3*)	[176]		
PtS	c	(−12.0)	[2415, 2625]	−21.6*	[323]	20.2*	[323]		
				−20.4	[229]	18.0	[1773]		
						12.2	[1685]		
PtS_2	c	(−26.3)	[2650]	−24.0	[2650]	17.85[1]	[2650]	15.75	[2650]
		(−20.6)	[2415, 2625]	−25.6*	[323]	17.8*	[323]		
				−27.3*	[229]	17.4	[1685]		
						20.2*	[1794]		
PtSe	c	−14.0*	[579]			24.1*	[579]		
$PtSe_2$	c					24.5*	[2650]		
PtTe	c					19.41[1]	[1406]	11.93	[1406]
						20.0*	[1406]		
		−11.0*	[579]			26.1*	[579]		
$PtTe_2$	c					28.92[1]	[2650]	18.03	[2650]
Pt_3O_4	c	−40.8*	[35]	−14.3*	[229]				
		−64*	[887]						
$H_2Pt(OH)_4$	c			−180.86*	[6]				
$H_4Pt(OH)_6$	c			−294.16*	[6]				
Pu	g			(74.93)	[1589]	42.3196	[827]		
Pu, *α*	c					12.3	[1589]	7.65	[1088, 1589]
						12.1*	[323]	8.0	[2270]
						17.2*	[1773]	8.48[2]	[1672]
Pu^{3+}	d			−140.5*	[323]	−39*	[323]		
						−30.9	[888]		
Pu^{4+}	d	−138.6	[1263]	−356	[1087]				
$PuBr_3$	c	(−187.8)	[2640]	−182.4*	[323]	49*	[323]		
		(−188)	[888]	−181.3*	[227]				
$PuC_{0.77}$	c	3.7	[1578, 2662]	2.5	[1578]	17*	[1578]		
$PuC_{0.85}$	c	−25	[888, 1126]	2.5	[1578]				
PuC_2	c	95.1[3]	[1998]						
$PuCl_3$	c	(−230)	[2668]	−214*	[323]	38*	[323]		

		(−226.8)	[1263]	−213.4*	[227]				
$PuCl_4$	c	−330	[888]						
$PuClO$	c	(−222.8)	[2669]						
		(−219.7)	[1263]						
PuD_2[4]	c	−35.5	[2000]						
PuF_3	c	−375	[2654]	−357*	[227]				
PuF_4	c	−400	[1069]	−400	[1087]				
PuF_6	g					88.39	[2483]	30.99	[2483]
						88.232	[2019]	30.926	[2019]
PuH_2[4]	c	(−37.4)	[2000]	−21.9*	[227]	12*	[323]		
PuI_3	c	(−133)	[888]	−133.6*	[323]	56*	[323]		
				−132.2*	[227]				
PuN	c	−95	[2000]						
		−78	[700]						
		⩽−64	[2076]			−22*[5]	[2076]		
PuO	c	−135	[2000]						
$PuO_{1.51}$, hexagonal	c					18.6	[2662]		
$PuO_{1.6}$, cubic	c					19.5	[2662]		
$Pu(OH)_3$	c			−280.2*	[323]				
$Pu(OH)_4$	c			−340*	[323]				
PuO_2	c	(−251)	[888]	−237.8	[229]	19.7	[1685, 2078]		
		(−252.4)	[2654]	−233.5*	[1045]	16.4	[2269]		
		(−246*)	[887]						
PuO_2, cubic	c					20.2	[2662]		
PuO_2^+	d					−19.2	[1685]		
PuO_2^{2+}	d					−28.9	[1685]		
PuO_2OH	c			−246.7*	[323]				
$PuO_2(OH)_2$	c			−278.9*	[323]				
Pu_2C_3	c	−1.7	[1578, 2662]	−2.6	[1578]	25*	[1578]		
				0.8	[2662]				
Pu_2O_3	c	−387	[888]						
Pu_2S_3	c	−256	[888]						
Ra	g	(38.700)	[2479]	(31.201)	[2479]	(42.15*)	[244]		
		(37.0*)	[402]						
	c					(17.00)	[2479]	(6.49)	[2479]
								(6.50)	[1685]
Ra^{2+}	g					42.16	[66]		
$Ra(BrO_3)_2$	c					62.5*	[699]		

1. $t = 5\,^\circ C$. 2. $T = 300\,^\circ K$. 3. $(\Delta H^\circ_{298})_{subl}$. 4. Solid solution. 5. ΔS°_{298}.

1	2	3		4		5		6
$RaBr_2$	c	−195	[890]			34*	[890]	
		−185*	[230]			37.9*	[698]	
		−184*	[2683]					
$Ra(CN)_2$	c	−52*	[2683]					
$Ra(CNS)_2$	c	−97*	[2683]					
$RaCO_3$	c	−300*	[218]			28.1*	[699]	
$Ra(ClO_3)_2$	c	−188*	[2683]			58.8*	[699]	
$Ra(ClO_4)_2$	c	−202*	[2683]			63.5*	[699]	
$RaCl_2$	c	−212	[890]			(29*)	[890]	
		−208*	[230, 2683]			(32.2*)	[698]	
$RaCl_2 \cdot H_2O$	c	(−280*)	[230]					
$RaCl_2 \cdot 4H_2O$	c	−484*	[230]					
$RaCl_2 \cdot 6H_2O$	c	−620*	[230]					
RaF_2	c	−287	[890]			23*	[890]	
		−290	[230]			25.4*	[698]	
		−292*	[2683]					
$Ra(HCO_3)_2$	c	−473*	[2683]					
$Ra(HS)_2$	c	−131*	[2683]					
$Ra(HSO_4)_2$	c	−556*	[2683]					
RaH_2	c	−36*	[2683]					
RaI_2	c	−167	[890]			37*	[890]	
		−149*	[230]			40.5*	[698]	
		−153*	[2683]					
$Ra(MnO_4)_2$	c					73.0*	[699]	
$RaMoO_4$	c	−375.0*	[172, 203]	−351.9*	[172, 203]			
$Ra(NH_2)_2$	c	−79*	[2683]					
$Ra(NO_2)_2$	c	−185*	[2683]					
$Ra(NO_3)_2$	c					(53.2*)	[699]	
RaO	c	(−130*)	[887]	−117.5*	[323]	16.3*	[323]	
		(−134*)	[358]	−123*	[1045]	17.6*	[698]	
$Ra(OH)_2$	c	−227*	[1683]			26.9*	[699]	
RaO_2	c	−143*	[2683]					
$RaReO_4$	c	−518*	[2683]					
RaS	c	−106*	[2683]			22.1*	[698]	
$RaSO_3$	c	−282*	[2683]					
		−281.6*	[1172]					
$RaSO_4$	c			(−325.99*)	[177]	(35.4)[1]	[177]	
						(32.1)	[699]	

RaSe	c					25.7	[698]		
$RaSeO_4$	c	−282.1*[2]	[621]			25.8	[498]		
		−281.0*	[499]						
		−281	[2683]						
$RaSiO_3$	c	−377*	[2683]						
RaTe	c					28.1*	[698]		
$RaWO_4$	c	−404.7*	[170, 172]	−380.4*	[170, 172]				
Rb	g	(19.600)	[2479]	(12.918)	[2479]	(40.63)	[1685]		
		(19.6)[3]	[570]			(40.6285)	[570]		
		(19.90)[4]	[1589]						
	c					(18.22)	[570, 2479]	(7.50)	[2479]
						(18.3)	[1079]	(7.38)	[570, 1079]
						(18.10)	[1589]	(7.36)	[1589, 1685]
						(18.1)	[1685]	(7.424)	[1215]
Rb^+	g					39.26	[66]		
						39.2511	[570]		
	d					(28.7)	[1685]		
Rb_2	g	(29.36)	[1185]	18.80	[1185]	64.690	[1185]	9.061	[1185]
		(27.550)	[2479]	19.127	[2479]	64.7	[1685]	8.75	[1685]
		(29.6)	[2243]			63.1	[1680]	8.93	[1679]
		(28.50)[4]	[1685]						
RbAt	c					31.27*[5]	[304a]	11.87*[6]	[304a]
$RbBH_4$	c	−59*	[724]						
$RbBO_3$	c	−88.90	[875]	−68.07	[875]	37.9	[875]		
RbBr	g	−44	[2243]			62.1	[1685, 2243]	8.78	[1685]
	c			−82.8[7]	[250]	(26.3)	[1685]	(12.60)	[1685]
						(26.0)	[995]		
						(26.0*)	[698]		
$RbBrO_3$	c	−88.90	[875]	−68.07	[875]	37.9	[875]		
						38.4*	[699]		
RbCN	c	−19*	[2683]						
		−26*	[2182]						
RbCNO	c	95*	[693]						
RbCNS	c	(−50.4*)	[689]						
RbCl	g	−56	[2243]			59.6	[698, 1685]	8.71	[1685]
	c			−96.8*	[323]	22.6*	[323]	(11.68)[5]	[1668]

1. $t = 20\,°C$. 2. Average of −282.6 and −281.5 [621]. 3. $\Delta H_0^\circ = 19.909$ [570]. 4. ΔH_0°. 5. $T = 300\,°K$. 6. C_v; $T = 300\,°K$. 7. Recalculated [234] from $\Delta H_{298}^\circ = -95.83$ [842] to −93.03 [2245].

1	2	3		4		5		6	
RbCl	c			-97.0*	[227]	21.9	[1794, 2063]		
				-96.5*[1]	[250]	23.1*	[698]		
						21.2	[2243]		
						23.0	[1685]		
$2RbCl\cdot TiCl_4$	c	-35	[1165]			90.2	[1771]		
$RbClO_3$	c					(36.6*)	[699]		
$RbClO_4$	c			(-73.57)	[177]	(39.6*)	[177]		
						(39.1*)	[699]		
RbCs	g					67.7	[1685]	8.79	[1685]
RbD	g					51.3	[1685]		
RbF	g					57.1	[1685]	8.50	[1685]
						57.2	[1680]		
	c			-124.3*	[323]	17.4*	[323]	(11.43)[2]	[1668]
				-125.1*	[227]	18.0	[1773]		
				-125.17[3]	[250]	19.6*	[698]		
						20.0*	[890]		
						19.2	[1685]		
RbF·HF	c					28.70	[912]	18.97	[911]
RbH	g			27.4*	[227]	49.81	[1685]	7.45	[1685]
	c	12.98	[1501]	-7.3*	[323]				
		8*	[2683]	-8.1*	[229]				
$RbHCO_3$	c	-155*	[693]	-204.4*	[323]	29.3*	[323]		
				-206.5*	[229]				
$RbHSO_4$	c			-246.2*	[229]				
RbI	g	(-32)	[2243]			63.8	[1685, 2243]	8.82	[1685]
	c			-77.0*[4]	[250]	(28.2*)	[698]	(11.84)[2]	[1668]
						(28.4)	[1685]	(12.52)	[1685]
$RbMnO_4$	c					43.8*	[699]		
$RbNO_2$	c	-86*	[693, 2683]						
$RbNO_3$	c	(-106.25)	[1997]	-93.3*	[323]	33.6*	[323]	23.2[5]	[2012]
		(-138*)	[358]	-93.4*	[227]	33.8*	[699]		
$RbNbCl_6$	c	-12.5[6]	[547]						
RbOH	c					20.3*	[699]		
						19.9*	[161]		
RbOH, II	c			-87.1*	[323]	16.9*	[323]		
				-88.9*	[229]				
RbO_2	c	-68.0	[887, 1109]	-52.5*	[1045]				
$RbPF_6$	c					53.02	[2442]	35.44[2]	[2442]

$Rb[PtNH_3Cl_3]$	c	−183.8	[423]						
$RbTaCl_6$	c	−17.6[7]	[423]						
Rb_2CO_3	c			−249.3*	[323]	23.3*	[323]		
				−250.0*	[227]				
	d			−261.2*	[323]	40.9*	[699]		
Rb_2CrO_4	c					52.6*	[669]		
Rb_2MoO_4	c	−356	[2683]						
Rb_2O	c			−69.5*	[323, 1045]	26.2*	[323]	20*	[683]
				−72.3*	[229]				
Rb_2O_2	c			−83.6*	[323]	24.8*	[323]		
				−84.7*	[229]				
				−86.5*	[1045]				
Rb_2O_3	c	(−126.0)	[887]	−92.4*	[323]	25.3*	[323]		
				−91.8*	[229]				
				−95.5*	[1045]				
Rb_2O_4	c			−94.6	[323]	27.8*	[323]		
				−93.7*	[229]				
$Rb_2[PtCl_4]$	c	−255.4	[423]						
Rb_2S	c			−80.6*	[323]	32*	[323]		
				−82.2*	[229]				
Rb_2SO_3	c	−269*	[2683]						
		−263.8*	[1172]						
Rb_2SO_4	c			−312.8*	[323]	45.8*	[323]		
				−313.6*	[229]	46.9*	[699]		
Rb_2Se	c	−68*	[693]						
Rb_2SeO_4	c	−270*	[2683]			41.4*	[498]		
		−269.7	[520]						
Rb_2SiO_3	c	−353*	[2683]						
		−366.4*	[364]						
$Rb_2Si_2O_5$	c	−587.5*	[364]						
$Rb_2Si_4O_9$	c	−1030*	[364]						
Rb_2SnBr_6	c					106.4	[1980]	54.54[2]	[1980]
Rb_2SnCl_6	c					90.25	[1980]	54.27[2]	[1980]
Rb_2UO_4	c	−487	[192]						
Rb_2WO_4	c	−390*	[2683]						
Rb_3VCl_6	c	−19.8[8]	[93]						
$Rb_3V_2Cl_9$	c	−26.7[8]	[93]						

1. Recalculated [234] from $\Delta H^\circ_{298} = -105.08$ [842] to −102.91 [2245]. 2. $T = 300°K$. 3. Recalculated [234] from $\Delta H^\circ_{298} = -133.24$ [842] to −131.28 [2245]. 4. Recalculated [234] from $\Delta H^\circ_{298} = -81.03$ [842] to −78.5 [2245]. 5. Extrapolated [234] from the equation recommended [2012] for use between 50 and 160°C. 6. From RbCl and $NbCl_5$. 7. From RbCl and $TaCl_5$. 8. From RbCl(c) and VCl_3(c).

1	2	3		4		5		6	
Re	g	(185.650)	[2479]	(174.845)	[2479]				
		(186.1)[1]	[1589]	(175.29)	[1519]				
		(186.9*)	[402]						
	c					(8.89)	[1589, 1685, 2479]	(6.143)	[2479]
								(6.0)[2]	[2521]
						(8.74)	[2147]	(6.16)	[1589]
								(6.14)	[1685]
Re^-				9.2	[323]				
$ReAs_2$	c	(−5.9)	[2625]			24.0	[1773]		
$ReBrO_3$	c					81.913[3]	[2198]	19.610[3]	[2198]
$ReBr_3$	c	−39.3	[1739]	−33.6	[1739]	44*	[1739]		
$ReClO_3$	c					78.049[3]	[2198]	19.156[3]	[2198]
$ReCl_3$	c	−63.0	[1739]	−47.8	[1739]	38*	[1739]		
$ReCl_6^-$	d					59.8	[921]		
ReF_5	g					84.1	[1685]	28.55	[1685]
ReF_6	g					85.19	[2483]	29.48	[2483]
						86.492	[2198]	29.270	[2198]
	c	(−278.0)	[890]						
ReO_2	c	−101.3	[874]	−89.2*	[874]	17.4*	[874]		
				−90.2*	[323]				
ReO_3	c	(−146.0)	[874]	−127.3	[874]	19.8	[874]		
		(−147*)	[887]	−128*	[1045]	19.3	[1685]		
				−126.0*	[232]				
ReO_4^-	d	(−189.2)	[874]	−167.1	[1002]	48.3	[1002, 1685]		
				−168.3*	[323]	50*	[323]		
ReS_2	c	(−33.2)	[2415, 2625]	−45.8*	[323]	20*	[323, 1794]		
		(−42.7)	[1851]	−41.5	[1851]				
				−43.5	[229]				
$ReSi_2$	c	−54.8*	[2351]			15.5	[2351]		
Re_2O_7	g					105.0	[918, 1685]		
	c	(−295.9)	[874]	−258.7	[874]	44.0*	[874]		
		(−297*)	[887]	−251.2*	[229]	38.6	[380]	44.6	[887]
				−255.0	[918]	49.54	[918]	39.73	[918]
				−249.6*	[232]	49.5	[1685]	37.93	[1685]
				−252	[1045]				
Re_2O_8	c	(−308.5*)	[1045]	−257	[1045]				
Re_2S_7	c	−107.9	[1851]	−101.0	[1851]				
$HReO_4$	c	−182.2	[370]	−157.0	[918]	36.4	[918]		

				−156.1*	[229]	36.3	[1685]		
	d	(−189.2)	[874]	−167.1	[874]				
H_2ReCl_6	c	−152.1	[203]						
	d	−282.1	[203]						
Rh	g	(133.1)[4]	[1589]	(122.11)	[1589]			(5.02)	[1685]
		(133.000)	[2479]	(122.031)	[2479]				
		(134.2)	[756, 1125]						
		(132.5)	[1471]						
		(132.8)	[2093]						
		(135)	[1125]						
	c					(7.53)	[1589, 1685]	(5.97)	[1589]
						(7.56)	[996]		
Rh^{3+}	d			55.3*	[323]				
$RhBr_2$	c	−16*	[230]						
$RhBr_3$	c	−50.0	[890]			45.0	[890]		
RhCl	c	(−20.0)	[890]	−11.4*	[227]	20.0	[890]		
				−12.4*	[323]				
$RhCl_2$	g	30.3	[817]			68.9	[817]		
	c	(−39.3)	[890]	−26.7*	[227]	29.0	[890]		
				−26.4*	[323]	29*	[323]		
$RhCl_3$	g	16.0	[817]			89.3	[817]		
	c	(−55.0)	[890]	−42.1*	[227]	38.0	[890]		
				−39.6*	[323]	33*	[323]		
		−71.5*	[817]			27.1	[817]		
$RhCl_6^{3-}$	d			−158.3*	[323]	50*	[323]		
RhF	c			−125.1*	[323]				
RhI_2	c	10*	[230]						
RhO	c			−16*	[323]	13*	[323]		
				−16.1*	[229]				
				−16.0*	[1045]				
RhTe	c					20.0*	[1406]		
$RhTe_2$	c					29.5*	[1406]		
Rh_2O	c			−19.1*	[323]	27.4*	[323]		
				−19*	[1045]				
Rh_2O_3	c			−50.0*	[323]	26.5*	[323]		
				−48.4*	[229]				
				−50*	[1045]				
Rh_8S_{15}	c					120*	[1406]		
Rh_9S_8	c					118.8*	[1406]		

1. $\Delta H_0^\circ = 185.9$ [1589]. 2. $T = 300–2200\,^\circ K$. 3. $T = 300\,^\circ K$. 4. $\Delta H_0^\circ = 132.79$ [1589].

1	2	3		4		5		6	
Rn	g					(40.096)	[568]		
						(42.09)	[2358]		
Rn^+	g	(247.865)[1]	[568]			44.849	[568]		
		(249.34)[2]	[2358]						
Ru	g	(144.000)	[2479]	(132.774)	[2479]	(44.55)	[1685, 2479]	5.14	[1685, 2479]
		(155.0)[3]	[1589]	(143.75)	[1589]				
		(154.9)	[2091]						
		(151.5)	[2128]						
	c					(6.82)	[1000, 1589, 1685]	(5.68)[4]	[1000]
								(5.75)	[1589]
								(5.80)	[1685]
								(5.70)	[2479]
$RuBr_3$	g	−33*	[643]	−29*	[643]				
	c	−44.2[5]	[643]	−30[5]	[643]				
$RuCl_2$	c	(−49*)	[641]	−35*	[641]	40*[6]	[641]		
		(−46.0)	[890]			38.0*	[890]		
$RuCl_3$	g	−12.4	[261]			80.8	[261]		
						95.1	[815]		
	c	(−60.5)	[814, 815]	−48.9*	[227]	30.5	[815]		
				−46.9*	[323]	33.5*	[323]		
$RuCl_4$	g	−22.3	[815]			89.5	[815]		
		−0.3	[261]			99.3	[261]		
$RuCl_5^{2-}$	d			−129*	[323]	30.5	[814]		
$RuCl_5OH^{2-}$	d			−158*	[323]				
RuF_5	c	−213.4	[2171]						
RuI_3	c	−23*	[642]			25*	[642]		
RuO_2	g	40*	[407]	38*	[407]				
	c	(−56.5*)	[1045]	−44.0	[1045]	14.5*	[1794]		
		(−73.1)[7]	[661]	−60.6	[661]				
		(−71)	[2289]	−40.7*	[323]	16.5*	[323]		
		(−72.2)	[816]	−39.3*	[229]	12.2	[816]		
RuO_3	g	−18.0	[816]			63.7	[816]		
		−12.7	[2292]						
	c	−60*	[407]	−42*	[407]	19*	[407]		
RuO_4	g	−46.7	[816]	−33*	[323]	65.5	[816]		
		−43.2	[2292]			69.60	[2077]	18.14	[2077]

		−46*	[407]						
	l	−55.0	[406]						
	c	−57.6	[406, 407]						
		−59	[406]						
RuO_4[8]	c	−52.0*	[887]	−32*	[887]				
RuO_4				2.563[9]	[404]	44.3[11]	[404]		
		13.20[9]	[404]	2.558[10]	[404]	35.6[12]	[404]		
		10.6[10]	[404]			8.7[14]	[404]		
		2.6[13]							
RuS_2	c	(−53.0*)	[2650]	−49.5*	[2650]	10.4*	[2650]		
		(−48.1)	[2415, 2625]	−46.7*	[323]	17.5*	[323, 1794]		
				−47.3*	[229]	12.5	[1685]		
$RuSe_2$	c					19.5*	[2077]		
$RuTe_2$	c					24.0	[2077]		
S	g	(66.636)[15]	[2358]	(56.949)	[2358]	(40.094)	[2358]	(5.658)	[569, 2358]
		(56.900)	[2479]	(47.218)	[2479]	(40.09)	[1685]		
		(53.54)	[1188]	(43.96)	[1188]				
		(66.4408)[16]	[1830]			(40.0861)	[570, 1830]	(5.6587)	[1830]
		(65.222)[17]	[569]			(40.084)	[569]		
		(65.225)[18]	[570]						
		(53.0)	[886, 2227]						
		(65.9)	[1879]						
		(65.651)	[1618a]	(55.975)	[1618a]	(40.086)	[1618a]	(5.659)	[1618a]
	l	0.336	[1618a]	0.093	[1618a]	8.444	[1618a]	7.579	[1618a]
S, monoclinic	c	(0.090)[19]	[569]	(0.045)	[569]	(7.78)	[569, 1685]	(5.65)	[569, 1685]
		(0.08)	[2358]						
S, rhombic	c	−0.072[20]	[754]			(7.60)	[2358]	(5.41)	[2358]
						(7.713)	[1830]	(5.401)	[1188, 1618a, 1830]
						(7.63)	[569]	(5.42)	[569]
						(7.631)	[1618a]	(5.44)[21]	[2638]
S^+	g	(305.508)[22]	[569]	(294.643)	[569]	39.082	[569]	4.968	[569]
		(306.97)[23]	[2358]						
S^{2+}	g	(842)[1]	[569]			39.027	[569]	7.013	[569]
		(848.2)[24]	[2358]						

1. ΔH_0°. 2. $\Delta H_0^\circ = (247.06)$ [2358]. 3. $\Delta H_0^\circ = 154.61$ [1589]. 4. $t = 0\,^\circ C$. 5. From $Br_2(g)$. 6. Calculated [234] from $\Delta S_{diss} = 47^*$ [641]. 7. The value −52.5 [2245] was stated to be erroneous [661]. 8. Unstable at room temperature. 9. $(\Delta H^\circ_{298})_{subl}$. 10. $(\Delta H^\circ_{298})_{vap}$. 11. $(\Delta S^\circ_{298})_{subl}$. 12. $(\Delta S^\circ_{298})_{vap}$. 13. $(\Delta H^\circ_{298})_f$. 14. $(\Delta S^\circ_{298})_f$. 15. $\Delta H_0^\circ = (66.1)$ [2358]. 16. $\Delta H_0^\circ = 65.9034$ [1830]. 17. $\Delta H_0^\circ = (64.685)$ [569]. 18. $\Delta H_0^\circ = 64.687$ [570]. 19. $\Delta H_0^\circ = (0.060)$ [569]. 20. For the process $S_{hex} \rightarrow S_{rhomb}$; $\Delta H_0^\circ = -0.300$ [745]. 21. $t = 30\,^\circ C$. 22. $\Delta H_0^\circ = 303.6$ [569]. 23. $\Delta H_0^\circ = 304.95$ [2358]. 24. $\Delta H_0^\circ = 844.8$ [2358].

1	2	3		4		5		6	
S^{3+}	g	(1645)[1]	[569]						
		(1657.9)[2]	[2358]						
S^{4+}	g	(2736)[1]	[569]						
		(2750)[3]	[2358]						
S^{5+}	g	(4408)[1]	[569]						
		(4422)[4]	[2358]						
S^{6+}	g	(6439)[1]	[569]						
		(6654)[5]	[2358]						
S^{7+}	g	(12921)[1]	[569]						
		(12935)[6]	[2358]						
S^{8+}	g	(20505)[1]	[569]						
		(20520)[7]	[2358]						
S^{9+}	g	29246[1]	[569]						
		29260[8]	[2358]						
S^{10+}	g	39584[1]	[569]						
S^{11+}	g	51244[1]	[569]						
S^{12+}	g	64340[1]	[569]						
S^{13+}	g	79370[1]	[569]						
S^{14+}	g	95640[1]	[569]						
S^{15+}	g	169900[1]	[569]						
S^{16+}	g	250200[1]	[569]						
S^-	g	17[1]	[569]						
		17.42[9]	[2358]						
S^{2-}	g					36.34	[66]		
	d	(8.56*)	[323]	(22.1*)	[323]	(−6.4*)	[323]		
		(7.9)	[2358]	(20.5)	[2358]	(−3.5)	[2358]		
		(7.8)	[1779]	(20.6)	[1779]	(−4)	[1685, 1779]		
S_2	g	(30.840)	[2479]	19.13	[2479]	54.51	[2358, 2479]	7.76	[569, 1685, 2358, 2479]
		(30.477)[10]	[569]	18.778	[569]	54.50	[569, 1685]		
		(30.68)[11]	[2358]	18.90	[2358]				
		(30.84)[12]	[1830]	21.0*	[229]	54.5100	[1618a, 1830]	7.7592	[1830]
		(30.632)[13]	[570]			54.504	[570]		
				19.138	[1618a]			7.759	[1618a]
		(30.84)[14]	[1618a, 1896]			54.50	[1896]		
		(31.0)	[886, 2227]						
		(28.7)[15]	[883]						
S_2^+	g	240[1]	[569]						

		255.5[16]	[2358]						
S_2^{2-}	d	(7.2)	[2358]	19.0	[2358]	6.8	[2358]		
		(7.8)	[1779]	20.6	[1779]	4	[1779]		
		(7.6)	[569]	21.8*	[323]	0*	[323]		
S_3	g	31.8	[569]						
		31.7	[2358]						
S_3^+	g	344	[2358]						
S_3^{2-}	d	6.2	[2358]	17.6	[2358]				
		6.8	[569]	21.1*	[323]	5*	[323]		
S_4	g	31.75	[883]			73.1	[883]		
		32.9	[569]						
		32.7	[2358]						
S_4^+	g	273[1]	[569]						
		334	[2358]						
S_4^{2-}	d	(5.5)	[2358]	16.5	[2358]	24.7	[2358]		
		(6.4)	[569]	19.4*	[323]	10*	[323]		
		(5.955)	[1928]	16.509	[1928]				
S_5	g	30.4	[569]						
		29.6	[2358]						
S_5^+	g	259	[2358]						
S_5^{2-}	d	5.1	[2358]	15.7	[2358]	33.6	[2358]		
		6.0	[569]						
		6.145	[1928]						
S_6	g	(27.45)	[883]	16.8*	[229]	89.8	[883]		
		(24.6)	[569]			91	[1685]	27.4	[1685]
		(24.5)	[2358]						
S_6^+	g	240[1]	[569]						
		247	[2358]						
S_7	g	27.0	[569]						
		27.1	[2358]						
S_7^+	g	248	[2358]						
S_8	g	(24.45)[17]	[2358]	11.87	[2358]	102.98	[2358]	37.39	[2358]
		(24.35)[18]	[1452]	11.89	[1452]	102.76	[1452]	37.17	[1460]
		(23.92)	[917]			102.7	[1685]	37.2	[1685]

1. ΔH_0°. 2. $\Delta H_0^\circ = 1653.0$ [2358]. 3. $\Delta H_0^\circ = 2743.6$ [2358]. 4. $\Delta H_0^\circ = 4415$ [2358]. 5. $\Delta H_0^\circ = 6445$ [2358]. 6. $\Delta H_0^\circ = 12925$ [2358]. 7. $\Delta H_0^\circ = 20508$ [2358]. 8. $\Delta H_0^\circ = 29247$ [2358]. 9. $\Delta H_0^\circ = 18.36$ [2358]. 10. $\Delta H_0^\circ = 30.4$ [569]. 11. $\Delta H_0^\circ = 30.647$ [2358]. 12. $\Delta H_0^\circ = 30.8068$ [1830]. 13. $\Delta H_0^\circ = 30.870$ [570]. 14. $\Delta H_0^\circ = 30.805$ [1618a]. 15. $t = 0°C$. 16. $\Delta H_0^\circ = 254$ [2358]. 17. $\Delta H_0^\circ = 25.35$ [2358]. 18. $\Delta H_0^\circ = 25.23$ [1452].

1	2	3		4		5		6	
S_8		(24.1)	[1896]			109	[1896]		
		(30.0)	[883]			112.5	[883]		
		(24.350)	[2479]						
		(23.85)[1]	[994]						
		(23.06)[2]	[994]						
		(23.11)[3]	[994]						
		(24.35)[4]	[569]						
		(25.2)[5]	[829]	11.77[5]	[829]	44.18[6]	[829]		
		(24.2)[7]	[1618a]	11.745	[1618a]	102.823	[1618a]	37.296	[1618a]
S_8^+	g	230[8]	[569]						
		247[9]	[2358]						
SCl	g	30.335[10]	[569]	23.501	[569]	57.2	[569]	8.2	[569]
		32[11]	[1830]			57.2534	[1830]	8.1925	[1830]
SCl_2	g	−20.68[12]	[1885]	−16.77[5]	[1885]	67.45	[569, 1881]	12.23	[569, 1881]
						67.1958	[1830]	12.1691	[1830]
						67.5	[1685]	12.17	[1685]
		−12	[2358]						
		−4.7	[2358]						
	l	−28	[890]	−19*	[229]				
		−11.8	[569]						
		−5.15[13]	[1830]						
SCl_4	l	(−13.4)	[569]	1.0*	[323]				
SD	g	34.619[14]	[569]	27.702	[569]	48.14	[569]	7.76	[569]
						48.18[15]	[1455]	7.757	[1455]
SF	g	18.196[16]	[569]	11.444	[569]	54.5	[569]	7.6	[569]
		18.20[17]	[570]			54.462	[570]		
				7.284[18]	[1830]	54.330	[1830]	7.5597	[1830]
SF_2	g	−32.83[19]	[569]			61.4	[569]	10.6	[569]
						60.9154	[1830]	10.4192	[1830]
		−32.823*[20]	[570]	−51.87[21]	[1830]	61.418	[570]		
SF_4	g	−171.7	[2580]			69.2733[5]	[2199]	17.0159[5]	[2199]
		−170.2[22]	[1830]			70.0518	[1830]	17.4729	[1830]
						70.085	[570]		
		−184[23]	[569]	−173.484	[569]	69.26	[569]	16.95	[569]
		−171.7[24]	[1134]	−174.8	[2358]	69.77	[2358]	17.45	[2358]
		−185.2[25]	[2358]			69.814	[1685]		
SF_5	g	−230	[569]			76.38	[569]	24.87	[569]
						76.26	[2358]	24.9	[2358]

SF_5^-	g	-301.8[8]	[569]						
SF_5Cl	g	-250.5[26]	[2358]	-226.9	[2358]	292.926[27]	[1985]	98.272[27]	[1985]
		-245	[1796]						
		-247[28]	[569]	-223.44	[569]				
	l	-254.7	[2358]						
		-251.2	[569]						
SF_6	g	(-289)[29]	[2358]	(-264.1)	[2358]	(69.72)	[2358]	23.25	[2358]
		(-288.5)[30]	[1830]			(69.7137)	[1830]	23.2616	[1830]
		(-288.5)[31]	[1618a]			(69.734)	[570]	23.01	[1685]
				(-263.676)	[1618a]	(69.713)	[1618a]		
				(-263.67)	[569]	(69.7)	[569]	23.3	[569]
SF_6^+	g	87.2[8]	[569]						
SF_6^-	g	-319.2[8]	[569]						
SO	g	(1.496)[32]	[2358]	-4.742	[2358]	(53.02)	[2358]	7.21	[2358]
		(0.097)[33]	[570]	(13.05)	[1045]	(53.023)	[570, 1618a]	7.23	[1188, 1685]
		(1.3112)[34]	[1830]			(53.0252)	[1830]	7.2123	[1830]
		(15.40)[8]	[1102]			(53.05)	[1685]		
		(19.30)	[1188]			(53.08)	[1188]		
		(-6.0)	[2145, 2227]			(53.096)[5]	[2106]	7.232[5]	[2106]
		(0.5)	[1879]						
		(0.519)[35]	[1618a]	-5.709	[1618a]			7.212	[1618a]
		(0.1)[36]	[569]	(-6.128)	[569]	(53.02)	[569]	7.21	[569]
SO^+	g	279[8]	[569]						
SO^-	g	-25.3[8]	[569]						
$SoBr_2$	g	-17.7	[2358]			79.54	[569]	16.66	[569, 1685]
SOCl	g	-24.5*[37]	[1830]			66.1689	[1830]	10.8672	[1830]
				-27.391	[569]	66.2	[569]	10.9	[569]
		-25.178[38]	[569]			66.58	[569]		
						66.6	[1685]		

1. α-Modification between 0 and 40°C. 2. β-Modification between 0 and 40°C. 3. γ-Modification between 0 and 60°C. 4. $\Delta H_0^\circ = 25.292$ [569]. 5. $t = 300$°C. 6. ΔS_{298}°. 7. $\Delta H_0^\circ = 25.137$ [1618a]. 8. ΔH_0°. 9. $\Delta H_0^\circ = 247$ [2358]. 10. $\Delta H_0^\circ = 30.276$ [569]. 11. $\Delta H_0^\circ = 31.9432$ [1830]. 12. For the reaction $\frac{1}{2}S_2(g) + Cl_2(g) = SCl_2(g)$. ($\Delta H_0^\circ = -20.41$). 13. $\Delta H_0^\circ = -4.8763$ [1830]. 14. $\Delta H_0^\circ = 34.5$ [569]. 15. $T = 300$°K. 16. $\Delta H_0^\circ = 18.185$ [569]. 17. $\Delta H_0^\circ = 18.187$ [570]. 18. $\Delta H_0^\circ = 7.2752$ [1830]. 19. $\Delta H_0^\circ = -32.315$ [569]. 20. $\Delta H_0^\circ = -32.313$* [570]. 21. $\Delta H_0^\circ = -51.2997$ [1830]. 22. $\Delta H_0^\circ = -168.4117$ [1830]. 23. $\Delta H_0^\circ = -182.104$ [569]. 24. $\Delta H_0^\circ = -169.914$ [570]. 25. $\Delta H_0^\circ = -183.4$ [2358]. 26. $\Delta H_0^\circ = -247.48$ [2358]. 27. $T = 300$°K; in *joules/mole*·°C. 28. $\Delta H_0^\circ = -243.968$ [569]. 29. $\Delta H_0^\circ = -285.7$ [2358]. 30. $\Delta H_0^\circ = -285.1739$ [1830]. 31. $\Delta H_0^\circ = -288.175$ [570]; -285.173 [1618a]. 32. $\Delta H_0^\circ = 1.5$ [2358]. 33. $\Delta H_0^\circ = 0.100$ [570]. 34. $\Delta H_0^\circ = 1.3149$ [1830]. 35. $\Delta H_0^\circ = 0.522$ [1618a]. 36. $\Delta H_0^\circ = 0.092$ [569]. 37. $\Delta H_0^\circ = -24.0397$ [1830]. 38. $\Delta H_0^\circ = -24.739$ [569].

1	2	3		4		5		6	
$SOCl_2$	g	−50.75[1]	[569]	−47.224	[569]	73.60	[569]	15.94	[569]
		−50.8[2]	[2358]	−47.4	[2358]	74.01	[2358]	15.9	[2358]
		−50.37[3]	[1830]			73.6185	[1830]	15.9184	[1830]
						73.2	[1685]	15.88	[1685]
	l	(−58.7)	[2358]			66.579	[570]	29	[2358]
		(−59.0)	[569]			66.5794	[1830]	28.8	[569]
		(−58.5)	[2039]						
SOF	g	−29.9[4]	[1830]			62.8741	[1830]	9.9522	[1830]
						62.9	[569]	10.0	[569]
SOF_2	g	−170.534[5]	[569]	−166.359	[569]			13.58	[569, 1685]
		−162[6]	[570]					13.5833	[1830]
						65.53[8]	[2087]		
SOF_4	g	−97.11[7]	[1830]			73.5177[9]	[2199]	20.1112[9]	[2199]
						73.43	[569]	20.05	[569]
SO_2	g	−85.75[10]	[1188]	(−71.74)	[1188]	(59.29)	[569, 1188, 1685]	9.53	[569, 1618a, 1188, 1685]
		(−70.944)[11]	[2358]	(−71.749)	[2358]	(59.30)	[2358]		
		(−70.947)[12]	[1188, 1830]			(59.2967)	[1830]	(9.5290)	[1830]
		(−70.96)[13]	[569]	(−71.752)	[569]	(59.019)	[2033]		
				(−71.741)	[1618a]	(59.298)	[1618a]		
		(−70.960)[14]	[570]			(59.296)	[570]	(9.514)	[570]
	l	−76.6	[2358]						
	d	−77.194	[2358]	−71.872	[2358]	38.7	[2358]		
SO_2^+	g	207	[1214]						
		215.1[15]	[2358]						
		−214.2[10]	[569]						
SO_2^-	g	−98[10]	[569]						
$SO_2 \cdot HCl$	g	−96.5	[2358]						
		−96.4	[569]						
$SO_2 \cdot HF$	g	−139.2	[2358]						
		−139	[569]						
SO_2Cl_2	g	−87.0[16]	[2358]	−76.5	[2358]	74.53	[2358]	18.4	[2358]
		−86.2[17]	[569]	−75.607	[569]	74.4	[569, 1685]	18.43	[1685]
				−73.6*	[323]			18.5	[569]
	l	(−93.5)	[569]	−72.9*	[323]	51.7	[1685]	(31.4)	[569]
		(−94.2)	[2358]			51.9	[1680]	(32)	[2358]
		(−93.3)	[2039]						
SO_2F_2	g	−205*[18]	[570, 1618a]			68.884	[570]		

				-194.207	[1618a]	68.883	[1618a]	16.356	[1618a]
						67.86	[2358]	15.78	[2358]
		-205[19]	[1830]			67.7473	[1830]	15.7245	[1830]
$SO_2F_2^+$	g	-104[10]	[569]						
SO_3	g	(-94.58)[20]	[2358]	(-88.69)	[2358]	(61.34)	[2358]	(12.11)	[569, 1819, 2358]
		(-94.47)[21]	[1830]			(61.3445)	[1830]	(12.1085)	[1830]
		(-94.400)[22]	[570]			(61.527)	[570]		
		(-94.61)[23]	[569]	(-88.71)	[569]	(61.35)	[569, 1819]		
						(61.322)	[1759]	(12.121)	[1759]
						(61.2)	[1685]		
						(61.19)	[1188]		
	l	(-105.41)	[2358]	-88.04	[2358]	22.85	[2672]		
		(-104.92)	[569]	-89.15	[1045]	29.1	[1680, 1685]	43.0	[569]
		(-104.6)	[2245]						
SO_3, low-melting	c	(-108.63)[24]	[2358]	-88.19[24]	[2358]	12.5[24]	[2358]		
				-87.8*	[229]				
				-89.2	[1045]				
SO_3, high-melting	c			-90.7*	[229]				
				-89.8	[1045]				
SO_3^{2-}	d	(-151.9*)	[323]	(-116.1*)	[323]	(-7*)	[323]		
		(-151.9)	[2358]	(-116.3)	[2358]	(-7)	[2358]		
		(-153.2)	[569]						
$SO_3 \cdot SeO_3$	c	-166.6	[569]	-134.0	[229]				
		-164.7	[2358]						
SO_3F	d	-193.0	[2358]						
SO_4^{2-}	g	(-177*)	[569, 1789a]						
	d	(-217.32)	[2358]	(-177.97)	[2358]	(4.8)	[2358]	-70	[2358]
		(-217.73)	[569]			(3.85)[25]	[2379]		
ST	g	34.625[26]	[569]	27.765	[569]	48.95	[560]	7.81	[560]
						49.07	[1455]	7.716	[1455]
S_2Br_2	l	(-3)	[2358]						
		(-3.6)	[569]						

1. $\Delta H_0^\circ = -50.028$ [569]. 2. $\Delta H_0^\circ = -50.07$ [2358]. 3. $\Delta H_0^\circ = -49.6435$ [1830]. 4. $\Delta H_0^\circ = -29.3089$ [1830]. 5. $\Delta H_0^\circ = -169.33$ [569]. 6. $\Delta H_0^\circ = -160.798$ [570]. 7. $\Delta H_0^\circ = -95.9084$ [1830]. 8. $T = 273.15\,°K$. 9. $t = 300\,°C$. 10. ΔH_0°. 11. $\Delta H_0^\circ = -70.336$ [2358]. 12. $\Delta H_0^\circ = -70.3398$ [1830]; -70.341 [1618a]. 13. $\Delta H_0^\circ = -70.352$ [569]. 14. $\Delta H_0^\circ = -70.353$ [570]. 15. $\Delta H_0^\circ = -214.2$ [2358]. 16. $\Delta H_0^\circ = -85.50$ [2358]. 17. $\Delta H_0^\circ = -84.717$ [569]. 18. $\Delta H_0^\circ = -203.168^*$ [570]; -203.169 [1618a]. 19. $\Delta H_0^\circ = -202.9859$ [1830]. 20. $\Delta H_0^\circ = -93.21$ [2358]. 21. $\Delta H_0^\circ = -93.1000$ [1830]. 22. $\Delta H_0^\circ = -93.061$ [570]. 23. $\Delta H_0^\circ = -93.241$ [569]. 24. SO_3, I, β. 25. Average of 4.12, 3.48, 3.66 and 4.13 [2379]. 26. $\Delta H_0^\circ = 34.5$ [569].

1	2	3		4		5		6	
S_2Cl_2	g	-4.4^{1}	[2358]	−7.6	[2358]	79.2	[2358]	17.6	[2358]
		-4.0^{2}	[569]	−6.429	[569]	76.7	[569]	17.4	[569]
		-4.75^{3}	[1830]			76.4860	[1830]	17.4169	[1830]
						76.4	[1685]	17.42	[1685]
						76.39	[1881]	17.60	[1881]
	l	(−13.9)	[569, 1208, 2468]	−5.9*	[323]	40*	[323]	(29.7)	[569]
		(−14.2)	[2358]	−9.1*	[229]				
		$(-38.51)^{4}$	[1885]	-33.45^{4}	[1885]				
S_2Cl_4	l			−9.4	[229]				
S_2F_2	g	-54.5320^{5}	[1830]			69.2958	[1830]	15.2929	[1830]
S_2F_{10}	g	−510	[569]						
S_2O	g	-26^{6}	[569]	−33.182	[569]	63.85	[569]	10.58	[569]
		-26.111^{7}	[570]			63.855	[570]		
		−22.7	[2460]						
		−17	[1458]						
		−13	[866]						
$S_2O_3^{2-}$	d	(−154.0)	[1949]	(−122.7)	[1949]	(15.0*)	[323]		
		(−145.7*)	[323]	(−124.0*)	[323]	8*	[323]		
		(−153.6)	[569]			(15.0)	[1685]		
		(−155.9)	[2358]						
$S_2O_4^{2-}$	d	(−178.3*)	[323]	(−143.4*)	[323]	(28*)	[323]		
		(−180.1)	[2358]	(−143.5)	[2358]	(22)	[2358]		
		(−185.2)	[569]						
$S_2O_5^{2-}$	d	(−232.6)	[569]	−189*	[323]	25*	[323]		
$S_2O_5Cl_2$	g	−153.2	[2358]						
	l	−168.7	[2358]					56	[2358]
$S_2O_6^{2-}$	d	(−281.4)	[569]	−231*	[323]	30*	[323]		
		(−286.4)	[2358]						
S_2O_7	c			−148.0*	[229]				
				−149.0*	[1045]				
$S_2O_7^{2-}$	d	−334.9	[2358]						
$S_2O_8^{2-}$	d	(−320.0)	[2358]	−265.4	[2358]	59.3	[2358]		
		(−320.56)	[2524]	−266.01	[2524]	59.5	[2524]		
		(−321.9)	[569]			35*	[323]		
						35	[1685]		
S_3Cl_2	l	−12.4	[2468, 1208]						
$S_3O_6^{2-}$	d	(−286.7)	[2358]	−229*	[323]	33*	[323]		

S_3O_9	g	-314	[569]						
S_4Cl_2	l	-10.2	[2468, 1208]						
$S_4O_6^{2-}$	d	(-288.4)	[569]	(-244.3)	[323]	(36*)	[323]		
		(-292.58)	[2358]			120.5*	[1685]		
S_4N_4	g	110	[779]						
S_5Cl_2	l	-8.8	[2468, 1208]						
$S_5O_6^{2-}$	d	(-295.5)	[2358]	-228.5*	[323]	40*	[323]		
S_6Cl_2	l	-7.0*	[2468, 1208]						
S_7Cl_2	l	-5.3*	[2468, 1208]						
S_8Cl_2	l	-3.5	[2468, 1208]						
DTS	g					53.54	[1454]	8.69	[1454]
		-5.683[8]	[569]	-8.736	[569]	53.49	[569]	8.68	[569]
D_2S	g	-5.8[9]	[569]	-8.527	[569]	51.40	[569]	8.55	[569]
		-5.71	[206]	-8.48	[206]	52.55	[1454]	5.56	[1454]
						52.354	[2032]	8.464	[2032]
D_2SO_4	g	-179.587[10]	[569]	-159.712	[569]	73.6	[569]	20.4	[569]
						73.60	[1429]	20.43	[1429]
HDS	g					68.44	[1429]	16.94	[1429]
						51.72	[1454]	8.31	[1454]
		-5.398[11]	[569]	-8.717	[569]	51.67	[569]	8.30	[569]
HS	g	34.10[12]	[2358]	27.08	[2358]	46.74	[2358]	7.72	[2358]
						46.79[13]	[1455]	7.723[13]	[1455]
		34.8[14]	[569]	27.79	[569]	46.74	[569]	7.73	[569]
		38.4	[1246]			46.746	[570]		
		36.2377[15]	[1830]			46.7445	[1830]	7.7271	[1830]
		32.0[16]	[1618a]	24.99	[1618a]	46.745	[1618a]	7.728	[1618a]
		34.6	[1867]						
		35.029[17]	[570]						
		34.9	[1868]						
HS^+	g	277[18]	[569]						
HS^-	g	-18.3[18]	[569]						
	d	(-4.10)	[1779]	(3.00)	[1779]	(15.0)	[1779, 2358]		
		(-4.2)	[2358]	(-2.88)	[2358]				
HSO_3^-		(-149.67)	[2358]	(-126.15)	[2358]	(33.4)	[2358]		
	d	(-151.9*)	[323]			(26*)	[323]		

1. $\Delta H_0^\circ = -4.18$ [2358]. 2. $\Delta H_0^\circ = -3.648$ [569]. 3. $\Delta H_0^\circ = 4.3917$ [1830]. 4. For the reaction $S_2(g) + Cl_2(g) = S_2Cl_2(g)$ ($\Delta H_0^\circ = -38.33$). 5. $\Delta H_0^\circ = -53.6634$ [1830]. 6. $\Delta H_0^\circ = -25.527$ [569]. 7. $\Delta H_0^\circ = -25.639$ [570]. 8. $\Delta H_0^\circ = -5.0$ [569]. 9. $\Delta H_0^\circ = -5.109$ [569]. 10. $\Delta H_0^\circ = -176.5$ [569]. 11. $\Delta H_0^\circ = -4.7$ [569]. 12. $\Delta H_0^\circ = 34$ [2358]. 13. $T = 300\,^\circ K$. 14. $\Delta H_0^\circ =$ $= 34{,}692$ [569]. 15. $\Delta H_0^\circ = 36.1318$ [1830]. 16. $\Delta H_0^\circ = 31.894$ [1618a]. 17. $\Delta H_0^\circ = 34.919$ [570]. 18. ΔH_0°.

1	2	3		4		5		6	
HSO_3Cl	g					74.09	[2358]	19.0	[2358]
	l	(−143.7)	[2358]					0.28[1]	[336]
		(−132.7)	[1098, 2707]						
HSO_3F	g	−181.9	[336]			71.4	[569]	17.6	[569]
	l	−184.2	[2707]						
		−190.3	[336]						
		−185.0	[569]						
		−186	[2358]						
	d	−190.2	[2707]						
		−191.9	[2358]						
HSO_4^-	d	(−212.08)	[2358]	(−180.69)	[2358]	(31.5)	[2358]	−20	[2358]
		(−212.53)	[569]						
$HS_2O_4^-$	d			−140.0*	[323]				
				−146.9	[2358]				
HTS	g	−5.596[2]	[569]	−8.838	[569]	52.41	[569]	8.41	[569]
						51.52	[1454]	8.42	[1454]
H_2S	g	(−4.93)[3]	[2358]	(−8.02)	[2358]	(49.16)	[569, 2358]	(8.18)	[569, 1454, 2358]
		(−5.0)[4]	[569]	(−8.081)	[569]	(49.17)	[1188]	(8.19)	[1188]
		(−4.820)[5]	[1830]			(49.1628)	[1830]	(8.1831)	[1830]
		(−4.87)[6]	[570]			(49.166)	[570]		
		−19.53[7]	[1454]	(−7.91)	[1454]	(49.18)	[1454]		
		(−4.94)	[206]	(−8.02)	[206]	(49.022)	[2032]	(8.144)	[2032]
		(−4.815)[8]	[1618a]	(−7.89)	[1618a]	(49.152)	[1618a]	(8.17)	[1618a]
		(−4.1)	[157]						
	d	(−9.5)	[2358]	(−6.66)	[2358]	(29)	[2358]		
H_2S^+	g	236	[1214]						
		237.1[7]	[569]						
		237.8	[2358]						
H_2SO_3	d	(−145.51)	[2358]	(−128.56)	[2358]	(55.5)	[2358]		
		(−145.5*)	[323]	(−128.59*)	[323]	(56*)	[323]		
		(−146.61)	[569]						
H_2SO_4	g	−177.8[9]	[569]	−158.44	[569]	(71.9)	[569]	19.3	[569]
						(65.48)	[2611]	16.22	[2611]
						(67.85)	[1429]	19.29	[1429]
						(71.93)	[1429]		
	l	(−194.6)	[569]	−164.983	[569]	37.50	[569]	(33.20)	[569, 1306]

		(-194.548)	[2358]	-164.942	[2358]	37.501	[1306]		
				-144.2*	[323]	37.49	[1618a, 2250]	(34.1)[10]	[2250]
		-193.91	[1618a]	-164.283	[1618a]			(33.18)	[1618a]
	c	-194.019[7]	[2358]						
	d	(-217.32)	[2358]	(-177.97)	[2358]	(4.8)	[2358]	(-70)	[2358]
		(-217.3)	[569]						
$H_2SO_4 \cdot H_2O$	l	(-269.72)	[569]	-227.391	[569]	50.56	[569]	51.35	[569, 1306]
		(-269.58)	[2358]	-227.186	[2358]	50.555	[1306]		
						50.49	[2250]	51.3	[2250]
$H_2SO_4 \cdot H_2O$, monoclinic	c	-269.449[7]	[569]						
$H_2SO_4 \cdot 2H_2O$	l	-341.085	[2358]	-286.777	[2358]	66.06	[569]	62.34	[569, 1306]
						66.063	[1306]		
						66.14	[2250]	62.4	[2250]
$H_2SO_4 \cdot 3H_2O$	c	-411.186	[2358]	-345.185	[2358]	82.549	[1306]	76.23	[1306, 2358]
						82.55	[569]	76.26	[569]
						82.55	[1544]	76.35*	[1544]
$H_2SO_4 \cdot 4H_2O$	c	-480.688	[2358]	-403.011	[2358]	99.09	[569]	91.35	[569, 1306]
						99.091	[1306]		
						99.07	[1544]		
$H_2SO_4 \cdot 6.5H_2O$	c	-653.264	[2358]	-546.413	[2358]	140.51	[2358]		
						140.5	[569]	136.3	[569]
						140.512	[1306]	136.30	[1306]
$H_2SO_4 \cdot 115H_2O$	l	-212.17	[1332]						
		-212.24	[1918]						
		-212.205	[2495]						
$H_2SO_4 \cdot 2500H_2O$	l	-213.92	[1632]						
		-213.91	[2498]						
		-214.33	[1644]						
		-214.09	[569]						
H_2S_2	g	-27.01[13]	[1881]	-20.03	[1881]	62.28	[1881]	12.29	[1881]
		3.65[11]	[569]	-1.074	[569]	62.3	[569]	12.3	[569, 2358]
		2.53	[2358]						
		3.9	[1879]						
		3.83	[1209]						
	l	(-5.51)	[2358]					20.1	[2358]
		(-4.37)	[569]					22.2	[569]
		(-4.21)	[1209]					0.333[12]	[1207]

1. In *cal/g*·°C. 2. $\Delta H_0^\circ = -4.9$ [569]. 3. $\Delta H_0^\circ = -4.381$ [2358]. 4. $\Delta H_0^\circ = -4.306$ [569]. 5. $\Delta H_0^\circ = -4.1220$ [1830]. 6. $\Delta H_0^\circ = -4.178$ [570]. 7. ΔH_0°. 8. $\Delta H_0^\circ = -4.119$ [1618a]. 9. $\Delta H_0^\circ = -174.527$ [569]. 10. $T = 280$ °K. 11. $\Delta H_0^\circ = 4.747$ [569]. 12. Specific at 20 °C. 13. From S_2(g).

1	2	3		4		5		6	
$H_2S_2^+$	g	240[1]	[569]						
		239	[2358]						
$H_2S_2O_4$	d			−140.0*	[323]				
				−147.4	[2358]				
$H_2S_2O_6$	d	−286.4	[2358]						
$H_2S_2O_7$	l	(−304.1)	[569]					64.3	[1072]
	c	−304.4	[2358]					27	[2358]
$H_2S_2O_8$	d	−320.0	[2358]	−265.4	[2358]	59.3	[2358]		
						35*	[323]		
H_2S_3	g	7.38	[1209]						
		7.21	[569]						
		7.27	[2358]						
	l	−3.60	[569]					29.5	[569]
		−3.51	[2358]					0.298[2]	[1207]
		−3.45	[1209]						
H_2S_4	g	10.61	[1209]						
		10.48	[569]						
		5.71	[2358]						
	l	−3.01	[569]					36.8	[569]
		−2.87	[1209]					0.284[3]	[1207]
		−7.85	[2358]						
H_2S_5	g	(13.85)	[1209]						
		(13.74)	[569]						
		(7.98)	[2358]						
	l	(−2.50)	[569]					44.2	[569]
		(−2.0*)	[323]					0.276[3]	[1207]
		(−2.37)	[1209]						
		(−8.35)	[2358]						
H_2S_6	g	17.08	[1209]						
	l	−1.87	[1209]					0.260[3]	[1207]
		−1.99	[569]					51.5	[569]
		−8.85	[2358]						
T_2S	g	−6.171[4]	[569]	−8.726	[569]	52.82	[569]	8.86	[569]
						52.88	[1454]	8.88	[1454]
Sb	g	(62.7)[5]	[2358]	(53.1)	[2358]				
		(62.70)	[2479]	(52.12)	[2479]				
		(62.6)[1]	[1589]						

		(62.36)	[2238]						
		(61.46)	[2238]						
		(49.21)	[712]						
Sb, III	c					(10.92)	[1099, 1589]	(6.03)	[1589, 2479]
								(6.1)[6]	[686]
Sb, IV, explosive form	v	2.54	[2358]						
Sb^+	g	(263.46)[7]	[2358]						
Sb^{2+}	g	(646.1)[8]	[2358]						
Sb^{3+}	g	(1231.6)[9]	[2358]			40.31	[66]		
Sb^{4+}	g	(2251.4)[10]	[2358]						
Sb^{5+}	g					40.31	[66]		
Sb^{6+}	g	(6021)[11]	[2358]						
Sb_2	g	(56.40)	[2479]	(44.75)	[2479]	(60.90)	[2358, 2479]	(8.69)	[1685, 2479]
		(56.3)[12]	[2358]	(44.7)	[2358]	(60.9)	[2685]	(8.70)	[1589, 2358]
		(56.8)[1]	[1589]						
		(50.4)[13]	[1093]						
		(49.83)	[2238]						
		(49.45)	[2238]						
Sb_4	g	(49.00)	[2479]	37.08	[2479]	(83.65)	[2479]	19.35	[1685, 2479]
		(49.0)[14]	[2358]	33.3*	[229]	(84)	[2358]		
		50.2[1]	[1589]			(83.6)	[1685]		
	c	49.78[15]	[868]			40.33[16]	[868]		
		67.5[17]	[868]						
$SbBr_3$	g	−46.5[18]	[2358]	−53.5	[2358]	89.09	[2358]	19.17	[2358, 2484]
						88.8	[1685]	19.18	[1685]
						89.03	[2484]		
	c	(−62.0)	[2358]	−57.2	[2358]	49.5	[2358]		
				−54.4*	[323]	40.2*	[323]		
				−57.7*	[227]				
SbCl	g	−6.22[19]	[2358]						
$SbCl_2$	g	−18.5[20]	[2358]						
$SbCl_3$	g	(−75.0)[21]	[2358]	(−72.0)	[2358]	(80.71)	[2358]	(18.33)	[1685, 2358]
						(80.70)	[2484]	(18.34)	[2484]
						(80.6)	[1685]		
	c	−91.34	[2358]	−77.37	[2358]	44.0	[2358]	25.8	[2358]
						42.2	[161]		

1. ΔH_0°. 2. In $cal/g \cdot {}^\circ C$ at 20.8°C. 3. In $cal/g \cdot {}^\circ C$ at 20°C. 4. $\Delta H_0^\circ = -5.5$ [569]. 5. $\Delta H_0^\circ = 62.63$ [2358]. 6. Per *g-atom* between 20 and 590°C. 7. $\Delta H_0^\circ = 261.91$ [2358]. 8. $\Delta H_0^\circ = 643.1$ [2358]. 9. $\Delta H_0^\circ = 1227.1$ [2358]. 10. $\Delta H_0^\circ = 2245.4$ [2358]. 11. $\Delta H_0^\circ = 6012$ [2358]. 12. $\Delta H_0^\circ = 56.76$ [2358]. 13. Calculated [234] from $(\Delta H_{298}^\circ)_{diss} = 71.2$ [1093]; $\Delta H_0^\circ = 51$. 14. $\Delta H_0^\circ = 50.2$ [2358]. 15. $(\Delta H_{298}^\circ)_{subl}$. 16. $(\Delta S_{298}^\circ)_{subl}$. 17. $Sb_4 \rightarrow 2Sb_2$. 18. $\Delta H_0^\circ = -41.03$ [2358]. 19. $\Delta H_0^\circ = -6$ [2358]. 20. $\Delta H_0^\circ = -18$ [2358]. 21. $\Delta H_0^\circ = -74.57$ [2358].

1	2	3		4		5		6	
$SbCl_5$	g	−94.25[1]	[2358]	−79.91	[2358]	96.04	[2358]	28.95	[2358]
				−73.8*	[229]				
	l	(−105.2)	[2358]	−83.7	[2358]	72	[2358]		
				−86.1*	[229]				
$SbDH_2$	g					58.86	[1087a]	10.29	[1087a]
						58.89	[589]	10.37	[589]
$SbDT_2$	g					62.49	[1087a]	12.41	[1087a]
SbD_2H	g					59.85	[1087a]	10.83	[1087a]
						59.91	[589]	10.91	[589]
SbD_2T	g					61.48	[1087a]	11.78	[1087a]
SbD_3	g					63.28	[588]	11.52	[588]
						58.62	[2482]	11.45	[2482]
						58.63	[1685]	11.44	[1685]
SbF	g	(−11.29)[2]	[2358]	−6.0*	[227]				
SbF_3	c	(−218.8)	[2358]	−199.8*	[323]	25.2*	[323]		
				−186*	[227]				
SbF_5	g					84.46	[1296]	25.71	[1296]
						84.9	[2021]	25.740	[2021]
$SbHT_2$	g					61.27	[1087a]	11.48	[1087a]
SbH_2T	g					59.77	[1087a]	10.76	[1087a]
SbH_3	g	34.681[3]	[2358]	35.31	[2358]	55.61	[1685, 2358, 2482]	9.81	[2358]
		34.64	[1442]	35.42	[1442]	55.65	[1442]	9.89	[588, 1442]
		34.7	[1437a]	35.3*	[323]	53*	[323]	9.83	[2482]
		36.9[4]	[589]			55.68	[588]	9.80	[1685]
		34.6	[1221]						
SbI_3	c	(−24.0)	[2358]	−22.5*	[323]	50.7*	[323]		
				−24.3*	[227]				
	d	(−23.6)	[2358]						
SbI_4	c			−33.3*	[227]				
SbN	g	(63.66)[5]	[2358]			55.2	[1685]	7.42	[1685]
SbO	g	(47.67)[4]	[2358]	38.1*	[227]	57.0	[1685]	7.60	[1685]
				39.7*	[229]				
SbO^+	d			(−42.33)	[2358]				
SbOCl	g	−25.5[6]	[2358]						
	c	(−89.4)	[2358]	−80.1*	[229]				
SbOF	d			−116.5	[2358]				
$Sb(OH)_2F$	d			−173.2	[2358]				

$Sb(OH)_3$	c	−183.7*	[232]	−152.62*	[176]				
				−163.8	[2358]				
	d	−184.9	[2358]	−154.1	[2358]	27.8	[2358]		
SbO_2	c	−96.0	[887]			15.2	[887]		
SbO_2^+	d			−81.32	[2358]				
SbO_2^-	d			−82.5*	[323]				
SbS_3^{2-}	d			−32*	[323]				
$Sb_{0.33}Sr_{0.67}$	c	-26.0^7	[1589]						
$Sb_{0.40}Sr_{0.60}$	c	-23.7^8	[1589]						
$Sb_{0.50}Sr_{0.50}$	c	-23.3^9	[1589]						
SbT_3	g					60.69	[2482]	12.55	[2482]
Sb_2Cl_5	l			−86.1*	[229]				
Sb_2H_4	g	57.2	[2260]						
Sb_2O_3	c	(−167.0)	[887]						
Sb_2O_3, valentinite	c					33.71	[145]	26.83	[145]
Sb_2O_3, cubic, orthorhombic	c	−169.9	[1045]	−150.0	[1045]	29.4	[1680, 1685]	24.23	[1685]
		−169.4	[1898]	−150.2	[1898]				
Sb_2O_3, orthorhombic	c	−168.5	[1045]	−149.1	[1045]				
Sb_2O_3, senarmontite						31.65	[145]	25.08	[145]
Sb_2O_3	d	(−164.9)	[2358]						
Sb_2O_4	c	(−216.9)	[1898, 2358]	(−190.2)	[1898, 2358]	(30.4)	[1685, 2358]	(27.39)	[1685, 2358]
		(−193.3*)	[323]	(−165.9*)	[323]				
		(−209*)	[1045]	(−182.5*)	[1045]				
Sb_2O_5	c	(−229*)	[1045]	(−195.5*)	[1045]			28.11	[1685]
		(−232.3)	[2358]	(−198.2)	[2358]				
		(−215*)	[887]						
	d	(−228.7)	[2358]						
$Sb_2S_2^-$	d			−13*	[323]				
Sb_2S_3, orange	c	(−35.2)	[2358]	−35.1*	[229]	43.2	[480]	29.45	[480]
Sb_2S_3, black	c	(−41.8)	[2358]	−41.5	[2358]	43.5	[2358]	28.65	[2358]
		(−40.5)	[2625]	−42.7*	[229]	30.3*	[1773]		
						39.6	[1685]		
Sb_2S_3	v			−32.0*	[323]	30.3*	[323]		
$Sb_2S_4^{2-}$	d	−52.4	[2358]	−23.8	[2358]	−12.5	[2358]		
$Sb_2(SO_3)_3$	c	−424.8*	[1172]	−499.0*	[229]				
$Sb_2(SO_4)_3$	c	(−574.2)	[2358]						
Sb_2Se_3	c	−24.5	[180]						

1. $\Delta H_0^\circ = -93.70$ [2358]. 2. $\Delta H_0^\circ = -11$ [2358]. 3. $\Delta H_0^\circ = 36.625$ [2358]. 4. $\Delta H_0^\circ = 48$ [2358]. 5. $\Delta H_0^\circ = 64$ [2358]. 6. $\Delta H_0^\circ = -25$ [2358]. 7. $SbSr_2$ phase. 8. Sb_2Sr_3 phase. 9. SbSr phase.

1	2	3		4		5		6	
Sb_2Te_3	c	-14.30[1]	[686]	-14.75[1]	[686]	67.0	[180]		
		-13.5	[2358]	-13.2	[2358]	56	[2358]		
$Sb_4O_5Cl_2$	c	-346.9	[2358]						
Sb_4O_6	g					102	[1685]		
Sb_4O_6, II, cubic	c	(-344.3)	[2358]	(-303.1)	[2358]	(52.8)	[2358]		
Sb_6O_{13}	c	(-670.6)	[2358]	-566*	[1045]				
	c	(-653*)	[1045]	-583.9*	[229]				
$HSb(OH)_4$	c			-209.27*	[6]				
$HSb(OH)_6$	d	-353.4	[2358]						
$HSbO_2$	d	-116.6	[2358]	-97.4	[2358]	11.1	[2358]		
				-97.5*	[323]				
H_3SbF_6	d	(-448.4)	[2358]						
$H_3Sb(OH)_6$	c			-322.57*	[6]				
H_3SbO_4	d	(-216.8)	[2358]						
Sc	g	(82.000)	[2479]	72.235	[2479]	(41.75)	[1685]	(5.28)	[1685]
		(80*)	[1539]	71.9*	[1589]				
		(82.28)	[238]						
		(91.2)	[1764]						
		(91.1)	[1764]						
		(90.98)[2]	[1456]						
	c					9.00	[2479]	(6.01)	[2479]
						9.0	[1685]	(6.00)	[1685]
						8*	[323]		
						8.20	[1589]		
Sc^{3+}	g					37.35	[66]		
	d			(-143.7*)	[323]	-56*	[323]		
$ScBr_3$	c	(-170)	[1773]	-171.5*	[323]	36.7*	[323]		
				-173.0*	[227]				
$ScCl_2$	c	-145*	[443, 444]						
		-145	[445]						
$ScCl_3$	c	(-215)	[1773]	-205.7*	[323]	30.4*	[323]		
		(-186*)	[358]	-204.0*	[227]				
ScF_3	c	-370*	[230]						
ScF_6^{3-}	d			-565*	[323]				
ScI_3	c	-128*	[230]						
ScN	c	-68	[2048]						

ScO	g			3*	[1045]	53.5	[1685]	7.38	[1685]
$ScO_{1.5}$, body-centered	c			−217.4	[2662]				
$Sc(OH)_3$	c	−362.5*	[232]	−293.5*	[323]				
				−294.66*	[176]				
Sc_2O_3	c	−456.16	[1560]	−458.3	[1560]	19.4	[443]	21.2*[3]	[1976]
		−447.28	[1897]	−425.8	[1897]	15*	[1187]		
		−411*	[887]	−389*	[1045]	18.4	[2633]		
		−410*	[1773]						
Sc_2S_3	c	−234*	[1480]						
$HSc(OH)_4$	c			−351.31*	[6]				
$H_3Sc(OH)_6$	c			−464.61*	[6]				
Se	g	(54.412)[4]	[569]	(44.829)	[569]	(42.212)	[569]	4.976	[569]
		(49.16)[5]	[2358]			(42.22)	[2358]	5.02	[2358]
		(49.400)	[2479]	(39.841)	[2479]	(39.02)	[66]	5.59[6]	[1759]
Se, III, hexagonal	c					(10.15)	[1097]	(6.062)	[1097, 2358]
						(10.07)	[569]	(6.06)	[569, 1685]
						(10.14)	[1685]	(6.09)	[2479]
						(11.7)	[1288]	(6.7)	[1288]
						(10.144)	[2358]		
Se, monoclinic	c	1.6	[1288, 2358]			11.7	[1288]	8.5	[1288]
		1.5	[569]					6.5	[569]
Se	v	(1.3)	[1289]			11.5	[1289]	(8.6)	[1289]
		(1.3)[7]	[569]	0.635	[569]			(7.0)	[569]
		(1.2)	[2358]						
Se, red	v	3.9	[1289]			12.5	[1289]	9.7	[1289]
		3.1	[569]			12.3	[569]	7	[569]
Se^+	g	(280.743)[8]	[569]	269.805	[569]	39.025	[569]	5.062	[569]
Se^{2+}	g	(768)[9]	[569]						
Se^{3+}	g	(1506)[9]	[569]						
Se^{4+}	g	(2496)[9]	[569]						
Se^{5+}	g	(4071)[9]	[569]						
Se^{6+}	g	(5964)[9]	[569]						
Se^{7+}	g	(9540)[9]	[569]						
Se^-	g	6*[9]	[569]						
Se^{2-}	d	(17.7)	[569]	(30.9)	[2358]	(41.5)	[1685]		
		(23)	[1773]						

1. $t = 400\,°C$. 2. $\Delta H_0^\circ = 90.55$ [1456]. 3. Average between 273 and 373 °K. 4. $\Delta H_0^\circ = (54.25)$ [569]. 5. $\Delta H_0^\circ = (49)$ [2358]. 6. $t = 300\,°C$. 7. $\Delta H_0^\circ = 1.269$ [569]. 8. $\Delta H_0^\circ = (279.1)$ [569]. 9. ΔH_0°.

1	2	3		4		5		6	
Se_2	g	(33.136)[1]	[569]	(21.186)	[569]	(60.22)	[569]	(8.46)	[569]
		(34.120)	[2479]	(22.214)	[2479]	(60.2)	[1685]	(8.47)	[1685, 2479]
		(33.3)	[1896]			(60.3)	[1896]		
		(34.9)	[2358]						
Se_6	g	35.380	[2479]	20.739	[2479]	110.00	[2479]	29.00	[2479]
		48.7	[2358]			110	[1685]	29.0	[1685]
		35.7	[569]						
$SeBr_2$	g	−5	[2358]						
$SeCl_2$	g	(−9)	[569]	−21.5*	[229]	70.1	[579]		
		(−7.6)	[2358]						
	l			−12.6*	[229]				
$SeCl_4$	c	(−45.3)	[569]	−23.3*	[323]	44*	[323]		
		(−43.8)	[2358]	−25.6*	[229]				
SeF_6	g	(−246)[2]	[569]	(−222.023)	[569]	(75.0)	[569]	26.4	[569, 2358]
		(−267)[3]	[2358]	(−243)	[2358]	(74.99)	[2358]	26.29	[1685]
SeO	g	(13.047)[4]	[2358]	6.66	[569]	56.00	[569]	7.44	[569]
				14*	[229]	59.5	[1685]	7.46	[1685]
						55.939[5]	[2106]	7.467[5]	[2106]
$SeOCl_2$	g	−6	[2358]						
$Se(OH)_3ClO_4$	c	(−146.0)	[569]						
		(−147.4)	[2358]						
SeO_2	g	−40.3[6]	[569]	−31.559	[569]	63.3	[569]	10.2	[569]
						63.307	[2033]	10.233	[2033]
SeO_2, tetragonal	c	(−57.5)	[2310]	−41.5*	[323]	13.6*	[323]		
		(−56.4)	[887, 2311]	−41.8*	[229]				
		(−53.35)	[100]						
		(−53.9)[7]	[1287]						
		(−55.2)[8]	[1287]						
		(−55.4)[9]	[1287]						
		(−57.0)[10]	[1287]						
		(−57.1)[11]	[1287]						
		(−53.9)	[569]						
		(−53.86)	[2358]						
SeO_2	d	(−52.97)	[2358]						
SeO_3, tetragonal	c	−44.1	[1990]			20.1*	[1480]		
		−41.4	[569]						
		−39.9	[2358]						
SeO_3^{2-}	d	(−121.7)	[2358]	(−88.4)	[2358]	(3)	[2358]		

		(−121.3)	[569]			(3.9)	[1685]		
						(4.4)	[339]		
						(3.92)	[511]		
						(4.08)	[340]		
						(4.07)	[509]		
SeO_4^{2-}	g	−120	[569, 1789a]						
		−124	[502]						
		−104*	[506]						
	d	(−143.2)	[2358]	(−105.5)	[2358]	(5.48)	[501]		
		(−143.5)	[569]			(0.9)	[504]		
						(5.5)	[503, 505]		
						(12.9)	[2358]		
Se_2Br_2	g	7	[2358]						
Se_2Cl_2	g	4	[2358]						
	l	(−20.4)	[569]	−11.60*	[323]	45*	[323]		
		(−19.7)	[2358]						
Se_2O_5	c	−99.3	[569]						
		−97.6	[2358]						
Se_4N_4	g	147.7	[779]						
DHSe	g	7.753[12]	[569]	4.222	[569]	54.82	[569]	8.48	[569]
D_2Se	g	(7.766)[13]	[569]	4.824	[569]	54.56	[569]	8.77	[569]
		(18.55)	[207]	15.37	[207]	54.557	[2032]	8.773	[2032]
HSe^-	d	(3.8)	[2358]	(10.5)	[2358]	(19)	[2358]		
		(4.2)	[569]			(22*)	[323]		
						(50.6)	[1685]		
$HSeO_3^-$	d	(−122.98)	[2358]	(−98.36)	[2358]	(33.1)	[2358]		
		(−122.5)	[569]						
$HSeO_4^-$	d	(−139.0)	[2358]	(−108.1)	[2358]	(35.7)	[2358]		
		(−137.9)	[569]						
H_2Se	g	(7.1)[14]	[2358]	(3.8)	[2358]	(52.32)	[2358]	8.30	[2358]
		(8)[15]	[569]	(4.71)	[569]	(52.30)	[569]	8.28	[569]
		(18.67)	[208]	(14.88)	[208]	(54.0)	[208]	8.22	[224]
		(18.16)	[207]	(14.67)	[207]	(52.303)	[2032]	8.282	[2032]
		(19.2)	[157]						
		(18.9)	[1760, 2247]						
	d	(4.6)	[2358]	(5.3)	[2358]	(39.1)	[2358]		
H_2Se^+	g	248	[1214]						
		237	[569]						

1. $\Delta H_0^\circ = 33.5$ [569]. 2. $\Delta H_0^\circ = -243.088$ [569]. 3. $\Delta H_0^\circ = -264.1$ [2358]. 4. $\Delta H_0^\circ = (13.235)$ [569]. 5. $t = 300$℃. 6. $\Delta H_0^\circ = -29.521$ [569]. 7. From hexagonal Se. 8. From vitreous Se. 9. From monoclinic Se. 10. From red amorphous Se. 11. From black amorphous Se. 12. $\Delta H_0^\circ = 8.7$ [569]. 13. $\Delta H_0^\circ = 8.7$ [569]. 14. $\Delta H_0^\circ = 8.05$ [2358]. 15. $\Delta H_0^\circ = 8.949$ [569].

1	2	3		4		5		6	
H_2SeO_3	c	(−125.42)	[569]						
		(−125.35)	[2358]						
	d	(−121.29)	[2358]	(−101.87)	[2358]	(49.7)	[2358]		
		(−143.5)	[569]						
H_2SeO_4	c	(−127.3)	[569]						
		(−126.7)	[2358]						
$H_2SeO_4 \cdot H_2O$	c	(−201.4)	[569]						
		(−200.9)	[2358]						
Si	g	(112)[1]	[1830]			(40.1231)	[1830]	(5.3188)	[1830]
		(105.000)	[2479]	(94.388)	[2479]	(40.12)	[1685]	(5.32)	[1685]
		(112.035)[2]	[570]			(40.1245)	[570]		
		(113)	[1129]						
		(89.9*)	[798]						
		(108.4)	[1085]						
		(106.0)[3]	[1618a]	(95.378)	[1618a]	(40.123)	[1618a]	(5.319)	[1618a]
	l	12.092	[1618a]	10.071	[1618a]	11.275	[1618a]	6.13	[1618a]
	c	(90.6*)[4]	[591]			(4.497)	[1618a, 1830]	(4.782)	[1830]
								(4.783)	[1618a]
						(4.50)	[570, 1239]	(4.73)	[570, 1685]
						(4.51)	[1685]	(5.80)[5]	[1239]
						(4.53)	[2479]	(4.82)	[530]
								(4.823)	[531]
								(4.98)	[189]
								(4.8)	[1356]
Si^{4+}	g					35.94	[66]		
Si_2	g	147.6061[6]	[1830]			54.9272	[1830]	8.2227	[1830]
		148.881*[7]	[570]			53.167	[570]		
		130.9[8]	[1618a]	117.208	[1618a]	54.917	[1618a]	8.22	[1618a]
Si_3	g	158.5323[9]	[1830]			60.6356	[1830]	12.9216	[1830]
		133.16[10]	[1618a]	119.104	[1618a]	60.635	[1618a]	12.921	[1618a]
SiBr	g					58.7	[1685]	9.22	[1685]
$SiBrCl_3$	g					84.49	[1959a]	22.01	[1959a]
$SiBrH_3$	g					62.76	[1946]	12.69	[1946]
						62.65	[1959a]	12.63	[1959a]
$SiBr_2Cl_2$	g					88.43	[1959a]	22.43	[1959a]
$SiBr_2H_2$	g					73.92	[1946]	15.68	[1946]
						74.18	[1959a]	15.77	[1959a]

$SiBr_3Cl$	g					89.99	[1959a]	22.81	[1959a]
$SiBr_3H$	g	−69.3	[2700]	−72.4	[2700]	83.24	[1959a]	19.31	[1959a]
						80.633[5]	[2585]	15.6992[5]	[2585]
	l	−78.3	[2700]	−74.3	[2700]				
$SiBr_3I$	g					96.582	[2016]	23.393	[2016]
$SiBr_4$	g	(−92.6)	[2700]	−96.3	[2700]	90.3	[1685]	23.20	[1685]
						90.24	[1959a]	23.21	[1959a]
						90.6*	[249]		
	l	(−103.0)	[2245, 2700]	99.0	[2700]				
				−75.0*	[229]				
	c	−100.7	[1176]						
SiC	g	179.018[11]	[570]			52.042	[570]		
	c	(−12.4)	[2226]	(−12.3*)	[2226]			(6.60)	[189]
		(−11.8)[12]	[570]						
		(−18.22)[13]	[2400]						
		(−15.0*)	[1086]						
SiC, *α*, hexagonal	c			−10.8[13]	[1741]	(3.935)	[570]	(6.39)	[570]
						(3.94)	[1685]	(6.38)	[1685]
SiC, *β*, cubic	c	−15.8	[1095]	−13.3	[1095]	(3.97)	[1685]	(6.42)	[1685]
		−15.6	[2220]						
SiC_2	g	151.463[14]	[570]			55.749	[570]		
						56.108	[2035]	10.698	[2035]
SiCl	g	48.045*[15]	[570]			56.814	[570]		
		47.7098[16]	[1830]			56.7253	[1830]	8.5542	[1830]
		48.1*[17]	[1618a]	40.46	[1618a]	56.7	[1618a]	8.55	[1618a]
						56.4	[1685]	8.53	[1685]
$SiClD_3$	g					64.968	[2025]	14.021	[2025]
$SiClF_3$	g	−315*	[1618a]	−306.057*	[1618a]	73.571*	[1618a]	18.971	[1618a]
$SiClH_3$	g	43.2*	[19]			59.83*	[956]	12.05*	[956]
						62.984	[2025]	12.018	[2025]
						59.85	[1959a]	12.20	[1959a]
		−48.0[18]	[1618a]	−42.633	[1618a]	59.885	[1618a]	12.199	[1618a]
$SiClI_3$	g					96.84	[1959a]	23.49	[1959a]
$SiCl_2$	g	−37.2[19]	[1830]			67.0662	[1830]	12.2947	[1830]
		−38.066[20]	[570]			66.614	[570]		
		−29.9	[2288]			71.1	[2288]		
		−125*[21]	[129]			71.0	[1685]		

1. $\Delta H_0^\circ = (110.9643)$ [1830]. 2. $\Delta H_0^\circ = (111.00)$ [570]. 3. $\Delta H_0^\circ = (104.964)$ [1618a]. 4. ΔH_0°. 5. $T = 300$ °K. 6. $\Delta H_0^\circ = 146.9285$ [1830]. 7. $\Delta H_0^\circ = 148$ [570]. 8. $\Delta H_0^\circ = 130.223$ [1618a]. 9. $\Delta H_0^\circ = 157.8928$ [1830]. 10. $\Delta H_0^\circ = 132.521$ [1618a]. 11. $\Delta H_0^\circ = 177.585$ [570]. 12. $\Delta H_0^\circ = (-11.573)$ [570]. 13. From Si (l). 14. $\Delta H_0^\circ = 150.17$ [570]. 15. $\Delta H_0^\circ = 47.55^*$ [570]. 16. $\Delta H_0^\circ = 47.2727$ [1830]. 17. $\Delta H_0^\circ = 47.591^*$ [1618a]. 18. $\Delta H_0^\circ = -45.844$ [1618a]. 19. $\Delta H_0^\circ = -37.2249$ [1830]. 20. $\Delta H_0^\circ = -38.00$ [570]. 21. From Si(g); $\Delta H_0^\circ = -131^*$ [1129].

1	2	3		4		5		6	
$SiCl_2$	g	−37.66[1]	[1618a]	−40.438	[1618a]	67.036	[1618a]	12.157	[1618a]
$SiCl_2^+$	g	204	[1214]						
$SiCl_2H_2$	g	76.3*	[19]			68.06	[1496]	14.83	[1567, 1959a]
						68.47	[1959a]		
		−75*[2]	[1618a]	−69.909*	[1618a]	66.498	[1618a]	14.831	[1618a]
$SiCl_3$	g	−87.322*[3]	[570]			75.648	[570]		
		−86.1	[810]						
$SiCl_3^+$	g	209	[1214]						
$SiCl_3F$	g	−201*[4]	[1618a]	−192.565*	[1618a]	80.295	[1618a]	21.53	[1618a]
$SiCl_3H$	g	−117.4	[2699]	−109.6	[2699]	(71.9747)[5]	[2585]	(14.5847)[5]	[2585]
		−112*[7]	[1618a, 2211]	−104.524*	[1618a]	(75.00*)	[956]	(18.12*)	[956]
						(74.892)	[1618a]	(18.041)	[1618a]
						(74.85)	[1959a]	(18.04)	[1959a]
	l	123.9	[2699]	−109.7	[2699]				
$SiCl_3I$	g					86.75	[1959a]	22.26	[1959a]
$SiCl_4$	g	(−151.8)	[2699]	(−142.3)	[2699]	(70.06*)	[955]	(21.63*)	[955]
		(−151.8)[6]	[1830]			(79.0646)	[1830]	(21.6446)	[1830]
		(−150.997)[8]	[570]			(79.004)	[570]		
		(−157.1)[9]	[1618a]	(−147.557)	[1618a]	(79.068)	[1618a]	(21.576)	[1618a]
		(−163.2)	[810]			(79.1)	[1685]	(21.65)	[1685]
		(−145.7)	[1176]			(79.01)	[1959a]	(21.63)	[1959a]
	l	−158.9	[2699]	(−143.0)	[2699]	(60.363)	[2022]	10.478	[2022]
		(−170.2)	[810]			(60.3997)	[1830]	10.4872	[1830]
		(−160.5)	[2245]			(60.759)	[570]		
						(57.3)	[1685]	(34.73)	[1683]
$SiCl_4^+$	g	222	[1214]						
SiD	g					48.7	[1685]	7.3	[1685]
$SiDF_3$	g					65.405	[2583]	15.203[10]	[2583]
						66.90	[1959a]	16.03	[1959a]
$SiDH_3$	g					52.58	[257]	10.77	[1205]
						52.61	[256]		
$SiDT_3$	g					56.48	[256]	13.54	[256]
SiD_2F_2	g					64.00	[1959a]	14.52	[1959a]
SiD_2H_2	g					54.23	[1959a]	11.26	[1959a]
						54.27	[256, 257]	11.33	[1205]
SiD_2T	g					57.07	[256]	13.18	[256]
SiD_3F	g					59.29	[1959a]	13.43	[1959a]
						59.892	[2025]	13.146	[2025]

SiD_3H	g					54.27	[1959a]	11.85	[1205, 1959a]
						54.29	[256, 257]		
SiD_3I	g					66.947	[2025]	14.999	[2025]
SiD_3T	g					55.70	[256]	12.83	[256]
SiD_4	g					52.36	[257]	12.47	[257]
						52.34	[1959a]	12.46	[1959a]
SiF	g	4.935*[11]	[570]			53.941	[570]		
		4.75[12]	[1830]			53.9432	[1830]	7.8046	[1830]
		-1.0[13]	[1618a]	-8.519	[1618a]	53.939	[1618a]	7.804	[1618a]
						53.9	[1685]	7.79	[1685]
$SiFH_3$	g					59.094	[2025]	11.333	[1618a, 2025]
						56.95	[1959a]	11.33	[1959a]
		129.5	[1163]			66.202	[2420]	15.058	[2420]
		-105.0[14]	[1618a]	-99.505	[1618a]	57.035	[1618a]		
SiF_2	g	-125.5[15]	[1830]	-284	[1163]				
		-148*	[1923]						
		-168.28[16]	[570]						
		-149.0[17]	[1618a]	-151.223	[1618a]	60.399	[1618a]	10.487	[1618a]
SiF_2H_2	g					62.62	[1959a]	12.87	[1959a]
		-194.0*[18]	[1618a]	-187.5*	[1618a]	62.282	[1618a]	12.191	[1618a]
SiF_3	g	-250.896[19]	[570]			66.456	[2420]	11.327	[2420]
		-267.5[20]	[1618a]	-264.458	[1618a]	66.963	[1618a]	14.894	[1618a]
						56.966	[570]		
SiF_3H	g					64.887[21]	[2583]	14.478[21]	[2583]
						66.26	[1959a]	15.17	[1959a]
		-283.0[22]	[1618a]	-275.133	[1618a]	66.317	[1618a]	15.12	[1618a]
SiF_4	g	(-356.02)[23]	[1830, 2694]	(-359.9*)	[232]	(67.4343)	[1830]	(17.5655)	[1830]
		(-370.8)	[2249]	(-360.5)	[2249]	(66.05)	[2616]	(16.88)	[2616]
		(-374)	[2245, 2249]			(67.77)	[2597]	(17.56)	[2597]
		(-385.98)[24]	[2695, 1618a]	(-375.855)	[1618a]	(67.3)	[1685]	(17.43)	[1685]
						(67.433)	[1618a]	(17.565)	[1618a]
						(67.43)	[1959a]	(17.57)	[1959a]
		(-372.5)[25]	[570]			(67.435)	[570]		
		(-372.4)	[87]			(59.85)[26]	[2086]		
SiF_6^{2-}	d			-511*	[323]	30.3	[2452]		

1. $\Delta H_0^\circ = -37.688$ [1618a]. 2. $\Delta H_0^\circ = -73.22$* [1618a]. 3. $\Delta H_0^\circ = -87$* [570]. 4. $\Delta H_0^\circ = -200.49$* [1618a]. 5. $T = 300$°K. 6. $\Delta H_0^\circ = -151.2894$ [1830]. 7. $\Delta H_0^\circ = -110.8$* [1618a]. 8. $\Delta H_0^\circ = -150.472$ [570]. 9. $\Delta H_0^\circ = -156.58$ [1618a]. 10. $t = 0$°C. 11. $\Delta H_0^\circ = 4.5$* [570]. 12. $\Delta H_0^\circ = 4.3193$ [1830]. 13. $\Delta H_0^\circ = -1.437$ [1618a]. 14. $\Delta H_0^\circ = -102.77$ [1618a]. 15. $\Delta H_0^\circ = -125.2513$ [1830]. 16. $\Delta H_0^\circ = -168$* [570]. 17. $\Delta H_0^\circ = -148.751$ [1618a]. 18. $\Delta H_0^\circ = -191.898$* [1618a]. 19. $\Delta H_0^\circ = -250$* [570]. 20. $\Delta H_0^\circ = -266.899$ [1618a]. 21. $t = 0$°C. 22. $\Delta H_0^\circ = -281.316$ [1618a]. 23. $\Delta H_0^\circ = -384.6910$ [1830]. 24. $\Delta H_0^\circ = -384.65$ [1618a]. 25. $\Delta H_0^\circ = -371.168$ [570]. 26. $T = 186.35$°K.

1	2	3		4		5		6	
SiH	g	89.4269[1]	[1830]			47.3195	[1830]	7.1810	[1830]
		89.039[2]	[570]			47.309	[570]		
						47.27	[1685]	7.17	[1685]
		114.0[3]	[1618a]	105.835	[1618a]	47.419	[1618a]	6.982	[1618a]
SiH^+	g	267	[1214]						
$SiHT_3$	g					55.64	[256]	12.98	[256]
SiH_2^+	g	311	[1214]						
		285	[2444]						
SiH_2T_2	g					55.29	[256]	12.07	[256]
SiH_3	g	49.2	[2444]						
SiH_3^+	g	214	[1214]						
SiH_3I	g					64.536	[2025]	12.863	[2025]
SiH_3T	g					53.16	[256]	12.98	[256]
						48.8858	[1830]	11.16	[1830]
SiH_4	g	(7.8)	[901, 2259]	(12.5)[4]	[901]	(48.88)	[722]	(10.22)	[722]
		(7.3)	[1437, 1437a]			(48.79)	[955]	(10.24)	[955, 1685]
		(9.9)[5]	[157]			(48.87)	[1959a]	(10.23	[1959a]
		(11.3)	[1205]			(60.04)	[1205]	(10.25)	[1205]
		(11.3)[6]	[1205]			(48.89)	[257, 1685]		
		(7.8)[7]	[1618a, 1830]	(13.184)	[1618a]	(48.789)	[1618a]	(10.236)	[1618a]
SiH_4^+	g	266	[1214]						
SiI_4	g	−47.7	[1176]			98.76	[17]	24.01	[17, 1959a]
						96.85	[1959a]		
						78.4	[1685]		
	c	(−38.5)	[2245]	−33.3*	[227]				
SiN	g	119.8258[8]	[1830]			51.7949	[1830]	7.2105	[1830]
		110.818*[9]	[570]			51.788	[570]		
						51.78	[1685]	7.21	[1618a, 1685]
		121.0[10]	[1618a]	113.7	[1618a]	51.793	[1618a]		
SiO	g	(−21.411)[11]	[1830]			(50.5473)	[1830]	7.1469	[1830]
		(−21.41)	[891]			(50.53)	[891]		
		(−21.725)[12]	[570]			(50.543)	[570]		
		(−21.8)	[1597]	(−28.2*)	[1597]	(50.55)	[1680]		
		(−23.0)	[730]	(−29.4)	[730]				
		(−29*)	[1425]						
		(−22.2)	[1773]						
		(−19*)	[863]						
		(−21.16)	[895]						

		(−21.27)	[2558]						
		(−20.53*)	[399]						
		(−21.411)[12]	[2282]						
		(−23.3)	[2282]						
		(−24.6)	[112]						
		(−24.04)	[2695]						
		(−24.2)[13]	[1618a]	(−30.624)	[1618a]	(50.546)	[1618a]	7.146	[1618a]
	c	−108.5	[57]						
$SiOF_2$	g	−231.0[14]	[1618a]	−227.231	[1618a]	64.806	[1618a]	12.832	[1618a]
SiO_2	g	−74.18[15]	[570]			54.368	[570]		
		−82[16]	[1830]			54.6173	[1830]	10.6609	[1830]
		−76.2[17]	[1618a]	−76.548	[1618a]	54.67	[1618a]	10.661	[1618a]
	l	−215.948	[1618a]	−203.342	[1618a]	11.22	[1618a]	10.596	[1618a]
SiO_2, quartz	c	−217.5[18]	[1298, 1331, 1618a]	−204.53	[1618a]	10.0	[1618a]	10.634	[1618a]
		−215.8	[1004]						
		−210.0[19]	[570]						
SiO_2, α-quartz	c	(−210.25)	[1896]	−197.3	[1896]			(11.0)	[189]
		(−208.3)	[2249]						
		(−210.26)	[1594]						
		(−210.2)	[1594, 2245, 2249]						
		(−217.72)	[2695]						
SiO_2, β-quartz	c	(−210.26)	[2324]			(10.00)	[570]	(10.63)	[570]
SiO_2, α-cristoballite	c	(−209.9)	[1045]	(−196.9)	[1045]				
		(−209.55)	[1045, 1594]	(−196.65)	[1045, 1594]				
		(−208.02)[20]	[891]						
SiO_2, β-cristoballite	c	(−206.6)	[2249]			10.20	[1685]		
		(−208.46)	[2324]						
		(−209.3)	[1594, 2245, 2249]						
SiO_2, tridymite	c	−207.63[21]	[891]			10.4	[1685]		
SiO_2, α-tridymite	c	(−209.4)	[1045]	(−196.5)	[1045]	8.6[21]	[1685]		
SiO_2, γ-tridymite	c	−208.94	[2324]						
SiO_2	v	(−205.3)	[2249]						
		(−207.99)	[2324]						
		(−215.94)	[2695]						

1. $\Delta H_0^\circ = 89.0227$ [1830]. 2. $\Delta H_0^\circ = 88.632$ [570]. 3. $\Delta H_0^\circ = 113.699$ [1618a]. 4. Calculated [234] from $K = 1.9 \cdot 10^{-10}$ [901]. 5. ΔH_0°. 6. $t = 20°C$. 7. $\Delta H_0^\circ = 10.085$ [1618a]; 10.0977 [1830]. 8. $\Delta H_0^\circ = 119.5438$ [1830]. 9. $\Delta H_0^\circ = 119.536*$ [570]. 10. $\Delta H_0^\circ = 120.705$ [1618a]. 11. $\Delta H_0^\circ = (-21.6876)$ [1830]. 12. $\Delta H_0^\circ = (-21.695)$ [2302]. 13. $\Delta H_0^\circ = (-24.476)$ [1618a]. 14. $\Delta H_0^\circ = -229.953$ [1618a]. 15. $\Delta H_0^\circ = -73.812$ [570]. 16. $\Delta H_0^\circ = -81.6889$ [1830]. 17. $\Delta H_0^\circ = -75.888$ [1618a]. 18. $\Delta H_0^\circ = -216.311$ [1618a]. 19. $\Delta H_0^\circ = -208.812$ [570]. 20. ΔH_0°. 21. Coesite.

1	2	3		4		5		6	
SiO_2, aerosil	v	−206.85	[2324]						
SiO_3^{2-}	c			−212	[323]				
SiP	c	−15.0	[2628]			6.8	[1773]		
		−16.5	[2625]						
SiS	g	29.1799[1]	[1830]			53.4346	[1830]	7.7134	[1830]
		16.926	[1618a]	4.593	[1618a]	53.427	[1618a]	7.711	[1618a]
						53.43	[1685]	7.70	[1685]
SiS_2	l	−37.303	[1618a]	−37.878	[1618a]	21.621	[1618a]	11.04	[1618a]
	c	(−49)	[1293, 2236]	−34.0*	[229]				
		(−43)	[1618a]	−41.899	[1618a]	16.0	[1618a]	14.99	[1618a]
SiSe	g					56.2	[1685]	8.03	[1685]
$SiSe_2$	c	−12.0	[1293]			19.2*	[889]		
SiT_4	g					53.92	[256]	13.90	[256]
SiTe	g					58.2	[1685]	8.25	[1685]
Si_2C	g	137.554[2]	[570]			57.790	[570]		
Si_2H_6	g	15.1	[2260]						
		17.1	[1437, 1437a]						
	l	−36.2	[1205]						
		−35.8[3]	[1206]						
Si_3H_8	g	25.9	[1440]						
	l	−54.1[3]	[1206]						
		−54.4	[1205]						
Si_3N_4	c	(−179)	[1773]			(22.8)	[1618a, 1680, 1685]		
		(−179.25)	[1618a]	−154.799	[1618a]			23.87	[1618a]
						(25.6)[4]	[2133]		
Si_4H_{10}	l	−70.4[3]	[1206]						
		−70.8	[1205]						
H_2SiF_6	d	(−556.2)	[2249]						
		(−554.6)	[211]						
$H_2SiF_6 \cdot 213H_2O$	d	−567.1	[1331]						
H_2SiO_3	c			−244.5*	[323]				
				−243.4*	[229]				
H_2SiO_4	c			−298.6*	[229]				
$H_2Si_2O_5$	c	−493.39	[2324]						
Sm	g	(50.000)	[2479]	41.819	[2479]	(43.75)	[1685]	(7.25)	[1685]
		(49.56)[5]	[1589]	41.48	[1589]	(54.65)	[2302]	(10.80)	[2302]

		(49.9*)	[2275]			(50.52)	[2302]		
		(50.0)	[2679]						
		(48.52)[6]	[445]						
	c					16.3	[1685]	6.50	[1685]
						13.95*	[323]	5.9*	[323]
						16.61	[1589]	7.06	[1589]
						16.28	[2479]	6.49	[2479]
						16.64[7]	[2423]	6.76	[2423]
						12.3	[1680]		
						16.32*	[2396]		
Sm^{2+}	d			-123	[1976]	-18	[1976]		
				-122*	[1977]				
Sm^{3+}	d			(-159)	[1976]	-50	[1976]		
				(-158*)	[1977]	-42.3*	[323]		
				(-167.0)	[229]				
SmB_6	c	-108.6	[455]						
$SmBr_3$	c	-207*	[230]						
		-209*	[2663]						
$SmCl(OH)_2$	c			-296.5	[14]				
$SmCl_2$	c	-195.6	[1865]	-183.9*	[234]				
		-192*	[442]	-184	[1976]				
		-203	[445, 446]	-183*	[1977				
$SmCl_3$	c	(-243)	[446]	-232.9*	[227]	34	[446]		
		(-244.18)	[1977]	-226*	[1977]				
		(-243*)	[442]	-231.9*	[323]	34.8*	[323]		
				-227	[1976]				
$SmCl_3 \cdot 6H_2O$	c			-585	[1976]	91.1	[2422]		
				-584*	[1977]				
SmI_3, β	c	(-149)	[1976]	-147	[1976]				
				-152.1*	[323]	51.6*	[323]		
				-152.3*	[227]				
				-146*	[1977]				
SmO	c					15.7*	[2523]		
$SmO_{1.5}$	c	-216.95	[2523]	-206.4	[2523]				
SmOCl	c	-238	[1976]	-225	[1976]				
$Sm(OH)_3$	c	-358.8*	[229]	(-308.7*)	[323]				
				(-314.0)	[14]				
Sm_2O_3	c	-433.90	[1659]	-412.85	[1659]	33.22[8]	[1659]	27.37	[1659]

1. $\Delta H_0^\circ = 28.8677$ [1830]. 2. $\Delta H_0^\circ = 136.585$ [570]. 3. $t = 20\,^\circ$C. 4. $S_{298}^\circ - S_0^\circ$. 5. $\Delta H_0^\circ = 49.42$ [1589]. 6. $\Delta H_0^\circ = 48.45$ [445]. 7. $S_{298}^\circ - S_0^\circ$. 8. $S_{298}^\circ - S_{10}^\circ$.

1	2	3		4		5		6	
Sm_2O_3	c	−430*	[1045]	−410.5*	[1045]	36.1	[1659, 2523, 2679]		
		−433.8[1]	[2679]	−410*	[229]	35.4	[2523]		
		−433.89	[1580]	−412	[1976]				
				−411*	[1977]				
Sm_2S_3	c	−253*	[2683]						
$Sm_2(SO_4)_3$	c	−928.5	[1977]	−845*	[1977]				
				−846	[1966]				
$Sm_2(SO_4)_3 \cdot 8H_2O$	c	−1509.7	[1977]	−1316*	[1977]	160.9	[1685]	144.9	[1685]
		−1522*	[323]			154.1	[323]		
		−1526*	[229]						
Sn	g	(72.000)	[2479]	(63.667)	[2479]				
		(72.20)[2]	[1589]	(63.88)	[1589]				
Sn, white	c					(12.32)	[1589]	(6.45)	[1589]
						(12.29)	[1685]		
Sn, gray	c	(0.5)[3]	[1770]						
Sn^{2+}	g					40.24	[66]		
	d	−2.39	[323]	−6.28	[323]	15.0	[202]		
						−4.9	[1685]		
Sn^{4+}	g					40.24	[66]		
	d			0.65*	[323]				
Sn_2	g	96*	[1598]					7.06	[1625]
		97.0*	[402]						
$SnBr_2$	c			−59.6*	[323]	34.9*	[323]		
				−60.3*	[227]				
$SnBr_4$	g					98.62	[729]	24.71	[729, 1685]
						98.2	[1685, 1773]		
	l	−108.4	[2280]						
	c			−76.9	[229]				
$Sn(CN)_2$	c	43*	[696, 2683]						
$Sn(CNS)_2$	c	20*	[696]						
		23*	[2683]						
$SnCO_3$	c	−167*	[696]						
		−177*	[2683]						
SnCl	g					60.1	[1685]	8.53	[1685]
$SnCl_2$	c					−72.2*	[323]	29.3*	[323]
						−73.6*	[227]		

$SnCl_2 \cdot 2H_2O$	c			−188.3*	[229]				
$SnCl_2 \cdot 4H_2O$	c	−366*	[230]						
$SnCl_2 \cdot 6H_2O$	c	−505*	[230]						
$SnCl_4$	g					87.20	[729]	23.53	[729, 1685]
						87.2	[1685]		
$[SnCl_6]^{2-}$	d	−235*	[331]						
	l	(−163.9)	[2280]						
$Sn(ClO_3)_2$	c	−46*	[2683]			(62.5)	[1685]	(39.49)	[1685]
$Sn(ClO_4)_2$	c	−54*	[2683]						
SnF	g					57.4	[1685]	8.04	[1685]
SnF_2	c	−155*	[230]						
		−152*	[583]						
SnF_4	g					76.2*	[249]		
						75.0	[1685]		
SnF_6^{2-}	d			−420*	[323]	0*	[323]		
SnH	g					50.92	[1685]	7.02	[1685]
$Sn(HCO_3)_2$	c	−353	[2683]						
$Sn(HS)_2$	c	−3*	[2683]						
$Sn(HSO_4)_2$	c	−424*	[2683]						
SnH_2	c	−17*	[2683]						
SnH_4	g	38.9	[1437, 1437a]						
		35.0^{4}	[2259]						
SnI	g					65.5	[1683]		
SnI_2	c			−34.4	[323]	40.3*	[323]		
				−34.9	[227]				
SnI_4	g					106.6	[1685]	25.18	[1685]
						106.66	[729]	25.17	[729]
	c	−47.6	[2280]						
$SnMoO_4$	c	−258*	[2683]						
$Sn(NH_2)_2$	c	−13*	[2683]						
$Sn(NO_2)_2$	c	−67*	[2683]						
$Sn(NO_3)_2$	c	−106*	[2683]						
		−109*	[696]						
SnO	g	−1*	[895]	−6.5	[1045]	(55.46)	[1685]	(7.58)	[1685]
	c	(−68.4)	[970]	(−61.5)	[970]	(13.5)	[970, 1685]	(10.59)	[1685]
		(−68.35)	[1596]						

1. $\Delta H_0^\circ = -432.2$ [2679]. 2. $\Delta H_0^\circ = 72.22$ [1589]. 3. $t = 13\,^\circ C$. 4. ΔH_0°.

1	2	3		4		5		6	
$Sn(OH)_2$	c	(−121*)	[696]	(−115.96*)	[176]	(21.6*)	[176]		
$Sn(OH)_4$	c			−225.81*	[176]	20.7*	[176]		
				−227.5*	[323]	29*	[323]		
				−229.0*	[229]				
$Sn(OH)_6^{2-}$	d			−310.5*	[323]				
SnO_2	c	(−138.7)	[2162]	(−123.9)	[2162]	(11.6)	[2162]		
		(−138.82)	[1596]						
$SnReO_4$	c	−401*	[2683]						
SnS	g					57.9	[1685]	8.24	[1685]
	c	(−24.34)	[2223]	(−24.19)	[2223]	(19.4)	[2223]		
		(−25.1)	[2223]	(−24.6)	[970]	(18.4)	[970, 1685, 1732]	11.77	[1685, 1732]
		52.6[1]	[1012]	(−23.9*)	[232]	(18.2*)	[247]		
				(−23.09)	[176]				
$SnSO_3$	c	−148*	[2683]						
$Sn(SO_3)_2$	c	−299.2*	[1172]						
$SnSO_4$	c	−211*	[696]						
		−220*	[2683]						
$Sn(SO_4)_2$	c			−346.8*	[323]	37.1*	[323]		
				−344.6*	[229]				
SnS_2	c	−40.0	[125]			20.9	[1685, 1732]	16.76	[1685, 1732]
		−51.5	[125]						
SnSe	g	52.4[1]	[1527]			60.8	[1685]	8.57	[1685]
		50.35[1]	[1527]			21.3*[1]	[180]		
	c	−16.4	[970]	−16.4	[970]	22.5	[970]		
		−16.5	[1773]			20.6*	[247]		
SnSe, white, hexagonal	c	−21.7	[101]						
$SnSeO_4$	c	−152*	[2683]						
$SnSiO_3$	c	−274*	[2683]						
SnTe	g	53.13[1]	[1527]			62.7	[1685]	8.70	[1685]
		53.9[1]	[1527]			24.2*[1]	[180]		
	c	−14.6	[2625]			24.2	[1680, 1685]		
$SnWO_4$	c	−278*	[2683]						
Sn_2H_6	g	65.6	[2260]						
Sn_2S_2	g	56.5[2]	[1012]						
Sn_2S_3	c			−85.0	[125]				
Sn_2S_5	c			−157.5	[125]				
$HSn(OH)_3$	c			−172.61	[6]				

$[HSn(OH)_4]^-$	d			−201.80*	[6]				
$HSnO_2^-$	d			(−98.0*)	[323]				
$H_2Sn(OH)_4$	c			−229.25*	[6]				
$H_2Sn(OH)_6$	c			−339.30*	[6]				
$H_4Sn(OH)_6$	c			−342.56*	[6]				
Sr	g	(39.30)	[1589]	(31.30)	[1589]	(32.3239)	[77]		
		(39.131)[3]	[570]			(39.3251)	[570]		
		(39.100)	[2479]	(31.104)	[2479]	(39.32)	[1685]		
		(36.1)	[867]						
	c					(12.7)	[570]	(6.50)	[570]
						(12.5*)	[244, 1589, 1984]	(6.3*)	[1589]
						(12.5)	[1685]	(6.30)	[1685, 2479]
Sr^+	g	(171.925)[4]	[570]			40.7026	[570]		
Sr^{2+}	g					39.33	[66]		
	d					(−6.3)	[185]		
						(−7.3)	[1685]		
SrB_6	c	50.4*	[494]						
$Sr(BF_4)_2$		43.2[5]	[2100]						
		38.5	[1153]						
SrBr	g	−51.7[6]	[1170]			62.5	[1685]	8.78	[1685]
SrBrH	c	−110.8	[1166]						
$SrBr_2$	g					75.99*	[297]	14.536*	[297]
	c	(−171.2)	[1166]	−166.3*	[323]	33.8*	[323]		
				−166.0*	[227]	32.40	[2518]	(18.01)	[2518]
						35.0	[1685]		
						33.7*	[698]		
						34*	[2243]		
$Sr(BrO_3)_2$	c					58.1*	[699]		
$Sr(CN)_2$	c	−49*	[2683]						
$Sr(CNO)_2$	c	−203*	[693]						
$Sr(CNS)_2$	c	−87*	[693, 2683]						
$SrCO_3$	c			(−272.02*)	[177]	(23.5*)	[177]		
						(23.8*)	[699]		
						(22.7*)	[228]		
SrCl	g	−64.8[6]	[1170]	2.8*	[227]	59.8	[1685]	8.63	[1685]
SrClH	c	−125.5	[1166]						
$SrCl_2$	g					70.51*	[297]	14.224*	[297]

1. $(\Delta H^\circ_{298})_{subl}$. 2. $2SnS(c) \rightarrow Sn_2S_2(g)$. 3. $\Delta H^\circ_0 = 39.2$ [570]. 4. $\Delta H^\circ_0 = 170.513$ [570]. 5. $T = 550^\circ K$. 6. ΔH°_0.

1	2	3		4		5		6	
$SrCl_2$	c	(−210.0)	[2375]			(27)	[2243]		
		(−198.2)	[1166]			(28.0*)	[698]		
						(30.0)	[1685]		
$SrCl_2 \cdot H_2O$	c			−248.2*	[229]				
$SrCl_2 \cdot 2H_2O$	c			−306.1*	[229]				
$SrCl_2 \cdot 4H_2O$	c	−482*	[230]						
$SrCl_2 \cdot 6H_2O$	c	(−624*)	[230]	−533.1*	[229]				
				−532.22	[190]	83.73	[190]		
$SrCl_2 \cdot SrF_2$	c	−498.0	[96]	−481.4*	[229]				
		−499.4	[2243]						
$Sr(ClO_3)_2$	c	−172.5*	[689]			54.5*	[699]		
		−173*	[2683]						
		−183	[481]						
$Sr(ClO_4)_2$	c	−177*	[693]			59.2*	[699]		
		−187*	[2683]						
$Sr(CrO_2)_2$	c					32.4*	[251]		
$SrCrO_4$	c	(−332*)	[232]	−308.06[1]	[177]	34.6*	[699]		
		(−326)	[481]						
SrD	g					52.1	[1685]	7.35	[1685]
SrF	g	−88.5[2]	[1170]	−10.9*	[227]	57.0	[1685]	8.22	[1685]
SrF_2	g	−186.6[3]	[1370]			65.26*	[297]	13.603*	[297]
		−211.7[4]	[1809]						
	c	(−289.0)	[890]	−277.0*	[176]	16.9*	[176]	16.3*	[228]
				−277.8*	[323]	21.4*	[323]		
				−277.4*	[227]	19.5*	[225]		
						18*	[890]		
						20.9*	[698]		
						19.5	[1685]		
SrH	g			(34.13)	[77]	(50.822)	[77]		
						(50.78)	[1685]	(7.18)	[1685]
$Sr(HCO_3)_2$	c	(−467*)	[232, 2683]	−421.65*	[177]				
		(−464*)	[693]						
SrHI	c	−92.3	[1166]						
$SrHPO_4$	c	(−432.87)	[709]	−399.7*	[323]	31.2*	[323]		
				−401.8*	[229]				
$Sr(HS)_2$	c	−114*	[693]						
		−120*	[2683]						
$Sr(HSO_4)_2$	c	−546*	[2683]						

$SrHfO_3$	c	−425.7	[353]						
SrI	g	−49.8[2]	[1170]			64.4	[1685]	8.83	[1685]
$Sr(IO_3)_2$	c	−245.0	[61]						
$Sr(IO_3)_2 \cdot 2H_2O$	c	−316.3	[615]						
SrI_2	g					79.62*	[297]	14.659*	[297]
	c	(−133.8)	[1166]	−135*	[323]	39.2*	[323]		
				−134.4*	[227]	37.8	[698]		
				−124.2*	[229]	38	[2243]		
						38	[1685]		
$SrI_2 \cdot 2H_2O$	c	−283*	[234]						
$SrI_2 \cdot 4H_2O$	c	−424*	[230]						
$Sr(MnO_4)_2$	c	−357*	[693]			68.6*	[699]		
$SrMoO_3$	c	−308.6	[171]	−284.9	[171]				
$SrMoO_4$	c	−372.2	[170]	−346.2	[170]	29.97	[170]		
		−369.1*	[172]	−345.6*	[172]				
		−367*	[2683]						
$Sr(NO_2)_2$	c			−145.1*	[323]	42*	[323]		
				−149.52*	[177]				
$Sr(NO_3)_2$	c			−186*	[323]	47.4*	[323]		
				−186.0*	[229]	48.8*	[699]		
						48.5*	[161]		
						46.72	[2518]	(35.91)	[2518]
$Sr(NO_3)_2 \cdot 4H_2O$	c			−412.4	[190]	86.91	[190]		
				−411.4*	[229]				
$Sr(N_3)_2$	c	(1.72)	[1356]	35.63	[1356]	35.5	[1356]		
		(0.1)	[37a]			46*	[323]		
SrO	g	−14.2[5]	[366]	105.10	[77]	54.960	[77]		
		−14.24[6]	[570]			54.961	[570]		
		5.7[2]	[1015]			54.95	[1685]	7.89	[1685]
	c	(−141.1)[7]	[570]	(−137.07*)	[250]	(13.3*)	[698]	10.64	[570]
		(−139.9)	[575]						
		(−144.44)	[1902]						
		(−144.4)	[1900]	(−137.3)	[1900]				
$SrO \cdot Al_2O_3$	c	−560.5	[903]						
		−541.9	[178a]	−549.5	[178a]	25.62	[178a]		
		−557.4	[147]						
$3SrO \cdot Al_2O_3$	c	−847.2	[903]						
		21.04[8]	[1940]						

1. $t = 15\,^\circ C$. 2. ΔH_0°. 3. Calculated [245] from $(\Delta H_{296}^\circ)_{subl} = 103.7$ [1370] and $(\Delta H_{298}^\circ)S_2F_2(c) = -290.3$ [2245]. 4. Calculated [245] from $(\Delta H_{298}^\circ)_{subl} = 78.6$ [1809] and $(\Delta H_{298}^\circ)SrF_2(c) = -290.3$ [2245]. 5. $\Delta H_0^\circ = -13.8$ [366]. 6. $\Delta H_0^\circ = -13.813$ [570]. 7. $\Delta H_0^\circ = -140.553$ [570]. 8. From SrO(c) and Al_2O_3(c).

1	2	3		4		5		6	
$4SrO \cdot (Al_2O_3)_{0.65}$, β	c	13.65[1]	[1938]						
$4SrO \cdot Al_2O_3$, α	c	−984.4	[903]						
		11.2[1]	[1938]						
$4SrO \cdot Al_2O_3$, β	c	−987.1	[903]						
		10.2[1]	[1938]						
$4Sr \cdot (Al_2O_3)_{1.13}$, β	c	15.0[1]	[1938]						
$SrO \cdot 6Fe_2O_3$	c	18*[2]	[1941]						
$7/5\,SrO \cdot Fe_2O_3$	c	12.2[2]	[1941]						
		−410.9	[1941]						
$2SrO \cdot Fe_2O_3$	c	30.9[2]	[1941]						
		−516.2	[1941]						
$3SrO \cdot Fe_2O_3$	c	64.8[2]	[1941]						
		−694.5	[1941]						
$Sr(OH)_2$	c			−207.1*	[249]	20.7*	[249]		
				−207.8*	[323]	21*	[323]		
				−208.0*	[229]	22.3*	[698]		
SrO_2	c	(−150.80)	[76]	−139*	[323]	13*	[323]		
				−140.4*	[229]				
				−141.0*	[1045]				
$Sr(ReO_4)_2$	c	−500*	[2683]						
SrS	g	30.0[3]	[1015]						
	c	(−113.1*)	[1480]	−97.4*	[323]	17*	[323]		
		(−108.1*)	[1015]	−106.8*	[229]	17.0*	[247]		
		(−113.1)	[1015]	−107.0	[1734]	16.3	[1685, 1734]	11.64	[1685, 1734]
						16.5*	[1773]		
						17.9*	[698]		
$SrSO_3$	c	−279.7*	[1172]						
		−279.4	[614]						
		−274*	[2683]						
$SrSO_4$	c	(−346.8)	[614]	(−319.48*)	[177]	(32.0*)	[177]		
		(−346.75)	[614]	(−318.4*)[4]	[250]	(28.2*)	[1680]		
				(−318.94)	[500]	(28.2)	[1685]		
						(28.6)	[699]		
SrSe	c			−77.7*	[229]	19.1*	[228]		
						21.5*	[698]		
$SrSeO_3$	c	−250.55	[509]	−230.84	[509]	30.36	[509]		
		−247.55	[507]						
$SrSeO_4$	c	−275.37	[501]	−244.71	[501]	18.12	[501]		

		-274.88	[185]	-248.6*	[232]	20.17	[185]		
				-244.7**	[232]	18.3*	[498]	22.22*	[498]
SrSi	c			-111.4*	[229]				
$SrSiO_3$	c	(-31.25)[5]	[1681]	-31.3[5]	[1681]	23.7*	[251]		
		(-382.6)	[776]	-350.8*	[323]	22.5*	[323]		
				-350.7*	[227]				
SrTe	c	-62.0*	[1773]			24.0*	[698]	23.51	[2554]
$SrTiO_3$	c	-399.0	[2243, 2552]	-378.8	[2243]	26.0	[1685]	23.51	[1685]
		-398.9	[428]	-379.0	[2552]	25.99	[2554]	34.31	[2555]
$SrWO_4$	c	(-393.0)	[329]	-366.0	[329]	28.3	[329]		
		(-398.2*)	[170, 172]	-373.7*	[170, 172]				
				-372.8*	[172]				
				-366.5*	[323]	37.8*	[323]		
				-373.9*	[229]				
$SrZrO_3$	c	-418.3	[350, 351]	-398.1	[350, 351]	27.5	[1733]	24.71	[1733]
Sr_2O	c			-147.4*	[229]				
Sr_2SiO_4	c	(-50.01)[5]	[1681]	-50.1[5]	[1681]	35.0*	[251]	34.34	[2555]
		(-542.5)	[776]	-495.7*	[323]	43*	[323]		
				-494.4*	[229]				
Sr_2TiO_4	c	-545.6	[2243, 2552]	-517.8	[2243]	38.0	[1685, 2555]	34.34	[1685]
				-518.0	[2552]				
$Sr_3(AsO_4)_2$	c			-770.1*	[323]	74.6*	[323]		
				-751.9	[229]				
Sr_3As_2	c	-144	[32]						
Sr_3N_2	c			-81.9*	[229]	29.5*	[1773]		
$Sr_3(PO_4)_2$	c			-932.1*	[323]	70*	[323]		
				-935.9*	[229]				
Sr_3P_2	c	-160.03	[647]						
Sr_3SiO_5	c	-702*	[148]						
Ta	g	(186.90)[6]	[1589]	(176.67)	[1589]			(4.99)	[1589, 1685]
		(186.800)	[2479]	(176.561)	[2479]				
		(168.4)	[756]						
		(153)	[758]						
	c					(9.90)	[997]	(6.023)[7]	[997]
						(9.92)	[1589, 1685, 2459]	(6.045)	[2459]
								(6.06)	[1589, 1685]
								(6.08)	[2479]

1. From SrO(c) and Al_2O_3(c). 2. From SrO(c) and Fe_2O_3(c). 3. ΔH_0°. 4. Recalculated [234] from $(\Delta H_{298}^\circ)_{diss} = 126.6$ [250] to 133.24 [2245] using the values of ΔG_{298}° for SO_3 and SrO.
5. From SrO and $SiO_2(\alpha)$. 6. $\Delta H_0^\circ = 186.76$ [1589]. 7. $t = 0$°C.

1	2	3		4		5		6	
TaB	c					13.1*	[1959]	11.30	[1959]
TaB_2	c	-45.5	[1800]			11.3*	[1959]	13.98	[1959]
$TaBr_3O$	c	-204*	[21]						
$TaBr_5$	c	-142.96*	[1421]						
		-164*	[20]			73.0*	[20]		
		-164.0	[668]						
$TaC_{0.40}$	c	-15.5	[546]	-15.3	[546]	9.72	[546]		
$TaC_{0.455}$		-96	[669]						
		-23.3[1]	[283]						
$TaC_{0.50}$	c	-17.0	[546]	-16.8	[546]	9.93	[546]		
$TaC_{0.507}$	c	-25.1[1]	[283]						
$TaC_{0.60}$	c	-18.7	[546]	-18.6	[546]	10.27	[546]		
$TaC_{0.70}$	c	-21.5	[546]	-21.4	[546]	10.46	[546]		
$TaC_{0.71}$	c	-31	[2710]			1.6[2]	[2710]		
$TaC_{0.80}$	c	-25.5	[546]	-25.4	[546]	10.53	[546]		
$TaC_{0.90}$	c	-31.7	[546]	-31.5	[546]	10.36	[546]		
$TaC_{0.982}$	c	-33.7	[285]						
$TaC_{0.99}$	c	-35.6	[2710]			-1.6[2]	[2710]		
TaC	c	-36.0*	[546]	-35.7*	[546]	(10.14)	[546]		
		-38.5	[1594]	-38.1	[1594]	(10.11)	[1685]		
		-34.3	[285]	-37.4*	[232]				
		-34.6	[1571]						
$TaClO_2$	c	-250*	[21]			23.4*	[21]		
$TaCl_2$	c	-93*; -96*	[669]						
$TaCl_3$	c	-130.5	[2284]			37	[2284]	22.3*	[2284]
		-139.2	[645]						
$TaCl_3O$	g	-187.2	[2290]			86.5	[2290]		
	c	-213.3	[2290]			42.4	[2290]		
		-232*	[21]			26.1	[21]		
$TaCl_4$	g	-136.3	[2284]			92	[2284]	23.6*	[2284]
		30.2	[644]			40.4[2]	[644]		
	c	-168.8	[2284]			46	[2284]	28.7*	[2284]
		-172.6	[645]						
$TaCl_5$	g	-182.7	[2284]			101.4	[2284]	27.5*	[2284]
		22.7[3]	[644]			45.2[2]	[644]		
						103*	[1634]		
	c	-205.0	[2283]	-180.1*	[234]	56	[2284]	34.5*	[2284]
		-205.5*	[20, 1420]			59.4*	[20]	59.4	[20]

		-220*	[623]						
		-206.0*	[668]						
$TaFO_2$	c	-282*	[21]			23.2*	[21]		
TaF_2O	c	-347*	[21]			25.7*	[21]		
TaF_5	c	-454.97	[1379]	-428.02	[1379]				
		-380*	[20]			40.6*	[20]		
TaI_3O	c	-173	[21]						
TaI_5	c	-117*	[20]			82.0*	[20]		
TaN	c	(-60.0)	[1907]	-53.2	[1907]	12.2*	[1773]		
		(-59.0)	[1772, 1907]	-53.7*	[232]				
				-52.0*	[229]				
TaO	g	63.0; 62	[1764a]						
TaO_2	g	-48.5; -44	[1764a]						
TaS_2	c	-116	[1487]						
$TaSi_2$	c	-27.8	[2232]						
Ta_2C	c	-47.2	[1571]			-0.5*[2]	[2709]		
Ta_2H						9.47	[2262]	10.870	[2262]
Ta_2N	c	-64.7	[2459]						
Ta_2O_5, *a*	c	(-488.8)	[1593]	(-456.5)	[1593]				
		(-489.0)	[887]	(-455.7)	[232]				
		(-489.3)	[284, 286]						
Ta_2Si_5	c	-86.4*	[2350]						
		-76.0*	[2230]						
Ta_5S_3	c	-75.9	[2232]						
Tb	g	(86.9); (87.2)	[2678]	77.4*	[229]				
		(93.96)[4]	[1456]						
	c					17.57	[1589]	6.91	[1589]
						17.5	[1628, 1685]	6.92	[1685]
						17.46	[2479]	6.54	[2479]
						17.50*	[2396]		
						14.15*	[323]		
Tb^{3+}	d			(-165.4*)	[323]	-42.8*	[323]		
TbB_6	c	-117.8	[455]						
$TbBr_3$	c	-200*	[230]						
$TbCl_{0.5}(OH)_{2.5}$	c			-305.36	[10]				
TbClO	c	-234*	[46]						
$TbCl(OH)_2$	c			-206.21	[10]				

1. In *kcal/gram-formula weight.* 2. ΔS°_{298}. 3. High temperatures. 4. $\Delta H^\circ_0 = 94.39$ [1456].

1	2	3		4		5		6	
$TbCl_2$	c	−118*	[442]						
$TbCl_3$	g	−163.8*[1]	[441]						
$TbCl_3$, β	c	(−237*)	[691]	−223.7*	[323]	34.9*	[323]		
		(−236*)	[442]	−224.8*	[227]				
TbI_3	c	−147*	[230]						
$TbO_{1.5}$	c	−218.4	[2473]	−207.7	[2662]				
$TbO_{1.71}$	c	−223.3	[2473]	−210	[1976]				
$TbO_{1.72}$	c			−211.2	[2662]	19.3	[2662]		
$TbO_{1.80}$	c	−226.4	[2473]	−213	[1976]				
$TbO_{1.84}$	c			−213.8	[2662]	19.4	[2662]		
$Tb(OH)_3$	c			−305.7*	[323]				
				−314.04	[10]				
TbO_2	c	−231*	[2662]	−217*	[2662]	19.8	[2662]		
				−216	[1976]				
Tb_2O_3	c	−436.8	[2473]	−414	[1976]	37.5	[2662]		
$Tb_2(SO_4)_3 \cdot 8H_2O$	c	−1517.3*	[323]			155.8*	[323]		
		−1521*	[229]						
Tb_4O_7	c	−899.2	[1976]	−844	[1976]				
Tc	g	155.000	[2479]	144.490	[2479]	43.25	[1685, 2479]		
		136.0*	[402]	91.2	[1045]				
	c					(8.00)	[2479]	5.80	[1685, 2479]
						(8.0)	[1685]		
						(7.5*)	[1773]		
TcO_2	c	−103.72	[2413]	−91.35*	[2413]	14.9*	[2413]		
				−90.5*	[232]	15.0*	[1773]		
TcO_3	c	−129.0	[2413]	−110.2	[2413]	17.3	[2413]		
		−129	[887]	−109.1*	[232]				
TcO_4^-	d	−173.0	[2413]	−150.63	[2413]	−75.0	[2413]		
Tc_2O_7	c	−266.1	[2413]	−224.1	[2413]	44.0*	[1773]		
				−219.8*	[229]				
$HTcO_4$	c	−167.42	[2413]	−141.27*	[2413]	33.3	[2413]		
				−141.8*	[232]				
Te	g	(45.821)[2]	[569]	(36.336)	[569]	(43.642)	[569]	5.81[4]	[1759]
		(45.52)[3]	[2358]	(36.05)	[2358]	(43.65)	[2358]		
		(46.500)	[2479]	(37.031)	[2479]	(43.64)	[1685]		
Te, I, hexagonal	c					(11.83)	[569]	(6.16)	[569]
						(11.88)	[1685, 2358]	(6.15)	[2358]
								(6.14)	[1685]

Te	v	(2.7)	[2358]						
Te^+	g	(255.102)[5]	[569]	244.262	[569]	43.198	[569]		
		(254.76)[6]	[2358]						
Te^{2+}	g	683[7]	[569]			40.444	[569]		
		685[8]	[2358]						
Te^{3+}	g	1348[7]	[569]						
		1393[9]	[2358]						
Te^{4+}	g	2210[7]	[569]						
		2266[10]	[2358]						
Te^{5+}	g	3565[7]	[569]						
		3658[11]	[2358]						
Te^{6+}	g	5195[7]	[569]						
		5327[12]	[2358]						
Te^{7+}	g	8360[7]	[569]						
		8494[13]	[2358]						
Te^{2-}	d			52.7*	[323]				
Te_2	g	(40.062)	[569]	(28.013)	[569]	64.07	[569]	8.74	[569]
		(39.600)	[2479]	(27.572)	[2479]	64.1	[1685]		
		(40.2)[14]	[2358]						
Te_2^{2-}	d			38.75	[323]				
$TeBr_4$	c	(-46.6)	[569]	-30.3*	[229]	17.0*	[1773]		
		(-45.5)	[2358]						
$TeCl_4$	g	-49.4	[569]						
	c	(-77.4)	[569]	-56.7*	[323]	50*	[323]		
		(-78.0)	[2358]	-57.1*	[229]				
TeF_6	g	(-315)[15]	[569]	(-292.078)	[569]	(80.3)	[569, 1685]	28.1	[569]
		(-315)	[2358]			(80.67*)	[323]	28.08	[1685]
		8.555[16]	[2359]						
TeI_4	c	-15	[234]						
TeO	g	(41.563)[17]	[569]	35.252	[569]	57.5	[569]	7.6	[569]
		(41.6)[7]	[2358]	47.1*	[323]	55.8	[1685]	7.62	[1685]
				36.5	[1045]	57.563[4]	[2106]	7.632[4]	[2106]
$Te(OH)_3^+$	d	-145.4	[2358]	-118.6	[2358]	26.7	[2358]		
$TeOOH^+$	d			-61.78*	[323]				
TeO_2	c	(-77.1)	[2358]	(-64.6)	[2358]	(19)	[2358]	(15.52)	[2181]
		(-76.9)	[2314]	(-63.236)	[569]	(14.0)	[569]	(15.3)	[569]

1. Calculated [234] from $(\Delta H^\circ_{296})TbCl_3(c) = -241.6$ [441] and $(\Delta H^\circ_0)_{vap} = 77.8$ [441]. 2. $\Delta H^\circ_0 = 45.8$ [569]. 3. $\Delta H^\circ_0 = 45.5$ [2358]. 4. $t = 300$°C. 5. $\Delta H^\circ_0 = 253.6$ [569]. 6. $\Delta H^\circ_0 = 253.26$ [2358]. 7. ΔH°_0. 8. $\Delta H^\circ_0 = 682$ [2358]. 9. $\Delta H^\circ_0 = 1388$ [2358]. 10. $\Delta H^\circ_0 = 2260$ [2358]. 11. $\Delta H^\circ_0 = 3650$ [2358]. 12. $\Delta H^\circ_0 = 5318$ [2358]. 13. $\Delta H^\circ_0 = 8483$ [2358]. 14. $\Delta H^\circ_0 = 40.7$ [2358]. 15. $\Delta H^\circ_0 = -312.532$ [569]. 16. $(\Delta H^\circ_{298})_{subl}$; $t = 37.4$°C. 17. $\Delta H^\circ_0 = 41.935$ [569].

1	2	3		4		5		6	
TeO_2	c					(14)	[1958]	(15.28)[1]	[1958]
						(16.8)	[1680, 1685]		
TeO_2, tetragonal	c	(90.6)	[104]						
$2(TeO_2)_2SO_3$	c	(−291.5)	[569]						
TeO_3	g	−12.4[2]	[569]	−13.73	[569]	65.3	[569]	10.6	[569]
	c					22*	[1480]		
TeO_3^{2-}	d	(−127.3)	[569]	−108.0*	[323]				
		(−142.6)	[2358]						
TeO_4^{2-}	d	(−171.5)	[569]						
		(−143*)	[506]						
TeSe	g	41.6	[2358]						
HTe^-	d			37.7*	[323]				
H_2Te	g	(23.83)[3]	[569]			(54.69)	[569]	8.50	[569]
		(23.8)	[2358]			(58.4*)	[249]	8.35*	[224]
		(38.1)	[157]						
	d			34.1*	[323]				
H_2Te^+	g	235.6[4]	[569]						
H_2TeO_3	c	(−146.5)	[569]						
				(−76.2)	[2358]				
	d	(−146.5)	[569]						
$H_2TeO_3 \cdot H_2O$	c	(−216.1)	[569]						
$H_4TeO_6^{2-}$	d	−289.1	[569]						
		−292.1	[2358]						
$H_5TeO_6^-$	d	−298.5	[569]						
		−301.5	[2358]						
H_6TeO_6, monoclinic	c	(−307.7)	[569]	−167.9*	[323]				
		(−310.4)	[2358]						
	d	−304.3	[569]						
		−307.0	[2358]						
Th	g	137.50[5]	[1589]	127.76	[1589]				
		137.3	[1077]						
		136.6	[1077]						
	c					(12.76)	[1397, 1589]	(6.532)	[1397]
								(6.53)	[1589]
						(12.8)	[1685]	(6.58)	[1685]
								(5.80)[6]	[370]
								(6.56)	[2609]

Th^{4+}	d	(−184.4)	[1190]	−175.2*	[323]	−75*	[323]		
$ThBr_2O$	c	−268.4*	[2276]	−257	[2276]	35.8	[2276]		
$ThBr_4$	c			−218.0*	[325]	55.9*	[323]		
				−218.9*	[227]	56.0*	[887]		
						59.0	[1685]		
ThC	c	−7	[1578]	−6.4	[1578]	12*	[1578]		
$ThC \cdot ThH_2$, hexagonal	c	−48.4[7]	[2142]						
$ThC \cdot 2ThH_2$, monoclinic	c	−38.3[8]	[2142]						
$ThC_{1.93}$	c	−31.2	[2671]			16.38	[2671]	13.55	[2671]
ThC_2	g	165[9]	[1606]						
	c	(−44.8)	[1752]	−44.8*	[227]	19.3	[1752]		
		(−30); (−33)	[1762]	−32.5	[1578, 1762]	19.6	[1578]		
		(−36.0)	[2709]			15.1	[1763]		
		(−31)	[1578]						
		(−46*)	[1816]						
		(−37.1)[10]	[1161]						
		(−38.7)	[1607]						
		(−48); (−44.6)	[1606]						
$ThCl_2O$	g	−185*	[687]			70.0	[687]		
	c	(−295.4)	[687]			27.3	[687]		
				−277.9	[2276]	31.8	[2276]		
$ThCl_3$	c	−190	[1069]						
$ThCl_4$	c	(−284.5)	[1190]	−263.9*	[323]	48.3*	[323]		
				−263.2*	[227]	46.8*	[224]		
				−232.4[11]	[1162]				
$ThCl_4 \cdot 2H_2O$	c			−390.4*	[229]				
$ThCl_4 \cdot 4H_2O$	c			−514.0*	[229]				
$ThCl_4 \cdot 7H_2O$	c			−688.4*	[229]				
$ThCl_4 \cdot 8H_2O$	c			−746.0*	[229]				
ThF_2O	c			−380.6	[2276]	24.8	[2276]		
ThF_4	c	(−482.4)	[1076]	−459.9	[1076]	33.9	[1076]		
				−454.7*	[323]	35.9*	[323]		
				−453.3*	[227]	33.95	[1685, 1811]	26.46	[1685, 1811]
ThH_4	c			−23.6*	[229]				
ThI_2O	c	(−237.4)	[2276]	−230.0	[2276]	40.3	[2276]		
ThI_3	c	−156	[1497]						

1. $(\Delta H^\circ_{298})_{subl}$; $t = 37.4$°C. 2. $\Delta H^\circ_0 = -11.529$ [569]. 3. $\Delta H^\circ_0 = 24.9$ [569]. 4. ΔH°_0. 5. $\Delta H^\circ_0 = 137.58$ [1589]. 6. $t = 50$°C. 7. From Th, H_2 and ThC. 8. From Th, H_2 and $ThC \cdot ThH_2$. 9. Calculated from ΔH for Th(c) [1606] and $(\Delta H^\circ_{298})_{subl} = 213$ [1606]. 10. Between 760 and 1000°C. 11. $t = 400$°C.

1	2	3		4		5		6	
ThI_4	c	(−155*)	[230]	−131*	[323]	67.9*	[323]		
		(−154*)	[1685]	−130.9*	[227]	65.0	[1685]		
		(−206)	[1069]			63.0	[1773]		
		(−160*)	[2569]						
ThO, cubic	c	−145	[887]			15.0	[2662]		
$Th(OH)_3$	c			−91.9*	[229]				
$Th(OH)_4$	c			−379*	[323]	32*	[323]		
				−379.0*	[229]				
ThO_2, cubic	c	(−293.2)	[1579]	−280.0*	[229]	16.9*	[229]		
		(−294.1)	[543]	−278.4*	[323]	15.39	[1685, 2078]	(14.76)	[1685, 2078, 2594]
				−279.2	[1045]	15.593[1]	[2594]		
						17.0	[2662]		
ThS	c	−100	[1773]						
$Th(SO_3)_2$	c	−490.2*	[1172]						
$Th(SO_4)_2$	c	(−607.4)	[1945]	−551.2	[1945]	35.4	[1945]	(41.4)	[1945]
		(−608.06)	[1675]	−548.9	[229]	34.80	[1675]		
$Th(SO_4)_2 \cdot 4H_2O$	c			−756.4*	[229]				
$Th(SO_4)_2 \cdot 8H_2O$	c			−1000*	[229]				
ThS_2	c	−110*	[1773]			23.0	[1685]	16.80	[1685]
$ThSi_2$	c	−41.6	[2232]						
Th_2S_3	c	(−258.6)	[1197]	−257.7*	[323]	35.7*	[323]		
				−258.9*	[229]				
Th_3N_4	c	(−310.0)	[2625]	−280.2*	[229]	42.7*	[1678]		
Ti	g	(112.600)	[2479]	(101.944)	[2479]	(43.068)	[1315, 1618a, 1757]	(5.8386)	[1315, 1757]
		(112.74)[2]	[1589]	(102.14)	[1589]				
		(112.49)[3]	[1618a]	(101.835)	[1618a]			(5.838)	[1618a]
		(113.41)[4]	[2243]	102.76)	[2243]				
		(113.2)	[1686]	(102.65)	[1686]				
	l	3.878	[1618a]	3.533	[1618a]	8.486	[1618a]	8.00	[1618a]
	c					7.33	[1618a, 1760]	(5.976)	[1760]
								(5.97)	[1618a]
								(25.4)[5]	[1755]
						(7.30)	[1589, 1685]	(5.98)	[1589, 1685]
						(7.37)	[990]	(5.998)	[990]
						(7.34)	[2432]	(5.976)	[2432]
Ti, *a*	c							0.1247[6]	[532]

Ti, β	c							0.167[7]	[532]
Ti^{2+}	d			-75.1*	[323]				
Ti^{3+}	g					40.29	[66]		
	d			-83.6*	[323]				
Ti^{4+}	g					37.53	[66]		
TiAs	c	-35.8	[649]						
$TiB_{1.94}$	c	-66.77	[678]						
$TiB_{1.98}$	c	-63.75	[678]						
TiB_2	l	-60.38	[1618a]	-60.166	[1618a]	9.327	[1618a]	10.66	[1618a]
	c	-70	[1618a]	-68.952	[1618a]	6.60	[1618a]	10.66	[1618a]
		-70.00	[306]	-69.11	[306]	7.50	[306]		
		-32*	[2307]			6.2*	[1959]	13.02	[1959]
		-50	[2688]						
		-52	[2306, 2688]						
		-72.00	[892]						
		-70.04	[491]						
		-66.85	[678]						
		-430[8]	[2306]						
$TiB_{2.16}$	c	-65.63	[678]						
TiBr	g	110.2*	[1618a]	99.306	[1618a]	62.062	[1618a]	8.702	[1618a]
$TiBr_2$	g	-53.2[9]	[1618a]	-62.567	[1618a]	75.131	[1618a]	14.347	[1618a]
	c	(-93.4)	[1618a]	-89.639	[1618a]	31.101	[1618a]	18.807	[1618a]
		(-95.3)	[1463]	-88*	[227]	30*	[1463]	18.6*	[1463]
		(-103.3)	[1686]	-92.45	[1686]	29.5	[1685, 1686]		
				-91.4*	[323]	31.6*	[323]		
		(-97.3)	[1771]			28.6	[1771]		
		(-104.5)	[629]						
$TiBr_3$	g	-85.7[10]	[1618a]	-92.693	[1618a]	85.361	[1618a]	18.068	[1618a]
		-87.7	[1771]			87.0	[1771]		
		-104.3	[1686]	-100.1	[1686]				
	c	(-131.5)[11]	[1618a]	-125.616	[1618a]	42.171	[1618a]	24.308	[1618a]
		(-142.3)	[1686]	-126.45	[1686]	42.2	[1685, 1686]	24.33	[1685]
		(-130.8)	[1464]	-124.6*	[323]	36.8*	[323]		
		(-130.6)	[1462]	-126.5*	[227]	43.4	[1462]		
		(-131.4)	[2243]	-123.3	[2243]	41.0	[1771]		
		(-144.8)	[629]						
$TiBr_4$	g	-131.6[12]	[1618a]	-136.117	[1618a]	95.249	[1618a]	24.071	[1618a]

1. $S^\circ_{298}-S^\circ$. 2. $\Delta H^\circ_0=112.08$ [1589]. 3. $\Delta H^\circ_0=111.838$ [1618a]. 4. $\Delta H^\circ_0=112.76$ [2243]. 5. $T=320°K$; in *joules/g-atom* · °C. 6. Specific. 7. $t=273°C$. 8. $(\Delta H^\circ_{298})_{subl}$. 9. $\Delta H^\circ_0=$ $=-49.806$ [1618a]. 10. $\Delta H^\circ_0=-80.0$ [1618a]. 11. $\Delta H^\circ_0=-127.052$ [1618a]. 12. $\Delta H^\circ_0=-124.445$ [1618a].

1	2	3		4		5		6	
$TiBr_4$	g	−131.3	[2243]	−135.8	[2243]	95.9*	[249]	23.29	[2243]
		−146.7	[1686]	−137.9	[1686]	95.0	[1686]		
		−131.7	[1771]			94.6	[1771]		
						94.9	[1685]	24.01	[1685]
	l	−144.581	[1618a]	−140.951	[1618a]	67.922	[1618a]	36.30	[1618a]
	c	(−147.6)	[1618a]	−141.079	[1618a]	58.227	[1618a]	31.43	[1618a, 1685]
		(−162.8)	[1686]	−142.95	[1686]	58.0	[1685, 1686]	28.0	[864]
		(−148.1)	[1418]	−146*	[323]	49.8*	[323]		
		(−147.9)	[2309]	−148*	[227]	57.4	[464, 1680]		
		(−147.4)	[2040]			57.2	[1771]		
		(−148.0)	[1417, 2243, 2309]	−140.6	[2243]				
		(−155)	[2243]						
$TiBr_4 \cdot H_2S$	c	−183	[2243]						
$TiBr_4 \cdot 2H_2S$	c	−195	[2243]						
$TiBr_4 \cdot PH_3$	c	−184	[2243]						
$TiBr_4 \cdot 2PH_3$	c	−193	[2243]						
$TiC_{0.79}$	c	−43.7	[384]						
$TiC_{0.91}$	c	−49.4	[384]						
TiC	l	−28.842	[1618a]	−29.315	[1618a]	10.274	[1618a]	8.11	[1618a]
	c	(−44.5)	[1618a]	(−43.639)	[1618a]	5.801	[1618a]	8.11	[1618a]
		(−44.921)	[1686]	(−43.25)	[1686]	5.79	[1685]		
		(−43.55)[1]	[2243]	(−42.98)	[2242]				
		(144.758)[2]	[1265]	(−43.0); (−43.85)	[1591]				
		(−46.0)[3]	[384]						
		(143.8)[4]	[1265]						
$Ti(CN)_2$	c	8*	[2683]						
$Ti(CNS)_2$	c	−10*	[2683]						
$TiC_{0.23}O_{0.12}$	c	−24.5	[384]						
$TiC_{0.42}O_{0.118}$	c	−39.8	[384]						
$TiC_{0.46}O_{0.114}$	c	−39.7	[384]						
$TiC_{0.61}O_{0.083}$	c	−42.8	[384]						
$TiC_{0.74}O_{0.059}$	c	−47.1	[384]						
$TiCO_3$	c	−224*	[2683]						
TiCl	g	111.2*[5]	[1618a]	103.621*	[1618a]	59.394	[1618a]	8.521	[1618a]
				113.6*	[229]	56.1	[721]	8.30[6]	[721]
TiClO	g	−58.38[7]	[1618a]	−59.726	[1618a]	62.992	[1618a]	12.346	[1618a]
	c	−182	[2294]			17.5	[2294]		

$Ti(ClO_3)_2$		-82*	[2683]						
$Ti(ClO_4)_2$	c	-92*	[2685]						
$TiCl_2$	g	-72.3[8]	[1618a]	-74.464	[1618a]	67.878	[1618a]	13.744	[1618a]
		-71.4	[1686]	-71.8	[1686]	69.0*	[1773]		
		-69.4	[721]	-68.4*; -71.0**	[232]	65.9	[721]	12.3[2]	[721]
		-54.5	[1771]			67.0	[1771]		
		-73.0[9]	[2386]	-75.4	[2243]	68.5	[2243]		
		-69.5[10]	[2386]	-64.4	[1775]	70.8*	[1775]		
		-50.8*	[1422]						
	c	(-123.5)[11]	[1618a, 2243]	-112.97	[1618a]	25.3	[1618a]	17.368	[1618a]
		(-121)	[1486]	-112.6	[2243]	26.2	[442]		
		(-122.7)	[1771]	-103.5*	[227]	24.1	[1771]		
		(-123.0)	[1686]	-112.2	[1686]	24.4	[1686]		
		(-120.6)	[721]			24.7	[721]		
		(-120.1)	[1761]	-96*	[323]	26*	[323]		
		(-123.3)	[988]			27.8*	[1775]		
		(-122.4)	[1498]			24.0	[1498]		
		(-118.3)[12]	[2386]			23.8*	[536]		
		(-123*)	[536]			24.3	[1685]		
						22.6	[1588]		
$TiCl_2O$	g	-130.39[13]	[1618a]	-127.878	[1618a]	76.697	[1618a]	17.197	[1618a]
$TiCl_3$	g	-129.3[14]	[1618a]	-126.015	[1618a]	76.246	[1618a]	16.909	[1618a]
		-129.5	[1771]	-129.5	[1771]	74.5	[1771]		
		-128.7	[721]	-122.2*; -125.0**	[232]	74.9	[721]	17.3[15]	[721]
		-129.8[16]	[2243]	-127.0; -126.2	[2243]	73.8	[2271]		
		-130.2	[2271]	-125.1	[1775]				
		-131.5	[1686]	-127.3	[1686]				
		-129*	[1196]						
		-128.0[17]	[2386]						
	c	(-172.0)[18]	[2243]	-156.3	[2243]	31.1	[2243, 2386]		
		(-172.4)[19]	[1618a, 1636]	-156.341	[1618a]	33.401	[1618a]	23.222	[1618a]
		(-171.6)	[1771]	-149.4*	[227]	33.0	[1771]		
		(-170.7)	[721]			34.4	[721]		
		(-170.0)[20]	[2386]	-155.0*	[232]	33.3; 32.1	[2271]		
		(-170*)	[536]	-154.9**	[232]	30.6*	[536]		
		(-161.35)	[2278]	-155.95	[1686]	33.4	[1685, 1686]	23.22	[1685]
		(-169.1)	[1761]	-148*	[323]	30.5*	[323]		

1. ΔH_0°. 2. TiC(c) = C(graphite) + Ti (g). 3. Synthesis at 1900°C. 4. $(\Delta H_0^\circ)_{subl}$. 5. $\Delta H_0^\circ = 111.161$ [1618a]. 6. $T = 300$°K. 7. $\Delta H_0^\circ = -57.998$ [1618a]. 8. $\Delta H_0^\circ = -72.193$* [1618a]. 9. $\Delta H_0^\circ = -72.7$ [2243]. 10. $\Delta H_0^\circ = -69.1$ [2386]. 11. ΔH_0° [2243]. 12. $\Delta H_0^\circ = -118.7$ [2386]. 13. $\Delta H_0^\circ = -130.002$ [1618a]. 14. $\Delta H_0^\circ = -128.58$ [1618a]. 15. $T = 300$°K. 16. $\Delta H_0^\circ = -129.6$ [2243]. 17. $\Delta H_0^\circ = -127.7$ [2386]. 18. $\Delta H_0^\circ = -172.1$ [2243]. 19. $\Delta H_0^\circ = -172.959$ [1618a]. 20. $\Delta H_0^\circ = -170.1$ [2386].

1	2	3	ref	4	ref	5	ref	6	ref
$TiCl_3$	c	(−172.2)	[987]						
		(−171.1)	[2243, 2278]						
		(−172.3)	[1498]			34.0	[1498]		
$TiCl_4$	g	-182.41^{1}	[1618a]	−173.548	[1618a]	(84.186)	[1618a]	(22.815)	[1618a]
		−182.2	[1686]	−173.35	[1686]	(84.13)	[1494]	(22.82)	[1494]
		−182.4	[1588]	−170.4*; −169.7	[292]	(83.721)	[2031]	(22.890)	[2031]
		−182.9	[1197]	−173.6*	[232]	(82.1)	[2005]		
		-183.0^{2}	[2386]	−171.5	[1775]	(84.4)	[2271]		
		−182.4	[1641]	−174.2	[2243]	(84.3)	[1680, 1685]		
		−181.7	[1771]						
		−181.6	[721]						
	l	(−192.3)	[1618a, 1641]	(−176.319)	[1618a]	(60.306)	[1618a]	34.704	[1618a]
		(−192.1)	[988, 2243]	(−176.1)	[2243]	(60.3)	[1680]		
		(−191.6)	[1771]	(−175.9)	[1686]	(59.5)	[1685, 1686]	35.73	[1685]
		$(7.71)^{3}$	[2130]	$(2.39)^{1}$	[2130]	(59.6)	[1680, 2298]		
		(−191.2)	[721]			(60.4)	[721]		
		(−192.5)	[1197]						
		(−190.0)	[1761]						
		(−191.5)	[1418]						
		(−190.3)	[1416]						
		(−192.9)	[2386]						
		(−191.5)	[2243]						
	c	-194.904^{4}	[1618a]	−175.828	[1618a]	49.927	[1618a]	30.943	[1618a]
		−195*	[230]						
		-196.4^{5}	[2386]						
$TiCl_4 \cdot H_2S$	c	−206.6	[2243]						
$TiCl_4 \cdot 2H_2S$	c	−218.9	[2243]						
$TiCl_4 \cdot PH_3$	c	−207.1	[2243]						
$TiCl_4 \cdot 2PH_3$	c	−215.7	[2243]						
TiF	g	93.4^{*6}	[1618a]	85.941*	[1618a]	56.572	[1618a]	8.040	[1618a]
TiFO	g	-103.54^{7}	[1618a]	−104.682	[1618a]	59.887	[1618a]	11.585	[1618a]
TiF_2	g	-156.2^{8}	[1618a]	−158.162	[1618a]	62.358	[1618a]	12.638	[1618a]
	c			−187.1*	[323]	19.2*	[323]		
				−187*	[2243]	19.2	[2243]		
				−187.0*	[227]	18.0	[1685]		
TiF_2O	g	-221.05^{9}	[1618a]	−217.394	[1618a]	68.016	[1618a]	15.005	[1618a]
TiF_3	g	-278.2^{10}	[1618a]	−274.768	[1618a]	68.488	[1618a]	14.121	[1618a]
								18.9	[863]

	c	(-337.5)	[1618a]	-320.953	[1618a]	24.5	[1618a, 1685]	21.994	[1618a]
		(-335.2)	[1771]	-298.1*	[227]	28.4	[1771]		
				-290.9*	[323]	21.8*	[323]		
				-298	[2243]	21.8	[2243]		
						18.9	[863]		
TiF_4	g	-371.04[11]	[1618a]	-362.229	[1618a]	74.673	[1618a]	20.288	[1618a]
		-369.6	[1771]			73.2	[1771]	19.8	[863]
						72.0	[1685]		
	c	(-394.19)[12]	[1618a]	-372.661	[1618a]	32.016	[1618a]	27.31	[1175, 1618a]
		(-392.5)	[1771]	-348*	[2243]	29.8	[2243]		
				-346.3*	[323]	29.8*	[323]		
				-360.3	[1175]	32.02	[1175]		
				-348.4*	[227]	31.3	[1464]		
	v	-394.19	[1381]	-372.66	[1381]	42*	[50]		
$TiF_4 \cdot 2HF$	d	-555.1	[2243]						
TiF_6^{2-}	d			-506.3*	[323]	20*	[323]		
$Ti(HCO_3)_2$	c	-396*	[2683]						
$Ti(HS)_2$	c	-40*	[2683]						
$Ti(HSO_4)_2$	c	-464*	[2683]						
$TiH_{1.607}$	c	-27.3[13]	[2433]			7.29	[2433]	7.28	[2433]
$TiH_{1.718}$	c	-28.0[14]	[2433]			7.24	[2433]	7.30	[2433]
$TiH_{1.851}$	c	-28.7	[2433]						
$TiH_{1.974}$	c	-29.5[15]	[2433]			7.10	[2433]		
TiH_2	c	-34.5[16]	[1618a]	-25.127	[1618a]	7.101	[1618a]	7.191	[1618a]
		-5.17	[1307]			7.10	[2431]	7.19	[2431]
TiI	g	-113.3*[17]	[1618a]	100.51*	[1618a]	64.106	[1618a]	8.809	[1618a]
TiI_2	g	-13.8[18]	[1618a]	-26.807	[1618a]	78.713	[1618a]	14.477	[1618a]
		3.2	[1771]			72.5	[1771]		
	c	(-64.50)	[1618a]	-64.563	[1618a]	35.301	[1618a]	20.609	[1618a]
		(-47.0)	[1771]			35.0	[1771]		
		(-81.0)	[1686]	-69.95	[1686]	32.5	[1685, 1686]		
		(-63.5*)	[1773]	-61.0	[227]	36.0*	[1773]		
				-61.6*	[323]	37*	[323]		
TiI_3	g	(-35.9)	[1618a]	-48.396	[1618a]	90.878	[1618a]	18.418	[1618a]
		(-68.0)	[1686]	-63.9	[1686]				
	c	(-81.4)	[1618a]	-80.515	[1618a]	46.0	[1618a]	27.909	[1618a]

1. $\Delta H_0^\circ = -181.992$ [1618a]. 2. $\Delta H_0^\circ = -182.6$ [2386]. 3. $(\Delta H_{298}^\circ)_{vap}$. 4. $\Delta H_0^\circ = -195.803$ [1618a]. 5. ΔH_0°. 6. $\Delta H_0^\circ = 93.425$* [1618a]. 7. $\Delta H_0^\circ = -102.996$ [1618a]. 8. $\Delta H_0^\circ = -155.811$ [1618a]. 9. $\Delta H_0^\circ = -219.998$ [1618a]. 10. $\Delta H_0^\circ = -276.993$ [1618a]. 11. $\Delta H_0^\circ = -370.122$ [1618a]. 12. $\Delta H_0^\circ = -393.661$ [1618a]. 13. $\Delta H_0^\circ = -25.3$ [2433]. 14. $\Delta H_0^\circ = -26.0$ [2433]. 15. $\Delta H_0^\circ = -27.5$ [2433]. 16. $\Delta H_0^\circ = -32.508$ [1618a]. 17. $\Delta H_0^\circ = -113.63$* [1618a]. 18. $\Delta H_0^\circ = -13.204$ [1618a].

1	2	3		4		5		6	
TiI_3	c	(−105.0)	[1686]	−88.7	[1686]	46.0	[1685, 1686]		
				−76.5*	[323]	47.3*	[323]		
				−80.3*	[227]				
TiI_4	g	(−68.60)[1]	[1618a]	−80.716	[1618a]	103.483	[1618a]	24.918	[1618a]
		(−100.0)	[1686]	−91.3	[1686]	102.6	[1686]		
		(−70.0)	[1771]			102.4	[1771]		
	l	−85.516	[1618a]	−88.952	[1618a]	74.369	[1618a]	37.40	[1618a]
	c	(−92.0)[2]	[1618a]	−90.803	[1618a]	58.831	[1618a]	30.026	[1618a]
		(−122.0)	[1686]	−101.5	[1686]	63.0	[1686]		
		(−92.2)	[1635]	−102.4*	[227]	60.5	[1685]	30.03	[1685]
		(−100*)	[1773]	−91.9	[2243]	62.2	[1773]		
				−102*	[323]	61.8*	[323]		
$TiMoO_4$	c	−300*	[2683]						
TiN	l	−65.242	[1618a]	−59.064	[1618a]	9.49	[1618a]	13.50	[1618a]
	c	(−80.5)[3]	[1591, 1618a]	−73.637	[1618a]	7.193	[1618a]	8.966	[1618a]
		(−80.7)	[1686]	−73.85	[1686]	7.24	[1685]		
		(−79.4)[4]	[1530]	−73.65	[1591]				
		(−80.47)[5]	[2243]	−73.62	[2242]				
$Ti(NH_2)_2$	c	−52*	[2683]						
$Ti(NO_2)_2$	c	−108*	[2683]						
$Ti(NO_3)_2$	c	−146*	[2683]						
TiO	g	(15.1)[6]	[1618a]	7.954	[1618a]	55.802	[1618a]	7.483	[1618a]
		(11.1)[7]	[2243]	3.9	[1045, 2243]	55.80	[1680, 1685]	7.48	[1685]
		(11.1)	[1045]			55.758[8]	[2105]	7.646[8]	[2105]
		(11.35)	[1686]	4.2	[1686]				
		(11*)	[1423]						
	l	−108.682	[1618a]	−103.349	[1618a]	13.950	[1618a]	14.50	[1618a]
	c	−123.9[9]	[1618a]	−116.892	[1618a]	8.33	[1618a]	9.556	[1618a]
		−123.91	[1590]	−116.9*	[476]				
		−124.15	[1686]	−117.15	[1686]				
		−125.4	[34]	−117.3	[229]				
		−123.20[10]	[2374]						
TiO^{2+}	d			−138*	[323]				
$Ti(OH)_2$	c	−186*	[2683]						
$Ti(OH)_3$	c	−284*	[2683]						
$TiO(OH)_2$	c			−253	[323]				
TiO_2	g	−79.8	[1618a]	−79.829	[1618a]	56.438	[1618a]	11.076	[1618a]
		−79*	[1423]						

		-173.1[11]	[2243]						
	l	-212.32	[1618a]	-200.122	[1618a]	15.43	[1618a]	19.0	[1618a]
	c	(-224.9)	[34]						
TiO_2, anatase	c	-218.1[12]	[1618a, 2243]	-204.859	[1618a]	11.93	[1618a]	13.23	[1618a]
				-204.9	[2243]			13.22	[2243]
TiO_2, rutile	c	(-225.5)[13]	[1618a]	(-212.283)	[1618a]	(12.01)	[1618a]	13.196	[1618a]
		(-225.52)[14]	[2243]	(-212.31)	[2243]	(12.04)	[1685]	13.14[15]	[565a]
		(-222.75)	[1686]	(-212.55)	[1686]			13.16	[2249]
TiO_2	v	(-225.5)	[1590]	-212.3	[1590]				
				-193.8*	[229]				
TiP	c	-63.4	[649]						
$Ti(ReO_4)_2$	c	-432*	[2683]						
TiS	c	127.8[16]	[1248]			11.7	[1685]		
		132.6[16]	[1248]						
		-63*	[2683]						
$TiSO_3$	c	-194*	[2683]						
$TiSO_4$	c	-263*	[2683]						
TiS_2	c	-80.0*	[1773]			18.73	[1685, 2551]	16.23	[1685, 2551]
		-84*	[1480]						
TiSb	c	-67.2	[649]						
$TiSeO_4$	c	-195*	[2683]						
TiSi	c	-39.2	[138]						
		-31.0	[2232]						
$TiSiO_3$	c	-320*	[2683]						
$TiSi_2$	c	-42.9	[138]						
		-32.2	[2232]						
$TiWO_4$	c	-321*	[2683]						
$Ti_{0.50}Zr_{0.50}$	c							6.14	[1589]
Ti_2N	c	-19.6	[1775]						
Ti_2O_3	l	-334.661	[1618a]	-316.114	[1618a]	25.97	[1618a]	36.0	[1618a]
Ti_2O_3, α	c	(-362.9)	[1590]	(-342.23)	[1590]				
		(-362.8)	[34]						
Ti_2O_3, II	c	(-363.4)	[1686]	(-342.75)	[1686]				
		(-360.96)[17]	[1590]						
$Ti_2(SO_4)_3$	c	-809*	[2683]						
Ti_2S_3	c	-147*	[2683]			28.9	[1685]		

1. $\Delta H_0^\circ = -67.311$ [1618a]. 2. $\Delta H_0^\circ = -91.507$ [1618a]. 3. $\Delta H_0^\circ = -79.625$ [1618a]. 4. $\Delta H_0^\circ = -78.5$ [1530]. 5. $\Delta H_0^\circ = -79.60$ [2253]. 6. $\Delta H_0^\circ = 15.037$ [1618a]. 7. $\Delta H_0^\circ = 17.8$ [2243]. 8. $T = 300\,^\circ K$. 9. $\Delta H_0^\circ = -123.186$ [1618a]. 10. ΔH_0°. 11. ΔH_0° [2374]. 12. $\Delta H_0^\circ = -217.0$ [2243]; -216.945 [1618a]. 13. $\Delta H_0^\circ = -224.347$ [1618a]. 14. $\Delta H_0^\circ = -224.37$ [2243]. 15. $T =$ $= 297.7\,^\circ K$. 16. $(\Delta H_{298}^\circ)_{subl}$. 17. ΔH_0° [2232].

1	2	3		4		5		6	
Ti_3O_5	c	(−587.65)^{1}	[1618a]	(−553.781)	[1618a]	30.9	[1685]	44.27	[1618a]
		(−588.16)	[467]	(−555.51)	[467]				
		(−586.7)	[1590]	(−553.1)	[1590]				
		(−587.65)	[1686]	(−553.75)	[1686]				
		(−586.91)^{2}	[2243]	(−553.04)	[2242]	30.92	[1618a, 2243]		
		(−587.0)	[34, 887]						
Ti_5Si_3	c	−147*	[138]						
		−138.6*	[2232]						
Tl	g	(43.55)^{3}	[1589]	(35.24)	[1589]				
		(43.000)	[2479]	(34.687)	[2479]				
		(42.85)	[712]						
		(43.15)^{4}	[153]						
		(43.12)^{4}; (42.79)^{4}	[122]						
		(44.87)^{4}; (42.40)	[663]						
	c					(15.35)	[1685, 2479]	(6.29)	[1589, 1685, 2479]
						(15.34)	[1589]		
Tl^{+}	g					41.86	[66]		
	d					(30.5)	[1685]		
Tl^{3+}	g					41.86	[66]		
	d	(46.8*)	[323]			(−42*)	[323]		
TlBr	g	−8.7^{5}	[2513]			(64.0)	[1685]		
						(63.99)	[786]		
	c	(32.34)^{4}	[786]	(−39.4*)	[250]	(29.9); (30.4)	[786]		
				(−39.66*)	[176]	(28.4*)	[176]		
						(29.5)	[1685]		
$TlBr_3$	c			−54.7*	[227]				
$TlBrO_3$	c			−217.8*	[229]	42.3*	[245]		
TlCN	c	21*	[2683]						
TlCNS	c	6*	[2683]						
TlCl	g	(−16.35)^{6}	[782]			(61.29)	[786]		
						(61.3)	[1685]		
	c	(−48.8)	[789]	(−44.2)	[789]	(26.59)	[789, 1685]	12.17	[789, 1685]
		(32.35)^{7}	[786]	(−43.99*)	[229]	(27.1)	[786]		
						(25.3*)	[176]		
$TlClO_3$	c	−29*	[2683]			40.4*	[245]		
		−32.1	[481]						

$TlClO_4$	c	-33*	[2683]						
$TlCl_3$	c			-69.5*	[227]				
$TlCl_3 \cdot 2H_2O$	c	-228*	[230]						
$TlCl_3 \cdot 4H_2O$	c			-297.2*	[229]				
$TlCl_3 \cdot 6H_2O$	c	-506*	[230]						
TlF	g	(33.95)[7]	[786]	-29.7*	[232]	58.39	[786]		
				-28.4**	[232]	58.6	[1685]	8.27	[1685]
				-38.4*	[227]				
	c	-72*	[230]	-66*	[227]	20.9	[362]		
		-69.6*	[583]			19.9	[786]		
		-74.0	[950]			22.0	[1685]		
		-77.8	[1066]			25.9	[1066]		
$(TlF)_2$		35.6[7]	[1066]						
TlF_3	c	-136.9	[2706]	-122.6*	[234]				
TlH	g					(51.35)	[1685]	7.08	[1685]
	c	-8*	[2683]						
$TlHCO_3$	c	-176*	[2683]						
$TlHF_2$	c					34.92	[913]	21.25	[913]
TlHS	c	-5*	[2683]						
$TlHSO_4$	c	-215*	[2683]						
TlI	g					(63.9*)	[249]		
						(65.8)	[1685]		
						(65.79)	[786]		
	c	(-29.6)	[1066]	(-30.1)	[2513]	(30.52)	[2513]	12.74	[2513]
				(-29.97*)	[176]	(29.6*)	[176]		
		(33.45)[7]	[786]	(-30.3)[8]	[250]	(30.0); (30.5)	[786]		
						(30.7)	[1064]		
						(31.0)	[1685]		
$TlIO_3$	c	-65.7*	[323]	(-47.45*)	[177]	40.9*	[323]		
		-65*	[229]			42.9*	[245]		
		-65.7	[2457]						
TlI_3	c	-27*	[2683]						
$TlNH_2$	c	0.5*	[2683]						
$TlNO_2$	c	-34	[2683]						
$TlNO_2$	c					(38.4)	[1685]	23.78	[1685]
TlN_3	c	(55.78)	[1356]	70.97	[1356]	31.19	[1356]		
		(55.34)	[1862]	69.0*	[232]				

1. $\Delta H_0^\circ = -584.523$ [1618a]. 2. $\Delta H_0^\circ = -583.50$ [1243]. 3. $\Delta H_0^\circ = 43.70$ [1589]. 4. $(\Delta H_{298}^\circ)_{subl}$. 5. Calculated from $(\Delta H_{298}^\circ)TlBr(c) = -41.2$ and $(\Delta H_{298}^\circ)_{vap} = 32.5$ [2513]. 6. Calculated [234] from $(\Delta H_{298}^\circ)_{subl} = 32.64$ [782] and $(\Delta H_{298}^\circ)TlCl(c) = -48.99$ [2245]. 7. $(\Delta H_{298}^\circ)_{subl}$. 8. Recalculated [234] from $\Delta H_{298}^\circ = -31.1$ [842] to -30.7 [2245].

1	2	3		4		5		6	
TlOH	g					61.20	[1144]		
	c			(−45.55*)	[176]	(17.4*)	[176]		
						(26.59)	[1144]		
$Tl(OH)_3$	c			−123.0*	[323]	24.4*	[323]		
				−91.9*	[229]				
$TlReO_4$	c	−207*	[2683]						
TlTe	c	−17.70	[2527]	−12.67	[2527]	10.4	[2527]		
Tl_2CO_3	c	−167.268	[2263]	−147.00	[2263]	37.9	[2263]		
		−168.1	[1284]	−149.2*	[232]	34.3[1]	[1284]		
Tl_2CS_3	c	−21.0	[1284]			32.6[1]	[1284]		
Tl_2CrO_4	c	−223.290	[2502]	−203.300	[2502]	67.48	[2502]		
				−197.5*	[229]				
				−201.3*	[232]				
Tl_2MnO_4	c	−255*	[2683]						
Tl_2O	c	(−43.2)	[250, 1045]	(−36.6)	[1045]				
		(−41.9)	[887]	(−37.3*)	[251]	(38.5*)	[251]		
Tl_2O_2	c	−43*	[2683]						
Tl_2O_3	c	−97.5*	[1045]	−76*	[1045]	35.4*	[1480]		
		−84.5	[887]	−76.8	[2303]				
Tl_2O_4	c	−114.5*	[1045]	−86.5*	[1045]				
Tl_2S	c			−21*	[323]	39*	[323]		
				−20.4*	[229]	39.0	[1283]		
Tl_2SO_3	c	−147	[2683]						
		−159.9*	[1172]						
Tl_2SO_4	c			−196.8*	[323]	52.8*	[323]		
				−195.9*	[229]	58.2	[1678]		
Tl_2Se	c			−19.8*	[323]	46.8*	[323]		
				−17.6*	[229]				
Tl_2SeO_4	c	−152.84	[497]	−126.38	[497]	50.0*	[498]	30.80*	[498]
						51.70	[505]		
Tl_2SiO_3	c	−265*	[2683]						
Tl_2Te	c	(−38.03)	[2527]	−26.34	[2527]	27.3	[2527]		
				−8.4*	[323]	47.3*	[323]		
				−6.8*	[229]				
Tl_2WO_4	c	−277*	[2683]						
$HTl(OH)_4$	c			−179.18*	[6]				
$H_3Tl(OH)_6$	c			−292.48*	[6]				

Tm	g	57.6	[2275]	48.85*	[1589]	72.682[3]	[1626]	27.02[3]	[1626]
		59.10[2]	[1456]						
	c					17.1	[1685]	6.45	[1685, 2479]
						17.06	[2479]		
						14.4*	[323]		
						17.10	[2396]		
Tm^{3+}	d			(−157.6*)	[323]	−44.8*	[323]		
TmB_6	c	−129.0	[455]						
$TmBr_3$	c	−190*	[230]						
TmClO	c	−230*	[46]						
$TmCl_2$	c	−159*	[442]						
$TmCl_3$	c	−226*	[442]						
$TmCl_3$, γ	c	−154.1[4]	[441]	−211.7*	[323]	35.2*	[323]		
				−212.9*	[227]				
TmH_2	c	−45	[1566]						
TmI_3, β	c			−136.6*	[323]	52.1*	[323]		
				−137.0*	[227]				
TmN, k	c	−75	[1566]						
$Tm(OH)_3$	c			−302.4*	[323]				
Tm_2O_3	c	−451.4	[1566]			36.5	[2662]		
U	g	(117.160)	[2479]	106.515	[2479]	47.73	[1685, 2479]	5.66	[1685, 2479]
		(128.12)[5]	[1589]	117.47	[1589]	47.726	[1690]	5.663	[1690]
		(114.3); (115.2)	[2663]			48.1	[2663]		
		(122); (117.7)	[2663]						
		(126)[6]	[1092]						
		(119.8)	[1801]						
		(121.4)[(125.5)	[1131]						
	c					(12.03)	[1656, 1685]	(6.57)	[1656]
						(12.00)	[1234, 1589]	(6.61)	[1234, 1589]
								(6.38)[7]	[370]
								(6.64)	[2479]
								(6.58)	[1685]
U^{3+}	d	(−122.6)	[2207]			(−35*)	[2207]		
U^{4+}	d	(−146.3)	[2207]			(−81*)	[2207]		
UB_2	c	−35.3	[2207]			15.8	[2207]		
UB_4	c	−58.7	[2207]			17.0	[2207]		

1. ΔS°_{298}. 2. $\Delta H^\circ_0 = 59.41$ [1456]. 3. In *joules/g-atom* · °C. 4. Calculated [234] from $(\Delta H^\circ_{298})TmCl_3(c) = -229.5$ [2245] and $(\Delta H^\circ_{298})vap = 75.4$ [441]. 5. $\Delta H^\circ_0 = 128.09$ [1589]. 6. ΔH°_0. 7. $t = 50$ °C.

1	2	3		4		5		6	
UB_{12}	c	−103.5	[2207]			33.4	[2207]		
UBi	c	−28.3	[2207]			15.1	[2207]		
UBi_2	c	−26.3	[2207]			29.1	[2207]		
UBi_3	c	−172.3	[2207]			45	[2207]		
UBi_4	c	−197.5	[2207]			56	[2207]		
UBr_2O	c	−426.9	[1383]	−236.4	[1383]	37.66	[1383, 1685]	23.42	[1383, 1685]
		−240	[2207]	−238.3*	[232]	37.7	[2207]		
						34.9*	[21]		
UBr_2O_2	c	−276.5	[2207]			40.5	[2207]		
	c	−274.3	[625]						
	d	(−307.6)	[627]						
$UBr_2O_2 \cdot H_2O$	c	−358.8[1]	[627]						
$UBr_2O_2 \cdot 3H_2O$	c	−498.3[1]	[627]						
UBr_3O	c	−236.0	[2207]						
		−233.8	[625]			49	[2207]		
UBr_4	c	(−214.9)	[626]						
UBr_5	c	−205*	[230]	−195*	[227]				
		−209.0*	[21]						
UBr_6	c	−212*	[230]	−201*	[227]				
UC	c	−20.8	[1578, 1991]	−20.5	[1991]	12.5	[1991]	12.0[2]	[1992]
		−20	[1126]	−20.1	[1578]	11.3	[1578]		
		−21.7	[2523]			14.3	[2523]	12.1	[2523]
		−28	[1162]			14.03	[735]	11.84	[735]
		−21.0	[1200]			11.5	[2207]		
$UC_{1.86}$	c	−18	[1578, 2207]	−19	[1578]	19*	[1578]		
		−27	[1763]			16.8	[2207]		
		−30	[2206]						
$UC_{1.90}$	c	−21.1	[1568]						
$UC_{1.91}$	c	−23	[2527a]			16.31	[735]	14.50	[735]
UC_2	c	(−38.8)	[1773]			(24.3)	[1773]	14.8	[302]
		(−25*)	[1816]			(18.88)	[1801]		
$UClO_2$	c	−284*	[438]						
UCl_2	c	−18.0	[1991]	−19.2	[1991]	(19.0*)	[1991]		
UCl_2O	g	−149*	[687]						
	c	−261.7	[1383]	−244.8	[1383]	33.06	[1383, 1685]	22.72	[1383, 1685]
		−255.9	[544]	−243.7*	[232]	49.2	[544]		
		−260	[2207]			33.1	[2207]		
						32.1*	[21]		

UCl_2O_2	c	(−300)	[1382]	−277	[1382]	35.977	[1382]	25.78	[1382, 1685]
		(−301.9)	[631]			35.98	[1685]		
		(−302.9)	[2207]			36.0	[2207]		
	d	−325.7	[627]						
$UCl_2O_2 \cdot H_2O$	c	−380.8	[627]						
		−381.8	[2207]						
$UCl_2O_2 \cdot 3H_2O$	c	−520.7	[627]						
		−521.6	[2207]						
UCl_3	c			−168.2[3]	[1162]	16.12	[2523]		
UCl_3O	c	−284.2	[2207]			42	[2207]		
		−283.4	[631]						
		−281.4	[128]						
UCl_5	c	(−261.5)	[2207]			(58.0)	[2207]		
UCl_6	c	(−270.7)	[2207]						
UD_3	c	−29.00[4]	[702]	−17.08	[702]	17.20	[702, 2207]	15.53	[702]
		−31.0	[2207]						
		−31.021	[701]						
		−30.1	[437]						
UF_2O_2	c	−391.4[5]	[453]			(33.4)	[1685]	(24.67)	[1685]
		−399	[2207]			(32.4)	[2207]		
						(31.6*)	[21]		
UF_3	c	(−345)	[2207]			(28)	[2207]		
UF_3O	c	−437.0*	[21]						
UF_4	c	(−460)	[230]			(36.9)	[2079]	(27.73)	[917, 2079]
		(−449.3)	[359]			(36.2)	[1685]	(27.91)	[1685]
		(−450)	[2207]			(36.3)	[2207]		
						(36.25)	[917]		
$UF_4 \cdot 2.5H_2O$	c	−629	[2207]						
$UF_{4.25}$	c	−461.5	[2207]			37.7	[2207]		
$UF_{4.5}$	c	−472.5	[2207]			39.4	[2207]		
UF_5	c	(−491.5)	[2207]			(45.0)	[2207]		
UF_6	g	(−510.77)	[2363]	(−491.96)	[2363]	(90.002)	[2019]	30.974	[2019]
		(−492)[6]	[2628]			(90.27)	[2483]	31.04	[2483]
						(89.8)	[1685]	30.93	[1685]
		(−511)	[2207]			(90.4)	[2207]		
	c	(−522.64)	[2363]	−490.79	[2363]	(54.4)	[1685]	39.85	[1685]
		(−523)	[2207]						
UFe_2	c	−7.7	[186]			25	[2207]		

1. From gaseous bromine. 2. $t = 100\,^\circ C$. 3. $t = 400\,^\circ C$. 4. ΔH_0°. 5. $t = 32\,^\circ C$. 6. Calculated [234] from the value of ΔH_0° of vaporization of UF_6 (12.965) [2628] and ΔH_{298}° for UF_6(c)(−505) [2245].

1	2	3		4		5		6	
UGa_3	c	−37.4	[2207]			40.1	[2207]		
UGe	c	−14.7	[2207]			21.6	[2207]		
UGe_2	c	−20.9	[2207]			31.2	[2207]		
UGe_3	c	−25.5	[2207]			40.8	[2207]		
UGe_5	c	−57.3	[2207]			84.1	[2207]		
UH_3	c	(−27.945)[1,2]	[1235]	−17.353[2]	[1235]	15.24[2]	[1235, 1685]	11.78[2]	[1235, 1685]
		(−30.4)	[2207]	−15.8*	[229]	15.2	[2207]		
		(−30.352*)	[701]						
		(−30.5)	[840]						
		(−29.1)	[1101]						
UHg_2	c	−0.1	[2207]			53.4	[2207]		
UHg_3	c	−0.6	[2207]			72.9	[2207]		
UHg_4	c	−1.6	[2207]			91.0	[2207]		
UIn_4	c	−24.4	[2207]			45.3	[2207]		
UI_3	c	(−114.2)	[2207]			(57)	[2207]		
UI_3O	c	−204.0*	[21]						
UI_4	c	(−126.5)	[2207]			(67)	[2207]		
UI_5	c	−130*	[230]	−131*	[227]				
		−151.2*	[21]						
UI_6	c	−133*	[230]	−135*	[227]				
		(−70.4)	[2207]			(13.0)	[2207]		
		(−69.6)	[1414]						
UO, cubic	c	−129	[887]			18.9; 16.2	[2662]		
$U(OH)_3$	c			−263.2*	[323]				
$U(OH)_4$	c			−351.6*	[323]	16*	[1685]		
UOTe	c					26.69	[2435]	19.27	[2435]
UO_2	c	(−259.5)	[2662]	(−246.9)	[2662]	(18.63)	[1135, 1656, 1685, 2662, 2665]	15.33	[1685, 2662]
		(−259.2)	[1579, 1656]	(−246.6)	[1656]			15.31*	[1656]
		(−259.0)	[2207]	(−246.0*)	[232]	(18.6)	[2207]		
		(−270.0)	[1135]			(18.41)	[2528a]	12.20	[2528a]
UO_2^+	g					61.5	[728]		
UO_2^{2+}	d	−242.2	[1036]			(−20*)	[2207]		
						(−17*)	[1685]		
$UO_2(NO_3)_2$	c	(−332*)	[2207]			(50*)	[2207]		
$UO_2(NO_3)_2 \cdot 2H_2O$	c	(−470.4)[3]	[75]	(−389.4)[3]	[75]	(100)[3]	[75]		
		(−475)	[2207]			(77*)	[2207]		
$UO_2(NO_3)_2 \cdot 3H_2O$	c	(−551.1)[3]	[75]	(−454.3)[3]	[75]	(98)[3]	[75]		

		(−547)	[2207]			(88)	[2207]		
		(−550.5)	[1036]						
$UO_2(NO_3)_2 \cdot 6H_2O$	c	(−764.4)[3]	[75]	(−626.6)[3]	[75]	(126)[3]	[75]		
		(−759)	[2207]			(120.9)	[2207]		
		(−762.3)	[1036]			(120.8)	[1685]	111.6	[1685]
UO_2SO_4	c	(−451.2)	[2084]	(−412.5)	[2084]	(37)	[2084]		
		(−449)	[2207]						
$UO_2SO_4 \cdot H_2O$	c	−519.9	[2084]	−470	[2084]				
		−519	[2207]						
$UO_2SO_4 \cdot 3H_2O$	c	−661	[2207]						
$UO_{2.25}$, cubic	c					19.7	[2662]		
$UO_{2.25}$	c	−270	[2662]	−256	[2662]	20.07	[2662]	17.53	[2662]
$UO_{2.33}$, trigonal	c							20.5	[2662]
$UO_{2.33}$, α	c	−273*	[2662, 2664]	−258	[2662]	19.73	[2662, 2664]	17.03	[2662, 2664]
				−256	[2664]				
$UO_{2.33}$, β	c	−273*	[2662, 2664]	−258	[2662, 2664]	19.96	[2662, 2664]	17.17	[2662, 2664]
$UO_{2.67}$	c	−284.8	[2662]	−268.5	[2662]	22.51	[2662]	18.96	[2662]
$UO_{2.67}$, orthorhombic						22.7	[2662]		
$UO_{2.92}$	c	−292.0	[1036]						
UO_3	c	(−291.6)	[1656]	(−273.1)	[1656]	(23.57)	[1656, 2662]	20.26*	[1656]
		(−292.0)	[887]	(−271.7*)	[232]	(23.58)	[1685]	20.25	[1685]
				(−272.5*)	[1045]	(22.6)	[1480]		
UO_3, α	c	−294.11	[2662]	−275.5	[2662]			20.16	[2662]
		−291.8	[1036]						
UO_3, β	c	−292.6	[1036]						
UO_3, γ	c	−295.80	[80]						
		−293.5	[1036, 1037]						
		−293	[2207]			23.6	[2207]		
		−291.6; −293	[2663]						
UO_3, δ	c	−290	[1036]						
UO_3, ϵ	c	−291.8	[1036]						
UO_3, A	c	−289.6	[1036]						
UO_3, hexagonal	c					23.0	[2662]		
UO_3	v	−290	[2663]						
α-$UO_3 \cdot 0.85H_2O$	c	−357.4	[1036]						
$UO_3 \cdot H_2O$	c	(−367.5)	[2207]	(−343*)	[323]	33*	[323]		
β-$UO_3 \cdot H_2O$	c	−367.4	[1036]						
ϵ-$UO_3 \cdot H_2O$	c	−366.8	[1036]						

1. ΔH_0°. 2. β-crystals. 3. Calculated [234] from data in [2245].

1	2	3		4		5		6	
$UO_3 \cdot 2H_2O$, I	c	(−437.3)	[2207]						
UPb	c	−9.0	[2207]			26.9	[2207]		
UPb_3	c	−17.2	[2207]			55.3	[2207]		
US	c	−93	[2207]			18.6*	[2207]		
		−90	[949]						
		−83	[1131]						
US, cubic	c			−112	[2662]	20.4; 18.63	[2662]	12.08	[2662]
$U(SO_3)_2$	c	−455.8*	[1172]						
$U(SO_4)_2$	c	−540*	[2207]	−510.3*	[229]	38.5*	[2207]		
				−515.6*	[323]	64*	[323]		
$US_{1.5}$, cubic	c			−120	[2662]	22.01	[2662]		
$US_{1.67}$, orthorhombic	c					23.3	[2662]		
$US_{1.9}$, tetragonal	c					24.2	[2662]		
US_2, orthorhombic	c	−120*	[2207]			26.4*	[2207]		
				−127.1	[2662]	25.3; 26.42	[2662]	17.84	[2662]
US_3, monoclinic	c	−125*	[2207]			33.1	[2207, 2662]		
						33.08	[2662]	22.85	[2662]
USe	c					23.67	[2514]	13.10	[2514]
USe, cubic	c					24.1	[2662]		
$USe_{1.33}$, cubic	c					26.7	[2662]		
$USe_{1.5}$, orthorhombic	c					27.9	[2662]		
$USe_{1.67}$, orthorhombic	c					29.0	[2662]		
$USe_{1.9}$, tetragonal	c					31.3	[2662]		
USe_3, monoclinic	c					42.3	[2662]		
USi	c	20.2	[2207]			15.9	[2207]		
USi_2	c	−31.0	[2207]			19.6	[2207]		
USi_3	c	−31.2	[2207]			25.4	[2207]		
USn_3	c	23.1	[2207]			48.2	[2207]		
UT_3	c	−31.1	[2207]			26	[2207]		
UT_3	c	−31.141	[701]						
UTe, cubic	c					26.7	[2662]		
$UTe_{1.33}$, cubic	c					30.1	[2662]		
$UTe_{1.5}$	c					31.7	[2662]		
UTe_2	c					36.2	[2662]		
$UTe_{2.5}$	c					41.0	[2662]		
UTe_3, monoclinic	c					45.7	[2662]		
UTl_3	c	10.3	[2207]			51.5	[2207]		
U_2C_3	c	−49	[1578, 2207]	−48	[1578]	25	[1578]		

		-46	[1762]			24.7	[2207]	26.0	[2645]
						32.91	[735]	25.69	[735]
U_2N_3	c	(−169.4)	[2207]			30.4	[2207]		
		(−29.15)	[1414]						
U_2O_5	c	−565*	[21]						
U_2S_3	c	−224*	[2207]			45*	[2207]		
U_2Si	c	−22*	[2207]			40*	[2207]		
U_2Zn_{17}	c	81.4	[2207]			157	[2207]		
U_3O_7	c	−815.7; −821.1	[1569]			62.39	[2436]	54.2^{1}	[1924]
		−11.3	[2301, 2446]						
U_3O_8	c	(−903.2)	[1135]	−845.0*	[229]	60.2	[1135]	57.2*^{2}	[2723]
		(−856.5)	[2661]	−804.0	[1045]	67.534	[2659]	56.87	[1685, 2659]
		(−854.1)	[2207]			67.5	[1685, 2207]	0.0785^{3}	[590]
		(−853.5)	[1579]						[1135]
U_3Si_2	c	40.8	[2207]			47.2	[2207]		
U_3Si_5	c	84.7	[2207]			55.3	[2207]		
U_3Sn_2	c	32.6	[2207]			59.1	[2207]		
U_3Sn_5	c	52.1	[2207]			95.1	[2207]		
U_4O_8	c	−1080	[1135]			74.52	[1135]		
U_4O_9	c	−1113.4	[1135]			92.97	[1135]	70.59^{4}	[2672]
		−1078	[2207]			80.3	[1685, 2207]	70.11	[1685]
		−1076	[1924]			80.29	[2080]	71.2	[1345]
		−1080	[887]						
U_5O_{12}	c	−3.3	[2446]						
U_6Fe	c	9.4	[2207]			78.5	[2207]		
		3.9	[186]						
V	g	(123.17)^{5}	[1589]	(112.21)	[1589]			70.11	[2080]
				(111.856)	[2479]			(5.32)	[140]
	c							(5.85)	
						(6.85)	[994]	(5.79)^{6}	[994]
						(6.79)	[1589]	(5.90)	[1589, 1685]
						(7.02)	[1685]	(24.6)^{7}	[1755]
						(6.88)	[844]	(5.97)	[844]
						(7.01)	[2479]		
V^{2+}	g	(122.750)	[2479]			40.48	[66]		
	d			−54.7*	[323]				
V^{3+}	g					40.99	[66]		
	d			−60.6*	[323]				

1. $t = 100°C$. 2. Between 20 and 100°C. 3. $t = 368°C$ (*cal/g·°C*). 4. $T = 300.82°K$. 5. $\Delta H_0^\circ = 122.37$ [1589]. 6. $t = 0°C$. 7. $T = 300°K$; in *joules/g-atom·°C*.

1	2	3		4		5		6	
V^{4+}	g					40.48	[66]		
V^{5+}	g					37.72	[66]		
VBr_2	c	-83^{1}	[675]			30^{1}	[675]		
VBr_3	c	−107.8	[632a]			34^{1}	[675]		
		−118	[675]						
		50.5^{2}	[1831]						
VBr_3O	c	−154*	[21]						
VBr_4	g	−118.5	[675]			80^{1}	[675]		
	l	-94^{1}	[675]						
	c					34^{1}	[675]		
VC	c	−12.5	[2226]	−23.95	[1901]			(5.91)	[2479]
		−24.35	[1902]	−12*	[2226]				
		−22.7	[1267]						
$VC_{0.5-0.7}$		$4.7 + 128.3^{3}$	[83]						
$VC_{0.58-0.88}$, cubic	c	−102.5	[82]						
$VC_{0.73}$	c	−22.2	[2710]			-1.5^{4}	[2710]		
$VC_{0.88}$	c	−24.1	[2710]			-1.5^{4}	[2710]		
$VC_{0.91}O_{0.04}$	c	−43*	[156]						
VCl_2	c	(−110)	[657]						
		(−121)	[1773]						
VCl_3	c	(−187)	[694]			31.3	[1685]	22.27	[1685]
		(−165)	[1773]						
		(−143)	[633]						
		(−143*)	[537]						
		$(47.6)^{5}$	[1831]						
VCl_3O	g					82.147	[2023]	21.607	[2023]
						82.2	[1685]	21.49	[1685]
	l	−177.2	[438]						
	c			−150.8*	[323]				
VCl_4	g					84.001	[2031]	22.995	[2031]
	l	(−166)	[1773]	−122.7*	[229]	56.2	[1773]		
		(−136.2)	[1413]						
	c	−149	[633]						
		−145	[537]						
VCl_5	c	−166*	[358]						
		−145*	[2285]						
VF_3	c	−319*	[953]			23.5	[1685]	21.60	[1685]

VF_3O	c	-297*	[21]						
VF_4	g	-321	[952]						
VF_5	g	-352	[952]						
$VH_{0.739}$	c					8.28	[844]	8.04	[844]
VI_2	c	-63*	[571]			34.2*	[571]		
VI_3	c	-67*	[571]			51.5*	[571]		
		-54*	[2683]						
VI_3O	c	-126*	[21]						
VN	c	(-51.9)	[1515]	(-45.7)	[1515]				
		(-51.88)	[1902]						
$VO_{0.064}$	c	-7.8	[381]						
$VO_{0.268}$	c	-24.3	[381]						
$VO_{0.388}$	c	-41.6	[381]						
$VO_{0.430}$	c	-46.8	[381]						
$VO_{0.473}$	c	-53.3	[381]						
$VO_{0.505}$	c	-55.6	[381]						
$VO_{0.586}$	c	-61.9	[381]						
$VO_{0.770}$	c	-80.4	[381]						
$VO_{0.855}$	c	-90.5	[86]						
$VO_{0.870}$	c	-92.5	[381]						
$VO_{0.904}$	c	-94.0	[86]						
$VO_{0.945}$	c	-97.1	[86]						
$VO_{0.982}$	c	-101.8	[381]						
VO	g	(60.0*)	[658]	(46.6)	[229]				
				(45.0*)	[1045]				
	c	-100.0*	[1045]	-93.5*	[1045]	9.3	[1685, 2549]	10.86	[1685, 2549]
		-103	[381]						
		-120	[604]						
		-102	[86]						
VO^{2+}	d			-109*	[323]	-26	[1685]		
$V(OH)_3$	c	-253*	[2683]						
$V(OH)_4^+$	d			-256*	[323]				
$VO_{1.047}$	c	-108.0	[86]						
$VO_{1.094}$	c	-110.9	[86]						
$VO_{1.142}$	c	-117.8	[381]						
$VO_{1.176}$	c	-118.7	[86]						
$VO_{1.188}$	c	-119.6	[86]						
$VO_{1.230}$	c	-124.3	[86]						

1. At 250–650°C. 2. $(\Delta H^\circ_{298})_{subl}$; $(\Delta H^\circ_0)_{subl} = 52.9$ [1831]. 3. In *kjoules/g-atom* V. 4. ΔS. 5. $(\Delta H^\circ_{298})_{subl}$; $(\Delta H^\circ_0)_{subl} = 50.0$ [1831].

1	2	3		4		5		6	
$VO_{1.280}$	c	−131.8	[86]						
$VO_{1.322}$	c	−134	[86]						
$VO_{1.509}$	c	−150	[86]						
VO_2	g					57.7	[1685]	10.57	[1685]
	c	−171.0	[86]			12.3	[1680, 1685]	13.98	[1685]
VO_2^{2+}	d	−113	[951]	−109	[951]	−13.4[1]	[951]		
						−5.5	[1685]		
$VO_{2.5}$	c	−186.5	[381]						
VO_4^-	d			−203.9*	[323]				
VSi_2	c	−75*	[139]						
V_2C	c	−35.2	[2710]			−1.0*[1]	[2709]		
V_2O_2	c			−189*	[323]	24*	[323]		
				−186.8	[229]				
V_2O_3	c	(−296*)	[1045]	(−277*)	[1045]	(23.5)	[1685]	(24.67)	[1685]
		(−300)	[86]						
		(−294)	[1772]						
V_2O_5	c	(−376)	[86]	(−341.5)	[1045]	31.3	[1685]	30.51	[1685]
		(−371.8)	[1772]						
		(−370.1)	[139]						
		(−778)[2]	[82]						
		(−777.5)[2]	[83]						
$V_2(SO_4)_3$	c	−744*	[2683]						
V_2S_3	c	−230	[1487]						
V_2Si	c	(−36.9)	[2543]						
V_3Si	c	−27*	[139]						
V_5Si_3	c	−96*	[139]						
V_6O_{13}	c	−1064*	[1045]	−980.5*	[1045]				
$HV_6O_{17}^{3-}$	d			(−1132*)	[323]				
$H_2V_6O_{17}^{2-}$	d			(−1135*)	[323]				
W	g	(201.799)[3]	[1618a]	(191.745)	[1618a]	41.551	[1618a]	5.092	[1618a]
		(202.40)[4]	[1589]	(192.38)	[1589]				
		(200.000)	[2479]	(190.009)	[2479]	(35.64)[1]	[2512]		
	l	(203.5)[5]	[2512]	6.64	[1618a]	9.716	[1618a]	5.797	[1618a]
	c	7.202	[1618a]					(5.73)[3]	[991]
						(7.83)	[991, 1618a]	(5.797)	[1618a]
						(7.80)	[1685]	(5.84)	[1685]

						(7.806)	[253]	(5.806)	[253]
						(8.04)	[2479]	(5.92)	[1589, 2479]
						(7.95)	[1589]	(5.828)[6]	[252]
WB	c					13.2*	[1959]	8.01	[1959]
WBr_2	c			-16.7*	[323]	36.8*	[323]		
				-16.5*	[227]				
WBr_2O_2	c	-179.7	[640]						
WBr_3	c			-27.2*	[227]				
WBr_4	c			-27.4*	[323]	55*	[323]		
				-30.0*	[323]				
WBr_4O	c	-139.2	[640]						
WBr_5	g	-68.5	[1618a]	-72.021	[1618a]	110.6	[1618a]	30.76	[1618a]
	l	-81.66	[1618a]	-78.681	[1618a]	88.8	[1618a]	39.0	[1618a]
	c	(-87.00)	[1618a]	-81.398	[1618a]	80.0	[1618a]	34.875	[1618a]
		(-84.6)	[639]	-35.8*	[227]				
WBr_6	g	-69.0[7]	[1618a]	-67.79	[1618a]	112.923	[1618a]	35.724	[1618a]
	c	(-92)	[638, 1618a]	-78.56	[1618a]	72.0	[1618a]	40.51	[1618a]
		(-92.1)	[639]	-36.5*	[227]				
WC	c	(-8.4)	[1581]	-9.6*	[227]	8.5*	[1773]	58.06	[604]
$W(CO)_6$	g	-209.6	[1042]	-197.4*	[229]	1.0*[1]	[2709]		
	c	-219.29	[603]						
		-227.2	[1042]						
		-226.3	[603, 1042]						
WCl_2	g	42.0[8]	[1618a]	38.002	[1618a]	74.529	[1618a]	13.193	[1618a]
		42*	[654]						
	c	(-60)	[1618a]	-51.056	[1618a]	31.119	[1618a]	16.866	[1618a]
		(-60*)	[654]	-27*	[323]	31.2*	[323]		
				-28.7*	[227]				
WCl_2O	g	-176	[671]			49	[671]		
		-163*	[438]						
	c	-199	[671]			20	[671]		
WCl_2O_2	g	-176.7[9]	[1618a]	-166.402	[1618a]	75.585	[1618a]	18.221	[1618a]
		-173	[563]			57	[563]		
		-176	[676]			49	[676]		
		-179*	[654]						
WCl_2O_2	c	-199.7	[632, 1618a]	-180.164	[1618a]	44.6	[1618a]	24.518	[1618a]
		-199	[414]			20	[563, 676]		
		-200*	[654]						

1. ΔS°_{298}. 2. In *kjoules/g-atom* V. 3. $\Delta H^{\circ}_0 = 201.493$ [1618a]. 4. $\Delta H^{\circ}_0 = 202.13$ [1589]. 5. $T = 298°K$. 6. $t = 0°C$. 7. $\Delta H^{\circ}_0 = -58.402$ [1618a]. 8. $\Delta H^{\circ}_0 = 42.016$ [1618a]. 9. $\Delta H^{\circ}_0 = -174.923$ [1618a].

1	2	3		4		5		6	
WCl_4	g	(−82.0)[1]	[1618a]	−72.437	[1618a]	82.333	[1618a]	21.270	[1618a]
		(−94)	[563]			93	[563]		
		(−82*)	[654]						
	c	(−121)	[1618a]	−101.62	[1618a]	49.408	[1618a]	28.019	[1618a]
		(−133)	[563]	−52.4*	[227]	44*	[563]	26.52	[1662]
		(−121*)	[654]	−51*	[323]	47.4*	[323]		
WCl_4O	g	−159.2[2]	[1618a]	−143.219	[1618a]	85.311	[1618a]	23.744	[1618a]
		−161	[563]			74	[563]		
		−163	[671, 676]			72	[671, 676]		
		−159*	[654]						
	c	−177.5	[632, 1618a]	−150.693	[1618a]	49.0	[1618a]	32.242	[1618a]
		−185	[671, 676]			26	[671, 676]		
		−177	[414]						
		−178*	[654]						
		−184	[563]			28	[563]		
WCl_5	g	−118.99[3]	[1618a]	−107.689	[1618a]	103.15	[1618a]	28.685	[1618a]
		−119	[563]						
		−119*	[654]						
	l	−131.757	[1618a]	−113.331	[1618a]	79.25	[1618a]	36.20	[1618a]
	c	(−136.5)	[1618a]	−115.331	[1618a]	70.05	[1618a]	33.575	[1618a]
		(−137*)	[654]	−59*	[323]	58*	[323]		
		(−137)	[563]	−60.9*	[227]	68	[563]		
WCl_6	g	−141.86[4]	[1618a]	−121.173	[1618a]	98,314	[1618a]	33.741	[1618a]
		−143	[671, 676]			95	[671, 676]		
		−140*	[654]						
	l	−157.4	[1618a]	−128.749	[1618a]	71.6	[1618a]	39.13	[1618a]
	c	−163.1	[632, 1618a]	−131.199	[1618a]	60.7	[1618a]	39.13	[1618a]
		−97.0	[890]	−70*	[323]	69*	[323]		
		−163	[654, 671]	−71.0*	[227]	61	[671, 676]		
WCl_6, α	c	−141	[563]						
WCl_6, β	c	−160	[563]			68	[563]		
		−157*	[654]						
WF	g	97.896[5]	[1618a]	89.566	[1618a]	59.994	[1618a]	7.681	[1618a]
WF_4O	g	−337.58[6]	[1618a]	−322.208	[1618a]	77.668	[1618a]	20.819	[1618a]
	l	−354.08	[1618a]	−327.74	[1618a]	40.88	[1618a]	36.0	[1618a]
	c	−356.0	[1618a]	−328.205	[1618a]	36.0	[1618a]	31.80	[1618a]
WF_6	g	−421.0[7]	[1618a]	−399.633	[1618a]	81.507	[1618a]	28.449	[1618a]
		−416	[2014]			89.0*	[1773]		

						81.82	[2483]	28.53	[2483]
						81.488	[2019]	28.458	[2019]
						81.8	[1685]	28.47	[1685]
	l	-427.0	[1618a]	-399.343	[1618a]	60.41	[1618a]	42.0	[1618a]
		-422	[2014]	-397	[2014]	60.0	[2014]		
WI_2	c			-2.7*	[323]	41.9*	[323]		
				-2.1*	[227]				
WI_4	c			-1*	[323]	67*	[323]		
				-2.2*	[227]				
WI_5	c			18.7	[227]				
WO	g	105.0[8]	[1618a]	96.378	[1618a]	61.251	[1618a]	7.615	[1618a]
WO_2	g	21.00[9]	[1618a]	18.299	[1618a]	65.893	[1618a]	10.814	[1618a]
	c	(-140.94)[10]	[1618a, 1895]	-127.597	[1618a]	12.081	[1618a]	13.414	[1618a]
		(-140.95)	[1737]	-127.6	[1737]	12.08	[1685, 1737]	13.32	[1685, 1737]
		(-136.6)	[124]	-124.2	[124]	16.0*	[887]	15.0	[124]
		(-135)	[1891]	-124.4*	[323]	17*	[323]		
		(-134.0)	[1401]	-123.1*	[229]	19.7	[1401]		
		(-134.8)	[380]	-124.6*	[1045]				
		(-137)	[1400]						
$WO_{2.67}$	c	-175.5	[1400]						
$WO_{2.72}$	c	(-180.3)	[1401]			25.0	[1401]		
		(-183.1)	[1400]						
$WO_{2.90}$	c	(-193.1)	[1401]			23.6	[1401]		
		(-193)	[1400]						
		(-191*)	[872]			24*	[872]		
WO_3	g	-70.0[11]	[1618a]	-66.21	[1618a]	68.624	[1618a]	14.936	[1618a]
	l	-187.801	[1618a]	-171.144	[1618a]	25.468	[1618a]	17.62	[1618a]
WO_3, yellow	c	(-201.46)[12]	[1618a, 1895]	(-182.619)	[1618a]	(18.144)	[1618a]	17.63	[1618a]
		(-203.0)	[68]	(-184.7)	[68]	(20.0)	[68]		
		(-202.8)	[140]			(19.1)	[140]		
		(-201.45)	[1737]	(-182.65)	[1737]	(18.15)	[1685, 1737]	17.66	[1685, 1737]
		(-199)	[1400]						
		(-200.16)	[1581]						
		(-200)	[887]						
$(WO_3)_3$	g	-468.51	[1618a]	-434.462	[1618a]	129.81	[1618a]	54.804	[1618a]
$(WO_3)_4$	g	-648.74	[1618a]	-599.064	[1618a]	158.73	[1618a]	75.802	[1618a]
$WO_3 \cdot H_2O$	c			-247.5*	[229]				

1. $\Delta H_0^\circ = -80.754$ [1618a]. 2. $\Delta H_0^\circ = -157.307$ [1618a]. 3. $\Delta H_0^\circ = -112.325$ [1618a]. 4. $\Delta H_0^\circ = -141.216$ [1618a]. 5. $\Delta H_0^\circ = 98.0$ [1618a]. 6. $\Delta H_0^\circ = -335.194$ [1618a]. 7. $\Delta H_0^\circ = -418.925$ [1618a]. 8. $\Delta H_0^\circ = 105.094$ [1618a]. 9. $\Delta H_0^\circ = 21.562$ [1618a]. 10. $\Delta H_0^\circ = -139.772$ [1618a]. 11. $\Delta H_0^\circ = -69.003$ [1618a]. 12. $\Delta H_0^\circ = -200.12$ [1618a].

1	2	3		4		5		6	
WO_4^{2-}	d	(−266.6)	[1350]	−220*	[323]	15*	[323]		
WS_2	c	(−48.4)	[1772]			(20.0)	[1772]		
		(−47.9)	[1487]						
WSi_2	c	−22.2	[2232]						
W_2B	c					28.2*	[1959]	15.36	[1959]
W_2B_5	c					21*	[1959]	21.09	[1959]
W_2C	c	−6.3	[1903]			2.0*[1]	[2709]		
W_2O_5	c			−306.9*	[323]				
				−304.8*	[229]				
W_2O_8	c	−533.5	[887]						
W_4O_{11}	c	−741.5*	[1045]	−674.0*	[1045]				
$W_{10}O_{29}$	c	−1934*	[887]						
H_2WO_4	g	−216.6[2]	[1618a]	−200.807	[1618a]	84.076	[1618a]	24.571	[1618a]
	c	(−280.21)[3]	[1618a]	−247.698	[1618a]	28.0	[1618a]	28.66	[1618a]
		(−268.407)	[557]						
Xe	g					(40.5304)	[570]		
						(40.529)	[568]		
						(40.5290)	[2358]		
	d	−4.2	[2358]	3.2	[2358]	15.7	[2358]		
Xe^+	g	(281.202)[4]	[568]						
		(281.2)[5]	[2358]						
Xe^{2+}	g	(769.8)[6]	[568]						
		(771.8)[7]	[2358]						
Xe^{3+}	g	(1510)[6]	[568]						
		(1514.1)[8]	[2358]						
Xe · HCl	g	−23.5[9]	[568]						
XeF_2	g	−37	[2504]						
XeF_2O_2	g	56	[1432]						
XeF_4	g	−44.8	[568]						
	c	−55	[1444]						
		−53	[2504]						
XeF_4, monoclinic	c	−60	[568]						
		−62.5	[2358]						
XeF_4O	g	−6	[1432]						
XeO_3	c	96	[1431]						
XeO_4	g	153.5	[1432]						
Y	g	(102.000)	[2479]	92.497	[2479]				

		(101.70)[10]	[1589]	92.09	[1589]				
		(101.52)[11]	[1456]	93.1*	[229]				
		(97.72); (86.27)	[237]						
		(99.0)	[2679]						
		(85.71)	[239, 394]						
	c					11.0	[1685]	6.00	[1685]
						11.00	[2479]	6.01	[2479]
						10.62	[1627]	6.34	[1589, 1627]
						59.88[12]	[1304]	26.72[12]	[1304]
						11.3*	[323]	5.87	[2636]
						10.5*	[244]		
Y^{3+}	g					39.38*	[66]		
	d	(−161.31)	[2422]	−164.1*	[323]	−48*	[323]		
				−155*	[1976]	−55*	[1976]		
YBr_3	c	−195*	[230]	−137.5*	[227]				
		−196*	[2683]						
$YCl_{0.5}(OH)_{2.5}$	c			−304.4	[13]				
$YCl(OH)_2$	c			−294.2	[13]				
$YCl_{1.25}(OH)_{1.75}$	c			−291.2	[13]				
YCl_3	c	(−232.69)	[2422]	−215.2	[2422]	32.7	[2422]		
		(−256*)	[358]	−215.0*	[232]	32.7*	[323]		
				−218.2*	[229]				
				−215*	[1976]				
$YCl_3 \cdot 6H_2O$	c	−679.87	[1336]	−581.1	[1336]	89.1	[1336]		
				−571.7*	[232]				
				−579*	[1976]				
YD_2	c					10.294	[1237, 2523]		
YD_3	c					12.028	[1238]	13.727	[1238]
YF_3	c	−410.7	[2253]	−393.6	[2253]				
		−382*	[230]						
YH_2	c	−44.4	[2523]			9.175	[1237, 2523]	8.243	[1237, 2523]
YH_2[13]	c	−44.42	[1825]			−27.07[1]	[1825]		
YH_3						10.019	[1238]	10.363	[1238]
YI_3	c	(−136.0)	[1773]	−127.1*	[229]	47.5*	[323]		
				−136*	[1976]				
YN	c	−71.5	[2048]						

1. ΔS°_{298}. 2. $\Delta H^\circ_0 = -214.292$ [1618a]. 3. $\Delta H^\circ_0 = -280.21$ [1618a]. 4. $\Delta H^\circ_0 = (279.721)$ [568]. 5. $\Delta H^\circ_0 = (279.72)$ [2358]. 6. ΔH°_0. 7. $\Delta H^\circ_0 = (768.8)$ [2358]. 8. $\Delta H^\circ_0 = (1509.6)$ [2358]. 9. $T = 240\,°K$. 10. $\Delta H^\circ_0 = 101.49$ [1589]. 11. $\Delta H^\circ_0 = 101.31$ [1456]. 12. In *joules/g-atom* · °C. 13. From saturated solution of H_2 in Y.

1	2	3		4		5		6	
Yo	g					56.3	[1685]	7.53	[1685]
$Y(OH)_3$	c			(−307.1*)	[323]	23*	[323]		
				(−309.61*)	[176]				
				(−310.3)	[13]				
$YO_{1.5}$, body-centered	c			−217.6	[2662]	23.69	[2662]		
Y_2O_3	c	−455.54[1]	[2679]	−434*	[1976]	23.7	[2679]	(23.2*)[2]	[1976]
		−420*	[887]	−429.7*	[234]	23.693	[1326]	(24.50)	[1326]
		−455.45	[1564]			23.6	[1685]	(24.58)	[1685]
						26.0*	[1773]		
						22.4	[2662]		
$Y_2(SO_4)_3$	c	−914*	[2683]						
$Y_2(SO_4)_3 \cdot 8H_2O$	c					140.6*	[323]		
Y_2S_3	c	−276*	[1480]						
		−282*	[2683]						
Yb	g	(42.900)	[2479]	35.044	[2479]	(41.35)	[1589, 1685, 2479]		
		(40.0)	[2275]						
		(36.33)[3]	[1456]						
	c					15.00	[2479]	6.00	[1685, 2479]
						15.0	[1685]		
						14.45*	[323]		
						59.88[4]	[1476]		
Yb^{2+}	d			(−122*)	[1976]	−18*	[1976]		
Yb^{3+}	d			(−156.8*)	[323]	−45.4*	[323]		
				(−149*)	[1976]	−53*	[1976]		
YbB_6	c	−131.5	[455]						
$YbBr_3$	c	−194*	[232]						
$YbCl_{0.5}(OH)_{2.5}$	c			−296.6	[16]				
YbCl	g					62.2	[1685]	8.65	[1685]
YbClO	c	−229*	[46]						
$YbCl(OH)_2$	c			−288.5	[16]				
$YbCl_2$	c	−184.5	[1865]	−173.0*	[234]				
		−185*	[442]	−174*	[1976]				
		−186	[445, 446]			32*	[446]		
$YbCl_3$, γ	c	(−230*)	[691]	−210.9*	[323]	35.3*	[323]		
		(−223*)	[442, 446]	−212.2	[227]	33*	[446]		
		(79.4)[5]	[441]	−206*	[1976]				

$YbCl_3 \cdot 6H_2O$	c			-57.3*	[1976]	91.6	[2422]		
YbI_3	c	-130*	[1976]	-128*	[1976]				
$Yb(OH)_3$	c			-301.7*	[323]				
				-305.89	[8]				
Yb_2O_3	c	-433.68	[1562, 1659]	-412.31	[1659]	29.02[6]; 31.8	[1659]	27.57	[1659]
				-410*	[1976]	34.5; 31.8	[2662]	25.6*[7]	[1976]
				-411.1*	[234]				
								28.1	[592]
$Yb_2(SO_4)_3 \cdot 8H_2O$	c	-1502*	[229]			156.6*	[323]		
Zn	g	(31.245)[8]	[1589]	(22.750)	[1589]				
		(30.73); (31.18)	[2238]	(22.682)	[2479]				
		(31.01)	[712]						
		(31.14)	[1033]						
		(30.30)[9]	[393]						
		(31.18)	[784]						
		(30.05)[9]	[1914]						
		(30.85)	[1370a]						
	c					(9.94)	[1168]	(6.07)	[1685, 2479]
Zn^{2+}	g					38.46	[66]		
	d					(-25.8)	[1685]		
$Zn(CN)_2$	c			29*	[323]	22.9*	[323]		
$Zn(CN)_4^{2-}$	d			100.4*	[323]				
$Zn(CNS)_2$	c	9*	[696]						
		6*	[2683]						
$ZnCO_3$	c	(-193.772)	[2263]	(-175.067)	[2263]	(22.1)	[2263]		
				(-175.04*)	[177]	(20.6*)	[177]		
				(-175.4*)	[232]	(19.05)	[1685]		
$ZnCl_{0.5}(OH)_{1.5}$	c			-125.51*	[11]				
$Zn(ClO_3)_2$	c	-60*	[2683]						
$Zn(ClO_4)_2$	c	-68*	[2683]	-29.19	[190]				
$Zn(ClO_4)_2 \cdot 6H_2O$	c	-510.6	[23]						
$ZnCl_2$	c			(26.5)	[1685]				
$ZnCl_2 \cdot 2Zn(OH)_2$	c	-420.7*	[229]	-367.82*	[587]				
ZnD	g					50.2	[1685]		
ZnF	g					55.6	[1685]	7.94	[1685]
ZnF_2	c	-182.7	[2254]	-170.5	[2254]	17.61	[1685]	15.69	[1685, 2465]

1. $\Delta H_0^\circ = 453.6$ [2679]. 2. Average between 273 and 373 °K. 3. $\Delta H_0^\circ = 36.45$ [1456]. 4. In *joules/mole* °C. 5. $(\Delta H_0^\circ)_{vap}$. 6. $S_{298}^\circ - S_{10}^\circ$. 7. Average between 273 and 373 °K. 8. $\Delta H_0^\circ = 31.110$ [1589]. 9. ΔH_0°.

1	2	3		4		5		6	
ZnF_2		-176*	[890]	-165*	[229]	17.6	[2465]		
$Zn_{0.1}Fe_{2.9}O_4$	c	-266.6	[450]	-240.0	[450]	34.00	[450]		
$Zn_{0.3}Fe_{2.7}O_4$	c	-269.3	[450]	-241.0	[450]	33.3	[450]		
$Zn_{0.5}Fe_{2.5}O_4$	c	-273.8	[450]	-246.0	[450]	33.0	[450]		
$Zn_{0.7}Fe_{2.3}O_4$	c	-275.0	[450]	-250.0	[450]	30.40	[450]		
$ZnFe_2O_4$	c	-286.5	[464]	-260.1	[464]	32.2[2]	[1720]	32.99	[1720]
		-286.7[1]	[419]			31.5*	[419]		
		-283.5	[450]	-255.5	[450]	30.78	[450]		
						36.2	[1685]	34.17	[1685]
						36.01	[2660]		
ZnH	g							(7.03)	[1685]
$Zn(HCO_3)_2$	c	-369*	[2683]						
$Zn(HS)_2$	c	-19*	[2683]						
$Zn(HSO_4)_2$	c	-439*	[2683]						
ZnH_2	c	-44*	[2683]						
ZnI_2	c					(38.5)	[1680]		
						(35.0)	[1685]		
$ZnMoO_4$	c	-272.4*	[170, 172]	-249.4*	[170, 172]	31.5*	[414]		
$Zn(NH_2)_2$	c	-33*	[2683]						
$Zn(NH_3)_2CS_3$	c	-82.4	[1285]			43.1	[1285]		
$[Zn(NH_3)_4]^{2+}$	d	-16.18	[2102]	-12.82	[2102]				
	d			-73.5*	[323]				
$Zn(NO_2)_2$	c	-83*	[2683]						
$Zn(NO_3)_2$	c	(-123)[3]	[694]	-71.42*	[323]	46.3*	[323]		
		(-121*)	[696]	-70.1*	[227]				
$Zn(NO_3)_2 \cdot 2H_2O$	c			-192.8*	[229]				
$Zn(NO_3)_2 \cdot 4H_2O$	c			-302.7*	[229]				
$Zn(NO_3)_2 \cdot 6H_2O$	c			-420.0	[190]	98.03	[190]		
				-416.9*	[229]				
$Zn(NO_3)_2 \cdot 4Zn(OH)_2$	c	-737.5*	[229]	-623.75*	[587]				
ZnO	g			-92.18	[2305]	53.7	[1685]	7.82	[1685]
	c								
						(10.43)	[1685]		
$3ZnO \cdot ZnSO_4$	c			-437	[2621]				
$ZnOH^+$	d			-78.8*	[323]				
$Zn(OH)_2$	c			-132.66*	[176]	(20.3*)	[176]		
				-132.6	[229, 323]	(19.9*)	[323]		
				-136.59	[11]	(18.2*)	[249]		

$Zn(OH)_2$, β	c			−132.53	[2305]				
$Zn(OH)_2$, γ	c			−132.56	[2305]				
$Zn(OH)_2$, ε	c			−132.83	[2305]				
$Zn(OH)_4^{2-}$	d			−206.25*	[6]				
				−216.40	[7]				
ZnO_2	c	−83*	[2683]						
ZnO_2^{2-}	d			−93.03*	[323]				
$Zn(ReO_4)_2$	c	−419*	[2683]						
ZnS, wurtzite	c	(−45.9)	[704]	−44.7	[704]	13.8	[1685]	11.00	[1685]
				−44.2*	[323]	13.8*	[323]		
				−44.7*	[229]				
ZnS, β	c	(−49.2)	[2224]	(−47.85*)	[176]	(15.6*)	[176]		
$ZnSO_3$	c	−162*	[2683]						
		−179.2*	[1172]						
$ZnSO_4$	c			(−207.0*)[4]	[250]	(32.99)	[2660]	(36.1)	[2469]
						(30.6)	[1680]		
						(27.0)	[1685]		
$ZnSO_4 \cdot 6H_2O$	c					(86.9)	[1685]	(85.02)	[1685]
						(85.1)	[778]		
$ZnSO_4 \cdot 7H_2O$	c					(93.0)	[778, 1685]	(90.0*)	[778]
								(91.17)	[1685]
$ZnSO_4 \cdot Zn(OH)_2$	c	−392.7*	[229]	−349.57*	[587]				
ZnSb	c	−2.065[5]	[167]	−17.8	[652]	−0.26[6]	[167]		
		−3.55	[1526]			21.4	[1680, 1685]		
ZnSe	c	(−31*)	[282]	−34.7*	[323]	22.3*	[323]		
				−33.5*	[229]	15.7*	[247]		
		(47*)	[2712]			14.6	[2712]		
$ZnSeO_3$	c	32[8]	[48a]	23[8]	[48a]	33[7]	[48a]		
$ZnSeO_3 \cdot H_2O$	c	−222.92	[507]						
		−223.0	[343]						
$ZnSeO_4$	c	−163.48	[515]			20.6*	[498]		
		−167*	[2683]						
$ZnSeO_4 \cdot H_2O$	c	−239.52	[515]						
$ZnSeO_4 \cdot 6H_2O$	c	−592.18	[515]						
$ZnSeO_4 \cdot 7H_2O$	c	−665.0*	[499]	−611.42	[190]	90.81	[190]		
$ZnSiO_3$	c			−274.8*	[323]	21.4	[323]		
				−262.4*	[246]	20.2*	[246]		
				−274.6	[227]				

1. Calculated [234] from the heat of formation from oxides 7.0 [419]. 2. $S^\circ_{298} - S^\circ_0$. 3. It was pointed out [694] that the value −115.1 [2245] is erroneous. 4. Recalculated [234] from $(\Delta H^\circ_{298})_{diss}$ = 79.0 [250] to 79.74 [2245], using the values of ΔG°_{298} for SO_3 and ZnO. 5. In *cal/g-atom*. 6. ΔS°_{298}; per *g-atom* at 420–500°C. 7. ΔS°_T (T = 693–773°K). 8. $ZnSeO_3 = ZnO + SeO_2$.

1	2	3		4		5		6	
ZnTe	c	(−28.8)	[2625]			(18.9)	[1685]		
		(−48.65)[1]	[281]						
$ZnTiO_3$	c	−309.1	[430]						
$ZnWO_4$	c	−295.8[2]	[173]	−262.4[2]	[173]	33.8	[173]		
		−294.0*	[172]	−270.1*	[172]				
		−293*	[2683]	−270.4	[203]				
$Zn_2Cl(OH)_3$	c			−251.02	[11]				
$Zn_2Fe(CN)_6$	c	78.6	[2234]						
$Zn_2P_2O_7$	c	−56.0[3]	[1170]						
		−694.5	[1947]						
	v	45.4[3]	[1170]						
Zn_2SiO_4	c	(−7.0)[4]	[1681]	−7.1[4]	[1681]				
		(−383.2*)[5]	[32]	−351.6	[2543]	31.4	[1685, 2543]	29.48	[2543]
		(−379.5)	[1727]	−337.0*	[229]	29.8	[419]		
		(−378.7)	[1712]						
Zn_2TiO_4	c	−391.6	[430]			32.8	[1716]	32.8	[1716]
		−393.5	[2552]	−366.8	[2552]	34.2	[1685]	32.82	[1685]
Zn_3As_2	c	−29*	[637]						
		−30.5	[763]						
Zn_3N_2	c	(−3.5)	[637]	1.1*	[229]				
		(−5.3)	[2625]						
$Zn_3(PO_4)_2$	v	−84.8[6]	[1170]						
Zn_3P_2	c	−55.03	[236]						
		−53.37	[236a]						
		−98	[637]						
		−53.4	[1670a]						
$Zn_3P_4O_{13}$	v	−102.5[6]	[1170]						
Zn_3Sb_2	c	−7.3	[2625]	−48.0	[652]	53.4	[2625]		
						63.6	[1685]		
Zn_4Sb_3	c					73.5	[1685]		
$Zn_5(P_3O_{10})_2$	v	−167.2[6]	[1170]						
$[HZn(OH)_4]^-$	d			−222.61*	[6]				
$H_2Zn(OH)_4$	c			−245.96*	[6]				
$H_4Zn(OH)_6$	c			−359.26*	[6]				
	g	(145.417)[7]	[1618a]	(135.270)	[1618a]	(43.317)	[1618a]	(6.368)	[1618a]
Zr		(146.000)	[2479]	(135.853)	[2479]	(43.3170)	[1758]	(6.36770)	[1758]
		(145.76)[8]	[1589]	(135.614)	[1589]	(43.32)	[1685]	(6.37)	[1685]
		(145.316)[9]	[570]			(43.3168)	[570]		

		(141.8)	[2566]						
	l	(5.269)	[1618a]	4.463	[1618a]	12.015	[1618a]	6.137	[1618a]
Zr, a	c					(9.290)	[1112]	6.197	[1112]
						(9.32)	[1685]	6.12	[1685]
						(9.31)	[1618a]	6.138	[1618a]
Zr, II	c					(9.28)	[2542]	6.186	[2542]
						(9.29)	[570, 2385]	6.01	[570, 1589, 2479]
								6.30[10]	[1117]
Zr^{2+}	g					42.72	[66]		
Zr^{4+}	g					39.45	[66]		
	d			-141*	[323]				
ZrB_2	g	-46.7	[1570]	-75.4	[2658]	8.59	[2658]	11.53	[2658]
						8.5	[1959]	13.12	[1959]
						8.58	[2646]		
	l	-60.627	[1618a]	-60.518	[1618a]	11.727	[1618a]	11.644	[1618a]
	c	-77.2	[1569]	-70.472	[1618a]	8.646	[1618a]	11.645	[1618a]
						7.94	[2576]	11.53	[2576]
$ZrB_{2.05}$	c	-75.02	[678]	-71.5	[1618a]				
				-71.6	[1327]				
				-72.1	[2566]				
$ZrBr_2$	g	-43.635[11]	[1618a]	-53.553	[1618a]	78.96	[1618a]	13.563	[1618a]
	l	-95.241	[1618a]	-92.536	[1618a]	36.621	[1618a]	20.50	[1618a]
	c	(-100*)	[1618a, 1826]	-95.768	[1618a]	31.5	[1618a]	20.50	[1618a]
				-116.5*	[323]	33.9*	[323]		
				-115.8*	[227]				
$ZrBr_3$	g	-103.0[12]	[1618a]	-110.424	[1618a]	88.787	[1618a]	18.988	[1618a]
	c	(-152.0)[13]	[1618a]	-145.213	[1618a]	41.122	[1618a]	23.777	[1618a]
		(-151*)	[1826]	-166.6*	[323]	39.1*	[323]		
				-167.7*	[227]				
$ZrBr_4$	g	-153.6[14]	[1618a]	-158.697	[1618a]	99.173	[1618a]	24.511	[1618a]
						97.0	[1685]		
	c	(-181.6)[15]	[1618a, 2569]	-173.14	[1618a]	53.702	[1618a]	29.829	[1618a]
				-172.5	[2569]	52.1*	[323, 2569]		
				-183.1*	[323]	55.5	[1685]		
				-184.3*	[227]				
$ZrC_{0.710}$	c	-33.1	[1905]						

1. $t = 520-720°C$. 2. Calculated [234] from heat of formation ΔH°_{298} from Zn(g) [173]. 3. From oxides. 4. From ZnO and $SiO_2(a)$. 5. Calculated [234] from heat of formation from oxides 11.5 [419]. 6. From ZnO (c) and P_2O_5(c) at 35°C. 7. $\Delta H^\circ_0 = 145.105$ [1618a]. 8. $\Delta H^\circ_0 = 145.44$ [1589]. 9. $\Delta H^\circ_0 = 145$ [570]. 10. Average heat capacity between 0 and 100°C. 11. $\Delta H^\circ_0 = -40.021$ [1618a]. 12. $\Delta H^\circ_0 = -97.508$ [1618a]. 13. $\Delta H^\circ_0 = -147.242$ [1618a]. 14. $\Delta H^\circ_0 = -146.527$ [1618a]. 15. $\Delta H^\circ_0 = -175.296$ [1618a].

1	2	3		4		5		6	
$ZrCo_{0.71}O_{0.08}$	c	−53.8	[318]			7.0	[1773]		
ZrC	g	−354.7; −361.7	[1828]			12.05	[1828]		
	l	−28.286	[1618a]	−29.515	[1618a]	18.108	[1618a]	11.265	[1618a]
	c	(−47.0)	[1618a, 1905]	−46.194	[1618a]	7.964	[1618a]	9.058	[1618a]
		(−47.7)	[2164]	−38.9	[2164]	7.90	[2657]	9.13	[2657]
		(−44.1)	[1906]	−36.5	[2226]	8.5*	[1773]		
				−43.9*	[227]	9.3	[1685]		
ZrCl	g	138.2[1]	[1618a]	130.611	[1618a]	61.409	[1618a]	8.521	[1618a]
	c	−48*	[482]						
$ZrCl_2$	g	−78.0[2]	[1618a]	−81.251	[1618a]	73.502	[1618a]	13.313	[1618a]
	l	−127.661	[1618a]	−117.777	[1618a]	29.448	[1618a]	23.0	[1618a]
	c	(−132)	[1618a]	−121.386	[1618a]	27.0	[1618a]	18.522	[1618a]
		(−136)	[2571]	−134.1*	[227]	28.3	[2571]		
		(−127*)	[2285]	−134.8*	[323]	28.3*	[323]		
		(−124.3*)	[1578]			26.4*	[483, 484]	17.8*	[483]
$ZrCl_2O \cdot 2H_2O$	c			−375.5*	[229]				
$ZrCl_2O \cdot 3.5H_2O$	c			−452.3*	[229]				
$ZrCl_2O \cdot 6H_2O$	c			−604.6*	[229]				
$ZrCl_2O \cdot 8H_2O$	c			−713.9*	[229]				
$ZrCl_3$	g	−144.0[3]	[1618a]	−141.394	[1618a]	80.504	[1618a]	18.276	[1618a]
	c	(−206.0)[4]	[1618a]	−188.724	[1618a]	31.299	[1618a]	22.78	[1618a]
		(−183*)	[2285]	−191.7*	[227]	32.5*	[483, 484]	23.9*	[483]
		(−178.6*)	[1826]	−191*	[323]	32.8*	[323]		
		(−186)	[2571]						
$ZrCl_4$	g	−207.03[5]	[1618a]	−198.795	[1618a]	88.268	[1618a]	23.588	[1618a]
						86.5	[1685]	23.36	[1685]
	c	(−234.7)[6]	[1417, 1618a]	(−212.477)	[1618a]	(41.353)	[1618a]	28.646	[1618a]
		(−234.35)	[111]	(−213.4)	[2569]	(44.5)	[1685, 2542]	28.65	[1685, 2542]
		(−231.9)	[2376]	(−211.0)	[229]				
$ZrD_{1.58}$	c							7.7*	[2557]
ZrD_2	c	−41.5	[1236]	−31.2	[1236]	9.17	[1236]	9.63	[1236]
		−40.5	[2523]	−30.0	[2523]	9.168	[2523]	9.631	[2523]
		−40.22	[1254]	−29.86	[1254]				
ZrF	g	116.70[7]	[1618a]	109.248	[1618a]	58.528	[1618a]	8.128	[1618a]
ZrF_2	g	−146.7*[8]	[1618a]	−147.764*	[1618a]	61.327	[1618a]	11.361	[1618a]
	l	−220.38	[1618a]	−210.168	[1618a]	23.505	[1618a]	30.0	[1618a]
	c	−230*	[1618a]	−219.041	[1618a]	21	[1618a]	22.739	[1618a]
				−219.2*	[323]	21.5*	[323]		

				-218.3	[227]				
ZrF_3	g	-284[9]	[1618a]	-281.143	[1618a]	72.399	[1618a]	16.362	[1618a]
	c	-361.0[10]	[1618a]	-341.425	[1618a]	16.325	[1618a]	19.126	[1618a]
				-332.8*	[323]	24.1*	[323]		
				-332.5*	[227]				
ZrF_4	g	-397.2[11]	[1618a]	-389.014	[1618a]	78.748	[1618a]	21.115	[1618a]
						74.3	[1685]		
	l							29*	[1854]
	c	(-456.80)[12]	[1380, 1618a]	-432.60	[1380, 1618a]	25.024	[1618a]	24.754	[1618a]
		(-390*)	[230]	-424.3*	[323]	32.1*	[323]	24.81[13]	[1854]
				-421.9*	[227]	32.5*	[890, 1794]		
						30.0	[1685]		
						22.2*	[60]		
ZrF_4, β	c			-432.6	[2644]	25.00	[2644]	24.79	[2644]
$ZrH_{0.25}$	c					9.27	[1112]	6.54	[1112]
$ZrH_{0.324}$	c							6.73	[1117]
$ZrH_{0.50}$	c					9.23	[1112]	6.75	[1112]
$ZrH_{0.556}$	c							6.95	[1117]
$ZrH_{0.57}$	c					9.22	[1112]	6.81	[1112]
$ZrH_{0.701}$	c							7.12	[1117]
$ZrH_{0.75}$	c					9.20	[1112]	6.97	[1112]
$ZrH_{0.999}$	c							7.44	[1117]
ZrH	g	123.4[14]	[1618a]	115.432	[1618a]	51.638	[1618a]	7.096	[1618a]
	c					9.16	[1112]	7.18	[1112]
$ZrH_{1.071}$	c							7.51	[1117]
$ZrH_{1.23}$	c	-25.3	[2570]						
$ZrH_{1.25}$	c					9.12	[1112]	7.39	[1112]
$ZrH_{1.43}$	c	-30.05	[2570]						
$ZrH_{1.58}$	c							9.7*	[2557]
$ZrH_{1.70}$	c	-34.7	[2570]						
$ZrH_{1.85}$	c	-38.2	[2570]						
ZrH_2	c	-39.3	[2523]	-29.7	[2523]	8.374	[2523]	7.396	[2523]
		-40.5	[1236]	-30.9	[1236]	8.37	[1236]	7.40	[1236]
		-38.90	[1254]	-29.32	[1254]				
		-39.7	[2570]						
ZrI	g	141.30[15]	[1618a]	128.575	[1618a]	65.868	[1618a]	8.823	[1618a]
ZrI_2	g	-15.928[16]	[1618a]	-29.438	[1618a]	82.38	[1618a]	13.681	[1618a]

1. $\Delta H_0^\circ = 138.311$ [1618a]. 2. $\Delta H_0^\circ = -77.899$ [1618a]. 3. $\Delta H_0^\circ = -143.602$ [1618a]. 4. $\Delta H_0^\circ = -205.975$ [1618a]. 5. $\Delta H_0^\circ = -206.765$ [1618a]. 6. $\Delta H_0^\circ = -234.896$ [1618a]. 7. $\Delta H_0^\circ = 116.876$ [1618a]. 8. $\Delta H_0^\circ = -146.054$ [1618a]. 9. $\Delta H_0^\circ = -283.116$ [1618a]. 10. $\Delta H_0^\circ = -359.455$ [1618a]. 11. $\Delta H_0^\circ = -396.422$ [1618a]. 12. $\Delta H_0^\circ = -455.445$ [1618a]. 13. $t = 300°C$. 14. $\Delta H_0^\circ = -123.652$ [1618a]. 15. $\Delta H_0^\circ = 141.783$ [1618a]. 16. $\Delta H_0^\circ = -15.117$ [1618a].

1	2	3		4		5		6	
ZrI_2	l	-55.985	[1618a]	-58.199	[1618a]	44.494	[1618a]	22.50	[1618a]
	c	(-62.0)	[1618a]	-61.652	[1618a]	35.9	[1618a]	22.50	[1618a]
		(-68*)	[1826]	-90.7*	[323]	39.3*	[323]		
				-89.5*	[227]				
ZrI_3	g	-53.0[1]	[1618a]	-66.148	[1618a]	95.047	[1618a]	19.317	[1618a]
	c	-95.0[2]	[1618a]	-94.389	[1618a]	48.897	[1618a]	24.813	[1618a]
		-103*	[1826]	-128*	[323]	49.6*	[323]		
				-127.4*	[227]				
ZrI_4	g	-84.9	[1618a]	-97.007	[1618a]	106.775	[1618a]	25.09	[1618a]
						107.7	[17]	25.20	[17]
						107.0	[1685]		
	c	(-115.9)[3]	[1618a, 2569]	-114.882	[1618a]	61.412	[1618a]	29.543	[1618a]
		(-141*)	[230]	-116.6*	[2569]	67.5*	[2569]		
				-130*	[323]	64.1*	[323]		
				-129.9*	[227]	63.0	[1685]		
$ZrN_{0.56}$	c	-56.1	[541]	-52.3*	[541]	9.4*	[541]		
$ZrN_{0.69}$	c	-68.7	[541]	-64.1*	[541]	9.7*	[541]		
$ZrN_{0.74}$	c	-72.2	[541]	-67.3*	[541]	9.7*	[541]		
$ZrN_{0.89}$	c	-82.4	[541]	-76.3*	[541]	9.3*	[541]		
ZrN	g	170.50[4]	[1618a]	163.468	[1618a]	55.78	[1618a]	7.567	[1618a]
	l	-69.489	[1618a]	-64.332	[1618a]	14.899	[1618a]	9.666	[1618a]
	c	(-87.3)[5]	[1618a, 1785]	(-80.47)	[1618a]	(9.288)	[1618a]	9.67	[1618a]
		(-87.9)	[541]	(-81.1*)	[541]	(9.3*)	[541]	9.66	[1618a]
		(-80.43)[6]	[1530]	(-80.5)	[1530]	(9.29)	[1685, 2542]	9.655	[2542]
		(-72.0)	[31]	(-79.9*)	[232]				
$Zr(NO_3)_2$	c	(-123*)	[694]						
		(-125)	[481]						
ZrO	g	21.1[7]	[1618a]	14.166	[1618a]	57.069	[1618a]	8.62	[1618a]
		22.636[8]	[570]			56.086	[570]		
						56.25	[1685]	8.58	[1685]
$Zr(OH)_4$	c			-370*	[323]	31*	[323]		
				-368.8*	[229]				
$ZrO(NO_3)_2 \cdot 2H_2O$	c			-388.8*	[229]				
$ZrO(NO_3)_2 \cdot 3H_2O$	c			-444.7*	[229]				
$ZrO(NO_3)_2 \cdot 3.5H_2O$	c			-477.4*	[229]				
$ZrO(NO_3)_2 \cdot 6H_2O$	c			-614.5*	[229]				
$ZrOOH^+$	d	-270.7	[2569]						
$ZrO(OH)_2$	c			-311.5*	[323]	22*	[323]		

				−309.8*	[229]				
$ZrO_{1.58}$	c			9.7[9]	[2557]				
ZrO_2	g	−82.50[10]	[1618a]	−82.535	[1618a]	58.431	[1618a]	11.332	[1618a]
		−83.942[11]	[570]			58.070	[570]		
	l	−245.518	[1618a]	−232.136	[1618a]	13.432	[1618a]	20.0	[1618a]
	c	(−261.5)[12]	[1593, 1618a]	(−247.704)	[1618a]	(12.04)	[1618a]	13.397	[1618a]
		(−261.5)[13]	[570]	(−247.7)	[1593]	(12.12)	[570, 1685]	13.40	[570]
		(−259.5)	[887, 2245]	(−247.3*)	[232]			13.42	[1685]
		(−260.3)	[2569]						
		(−263.1)	[1569]						
$Zr(SO_3)_2$	c	−478.4*	[1172]						
$Zr(SO_4)_2$	c			−538.9*	[323]	24.1*	[323]		
				−544.4*	[229]				
$ZrSO_4 \cdot H_2O$	c			−632.7	[229]				
$ZrSO_4 \cdot 4H_2O$	c			−802.8*	[229]				
ZrS_2	c	−148*	[1480]						
ZrSI	c	−35.3	[2232]						
		−62	[143]						
$ZrSi_{1.62}$	c	−47	[143]						
$ZrSi_2$	c	−35.8	[2232]						
		17.9	[2356]						
$ZrSiO_4$	c					(20.2)	[1685]	(12.56)	[1685]
$ZrTiO_3$	c	−3*[14]	[60]			22.2*	[60]		
$ZrZn_2$	c	−35.3	[2406]			12.1	[2406]		
Zr_2Si	c	50.0	[2232]						
		−81	[143]						
Zr_5Si_3	c	40.7	[2386]						
		−146.5	[2232]						
		−216	[143]						
Zr_6Si_5	c	−253	[143]						
$HZrO_3$	c			−287.7*	[323]				

1. $\Delta H_0^\circ = -51.828$ [1618a]. 2. $\Delta H_0^\circ = -94.774$ [1618a]. 3. $\Delta H_0^\circ = -115.414$ [1618a]. 4. $\Delta H_0^\circ = 169.418$ [1618a]. 5. $\Delta H_0^\circ = -86.522$ [1618a]. 6. $\Delta H_0^\circ = -79.53$ [1530]. 7. $\Delta H_0^\circ = 21.119$ [1618a]. 8. $\Delta H_0^\circ = 23$ [570]. 9. From graphite. 10. $\Delta H_0^\circ = 81.817$ [1618a]. 11. $\Delta H^\circ = -83.212$ [570]. 12. $\Delta H_0^\circ = -260.198$ [1618a]. 13. $\Delta H_0^\circ = -260.212$ [570]. 14. From oxides.

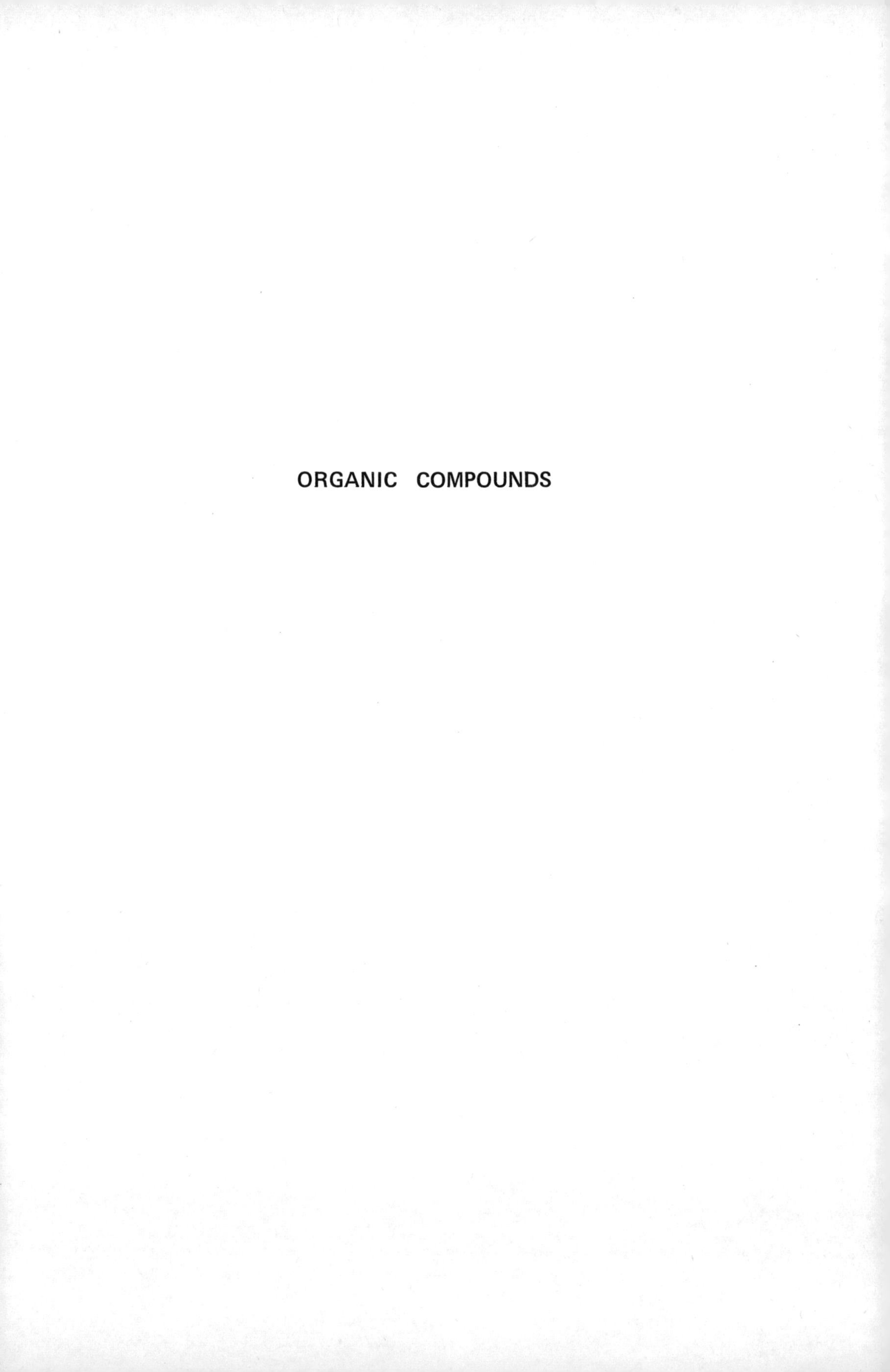

ORGANIC COMPOUNDS

Formula	Name of compound	Phase	ΔH°_{298}, $\frac{kcal}{mole}$	ΔG°_{298}, $\frac{kcal}{mole}$	S°_{298}, $\frac{cal}{mole \cdot {}^\circ C}$	Cp°_{298}, $\frac{cal}{mole \cdot {}^\circ C}$
1	2	3	4	5	6	7
			1, I			
CH	Methine radical	g	(142.3847)[1] [1830]		43.7164 [1830]	6.97 [1830]
			(142.006)[2] [1618a]	134.028 [1618a]	43.722 [1618a]	6.972 [1618a]
			(142.035)[3] [570]		43.725 [570]	
			(142.1) [2511]			
			(142.4)[4] [2358]			
			(103) [1001]			
CH^+	Positively charged methine ion	g	400.4[5] [2358]			
			355* [1214]			
CH_2	Methylene radical	g	95*[6] [1618a]	91.809 [1618a]	43.271 [1618a]	7.492 [1618a]
			68.9504[7] [1830]		43.1956 [1830]	7.1965 [1830]
			65.853[8] [570]		43.430 [570]	
			93.7[9] [2358]		44.87 [2726]	
			95 [2185]			
CH_2^+	Positively charged methylene ion	g	334.9[10] [2358]			
			335* [1214]			
			339[11] [1909]			
CH_2^-	Negatively charged methylene ion	g	92.24 [1807]			
			95 [2511]			
			100 [1909]			
			233.06 [1807]			
CH_3	Methyl radical	g	(31.94)[12] [1618a]	32.546 [1618a]	46.137 [1618a]	8.773 [1618a]
			(33.4908)[13] [1830]		46.3923 [1830]	9.2665 [1830]
			(33.0)[14] [570]		47.408 [570]	
			(31.5) [2511]		47.4 [1612]	8.5 [1612]
			(32.5) [2387]		47.35 [2726]	
			(33.2)[15] [2358]		46.43 [2195]	
			(32.05) [1807]			
			(34.1) [1325a]			
CH_3	Positively charged methyl ion	g	261.7[16] [2358]			
			268.96 [1807]			

1. $\Delta H^\circ_0 = 141.5882$ [1830]. 2. $\Delta H^\circ_0 = 141.183$ [1618a]. 3. $\Delta H^\circ_0 = 141.217$ [570]. 4. $\Delta H^\circ_0 = 141.6$ [2358]. 5. $\Delta H^\circ_0 = 398.1$ [2358]. 6. $\Delta H^\circ_0 = 95.18$ [1618a]. 7. $\Delta H^\circ_0 = 69.1407$ [1830]. 8. $\Delta H^\circ_0 = 66$* [570]. 9. $\Delta H^\circ_0 = 93.0$ [2358]. 10. $\Delta H^\circ_0 = 333.6$ [2358]. 11. Apparent. 12. $\Delta H^\circ_0 = 32.805$ [1618a]. 13. $\Delta H^\circ_0 = 34.2892$ [1830]. 14. $\Delta H^\circ_0 = 33.9$ [570]. 15. $\Delta H^\circ_0 = 34.0$ [2358]. 16. $\Delta H^\circ_0 = 261.0$ [2358].

1	2	3	4		5		6		7	
CH_4	Methane	g	−17.895[1]	[1618a]	−12.145	[1618a]	44.490	[1618a]	8.518	[1618a]
			−17.889[2]	[1830, 2244]	−12.14	[2244, 2605]	44.50	[2244, 2605]	8.536	[2244, 2605]
							44.5062	[1830]	8.5187	[1830]
			−17.88[3]	[2358]	−12.13	[2358]	44.492	[2358]	8.439	[2358]
			−17.88[4]	[570]			44.507	[570]		
			−15.9	[157]			44.51	[257]	8.52	[257, 1654]
							44.2148	[1861]	8.5335	[1861]
							50.00[5]	[1654]		
CH_4^+	Positive methane ion	g	(285)	[1214]						
			(276.7)[6]	[2358]						
CBr_4	Carbon tetrabromide	g	12[7]	[1618a]	8.59	[1618a]	85.563	[1618a]	21.793	[1618a]
			19[8]	[2358]	16	[2358]	85.55	[2358]	21.79	[2358]
			20*[9]	[570]			85.581	[570]		
			20	[679]			85.53	[1301]	21.80	[1301]
		l					74.30	[1336]	35.47[10]	[313]
									30.86[11]	[1929]
CCl	Carbon monochloride (free radical)	g	132[12]	[1618a]	124.315	[1618a]	53.780	[1618a]	7.742	[1618a]
			122.4050[13]	[1830]			53.6451	[1830]	7.7055	[1830]
			119.048[14]	[570]			53.641	[570]		
							53.88	[1339]	7.740	[1339]
CCl^+	Positive ion of carbon monochloride	g	340*	[1214]						
CCl_2	Carbon dichloride (free radical)	g	75.0[15]	[1618a]	72.309	[1618a]	63.673	[1618a]	10.826	[1618a]
			46.263[16]	[570]			63.282	[570]		
CCl_2^+	Positive ion of carbon dichloride	g	345	[1214]						
CCl_3	Carbon trichloride (free radical)	g	35*	[1618a]	38.14	[1618a]	70.76	[1618a]	14.884	[1618a]
			12	[679]			71.9	[1612]	15.0	[1612]
			14.5	[2387]			71.745	[570]		
			19.7	[824]						
CCl_3^+	Positive ion of carbon trichloride	g	310*	[1214]						
CCl_4	Carbon tetrachloride	g	(−25.94)[17]	[1618a]	−15.833	[1618a]	(74.039)	[1618a]	(19.866)	[1618a]
			(−24.6)[18]	[2358]	−14.49	[2358]	(74.03)	[1888, 2358]	(19.91)	[2358]
			(−25.5)[19]	[1830]			(74.0395)	[1830]	(19.8658)	[1830]
			(−24.97)[20]	[321]	−15.37	[321]	(74.30)	[1339]	20.09	[1339]

			(−22.0)[21]	[2408]			(73.92)	[1516]	(19.94)	[1888]
			(−24.7)	[679]			(73.94)	[1301]	(19.92)	[1301]
			(−24.5)	[2042]			(74.25)[22]	[710]	(20.08)[21]	[710]
			(−24.7)[23]	[570]			(74.107)	[570]		
			(−24.6)	[47, 48]						
		l	(−33.3)	[321]	−16.40	[321]	(51.25)	[321]	(31.49)	[321]
			(−29.8)[24]	[2408]			(51.67)	[1516]	(31.26)[24]	[313]
			(−32.3)	[2042]					(31.46)	[2717]
			(−32.5)	[679]						
CCl_4^+	Positive ion of carbon tetrachloride	g	230*	[1214]						
CD_4	Tetradeuteromethane	g					56.27[25]	[1654]	9.69	[257, 1654]
							47.54	[257]		
CF	Carbon monofluoride (free radical)	g	74.400[26]	[1618a]	66.855	[1618a]	50.889	[1618a]	7.184	[1618a]
			74.6954[27]	[1830]			50.8904	[1830]	7.1843	[1830]
			80.963[28]	[570]			50.889	[570]		
			74.48	[1807]						
CF^+	Positive ion of carbon monofluoride	g	295.17	[1807]						
CF_2	Carbon difluoride (free radical)	g	−30*	[1618a]	−32.911	[1618a]	59.570	[1618a]	9.127	[1618a]
			−30[29]	[1830]			57.2225	[1830]	9.1676	[1830]
			−29.880	[570]			57.486	[570]		
			−35	[894, 1921]						
			−50	[1348]						
		g	−41*[30]	[2180]						
			−36.90	[1807]						
CF_2^+	Positive ion of carbon difluoride	g	−232.91	[1807]						
CF_3	Carbon trifluoride (free radical)	g	−115.7[31]	[1618a]	−112.218	[1618a]	62.350	[1618a]	12.157	[1618a]
			−119.5[32]	[1830]			61.4904	[1830]	11.3004	[1830]
			−119.651[33]	[570]			63.084	[570]		

1. $\Delta H_0^\circ = -15.991$ [1618a]. 2. $\Delta H_0^\circ = -15.9824$ [1830]; -15.987 [2244]. 3. $\Delta H_0^\circ = -15.970$ [2358]. 4. $\Delta H_0^\circ = -16.005$ [570]. 5. Including nuclear spin. 6. $\Delta H_0^\circ = 277.1$ [2358]. 7. $\Delta H_0^\circ = = 19.097$ [1618a]. 8. $\Delta H_0^\circ = 26.10$ [2358]. 9. $\Delta H_0^\circ = 27.078$ [570]. 10. Interpolated [234] with the aid of the equation given in the original paper. 11. $t = 27.42°C$. 12. $\Delta H_0^\circ = 131.099$ [1618a]. 13. $\Delta H_0^\circ = 121.5082$ [1830]. 14. $\Delta H_0^\circ = 80*$ [570]. 15. $\Delta H_0^\circ = 74.689$ [1618a]. 16. $\Delta H_0^\circ = 46*$ [570]. 17. $\Delta H_0^\circ = -25.419$ [1618a]. 18. $\Delta H_0^\circ = -24.08$ [2358]. 19. $\Delta H_0^\circ = -24.9808$ [1830]. 20. ΔH_0°. 21. Interpolated [234] with the aid of the equation given in the original paper. 22. $T = 300°K$. 23. $\Delta H_0^\circ = -24.208$ [570]. 24. Interpolated [234] with the aid of the equation given in the original paper. 25. Including nuclear spin. 26. $\Delta H_0^\circ = 73.536$ [1618a]. 27. $\Delta H_0^\circ = 73.8308$ [1830]. 28. $\Delta H_0^\circ = 80.085$ [570]. 29. $\Delta H_0^\circ = -30.1046$ [1830]. 30. $+37 \geqslant \Delta H \geqslant 45$. 31. $\Delta H_0^\circ = = 115.077$ [1618a]. 32. $\Delta H_0^\circ = -118.7361$ [1830]. 33. $\Delta H_0^\circ = -119$ [570].

1	2	3	4		5		6		7	
CF_3	Carbon trifluoride (free radical)	g	−105	[2568]			64.1	[1612]	12.1	[1612]
			−118	[2387]						
			−120	[679]						
			−123.37	[1807]						
CF_3^+	Carbon trifluoride (positive ion)	g	85.78[1]	[1807]						
			117.84[2]	[1807]						
CF_4	Carbon tetrafluoride	g	(−220.5)[3]	[1618a]	(−209.827)	[1618a]	(62.457)	[1618a]	14.594	[1618a]
			(−221)[4]	[2358]	(−210)	[2358]	(62.50)	[2358]	14.60	[2358]
			(−217.2)[5]	[1830]			(62.4995)	[1830]	14.6958	[1830]
			(−220)[6]	[570]			(62.472)	[570]		
			(−216.6)[7]	[321]	(−207.27)	[321]	(62.62)	[1090]	14.63	[1090]
			(−225.63)[8]	[1056]			(62.416)	[2028]	14.578	[2028]
			(−218)	[433]			(62.60)[14]	[710]	14.73[14]	[710]
			(−220.1)	[47, 48]			(62.48)	[1301]	14.61	[1301]
			(−231)	[2618]						
			(−218*)	[1740]						
			(−220.4)[9,10]	[1629]						
			(−218.3)[11]	[2337]						
			(−212.7)	[1168]						
			(−217.1)[12]	[2043]						
			(−219.2)[13]	[95]						
			(−225.4)	[1337]						
CI_4	Carbon tetraiodide	g	−59*	[230]			93.38	[495]	22.62	[495]
			−73*	[361a]			93.60	[1368]	22.91	[1378, 2358]
							93.65	[2358]		
CN	Cyanide (free radical)	g	109*	[1618a]	101.796	[1618a]	(48.406)	[1618a]	6.969	[1618a]
			96.3547[15]	[1830]			(48.4089)	[1830]	6.9686	[1830]
			88.803[16]	[570]			(48.407)	[570]		
			89	[1104, 1502]			(45.2)	[1797]		
			70	[679]						
			109	[830]						
CN^+	Cyanide cation	g	423	[1104]						
CN^-	Cyanide anion	g	15	[830, 1502]						
		d	36.0	[2358]	41.2	[2358]	22.5	[2358]		
CN_4	Cyanazide	g			−73.4*	[229]				
		c	92.6	[2358]						

$\frac{1}{n}(CN_4)_n$	Cyanazide polymer	c	82.2	[2358]						
CS	Carbon monosulfide (free radical)	g	55*[17]	[1618a]	42.684*	[1618a]	50.299	[1618a]	7.122	[1618a]
			54.6697[18]	[1830]			50.3020	[1830]	7.1227	[1830]
			59.294[19]	[570]			50.298	[570]		
			60*	[2295]	80*	[2295]				
			55	[1879]						
CS_2	Carbon disulfide	g	(27.98)[20]	[1333, 1618a]	15.991	[1618a]	(56.832)	[570, 1618a]	(10.875)	[1618a]
			(28.04)[21]	[2358]	16.05	[2358]	(56.82)	[2358]	(10.85)	[2358]
			(28.6)	[2601]	-3.15[32]	[2601]	(56.836)	[2601]	(10.876)	[2601]
			(27.980)[22]	[1830]			(56.8301)	[1830]	(10.8692)	[1830]
			(27.209)[23]	[570]			(56.84)[24]	[2103]	(10.89)	[2103]
			(27.7)	[1428]						
			(26.1)	[1214]						
		l	21.3_7	[1291]			36.17	[2358]	18.1	[2358]
CT_4	Tetratritiomethane	g					55.17[25]	[1654]	10.72	[256, 1654]
							49.65	[256]		

1, II

$CHBr_3$	Bromoform	g	(4)[26]	[2358]	2	[2358]	(79.07)	[2358]	(17.02)	[2358]
			(10)[27]	[570]			(79.081)	[570]		
			(10)	[679]			(79.03)	[1301]		
							(78.92)		(16.99)	[1301]
							(80.08)	[362]	(17.44)	[362]
		l	-6.8	[2358]	-1.2	[2358]	52.8	[2358]	31	[2358]
									31.21[28]	[713]
$CHCl_3$	Chloroform	g	(-25.0)[29]	[1618a]	-17.179	[1618a]	(70.665)	[1618a]	(15.730)	[1618a]
			(-24.65)[30]	[2358]	-16.82	[2358]	(70.65)	[2358]	(15.70)	[2538]
			(-22.84)[31]							
			(-22.835)[31]	[321]			(70.66)	[1301]	(15.71)	[1301]

1. In alkenes. 2. In alkanes. 3. $\Delta H_0^\circ = -219.071$ [1618a]. 4. $\Delta H_0^\circ = -219.6$ [2358]. 5. $\Delta H_0^\circ = -215.779$ [1830]. 6. $\Delta H_0^\circ = -218.588$ [570]. 7. $\Delta H_0^\circ = -216.57$ [321]. 8. $\Delta H_0^\circ = -218.56$ [1056]. 9. $t = 320°C$. 10. $\Delta H_0^\circ = -218.7$; recalculated [1056]. 11. According to the authors [679] this is one of the most reliable values. 12. $\Delta H_0^\circ = -224.2$; recalculated [1056]. 13. $\Delta H_0^\circ = -226.7$; recalculated [1056]. 14. $T = 300°K$. 15. $\Delta H_0^\circ = 95.5693$ [1830]. 16. $\Delta H_0^\circ = 88$ [570]. 17. $\Delta H_0^\circ = 54.224$ [1618a]. 18. $\Delta H_0^\circ = 53.8932$ [1830]. 19. $\Delta H_0^\circ = 58.5$ [570]. 20. $\Delta H_0^\circ = 27.787$ [1618a]. 21. $\Delta H_0^\circ = 27.86$ [2358]. 22. $\Delta H_0^\circ = 27.7900$ [1830]. 23. $\Delta H_0^\circ = 27$ [570]. 24. $t = 26.1°C$. 25. Including nuclear spin. 26. $\Delta H_0^\circ = 10.24$ [2358]. 27. $\Delta H_0^\circ = 16.219$ [570]. 28. Interpolated [234] with the aid of equation given in the original paper. 29. $\Delta H_0^\circ = 23.837$ [1618a]. 30. $\Delta H_0^\circ = -23.486$ [2358]. 31. ΔH_0°. 32. From S_2 (g).

1	2	3	4		5		6		7	
$CHCl_3$	Chloroform	g	(−24.9)[1]	[570]			(70.723)	[570]		
			(−24.9)[2]	[2408]			(70.62)	[1888]	(15.63)	[1888]
			(−24*); (−23*)	[361a]						
		l	(−32.14)	[2358]	−17.62	[2358]	48.2	[2358]	(27.2)	[2358]
			(−32.4)[2]	[2408]					(27.9)	[538]
CHD_3	Trideuteromethane	g					57.52	[1654]	9.32	[257, 1654]
							49.67	[257]		
CHF	Fluoromethylene (free radical)	g	8.084[3]	[570]			52.997	[570]		
			7.70	[1807]						
CHF^+	Positive ion of fluoromethylene	g	279.81	[1807]						
CHF_2	Difluoromethyl (free radical)	g	−67.851[4]	[570]			60.567	[570]		
			−61.57	[1807]						
CHF_2^+	Positive ion of difluoromethyl	g	142.28[5]	[1807]						
			154.96[6]	[1807]						
CHF_3	Fluoroform	g	−165.1[7]	[1618a]	−156.874	[1618a]	62.043	[1618a]	12.197	[1618a]
			−164.5[8]	[2358]	−156.3	[2358]	62.04	[1301, 2358]	12.20	[13.01, 2358]
			−170[9]	[570]			62.040	[570]		
			−169.0	[836, 1199]			62.21	[362]	12.49	[362]
			−162.60	[2047]			62.09	[1090]	12.21	[1090]
			−162.1	[2042]			62.045	[1232, 2575]	12.198	[1232, 2575]
			−170	[679]						
			−160.94[10]							
			−160.935[10]	[321]						
			−162.6	[190]						
			−164*, −161*	[361a]						
CHI_3	Iodoform	g	51[11]	[570]			85.102	[570]		
			51	[679]			85.41	[495]	17.96	[495]
			50*	[361a]			85.1	[2358]	17.92	[2358]
		l	38	[679]						
		c	(34)	[679]						
			(33.7)	[2358]						
CHN	Hydrogen cyanide	g	(31.2)[12]	[1618a]	28.704	[1618a]	(48.213)	[1618a]	8.594	[1618a]
			(32.3)[13]	[2358]	29.8	[2358]	(48.20)	[2358]	8.57	[2358]
			(31.1895)[14]	[1830]			(48.2117)	[1830]	8.5701	[1830]
			(30.5)[15]	[570]			(48.211)	[570]		
			(31.09)[16]	[880]			(48.22)	[2437]	8.58	[2437]
		l	26.02	[2358]	29.86	[2358]	26.97	[2358]	16.88	[2358]

		d	36.0	[2358]	41.2	[2358]	22.5	[2358]		
CHO	Formyl (free radical)	g	-2.9*[17]	[1618a]	-6.543	[1618a]	53.683	[1618a]	8.264	[1618a]
			-3.2241[18]	[1830]			53.6735	[1830]	8.2643	[1830]
			-5.3[19]	[570]			53.617	[570]		
			-0.3	[2364]			53.68	[2358]	8.26	[2358]
			0	[2443]						
			-4	[1984]						
CHO_2	Formaldehyde	g	-22*	[2387]						
CHO_2^-	Formate ion	d	-101.71	[2358]	-83.87	[2358]	22	[2358]	-21.0	[2358]
CHT_3	Tritritiomethane	g					56.78	[1654]	9.98	[1664]
							51.36	[256]	10.17	[256]
CH_2Br	Bromomethyl (free radical)	g							28.1*	[826a]
CH_2Br_2	Dibromomethane	g	(1*)[20]	[570]			70.118	[570]		
			(1)	[679]			70.02	[1301]	13.09	[1301]
			(−2.9*);							
			(-1*)	[361a]			70.06	[2358]	13.07	[2358]
		l							28.84[2]	[313]
CH_2Cl_2	Dichloromethane	g	(-22.4)[21]	[1618a]	-16.059	[1618a]	(64.587)	[1618a]	(12.226)	[1618a]
			(-22.10)[22]	[2358]	-15.75	[2358]	(64.56)	[2358]	(12.18)	[2089, 2358]
			(-22.5)[23]	[570]			(64.602)	[570]		
			(-22.5)[24]	[2408]			(64.53)	[2089]		
			(-19.36)[10]	[321]			(64.59)	[1301]	(12.22)	[1301]
			(-22*)	[361a]						
		l	(-29.03)	[2358]	-16.09	[2358]	42.5	[2358]	(23.9)	[2358]
			(-32.4)	[679]					(27.38)[25]	[313]
CH_2D_2	Dideuteromethane	g					56.79[26]	[1654]	9.00	[1654]
							49.69	[257]	9.01	[257]
CH_2F	Fluoromethyl (free radical)	g	-17.905[27]	[570]			54.565	[570]		
			-0.95[28]	[1807]						
			-21.91	[1807]						

1. $\Delta H_0^\circ = -23.769$ [570]. 2. Calculated [679] from the data of [2408]. 3. $\Delta H_0^\circ = 8^*$ [570]. 4. $\Delta H_0^\circ = -67^*$ [570]. 5. In alkenes. 6. In alkanes. 7. $\Delta H_0^\circ = -163.435$ [1618a]. 8. $\Delta H_0^\circ = -162.84$ [2358]. 9. $\Delta H_0^\circ = -168.354$ [570]. 10. ΔH_0°. 11. $\Delta H_0^\circ = 52.895$ [570]. 12. $\Delta H_0^\circ = 31.291$ [1618a]. 13. $\Delta H_0^\circ = 32.39$ [2358]. 14. $\Delta H_0^\circ = 31.2814$ [1830]. 15. $\Delta H_0^\circ = 30.570$ [570]. 16. ΔH_0°. 17. $\Delta H_0^\circ = -2.986$ [1618a]. 18. $\Delta H_0^\circ = -3.3110$ [1830]. 19. $\Delta H_0^\circ = -5.392$ [570]. 20. $\Delta H_0^\circ = 6.096$ [570]. 21. Interpolated [234] with the aid of equation given in the original paper; $\Delta H_0^\circ = -20.765$ [1618a]. 22. $\Delta H_0^\circ = -20.462$ [2358]. 23. $\Delta H_0^\circ = -20.888$ [570]. 24. Calculated [679] from the data of [2408]. 25. Interpolated [234] with the aid of equation given in the original paper. 26. Including nuclear spin. 27. $\Delta H_0^\circ = -17^*$ [570]. 28. In *eV/mole.*

1	2	3	4		5		6		7	
CH_2F^+	Positive fluoromethyl ion	g	−195.78	[1807]						
CH_2F_2	Difluoromethane	g	−107.2[1]	[1618a]	−100.618	[1618a]	58.938	[1618a]	10.246	[1618a]
			−106.8[2]	[2358]	−100.2	[2358]	58.94	[2358]	10.25	[2358]
			−118*[3]	[570]			58.940	[570]		
			−105.5	[2047]			58.92	[1301]	10.28	[1301
			−118[3]	[679]						
			−110*	[1823a]						
			−103.672[4]	[321]						
			−105.5	[433]						
			−115*; −112*	[361a]						
CH_2I	Iodomethyl (free radical)	g					90.2*	[826a]	28.5*	[826a]
CH_2I_2	Diiodomethane	g	27.0[5]	[2358]	22.9	[2358]	74.0	[2358]	13.79	[2358]
			27[6]	[570]			74.115	[570]		
			28*; 27*	[361a]			76.84	[2616]	13.81	[2616]
			27	[679]			73.88	[1301]	13.88	[1301]
		l	(16.0)	[2358]	21.6	[2358]	41.6	[2358]	32	[2358]
			(16)	[679]					30.00[7]	[313]
CH_2N_2	Diazirine	g					56,87	[2358]	10.19	[2358]
CH_2N_2	Diazomethane	g					58.02	[2358]	12.55	[2358]
CH_2N_2	Cyanamide	c	14.1	[2358]						
CH_2N_4	Tetrazole	c	56.7	[2538]						
CH_2O	Formaldehyde	g	−27.72[8]	[1618a]	(−26.266)	[1618a]	(52.261)	[1618a]	(8.461)	[1618a]
			−28[9]	[2358]	(−27)	[2358]	(52.26)	[1138, 1360, 2358]	(8.46)	[2358]
			−27.7	[1360]	(−26.3)	[1360]	(52.28)	[2726]	(8.45)	[2726]
			−27.7[10]	[570]			(52.260)	[570]	(3.44)	[1138]
					(−26.2*)	[323]	(52.26*)	[323]		
		d	−35.9[11]	[2358]	−31.0*	[323]				
CH_2O_2	Formic Acid	g	(−90.49)	[1360, 1362]	(−83.89)	[1362]	(59.45); (59.446)	[1362]	10.81 10.807	[1382]
			(−84.83)[4]	[821, 1657]	(−80.10)	[1967]	(59.43)	[1967]	12.40	[1967]
			(−90.03)	[2616]	(−83.64)	[2616]	(60.13)	[2616]		
			(−90.48)	[2358]						
		l	(−101.51)	[2358]	(−86.38)	[2358, 2380]	(30.82)	[1360, 2358]	23.67	[2358]
			(−101.06)	[2616]	(−86.27)	[2616]	(30.08)	[2616]		
			(−102.52)	[1360, 2380]	(−86.39)	[1360]				
		l	(−101.70)	[328]						

		d	−101.68[12]	[2358]	−88.98[1]	[2358]	39[1]	[2358]		
			−101.71[13]	[2358]	−83.87[2]	[2358]	22[2]	[2358]	−21.0[13]	[2358]
$CH_2O_2^+$	Positive ion of formic acid	g	165.80	[2358]						
CH_2S_3	Trithiocarbonic acid	l	6.0	[1291, 2358]	7.0	[2358]	52	[2358]	35.8	[2358]
			6.1	[1291]			53.3	[1290, 1291]		
			5.6	[1290]						
CH_2T_2	Ditritiomethane	g					50.98	[256]	9.62	[256]
							56.35[14]	[1654]	9.36	[1654]
CH_3Br	Methyl bromide	g	(−8.4)[15]	[2358]	−6.2	[2358]	(58.86)	[2358]	(10.14)	[1301, 2358]
			(−8.6)[16]	[570]			(58.767)	[570]		
			(−8.6)	[679]			(58.82)	[1301]		
			(−8.97)	[1080, 1243]						
			(−10*); (−9*)	[361a]						
		l	−2.3	[679]					27.95[17]	[313]
CH_3Br^+	Positive ion of methyl bromide	g	237	[1214]						
CH_3Cl	Methyl chloride	g	(−20.66)[18]	[1618a]	(−15.046)	[1618a]	(55.987)	[1618a]	(9.726)	[1618a]
			(−19.32)[19]	[2358]	(−13.72)	[2358]	(56.04)	[2358]	(9.74)	[2358]
			(−18.73)[4]	[321]	(−14.96)	[321]	(55.80)	[1301]	(9.73)	[1301]
			(−20.62)[20]	[570]			(56.021)	[570]		
			(−20.63)	[1080, 1785]						
			(−20*); (−19*)	[361a]						
		d	−24.3	[2358]	−12.3	[2358]	34.6	[2358]		
CH_3Cl^+	Positive ion of methyl chloride	g	241	[1214]						
			243	[762]						
CH_3D	Monodeuteromethane	g					54.39[21]	[1654]	8.74	[1654]
							48.10	[257]	8.75	[257]
CH_3F	Methyl fluoride	g	−56*	[1618a]	−50.293	[1618a]	(53.252)	[1618a]	(8.963)	[1618a]
			−68*[22]	[570]			(53.243)	[570]		
			−67*; −64*	[361a]			(53.25)	[2358]	(8.96)	[2358]
			−58.5	[540]			(52.34)	[1301]	(8.94)	[1301]
			−68	[679]						
			−60*	[1823a]						

1. $\Delta H_0^\circ = -105.369$ [1618a]. 2. $\Delta H_0^\circ = -104.97$ [2358]. 3. $\Delta H_0^\circ = -116.191$ [570]. 4. ΔH_0°. 5. $\Delta H_0^\circ = 29.26$ [2358]. 6. $\Delta H_0^\circ = 29.251$ [570]. 7. Interpolated [234] with the aid of the equation given in the original paper. 8. $\Delta H_0^\circ = -26.782$ [1618a]. 9. $\Delta H_0^\circ = -27.1$ [2358]. 10. $\Delta H_0^\circ = -26.824$ [570]. 11. Nonhydrolized. 12. Nonionized. 13. Ionized. 14. Including nuclear spin. 15. $\Delta H_0^\circ = -4.72$ [2358]. 16. $\Delta H_0^\circ = -4.944$ [570]. 17. Interpolated [234] with the aid of the equation given in the original paper. 18. $\Delta H_0^\circ = -18.764$ [1618a]. 19. $\Delta H_0^\circ = -17.426$ [2358]. 20. $\Delta H_0^\circ = -18.51$ [570]. 21. Including nuclear spin. 22. $\Delta H_0^\circ = -66.103$ [570].

1	2	3	4		5		6		7	
CH_3I	Methyl iodide	g	(3.1)[1]	[2358]	3.5	[2358]	60.71	[2358]	10.54	[1210, 2358]
			(4.1)[2]	[570]			60.677	[570]	19.55[3]	[1820]
			(4.6)	[679]			60.47	[1301]	10.55	[1301]
			(3.28)	[1325a]			60.66	[1210]		
			(3.40)	[1347]						
			(5*)	[361a]						
		l	(−2.3)	[679]			39.0	[2358]	30	[2358]
									30.41[4]	[313]
CH_3N_5	5-Aminotetrazole	c	49.7	[2358]						
									28.7*	[826a]
CH_3O	Methoxy radical	g	−2.1*	[1883]			64.94*	[1883]		
			3	[759a]			54.2	[1613]	8.9	[1613]
CH_3O^+		g	223	[1214]						
			202	[2004]						
CH_3S	Methyl sulfide (free radical)	g	30.5*	[1867]						
			33.0*	[1246]						
CH_3S^+	Positive ion of methyl sulfide	g	222.2	[1246]						
			224	[1917]						
CH_3T	Tritiomethane	g					54.21	[1654]	8.86	[1654]
							48.10	[256]	9.07	[256]
CH_4N	Aminomethyl (free radical)	g	19.8	[826a]			88.2*	[826a]	29.7*	[826a]
CH_4N_2	Ammonium cyanide	c	0.10	[2358]					32	[2358]
			3*	[2683]						
		d	4.3	[2358]	22.2	[2358]	49.6	[2358]		
CH_4O	Methanol	g	(−47.96)[5]	[2358]	−38.72	[2358]	(57.29)	[1360, 1365, 1604, 2358]	(10.49)	[1365, 1604, 2358]
			(−48.08)[6]	[1604]	−38.84	[1360, 1604]	(57.55)	[179]	[10.53)	[179]
			(−47.94)	[1365]	−38.70	[1365]	(60.42)	[2635]	(11.46)[7]	[2635]
			(−48.08)	[1360]						
		l	−57.04	[2358]	−39.76	[2358]	30.3	[1360, 2358]	19.5	[2358]
			−57.02	[2245]	−39.73	[1360]			(19.8)[8]	[1545]
			−57.01	[1365]						
			−57.24	[961]						
		d	−58.779	[2358]						
CH_4O^+	Positive ion of methanol	g	203	[1214]						
CH_4O_3	Methanol peroxide	g	−13*	[823]						

CH_4O_4	Methanol ozonide	g	6*	[823]						
CH_4S	Methanethiol (methyl mercaptan)	g	-20.88[9,21]	[2342]	-11.91[21]	[2342]	(60.96)	[2342, 2358]	12.01	[2342, 2358]
			-5.34[10]	[2358]	-2.23	[2358]				
			-20.89[11,21]	[1663a]	-11.92[21]	[1663a]	(60.94)	[1663a]	12.05	[1663a]
			-6.84	[1883]			(68.10)	[1883]		
			-17.17[12,21]	[848]	-8.919[21]	[849]	(60,86)	[848]	12.12	[848]
			-5.46	[1333, 1879]						
		l	-11.08[21]	[2358]	-1.85[21]	[2358]	40.44	[2358]	21.64	[2358]
			-0.9*	[323]	-0.4*	[323]				
			-11.15[21]	[1879]	0.76	[849]				
CH_5N	Methylamine	g	-5.49	[2358]	7.67	[2358]	58.15	[2358]	12.7	[2358]
							58.04	[2356]	11.77	[2356]
							57.93	[74]	11.91	[74]
		l	-11.3	[2358]	8.5	[2358]	35.90	[2358]		
		d	-16.77[13]	[2358]	4.94	[2358]	29.5	[2358]		
CH_6N_2	Methylhydrazine	g	22.55[14]	[2358]	44.66	[2358]	66.61	[750, 2358]	17.0	[750, 2358]
		l	12.9	[2358]	36.2	[2358]	39.66	[2358]	32.25	[2358]
CH_6Si	Methylmonosilane	g					61.26	[2421]	15.66	[2421]
$CBrCl_3$	Bromotrichloromethane	g	-11.0[15]	[2358]	-5.1	[2358]	79.55	[1888, 2358]	20.38	[1888, 2358]
			-10.448[16]	[570]			79.582	[570]		
			-10.3	[679]			77.45	[1301]	20.42	[1301]
			-8.7	[824]			79.66	[362]	20.80	[362]
			-16*	[361a]						
$CBrF_3$	Bromotrifluoromethane	g	-153.6[17]	[2358]	-147.3	[2358]	71.14	[2358]	16.57	[2358]
			-158[18]	[570]			71.112	[570]		
			-158	[679]			71.19	[1863]	16.58	[1863]
			-156*	[361a]			71.09	[1301]	16.54	[1301]
							71.37	[362]	16.53	[362]
$CBrI_3$	Bromotriiodomethane	g	59	[679]						
			58*	[361a]						
$CBrN$	Bromide cyanide	g	44.5[19]	[2358]	39.5	[2358]	(59.32)	[2358]	11.22	[2358]
			43.3[20]	[1618a]	38.268	[1618a]	(59.314)	[1618a]	11.227	[1618a]
			56.1	[1817]	38.3	[1817]	(59.07)	[321, 1817]		
			32.5	[321]	30.86	[321, 1817]				
		c	33.58	[2358]						

1. $\Delta H_0^\circ = 5.38$ [2358]. 2. $\Delta H_0^\circ = 6.364$ [570]. 3. $T = 303.2°K$. 4. Interpolated [234] with the aid of the equation given in the original paper. 5. $\Delta H_0^\circ = -45.355$ [2358]. 6. $\Delta H_0^\circ = -45.48$ [1604]. 7. $T = 345.6°K$. 8. $t = 40°C$ (extrapolated). 9. $\Delta H_0^\circ = -18.41$[21] [2342]. 10. $\Delta H_0^\circ = -2.885$ [2358]. 11. $\Delta H_0^\circ = -18.42$[21] [1663a]. 12. ΔH_0°[21]. 13. Nonionized. 14. $\Delta H_0^\circ = 27.507$ [2358]. 15. $\Delta H_0^\circ = -8.81$ [2358]. 16. $\Delta H_0^\circ = -8.18$ [570]. 17. $\Delta H_0^\circ = -151.21$ [2358]. 18. $\Delta H_0^\circ = -155.120$ [570]. 19. $\Delta H_0^\circ = 46.07$ [2358]. 20. $\Delta H_0^\circ = 44.87$ [1618a]. 21. From S_2 (g).

1	2	3	4		5		6		7	
CBr_2Cl_2	Dibromodichloromethane	g	−1*[1]	[570]			83.266	[570]		
			−1	[679]			83.27	[1301]	20.88	[1301]
			−7*	[361a]			83.1	[2358]	20.81	[2538]
							83.52	[362]	20.80	[1084a]
CBr_2D_2	Dibromodideuteromethane	g					71.04	[1120]	14.53	[1120]
CBr_2F_2	Dibromodifluoromethane	g	−99[2]	[570]			77.754	[570]		
			−99	[679]			77.72	[1301]	18.45	[1301]
			−100*	[361a]			77.66	[1091]	18.40	[1091]
							77.71	[2358]	18.41	[2358]
CBr_2I	Dibromoiodomethyl (radical)	g	49.1*	[360]						
CBr_2I_2	Dibromodiiodomethane	g	46	[679]						
			43	[361a]						
CBr_2O	Dibromoformaldehyde	g	−23.0	[2358]			73.82	[2083]	14.78	[2083]
	(carbon oxydibromide)	l	−30.4	[2358]						
CBr_3Cl	Tribromochloromethane	g	10*[3]	[570]			85.468	[570]		
			10*	[679]			85.36	[1301]	21.35	[1301]
			3*	[361a]			85.48	[362]	21.34	[362]
							85.5	[2358]	21.36	[2358]
CBr_3D	Tribromodeuteromethane	g					79.34	[877, 1211]	17.17	[877, 1211]
CBr_3F	Tribromofluoromethane	g	−41*[4]	[570]			82.614	[570]		
			−41	[679]			82.65	[1301]	20.18	[1301]
			−44*	[361a]			82.96	[362]	20.13	[362]
							82.64	[2358]	20.17	[2358]
CBr_3I	Tribromoiodomethane	g	−32	[679]						
			−27	[361a]						
$CClF_2$	Chlorodifluoromethyl (radical)	g	−69*	[1670]						
$CClF_3$	Chlorotrifluoromethane	g	−171.3[5]	[570]			68.169	[570]		
			−161	[2620]			68.23	[1301]	15.97	[1301]
			−171.3	[1948]			67.58	[2299]	15.38	[2299]
			−171*	[1740]			68.29	[362]	15.95	[362]
			−168.77[7]	[321]	−161.3	[321]	68.38[3]	[710]	16.13[6]	[710]
			−171.8	[269]			68.09	[1090]	15.96	[1090]
			−172.0	[265, 268]						
			−167	[433]						
			−166.2	[48]						
$CClI_2$	Chlorodiiodomethyl (radical)	g	55.3*	[360]						
$CClI_3$	Chlorotriiodomethane	g	49	[679]						

			49*	[361a]						
CClN	Chlorine cyanide	g	32.2[8]	[1618a]	30.548	[1618a]	56.423	[1618a]	10.753	[1618a]
			32.97	[2358]	31	[2358]	56.42	[2358]	10.75	[2358]
			31.641[9]	[1830]			56.3995	[1830]	10.7216	[1830]
			31.6	[321, 1817]	29.99	[321, 1817]	56.28	[321, 1817]		
					30.0	[1817]				
$CClN^+$	Positive ion of chlorine cyanide	l	26.79	[2358]						
		g	(31.6)	[1817]						
CClO	Carbon oxychloride (free radical)	g	-3.7[10]	[570]			62.844	[570]		
CCl_2D_2	Dichlorodideuteromethane	g					65.44	[2089]	13.45	[2089]
CCl_2F_2	Dichlorodifluoromethane	g	-110.99[11]	[321]	-102.65	[321]	71.92	[1937]	17.41	[1937]
			-119.1[12]	[570]			71.921	[570]	17.28	[1191]
			-112*	[1740]			72.02[13]	[710]	17.45[13]	[710]
			-110	[1891, 2620]			71.84	[1301]		
			-119.1	[1948]			72.10	[362]		
			-112	[433]						
			-112.1	[269]						
			-113.3	[265, 268]						
			-114[14]	[2358]	-105	[2358]	71.86	[2358]	17.27	[2358]
			-115[15]	[1618a]	-105.7	[1618a]	71.913	[1618a]	17.307	[1618a]
			-119*	[361a]						
CCl_2I_2	Dichlorodiiodomethane	g	23	[679]						
			24*	[361a]						
CCl_2O	Dichloroformaldehyde (phosgene)	g	-52.6[16]	[1618a]	-49.221	[1618a]	(67.816)	[1618a]	(13.790)	[1618a]
			-52.3[17]	[2358]	-48.9	[2358]	(67.74)	[2358]	(13.78)	[2358]
			-53.3	[321]	-50.32	[321]	(66.74)[20]	[2315]	(14.51)	[321]
			-53.3[18]	[1830]			(67.8174)	[1830]	(13.8070)	[1830]
			-52[19]	[570]			(67.78)	[570]		
			-53.10[21]	[1343]			(69.17)	[1343]	(11.01)	[1343]
							(67.81)	[1307]	(13.79)	[1307]
		l	(-51.5)	[2492]						
CCl_2S	Thiophosgene	g					70.19	[2726]	15.45	[2726]
CCl_3F	Trichlorofluoromethane	g	-68.0[22]	[1618a]	-58.605	[1618a]	(74.005)	[1618a]	(18.647)	[1618a]
			-66[23]	[2358]	-57	[2358]	(74.05)	[2358]	(18.66)	[2358]
			-70.9[24]	[570]			(74.007)	[570]		

1. $\Delta H_0^\circ = 2.820$ [570]. 2. $\Delta H_0^\circ = -94.687$ [570]. 3. $\Delta H_0^\circ = 15.440$ [570]. 4. $\Delta H_0^\circ = -35.286$ [570]. 5. $\Delta H_0^\circ = -170.097$ [570]. 6. $T = 300°K$. 7. ΔH_0°. 8. $\Delta H_0^\circ = 32.031$ [1618a]. 9. $\Delta H_0^\circ = 31.4779$ [1830]. 10. $\Delta H_0^\circ = -3.979$ [570]. 11. ΔH_0°. 12. $\Delta H_0^\circ = -118.116$ [570]. 13. $T = 300°K$. 14. $\Delta H_0^\circ = -113.0$ [2358]. 15. $\Delta H_0^\circ = -113.998$ [1618a]. 16. $\Delta H_0^\circ = -52.192$ [1618a]. 17. $\Delta H_0^\circ = -51.89$ [2358]. 18. $\Delta H_0^\circ = -52.8962$ [1830]. 19. $\Delta H_0^\circ = -51.609$ [570]. 20. $T = 280.66°K$. 21. ΔH_0°. 22. $\Delta H_0^\circ = -567.241$ [1618a]. 23. $\Delta H_0^\circ = -65.2$ [2358]. 24. $\Delta H_0^\circ = -70.158$ [570].

1	2	3	4		5		6		7	
CCl_3F	Trichlorofluoromethane	g	−70*	[1740]			(73.96)	[838, 1301]	(18.61)	[1301]
			−70.9	[1948]			(74.02)	[362]	(18.60)	[362]
			−66.2	[2042]			(74.25)[1]	[710]	(18.81)[1]	[710]
			−69.23	[321]	−60.58	[321]			(18.62)	[838
			−66	[433]						
			−66.4	[47, 48]						
			−72*	[361a]						
			−62	[2620]						
		l	−72.02	[2358]	−56.61	[2358]	53.86	[2358]	29.05	[2358]
CCl_3I	Trichloroiodomethane	g	0	[679]						
			−0.8	[361a]						
CDF_3	Deuterotrifluoromethane	g					62.33	[2166]	12.76	[2166]
							62.37	[1090]	12.80	[1090]
CDT_3	Deuterotritritiomethane	g					58.21[2]	[1654]	10.43	[1654]
							51.91	[256]	10.46	[256]
CD_2O	Dideuteroformaldehyde	g					53.79	[2670]	9.17	[2670]
CD_2T_2	Dideuteroditritiomethane	g					59.32[2]	[1654]	10.16	[1654]
							52.20	[256]	10.21	[256]
CD_3I	Trideuteroiodomethane	g					62.52	[1210]	12.07	[1210]
CD_3T	Trideuterotritiomethane	g					57.86[3]	[1654]	9.90	[1654]
							50.88	[256]	9.95	[256]
$CFCl_2$	Fluorodichloromethyl (free radical)	g	−24*	[1670]						
CFI_3	Fluorotriiodomethane	g	0	[679]						
			−2*	[361a]						
CFN	Fluorine cyanide	g	−3*[4]	[1618a]	−4.622	[1618a]	53.902	[1618a]	10.143	[1618a]
			−17[5]	[570]			54.010	[570]		
							45.69	[1822]	10.18	[1822]
CFO	Carbon oxyfluoride (free radical)	g	−45*[6]	[570]			59.548	[570]		
	Difluoroiodomethyl (free radical)	g	−50.2*	[360]						
CF_2I_2	Difluorodiiodomethane	g	−73*[7]	[570]			81.451	[570]		
			−73	[679]						
			−70*	[361a]						
CF_2O	Difluoroformaldehyde (carbon oxydifluoride)	g	−151.7[8]	[1618a]	−147.986	[1618a]	61.852	[1618a]	11.294	[1618a]
			−151.7[9]	[2358]	−148.0	[2358]	61.78	[2358]	11.19	[2358]

		g	-150.4[10]	[1830]			61.8529	[1830]	11.2945	[1830]
			-149.5[11]	[570]			61.835	[570]		
			-166.6	[1136]			58.5	[1773]		
			-150.35	[2618]						
CF_3I	Trifluoroiodomethane	g	-144[12]	[570]			73.433	[570]		
			-144	[679]			73.50	[1863]	16.95	[1863]
			-141*	[361a]			73.32	[1301]	16.90	[1301]
							73.44	[2358]	16.94	[2358]
CF_4O	Trifluoromethyl hypofluorite	g	-184.0[13]	[1618a]	-169.335	[1618a]	73.570	[1618a]	18.860	[1618a]
CIN	Iodine cyanide	g	(38.3)	[1817]	(45.5)	[1817]	61.33	[1817]		
			(53.9)[14]	[2358]	(47.0)	[2358]	61.35	[2358]	11.54	[2358]
			(52.40)[15]	[1618a]	(45.473)	[1618a]	61.356	[1618a]	11.545	[1618a]
		c	39.71	[2358]	44.22	[2358]	23.0	[2358]		
		d	42.5	[2358]	44.95	[2358]	29.9	[2358]		
CN_4O_8	Tetranitromethane	l	8.8	[1281, 2358]						
COS	Carbon oxysulfide	g	-33.08[16]	[1618a]	-39.589	[1618a]	55.323	[1618a]	9.918	[1618a]
			-33.96[17]	[2358]	-40.47	[2358]	55.32	[2358]	9.92	[2358]
			-32.8[18]	[1830]			55.3231	[1830]	9.9165	[1830]
			-33.952[19]	[570]			55.324	[570]		

1, III

$CHBrCl_2$	Bromodichloromethane	g	-13*[20]	[570]			75.633	[570]		
			-13	[679]			75.58	[1301]	16.16	[1301]
			-14*	[361a]			76.55	[362]	16.55	[362]
							75.56	[2165]	16.10	[2165]
							75.6	[2358]	16.11	[2358]
$CHBrD_2$	Bromodideuteromethane	g					62	[1119]	11.33	[1119]
CHBrF	Bromofluoromethyl (radical)	g	-15.5*	[360]						
$CHBrF_2$	Bromodifluoromethane	g	-110*[21]	[570]			70.544	[570]		
			-110*	[679]			69.71	[1301]	13.78	[1301]
			-108*; -105*	[361a]			71.00	[362]	14.36	[362]
							70.5	[2358]	14.04	[2358]
CHBrI	Bromoiodomethyl (radical)	g	47.8*	[360]						

1. $T = 300°K$. 2. Including nuclear spin. 3. Including nuclear spin. 4. $\Delta H_0^\circ = -3.12$ [1618a]. 5. $\Delta H_0^\circ = -17.155$ [570]. 6. $\Delta H_0^\circ = -45.138$ [570]. 7. $\Delta H_0^\circ = -71.594$ [570]. 8. $\Delta H_0^\circ = -150.958$ [1618a]. 9. $\Delta H_0^\circ = -150.95$ [2358]. 10. $\Delta H_0^\circ = -149.6593$ [1830]. 11. $\Delta H_0^\circ = -148.776$ [570]. 12. $\Delta H_0^\circ = -142.591$ [570]. 13. $\Delta H_0^\circ = -182.276$ [1618a]. 14. $\Delta H_0^\circ = 54.04$ [2358]. 15. $\Delta H_0^\circ = 52.541$ [1618a]. 16. $\Delta H_0^\circ = -33.111$ [1618a]. 17. $\Delta H_0^\circ = -33.990$ [2358]. 18. $\Delta H_0^\circ = -32.8306$ [1830]. 19. $\Delta H_0^\circ = -34$ [570]. 20. $\Delta H_0^\circ = -10.153$ [570]. 21. $\Delta H_0^\circ = -106.864$ [570].

1	2	3	4		5		6		7	
$CHBrI_2$	Bromodiiodomethane	g	36	[679]						
			35	[361a]						
$CHBr_2Cl$	Dibromochloromethane	g	-2*[1]	[570]			78.389	[570]		
			-2	[679]			78.39	[1301]	16.60	[1301]
			-5*; -4*	[361a]			78.94	[362]	16.98	[362]
							78.31	[2167]	16.53	[2167, 2358]
							78.3	[2358]		
$CHBr_2D$	Dibromodeuteromethane	g					71.95	[1120]	13.81	[1120]
$CHBr_2F$	Dibromofluoromethane	g	-50*[2]	[570]			75.754	[570]		
			-50	[679]			75.70	[1301]	15.57	[1301]
			-50*; -52*	[361a]			75.78	[362]	15.77	[362]
							75.7	[2358]	15.56	[2358]
$CHBr_2I$	Dibromoiodomethane	g	-22*	[779]						
			-20*; -21*	[361a]						
$CHClF_2$	Chlorodifluoromethane	g	-113.0*[3]	[1618a]	-105.566	[1618a]	67.121	[1618a]	13.350	[1618a]
			-121*[4]	[570]			67.165	[570]		
			-121	[679]			67.13	[1301, 2629]	13.35	[1301, 2358]
			-110*	[540]			67.11	[2358]	13.34	[2629]
			-111*; -117*	[361a]			67.72	[362]	13.78	[362]
CHClI	Chloroiodomethyl (radical)	g	40.4*	[360]						
$CHClI_2$	Chlorodiiodomethane	g	25	[679]						
			25*; 26*	[361a]						
$CHCl_2D$	Dichlorodeuteromethane	g					66.43	[1909]	12.79	[1909]
$CHCl_2F$	Dichlorofluoromethane	g	-69*[5]	[1618a]	-61.711	[1618a]	70.027	[1618a]	14.567	[1618a]
			-73*[6]	[570]			70.077	[570]		
			-66*; -70*	[361a]			69.99	[2629]	14.56	[2358, 2629]
			-73	[679]			70.00	[1301]	14.57	[1301]
			-66.5	[540]			70.10	[362]	14.75	[362]
							70.02	[2358]		
$CHCl_2I$	Dichloroiodomethane	g	0	[679]						
			1*; -1.5*	[361a]						
$CHCsO_2$	Cesium formate	c	-156.8*	[1984]						
CHD_2I	Dideuteroiodomethane	g					64.19	[1106]	11.53	[1106]
$CHFI_2$	Fluorodiiodomethane	g	-24	[679]						
			-21*; -22*	[361a]						
CHFO	Formyl fluoride	g	-90[7]	[1618a]	-87.994	[1618a]	58.961	[1618a]	9.659	[1618a]
CHF_2I	Difluoroiodomethane	g	-96*[8]	[570]			72.981	[570]		
			-96	[679]						

			-90*; -92*	[361a]						
$CHKO_2$	Potassium formate	c			-141.3	[323]	25.2	[323]		
$CHLiO_2$	Lithium formate	c	-164.9*	[689]						
			-155.2*	[1984]						
CHNO	Cyanic acid	g					10.73	[1824]	56.92	[1824]
	Cyanic acid, ionized	d	-34.9	[2358]	-23.3	[2358]	25.5	[2358]		
	Cyanic acid, nonionized	d	(-36.90)	[2358]	(-28.0)	[2358]	(33.9)	[2358]		
	Isocyanic acid	g	-27.90[9]	[1618a]	-25.681	[1618a]	56.909	[1618a]	10.724	[1618a]
							56.85	[2358]	10.72	[2358]
CHNS	Isothiocyanic acid	g	30.5	[2358]	27.0	[2358]	59.2	[2358]	11.2	[2358]
			27	[2365]						
	Thiocyanic acid, nonionized	d			23.31	[2358]				
	Thiocyanic acid, ionized	d	18.27	[2358]	22.15	[2358]	34.5	[2358]	-9.6	[2358]
CHN_3O_6	Trinitromethane	l	-5.1	[2358]						
			18.63	[1534]						
$CHNaO_2$	Sodium formate	c	-155.03	[2670]	-179.12	[2670]	24.80	[2670]	19.76	[2670]
CHO_2Rb	Rubidium formate	c	-156.8*	[1984]						
			-86*	[2358]						
CHO_2Tl	Thallium formate	c	-103*	[2358]						
CH_2BrCl	Bromochloromethane	g	-12*[10]	[570]			68.704	[570]		
			-12*	[351a, 679]			68.71	[1301]	12.65	[362, 1301]
			-11*	[361a]			68.7	[2358]	12.60	[2358]
							68.84	[362]		
							68.67	[1863]		
CH_2BrD	Bromodeuteromethane	g					61.53	[1119]	10.67	[1119]
CH_2BrF	Bromofluoromethane	g	-60*[11]	[570]			66.041	[570]		
			-60*	[679]			65.97	[1301]	11.76	[2358, 1301]
			-56*; -59*	[361a]			66.17	[362]	11.68	[362]
							66.0	[2358]		
CH_2BrI	Bromoiodomethane	g	12*[12]	[570]			73.558	[570]		

1. $\Delta H_0^\circ = -2.545$ [570]. 2. $\Delta H_0^\circ = -45.280$ [570]. 3. $\Delta H_0^\circ = -111.485$ [1618a]. 4. $\Delta H_0^\circ = -119.505$* [570]. 5. $\Delta H_0^\circ = -67.658$ [1618a]. 6. $\Delta H_0^\circ = -71.678$ [570]. 7. $\Delta H_0^\circ = -89.139$ [1618a]. 8. $\Delta H_0^\circ = -94.358$ [570]. 9. $\Delta H_0^\circ = -27.179$ [1618a]. 10. $\Delta H_0^\circ = -8.640$ [570]. 11. $\Delta H_0^\circ = -56.540$ [570]. 12. $\Delta H_0^\circ = 15.666$ [570].

1	2	3	4		5		6		7	
CH_2BrI	Bromoiodomethane	g	12	[679]			73.49	[362, 1301]	13.47	[1301]
			12*; 13*	[361a]			73.5	[2358]	13.46	[362, 2358]
CH_2ClF	Chlorofluoromethane	g	−64.5[1]	[1618a]	−58.459	[1618a]	63.173	[1618a]	11.242	[1618a]
			−72*[2]	[570]			63.175	[570]		
			−72*	[679]			63.16	[1301]	11.25	[362, 1301]
			−63	[540]			63.17	[2358]	11.24	[2358]
			−66*; −68*	[361a]			63.23	[362]		
CH_2ClI	Chloroiodomethane	g	2*[3]	[570]			70.804	[570]		
			2	[679]			70.78	[1301]	13.02	[362, 1301, 2358]
			3	[361a]			70.92	[362]		
							70.7	[2358]		
CH_2FI	Fluoroiodomethane	g	−47*[4]	[570]			68.421	[570]		
			−47*	[679]						
			−42*; −44*	[361a]						
$CH_2NO_2^-$	Nitromethane ion (nitroform)	d	−20.3	[2358]						
CH_2N_4O	5-Hydroxytetrazole	c	1.5	[2358]						
$CH_2N_6O_2$	Nitroguanyl azide	c	71.3	[2358]						
CH_2O_4S	Methylene sulfate	c	−164.6	[2358]						
$CH_3{}^{10}BO$	Methylboryl	g					59.42	[2486]	14.17	[2486]
							59.5	[1685]	13.87	[1685]
$CH_3{}^{11}BO$		g					59.61	[2486]	14.24	[2486]
CH_3Cl_3Si	Trichloromethylsilane	g	−126.4	[1618a]	−111.898	[1618a]	83.90	[1618a]	24.470	[1618a]
CH_3D_3Si	Trideuteromethylsilane	g					63.75	[2421]	17.92	[2421]
CH_3F_3Si	Trifluoromethylsilane	g	−294.625	[1618a]	−279.656	[1618a]	75.07	[1618a]	21.72	[1618a]
CH_3NO	Formamide	g					59.41	[2358]	10.84	[1174, 1179, 2358]
							59.53	[1174, 1179]		
							59.56	[2356]	11.05	[2356]
		l	−60.7	[2358]						
CH_3NO_2	Nitromethane	g	(−17.86)	[2358]	−1.65	[2358]	65.69	[2358]	13.70	[1848, 2358]
			(−17.86)[5]	[1848]	−1.66	[1848]	65.73	[1848]		
		l	−27.03	[2358]	−3.47	[2358]	41.05	[2358]	(25.33)	[2358]
			−21.28	[1534]					(25.75)[6]	[1545]
	Methyl nitrite	g	−14.93	[1354]	−0.45	[1354]	71.5	[1354]		
			−15.64	[2212]			60.81	[2212]		
			−16.8	[1300]			68.0*	[826a]		

			−16.5	[2358]						
		l	(−20.33)	[761]					19.9*	[826a]
CH_3NO_3	Methyl nitrate	g	−29.4	[1355]						
			−29.2	[2215]						
			−29.8	[2358]						
		l	−37.2	[1355, 2674]	−9.56	[1355]	51.86	[1355]	37.57	[1355]
			−38.0	[2358]						
CH_3O_2S	Methyl sulfone (free radical)	g	−60*	[1867]						
$CH_3N_3O_3$	Nitrourea	c	−67.5	[2358]						
CH_4N_2O	Urea	g					64.61	[28]	13.23	[28]
		g					72.51	[1157]	22.31	[1157]
		c	−79.56	[2358]	−47.04	[2358]	25.00	[2358]	22.26	[2358]
			−79.634	[53]	−47.12	[53]				
		d	−76.117	[2358]						
	Ammonium cyanate	c	−72.75	[2358]						
		d	−66.6	[2358]	−42.3	[2358]	52.6	[2358]		
CH_4N_2S	Thiourea	g	−6.0*[7]	[1879]			72.44	[1881]	17.69	[1881]
		c	−21.4[7]	[1879]						
			−21.1	[2358]						
CH_4N_2S	Ammonium thiocyanate	c	−18.8	[2358]						
		d	−13.40	[2358]	3.18	[2358]	61.6	[2358]	9.5	[2358]
$CH_4N_4O_2$	Nitroguanidine	c	−22.13	[2358]						
$CH_4N_6O_3$	Guanylazide nitrate	c	3.8	[2358]						
	5-Aminotetrazole nitrate	c	−6.6	[2358]						
CH_5NO_2	Ammonium formate	c	−131*; −135.63	[2683]						
		d	−133.38	[2358]	−102.81	[2358]	49	[2358]	−1.9	[2358]
CH_5N_3O	Semicarbazide (Aminourea)	d	−39.9	[2358]	−9.7	[2358]	71.2	[2358]		
$CH_5N_3O_4$	Urea nitrate	c	−131.8	[2358]						
CH_5N_3S	Thiosemicarbazide	c	5.7[7]	[1879]						
$CH_5N_5O_2$	Nitroaminoguanidine	c	5.3	[2358]						
CH_6ClN	Methylamine hydrochloride	c	−71.20	[2358]	−37.99	[2358]	33.13	[2358]	21.72	[2358]
		d	−69.82	[2358]	−40.92	[2358]	47.6	[2358]		
$CH_6N_2O_2$	Ammonium carbamate	c	−154.17	[2358]	−107.09	[2358]	31.9	[2358]		
		d	−150.4	[2358]						
$CH_6N_2O_3$	Methylamine nitrate	c	−84.7	[2358]						
			−80.7	[1044]						

1. $\Delta H_0^\circ = -62.761$ [1618a]. 2. $\Delta H_0^\circ = -70.284$ [570]. 3. $\Delta H_0^\circ = 3.934$ [570]. 4. $\Delta H_0^\circ = -45.464$ [570]. 5. $\Delta H_0^\circ = -14.55$ [1848]. 6. $t = 30°C$; extrapolated. 7. $T = 293.15°K$.

1	2	3	4		5	6		7	
$CH_6N_4O_3$	Guanidine nitrate	c	−92.5	[2358]					
			−93.00	[308]					
$CH_8N_6O_3$	Diaminoguanidine nitrate	c	−37.6	[2358]					
$CB_{10}D_3O$	Trideuteromethylboryl	g				61.83	[2486]	15.89	[2486]
$CB_{11}D_3O$		g				62.00	[2486]	15.97	[2486]
$CBrClF_2$	Bromochlorodifluoromethane	g	−111*[1]	[570]		76.182	[570]		
			−111	[679]		76.14	[1301]	17.82	[1301, 2358]
			−110*	[361a]		76.23	[362]	17.86	[362]
						76.1	[2358]		
$CBrClF_2 \cdot 17H_2O$	Bromochlorodifluoromethane, crystalline hydrate	c				216.6[2]	[1322]	167.1[2]	[1322]
$CBrClI_2$	Bromochlorodiiodomethane	g	34	[679]					
			33*	[361a]					
$CBrClO$	Bromochloroformaldehyde	g				72.04	[2083]	14.28	[2083]
$CBrCl_2D$	Bromodichlorodeuteromethane	g	−17.3*	[826a]		75.90	[2165]	16.83	[2165]
$CBrCl_2F$	Bromodichlorofluoromethane	g	−63*[3]	[570]		79.129	[570]		
			−63*	[361a]		79.05	[1301]	19.22	[1301]
			−63	[679]		78.87	[1312]	19.13	[1312, 2358]
						79.0	[2358]		
						79.22	[362]	19.08	[362]
$CBrCl_2I$	Bromodichloroiodomethane	g	10*	[679]					
			9*	[361a]					
$CBrFI_2$	Bromofluorodiiodomethane	g	−14	[679]					
			−14*	[361a]					
$CBrF_2I$	Bromodifluoroiodomethane	g	−87*[4]	[570]		81.772	[570]		
			−87	[679]					
			−85*	[361a]					
CBr_2ClD	Dibromochlorodeuteromethane	g				78.69	[2167]	17.32	[2167]
CBr_2ClF	Dibromochlorofluoromethane	g	−52*[5]	[570]		82.022	[570]		
			−52	[679]		81.95	[1301]	19.73	[1301]
			−54*	[361a]		81.97	[362]	19.66	[362]
						81.89	[1312]	19.67	[1312]
CBr_2ClI	Dibromochloroiodomethane	g	21	[679]					
			18*	[361a]					
CBr_2FI	Dibromofluoroiodomethane	g	−27	[679]					
			−29*	[361a]					
$CClDF_2$	Chlorodeuterodifluoromethane	g				67.47	[2629]	14.02	[2629]
$CClFI$	Chlorofluoroiodomethyl (free radical)	g	−8*	[360]					

$CClFI_2$	Chlorofluorodiiodomethane	g	-25	[679]				
			-23	[361a]				
$CClFO$	Chlorofluoroformaldehyde	g	-102.0*[6]	[1618a]	66.184	[1618a]	12.523	[1618a]
			-101.85[7]	[1830]	66.1472	[1830]	15.5233	[1830]
			-101[8]	[570]	66.125	[570]		
$CClF_2I$	Chlorodifluoroiodomethane	g	-98*[9]	[570]	78.544	[570]		
			-98	[679]				
			-94*	[361a]				
$CClN_3O_6$	Trinitrochloromethane	l	-5.6	[2358]			39.0	[2358]
			-5.57	[2729]				
CCl_2DF	Dichlorodeuterofluoromethane	g			70.35	[2629]	15.28	[2629]
CCl_2FI	Dichlorofluoroiodomethane	g	-50	[679]				
			-48*	[361a]				

1, IV

$CHBrClF$	Bromochlorofluoromethane	g	-62*[10]	[570]	72.970	[570]		
			-62	[679]	72.88	[1301]	15.11	[1301]
			-61*; -62*	[361a]	73.17	[362]	14.99	[362]
$CHBrClI$	Bromochloroiodomethane	g	11	[679]				
			10*; 11*	[361a]				
$CHBrFI$	Bromofluoroiodomethane	g	-37	[679]				
			-36*; -38*	[361a]				
$CHClFI$	Chlorofluoroiodomethane	g	-48	[679]				
			-46*; -48*	[361a]				
$CH_5N_3O_3S$	Thiourea nitrate	c	-73.1	[2358]				
CH_6ClN_3O	Semicarbazide hydrochloride	c					34	[2358]
$CH_6ClN_3O_4$	Guanidine perchlorate	c	-74.8	[2358]				
			-74.10	[308]				
		d	-64.4	[2358]				
$CBrClFI$	Bromochlorofluoroiodo-methane	g	-38	[679]				
			-38*; 36*	[361a]				

1. $\Delta H_0^\circ = 108.337$ [570]. 2. $t = 0°C$. 3. $\Delta H_0^\circ = -60.599$ [570]. 4. $\Delta H_0^\circ = -84.189$ [570]. 5. $\Delta H_0^\circ = -47.946$ [570]. 6. $\Delta H_0^\circ = -101.404$* [1618a]. 7. $\Delta H_0^\circ = -101.2550$ [1830]. 8. $\Delta H_0^\circ = -100.421$ [570]. 9. $\Delta H_0^\circ = -96.833$ [570]. 10. $\Delta H_0^\circ = -58.983$ [570].

1	2	3	4		5		6		7	
1, V										
CHBBrClO	Bromochloromethylboryl	l	−51.8*	[361]						
CHBBrIO	Bromoiodomethylboryl	l	−85.7*	[361]						
CHBClIO	Chloroiodomethylboryl	l	−69*	[361]						
2, I										
C_2H	Ethynyl radical	g	116.798[1]	[570]			49.685	[570]		
			112	[1001]						
C_2H^+	Positive ethynyl ion	g	415	[1214]						
C_2H_2	Acetylene	g	54.190[2]	[1618a]	49.993	[1618a]	48.004	[1618a]	10.539	[1618a]
			54.194[3]	[1830, 2244]			48.0026	[1830]	10.5342	[1830]
					50.00	[2244]	49.997	[2244]	10.499	[2244]
			54.2[4]	[570]			48.00	[570]		
							48.002	[1342]	10.531	[1342]
C_2H_2	Ethynyl radical	g	54.19	[1807]						
C_2H_2	Positive ethine ion	g	317.08	[1807]						
			317	[1214]						
			337	[1528]						
C_2H_3	Ethenylene radical	g	65*	[1478]						
			65.26	[1807]						
$C_2H_3^+$	Positive ethenylene ion	g	283.18	[1807]						
			282	[1214]						
			283	[1478]						
			288	[1528]						
C_2H_4	Ethylene	g	12.496[5]	[1618a, 1830, 2244]	16.284	[1618a]	52.447	[1618a]	10.412	[1618a]
					16.282	[2444]	52.45	[2444]	10.41	[2444]
							52.4493	[1830]	10.4117	[1830]
			12.5[6]	[570]			52.412	[570]		
$C_2H_4^+$	Positive ethylene ion	g	257	[1214]						
		g	213	[1214]						
C_2H_5	Ethyl (free radical)	g	24.5	[2511]			59.22	[2195]		
			25.5	[2387]						
			25.3	[1481]						
$C_2H_5^+$	Positive ethyl ion	g	225	[1214]						
			223.5	[1867]						

C_2H_6	Ethane	g	-20.236[7]	[2244]	-7.86	[2244]	54.85	[2244]	(12.585)	[2244]
									(12.51)[8]	[1245]
									(12.58)	[321]
$C_2H_6^+$	Positive ethane ion	g	249	[1214]						
C_2Br_4	Tetrabromoethylene	g					92.48	[1912]	24.54	[1912]
							92.35*	[803a]	24.73	[803a]
C_2Br_6	Hexabromoethane	g					105.59	[935]	33.30	[935]
C_2Cl_4	Tetrachloroethylene	g	-4.1[9]	[570]			81.482	[570]	22.98	[2560a]
							81.45	[1912]	22.69	[1912]
							82.08	[803a]	22.41	[803a]
							81.60	[2560a]	33.41[10]	[313]
C_2Cl_6	Hexachloroethane	g	-36.0[11]	[1750]	-15.78	[1750]	94.77	[935, 1750]	32.66	[1750]
C_2F	Fluoroethynyl radical	g	65.677[12]	[570]			55.479	[570]	32.59	[935]
C_2F_2	Difluoroacetylene	g	-51.3*[13]	[1618a]	-54.006	[1618a]	60.248	[1618a]	14.595	[1618a]
			-45*[14]	[570]			59.836	[570]		
C_2F_3	Trifluoroethenyl radical	g	-25.37	[1807]						
$C_2F_3^+$	Positive ion of trifluoro- ethenyl	g	198.09	[1807]						
C_2F_4	Tetrafluoroethylene	g	-155.0[15]	[1618a]	-146.672	[1618a]	71.681	[1618a]	19.23	[1618a]
			-162	[1740]	-282.4	[1740]	79.27	[1740]		
			-152[16]	[570]			71.688	[570]		
			-151.7	[2043]			70.47*	[803a]	19.29	[803a]
			-151.3	[1136]						
			-162	[2620]						
			-152	[433]						
			-151.9	[266]						
$\frac{1}{n}(C_2F_4)_n$	Tetrafluoroethylene polymer	c	-193.5	[433]						
C_2F_6	Hexafluoroethane	g	(-303*)	[433, 1740]			79.06	[935]	25.15	[935]
C_2I_4	Tetrafluoroethylene polymer	g					99.96*; 100.76*	[803a]	26.25*	[803a]

1. $\Delta H_0^\circ = 116$ [570]. 2. $\Delta H_0^\circ = 54.325$ [1618a]. 3. $\Delta H_0^\circ = 54.3270$ [1830]. 4. $\Delta H_0^\circ = 54.294$ [1830]. 5. $\Delta H_0^\circ = 14.5204$ [1830]; 14.520 [1618a]; 14.522 [2244]. 6. $\Delta H_0^\circ = 14.490$ [570]. 7. $\Delta H_0^\circ = -16.517$ [2244]. 8. $t = 25.8°C$. 9. $\Delta H_0^\circ = -3.931$ [570]. 10. Interpolated [234] with the aid of the equation given in the original paper. 11. $\Delta H_0^\circ = -35.4$ [1750]. 12. $\Delta H_0^\circ = 64.670$ [570]. 13. $\Delta H_0^\circ = -51.93$ [1618a]. 14. $\Delta H_0^\circ = -45.585$ [570]. 15. $\Delta H_0^\circ = -154.179$ [1618a]. 16. $\Delta H_0^\circ = -151.213$ [570].

1	2	3	4		5		6		7	
C_2N	Radical	g	123	[1104]						
C_2N^+	Ion	g	419	[1104]						
C_2N_2	Cyanogen	g	73.87[1]	[1618a]	71.117	[1618a]	57.711	[1618a]	13.563	[1618a]
			73.840[2]	[1830]			57.7889	[1830]	13.5815	[1830]
			73.83[3]	[570]			57.712	[570]		
							57.91	[2726]	13.60	[2726]
$C_2O_4^{2-}$	Oxalate anion	d			−159.4*	[323]	(10.6*)	[323]		
							(15)	[219]		
							(11)	[216]		
					2, II					
C_2HBr_3	Tribromoethylene	g					85.69[4]	[1181]	20.51[4]	[1181]
							85.94*	[803a]	20.61*	[803a]
									20.77	[362]
C_2HCl_3	Trichloroethylene	g	−1.4*	[361a]			78.26	[361a]	18.96	[361a]
			−1.8[5]	[570]			77.673	[570]		
		l							29.09[6]	[313]
C_2HCl_5	Pentachloroethane	g	−35.4[7]	[1750]	−16.93	[1750]	90.94	[1750]	28.17	[1750]
							90.95	[2061]	28.14	[2061]
									46.95[6]	[313]
C_2HF	Fluoroacetylene	g	5*[8]	[570]			55.381	[570]		
C_2HF^{+2}	Positive ion of fluoro-acetylene	g	295.17	[1807]						
$C_2HF_2^+$	Positive ion of difluoro-ethylene	g	249.05	[1807]						
C_2HF_3	Trifluoroethylene	g	−114.6[9]	[570]			69.944	[570]		
			−113.3	[273]			69.97*	[803a]	16.38*	[803a]
			−110.4*	[361a]						
C_2HI_3	Triiodoethylene	g					89.96*	[803a]	21.93*	[803a]
$C_2HO_4^-$	Oxalate anion	d			−165.12*	[323]				
$C_2H_2Br_2$	1.1-Dibromoethylene	g					76.46*	[803a]	16.61	[803a]
	trans-Dibromoethylene	g					75.96*	[803a]	16.79	[1121, 803a]
							74.90	[1121]	11.00[10]	[1181]
							75.74*	[803a]	16.73	[803a]
	cis-Dibromoethylene	g					75.80[10]	[1181]	16.53[10]	[1181]
							74.38	[1121]	16.44	[1121]
									17.5	[362]

$C_2H_2Br_4$	Tetrabromoethane	g	-9.6	[2387]						
	1, 1, 2, 2-Tetrabromoethane	l							39.52[11]	[313]
$C_2H_2Cl_2$	1, 1-Dichloroethylene	g					68.72*	[803a]	15.51*	[803a]
		l	-6.0	[2384]					16.7*	[826a]
	1, 2-Dichloroethylene	g	5.4*	[826a]						
	trans-Dichloroethylene	g					69.29	[2159]	15.93	[2159]
							70.20*	[803a]	15.69*	[803a]
									16.57	[362]
	cis-Dichloroethylene	g	0.6[12]	[570]			69.190	[570]		
			0.8*	[361a]			69.13	[2159]	15.55	[2159]
							70.74*	[803a]	15.63*	[803a]
									26.79[13]	[313]
$C_2H_2Cl_4$	1, 1, 1, 2-Tetrachloroethane	g					85.07	[2061]	24.55	[2061]
							85.10	[1750]	24.57	[1750]
	1, 1, 2, 2-Tetrachloroethane	g	-33.0[14]	[1750]	-16.96	[1750]	86.09	[1750]	24.09	[1750]
		l							38.98[13]	[313]
C_2H_2F	Fluoroethenylene (free radical)	g	27.52	[1807]						
$C_2H_2F^+$	Positive ion of fluoro-ethenylene	g	239.59	[1807]						
$C_2H_2F_2$	1, 1-Difluoroethylene	g	-77.5[15]	[570]			63.384	[570]		
			-77.5	[433, 1740]			64.01	[803a]	14.45*	[803a]
			-79.6	[273]						
			-69*	[361a]						
	trans-Difluoroethylene	g					67.49*	[803a]	14.63*	[803a]
	cis-Difluoroethylene	g					67.77*	[803a]	14.57*	[803a]
$\frac{1}{n}(C_2H_2F_2)_n$	Difluoroethylene polymer	c	-113.32	[55]						
$C_2H_2F_4$	Tetrafluoroethane	g					75.849	[2614]	20.817	[2614]
$C_2H_2I_2$	1, 1-Diiodoethylene	g					79.69*	[803a]	17.49*	[803a]
	trans-Diiodoethylene	g					79.96*	[803a]	17.59*	[803a]
	cis-Diiodoethylene	g					79.49*	[803a]	17.53*	[803a]
C_2H_2O	Ketene	g	-14.60[16]	[150]	-14.20	[150]	57.14	[150]	11.43	[150]
							57.03	[2487]	11.46	[2487]
							57.77	[1978]	12.36	[1978]

1. $\Delta H_0^\circ = 73.428$ [1618a]. 2. $\Delta H_0^\circ = 73.3876$ [1830]. 3. $\Delta H_0^\circ = 73.352$ [570]. 4. $T = 300°K$. 5. $\Delta H_0^\circ = -1.008$ [570]. 6. Interpolated [234] with the aid of equation given in the original paper. 7. $\Delta H_0^\circ = -33.6$ [1750]. 8. $\Delta H_0^\circ = 4.789$ [570]. 9. $\Delta H_0^\circ = -113.380$ [570]. 10. $T = 300°K$. 11. Interpolated [234] with the aid of equation given in the original paper. 12. $\Delta H_0^\circ = 1.992$ [570]. 13. Interpolated [234] with the aid of equation given in the original paper. 14. $\Delta H_0^\circ = -31.0$ [1750]. 15. $\Delta H_0^\circ = -75.847$ [570]. 16. $\Delta H_0^\circ = -13.71$ [150].

1	2	3	4		5		6		7	
$C_2H_2O_2^+$	Positive glyoxal ion	g	207	[1214]						
$C_2H_2O_2$	Glyoxal	g					64.09	[129]	14.07	[129]
$C_2H_2O_4$	Oxalic acid	c	−196.7	[1360]	−165.9	[1360]	28.7	[1360]		
			−198.36	[2685]			28.7*	[323]		
		d	−195.57*	[323]	−166.8	[323]				
C_2H_3Br	Vinyl bromide	g	18.68	[1786]	19.26	[1786]	65.8	[1786]	13.3	[1786]
							65.89*	[803a]	13.41	[803a]
									13.72	[362]
									13.44	[1913]
$C_2H_3Br_3$	Tribromoethane	g							39.51[1]	[1103, 2717]
C_2H_3Cl	Vinyl chloride	g	(8.89)	[1785]	12.80	[1785]	63.03	[1785]	13.19	[1785]
			(8.9)[2]	[570]			63.088	[570]		
			(8.072)	[765]			62.95*	[803a]	12.85	[803a]
			(7*); (8.5*)	[361a]						
$C_3H_3Cl_3$	1,1,1-Trichloroethane	g					77.09	[1750, 2158]	22.35	[1750]
									22.17	[2158]
		l					54.37	[321]	34.5	[321]
	1,1,2-Trichloroethane	g	−45.0[3]	[1750]	−30.42	[1750]	80.57	[1750]	21.27	[1750]
C_2H_3F	Vinyl fluoride	g	−28*	[361a]			60.50*	[803a]	12.33*	[803a]
			−33*[4]	[570]			60.390	[570]		
$C_2H_3F_3$	1,1,1-Trifluoroethane	g	−174.1	[273]			68.47	[2060]	18.75	[2060]
							63.87	[321]		
	1,1,2-Trifluoroethane	g	−172.4	[272]						
C_2H_3I	Vinyl iodide	g					67.96*	[803a]	17.53*	[803a]
C_2H_3N	Acetonitrile	g	22.70[5]	[321]			(58.67)	[2197]	(21.81)	[2197]
							(58.01)	[1446, 2197]	(12.40)	[1446]
							(58.15)	[2726]	(12.49)	[2726]
							(58.19)	[2155]	(12.48)	[2155]
		l					(35.76)	[2197]		
	Methyl isocyanide	g	37.48[5]	[321]			(58.98)	[2155]	(12.80)	[2155]
C_2H_3O	Acetyl radical	g	−10.8	[2511]						
$C_3H_3O_2$	Acetate radical	g	−45	[2387]						
			−11	[938, 2510]						
			−39*	[1984]						
$C_2H_3O_2^-$	Acetate anion	d			−89.02*	[323]				

$C_2H_3S^*$	Positive ion of cyclo-thiapropene	g	271	[1528]						
$C_2H_4Br_2$	1, 2-Dibromoethane	g	-9.3	[1453]	-2.52	[1453]	78.81	[1453]	32.22[6]	[1103, 2717]
							79.6*	[826a]	18.2*	[826a]
		l	-19.3	[321]	-4.94	[321]	53.37	[321]	(32.51)	[321]
									(32.23)[7]	[313]
$C_2H_4Cl_2$	*trans*-Ethylene chloride	l							30.46[7]	[313]
	cis-Ethylene chloride	l					50.61	[1806]	29.36[7]	[313]
	1, 1-Dichloroethane	g					72.82	[1806]	18.22	[1806]
							72.69	[1070]	18.15	[1070]
		l	-39.6	[2384]	-20.2	[2384]	50.61	[1806]	30.18	[1806]
	1, 2-Dichloroethane	g	(-31.3)[8]	[1750]	(-18.0)	[1750]	(73.81)	[1750]	(19.00)	[1750]
			(-30.3)	[2408]			(73.9)	[1453]	(18.8)	[1453]
							(72.82)	[1806]	(17.6*)	[826a]
		l	-39.6	[2384]	-20.2	[2384]	49.84	[2384]	18.22	[1806]
$C_2H_4F_2$	1, 1-Difluoroethane	g	-113.6	[272]						
$C_2H_4I_2$	1, 2-Diiodoethane	g	15.9	[825]			83.3	[825]	19.2	[825]
$C_2H_4N_4$	Cyanoguanidine (dicyanamide)	g	5.96	[2448]	43.50	[2448]	30.90	[2448]		
C_2H_4O	Ethylene oxide	g	-22.02	[1363]	-5.60	[1363]	67.15	[1363]	17.34	[1363]
			-12.19	[371, 1360, 1445]	-2.79	[1360]	58.13	[1360]		
					-2.82	[1445]	58.24	[1445]	11.60	[1445]
			-9.199[5]	[1618a]	-2.771	[1618a]	58.057	[1618a]	11.449	[1618a]
			-12.58	[2134]			58.03	[2485]	11.45	[2485]
	Acetaldehyde	g	-39.67	[67, 1360]	-31.74	[67]	63.0	[67]	13.22	[67]
			-37.15[5]	[321]	-31.77	[1360]	63.15	[1360]	14.8	[1011]
			-41.18	[1883]			71.14	[1883]		
			-39.67	[2161]			58.13	[130]	11.51	[130]
							58.03	[1195]	11.45	[1195]
							63.50	[30]	13.18	[30]
		l					-117.3	[1748]	65.6	[1748]
		d	-49.88*	[323]						
$C_2H_4O_2$	Acetic acid (monomer)	g	-104.53[9]	[2634]	75.41	[2634]	67.52	[2634]	15.90	[2634]
			-103.8	[1360]	-89.9	[1360]	67.5	[1360]		
									17.7*; 13.8*	[826a]
			-106	[1883]			77.5	[1883]		
			-100.48[5]	[321]						

1. $t = 20°C$. 2. $\Delta H_0^\circ = 10.669$ [570]. 3. $\Delta H_0^\circ = -42.44$ [1750]. 4. $\Delta H_0^\circ = -31.160$ [570]. 5. ΔH_0°. 6. $t = 20°C$. 7. Interpolated [234] with the aid of equation given in the original paper. 8. $\Delta H_0^\circ = -22.18$ [1750]. 9. $\Delta H_0^\circ = -101.20$ [2634].

1	2	3	4	5	6	7
$C_2H_4O_2$	Acetic acid (monomer)	l	(−115.7) [1360]	−93.1 [1360]	38.2 [1360, 2113]	29.5 [2113]
			(−115.72) [1178]			
		d	(−115.80) [328]	(−95.51*) [323]	69.7 [971]	16.8 [971]
			−103.1[1] [971]		84.6 [1360]	
	Methyl formate	g	−81.0 [1360]	−72.0 [1360]	69.95 [30]	
			−80.08[2] [321]		69.1*; 70.1* [826a]	16.36 [30]
						14.3* [2592a]
		l	−88.6 [1360]			
$C_2H_4O_4$	Dimer of formic acid	g	−194.20 [2616]	−170.69 [2616]	83.35 [2616]	
			−195.12 [1360, 1362]	−171.19 [1360, 1362]	82.89 [1360, 1362]	
C_2H_4S	Cyclothiapropane	g	19.93 [1879]	13.93 [1451]	61.01 [1451]	12.83 [1451]
			13.31 [1567]			
			6.82[3,14] [1451]			
		l	12.05 [1451]	22.16 [1451]		
			12.38 [1879, 2495]			
	Ethylene sulfide	l	19.52 [1214]		43.30* [323]	
C_2H_5Br	Ethyl bromide	g	−15.3 [1792]			17 [1792]
			−14.79 [1243]		68.7* [826a]	15.3* [826a]
			−14.89 [1080]			
		l	−23.0 [746]			24.09[4] [313]
C_2H_5Cl	Ethyl chloride	g	(−25.7)[5] [1750]	(−13.26) [1750]	(65.67) [1070]	(14.90) [1070]
			(−25.74) [1785]			(14.80) [1785]
			(−26.7) [1787]			
			(−24) [943]			
			(−23.7)[6] [943]			
			(−26.01) [1080]			
		l				26.56[7] [313]
$C_2H_5Cl^+$	Positive ion of ethyl chloride	g	226 [1214]			
			230 [762]			
C_2H_5I	Ethyl iodide	g	−10.93 [197]	1.25 [197]	70.88 [197]	15.97 [197]
		l	−9.6 [746]			(27.54)[7] [313]
$C_2H_5I^+$	Positive ion of ethyl iodide	g	215 [1214]			
			−14.0 [327]			
C_2H_5Li	Ethyllithium	c	−6 [759a]			
C_2H_5O	Ethoxy radical	g	25.5 [1867]			
C_2H_5S	Ethyl sulfide (free radical)	g	25.0* [1246]			
$C_2H_5S^+$	Positive ion of ethyl sulfide	g	213 [1214]			
			212.8 [1246]			

C_2H_6Cd	Dimethylcadmium	g	9.528[8]	[1390]			72.40	[1804]	31.5	[1804]
		l					48.25	[1804]		
C_2H_6Hg	Dimethylmercury	g	14.3	[1484]						
			8.264[8]	[1390]						
		l	(14.3)	[922]						
C_2H_6O	Ethanol	g	-56.17	[1364]	-40.27	[1364]	67.58	[1360, 1364]	15.64	[1364]
			-56.24	[1360]	40.35	[1360]	67.54	[1365]	16.0*	[826a]
			-51.957[9]	[321]						
		l	-66.36	[1360]	-41.77	[1360]	38.40	[1360]		
			-66.35	[1365]			38.53	[1364]	26.76	[1364]
			-66.20	[961]						
		d			-42.4*	[323]				
	Dimethyl ether	g	(-44.3)[10]	[2355]	(-27.27)	[1360, 2355]	(63.74)	[1360, 2355]	(15.77)	[2355]
			(-43.99)	[2150]			(63.746)	[765]	(15.729)	[765]
			(-44.3)	[1360]			(63.73)	[1935]	(15.29)	[1935]
		l	-50.05	[1692]	-27.45	[1692]	44.98	[1692]		
$C_2H_6O_2$	Dimethyl peroxide	g	-30.0	[759a]						
			-32	[823]						
$C_2H_6O_2$	Ethylene glycol	g	-92.8[11]	[162]	-71.52	[162]	77.33	[162, 1360]	18.8	[162]
			-95.10	[1360]	-74.82	[1360]	76.8	[826a]	18.8*	[826a]
		l	-108.74	[1360]	-77.3	[1360]	39.9	[1360]		
	Ethyl hydroperoxide	l	-58*	[1360]						
$C_2H_6O_3$	Dimethyl peroxide	g	-13*	[823]						
$C_2H_6O_4$	Dimethyl ether ozonide	g	6*	[823]						
C_2H_6S	Dimethyl sulfide (free radical)	g	-11.0*	[1867]						
C_2H_6S	2-Thiopropane (dimethyl sulfide)	g	-24.36[12,14]	[1843, 2342]	-7.88[14]	[2342]	(68.32)	[1843, 2342]	17.71	[1843, 2342]
			-24.40[14];	[1843]	-7.91[14]	[1843]			17.36	[1846]
			-8.94	[1897]	4.435	[849]	(68.25)	[848]	17.00	[848]
					-5.344[14]					
			-20.17[9,14]	[848]						
		l	-15.64[14]; -8.98	[1843, 1879]	1.37[14]; 1.65[14]	[1843]				
			-14.4	[1110]						
	Ethanethiol (ethyl mercaptan)	g	-26.41[13,14]	[2342]	-10.66[14]	[2342]	70.77	[1663a, 1843, 2342]	17.37	[1663a, 1843, 2342]

1. $\Delta H_0^\circ = -100.1$ [971]. 2. ΔH_0° [1242]. 3. ΔH_0° 14. 4. Interpolated [234] with the aid of equation given in the original paper. 5. $\Delta H_0^\circ = -26.46$ [1750]. 6. $t = 20°C$. 7. Interpolated [234] with the aid of equation given in the original paper. 8. ΔH_{vap}. 9. ΔH_0°. 10. $\Delta H_0^\circ = -40.11$ [2355]. 11. $\Delta H_0^\circ = -95.10$ [162]. 12. $\Delta H_0^\circ = -20.47$ (from S_2(g)) [1843, 2342]. 13. $\Delta H_0^\circ =$ $= -22.3814$ [2342]. 14. From S_2(g).

1	2	3	4		5		6		7	
C_2H_6S	Ethanethiol (ethyl mercaptan)	g	−26.45[1,11]	[1843]	−10.7[11]	[1843]				
			−26.60[2,11]	[1663a]	−10.84[11]	[1663a]				
					−10.70[11]	[1846, 2329]				
		g	−12.93	[1883]			81.46	[1883]		
			−10.90	[1879]						
			−11.03	[1843]						
		l	−17.61	[1843]	−1.13[11]; −1.36[11]	[1843]	49.48	[1846]		
			−17.62	[1879]						
$C_2H_6S_2$	2, 3-Dithiabutane (dimethyl disulfide)	g	−36.55[3,11]	[1552, 2342]	−15.56[11]	[2342]	80.46	[2342]	22.54	[2342]
			−5.71	[1879]	−15.60[11]	[1552]	80.51	[2327a]		
			−7.40	[1883]			93.88	[1883]		
			−7.2	[1246]						
		l	−14.89	[1879]			56.26	[2327a]		
			−16.4	[1246]						
	3, 4-Dithiabutane	g	−17.78	[1879]						
		l	−28.64	[1879]						
	1, 4-Ethanedithiol	g	−12.03	[1917]						
C_2H_6Zn	Dimethylzinc	g	7.058[4]	[1390]						
C_2H_7N	Dimethylamine	g					(65.24)	[749]	16.62	[749]
							(65.50)	[2356]	16.92	[2356]
							(65.3)	[53]	16.58	[53]
		l	−13.9	[749]	13.91	[749]	43.58	[749]	28.5	[228]
	Ethylamine	g					68.5*	[826a]		
C_2AgO_4	Silver (II) oxalate	c	(−168.7*)	[232]	−144.47*	[177]				
$C_2Ag_2O_4$	Silver (I) oxalate	c			−137.2*	[323]	48*	[323]		
C_2BaO_4	Barium oxalate	c	−327.6	[209]	−309.87*	[177]				
					−307*	[229]				
$C_2BaO_4 \cdot 2H_2O$	Barium oxalate dihydrate	c	−416.3*	[323]						
C_2BeO_4	Beryllium oxalate	c	−288*	[2683]						
$C_2Br_2D_2$	*trans*-Dibromodideutero-ethylene	g					76.07	[1121]	18.21	[1121]
	cis-Dibromodideutero-ethylene	g					75.56	[1121]	19.67	[1121]

$C_2Br_2D_4$	1,1-Dibromotetradeutero-ethane	g							35.29[1]	[1103, 2717]
$C_2Br_2F_2$	Dibromodifluoroethylene	g					87.194	[2062]	22.904	[2062]
$C_2Br_2F_4$	1, 2-Dibromo-1, 1, 2, 2-tetra-fluoroethane	g	-183	[433]						
$C_2Br_3D_3$	1, 1, 2-Trideuterotribromo-ethane	g							42.74[5]	[1103, 2717]
C_2CaO_4	Calcium oxalate	c	-325.2	[209]	(-310.28*)	[177]	(32.0*)	[699]		
					(-299.6*)	[299]				
C_2CdO_4	Cadmium oxalate	c	-217.4	[213]	-195.62*[6]	[177]				
C_2ClF_3	Chlorotrifluoroethylene	g	-127[7]	[570]			77.070	[570]		
			-126*	[1740]			73.18	[2075]		
			-115	[2620]						
			-120	[433]						
			-130.2	[267]						
			-114*	[361a]						
		l					52.74[8]	[2075]	29.26[8]	[2075]
C_2ClF_5	Chloropentafluoroethane	g					85.47	[753]		
$C_2Cl_2F_2$	*trans*-Dichlorodifluoro-ethylene	g	-78[9]	[570]			78.278	[570]		
			-77*	[361a]						
	sym-Dichlorodifluoroethylene	g			-78	[2620]				
	as-Dichlorodifluoroethylene	g	-76	[2620]			72.89	[1806]		
$C_2Cl_2F_4$	1,2-Dichloro-1,1, 2, 2-tetrafluoroethane	g	-213*	[1740]						
			-209	[433]						
C_2Cl_3F	Trichlorofluoroethylene	g	-38*[10]	[570]			81.872	[570]		
			-40*	[361a]			81.84	[1913]	21.76	[1913]
$C_2Cl_3F_3$	1,1, 2-Trichlorotrifluoro-ethane	g					92.78; 92.68	[1748]	30.29; 30.23	[1748]
	1, 2, 2-Trichlorotrifluoro-ethane	g	-169	[570]						
C_2Cl_3N	Trichloroacetonitrile	g					80.31	[1083]	22.95	[1083]
C_2Cl_4O	Trichloroacetyl chloride	g	-60.5	[2183]						
		l	-68.5	[2183]						
C_2CoO_4	Cobalt oxalate	c	-211	[2683]						
$C_2Cs_2O_4$	Cesium oxalate	c	-318*	[2683]						
C_2CuO_4	Cupric oxalate	c	-183*	[232]	-161.38*	[177]				
$C_2CuO_4^-$	Cupric oxalate ion	d			-317.5*	[323]				

1. $\Delta H_0^\circ = -22.42$ (from S_2 (g)) [1843]. 2. $\Delta H_0^\circ = -22.57$ (from S_2 (g)) [1663a]. 3. $\Delta H_0^\circ = -32.61$ (from S_2 (g)) [1552, 2342]. 4. ΔH_{vap}. 5. $t = 20$°C. 6. $t = 18$°C. 7. $\Delta H_0^\circ = -126.363$ [570]. 8. $T = 244.80$°K. 9. $\Delta H_0^\circ = -77.535$ [570]. 10. $\Delta H_0^\circ = -37.663$ [570]. 11. From S_2 (g).

1	2	3	4		5		6		7	
C_2D_2O	Deuteroketene	g					58.72	[2487]	12.50	[2487]
C_2D_4O	Deutero-substituted ethylene oxide	g					60.17	[1195, 2485]	13.89	[1195, 2485]
C_2F_3N	Trifluoroacetonitrile	g					71.26	[2085]		
C_2FeO_4	Ferrous oxalate	c	-218*	[232]	-195.79*	[177]				
			-219*	[2683]						
C_2HgO_4	Mercuric oxalate	c			-126.2*	[323]	33.1*	[323]		
$C_2Hg_2O_4$	Mercurous oxalate	c	-168*	[232]	-140.7*	[323]				
			-163*	[2683]	-146.85*[1]	[177]				
$C_2K_2O_4$	Potassium oxalate	c			-296.7*	[323]	40.4*	[323]		
C_2MgO_4	Magnesium oxalate	c	-302.5	[209]	-277.2*	[229]				
			-308*	[2683]	-280.92*	[177]				
					-273.9*	[254]				
C_2MnO_4	Manganese oxalate	c			-234.2*	[323]	28*	[323]		
$C_2N_2S_2$	Dithiocyanogen	g			77.9*	[323]				
$C_2Na_2O_4$	Sodium oxalate	c			-308*	[323]	37*	[323]		
$C_2NpO_4^{2-}$	Complex ion[2]	d	0	[1426]						
C_2O_4Pb	Lead oxalate	c	(-206.24)	[219]	(-180.91)	[219]	34.9	[219]	24.8*	[219]
			(-206.2)	[216]	(-179.3)	[216]	31.23	[216, 2338]		
			(-203.2)	[2338]	(-180.3*)	[323]	33.2*	[323]		
			(-208*)	[232]	(-178.9*)	[232]				
			(-200.5)	[221]	(-186.60*)[3]	[177]				
			(-210*)	[2683]						
C_2O_4Pd	Palladium oxalate	c	-175*	[2683]						
C_2O_4Ra	Radium oxalate	c	-337*	[2683]						
C_2O_4Rb	Rubidium oxalate	c	-317*	[2683]						
C_2O_4Sn	Stannous oxalate	c	-218*	[2683]						
C_2O_4Sr	Strontium oxalate	c	(-327.7)	[209]	(-307.0*)	[229]				
			(-333*)	[2683]	(-309.47*)	[177]				
					(-332*)	[232]				
C_2O_4Ti	Titanium (II) oxalate	c	-264*	[2683]						
$C_2O_4Tl_2$	Thallium oxalate	c	-211*	[2683]						
C_2O_4Yb	Ytterbium oxalate	c	-352*	[232]	-328.60	[177]				
C_2O_4Zn	Zinc oxalate	c	-236*	[232]	-213.66*	[177]				
			-233	[2683]						

C_2HBrF_2	Bromodifluoroethylene	g					75.24	[2529]	17.63	[2529]
C_2HBrF_4	Bromotetrafluoroethane	g	−196	[433]						
C_2HClF_2	2-Chloro-1, 1-difluoroethylene	g	-77.5^{4}	[570]			72.366	[570]		
			−73*	[361a]						
C_2HCl_2F	2, 2-Dichloro-1-fluoroethylene	g	-39^{*5}	[570]			75.492	[570]		
			−36*	[361a]						
$C_2H_2BeO_4$	Beryllium formate	c	−274*	[2683]						
$C_2H_2BrF_3$	Bromotrifluoroethane	g					80.593	[2614]	21.668	[2614]
$C_2H_2Br_2D_2$	Dibromodideuteroethane	g							34.10^{6}	[1103, 2717]
									33.86^{6}	
$C_2H_2Br_3D$	Tribromodeuteroethane	g							$(40.54)^{6}$	[177]
									40.49^{6}	[1103, 2717]
$C_2H_2CaO_4$	Calcium formate	c			−300.8*	[323]	37.3*	[323]		
$C_2H_2CdO_4$	Cadmium formate	c	−215*	[696]						
			−207*	[1984]						
			−212	[2683]						
C_2H_2ClF	1-Chloro-1-fluoroethylene	g	-35^{*7}	[570]			67.694	[570]		
			−32*	[361a]						
$C_2H_2ClF_3$	Chlorotrifluoroethane	g					78.092	[2614]	21.306	[2614]
$C_2H_2CoO_4$	Cobalt formate	c	−209.66	[690]	−175.4	[229]				
			−206*	[2683]						
$C_2H_2F_3I$	Trifluoroiodoethane	g					82.318	[2614]	21.777	[2614]
$C_2H_2FeO_4$	Ferrous formate	c	−208*	[694]						
			−210*	[2683]						
$C_2H_2HgO_4$	Mercuric formate	c	−155*	[2683]						
$C_2H_2Hg_2O_4$	Mercurous formate	c	−110*	[2683]						
$C_2H_2MgO_4$	Magnesium formate	c	−300*	[1984]						
			−295*	[2683]						
$C_2H_2MnO_4$	Manganese formate	c			−212.0*	[323]	38.3*	[323]		
$C_2H_2NiO_4$	Nickel formate	c	−208.48	[690]	−174.3*	[229]				
			−202*	[2683]						
$C_2H_2O_4Pb$	Lead formate	c					35.5*	[323]		

1. $t=18°C$. 2. $NpO_2 \cdot (COO)_2^-$. 3. $t=18°C$. 4. $\Delta H_0^\circ=-76.384$ [570]. 5. $\Delta H_0^\circ=-38.103$ [570]. 6. $t=20°C$. 7. $\Delta H_0^\circ=-33.511$ [570].

1	2	3	4		5		6		7	
$C_2H_2O_4Pd$	Palladium formate	c	−168*	[2663]						
$C_2H_2O_4Ra$	Radium formate	c	−329*	[2683]						
$C_4H_2O_5Sn$	Tin formate	c	−205*	[696]						
$C_2H_2O_4Sr$	Strontium formate	c			−295*	[323]	40*	[323]		
$C_2H_2O_4Ti$	Titanium (II) formate	c	−253	[2683]						
$C_2H_3AgO_2$	Silver acetate	c			−74.2*	[323]	33.8*	[323, 2156]		
					−74.58*	[777]				
$C_2H_3AuO_2$	Gold acetate	c			−70.4	[1617]				
C_2H_3BrO	Acetyl bromide	l	(−53.9)	[941]						
$C_2H_3Br_2D$	Dibromodeuteroethane	g							32.90[1]	[1103, 2717]
C_2H_3ClO	Acetyl chloride	g	(−65.8)	[941]			71.22	[30]	16.21	[30]
			(−66.2)	[2183]						
		l	−59.4	[2183]						
$C_2H_3Cl_3Si$	Vinyltrichlorosilane	g					284.1[2]	[152]	175.0[2]	[152]
$C_2H_3CsO_2$	Cesium acetate	c	−172.4*	[1984]						
			−171*	[693]						
C_2H_3FO	Acetyl fluoride	g	−104.4	[433, 2184]						
		l	−110.7	[433, 2184]						
			−110.6	[941]						
$C_2H_3FO_2$	Monofluoroacetic acid	c	−160.9	[433]						
$C_2H_3F_3O$	2, 2, 2-Trifluoroethanol	l	−205.0	[270]						
C_2H_3IO	Acetyl iodide	l	(−39.7)	[941]						
$C_2H_3LiO_2$	Lithium acetate	c	−180.3*	[689]						
			−169.7*	[1984]						
			−177*	[2683]						
			−179	[481]						
C_2H_3NS	Methyl thiocyanate	g		[1885]	−18.86[3]	[1885]				
			−11.97[3]							
			27.1	[2492]						
		c	18.7	[2492]						
	Methyl isothiocyanate	g					69.29	[1881]	15.65	[1881]
		c	19.02	[2495]						
$C_2H_3O_2Rb$	Rubidium acetate	c	−172.3	[1984]						
			−171*	[693]						

			-176	[481]						
$C_2H_3O_2Tl$	Thallium acetate	c	-120*	[2683]						
$C_2H_4F_2O$	Difluoroethanol	l	-161.4	[433]						
$C_2H_4N_2O_2$	Oxamide, triclinic	c					28.23	[1157]	27.22	[1157]
C_2H_4OS	Thioacetic acid	g	-58.07[3]	[1881]	-45.54[3]	[1881]	74.86	[1881]	19.33	[1881]
			-42.6*	[1879]						
		l	-51.58	[2494]						
			-52.3	[2499]						
			-52.42	[2495]						
			-51.5	[1879]						
C_2H_5ClO	2-Chloroethanol	g					76.9*	[826a]	18.5*	[826a]
$C_2H_5Cl_3Si$	Ethyltrichlorosilane	l	-132	[99]						
C_2H_5FO	Monofluoroethanol	l	-66.4	[433]						
C_2H_5NO	Acetamide	g					68.92	[28]	15.57	[28]
$C_2H_5NO_2$	Nitroethane	l	-33.48	[1534]						
	Ethyl nitrite	g	-30.15	[761]			24.74	[1598]	23.71	[1598]
	Glycine (α-aminoacetic acid)	c	-128.4	[1599]	-90.3	[1599]				
		l							23.7	[53]
$C_2H_5NO_3$	Ethyl nitrate	g	-37.0	[1339]					25.3*	[826a]
		l	(-45.7)	[1339]	-10.5	[1339]	59.08[4]	[1339]		
			(-45.51)	[1353]						
			(-45.5)	[2389]						
$C_2H_6Cl_2Si$	Dimethyldichlorosilane	g	(-15.0)	[1086]			80.16[5]	[2370]	24.17[5]	[2370]
$C_2H_6N_2O_5$	Glycine nitrate	g	-173.6	[1044]						
C_2H_6OS	Dimethyl sulfoxide	g	-49.91[3]	[1878]	-27.65[3]	[1878]	73.20	[1878]	21.256	[1878]
			-35.1	[1111]						
			-34.57	[1879]						
		l	-30.3*	[323]	-18.9*	[323]				
			-47.21[3]	[1879]						
			-47.7[3]	[1110]						
$C_2H_6O_2S$	Dimethyl sulfone	g	-89.9	[929, 1879]			76	[929]		
		l	-81.4*	[323]	-64.7*	[323]				
		c	-108.3	[926, 1879]						
			-106.7	[1110]						
$C_2H_7NO_2$	Ammonium acetate	c	-146*	[2683]						
$C_2H_8N_2O_3$	Dimethylamine nitrate	c	-79.0	[1044]						
$C_2H_8N_2O_3$	Ethylamine nitrate	c	-86.9	[1044]						
$C_2H_8N_2O_4$	Ethanolamine nitrate	c	-137.6	[1044]						
	Ammonium oxalate	c	-267*	[2683]						

1. $t = 20°C$. 2. In *joules/mole* · °C. 3. From S_2 (g). 4. $S^\circ_{298} - S^\circ_0$. 5. $T = 300°K$.

	2	3	4		5		6		7	
$C_2H_{11}B_2N$	Dimethylaminodiborane	g	−36.22	[1637]			74.93	[1910]	28.14	[1910]
							72.25[1]	[1271]		
									21.77[2]	[2530]
C_2BrClF_2	Bromochlorodifluoroethylene	g					82.35[2]	[2530]	20.09	[1336]
$C_2Br_2ClF_3$	Dibromochlorotrifluoro-ethane	g	−145	[433]						
				2, IV						
$C_2HBrClF_3$	Bromochlorotrifluoroethane	g	−158	[433]						
$C_2H_{12}N_6O_4S$	Diguanidine sulfate	c	−287.0	[308]						
			−288.0	[2358]						
		d	−281.2	[2358]						
				3, I						
C_3H^+	Positive propenylidene ion	g	322	[1748]						
$C_3H_2^+$	Positive propenylene ion	g	363; 379	[1748]						
$C_3H_3^+$	Positive propenyl ion	g	281	[1748]						
			271	[2680]						
C_3H_4	Propyne	g	44.319[3]	[2604]	46.313	[2604]	59.30	[2604]	14.50	[2604]
	Propadiene (allene)	g	45.92[4]	[1707]	48.37	[1707]	58.30	[1707]	14.10	[1707]
$C_3H_4^+$	Positive propadiene ion	g	298	[1748]						
$C_3H_5^+$	Positive allyl ion	g	253	[1748]						
$C_3H_5^-$	Negative allyl ion	g	−34.0	[929]						
C_3H_6	Propene	g	4.879[5]	[1708]	14.99	[1708]	(63.80)	[1708]	(15.27)	[1708]
							(63.85)	[1264]	(15.36)	[1264]
									(15.18)	[1798]
	Cyclopropane	g	12.74[6]	[321]	24.94	[321]	56.81	[321]	13.2	[321]
$C_3H_6 \cdot 17H_2O$	Cyclopropane hydrate	g	30.23[7]	[980]						
C_3H_7	Propyl radical	g					69.32	[2195]		
C_3H_8	Propane	g	−24.82[8]	[2192]	−25.614	[2192]	64.51	[2192]	17.57	[2192]
C_3F_6	Hexafluoropropene (perfluoropropene)	g	−259	[433]						

C_3N	Radical	g	131	[1104]						
C_3N^+	Positive ion	g	461	[1104]						
C_3O_2	Carbon suboxide	g	-23.38	[1780]			62.12[10]	[1859]		
			-8.30[9]	[1618a]	-10.726	[1618a]	61.236	[1618a]	15.70	[1618a]

3, II

$C_3H_2N_2$	Malonic acid dinitrile	g					69.05	[1468]	17.32	[1468]
$C_3H_3F_5$	1, 1, 1, 2, 2-Pentafluoropropane	g					86.12	[736]	28.71	[730]
C_3H_3N	Vinyl cyanide	g	45.65	[321]						
	Acrylonitrile	g	44.04	[1469]	46.50	[1469]	65.47	[1469]	15.24	[1469]
$C_3H_4N_2$	Imidazole (glyoxaline, 1, 3-diazole)	g	30.6	[807]						
		c	14.6	[807]						
	Pyrazole (1, 2-diazole)	g	43.3	[807]						
		c	28.3	[807]						
$C_3H_4O_2$	Malonic acid	c	-212.7	[1360]						
			-212.97	[2685]						
C_3H_5N	Propionic acid nitrile	g					68.75	[2622, 2623]		
							67.81	[1133]	17.23	[1133]
							45.497[11]	[2622]	28.61[10]	[2622, 2623]
		l					45.25	[2623]		
$C_3H_5S^+$	Positive ion of methyl vinyl sulfide	g	226	[1748]						
C_3H_6Br	Isopropyl bromide	g	14.8*	[360]						
C_3H_6F	Isopropyl fluoride	g	-34.8*	[360]						
C_3H_6I	Isopropyl iodide	g	52.4*	[360]						
$C_3H_6I_2$	1, 2-Diiodopropane	g	8.6	[477]			94.6	[825]	24.1	[825]
	1, 3-Diiodopropane	g	10.6*	[825]			93.0*	[825]	24.7*	[825]
$C_3H_6N_6$	Melamine (2, 4, 6-triamino-1, 3, 5-triazine)	g	-17.13	[2448]	42.33	[2448]	74.10	[2448]	20.93	[2448]
C_3H_6O	Trimethylene oxide	g	-19.95	[2134]			63.40	[1360]		
	α-Propylene oxide	g	-22.17	[2070, 2382]	-6.17	[2070]	68.69; 68.53	[2070]	17.29	[2070]
			-22.02	[1360]	-3.60	[1360]	67.15	[1360]		
		l	-28.84	[2382]			46.91	[2070]	28.77	[2070]

1. $T = 271.60°K$. 2. $T = 350°K$. 3. $\Delta H_0^\circ = 46.017$ [321]. 4. $\Delta H_0^\circ = 47.70$ [321]. 5. $\Delta H_0^\circ = 8.468$ [321]. 6. $\Delta H_0^\circ = 16.836$ [321]. 7. ΔH_0° for the reaction $C_3H_6 \cdot 17H_2O(c) = C_3H_6(g) + 17H_2O(l)$. 8. $\Delta H_0^\circ = -18.482$ [321]. 9. $\Delta H_0^\circ = -8.722$ [1618a]. 10. $T = 230°K$. 11. $T = 300°K$.

1	2	3	4		5		6		7	
C_3H_6O	Propionaldehyde	g	−45.9	[2540]						
		l	−52.95	[2540]						
	Acetone	g	−51.72[1]	[1360]	−36.30	[1360]	70.49	[1360]	17.90	[2137]
		l	−59.34	[1360]	−37.19	[1360]	47.9	[1360]	30.22[2]	[1820]
			−59.20	[2137]	−37.02	[2137]	47.82	[2137]	30.1	[2137]
$C_3H_6O_2$	Propionic acid	l	−121.3	[1360, 2308]						
			−122.08	[328]						
	Methyl acetate	l	−106.2	[1360]						
	1, 3-Dioxolan	l	−79.5[1]; −80.7[3]	[1360]						
$C_3H_6O_3$	Dimethyl ester of carbonic acid	g	3179[4]	[1942]						
	Lactic acid (α-hydroxy-	l	−161.1	[1360]	−123.7	[1360]	45.9	[1360]		
	propionic acid)	c	−165.89	[1360]	−125.0	[1360]	34.0	[1360]		
C_3H_6S	Cyclothiabutane	g	16.32	[2331]	16.32	[2321, 2342]	68.14	[2331]	16.57	[2331, 2342]
			14.63	[1879]						
			−0.62[5,14]	[2331]						
		l	5.77	[1879, 2495]						
			6.04	[1879]						
	2-Methylcyclothiapropane	g	10.99	[1879]						
		l	2.74	[1879, 2495]						
$C_3H_6S^+$	Positive ion of propenthiol	g	217	[1748]						
C_3H_7Br	1-Bromopropane	g	−22.02	[855]						
			−19.82	[1080]						
	Isopropyl bromide	g	−23.190[6]	[478]			75.7	[478]	21.35	[2804]
			−23.60	[855]			79.76	[477]	20.76	[477]
			−22.71	[1080]						
			−26.915	[479]	−6.955	[479]	75.71	[479]	21.35	[479]
C_3H_7Cl	1-Chloropropane	g	−31.06	[196]	−12.47	[196]	76.17	[196]	20.66	[196]
			−30.94	[1080]						
	Isopropyl chloride	g	−34.56	[1546]	−14.92	[1546]	74.10	[1546]	20.93	[1546]
			−32.93	[1080]						
$C_3H_7Cl^+$	Positive ion of n-chloro-propane	g	217	[762]						
$C_3H_7Cl^+$	Positive ion of isopropyl chloride	g	214	[762]						
C_3H_7F	1-Fluoropropane	g	−66.1	[433]						

	2-Fluoropropane	g	-67.9	[433]						
C_3H_7I	1-Iodopropane	g	15.97	[197]	3.11	[197]	80.95	[197]	21.08	[197]
	2-Iodopropane	g	18.37	[197]	1.60	[197]	77.62	[197]	21.68	[197]
C_3H_7S	*n*-Thiopropyl radical	g	20*	[1867]						
	Thioisopropyl radical	g	18	[1867]						
C_3H_8O	*n*-Propanol	g	-61.92	[1942]	-39.32	[1942]	77.63	[1942]	20.82	[1942]
			-62.22[7]	[321]	-39.509	[321]	77.25	[321]		
			-61.84	[1365]	-39.21	[1365]	77.59	[1365]		
			-61.85	[1359, 1360]	-39.13	[1360]	76.19	[162, 1360]	0.15775[8]	[1934]
			-61.87	[2417]			77.1	[1360]		
		l	-73.37	[321]	-41.37	[321]			31.35	[321]
			-73.20	[1360]	-41.2	[1360]	46.1	[1360, 2113]		
			-72.31	[2417]						
			-72.79	[961]						
	Isopropanol	g	-65.56	[321]	-42.21	[321]	75.1	[321]	18.4	[321]
			-65.42	[1360]	-41.71	[1360]	73.92	[1360]		
			-65.28	[1360]			73.71	[1360]		
			-64.22[9]	[2572]	-41.75[1]	[2572]	73.2	[3194]		
			-65.07	[2417]			74.07	[1367]	21.21	[1367]
		l	-76.18	[1360, 2120]	-43.26	[3160]	43.0	[3160]		
			-76.04	[2417]			43.16	[733]	36.91	[733]
			-75.77	[2135]					39.4	[321]
	Methyl ethyl ether	g	-51.73	[2150]						
$C_3H_8O_2$	Dimethoxymethane	g					80.24	[1141]		
		l					58.319	[1141]	38.67[9]	[1141]
	1, 2-Propanediol	l	-118.9[10]	[1360]						
$C_3H_9O_3$	Glycerol	l	-159.80	[1360, 2124]	-114.01	[1360]	48.87	[707, 1360]	35.9	[321]
C_3H_8S	1-Propanethiol	g	-31.61[11,14]	[2342]	-9.02[14]	[1342]	80.40	[2138, 2342]	22.65	[2138, 2342]
			-31.46[12,14]	[2138]	-8.87[14]	[2138]				
			-16.19	[1879]						
		l	-23.84	[1879]						
	2-Propanethiol	g	-33.46[14]	[2138]	-10.0[14]	[2138]	77.51	[2138]	22.94	[3273]
			-18.19	[1879]						
		l	-25.27	[1879]						
	2-Thiabutane (methyl ethyl sulfide)	g	-29.64[13,14]	[2342]	-6.81[14]	[2342]	79.62	[2333, 2342]	22.73	[2342]
			-14.22	[1879]					22.72	[2333]

1. $\Delta H_0^\circ = -47.440$ [321]. 2. $T = 300°K$. 3. $t = 20°C$. 4. ΔH°_{comb} *(cal/gram)*. 5. $\Delta H_0^\circ = 3.91$ [2331]. 6. $\Delta H_0^\circ = -22.009$ [478]. 7. $\Delta H_0^\circ = -56.644$ [321]. 8. *BtU/(eV·°K)* or BET/eq·vol.–°K. 9. $T = 300°K$. 10. $t = 17°C$. 11. $\Delta H_0^\circ = -26.32$ (from $S_2(g)$) [2342]. 12. $\Delta H_0^\circ = -26.1714$ [2138]. 13. $\Delta H_0^\circ = 24.30$ (from $S_2(g)$) [2342]. 14. From $S_2(g)$.

1	2	3	4	5	6	7
C_3H_8S	2-Thiabutane (methyl ethyl sulfide)	l	−21.86 [1879]			
$C_3H_8S_2$	1,3-Propanedithiol	g	−7.03 [1917]			
		l	−18.90 [1917]			
C_3H_9Al	Trimethylaluminium	l	−36.1 [1987]		50.05 [1844]	37.19 [1844]
C_3H_9B	Trimethylboron	g	−29.96 [1639]			
		l	−34.79 [1639]			
			−31.4 [323]			
C_3H_9N	Trimethylamine	g			68.98 [2356]	21.73 [2356]
		l	10.90 [752]	45.96 [752]	49.82 [752]	32.0 [752]
C_3H_9P	Trimethylphosphorus	l	−30.1 [1813]			
C_3H_9Si	Trimethylsilicon		−22* [1504]			
$C_3Cl_2F_6$	1,3-Dichlorohexafluoropropane	g			97.10 [736]	37.28 [736]

3, III

1	2	3	4	5	6	7
C_3H_5NS	Ethyl isothiocyanate	g	22* [2365]			
$C_3H_5O_2S$	Allyl sulfone radical	g	−44.0* [1867]			
$C_3H_6N_2O_4$	1,1-Dinitropropane	l	−40.78 [1534]			
	1,3-Dinitropropane	l	−53.51 [1534]			
	2,2-Dinitropropane	c	−44.87 [1534]			
$C_3H_7NO_2$	1-Nitropropane	l	−40.05 [1534]			
	2-Nitropropane	l	−43.78 [1534]			
	L-Alanine	c	−134.5 [2410]	−88.5 [2410]	30.88 [1598]	
$C_3H_7N_3S$	Acetaldehyde thiosemicarbazone	c	15.0[1] [1879]			
$C_3H_7O_2S$	Isopropyl sulfone radical	g	−74.7 [1867]			
$C_3H_8O_2S$	Methyl ethyl sulfone	g	−98.7 [928, 929, 1879]			
		l	−117.0 [926, 1879]			
			2.4[2] [928]			
			15.9[3] [928]			
C_3H_9BrSn	Trimethylbromotin	l	−52.76 [2132]			
			−43.8 [1081]			
C_3H_9ISn	Trimethyliodotin	l	−39.66 [2132]			
			−30.7 [1081]			

$C_3H_{10}N_2O_3$	Trimethylamine nitrate	c	71.1	[1212]						
$C_3H_{16}B_3N$	Trimethylaminotriborane	c					54.60	[1803]	51.98	[1803]

3, IV

$C_3H_6Cl_3GaO$	Complex compound of acetone with $GaCl_3$	c	−15.3	[1386]						

4, I

C_4H_2	Diacetylene (butadiyne)	g					59.76	[1100]	17.60	[1100]
C_3H_6	1, 2-Butadiene	g	38.77[4]	[2244]	47.43	[2244]	70.03	[2244]	19.15	[2244]
	1, 3-Butadiene (divinyl)	g	26.33[5]	[2244]	36.01	[2244]	66.62	[2244]	19.01	[2244]
							66.63	[496]	19.27	[496]
		l	21.21	[2244]						
	Butyne-1 (ethylacetylene)	g	39.48[6]	[2244]	48.30	[2244]	69.51	[2244]	19.46	[2244]
	Butyne-2 (dimethylacetylene)	g	34.97[7]	[2244]	44.32	[2244]	67.71	[2244]	18.36	[2244]
C_4H_8	Butene-1 (*a*-butylene)	g	−0.03[8]	[2244]	17.09	[2244]	73.04	[2244]	20.47	[2244]
	trans-Butene-2	g	−2.67[9]	[2244]	15.05	[2244]	70.86	[2244]	20.99	[2244]
	cis-Butene-2	g	−1.67[10]	[2244]	15.74	[2244]	71.90	[2244]	18.86	[2244]
	2-Methylpropene (isobutene)	g	−4.04[11]	[2244]	13.88	[2244]	70.17	[2244]	21.30	[2244]
	Cyclobutane	g	6.38[12]	[321]	26.31	[321]	63.43	[321]	17.26	[321]
		l	0.715	[1663]			67.55	[2195]		
C_4H_9	Isobutyl radical	g					70.8	[39, 94]		
	tert-Butyl radical	g	6.7	[2525]						
$C_4H_9^+$	Positive isobutyl ion	g	168	[1246]						
C_4H_{10}	Butane	g	−30.15	[321, 1685]	−4.10	[321, 1685]	74.12	[321, 1685]		
			−23.67[13]	[2244]					23.29	[2244]
		l	−35.21	[2244]						
			−25.30[13]	[321]						
	2-Methylpropane (isobutane)	g	−32.15[14]	[2244]	−5.00	[2244]	70.42	[2244]	23.14	[2244]
		l	−37.87	[2244]						
C_4F_9	Perfluorocyclobutane	g	−352	[433]					28.95[15]	[1933]
			−350	[279]						

1. $T = 293.15\,°K$. 2. ΔH_f. 3. ΔH_{vap}. 4. $\Delta H_0^\circ = 42.00$ [2244]. 5. $\Delta H_0^\circ = 29.74$ [2244]. 6. $\Delta H_0^\circ = 42.74$ [2244]. 7. $\Delta H_0^\circ = 38.09$ [2244]. 8. $\Delta H_0^\circ = 4.96$ [2244]. 9. $\Delta H_0^\circ = 2.24$ [2244]. 10. $\Delta H_0^\circ = 3.48$ [2244]. 11. $\Delta H_0^\circ = 0.98$ [2244]. 12. $\Delta H_0^\circ = 12.18$ [321]. 13. ΔH_0°. 14. $\Delta H_0^\circ = -25.30$ [2244]. 15. $T = 360\,°K$.

1	2	3	4		5		6		7	
C_4N	Free radical	g	530	[1104]						
C_4N_2	Dicyanoacetylene	l	119.6; 126.5	[738]						
	Carbon subnitride (dinitrile of acetylenedicarboxylic acid)	g					64.102	[2038]	20.528	[2038]
	Tetracarbon dinitride	g	127.5[1]	[1618a]	122.098	[1618a]	69.314	[1618a]	20.528	[1618a]
					4, II					
$C_4H_2O_3$	Maleic acid anhydride	c	−112.23	[1360]						
			−112.43	[2685]						
$C_4H_4N_2$	Pyrazine (1, 4-diazine)	g	46.86	[2541]						
		l	33.41	[2541]						
	Pyridazine (1, 2-diazine)	g	66.53	[2541]						
		l	53.75	[2541]						
	Pyrimidine (1, 2-diazine)	g	46.99	[2541]						
		l	35.04	[2541]						
$C_4H_4N_2$	Succinic acid dinitrile	g					79.04	[2714]		
		c					45.79	[2714]	34.80	[2714]
C_4H_4O	Furane	g	−8.293	[1360]	0.208	[1360]	63.86	[1360]		
			−5.156[1]	[321]						
		l	−14.903	[1360]	0.050	[1360]	42.22	[1360]		
$C_4H_4O_3$	Succinic acid anhydride	c	−143.2	[1360]						
$C_4H_4O_4$	Maleic acid	c	−188.28	[1360]	−150.2	[1360]	38.1	[1360]	32.36	[2322]
			−188.95	[2685]						
					−150.2	[1360]	39.7	[1360]		
	Fumaric acid	c	−193.83	[1360]	−156.21	[2322]	33.9	[2322]		
			−193.84	[2685]						
C_4H_4S	Thiophene	g	27.49	[1558]	34.78	[1558]	66.65	[1558]	17.42	[1558]
			27.82	[1879]						
			27.5	[1246]						
			15.02[2,5]	[321]						
		l	12.07[3,5]	[1558]	20.56[5]; 28.80[5]	[1558]	43.30	[1558]		
			19.20	[1246]						
			19.52	[1879]						
			19.35	[2495]						

C_4H_5N	*trans*-Crotonic acid nitrile	g	35.77[4]	[2719]	46.22	[2719]	71.31	[2719]	19.62	[2719]
C_4H_6O	Divinyl ether	g	-3.03	[2151]						
	Crotonaldehyde	l	-34.45	[1360, 2539]						
$C_4H_6O_2$	2, 3-Butanedione (diacetyl)	l	-87.5	[1360]						
	Crotonic acid	c	-83	[1360]						
$C_4H_6O_3$	Acetic acid anhydride	l	-149.20	[1360]						
			-117.3	[1748]						
$C_4H_6O_4$	Diacetyl peroxide	l	-161.0	[1360]						
	Succinic acid	c	-224.77	[1360]	-178.5	[1360]	42.0	[1360]		
			-224.92	[1586]	-178.68	[1586]			35.8	[1586]
			-224.87	[2685]						
$C_4H_6O_5$	*L*-Malic acid	c	-263.78	[2685]						
	DL-Malic acid	c	-264.27	[2685]						
$C_4H_6O_6$	*D*-Tartaric acid	c	-373.8	[1360]						
	L-Tartaric acid	c	-368.7	[1360]						
	meso-Tartaric acid	c	-369.3	[1360]						
C_4H_7N	Propyl cyanide	g					77.42	[72]	22.94	[72]
C_4H_7NO	*α*-Pyrrolidone	c	-68.21	[321]	-29.64	[321]	32.7	[321]		
$C_4H_8Br_2$	1, 2-Dibromobutane	g	-24.54	[855]						
C_4H_8O	2-Methylpropanal	g	-52.1	[2540]						
		l	-59.81	[2540]						
C_4H_8O	Vinyl ethyl ether	g	-33.50	[2151]						
	Tetrahydrofurane	g	-43.5	[1360]						
			-44.03	[2134]						
		l	-51.1	[1360]						

1. $\Delta H_0^\circ = 126.341$ [1618a]. 2. $\Delta H_0^{\circ 5}$. 3. $\Delta H_0^\circ = 15.02^5$ [1558]. 4. $\Delta H_0^\circ = 39.04$ [2719]. 5. From S_2(g).

1	2	3	4		5		6		7	
C_4H_8O	Butanone-2 (methyl ethyl ketone)	g	-56.97	[2383]	-34.92	[2383]	80.81	[2383]	24.59	[2383]
			-58.37[1]	[2058]	-36.82	[2058]	82.51; 91.61	[2058]	24.56; 28.91	[2058]
							81.7*	[826a]	23.3*	[826a]
		l	-66.60	[2429]	-37.71	[2429]	57.7	[2429]	38.5	[2429]
		g	-66.68	[1360]	-37.73	[1360]	57.71	[1360]		
			-65.31	[2383]			57.08	[2383]	37.98	[2383]
	Butyraldehyde	g	-51.04	[321]	71.0*	[826a]	24.0*	[826]		
		l	-57.2	[1360]	-28.6	[1360]	59.0	[1360, 2114]		
			-58.94	[2114]	-30.38	[2114]				
			-57.06	[2539]						
	Butylene oxide	l	-39.7[2]	[1360]						
$C_4H_8O_2$	Methyl propionate	l	-111.6	[1360]						
	1, 3-Dioxane (1, 3-diethylene dioxide)	g	-81.5	[2417]						
		l	-90.01	[2417]						
			-92.1[3]; -94.5	[1360]						
			-95.08	[289]						
	1, 4-Dioxane (1, 4-diethylene dioxide)	g	-75.95	[2412]						
			-85.47	[289]						
		l	-95.5	[1360]	-55.1	[1360]	47.0	[1360, 1608]		
			-95.08	[289]	-55.63	[1608]			36.5	[1608]
			-84.5	[2417]						
	Butyric acid	l	-127.2	[1360]	-89.9	[1360]	54.1	[1360, 2113]		
			-128.08	[321]	-90.75	[321]			42.1	[321]
			-127.61	[328]						
	Ethyl acetate	g	-103.44	[73]	-78.86	[73]	90.11	[73]	29.0*	[73]
			-103.4	[1360]	-76.8	[1360]	90.1	[1360]		
							90.0*	[826a]	24.5*[4]	[826a]
		l	-106.2; -113.9; -111.6	[1360]	-71.2	[1360]	62.0	[1360]		
			-112.57	[321]	-77.6	[321]			40.4	[321]
$C_4H_8O_4$	Dimer of acetic acid	g	-223.0	[1360]	-183.7	[1360]	(96.7)	[1360]		
			-224.26[5]	[2634]			(96.44)	[2634]	(34.99)	[2634]
C_4H_8S	Cyclothipentane	g	-23.5[6]	[1553]	1.4	[1553]	73.94	[1553]	21.72	[1553]
			-7.57; -8.17	[1879]						
		l	-17.39	[1879, 2495]						
			-17.40	[1879]						

	2, 2-Dimethylcyclothia-	g	2.73	[1879]						
	propane	l	−5.82	[1879, 2495]						
	trans-2, 3-Dimethylcyclothia-	g	0.89	[1879]						
	propane	l	−7.06	[1879, 2495]						
	cis-2, 3-Dimethylcyclothia-	g	2.73	[1879]						
	propane	l	−5.82	[1879, 2495]						
	Tetrahydrothiophene	g	−8.02	[1082]						
		l	−17.40	[1082]						
C_4H_9Br	Butyl bromide	g	−29.3	[26]	−3.4	[26]	88.57	[26]	26.6	[26]
			−25.17	[856]						
		l	−34.47	[856]						
	2-Bromobutane	g	−28.69	[855]						
C_4H_9Cl	Butyl chloride	g	−36.95	[26]	−11.0	[26]	85.78	[26]	26.5	[26]
							84.8*	[826a]	25.9*	[826a]
	Isobutyl chloride	g	−14.47	[1745]						
	tert-Monochlorobutane	g	−42.99	[1546]	−14.52	[1546]	77.04	[1546]	27.30	[1546]
$C_4H_9Cl^+$	Positive ion of *n*-monochlorobutane	g	205	[762]						
	Positive ion of *iso*-monochlorobutane	g	204	[762]						
	Positive ion of *sec*-monochlorobutane	g	203	[762]						
	Positive ion of *tert*-monochlorobutane	g	195	[762]						
C_4H_9I	2-Iodobutane (*d*-isomer)	g	−23.42	[197]	3.25	[197]	87.44	[197]	26.84	[197]
	Butyl iodide	g	−21.25	[26]	4.6	[26]	90.56	[26]	26.8	[26]
	tert-Monoiodobutane	g	−17.2	[826]						
C_4H_9Li	Butyllithium	l	−31.4	[1244]						
			−32.0	[327]						
C_4H_9N	Pyrrolidine	g	−0.82	[1519]	27.45	[1519]	74.01	[1519]	19.66	[1519]
C_4H_9O	*tert*-Butoxy radical	g	−22	[759a]						
C_5H_9S	Butyl sulfide (free radical)	g	15*	[1867]						
$C_4H_{10}Hg$	Diethylmercury	l	−9.9	[1485]						
$C_4H_{10}N_2$	Piperazine	c	−10.90	[804]						
	Diethylene diamine	c	−3.2	[2125]	57.4	[2125]	20.5	[2125]		

1. $\Delta H_0^\circ = -53.21$ [2058]. 2. $t = 17°C$. 3. $t = 20°C$. 4. $T = 300°K$. 5. $\Delta H_0^\circ = -217.74$ [2634]; -216.30 [321]. 6. From S_2 (g).

1	2	3	4		5		6		7	
$C_4H_{10}O$	*n*-Butanol	g	−66.92	[1360]	−38.12	[1360]	89.42	[1360]		
			−67.54[1]	[321]	−39.09	[321]	84.7*, 86.1*	[826a]	26.5*; 27.0*	[826a]
			−67.89	[162]	−39.08	[162]				
			−66.1	[2393]	−37.37	[1365]	86.90	[1365]	26.29	[1365]
			−65.81	[1430]			86.8	[1052]		
			−66.92	[1359]			89.42	[162]		
		l	−79.54	[1360]	−40.33	[1360]	54.5	[321, 1360, 2113]		
			−79.34	[321]	−40.13	[321]			43.8	[321]
			−78.09	[1430]			53.95	[1052]	42.31	[1052]
			−79.55	[2539]						
			−79.54	[1359]						
			−78.49	[2393]						
			−77.87	[961]						
	Isobutanol-1	g	−67.9	[1360, 2393]			83.5*	[826a]	26.6*	[826a]
		l	−80.00	[1360, 2393]						
			−81.90	[961]						
	Butanol-2	g	−69.84	[835]	−46.94	[835]	85.81	[835]	27.08	[835]
			−70.1	[1360, 2393]						
		l	−81.88	[1360, 2393]						
	Isobutanol-2	g	−74.9	[1360, 2393]	−42.3	[1360]	76.8	[1360]		
			−77.59	[321]						
		l	−88.69	[321]	−46.74	[321]	45.3	[321, 1360, 2113]	53.8	[321]
			−85.0	[2512a]	−44.1	[2512a]				
			−85.87	[1360, 2393]	−43.92	[1360]				
	2-Methylpropanol-2	g	−74.72	[841]	−67.48	[841]	77.98	[841]	27.10	[841]
		l					40.84	[2069]	34.92	[2069]
	Diethyl ether	g	−59.70	[289]	−28.09	[289]	84.4*	[289]		
			−60.28	[2151]			80.816	[765]	26.758	[765]
							83.7*	[826a]	25.9*	[826a]
		l	−65.30	[321]	−27.88	[321]	60.5	[321]	40.8	[321]
	Methyl propyl ether	g	−56.82	[2150]						
	Methyl isopropyl ether	g	−60.24	[2150]						
$C_4H_{10}O_2$	Butanediol-1, 2	g					93.3*	[826a]	30.4*	[826a]
		l	−124.4[2]	[1360]						
	Butanediol-1, 3	g					93.3*	[826a]	30.4*	[826a]

		l	-122.3[2]	[1360]						
	Butanediol-2, 3	g					88.2*	[826a]	31.0*	[826a]
		l	-128.7	[1360]						
	Isobutanediol-1, 2	l	-128.2[2]	[1360]						
	Diethyl peroxide	g	-45.6	[759a]			91.6*; 94.3*	[826a]	29.0*; 31.7*	[826a]
		l	-55.6	[1360]						
			-53.4	[759a]						
	tert-Butyl hydroperoxide	l	-63.8	[1360]						
$C_4H_{10}O_3$	Diethylene glycol	g					105.4*	[826a]	32.3*	[826a]
		l	-149.3[2]	[1360]						
$C_4H_{10}O_3$	Erythritol	c	-217.61	[1360]	-152.71	[1360]	39.9	[1360]		
$C_4H_{10}S$	Butanethiol-1	g	-36.44[3,10]	[1663a, 2342]	-6.90[10]	[2342]	89.68	[2342]	28.24	[1663a, 2334, 2342]
			-36.29[4,10]	[2334]	-6.75[10]	[2334]	89.69	[2334]		
			-21.02	[1879]	-6.88	[1663a]	89.62	[1663a]		
		l	-29.76	[1879]						
	Butanethiol-2	g	-23.12	[1879]	-1.32	[1841]	87.67	[1841]		
		l	-38.54[10]	[1842]	-0.02	[1841]	64.87	[1841]	40.92	[1841]
		l	-31.25	[1879]						
	2-Methylpropanethiol-1	g	-38.48[5,10]	[2345]	-8.06[10]	[2345]	86.73	[2345]	28.28	[2345]
			-38.63[10]	[1842]						
			-23.21	[1879]						
		l	-31.51	[1879]						
	2-Methylpropanethiol-2	g	-41.79[7,10]	[1847]	-9.60[10]	[1847]	80.79	[1847]	28.91	[1847]
			-26.14	[1879]						
		l	-33.53	[1879]						
	3-Methyl-2-thiabutane (methyl isopropyl sulfide)	g	-21.58	[1879]	-9.26	[1840]	85.87	[1840]	28.70	[1840]
			-36.83[6,10]	[2334]						
		l	-29.76	[1879]	2.09	[1840]	62.88	[1840]	41.20	[1840]
	2-Thiapentane (methyl propyl sulfide)	g	-34.93[8,10]	[2342]	-5.14[10]	[2342]	88.84	[2334, 2342]	28.05	[2334, 2342]
			-34.78;[10]	[2334]	-4.99[10]	[2334]				
			-19.51	[1879]						
		l	-28.18	[1889]						
	3-Thiapentane (diethyl sulfide)	g	-35.34[9,10]	[2342]	-5.29[10]	[2342]	87.96	[2330, 2342]	27.97	[2330, 2342]

1. $\Delta H_0^\circ = -60.69$ [321]. 2. $t = 17°C$. 3. $\Delta H_0^\circ = -29.88$ (from S_2 (g)) [1663a]; -29.99 (from S_2 (g)) [2342]. 4. $\Delta H_0^\circ = -29.84$ (from S_2 (g)) [2334]. 5. $\Delta H_0^\circ = -31.53$ (from S_2 (g)) [2345]. 6. $\Delta H_0^\circ = -30.06$ (from S_2 (g)) [2334]. 7. $\Delta H_0^\circ = -34.77$ (from S_2 (g)) [1847]. 8. $\Delta H_0^\circ = -28.35$ (from S_2 (g)) [2334, 2342]. 9. $\Delta H_0^\circ = -28.61$ (from S_2 (g)) [2342]. 10. From S_2 (g).

1	2	3	4		5		6		7	
$C_4H_{10}S$	3-Thiapentane (diethyl sulfide)	g	–30.3[7]	[1872]	–5.30[7]	[2330]				
			–19.92	[1879]						
		l	–41.1[7]	[1872]						
			–28.49	[1879]						
$C_4H_{10}S_2$	3,4-Dithiahexane (diethyl disulfide	g	–48.62[1,7]	[2342]	–13.76[7]	[2342]	99.07	[2342]	33.78	[2342]
			–48.26[2,7]	[1552]	–13.40[7]	[1552, 2332]	98.99	[2332]	34.24	[2332]
			–47.05[7]	[1879]						
			–20.51	[1883]			119.8	[1883]		
			–20.0	[1246]						
		l	–59.76[7]	[1879]						
			–32.5	[1246]						
$C_4H_{11}Al$	Diethyl aluminium hydride	l	–73.5	[607]						
$C_4H_{12}Ge$	Tetramethylgermanium	g					91.99	[1808]	31.98	[1808]
$C_4H_{12}Pb$	Tetramethyllead	g	23.2	[1808]	35.6	[1808]	99.86	[1808]	34.42	[1808]
			32.6	[1336]	64.7	[1336]	100.5	[1336]		
		l	23.5	[1336]	62.8	[1336]	76.5	[1336]		
$C_4H_{12}Si$	Tetramethylsilane	g	–68.50	[1608a]	–35.456	[1618a]	86.30	[1618a]	31.12	[1618a]
							83.23[3]	[2431]	31.64[3]	[2431]
							85.79	[2346]	34.39	[2346]
$C_4H_{12}Sn$	Tetramethyltin	g	–13.6	[1808]	19.0	[1808]	96.11	[1808]	33.34	[1808]
			–11.0	[49]						
		l	–19.2	[49]						
			–21.4*	[1808]						
			–12.5	[1081]						
$C_4Ce_2O_8 \cdot 9H_2O$	Cerium oxalate (hydrate)	c	–1550.93	[2424]	–1349.08	[2424]	155	[2424]		
					–1351*	[1976]				

4.III

1	2	3	4		5		6		7	
$C_4H_2F_2N_2$	*trans*-1,2-Difluorodiazine	g					26.70[4]	[2258]	6.029[5]	[2258]
$C_4H_6BaO_4$	Barium acetate	c					73*	[683]		
$C_4H_6BeO_4$	Beryllium acetate	c	–302*	[2683]						
$C_4H_6CaO_4$	Calcium acetate	c			–309.7*	[323]	47.3*	[323]		
							61.5*	[683]		
$C_4H_6CdO_4$	Cadmium acetate	c	–231*	[1984]						
			–245*	[696]						
$C_4H_6CoO_4$	Cobalt acetate	c	–236*	[2683]						

$C_4H_6CuO_4$	Cupric acetate	c					61*	[683]		
$C_4H_6FeO_4$	Ferrous acetate	c	–243	[2683]						
$C_4H_6HgO_4$	Mercuric acetate	c			–155.5	[1617]				
$C_4H_6Hg_2O_4$	Mercurous acetate	c			–162.78*	[177]				
$C_4H_6MgO_4$	Magnesium acetate	c	–336*	[1984]	–154.5	[323]				
			–324*	[2683]						
$C_4H_6MnO_4$	Manganese acetate	c					–222.6	[323]	48.3*	[323]
$C_4H_6NiO_4$	Nicel acetate	c	–235*	[2683]						
$C_4H_6O_2S$	Butadiene sulfone	g	–61.1	[1876]						
			–61.1*	[1879]						
		c	–76.1	[1876, 1879]						
$C_4H_6O_4Pb$	Lead acetate	c					40*	[323]		
$C_4H_6O_4Pd$	Palladium acetate	c	–202*	[2683]						
$C_4H_6O_4Ra$	Radium acetate	c	–358*	[2683]						
$C_4H_6O_4Sn$	Stannous acetate	c	–243*	[2683]						
			–235*	[696]						
$C_4H_6O_4Ti$	Titanium acetate	c	–285*	[2683]						
C_4H_7NO	Dimethylformamide	l					28.5	[119]	37.45	[119]
$C_4H_8O_2S$	Methyl allyl sulfone	g	–73.5	[929, 1879]						
		l	–92.3	[926, 1879]						
$C_4H_9NO_2$	1-Nitrobutane	l	–46.03	[1534]						
	2-Nitrobutane	l	–49.61	[1534]						
$C_4H_9N_3O_2$	Creatine (N-methyl-guanidine acetic acid, guanidine methylglycine)	c	–128.42	[321]	–63.35	[321]	45.3	[321]		
$C_4H_9N_3S$	Acetone thiosemicarbazone	c	4.6[6]	[1879]						
$C_4H_9O_2S$	*n*-Butyl sulfone radical	g	–80.5*	[1867]						
	tert-Butyl sulfone (free radical)	g	–82.8*	[1867]						
$C_4H_{10}OS$	Diethyl sulfide oxide	g	–49.0	[1877, 1879]						
		l	–63.9	[1877, 1879]						
$C_4H_{10}O_2S$	Diethyl sulfone	g	–103.8	[1874]						
		c	–124.0	[1874]						
	Methyl isopropyl sulfone	g	–104.2	[929, 1879]						
		l	–121.3	[929, 1879]						

1. $\Delta H_0^\circ = -42.17^7$ [2342]. 2. $\Delta H_0^\circ = -41.81^7$ [1552]. 3. $t = 0\ ^\circ C$. 4. $T = 300\ ^\circ K$; S/R. 5. $T = 300\ ^\circ K$; C_p/R. 6. $T = 293.15\ ^\circ K$. 7. From $S_2(g)$.

1	2	3	4		5		6		7	
$C_4H_{12}BrN$	Tetramethylammonium bromide						47.99	[958]	38.64	[958]
$C_4H_{12}ClN$	Tetramethylammonium chloride						45.58	[958]	37.51	[958]
$C_4H_{13}Cl_2N$	Tetramethylammonium chloride hydrochloride						60.63	[959]	49.07	[959]
				4, IV						
$C_4H_8N_2NiO_4$	*bis*-Glycine nickel (II)	c			−290.57	[416]				
				5, I						
C_5H_8	Pentadiene-1, 2	g	34,80[1]	[2244]	50.29	[2244]	79.7	[2244]	25.2	[2244]
			33.61	[321]	49.10	[321]				
	trans-Pentadiene-1,3 (*trans*-piperylene)	g	18.60[2]	[2244]	35.07	[2244]	76.4	[2244]	24.7	[2244]
			18.11	[321]	34.58	[321]				
	cis-Pentadiene-1,3 (*cis*-piperylene)	g	18.70[3]	[2244]	34.88	[2244]	77.5	[2244]	22.6	[2244]
			19.77	[321]	35.92	[321]				
	Pentadiene-1,4	g	25.20[4]	[2244]	40.69	[2244]	79.7	[2244]	25.1	[2244]
			25.41	[321]	40.90	[321]				
	Pentadiene-2,3	g	33.10[5]	[2244]	49.22	[2244]	77.6	[2244]	24.2	[2244]
			31.79	[321]	47.91	[321]				
	2-Methylbutadiene-1,3 (isoprene)	g	18.10[6]	[2244]	34.87	[2244]	75.44	[2244]	25.0	[2244]
			18.09	[321]	34.85	[321]				
		l	11.80	[2244]						
	3-Methylbutadiene-1,2	g	31.00[7]	[2244]	47.47	[2244]	76.4	[2244]	25.2	[2244]
	Cyclopentene	g	7.87[8]	[2244]	26.48	[2244]	69.23	[2244]	17.95	[1171, 2244]
			1.16	[1171]	19.77	[1171]	59.23	[1171]		
		l	−5.55	[1171]	19.36	[1171]			29.24	[1171]
			1.16	[2244]			48.10	[2244]		
	Pentyne-1	g	34.50[9]	[2244]	50.16	[2244]	78.82	[2244]	25.18	[2244]
							79.10	[2604]	25.50	[2604]
	Pentyne-2	g	30.80[10]	[2244]	46.41	[2244]	79.30	[2244]	23.59	[2244]
	3-Methylbutyne-1	g	32.60[11]	[2244]	49.12	[2244]	76.23	[2244]	25.02	[2244]
	Spiropentene	g	44.23[12]	[321]	63.37	[321]	67.46	[321]	21.06	[321]
		l	37.63	[2328]	62.556	[2328]	46.29	[2328]	32.15	[2328]
C_5H_{10}	Pentene-1	g	−5.00[13]	[2244]	18.96	[2244]	82.65	[2244]	26.19	[2244]

		l					63.75	[2556]	37.12	[2556]
	trans-Pentene-2	g	−7.59[14]	[2244]	16.76	[2244]	81.36	[2244]	25.92	[2244]
		l	−14.86	[2556]	15.22	[2556]	61.31	[2556]	37.52	[2556]
	cis-Pentene-2	g	−6.71[15]	[1709, 2244]	17.17	[1709, 2244]	82.76	[1709, 2244]	24.32	[1709, 2244]
		l	−14.86	[2556]	15.43	[2556]	61.81	[2556]	36.26	[2556]
	2-Methylbutene-1	g	−8.68[16]	[2244]	15.51	[2244]	81.73	[2244]	26.69]	[2244]
					15.68	[1845]	81.15	[1845]	26.28	[1845]
	3-Methylbutene-1	g	−6.92[17]	[2244]	17.87	[2244]	79.70	[2244]	28.35	[2244]
		l	−15.20	[2556]	15.11	[2556]	60.54	[2556]	37.30	[2556]
	2-Methylbutene-2	g	−10.17[18]	[2244]	14.26	[2244]	80.92	[2244]	25.10	[2244]
		l					60.0	[2556]	35.52	[2556]
	Cycloptentane	g	−18.46[19]	[1710, 2244]	9.23	[1710, 2244]	70.00	[1710, 2244]	19.82	[1710, 2244]
							65.13	[1195, 2485]	21.46	[1195, 2485]
		l	−25.30	[2244]	8.70	[2244]	48.82	[2244]	30.80	[2244]
C_5H_{12}	*n*-Pentane	g	−35.00	[321]	−2.00	[321]	83.40	[321]	28.73	[321]
			−27.23[20]	[2244]						
		l	−41.36	[2244]	−2.25	[2244]	62.92	[2244]		
	2-Methylbutane (isopentane)	g	−36.92[21]	[2244]	−3.50	[2244]	82.12	[2244]	28.39	[2244]
		l	−42.85	[2244]	−3.59	[2244]	62.52	[2244]		
							62.24	[2345a]		
	2.2-Dimethylpropane	g	−39.67[22]	[2244]	−3.64	[2244]	73.23	[2244]	29.07	[2244]
	(neopentane)	l	−44.98[23]	[2244]	−3.37	[2244]	54.5	[2244]		
C_5D_{10}	Perdeuterocyclopentane	g					69.95	[1195, 2485]	28.48	[1195, 2485]

5, II

C_5HN_3	Tricyanoethylene	g	123.9	[876]
		l	108.2	[876]
		c	105.0	[876]
$C_5H_4O_2$	Furfural	l	−46.4	[1360]

1. $\Delta H_0^\circ = 39.32$ [2244]. 2. $\Delta H_0^\circ = 23.39$ [2244]. 3. $\Delta H_0^\circ = 23.73$ [2244]. 4. $\Delta H_0^\circ = 29.63$ [2244]. 5. $\Delta H_0^\circ = 37.77$ [2244]. 6. $\Delta H_0^\circ = 22.98$ [2244]. 7. $\Delta H_0^\circ = 35.64$ [2244]. 8. $\Delta H_0^\circ = 13.76$ [2244]. 9. $\Delta H_0^\circ = 38.90$ [2244]. 10. $\Delta H_0^\circ = 35.48$ [2244]. 11. $\Delta H_0^\circ = 37.37$ [2244]. 12. $\Delta H_0^\circ = 49.842$ [321]. 13. $\Delta H_0^\circ = -1.13$ [2244]. 14. $\Delta H_0^\circ = -1.25$ [2244]. 15. $\Delta H_0^\circ = -0.18$ [2244]. 16. $\Delta H_0^\circ = -2.30$ [2244]. 17. $\Delta H_0^\circ = -0.68$ [2244]. 18. $\Delta H_0^\circ = -3.63$ [2244]. 19. $\Delta H_0^\circ = -10.68$ [2244]. 20. ΔH_0°. 21. $\Delta H_0^\circ = -28.81$ [2244]. 22. $\Delta H_0^\circ = -31.30$ [2244]. 23. Under saturation pressure.

1	2	3	4		5		6		7	
$C_5H_4O_3$	Furanecarboxylic acid	l	−119.1	[1360]						
C_5H_5N	Pyridine	g	33.5	[1834]	45.47	[1834]	67.59	[1834]	18.67	[1834]
			33.63	[1054]						
			37.52[1]	[321]						
		l	23.89	[1554]	42.33	[1834]	42.52	[1834]	31.72	[1834]
C_5H_6O	2-Methylfurane (silvane)	l					51.12	[934]	34.37	[934]
$C_5H_6O_2$	Furyl alcohol	l	−66.05	[1360]	−36.88	[1360]	51.6	[1360, 2114]		
			−66.03	[2114]	−36.86	[2114]				
$C_5H_6O_4$	Itaconic acid	c	−201.03	[2684]						
	Citraconic acid	c	−197.04	[2684]						
$C_5H_6O_5$	α-Ketoglutaric acid	c	−245.35	[2684]						
C_5H_6S	2-Methylthiophene	g	15.60	[2136]	24.97	[2136]	76.62	[2136]	22.80	[2136]
			4.74[2,6]	[1558, 2136]	19.97[6]	[1558, 2136]				
			20.16	[1879]						
		l	10.86	[1879]	27.51	[2136]	52.22	[2136]		
	3-Methylthiophene	g	19.94	[1849]	29.26	[1849]	76.79	[1558, 1849, 2136]	22.67	[1558, 1849, 2136]
			4.54[3,6]	[1558, 1849]	19.72	[1558, 1849]				
		l	10.49	[1849]	27.15	[1849]	15.185	[1849]		
$C_5H_8Br_4$	Pentaerythrityl bromide	c					69.58	[984, 2643]	51.10	[2643]
									52.24	[984]
$C_5H_8Cl_4$	Pentaerythrityl chloride	c					61.54	[984, 2643]	47.44	[2643]
$C_5H_8F_4$	Pentaerythrityl flurodide	c					69.35	[2643]	50.80	[2643]
							69.31	[2564]	50.71	[2564]
$C_5H_8I_4$	Pentaerythrityl iodide	c					75.70	[2643]	49.64	[2643]
							75.75	[984]	50.12	[984]
C_5H_8O	Cyclopentanone	g	−46.31	[2360]						
		l	−56.52	[2360]						
			−57.6[4]	[1360]						
$C_5H_8O_2$	4-Pentenic acid (allylacetic acid]	l	−101.8	[1360]						
	Pentadione-2.4	g					95.1*	[826a]	28.7*	[826a]
		l	−101.33	[1360]						
	Methyl isocrotonate	l	−90.6	[1360]						
	Propylideneacetic acid	l	−105.6	[1360]						

$C_5H_8O_4$	Glutaric acid (propane-1, 3-dicarboxylic acid)	c	−229.44	[2685]						
	Ethylmalonic acid	c	−226.3	[1360]						
C_5H_9N	Butyl cyanide	g					86.70	[72]	28.38	[72]
	β-Ethylidenepropionic acid	l	−102.8	[1360]						
$C_5H_{10}O$	Tetrahydropyrane	g	−50.7;	[1360]						
			−53.98							
			−52.56	[2417]						
			−53.50	[2134]						
		l	−59.1;	[1360]						
			−61.33							
			−60.91	[2417]						
	Pentanone-2	l					65.11	[2071]	44.06	[2071]
	Cyclopentanol	g	−57.63	[2360]						
		l	−71.37	[2360]						
			−71.77	[805, 1360]	−30.6	[1360]	49.3	[1360, 2114]		
			−71.74	[2114]	−30.58	[2114]				
$C_5H_{10}O_2$	Valeric acid	g					105.12	[1858]		
		l	−133.90	[328]			62.10	[1858]	50.48[5]	[1858]
			−131.2;	[1360]						
			−133.6							
	Isovaleric acid	l	−134.8	[1360]						
	α-Methylbutyric acid	l	−133.1	[1360]						
	Trimethylacetic acid	c	−135.5	[1360]						
	Tetrahydrofuryl alcohol	l	−102.0	[1360]						
	trans-Cyclopentanediol-1,2	c	−117.2	[1360]						
	cis-Cyclopentanediol-1,2	c	−115.2	[1360]						
	4-Methyl-1,3-dioxane	l	−102.2	[1360]						
	Propyl acetate	l	−119.3	[1360]						
	Isopropyl acetate	l	−122.0	[1360]						

1. ΔH_0°. 2. $\Delta H_0^\circ = 8.93^6$ [1558, 2136]. 3. $\Delta H_0^\circ = 8.81$ (from S_2(g)) [1558, 1849]. 4. $t = 20$ °C. 5. $T = 300$ °K. 6. From S_2(g).

1	2	3	4		5		6		7	
	Ethyl propionate	g					100.0*	[826a]		
		l	−119.9	[1360]						
	Methyl butyrate	l	−117.2	[1360]						
$C_5H_{10}S$	4-Thiahexene-1	g	−4.3	[1879]						
			−5.06	[1879]						
	Trimethyl cyclothiapropane	g	−5.09	[1879]						
		l	−14.49	[1879, 2495]						
	Cyclothiahexane	g	−30.38[4]	[1836]	3.27	[1836]	77.26	[1836]	25.86	[1836]
			−14.91;	[1879]						
			−14.96							
		l	−25.18	[1879]						
			−25.41	[1879, 2495]						
	Cyclopentanethiol	g	−11.42	[1879]						
		l	−21.35	[1879]						
$C_5H_{11}Br$	Amyl bromide	g	−34.2	[26]	−1.3	[26]	97.85	[26]	31.9	[26]
			−31.2	[856]						
		l	−40.72	[856]						
	2-Bromopentane	g	−36.9	[26]	−3.5	[26]	96.05	[26]	32.0	[26]
$C_5H_{11}Cl$	Amyl chloride	g	−41.80	[26]	−8.86	[26]	95.06	[26]	31.8	[26]
	2-Chloropentane	g	−44.80	[26]	−11.4	[26]	93.14	[26]	31.7	[26]
	Amyl iodide	g	−26.10	[26]	6.7	[26]	99.84	[26]	32.2	[26]
$C_5H_{11}I$	2-Iodopentane	g	−28.5	[26]	5.35	[26]	96.72	[26]	32.3	[26]
$C_5H_{11}N$	Piperidine	l	−21.06	[804]						
$C_5H_{12}O$	*n*-Amyl alcohol	g	−73.41	[2241]	−35.40	[1365]	96.21	[1365]	31.76	[1365]
			−71.85	[1359, 1360]						
	Pentanol-1	l	−85.65	[1359, 1360]	−38.63	[1360]	60.9	[1359, 1360]		
			−85.86	[321]	−38.85	[321]			50.0	[321]
			−85.55	[961]						

	Pentanol-2	l	–87.75	[961]						
	Pentanol-3	l	–96.1	[1360, 1835]	–47.3	[1360]	54.8	[1360, 2112]		
			–88.51	[961]						
$C_5H_{12}O$	2-Methylbutanol-1	l	–85.24	[961]						
	2-Methylbutanol-2	l	–95.56	[321]	–46.71	[321]	54.7	[321]		
			–90.71	[961]						
	3-Methylbutanol-1	l	–85.18	[261]						
	3-Methylbutanol-2	l	–87.63	[961]						
$C_5H_{12}O_2$	2,2-Dimethoxypropane	l	–109.92	[2455]						
$C_5H_{12}O_4$	Pentaerythritol						47.34	[2643]	45.51	[2643]
$C_5H_{12}O_5$	Xylitol	c	–267.34	[417]						
$C_5H_{12}S$	Pentathiol-1(*n*-amyl mercaptan)	g	–41.86[1,4]	[1663a]	–5.43	[1663a]	99.05	[1663a]	33.71	[1663a]
			–41.30[2,4]	[2432]	–4.92	[2329, 2342]	99.98	[2329]	33.75	[2342]
			–25.88; –26.7	[1879]			99.18	[1225]	33.6*	[826a]
							99.19	[72]	33.86	[72]
		l	–36.11; –36.2	[1879]						
			–36.06	[2495]						
	2-Methyl-3-thiapentane (ethyl isopropyl sulfide)	g	–28.0	[1872, 1879]						
			–37.3[4]	[1872]						
			–37.28[4]	[1879]						
	3.3-Dimethyl-2-thiabutane (methyl isobutyl sulfide)	g	–44.35[4]	[2336]	–4.95	[2336]	89.21	[2336]		
			–28.93	[764, 1879, 2336]	–4.61	[1788]	92.92	[1788]		
					–4.49	[764]				
		l	–37.49	[764, 1879, 2336]	2.96	[764, 2336]	66.0	[764, 2336]	47.79	[764, 2336]
	2-Thiahexane (methyl butyl sulfide)	g	–39.81[3,4]	[2342]	–3.17	[2342]	98.43	[2342]	33.64	[2342]
			–24.2	[1872]						
			–34.29[4]; –34.39[4]	[1879]						
		l	–34.0	[1872, 1879]						
			–34.12	[1879]						
	3-Thiahexane (ethyl propyl sulfide)	g	–40.39[4]	[2342]	3.91	[2342]	98.97	[2342]	33.25	[2342]
			–24.97	[1879]						
		l	–34.55	[1879]						

1. $\Delta H_0^\circ = -34.92$ (from S_2(g)) [1663a]. 2. $\Delta H_0^\circ = -33.58$ (from S_2(g)) [2342]. 3. $\Delta H_0^\circ = -32.06$ (from S_2(g)) [2342]. 4. From S_2(g).

1	2	3	4		5		6		7	
$C_5H_{12}S$	2-Methylbutanethiol-1	g	−42.83	[1842]						
	2-Methylbutanethiol-2	g	−45.75[1]	[1020, 2336]	−7.33[1]	[2336]	92.48	[2336]	34.30	[2336]
			−45.76[1]	[1842]						
			−30.33	[764]	2.23	[764]	92.48	[764]	34.30	[764]
			−30.34	[1879]						
			−38.87	[764, 1879, 2326]	0.59	[764, 2326]	69.34	[764, 2326]	47.30	[764, 2326]
	3-Methylbutanethiol-1	g	−27.41	[1879]						
		l	−36.84	[1879]						
	4-Thiahexene-1 (ethyl allyl sulfide)	g	4.3	[1873]						
		l	−16.1	[1081]						
$C_5H_{14}Sn$	Trimethylethyltin	g	−475.78	[1338]	−422.10	[1338]	116.10	[1338]		
$C_5F_{11}N$	Perfluoropiperidine		−475.8	[1335]						
		l	−482.94	[1338]	−422.67	[1338]	94.02	[1338]	70.93	[1338]
			−482.9	[1335]						
					5, III					
C_5H_9NO	α-Piperidone	c	−73.08	[321]	−26.79	[321]	39.4	[321]		
$C_5H_{10}OS$	Ethyl allyl sulfoxide	g	−24.7	[1877, 1879]						
		l	−41.8	[1877, 1879]						
$C_5H_{10}O_2S$	Ethyl allyl sulfone	g	−78.4	[1879]						
		l	−98.3	[1879]						
$C_5H_{11}NO_2$	*L*-Valine (α-amino-isovaleric acid)		−147.7	[1599]	−85.8	[1599]	42.75	[1599]	40.35	[1599]
$C_5H_{12}O_2S$	Methyl *n*-butyl sulfone	g	−110.5	[1874]						
			−110.0	[1879]						
			−112.3	[928]						
			−18.0[2]	[928]						
		c	−128.9	[1874, 1879]						
	Methyl isobutyl sulfone	c	−133.7	[926]						
			3.3[3]	[926]						
	Methyl *tert*-butyl sulfone	g	−112.3	[929, 1879]						
		l	−133.7	[1879]						

5, IV

$C_5H_5BBr_3N$	Complex of pyridine with BBr_3	l	–45.6	[100]						
$C_5H_{10}Cl_5OSb$	Complex of pentanone-3 with $SbCl_5$	l	16.53	[2075a]						
$C_5H_{11}BBr_3N$	Complex of piperidine with BBr_3	l	–114.5	[100]						

6, I

C_6H_5	Phenyl radical	g	70	[2387]						
C_6H_6	Benzene	g	19.820[4]	[2244]	30.989	[2244]	63.34	[2244]	19.52	[2244]
		l	11.718	[2244]	29.756	[2244]	41.30	[2244]		
C_6H_8	Cyclohexadiene-1,3	g	25.6*	[1621]	44.72*	[1621]	68.9*	[1621]		
C_6H_{10}	Cyclohexene	g	–9.60	[1171]	17.12	[1171]	74.2	[1171]	25.10	[1171]
			–1.70[5]	[2244]						
		l	–17.60	[1171]	15.96	[1171]	51.67	[1171]	34.9	[1171]
	1-Methylcyclopentene	g					78.0	[2244]	24.1	[2244]
C_6H_{10}	3-Methylcyclopentene	g					79.0	[2244]	23.9	[2244]
	4-Methylcyclopentene	g					78.6	[2244]	23.9	[2244]
	Hexyne-1	g	29.55[6]	[2244]	52.17	[2244]	88.13	[2244]	30.65	[2244]
C_6H_{12}	Methylcyclopentane	g	25.50[7]	[2244]	8.55	[2244]	81.24	[2244]	26.24	[2244]
		l	–33.07	[2244]	7.53	[2244]	59.26	[2244]	37.61	[321]
	Cyclohexane	g	–29.43[8]	[1743, 2244]	7.59	[2244]	71.28	[2244]	25.40	[2244]
		l	–37.34	[2244]	6.37	[2244]	48.85	[2244]	37.4	[1642]
	Hexene-1	g	–9.96[9]	[2244]	20.94	[2244]	91.93	[2244]	31.63	[2244]
		l	–2.64	[321]	35.59	[321]	70.55	[321]	43.81	[321]
	trans-Hexene-2	g	–12.56[10]	[2244]	18.63	[2244]	90.97	[2244]	31.64	[2244]
	cis-Hexene-2		–11.56[11]	[2244]	19.16	[2244]	92.37	[2244]	30.04	[2244]
	trans-Hexene 3		–12.56[12]	[2244]	19.04	[2244]	89.59	[2244]	31.75	[2244]
	cis-Hexene-3	g	–11.56[13]	[2244]	19.66	[2244]	90.73	[2244]	29.55	[2244]
	2-Methylpentene-1	g	–13.56[14]	[2244]	17.47	[2244]	91.34	[2244]	32.41	[2244]
	3-Methylpentene-1	g	–11.02[15]	[2244]	20.40	[2244]	90.06	[2244]	34.64	[2244]
	4-Methylpentene-1	g	–11.66[16]	[2244]	20.45	[2244]	87.89	[2244]	30.23	[2244]
	2-Methylpentene-2	g	–14.96[17]	[2244]	16.34	[2244]	90.45	[2244]	30.26	[2244]
	trans-3-Methylpentene-2	g	–14.32[18]	[2244*]	16.74	[2244]	91.26	[2244]	30.26	[2244]
	cis-3-Methylpentene-2	g	–16.32[19]	[2244]	16.98	[2244]	90.45	[2244]	30.26	[2244]
							90.8*[20]	[826a]		

1. From S_2(g). 2. ΔH_{vap}. 3. ΔH_f. 4. $\Delta H_0^\circ = 24.000$ [2244]. 5. $\Delta H_0^\circ = 5.76$ [2244]. 6. $\Delta H_0^\circ = 35.26$ [2244]. 7. $\Delta H_0^\circ = -16.62$ [2244]. 8. $\Delta H_0^\circ = -20.0$ [2244]. 9. $\Delta H_0^\circ = -2.54$ [2244]. 10. $\Delta H_0^\circ = -5.08$ [2244]. 11. $\Delta H_0^\circ = -3.89$ [2244]. 12. $\Delta H_0^\circ = -4.91$ [2244]. 13. $\Delta H_0^\circ = -3.66$ [2244]. 14. $\Delta H_0^\circ = -6.04$ [2244]. 15. $\Delta H_0^\circ = -3.48$ [2244]. 16. $\Delta H_0^\circ = -3.49$ [2244]. 17. $\Delta H_0^\circ = -6.99$ [2244]. 18. $\Delta H_0^\circ = -6.35$ [2244]. 19. $\Delta H_0^\circ = -6.35$ [2244]. 20. 3-Methyl-2-pentene.

1	2	3	4		5		6		7	
C_6H_{12}	*trans*-4-Methylpentene-2	g	−14.26[1]	[2244]	17.77	[2244]	88.02	[2244]	33.80	[2244]
	cis-4-Methylpentene	g	−13.26[2]	[2244]	18.40	[2244]	89.23	[2244]	31.92	[2244]
	3-Ethylbutene-1	g	−12.92[3]	[2244]	18.51	[2244]	90.01	[2244]	31.92	[2244]
	2,3-Dimethylbutene-1	g	−14.78[4]	[2244]	17.43	[2244]	87.39	[2244]	34.29	[2244]
	3,3-Dimethylbutene-1	g	−14.25[5]	[2244]	19.53	[2244]	86.12	[2244]	30.23	[2244]
	2.3-Dimethylbutene-2	g	−15.91[6]	[2244]	16.52	[2244]	86.17	[2244]	40.48	[2244]
	1,1,2-Trimethylcyclopropane	l	−954.4*[7]	[241]						
C_6H_{14}	*n*-Hexane	g	−39.96[8]	[2244]	−0.07	[2244]	92.83	[2244]	34.20	[2244]
		l	−47.52	[2244]	−1.03	[2244]	70.72	[2244]	45.2	[2244]
	2-Methylpentane	g	−41.66[9]	[2244]	−1.20	[2244]	90.95	[2244]	34.46	[2244]
		l	−48.82	[2244]	−1.97	[2244]	69.51	[2244]		
	3-Methylpentane	g	−41.02[10]	[2244]	−0.51	[2244]	90.77	[2244]	34.20	[2244]
		l	−48.28	[2244]	−1.34	[2244]	69.22	[2244]		
	2,2-Dimethylbutane	g	−44.35[11]	[2244]	−2.37	[2244]	85.62	[2244]	33.91	[2244]
		l	−51.00	[2244]	−2.90	[2244]	65.08	[2244]		
	2,3-Dimethylbutane	g	−42.49[12]	[2244]	−0.98	[2244]	87.42	[2244]	33.59	[2244]
		l	−49.48	[2244]	−1.69	[2244]	66.36	[2244]		
C_6Cl_6	Hexachlorobenzene	c	−31.30	[1515]	0.3	[1515]	62.20	[1515]	48.11	[1515]
C_6F_6	Hexafluorobenzene	g	−220.43	[1051]	−201.97	[1051]	91.59	[1051]	37.43	[1051]
			−220.4	[1055]						
		l	−229.04	[1055]			66.90	[1051]	52.96	[1051]
C_6F_{10}	Decafluorocyclohexene	g	−449.6	[1055]						
		l	−456.93	[1055]						
C_6N_4	Tetracyanoethylene	g	168.5	[876]						
		c	149.1	[876]						
					6, II					
$C_6H_4F_2$	1,2-Difluorobenzene	g	−67.64	[2347]	−55.09	[2347]	76.94	[2347]	25.46	[2347]
			−67.65[13]	[1334, 1335, 1369]	−55.22	[1369]	77.32	[1369]	25.41	[1369]
		l	−76.30	[1334]			53.20	[2347]	38.01	[2347]
			−76.29	[1335]						
	1,3-Difluorobenzene	g	−71.37[14]	[1335, 1369]	−58.71	[1369]	76.57	[1369]	25.40	[1369]
			−71.35	[1334]						
		l	−79.64	[1334]						
			−79.63	[1335]						

	1,4-Difluorobenzene	g	−70.70[15]	[1335, 1369]	−57.70	[1369]	75.43	[1369]	25.53	[1369]
			−70.69	[1334]						
		l	−79.24	[1334]						
			−79.23	[1335]						
$C_6H_4Cl_2$	1,2-Dichlorobenzene	g					81.59	[131]	27.10	[131]
		l	−4.20	[1557]						
	1,3-Dichlorobenzene	g					82.14; 82.16	[131]	27.34	[131]
		l	−4.89	[1557]						
	1,4-Dichlorobenzene	g					79.94	[131]	27.26	[131]
		l	−10.12	[1557]						
$C_6H_4O_2$	*p*-Quinone	g					76.653; 78.926	[803]	25.666; 26.654	[803]
		c	−44.10	[2117]	−20.0	[2117]	38.9	[2117]		
C_6H_5Br	Bromobenzene	g	21.62[16]	[2675]	29.56	[2675]	77.76	[2675]	23.83	[2675]
		l	11.60	[2477]	27.82	[2477]	49.7*	[2477]	37.17	[2477]
C_6H_5Cl	Chlorobenzene	g	12.21	[2210]	23.53	[2210]	74.86	[132, 2210]	23.20	[132, 2210]
			12.21[17]	[321]						
		l	2.55	[321]	22.12	[321]	47.2*	[321]	35.9	[321]
C_6H_5F	Fluorobenzene	g	−26.48	[570, 2443]	−5.10	[2443]	72.33	[2443]	22.57	[2443]
		l	−34.75	[570, 2443]	−16.50	[2443]	72.33	[2443]	22.57	[2443]
C_6H_5I	Iodobenzene	g					79.85	[2675]	24.08	[2675]
		l	27.40	[2477]			49.1*	[2477]	37.95	[2477]
$C_6H_5O_7^{3-}$	Citrate anion				−277.69	[1177]				
					−278.8	[915]				
C_6H_6O	Phenol	g	−22.50	[321]	−8.22	[321]	78.5	[321]	23.7	[321]
			−23.05[18]	[731, 1360, 1361]	−7.88	[1361]	75.43	[1361]	24.75	[1361]
			−23.03	[1053]	−7.89	[1360]	75.44	[1360]		
		l					30.42; 30.545[19]	[732]	30.46	[732]
		c	−38.90	[2117]	−11.38	[2117]	34.0	[2117]	32.2	[2117]
			−39.46	[731, 1360]	−12.45	[1360]	35.71	[1360, 1361]		
			−39.44	[1053]						
	Furylethylene	l	−0.3	[1360]						
$C_6H_6O_2$	Hydroquinone	c	−86.75	[321]	−49.48	[321]	33.5	[321]	33.9	[321]

1. $\Delta H_0^\circ = -6.67$ [2244]. 2. $\Delta H_0^\circ = -5.42$ [2244]. 3. $\Delta H_0^\circ = -5.17$ [2244]. 4. $\Delta H_0^\circ = -7.10$ [2244]. 5. $\Delta H_0^\circ = -5.82$ [2244]. 6. $\Delta H_0^\circ = -7.96$ [2244]. 7. $(\Delta H^\circ_{comb})_{298}$. 8. $\Delta H_0^\circ = -30.91$ [2244]. 9. $\Delta H_0^\circ = -32.08$ [2244]. 10. $\Delta H_0^\circ = -31.97$ [2244]. 11. $\Delta H_0^\circ = -34.65$ [2244]. 12. $\Delta H_0^\circ = -32.73$ [2244]. 13. $\Delta H_0^\circ = -64.42$ [1369]. 14. $\Delta H_0^\circ = -68.04$ [1369]. 15. $\Delta H_0^\circ = -67.41$ [1369]. 16. $\Delta H_0^\circ = 21.62$ [321]. 17. ΔH_0°. 18. $\Delta H_0^\circ = -18.63$ [1361]. 19. $T = 298.78$ °K.

1	2	3	4		5		6		7	
	Pyrocatechol	c	−84.45	[289]	−50.20	[289]	35.9	[289]	31.6	[289]
	Resorcinol	c	−86.46	[289]	−50.00	[289]	35.3	[289]	31.3	[289]
$C_6H_6O_6$	*trans*-Aconitic acid	c	−294.63	[2684]						
	cis-Aconitic acid	c	−292.7	[2684]						
C_6H_6S	Thiophenol	g	11.24^{6}	[2344]	32.58^{6}; 25.71^{6}	[2344]	80.51; 80.91	[2344]	25.07	[2344]
			21.9	[1868]						
			26.66	[1879, 2314]						
			15.44^{1,6}	[321]						
		l	15.02	[321, 2344]	31.77^{6}	[2344]	53.25	[2344]	41.40	[2344]
			9.55^{6}	[1868]						
C_6H_7N	Aniline	g	20.80	[1491]	33.90	[1491]	76.28	[1491]	25.91	[1491]
			20.90	[289]						
		l	8.44	[289]	36.62	[289]	45.8	[282]	45.6	[282]
			7.47	[1491]	35.68	[1491]	45.721	[1491]	45.90	[1491]
	α-Picoline	g	24.38	[1054]						
			23.65^{2}	[2341]	42.31	[2341]	77.68	[2341]	23.90	[2341]
			27.16	[1054]						
		l	13.50	[2341]	39.80	[2341]	52.07	[2341]	37.86	[2341]
C_6H_7N	β-Picoline	g	25.37^{3}	[2335]	44.03	[2335]	77.67	[2335]	23.80	[2335]
			24.43	[1054]						
		l	14.75	[2335]	41.16	[2335]	51.70	[2335]	37.93	[2335]
$C_6H_8O_7$	Citric acid	c	−374.4	[1951]	−295.5	[1951]	39.73	[1951]		
			−369.0	[2685]						
$C_6H_8O_7 \cdot H_2O$	Citric acid monohydrate	c	−439.2	[1360]	−352.0	[1177]	67.74	[1177]	1.276^{4}	[1177]
C_6H_8S	2,5-Dimethylthiophene	l					58.49	[933]	42.62	[933]
$C_6H_{10}Br_2$	1,2-Dibromocyclohexane	l	−38.46	[855]						
$C_6H_{10}O$	Cyclohexanone	g	−54.09	[2360]						
		l	−64.86	[2360]						
			−60.7	[463]						
			69.5^{5}	[1360]						
$C_6H_{10}O_2$	Ethyl isocrotonate	l	−99.1	[1360]						
$C_6H_{10}O_4$	Propylmaleic acid	c	−232.1	[1360]						
	Dipropionyl peroxide	l	−148.2	[1360]						

$C_6H_{11}N$	Amyl cyanide	g					96.13	[1133]	33.85	[1133]
$C_6H_{12}O$	Cyclohexanol	g	−68.41	[2360]						
		l	−83.45	[331, 1360, 2120]	−32.1	[1360]	47.7	[1360, 1677]		
			−83.23	[2360]	−32.07	[321]			49.93	[321]
			−83.6	[463]						
$C_6H_{12}O_2$	Caproic acid (*n*-hexanoic acid)	l	−139.98	[328]						
	trans-1-Methylcyclo-pentanediol-1,2	l	−128.3	[1360]						
	cis-1-Methylcyclo-pentanediol-1,2	l	−126.0	[1360]						
	trans-Cyclohexanediol-1,2	c	−130.7	[1360]						
	cis-Cyclohexanediol-1,2	c	−131.7	[1360]						
	Butyl acetate	l	−125.5	[1360]						
	Isobutyl acetate	l	−127.5	[1360]						
	Propyl propionate	l	−124.9	[1360]						
	Isopropyl propionate	l	−128.2	[1360]						
	Ethyl butyrate	l	−126.3	[1360]						
$C_6H_{12}S$	Cyclothiaheptane	g	−15.7	[1879]						
		l	−27.00	[1879, 2495]						
	Tetramethylcyclothia-propane	c	−19.88	[1879, 2495]						
	Cyclohexanethiol	g	−22.90	[1879]						
		l	−33.58	[1879]						
$C_6H_{13}Br$	1-Bromohexane	g	−34.97, −35.88	[856]						

1. $\Delta H_0^{\circ 6}$. 2. $\Delta H_0^\circ = 29.04$ [2341]. 3. $\Delta H_0^\circ = 30.76$ [2335]. 4. *abs·joules*/°C. 5. $t = 20$ °C. 6. From S_2(g).

1	2	3	4		5		6		7	
$C_6H_{13}Br$	1-Bromohexane	l	–45.57; –46.48	[856]						
$C_6H_{14}O$	1-Hexanol	g	–78.92	[2241]	–33.33	[1365]	105.52	[1365]	37.23	[1365]
			–76.75	[1359, 1360]						
		l	–91.75	[1359, 1360]	–37.3	[1360]	68.6	[767, 1360]		
			–91.97	[321]	–37.55	[321]			55.57	[321]
			–90.67	[961]						
	Diisopropyl ether	g	–73.2	[2572]			104.1	[2572]		
		l	–83.94	[1360, 2116]	–21.1	[1360]	70.4	[1360, 2112]		
	Dipropyl ether	g	–70.14	[1020]			97.89	[765]	37.79	[765]
$C_6H_{14}O_2$	Dipropyl peroxide	l	–76*	[1360]						
$C_6H_{14}O_4$	Triethylene glycol	l	–191.0[1]	[1360]						
$C_6H_{14}O_6$	Dulcitol	c	–321.90	[1360]	–227.2	[1360]	56.0	[432, 1360]		
			–316.62	[432]	–221.91	[[432]				
	Mannitol	c	–312.42	[432]	–221.01	[432]				
			–319.61	[1360]	–225.2	[1360]	57.0	[432, 1360]		
$C_3H_{14}S$	1-Hexanethiol	g	–46.22[2,10]	[2342]	–2.91[10]	[2342]	108.58	[2342]	39.21	[2342]
			–46.64[3,10]	[1663a]	–3.27[10]	[1663a]	108.46	[1663a]	39.18	[1663a]
							108.54	[72]	39.36	[72]
	2-Thiaheptane (methyl pentyl sulfide)	g	–44.73[4,10]	[2342]	–1.16[10]	[2342]	107.73	[2342]	39.10	[2342]
			–29.1	[1872, 1879]						
		l	–39.9	[1872, 1879]						
	3-Thiaheptane (ethyl butyl sulfide)	g	–45.31[5,10]	[2342]	–1.90[10]	[2342]	108.27	[2342]	38.71	[2342]
			–30.3	[1879]						
		l	–41.14	[1879]						
	4-Thiaheptane(dipropyl sulfide)	g	–45.35[6,10]	[2342]	–1.62[10]	[2342]	107.22	[2342]	38.53	[2342]
			–40.59	[1879]						
		l	–29.93	[1879]						
	2,2-Dimethyl-3-thiapentane (ethyl isobutyl sulfide)	g	–35.3	[1872, 1879]						
		l	–44.7	[1872]						
			–44.73	[1879]						
	2,4 Dimethyl-3-thiapentane (diisopropyl sulfide)	g	–34.1	[1872]						
			–33.84	[1879]						
		l	–43.5	[1872]						
			–43.32	[1879]						
$C_6H_{14}S_2$	4,5-Dithiaoctane (dipropyl disulfide)	g	–58.79[7,10]	[1552, 2342]	–10.24[10]	[1552, 2342]	118.30	[2342]	44.30	[2342]
			–27.95	[1879]						
		l	–40.89	[1879]						

$C_6H_{15}Al$	Triethylaluminum	l	-51.9	[607]						
$C_6H_{15}B$	Treithylboron	g	-38.4	[1639]						
			-36.6	[2168]						
		l	-47.2	[1639]						
			-45.4	[2168]						
$C_6H_{16}Sn$	Trimethylpropyltin	l	4.35	[2131]						
			13.2	[1081]						
$C_6H_{18}Al_2$	Trimethylaluminum, dimer	g	125.45	[1844]						
$C_6H_{18}Si_2$	Permethyldisilane		-129*	[884]						
$C_6Ce_2O_{12}$	Cerium oxalate	c			-879.15*	[177]				
$C_6Ga_2O_{12}$	Gallium oxalate	c					64*	[323]		
$C_6La_2O_{12}$	Lanthanum oxalate	c	-952*	[232]	-882.71*[8]	[177]				
$C_6Nd_2O_{12}$	Neodymium oxalate	c	-942*	[232]	-872.65*	[177]				
			-164.60	[2424]						
$C_6Nd_2O_{12}\cdot10H_2O$	Neodymium oxalate decahydrate	c	-1661.62	[2424]	(-1396.05)	[2424]	165	[2424]		
					(-13.98*)	[1976]				

6, III

C_6HCl_5O	Pentachlorophenol	c	-70.6	[1515]	-34.40	[1515]	60.21	[1515]	48.27	[1515]
$C_6H_4N_2O_4$	1,2-Dinitrobenzene	c	2.06	[432]	50.56	[432]	51.7	[432]		
	1,3-Dinitrobenzene	c	-4.04	[432]	44.13	[432]	52.8	[432]		
$C_6H_5Cl_3Si$	Trichlorophenylsilane	l					314.7[9]	[151]	220.7[9]	[151]
$C_6H_5NO_2$	Nitrobenzene	g	15.48	[289]						
		l	3.80	[2122, 2192]	34.95	[2122, 2192]	53.6	[2122, 2192]	44.4	[2122]
$C_6H_5N_3O_4$	2,3-Dinitroaniline	l	-2.8	[1864]						
	2,4-Dinitroaniline	l	-15.7	[1864]						
	2,5-Dinitroaniline	l	-10.6	[1864]						
	2,6-Dinitroaniline	l	-12.1	[1864]						
	3,4-Dinitroaniline	l	-7.8	[1864]						
	3,5-Dinitroaniline	l	-9.3	[1864]						
$C_6H_6N_2O_2$	*o*-Nitroaniline	c	-3.45	[432]	42.60	[432]	42.1	[432]	39.3	[432]
	m-Nitroaniline	c	-4.46	[432]	41.60	[432]	42.1	[432]	40.2	[432]

1. $t = 17°C$. 2. $\Delta H_0^\circ = -37.22^{10}$ [2342]. 3. $\Delta H_0^\circ = -37.52^{10}$ [1663a]. 4. $\Delta H_0^\circ = -35.70^{10}$ [2342]. 5. $\Delta H_0^\circ = -36.04^{10}$ [2342]. 6. $\Delta H_0^\circ = -36.10^{10}$ [2342]. 7. $\Delta H_0^\circ = -49.82^{10}$ [1552, 2342]. 8. $t = 18\ °C$. 9. In *joules/mole* · °C. From $S_2(g)$.

1	2	3	4		5		6		7	
$C_6H_6N_2O_2$	*p*-Nitroaniline	c	−9.92	[1010]	36.10	[1010]	42.1	[1010]	40.4	[1010]
$C_6H_6N_4O_7$	Ammonium picrate	c	−88.42	[92]						
$C_6H_8N_2O_3$	Aniline nitrate	c	42.5	[1044]						
$C_6H_9AlO_6$	Aluminum acetate	c	−451.8	[1987]						
$C_6H_{11}NO$	ε-Caprolactam	c	−78.54	[321]	−22.72	[321]	40.3	[321]		
$C_6H_{12}F_4N_2$	1,2-*bis*-Difluoroamino-	g	−49.58	[1329]						
	-4-methylpentane	l	−60.09	[1329]						
$C_6H_{13}NO_2$	*L*-Leucine	c	−154.6	[1599]	−85.4	[1599]	50.62	[1599]	48.03	[1599]
	L-Isoleucine	c	−152.5	[1599]	−83.0	[1599]	49.71	[1599]	45.00	[1599]
$C_6H_{14}OS$	Ethyl *tert*-butyl sulfoxide	g	−65.5	[1877, 1879]						
		l	−83.3	[1877, 1879]						
	1-(Propylsulfinyl)-propane	g	−60.9	[1877, 1879]						
		l	−78.7	[1877, 1879]						
$C_6H_{14}O_2S$	Ethyl *tert*-butyl sulfone	g	−117.6	[1874]						
		c	−138.7	[1874]						
	Dipropyl sulfone	g	−112.1	[1874]						
		l	−131.8	[1874]						
$C_6H_{15}BO_2$	Diisopropylhydroxyborine	l	−183.85	[822]						
$C_6H_{16}N_2O_3$	Triethylamine nitrate	c	97.3	[1044]						
$C_6H_{16}O_3Si$	Triethoxysilane	l	−221.1	[390]						
$C_6H_{18}OSi_2$	Hexamethyldisiloxane	l	−194.7	[1331]	−129.5	[1331]	103.69	[2346]	74.42	[2346]

6, IV

1	2	3	4		5		6		7	
$C_6H_2KN_3O_7$	Potassium picrate	c	−108.37	[92]						
$C_6H_2LiN_3O_7$	Lithium picrate	c	−113.94	[92]						
$C_6H_2N_3NaO_7$	Sodium picrate	c	−118.45	[3375]						
$C_6H_8BrCl_3O_2$	1-Bromopropyl 2-ether of trichloropropionic acid	g					140.7*	[826a]		
$C_6H_{10}O_2N_3Cl$	Histidine hydrochloride	c					65.99	[1007]	59.64	[1007]
$C_6H_{12}Cl_5OSb$	Complex of isopropyl ethyl ketone with $SbCl_5$	l	−16.16	[2075a]						

$C_6H_{15}ClN_2O_2$	l-Lysine hydrochloride	c					63.21	[1007]	57.10	[1007]
$C_6H_{15}ClN_4O_2$	l-Arginine hydrochloride	c					68.43	[1007]	62.37	[1007]
$C_6H_{18}Cl_2NiO_6$	Complex of hexamethyl-nickel[1]	c	−214.2*	[689]						

7, I

C_7H_7	Benzyl radical	g	39.7	[747]						
			43.1	[929]						
		l	12.6	[747]						
		c	−36.80	[2118]						
C_7H_8	Toluene	g	11.950[2]	[2244, 2522]	29.228	[2244]	76.42	[2244, 2522]	24.80	[2244, 2522]
					29.23	[2522]	76.64	[2340]	24.77	[2340]
		l	2.87	[2189]	27.30	[2189]	52.4	[2189]	37.3	[2189]
							52.81	[2340]	37.58	[2340]
	Cycloheptatriene	g	43.47	[1224]	61.04	[1224]	75.44	[1224]		
		l	34.22	[1224]	58.09	[1224]	51.30	[1224]	38.90	[1244]
C_7H_{12}	Heptyne-1	g	24.62[3]	[2244]	54.18	[2244]	97.44	[2244]	36.11	[2244]
C_7H_{12}	1,2-Dimethylcyclopentene	g					84.0	[2244]	30.3	[2244]
	1,3-Dimethylcyclopentene	g					86.4	[2244]	30.1	[2244]
	1,4-Dimethylcyclopentene	g					87.4	[2244]	30.0	[2244]
	1,5-Dimethylcyclopentene	g					86.4	[2244]	30.1	[2244]
	3,3-Dimethylcyclopentene	g					83.2	[2244]	29.4	[2244]
	trans-3,4-Dimethylcyclo-pentene	g					86.8	[2244]	30.0	[2244]
	cis-3,4-Dimethylcyclo-pentene	g					86.4	[2244]	29.8	[2244]
	trans-3,5-Dimethylcyclo-pentene	g					84.6	[2244]	30.0	[2244]
	cis-3,5-Dimethylcyclo-pentene	g					84.6	[2244]	30.0	[2244]
C_7H_{14}	Cycloheptane	g	−28.52	[1224]	15.06	[1224]	81.82	[1224]		
		l	−37.73	[1224]	12.96	[1224]	57.97	[1224]	43.20	[1224]
	Heptene-1	g	−14.89[4]	[2244]	22.95	[2244]	101.24	[2244]	37.10	[2244]
		l	−23.58	[1835]	19.20	[1835]	78.31	[1835]	50.62	[1835]

1. $Ni(ClO_3)_2 \cdot 6CH_3$. 2. $\Delta H_0^\circ = 17.500$ [2244]. 3. $\Delta H_0^\circ = 31.61$ [2244]. 4. $\Delta H_0^\circ = -6.18$ [2244].

1	2	3	4		5		6		7	
C_7H_{14}	*cis*-1-Heptene-2	g	−16.76	[231]						
	1,1-Dimethyl-2-ethyl-cyclopropane	l	−21.6	[241]						
	Methylcyclohexane	g	−36.99[1]	[2244]	6.52	[2244]	82.06	[2244]	32.27	[2244]
	Methylcyclohexane	l	−45.45	[2244]	4.86	[2244]	59.26	[2244]		
	Ethylcyclopentane	g	−30.37[2]	[2244]	10.66	[2244]	90.42	[2244]	31.49	[2244]
		l	−39.10	[2244]	8.92	[2244]	67.00	[2244]		
	1,1-Dimethylcyclopentane	g	−33.05[3]	[2244]	9.33	[2244]	85.87	[2244]	31.86	[2244]
		l	−41.14	[2244]	7.96	[2244]	63.34	[2244]		
	trans-1,2-Dimethylcyclo-	g	−32.67[4]	[2244]	9.17	[2244]	87.67	[2244]	32.14	[2244]
	pentane	l	−40.94	[2244]	7.70	[2244]	64.86	[2244]		
	cis-1,2-Dimethylcyclo-	g	−30.96[5]	[2244]	10.93	[2244]	87.51	[2244]	32.06	[2244]
	pentane	l	−39.52	[2244]	9.29	[2244]	64.33	[2244]		
	trans-1,3-Dimethylcyclo-	g	−32.47[6]	[2244]	9.37	[2244]	87.67	[2244]	32.14	[2244]
	pentane	l	−40.68	[2244]	7.93	[2244]	64.90	[1411a]		
	cis-1,3-Dimethylcyclo-	g	−31.93[7]	[2244]	9.91	[2244]	87.67	[2244]	32.14	[2244]
	pentane	l	−40.19	[2244]	8.45	[2244]	64.88	[2244]		
C_7H_{16}	Heptane	g	−44.89[8]	[2244]	1.94	[2244]	102.24	[2244]	39.67	[2244]
			−44.48	[1587]	1.91	[1587]	102.27	[1587]		
		l	−53.63	[2244]	0.27	[2244]	78.52	[2244]		
					0.24	[1587]	78.53	[1587]	53.76	[1587]
	2-Methylhexane	g	−46.60[9]	[2244]	0.77	[1587, 2244]	100.35	[2244]		
			−46.59	[1587]			100.38	[1587]		
		l	−54.93	[2244]	−0.68	[2244]	77.29	[2244]		
					−0.69	[1587]	77.28]	[1587]	53.28	[1587]
	3-Methylhexane	g	−45.96[10]	[2244]	1.10	[2244]	101.37	[2244]		
		l	−54.35	[2244]	−0.39	[2244]	78.23	[2244]		
	3-Ethylpentane	g	−45.34[11]	[2244]	2.57	[2244]	98.30	[2244]		
			−45.33	[1587]	2.63	[1587]	98.35	[1587]		
		l	−53.77	[2244]	1.04	[2244]	75.16	[2244]		
					1.10	[1587]	75.18	[1587]	52.48	[1587]
	2,2-Dimethylpentane	g	−49.29[12]	[2244]	0.02	[1587, 2244]	93.85	[2244]		
			−49.27	[1587]			93.90	[1587]		
		l	−57.05	[2244]	−1.15	[2244]	71.65	[2244]		
					−1.16	[1587]	71.77	[1587]	52.85	[1587]
	2,3-Dimethylpentane	g	−47.62[13]	[2244]	0.16	[2244]	98.96	[2244]	39.2*	[2244]
		l	−55.81	[2244]	−1.27	[2244]	76.27	[2244]		
	2,4-Dimethylpentane	g	−48.30[14]	[2244]	0.72	[2244]	94.80	[2244]		

			−48.28	[1587]	0.73	[1587]	94.82	[1587]		
		l	−56.17	[2244]	−0.49	[1587, 2244]	72.47	[2244]		
							72.46	[1587]	53.59	[1587]
	3,3-Dimethylpentane	g	−48.17[15]	[2244]	0.63	[2244]	95.53	[2244]	45.5*	[2244]
		l	−56.07	[2244]	−0.69	[2244]	73.44	[2244]		
	2,2,3-Trimethylbutane	g	−48.96[16]	[2244]	1.02	[1587, 2244]	91.60	[2244]	39.33	[2244]
			−48.95	[1587]			91.61	[1587]		
		l	−56.63	[2244]	−0.17	[1587, 2244]	69.87	[2244]		
							69.85	[1587]	51.03	[1587]
C_7F_{16}	*n*-Perfluoroheptane	g	−789.0	[433]						
		l	−791.9	[433]						

7, II

$C_7H_5F_3$	Benzotrifluoride	g	−138.87	[433]						
	(α-Triluorotoluene)		−148.20	[1331]						
			−134.20[17]	[321]						
		l	−147.85	[433]						
			−148.29	[1331]						
C_7H_6O	Benzldehyde	g	−6.0*	[1360]						
		l	−17.8*	[1360]						
$C_7H_6O_2$	Benzoic acid	c	−91.91	[289]	−58.7	[289]	40.8	[289]	34.7	[289]
			−91.812	[1360]	−59.11	[1360]	40.04	[1360]	34.97	[1360]
	o-Hydroxybenzaldehyde	l	−67.0*[18]	[1360]						
	m-Hydroxybenzaldehyde	l	−70.3[18]	[1360]						
	p-Hydroxybenzaldehyde	l	−74.3[18]	[1360]						
$C_7H_6O_3$	*o*-Hydroxybenzoic acid	c	−140.0	[1360]	−100	[1360]	42.6	[1360]		
			−140.64	[2115]	−100.7	[2115]			38.03	[2115]
	m-Hydroxybenzoic acid	c	−141.1	[1360]	−101.0	[1360]	42.3	[1360]		
			−140.49	[2115]	−100.4	[2115]			37.59	[2115]
	p-Hydroxybenzoic acid	c	−142.0	[1360]	−101.1	[1360]	42.0	[1360]		
			−141.38	[2115]	−101.2	[2115]			37.08	[2115]
	2-Furaneacrylic acid	l	−107.3	[1360]						

1. $\Delta H_0^\circ = -26.30$ [2244]. 2. $\Delta H_0^\circ = -20.23$ [2244]. 3. $\Delta H_0^\circ = -22.69$ [2244]. 4. $\Delta H_0^\circ = -22.39$ [2244]. 5. $\Delta H_0^\circ = -20.66$ [2244]. 6. $\Delta H_0^\circ = -22.19$ [2244]. 7. $\Delta H_0^\circ = -21.65$ [2244]. 8. $\Delta H_0^\circ = -34.55$ [2244]. 9. $\Delta H_0^\circ = -35.77$ [2244]. 10. $\Delta H_0^\circ = -34.96$ [2244]. 11. $\Delta H_0^\circ = -34.10$ [2244]. 12. $\Delta H_0^\circ = -38.00$ [2244]. 13. $\Delta H_0^\circ = -36.29$ [2244]. 14. $\Delta H_0^\circ = -36.98$ [2244]. 15. $\Delta H_0^\circ = -36.92$ [2244]. 16. $\Delta H_0^\circ = -37.71$ [2244]. 17. ΔH_0°. 18. $t = 20°C$.

1	2	3	4	5	6	7
C_7H_7Br	Benzyl bromide	g	15.1 [747]			
		l	3.8 [747]			
			7.1 [1244]			
C_7H_7F	4-Fluorotoluene	g	−34.01 [1334]			
			−34.0 [1335]			
		l	−43.43 [1334, 1335]			
C_7H_7I	Benzyl iodide	g	23.9 [747]			
C_7H_8O	*o*-Cresol	g	−30.74[1] [731, 1360, 1366]	−8.86 [1366]	85.47 [1366]	31.15 [1366]
			−30.67 [1053]			
		c	−48.84 [1053]			
			−48.91 [731, 1360]			
	m-Cresol	g	−31.63[2] [1366]	−9.69 [1366]	85.27 [1366]	29.75 [1366]
			−31.44 [1053]			
			−31.63 [731, 1360]			
		l	−46.19 [1050]			
			−46.38 [731, 1360]			
	p-Cresol	g	−29.97[2] [731, 1360, 1366]	−7.67 [1366]	83.09 [1366]	29.75 [1366]
			−29.94 [1053]			
		c	−47.61 [1053]			
			−47.64 [731, 1310]			
	Benzylic alcohol	g	−22.39 [321]			
	(phenyl carbinol)	l	−38.49 [1360, 2117]	−7.47 [2117]	50.7 [2117]	
				−6.6 [1360]	51.8 [1360, 2122]	
	Anisole	l	−29.61 [759, 1360]			
C_7H_8S	Thiobenzylic alcohol	g	21.9 [1868]			
		l	9.55 [1868]			
	Phenyl methyl sulfide	g	23.5 [1871, 1873, 1879]			
		l	11.47 [1871, 1879]			
C_7H_9N	2,5-Lutidine	g	15.67 [1054]			
	2,6-Lutidine	g	13.43 [1054]			
$C_7H_{12}O$	Cycloheptanone	l	−71.1[4] [1360]			

$C_7H_{12}O_2$	Propyl isocrotonate	l	–104.6	[1360]						
	Isopropyl isocrotonate	l	–107.8	[1360]						
	Ethyl ester of 4-pentenoic acid	l	–102.0	[1360]						
$C_7H_{12}O_4$	Pimelic acid	c	–242.75	[1360]						
	Butylmalonic acid	c	–239.5	[1360]						
$C_7H_{13}N$	Hexyl cyanide	g					105.54	[72]	39.32	[72]
$C_7H_{14}O$	Cyclopentanol	l	-94.0^4	[1360]						
			–94.0	[2399]						
	Cyclohexylmethanol	c	–102.0	[1360, 1791]						
	trans-2-Methylcyclohexanol	l	–100.93	[1360, 2394]						
	cis-2-Methylcyclohexanol	l	–94.85	[1360, 2394]						
	trans-3-Methylcyclohexanol	l	–95.82	[1360, 2394]						
	cis-3-Methylcyclohexanol	l	–101.02	[1360, 2394]						
	trans-4-Methylcyclohexanol	l	–105.07	[1360, 2394]						
	cis-4-Methylcyclohexanol	l	–100.24	[1360, 2394]						
	Enanthic aldehyde (*n*-heptyl aldehyde)	l	–74.5	[1360]	–24.1	[1360]	83.3	[1360, 2114]		
$C_7H_{14}O_5$	Oenanthic acid	l	–146.15	[328]						
	trans-1-Methylcyclohexanediol-1,2	c	–140.5	[1360]						
	cis-1-Methylcyclohexanediol-1,2	c	–143.0	[1360]						
	Isoamyl acetate	l	–133.6	[1360]						
	Butyl propionate	l	–130.1	[1360]						

1. $\Delta H_0^\circ = -25.25$ [1366]. 2. $\Delta H_0^\circ = -25.84$ [1366]. 3. $\Delta H_0^\circ = -24.21$ [1366]. 4. $t = 20$ °C.

1	2	3	4	5	6	7
$C_7H_{14}O_2$	Isobutyl propionate	l	−133.7 [1360]			
	Propyl butyrate	l	−132.1 [1360]			
	Isopropyl butyrate	l	−133.9 [1360]			
	Ethyl valerate	l	−130.8 [1360]			
$C_7H_{14}S$	Allyl *tert*-butyl sulfide	g	−11.0 [1873]			
	4-Thia-5,5-dimethyl-hexene-1	g	−11.0 [1879]			
		l	−21.67 [1879]			
$C_7H_{15}Br$	1-Bromoheptane	g	−40.69 [856]			
		l	−52.24 [856]			
$C_7H_{16}O$	Heptanol-1	g	−81.65 [1359, 1360]	−31.29 [1365]	114.83 [1365]	42.70 [1365]
					114.4* [826a]	42.9* [826a]
		l	−97.22 [2114]	−35.85 [2114]	77.9 [1360, 2114]	
			−97.85 [1359, 1360]	−36.5 [1360]		
			−95.31 [961]			
$C_7H_{16}O_2$	2,2-Diethoxypropane	l	−128.15 [2455]			
$C_7H_{16}S$	Heptanethiol-1	g	−51.15[1,12] [2342]	−0.90[12] [2342]	117.89 [2342]	44.68 [2342]
			−51.57[2,12] [1663a]	−1.26[12] [1663a]	117.77 [1663a]	44.65 [1663a]
					117.88 [72]	44.85 [72]
	2-Thiaoctane (methyl hexyl sulfide)	g	−49.65[12] [2342]	0.84[12];	[2342] 117.04 [2342]	44.57 [2342]
			−49.66[3,12]	0.85[12]		
	3-Thiaoctane (ethyl pentyl sulfide)	g	−50.24[4,12] [2342]	0.10[12]; 0.11[12] [2342]	117.58 [2342]	44.18 [2342]
	4-Thiaoctance (propyl butyl sulfide)	g	−50.27[5.12] [2342]	−0.01[12] [2342]	117.90 [2342]	43.99 [2342]

7, III

1	2	3	4	5	6	7
$C_7HF_5O_2$	Pentafluorobenzoic acid	c	−289.66 [1055]			
$C_7H_5FO_2$	*m*-Fluorobenzoic acid	c	−137.84 [433]			
	o-Fluorobenzoic acid	c	−134.38 [433]			
	p-Fluorobenzoic acid	c	−138.95 [433]			
			−138.50 [1055]			

Formula	Substance	State								
$C_7H_5NO_4$	*m*-Nitrobenzoic acid	c	−100.25	[432]	−52.71	[432]	49.0	[432]		
	o-Nitrobenzoic acid	c	−94.25	[432]	−46.95	[432]	49.8	[432]		
	p-Nitrobenzoic acid	c	−101.25	[432]	−53.07	[432]	50.2	[432]	43.3	[432]
$C_7H_5NaO_2$	Sodium benzoate	c	−142.3	[1802]						
$C_7H_7O_2S$	Benzylsulfonyl (free radical)	g	−38.5	[1867]						
$C_7H_8O_2S$	Methyl phenyl sulfone	g	−68.0	[929]						
			−63.4*	[1879]						
		c	−83.3	[1879]						
$C_7H_{10}N_2O_3$	Benzylamine nitrate	c	57.2	[1044]						
$C_7H_{13}NO$	*α*-Oenantholactam	c	−83.02	[321]	−19.10	[321]	45.4	[321]		

7, IV

Formula	Substance	State		
$C_7H_{14}Cl_5OSb$	Complex of diisopropyl ketone with $SbCl_5$	c	−16.20	[2075a]
	Complex of *tert*-butyl ethyl ketone with $SbCl_5$	c	−14.58	[2075a]

8, I

Formula	Substance	State								
C_8H_8	Styrene	g	35.22^{6}	[2244]	51.10	[2244]	82.48	[2244]	29.18	[2244]
		l	24.83	[2244]	48.37	[2157]	56.76	[2157]	43.64	[2157]
	Cyclooctatetraene	g	71.12	[2339]	88.30	[2339]	78.10	[2339]	21.16	[2339]
		l	60.82	[2190]	85.59	[2190]	52.65	[2190]		
C_8H_{10}	Ethylbenzene	g	7.120^{7}	[2244]	31.208	[2244]	86.15	[2244]	30.69	[2244]
		l	−2.977	[2244]	28.614	[2244]	60.99	[2244]	44.56	[2244]
	o-Xylene	g	4.540^{8}	[1489, 2244]	29.177	[2244]	84.31	[2244]	31.85	[2244]
					29.173	[1489]	84.34	[1489]	31.93	[1489]
		l	−5.84	[2189, 2244]	26.37	[2244]	58.91	[2244]	44.9	[2244]
	m-Xylene	g	4.120^{9}	[2244]	28.405	[2244]	85.49	[2244]	30.49	[2244]
		l	−6.075	[2244]	25.73	[2244]	60.27	[2244]	43.8	[2244]
	p-Xylene	g	4.290^{10}	[2244]	28.952	[2244]	84.23	[2244]	30.32	[2244]
		l	−5.838	[2244]	26.31	[2244]	59.12	[2244]		
C_8H_{12}	Vinylcyclohexene	g	16.80	[1132]	47.14	[1132]	96.4	[1132]		
C_3H_{14}	Octyne-1	g	19.70^{11}	[2244]	56.19	[2244]	106.75	[2244]	41.58	[2244]

1. $\Delta H_0^\circ = -40.86^{12}$ [2342]. 2. $\Delta H_0^\circ = -41.16^{12}$ [1663a]. 3. $\Delta H_0^\circ = -39.34^{12}$ [2342]. 4. $\Delta H_0^\circ = -39.68^{12}$ [2342]. 5. $\Delta H_0^\circ = -39.74^{12}$ [2342]. 6. $\Delta H_0^\circ = 40.34$ [2244]. 7. $\Delta H_0^\circ = 13.917$ [2244]. 8. $\Delta H_0^\circ = 11.096$ [2244]. 9. $\Delta H_0^\circ = 10.926$ [2244]. 10. $\Delta H_0^\circ = 11.064$ [2244]. 11. $\Delta H_0^\circ = 27.97$ [2244]. 12. From S_2(g).

1	2	3	4		5		6		7	
C_8H_{16}	*n*-Propylcyclopentane	g	−35.39[1]	[2244]	12.56	[2244]	99.73	[2244]	36.96	[2244]
		l	−45.21	[2244]	10.12	[2244]	74.98	[2244]		
							74.29	[1955]	51.69	[1955]
	Octene-1	g	−19.82[2]	[2244]	24.96	[2244]	110.55	[2244]	42.56	[2244]
		l					86.15	[1835]	57.65	[1835]
	Cyclooctane	g	−30.06	[1224]	21.50	[1224]	62.62	[1224]		
		l	−40.42	[1224]	18.60	[1224]	87.66	[1224]	51.50	[1224]
	cis-1-Octene-2	g	−21.60	[231]						
	1,1-Dimethyl-2-propyl cyclopropane	l	−27.8	[241]						
	Ethyl cyclohexane	g	−41.05[3]	[2244]	9.38	[2244]	91.44	[2244]	37.96	[2244]
		l	−50.72	[2244]	6.96	[2244]	67.12	[2244]		
	1,1-Dimethylcyclohexane	g	−43.26[4]	[2244]	8.42	[2244]	87.24	[2244]	36.9	[2244]
		l	−52.31	[2244]	6.34	[2244]	63.89	[2244]		
	trans-1,2-Dimethyl	g	−43.02[5]	[2244]	8.24	[2244]	88.65	[2244]	38.0	[2244]
	cyclohexane	l	−52.19	[2244]	6.06	[2244]	65.20	[2244]		
	cis-1,2-Dimethylcyclo-	g	−41.15[6]	[2244]	9.85	[2244]	89.51	[2244]	37.4	[2244]
	hexane	l	−50.64	[2244]	7.50	[2244]	65.56	[2244]		
	trans-1,3-Dimethyl-	g	−42.20[7]	[2244]	8.68	[2244]	89.92	[2244]	37.6	[2244]
	cyclohexane	l	−51.57	[2244]	6.44	[2244]	65.99	[2244]		
	cis-1,3-Dimethylcyclo-	g	−44.16[8]	[2244]	7.13	[2244]	88.54	[2244]	37.6	[2244]
	hexane	l	−53.30	[2244]	5.02	[2244]	64.98	[2244]		
	trans-1,4-Dimethyl-	g	−44.12[9]	[2244]	7.58	[2244]	87.19	[2244]	37.7	[2244]
	cyclohexane	l	−53.18	[2244]	5.50	[2244]	63.80	[2244]		
C_8H_{18}	*cis*-1,4-Dimethylcyclo-	g	−42.22[10]	[2244]	9.07	[2244]	88.54	[2244]	37.6	[2244]
	hexane	l	−51.55	[2244]	6.85	[2244]	64.70	[2244]		
	n-Octane	g	−49.82[11]	[2244]	3.95	[2244]	111.55	[2244]	45.14	[2244]
		l	−59.74	[2244]	1.58	[2244]	86.23	[2244]	60.74	[2244]
	2-Methylheptane	g	−51.50[12]	[2244]	3.06	[2244]	108.81	[2244]		
		l	−60.98	[2244]	0.92	[2244]	84.16	[2244]		
	3-Methylheptane	g	−50.82[13]	[2244]	3.29	[2244]	110.32	[2244]		
		l	−60.34	[2244]	1.12	[2244]	85.66	[2244]		
	4-Methylheptane	g	−50.69[14]	[2244]	4.00	[2244]	108.35	[2244]		
		l	−60.17	[2244]	1.86	[2244]	83.72	[2244]		
	3-Ethylhexane	g	−50.40[15]	[2244]	3.95	[2244]	109.51	[2244]		
		l	−59.88	[2244]	1.80	[2244]	84.95	[2244]		
	2,2-Dimethylhexane	g	−53.71[16]	[2244]	2.56	[2244]	103.06	[2244]		
		l	−62.63	[2244]	0.72	[2244]	79.33	[2244]		
	2,3-Dimethylhexane	g	−51.13[17]	[2244]	4.23	[2244]	106.11	[2244]		
		l	−60.40	[2244]	2.17	[2244]	81.91	[2244]		

	2,4-Dimethylhexane	g	−52.44[18]	[2244]	2.80	[2244]	106.51	[2244]		
		l	−61.47	[2244]	0.89	[2244]	86.62	[2244]		
	2,5-Dimethylhexane	g	−53.21[19]	[2244]	2.50	[2244]	104.93	[2244]		
		l	−62.26	[2244]	0.59	[2244]	80.96	[2244]		
	3,3-Dimethylhexane	g	−52.61[20]	[2244]	3.17	[2244]	104.70	[2244]		
		l	−61.58	[2244]	2.23	[2244]	81.12	[2244]		
	3,4-Dimethylhexane	g	−50.91[21]	[2244]	4.14	[2244]	107.15	[2244]		
		l	−60.23	[2244]	2.03	[2244]	82.97	[2244]		
	2-Methyl-2-ethylpentane	g	−50.48[22]	[2244]	5.08	[2244]	105.43	[2244]		
		l	−59.69	[2244]	3.03	[2244]	81.41	[2244]		
	3-Methyl-3-ethylpentane	g	−58.38[23]	[2244]	4.76	[2244]	103.48	[2244]		
		l	−60.46	[2244]	2.69	[2244]	79.97	[2244]		
	2,2,3-Trimethylpentane	g	−52.61[24]	[2244]	4.09	[2244]	110.62	[2244]		
		l	−61.44	[2244]	2.22	[2244]	78.30	[2244]		
	2,2,4-Trimethylpentane	g	−53.57[25]	[2244]	3.27	[2244]	101.15	[2244]		
		l	−61.97	[2244]	1.65	[2244]	78.40	[2244]		
	2,3,3-Trimethylpentane	g	−51.73[26]	[2244]	4.52	[2244]	103.14	[2244]		
		l	−60.63	[2244]	2.54	[2244]	79.93	[2244]		
	2,3,4-Trimethylpentane	g	−51.97[27]	[2244]	4.52	[2244]	102.31	[2244]		
		l	−60.98	[2244]	2.54	[2244]	78.71	[2244]		
	2,2,3,3-Tetramethylbutane	g	−53.99[28]	[2244]	5.27	[2244]	93.06	[2244]		
							86.23	[321]	60.74	[321]
		l	−64.23	[2244]	3.13	[2244]	65.89	[2244]	46.03	[2244]

8, II

$C_8H_4O_3$	Phthalic anhydride	c	−110.03	[1360]	−79.1	[1360]	42.9	[1360]	38.5	[321]
$C_8H_6Cl_4$	2,3,5,6-Tetrachloro-*p*--xylene	c	−42.06	[2411]						
$C_8H_6O_4$	*o*-Phthalic acid	c	−186.88	[321, 1360]	141.32	[321]	49.7	[321, 1360]	45.0	[321]
			−186.93	[2323]	−61.30	[1360]				
	m-Phthalic acid	c	−191.23	[2323]						

1. $\Delta H_0^\circ = -23.98$ [2244]. 2. $\Delta H_0^\circ = -9.83$ [2244]. 3. $\Delta H_0^\circ = -28.94$ [2244]. 4. $\Delta H_0^\circ = -30.93$ [2244]. 5. $\Delta H_0^\circ = -30.91$ [2244]. 6. $\Delta H_0^\circ = 28.95$ [2244]. 7. $\Delta H_0^\circ = -30.06$ [2244]. 8. $\Delta H_0^\circ = -32.02$ [2244]. 9. $\Delta H_0^\circ = -31.99$ [2244]. 10. $\Delta H_0^\circ = -30.08$ [2244]. 11. $\Delta H_0^\circ = -38.20$ [2244]. 12. $\Delta H_0^\circ = -39.42$ [2244]. 13. $\Delta H_0^\circ = -38.64$ [2244]. 14. $\Delta H_0^\circ = -38.43$ [2244]. 15. $\Delta H_0^\circ = -37.71$ [2244]. 16. $\Delta H_0^\circ = -41.23$ [2244]. 17. $\Delta H_0^\circ = -33.76$ [2244]. 18. $\Delta H_0^\circ = -39.74$ [2244]. 19. $\Delta H_0^\circ = -40.61$ [2244]. 20. $\Delta H_0^\circ = -39.90$ [2244]. 21. $\Delta H_0^\circ = -38.61$ [2244]. 22. $\Delta H_0^\circ = -37.96$ [2244]. 23. $\Delta H_0^\circ = -38.68$ [2244]. 24. $\Delta H_0^\circ = -39.77$ [2244]. 25. $\Delta H_0^\circ = -40.73$ [2244]. 26. $\Delta H_0^\circ = -39.01$ [2244]. 27. $\Delta H_0^\circ = -39.12$ [2244]. 28. $\Delta H_0^\circ = -42.24$ [2244].

1	2	3	4	5	6	7
$C_8H_6O_4$	*p*-Phthalic acid (terephthalic acid)	c	−195.07 [2323]			
C_8H_8O	Acetophenone	l	−34.06 [1018, 1360]			
$C_8H_8O_2$	*o*-Toluic acid (*o*-methylbenzoic acid)	c	−99.55 [1023]			
	m-Toluic acid (*m*-methylbenzoic acid)	c	−101.90 [1360]			
			−101.84 [1023]			
			−99.5 [1360]			
	p-Toluic acid (*p*-methylbenzoic acid)	c	−102.58 [1029, 1360]			
	o-Methoxybenzaldehyde	l	−62.6[1] [1360]			
	m-Methoxybenzaldehyde	l	−64.9[1] [1360]			
	p-Methoxybenzaldehyde	l	−62.8[1] [1360]			
	Furylideneacetone	l	−72.40 [[688]			
$C_8H_8O_3$	3-Hydroxy-4-methoxy-benzaldehyde	l	−107.3[1] [1360]			
$C_8H_{10}O$	*o*-Ethylphenol	g	−34.75 [843]			
		l	−49.92 [843]			
	m-Ethylphenol	g	−34.94 [843]			
		l	−51.22 [843]			
	p-Ethylphenol	g	−34.48 [843]			
		l	−53.64 [843]			
	Ethyl phenyl ether	l	−37.67 [1360]			
	Methyl *o*-tolyl ether	l	−36.69 [1360]			
	2,3-Xylenol	g	−37.59 [731, 1360]			
		c	−57.67 [731, 1360]			
	2,4-Xylenol	g	−38.95 [731, 1360]			
		l	−54.69 [731, 1360]			
	2,5-Xylenol	g	−38.65 [731, 1360]			
		c	−58.96 [731, 1360]			
	2,6-Xylenol	g	−38.68 [731, 1360]			
		c	−56.75 [731, 1360]			
	3,4-Xylenol	g	−37.44 [731, 1360]			
		c	−57.93 [731, 1360			
	3,5-Xylenol	g	−38.63 [731, 1360]			

		c	−58.43	[731, 1360]				
$C_8H_{10}O_2$	*o*-Dimethoxybenzene	l	−89.5	[1360]				
	p-Xylene-*α*, *α*′-diol	c	−94.17	[2118]				
$C_8H_{10}S$	Benzyl methyl sulfide	g	19.0	[1871, 1873, 1879]				
		l	6.21	[1871, 1879]				
	Phenyl ethyl sulfide	g	18.4	[1871, 1873, 1879]				
			5.23	[1871, 1879]				
$C_8H_{12}S_6$	1,3,5,7-Tetramethyl-2,4,6,8,9,10-hexathia-adamantane	c			76.75	[960]	72.09	[960]
$C_8H_{14}O$	2-Ethylhexene-2-al	l	−62.46	[1360]				
$C_8H_{14}O_2$	Butyl isocrotonate	l	−110.2	[1360]				
	Isobutyl isocrotonate	l	−112.7	[1360]				
	sec-Butyl isocrotonate	l	−112.9	[1360]				
	Propyl ester of 4-pentenoic acid	l	−105.4	[1360]				
	Isopropyl ester of 4-pentenoic acid	l	−109.2	[1360]				
$C_8H_{15}N$	Heptyl cyanide	g			114.85	[72]	44.78	[72]
$C_8H_{16}O$	Octanone-2	l			89.35	[2071]	65.31	[2071]
	trans-3-*cis*-5-Dimethyl-cyclohexanol	l	−115.4	[1360]				
$C_8H_{16}O$	*cis*-3-*trans*-5-Dimethyl-cyclohexanol	l	−121.3	[1360]				
	cis-3-*cis*-5-Dimethyl-cyclohexanol	l	−100.9	[1360]				
	2-Ethylcaproaldehyde	l	−83.32	[1360]				
$C_8H_{16}O_2$	Caprylic acid (octanoic acid)	l	−152.22	[328]				
	Isoamyl propionate	l	−139.0	[1360]				
	Butyl butyrate	l	−138.1	[1360]				

1. $t = 17.°C$.

1	2	3	4	5	6	7
$C_8H_{16}O_2$	Isobutyl butyrate	g			125.6* [826a]	
		l	−139.8 [1360]			
	Sec-Butyl butyrate	l	−136.0 [1360]			
	Propyl valerate	l	−137.3 [1360]			
	Isopropyl valerate	l	−140.0 [1360]			
$C_8H_{17}Br$	1-Bromooctane	g	−46.26 [856]			
		l	−58.61 [856]			
$C_8H_{18}O$	Dibutyl ether	l	−96.1 [2416]			
$C_8H_{18}O$	Octanol-1	g	−86.56 [1359, 1360]	−29.27 [1365]	124.14 [1365]	48.17 [1365]
			−89.66 [2241]			
		l	−103.96 [1359, 1360]			
			−101.62 [961]			
			−103.61 [321]			
	n-Butyl ether	l	−156.1 [109]			
		g	−79.84 [1020]		114.96 [765]	48.82 [765]
			−87.2 [2416]			
	Di-sec-butyl ether	g	−86.28 [1020]			
	2-Thianone(methyl heptyl sulfide)	l	−103.46 [1360]			
		g	−66* [823]			
$C_8H_{18}O_2$	*Di-tert*-butylperoxide	g	−81.6 [759a]			
			−85* [823]			
		l	−91.1 [759a]			
			−94.0 [1360]			
		g	−59 [823]			
$C_8H_{18}O_4$	Dibutyl ether-ozonide	g	−47* [823]			
$C_8H_{18}S$	Octanethiol-l	g	−56.07[1,10] −56.08[2,10] [2342]	1.10[10]; 1.11[10] [2342]	127.20 [2342]	50.14; 50.15 [2342]
			−56.50[3,10] [1663a]	0.74[10] [1663a]	127.08 [1663a]	50.11 [1663a]
					127.22 [72]	50.34 [72]
	Z-Thianone(methyl heptyl sulfide)	g	−54.58[3,10]; −54.59[4,10] [2342]	2.85[10]; 2.86[10] [2342]	126.35 [2342]	50.03; 50.04 [2342]
	3-Thianone(ethyl hexyl sulfide)	g	−55.16[5,10]; −55.18[6,10] [2342]	2.11[10]; 12[10] [2342]	126.89 [2342]	49.64; 49.65 [2342]
	4-Thianone(propyl pentyl sulfide)	g	−55.20[7,10] [2342]	1.99[10] [2342]	127.21 [2342]	49.64 [2342]

	5-Thianonane	g	−55.38[8,10]	[2342]	2.22[10]	[2342]	125.84	[2342]	49.46	[2342]
			−39.96	[1247]						
		l	−52.7; −52.71	[1879]						
			−52.76	[2495]						
	2.6-Dimethyl-4-thiaheptane	g	−42.9	[1872, 1879]						
	(*di*(2-methylpropyl)	l	−54.8	[1872]						
	sulfide)		−54.79	[1879]						
	2,2,4,4-Tetramethyl-3-	g	−49.6	[1872, 1879]						
	-thiapentane	l	−60.39	[1879]						
			−60.4	[1872]						
$C_8H_{18}S_2$	5,6-Dithiadecane (dibutyl	g	−68.64[9,10]	[2342]	−6.22[10]	[2342]	136.91	[2342]	55.23	[2342]
	disulfide)		−37.63*	[1879]						
		l	−53.03	[1879]						
	2,7-Dimethyl-4,5-dithia-	g	−40.61	[1869, 1879]						
	octane (*di*-(1-isobutyl)	l	−55.40	[1869, 1879]						
	disulfide)									
	2,2,5,5-Tetramethyl-3,4-	g	−47.05	[1869, 1879]						
	-dithiahexane (*di-tert*-	l	−59.76	[1869, 1879]						
	-butyl disulfide)									
$C_8H_{19}Al$	Diisobutyl aluminum hybride	l	−96.1	[607]						
$C_8H_{19}N$	*n*-Butylisobutylamine	g	−41.8	[807]						
		l	−51.6	[807]						
$C_8H_{20}Ge$	Tetraethylgermanium	g	−34.6	[2170]						
			−40.2	[462]						
		l	−43.35	[2170]						
			−50.3	[462]						
			−50.0	[847]						
$C_8H_{20}Pb$	Tetraethyllead	l	(12.8)	[2338]	80.4	[2338]	112.92	[2338]		
$C_8H_{20}Sl$	Tetraethylsilane	g	−38	[567]						
		l	−49	[567]						
$C_8H_{20}Sn$	Tetraethyltin	g	−12	[1223]			132.6	[2194]		
			−16.7	[49]						
		l	−24	[461]						
			−28.8	[49]						
			−22.9	[1081]						

1. $\Delta H_0^\circ = -44.51^{10}$ [2342]. 2. $\Delta H_0^\circ = -44.50^{10}$ [2342]. 3. $\Delta H_0^\circ = -42.99^{10}$ [2342]. 4. $\Delta H_0^\circ = -42.98^{10}$ [2342]. 5. $\Delta H_0^\circ = -43.33^{10}$ [2342]. 6. $\Delta H_0^\circ = -43.32^{10}$ [2342]. 7. $\Delta H_0^\circ = -43.88^{10}$; -43.39^{10} [2342]. 8. $\Delta H_0^\circ = -43.57^{10}$ [2342]. 9. $\Delta H_0^\circ = -57.10^{10}$ [2342]. 10. From S_2(g).

1	2	3	4	5	6	7
			8, III			
$C_8H_5F_3O_2$	*m*-Trifluorotoluic acid	c	–251.78 [1334]			
$C_8H_5MnO_3$	Manganese cyclopentadienyl-tricarbonyl	c	–125.5 [165]			
$C_8H_{10}O_2S$	Methyl benzyl sulfone	g	–68.0 [926, 929]			
			–63.4* [879]			
		c	–89.5 [926]			
		l	–83.3 [1879]			
	Methyl *p*-tolyl sulfone	g	–71.6* [1879]			
		c	–93.2 [1879]			
$C_8H_{18}O_2S$	*Di-tert*-butyl sulfone	g	–129.7 [1874]			
		c	–154.0 [1874]			
	Di-isobutyl sulfone	g	–126.3 [1874]			
		c	–150.3 [1874]			
	Di-n-butyl sulfone	g	–122.2 [1874]			
		c	–146.7 [1874]			
$C_8H_{20}BN$	*Di-n*-butyl (amino) boron	l	–95.2 [107]			
$C_8H_{20}O_4Si$	Tetraethoxysilane	l	–318.9 [390]			
			–317.8 [390a]			
			8, IV			
$C_8H_{16}Cl_5OSb$	Complex of *tert*-butyl isopropyl ketone with $SbCl_5$	l	–11.34 [2075a]			
			9, I			
C_9H_8	Indene	g			51.19 [2480]	44.68 [2480]
C_9H_{10}	*α*-Methylstyrene (isopropenylbenzene)	g	27.00[1] [2244]	49.84 [2244]	91.7 [2244]	34.7 [2244]
	trans-β-Methylstyrene	g	28.00[2] [2244]	51.08 [2244]	90.9 [2244]	34.9 [2244]
						34.7 [1707]
	cis-β-Methylstyrene	g	29.00[3] [2244]	51.84 [2244]	91.7 [2244]	34.7 [1707]
	m-Methylstyrene	g	27.60[4] [2244]	50.02 [2244]	93.1 [2244]	34.7 [2244]

	o-Methylstyrene	g	28.30[5]	[2244]	51.14	[2244]	91.7	[2244]	34.7	[2244]
	p-Methylstyrene	g	27.40[6]	[2244]	50.24	[2244]	91.7	[2244]	34.7	[2244]
	Phenylcyclopropane	l	19.0	[258]						
	Indane (hydrindene)	g					56.01	[2480]	45.47	[2480]
C_9H_{12}	*n*-Propylbenzene	g	1.870[7]	[2244]	32.81	[2244]	95.76	[2244]	36.41	]2244]
							95.74	[2522]	36.73	[2523]
		l	−9.178	[2244]	29.600	[2244]	69.44	[2244]		
			11.020[8]	[1955a]			68.78	[1955a]	51.32	[1955a]
	Isopropylbenzene	g	0.940[9]	[2244]	32.738	[2244]	92.87	[2244]	36.26	[2244]
		l	−9.848	[2244]	29.708	[2244]	66.87	[2244]		
	1-Methyl-2-ethylbenzene	g	0.290[10]	[2244]	31.323	[2244]	95.42	[2244]	37.74	[2244]
		l	−11.110	[2244]	27.973	[2244]	68.42	[2244]		
	2-Methyl-3-ethylbenzene	g	−0.460[11]	[2244]	30.217	[2244]	96.60	[2244]	36.38	[2244]
		l	−11.670	[2244]	26.977	[2244]	69.90	[2244]		
	1-Methyl-4-ethylbenzene	g	−0.780[12]	[2244]	30.281	[2244]	95.34	[2244]	36.22	[2244]
		l	−11.920	[2244]	27.041	[2244]	68.84	[2244]		
	1,2,3-Trimethylbenzene	g	−2.290[13]	[2244]	29.319	[2244]	93.50	[2244]	36.85	[2244]
			5.48[14]	[321]	29.828	[1489]	91.79	[1489]	37.74	[1489]
		l	−14.013	[2244]	25.679	[2244]	66.40	[2244]		
	1,2,4-Trimethylbenzene	g	−3.330[15]	[2244]	27.912	[2244]	94.73	[2244]	37.10	[2244]
			4.503[14]	[321]	27.968	[1489]	94.59	[1489]	36.81	[1489]
		l	−14.785	[2244]	24.462	[2244]	67.93	[2244]		
					24.507	[2196]	67.73	[2196]	51.38	[2196]
	1,3,5-Trimethylbenzene	g	−3.840[16]	[2244]	28.172	[2244]	92.15	[2244]	35.91	[2244]
					28.19	[2519]	92.09	[2519]	35.92	[2519]
		l	−15.184	[2244]	24.832	[2244]	65.35	[2244]		
					24.81	[2519]	65.38	[2519]		
C_9H_{16}	Spiro-(4,4)-nonane	l	−34.4	[259]						
	Nonyne-1	g	14.77[17]	[2244]	58.20	[2244]	116.06	[2244]	47.04	[2244]
	Nonene-1	g	−24.74[18]	[2244]	26.97	[2244]	119.86	[2244]	48.03	[2244]
C_9H_{18}							93.90	[1835]		
	cis-1-Nonene-2	g	−26.56	[231]						
	n-Propylcyclohexane	g	−46.20[19]	[2244]	11.31	[2244]	100.27	[2244]	44.03	[2244]
							100.35	[1223]		

1. $\Delta H_0^\circ = 33.33$ [2244]. 2. $\Delta H_0^\circ = 34.45$ [2244]. 3. $\Delta H_0^\circ = 35.33$ [2244]. 4. $\Delta H_0^\circ = 33.93$ [2244]. 5. $\Delta H_0^\circ = 34.63$ [2244]. 6. $\Delta H_0^\circ = 33.73$ [2244]. 7. $\Delta H_0^\circ = 9.810$ [2244]. 8. $\Delta H_{\mathrm{vap}_{298}}$. 9. $\Delta H_0^\circ = 9.250$ [2244]. 10. $\Delta H_0^\circ = 8.092$ [2244]. 11. $\Delta H_0^\circ = 7.593$ [2244]. 12. $\Delta H_0^\circ = 7.241$ [2244]. 13. $\Delta H_0^\circ = 5.527$ [2244]. 14. ΔH_0°. 15. $\Delta H_0^\circ = 4.468$ [2244]. 16. $\Delta H_0^\circ = 4.241$ [2244]. 17. $\Delta H_0^\circ = 24.32$ [2244]. 18. $\Delta H_0^\circ = -13.47$ [2244]. 19. $\Delta H_0^\circ = -33.62$ [2244].

1	2	3	4	5	6	7
C_9H_{18}	*n*-Propylcyclohexane	l	−56.98 [2244]	8.22 [2244]	74.48 [2244]	
					74.54 [1223]	57.85 [1223]
	1,1-Dimethyl-2-butyl-cyclopropane	l	−33.9 [241]			
	n-Butylcyclopentane	g	−40.22[1] [2244]	14.67 [2244]	109.04 [2244]	42.42 [2244]
		l	−51.22 [2244]		82.18 [1955]	58.86 [1955]
C_9H_{20}	*n*-Nonane	g	−54.74[2] [2244]	5.96 [2244]	120.86 [2244]	50.60 [2244]
		l	−65.84 [321]	3.84 [321]	94.09 [321]	67.97 [321]
	2-Methyloctane	g	−56.51 [231]			
	3-Methyloctane	g	−56.00 [231]			
	2,2-Dimethylheptane	g	−59.05 [231]			
	2,3-Dimethylheptane	g	−55.98 [231]			

9, II

1	2	3	4	5	6	7
C_9H_7N	Quinoline	l	37.33 [2122]	65.90 [2122]	51.9 [2122]	
$C_9H_8O_2$	*trans* Cinnamic acid	c	−80.54 [2118]			
	cis-Cinnamic acid[3]	c	−73.9 [1360]			
	cis-Cinnamic acid[4]	c	−75.3 [1360]			
	cis-Cinnamic acid[5]	c	−71.5 [1360]			
$C_9H_{10}O$	1-Phenylpropanone-2	l	−36.4 [1360]			
	Propiophenone (ethyl phenyl ketone)	l	−39.95 [1018, 1360]			
$C_9H_{11}O_2$	2.3-Xylylic acid (2,3-di-methylbenzoic acid)	c	−107.65 [1023, 1360]			
	2,4-Xylylic acid (2,4-di methylbenzoic acid)	c	−109.58 [1023, 1360]			
	2,6-Xylylic acid (2,6-di-methylbenzoic acid)	c	−105.33 [1023, 1360]			
	3,4-Xylylic acid (3,4-di-methylbenzoic acid)	c	−112.04 [1023, 1360]			
	3,5-Xylylic acid (3,5-di-methylbenzoic acid)	c	−111.48 [1023, 1360]			
	Isoxylylic acid	c	−109.02 [1023, 1360]			
	trans-Indanediol-1,2	c	−88.5 [1360]			

	cis-Indanediol 1,2	c	−88.7	[1360]						
$C_9H_{12}S$	Benzyl ethyl sulfide	g	12.4	[1871, 1873, 1879]						
		l	−1.25	[1871, 1879]						
$C_9H_{14}S$	Thiaadamantane	c	−34.29	[1788]						
$C_9H_{14}Sn$	Trimethylphenyltin	l	6.65*	[2131]						
			13.6	[1081]						
$C_9H_{16}O_2$	Isoamyl isocrotonate	l	−117.6	[1360]						
	Butyl ester of 4-pentenoic acid	l	−113.8	[1360]						
	sec-Butyl ester of 4-pentenoic acid	l	−116.8	[1360]						
	Isobutyl ester of 4 pentenoic acid	l	−114.8	[1360]			124.16	[72]	50.25	[72]
$C_9H_{17}N$	Octyl cyanide	g					124.16	[72]	50.25	[72]
$C_9H_{18}O$	3 3,5-Trimethylcyclo-hexanol	l	−109.2	[1360, 2056]						
$C_9H_{18}O_2$	Pelargonic acid	l	−158.20	[328]						
	Isobutyl valerate	l	−147.2	[1360]						
	Butyl valerate	l	−145.1	[1360]						
	sec-Butyl valerate	l	−148.3	[1360]						
	Isoamyl butyrate	l	−146.0	[1360]						
	Nonanol-1	g	−91.47	[1359, 1360]	−27.24	[1365]	133.45	[1365]	53.64	[1365]
$C_9H_{20}O$		l	−110.07	[1359, 1360]						
			−109.75	[961]						
	Nonanethiol-1	g	−61.00[6,11]	[2342]	3.11[11]; 3.12[11]	[2342]	136.51	[2342]	55.61; 55.62	[2342]
$C_9H_{20}S$			−61.01[7,11]	[2342]			136.56	[72]	55.84	[72]
			−61.42[8,11]	[1663a]	2.75[11]	[1663a]	136.39	[1663a]	55.58	[1663a]
	2-Thiadecane	g	−59.51[9,11]; −59.52[10,11]	[2342]	4.86[11]; 4.87[11]	[2342]	135.66	[2342]	55.50; 55.51	[2342]

1. $\Delta H_0^\circ = -27.52$ [2244]. 2. $\Delta H_0^\circ = -41.84$ [2244]. 3. Mp 58 °C. 4. Mp 42 °C. 5. Mp 68 °C. 6. $\Delta H_0^\circ = -48.15$[11] [2342]. 7. $\Delta H_0^\circ = -48.14$[11] [2342]. 8. $\Delta H_0^\circ = -48.45$[11] [1663a]. 9. $\Delta H_0^\circ = -46.63$[11] [2342]. 10. $\Delta H_0^\circ = -46.62$[11] [2342]. 11. From S_2(g).

1	2	3	4		5		6		7	
$C_9H_{20}S$	3-Thiadecane	g	−60.09[1,20] – 60.10[2,20]	[2342]	4.12[20]; 4.13[20]	[2342]	136.20	[2342]	55.11; 55.12	[2342]
	4-Thiadecane	g	−60.12[3,20] – 60.13[4,20]	[2342]	3.99[20]; 4.00[20]	[2342]	136.52	[2342]	54.92; 54.93	[2342]
	5-Thiadecane	g	−60.31[5,20]	[2342]	3.82[20]	[2342]	136.52	[2342]	54.92	[2342]
$C_9H_{21}B$	Tripropylboron	g	−52.3	[1639]						
		l	−67.3	[108]						
	Triisopropylboron	g	−57.4	[1639]						
		l	−71.1	[108]						
					9, III					
$C_9H_9NO_3$	Hippuric acid	c	−145.54	[1554]						
$C_9H_{11}NO_2$	β-Phenyl-l-alanine	c	−111.6	[1006]	−50.6	[1006]	51.06	[1006]	48.52	[1006]
$C_9H_{11}NO_3$	*L*-Tyrosine	c								
			−160.5	[1006]	−92.2	[1006]	51.15	[1006]	51.73	[1006]
$C_9H_{15}AlO_9$	Aluminum trilactate	c	−622	[1671]						
					9, IV					
$C_9H_{18}Cl_5OSb$	Complex of *tert*-dibutyl ketone with $SbCl_5$	c	−10.30	[2075a]						
					10, I					
$C_{10}H_8$	Naphthalene	g	36.33[6]	[321]	53.63	[321]	80.43	[321]	32.08	[321]
			36.12	[1963]	53.58	[1963]				
			36.25	[1147]	53.55	[1147]				
		c	18.75	[1963]	48.10	[321]	40.01	[321]	39.60	[321]
			16.42	[1882]						
$C_{10}H_{12}$	1,2,3,4-Tetrahydro-naphthalene (etralin)	g	6.65*	[1147]	40.38*	[1147]	87.7	[1147]		
$C_{10}H_{14}$	1-Methyl-4-isopropyl-benzene (*p*-cymene)	g	6.90	[321]					40.6	[2471]
		l	−18.73	[2189]	28.61	[2189]	73.3	[2189]	56.6	[2189]
									50.6[13]	[2471]
	n-Butylbenzene	g	−3.30[7]	[2244]	34.58	[2244]	105.04	[2244]	41.85	[2244]

							161.1	[1955a]	42.42	[321]
		l	−15.28	[2189]	30.99	[2189]	76.9	[2189]	57.4	[2189]
			−15.58	[1955a]			123.4	[1955a]		
	1,2,3,4-Tetramethylbenzene	g	−10.02[8]	[321]	29.496	[321]	99.55	[321]	45.31	[321]
	1 2,3,5-Tetramethylbenzene	g	−10.71[9]	[321]	28.377	[321]	100.99	[321]	44.39	[321]
	l	l	−23.54	[321]	23.57	[321]	74.1	[321]	57.5	[321]
	1,2,4,5-Tetramethylbenzene	g	−10.82[10]	[321]	28.553	[321]	100.03	[321]	44.58	[321]
		c	−23.58	[321]	28.12	[321]	58.7	[321]	51.6	[321]
			−29.48	[870]						
$C_{10}H_{18}$	Decyne-1	g	−9.85[11]	[2244]	60.20	[2244]	125.36	[2244]	52.51	[2244]
	Spiro-(4,5)-decane	c	−47.9	[259]						
	cis-Decalin	g	−40.38	[1972]	20.51	[1972]	90.28	[1972]	39.84	[1972]
			−43.54	[1147]	17.58	[1147]				
			−25.777[12]	[321]						
		l	−52.45	[321]	16.47	[321]	63.34	[321]	55.45	[321]
	trans-Decalin	g	−43.57	[1972]	17.55	[1972]	89.52	[1972]	40.04	[1972]
			−40.45	[1147]	20.44	[1147]				
			−29.025[14]	[321]						
		l	−55.14	[321]	13.79	[321]	63.32	[321]	54.61	[321]
$C_{10}H_{20}$	Decene-1	g	−29.67[15]	[2244]	28.98	[2244]	129.17	[2244]	53.49	[2244]
							101.58	[1835]	71.78	[1835]
	cis-1-Decene-2	g	−31.49	[231]						
	n-Pentylcyclopentane	g	−45.15[16]	[2244]	16.68	[2244]	118.35	[2244]	47.89	[2244]
	n-Butylcyclohexane	g	−50.95[17]	[2244]	13.49	[2244]	109.58	[2244]	49.50	[2244]
							109.89	[1223]		
		l	−62.91	[2244]	9.69	[2244]	82.21	[2244]		
	1 1-Dimethyl-2-amyl-cyclopropane	l	−40.0	[241]			82.45	[1223]	64.78	[1223]
	Cyclodecane	l	−6586.2[18]	[1031]						
$C_{10}H_{22}$	*n*-Decane	g	−59.67[19]	[2244]	7.97	[2244]	130.17	[2244]	56.07	[2244]
		l	−71.95	[321]	4.19	[321]	101.70	[321]	75.16	[321]
	2-Methylnonane	g	−61.44	[231]						
	3-Methylnonane	g	−60.85	[231]						
	2,2-Dimethyloctane	g	−64.01	[231]						

1. $\Delta H_0^\circ = -46.97^{20}$ [2342]. 2. $\Delta H_0^\circ = 46.96^{20}$ [2342]. 3. $\Delta H_0^\circ = -47.03^{20}$ [2342]. 4. $\Delta H_0^\circ = -47.62^{20}$ [2342]. 5. $\Delta H_0^\circ = -47.21^{20}$ [2342]. 6. $\Delta H_0^\circ = 41.852$ [321]. 7. $\Delta H_0^\circ = 5.93$ [2244]. 8. $\Delta H_0^\circ = -1.155$ [321]. 9. $\Delta H_0^\circ = -1.782$ [321]. 10. $\Delta H_0^\circ = -2.104$ [321]. 11. $\Delta H_0^\circ = 20.68$ [2244]. 12. ΔH_0°. 13. $t = 20\,^\circ C$. 14. ΔH_0°. 15. $\Delta H_0^\circ = -17.12$ [2244]. 16. $\Delta H_0^\circ = -21.16$ [2244]. 17. $\Delta H_0^\circ = -36.09$ [2244]. 18. $(\Delta H^\circ_{comb})_{298}$ in *joules/mole*. 19. $\Delta H_0^\circ = -45.49$ [2244]. 20. From S_2(g).

1	2	3	4		5		6		7	
	10, II									
$C_{10}H_8O$	1-Naphthol (*α*-naphthol)	c	−26.4	[1360, 1799]						
	2-Naphthol (*β*-naphthol)	c	−29.3	[1360, 1799]						
$C_{10}H_{10}Fe$	Ferrocene (*bis*-(cyclopenta-dienyl)-iron)	g					87.51	[1145, 1146]		
							87.4	[1146]		
		c					51.68	[1146]	46.82	[1146]
$C_{10}H_{12}O$	*n*-Propyl phenyl ketone	l	−45.13	[1360]						
$C_{10}H_{12}O_2$	*cis*-1,2,3,4-Tetrahydro-naphthalenediol-1,2	c	−98.5	[1360]						
	trans-1,2,3,4-Tetrahydro-napthalenediol-1,2	c	−99.8	[1360]						
	cis-1,2,3,4-Tetrahydro-naphthalenediol-2,3	c	−98.5	[1360]						
	trans-1,2,3,4-Tetrahydro-naphthalenediol-2,3	c	−98.9	[1360]						
	2,3,4-Trimethylbenzoic acid	c	−116.30	[1025]						
	2,3,5-Trimethylbenzoic acid	c	−116.79	[1025]						
	2,3,6-Trimethylbenzoic acid	c	−113.68	[1025]						
	2,4,5-Trimethylbenzoic acid	c	−118.46	[1025]						
	2,4,6-Trimethylbenzoic acid	c	−114.20	[1025]						
	3,4,5-Trimethylbenzoic acid	c	−119.71	[1025]						
$C_{10}H_{12}O_4$	Glycerol 1-monobenzoate	c	−185.80	[2377]						
	Glycerol 2-monobenzoate	c	−184.72	[2377]						
$C_{10}H_{19}N$	Nonyl cyanide	g					133.47	[72]	55.72	[72]
$C_{10}H_{22}O$	Diamyl ether	g					132.03	[765]	59.85	[765]
	Decanol-1	g	−96.36	[1359, 1360]	−25.22	[1365]	142.76	[1365]	59.11	[1365]

		l	−116.18	[1359, 1360]						
			−114.66	[961]						
	Pentaethylene glycol	c	−233.1[1]	[1360]						
$C_{10}H_{22}O_2$	Decanediol-1,10	c	−165.77	[2118]						
$C_{10}H_{22}S$	Decanethiol-1	g	−65.93[2,16]; −65.94[3,16]	[2342]	5.12[16]; 5.13[16]	[2342]	145.82	[2342]	61.08; 61.09	[2342]
			−66.35[4,16]	[1663a]	4.76	[1663a]	145.70	[1663a]	61.04	[1663a]
							145.91	[72]	61.33	[72]
	2.8-Dimethyl-5-thianonane (*di*-(methylbutyl) sulfide)	g	−53.0	[1872, 1879]						
		l	−67.4	[1872, 1879]						
	2-Thiaundecane (methyl nonyl sulfide)	g	−64.44[5,16]	[2342]	6.87[16]; 6.88[16]	[2342]	144.97	[2342]	60.97; 60.98	[2342]
			−64.45[6,16]	[2342]						
	3-Thiaundecane (ethyl octyl sulfide)	g	−65.02[7,16]	[2342]	6.13[16]; 6.14[16]	[2342]	145.51	[2342]	60.58; 60.59	[2342]
			−65.03[8,16]	[2342]						
	4-Thiaundecane (propyl heptyl sulfide)	g	−65.05[9,16]	[2342]	6.00[16]; 6.01[16]	[2342]	145.83	[2342]	60.39; 60.40	[2342]
			−65.06[10,16]	[2342]						
	5-Thiaundecane (butyl hexyl sulfide)	g	−65.23[11,16]; 65.24[16]	[2342]	5.82[16]	[2342]	145.83	[2342]	60.39	[2342]
	6-Thiaundecane (diamyl sulfide)	g	−64.21[12.16]	[2342]	6.23[16]	[2342]	144.45	[2342]	60.39	[2342]
			−49.0	[1872, 1879]						
		l	−63.7	[1872, 1879]						
$C_{10}H_{22}S_2$	6,7-Dithiadodecane (dipentyl disulfide)	g	−78.49[13.16]	[2342]	−2.20[16]	[2342]	155.53	[342]	66.16	[2342]

11, I

$C_{11}H_{10}$	1-Methylnaphthalene	g					90.21	[1965]	38.13	[1965]
		l					60.90	[1838]	53.63	[1838]
	2-Methylnaphthalene	g					90.83	[1965]	38.19	[1965]
		c	7.99	[1838]	43.30	[1838]	52.58	[1838]	46.84	[1838]
$C_{11}H_{16}$	*n*-Amylbenzene	g	−8.23[14]	[2244]	36.54	[2244]	114.47	[2244]	47.32	[2244]
	Pentamethylbenzene	g	−17.18	[1489]	29.447	[1489]	106.09	[1489]	51.74	[1489]
			−7.608[15]	[321]						
		c	−32.44	[2114]	25.51	[2114]	70.3	[2114]		
			−31.93	[870]						

1. $t = 17$ °C. 2. $\Delta H_0^\circ = -51.80$[16] [2342]. 3. $\Delta H_0^\circ = -51.78$[16] [2342]. 4. $\Delta H_0^\circ = -52.10$[16] [1663a]. 5. $\Delta H_0^\circ = -50.28$[16] [2342]. 6. $\Delta H_0^\circ = -50.26$[16] [2342]. 7. $\Delta H_0^\circ = -50.62$[16] [2342]. 8. $\Delta H_0^\circ = -50.60$[16] [2342]. 9. $\Delta H_0^\circ = -50.67$[16] [2342]. 10. $\Delta H_0^\circ = -50.66$[16] [2342]. 11. $\Delta H_0^\circ = -50.85$[16] [2342]. 12. $\Delta H_0^\circ = -50.85$[16] [2342]. 13. $\Delta H_0^\circ = -64.39$[16] [2342]. 14 $\Delta H_0^\circ = = 2.28$[16] [2244]. 15. ΔH_0°. 16. From S_2(g).

1	2	3	4		5		6		7	
$C_{11}H_{29}$	Undecyne-1	g	–4.92[1]	[2244]	62.21	[2244]	134.67	[2244]	57.98	[2244]
	Spiro-(5,5)-undecane	l	–59.3	[259]						
	1,1-Dimethyl-2-hexyl-cyclopropane	l	–1740*[2]	[240]						
			–46.2	[241]						
$C_{11}H_{23}$	*n*-Pentocyclohexane	g	–55.88[3]	[2244]	18.80	[2244]	118.89	[2244]	54.90	[2244]
	n-Hexylcyclopentane	g	–50.07[4]	[2244]	18.69	[2244]	127.66	[2244]	53.35	[2244]
	Undecene-1	g	–34.60[5]	[2244]	30.98	[2244]	138.48	[2244]	58.96	[2244]
							109.31	[1360]	78.86	[1360]
	Cycloundecane	l	–7236.7[6]	[1031]						
$C_{11}H_{24}$	*n*-Undecane	g	–64.60[7]	[2244]	9.98	[2244]	139.48	[2244]	61.53	[2244]
		l	–78.06	[1222]	5.42	[1222]	109.50	[1222]	82.47	[1222]
	2-Methyldecane	g	–66.37	[231]						
	3-Methyldecane	g	–65.81	[231]						
	2,2-Dimethylnonane	g	68.94	[231]						

11, II

1	2	3	4		5		6		7	
$C_{11}H_{14}O$	Isobutyl phenyl ketone		–52.62	[1018, 1360]						
	tert-Butyl phenyl		–49.91	[1018, 1360]						
	2,4,5-Trimethylacetophenone	l	– 61.4	[1360]						
	2,4,6-Trimethylacetophenone	l	–65.0	[1360]						
$C_{11}H_{14}O_2$	2,3,4,5-Tetramethylbenzoic acid	c	–122.94	[1024]						
	2,3,4,6-Tetramethylbenzoic acid	c	–121.33	[1024]						
	2,3,5,6-Tetramethylbenzoic acid	c	–120.95	[1024]						
	cis-1-Phenylcyclopentane-diol-1,2	c	–97.5	[1360]						
$C_1\ H_{21}N$	Decyl cyanide	g					142.78	[72]	61.18	[72]
$C_{11}H_{24}O$	Undecanol-1	g	–101.27	[1365]	–23.20	[1365]	152.07	[1365]	64.58	[1365]
		l	–122.29*	[1365]						
$C_{11}H_{24}S$	Undecanethiol-1	g	–70.85[8,23]	[2342]	7.13[23] 7.14[23]	[2342]	155.13	[2342]	66.54; 66.56	[2342]
			–70.87[9,23]	[2342]			155.25	[72]	66.83	[72]
	2-Thiadodecane (methyl decyl sulfide)		–69.36[10,23]	[2342]						
			–69.38[11,23]	[2342]	8.88[23]; 8.89[23]	[2342]	154.28	[2342]	66.43; 66.45	[2342]

	3-Thiadodecane (ethyl nonyl sulfide)	g	−69.94[12,23]	[2342]	8.14[23]; 8.15[23]	[2342]	154.82	[2342]	66.04; 66.06	[2342]
			−69.96[13,23]	[2342]						
	4-Thiadodecane (propyl octyl sulfide)	g	−69.98[14,23]	[2342]	8.01[23]; 8.02[23]	[2342]	155.14	[2342]	65.86; 65.87	[2342]
			−69.99[15,23]	[2342]						
	5-Thiadodecane (butyl heptyl sulfide)	g	−70.16[16,23]	[2342]	7.83[23]	[2342]	155.14	[2342]	65.86	[2342]
			−70.17[23]	[2342]						
11, III										
$C_{11}H_{12}N_2O_2$	*L*-Tryptophane	c	−99.2	[1106]	−28.5	[1106]	60.00	[1106]	56.92	[1106]
$C_{11}H_{26}N_2O$	Product of addition of decane to urea	c							30.23	[2135]
12, I										
$C_{12}H_8$	Acenaphthylene	g	61.7	[876a]						
		c	44.7	[876a]						
	Diphenylene	c	−84.4	[806]						
$C_{12}H_{10}$	Diphenyl	g	41.30	[289]	67.86	[289]	83.3	[289]		
		c	23.10	[321]	59.83	[321]	49.2	[321]	47.1	[321]
			23.14	[1882]						
	Acenaphthene	g	37.4	[876a]						
		c	16.8	[876a]						
$C_{12}H_{18}$	*n*-Hexylbenzene	g	−13.15[17]	[2244]	38.55	[2244]	123.78	[2244]	52.79	[2244]
	Hexamethylbenzene	g	−25.26	[1489]	33.909	[1489]	108.12	[1489]	59.42	[1489]
			−13.15[19]	[321]	38.55	[321]	123.78	[321]	52.79	[321]
							72.647[18]	[1247]	59.03[2]	[1247]
		c	−38.59	[870]						
			−33.19	[2124]	30.04	[2124]	74.0	[2124]	61.5	[2124]
$C_{12}H_{22}$	Dodecyne-1	g	−0.01[20]	[2244]	64.22	[2244]	143.98	[2244]	63.44	[2244]
	Spiro-(5,6)-dodecane	l	−60.5	[259]						
	n-Hexylcyclohexane	g	−60.80[21]	[2244]	17.51	[2244]	128.20	[2244]	60.43	[2244]
$C_{12}H_{24}$	*n*-Heptylcyclopentane	g	−55.00[22]	[2244]	20.70	[2244]	136.96	[2244]	58.82	[2244]

1. $\Delta H_0^\circ = 17.04$ [2244]. 2. $\Delta H_0^\circ \Delta H_{comb}$. 3. $\Delta H_0^\circ = -39.73$ [2244]. 4. $\Delta H_0^\circ = -34.81$ [2244]. 5. $\Delta H_0^\circ = -20.76$ [2244]. 6. $(\Delta H^\circ_{comb})_{298}$ in *kjoules/mole*. 7. $\Delta H_0^\circ = -49.13$ [2244]. 8. $\Delta H_0^\circ = -55.44$ [2342]. 9. $\Delta H_0^\circ = -55.42$ [2342]. 10. $\Delta H_0^\circ = -53.92$ [2342]. 11. $\Delta H_0^\circ = -53.90$ [2342]. 12. $\Delta H_0^\circ = -54.26$[23] [2342]. 13. $\Delta H_0^\circ = -54.24$[23] [2342]. 14. $\Delta H_0^\circ = -54.32$[23] [2342]. 15. $\Delta H_0^\circ = -54.30$[23] [2342]. 16. $\Delta H_0^\circ = -54.49$[23] [2342]. 17. $\Delta H_0^\circ = -1.36$ [2244]. 18. $T = 303.15$ °K. 19. $\Delta H_0^\circ = -13.835$ [321]. 20. $\Delta H_0^\circ = 13.39$ [2244]. 21. $\Delta H_0^\circ = -43.38$ [2244]. 22. $\Delta H_0^\circ = -38.45$ [2244]. 23. From $S_2(g)$.

1	2	3	4		5		6		7	
$C_{12}H_{24}$	Dodecene-1	g	–39.52[1]	[2244]	32.99	[2244]	147.78	[2244]	64.43	[2244]
		l					117.08	[1835]	86.02	[1835]
	Cyclododecane	c	–7844.8[2]	[1031]						
$C_{12}H_{26}$	*n*-Dodecane	g	–62.52[3]	[2244]	11.98	[2244]	148.79	[2244]	67.00	[2244]
		l	–84.16	[321]	6.71	[321]	117.27	[321]	89.86	[321]
	2-Methylundecane	g	–71.29	[231]						
	3-Methylundecane	g	–70.74	[231]						

12, II

1	2	3	4		5		6		7	
$C_{12}H_8Cl_2$	2,2'-Dichlorodiphenyl	g	30.4	[2410]						
		c	7.39	[2410]						
	4,4'-Dichlorodiphenyl	g	28.8	[2410]						
		c	3.95	[2410]						
$C_{12}H_8F_2$	2,2'-Difluorodiphenyl	g	–45.4	[2410]						
		c	–68.09	[2410]						
	4,4'-Difluorodiphenyl	g	–46.5	[2410]						
		c	–68.27	[2410]						
$C_{12}H_8O$	Dibenzofurane (diphenylene oxide)	c	–1.4	[1360]						
$C_{12}H_8S_2$	Thianthrene	c	43.56	[2495]						
$C_{12}H_{10}Cr$	Diphenylchromium	c	21	[1227]						
$C_{12}H_{10}O_4$	Quinhydrone	c	–19.79	[432]	–77.19	[432]	77.9	[432]	66.2	[432]
$C_{12}H_{10}S$	Diphenyl sulfide	g	55.3	[1873, 1879]						
		l	39.14	[1879]						
$C_{12}H_{10}S_2$	Diphenyl disulfide	g	58.4	[1873]						
			59.8*	[1879]						
		l	35.69	[1879]						
$C_{12}H_{16}O_2$	Pentamethylbenzoic acid	c	–128.12	[3405]						
	trans-1-Phenylcyclohexanediol-1,2	c	–109.8	[1360]						
	cis-1-Phenylcyclohexanediol-1,2	c	–110.6	[1360]						
$C_{12}H_{22}O_{11}$	Saccharose	c	–532.0	[979]	–370.0	[979]	86.1	[979]		
$C_{12}H_{23}N$	Undecyl cyanide	g					152.09	[72]	66.25	[72]

$C_{12}H_{26}O$	Dihexyl ether	g					149.10	[765]	70.88	[765]
	Dodecanol-1	g	–106.18	[1365]	–21.18	[1365]	161.38	[1365]	70.05	[1365]
		l	–128.10*	[1365]						
$C_{12}H_{26}S$	Dodecanethiol-1	g	–75.78[4,16]	[2342]	9.14[16]; 9.15[16]	[2342]	164.44	[2342]	72.01; 72.03	[2342]
			–75.80[5,16]	[2342]			164.59	[72]	72.32	[72]
	2-Thiatridecane (methyl undecyl sulfide)	g	–74.29[6,16]	[2342]	10.89[16]; 10.90[16]	[2342]	163.59	[2342]	71.90; 71.98	[2342]
			–74.31[7,16]	[2342]						
	3-Thiatridecane (ethyl decyl sulfide)	g	–74.87[8,16]	[2342]	10.15[16]; 10.16[16]	[2342]	164.13	[2342]	71.51; 71.53	[2342]
			–74.82[9,16]	[2342]						
	4-Thiatridecane (propyl nonyl sulfide)	g	–74.90[10,16]	[2342]	10.02[16]; 10.03[16]	[2342]	164.45	[2342]	71.32; 71.34	[2342]
			–74.92[11,16]	[2342]						
	5-Thiatridecane (butyl octyl sulfide)	g	–75.08[12,16]	[2342]	9.84[16]	[2342]	164.45	[2342]	71.32	[2342]
			–75.10[13,16]	[2342]						
	7-Thiatridecane (dihexyl sulfide)	g	–75.08[14,16]	[2342]	10.25[16]	[2342]	163.07	[2342]	71.32	[2342]
$C_{12}H_{26}S_2$	7,8-Dithiatetradecane (dihexyl disulfide)	g	–88.34[15,16]	[2342]	1.81[16]; 1.82[16]	[2342]	174.15	[2342]	77.09	[2342]
$C_{12}H_{27}Al$	Triisobutylaluminum	l	–69.9	[607]						
$C_{12}H_{27}B$	Tributylboron	g	–69.4	[1639]						
		l	–83.2	[1639]						
	Tri-*tert*-butylboron	g	–85.6	[1639]						
	Tri-*sec*-butylboron	g	–72.6	[1639]						
	Triisobutylboron	l	–92.6	[108]						
			–81.9	[2168]						
		g	–74.5	[1639]						
			–68.1	[2168]						
$C_{12}H_{28}Ge$	Tetrapropylgermanium	g	–54.9	[2170]						
		l	–69.60	[2170]						
$C_{14}H_{28}Sn$	Tetrapropyltin	g	–48.6	[2430]						
		l	–50.6	[1081]						

1. $\Delta H_0^\circ = -24.40$ [2244]. 2. $(\Delta H^\circ_{comb})_{298}$ in *kjoules/mole*. 3. $\Delta H_0^\circ = -52.77$ [2244]. 4. $\Delta H_0^\circ = -59.08$[16] [2342]. 5. $\Delta H_0^\circ = -59.06$[16] [2342]. 6. $\Delta H_0^\circ = -57.56$[16] [2342]. 7. $\Delta H_0^\circ = -57.54$[16] [2342]. 8. $\Delta H_0^\circ = -57.90$[16] [2342]. 9. $\Delta H_0^\circ = -57.88$[16] [2342]. 10. $\Delta H_0^\circ = -57.96$[16] [2342]. 11. $\Delta H_0^\circ = -57.94$[16] [2342]. 12. $\Delta H_0^\circ = -58.14$[16] [2342]. 13. $\Delta H_0^\circ = -58.13$[16] [2342]. 14. $\Delta H_0^\circ = -58.14$[16] [2342]. 15. $\Delta H_0^\circ = -71.68$[16] [2342]. 16. From S_2 (g).

1	2	3	4	5	6	7
				12, III		
$C_{12}H_{10}OS$	Diphenyl sulfoxide	g	25.6* [1879]			
			25.6 [1877]			
		l	2.4 [1877, 1879]			
$C_{12}H_{10}O_2S$	Diphenyl sulfone	g	−28.7 [1879]			
		l	−54.1 [1879]			
$C_{12}H_{10}O_4S_2$	Diphenyl disulfone	g	−93* [1879]			
			−114.9 [1884]			
		c	−126.2 [1879]			
			−153.63 [1884]			
$C_{12}H_{27}BO_2$	Di-*n*-butyl ester of *n*-butylboric acid	l	−224.7 [110]			
$C_{12}H_{27}BO_3$	*n*-Tributyl borate	l	−284.7 [106]			
$C_{12}H_{27}BrSn$	Tributylbormotin	l	−85.5 [806]			
$C_{12}H_{28}BN$	Di-*n*-butyl (*n*-butyl-amino)-boron	l	−108.1 [107]			
				13, I		
$C_{13}H_{12}$	Diphenylmethane	g			76.25[1] [2194]	26.34[1] [2194]
		l	21.25 [321]	66.19 [321]	57.2 [321]	55.7 [321]
$C_{13}H_{20}$	*n*-Heptylbenzene	g	−18.08[2] [2244]	40.56 [2244]	133.09 [2244]	58.25 [2244]
$C_{13}H_{24}$	Tridecyne-1	g	−4.93[3] [2244]	66.23 [2244]	153.29 [2244]	68.91 [2244]
$C_{13}H_{26}$	*n*-Heptylcyclohexane	g	−65.73[4] [2244]	19.52 [2244]	137.51 [2244]	65.89 [2244]
	n-Octylcyclopentane	g	−59.92[5] [2244]	22.71 [2244]	146.27 [2244]	64.29 [2244]
	Tridecene-1	g	−44.45[6] [2244]	35.00 [2244]	157.09 [2244]	69.89 [2244]
		l			124.78 [1835]	
	Cyclotridecane	l	−8521.1[7] [1031]			
$C_{13}H_{28}$	*n*-Tridecane	g	−74.45[8] [2244]	13.99 [2244]	158.09 [2244]	72.47 [2244]
	2-Methyldodecane	g	−76.22 [1807]			
				13, II		
$C_{13}H_{10}O$	Benzophenone	c	−8.1 [1360]	33.5 [1360]	58.6 [1360]	
			−7.6 [289]	34.0 [289]		
	Xanthene	c	−15.3 [1360]			

$C_{13}H_{25}N$	Dodecyl cyanide	g					161.40	[72]	72.11	[72]
$C_{13}H_{26}O_4$	Glycerol 1-monocaprate	c	−265.06	[2377]						
	Glycerol 2-monocaprate	c	−261.90	[2377]						
$C_{13}H_{28}S$	Tridecanethiol-1	g	80.70[9,21]	[2342]	11.15[21]; 11.16[21]	[2342]	173.75	[2342]	77.47; 77.50	[2342]
			−80.73[10,21]	[2342]			173.94	[72]	77.81	[72]
	2-Thiatetradecane (methyl dodecyl sulfide)	g	−79.21[11,21]	[2342]	12.90[21]; 12.91[21]	[2342]	172.90	[2342]	77.36; 77.39	[2342]
			−79.24[12,21]	[2342]						
	3-Thiatetradecane (ethyl undecyl sulfide)	g	−79.79[13,21]	[2342]	12.16[21]; 12.17[21]	[2342]	173.44	[2342]	76.97; 77.0	[2342]
			−79.82[14,21]	[2342]						
	5-Thiatetradecane (butyl nonyl sulfide)	g	−80.01[15,21]	[2342]	11.85	[2342]	173.76	[2342]	76.79	[2342]
			−80.03[16,21]	[2342]						

13, III

$C_{13}H_{30}N_2O$	Product of addition of urea to dodecane	c							29.88	[2135]

14, I

$C_{14}H_{10}$	Phenanthrene	g	48.2	[1666a]						
		c	27.00	[819]	64.12	[819]	50.6	[819]		
			27.5	[1890a, 2387a]						
	Anthracene	c	27.8	[1882]						
			30.60	[321]	68.02	[321]	49.6	[321]	49.7	[321]
$C_{14}H_{14}$	Dibenzyl	g					115.1*	[826a]		
		c	10.53	[2124]	62.15	[2124]	64.4	[2124]	61.0	[2124]
$C_{14}H_{20}$	Cyclotetradecaciyne-1,8	c	35.51	[1259]						
$C_{14}H_{22}$	*n*-Octylbenzene	g	−23.00[17]	[2244]	42.57	[2244]	142	[2244]	63.72	[2244]
$C_{14}H_{26}$	Tetradecyne-1	g	−9.86[18]	[2244]	68.24	[2244]	162.60	[2244]	74.37	[2244]
$C_{14}H_{28}$	*n*-Nonylcyclopentane	g	−64.85[19]	[2244]	24.72	[2244]	155.58	[2244]	69.75	[2244]
	n-Octylcyclohexane	g	−70.65[20]	[2244]	21.53	[2244]	146.82	[2244]	71.36	[2244]

1. $T = 303\ °K$. 2. $\Delta H_0^\circ = -5.01$ [2244]. 3. $\Delta H_0^\circ = 9.75$ [2244]. 4. $\Delta H_0^\circ = -47.02$ [2244]. 5. $\Delta H_0^\circ = -42.10$ [2244]. 6. $\Delta H_0^\circ = -28.05$ [2244]. 7. $(\Delta H^\circ_{comb})_{298}$ in *joules/mole*. 8. $\Delta H_0^\circ = -56.42$ [2244]. 9. $\Delta H_0^\circ = -62.73$[21] [2342]. 10. $\Delta H_0^\circ = -62.70$[21] [2342]. 11. $\Delta H_0^\circ = -61.21$[21] [2342]. 12. $\Delta H_0^\circ = -61.18$[21] [2342]. 13. $\Delta H_0^\circ = -61.55$[21] [2342]. 14. $\Delta H_0^\circ = -61.52$[21] [2342]. 15. $\Delta H_0^\circ = -61.78$[21] [2342]. 16. $\Delta H_0^\circ = -63.77$[21] [2342]. 17. $\Delta H_0^\circ = -8.65$ [2244]. 18. $\Delta H_0^\circ = 6.10$ [2244]. 19. $\Delta H_0^\circ = -45.74$ [2342]. 20. $\Delta H_0^\circ = -50.67$ [2342]. 21. From S_2(g).

1	2	3	4	5	6	7
	Tetradecene-1	g	−49.36[1] [2244]	37.01 [2244]	166.40 [2244]	75.36 [2244]
		l			132.50 [1835]	
	Cyclotetradecane	c	−9135.7[2] [1031]			
			−88.94 [1259]			
$C_{14}H_{30}$	2-Methyltridecane	g	−81.15 [1807]			
	n-Tetradecane	g	−79.38[3] [2244]	16.00 [2244]	167.40 [2244]	77.93 [2244]
		l	−96.38 [321]	9.30 [321]	132.75 [321]	104.79 [321]

14, II

1	2	3	4	5	6	7
$C_{14}H_{10}O_2$	Benzil (dibenzoyl)	c	−42.7 [1360]			
			−36.80 [2118]			
$C_{14}H_{10}O_4$	Benzoyl peroxide	c	−106 [461]			
			−93.5 [1360]			
$C_{14}H_{12}O$	Desoxybenzoin	c	−16.99 [2118]			
	p-Methylbenzophenone	c	−184.0 [1360]			
$C_{14}H_{12}O_2$	Benzoin	c	−59.24 [2118]			
$C_{14}H_{14}S$	Dibenzyl sulfide	g	46.1 [1873]			
			46.1* [1879]			
		l	23.73 [1879]			
$C_{10}H_{16}S_4$	1, 3, 5, 7-Tetramethyl-2, 4, 6, 8-tetrathiaadamantane	c			71.90 [960, 1031]	70.71 [960, 1031]
$C_{14}H_{27}N$	Tridecyl cyanide	c			170.71 [72]	77.58 [72]
$C_{14}H_{30}O$	Diheptyl ether				166.17 [765]	81.91 [765]
$C_{14}H_{30}S$	Tetradecandiol-1	g	−85.63[4,23] [2342]	13.16[23]; 13.17[23] [2342]	183.06 [2342]	82.94; 82.97 [2342]
		g	−85.66[5,23] [2342]		183.28 [72]	83.31 [72]
	2-Thiapentadecane (methyl		−84.14[6,23] [2342]	14.91[23]; 14.92[23] [2342]	182.21 [2342]	82.83; 82.86 [2342]
	tridecyl sulfide)	g	−84.17[7,23] [2342]			
	3-Thiapentadecane (ethyl		−84.72[8,23] [2342]	14.17[23]; 14.18[23] [2342]	182.75 [2342]	82.44; 82.47 [2342]
	dodecyl sulfide)	g	−84.75[9,23] [2342]			
	4-Thiapentadecane (propyl		−84.75[10,23] [2342]	14.04[23]; 14.05[23] [2342]	183.07 [2342]	82.25; 82.28 [2342]
	undecyl sulfide)	g	−84.78[11,23] [2342]			
	5-Thiapentadecane (butyl		−84.94[12,23] [2342]	13.86[23] [2342]	183.07 [2342]	82.25 [2342]
	decyl sulfide)		−84.96[13,23] [2342]			

	8-Thiapentadecane (diheptyl sulfide)	g	−84.93[14,23]	[2342]	14.27[23]	[2342]	181.69	[2342]	82.25	[2342]
$C_{14}H_{30}S_2$	8, 9-Dithiahexadecane (diheptyl disulfide)	g	−98.19[15,23]	[2342]	5.83[23]; 5.84[23]	[2342]	192.77	[2342]	88.02	[2342]
			14, III							
$C_{14}H_{14}O_2S$	Benzyl sulfone	g	−36.8	[1879]						
		c	−64.1	[1879]						
	Di-*p*-tolyl sulfone	g	−49.0*	[1879]						
		c	−75.2	[1879]						
			15, I							
$C_{15}H_{14}$	1,1-Diphenylcyclopropane	l	44.3	[258]						
	trans-1, 2-Diphenylcyclopropane	l	39.7	[258]						
	cis-1, 2-Diphenylcyclopropane	l	42.7	[258]						
$C_{15}H_{24}$	*n*-Nonylbenzene	g	−27.33[16]	[2244]	44.58	[2244]	151.71	[2244]	69.18	[2244]
$C_{15}H_{28}$	Pentadecyne-1	g	−14.78[17]	[2244]	70.25	[2244]	171.91	[2244]	79.84	[2244]
$C_{15}H_{30}$	*n*-Decylcyclopentane	g	−69.78[18]	[2244]	26.72	[2244]	164.89	[2244]	75.22	[2244]
		l					128.71	[1955]	101.94	[1955]
	n-Nonylcyclohexane	g	−75.58[19]	[2244]	23.54	[2244]	156.12	[2244]	76.83	[2244]
	Pentadecene-1	g	−54.31[20]	[2244]	39.02	[2244]	175.71	[2244]	80.82	[2244]
		l					140.23	[1835]		
	Cyclopentadecane	c	−9813.3[21]	[1031]						
$C_{15}H_{32}$	2-Methyltetradecane	g	−86.07	[231]						
	n-Pentadecane	g	−84.31[22]	[2244]	18.01	[2244]	176.71	[2244]	83.40	[2244]
		l	−102.49	[321]	10.63	[321]	140.42	[321]	112.32	[321]

1. $\Delta H_0^\circ = -31.69$ [2244]. 2. $(\Delta H^\circ_{comb})_{298}$ in *kjoules/mole.* 3. $\Delta H_0^\circ = -60.06$ [2244]. 4. $\Delta H_0^\circ = -66.37^{23}$ [2342]. 5. $\Delta H_0^\circ = -66.34^{23}$ [2342]. 6. $\Delta H_0^\circ = -64.85^{23}$ [2342]. 7. $\Delta H_0^\circ = -65.82^{23}$ [2342]. 8. $\Delta H_0^\circ = -65.19^{23}$ [2342]. 9. $\Delta H_0^\circ = -65.16^{23}$ [2342]. 10. $\Delta H_0^\circ = -65.25^{23}$ [2342]. 11. $\Delta H_0^\circ = -65.22^{23}$ [2342]. 12. $\Delta H_0^\circ = -65.43^{23}$ [2342]. 13. $\Delta H_0^\circ = -65.41^{23}$ [2342]. 14. $\Delta H_0^\circ = -65.43^{23}$ [2342]. 15. $\Delta H_0^\circ = -78.97^{23}$ [2342]. 16. $\Delta H_0^\circ = -12.30$ [2244]. 17. $\Delta H_0^\circ = 2.46$ [2244]. 18. $\Delta H_0^\circ = -49.38$ [2244]. 19. $\Delta H_0^\circ = -54.31$ [2244]. 20. $\Delta H_0^\circ = -35.34$ [2244]. 21. $(\Delta H^\circ_{comb})_{298}$ in *kjoules/mole.* 22. $\Delta H_0^\circ = -60.71$ [2244]. 23. From S_2 (g).

1	2	3	4	5	6	7
15, II						
$C_{15}H_{12}O_2$	1, 3-Diphenylpropane-dione-1, 3	c	−53.14 [2118]			
$C_{15}H_{14}O$	1, 3-Diphenylpropanone-2	c	−20.3 [1360]			
	p-Ethylbenzophenone	l	−243.0 [1360]			
$C_{15}H_{29}N$	Tetradecyl cyanide	g			180.02 [72]	83.05 [72]
$C_{15}H_{30}O_4$	Glyceryl 1-monolaurate	c	−277.47 [2377]			
	Glyceryl 2-monolaurate	c	−275.48 [2377]			
$C_{15}H_{32}S$	Pentadecanethiol-1	g	−90.56[1,24] [2342]	15.17[24]; 15.18[24] [2342]	192.37 [2342]	88.41; 88.44 [2342]
			−90.59[2,24] [2342]		192.62 [72]	88.80 [72]
	2-Thiahexadecane (methyl tetradecyl sulfide)	g	−89.07[3,24] [2342]	16.92[24]; 16.93[24] [2342]	191.52 [2342]	88.30; 88.33 [2342]
			−89.10[4,24] [2342]			
	3-Thiahexadecane (ethyl tridecyl sulfide)	g	−89.65[5,24] [2342]	16.18[24]; 16.19[24] [2342]	192.06 [2342]	87.91; 87.94 [2342]
			−89.68[6,24] [2342]			
	4-Thiahexadecane (propyl dodecyl sulfide)	g	−89.68[7,24] [2342]	16.05[24]; 16.06[24] [2342]	192.38 [2342]	87.72 [2342]
			−89.71[8,24] [2342]			87.75 [2342]
	5-Thiahexadecane (butyl undecyl sulfide)	g	−89.86[9,24] [2343]	15.87[24] [2342]	192.38 [2342]	87.72 [2342]
			−89.89[10,24] [2342]			
16, I						
$C_{16}H_{10}$	Pyrene	c	26.55 [2123]	64.25 [2123]	51.4 [2123]	56.4 [2123]
	Fluoranthene	g	70.4 [876a]			
		c	46.0 [876a]			
$C_{16}H_{14}$	2, 7-Dimethylphenanthrene	g	34.2 [1666a]			
		c	8.69; 8.7 [1258]			
	4, 5-Dimethylphenanthrene	g	46.3 [1666a]			
		c	21.25; 21.3 [1258]			
$C_{16}H_{26}$	*n*-Decylbenzene	g	−32.86[11] [2244]	46.58 [2244]	161.02 [2244]	74.65 [2244]
		l	−59.23 [2522]	41.27 [2522]	184.05 [2522]	90.68 [2522]
$C_{16}H_{30}$	Hexadecyne-1	g	−19.71[12] [2244]	72.26 [2244]	181.22 [2244]	85.31 [2244]
$C_{16}H_{32}$	Hexadecene-1	g	−59.23[13] [2244]	41.03 [2244]	185.02 [2244]	86.29 [2244]
		l			147.91 [1835]	

	n-Decylcyclohexane	g	−80.51[14]	[2244]	25.54	[2244]	165.43	[2244]	82.29	[2244]
							165.97	[1223]		
		l					129.10	[1223]	108.09	[1223]
	n-Undecylcyclopentane	g	−74.70[15]	[2244]	28.73	[2244]	174.20	[2244]	80.68	[2244]
	Cyclohexadecane	c	−10465.2[16]	[1031]						
$C_{16}H_{34}$	*n*-Hexadecane	g	−89.23[17]	[2244]	20.02	[2244]	186.02	[2244]	88.86	[2244]
		l	−89.23	[321]	20.2	[321]	186.02	[321]	88.86	[321]
	2-Methylpentadecane	g	−91.00	[231]						
				16, II						
$C_{16}H_{12}O_2$	Dibenzoylethylene	c	−27.55	[1360]	26.3	[1360]	77.6	[1360]		
$C_{16}H_{14}O_2$	Dibenzoylethane	c	−61.24	[1360]	2.3	[1360]	76.3	[1360]		
$C_{16}H_{14}O_4$	Di-*p*-Toluyl peroxide	l	−107.7	[1360]						
	Di-*o*-toluyl peroxide	l	−119.4	[1360]						
$C_{16}H_{16}O$	*p*-Isopropylbenzophenone	l	−520.5	[1360]						
$C_{16}H_{31}N$	Pentadecyl cyanide	g					189.33	[321]	88.51	[321]
$C_{16}H_{32}O_2$	Palmitic acid (hexadecanoic	l	−201.0	[328]						
	acid)	c	−211.2	[1360]	−75.1	[1360]	104.8	[1360]		
$C_{16}H_{34}O$	Dioctyl ether	g					183.24	[765]	92.94	[765]
	Cetyl alcohol (hexadecylic	l	−151.86	[1360]	−23.08	[1360]	145.0	[1360, 2114]		
	alcohol)		−151.73	[2114]	−22.97	[2114]				
		c	−163.55	[1360, 2120]	−23.74	[1360]	108.0	[1360, 2114]		
			−163.42	[2114]	−23.62	[2114]				
$C_{16}H_{34}S$	Hexadecanethiol-1	g	−95.48[18,24]	[2342]	17.17[24]; 17.19[24]	[2342]	201.67; 201.68	[2342]	93.87; 93.91	[2342]
			−95.52[19,24]	[2342]			201.97	[72]	94.30	[72]
	2-Thiaheptadecane (methyl	g	−93.99[20,24]	[2342]						
	pentadecyl sulfide)		−94.03[21,24]	[2342]	18.92[24]; 18.94[24]	[2342]	200.82; 200.83	[2342]	93.76; 93.80	[2342]
	3-Thiaheptadecane (ethyl	g	−94.57[22,24]	[2342]	18.18[24]; 18.20[24]	[2342]	201.36; 201.37	[2342]	93.37; 93.41	[2342]
	tetradecyl sulfide)		−94.61[23,24]	[2342]						

1. $\Delta H_0^\circ = -70.02$[24] [2342]. 2. $\Delta H_0^\circ = -69.98$[24] [2342]. 3. $\Delta H_0^\circ = -68.50$[24] [2342]. 4. $\Delta H_0^\circ = -68.46$[24] [2342]. 5. $\Delta H_0^\circ = -68.84$[24] [2342]. 6. $\Delta H_0^\circ = -68.80$[24] [2342]. 7. $\Delta H_0^\circ = -68.89$[24] [2342]. 8. $\Delta H_0^\circ = -68.86$[24] [2342]. 9. $\Delta H_0^\circ = -69.07$[24] [2342]. 10. $\Delta H_0^\circ = -69.05$[24] [2342]. 11. $\Delta H_0^\circ = -15.94$[24] [2244]. 12. $\Delta H_0^\circ = -1.18$ [2244]. 13. $\Delta H_0^\circ = -39.98$ [2244]. 14. $\Delta H_0^\circ = -57.95$ [2244]. 15. $\Delta H_0^\circ = -53.03$ [2244]. 16. $(\Delta H^\circ_{comb})_{298}$ in *kjoules/mole.* 17. $\Delta H_0^\circ = -67.35$ [2214]. 18. $\Delta H_0^\circ = -73.66$[24] [2342]. 19. $\Delta H_0^\circ = -73.62$[24] [2342]. 20. $\Delta H_0^\circ = -72.14$[24] [2342]. 21. $\Delta H_0^\circ = -72.10$[24] [2342]. 22. $\Delta H_0^\circ = -72.48$[24] [2342]. 23. $\Delta H_0^\circ = -72.50$[24] [2342]. 24. From S_2 (g).

1	2	3	4		5		6		7	
$C_{16}H_{34}S$	4-Thiaheptadecane (*n*-propyl tridecyl sulfide)	g	−94.61[1,21]	[2342]	18.06[21]; 18.07[21]	[2342]	201.69	[2342]	93.19; 93.22	[2342]
			−94.64[2,21]	[2342]						
	5-Thiaheptadecane (*n*-butyl dodecyl sulfide)	g	−94.79[3,21]	[2342]	17.88[21]	[2342]	201.69	[2342]	93.19	[2342]
			−94.82[4,21]	[2342]						
	9-Thiaheptadecane (dioctyl sulfide)	g	−94.78[5,21]	[2342]	18.29[21]	[2342]	200.31	[2342]	93.19	[2342]
$C_{16}H_{34}S_2$	9,10-Dithiaoctadecane (dioctyl disulfide)	g	−108.05[6,21]; −108.03[21]	[2342]	9.85[21]; 9.86[21]	[2342]	211.39	[2342]	98.96; 98.95	[2342]
$C_{16}H_{36}S_4$	Dimer of di-*tert*-butyl disulfide	g	−47.1	[1883]						
$C_{16}H_{36}Sn$	Tetrabutyltin	l	−72.7	[1081]						

16, III

1	2	3	4		5		6		7	
$C_{16}H_{31}NaO_2$	ω-Sodium palmitate	g					113.6	[2691]		
	β-Sodium palmitate	c					112.9	[2691]		
	δ-Sodium palmitate	c					112.2	[2691]		
$C_{16}H_{31}NaO_2\cdot 0.010H_2O$	δ-Sodium palmitate hydrate	c					113.0[7]	[2692]	110.6	[2692]
$C_{16}H_{31}NaO_2\cdot 0.12H_2O$	δ-Sodium palmitate hydrate	c					113.4[7]	[2691]	107.4	[2691]
$C_{16}H_{31}NaO_2\cdot 0.17H_2O$	ω-Sodium palmitate hydrate	c					113.8[7]	[2691]	118.3	[2691]
$C_{16}H_{31}NaO_2\cdot 0.409H_2O$	β-Sodium palmitate hydrate	c					119.3[7]	[2692]	115.0	[2692]
$C_{16}H_{31}NaO_2\cdot 0.482H_2O$	ε-Sodium palmitate hydrate	c					119.7[7]	[2692]	113.9	[2692]
$C_{16}H_{31}NaO_2\cdot 0.715H_2O$	ε-Sodium palmitate hydrate	c					123.9[7]	[2692]	119.9	[2692]
$C_{16}H_{36}B_2O$	Di-*n*-butylboric acid anhydride	c	−212.8	[106]						

17, I

$C_{17}H_{28}$	*n*-Undecylbenzene	g	−37.78[8]	[2244]	48.59	[2244]	170.32	[2244]	80.12	[2244]
$C_{17}H_{32}$	Heptadecyne-1	g	−24.64[9]	[2244]	74.27	[2244]	190.53	[2244]	90.77	[2244]
$C_{17}H_{34}$	Heptadecene-1	g	−64.15[10]	[2244]	43.01	[2244]	194.33	[2244]	91.76	[2244]
	n-Dodecylcylopentane	g	−79.63[11]	[2244]	30.74	[2244]	183.51	[2244]	86.15	[2244]
	n-Undecylcyclohexane	g	−85.43[12]	[2244]	27.55	[2244]	174.74	[2244]	87.76	[2244]
	Cycloheptadecane	c	−11117.5[13]	[1031]						
$C_{17}H_{36}$	*n*-Heptadecane	g	−94.15[14]	[2244]	22.03	[2244]	195.33	[2244]	94.33	[2244]
		l	−114.69	[2192]						

17, II

$C_{17}H_{18}O$	*p-tert*-Butylbenzo-phenone	l	−686.7	[1360]						
$C_{17}H_{33}N$	Hexadecyl cyanide	g					198.64	[72]	93.98	[72]
$C_{17}H_{34}O_4$	Glyceryl 1-mono-myristate (*α*-mono-myristin)	c	−292.31	[2377]						
	Glyceryl 2-mono-myristate	c	−289.89	[2377]						
$C_{17}H_{36}S$	Heptadecanethiol-1	g	−100.41[15,21]	[2342]	19.18[21]; 19.20[21]	[2342]	210.98; 210.99	[2342]	99.34; 99.38	[2342]
			−100.45[16,21]	[2342]			211.31	[72]	99.79	[72]
	2-Thiaoctadecane (methyl hexadecyl sulfide)	g	−98.92[17,21]	[2342]	20.93[21]; 20.95[21]	[2342]	210.13; 210.14	[2342]	99.23; 99.27	[2342]
			−98.96[18,21]	[2342]						
	3-Thiaoctadecane (ethyl pentadecyl sulfide)	g	−99.50[19,21]	[2342]	20.19[21]; 20.21[21]	[2342]	210.67; 210.68	[2342]	98.84; 98.88	[2342]
			−99.54[20,21]	[2342]						

1. $\Delta H_0^\circ = -72.54$[21] [2342]. 2. $\Delta H_0^\circ = -72.50$[21] [2342]. 3. $\Delta H_0^\circ = -72.71$[21] [2342]. 4. $\Delta H_0^\circ = -72.69$[21] [2342]. 5. $\Delta H_0^\circ = -72.72$[21] [2342]. 6. $\Delta H_0^\circ = -86.26$[21] [2342]. 7. $S_{298}^\circ - S_0^\circ$. 8. $\Delta H_0^\circ = -19.58$ [2244]. 9. $\Delta H_0^\circ = -4.83$ [2244]. 10. $\Delta H_0^\circ = -42.62$ [2244]. 11. $\Delta H_0^\circ = -55.67$ [2244]. 12. $\Delta H_0^\circ = -61.60$ [2244]. 13. $(\Delta H_{comb}^\circ)_{298}$ in *kjoules/mole*. 14. $\Delta H_0^\circ = -70.99$ [2244]. 15. $\Delta H_0^\circ = -77.30$[21] [2342]. 16. $\Delta H_0^\circ = -77.26$[21] [2342]. 17. $\Delta H_0^\circ = -75.38$[21] [2342]. 18. $\Delta H_0^\circ = -75.74$[21] [2342]. 19. $\Delta H_0^\circ = -76.12$[21] [2342]. 20. $\Delta H_0^\circ = -76.08$[21] [2342]. 21. From $S_2(g)$.

1	2	3	4		5		6		7	
$C_{17}H_{36}S$	4-Thiaoctadecane (propyl tetradecyl sulfide)	g	−99.53[1,24]	[2342]	20.07[24]; 20.08[24]	[2342]	210.99; 211.00	[2342]	98.65; 98.69	[2342]
			−99.57[2,24]	[2342]						
	5-Thiaoctadecane (butyl tridecyl sulfide)	g	−99.71[3,24]	[2342]						
			−99.75[4,24]	[2342]	19.89[24]	[2342]	210.99	[2342]	98.65	[2342]
					17, III					
$C_{17}H_{38}N_2O$	Product of addition of urea to hexadecane	c							30.61	[2135]
					18, I					
$C_{18}H_{12}$	1,2 Benzanthracene	g	65.6	[1666a]						
		c	40.6	[1890a]						
$C_{18}H_{18}$	Cyclooctadecanonaene	g	19.82	[811]						
		c	39.0	[811]						
	2,4,5,7-Tetramethyl-phenanthrene	g	31.1	[1666a]						
		c	3.8	[1666a]						
	3,4,5,6-Tetramethyl-phenanthrene	g	38.3	[1666a]						
		c	6.4	[1666a]						
$C_{18}H_{30}$	*n*-Dodecylbenzene	g	−42.71[5]	[2244]	50.60	[2244]	179.63	[2244]	85.58	[2244]
$C_{18}H_{34}$	Octadecyne-1	g	−29.56[6]	[2244]	76.28	[2244]	199.84	[2244]	96.24	[2244]
$C_{18}H_{36}$	*n*-Dodecylcyclohexane	g	−90.36[7]	[2244]	29.56	[2244]	184.05	[2244]	93.22	[2244]
	n-Tridecylcyclopentane	g	−84.55[8]	[2244]	32.75	[2244]	192.89	[2244]	91.62	[2244]
	Octadecene-1	g	−69.08[9]	[2244]	45.05	[2244]	203.64	[2244]	97.22	[2244]
$C_{18}H_{38}$	*n*-Octadecane	g	−99.08[10]	[2244]	24.04	[2244]	204.64	[2244]	99.80	[2244]
		l	−120.8	[1911]	13.67	[1911]	166.5	[1911]		
		c	−135.92	[1911]	12.80	[1911]	118.7	[1911]		
					18, II					
$C_{18}H_{13}P$	P-Phenyl-9-phosphafluorene	c	44.9	[808]						
$C_{18}H_{14}O_4$	Dicinnamoyl peroxide	c	−84.7	[1360]						
$C_{18}H_{15}As$	Triphenylarsenic	g	92	[1988]						
		l	−81.2	[851]						

		c	71.0	[1988]						
$C_{18}H_{15}Bi$	Triphenylbismuth	l	−100.1	[851]						
$C_{18}H_{15}P$	Triphenylphosphorus	c	54.3	[809, 1986]						
$C_{18}H_{35}N$	Heptadecyl cyanide	g					207.95	[72]	99.44	[72]
$C_{18}H_{36}O_2$	Stearic acid (octadecanoic acid)	l	−213.7	[328]						
$C_{18}H_{38}O$	Dinonyl ether	g					200.31	[765]	103.97	[765]
$C_{18}H_{38}S$	Octadecanethiol-1	g	−105.33[11,24]	[2342]	21.19[24]	[2342]	220.29; 220.30	[2342]	104.80; 104.85	[2342]
			−105.38[12,24]	[2342]			220.65	[72]	105.28	[72]
	2-Thianonadecane (methyl heptadecyl sulfide)	g	−103.84[13,24]	[2342]	22.94[24]; 22.96[24]	[2342]	219.44; 219.45	[2342]	104.69; 104.74	[2342]
			−103.89[14,24]	[2342]						
	3-Thianonadecane (ethyl hexadecyl sulfide)	g	−104.42[15,24]	[2342]	22.20[24]; 22.22[24]	[2342]	219.98; 219.99	[2342]	104.30; 104.35	[2342]
			−104.47[16,24]	[2342]						
	4-Thianonadecane (propyl pentadecyl sulfide)	g	−104.46[17,24]	[2342]	22.08[24]; 22.09[24]	[2342]	220.30; 220.31	[2342]	104.12; 104.16	[2342]
			−104.50[18,24]	[2342]						
	5-Thianonadecane (butyl tetradecyl sulfide)	g	−104.64[19,24]	[2342]	21.90[24]	[2342]	220.30	[2342]	104.12	[2342]
			−104.68[20,24]	[2342]						
	10-Thianonadecane (dinonyl sulfide)	g	−104.64[21,24]	[2342]	22.31[24]	[2342]	218.92	[2342]	104.12	[2342]
$C_{18}H_{38}S_2$	10,11-Dithiacicosane (dinonanyl disulfide)	g	−117.90[22,24]	[2342]	13.86[24]; 13.88[24]	[2342]	230.00; 230.01	[2342]	109.89; 109.88	[2342]
			−117.88[23,24]	[2342]						
	18, III									
$C_{18}H_{13}OP$	9-Phenyl-9-phosphofluorene oxide	c	−21.3	[808]						
$C_{18}H_{15}BrSn$	Triphenylbrominetin	c	46.5	[2169]						

1. $\Delta H_0^\circ = -76.18$[24] [2342]. 2. $\Delta H_0^\circ = -76.14$[24] [2342]. 3. $\Delta H_0^\circ = -76.36$[24] [2342]. 4. $\Delta H_0^\circ = -76.33$[24] [2342]. 5. $\Delta H_0^\circ = -23.23$ [2244]. 6. $\Delta H_0^\circ = -8.47$ [2244]. 7. $\Delta H_0^\circ = -65.24$ [2244]. 8. $\Delta H_0^\circ = -60.32$ [2244]. 9. $\Delta H_0^\circ = -46.27$ [2244]. 10. $\Delta H_0^\circ = -74.64$ [2244]. 11. $\Delta H_0^\circ = -80.95$[24] [2342]. 12. $\Delta H_0^\circ = -80.90$[24] [2342]. 13. $\Delta H_0^\circ = -79.43$[24] [2342]. 14. $\Delta H_0^\circ = -79.38$[24] [2342]. 15. $\Delta H_0^\circ = -79.77$[24] [2342]. 16. $\Delta H_0^\circ = -79.72$[24] [2342]. 17. $\Delta H_0^\circ = -79.83$[24] [2342]. 18. $\Delta H_0^\circ = -79.78$[24] [2342]. 19. $\Delta H_0^\circ = -80.00$[24] [2342]. 20. $\Delta H_0^\circ = -79.97$[24] [2342]. 21. $\Delta H_0^\circ = -80.01$[24] [2342]. 22. $\Delta H_0^\circ = -93.54$[24] [2342]. 23. $\Delta H_0^\circ = -93.55$[24] [2342]. 24. From S_2(g).

1	2	3	4	5	6	7
$C_{18}H_{15}OP$	Triphenylphosphine oxide	c	−15.6 [809, 1986]			

19, I

1	2	3	4	5	6	7
$C_{19}H_{16}$	Triphenylmethane	c	38.71 [2114]	98.60 [2114]	74.6 [2114]	70.5 [2114]
$C_{19}H_{32}$	*n*-Tridecylbenzene	g	−47.63[1] [2244]	52.61 [2244]	188.94 [2244]	91.05 [2244]
$C_{19}H_{36}$	Nonadecyne 1	g	−34.49[2] [2244]	78.29 [2244]	209.15 [2244]	101.70 [2244]
$C_{19}H_{38}$	*n*-Tridecylcyclohexane	g	−95.28[3] [2244]	31.57 [2244]	193.56 [2244]	98.69 [2244]
	n-Tetradecylcycloheptane	g	−89.48[4] [2244]	34.76 [2244]	202.13 [2244]	97.08 [2244]
	Nonadecene-1	g	−74.00[5] [2244]	47.06 [2244]	212.95 [2244]	102.69 [2244]
$C_{19}H_{40}$	*n*-Nonadecane	g	−104.00[6] [2244]	26.05 [2244]	213.95 [2244]	105.26 [2244]
		l	−126.9 [2192]			

19, II

1	2	3	4	5	6	7
$C_{19}H_{16}O$	Triphenylcarbinol		−0.80 [1360]	65.2 [1360]	78.7 [1360]	
$C_{19}H_{36}O_2$	Methyl elaidate	l	−175.3 [1360]			
	Methyl oleate	l	−173.7 [1360]			
$C_{19}H_{37}N$	Octadecyl cyanide	g			217.26 [72]	104.91 [72]
$C_{19}H_{38}O_4$	Glyceryl 1-monopalmitate	c	−306.30 [2377]			
	Glyceryl 2-monopalmitate	c	−303.25 [2377]			
$C_{19}H_{40}S$	Nonadecanethiol	g	−110.26[7,25] [2342]	23.20[25]; 23.22[25] [2342]	229.60; 229.61 [2342]	110.27; 110.31 [2342]
			−110.31[8,25] [2342]		222.99 [72]	110.78 [72]
	2-Thiaeicosane (methyl octadecyl sulfide)	g	−108.77[9,25] [2342]	24.95[25]; 24.97[25] [2342]	228.75; 228.76 [2342]	110.16; 110.21 [2342]
			−108.82[10,25] [2342]			
	3-Thiaeicosane (ethyl heptadecyl sulfide)	g	−109.35[11,25] [2342]	24.21[25]; 24.23[25] [2342]	229.29; 229.30 [2342]	109.77; 109.82 [2342]
			−109.40[12,25] [2342]			

	4-Thiaeicosane (propyl hexadecyl sulfide)	g	−109.38[13,25]	[2342]	24.08[25]; 24.10[25]	[2342]	229.61; 229.62	[2342]	109.58; 109.63	[2342]
			−109.43[14,25]	[2342]						
	5-Thiaeicosane (butyl pentadecyl sulfide)	g	−109.57[15,25]	[2342]	23.91[25]	[2342]	229.61	[2342]	109.58	[2342]
			−109.61[16,25]	[2342]						

20, I

$C_{20}H_{16}$	1',9-Dimethyl-1,2-benz-anthracene	g	60.1	[1666a]						
		c	33.20	[1258]						
	3',6-Dimethyl-1,2-benz-anthracene	g	45.1	[1666a]						
		c	18.20	[1258]						
$C_{20}H_{34}$	*n*-Tetradecylbenzene	g	−52.56[17]	[2244]	54.62	[2244]	198.25	[2244]	96.51	[2244]
$C_{20}H_{38}$	Eicosyne-1	g	−39.41[18]	[2244]	81.00	[2244]	218.46	[2244]	107.17	[2244]
	n-Tetradecylcyclohexane	g	−100.21[19]	[2244]	33.58	[2244]	202.67	[2244]	104.16	[2244]
	n-Pentadecylcyclopentane	g	−94.41[20]	[2244]	36.77	[2244]	211.44	[2244]	102.55	[2244]
	Eicosene-1	g	−78.93[21]	[2244]	49.09	[2244]	222.26	[2244]	108.15	[2244]
$C_{20}H_{42}$	*n*-Eicosane	g	−108.93[22]	[2244]	28.06	[2244]	223.26	[2244]	110.73	[2244]
		?	−133.01	[2192]						

20, II

$C_{20}H_{38}O_2$	Ethyl oleate	l	−184.7	[1360]						
	Ethyl elaidate	l	−184.1	[1360]						
$C_{20}H_{39}N$	Nonadecyl cyanide	g					226.57	[72]	110.38	[72]
$C_{20}H_{42}O$	Didecyl ether	g					217.38	[765]	115.00	[765]
$C_{20}H_{42}S$	Eicosanethiol-1	g	−115.19[23,25]	[2342]	25.21[25]; 25.23[25]	[2342]	238.91; 238.92	[2342]	115.74; 115.77	[2342]
			−115.24[24,25]	[2342]			239.34	[72]	116.27	[72]

1. $\Delta H_0^\circ = -26.87$ [2244]. 2. $\Delta H_0^\circ = -12.12$ [2244]. 3. $\Delta H_0^\circ = -68.89$ [2244]. 4. $\Delta H_0^\circ = -63.96$ [2241]. 5. $\Delta H_0^\circ = -49.91$ [2244]. 6. $\Delta H_0^\circ = -78.28$ [2244]. 7. $\Delta H_0^\circ = -84.52$[25] [2342]. 8. $\Delta H_0^\circ = -84.54$[25] [2342]. 9. $\Delta H_0^\circ = -83.07$[25] [2342]. 10. $\Delta H_0^\circ = -83.02$[25] [2342]. 11. $\Delta H_0^\circ = -83.36$[25] [2342]. 12. $\Delta H_0^\circ = -83.41$[25] [2342]. 13. $\Delta H_0^\circ = -83.47$[25] [2342]. 14. $\Delta H_0^\circ = -83.42$[25] [2342]. 15. $\Delta H_0^\circ = -83.65$[25] [2342]. 16. $\Delta H_0^\circ = -83.61$[25] [2342]. 17. $\Delta H_0^\circ = -30.52$ [2244]. 18. $\Delta H_0^\circ = -15.76$ [2244]. 19. $\Delta H_0^\circ = -72.53$ [2244]. 20. $\Delta H_0^\circ = -67.60$ [2244]. 21. $\Delta H_0^\circ = -53.56$ [2244]. 22. $\Delta H_0^\circ = -81.93$ [2244]. 23. $\Delta H_0^\circ = -88.24$[25] [2342]. 24. $\Delta H_0^\circ = -88.18$[25] [2342]. 25. From S_2(g).

1	2	3	4		5		6		7	
$C_{20}H_{42}S$	2-Thiaheneicosane (methyl nonadecyl sulfide)	g	−113.70[1,15]	[2342]	26.96[15]	[2342]	238.06	[2342]	115.63	[2342]
	3-Thiaheneicosane (ethyl octadecyl sulfide)	g	−114.28[2,15]	[2342]	26.22[15]	[2342]	238.60	[2342]	115.24	[2342]
	4-Thiaheneicosane (propyl heptadecyl sulfide)	g	−114.31[3,15]	[2342]	26.09[15]	[2342]	238.92	[2342]	115.05	[2342]
	5-Thiaheneicosane (butyl hexadecyl sulfide)	g	−114.49[4,15]	[2342]	25.91[15]	[2342]	238.92	[2342]	115.05	[2342]
	11-Thiaheneicosane (didecyl sulfide)	g	−114.49[5,15]	[2342]	26.32[15]	[2342]	237.54	[2342]	115.05	[2342]
$C_{20}H_{42}S_2$	11,12-Dithiadoeicosane (didecyl disulfide)	g	−127.75[6,15] −127.73[7,15]	[2342]	17.88[15]; 17.90[15]	[2342]	248.62; 248.63	[2342]	120.82; 120.81	[2342]
					21, I					
$C_{21}H_{36}$	*n*-Pentadecylbenzene	g	−57.49[8]	[2244]	56.63	[2244]	207.56	[2244]	101.98	[2244]
$C_{21}H_{42}$	*n*-Pentadecylcyclohexane	g	−105.14[9]	[2244]	37.60	[2244]	221.29	[2244]	109.62	[2244]
	n-Hexadecylcyclopentane	g	−99.33[10]	[2244]	38.78	[2244]	220.75	[2244]	108.01	[2244]
					21, II					
$C_{21}H_{40}O_2$	Propyl oleate	l	−188.5	[1360]						
	Propyl elaidate	l	−190.0	[1360]						
$C_{21}H_{41}N$	Eicosyl cyanide	g					236.88	[72]	115.84	[72]
$C_{21}H_{42}O_4$	Glyceryl 1-monostearate	c	−319.75	[2377]						
	Glyceryl 2-monostearate	c	−315.81	[2377]						
$C_{21}H_{45}B$	Triheptyl boron	l	−134.56	[821]						
					21, III					
$C_{21}H_{46}N_2O$	Product of addition of urea to eicosane	c							30.32	[2135]

22, I

$C_{22}H_{38}$	*n*-Hexadecylbenzene	g	−62.41[11]	[2244]	58.64	[2244]	216.87	[2244]	107.45	[2244]
$C_{22}H_{44}$	*n*-Hexadecylcyclohexane	g	−110.06[12]	[2244]	37.60	[2244]	221.29	[2244]	115.09	[2244]

22, II

$C_{22}H_{42}O_2$	Butyl oleate	l	−194.3	[1360]
	Butyl elaidate	l	−196.2	[1360]

24, II

$C_{24}H_{20}Ge$	Tetraphenylgermanium	g	103*	[566]
		c	−208.6	[852]
			82*	[566]
$C_{24}H_{20}Pb$	Tetraphenyllead	g	19.18[13]	[939]
			18.96[13]	[940]
$C_{24}H_{20}Si$	Tetraphenylsilane	g	98	[566]
		c	−80.0	[852]
			76*	[566]
$C_{24}H_{20}Sn$	Tetraphenyltin	g	15.85[13]	[939]
			15.8[14]	[940]
			137*	[566]
		c	116*	[566]
			−225.0	[852]
			98.5	[2169]
$C_{24}H_{51}B$	Trioctylboron	g	−149.25	[368]
		l	−153.04	[368]

1. $\Delta H_0^\circ = -86.72$[15] [2342]. 2. $\Delta H_0^\circ = -87.06$[15] [2342]. 3. $\Delta H_0^\circ = -87.11$[15] [2342]. 4. $\Delta H_0^\circ = -87.29$[15] [2342]. 5. $\Delta H_0^\circ = -87.29$[15] [2342]. 6. $\Delta H_0^\circ = -100.83$[15] [2342]. 7. $\Delta H_0^\circ = -100.84$[15] [2342]. 8. $\Delta H_0^\circ = -34.15$ [2244]. 9. $\Delta H_0^\circ = -76.17$ [2244]. 10. $\Delta H_0^\circ = -77.25$ [2244]. 11. $\Delta H_0^\circ = -37.80$ [2244]. 12. $\Delta H_0^\circ = -79.82$ [2244]. 13. $(\Delta H_{298}^\circ)_{subl}$. 14. ΔH_{subl}; 30–40 °C. 15. From S_2 (g).

1	2	3	4	5	6	7
			24, IV			
$C_{24}H_{51}NO_4S$	Tri-*n*-octylamine sulfate	c	−20.95 [2592a]			
			32, II			
$C_{32}H_{28}Si$	Tetra-*β*-styryl silane	c	−161.5 [2003, 2116]			
			34, II			
$C_{34}H_{25}P$	Pentaphenylcyclo-phosphapentadiene	c	93.7 [808]			
			34, III			
$C_{34}H_{25}OP$	Pentaphenylcyclo-phosphapentadiene oxide	c	52.8 [808]			

EXPLANATORY LIST OF ABBREVIATIONS OF U.S.S.R. INSTITUTIONS AND JOURNALS APPEARING IN THIS TEXT

Abbreviation	Full name (transliterated)	Translation
AN SSSR	Akademiya Nauk SSSR	Academy of Sciences of the USSR
AN AzSSR	Akademiya Nauk Azerbaidzhanskoi SSR	Academy of Sciences of the Azerbaidzhan SSR
AN KazSSR	Akademiya Nauk Kazakhskoi SSR	Academy of Sciences of the Kazakh SSR
DAN SSSR	Doklady Akademii Nauk SSSR	Proceedings of the Academy of Sciences of the USSR
DAN TadzhSSR	Doklady Akademii Nauk Tadzhikskoi SSR	Proceedings of the Academy of Sciences of the Tadzhik SSR
IONKh AN SSSR	Institut Obshchei i Neorganicheskoi Khimii im. N.S. Kurnakova	Kurnakov Institute of General and Inorganic Chemistry
Izd. VKhO	Izdatel'stvo Vsesoyuznogo Khimicheskogo Obshchestva im. D.I. Mendeleeva	D.I. Mendeleev All-Union Chemical Society Publishing House
Izv. AN SSSR	Izvestiya Akademii Nauk SSSR	Bulletin of the Academy of Sciences of the USSR
LGU	Leningradskii Gosudarstvennyi Universitet	Leningrad State University
MGU	Moskovskii Gosudarstvennyi Universitet	Moscow State University
OKhN	Otdelenie Khimicheskikh Nauk (Akademii Nauk SSSR)	Department of Chemical Sciences (of the Academy of Sciences of the USSR)
ZhFKh	Zhurnal Fizicheskoi Khimii	Journal of Physical Chemistry
ZhNKh	Zhurnal Neorganicheskoi Khimii	Journal of Inorganic Chemistry
ZhOKh	Zhurnal Obshchei Khimii	Journal of General Chemistry
ZhPKh	Zhurnal Prikladnoi Khimii	Journal of Applied Chemistry

BIBLIOGRAPHY

1. ABBASOV, A.S., A.V. NIKOL'SKAYA, Ya.I. GERASIMOV, and V.V. VASIL'EV. *DAN SSSR*, **156**, 118 (1964).
2. ABASOV, A.S., A.V. NIKOL'SKAYA, Ya.I. GERASIMOV, and V.V. VASIL'EV. *DAN SSSR*, **156**, 1140 (1964).
3. ABBASOV, A.S., A.V. NIKOL'SKAYA, Ya.I. GERASIMOV, and V.V. VASIL'EV. *DAN SSSR*, **156**, 1399 (1964).
4. AZERBAEVA, R.G. and N.L. TSEFT. *Trudy Instituta Metallurgii i Obogashcheniya AN KazSSR, Tsvetnaya Metalllurgiya*, **8**, 50 (1963).
5. AKISHIN, P.A., O.T. NIKITIN, and L.N. GOROKHOV. *DAN SSSR*, **129**, 1075 (1959).
6. AKSEL'RUD, N.V. *ZhFKh*, **29**, 2204 (1955).
7. AKSEL'RUD, N.V. *DAN SSSR*, **132**, 1067 (1960).
8. AKSEL'RUD, N.V. *ZhNKh*, **5**, 1910 (1960).
9. AKSEL'RUD, N.V. *ZhNKh*, **8**, 11 (1963).
10. AKSEL'RUD, N.V. and V.I. ERMOLENKO. *ZhNKh*, **6**, 777 (1961).
11. AKSEL'RUD, N.V. and V.B. SPIVAKOVSKII. *ZhNKh*, **3**, 269 (1958).
12. AKSEL'RUD, N.V. and V.B. SPIVAKOVSKII. *ZhNKh*, **4**, 56 (1959).
13. AKSEL'RUD, N.V. and V.B. SPIVAKOVSKII. *ZhNKh*, **5**, 327 (1960).
14. AKSEL'RUD, N.V. and V.B. SPIVAKOVSKII. *ZhNKh*, **5**, 340 (1960).
15. AKSEL'RUD, N.V. and V.B. SPIVAKOVSKII. *ZhNKh*, **5**, 348 (1960).
16. AKSEL'RUD, N.V. and V.B. SPIVAKOVSKII. *ZhNKh*, **5**, 547 (1960).
17. ALEKSANDROVSKAYA, A.M., Yu.A. ALESHONKOVA, L.N. SINITSYNA, and I.N. GODNEV. *Izvestiya Vysshikh Uchebnykh Zavedenii, Khimiya i Khimicheskaya Tekhnologiya*, No.1, 171 (1962).
18. ALEKSANDROVSKAYA, A.M., I.N. GODNEV, and A.S. SVERDLIN. *Izvestiya Vysshikh Uchebnykh Zavedenii, Khimiya i Khimicheskaya Tekhnologiya*, **6**, 165 (1963).
19. ALIKBEROV, S.S. and L.P. SHKLOVER. *ZhNKh*, **5**, 513 (1960).
20. AMOSOV, V.M. *Izvestiya Vysshikh Uchebnykh Zavedenii, Tsvetnaya Metallurgiya*, No.2, 103 (1963).
21. AMOSOV, V.M. *Izvestiya Vysshikh Uchebnykh Zavedenii, Tsvetnaya Metallurgiya*, No.2, 114 (1964).
22. AMOSOV, V.M. *Izvestiya Vysshikh Uchebnykh Zavedenii, Tsvetnaya Metallurgiya*, No.3, 123 (1964).
23. ANDREEV, S.N., V.G. KHALDIN, and E.V. STROGONOV. *ZhOKh*. **29**, 1798 (1959).
24. ANDREEVA, L.A. and M.Kh. KARAPET'YANTS. *ZhFKh*, **39**, 2410 (1965).
25. ANDREEVA, L.L. and A.A. KUDRYAVTSEV. *Trudy MKhTI im. D.I. Mendeleeva*, **49**, 25 (1965).
26. ANDREEVSKII, D.N. *Neftekhimiya*, **5**, 126 (1965).
27. ANTONOV, A.A. *ZhFKh*, **38**, 1713 (1964).
28. ANTONOV, A.A. *ZhOKh*, **34**, 2340 (1964).
29. ANTONOV, A.A., D.S. KOVAL'CHUK, and P.G. MASLOV. *Ukrainskii Khimicheskii Zhurnal*, **30**, 20 (1964).
30. ANTONOV, A.A. and P.G. MASLOV. *ZhFKh*, **38**, 600 (1964).
31. APIN, A.Ya., Yu.A. LEBEDEV, and O.I. NEFEDOVA. *ZhFKh*, **32**, 819 (1958).
32. ARIYA, S.M., KAN HO YN, Yu. BARBANEL', and G.M. LOGINOV. *ZhOKh*, **27**, 1743 (1957).
33. ARIYA, S.M., E.M. KOLBINA, and M.S. APURINA. *ZhNKh*, **2**, 23 1957.
34. ARIYA, S.M., M.P. MOROZOVA, and E. VOL'F. *ZhNKh*, **2**, 13 (1957).
35. ARIYA, S.M., M.P. MOROZOVA, and A.A. REIKHARDT. *ZhOKh*, **23**, 1455 (1953).
36. ARIYA, S.M., M.P. MOROZOVA, and HUANG CHI-T'AO. *ZhOKh*, **26**, 1813 (1956).
37. ARIYA, S.M., M.P. MOROZOVA, HUANG CHI-T'AO, and E. VOL'F. *ZhOKh*, **27**, 293 (1957).

37a. ARIYA, S.M. and E.A. PROKOF'EVA. *Sbornik statei po obshchei khimii (Collection of Papers on General Chemistry)*. Izd. AN SSSR, **1**, 9 1953.

38. ARIYA, S.M. and E.A. PROKOF'EVA. *ZhOKh*, **25**, 849 1955.
39. ARIYA, S.M., E.A. PROKOF'EVA, and I.I. MATVEEVA. *ZhOKh*, **25**, 634 (1955).
40. ARIYA, S.M., S.A. SHCHUKAREV, and V.B. GLUSHKOVA. *ZhOKh*, **23**, 1241 (1953).
41. ASTROV, D.N., E.S. ITSKEVICH, and K.A. SHARIFOV. *ZhFKh*, **29**, 424 (1955).
42. AKHACHINSKII, V.V. and L.M. KOPYTINA. *Atomnaya Energiya*, **9**, 504 (1960).
43. AKHACHINSKII, V.V., L.M. KOPYTINA, M.I. IVANOV, and N.S. PODOL'SKAYA. *Thermodynamics of Nuclear Materials*. International Atomic Energy Agency, p. 309, Vienna (1962).
44. AFANAS'EV, Yu.A., A.I. RYABININ, and T.I. KOROLEVA. *ZhFKh*, **39**, 2296 (1965).
45. BAEV, A.K. and G.I. NOVIKOV. *ZhNKh*, **6**, 2610 (1961).
46. BAEV, A.K. and G.I. NOVIKOV. *ZhNKh*, **10**, 2457 (1965).

47, BAIBUZ, V.F. *DAN SSSR*, **140**, 1358 (1961).
48. BAIBUZ, V.F. and V.A. MEDVEDEV. *Sbornik Trudov GIPKh*, **49**, 84 (1962).
48a. BAKSEVA, S.S., E.A. BUKETOV, and M.I. BAKSEV. *Trudy Instituta Metallurgii i Obogashcheniya AN KazSSR*, **11**, 163 (1964).
49. BALANDIN, A.A., E.I. KLABUNOVSKII, M.P. KOZINA, and O.D. UL'YANOVA. *Izv. AN SSSR, OKhN*, No.1, 12 (1958).
50. BAMBUROV, V.G. *Trudy Instituta Khimii Ural'skogo Filiala AN SSSR*, No.7, 27 (1963).
51. BARVINOK. M.S. *Informatsionnyi Byulleten' Voenno-Transportnoi Akademii*, No.9, 20 (1946).
52, BARVINOK, M.S. *ZhOKh*, **20**, 208 (1950).
53. BARON, N.M., E.P. KVYAT, E.A. PODGORNAYA, A.M. PONOMAREVA, A.A. RAVDEL', and Z.N. TIMOFEEVA. *Kratkii spravochnik fiziko-khimicheskikh velichin (Brief Handbook of Physicochemical Magnitudes)*. Goskhimizdat (1959).
54. BELYKH, L.P. and An.N. NESMEYANOV. *DAN SSSR*, **128**, 979 (1960).
55. BERG, L.G. and K.P. PRIBYLEV. *ZhNKh*, **10**, 1419 (1965).
56. BERGMAN, G.A. *ZhNKh*, **3**, 2422 (1958).
57. BERGMAN, G.A. and V.A. MEDVEDEV. *Sbornik Trudov GIPKh*, **42**, 158 (1959).
58. BERGMAN, G.A. and E.I. SHMUK. *Izv. AN SSSR, Metallurgiya i Toplivo*, No. 1, 60 (1962).
59, BERGMAN, G.A. and E.I. SHMUK, *Izv. AN SSSR, Metallurgiya i Gornoe Delo*, No. 3, 91 (1964).
60. BEREZHNOI, A.S. *DAN URSR*, No. 3, 387 (1962).
61. BRITSKE, E.V., A.F. KAPUSTINSKII, B.K. VESELOVSKII, L.M. SHAMOVSKII, L.G. CHENTSOVA, and B.I. ANVAER. *Termicheskie konstanty neorganicheskikh veshchestv (Thermal Constants of Inorganic Compounds)*. Izd. AN SSSR (1949).
62. BROUNSHTEIN, B.I., B.F. YUDIN, and O.S. LUKOVSKII. *ZhFKh*, **33**, 2773 (1959).
63. BAGLEY, K. *"Plutonium and its Alloys." Second Int. Conf. Peaceful Uses At. Energy*, **10**, 3 (1958).
64. Bya Re Seb Choson. *Vestn. AN KNDR*, No. 4, 67 (1954).
65. VASIL'EV, V.P. *ZhNKh*, **6**, 2241 (1961).
65a. VASIL'EV, V.P. and V.N. VASIL'EVA. *ZhFKh*, **36**, 2238 (1962).
65b. VASIL'EV V.P. and V.N. VASIL'EVA. *ZhFKh*, **39**, 2678 (1965).
66. VASIL'EV, V.P., E.K. ZOLOTAREV, and K.B. YATSIMIRSKII. *ZhFKh*, **33**, 328 (1959).
67. VASIL'EVA, I.A. and A.A. VVEDENSKII. *ZhFKh*, **39**, 2052 (1965).
68. VASIL'EVA, I.A., Ya.I. GERASIMOV, and Yu.P. SIMANOV. *ZhFKh*, **34**, 1811 (1960).
69. VASIL'KOVA, I.V., A.I. EFIMOV, and B.Z. PITIRIMOV. *ZhNKh*, **9**, 754 (1964).
70. VASIL'KOVA, I.V., N.D. ZAITSEVA, and Yu.S. SVALEV. *Vestn. LGU*, No. 16, 140 (1961).
71. VASIL'KOVA, I.V. and I.L PERFILOVA. *ZhNKh*, **10**, 2296 (1965).
72. VVEDENSKII, A.A. *Fiziko-khimicheskie konstanty organicheskikh soedinenii (Physicochemical Constants of Inorganic Compounds)*. Goskhimizdat (1961).
73 VVEDENSKII, A.A., P.Ya. IVANNIKOV, and V.A. NEKRASOVA. *ZhOKh*, **19**, 1094 (1949).
74. VVEDENSKII, A.A. and V.M. PETROV. *ZhFKh*, **39**, 1526 (1965).
75. VDOVENKO, V.M. and A.P. SOKOLOV. *Radiokhimiya*, **1**, 117 1959.
76. VEDENEEV, A.V., L.I. KAZARNOVSKAYA, and I.A. KAZARNOVSKII. *ZhFKh* **26**, 1808 (1952).
77. VEITS, I.V., L.V. GURVICH, and N.P. RTISHCHEVA. *ZhFKh*, **32**, 2532 (1958).
78. VECHER, R.A., V.A. GEIDERIKH, and Ya.I. GERASIMOV. *DAN SSSR*, **164**, 835 1965.
79. VECHER, R.A., V.A. GEIDERIKH, and Ya.I. GERASIMOV. *Izv. AN SSSR, Neorganicheskie Materialy*, **1**, 1722 (1965).
80. VIDAVSKII, L.M., N.I. BYAKHOVA, and E.A. IPPOLITOVA. *ZhNKh*, **10**, 1746 (1965).
80a. VOL, Yu.Ts. and N.A. SHISHAKOV. *Izv. AN SSSR, OKhN*, No.11, 1920 (1963).
81. VOLKENSHTEIN, N.V. and Yu.N. TSIOVKIN. *Fizika Metallov i Metallovedenie*, **15**, 465 (1963).
81a. VOLKOVA, N.M. and G.V. GAIDUKOV. *Izvestiya Sibirskogo Otdeleniya AN SSSR*, No. 6, 70 (1959).
82. VOLKOVA, N.M. and P.V. GEL'D. *Izvestiya Vysshikh Uchebnykh Zavedenii, Tsvetnaya Metallurgiya*, No.5, 89 (1963).
83. VOLKOVA, N.M. and P.V. GEL'D. *Izvestiya Vysshikh Uchebnykh Zavedenii, Tsvetnaya Metallurgiya*, No. 3, 77 (1965).
84. VOLODINA, N.A., A.A. SHIDLOVSKII, and A.A. VOSKRESENSKII. *ZhFKh*, **38**, 1703 (1964).
85. VOLOZHIN, Ya.S. *Trudy Vostochnogo Nauchno-Issledovatel'skogo Gornorudnogo Instituta i Gornogo Fakul'teta Sibirskogo Metallurgicheskogo Instituta*, **1**, 172 (1961).
86. VOL'F, E. and S.M. ARIYA. *ZhOKh*, **29**, 2470 (1959).
87. VOROB'EV, A.F. , V.P. KOLESOV. and S.M. SKURATOV. *ZhNKh*. **5**, 1402 (1960).
88. VOROB'EV, A.F., A.S. MONAENKOVA, N.M. PRIVALOVA, and S.M. SKUTATOV. *Vestn. MGU, Seriya Khimii*, No.3, 48 (1963).
89 VOROB'EV, A.F. and N.M. PRIVALOVA. *Vestn. MGU, Seriya Khimii*, No. 6, 22 (1963).
90. VOROB'EV, A.F., N.A. PRVALOVA, A.S. MONAENKOVA, and S.M. SKURATOV. *DAN SSSR*, **135**, 1388 (1960).
91. VOROB'EV A.F., N.M. PRIVALOVA. and S.M. SKURATOV. *Vestn. MGU, Seriya Khimmii*, No. 4, 39 (1963).
92. VOROB'EV, A.F., N.M. PRIVALOVA, L.V. STOROZHENKO, and S.M. SKURATOV. *DAN SSSR*, **135**, 113 (1960).
93. VOROB'EV, A.F., N.M. PRIVALOVA, and HUANG LI-TAO. *Vestn. MGU, Seriya Khimii*, No. 6, 27 (1963).
94. VOROB'EV, A.F. and S.M. SKURATOV. *ZhFKh*, **32**, 2580 (1958).
95. VOROB'EV, A.F. and S.M. SKURATOV. *ZhNKh*, **5**, 1398 (1960).
96. VOSKRESENSKAYA, N.K. and G.A. BUKHALOVA. *ZhOKh*, **21**, 1957 (1951).

97. VOSKRESENSKAYA, N.K., V.A. SOKOLOV, E.I. BONASHEK, and N.E. SCHMIDT. *Izvestiya Sektora Fiziko-Khimicheskogo Analiza IONKh AN SSSR*, **27**, 233 (1956).
98. VUKALOVICH, M.P., D.S. RASSKAZOV, V.N. POPOV, and Yu. M. BABIKOV. *Teploenergetika*, No.6, 56 (1964).
99. GADZHIEV, S.N. and M.Ya. AGARUNOV. *ZhFKh*, **39**, 239 (1965).
100. GADZHIEV, S.N. and K.A. SHARIFOV. *DAN AzSSR*, **15**, 667 (1959).
101. GADZHIEV, S.N. and K.A. SHARIFOV. *DAN AzSSR*, **16**, 659 (1960).
102. GADZHIEV, S.N. and K.A. SHARIFOV. *DAN SSSR*, **136**, 1339 (1961).
103. GADZHIEV, S.N. and K.A. SHARIFOV. *Voprosy metallurgii i fiziki poluprovodnikov (Problems in Physics and Metallurgy of Semiconductors)*, p.43. Izd. AN SSSR (1961).
104. GADZHIEV, S.N. and K.A. SHARIFOV. *Izv. AN AzSSR, Seriya Fiziko Matematicheskikh i Tekhnicheskikh Nauk*, No.1, 47 (1962).
105. GALKIN, N.P., B.N. SUDARIKOV, and V.A. ZAITSEV. *Trudy MKhTI im. D.I. Mendeleeva*, **43**, 64 (1963).
106. GAL'CHENKO, G.L., M.M. AMMAR, S.M. SKURATOV, Yu.N. BUBNOV, and B.N. MIKHAILOV. *Vestn. MGU, Seriya Khimii*, No.2, 3 (1965).
107. GAL'CHENKO, G.L., M.M. AMMAR, S.M. SKURATOV, Yu.N. BUBNOV, and B.M. MIKHAILOV. *Vestn. MGU, Seriya Khimii*, No.3, 10 (1965).
108. GAL'CHENKO, G.L. and R.M. VARUSHCHENKO. *ZhFKh*, **37**, 2513 (1963).
109. GAL'CHENKO, G.L., R.M. VARUSHCHENKO, Yu.N. BUBNOV, and B.M. MIKHAILOV. *ZhOKh*, **32**, 284 (1962).
110. GAL'CHENKO, G.L., R.M. VARUSHCHENKO, Yu.N. BUBNOV, and B.M. MIKHAILOV. *ZhOKh*, **32**, 2405 (1962).
111. GAL'CHENKO, G.L., D.A. GEDAKYAN, B.I. TIMOFEEV, and S.M. SKURATOV. *DAN SSSR*, **161**, 1081 (1965).
112. GAL'CHENKO, G.L., A.N. KORNILOV, and S.M. SKURATOV. *ZhNKh*, **5**, 2104 (1960).
113. GAL'CHENKO, G.L., A.N. KORNILOV, and S.M. SKURATOV. *ZhNKh*, **5**, 2651 (1960).
114. GAL'CHENKO, G.L., A.N. KORNILOV, B.I. TIMOFEEV, and S.M. SKURATOV. *DAN SSSR*, **127**, 1016 (1959).
115. GAL'CHENKO, G.L., B.I. TIMOFEEV, and S.M. SKURATOV. *ZhNKh*, **5**, 2645 (1960).
116. GAL'CHENKO, G.L., B.I. TIMOFEEV, and S.M. SKURATOV. *DAN SSSR*, **142**, 1077 (1962).
117. GANELINA, E.Sh. *ZhPKh*, **37**, 1358 (1964).
118. GARTMAN, Yu.M. and P.V. GEL'D. In: *Sbornik "Fiziko-khimicheskie osnovy proizvodstva stali"*, p.52, Izd. AN SSSR (1964).
119. GELLER, B.E. *ZhFKh*, **35**, 2210 (1961).
120. GEL'D, P.V. and M. KOCHNEV. *ZhPKh*, **21**, 1249 (1948).
121. GEL'D, P.V. and F.G. KUSENKO. *Izv. AN SSSR OTN, Metallurgiya i Toplivo*, No.2, 79 (1960).
122. GENOV, L.Kh., An.N. NESMEYANOV, and Yu.A. PRISELKOV. *DAN SSSR*, **140**, 158 (1961).
123. GERASIMENKO, L.N., V.A. ZAITSEV, L.N. LOZHKIN, and A.G. MORACHEVSKII. *ZhPKh*, **38**, 422 (1965).
124. GERASIMOV, Ya.I., I.A. VASIL'EVA, T.P. CHUSOVA, V.A. GEIDERIKH, and M.A. TIMOFEEVA. *DAN SSSR*, **134**, 1350 (1960).
125. GERASIMOV, Ya.I., E.V. KRUGLOVA, and N.D. ROZENBLYUM. *ZhOKh*, **7**, 1520 (1937).
126. GERTMAN, Yu.M. and P.V. GEL'D. *Izvestiya Vysshikh Uchebnykh Zavedenii, Chernaya Metallurgiya*, No.9, 15 (1959).
127. GINZBURG, P.I. In: *Sbornik "Problemy magmy i genezisa izverzhennykh gornykh porod"*, p.210, Izd. AN SSSR (1963).
128. KUO KAO-PIN. *Hwa Hsüeh Tung pao*, No.5, 9 (1959).
129. GODNEV, I.N. Thesis, Ivanovo, 1947. Cited in [321].
130. GODNEV, I.N. and V. MOROZOV. *ZhFKh*, **22**, 801(1948).
131. GODNEV, I.N. and A.S. SVERDLIN. *ZhFKh*, **24**, 670 (1950).
132. GODNEV, I.N., A.S. SVERDLIN, and M.S. SAVOGINA. *ZhFKh*, **24**, 807 (1950).
133. GODNEV, I.N., A.S. SVERDLIN, and N.I. USHANOVA. *Optika i Spektroskopiya*, **2**, 704 (1957).
134. GOLOMZIK, A.I. *Izvestiya Vysshikh Uchebnykh Zavedenii, Tsvetnaya Metallurgiya*, No. 2, 47 (1964).
135. GOLUBENKO, A.N. and T.N. REZUKHINA. *ZhFKh*, **38**, 2920 (1964).
136. GOLUBENKO, A.N. and T.N. REZUKHINA. *ZhFKh*, **39**, 1519 (1965).
137. GOLUBENKO, A.N., A.A. USTINOV, and T.N. REZUKHINA. *ZhFKh*, **39**, 1164 (1965).
138. GOLUTVIN, Yu.M. *ZhFKh*, **30**, 2251 (1956).
139. GOLUTVIN, Yu.M. and T.M. KOZLOVSKAYA. *ZhFKh*, **34**, 2350 (1960).
140. GOLUTVIN, Yu.M. and T.M. KOZLOVSKAYA. *ZhFKh*, **36**, 362 (1962).
141. GOLUTVIN, Yu.M., T.M. KOZLOVSKAYA, and E.G. MASLENNIKOVA. *ZhFKh*, **37**, 1362 (1963).
142. GOLUTVIN, Yu.M. and LIANG CHIN-K'UEI. *ZhFKh*, **35**, 129 (1961).
143. GOLUTVIN, Yu.M. and E.G. MASLENNIKOVA. *ZhFKh*, **39**, 3102 (1965).
144. GORGORAKI, E.A., A.K. MAL'TSEV, and V.A. TURDAKIN. *Trudy MKhTI im. D.I. Mendeleeva*, **49**, 16 (1965).
145. GORGORAKI, E.A. and V.V. TARASOV. *Trudy MKhTI im. D.I. Mendeleeva*, **49**, 11 (1965).
146. GORYSHKO, N.N., M.P. KOZINA, S.M. SKURATOV, N.A. BELIKOVA, and A.F. PLATE. *Vestn. MGU, Seriya Khimii*, No.4, 3 (1964).
147. GRADOVICH, A.A. In: *Sbornik "Materialy tret'ei nauchnoi konferentsii aspirantov,"* p.174, Izd. Rostovskogo Gosudarstvennogo Universiteta (1961).
148. GREBENSHCHIKOV, R.G. *ZhNKh*, **9**, 1038 (1964).
149. GREBENSHCHIKOV, R.G. and R.A. PASECHNOVA. *DAN SSSR*, **164**, 571 (1965).

150. GRYAZNOV, V.M., V.V. KOROBOV, and A.V. FROST. *Vestn. MGU, Seriya Khimii*, No.9, 51 (1948).
151. GUMBATOV, D.O. and V.N. KOSTRYUKOV. *ZhFKh*, **39**, 116 (1965).
152. GUMBATOV, D.O., V.N. KOSTRYUKOV, and Yu.Kh. SHAULOV. *Izv. AN AzSSR, Seriya Fiziko-Tekhnicheskikh i Matematicheskikh Nauk*, No.1, 53 (1965).
153. GURVICH, L.V. *ZhFKh*, **34**, 1690 (1960).
154. GURVICH, L.V., B.A. VOROB'EV, V.A. KVLIVIDZE, E.A. PROZOROVSKII, N.P. RTISHCHEVA, and V.S. YUNGMAN. *Sbornik Trudov GIPKh*, 49, 38 (1962).
155. GURVICH, L.V., V.A. KVLIVIDZE, E.A. PROZOROVSKII, and N.P. RTISHCHEVA. *Sbornik Trudov GIPKh*, **49**, 61 (1962).
156. GUREVICH, M.A. *ZhNKh*, 8, 2645 (1963).
157. DEVYATYKH, G.G. and A.S. YUSHIN. *ZhFKh*, **38**, 957 (1964).
158. DROBOT, D.V., B.G. KORSHUNOV, and L.V. DURININA. *Izv. AN SSSR, Neorganicheskie Materialy*, **1**, 2189 (1965).
159. DROBYSHEV, V.N., T.N. REZUKHINA, and L.A. TARASOVA. *ZhFKh*, **39**, 141 (1965).
160. DROBYSHEV, V.N. and T.N. REZUKHINA. *ZhFKh*, 39, 151 (1965).
161. DROZIN, N.N. *ZhFKh*, **35**, 1789 (1961).
162. DYATKINA, M.E. *ZhFKh*, **28**, 377 (1954).
163. EVSEEV, A.M. and G.V. POZHARSKAYA. *Vestn. MGU, Seriya Matematiki, Mekhaniki, Astronomii, Fiziki i Khimii*, No.1, 165 (1959).
164. EVSEEV, A.M., G.V. POZHARSKAYA, An.N. NESMEYANOV, and Ya.I. GERASIMOV. *ZhNKh*, **4**, 2189 (1959).
165. EVSTIGNEEVA, E. V. and G.O. SHMYREVA. *ZhFKh*, **39**, 1000 (1965).
166. EGOROV, A.M. and Z.P. TITOVA. *ZhNKh*, **7**, 275 (1962).
167. EREMENKO, V.N. and G.M. LUKASHENKO. *ZhNKh*, **8**, 8 (1963).
168. EREMENKO, V.N. and G.M. LUKASHENKO. *ZhNKh*, **9**, 1552 (1964).
169. EREMENKO, V.N. and G.M. LUKASHENKO. *Izv. AN SSSR, Neorganicheskie Materialy*, **1**, 1296 (1965).
169a. ERMOLENKO, E.N. and N.N. SIROTA. In: *Sbornik "Khimicheskaya svyaz' v poluprovodnikakh i tverdykh telakh"*, p.128, Izd. Nauka i Tekhnika, Minsk (1965).
170. ZHARKOVA, L.A. Summary of Candidate's Thesis. MGU (1960).
171. ZHARKOVA, L.A. and N.G. BARANCHEEVA. *ZhFKh*, **38**, 752 (1964).
172. ZHARKOVA, L.A. and Ya.I. GERASIMOV. *ZhFKh*, **35**, 2291 (1961).
173. ZHARKOVA, L.A., Ya.I. GERASIMOV, T.N. REZUKHINA, and Yu.P. SIMANOV. *DAN SSSR*, **128**, 992 (1959).
174. ZHELANKIN, V.I., V.S. KUTSEV, and B.F. ORMONT. *ZhFKh*, **35**, 2608 (1961).
175. ZHELANKIN, V.I. and V.S. KUTSEV. *ZhFKh*, **38**, 562 (1964).
176. ZHUK, N.P. *ZhFKh*, **28**, 1523 (1954).
177. ZHUK, N.P. *ZhFKh*, **28**, 1690 (1954).
178. ZHUKOVA, L.A., Ya.I. GERASIMOV, T.N. REZUKHINA, and Yu.P. SIMANOV. *DAN SSSR*, **131**, 1130 (1960).
178a. ZHUKOVETSKII, V.V. *Trudy Severo-Kavkazskogo Gorno-Metallurgicheskogo Instituta*, **15**, 210 (1957).
179. ZHURAVLEV, E.Z. and I.B. RABINOVICH. *Trudy po Khimii i Khimicheskoi Tekhnologii*, **3**, 475, Gor'kii (1959).
180. ZAINULLIN, G.G. and A.S. PASHINKIN. *Geokhimiya*, No.9, 843 (1963).
181. ZAIONCHKOVSKII, Ya.A. and E.V. RUBAL'SKAYA. *Izv. AN SSSR, Neorganicheskie Materialy*, **1**, 257 (1965).
182. ZAIONCHKOVSKII, Ya.A. and E.V. RUBAL'SKAYA. *Izv. AN SSSR, Neorganicheskie Materialy*, **1**, 1376 (1965).
183. ZAITSEVA, N.D. *ZhNKh*, **8**, 2365 (1963).
184. ZUBAREVA, N.D., A.P. OBEREMOK-YAKUBOVA, Yu.I. PETROV, E.I. KLABUNOVSKII, and A.A. BALANDIN. *Izv. AN SSSR, Seriya Khimicheskaya*, No.12, 2207 (1963).
185. ZUBOVA, G.A. *Tezisy dokladov nauchno-tekhnicheskoi konferentsii MKhTI im. D.I. Mendeleeva (Papers Read at the Scientific and Technological Conference of the Mendeleev Institute of Chemical Technology in Moscow)*, p.11 (1955).
186. IVANOV, M.I. and N.S. PODOL'SKAYA. *Atomnaya Energiya*, **13**, 572 (1962).
187. IVANOV, M.I. and V.A. TUMBAKOV. *Atomnaya Energiya*, **7**, 33 (1959).
188. IVANOV, M.I., V.A. TUMBAKOV, and N.S. PODOL'SKAYA. *Atomnaya Energiya*, **5**, 166 (1958).
189. IVANOVA, L.I. *ZhOKh*, **21**, 444 (1951).
190. IONIN, M.V. *ZhFKh*, **38**, 2684 (1964).
191. IONIN, M.V. and D.N. GEZGANOVA. *Trudy po Khimii i Khimicheskoi Tekhnologii*, **2(10)**, 183, Gor'kii (1964).
192. IPPOLITOVA, E.A., D.G. FAUSTOVA, and Vikt.I. SPITSYN. *Issledovaniya v oblasti khimii urana (Research on the Chemistry of Uranium)*, pp.145–147. Izd. MGU (1961).
193. ITSKEVICH, E.S. *ZhFKh*, **35**, 1813 (1961).
194. ITSKEVICH, E.S. and P.G. STRELKOV. *ZhFKh*, **33**, 1575 (1959).
195. ITSKEVICH, E.S. and P.G. STRELKOV. *ZhFKh*, **34**, 1312 (1960).
196. KABO, G.Ya. and D.N. ANDREEVSKII. *Neftekhimiya*, **5**, 132 (1965).
197. KABO, G.Ya. and D.N. ANDREEVSKII. *Izvestiya Vysshikh Uchebnykh Zavedenii, Khimiya i Khimicheskaya Tekhnologiya*, No4, 575 (1965).
198. KAZARNOVSKAYA, L.I. and I.A. KAZARNOVSKII. *ZhFKh*, **25**, 293 (1951).
199. KAZARNOVSKII, I.A. and S.I. RAIKHSHTEIN. *ZhFKh*, **21**, 245 (1947).
200. KALISHEVICH, G.I., P.V. GEL'D, and R.P. KRENTSIS. *Teplofizika Vysokikh Temperatur*, **2**, 16 (1964).
201. KAPUSTINSKII, A.F. *ZhFKh*, **15**, 220 (1941).
202. KAPUSTINSKII, A.F. *ZhFKh*, **15**, 645 (1941).

203. KAPUSTINSKII, A.F. and K.I. VASILEVSKII. *ZhNKh,* **2,** 2031 (1957).
204. KAPUSTINSKII, A.F. and Yu.M. GOLUTVIN. *Izv. AN SSSR, OKhN,* No.2, 192 (1951).
205. KAPUSTINSKII, A.F. and Yu.M. GOLUTVIN. *ZhFKh,* **25,** 719 (1951).
206. KAPUSTINSKII, A.F. and R.T. KAN'KOVSKII. *ZhFKh,* **32,** 2810 (1958).
207. KAPUSTINSKII, A.F. and R.T. KAN'KOVSKII. *ZhFKh,* **33,** 722 (1959).
208. KAPUSTINSKII, A.F., A.I. MAKOLKIN, and L.I. KRISHTALIK. *ZhFKh,* **21,** 125 (1947).
209. KAPUSTINSKII, A.F. and O.Ya. SAMOILOV. *Izv. AN SSSR, OKhN,* No.4, 337 (1950).
210. KAPUSTINSKII, A.F. and O.Ya. SAMOILOV. *Izv. AN SSSR, OKhN,* No.2, 218 (1952).
211. KAPUSTINSKII, A.F. and K.K. SAMPLAVSKAYA. *Trudy MKhTI im. D.I. Mendeleeva,* **22,** 47 (1957).
212. KAPUSTINSKII, A.F. and K.K. SAMPLAVSKAYA. *ZhNKh,* **6,** 2237 (1961).
213. KAPUSTINSKII, A.F. and K.K. SAMPLAVSKAYA. *ZhNKh,* **6,** 2241 (1961).
214. KAPUSTINSKII, A.F. and K.K. SAMPLAVSKAYA. *Trudy MKhTI im. D.I. Mendeleeva,* **38,** 7 (1962).
215. KAPUSTINSKII, A.F. and N.M. SELIVANOVA. *ZhFKh,* **23,** 1508 (1949).
216. KAPUSTINSKII, A.F., N.M. SELIVANOVA, and M.S. STAKHANOVA. *Trudy MKhTI im. D.I. Mendeleeva,* **22,** 30 (1956).
217. KAPUSTINSKII, A.F. and M.S. STAKHANOVA. *DAN SSSR,* **57,** 575 (1947).
218. KAPUSTINSKII, A.F. and M.S. STAKHANOVA. *Izv. AN SSSR, OKhN,* No. 6, 587 (1954).
219. KAPUSTINSKII, A.F., I.I. STRELKOV, V.E. GANENKO, A.V. ALAPINA, M.S. STAKHANOVA, and N.M. SELIVANOVA. *ZhFKh,* **34,** 1088 (1960).
220. KAPUSTINSKII, A.F. and A.A. SHIDLOVSKII. *Izvestiya Sektora Platiny IONKh AN SSSR,* **30,** 31 (1955).
221. KAPUSTINSKII, A.F., A.A. SHIDLOVSKII, and Yu.S. SHIDLOVSKAYA. *Izv. AN SSSR, OKhN,* No.4, 385 (1958).
222. KAPUSTINSKII, A.F. and K.B. YATSIMIRSKII. *ZhFKh,* **22,** 1271 (1948).
223. KARAVAEV, M.M. and G.A. SKVORTSOV. *ZhFKh,* **36,** 1072 (1962).
224. KARAPET'YANTS, M.Kh. *Khimicheskaya termodinamika (Chemical Termodynamics),* 2nd ed. Goskhimizdat (1953).
225. KARAPET'YANTS, M.Kh. *ZhFKh,* **27,** 775 (1953).
226. KARAPET'YANTS, M.Kh. *ZhFKh,* **28,** 186 (1954).
227. KARAPET'YANTS, M.Kh. *ZhFKh,* **28,** 353 (1954).
228. KARAPET'YANTS, M.Kh. *Trudy MKhTI im D.I. Mendeleeva,* **18,** 27 (1954).
229. KARAPET'YANTS, M.Kh. *Trudy MKhTI im. D.I. Mendeleeva,* **20,** 10 (1955).
230. KARAPET'YANTS, M.Kh. *ZhFKh,* **30,** 593 (1956).
231. KARAPET'YANTS, M.Kh. *Khimiya i Tekhnologiya Topliva,* No.9, 22 (1956).
232. KARAPET'YANTS, M.Kh. *Ph.D. Thesis. MKhTI im. D.I. Mendeleeva* (1957).
233. KARAPET'YANTS, M.Kh. *Tablitsy nekotorykh termodinamicheskikh svoistv razlichnykh veshchestv (Tables of Certain Thermodynamic Parameters of Different Substances).* Szechwan University (1959).
234. KARAPET'YANTS, M.Kh. and M.L. KARAPET'YANTS. Calculations carried out for inclusion in this book (1959–1966).
235. KARAPET'YANTS, M.Kh. and M.L. KARAPET'YANTS. *Tablitsy nekotorykh termodinamicheskikh svoistv razlichnykh veshchestv (Tables of Certain Thermodynamic Parameters of Different Substances). Trudy MKhTI im. D.I. Mendeleeva,* **34** (1961).
236. KARVYALIS, N. *Uchenya Zapiski Vil'nyusskogo Universiteta (khimiya),* **28,** 111 (1959).
236a. KARVYALIS, N. *Uchenya Zapiski Vil'nyusskogo Universiteta (khimiya),* **28,** 119 (1959).
237. KARELIN, V.V., An.N. NESMEYANOV, and Yu.A. PRISELKOV. *Izv. AN SSSR, Metallurgiya i Toplivo,* No.5, 117 (1962).
238. KARELIN, V.V. and An.N. NESMEYANOV. *DAN SSSR,* **144,** 352 (1962).
239. KARELIN, V.V., An.A. NESMEYANOV, Yu.A. PRISELKOV, and CHOU K'UN-YING. *Vestn. MGU, Seriya Khimii,* No.2, 40 (1962).
240. KACHINSKAYA, O.N. *Vestn. MGU, Seriya Khimii,* No.1, 69 (1961).
241. KACHINSKAYA, O.N., S.Kh. TOGOEVA, A.P. MESHCHERYAKOV, and S.M. SKURATOV. *DAN SSSR,* **132,** 119 (1960).
242. KINNE, G., A.F. VISHKAREV, and V.I. YAVOISKII. *Izvestiya Vysshego Uchebnego Zavedeniya, Chernaya Metallurgiya,* No.9, 92 (1962).
243. KIPNIS, A.Ya. *ZhNKh,* **7,** 1500 (1962).
244. KIREEV, V.A. *ZhFKh,* **20,** 339 (1946).
245. KIREEV, V.A. *ZhOKh,* **16,** 1199 (1946).
246. KIREEV, V.A. *ZhOKh,* **16,** 1391 (1946).
247. KIREEV, V.A. *ZhOKh,* **16,** 1569 (1946).
248. KIREEV, V.A. *ZhOKh,* **17,** 1229 (1947).
249. KIREEV, V.A. *Sbornik rabot po fizicheskoi khimii (Collection of Papers on Physical Chemistry),* p.181. Izd. AN SSSR (1947).
250. KIREEV, V.A. *Sbornik rabot po fizicheskoi khimii (Collection of Papers on Physical Chemistry),* p.197. Izd. AN SSSR (1947).
251. KIREEV, V.A. *ZhFKh,* **22,** 847 (1948).
252. KIRILLIN, V.A., A.B. SHEINDLIN, and V.Ya. CHEKHOVSKOI. *DAN SSSR,* **142,** 1323 (1962).
253. KIRILLIN, V.A., A.E. SHEINDLIN, V.Ya. CHEKHOVSKOI, and V.A. PETROVA. *ZhFKh,* **37,** 2249 (1963).

253a. KIRILLIN, V.A., A.E. SHEINDLIN, V.Ya. CHEKHOVSKOI, and I.A. ZHUKOVA. *Teplofizika Vysokikh Temperatur,* **3,** 860 (1965).

254. KISELEVA, E.V. *Tezisy dokladov nauchno-tekhnicheskoi konferentsee MKhTI im. D.I. Mendeleeva (Papers Read at the Scientific and Technological Conference of the Mendeleev Institute of Chemical Technology in Moscow),* p.10 (1960).

255. KLUSHINA, T.V., N.M. SELIVANOVA, and S.S. TITOV. *Trudy MKhTI im. D.I. Mendeleeva,* **49,** 28 (1965).

256. KOVAL'CHUK, D.S. and A.A. ANTONOV. *Ukrainskii Khimicheskii Zhurnal,* **30,** 169 (1964).

257. KOVAL'CHUK, D.S. and V.P. MOROZOV. *Trudy Dnepropetrovskogo Khimiko-Tekhnicheskogo Instituta im. F.E. Dzerzhinskogo,* **16,** 1 (1962).

258. KOZINA, M.P., M.Yu. LUKINA, N.D. ZUBAREVA, I.L. SAFONOVA, S.M. SKURATOV, and B.A. KAZANSKII. *DAN SSSR,* **138,** 843 (1961).

259. KOZINA, M.P., A.K. MIRZOEVA, I.E. SOSNINA, N.V. ELAGINA, and S.M. SKURATOV. *DAN SSSR,* **155,** 1123 (1964).

260. KOZLOV, N.A. and I.B. RABINOVICH. *Trudy po Khimii i Khimicheskoi Tekhnologii,* **2(10),** 189, Gor'kii (1964).

261. KOLBIN, N.I., V.M. SAMOILOV, and A.N. RYABOV. In: *Sbornik "Khimiya redkikh elementov,"* p.50, Izd. LGU (1964).

262. KOLBIN, N.I. and I.N. SEMENOV. *ZhNKh,* **9,** 203 (1964).

263. KOLBIN, N.I., I.N. SEMENOV, and Yu.M. SHUTOV. *ZhNKh,* **9,** 1029 (1964).

264. KOLBINA, E.M., Yu.A. BARBANEL', M.V. NAZAROVA, and S.M. ARIYA. *Vestn. LGU,* No.4, 122 (1960).

265. KOLESOV, V.P. and I.D. ZENKOV. *ZhFKh,* **36(9),** 2082 (1962).

266. KOLESOV, V.P., I.D. ZENKOV, and S.M. SKURATOV. *ZhFKh,* **36,** 89 (1962).

267. KOLESOV, V.P., I.D. ZENKOV, and S.M. SKURATOV. *ZhFKh.* **37,** 224 (1962).

268. KOLESOV, V.P., I.D. ZENKOV, and S.M. SKURATOV. *ZhFKh,* **36,** 2082 (1962).

269. KOLESOV, V.P., I.D. ZENKOV, and S.M. SKURATOV. *ZhFKh,* **37,** 720 (1963).

270. KOLESOV, V.P., I.D. ZENKOV, and S.M. SKURATOV. *ZhFKh,* **39,** 2474 (1965).

271. KOLESOV, V.P., A.M. MARTYNOV, and S.M. SKURATOV. *ZhNKh,* **6,** 2623 (1961).

272. KOLESOV, V.P., A.M. MARTYNOV, and S.M. SKURATOV. *ZhFKh,* **39,** 435 (1965).

273. KOLESOV, V.P., A.M. MARTYNOV, S.M. SHTEKHER, and S.M. SKURATOV. *ZhFKh,* **36,** 2078 (1962).

274. KOLESOV, V.P., I.E. PAUKOV, S.M. SKURATOV, and E.A. SEREGIN. *DAN SSSR,* **128,** 130 (1959).

275. KOLESOV, V.P., M.M. POPOV, and S.M. SKURATOV. *ZhNKh,* **4,** 1233 (1959).

276. KOLESOV, V.P., E.A. SEREGIN, and S.M. SKURATOV. *ZhFKh,* **36,** 647 (1962).

277. KOLESOV, V.P., and S.M. SKURATOV. *ZhNKh,* **6,** 1741 (1961).

278. KOLESOV, V.P., S.M. SKURATOV, and I.D. ZAIKIN. *ZhNKh,* **4,** 1237 (1959).

279. KOLESOV, V.P., O.G. TALAKIN, and S.M. SKURATOV. *ZhFKh,* **38,** 1701 (1964).

280. KONDAKOV, B.V., P.V. KOVTUNENKO, and A.A. BUNDEL'. *ZhFKh,* **38,** 190 (1964).

281. KORNEEVA, I.V., A.V. BELAEV, and A.V. NOVOSELOVA. *ZhNKh,* **5,** 3 (1960).

282. KORNEEVA, I.V., V.V. SOKOLOV, and A.V. NOVOSELOVA. *ZhNKh,* **5,** 241 (1960).

283. KORNILOV, A.N., I.D. ZAIKIN, S.M. SKURATOV, L.B. DUBROVSKAYA, and G.P. SHVEIKIN. *ZhFKh,* **38,** 702 (1964).

284. KORNILOV, A.N., V.Ya. LEONIDOV, and S.M. SKURATOV. *DAN SSSR,* **144,** 355 (1962).

285. KORNILOV, A.N., V.Ya. LEONIDOV, and S.M. SKURATOV. *Vestn. MGU,* No.6, 48 (1962).

286. KORNILOV, A.N., V.Ya. LEONIDOV, and S.M. SKURATOV. *ZhFKh,* **38,** 2008 (1964).

287. KORNILOV, A.N., V.Ya. LEONIDOV, and S.M. SKURATOV. *ZhFKh,* **38,** 2013 (1964).

288. KORNILOV, I.I. and N.M. MATVEEVA. *DAN SSSR,* **139,** 880 (1961).

289. KOROBOV, V.V. and A.V. FROST. *Svobodnaya energiya organicheskikh soedinenii (Free Energy of Organic Compounds).* Izd. VKhO im. D.I. Mendeleeva, Moscow Branch (1949).

290. KORSHUNOV, I.A. *ZhFKh,* **14,** 134 (1940).

291. KOSTRYUKOV, V.N. *ZhFKh,* **35,** 1759 (1961).

292. KOSTRYUKOV, V.N. and I.N. KALINKINA. *ZhFKh,* **38,** 780 (1964).

293. KOSTRYUKOV, V.N. and G.Kh. MOROZOVA. *ZhFKh,* **34,** 1833 (1960).

294. KOCHETKOVA, N.M. and T.N. REZUKHINA. In: *Sbornik "Voprosy metallurgii i fizika poluprovodnikov" (Problems in Physics and Metallurgy of Semiconductors),* pp.34–37. Izd. AN SSSR (1961).

295. KOCHNEV, M.I. *DAN SSSR,* **70,** 433 (1950) (cf. [1773]).

296. KRASNOV, K.S. *Radiokhimiya,* **2,** 668 (1960).

297. KRASNOV, K.S. and V.I. SVETTSOV. *Izvestiya Vysshikh Uchebnykh Zavedenii, Khimiya i Khimicheskaya Tekhnologiya,* No. 1, 167 (1963).

298. KRASOVSKII, V.P. and I.G. FAKIDOV. *Fizika Metallov i Metallovedenie,* **11,** 477 (1961).

299. KRENTSIS, R.P. and P.V. GEL'D. *Izvestiya Vysshikh Uchebnykh Zavedenii, Chernaya Metallurgiya,* No. 11, 12 (1962).

300. KRENTSIS, R.P. and P.V. GEL'D. *Fizika Metallov i Metallovedenie,* **13,** 319 (1962).

301. KRENTSIS, R.P. and P.V. GEL'D. In: *Sbornik "Fiziko-khimicheskie osnovy proizvodstva stali",* p.400. Izd. Nauka (1964).

302. KRENTSIS, R.P., P.V. GEL'D, and G.I. KALISHEVICH. *Izvestiya Vysshikh Uchebnykh Zavedenii, Chernaya Metallurgiya,* No. 9, 161 (1963).

303. KRENTSIS, R.P., P.V. GEL'D, and G.I. KALISHEVICH. *Izvestiya Vysshikh Uchebnykh Zavedenii, Chernaya Metallurgiya,* No. 11, 146 (1964).

304. KRENTSIS, R.P., P.V. GEL'D, and N.N. SEREBRENNIKOV. *Izvestiya Vysshikh Uchebnykh Zavedenii, Chernaya Metallurgiya*, No. 12, 5 (1960).
304a. KRESTOV, G.A. and V.A. LAPIN. *Radiokhimiya*, **7**, 311 (1965).
305. KRESTOVNIKOV, A.N. and M.S. VENDRIKH. *Trudy Moskovskogo Instituta Tsvetnykh Metallov i Zolota im. M.I. Kalinina*, No. 31, 426 (1958).
306. KRESTOVNIKOV, A.N. and M.S. VENDRIKH. *Izvestiya Vysshikh Uchebnykh Zavedenii, Tsvetnaya Metallurgiya*, No. 2, 54 (1959).
307. KRESTOVNIKOV, A.N. and M.S. VENDRIKH. *Izvestiya Vysshikh Uchebnykh Zavedenii, Chernaya Metallurgiya*, 3, 13 (1960).
308. KRIVTSOV, N.V., K.V. TITOVA, and V. Ya. ROSOLOVSKII. *ZhNKh*, **10**, 454 (1965).
309. KUZNETSOV, S.I. *ZhNKh*, **23**, 1187 (1950).
310. KUZNETSOV, F.A., V.I. BELYI, T.N. REZUKHINA, and Ya.I. GERASIMOV. *DAN SSSR*, **139**, 1405 (1961).
311. KUZNETSOV, F.A., T.N. REZUKHINA, and A.N. GOLUBENKO. *ZhFKh*, **34**, 2129 (1960).
312. KUL'BA, F.Ya. *ZhOKh*, **24**, 1700 (1954).
313. KURBATOV, V.Ya. *ZhOKh*, **18**, 372 (1948).
314. KUSENKO, F.G. and P.V. GEL'D. *Izvestiya Sibirskogo Otdeleniya AN SSSR*, No. 2, **46** (1960).
315. KUSENKO, F.G. and P.V. GEL'D. *Izvestiya Vysshikh Uchebnykh Zavedenii, Tsvetnaya Metallurgiya*, No. 4, 102 (1960).
316. KUSENKO, F.G. and P.V. GEL'D. *ZhOKh*, **30**, 3487 (1960).
317. KUSENKO, F.G. and P.V. GEL'D. In: *Sbornik "Fiziko-khimicheskie osnovy proizvodstva stali"*, p. 41, Izd. AN SSSR (1961).
318. KUTSEV, V.S., B.F. ORMONT, and V.A. EPEL'BAUM. *DAN SSSR*, **104**, 567 (1955).
319. LAVRENT'EV, V.I., Ya.I. GERASIMOV, and T.N. REZUKHINA. *DAN SSSR*, **133**, 374 (1960).
320. LAVRENT'EV, V.I., Ya.I. GERASIMOV, and T.N. REZUKHINA. *DAN SSSR*, **136**, 1372 (1961).
321. LAVRON, N.V., V.V. KOROBOV, and V.I. FILIPPOVA. *Termodinamika reaktsii gazifikatsii i sinteza iz gazov (Thermodynamics of Gasification Reaction and Syntheses from Gases)*. Izd. AN SSSR (1960).
322. LANDIYA, N.A. *ZhFKh*, **24**, 257 (1950).
323. LATIMER, W.M. *The Oxidation States of the Elements and Their Potentials in Aqueous Solutions*. Prentice–Hall, N.Y. (1952).
324. LEBEDEV, B.G. and V.A. LEVITSKII. *ZhFKh*, **36**, 630 (1962).
325. LEBEDEV, B.G. and V.A. LEVITSKII. *Izvestiya Vysshikh Uchebnykh Zavedenii, Chernaya Metallurgiya*, No. 7, 5 (1962).
326. LEBEDEV, B.G., V.A. LEVITSKII, and V.A. BURTSEV. *ZhFKh*, **36**, 877 (1962).
326a. LEONIDOV, V.Ya., Yu.P. BARSKII, and N.I. KHITAROV. *Geokhimiya*, No. 5, 414 (1964).
327. LEBEDEV, Yu.A., E.A. MIROSHNICHENKO, and A.M. CHAIKIN. *DAN SSSR*, **145**, 1288 (1962).
328. LEBEDEVA, N.D. *ZhFKh*, **38**, 2648 (1964).
329. LEVITSKII, V.A. and T.N. REZUKHINA. *ZhFKh*, **37**, 1135 (1963).
329a. LEVITSKII, V.A. and T.N. REZUKHINA. *Izv. AN SSSR, Neorganicheskie Materialy*, **2**, 145 (1965).
330. LEVITSKII, V.A., T.N. REZUKHINA, and A.S. GUZEI. *Elektrokhimiya*, **1**, 237 (1965).
331. LEVITSKII, V.A., T.N. REZUKHINA, and V.G. DNEPROVA. *Elektrokhimiya*, **1**, 933 (1965).
332. LEVITSKII, V.A., M.A. FRENKEL', and T.N. REZUKHINA. *Elektrokhimiya*, **1**, 1371. (1965).
333. LENEV, L.M. and I.A. NOVOKHATSKII. *Izv. AN SSSR, Metallurgiya i Gornoe Delo*, No. 6, 47 (1963).
334. LENEV, L.M. and I.A. NOVOKHATSKII. *Izv. AN SSSR, Metallurgiya i Gornoe Delo*, No. 4, 87 (1964).
335. LENEV, L.M. and I.A. NOVOKHATSKII. *ZhNKh*, **10**, 2400 (1965).
336. LENSKII, A.S., A.D. SHAPOSHNIKOVA, and E.S. SOKOLOVA. *ZhNKh*, **9**, 1147 (1964).
337. LETUN, S.M. and P.V. GEL'D. *Teplofizika Vysokikh Temperatur*, 3, 47 (1965).
338. LETUN, S.M., P.V. GEL'D, and N.N. SEREBRENNIKOV. *Izvestiya Vysshikh Uchebnykh Zavedenii, Chernaya Metallurgiya*, No. 4, 5 (1965).
338a. LETUN, S.M., P.V. GEL'D, and N.N. SEREBRENNIKOV. *ZhNKh*, **10**, 1263 (1965).
339. LESHCHINSKAYA, Z.L., M.A. AVERBUKH, and N.M. SELIVANOVA. *ZhFKh*, **39**, 2036 (1965).
340. LESHCHINSKAYA, Z.L. and N.M. SELIVANOVA. *Trudy MKhTI im. D.I. Mendeleeva*, **41**, 18 (1963).
341. LESHCHINSKAYA, Z.L. and N.M. SELIVANOVA. *Trudy MKhTI im. D.I. Mendeleeva*, **44**, 37 (1963).
342. LESHCHINSKAYA, Z.L. and N.M. SELIVANOVA. *Trudy MKhTI im. D.I. Mendeleeva*, **41**, 22 (1963).
343. LESHCHINSKAYA, Z.L. and N.M. SELIVANOVA. *ZhFKh*, **38**, 972 (1964).
344. LESHCHINSKAYA, Z.L. and N.M. SELIVANOVA. *ZhFKh*, **39**, 2430 (1965).
345. LESHCHINSKAYA, Z.L., N.M. SELIVANOVA, and I.S. STREL'TSOV. *ZhNKh*, **8**, 763 (1963).
346. LOVCHIKOV, V.S. *Izvestiya Vysshikh Uchebnykh Zavedenii, Tsvetnaya Metallurgiya*, No. 2, 76 (1964).
347. LUKASHENKO, G.M. and V.N. EREMENKO. *ZhNKh*, **9**, 2295 (1964).
348. LYUBIMOV, A.P. and Yu.N. LYUBITOV. *Trudy Moskovskogo Instituta Stali*, No. 36, 191 (1957).
349. LYUKSHIN, V.V. and Ya.A. ZAIONCHKOVSKII. *Izv. AN SSSR, Neorganicheskie Materialy*, **1**, 1602 (1965).
350. L'VOVA A.S. In: *Sbornik "Materialy chetvertoi nauchnoi konferentsii aspirantov"*, p. 154, Izd. Rostovskogo Gosudarstvennogo Universiteta (1962).
351. L'VOVA, A.S. and N.N. FEODOS'EV. *ZhFKh*, **38**, 28 (1964).
352. L'VOVA, A.S. and N.N. FEODOS'EV. *ZhNKh*, **9**, 2251 (1964).
353. L'VOVA, A.S. and N.N. FEODOS'EV. *ZhFKh*, **39**, 2049 (1965).
354. L'VOVA, A.S. and N.N. FEODOS'EV. *ZhNKh*, **10**, 2378 (1965).

355. LIANG CHIN-KUEI. *Ching Hsueh-pao. Acta phys.*, **17**, 567 (1961).
356. MAKOLKIN, I.A. *ZhFKh*, **14**, 110 (1940).
357. MAIER, A.I., N.M. SELIVANOVA, and L.A. TERENT'EVA. *ZhFKh*, **39**, 1746 (1965).
358. MAKSIMOVA, I.N. *Zhurnal Strukturnoi Khimii*, 3, 208 (1962).
359. MAL TSEV, V.A., Yu.V. GAGARINSKII, and M.M. POPOV. *ZhNKh*, **5**, 228 (1960).
360. MASLOV, P.G. *ZhFKh*, **35**, 1551 (1961).
361. MASLOV, P.G. *ZhOKh*, **33**, 1054 (1963).
361a. MASLOV, P.G. and Yu.P. MASLOV. *Khimiya i Tekhnologiya Topliv i Masel*, No. 10, 50 (1958).
361b. MASLOV, P.G. and Yu.P. MASLOV. *ZhOKh*, **35**, 2112 (1965).
362. MASLOV, Yu.P. and P.G. MASLOV. *ZhFKh*, **32**, 1715 (1958).
363. MATVEEV, M.A. *Trudy MKhTI im. D.I. Mendeleeva*, 18, 27 (1954);
MATVEEV, M.A. and G.M. MATVEEV. In: *Sbornik "Fiziko-khimicheskie osnovy keramiki"*, p. 504, Promstroiizdat (1956).
364. MATVEEV, M.A., B.N. FRENKEL', and G.M. MATVEEV. *Izv. AN SSSR, Neorganicheskie Materialy*, **1**, 1426 (1965).
365. MASHOVETS, V.P. and B.F. YUDIN. *Izvestiya Vysshikh Uchebnykh Zavedenii, Tsvetnaya Metallurgiya*, No. 4, 95 (1962).
366. MEDVEDEV, V.A. *ZhFKh*, **35**, 1481 (1961).
367. MEDVEDEV, V.A. *ZhFKh*, 37, 1403 (1963).
368. MEDVEDEVA, Z.S. and Ya.Kh. GRINBERG. *ZhNKh*, **9**, 491 (1964).
369. MINENKO, V.I. and V.S. IVANOVA. *Izvestiya Vysshikh Uchebnykh Zavedenii, Chernaya Metallurgiya*, No. 3, 58 (1959).
370. MIT'KINA, E.A. *Atomnaya Energiya*, No. 7, 163 (1959).
371. MIKHAILOV, M.A. *Izvestiya Sibirskogo Otdeleniya AN SSSR*, No. 9, 116 (1962).
371a. MISHCHENKO, K.P., T.A. TUMANOVA, and I.E. FLISS. *ZhAKh*, **15**, 211 (1960).
372. MISHCHENKO, K.P., I.E. FLISS, and V.A. KUSTODINA. *ZhPKh*, **33**, 2671 (1960).
373. MOROZOV, V.P., N.F. KOVALENKO, V.N. KHLEBNIKOVA, and Yu.K. FEDOROV. *Teoreticheskaya Eksperimental'naya Khimiya*, **1**, 462 (1965).
374. MOROZOV, A.N. and I.A. NOVOKHATSKII. *Izv. AN SSSR, OTN, Metallurgiya i Toplivo*, No. 6, 3 (1962).
375. MOROZOV, A.N. and I.A. NOVOKHATSKII. *Sbornik trudov NII Metallurgii Chelyabinskogo ekonomicheskogo raiona (Teoriya i praktika metallurgii)*, No. 6, 11 (1963).
376. MOROZOV, V.P. *Ukrainskii Khimicheskii Zhurnal*, **21**, 554 (1955).
377. MOROZOVA, M.P., G.A. BOL'SHAKOVA, and N.L. LUKINYKH. *ZhOKh*, **29**, 3144 (1959).
378. MOROZOVA, M.P., L.L. GETSKINA, and M. GOLOMOLZINA. *ZhOKh*, **27**, 1846 (1957).
379. MOROZOVA, M.P. and L.L GETSKINA. *ZhOKh*, **29**, 1049 (1959).
380. MOROZOVA, M.P. and L.L. GETSKINA. *Vestn. LGU*, No. 22, 128 (1959).
381. MOROZOVA, M.P. and G. EGER. *ZhOKh*, **30**, 3514 (1960).
382. MOROZOVA, M.P. and T.A. STOLYAROVA. *ZhOKh*, **30**, 3848 (1960).
383. MOROZOVA, M.P. and T.A. STOLYAROVA. *Vestn. LGU*, No. 16, 150 (1964).
384. MOROZOVA, M.P., M.K. KHRIPUN, and S.M. ARIYA. *ZhOKh*, **32**, 2072 (1961).
385. MURADOV, V.G. *ZhFKh*, **39**, 170 (1965).
386. MURATOV, F.Sh. and A.V. NOVOSELOVA. *DAN SSSR*, **143**, 599 (1962).
387. MCHEDLOV-PETROSYAN, O.P. and V.I. BABUSHKIN. *DAN SSSR*, **128**, 348 (1959).
388. NADZHAFOV, Yu.B., V.B. LOSEV, Yu.Kh. SHAULOV, A.F. MOISEEV, and V.S. TUBYANSKAYA. *ZhFKh*, **39**, 1220 (1965).
389. NADZHAFOV, Yu.B. and K.A. SHARIFOV. *Trudy Instituta Fiziki AN AzSSR*, **11**, 35 (1963).
390. NADZHAFOV, Yu.B. and Yu.Kh. SHAULOV. *ZhFKh*, **38**, 2975 (1964).
390a. NADZHAFOV, Yu.B. and Yu.Kh. SHAULOV. *Izv. AN AzSSR, Seriya Fiziko-Tekhnicheskikh i Matematicheskikh Nauk*, No. 1, 47 (1965).
391. NESMEYANOV, An.N. and L.P. BELYKH. *ZhFKh*, **34**, 841 (1960).
392. NESMEYANOV, An.N. and DE DYK MAN. *DAN SSSR*, **131**, 1383 (1960).
393. NESMEYANOV, An.N. and I.A. IL'ICHEVA. *ZhFKh*, **32**, 422 (1958).
394. NESMEYANOV, An.N., Yu.A. PRISELKOV, and V.V. KARENIN. *Techn. Repts. Internat. Atomic Energy Agency*, No. 14, 667 (1963).
395. NESMEYANOV, An.N. and L.A. SAZONOV. *ZhNKh*, **5**, 519 (1960).
396. NESMEYANOV, An.N., L.A. SMAKHTIN, and V.I. LEBEDEV. *DAN SSSR*, **112**, 700 (1958).
397. NESMEYANOV, An.N. and G. TRAPP. *ZhFKh*, **38**, 2931 (1964).
398. NESMEYANOV, An.N. and L.P. FIRSOVA. *ZhFKh*, **34**, 1032 (1960).
399. NESMEYANOV, An.N. and L.P. FIRSOVA. *ZhFKh*, **34**, 1907 (1960).
400. NESMEYANOV, An.N., L.P. FIRSOVA, and E.P. ISAKOVA. *ZhFKh*, **34**, 1200 (1960).
401. NESMEYANOV, An.N., L.P. FIRSOVA, and E.P. ISAKOVA. *ZhFKh*, **34**, 1699 (1960).
402. NESMEYANOV, An.N. and N.E. KHANDAMIROVA. *Vestn. MGU*, No.4, 28 (1960).
403. NIKOL'SKAYA, A.V., V.A. GEIDERIKH, and Ya.I. GERASIMOV. *DAN SSSR*, **130**, 1074 (1960).
404. NIKOL'SKII, A.B. *ZhNKh*, **8**, 1045 (1963).
405. NIKOL'SKII, A.B. *ZhNKh*, **10**, 290 (1965).

406. NIKOL'SKII, A.B. and A.N. RYABOV. *ZhNKh*, **9**, 7 (1964).
407. NIKOL'SKII, A.B. and A.N. RYABOV. *ZhNKh*, **10**, 3 (1965).
408. NIKOL'SKII, G.P., L.I. KAZARNOVSKAYA, Z.A. BAGDASARYAN, and I.A. KAZARNOVSKII. *DAN SSSR*, **72**, 713 (1950).
409. NICHKOV, I.F. *DAN SSSR*, **5**, 1113 (1961).
410. NOVIKOV, G.I. and N.V. GALITSKII, *ZhNKh*, **10**, 576 (1965).
411. NOVIKOV, G.I. and O.G. POLYACHENOK. *ZhNKh*, **7**, 1209 (1962).
412. NOVIKOV, G.I. and O.G. POLYACHENOK. *ZhNKh*, **8**, 1053 (1963).
413. NOVIKOV, G.I. and O.G. POLYACHENOK. *ZhNKh*, **8**, 1649 (1963).
414. NOVIKOV, G.I., S.A. SHCHUKAREV, I.V. VASIL'KOVA, A.V. SUVOROV, B.N. SHARUPIN, N.V. ANDREEVA, and A.K. BOEV. *VIII Mendeleevskii s"ezd po obshchei i prikladnoi khimii. Referaty dokladov i soobshchenii (Papers Read at the VIII Mendeleev Convention for Pure and Applied Chemistry)*, No. 4, 220 , Izd. AN SSSR (1959).
415. NOVOKHATSKII, I.A. *Izv. AN SSSR, OTN, Metallurgiya i Gornoe Delo*, No. 2, 3 (1963).
416. NOVOKHATSKII, I.A. and L.M. LENEV. *Izvestiya Vysshikh Uchebnykh Zavedenii, Tsvetnaya Metallurgiya*, No. 4, 68 (1965).
417. OBEREMOK-YAKUBOVA, A.P. and A.A. BALANDIN. *Izv. AN SSSR, OKhN*, No. 12, 2210 (1963).
418. OZHIGOV, E.P. *ZhOKh*, **34**, 3519 (1964).
419. OKUNEV, A.I. and N.P. DIEV. *Trudy Instituta Metallurgii Ural'skogo Filiala AN SSSR*, **1**, 71 (1957).
420. OSTROVSKII, Yu.P. and N.P. PENKIN. *Optika i Spektroskopiya*, No. 4, 719 (1958).
421. PALKIN, V.A., N.N. KUZ'MINA, and P.I. CHERNYAEV. *ZhNKh*, **10**, 41 (1965).
422. PALKIN, V.A., N.N. KUZ'MINA, and P.I. CHERNYAEV. *ZhNKh*, **10**, 49 (1965).
423. PALKIN, V.A., N.N. KUZ'MINA, and P.I. CHERNYAEV. *ZhNKh*, **10**, 1792 (1965).
424. PANIN, V.E., S.A. GRIBANOV and K.K. ZILING. *Izvestiya Vysshikh Uchebnykh Zavedenii, Fizika*, No. 2, 121 (1960).
425. PANKOVA, L.L. *Izvestiya Vysshikh Uchebnykh Zavedenii, Khimiya i Khimicheskaya Tekhnologiya*, **5**, 564 (1962).
426. PANKRATOV, A.V., A.N. ZERCHENINOV, O.G. TALAKIN, O.M. SOKOLOV, and N.A. KNYAZEVA. *ZhFKh*, **37**, 1399 (1963).
427. PANYUSHKIN, V.T. and V.S. MAL'TSEV. *Trudy Instituta Metallurgii i Obogashcheniya AN KazSSR*, **11**, 79 (1964).
428. PANFILOV, B.I. and N.N. FEODOS'EV. *ZhNKh*, **9**, 2685 (1964).
429. PANFILOV, B.I. and N.N. FEODOS'EV. *ZhNKh*, **9**, 2693 (1964).
430. PANFILOV, B.I. and N.N. FEODOS'EV. *ZhNKh*, **10**, 298 (1965).
431. PANFILOV, B.I. and N.N. FEODOS'EV. *ZhNKh*, **10**, 1844 (1965).
432. PARKS, G.S.and H.M. HUFFMAN. *Free Energy of Some Organic Compounds*. Reinhold Publ. New York (1932).
433. PATRICK, S. In: *Sbornik "Uspekhi khimii ftora"*, **1 – 11**, 336, Izd. Khimiya (1964).
434. PAUKOV, I.E. Summary of Candidate's Thesis, MGU (1960).
435. PAUKOV, I.E., P.G. STRELKOV, V.V. NOGTEVA, and V.I. BELYI. *DAN SSSR*, **162**, 543 (1965).
436. PAKHOMOVA, M.V. Summary of Candidate's Thesis. Leningradskii Khimiko-Tekhnologicheskii Institut im. Lensoveta, Leningrad. (1956).
437. PEPEKIN, V.I., T.N. DYMOVA, Yu.A. LEBEDEV, and A.Ya.APIN. *ZhFKh*, **38**, 1024 (1964).
438. PERFILOVA, I.P., I.V. KOZLOVA, S.A. SHCHUKAREV, and I.V. VASIL'KOVA. *Vestn. LGU*, No. 16, 130 (1961).
439. POZIN, M.E., B.A. KOPYLEV, and R.Yu. ZINYUK. *Izvestiya Vysshikh Uchebnykh Zavedenii, Khimiya i Khimicheskaya Tekhnologiya*, **6**, 98 (1963).
440. POLYACHENOK, O.G. *ZhNKh*, **10**, 1939 (1965).
441. POLYACHENOK, O.G. and G.I. NOVIKOV. *ZhNKh*, **8**, 1526 (1963).
442. POLYACHENOK, O.G. and G.I. NOVIKOV. *ZhNKh*, **8**, 1567 (1963).
443. POLYACHENOK, O.G. and G.I. NOVIKOV. *ZhNKh*, **8**, 2819 (1963).
444. POLYACHENOK, O.G. and G.I. NOVIKOV. *ZhOKh*, **33**, 2797 (1963).
445. POLYACHENOK, O.G. and G.I. NOVIKOV. *Vestnik LGU*, No. 16, 133 (1963).
446. POLYACHENOK, O.G. and G.I. NOVIKOV. *ZhNKh*, **9**, 773 (1964).
446a. PONOMAREV, V.V., T.A. ALEKSEEVA, and L.N. AKIMOVA. *ZhFKh*, **36**, 1083 (1962).
447. PONOMAREV, V.V., T.A. ALEKSEEVA, and L.N. AKIMOVA. *ZhFKh*, **37**, 227 (1963).
448. PONOMAREV, V.V., T.A. ALEKSEEVA, and L.N. AKIMOVA. *ZhFKh*, **36**, 872 (1962).
449. POPOV, G.P. *DAN SSSR*, **140** 1338 (1961).
450. POPOV, G.P., M.I. SIMANOVA, T.A. UGO'NIKOVA, and G.I. CHUFAROV. *DAN SSSR*, **148**, 357 (1963).
451. POPOV, G.P. and G.I. CHUFAROV. *ZhFKh*, **37**, 586 (1963).
452. POPOV, M.M. and V.P. KOLESOV. *ZhOKh*, **26**, 2385 (1956).
453. POPOV, M.M., F.A. KOSTYLEV, and T.F. KARPOVA. *ZhNKh*, **2**, 9 (1957).
454. POPOV. M.M. and F.I. TAZETDINOV. *Atommaya Energiya*, **8**, 420 (1960).
455. PORTNOI, K.N., V.A. TIMOFEEV, and E.N. TIMOFEEVA. *Izv. AN SSSR, Neorganicheskie Materialy*, **1**, 1513 (1965).
456. PRISELKOV, Yu.A. Yu.A. SAPOZHNIKOV, and A.V. TSEPLYAEVA. *Izv. AN SSSR, OTN, Metallurgiya i Toplivo*, No. 1, 106 (1959).
457. PRISELKOV, Yu.A., Yu.A. SAPOZHNIKOV, and A.V. TSEPLYAEVA. *Izv. AN SSSR, OTN, Metallurgiya i Toplivo*, No. 1, 134 (1960).
458. PROSHINA, Z.V. and T.N. REZUKHINA. *ZhNKh*, **5**, 1016 (1960).
459. PROSHINA, Z.V. and T.N. REZUKHINA. *ZhFKh*, **36**, 153 (1962).

460. PROSHINA, Z.V. and T.N. REZUKHINA. *ZhFKh*, **36**, 1749 (1962).
461. RABINOVICH, I.B., V.I. TEL'NOI, P.N. NIKOLAEV, and G.A. RAZUVAEV. *DAN SSSR*, **138**, 852 (1961).
462. RABINOVICH, I.B., V.I. TEL'NOI, N.V. KARYAKIN, and G.A. RAZUVAEV. *DAN SSSR*, **149**, 324 (1963).
463. RABINOVICH, I.B., V.I. TEL'NOI, L.M. TERMAN, A.S. KIRILLOVA, and G.A. RAZUVAEV. *DAN SSSR*, **143**, 133 (1962).
464. REZNITSKII, L.A. Summary of Candidate's Thesis. MGU (1960).
465. REZNITSKII, L.A. and K.G. KHOMYAKOV. *DAN SSSR*, **131**, 325 (1960).
466. REZNITSKII, L.A. and K.G. KHOMYAKOV. *Vestn. MGU*, No. 6, 24 (1961).
467. REZNICHENKO, V.A., F.B. KHALILEEV, and T.P. UKOLOVA. In: *Sbornik "Titan i ego svoistva"*, No. 9, 42, Izd. AN SSSR (1963).
468. REZUKHINA, T.N., V.I. LAVRENT'EV, V.A. LEVITSKII and F.A. KUZNETSOV. *ZhFKh*, **35**, 1367 (1961).
469. REZUKHINA, T.N. and V.A. LEVITSKII. *ZhFKh*, **37**, 2357 (1963).
470. REZUKHINA, T.N., V.A. LEVITSKII, and B.A. ISTOMIN. *Elektrokhimiya*, **1**, 467 (1965).
471. REZUKHINA, T.N., V.A. LEVITSKII, and N.M. KAZIMIROVA. *ZhFKh*, **35**, 2639 (1961).
472. REZUKHINA. T.N., V.A. LEVITSKII, and P. OZHEGOV. *ZhFKh*, **37**, 687 (1963).
473. REZUKHINA, T.N. and Z.V. PROSHINA. *ZhFKh*, **36**, 637 (1962).
474. RENGEVICH, E.N. and E.A. SHILOV. *Ukrainskii Khmicheskii Zhurnal*, **28**, 1080 (1962).
475. RESHETNIKOV. *ZhNKh*, **6**, 682 (1961).
476. ROZHDESTVENSKII, I.B. and E.V. SAMUILOV. In: *Sbornik "Fizika, gazodinamika, teploobmen i termodinamika gazov vysokikh temperatur"*, p. 103, Izd. AN SSSR (1962).
477. ROZHNOV, A.M. Summary of Candidate's Thesis, Kuibyshev (1963).
478. ROZHNOV, A.M. and D.N. ANDREEVSKII. *DAN SSSR*, **147**, 388 (1962).
479. ROZHNOV, A.M. and D.N. ANDREEVSKII. *Neftekhimiya*, **3**, 405 (1963).
480. ROMANOVSKII, V.A. and V.V. TARASOV. *Fizika Tverdogo Tela*, **2**, 1294 (1960).
481. RUDNITSKII, L.A. *ZhFKh*, **35**, 1853 (1961).
482. RUZINOV, L.P. and Yu.P. ADLER. *ZhFKh*, **39**, 3095 (1965).
483. RUZINOV, L.P. and S.F. BELOV. *Tsvetnye Metally*, No. 12, 71 (1959).
484. RUZINOV, L.P. and S.F. BELOV. *Izvestiya Vysshikh Uchebnykh Zavedenii, Tsvetnaya Metallurgiya*, No. 6, 104 (1960).
485. RUSIN, A.D. and V.M. TATEVSKII, *ZhFKh*, **37**, 716 (1963).
486. RUSIN, A.D. and V.M. TATEVSKII. *Teplofizika Vysokikh Temperatur*, **3**, 547 (1965).
487. RYSS, I.G. and D.T. DONSKAYA. *ZhFKh*, **33**, 107 (1959).
488. RYABCHIKOV, L.N. and G.F. TIKHVINSKII. *Fizika Metallov i Metallovedenie*, **10**, 635 (1960).
489. SAZYKINA, T.A. and N.M. SELIVANOVA. *Trudy MKhTI im. D.I. Mendeleeva*, **41**, 14 (1963).
490. SALNIS' K.Yu., K.P. MISHCHENKO and I.E. FLISS. *ZhNKh*, **2**, 1985 (1957).
491. SAMSONOV, G.V. *ZhPKh*, **28**, 1018 (1955).
492. SAMSONOV, G.V. *ZhFKh*, **30**, 2057 (1956).
493. SAMSONOV, G.V., V.S. NESHPOR, and Yu.B. PADERNO. In: *Sbornik 'Redkozemel'nye elementy,"* p. 22, Izd. AN SSSR (1963).
494. SAMSONOV, G.V., T.N. SEREBRYAKOVA, and A.S. BOLGAR. *ZhNKh*, **6**, 2243 (1961).
495. SVERDLIN, A.S. *ZhFKh*, **32**, 659 (1958).
496. SVERDLOV, L.M. and E.N. BOLOTINA. *ZhFKh*, **36**, 2765 (1962).
497. SELIVANOVA, N.M. *ZhFKh*, **32**, 1277 (1958).
498. SELIVANOVA, N.M. *ZhFKh*, **37**, 850 (1963).
499. SELIVANOVA, N.M. *ZhNKh*, **8**, 2024 (1963).
500. SELIVANOVA. N.M. and G.A. ZUBOVA. *Trudy MKhTI im. D.I. Mendeleeva*, **22**, 28 (1956).
501. SELIVANOVA, N.M. and G.A. ZUBOVA. *ZhFKh*, **33**, 141 (1959).
502. SELIVANOVA, N.M., G.A. ZUBOVA, I.I. ABRAMOV, A.V. KALINKINA, and T.A. SAZYKINA. *Trudy MKhTI im. Mendeleeva*, **38**, 21 (1962).
503. SELIVANOVA, N.M., G.A. ZUBOVA, and E.I. FINKEL'SHTEIN. *ZhFKh*, **33**, 2365 (1959).
504. SELIVANOVA, N.M. and A.F. KAPUSTINSKII. *ZhFKh*, **27**, 565 (1953).
505. SELIVANOVA N.M., A.F. KAPUSTINSKII, and G.A. ZUBOVA. *Izv. AN SSSR, OKhN*, No. 2, 187 (1959).
506. SELIVANOVA N.M. and M.Kh. KARAPET'YANTS. *Izvestyia Vysshikh Uchebnykh Zavedenii, Khimiya i Khimicheskaya Tekhnologiya*, No. 6, 891 (1962).
507. SELIVANOVA, N.M. and Z.L. LESHCHINSKAYA. *Tezisy dokladov vtoroi konferentsii po kalorimetrii (Papers Read at the Second Conference on Calorimetry)*. Leningrad (1963).
508. SELIVANOVA, N.M. and Z.L. LESHCHINSKAYA. *Trudy MKhTI im. D.I. Mendeleeva*, **38**, 37 (1962).
509. SELIVANOVA, N.M. and Z.L. LESHCHINSKAYA. *ZhNKh*, **8**, 563 (1963).
510. SELIVANOVA, N.M. and Z.L. LESHCHINSKAYA. *ZhNKh*, **9**, 259 (1964).
511. SELIVANOVA, N.M., Z.L. LESHCHINSKAYA, and T.V. KLUSHINA. *ZhFKh*, **36**, 1349 (1962).
512. SELIVANOVA, N.M., Z.L. LESHCHINSKAYA, A.I. MAIER, I.S. STREL'TSOV, and E.Yu. MUZALEV. *ZhFKh*, **37**, 1563 (1963); I. LESHCHINSKAYA, N.M. SELIVANOVA, A.I. MAIER, I.S. STREL'TSOV, and E.Yu. MUZALEV. *Zh. VKhO im. D.J. Mendeleeva*, **8**, 577 (1963).
513. SELIVANOVA, N.M., Z.L. LESHCHINSKAYA, A.I. MAIER, and E.Yu. MUZALEV. *Izvestiya Vysshikh Uchebnykh Zavedenii, Khimiya i Khimicheskaya Tekhnologiya*, **7**, 209 (1964).

514. SELIVANOVA, N.M., Z.L. LESHCHINSKAYA, and I.S. STREL'TSOV. *ZhFKh,* **37,** 668 (1963).
515. SELIVANOVA, N.M., A.I. MAIER, and T.A. LUK'YANOVA. *ZhNKh,* **8,** 2428 (1963).
516. SELIVANOVA, N.M., A.I. MAIER, and T.A. LUK'YANOVA. *ZhFKh,* **37,** 1588 (1963).
517. SELIVANOVA, N.M. and T.A. SAZYKINA. *ZhNKh,* **7,** 536 (1962).
518. SELIVANOVA, N.M. and T.A. SAZYKINA. *Tezisy dokladov konferentsii po kalorimetrii (Papers Read at the Conference on Calorimetry).* Leningrad (1964).
519. SELIVANOVA, N.M. and T.A. SAZYKINA. *Trudy MKhTI im. D.I. Mendeleeva,* **38,** 26 (1962).
520. SELIVANOVA, N.M. and T.A. SAZYKINA. *Izvestiya Vysshikh Uchebnykh Zavedenii, Khimiya i Khimicheskaya Tekhnologiya,* No.4, 531 (1963).
521. SELIVANOVA, N.M. and T.A. SAZYKINA. *ZhPKh,* **37,** 514 (1964).
522. SELIVANOVA, N.M., K.K. SAMPLAVSKAYA, and A.I. MAIER. *Trudy MKhTI im. D.I. Mendeleeva,* **38,** 30 (1962).
523. SELIVANOVA, N.M. and V.A. SHNEIDER. *Khimicheskaya Nauka i Promyshlennost,* **3,** 834 (1958).
524. SELIVANOVA, N.M. and V.A. SHNEIDER. *Izvestiya Vysshikh Uchebnykh Zavedenii, Khimiya i Khimicheskaya Tekhnologiya,* **2,** 475 (1959); *Nauchnye Doklady Vysshei Shkoly,* **2,** 651 (1959).
525. SELIVANOVA, N.M. and V.A. SHNEIDER. *ZhFKh,* **35,** 574 (1961).
526. SELIVANOVA, N.M., V.A. SHNEIDER, and T.A. SAZYKINA. *Izvestiya Vysshikh Uchebnykh Zavedenii, Khimiya i Khimicheskaya Tekhnologiya,* **5,** 183 (1962).
527. SELIVANOVA, N.M., V.A. SHNEIDER, and R.I. RYABOVA. *ZhNKh,* **6,** 27 (1961).
528. SEMENKEVICH, S.A. *ZhPKh,* **30,** 933 (1957).
529. SEMENKEVICH, S.A. *ZhPKh,* **33,** 1281 (1960).
530. SEREBRENNIKOV, N.N. and P.V. GEL'D. *DAN SSSR,* **87,** 1021 (1952).
531. SEREBRENNIKOV, N.N. and P.V. GEL'D. *DAN SSSR,* **115,** 354 (1957).
532. SEREBRENNIKOV, N.N. and P.V. GEL'D. *Izvestiya Vysshikh Uchebnykh Zavedenii, Tsvetnaya Metallurgiya,* No.4, 80 (1961).
533. SEREGIN, E.A., N.N. GORYSHKO, V.P. KOLESOV, N.A. BELIKOVA, S.M. SKURATOV, and A.F. PLATE. *DAN SSSR,* **159,** 138 (1964).
534. SEREGIN, E.A., V.P. KOLESOV, N.A. BELIKOVA, S.M. SKURATOV, and A.F. PLATE. *DAN SSSR,* **145,** 580 (1962).
535. SINEL'NIKOVA, V.S., V.A. PODERGIN, and V.N. RECHKIN. *Aluminidy (Aluminides).* Izd. Naukova Dumka, Kiev (1965).
535a. SIROTA, N.N. and N.N. YUSHKEVICH. In: *Sbornik "Khimicheskaya svyaz' v poluprovodnikakh i tverdykh telakh",* p. 122, Izd. Nauka i Tekhnika, Minsk (1965).
536. SKLYARENKO, S.I. and S.F. BELOV. *Sbornik nauchnykh trudov Giredmeta (1931–1956) (Collection of Scientific Works of Giredmet (1931–1956)),* **1,** 329. Tekhnologiya, Metallurgizdat (1959).
537. SKLYARENKO, S.I., L.P. RUZINOV, and Yu.U. SAMSONOV. *ZhNKh,* **7,** 2645 (1962).
538. SKURATOV, S.M. *Kolloidnyi Zhurnal,* **9,** 133 (1947).
539. SKURATOV, S.M., A.F. VOROB'EV, and N.M. PRIVALOVA. *ZhNKh,* **7,** 677 (1962).
540. SKURATOV, S.M. and V.P. KOLESOV. *ZhFKh,* **35,** 1156 (1961).
541. SMAGINA, E.I., V.S. KUTSEV, and B.F. ORMONT. *DAN SSSR,* **115,** 354 (1957); *Trudy Instituta im. L.Ya. Karpova,* **2,** 118 (1959).
542. SMAGINA, E.I. and B.F. ORMONT. *ZhFKh,* **25,** 224 (1955).
543. SMIRNOV, M.V. and L.E. IVANOVSKII. *ZhNKh,* **2,** 238 (1957).
544. SMIRNOV, M.V., I.F. NICHKOV, S.P. RASPOPIN, and M.V. PERFIL'EV. *DAN SSSR,* **130,** 581 (1960).
545. SMIRNOV, M.V. and N.Ya. CHUKREEV. *ZhNKh,* **3,** 2445 (1958).
546. SMIRNOVA, V.I. and B.F. ORMONT. *DAN SSSR,* **100,** 127 (1955).
547. SMIRNOVA, E.K., I.V. VASIL'KOVA, and N.F. KUDRYASHOVA. *ZhNKh,* **9,** 489 (1964).
548. SMIRNOVA, Z.G., V.V. ILLARIONOV, and S.I. VOL'FKOVICH. *ZhNKh,* **7,** 1779 (1962).
549. SOBOL', S.I. *ZhOKh,* **31,** 372 (1961).
550. SOBOLEVA, M.S. and Ya.V. VASIL'EV. *Vestn. LGU,* No.16, 153 (1962).
551. SOKOLOV, V.A. and G.A. SHARPATAYA. *ZhNKh,* **9,** 1542 (1964).
552. SOKOLOV, V.A. and N.E. SHMIDT. *Izvestiya Sektora Fiziko-Khimicheskogo Analiza IONKh AN SSSR,* **26,** 123 (1955).
553. SOKOLOV, V.A. and N.E. SHMIDT. *Izvestiya Sektora Fiziko-Khimicheskogo Analiza IONKh AN SSSR,* **27,** 217 (1956).
554. SOKOLOV, O.K. and A.N. BELYAEVA. *Izvestiya Vysshikh Uchebnykh Zavedenii, Tsvetnaya Metallurgiya,* No.5, 172 (1960).
555. SOKOLOVA, N.D., S.M. SKURATOV, A.M. SHEMONAEVA, and V.M. YULDASHEVA. *ZhNKh,* **6,** 774 (1961).
556. SPIVAKOVSKII, V.B. and L.P. MAISA. *ZhNKh,* **9,** 2287 (1964).
557. SPITSYN, Vikt.I. and N.N. PATSUKOVA. *ZhNKh,* **10,** 2396 (1965).
558. STEPIN, B.D., A.B. BABKOV, and T.M. SAS. *ZhNKh,* **10,** 1603 (1965).
559. STRELKOV, P.G., E.S. ITSKEVICH, V.N. KOSTYUKOV, and G.G. MIRSKAYA. *DAN SSSR,* **85,** 1085 (1952).
560. STREPIKHEEV, Yu.A., Yu.I. BARANOV, and O.A. BURMISTROVA. *Izvestiya Vysshikh Uchebnykh Zavedenii, Khimiya i Khimicheskaya Tekhnologiya,* No.2, 387 (1962).
561. STRUKOV, B.A. *Fizika Tverdogo Tela,* **6,** 2862 (1964).

562. STRUKOV, B.A. and M.N. DANILYCHEVA. *Fizika Tverdogo Tela,* **5**, 1724 (1963).
563. SUVOROV, A.V., G.I. NOVIKOV, R.B. DOBROTIN, and A.V. TARASOV. In: *Sbornik "Khimiya redkikh elementov,"* p.26, Izd. LGU (1964).
564. SUNG-YÜ-MIN and G.I. NOVIKOV. *ZhNKh,* **8**, 700 (1963).
565. TALAKIN, O.G., L.A. AKHANSHCHIKOVA, E.N. SOSNOVSKII, A.V. PANKRATOV, and A.N. ZERCHANINOV. *ZhFKh,* **36**, 1065 (1962).
565a. TARASOV, V.V., Kh.B. KHOKONOV, and N.A. CHERNOPLEKOV. In: *Sbornik "Fiziko-khimicheskie osnovy keramiki,"* p.170, Gosstroiizdat (1956).
566. TEL'NOI, V.I. and I.B. RABINOVICH. *ZhFKh,* **39**, 2314 (1965).
567. TEL'NOI, V.I., I.B. RABINOVICH, and G.A. RAZUVAEV. *DAN SSSR,* **159**, 1106 (1964).
568. GLUSHKO, V.P., V.A. MEDVEDEV, G.A. BERGMAN, L.V. GURVICH, V.S. YUNGMAN, A.F. VOROB'EV, V.P. KOLESOV, L.A. REZNITSKII, V.V. MIKHAILOV, G.L. GAL'CHENKO, and M.Kh. KARAPET'YANTS, editors. *Termicheskie konstanty veshchestv (Thermal Constants of Compounds).* Handbook No.1, VINITI AN SSSR (1965).
569. GLUSHKO, V.P., V.A. MEDVEDEV, G.A. BERGMAN, L.V. GURVICH, A.F. VOROB'EV, V.P. KOLESOV, L.A. REZNITSKII, G.L. GAL'CHENKO, V.S. YUNGMAN, and V.V. MIKHAILOV, editors. *Termicheskie konstanty veshchestv (Thermal Constants of Compounds).* Handbook, No.2, VINITI AN SSSR (1965).
570. GLUSHKO, V.P., L.V. GURVICH, G.A. KHACHKURUZOV, I.V. VEITS, and V.A. MEDVEDEV, editors. *Termodinamicheskie svoistva individual'nykh veshchestv (Thermodynamic Properties of Individual Substances),* 2nd edition, **1** and **2**. Izd. AN SSSR (1962).
571. TOLMACHEVA, T.A., V.M. TSINTSIUS, and L.V. ANDRIANOVA. *ZhNKh,* **8**, 553 (1963).
572. TOPORISHCHEV, G.A. and O.A. ESIN. *Izvestiya Vysshikh Uchebnykh Zavedenii, Chernaya Metallurgiya,* No.2, 16 (1963).
573. TOTSKII, E.E. and E.E. SHPIL'RAIN. *Teplogizika Vysokikh Temperatur,* **1**, 456 (1963).
574. TROITSKAYA, N.V. *Trudy Leningradskogo Tekhnologicheskogo Instituta,* **7**, 119 (1959).
575. TURKOVA, G.V., P.V. KOVTUNENKO, and A.A. BUNDEL'. *Trudy MKhTI im. D.I. Mendeleeva,* **39**, 72 (1962).
576. TURKOVA, G.V., P.V. KOVTUNENKO, and A.A. BUNDEL'. *Tezisy dokladov na nauchno-tekhnicheskoi konferentsii MKhTI (Papers Read at the Scientific and Technological Conference of MKhTI),* p.40 (1963).
577. FEDOROV, G.B. and E.A. SMIRNOV. *Thermodynamics of Nuclear Materials.* International Atomic Energy Agency, p.285, Vienna (1962).
578. FEDOROV, P.I., A.G. DUDAREVA, and N.F. DROBOT. *ZhNKh,* **8**, 1287 (1963).
579. FILIPPOV, A.A. and V.I. SMIRNOV. *Izvestiya Vysshikh Uchebnykh Zavedenii, Tsvetnaya Metallurgiya,* No.6, 55 (1960).
580. FLISS, I.E. Ph.D. Thesis. Leningradskii Khimiko-Tekhnicheskii Institut im. Lensoveta, Leningrad (1959).
581. FLISS, I.E. *ZhPKh,* **37**, 683 (1964).
582. FLISS, I.E., K.P. MISHCHENKO, and N.V. PAKHOMOVA. *ZhNKh,* **3**, 1781 (1958).
583. FOMIN, V.V. *ZhFKh,* **28**, 1896 (1954).
584. KHANDAMIROVA, N.E., A.M. EVSEEV, G.V. POZHARSKAYA, E.A. BORISOV, An.N. NESMEYANOV, and Ya.I. GERASIMOV. *ZhNKh,* **4**, 2192 (1959).
585. KHACHKURUZOV, G.A. *Trudy GIPKh,* **46**, 51 (1960).
586. KHVOROSTUKHINA, N.A., Yu.V. RUMYANTSEV, and I.K. SKOBEEV. *Trudy Vostochno-Sibirskogo Otdeleniya AN SSSR,* **41**, 67 (1962).
587. KHEIFETS, V.L. and A.L. ROTINYAN. *ZhOKh,* **24**, 930 (1954).
588. KHLEBNIKOVA, V.N. and V.P. MOROZOV. *Ukrainskii Khimicheskii Zhurnal,* **24**, 3 (1958).
589. KHLEBNIKOVA, V.N. and V.P. MOROZOV. *Ukrainskii Khimicheskii Zhurnal,* **27**, 550 (1961).
590. KHOMYAKOV, K.G., Vikt.I. SPITSYN, and S.A. ZHVANKO. In: *Sbornik "Issledovaniya v oblasti khimii urana,"* p.141, Izd. MGU (1961).
591. TSEPLYAEVA, A.V., Yu.A. PRISELKOV, and V.V. KARELIN. *Vestn. MGU,* No.5, 36 (1960).
592. TSAGAREISHVILI, D.Sh. and G.G. GVELESIANI. *ZhNKh,* **10**, 319 (1965).
593. CHERNYAEV, I.I., V.A. PALKIN, and R.A. BARANOVA. *ZhNKh,* **3**, 1512 (1958).
594. CHERNYAEV, I.I., V.A. PALKIN, and R.A. BARANOVA. *ZhNKh,* **5**, 821 (1960).
595. CHERNYAEV, I.I., V.A. PALKIN, R.A. BARANOVA, and N.N. KUZ'MINA. *ZhNKh,* **5**, 1428 (1960).
596. CHERNYAEV, I.I., V.A. SOKOLOV, N.E. SHMIDT, and G.S. MURAVEISKAYA. *DAN SSSR,* **62**, 235 (1948).
597. CHEKHOVSKOI, V.Ya. *Inzhenerno-Fizicheskii Zhurnal,* **5**, 43 (1962).
598. CHEKHOVSKOI, V.Ya. *Teplofizika Vysokikh Temperatur,* **2**, 296 (1964).
599. CHUFAROV, G.I. and L.I. LEONT'EV. *DAN SSSR,* **154**, 881 (1964).
600. SHARIFOV, K.A. and S.N. GADZHIEV. *ZhFKh,* **38**, 2070 (1964).
601. SHARIFOV, K.A., S.N. GADZHIEV, and M.Ya. AGARUNOV. *Izv. AN AzSSR, Seriya Fiziko-Tekhnicheskikh i Matematicheskikh Nauk,* No.2, 85 (1964).
602. SHARIFOV, K.A., S.N. GADZHIEV, and I.M. GARIBOV. *Izv. AN AzSSR, Seriya Fiziko-Matematicheskikh i Tekhnicheskikh Nauk,* No.2, 53 (1963).
603. SHARIFOV, K.A. and T.N. REZUKHINA. *Trudy Instituta Fiziki i Matematiki AN AzSSR, Seriya Fizicheskaya,* **6**, 53 (1953).
604. SHARIFOV, K.A. and S.M. SKURATOV. *DAN AzSSR,* **9**, 377 (1953).

605. SHARPATAYA, G.A. and V.A. SOKOLOV. *ZhNKh*, **10**, 992 (1965).
606. SHARPATAYA, G.A. and V.A. SOKOLOV. *ZhNKh*, **10**, 2235 (1965).
607. SHAULOV, Yu.Kh., G.O. SHMYREVA, and V.S. TUBYANSKAYA. *ZhFKh*, **39**, 105 (1965).
608. SHVEIKIN, G.P. *Sbornik Instituta Khimii Ural'skogo Filiala AN SSSR*, No.2, 45 (1958).
609. SHEMYAKINA, T.S., E.K. SMIRNOVA, T.P. POPOVA, and V.M. KUPTSOVA. *ZhNKh*, **9**, 2387 (1964).
610. SHEMYAKINA, T.S., E.K. SMIRNOVA, and S.A. SHCHUKAREV. *Vestn. LGU*, No.16, 155 (1962).
611. SHIDLOVSKII, A.A. *ZhFKh*, **36**, 1773 (1962).
612. SHIDLOVSKII, A.A. *ZhFKh*, **39**, 2163 (1965).
613. SHIDLOVSKII, A.A. and K.V. VALKINA. *ZhFKh*, **35**, 294 (1961).
614. SHIDLOVSKII, A.A. and A.A. VOSKRESENSKII. *ZhFKh*, **37**, 2062 (1963).
615. SHIDLOVSKII, A.A. and A.A. VOSKRESENSKII. *ZhFKh*, **39**, 1523 (1965).
616. SHIDLOVSKII, A.A. and A.A. VOSKRESENSKII. *ZhFKh*, **39**, 3097 (1965).
617. SHIDLOVSKII, A.A. and A.A. VOSKRESENSKII. *ZhFKh*, **40**, 2609 (1966).
618. SHIDLOVSKII, A.A., A.A. VOSKRESENSKII, I.A. KONDRASHINA, and E.S. SHITIKOV. *ZhFKh*, **40**, 1947 (1966).
619. SHIDLOVSKII, A.A., V.I. SEMISHIN, and L.F. SHMAGIN. *ZhPKh*, **35**, 756 (1962).
620. SHMIDT, N.E. and V.A. SOKOLOV. *ZhNKh*, **6**, 2613 (1961).
621. SHNEIDER, V.A. Summary of Candidate's Thesis, MKhTI im. D.I. Mendeleeva (1958).
621a. SHTEKHER, S.M., S.M. SKURATOV, V.N. DAUNSHAS, and R.Ya. LEVINA. *DAN SSSR*, **127**, 812 (1959).
622. SHCHERBAKOV, S.A., G.A. SEMENOV, and K.E. FRANTSEVA. *DAN SSSR*, **145**, 119 (1962).
623. SHCHUKAREV, S.A. *ZhOKh*, **28**, 845 (1958).
624. SHCHUKAREV, S.A., S.M. ARIYA, and G.A. LAKHTIN. *Vestn. LGU*, No.2, 121 (1953).
625. SHCHUKAREV, S.A., I.V. VASIL'KOVA, and V.M. DROZDOVA. *ZhNKh*, **3**, 2651 (1958).
626. SHCHUKAREV, S.A., I.V. VASIL'KOVA, V.M. DROZDOVA, and N.S. MARTYNOVA. *ZhNKh*, **4**, 33 (1959).
627. SHCHUKAREV, S.A., I.V. VASIL'KOVA, V.M. DROZDOVA, and K.E. FRANTSEVA. *ZhNKh*, **4**, 39 (1959).
628. SHCHUKAREV, S.A., I.V. VASIL'KOVA, and N.D. ZAITSEVA. *Vestn. LGU*, No.22, 127 (1961).
629. SHCHUKAREV, S.A., I.V. VASIL'KOVA, and D.V. KOROL'KOV. *ZhNKh*, **9**, 1810 (1964).
630. SHCHUKAREV, S.A., I.V. VASIL'KOVA, D.V. KOROL'KOV, and S.S. NIKOL'SKII. *Vestn. LGU*, No.4, 148 (1962).
631. SHCHUKAREV, S.A., I.V. VASIL'KOVA, N.S. MARTYNOVA, and Yu.G. MAL'TSEV. *ZhNKh*, **3**, 2647 (1958).
632. SHCHUKAREV, S.A., I.V. VASIL'KOVA, and G.I. NOVIKOV. *ZhNKh*, **3**, 2642 (1958).
632a. SHCHUKAREV, S.A., I.V. VASIL'KOVA, M.A. ORANSKAYA, V.M. TSINTSIUS, and N.A. SUBBOTINA. *Vestn. LGU*, No.16, 125 (1961).
633. SHCHUKAREV, S.A., I.V. VASIL'KOVA, I.L. PERFIL'EVA, and L.V. CHERNYKH. *ZhNKh*, **7**, 1509 (1962).
634. SHCHUKAREV, S.A., I.V. VASIL'KOVA, and B.N. SHARUPIN. *Vestn. LGU*, No.10, 112 (1960).
635. SHCHUKAREV, S.A., I.V. VASIL'KOVA, and B.N. SHARUPIN. *Vestn. LGU*, No.22, 130 (1961).
636. SHCHUKAREV, S.A., E. VOL'F, and M.P. MOROZOVA. *ZhOKh*, **24**, 1925 (1954).
637. SHCHUKAREV, S.A., G. GROSSMAN, and M.P. MOROZOVA. *ZhOKh*, **25**, 633 (1955).
638. SHCHUKAREV, S.A. and G.A. KOKOVIN. *ZhNKh*, **5**, 507 (1960).
639. SHCHUKAREV, S.A. and G.A. KOKOVIN. *ZhNKh*, **9**, 1309 (1964).
640. SHCHUKAREV, S.A. and G.A. KOKOVIN. *ZhNKh*, **9**, 1565 (1964).
641. SHCHUKAREV, S.A., N.I. KOLBIN, and A.N. RYABOV. *ZhNKh*, **3**, 1721 (1958).
642. SHCHUKAREV, S.A., N.I. KOLBIN, and A.N. RYABOV. *ZhNKh*, **6**, 1013 (1961).
643. SHCHUKAREV, S.A., N.I. KOLBIN, and A.N. RYABOV. *Vestn. LGU*, No.4, 100 (1961).
644. SHCHUKAREV, S.A. and A.R. KURBANOV. *Vestn. LGU*, No.10, 144 (1962).
645. SHCHUKAREV, S.A. and A.R. KURBANOV. *Izv. AN TadzhSSR, Otdelenie Geologo-Khimicheskikh i Tekhnicheskikh Nauk*, No.1(7), 56 (1962).
646. SHCHUKAREV, S.A., M.P. MOROZOVA, and M.M. BORTNIKOVA. *ZhOKh*, **28**, 3289 (1958).
647. SHCHUKAREV, S.A., M.P. MOROZOVA, and K'ANG HUO-YN. *ZhOKh*, **27**, 289 (1957).
648. SHCHUKAREV, S.A., M.P. MOROZOVA, K'ANG HUO-YN, and V.T. SHAROV. *ZhOKh*, No. 27, 290 (1957).
649. SHCHUKAREV, S.A., M.P. MOROZOVA, and LI MIAO-HSIU. *ZhOKh*, **29**, 2465 (1959).
650. SHCHUKAREV, S.A., M.P. MOROZOVA, and LI MIAO-HSIU. *ZhOKh*, **29**, 3142 (1959).
651. SHCHUKAREV, S.A., M.P. MOROZOVA, and G.F. PRON'. *ZhOKh*, **32**, 2069 (1962).
652. SHCHUKAREV, S.A., M.P. MOROZOVA, and Yu.P. SAPOZHNIKOV. *ZhOKh*, **26**, 304 (1956).
653. SHCHUKAREV, S.A., M.P. MOROZOVA, and T.A. STOLYAROVA. *ZhOKh*, **31**, 1773 (1961).
654. SHCHUKAREV, S.A.,G.I. NOVIKOV, I.V. VASIL'KOVA, A.V. SUVOROV, N.V. ANDREEVA, B.N. SHARUPIN, and A.K. BAEV. *ZhNKh*, **5**, 1650 (1960).
655. SHCHUKAREV, S.A. and M.A. ORANSKAYA. *ZhOKh*, **24**, 1926 (1954).
656. SHCHUKAREV, S.A., M.A. ORANSKAYA, T.A. TOLMACHEVA, and L.L. VANICHEVA. *ZhNKh*, **3**, 1478 (1958).
657. SHCHUKAREV, S.A., M.A. ORANSKAYA, T.A. TOLMACHEVA, and Yu.S. IL'INSKII. *ZhNKh*, **5**, 8 (1960).
658. SHCHUKAREV, S.A., M.A. ORANSKAYA, and V.M. TSINTSIUS. *ZhNKh*, **1**, 881 (1956).
659. SHCHUKAREV, S.A., M.A. ORANSKAYA, and T.S. SHEMYAKINA. *ZhNKh*, **1**, 17 (1956).
660. SHCHUKAREV, S.A., M.A. ORANSKAYA, and T.S. SHEMYAKINA. *ZhNKh*, **5**, 2135 (1960).
661. SHCHUKAREV, S.A. and A.N. RYABOV. *ZhNKh*, **5**, 1931 (1960).
662. SHCHUKAREV, S.A., G.A. SEMENOV, and I.A. RAT'KOVSKII. *ZhNKh*, **6**, 1973 (1961).

663. SHCHUKAREV, S.A., G.A. SEMENOV, and I.A. RAT'KOVSKII. *ZhNKh,* **7,** 469 (1962).
664. SHCHUKAREV, S.A., G.V. SEMENOV, I.A. RAT'KOVSKII, and V.A. PEREVOSHCHIKOV. *ZhOKh,* **31,** 2090 (1961).
665. SHCHUKAREV, S.A., G.A. SEMENOV, and K.E. FRANTSEVA. *Izvestiya Vysshikh Uchebnykh Zavedenii, Khimiya i Khimicheskaya Tekhnologiya,* No.5, 691 (1962).
666. SHCHUKAREV, S.A., E.K. SMIRNOVA, I.V. VASIL'KOVA, and N.I. BOROVKOVA. *ZhNKh,* **7,** 1213 (1962).
667. SHCHUKAREV, S.A., E.K. SMIRNOVA, I.V. VASIL'KOVA, and M.S. KOTOVA. *Vestn. LGU,* No.22, 174 (1963).
668. SHCHUKAREV, S.A., E.K. SMIRNOVA, I.V. VASIL'KOVA, and L.I. LAPPO. *Vestn. LGU,* No.16, 113 (1960).
669. SHCHUKAREV, S.A., E.K. SMIRNOVA, and A.R. KURBANOV. *DAN TadzhSSR,* **5,** No.4, 14 (1962).
[670. is omitted in the Russian bibliography.]
671. SHCHUKAREV, S.A. and A.V. SUVOROV. *ZhNKh,* **6,** 1488 (1961).
672. SHCHUKAREV, S.A., T.A. TOLMACHEVA, and M.A. ORANSKAYA. *ZhOKh,* **24,** 2093 (1954).
673. SHCHUKAREV, S.A., T.A. TOLMACHEVA, M.A. ORANSKAYA, and L.V. KOMANDROVSKAYA. *ZhNKh,* **1,** 8 (1956).
674. SHCHUKAREV, S.A., T.A. TOLMACHEVA, and Yu.L. PAZUKHINA. *ZhNKh,* **9,** 2507 (1964).
675. SHCHUKAREV, S.A., T.A. TOLMACHEVA, and V.M. TSINTSIUS. *ZhNKh,* **7,** 679 (1962).
676. SHCHUKAREV, S.A. and T.S. SHEMYAKINA. *ZhNKh,* **5,** 2135 (1960).
677. EITEL', V. *Termokhimiya silikatov (Thermochemistry of Silicates).* Promstroiizdat (1957).
678. EPEL'BAUM, V.A. and M.I. STAROSTINA. *Trudy konferentsii po khimii bora i ego soedinenii (Proceedings of the Conference on the Chemistry of Boron and Its Compounds),* p.97. Goskhimizdat (1958).
679. YUDIN, B.V. and G.A. KHACHKURUZOV. *Trudy GIPKh,* **42,** 132 (1959).
680. YUNGMAN, V.S., L.V. GURVICH, V.A. KVLIVIDZE, and N.P. RTISHCHEVA. *Trudy GIPKh,* **46,** 15 (1960).
681. YUNGMAN, V.S., L.V. GURVICH, and N.P. RTISHCHEVA. *Trudy GIPKh,* **49,** 20 (1963).
682. YAGFAROV, M.Sh. *DAN SSSR,* **127,** 615 (1959).
683. YAKERSON, V.I. *Izv. AN SSSR, Seriya Khimicheskaya,* No.6, 1003 (1963).
684. YAKOVLEVA, R.A. and T.N. REZUKHINA. *ZhFKh,* **34,** 819 (1960).
685. YAKUB'YAN, E.S., G.A. BUKHALOVA, and T.M. KHLIYAN. *ZhNKh,* **10,** 258 (1965).
686. GERASIMOV, Ya.I. and A.V. NIKOL'SKAYA. In: *Sbornik "Voprosy metallurgii i fiziki poluprovodnikov" (Problems in Metallurgy and Physics of Semiconductors),* p.30. Izd. AN SSSR (1961).
687. YEN KUNG-FAN, LI SHAO-CHUNG, and G.I. NOVIKOV. *ZhNKh,* **8,** 89 (1963).
688. YAPRINTSEVA, A.A. and A.V. FINKEL'SHTEIN. *Trudy Sibirskogo Tekhnologicheskogo Instituta,* **36,** 75 (1963).
688a. YATSIMIRSKII, K.B. *DAN SSSR,* **58,** 1407 (1947).
689. YATSIMIRSKII, K.B. *Izv. AN SSSR, OKhN,* No.5, 453 (1947).
690. YATSIMIRSKII, K.B. *Izv. AN SSSR, OKhN,* No.6, 590 (1948).
691. YATSIMIRSKII, K.B. *Izv. AN SSSR, OKhN,* No.6, 648 (1949).
692. YATSIMIRSKII, K.B. *Termokhimiya kompleksnykh soedinenii (Thermochemistry of Complex Compounds).* Izd. AN SSR (1951).
693. YATSIMIRSKII, K.B. *ZhOKh,* **26,** 2376 (1956).
694. YATSIMIRSKII, K.B. *ZhNKh,* **3,** 2244 (1958).
695. YATSIMIRSKII, K.B. *Izvestiya Vysshikh Uchebnykh Zavedenii, Khimiya i Khimicheskaya Tekhnologiya,* **2,** 480 (1959).
696. YATSIMIRSKII, K.B. *ZhNKh,* **6,** 518 (1961).
697. YATSIMIRSKII, K.B. and A.A. ASTASHEVA. *DAN SSSR,* **69,** 381 (1949).
698. YATSIMIRSKII, K.B. and G.A. KRESTOV. *ZhFKh,* **34,** 2263 (1960).
699. YATSIMIRSKII, K.B. and G.A. KRESTOV. *ZhFKh,* **34,** 2448 (1960).
700. ABRAHAM, B.M., N.R. DAVIDSON, and E.F. WESTRUM *Nat. Nucl. Energy Ser., Div. IV,* **14B,** *The Transuranium Elements,* p.60 (1949).
701. ABRAHAM, B.M. and H.E. FLOTOW. *J. Am. Chem. Soc.,* **77,** 1446 (1955).
702. ABRAHAM, B.M., D.W. OSBORNE, H.E. FLOTOW, and R.B. MARCUS. *J. Am. Chem. Soc.,* **82,** 1064 (1960).
703. ADAMI, L.H. and K.K. KELLEY. *Rept. Invest. Bur. Mines,* No. 6260, U.S. Dept. Interior (1963).
704. ADAMI, L.H. and E.G. KING. *Rept. Invest. Bur. Mines,* No. 6495, U.S. Dept. Interior (1964).
705. ADAMS, G.B. and H.L. JOHNSTON. *J. Am. Chem. Soc.,* **74,** 4788 (1952).
706. ADAMS, G.B., H.L. JOHNSTON, and E.C. KERR. *J. Am. Chem. Soc.,* **74,** 4784 (1952).
707. AHLBERG, BLANCHARD, and LUNDBERG. *J. Chem. Phys.,* **5,** 539 (1937).
708. AHLUWALIA, J.C. and J.W. COBBLE. *J. Am. Chem. Soc.,* **86,** 5377 (1964).
709. AIA, M.A. J.E. MATHERS, and R.W. MOONEY. *J. Chem. Eng. Data,* **9,** 355 (1964).
709a. AKERS, L.K., Ph.D. Thesis, Vanderbilt Univ., 1955 (cited in [2068a]).
710. ALBRICHT, L.F., W.C. GALAGAR, and K.K. INNES. *J. Am. Chem. Soc.,* **76,** 6017 (1954).
711. ALDRED, A.T., J.D. FILBY, and J.N. PRATT. *Trans. Faraday Soc.,* **55,** 2030 (1959).
712. ALDRED, A.T. and J.N. PRATT. *J. Chem. Eng. Data,* **8,** 429 (1963).
713. ALDRED, A.T. and J.N. PRATT. *J. Chem. Phys.,* **38,** 1085 (1963).
714. ALLEN, T.L. *J. Am. Chem. Soc.,* **78,** 5476 (1956).
715. ALLEN, T.L. and D.M. YOST. *J. Chem. Phys.,* **22,** 855 (1954).
716. ALTMAN, R.L. *J. Chem. Phys.,* **31,** 1035 (1959).
717. ALTMAN, R.L. *J. Chem. Phys.,* **32,** 615 (1960).

718. ALTMAN, R.L. *J. Chem. Eng. Data,* **8**, 534 (1963).
719. ALTMAN, R.L. *J. Phys. Chem.*, **67**, 366 (1963).
720. ALTMAN, R.L., *J. Phys. Chem.*, **68**, 3425 (1964).
721. ALTMAN, D., M. FARBER, and D.M. MASON. *J. Chem. Phys.*, **25**, 531 (1956).
722. ALTSHULLER, A.P. *J. Chem. Phys.*, **23**, 761 (1955).
723. ALTSHULLER, A.P. *J. Am. Chem. Soc.*, 77, 3480 (1955).
724. ALTSHULLER, A.P. *J. Am. Chem. Soc.*, 77, 5455 (1955).
725. ALTSHULLER, A.P. *J. Am. Chem. Soc.*, 77, 6187 (1955).
726. ALTSHULLER, A.P. *J. Am. Chem. Soc.*, 78, 4220 (1956).
727. ALTSHULLER, A.P. *J. Phys, Chem.*, **61**, 251 (1957).
728. ALTSHULLER, A.P. *J. Chem. Phys.*, **28**, 1254 (1958).
729. ANANTHANARAYANAN, V. *J. Sci. a. Ind. Res.*, **B21**, 89 (1962).
730. ANCEY-MORET, M.F., M. OLETTE, and F.D. RICHARDSON. *Mém. Sci. Rev. métallurgie*, **61**, 169 (1964).
731. ANDON, R.J.L., D.P. BIDDISCOMBE, J.D. COX, R. HANDLEY, D. HARROP. E.F.G. HERRINGTON, and J.F. MARTIN. *J. Chem. Soc.*, **1960**, 5246.
732. ANDON, R.J.L., J.F. COUNSELL, E.F.G. HERRINGTON, and J.F. MARTIN. *Trans. Faraday Soc.*, **259**, 830 (1946).
733. ANDON, R.J.L., J.F. COUNSELL, and J.F. MARTIN. *Trans. Faraday Soc.*, **59**, 1555 (1963).
734. ANDON, R.J.L., J.F. COUNSELL, H.M. McKERRELL, and J.F. MARTIN. *Trans. Faraday Soc.*, **59**, 2702 (1963).
735. ANDON, R.J.L., J.F. COUNSELL, J.F. MARTIN, and H.J. HEDGER. *Trans. Faraday Soc.*, **60**, 1030 (1964).
736. ANGELL, C.L. *J. Chem. Eng. Data,* **9**, 341 (1964).
737. ANOUS, M.M.T. *Rec. trav. chim.*, 78, 104 (1959).
738. ARMSTRONG, G.T. *J. Phys. Chem.*, 67, 2888 (1963).
739. ARMSTRONG, G.T. and R.S. JESSUP. *J. Res. Nat. Bur. Stand.*, **64A**, 49 (1960).
740. ARMSTRONG, G.T. and S. MARANTZ. Private communication. 1961.
741. ARMSTRONG, G.T. and S. MARANTZ. *J. Chem. Phys.*, 38, 169 (1963).
742. ARMSTRONG, G.T., S. MARANTZ, and C.F. COYLE. *J. Am. Chem. Soc.*, 81, 3798 (1959).
743. ARNOLD, H. *Z. phys. Chem.* (GDR), **225**, 45 (1964).
744. ARNOLD, M. *Z. phys. Chem.* (GDR), **226**, 146 (1964).
745. ARUMUGAM, K. and M. RADHAKRISHNAN. *Z. phys. Chem.* (GFR), 39, 262 (1963).
746. ASHCROFT, S.J., A.S. CARSON, W. CARTER, and P.G. LAYE. *Trans. Faraday Soc.*, **61**, 225 (1965).
747. ASHCROFT, S.J., A.S. CARSON, and J.B. PEDLEY. *Trans. Faraday Soc.*, 59, 2713 (1963).
748. ASHMORE, P.G. and B.J. TYLER. *J. Chem. Soc.*, **1961**, 1017.
749. ASTON, J.G., M.L. EIDINOFF, and W.S. FORSTER. *J. Am. Chem. Soc.*, **61**, 1539 (1939).
750. ASTON, J.G., H.L. FINKE, G.J. JANZ, and K.E. RUSSEL. *J. Am. Chem. Soc.*, **73**, 1939 (1951).
751. ASTON, J.G., O.W. ISSER, G.J. SZASZ, and R.M. KENNEDY. *J. Chem. Phys.*, **12**, 336 (1944).
752. ASTON, J.G. and M. SAGENKAHN. *J. Am. Chem. Soc.* **66**, 1171 (1944).
753. ASTON, J.G., P.E. WILLS, and T.P. ZOLKI. *J. Am. Chem. Soc.*, **77**, 3939 (1955).
754. AURIVILLIAS, K. and O. HEIDENSTAM. *Acta chem. scand.*, **15**, 1993 (1961).
755. AUSTIN, J.M. and A.D. MAIR. *J. Phys. Chem.*, **66**, 519 (1962).
756. BABELIOWSKY, T.P.J., BABELIOWSKY, T.P.J. *Physica*, **28**, 1160 (1962).
757. BABELIOWSKY, T.P. J. *J. Chem. Phys.*, 38, 2035 (1963).
758. BABELIOWSKY, T.P.J. and A.J.H. BOERBOOM. *Advances Mass-Spectrum*, **2**, Oxford–London–New York–Paris, Pergamon Press, 1963, 135; BABELIOWSKY, T.P.J., A.J.H. BOERBOOM, and J. KISTEMAKER. *Physica*, **28**, 1155 (1962).
759. BADOCHE. *Bull. Soc. chim. France*, **8**, 212 (1941).
760. BAKER, G., J.H.LITTLEFAIR, R. SHAW, and J.C.J. THYNNE. *J. Chem. Soc.*, **1965**, 6970.
760. BAKER, J.W. and W.T. TWEED. *J. Chem. Soc.*, **1941**, 796.
761. BALDREY, M., J.A. LOTZSGESELL, and D.W.C. STYLE. Private communication (cited in [1358]).
762. BALDWIN, A. MACCOLL, and S.I. MILLER. *J. Am. Chem. Soc.*, **86**, 4498 (1964).
763. BALDESDENT, D. *Compt. rend.*, **240**, 1884 (1955).
764. BANERJEE, S.C., D.C. BIGG, and L.K. DORAISWAMY. *J. Chem. Eng. Data*, **9**, 688 (1964).
765. BANERJEE, S.C., and L.K. DORAISWAMY. *Brit. Chem. Eng.*, **9**, 311 (1964).
766. BARBER, C.M. and E.F. WESTRUM. *J. Phys. Chem.*, 67, 2373 (1963).
767. BARROW. *J. Chem. Phys.*, **20**, 1739 (1952).
768. BANK, J.F. and A.B. GARRETT. *J. Electrochem. Soc.*, **106**, 612 (1959).
769. BARANOWSKI, B., and K. BOCHENSKA. *Z. phys. Chem.* (GFR), **45**, 140 (1965).
770. BARANY, R. *Bur. Mines Rept. Investig.*, No. 5466, U.S. Dept. Interior, Washington (1959).
771. BARANY, R. *Bur. Mines Rept. Investig.*, No. 5900, U.S. Dept. Interior, Washington (1962).
772. BARANY, R. *Bur. Mines Rept. Investig.*, No. 6143, U.S. Dept. Interior, Washington (1962).
773. BARANY, R. *Bur. Mines, Berkeley Thermodynam. Lab.*, Berkeley, California (1963).
774. BARANY, R. *Bur. Mines Rept. Investig.*, No. 6356, U.S. Dept. Interior, Washington (1964).
775. BARANY, R. and K.K. KELLEY. *Bur. Mines Rept. Investig.*, No. 5825, U.S. Dept. Interior, Washington (1961).
776. BARANY, R., E.G. KING, and S.S. TODD. *J. Am. Chem. Soc.*, 79, 3639 (1957).
777. BARANY, R., L.B. PANKRATZ, and W.W. WELLER. *Bur. Mines Rept. Investig.*, No. 6513, U.S. Dept. Interior, Washington (1964).

778. BARIEAU, R.E. and W.F. GIAUQUE, *J. Am. Chem. Soc.*, 72, 5676 (1950).
779. BARKER, C.K., A.W. CORDES, and J.L. MARGRAVE. *J. Phys. Chem.*, **69**, 334 (1965).
780. BARRETT, P., and N. GUENEBAUT-THEVENOT. *Bull. Soc. chim. France*, No. 3, 409 (1957).
781. BARRON, T.H.K., W.T. BERG, and J.A. MORRISON. *Proc. Roy. Soc.* **A250**, 70 (1959).
782. BARROW, R.F. *Proc. Roy. Soc.*, 75, 933 (1950).
783. BARROW, R.F. and A.D. CAUNT. *Proc. Roy. Soc.*, **A219**, 120 (1953).
784. BARROW, R.F., P.G. DODSWORTH, A.R. DOWNIE, E.A.N.S. JEFFRIES, A.C.P. PUGH, F.J. SMITH, and J.M. SWINSTEAD. *Trans. Faraday Soc.*, **51**, 1354 (1955).
785. BARROW, R.F., P.G. DODSWORTH, G. DRUMMOND, and E.A.N.S. JEFFRIES. *Trans. Faraday Soc.*, **51**, 1480 (1955).
786. BARROW, R.F., E.A.N.S. JEFFRIES, and J.M. SWINSTEAD. *Trans. Faraday Soc.*, **51**, 1650 (1955).
787. BARROW, R.F., J.W.C. JOHNS, and F.J. SMITH. *Trans. Faraday Soc.*, **52**, 913 (1956).
788. BARROW, R.F., A.C.P. PUGH, and F.J. SMITH. *Trans. Faraday Soc.*, **51**, 1657 (1955).
789. BARTKY, J.R. and W.F. GIAUQUE. *J. Am. Chem. Soc.*, **81**, 4169 (1959).
790. BARTON, L., S.K. WATSON, and R.F. PORTER. *J. Phys. Chem.*, **69**, 3160 (1965).
790a. BASTIUS, H. and A. LISSNER. *Z. phys. Chem.* (GDR), **207**, 111 (1957).
791. BAUDER, A. and H.H. GÜNTHARD. *Helv. chim. Acta*, **45**, 1698 (1962).
792. BAUER, S.H. *J. Am. Chem. Soc.*, **80**, 294 (1958).
793. BAUER, S.H., T. INO, and R.F. PORTER. *J. Chem. Phys.*, **33**, 685 (1960).
794. BAUER, S.H., A. SHEPP, and R.E. McCOY. *J. Am. Chem. Soc.*, **75**, 1003 (1953).
795. BAUER, T.W. and R.M. DORLAND. *Can. J. Res.*, **30**, 76 (1952).
796. BAUER, T.W. and H.L. JOHNSTON. *J. Am. Chem. Soc.*, **75**, 2217 (1953).
797. BAUER, T.W., H.L. JOHNSTON, and E.C. KERR. *J. Am. Chem. Soc.*, 72, 5174 (1950).
798. BAUGHAN, E.C. *Quart. Rev.*, **7**, 116 (1953).
799. BAUR, A. and A. LECOCQ. *Compt. rend.*, **257**, 1445 (1963).
800. BAUTISTA, R.G. and J.L. MARGRAVE. *J. Phys. Chem.*, 67, 2411 (1963).
801. BEAR, I.J. and A.G. TURNBULL. *J. Phys. Chem.*, **69**, 2828 (1965).
802. BECKER, G. and W.A. ROTH. *Ber.*, **67B**, 627 (1934).
803. BECKER, E.D., E. CHARNLEY, and T. ANNO. *J. Chem. Phys.*, **42**, 942 (1965).
803a. BECKWITH, W.F. and R.W. FAHIEN. *Chem. Eng. Progr. Sympos.*, Ser. **44**, 75 (1963).
804. BEDFORD, A.F., A.E. BEEZER, and C.T. MORTIMER. *J. Chem. Soc.*, **1963**, 2039.
805. BEDFORD, A.F., A.E. BEEZER, C.T. MORTIMER, and H.D. SPRINGELL. *J. Chem. Soc.*, **1963**, 3823.
806. BEDFORD, A.F., J.G. CAREY, I.T. MILLAR, C.T. MORTIMER, and H.D. SPRINGELL. *J.Chem.Soc.*, **1962**, 3895.
807. BEDFORD; A.F., P.B. EDMONDSON, and C.T. MORTIMER. *J. Chem. Soc.*, **1962**, 2927.
808. BEDFORD, A.F., D.M. HEINEKEY, I.T. MILLAR, and C.T. MORTIMER. *J.Chem.Soc.*, **1962**, 2932.
809. BEDFORD, A.F. and C.T. MORTIMER. *J. Chem. Soc.*, **1960**, 1622.
810. BEEZER, A.E. and C.T. MORTIMER. *J. Chem. Soc.*, **1964**, 2727.
811. BEEZER, A.E., C.T. MORTIMER, H.D. SPRINGALL, F. SONDHEIMER, and R. WOLOVSKY. *J. Chem. Soc.*, **1965**, 216.
812. BEEZER, A.E., C.T. MORTIMER, and E.G. TYLER. *J. Chem. Soc.*, **1965**, 447.
813. BELL, W.E., DICKLEY, RUST, and VAUGHAN. *Ind. Eng. Chem.*, **41**, 2597 (1949).
814. BELL, W.E., M.C. GARRISON, and U. MERTEN. *J. Phys. Chem.*, **64**, 145 (1960).
815. BELL, W.E., M.C. GARRISON, and U. MERTEN. *J. Phys. Chem.*, **65**, 517 (1961).
816. BELL, W.E. and M. TAGAMI. *J. Phys. Chem.*, **67**, 2432 (1963).
817. BELL, W.E., M. TAGAMI, and U. MERTEN. *J. Phys. Chem.*, **66**, 490 (1962).
818. BENYAMINS, E. and E.F. WESTRUM. *J. Am. Chem. Soc.*, 79, 287 (1957).
819. BENDER, P. and J. FARBER. *J. Am. Chem.* Soc., **74**, 1450 (1952).
820. BENKOWITZ, J., W.A. CHUPKA, D.G. BLUE, and J.L. MARGRAVE. *J. Phys. Chem.*, **63**, 644 (1959).
821, BENNETT, J.E. and H.A. SKINNER. *J. Chem. Soc.*, **1961**, 2472.
822. BENNETT, J.E., H.E. SKINNER. *J. Chem. Soc.*, **1962**, 2150.
823. BENSON, S.W. *J. Am. Chem. Soc.*, **86**, 3922 (1964).
824. BENSON, S.W. *J. Chem. Phys.*, **43**, 2044 (1965).
825. BENSON, S.W. and A. AMANO. *J. Chem. Phys.*, **36**, 3464 (1962).
826. BENSON, S.W. and A. AMANO. *J. Chem. Phys.*, 37, 197 (1962).
826a. BENSON, S.W. and J.H. BUSS. *J. Chem. Phys.*, **29**, 546 (1958).
827. BENTON, A. *J. Chem. Eng. Data*, **9**, 198 (1964).
828. BERG, W.T., D.W. SCOTT, W.N. HUBBARD, S.S. TODD, J.F. MESSERLY, I.A. HOSENLOPP, A. OSBORN, D.R. DOUSLIN, and J.P. McCULLOUGH, *J. Phys. Chem.*, **65**, 1425 (1961).
829. BERKOWITZ, J. and W.A. SHUPKA. *J. Chem. Phys.*, **40**, 287 (1964).
830. BERKOWITZ, J. *J. Chem. Phys*, **36**, 2533 (1962).
831. BERKOWITZ-MATTUCK, J.B. and A. BÜCHLER. *J. Phys. Chem.*, 67, 1386 (1963).
832. BERMAN, H.A. *J. Res. Nat. Bur. Stand.*, **69A**, 407 (1965).
833. BERMAN, H.A. and E.S. NEWMAN. *J. Res. Nat. Bur. Stand.*, **65A**, 197 (1960).
834. BERMAN, H.A. and E.S. NEWMAN. *J. Res. Nat. Bur. Stand.*, 67A, 1 (1963).
835. BERMAN, N.S. and J.J. Mc KETTA. *J. Phys. Chem.*, **66**, 1444 (1962).

835a. BERNECKER, R.R. and F.A. LONG. *J. Phys. Chem.*, **65**, 1565 (1961).
836. BERNSTEIN, H.J. Private communication (cited in [1199]).
837. BERNSTEIN, R.B. and J.J. KATZ. *J.Phys. Chem.*, **56**, 885 (1952).
838. BERNSTEIN, R.B., J.P. ZIETLOW, and F.F. CLEVELAND. *J. Chem. Phys.*, **21**, 1778 (1953).
839. BESENBRUCH, G., A.S. KANAAN, and J.L. MARGRAVE. *J. Phys. Chem.*, **69**, 3174 (1965).
840. BESSON, J. and J. CHEVALLIER. *Compt. rend.*, **258**, 5888 (1964).
841. BEYNON, E.T. and J.J. McKETTA. *J. Phys. Chem.*, **67**, 2761 (1963).
842. BICHOWSKY, F.R. and F.D. ROSSINI. *Thermochemisty of the Chemical Substances,* New York, Reinhold (1936).
843. BIDDISCOMBE, D.P., R. HANDLEY, D. HARROP, A.J. HEAD, G.B. LEWIS, J.F. MARTIN, and C.H.S. SPRAKE. *J. Chem. Soc.*, **1963**, 5764.
844. BIEGANSKI, Z. and B. STALINSKI. *Bull. Acad. polon. sci., Ser. sci. chim.*, **9**, 367 (1961).
845. BILLS, J.L. and F.A. COTTON. *J. Phys. Chem.*, **64**, 1477 (1960).
846. BILLS, J.L. and F.A. COTTON. *J. Phys. Chem.*, **68**, 802 (1964).
847. BILLS, J.L. and F.A. COTTON. *J. Phys. Chem.*, **68**, 806 (1964).
848. BINDER, J.L. *J. Chem. Phys.*, **17**, 499 (1949).
849. BINDER, J.L. *J. Chem. Phys.*, **18**, 77 (1950).
850. BIRKY, M.M. and L.G. HEPLER. *J. Phys. Chem.*, **64**, 686 (1960).
851. BIRR, K.-H. *Z. anorg allg. Chem.*, **311**, 92 (1961).
852. BIRR, K.-H. *Z. anorg. allg. Chem.*, **315**, 175 (1962).
853. BIRR, K.-H. and Ch. SAFARIDIS. *Z. anorg. allg. Chem.*, **311**, 97 (1961).
854. BISBEE, W.R., J.V. HAMILTON, R. RUSHWORTH, J.M. GERHAUSER, and T.J. HOUSER. *AIAA Bull.*, **2**, 114 (1965).
855. BJELLERUP, L. *"Thermodynamics". Proc. of the Symp. on Thermod., Aug., 1959,* London, Butterworth, 1961, p. 45.
856. BJELLERUP, L. *Acta chem. scand.*, **15**, 231 (1961).
857. BLACKBURN, P.E., M. HOCH, and H.L. JOHNSTON. *J. Phys. Chem.*, **62**, 769 (1958).
858. BLAUER, J. and M. FARBER. *J. Chem. Phys.*, **39**, 158 (1963).
859. BLAUER, J.A. and M. FARBER. *J. Phys. Chem.*, **68**, 2357 (1964).
860. BLAUER, J. and M. FARBER. *Trans. Faraday Soc.*, **60**, 301 (1964).
861. BLAUER, J., M.A. GREENBAUM, and M. FARBER. *J. Phys. Chem.*, **68**, 2332 (1964).
862. BLAUER, J.A., M.A. GREENBAUM, and M. FARBER. *J. Phys. Chem.*, **69**, 1069 (1965).
863. BLOCHER, J.N. and E.H. HALL. *J. Phys. Chem.*, **63**, 127 (1959).
864. BLOCHER, J.N., R.F. ROLSTEN, N.D. VILGEL, and I.E. CAMPBELL. *Batelle Memorial Inst., Report of July 1, 1955 to ONR* (cited in [2243]).
865. BLUE, G.D., J.W. GREEN, R.G. BAUTISTA, and J.L. MARGRAVE. *J. Phys. Chem.*, **67**, 877 (1963).
866. BLUKIS, U. and R.J. MYERS. *J. Phys. Chem.*, **69**, 1154 (1965).
867. BOERBOOM, A.J.H., H.W. REYN, and J. KISTEMAKER. *Physica*, **30**, 254 (1964).
868. BOERBOOM, A.J.H., H.W. REYN, H.F. VUGTS, and J. KISTEMAKER. *Physica*, **30**, 2137 (1964).
869. BOLLING, G.F. *J. Chem. Phys.*, **33**, 305 (1960).
870. BONED, M.L., M. COLOMINA, R. PÉREZ-OSSORIO, and C. TURRIÓN. *An. Real. soc. esp. fis. y. quim.*, **B60**, 459 (1964).
871. BONINO, MANZONI-ANSIDEI, and ROLLA. *Ricerca sci.*, **8**, 5 (1937).
872. BOUSQUET, J. and G. PETRACHON. *Compt. rend.*, **256**, 694 (1963).
873. BOUSQUET, J. and J.-C. REMY. *Bull. Soc. chim. France,* No.2, 211 (1964).
874. BOYD, G.E., J.W. COBBLE, and W.T. SMITH. *J. Am. Chem. Soc.*, **75**, 5783 (1953).
875. BOYD, G.E. and F. VASLOW. *J. Chem. Eng. Data*, 7, 237 (1962).
876. BOYD, R.H. *J. Chem. Phys.*, **38**, 2529 (1963).
876a. BOYD, R.H., R.L. CHRISTENSEN, and R. PUA. *J. Am. Chem. Soc.*, **87**, 3554 (1965).
877. BOYER, W.M. and R.B. BERNSTEIN. *J. Chem. Phys.*, **18**, 1073 (1950).
878. BOYLE, B.J., E.G. KING, and K.C. CONWAY. *J. Am. Chem. Soc.*, **76**, 3835 (1954).
879. BRADLAY, R.S. *Proc. Roy. Soc.*, **A205**, 553 (1951).
880. BRADLEY, J.C., L. HAAR, and A.S. FRIEDMAN. *J. Res. Nat. Bur. Stand.*, **56**, 197 (1956).
881. BRADY, A.P., O.E. MYERS, and J.K. CLAUSS. *J. Phys. Chem.*, **64**, 588 (1960).
882. BRAUN, M. and R. KOHLHAAS. *Z. Naturforsch.*, **19A**, 663 (1964).
883. BRAUNE, H., S. PETER, and V. NEVELING. *Z. Naturforsch.*, **6A**, 32 (1951).
884. BREAZEALE, J.D. *United Techn. Corp. Res. and Advanced Technol., Div. Sunnyvale, California,* 1963.
885. BREBRICK, R.F. *J. Chem. Phys.*, **41**, 1140 (1964).
886. BREWER, L. *Nat. Nuclear Energy Ser., Div. IV,* **19B**. *The Chemistry and Metallurgy of Miscellaneous Materials,* ed. L.L. Quill. New York, Toronto, London, 1950, p.60.
887. BREWER, L. *Chem. Rev.*, **52**, 1 (1953).
888. BREWER, L., L. BROMLEY, P.W. GILLES, and N.L. LOFGREN. *Natl. Nuclear Energy Ser., Div. IV,* **14B**, *The Transuranium Elements,* Research Papers. Pt. II, ed. G.T.SEABORG, J.J. KATZ, and W.M. MANNING. New York, Toronto, London, 1949, p.861.
889 BREWER, L., L. BROMLEY, P.W. GILLES, and N.L. LOFGREN. *Natl. Nuclear Energy Ser., Div. IV,* **19B**. *The Chemistry and Metallurgy of Miscellaneous Materials,* ed. L.L. QUILL, New York, Toronto, London, 1950, p.40.

890. BREWER, L., L. BROMLEY, P.W. GILLES, and N.L. LOFGREN. *Natl. Nuclear Energy Ser. Div. IV*, **19B**, *Chemistry and Metallurgy of Miscellaneous Materials*, ed. L.L. QUILL, New York, Toronto, London, 1950, p. 76.
891. BREWER, L. and R.K. EDWARDS. *J. Phys. Chem.*, **58**, 351 (1954).
892. BREWER, L. and H. HARALDSEN. *J. Electrochem. Soc.*, **102**, 399 (1955).
893. BREWER, L. and O. KRIKORIAN. *J. Electrochem. Soc.*, **103**, 38 (1956).
894. BREWER, L., J.L. MARGRAVE, R.F. PORTER, and K. WIELAND. *J. Phys. Chem.* **65**, 1913 (1961).
895. BREWER, L. and D.F. MASTICK. *J. Chem. Phys.*, **19**, 834 (1951).
896. BREWER, L. and A.W. SEARCY. *J. Am. Chem. Soc.*, **73**, 5308 (1951).
897. BREWER, L. and A.W. SEARCY. *Ann Rev. Phys. Chem.*, **7**, 259 (1956).
898. BRICKWEDDE, F.G., M. MOSKOW, and J.G. ASTON. *L. Res. Nat. Bur. Stand.*, **37**, 263 (1946).
899. BREITENBACH and DERKOSCH. *Monatsh.*, **81**, 689 (1950).
900. BREITENBACH and DERKOSCH. *Monatsh.*, **82**, 177 (1951).
901. BRIMM, E.O. and H.M. HUMPHREY. *J. Phys. Chem.*, **61**, 829 (1957).
902. BRISI, C. and F. ABBATISTA. *Ricerca sci.*, **29**, 1402 (1959).
903. BRISI, C. and F. ABBATISTA. *Ann. chimica*, **50**, 165 (1960).
904. BRISKE, C., N.H. HARTSHORNE, and D.R. STRANKS. *J. Chem. Soc.*, **1960**, 1200.
905. BRODALE, G. and W.F. GIAUQUE. *J. Am. Chem. Soc.*, **80**, 2042 (1958).
906. BROOKS, A.A. *J. Am. Chem. Soc.*, **75**, 2464 (1953).
907. BRUNAUER, S., D.L. KANTRO, and C.H. WEISE. *J. Phys. Chem.*, **60**, 771 (1956).
908. BUCK, T.M., W.E. WALLAGE, and R.M. RULON. *J. Am. Chem. Soc.*, **74**, 136 (1954).
909. BUES, W. and H. von WARTENBERG. *Z. anorg. allg. Chem.*, **266**, 281 (1951).
910. BURDESE. A. *Ann. chimica*, **49**, 1879 (1959).
911. BURDESE, A. and F. ABBATISTA. *Atti Acad. sci. Toronto*, **93**, 1958–1959.
912. BURNEY, G.A. *Doct. Dissert., Univ. Michigan*, 1953 (cited in [913]).
912a. BURNEY. G.A. *Dissert. Abstr.*, **14**, 1027 (1954) (cited in [2270]).
913. BURNEY, G.A. and E.F. WESTRUM. *J. Phys. Chem.*, **65**, 349 (1961).
914. BUROW, F. *Dissert., Univ. Kiel*, 1956 (cited in [1746]).
915. BURTON. *Biochem. J.*, **59**, 44 (1955) (cited in [1177]).
916. BURUS, W.C. and H.J. BERNSTAIN. *J. Chem. Phys.*, **18**, 1669 (1950).
917. BURUS, J.H., D.W. OSBORNE, and E.F. WESTRUM. *J. Chem. Phys.*, **33**, 387 (1960).
918. BUSEY, R.H. *J. Am. Chem. Soc.*, **78**, 3263 (1956).
919. BUSEY, R.H. *J. Phys. Chem.*, **69**, 3179 (1965).
920. BUSEY, R.H., R.B. BEVAN, and R.A. GILBERT. *J. Phys. Chem.*, **69**, 3471 (1965).
921. BUSEY, R.H., H.H. DEARMAN, and R.B. BEWAN. *J. Phys. Chem.*, **66**, 82 (1961).
922. BUSEY, R.H. and W.F. GIAUQUE. *J. Am. Chem. Soc.*, **74**, 3157 (1952).
923. BUSEY, R.H. and W.F. GIAUQUE. *J. Am. Chem. Soc.*, **74**, 4443 (1952).
924. BUSEY, R.H. and W.F. GIAUQUE. *J. Am. Chem. Soc.*, **75**, 806 (1953).
925. BUSEY, R.H. and W.F. GIAUQUE. *J. Am. Chem. Soc.*, **75**, 1791 (1953).
926. BUSFIELD, W.R., H. MACKLE, and P.A.G. O'HARA. *Trans. Faraday Soc.*, **57**, 1054 (1961).
927. BUSFIELD, W.K., K.J. IVIN, H. MACKLE, and P.A.G. O'HARA. *Trans. Faraday Soc.*, **57**, 1054 (1961).
928. BUSFIELD, W.K., K.J. IVIN, H. MACKLE, and P.A.G. O'HARA. *Trans. Faraday Soc.*, **57**, 1058 (1961).
929. BUSFIELD, W.K., K.J. IVIN, H. MACKLE, and P.A.G. O'HARA. *Trans. Faraday Soc.*, **57**, 1064 (1961).
930. BUTERA, R.A. and R.S. CRAIG. *J. Chem. Eng. Data*, **10**, 38 (1965).
931. CALDER, G.V. and W.F. GIAUQUE. *J. Phys. Chem.*, **69**, 2443 (1965).
932. CAMIN, D.L. and F.D. ROSSINI. *J. Phys. Chem.*, **60**, 1446 (1956).
933. CARLSON, H.G. and E.F. WESTRUM. *J. Phys. Chem.*, **69**, 1524 (1965).
934. CARLSON, H.G. and E.F. WESTRUM. *J. Chem. Eng. Data*, **10**, 134 (1965).
935. CARNEY, R.A., E.A. PIOTROWSKI, A.G. CARTER, J.H. BRAUN, and F.F. CLEVELAND. *J. Molec. Spectr.*, **7**, 209 (1961).
936. CARPENTER, J.H. and A.W. SEARCY. *J. Phys. Chem.*, **67**, 2144 (1963).
937. CARRERA, N.J., R.F. WALKER, and E.R. PLAUTE. *J. Res. Nat. Bur. Stand.*, **68A**, 325 (1964).
938. CARSON, A.S., B.M. CARSON, and B. WILMHURST. *Nature*, **170**, 320 (1952).
939. CARSON, A.S., R. COOPER, and D.R. STRANKS. *Trans. Faraday Soc.*, **58**, 2125 (1962).
940. CARSON, A.S., R. COOPER, and D.R. STRANKS. *Radioisotopes in the Physical Sciences and Industries*, **3**, Intern. Atomic Energy Agency, Vienna, 1965, p. 495.
941. CARSON, A.S. and H.A. SKINNER. *J. Chem. Soc.*, **1949**, 936.
942. CARUSO, R., F.J. LOPREST, and A. LUM. *J. Phys. Chem.*, **69**, 1716 (1965).
943. CASEY, D.W.H., and S. FORDHAM. *J. Chem. Soc.*, **1951**, 2513.
944. CASS, R.C., S.E. FLETCHER, C.T. MORTIMER, P.G. QUINCEY, and H.D. SPRINGALL. *J. Chem. Soc.*, **1958**, 2595.
945. CASS, R.C., S.E. FLETCHER, C.T. MORTIMER, H.D. SPRINGALL, and T.R. WHITE. *J. Chem. Soc.*. **1958**, 1406.
946. CASTLE, P., R. STOESSER, and E.F. WESTRUM. *J. Phys. Soc.*, **68**, 49 (1964).
947. CATALANO, E. and J.W. STOUT. *J. Chem. Phys.*, **23**, 1284 (1955).
948. CATALANO, E. and J.W. STOUT. *J. Chem. Phys.*, **23**, 1803 (1955).
948a. CATER, D., T.E. LEE, E.W. JOHNSON, E.G. RAUH, and H.A. EICK. *J. Phys. Chem.*, **69**, 2684 (1965).

949. CATER, E.D., P.W. GILLES, and R.J. THORN. *J. Chem. Soc.*, **35**, 608 (1961).
950. CAUNT, A.D. and R.F. BARROW. *Trans. Faraday Soc.*, **46**, 154 (1950).
951. CAVELL, R.G. and H.C. CLARK. *J. Chem. Soc.*, **1963**, 3890.
952. CAVELL, R.G. and H.C. CLARK. *Trans. Faraday Soc.*, **59**, 2706 (1963).
953. CAVELL, R.G. and H.C. CLARK. *J. Chem. Soc.*, **1965**, 444.
954. CELIN, R. and J. DROWART. *J. Phys. Soc.*, **68**, 428 (1964).
955. ČERNY, C. and E. ERDÖS. *Chem. Listy*, **47**, 1742 (1953).
956. ČERNY, C. and E. ERDÖS. *Chem. Listy*, **47**, 1745 (1953).
957. ČHAN, J.P. and W.F. GIAUQUE. *J. Phys. Chem.*, **68**, 3053 (1964).
958. CHANG SHU-SING, and E.F. WESTRUM. *J. Chem. Phys.*, **36**, 2420 (1962).
959. CHANG SHU-SING, and E.F. WESTRUM. *J. Chem. Phys.*, **36**, 2571 (1962).
960. CHANG SHU-SING, and E.F. WESTRUM. *J. Phys. Chem.*, **66**, 524 (1962).
960a. CHANG, Y.A. and R. HULTGREN. *J. Phys. Chem.*, **69**, 4162 (1965).
961. CHAO, J. and F.D. ROSSINI. *J. Chem. Eng. Data*, **10**, 374 (1965).
962. CHAPPEL and HAARE. *Trans. Faraday Soc.*, **54**, 367 (1958).
963. CHARLU, T.V. and M.R.A. RAO. *Proc. Indian Acad. Sci.*, **A60**, 31 (1964).
964. CHARNLEY, T. and H.A. SKINNER. *J. Chem. Soc.*, **1953**, 450.
965. CHARTIER, P. *Compt. rend.*, **256**, 1976 (1963).
966. CHARTIER, P. *Ber. Bunsenges, phys. Chem.*, **68**, 404 (1964).
967. CHEEK, C.H. and J.W. SWINNERTON. *J. Phys. Chem.*, **68**, 1427 (1964).
967a. CHERNICK, C.L. and H.A. SKINNER. *J. Chem. Soc.*, **1956**, 1401.
967b. CHERNICK, C.L., H.A. SKINNER, and C.T. MORTIMER. *J. Chem. Soc.*, **1955**, 3936.
968. CHICHE, R. *Ann. Chimica*, **7**, 361 (1952).
969. CHICHE, R. *Compt. rend.*, **234**, 830 (1952).
970. CHIKARA HIRAYAMA. *J. Chem. Eng. Data*, **9**, 65 (1964).
971. CHILD, W.C. and A.J. HAY. *J. Am. Chem. Soc.*, **86**, 182 (1964).
972. CHIOTTI, P. and G.R. KILP (cited in [2315]).
973. CHISHOLM, R.C. and J.W. STOUT. *J. Chem. Soc.*, **36**, 972 (1962).
974. CHRISTENSEN, J.J., R.M. IZATT, J.D. HALE, R.T. PACK, and G.D. WATT. *Inorg. Chem.*. **2**, 337 (1963).
975. CHUPKA, W.A. *Argonic Natl. Lab.*, Private communication, 1957 (cited in [1185]).
976. CHUPKA, W.A. and M.G. INGHRAM. *J. Phys. Chem.*, **59**, 100 (1955).
977. CLAASEN, H.H., B. WEINSTOCK, and J.G. MALM. *J. Chem. Phys.*, **28**, 285 (1958).
978. CLARK, C.J. *J. Chem. Eng. Data*, **8**, 532 (1963).
979. CLARK, T.H. and G. STEGEMAN. *J. Am. Chem. Soc.*, **61**, 1726 (1939).
980. CLARKE, E.C., R.W. FORD, and D.N. GLEW. *Can. J. Chem.*, **42**, 2027 (1964).
980a. CLAYDON, A.P., P.A. FOWELL, and C.T. MORTIMER. *J. Chem. Soc.*, **1960**, 3284.
981. CLAYDON, A.P. and C.T. MORTIMER. *J. Chem. Soc.*, **1962**, 3212.
982. CLEVELAND, F.F. and M. KLEIN. *J. Chem. Phys.*, **20**, 337 (1952).
983. CLEVER, H.L. and E.F. WESTRUM. *J. Phys. Chem.*, **69**, 1214 (1965).
984. CLEVER, H.L., WONG WEN-KUEI, and E.F. WESTRUM. *J. Phys. Chem.*, **69**, 1209 (1965).
985. CLEVER, H.L., WONG WEN-KUEI, C.A. WULFF, and E.F. WESTRUM. *J. Phys. Chem.*, **68**, 1967 (1964).
986. CLIFTON, D.G. *J. Chem. Phys.*, **41**, 3656 (1964).
987. CLIFTON, D.G. and G.E. MacWOOD. *J. Phys. Chem.*, **60**, 309 (1956).
988. CLIFTON, D.G. and G.E. MacWOOD. *J. Phys. Chem.*, **60**, 311 (1956).
989. CLOPATT. *Soc. Sci. Fennica, Commentations Phys. Mat.*, **6**, 1 (1932).
990. CLUSIUS, K. and P. FRANZOSINI. *Z. phys. Chem.* (FGR), **16**, 194 (1958).
991. CLUSIUS, K. and P. FRANZOZINI. *Z. Naturforsch.*, **14a**, 99 (1959).
992. CLUSIUS, K. and P. FRANZOSINI. *Z. Naturforsch.*, **17a**, 522 (1962).
993. CLUSIUS, K. and P. FRANZOSINI. *Gazz. chim ital.*, **93**, 221 (1963).
994. CLUSIUS, K., P. FRANZOSINI, and U. PIESBERGEN. *Z. Naturforsch.*, **15a**, 728 (1959).
995. CLUSIUS, K., J. GOLDMAN, and A. PERLICK. *Z. Naturforsch.*, **4a**, 424 (1949).
996. CLUSIUS, K. and C.G. LOSA. *Z. Naturforsch.*, **10a**, 545 (1955).
997. CLUSIUS, K. and C.G. LOSA. *Z. Naturforsch.*, **10a**, 939 (1955).
998. CLUSIUS, K. and L. SCHAHINGER. *Z. Naturforsch.*, **7a**, 185 (1952).
999. CLUSIUS, K. and L. SCHAHINGER. *Z. angew. Phys.*, **4**, 442 (1952).
1000. CLUSIUS, K., A. SPERANDIO, and U. PIESBERGEN. *Z. Naturforsch.*, **14a**, 793 (1959).
1001. COATS, F.H. and R.C. ANDERSON. *J. Am. Chem. Soc.*, **79**, 1340 (1957).
1002. COBBLE, J.W., G.D. OLIVER, and W.T. SMITH. *J. Am. Chem. Soc.*, **75**, 5786 (1953).
1003. COCHRAN, C.N. and L.M. FOSTER. *J. Electrochem. Soc.*, **109**, 144 (1962).
1004. COCHRAN, C.N. and L.M. FOSTER. *J. Phys. Chem.*, **66**, 380 (1962).
1005. COEL, N.S. and R.P. SINGH. *Indian Pure a. Appl. Phys.*, **1**, 343 (1963).
1006. COLE, A.G., J.O. HUTCHENS, and J.W. STOUT. *J. Phys. Chem.*, **67**, 1852 (1963).
1007. COLE, A.G., J.O. HUTCHENS, and J.W. STOUT. *J. Phys. Chem.*, **67**, 2245 (1963).
1008. COLE, L.G. and G.W. ELVERUM. *J. Chem. Phys.*, **20**, 1543 (1952).

1009. COLE, L.G., M. FARBER, and G.W. ELVERUM. *J. Chem. Phys.*, **20,** 586 (1952).
1010. COLE, L.G. and E.C. GILBERT. *J. Am. Chem. Soc.*, **73,** 5423 (1951).
1011. COLEMAN, C.F. and Th. DeVRIES. *J. Am. Chem. Soc.*, **71,** 2839 (1949).
1012. COLIN, R. and J. DROWART. *J. Chem. Phys.*, **37,** 1120 (1962).
1013. COLIN, R. and J. DROWART. *Trans. Faraday Soc.*, **60,** 673 (1964).
1014. COLIN, R., P. GOLDFINGER, and M. JEUNEHOMME. *Nature,* **187,** 408 (1960).
1015. COLIN, R., P. GOLDFINGER, and M. JEUNEHOMME. *Trans. Faraday Soc.*, **60,** 306 (1964).
1016. COLOMINA, M., CAMBEIRO, R.PERÉZ-OSSORIO, and C. LATORE. *Ann. real Soc. españ. fis. y. quim.*, **6,** 509 (1956).
1017. COLOMINA, M., C. LATORE, and R. PEREZ-OSSORIO. *Bull. Chem. Thermodynamics, I.U.P.A.C.*, No. 1, A19, (1958).
1018. COLOMINA, M., C. LATORE, and R. PEREZ-OSSORIO. *"Thermodynamics", Proc. of the Symp. on Thermod., 1959* London, Butterworth, 1961, p. 133.
1019. COLOMINA, M. and J. NICOLAS, *Ann. real Soc. españ. fis. y. quim.*, **458,** 137 (1949).
1020. COLOMINA, M. and A.S. PELL. Private communication (cited in [2150]).
1021. COLOMINA, M., R.PERÉZ-OSSORIO, and M.L. BONED. *Bull. Chem. Thermodynamics, I. U. P. A. C.*, No.2, 27 (1959).
1022. COLOMINA, M., R.PERÉZ-OSSORIO, and M.L. BONED. *Bull. Chem. Thermodynamics, I. U. P. A. C.*, No.3, 21 (1960).
1023. COLOMINA, M., R.PERÉZ-OSSORIO, M.L. BONED, M. PANEA, and C. TURRION. *Ann. real. Soc. españ. fis. y. quim.*, **B57,** 665 (1961).
1024. COLOMINA, M., R. PERÉZ-OSSORIO, C. TURRIÓN, and M.L. BONED. *Ann. real. Soc. españ. fis. y. quim.*, **B60,** 627 (1964).
1025. COLOMINA, M., C. TURRIÓN, M.L. BONED, and M. PANEA. *Ann. real Soc. españ. fis. y. quim.*, **B90,** 619 (1964).
1026. CONN, J.B., G.B. KISTIAKOWSKY, R.M. ROBERTS, and E.A. SMITH. *J. Am. Chem. Soc.*, **64,** 1747 (1942).
1027. CONNIC, R.E. and CHIA YUAN-TSAM. *J. Am. Chem. Soc.*, **81,** 1260 (1959).
1028. CONNIC, R.E. and W.H. McVEY. *J. Am. Chem. Soc.*, **73,** 798 (1951).
1029. COOPER, W.J. and J.F. MASI. *J. Phys. Chem.*, **64,** 682 (1960).
1030. COOPS, J., N. ADRIANCE, and K. van NES. *Rec. trav. chim.*, **75,** 237 (1956).
1030a. COOPS, J. and G.J. HOIJTINK. *Rec. trav. chim.*, **69,** 358 (1950).
1030b. COOPS, J., G.J. HOIJTINK, and Th. J.E. KRAMER. *Rec. trav. chim.*, **72,** 793 (1953).
1030c. COOPS, J., G.J. HOIJTINK, Th.J.E. KRAMER, and A.C. FABER. *Rec. trav. chim.*, **72,** 765 (1953).
1030d. COOPS, J., G.J. HOIJTINK, Th.J.E. KRAMER, and A.C. FABER. *Rec. trav. chim.*, **72,** 781 (1953).
1030e. COOPS, J., D. MULDER, J.W. DIENSKE, and J. SMITTENBERG. *Rec. trav. chim.*, **72,** 785 (1953).
1031. COOPS, J., H. VAN KAMP, W.A. LAMBREGTS, B.J. VISSER, and H. DEKKER, *Rec. trav. chim.*, **79,** 1226 (1960).
1032. CORBETT, J.D. and N.W. GREGORY. *J. Am.Chem.Soc.*, **76,** 1446 (1954).
1033. CORDES, H. and H. CAMMENGA. *Z. phys. Chem.* (GFR), **45,** 196 (1965).
1034. CORDES, H.F. and N.F. FETTER. *J. Phys. Chem.*, **62,** 1340 (1958).
1035. CORDES, H. and W. WITSCHEL. *Z. Phys. Chem.*, Neue Folge, **46,** 35 (1965).
1036. CORDFUNKE, E.H.P. *J. Phys. Chem.*, **68,** 3353 (1964).
1037. CORDFUNKE, E.H.P., and P. ALING. *Trans. Faraday Soc.*, **50** (1965).
1038. CORDFUNKE, E.H.P. and G. MEYER. *Rec. trav. chim.*, **81,** 495 (1962).
1039. CORDFUNKE, E.H.P. and G. MEYER. *Rec. trav. chim.*, **81,** 670 (1962).
1040. COSGROVE, L.A. and P.E. SNYDER. *J. Am. Chem. Soc.*, **75,** 1227 (1953).
1041. COSGROVE, L.A. and P.E. SNYDER. *J. Am. Chem. Soc.*, **75,** 3102 (1953).
1042. COTTON, F.A., A.K. FISCHER and G. WILKINSON. *J. Am. Chem. Soc.*, **78,** 5168 (1956).
1043. COTTON, F.A., A.K. FISCHER and G. WILKINSON. *J. Am. Chem. Soc.*, **81,** 800 (1959).
1044. COTTRELL, T.L., and J.E. GILL. *J. Chem. Soc.*, **1951,** 1798.
1045. COUGHLIN, J.P. *Heat and Free Energies of Formation of Inorganic Oxides. Contribution to the Data on Theoretical Metallurgy,* XII, *Bur. Mines, Bull.*, 542, Washington, 1954.
1046. COUGHLIN, J.P. *J. Am. Chem. Soc.*, **78,** 5479 (1956).
1047. COUGHLIN, J.P. *J. Am. Chem. Soc.*, **79,** 2397 (1957).
1048. COUGHLIN, J.P. *J. Am. Chem. Soc.*, **80,** 1802 (1958).
1049. COUGHLIN, J.P. *J. Phys. Chem.*, **62,** 419 (1958).
1050. COULTER, L.V., J.R. SINCLAIR, A.G. COLE, and G.C. ROPER. *J. Am. Chem. Soc.*, **81,** 2986 (1959).
1051. COUNSELL, J.F., J.H.S. GREEN, J.L. HALES, and J.F. MARTIN. *Trans. Faraday Soc.*, **61,** 212 (1965).
1052. COUNSELL, J.F., J.L. HALES, and J.F. MERTON. *Trans. Faraday Soc.*, **61,** 1869 (1965).
1053. COX, J.D. *"Thermodynamics", Proc. of the Symp. on Thermod., 1959,* London, Butterworth, 1961, p. 125.
1054. COX, J.D., A.R. CHALLONER, and A.D. MEETHAM. *J. Chem. Soc.*, **1954,** 265.
1055. COX, J.D., H.A. GUNDRY, and A.J. HEAD. *Trans. Faraday Soc.*, **60,** 653 (1964).
1056. COX, J.D., H.A. GUNDRY, and A.J. HEAD. *Trans. Faraday Soc.*, **61,** 1594 (1965).
1057. COX, J.D. and D. HARROP. *Trans. Faraday Soc.*, **61,** 1328 (1965).
1058. COX, W.P., E.W. HORNUNG, and W.F. GIAUQUE. *J. Am. Chem. Soc.*, **77,** 3935 (1955).
1059. CRAIG, R.S., C.A. KRIER, L.W. COFFER, E.A. BATES, and W.E. WALLAGE. *J. Am. Chem. Soc.*, **76,** 238 (1954).

1060. CROG and HUNT. *J. Phys. Chem.*, **46**, 1162 (1942).
1060a. CROWDER, G.A., G. GORIN, F.H. KRUSE, and D.W. SCOTT. *J. Molec. Spectrosc.*, **16**, 115 (1965).
1061. CSEJKA, D.A., F. MARTINEZ, J.A. WOJTOWICZ, and J.A. ZASLOWSKY. *J. Phys. Chem.*, **68**. 3878 (1964).
1062. CUBICIOTTI, D. *J. Phys. Chem.*, **64**, 791 (1960).
1063. CUBICIOTTI, D. *J. Phys. Chem.*, **64**, 1506 (1960).
1064. CUBICIOTTI, D. *J. Phys. Chem.*, **69**, 1410 (1965).
1064a. CUBICIOTTI, D. and H. EDING. *J. Phys. Chem.*, **69**, 2743 (1965).
1065. CUBICIOTTI, D. and H. EDING. *J. Phys. Chem.*, **69**, 3621 (1965).
1066. CUBBICIOTTI, D. and G.L. WITHERS. *J. Phys. Chem.*, **69**, 4030 (1965).
1067. CUFFEL, R.F., W. KOZICKI, and B.H. SAGE. *Can. J. Chem. Eng.*, **41**, 19 (1963).
1068. CULVER, R.V. and C.J. HAMDORF. *J. Appl. Chem.*, **5**, 383 (1955).
1069. CUNNINGHAM, B.B. *Proc. Intern. Conf. Peaceful Uses Atomic Energy*, Geneva, 7, 225 (1956).
1070. CURTIS, R.W. and P. CHIOTTI. *J. Phys. Chem.*, **67**, 1061 (1963).
1071. DAASCH, W., C.Y. LIANG, and J.K. NIELSEN. *J. Chem. Phys.*, **22**, 1293 (1954).
1072. DACRE, B. and P.A. WYATT. *Trans. Faraday Soc.*, **57**, 1281 (1961).
1073. DAINTON, F.S. and H.M. KIMBERLEY. *Trans. Faraday Soc.*, **46**, 912 (1950).
1074. DANIELE, G. *Gazz. chim. ital.*, **90**, 1587 (1960).
1075. DANIELE, G. *Gazz. chim. ital.*, **90**, 1597 (1960).
1076. DARNELL, A.J., *J. Inorg. Nucl. Chem.*, **15**, 359 (1960).
1077. DARNELL, A.J., W.A. McCOLLUM, and T.A. MILNE. *J. Phys. Chem.*, **64**, 341 (1960).
1078. DARNELL, A.J. and J. YOSIM. *J. Phys. Chem.*, **63**, 1813 (1959).
1079. DAUPHINEE, T.M., D.L. MARTIN, and H. PRESTON-THOMAS. *Proc. Roy. Soc.*, **233**, 214 (1955).
1080. DAVIES, J., J.R. LACHER, and J.D. PARK. *Trans. Faraday Soc.*, **61**, 2413 (1965).
1081. DAVIES, J.V., A.E. POPE, and H.A.SKINNER. *Trans. Faraday Soc.*, **59**, 2233 (1963).
1082. DAVIES, J.V. and S. SUNNER. *Acta chem. scand.*, **16**, 1870 (1962).
1083. DAVIES, M. and D.G. JENKIN. *J. Chem. Soc.*, **1954**, 2374.
1084. DAVIES, M.L. and E.F. WESTRUM. *J. Phys. Chem.*, **65**, 338 (1961).
1084a. DAVIS, A., F.F. CLEVELAND, and A.G. MEISTER. *J. Chem. Phys.*, **20**, 454 (1952).
1085. DAVIS, S.G., D.F. ANTHROP, and A.W. SEARCY – cited in [2353].
1086. DAVIS, S.G., D.F. ANTHROP,and A.W.SEARCY. *J. Chem. Phys.*, **34**, 659 (1961).
1087. DAWSON, J.K., M. ELLIOT, R. HURST and A.E. TRUSWELL. *J. Chem. Soc.*, **1954**, 558.
1087a. DAYKIN, P.N. and S. SUNDARAM. *Z. phys. Chem.* (GFR), **32**, 222 (1962).
1088. DEAN, D., A.E. KAY, B.W. LOWTHIAN, R.F. POWELL, and E. DEMPSEY – cited in [63].
1089. DEAR, D.J.A. and D.D. ELEY. *J. Chem. Soc.*, **1954**, 4684.
1090. DECKER, C.E., A.G. MEISTER, and F.F. CLEVELAND. *J. Chem. Phys.*, **19**, 784 (1951).
1091. DECKER, C.E., A.G. MEISTER, F.F. CLEVELAND, and R.B. BERNSTEIN. *J. Chem. Phys.*, **21**, 1781 (1953).
1092. De MARIA, G., R.P. BURNS, J. DROWART, and M.G. INGHRAM. *J. Chem. Phys.*, **32**, 1373 (1960).
1093. De MARIA, G., J. DROWART, and M.G. INGHRAM. *J. Chem. Phys.*, **31**, 1076 (1959).
1094. De MARIA, G., M. GUIDO, and L. MALAPINA. *Ann. chimica*, **53**, 1044 (1963).
1095. D'ENTREMANT, J.C. and J. CHIPMAN. *J. Phys. Chem.*, **67**, 499 (1963).
1096. De SORBO, W. *J. Chem. Phys.*, **21**, 876 (1953).
1097. De SORBO, W. *J. Chem. Phys.*, **21**, 1144 (1953).
1098. De SORBO, W. *J. Am. Chem. Soc.*, **75**, 1825 (1953).
1099. De SORBO, W. *Acta metallurg.*, **1**, 503 (1953).
1100. De SORBO, W. *J. Phys. Chem.*, **62**, 965 (1958).
1101. DESTRIAN, M. and J. SERIOT. *Compt. rend.*, **254**, 2982 (1962).
1102. DEWING, E.W. and F.D. RICHARDSON. *Trans. Faraday Soc.*, **54**, 679 (1958).
1103. D'HONT, M., and J.C. JUNGERS. *Bull. Soc. chim. belg.*, **58**, 196 (1949).
1104. DIBELER, V.H., R.M. REESE, and J.L. FRANKLIN. *J. Am. Chem. Soc.*, **83**, 1813 (1961).
1105. DICKSON, D.S., J.R. MYERS, and R.K. SAXER. *J. Phys. Chem.*, **69**, 4044 (1965).
1106. DITZEL, E.F., A.G. MEISTER, E.A. PIOTROWSKI, F.F. CLEVELAND, Y.A. SARMA, and S. SUNDARAM. *Can. J. Chem.*, **42**, 2841 (1964).
1107. DONOVAN, T.M., C.H. SHOMATE, and T.B. JOYNER. *J. Phys. Chem.*, **64**, 378 (1960).
1108. D'ORAZIO, L.A. and R.H. WOOD. *J. Phys. Chem.*, **67**, 1435 (1963).
1109. D'ORAZIO, L.A. and R.H. WOOD. *J. Phys. Chem.*, **69**, 2550 (1965).
1110. DOUGLAS, T.B. *J. Am. Chem. Soc.*, **68**, 1072 (1946).
1111. DOUGLAS, T.B. *J. Am. Chem. Soc.*, **70**, 2001 (1948).
1112. DOUGLAS, T.B. *J. Res. Nat. Bur. Stand.*, **67A**, 403 (1963).
1113. DOUGLAS, T.B. and J.L. DEVER. *J. Am. Chem. Soc.*, **76**, 4824 (1954).
1114. DOUGLAS, T.B. and J.L. DEVER. *J. Am. Chem. Soc.*, **76**, 4826 (1954).
1115. DOUGLAS, T.B., L.F. EPSTEIN, J.L. DEVER, and W.H. HOWLAND. *J. Am. Chem. Soc.*, **77**, 2144 (1955).
1116. DOUGLAS, T.B. and A.W. HARMAN. *J. Res. Nat. Bur. Stand.*, **60**, 117 (1958).
1117. DOUGLAS, T.B. and A.C. VICTOR. *J. Res. Nat. Bur. Stand.*, **61**, 13 (1958).
1118. DOUSLIN, D.R. and H.M. HUFFMAN. *J. Am. Chem. Soc.*, **68**, 1704 (1946).

1119. DOWLING, J.M. *J. Chem. Phys.*, **23**, 700 (1955).
1120. DOWLING, J.M. and A.G. MEISTER. *J. Chem. Phys.*, **22**, 1042 (1954).
1121. DOWLING, J.M., P.G. PARANIK, and A.G. MEISTER. *J. Phys. Chem.*, **26**, 233 (1957).
1122. DOWS, D.A. and G.C. PIMENTEL. *J. Chem. Phys.*, **23**, 1258 (1955).
1123. DREGER, L.H., V.V. DADAPE, and J.L. MARGRAVE. *J. Phys. Chem.*, **66**, 1556 (1962).
1124. DREGER, L.H. and J.L. MARGRAVE. *J. Phys. Chem.*, **64**, 1323 (1960).
1125. DREGER, L.H. and J.L. MARGRAVE. *J. Phys. Chem.*, **65**, 2106 (1961).
1126. DROEGE, J.W., A.W. LEMMON, and R.B. FILBERT. *Barrele Memorial Institute Report*, BMI–1313, ed. by A.B. Tripler, 1959, p. 38 (cited in [1578]).
1127. DROWART, J., F. DEGREVE, G. VERHAEGAN, and R. COLIN. *Trans. Faraday Soc.*, **61**, 1072 (1965).
1128. DROWART, J., G. De MARIA, R.P. BURNS, and M.G. INGHRAM. *J. Chem. Phys.*, **32**, 1366 (1960).
1129. DROWART, J., G. De MARIA, and M.G. INGHRAM. *J. Chem. Phys.*, **29**, 1015 (1958).
1130. DROWART, J. and R. HONIG. *Bull. Soc. chim. belg.* **66**, 411 (1957).
1131. DROWART, J., A. PATTORETT, and S. SMEES. *J. Nucl. Mater.*, **12**, 319 (1964).
1132. DUNCAN, N.E. and G.J. JANZ. *J. Chem. Phys.*, **20**, 1644 (1952).
1133. DUNCAN, N.E. and G.J. JANZ. *J. Chem. Phys.*, **23**, 434 (1955).
1133a. DUNKEN, H. and G. MARX. *Abhandl.Dtsch.Akad. Wissenschaften, Berlin, Kl.Math., Phys. und Techn.*, No.6, 101 (1964).
1134. *Du Pont's Information Bull. "Sulfur Tetrafluoride Techniques"* (cited by A.G. STRENG, *J. Am. Chem. Soc.*, **85**, 1380 (1963)).
1135. DUQUESNOY, A. and F. MARION. *Compt. rend.* **258**, 5657 (1964).
1135a. DUUS, H.C. *Report, E.I. du Pont de Nemours a. Co.*, presented at the Meeting of the Am. Chem. Soc. in New York, 15 Sept. 1954 (cited in [629]).
1136. DUUS, H.C. *Ind. Eng. Chem.*, **47**, 1445 (1955).
1137. DUUS, H.C. and D.P. MYDYTINK. *Symp. on Thermochem., Thermodynamics, Lund, 1963* (cited in [1217]).
1138. DWORJANYN, L.O. *Austral. J. Chem.*, **13**, 175 (1960).
1139. DWORKIN, A.S., D.J. SASMOR, and E.R. VAN ARTSDALEN. *J. Chem. Phys.*, **22**, 837 (1954).
1140. DWORKIN, A.S., B.J. SASMORE, and E.R. VAN ARTSDALEN. *J. Am. Chem. Soc.*, **77**, 1304 (1955).
1141. EACHERN, D.M. and J.E. KILPATRICK. *J. Chem. Phys.*, **41**, 3127 (1964).
1142. ECKSTEIN, P.H. and E.R. van ARTSDALEN. *J. Am. Chem. Soc.*, **80**, 1352 (1958).
1143. EDGELL, W.F. and W.E. WILSON – cited in [1797].
1144. EDING, H. and D. CUBICIOTTI. *J. Chem. Eng. Data*, **9**, 524 (1964).
1145. EDWARDS, J.W. and G.L. KINGTON. *Trans. Faraday Soc.*, **58**, 1323 (1962).
1146. EDWARDS, J.W. and G.L. KINGTON. *Trans. Faraday Soc.*, **58**, 1334 (1962).
1147. EGAN, C.J. *J. Chem. Eng. Data*, **8**, 532 (1963).
1147a. EGAN, E.P. and B.B. LUFF. *J. Phys. Chem.*, **65**, 523 (1961).
1148. EGAN, E.P. and Z.T. WAKEFIELD. *J. Am. Chem. Soc.*, **78**, 4245 (1956).
1149. EGAN, E.P. and Z.T. WAKEFIELD. *J. Am. Chem. Soc.*, **79**, 558 (1957).
1150. EGAN, E.P. and Z.T. WAKEFIELD. *J. Phys. Chem.*, **61**, 1500 (1957).
1151. EGAN, E.P. and Z.T. WAKEFIELD. *J. Phys. Chem.*, **64**, 1953 (1960).
1152. EGAN, E.P. and Z.T. WAKEFIELD. *J. Chem. Eng. Data*, **8**, 182 (1963).
1153. EGAN, E.P. and Z.T. WAKEFIELD. *J. Chem. Eng. Data*, **9**, 541 (1964).
1154. EGAN, E.P., Z.T. WAKEFIELD, and K.L. ELMORE. *J. Am. Chem. Soc.*, **73**, 5579 (1951).
1155. EGAN, E.P., Z.T. WAKEFIELD, and K.L. ELMORE. *J. Am. Chem. Soc.*, **73**, 5582 (1951).
1156. EGAN, E.P., Z.T. WAKEFIELD, and K.L. ELMORE. *J. Am. Chem. Soc.*, **78**, 1811 (1956).
1157. EGAN, E.P., Z.T. WAKEFIELD, and T.D. FARR. *J. Chem. Eng. Data*, **10**, 138 (1965).
1158. EGAN, E.P. Z.T. WAKEFIELD, and B.B. LUFF. *J. Phys. Chem.*, **65**, 1265 (1961).
1159. EGAN, E.P., Z.T. WAKEFIELD, and B.B. LUFF. *J. Phys. Chem.*, **65**, 1609 (1961).
1160. EGAN, E.P., Z.T. WAKEFIELD, and B.B. LUFF. *J. Chem. Eng. Data*, **8**, 184 (1963).
1161. EGAN, J.J. *J. Phys. Chem.*, **68**, 978 (1964).
1162. EGAN, J.J., W. McCOY, and J. BRACKER. *Thermodynamics of Nuclear Materials*, International Atomic Energy Agency, Vienna, 1962, p. 163.
1163. EHLERT, T.C. and J.L. MARGRAVE. *J. Chem. Phys.*, **41**, 1066 (1964).
1164. EHLERT, T.C. and J.L. MARGRAVE. *J. Am. Chem. Soc.*, **86**, 390 (1964).
1165. EHRLICH P. and E. FRAMM. *Z. Naturforsch.*, **9b**, 326 (1954).
1165a. EHRLICH, P., F.W. KOKNAT, and H.J. SEIFERT. *Z. anorg. allg. Chem.*, **341**, 281 (1965).
1166. EHRLICH, P., K. PEIK, and E. KOCH. *Z. anorg. allg. Chem.*, **324**, 113 (1963).
1167. EICHENAUER, W. and D. LIEBSCHER. *Naturforsch.*, **20a**, 160 (1965).
1168. EICHENAUER, W. and M. SCHULZE. *Z. Naturforsch.*, **14a**, 28 (1959).
1169. EISENLOHR and Ö. METZER. *Z. phys. Chem.*, **A178**, 339 (1937).
1170. EMONS, H.H. and G. ROEWER. *Z. phys. Chem.* (GDR), **222**, 65 (1963).
1171. EPSTEIN, M.B., G.M. BARROW, K.S. PITZER, and F.D. ROSSINI. *J. Res. Nat. Bur. Stand.*, 48, 245 (1945).
1172. ERDÖS, E. *Coll. Czech. Chem. Comm.*, **27**, 1428 (1962).
1173. ESPENSCHEID, W.F., M. KERKER, and E. MATIJEVIE. *J. Phys. Chem.*, **68**, 3093 (1964).
1174. ESTERMANN, J. and J.R. WEERTMAN. *J. Chem. Phys.*, **20**, 272 (1952).

1175. EULER, R.D. and E.F. WESTRUM. *J. Phys. Chem.*, **65**, 132 (1961).
1176. EVANS, D.F. and R.E. RICHARDS. *J. Chem. Soc.*, **1952**, 1292.
1177. EVANS, D.M., F.E. HAARE, and T.P. MELIA. *Trans. Faraday Soc.*, 58, 1511 (1962).
1178. EVANS, D.M. and H.A. SKINNER. *Trans. Faraday Soc.*, **55**, 260 (1959).
1179. EVANS, J.C. *J. Chem. Phys.*, **22**, 1228 (1954).
1180. EVANS, J.C. and H.J. BERNSTEIN. *Can. J. Chem.*, **34**, 1083 (1956).
1181. EVANS, J.C. and H.J. BERNSTEIN. *Can. J. Chem.*, **33**, 1171 (1955).
1182. EVANS, J.P. and P.G. MARDON. *Phys. a. Chem. Solids*, **10**, 311 (1959).
1183. EVANS, M.W. *Natl. Nuclear Energy Ser., Div. IV*, **14B**. *The Transuranium Elements, Research Papers*, Pt. 1, 1949, p. 282.
1184. EVANS, M.W. *Natl. Nuclear Energy Ser., Div. IV*, **19B**, *The Chemistry and Metallurgy of Miscellaneous Materials*, ed. L.L. QUILL, New York, Toronto, London, 1950, p. 312.
1185. EVANS, W.H., R. JACOBSON, T.R. MUNSON, and D.D. WAGMAN. *J. Res. Nat. Bur. Stand.*, **55**, 83 (1955).
1186. EVANS, W.H., T.R. MUNSON, and D.D. WAGMAN. *J. Res. Nat. Bur. Stand.*, **55**, 147 (1955).
1187. EVANS, W.H., E.J. PROSEN, and D.D. WAGMAN. *Thermodynamic and Transport Properties of Gases, Liquids and Solids*. Am. Soc. Mechan. Eng., New York, 1959, p. 226.
1188. EVANS, W.H. and D.D. WAGMAN. *J. Res. Nat. Bur. Stand.*, **49**, 141 (1952).
1189. EYRING, L., H.R. LOHR, and B.B. CUNNINGHAM. *J. Am. Chem. Soc.*, **74**, 1186 (1952).
1190. EYRING, L.R. and E.F. WESTRUM. *J. Am. Chem. Soc.*, **72**, 5555 (1950).
1191. EYRING, L.R. and E.F. WESTRUM. *J. Am. Chem. Soc.*, 75, 4802 (1953).
1192. FAKTOR, M.M. *J. Phys. Soc.*, **66**, 1003 (1962).
1193. FARBER, M. *J. Phys. Chem.*, **66**, 661 (1962).
1194. FARBER, M. *J. Phys. Chem.*, **66**, 1101 (1962).
1195. FARBER, M. and J. BLAUER. *Trans. Faraday Soc.*, **58**, 2090 (1962).
1196. FARBER, M. and A. DARNELL. *J. Phys. Chem.*, **59**, 156 (1955).
1197. FARBER, M. and A. DARNELL. *J. Chem. Phys.*, **23**, 1460 (1955).
1198. FARBER, M. and H.L. PETERSEN. *Trans. Faraday Soc.*, **59**, 836 (1963).
1199. FARMER, J.B., J.H.S. HENDERSON, F.P. LOSSING, and D.H. MARSDEN. *J. Chem. Phys.* **24**, 348 (1956).
1200. FARR, J.D., E.T. HUBER, E.L. HEAD, and C.E. HOLLEY. *J. Phys. Chem.*, **63**, 1455 (1959).
1201. FASOLINO, L.G. *J. Chem. Eng. Data*, **9**, 68 (1964).
1202. FASOLINO, L.G. *J. Chem. Eng. Data*, **10**, 371 (1965).
1203. FASOLINO, L.G. *J. Chem. Eng. Data*, **10**, 373 (1965).
1204. FEDER, H.M., W.N. HUBBARD, S.S. WISE, and J.L. MARGRAVE. *J. Phys. Chem.*, **67**, 1148 (1963).
1205. FEHÉR, F., G. JANSEN, and H. ROHMER. *Angew. Chem.*, **75**, 859 (1963).
1206. FEHÉR, F., G. JANSEN, and H. ROHMER. *Z. anorg. allg. Chem.*, **329**, 31 (1964).
1207. FEHÉR. F., and K. SÉYFRIED. *Z. anorg. allg. Chem.*, **322**, 1955 (1963).
1208. FEHÉR, F. and F. STRÄTER. *Z. anorg. allg. Chem.*, **322**, 172 (1963).
1209. FEHÉR, F. and G. WINKHAUS. *Z. anorg. allg. Chem.*, **292**, 210 (1957).
1210. FENLON, P.F., F.F. CLEVELAND, and A.G. MEISTER. *J. Chem. Phys.*, **19**, 1561 (1951).
1211. FERIGLE, S.M., F.F. CLEVELAND, W.M. BOYER, and R.B. BERNSTEIN. *J. Chem. Phys.*, **18**, 1075 (1950).
1212. FERIGLE, S.M. and A. WEBER. *J. Chem. Phys.*, **20**, 1654 (1952).
1213. FESCHOTTE, P. and O. KUBASCHEWSKI. *Trans. Faraday Soc.*, **60**, 1941 (1964).
1214. FIELD, F.H. and J.L. FRANKLIN. *Electron Impact Phenomena and the Properties of Gaseous Ions.*, New York (1957).
1215. FILBY, J.D. and D.L. MARTIN. *Proc. Roy. Soc.*, **284**, 83 (1965).
1216. FINCH, A. *Rec. trav. chim.*, **83**, 1325 (1964).
1217. FINCH, A. *Rec. trav. chim.*, **84**, 424 (1965).
1218. FINCH, A. and P.J. GARDNER. *J. Chem. Soc.*, **1964**, 2985.
1219. FINCH, A., P.J. GARDNER, and I.J. HYAMS. *Trans. Faraday Soc.*, **91**, 649 (1965).
1220. FINCH, A., P.J. GARDNER, and J.H. WOOD. *J. Chem. Soc.*, **1965**, 40.
1221. FINCH, A., P.J. GARDNER, and J.H. WOOD. *J. Chem. Soc.*, **1965**, 746.
1222. FINKE, H.L., M.E. GROSS, G. WADDINGTON, and H.M. HUFFMAN. *J. Am. Chem. Soc.*, **76**, 333 (1954).
1223. FINKE, H.L., J.F. MESSERLY, and S.S. TODD. *J. Phys. Chem.*, **69**, 2094 (1965).
1224. FINKE, H.L., D.W. SCOTT, M.E. GROSS, J.F. MESSERLY, and G. WADDINGTON. *J. Am. Chem. Soc.*, 78, 5469 (1956).
1225. FINKE, H.L., D.W. SCOTT, M.E. GROSS, G. WADDINGTON, and H.M. HUFFMAN. *J. Am. Chem. Soc.*, 74, 2804 (1952).
1226. FISCHER, A.K., F.A. COTTON, and G. WILKINSON. *J. Am. Chem. Soc.*, **79**, 2044 (1957).
1227. FISCHER, A.K., F.A. COTTON, and G. WILKINSON. *J. Phys. Chem.*, **63**, 154 (1959).
1228. FISCHER, E.O. and A. RECKZIEGEL. *Chem. Ber.*, **94**, 2204 (1962).
1229. FISCHER, E.O. and S. SCHREINER. *Chem. Rev.*, **91**, 2213 (1958).
1230. FITZGIBBON, G.C., C.E. HOLLEY, and I. WADSÖ. *J. Phys. Chem.*, **69**, 2464 (1965).
1231. FLAY, D.C. *Ph. D. Thesis, Univ. of California, Radiation Laboratory. Declassified Report* UCRL–2546. 1957 (cited in [1069]).
1232. FLEISCHER, D. and H. FREISER. *J. Phys. Chem.* **66**, 392 (1962).
1233. FLETCHER, S.E., C.T. MORTIMER, and H.D. SPRINGALL. *Bull. Chem. Thermodynamics I.U.P.A.C.*, No. **1**, A17 (1958).

1234. FLOTOW, H.E. and H.P. LOHR. *J. Phys. Chem.*, **64**, 904 (1960).
1235. FLOTOW, H.E., H.R. LOHR, E.M. ABRAHAM, and D.W. OSBORNE. *J. Am. Chem. Soc.*, **81**, 3529 (1959).
1236. FLOTOW, H.E. and D.W. OSBORNE. *J. Chem. Phys.*, **34**, 1418 (1961).
1237. FLOTOW, H.E., D.W. OSBORNE, and K. OTTO. *J. Chem. Phys.*, **36**, 866 (1962).
1238. FLOTOW, H.E., D.W. OSBORNE, K. OTTO, and B.M. ABRAHAM. *J. Chem. Phys.*, **38**, 2620 (1963).
1239. FLUBACHER, P., A.J. LEADBETTER, and J.A. MORRISON. *Phil. Mag.*, **4**, 273 (1959).
1240. FOLEY, W.T. and P.A. GIGNERE. *Can. J. Chem.*, **29**, 895 (1951).
1241. FONER, S.N. and R.L. HUDSON. *J. Chem. Phys.*, **28**, 719 (1958).
1242. FONTEYNE, R. *Acta chimica*, **1**, 65 (1944).
1242a. FORBES, G.S. and H.H. ANDERSON. *J. Am. Chem. Soc.*, **62**, 761 (1940).
1243. FOWELL, P., J.R. LACHER, and J.D. PARK. *Trans. Faraday Soc.*, **61**, 1324 (1965).
1244. FOWELL, P.A. and C.T. MORTIMER. *J. Chem. Soc.*, **1961**, 3793.
1245. FRANCK, E.U. and F. MEYER. *Z. Elektrochem.*, **63**, 571 (1959).
1245a. FRANK, G. *Ber. Bunsen-Gesellschaft phys. Chem.*, **69**, 119 (1965).
1246. FRANKLIN, J.L. and H.E. LUMPKIN. *J. Am. Chem. Soc.*, **74**, 1023 (1952).
1247. FRANKOSKY, M. and J.G. ASTON. *J. Phys. Chem.*, **69**, 3126 (1965).
1248. FRANZEN, H.F. and P.W. GILLES. *J. Chem. Phys.*, **42**, 1033 (1965).
1249. FRANZOSINI, P. *Ricerca sci.*, P. 2, sez. **A, 3**, 365 (1963).
1250. FRANZOSINI, P. and K. CLUSIUS. *Z. Naturforsch.*, **18a**, 1243 (1963).
1251. FRANZOSINI, P. and K. CLUSIUS. *Z. Naturforsch.*, **19a**, 1430 (1964).
1252. FRANZOSINI, P. and C.G. LOSA. *Z. Naturforsch.*, **19a**, 1348 (1964).
1253. FRASER, F.M. and E.J. PROSEN. *J. Res. Nat. Bur. Stand.*, **54**, 143 (1955).
1254. FREDERICKSON, D.R., R.L. NUTTALL, H.E. FLOTOW, and W.N. HUBBARD. *J. Phys. Chem.*, **67**, 1506 (1963).
1255. FREY, M.B. and N.W. GREGORY. *J. Am. Chem. Soc.*, **82**, 1068 (1960).
1256. FRIEDMAN, A.S. and L. HAAR. *J. Chem. Phys.*, **22**, 2051 (1954).
1257. FRIEDMAN, H.L. and M. KAHWEIT. *J. Am. Chem. Soc.*, **78**, 4243 (1956).
1258. FRISH, M.A., C. BARKER, J.L. MARGRAVE, and M.S. NEWMAN. *J. Am. Chem. Soc.*, **85**, 2356 (1963).
1259. FRISCH, M.A., R.G. BAUTISTA, J.L. MARGRAVE, Ch.G. PARSONS, and J.H. WOTIZ. *J. Am. Chem. Soc.*, **86**, 335 (1964).
1260. FRISCH, M.A., M.A. GREENBAUM, and M. FARBER. *J. Phys. Chem.*, **69**, 3001 (1965).
1261. FRISCH, M.A. and J.L. MARGRAVE. *J. Phys. Chem.*, **69**, 3863 (1965).
1262. FROSCH, C.J. and C.D. THURMOND. *J. Phys. Chem.*, **66**, 877 (1962).
1263. FUGER, J. and B.B. CUNNINGHAM. *J. Inorg. Nucl. Chem.*, **25**, 1423 (1963).
1264. FUHRER, H. and H.H. GÜNTHARD. *Helv. chim. acta*, **42**, 1298 (1959).
1265. FUJISHIRO, S. and N.A. GOKCEN. *J. Phys. Chem.*, **65**, 161 (1961).
1266. FUJISHIRO, S. and N.A. GOKCEN. *Trans. Metallurg. Soc., AIME*, **321**, 275 (1961).
1267. FUJISHIRO, S. and N.A. GOKCEN. *J. Electrochem. Soc.*, **109**, 835 (1962).
1268. FURUKAWA, G.T., T.B. DOUGLAS, R.E. McCOSKEY, and D.C. GINNINGS. *J. Res. Nat. Bur. Stand.*, **57**, 67 (1956).
1269. FURUKAWA, G.T., T.B. DOUGLAS, W.G. SABA, and A.C. VICTOR. *J. Res. Nat. Bur. Stand.*, **69A**, 423 (1965).
1270. FURUKAWA, G.T., D.C. GINNINGS, R.E. McCOSKEY, and R.A. NELSON. *J. Res. Nat. Bur. Stan.*, **46**, 195 (1951).
1271. FURUKAWA, G.T., R.E. McCOSKEY, M.L. REILLY, and A.W. HARMAN. *J. Res. Nat. Bur. Stand.*, **55**, 201 (1955).
1272. FURUKAWA, G.T. and R.P. PARK. *J. Res. Nat. Bur. Stand.*, **55**, 255 (1955).
1273. FURUKAWA, G.T., M.L. REILLY, and J.H. PICCIRELLI. *J. Res. Nat. Bur. Stand.*, **68A**, 381 (1964).
1274. FURUKAWA, G.T., M.L. REILLY, and J.H. PICCIRELLI. *J. Res. Nat. Bur. Stand.*, **68A**, 651 (1964).
1275. FURUKAWA, G.T., M.L. REILLY, J.H. PICCIRELLI, and M. TENENBAUM. *J. Res. Nat. Bur. Stand.*, **68**, 367 (1964).
1276. FURUKAWA, G.T. and W.G. SABA. *J. Res. Nat. Bur. Stand.*, **69A**, 13 (1965).
1277. GALBRAITH, H.J. *J. Chem. Phys.*, **22**, 1461 (1954).
1278. GALLAGHER, K., G. BRODALE, and T.E. HOPKINS. *J. Phys. Chem.*, **64**, 687 (1960).
1279. GAMSJÄGER, H., H.U. STUBER, and P. SCHINDLER. *Helv. chim. acta*, **48**, 723 (1965).
1280. GANCY, A.B. *J. Chem. Eng. Data*, **8**, 301 (1963).
1281. GARDNER, D.M. and J.C. GRIGGER. *J. Chem. Eng. Data*, **8**, 73 (1963).
1282. GARDNER, T.E. and A.R. TAYLOR. *Bur. Mines Rept. of Investig.*, 6435 (1964).
1283. GATTOW, G. – cited in [2313], p. 121.
1284. GATTOW, G. *Naturwis.*, **45**, 623 (1958).
1285. GATTOW, G. *Naturwis.*, **46**, 72 (1959).
1286. GATTOW, G. *Angew. Chem.*, **68**, 521 (1960).
1287. GATTOW, G. *Z. anorg. allg. Chem.*, **317**, 245 (1962).
1288. GATTOW, G. and G. HEINRICH. *Z. anorg. allg. Chem.*, **331**, 256 (1964).
1289. GATTOW, G. and G. HEINRICH. *Z. anorg. allg. Chem.*, **331**, 275 (1964).
1290. GATTOW, G. and B. KREBS. *Angew. Chem.*, **74**, 29 (1962).
1291. GATTOW, G. and B. KREBS. *Z. anorg. allg. Chem.*, **322**, 113 (1963).
1292. GATTOW, G. and A. SCHNEIDER. *Angew. Chem.*, **67**, 306 (1955).
1293. GATTOW, G. and A. SCHNEIDER. *Z. anorg. allg. Chem.*, **286**, 296 (1956).
1294. GATTOW, G. and A. SCHNEIDER. *Angew. Chem.*, **68**, 520 (1956).

1295. GAUNT, J. and J.B. AINSCOUGH. *Spectrochim. acta,* **10,** 52 (1957).
1296. GAUNT, J. and J.B. AINSCOUGH. *Spectrochim. acta,* **10,** 57 (1957).
1297. GEBALLE, T.H. and W.F. GIAUQUE. *J. Am. Chem. Soc.,* **74,** 2368 (1952).
1298. GEED, W.D. *J. Phys. Chem.,* **66,** 380 (1962).
1299. GEISELER, G. and M. RÄTZSCH. *Z. phys. Chem.,* (GDR), **207,** 138 (1957).
1300. GEISELER, G. and W. THIERFELDER. *Z. phys. Chem.* (GFR), **29,** 248 (1961).
1301. GELLES, E. and K.S. PITZER. *J. Am. Chem. Soc.,* **75,** 5259 (1953).
1302. GERKIN, R.E. and K.S. PITZER. *J. Am. Chem. Soc.,* **84,** 2662 (1962).
1303. GERSTEIN, B.C., M. GRIFFEL, L.D. JENNINGS, R.E. MILLER, R.E. SKOCHDOPOLE, and F.H. SPEDDING. *J. Chem. Phys.,* **27,** 394 (1957).
1304. GERSTEIN, B.C., J. MALLALY, E. PHILLIPS, R.E. MILLER, and F.H. SPEDDING. *J. Chem. Phys.,* **41,** 883 (1964).
1305. GERSTEIN, B.C., C.J. PENNEY, and F.H. SPEDDING. *J. Chem. Phys.,* **37,** 2610 (1962).
1306. GIAUQUE, W.F., E.W. HORNUNG, J.E. KUNZLER, and T.R. RUBIN. *J. Am. Chem. Soc.,* **82,** 62 (1960).
1307. GIAUQUE, W.E. and J.B. OTT. *J. Am. Chem. Soc.,* **82,** 2689 (1960).
1308. GIBB, T.R.P., J.J. McSHARRY, and R.W. BRAYDON. *J. Am. Chem. Soc.,* **73,** 1751 (1951).
1309. GIBSON, G., D.M. GRUEN, and J.J. KATZ. *J. Am. Chem. Soc.,* **74,** 2103 (1952).
1310. GIGUERE, P.-A. *Can. J. Res.,* **28,** 485 (1950).
1311. GIGUERE, P.-A. and J.D. LIU. *J. Am. Chem. Soc.,* **77,** 6477 (1955).
1312. GILBERT, R.L., E.A. PIOTROWSKI, J.M. DOWLING, and F.F. CLEVELAND. *J. Chem. Phys.,* **31,** 1633 (1959).
1313. GILLES, P.W. and H.G. KALSKY. *J. Chem. Phys.,* **22,** 232 (1954).
1314. GILLES, P.W. and J.L. MARGRAVE. *J. Phys. Chem.,* **60,** 1333 (1956).
1315. GILLES, P.W. and Q.L. De WHEATLEY. *J. Chem. Phys.,* **19,** 129 (1951).
1316. GILLILAND, A.A. *J. Res. Nat. Bur. Stand.,* **A66,** 447 (1962).
1317. GILLILAND, A.A. and W.H. JOHNSON. *J. Res. Nat. Bur. Stand.,* **65A,** 67 (1961).
1318. GILLILAND, A.A. and D.D. WAGMAN. *J. Res. Nat. Bur. Stand.,* **69A,** 1 (1965).
1319. GINNINGS, D.C. and CORRUCCINI. *Ind. Eng. Chem.,* **40,** 1990 (1948).
1320. GLEISER, M. and J. CHIPMAN. *J. Phys. Chem.,* **66,** 1539 (1962).
1321. GLEMSER, O. and H. SCHRÖDER. *Z. anorg. allg. Chem.,* **271,** 293 (1953).
1322. GLEW, D.N. *Can J. Chem.,* **38,** 208 (1960).
1323. GLOOR, M. and K. WIELAND. *Helv. chim. acta,* **44,** 1098 (1961).
1324. GOEL, N.S. and R.P. SINGH. *Indian J. Pure a. Appl. Phys.,* **1,** 343 (1963).
1325. GOKCEN, N.A. *Metals,* **7,** 1019 (1953).
1325a. GOLDEN, D.M., R. WALSH, and S.W. BENSON. *J. Am. Chem. Soc.,* **87,** 4053 (1965).
1326. GOLDSTEIN, H.W., E.F. NIELSON, P.N. WALSH, and D. WHITE. *J. Phys. Chem.,* **63,** 1445 (1959).
1327. GOLDSTEIN, H.W. and O.C. TRULSON. *Condensation and Evaporation of Solids,* New York–London, 1964, p. 319.
1328. GOLDSTEIN, H.W., P.N. WALSH, and D. WHITE. *J. Phys. Chem.,* **65,** 1400 (1961).
1329. GOOD, W.D., D.R. DOUSLIN, and J.P. McCULLOUGH. *J. Phys. Chem.,* **67,** 1312 (1963).
1330. GOOD, W.D., D.M. FAIRBROTHER, and G. WADDINGTON. *J. Phys. Chem.,* **62,** 853 (1958).
1331. GOOD, W.D., J.L. LACINA, B.L. De PRATER, and J.P. McCULLOUGH. *J. Phys. Chem.,* **68,** 579 (1964).
1332. GOOD, W.D., J.L. LACINA, and J.P. McCULLOUGH. *J. Am. Chem. Soc.,* **82,** 5589 (1960).
1333. GOOD, W.D., J.L. LACINA, and J.P. McCULLOUGH. *J. Phys. Chem.,* **65,** 2229 (1961).
1334. GOOD, W.D., J.L. LACINA, D.W. SCOTT, and J.P. McCULLOUGH. *J. Phys. Chem.,* **66,** 1529 (1962).
1335. GOOD, W.D. and D.W. SCOTT. *Bur. of Mines, Thermod. Labor.,* Bartlesville, Okla., U.S.A. (unpubl.); *"Thermodynamics, Proc. of the Symp. on Thermod., Aug. 1959,* London, Butterworth, 1961, p.77.
1336. GOOD, W.D., D.W. SCOTT, J.L. LACINA, and J.P. McCULLOUGH. *J. Phys. Chem.,* **63,** 1139 (1959).
1337. GOOD, W.D., D.W. SCOTT, and G. WADDINGTON. *J. Phys. Chem.,* **61,** 1080 (1956).
1338. GOOD, W.D., S.S. TODD, J.F. MESSERLY, J.L. LACINA, J.P. DAWSON, D.W. SCOTT, and J.P. McCULLOUGH. *J. Phys. Chem.,* **67,** 1306 (1963).
1339. GORDON, J.S. *J. Chem. Phys.,* **29,** 889 (1958).
1340. GORDON, J.S. *ARS Journal,* **29,** 445 (1959).
1341. GORDON, J.S. *J. Chem. Eng. Data,* **7,** 82 (1962).
1342. GORDON, J.S. *J. Chem. Eng. Data,* **8,** 294 (1963).
1343. GORDON, J.S. and D. COLAND. *J. Chem. Phys.,* **27,** 1223 (1957).
1344. GOTON and WHALLEY. *Can. J. Chem.,* **34,** 1506 (1956).
1345. GOTOO, K. and K. NAITO. *J. Phys. Chem. Solids,* **26,** 1673 (1965).
1346. GOTTSCHAL, A.J. *J. S. Afric. Chem. Inst.,* **11,** 45 (1958).
1347. GOY, C.A. and H.O. PRITCHARD. *J. Phys. Chem.,* **69,** 3040 (1965).
1348. GOZZO, F. and C.R. PATRICK. *Nature,* **202,** 80 (1964).
1349. GRAHAM, R.L. and L.G. HEPLER. *J. Am. Chem. Soc.,* **78,** 4846 (1956).
1350. GRAHAM, R.L. and L.G. HEPLER. *J. Am. Chem. Soc.,* **80,** 3538 (1958).
1351. GRAHAM, R.L. and L.G. HEPLER. *J. Phys. Chem.,* **63,** 723 (1959).
1351a. GRAY, P. *Trans. Faraday Soc.,* **52,** 344 (1956).
1352. GRAY, P. *Trans. Faraday Soc.,* **55,** 408 (1959).

1352a. GRAY, P. *Quart. Rev.*, **17**, 441 (1963).
1352b. GRAY, P., M.W.T. PRATT, and M.J. LARKIN. *J. Chem. Soc.*, **1956**, 210.
1353. GRAY, P. and M.W.T. PRATT. *J. Chem. Soc.*, **1957**, 2163.
1354. GRAY, P. and M.W.T. PRATT. *J. Chem. Soc.*, **1958**, 3403.
1355. GRAY, P. and P.L. SMITH. *J. Chem. Soc.*, **1953**, 2380.
1355a. GRAY, P. and P.L. SMITH. *J. Chem. Soc.*, **1954**, 769.
1356. GRAY, P. and T.C. WADDINGTON. *Proc. Roy. Soc.*, **A235**, 106 (1956).
1357. GRAY, P. and T.C. WADDINGTON. *Proc. Roy. Soc.*, **A235**, 461 (1956).
1358. GRAY, P. and A. WILLIAMS. *Chem. Rev.*, **59**, 239 (1959).
1359. GREEN, J.H.S. *Chem. a. Ind.*, **1960**, 1215.
1360. GREEN, J.H.S. *Quart. Rev.*, **15**, 125 (1961).
1361. GREEN, J.H.S. *J. Chem. Soc.*, **1961**, 2236.
1362. GREEN, J.H.S. *J. Chem. Soc.*, **1961**, 2241.
1363. GREEN, J.H.S. *Chem. a. Ind.*, **1961**, 369.
1364. GREEN, J.H.S. *Trans. Faraday Soc.*, **57**, 2133 (1961).
1365. GREEN, J.H.S. *J. Appl. Chem.*, **11**, 397 (1961).
1366. GREEN, J.H.S. *Chem. a. Ind.*, **1962**, 1575.
1367. GREEN, J.H.S. *Trans. Faraday Soc.*, **59**, 1559 (1963).
1368. GREEN, J.H.S. and D.J. HOLDEN. *J. Chem. Soc.*, **1962**, 1513.
1369. GREEN, J.H.S., W. KYNASTON, and H.M. PAISLEY. *J. Chem. Soc.*, **1963**, 473.
1370. GREEN, J.W., G.D. BLUE, T.C. EHLERT, and J.L. MARGRAVE. *J. Chem. Phys.*, **41**, 2245 (1964).
1370a. GREENBANK, J.C. and B.B. ARGENT. *Trans. Faraday Soc.*, **61**, 655 (1965).
1371. GREENBAUM, M.A., M.L. ARIN, and M. FARBER. *J. Phys. Chem.*, **67**, 1191 (1963).
1372. GREENBAUM, M.A., M.L. ARIN, M. WONG, and M. FARBER. *J. Phys. Chem.*, **68**, 791 (1964).
1373. GREENBAUM, M.A., J.A. BLAUER, M.R. ARSHADI, and M. FARBER. *Trans. Faraday Soc.*, **60**, 1592 (1964).
1374. GREENBAUM, M.A., J.N. FOSTER, M.L. ARIN, and M. FARBER. *Phys. Chem.*, **67**, 36 (1963).
1375. GREENBAUM, M.A., J.N. FOSTER, M.L. ARIN, and M. FARBER. *Phys. Chem.*, **67**, 703 (1963).
1376. GREENBAUM, M.A., HON CHANG KO, M. WONG, and M. FARBER. *J. Phys. Chem.*, **68**, 965 (1964).
1377. GREENBAUM, M.A., R. YATES, M.L. ARIN, M. ARSHADI, J. WEINER, and M. FARBER. Unpublished data (cited in [1374]).
1378. GREENBAUM, M.A., R.E. YATES, and M. FARBER. *J. Phys. Chem.*, **67**, 1802 (1963).
1379. GREENBERG, E., C.A. NATKE, and W.N. HUBBARD. *J. Phys. Chem.*, **69**, 2089 (1965).
1380. GREENBERG, E., J.L. SETTLE, H.M. FEDER, and W.N. HUBBARD. *J. Phys. Chem.*, **65**, 1168 (1961).
1381. GREENBERG, E., J.L. SETTLE, and W.N. HUBBARD. *J. Phys. Chem.*, **66**, 1345 (1962).
1382. GREENBERG, E. and E.F. WESTRUM. *J. Am. Chem. Soc.*, **78**, 4526 (1956).
1383. GREENBERG, E. and E.F. WESTRUM. *J. Am. Chem. Soc.*, **78**, 5144 (1956).
1384. GREENBERG, S.A. and L.E. COPELAND. *J. Phys. Chem.*, **64**, 1057 (1960).
1385. GREENSHIELD, S. and F.D. ROSSINI. *J. Phys. Chem.*, **62**, 271 (1958).
1386. GREENWOOD, N.N. and P.G. PERKINS. *J. Chem. Soc.*, **1960**, 356.
1387. GREENWOOD, N.N. and P.G. PERKINS. *"Thermodynamics," Proc. of the Symp. on Thermod., Aug. 1959,* London, Butterworth, 1961, p.55.
1388. GREENWOOD, N.N., P.G. PERKINS, and K. WADE. *J. Chem. Soc.*, **1957**, 4345.
1389. GREGOR, L.V. and K.S. PITZER. *J. Am. Chem. Soc.*, **84**, 2664 (1962).
1390. GREGOR, L.V. and K.S. PITZER. *J. Am. Chem. Soc.*, **84**, 2671 (1962).
1391. GREGORY, N.W. and T.R. BURTON. *J. Am. Chem. Soc.*, **75**, 6054 (1953).
1392. GREGORY, N.W. and R.O. McLAREN. *J. Phys. Chem.*, **53**, 110 (1951).
1393. GREGORY, N.W. and B.A. THACKREY. *J. Am. Chem. Soc.*, **72**, 3176 (1950).
1394. GRENIER, G. and E.F. WESTRUM. *J. Am. Chem. Soc.*, **78**, 6226 (1956).
1395. GRENIER, G. and E.F. WESTRUM. *J. Am. Chem. Soc.*, **79**, 1802 (1957).
1396. GREY, N.R. and L.A.K. STAVELEY. *Molec. Phys.*, 7, 83 (1963–1964).
1397. GRIFFEL, M. and R.E. SKOCHDOPOLE. *J. Am. Chem. Soc.*, **75**, 5250 (1953).
1398. GRIFFEL, M., R.E. SKOCHDOPOLE, and F.H. SPEDDING. *Phys. Rev.*, **93**, 657 (1954).
1399. GRIFFEL, M., R.E. SKOCHDOPOLE, and F.H. SPEDDING. *J. Chem. Phys.*, **25**, 75 (1956)
1400. GRIFFIS, R.C. *J. Electrochem. Soc.*, **105**, 398 (1958).
1401. GRIFFIS, R.C. *J. Electrochem. Soc.*, **106**, 418 (1959).
1402. GRIFFITHS, J.E., T.N. SRIVASTAVA, and M. ONYSZCHUK. *Can. J. Chem.*, **40**, 579 (1962).
1403. GRISARD, J.W., H.A. BERNHARDT, and G.D. OLIVER. *J. Am. Chem. Soc.*, **74**, 5725 (1951).
1404. GRJOTHEIM, K., O. HERSTAD, S. PETRUCCI, R. SCARBÖ, and J. TOGURI. *Rev. Chim. Acad. RPR*, 7, 217 (1962).
1405. GRÖNWOLD, F. and T.THURMAN-MEE. *Acta chem. Scand.*, **14**, 634 (1960).
1406. GRÖNWOLD, F. and T. THURMAN-MEE. *J. Phys. Chem.*, **35**, 1665 (1961).
1407. GRÖNWOLD, F. and E.F. WESTRUM. *Acta chem. Scand.*, **13**, 241 (1959).
1408. GRÖNWOLD, F. and E.F. WESTRUM. *J. Am. Chem. Soc.*, **81**, 1780 (1959).
1409. GRÖNWOLD, F. and E.F. WESTRUM. *Inorg. Chem.*, **1**, 36 (1962).
1410. GRÖNWOLD, F. and E.F. WESTRUM. *Z. anorg. allg. Chem.*, **328**, 272 (1964).

1411. GRÖNWOLD, F., E.F. WESTRUM, and CHOU CHIEN. *J. Chem. Phys.*, **30**, 528 (1959).
1411a. GROSS, M.E., G.D. OLIVER, and H.M. HUFFMAN. *J. Am. Chem. Soc.*, **75**, 2801 (1953).
1412. GROSS, P., C.S. CAMPBELL, P.J.C. KENT, and D.L. LEVI. *Disc. Faraday Soc.*, **4**, 206 (1948).
1413. GROSS, P. and C. HAYMAN. *Trans. Faraday Soc.*, **60**, 45 (1964).
1414. GROSS, P., C. HAYMAN, and H. CLAYTON. *Thermodynamics of Nuclear Materials*, International Atomic Energy Agency, Vienna, 1962, p.653.
1415. GROSS, P., C. HAYMAN, and D.L. LEVI. *Trans. Faraday Soc.*, **50**, 477 (1954).
1416. GROSS, P., C. HAYMAN, and D.L. LEVI. *Trans. Faraday Soc.*, **51**, 626 (1955).
1417. GROSS, P., C. HAYMAN, and D.L. LEVI. *Trans. Faraday Soc.*, **53**, 1285 (1957).
1418. GROSS, P., C. HAYMAN, and D.L. LEVI. *Trans. Faraday Soc.*, **53**, 1601 (1957).
1419. GROSS, P., C. HAYMAN, D.L. LEVI, and M.C. STUART. *Fulmer Research Institute Report*, No. R146/4/23, 1960 (cited in [2696]).
1420. GROSS, P., C. HAYMAN, D.L. LEVI, and G.L. WILSON. *Trans. Faraday Soc.*, **56**, 318 (1960).
1421. GROSS, P., C. HAYMAN, D.L. LEVI, and G.L. WILSON. *Trans. Faraday Soc.*, **58**, 890 (1962).
1422. GROSS, P. and D.L. LEVI. *Inter. Congr. Pure a. Appl. Chem., Paris, 1957* (cited in [1773]).
1423. GROVES, W.O., M. HOCH, and H.L. JOHNSTON. *J. Phys. Chem.*, **59**, 127 (1955).
1424. GRUBE, G. and M. FLAD – cited in [1773].
1425. GRUBE, G. and H. SPEIDEL. *Z. Elektrochem.*, **53**, 341 (1949).
1426. GRUEN, D.M. and J.J. KATZ. *J. Am. Chem. Soc.*, **75**, 3772 (1953).
1427. GRUDZINOWICZ, B.J., R.H. CAMPBELL, and J.S. ADAMS. *J. Chem., Eng. Data*, **8**, 201 (1963).
1428. GNERIN, H. and J. ADAM-GIRONNE. *Bull. Soc. chim. France*, **1949**, 607.
1429. GUGNERE, P.A. and R. SAVOIE. *J. Am. Chem. Soc.*, **85**, 287 (1963).
1430. GUNDRY, H.A., A.J. HEAD, and G.B. LEWIS. *Trans. Faraday Soc.*, **58**, 1309 (1962).
1431. GUNN, S.R. In: *Noble Gas Compounds*, ed. H.H. Hyman, Univ. of Chicago Press, Chicago, Ill., 1963, p. 149 (cited in [1432]).
1432. GUNN, S.R. *J. Am. Chem. Soc.*, **87**, 2290 (1965).
1433. GUNN, S.R. *J. Phys. Chem.*, **69**, 1010 (1965).
1434. GUNN, S.R. and B.B. CUNNINGHAM. *J. Am. Chem. Soc.*, **79**, 1563 (1957).
1435. GUNN, S.R. and L.G.-R. GREEN. *J. Am. Chem. Soc.*, **80**, 4782 (1958).
1436. GUNN, S.R. and L.G.-R. GREEN. *J. Phys. Chem.*, **64**, 61 (1960).
1437. GUNN, S.R. and L.G.-R. GREEN. *J. Phys. Chem.*, **65**, 178 (1961).
1437a. GUNN, S.R. and L.G.-R. GREEN. *J. Phys. Chem.*, **65**, 779 (1961).
1438. GUNN, S.R. and L.G.-R. GREEN. *J. Phys. Chem.*, **65**, 2173 (1961).
1439. GUNN, S.R. and L.G.-R. GREEN. *J. Chem. Phys.*, **36**, 1118 (1962).
1440. GUNN, S.R. and L.G.-R. GREEN. *J. Phys. Chem.*, **68**, 946 (1964).
1441. GUNN, S.R. L.G.-R. GREEN, and A.I. von EGIDY. *J. Phys. Chem.*, **63**, 1787 (1959).
1442. GUNN, S.R., W.L. JOLLEY, and L.G.-R. GREEN. *J. Phys. Chem.*, **64**, 1334 (1964).
1443. GUNN, S.R. and R.H. SANBORN. *J. Chem. Phys.*, **33**, 955 (1960).
1444. GUNN, S.R. and S.M. WILLIAMSON. *Science*, **140**, 177 (1963).
1445. GÜNTHARD, H.H. and E. HEILBRONNER. *Helv. chim. acta*, **31**, 2128 (1948).
1446. GÜNTHARD, H.H. and E. KOVATZ. *Helv. chim acta*, **35**, 1190 (1952).
1447. GÜNTHARD, H.H., MESIKOMMER, and KOHLER. *Helv. chim acta*, **33**, 1809 (1950).
1447a. GUPTA, R.B. and B. DAYAL. *Phys. status solidi*, **9**, 87 (1965).
1448. GUPTA, S.R., G.J. HILLS, and D.J.G. IVES. *Trans. Faraday Soc.*, **59**, 1874 (1963).
1449. GUPTA, S.R., G.J. HILLS, and D.J.G. IVES. *Trans. Faraday Soc.*, **59**, 1886 (1963).
1450. GUTHRIE, G.B., D.W. SCOTT, W.N. HUBBARD, C. KATZ, J.P. McCULLOUGH, M.E. GROSS, K.D. WILLIAMSON, and G. WADDINGTON. *J. Am. Chem. Soc.*, **74**, 4662 (1952).
1451. GUTHRIE, G.B., D.W. SCOTT, and G. WADDINGTON. *J. Am. Chem. Soc.*, **74**, 2795 (1952).
1452. GUTHRIE, G.B., D.W. SCOTT, and G. WADDINGTON. *J. Am. Chem. Soc.*, **76**, 1488 (1954).
1453. GWINN, W.D. and K.S. PITZER. *J. Chem. Phys.*, **16**, 303 (1948).
1454. HAAR, L., J.C. BRADLEY, and A.S. FRIEDMAN. *J. Res. Nat. Bur. Stand.*, **55**, 285 (1955).
1455. HAAR, L. and A.S. FRIEDMAN. *J. Chem. Phys.*, **23**, 869 (1955).
1456. HABERMAN, C.E. and A.H. DAANE. *J. Chem. Phys.*, **41**, 2818 (1964).
1457. HADZI. *Compt. rend.*, **239**, 349 (1954).
1458. HAGEMANN, R. *Compt. rend.*, **255**, 1102 (1962).
1459. HAHN, H. and F. BUROW. *Angew. Chem.*, **68**, 382 (1956).
1460. HAHN, H. and E. GILBERT. *Z. anorg. allg. Chem.*, **258**, 77 (1949).
1461. HAHN, H. and A. KONRAD. *Z. anorg. allg. Chem.*, **264**, 181 (1951).
1461a. HALFORD, J.O. *J. Chem. Phys.*, **9**, 859 (1941).
1462. HALL, E.H. and J.M. BLOCHER. *J. Electrochem. Soc.*, **105**, 40 (1958).
1463. HALL, E.H. and J.M. BLOCHER. *J. Phys. Chem.*, **63**, 1525 (1959).
1464. HALL, E.H., J.M. BLOCHER, and J.E. CAMPBELL (cited in [1773]).
1465. HALLE, F. *Z. phys. Chem.*, (GFR), **32**, 267 (1962).
1466. HALLE, F. *Monatsh. Chem.*, **93**, 946 (1962).

1467. HALLETT, N.C. and H.L. JOHNSTON. *J. Am. Chem. Soc.*, **75**, 1496 (1953).
1468. HALVERSON, F. and R.J. FRANCEL. *J. Chem. Phys.*, **17**, 694 (1949).
1469. HALVERSON, F., R.F. STAMM, and J.J. WHALEN. *J. Chem. Phys.*, **16**, 808 (1948).
1470. HAMMER, R.R. and J.A. PASK. *J. Am. Ceram. Soc.*, **47**, 264 (1964).
1471. HAMPSON, R.F. and R.F. WALKER. *J. Res. Nat. Bur. Stand.*, **65A**, 289 (1961).
1472. HAMPSON, R.F. and R.F. WALKER. *J. Res. Nat. Bur. Stand.*, **66A**, 177 (1962).
1473. HANCOCK, WATSON, and GILBY. *J. Phys. Chem.*, **58**, 127 (1954).
1474. HANSEN, W.N. and M. GRIFFEL. *J. Chem. Phys.*, **28**, 902 (1958).
1475. HARMONY, M.D. and R.J. MYERS. *J. Chem. Phys.*, **37**, 636 (1962).
1476. HARNESS, J.P., J.C. MATTHEWS, and N. MORTON. *Brit. J. Appl. Phys.*, **15**, 963 (1964).
1477. HARRIS. *Proc. Roy. Soc.*, **A173**, 126 (1939).
1478. HARRISON, A.G. and F.P. LOSSING. *J. Am. Chem. Soc.*, **82**, 519 (1960).
1479. HARRISON, R.H. and K.A. KOBE. *Chem. Eng. Progr.*, **49**, 349 (1953).
1480. HART, D. *J. Phys. Chem.*, **56**, 202 (1952).
1480a. HARTLEY, D.B., ALBRIGHT, and WILSON – cited in [4209].
1481. HARTLEY, D.B. and S.W. BENSON. *J. Chem. Phys.*, **39**, 132 (1963).
1482. HARTLEY, S.B. and J.C. McCOUBROY. *Nature*, **198**, 476 (1963).
1482a. HARTLEY, S.B., W.S. HOLMES, J.K. JACQUES, M.F. MOLE, and J.C. McCOUBREY. *Quart. Rev.*, **17**, 204 (1963).
1483. HARTLEY, S.B., N.L. PADDOCK, and H.T. SEARLE. *J. Chem. Soc.*, **1961**, 430.
1484. HARTLEY, K., H.O. PRITCHARD, and H.A. SKINNER. *Trans. Faraday Soc.*, **46**, 1019 (1950).
1485. HARTLEY, K., H.O. PRITCHARD, and H.A. SKINNER. *Trans. Faraday Soc.*, **47**, 254 (1951).
1486. HARTMANN, H. and G. RINK. *Z. phys. Chem.* (GFR), **11**, 211 (1957).
1487. HARTMANN, H. and G. WAGNER. *Abhandl. Braunschweig. wiss. Ges.*, **14**, 13 (1962).
1488. HASKELL, R.W. and R.C. DeVRIES. *J. Am. Ceram. Soc.*, **47**, 202 (1964).
1489. HASTINGS, S.H. and D.E. NICHELSON. *J. Phys. Chem.*, **61**, 730 (1956).
1490. HARTON, W.E., D.L. HILDENBRAND, G.C. SINKE, and D.R. STULL. *J. Am. Chem. Soc.*, **81**, 5028 (1959).
1491. HATTON, W.E., D.L. HILDENBRAND, G.C. SINKE, and D.R. STULL. *J. Chem. Eng. Data*, **7**, 229 (1962).
1492. HAWKINS, D.T., M. ONILLON, and R.L. ORR. *J. Chem. Eng. Data*, **8**, 628 (1963).
1493. HAWKINS, D.T. and R.L. ORR. *J. Chem. Eng. Data*, **9**, 505 (1964).
1494. HAWKINS, N.J. and D.R. CARPENTER. *J. Chem. Phys.*, **23**, 1700 (1955).
1495. HAWKINS, N.J., H.C. MATTRAW, N.W. SABOL, and D.R. CARPENTER. *J. Chem. Phys.*, **23**, 2422 (1960).
1496. HAWKINS, N.J., S.R. POLE, and M.K. WILSON. *J. Chem. Phys.*, **21**, 1122 (1953).
1497. HAYEK, E., T. RECHER, and A. FRANK. *Monatsh. Chem.*, **82**, 575 (1951).
1498. HEAD, R.B. *Austral. J. Chem.*, **13**, 332 (1960).
1499. HEPLER, L.G. *J. Am. Chem. Soc.*, **80**, 6181 (1958).
1500. HEPLER, L.G., J.R. SWEET, and R.A. JESSER. *J. Am. Chem. Soc.*, **82**, 304 (1960).
1501. HEROLD, A. *Compt. rend.*, **228**, 686 (1949).
1502. HERRON, J.T. and V.H. DIBELER. *J. Am. Chem. Soc.*, **82**, 1555 (1960).
1503. HERREN, J.T. and V.H. DIBELER. *J. Res. Nat. Bur. Stand.*, **65A**, 405 (1961).
1504. HESS, G.G., F.W. LAMPE, and J.H. SOMMER. *J. Am. Chem. Soc.*, **86**, 3174 (1964).
1505. HICKS, W.T. *J. Chem. Phys.*, **38**, 1873 (1963).
1506. HIGGINS, T.L. *Dissert. Abstracts*, **17**, 1231 (1957) (cited in [742]).
1507. HIGGINS, T.L. and E.F. WESTRUM. *J. Phys. Chem.*, **65**, 830 (1961).
1508. HILDENBRAND, D.L. and W.F. GIAUQUE. *J. Am. Chem. Soc.*, **75**, 2811 (1953).
1509. HILDENBRAND, D.L. and W.F. HALL. *J. Phys. Chem.*, **66**, 754 (1962).
1510. HILDENBRAND, D.L. and W.F. HALL. *J. Phys. Chem.*, **67**, 888 (1963).
1511. HILDENBRAND, D.L. and W.F. HALL. *Condensation and Evaporation of Solids*, New York, London, 1964, p. 400.
1512. HILDENBRAND, D.L. and W.F. HALL. *J. Phys. Chem.*, **68**, 989 (1964).
1513. HILDENBRAND, D.L., W.F. HALL, and N.D. POTTER. *J. Chem. Phys.*, **40**, 2882 (1964).
1514. HILDENBRAND, D.L., W.R. KRAMER, R.A. McDONALD, and D.R. STULL. *J. Am. Chem. Soc.*, **80**, 4129 (1958).
1515. HILDENBRAND, D.L., W.R. KRAMER, and D.R. STULL. *J. Phys. Chem.*, **62**, 958 (1958).
1516. HILDENBRAND, D.L. and R.A. McDONALD. *J. Phys. Chem.*, **63**, 1521 (1959).
1517. HILDENBRAND, D.L. and E. MURAD. *J. Chem. Phys.*, **43**, 1400 (1965).
1518. HILDENBRAND, D.L. and N.D. POTTER. *J. Phys. Chem.*, **67**, 2231 (1963).
1519. HILDENBRAND, D.L., G.C. SINKE, R.A. McDONALD, W.R. KRAMER, and D.R. STULL. *J. Chem. Phys.*, **31**, 650 (1959).
1520. HILDENBRAND, D.L. and L.P. THEARD. *Aeronutron. Newport Beach*, California, 1963.
1521. HILDENBRAND, D.L. and L.P. THEARD. *J. Chem. Phys.*, **42**, 3231 (1965).
1522. HILDENBRAND, D.L., L.P. THEARD, and A.M. SAUL. *J. Chem. Phys.*, **39**, 1973 (1963).
1523. HILL, R.A.W. and J.F. WILLIAMSON. *J. Chem. Soc.*, **1957**, 2417.
1524. HILL, R.W. and P.L. SMITH. *Phil. Mag.*, **44**, 636 (1953).
1525. HIRAYAMA, C. *J. Phys. Soc.*, **66**, 1563 (1962).
1526. HIRAYAMA, C. *J. Electrochem. Soc.*, **110**, 88 (1963).
1527. HIRAYAMA, C., Y. ISHIKAWA, and A.M. De ROO. *J. Phys. Chem.*, **67**, 1039 (1963).

1528. HOBROCK, B.G. and R.W. KISER. *J. Phys. Chem.*, **66**, 1551 (1962).
1529. HOCH, M. *J. Appl. Phys.*, **29**, 1588 (1958).
1530. HOCH, M., D.P. DINGLEDY, and H.L. JOHNSTON. *J. Am. Chem. Soc.*, 77, 304 (1955).
1531. HOCH, M. and K.S. HINGA. *J. Chem. Phys.*, **35**, 451 (1961).
1532. HOCH, M. and D. WHITE. *ASTIA Unclas. Rep.* 142616, Oct. 29, 1956; *Techn. Res. Rep.* MCC–1023–TR–216, Ohio State Univ., Res. Foundat., Oct. 29, 1956 (cited in [1123]).
1533. HIHMANN, E. and H. BOMMER. *Z. anorg. allg. Chem.*, **248**, 383 (1941).
1534. HOLCOMB, D.E. and C.L. DORSEY. *Ind. Eng. Chem.*, **41**, 2788 (1949).
1535. HOLLEY, C.E. and E.G. HUBER. *J. Am. Chem. Soc.*, 73, 5577 (1951).
1536. HOLLEY, C.E., E.J. HUBER, and E.H. MEIERKORD. *J. Am. Chem. Soc.*, **74**, 1084 (1952).
1537. HOLMES, W.S. *Trans. Faraday Soc.*, **58**, 1916 (1962).
1538. HON CHUNG KO, M.A. GREENBAUM, J.A. BLAUER, and M. FARBER. *J. Phys. Chem.*, **69**, 2311 (1965).
1539. HONIG, R.E. *J. Chem. Phys.*, **22**, 1610 (1954).
1540. HONIG, R.E. *R.C.A. Rev. a. Techn. J.*, **28**, 195 (1957) (cited in [402]).
1541. HOPKINS, H.P. and C.A. WULFF. *J. Phys. Chem.*, **69**, 6 (1965).
1542. HOPKINS, H.P. and C.A. WULFF. *J. Phys. Chem.*, **69**, 9 (1965).
1543. HÖRBE, R. and O. KNACKE. *Z. Erzbergbau u. Metallhüttenwesen*, **12**, 321 (1959).
1544. HORNUNG, E.W. and W.F. GIAUQUE. *J. Am. Chem. Soc.*, 77, 2983 (1955).
1545. HOUGH, E.W., D.M. MASON, and B.H. SAGE. *J. Am. Chem. Soc.*, **72**, 5775 (1950).
1546. HOWLETT, K.E., *J. Chem. Soc.*, **1955**, 1784.
1547. HOY, Y.C. and J.J. MARTIN. *A.I. Ch. E. Journal*, **5**, 125 (1959).
1547a. HROSTOWSKI, H.J. and G.C. PIMENTEL. *J. Am. Chem. Soc.*, **75**, 539 (1953).
1548. HU, J.H. and H.L. JOHNSTON. *J. Am. Chem. Soc.*, 73, 4550 (1951).
1549. HU, J.H. and H.L. JOHNSTON. *J. Am. Chem. Soc.*, **74**, 4771 (1952).
1550. HU, J.H. and H.L. JOHNSTON. *J. Am. Chem. Soc.*, **75**, 2471 (1953).
1551. HU, J.H., D. WHITE, and H.L. JOHNSTON. *J. Am. Chem. Soc.*, **75**, 1232 (1953).
1552. HUBBARD, W.N., D.R. DOUSLIN, J.P. McCULLOUGH, D.W. SCOTT, S.S. TODD, J.F. MESSERLY, I.A. HASSENLOPP, and G. WADDINGTON. *J. Am. Chem. Soc.*, **80**, 3547 (1958).
1553. HUBBARD, W.N., H.L. FINKE, D.W. SCOTT, J.P. McCULLOUGH, C. KATZ, M.E. GROSS, J.F. MESSERLY, R.E. PENNINGTON, and G. WADDINGTON. *J. Am. Chem. Soc.*, **74**, 6025 (1952).
1554. HUBBARD, W.N., F.R. FROW, and G. WADDINGTON. *J. Phys. Chem.*, **65**, 1326 (1961).
1555. HUBBARD, W.N., W.D. GOOD, and G. WADDINGTON. *J. Phys. Chem.*, **62**, 614 (1958).
1556. HUBBARD, W.N., C. KATZ, and G. WADDINGTON. *J. Phys. Chem.*, **58**, 142 (1954).
1557. HUBBARD, W.N., J.W. KNOWLTON, and H.M. HUFFMAN. *J. Phys. Chem.*, **58**, 396 (1954).
1558. HUBBARD, W.N., D.W. SCOTT, F.R. FROW, and G. WADDINGTON. *J. Am. Chem. Soc.*, 77, 5855 (1955).
1559. HUBBARD, W.N. and G. WADDINGTON. *Rec. trav. chim.*, 73, 910 (1954).
1560. HUBER, E.J., G.C. FITZGIBBON, E.L. HEAD, and C.E. HOLLEY. *J. Phys. Chem.*, **67**, 1731 (1963).
1561. HUBER, E.J., G.C. FITZGIBBON, and C.E. HOLLEY. *J. Phys. Chem.*, **68**, 2720 (1964).
1562. HUBER, E.J., E.L. HEAD, and C.E. HOLLEY. *J. Phys. Chem.*, **60**, 1457 (1956).
1563. HUBER, E.J., E.L. HEAD, and C.E. HOLLEY. *J. Phys. Chem.*, **60**, 1582 (1956).
1564. HUBER, E.J., E.L. HEAD, and C.E. HOLLEY. *J. Phys. Chem.*, **61**, 497 (1957).
1565. HUBER, E.J., E.L. HEAD, and C.E. HOLLEY. *J. Phys. Chem.*, **61**, 1021 (1957).
1566. HUBER, E.J., E.L. HEAD, and C.E. HOLLEY. *J. Phys. Chem.*, **64**, 379 (1960).
1567. HUBER, E.J., E.L. HEAD, and C.E. HOLLEY. *J. Phys. Chem.*, **64**, 1768 (1960).
1568. HUBER, E.J., E.L. HEAD, and C.E. HOLLEY. *J. Phys. Chem.*, **67**, 1730 (1963).
1569. HUBER, E.J., E.L. HEAD, and C.E. HOLLEY. *J. Phys. Chem.*, **68**, 3040 (1964).
1570. HUBER, E.J., E.L. HEAD, and C.E. HOLLEY – cited in [1800].
1571. HUBER, E.J., E.L. HEAD, C.E. HOLLEY, and A.L. BOWMAN. *J. Phys. Chem.*, **67**, 793 (1963).
1572. HUBER, E.J., E.L. HEAD, C.E. HOLLEY, E.K. STORMS, and N.H. KRIKORIAN. *J. Phys. Chem.*, **65**, 1846 (1961).
1573. HUBER, E.J. and C.E. HOLLEY. *J. Am. Chem. Soc.*, **74**, 5530 (1952).
1574. HUBER, E.J. and C.E. HOLLEY. *J. Am. Chem. Soc.*, **75**, 3645 (1953).
1575. HUBER, E.J. and C.E. HOLLEY. *J. Am. Chem. Soc.*, **75**, 5594 (1953).
1576. HUBER, E.J. and C.E. HOLLEY. *J. Am. Chem. Soc.*, 77, 1444 (1955).
1577. HUBER, E.J. and C.E. HOLLEY. *J. Phys. Chem.*, **60**, 498 (1956).
1578. HUBER, E.J. and C.E. HOLLEY. *Thermodynamics of Nuclear Materials.* International Atomic Energy Agency, Vienna, 1962, p. 581.
1579. HUBER, E.J., C.E. HOLLEY, and E.H. MEIERKORD. *J. Am. Chem. Soc.* **74**, 3406 (1952).
1580. HUBER, E.J., C.O. MATTHEWS, and C.E. HOLLEY. *J. Am. Chem. Soc.*, 77, 6493 (1955).
1581. HUFF, G., E. SQUITIERI, and P.E. SNYDER. *J. Am. Chem. Soc.*, **70**, 3380 (1948).
1582. HUFF, V.N., S. GORDON, and V.E. MORRELL. *Natl. Advisory Comm. Aeronaut.*, Rept. No. 1037, (1952).
1583. HUFFMAN, H.M. and E.L. ELLIS. *J. Am. Chem. Soc.*, **57**, 41 (1935).
1584. HUFFMAN, H.M., E.L. ELLIS, and H. BORSOOK. *J. Am. Chem. Soc.*, **62**, 297 (1940).
1585. HUFFMAN, H.M., H.L ELLIS, and S.W. FOX. *J. Am. Chem. Soc.*, **58**, 1728 (1936).
1586. HUFFMAN, H.M. and S.W. FOX. *J. Am. Chem. Soc.*, **60**, 1400 (1938).

1587. HUFFMAN, H.M., M.E. GROSS, D.W. SCOTT, and J.P. McCULLOUGH. *J. Phys. Chem.*, **65**, 495 (1961).
1588. HUGUS, Z.Z. *J. Am. Chem. Soc.*, 73, 5459 (1951).
1589. HULTGREN, R., R.L. ORR, P.D. ANDERSON, and K.K. KELLEY. *Selected Values of Thermodynamic Properties of Metals and Alloys.* Dept. of Mineral Technology, Univ. of California, Berkeley (1963).
1590. HUMPHREY, G.L. *J. Am. Chem. Soc.*, 73, 1587 (1951).
1591. HUMPHREY, G.L. *J. Am. Chem. Soc.*, 73, 2261 (1951).
1592. HUMPHREY, G.L. *J. Am. Chem. Soc.*, **75**, 2806 (1953).
1593. HUMPHREY, G.L. *J. Am. Chem. Soc.*, **76**, 978 (1954).
1594. HUMPHREY, G.L. and E.G. KING. *J. Am. Chem. Soc.*, **74**, 2041 (1952).
1595. HUMPHREY, G.L., E.G. KING, and K.K. KELLEY. *U.S. Bur. Mines Rept. Investig.*, No. 4870 (1952) (cited in [1045]).
1596. HUMPHREY, G.L. and C.J. O'BRIEN. *J. Am. Chem. Soc.*, **75**, 2805 (1953).
1597. HUMPHREY, G.L., S.S. TODD, J.P. COUGHLIN, and E.G. KING. *U.S. Bur. Mines Rept. Investig.*, No. 4883 (1952) (cited in [1045]).
1598. HUTCHENS, J.O., A.G. COLE, and J.W. STOUT. *J. Am. Chem. Soc.*, **82**, 4813 (1960).
1599. HUTCHENS, J.O., A.G. COLE, and J.W. SCOTT. *J. Phys. Chem.*, **67**, 1128 (1963).
1600. INANI, S.H., W.A. ROSSER, and H. WISE. *J. Phys. Chem.*, **67**, 1077 (1963).
1601. *Inter. Thermochemical Tables. U.S. Joint Army–Navy–Air Force. Thermochemical Panel.* Tables prepared at Thermal Laboratory, Dow Chemical Co., Midland, Michigan.
1602. IRMAUN, F. *Helv. chim. acta*, **31**, 1584, 2263 (1948).
1603. IRVING, R.J. and J. WADSÖ. *Acta chem. scand.*, **18**, 195 (1964).
1603a. ISMAT ABU-ISA, and M. DOLE. *J. Phys. Chem.*, **69**, 2668 (1965).
1604. IVASH, E.V., C.M. LI, and K.S. PITZER. *J. Chem. Phys.*, **23**, 1814 (1955).
1605. IVIN, K.J., W.A. KEITH, and H. MACKLE. *Trans. Faraday Soc.*, **55**, 262 (1959).
1606. JACKSON, D.D., G.W. BARTON, O.H. KRIKORIAN, and R.S. NEWBURY. *Thermodynamics of Nuclear Materials*, International Atomic Energy Agency, Vienna, 1962, p. 529.
1607. JACKSON, D.D., G.W. BARTON, O.H. KRIKORIAN, and R.S. NEWBURY. *J. Phys. Chem.*, **68**, 1516 (1964).
1608. JACOWS, C.J. and G.S. PARKS. *J. Am. Chem. Soc.*, **56**, 1513 (1934).
1609. JACQUES, J.K. *J. Chem. Soc.*, **1963**, 3820.
1610. JACQUES, J.K. *J. Chem. Soc.*, **1963**, 4297.
1610a. JACQUES, ROBERTS, SZWARC – cited in [1482a].
1611. JAFFE, L., E.J. PROSEN, and M. SZWARC. *J. Chem. Phys.*, **27**, 416 (1957).
1612. JAIN, D.V.S. and M.M. KAPOOR. *Proc. Nat. Inst. Sci. India*, **A27**, 101 (1961).
1613. JAIN, D.V.S. and M.M. KAPOOR. *Proc. Nat. Inst. Sci. India*, **A27**, 106 (1961).
1614. JAKEŠ, J. and D. PAPOUSEK. *Coll. Czech. Chem. Comm.*, **26**, 2110 (1961).
1615. JAKUSZEWSKI, B. and Z. KOZTOASKI. *Soc. Sci. Lodz. acta chim.*, **3**, 5 (1958).
1616. JAKUSZEWSKI, B. *Soc. Sci. Lodz. acta chim.*, **4**, 5 (1960).
1617. JAKUSZEWSKI, B. and J. BADECKA-JEDRZEJEWSKA. *Rochn. chemii*, **39**, 907 (1965).
1618. *JANAF Thermochemical Tables*, The Dow Chemical Co., Midland, Michigan, 1960 (cited by STRENG, A.G. *J. Chem. Soc.*, **85**, 1380 (1963)).
1618a. *JANAF thermochemical Tables*, PB-168370, Clearinghouse, U.S. Depart. of Commerce (Nat. Bur. Stand.), Aug., 1965.
1619. JANGG, G. and W. GRÖLL. *Z. Metallkunde*, **56**, 232 (1965).
1620. JANZ, G.J. and F.J. KELLY. *J. Phys. Chem.*, **67**, 2848 (1963).
1621. JANZ, L.J. *J. Chem. Phys.*, **22**, 751 (1954).
1622. JEFFES, J.H.E., F.D. RICHARDSON, and J. PEARSON. *Trans. Faraday Soc.*, **50**, 364 (1954).
1623. JEKEL, E.C., M. CRISS, and J.W. COBBLE. *J. Am. Chem. Soc.*, **86**, 5464 (1964).
1624. JELLINEK, H.H.G. *Trans. Faraday Soc.*, **40**, 1 (1944).
1625. JENNINGS, L.D., E.D. HILL, and F.H. SPEDDING. *J. Chem. Phys.*, **31**, 1240 (1959).
1626. JENNINGS, L.D., E. HILL, and F.H. SPEDDING. *J. Chem. Phys.*, **34**, 2082 (1961).
1627. JENNINGS, L.D., R.E. MILLER, and F.H. SPEDDING. *J. Chem. Phys.*, **33**, 1849 (1960).
1628. JENNINGS, L.D., R.M. STANTON, and F.H. SPEDDING. *J. Chem. Phys.* **27**, 909 (1957).
1629. JESSUP, R.S., R.E. McCOSKEY, and R.A. NELSON. *J. Am. Chem. Soc.*, **77**, 244 (1955).
1630. JOHNSON, F.A. and Ch.B. COLBURN. *Inorg. Chem.*, **2**, 24 (1963).
1631. JOHNSON, R.G., D.E. HUDSON, W.C. CALDWELL, F.H. SPEDDING, and W.R. SAVAGE. *J. Chem. Phys.*, **25**, 917 (1956).
1632. JOHNSON, W.H. and J.R. AMBROSE. *J. Res. Nat. Bur. Stand.*, **67A**, 427 (1963).
1633. JOHNSON, W.H. and A.A. GILLILAND. *J. Res. Nat. Bur. Stand.*, **65A**, 59 (1961).
1634. JOHNSON, W.H. and A.A. GILLILAND. *J. Res. Nat. Bur. Stand.*, **65A**, 63 (1961).
1635. JOHNSON, W.H., A.A. GILLILAND, and E.J. PROSEN. *J. Res. Nat. Bur. Stand.*, **63A**, 161 (1959).
1636. JOHNSON, W.H., A.A. GILLILAND, and E.J. PROSEN. *J. Res. Nat. Bur. Stand.*, **64A**, 515 (1960).
1637. JOHNSON, W.H., J. JAFFE, and E.J. PROSEN. *J. Res. Nat. Bur. Stand.*, **65A**, 71 (1961).
1638. JOHNSON, W.H., M.V. KILDAY, and E.J. PROSEN. *J. Res. Nat. Bur. Stand.*, **64A**, 521 (1960).
1639. JOHNSON, W.H., M.V. KILDAY, and E.J. PROSEN. *J. Res. Nat. Bur. Stand.*, **65A**, 215 (1961).
1640. JOHNSON, W.H., R.G. MILLER, and E.J. PROSEN. *J. Res. Nat. Bur. Stand.*, **62**, 213 (1959).

1641. JOHNSON, W.H., R.A. NELSON, and E.J. PROSEN. *J. Res. Nat. Bur. Stand.*, **62**, 49 (1959).
1642. JOHNSON, W.H., E.J. PROSEN, and F.D. ROSSINI. *J. Res. Nat. Bur. Stand.*, **36**, 463 (1946); **37**, 51 (1946).
1643. JOHNSON, W.H., R.H. SCHUMM, J.H. WILSON, and E.J. PROSEN. *J. Res. Nat. Bur. Stand.*, **65a**, 97 (1961).
1644. JOHNSON, W.H. and S. SUNNER. *Acta chem. scand.*, **17**, 1916 (1963).
1645. JOHNSTON, H.L. and T.W. BAUER. *J.Am. Chem. Soc.*, **73**, 1119 (1951).
1646. JOHNSTON, H.L. and H.J. BERLIN. *J. Am. Chem. Soc.*, **81**, 6402 (1959).
1647. JOHNSTON, H.L. and N.C. HALLET. *J. Am. Chem. Soc.*, **75**, 1467 (1953).
1648. JOHNSTON, H.L., H.N. HERSH, and E.C. KERR. *J. Am. Chem. Soc.*, **73**, 1112 (1951).
1649. JOHNSTON, H.L., J.H. HU, and W.S. HORTON. *J. Am. Chem. Soc.*, **75**, 3922 (1963).
1650. JOHNSTON, H.L. and E.C. KERR. *J. Am. Chem. Soc.*, **72**, 4333 (1950).
1651. JOLLY, W.L. and W.M. LATIMER. *J. Am. Chem. Soc.*, **74**, 5757 (1952).
1652. JOLLY, W.L. and W.M. LATIMER. *J. Am. Chem. Soc.*, **74**, 5757 (1952) [Repetition in Russian Source.]
1653. JONES, L.H. *J. Chem. Phys.*, **25**, 1069 (1956).
1654. JONES, L.H. and R.S. McDOWELL. *J. Molec. Spectrosc.*, **3**, 632 (1959).
1654a. JONES, M.M., B.J. YOW, and W.R. MAY. *Inorg. Chem.*, **1**, 166 (1962).
1655. JONES, W.A. *J. Chem. Phys.*, **16**, 1077 (1948).
1656. JONES, W.M., J. GORDON, and E.A. LONG. *J. Chem. Phys.*, **20**, 695 (1952).
1657. JUNGERS, J.C. *Bull. Soc. chim. belg.*, **58**, 196 (1949).
1658. JUSTICE, B.H. and E.F. WESTRUM. *J. Phys. Chem.*, **67**, 339 (1963).
1659. JUSTICE, B.H. and E.F. WESTRUM. *J. Phys. Chem.*, **67**, 345 (1963).
1660. JUZA, R. and P. LAURER. *Z. anorg. allg. Chem.*, **275**, 79 (1953).
1661. JUZA, R. and W. UPHOFF. *Z. anorg. allg. Chem.*, **287**, 113 (1956).
1662. JUZA, R., G. WAINHOFF, and W. UPHOFF. *Z. anorg. allg. Chem.*, **296**, 157 (1958).
1663. KAARSEMAKER, S. and J. COOPS. *Rec. trav. chim.*, **71**, 261 (1952).
1663a. KANGRO, W. *J. Chem. Eng. Data*, **7**, 618 (1961).
1664. KANGRO, W. and E. PETERSEN. *Z. anorg. allg. Chem.*, **264**, 157 (1950).
1665. KANGRO, W. and T. WAINGÄRTNER. *Z. Elektrochem.*, **58**, 504 (1954).
1666. KARASZ, F.E., H.E. BAIR, and J.M. O'REILLY. *J. Phys. Chem.*, **69**, 2657 (1965).
1666a. KARNES, H.A., B.D. KYBETT, M.H. WILSØN, J.L. MARGRAVE, and M.S. NEWMAN. *J. Am. Chem. Soc.*, 87, 5554 (1965).
1667. KARO, A.M. *J. Chem. Phys.*, **31**, 1489 (1960).
1668. KARO, A.M. *J. Chem. Phys.*, **33**, 7 (1961).
1669. KASCHIO, W. *J. Inorg. Nucl. Chem.*, **27**, 750 (1965).
1670. KAUFMAN, E.D. and J.F. REED. *J. Phys. Chem.*, **67**, 896 (1963).
1670a. KAVELIS. *Vilnius Univ. Mokslo Darbai, Chem.*, **28**, 110 (1959) (cited in [1482a]).
1671. KAWASAKI, Y., T. TANAKA, and R. OKAWARA. *Technol. Repts. Osaka Univ.*, **13**, 217 (1963).
1672. KAY, A.E. and R.G. LOASBY. *Phil. Mag.*, **9**, 37 (1964).
1673. KEFFLER, L.J.P., *J. Phys. Chem.*, **41**, 715 (1937).
1674. KEFFLER, L.J.P. and G.B. GUTHRIE. *J. Phys. Chem.*, **31**, 65 (1927).
1675. KELLEY, H.H. *Trans. Metallurg. Soc. AIME*, **230**, 1622 (1964).
1676. KELLEY, K.K. *J. Am. Chem. Soc.*, **51**, 1145 (1929).
1677. KELLEY, K.K. *J. Am. Chem. Soc.*, **51**, 1400 (1929).
1678. KELLEY, K.K. *Bull. U.S. Bur. Mines*, No. 406 (1937).
1679. KELLEY, K.K. *Bull. U.S. Bur. Mines*, No. 476 (1940).
1680. KELLEY, K.K. *Bull. U.S. Bur. Mines*, No. 477 (1950).
1681. KELLEY, K.K. *Bur. Mines Rept. of Investig.*, 5901, Wash., 1962.
1682. KELLEY, K.K., L.H. ADAMI, and E.G. KING. *Bur. Mines Rept. of Investig.*, 6197, Washington, 1963.
1683. KELLEY, K.K. and C.T. ANDERSON. *Bull. U.S. Bur. Mines*, No. 384 (1935).
1684. KELLEY, K.K., R. BARANY, E.G. KING, and A.U. CHRISTENSEN. *Bur. Mines Rept. of Investig.*, 5436, 1959; (cited in [1681]).
1685. KELLEY, K.K. and E.G. KING. *Contribution to the Data on Theoretical Metallurgy. XIV. Entropies of the Elements and Inorganic Compounds. Bur. Mines Bull.*, 592, Wash. (1961).
1686. KELLEY, K.K. and A.D. MAH. *Metallurgical Thermochemistry of Titanium. Bur. Mines Rept. of Investig.*, 5490, Wash., 1959.
1687. KELLEY, K.K., S.S. TODD, R.L. ORR, E.G. KING, and K.R. BONNICKSON. *Bur. Mines Rept. of Investig.*, 4955, Wash., 1953.
1688. KELLEY, K.K. and W.W. WELLER. *Bur. Mines Rept. of Investig.*, 5810, Wash., 1961 (cited in [775]).
1689. KELLY, J.C.R. and P.E. SNYDER. *J. Am. Chem. Soc.*, **73**, 4114 (1951).
1690. KENDALL, W.B. *J. Chem. Eng. Data*, **7**, 540 (1962).
1691. KENDALL, W.B., R. L'ORR, and R. HULTGREN. *J. Chem. Eng. Data*, **7**, 516 (1962).
1692. KENNEDY, S.M., M. SAGENKAHN, and J.G. ASTON. *J. Am. Chem. Soc.*, **63**, 2267 (1941).
1693. KENNELLEY, J.A., J.W. VARWIG, and H.W. MYERS. *J. Phys. Chem.*, **64**, 703 (1960).
1694. KENESHEA, F.J. and D.D. CUBICCIOTTI. *J. Chem. Phys.*, **40**, 1778 (1964).
1695. KENESHEA, F.J. and D.D. CUBICCIOTTI. *J. Phys. Chem.*, **69**, 3910 (1965).

1696. KERR, A.A. and J.G. CALVERT. *J. Phys. Chem.*, **69**, 1022 (1955).
1697. KERR, E.C., N.C. HALLETT, and H.L. JOHNSTON. *J. Am. Chem. Soc.*, **73**, 1117 (1951).
1698. KERR, E.C., H.N. HERSH, and H.L. JOHNSTON. *J. Am. Chem. Soc.*, **72**, 4738 (1950).
1699. KERR, E.C., H.L. JOHNSTON, and N.C. HALLETT. *J. Am. Chem. Soc.*, **72**, 4710 (1950).
1700. KETCHEN, E.E. and W.E. WALLAGE. *J. Am. Chem. Soc.*, **73**, 5810 (1951).
1701. KETCHEN, E.E. and W.E. WALLAGE. *J. Am. Chem. Soc.*, **76**, 4736 (1954).
1702. KIHIRA, A. *Res. Repts. Fac. Eng. Nagoja Univ.*, 3, 39 (1950).
1703. KILDAY, M.V., W.H. JOHNSON, and E.J. PROSEN. *J. Res. Nat. Bur. Stand.*, **65A**, 101 (1961).
1704. HILDAY, M.V., W.H. JOHNSON, and E.J. PROSEN. *J. Res. Nat. Bur. Stand.*, **65A**, 435 (1961).
1705. KILDAY, M.V. and E.J. PROSEN. *J. Am. Chem. Soc.*, **82**, 5508 (1960).
1706. KILDAY, M.V. and E.J. PROSEN. *J. Res. Nat. Bur. Stand.*, **68A**, 127 (1964).
1707. KILPATRIK, J.E., C.W. BECKETT, E.J. PROSEN, K.S. PITZER, and F.D. ROSSINI. *J. Res. Nat. Bur. Stand.*, **42**, 225 (1949).
1708. KILPATRIK, J.E. and K.S. PITZER. *J. Res. Nat. Bur. Stand.*, **37**, 163 (1946).
1708a. KILPATRIK, J.E. and K.S. PITZER. *J. Am. Chem. Soc.*, **68**, 1066 (1946).
1709. KILPATRIK, J.E., E.J. PROSEN, K.S. PITZER, and F.D. ROSSINI. *J. Res. Nat. Bur. Stand.*, **36**, 559 (1946).
1710. KILPATRIK, J.E., H.G. WERNER, C.W. BECKETT, K.S. PITZER, and F.D. ROSSINI. *J. Res. Nat. Bur. Stand.*, **39**, 523 (1947).
1711. KING, E.G. *Ind. Eng. Chem.*, **41**, 1298 (1949).
1712. KING, E.G. *J. Am. Chem. Soc.*, **73**, 656 (1951).
1713. KING, E.G. *J. Am. Chem. Soc.*, **74**, 4446 (1952).
1714. KING, E.G. *J. Am. Chem. Soc.*, **76**, 3289 (1954).
1715. KING, E.G. *J. Am. Chem. Soc.*, **76**, 5849 (1954).
1716. KING, E.G. *J. Am. Chem. Soc.*, **77**, 2150 (1955).
1717. KING, E.G. *J. Am. Chem. Soc.*, **77**, 2192 (1955).
1718. KING, E.G. *J. Am. Chem. Soc.*, **77**, 3189 (1955).
1719. KING, E.G. *J. Phys. Chem.*, **59**, 218 (1955).
1720. KING, E.G. *J. Phys. Chem.*, **60**, 410 (1956).
1721. KING, E.G. *J. Am. Chem. Soc.*, **79**, 2056 (1957).
1722. KING, E.G. *J. Am. Chem. Soc.*, **79**, 2399 (1957).
1723. KING, E.G. *J. Am. Chem. Soc.*, **79**, 5437 (1957).
1724. KING, E.G. *J. Am. Chem. Soc.*, **80**, 1799 (1958).
1725. KING, E.G. *J. Am. Chem. Soc.*, **80**, 2400 (1958).
1726. KING, E.G. *J. Am. Chem. Soc.*, **81**, 799 (1959).
1727. KING, E.G. cited in [677].
1728. KING, E.G. and A.U. CHRISTENSEN. *J. Phys. Chem.*, **62**, 499 (1958).
1729. KING, E.G. and A.U. CHRISTENSEN. *Bur. Mines Report of Investig.*, 5510, U.S. Dept. of Interior, Wash., 1959 (cited in [2648]).
1730. KING, E.G. and E.R. LIPPINCOTT. *J. Am. Chem. Soc.*, **78**, 4192 (1956).
1731. KING, E.G., R.L. ORR, and K.R. BONNICKSON. *J. Am. Chem. Soc.*, **76**, 4320 (1954).
1732. KING, E.G. and S.S. TODD. *J. Am. Chem. Soc.*, **75**, 3023 (1953).
1733. KING, E.G. and W.W. WELLER. *Bur. Mines Report of Investig.*, 5571, U.S. Dept. of Interior, Wash., 1960.
1734. KING, E.G. and W.W. WELLER. *Bur. Mines Report of Investig.*, 5590, U.S. Dept. of Interior, Wash., 1960.
1735. KING, E.G. and W.W. WELLER. *Bur. Mines Report of Investig.*, 5855, U.S. Dept. of Interior, Wash., 1961.
1736. KING, E.G. and W.W. WELLER. *Bur. Mines Report of Investig.*, B6001, U.S. Dept. of Interior, Wash., 1962.
1737. KING, E.G., W.W. WELLER, and A.U. CHRISTENSEN. *Bur. Mines Report of Investig.*, 5664, U.S. Dept. of Interior, Wash., 1960.
1738. KING, E.G., W.W. WELLER, and L.B. PANKRATZ. *Bur. Mines Report of Investig.*, 5857, U.S. Dept. of Interior, Wash., 1961.
1739. KING, J.P. and J.W. COBBLE. *J. Am. Chem. Soc.*, **82**, 2111 (1960).
1739a. KIRKBRIDE, F.W. *J. Appl. Chem.*, **6**, 11 (1956).
1740. KIRKBRIDE, F.W. and F.G. DAVIDSON. *Nature*, **174**, 79 (1954).
1741. KIRKWOOD, D.H. and J. CHIPMAN. *J. Phys. Soc.*, **65**, 1682 (1961).
1742. KIRSCHENBAUM, A.D., A.V. GROSSE, and J.G. ASTON. *J. Am. Chem. Soc.*, **81**, 6398 (1959).
1743. KIRSCHNING, H.J., K. PLIETH, and J.N. STRANSKI. *Z. Kristallogr.*, **106**, 172 (1954).
1744. KISTIAKOWSKY, G.B. and W.W. RICE. *J. Chem. Phys.*, **8**, 610 (1940).
1745. KISTIAKOWSKY, G.B. and C.H. STAUFFER. *J. Am. Chem. Soc.*, **59**, 165 (1937).
1746. KLANBERG, F. and H. SPANDAU. *J. Inorg. Nucl. Chem.*, **19**, 180 (1962).
1747. KLEPPA, O.J. *J. Am. Chem. Soc.*, **77**, 897 (1955).
1748. KNOPP, J.A., W.S. LINKELL, and W.C. CHILD. *J. Phys. Chem.*, **66**, 1513 (1962).
1748a. KNOWLTON, J.W. and H.M. HUFFMAN. *J. Am. Chem. Soc.*, **66**, 1492 (1944).
1749. KO, H.C. and L.G. HEPLER. *J. Chem. Eng. Data*, **8**, 59 (1963).
1750. KOBE, K.A. and R.H. HARRISON. *Petr. Refiner*, **36**, 155 (1957).
1751. KOBE, K.A., R.H. HARRISON, and R.E. PENNINGTON. *Petr. Refiner*, **30**, 119 (1951).
1752. KOEHLER, M.F. and J.P. COUGHLIN. *J. Phys. Chem.*, **63**, 605 (1959).

1753. KOEHLER, Mary F., L.B. PANKRATZ, and R. BARANY. *Bur. Mines Report of Investg.*, 5973, U.S. Dept. of Interior, Wash., 1962.
1754. KOERNER, W.E. and F. DANIELS. *J. Chem. Phys.*, **20**, 113 (1952).
1755. KOHLHAAS, R., M. BRAUN, and O. VILLMER. *Z. Naturforsch.*, **20a**, 1077 (1965).
1756. KOKICHI SANO. *Sci. Repts. Tohoku Univ.*, **37**, Ser. 1, No. 1, 1 (1953).
1757. KOLSKY, H.G. and P.W. GILLES. *J. Chem. Phys.*, **22**, 232 (1954).
1758. KOLSKY, H.G. and P.W. GILLES. *J. Chem. Phys.*, **24**, 828 (1956).
1759. KOTHARI, L.S. and V.K. TEWARY. *J. Chem. Phys.*, **38**, 417 (1963).
1760. KOTHEN, C.W. and H.L. JOHNSTON. *J. Am. Chem. Soc.*, **75**, 3101 (1953).
1761. KRIEVE, W.F., S.P. VANGO, and D.M. MASON. *J. Chem. Phys.*, **25**, 519 (1956).
1762. KRIKORIAN, O.H. *Univ. of California Radiation Labor. Report,* UCRL-2888, 1955 (cited in [1578]).
1763. KRIKORIAN, O.H. *Univ. of California Radiation Labor. Report,* UCRL-6785, 1962; (cited in [472]).
1764. KRIKORIAN, O.H. *J. Phys. Chem.*, **67**, 1586 (1963).
1764a. KRIKORIAN, O.H. and J.H. CARPENTER. *J. Phys. Chem.*, **69**, 4399 (1965).
1765. KRISHNA PILLAI, M.G. and A. PERUMAL. *Bull. Soc. chim. belg.*, **74**, 29 (1964).
1766. KRÖGER, C. and W. JANETZKO. *Z. anorg. allg. Chem.*, **284**, 83 (1956).
1767. KRUGER, O.L. and H. SAVAGE. *J. Chem. Phys.*, **40**, 3324 (1964).
1768. KRUIS, A. *Z. Naturforsch.*, **3a**, 596 (1948).
1769. KUAN PAN. *J. Chinese Soc.* (Taiwan), Ser. II, **1**, 1, 16, 26 (1954); *Chem. Abstr.*, **49**, 7419g (1955).
1770. KUBASCHEWSKI, O. *Z. Elektrochem.*, **54**, 275 (1950).
1771. KUBASCHEWSKI. O. *Angew. Chem.*, **72**, 255 (1960).
1772. KUBASCHEWSKI, O. and J.A. CATTERALL. *Thermodynamic Data of Alloys.* Pergamon Press, London, New York, 1956.
1772a. KUBASCHEWSKI. O and W.A. DENCH. *Acta metallurg.*, **3**, 339 (1955).
1773. KUBASCHEWSKI, O. and E.L. EVANS. *Metallurgical Thermochemistry,* Pergamon Press, London, New York, Paris, Los Angeles, 3, ed. 1958.
1774. KUBASCHEWSKI, O. and H. VILLA. *Z. Elektrochem.*, **53**, 32 (1949).
1775. KUBASCHEWSKI, O., H. VILLA, and W.A. DENCH. *Trans. Faraday Soc.*, **52**, 214 (1956).
1776. KUČIREK, J. and D. PAPOUŠEK. Coll. Czech, Chem. Comm., **25**, 31 (1960).
1777. KUČIREK, J. and D. PAPOUŠEK. Coll. Czech. Chem. Comm., **26**, 1458 (1961).
1778. KURY, J.W. *U.S. Atomic Energy Comm., Tech. Inform. Service,* Oak Ridge, Tenn., UCRL-2271, 1953; *Chem. Abstr.*, **48**, 3833c (1954).
1779. KURY, J.W., A.J. ZIELEN, and W.M. LATIMER. *J. Electrochem. Soc.*, **100**, 468 (1953).
1780. KYBETT, B.D., G.K. JOHNSON, C.K. BARKER, and J.L. MARGRAVE. *J. Phys. Chem.*, **69**, 3603 (1965).
1781. LABBAUF, A. and F.D. ROSSINI. *J. Phys. Chem.*, **65**, 476 (1961).
1782. LABOWITZ, L.C. and E.F. WESTRUM. *J. Phys. Chem.*, **65**, 403 (1961).
1783. LABOWITZ, L.C. and E.F. WESTRUM. *J. Phys. Chem.*, **65**, 408 (1961).
1784. LACHER, J.R., L. CASALI, and J.D. PARK. *J. Phys. Chem.*, **60**, 608 (1956).
1785. LACHER, J.R., E. EMERY, E. BOHMFALK, and J.D. PARK. *J. Phys. Chem.*, **60**, 492 (1956).
1786. LACHER, J.K., A. KIANPOUR, P. MONTGOMERY, H. KNEDLER, and J.D. PARK. *J. Phys. Chem.*, **61**, 1125 (1957).
1787. LACHER, J.R., A. KIANPOUR, F. OETTING, and J.D. PARK. *Trans. Faraday Soc.*, **52(11)**, 1500 (1956).
1788. LACINA, J.L., W.D. GOOD, and J.P. McCULLOUGH. *J. Phys. Chem.*, **65**, 1026 (1961).
1789. LADD, M.F.C. and W.H. LEE. *J. Inorg. Nucl. Chem.*, **19**, 218 (1960).
1789a. LADD, M.F.C. and W.H. LEE. *J. Inorg. Nucl. Chem.*, **21**, 216 (1961).
1790. LAGEMANN, R.T. and C.H. KNOWLES. *J. Chem. Phys.*, **32**, 561 (1960).
1791. LANDRIEU, BAYLOCQ, and JOHNSON. *Bull. Soc. chim. France,* **45**, 36 (1929).
1792. LANE, M.R., J.W. LINNETT, and H.G. OSWIN. *Proc. Roy. Soc.*, **A216**, 361 (1953).
1793. LARMANN, J.P., D.E. MARTIRE, and L.Z. POLLARA. *J. Chem. Eng. Data,* **6**, 330 (1961).
1794. LATIMER, W.M. *J. Am. Chem. Soc.*, **73**, 1480 (1951).
1795. LAUBENGAUER, A.W. and D.C. SEARS. *J. Am. Chem. Soc.*, **67**, 164 (1945).
1796. LEACH, H.F. and H.L. ROBERTS. *J. Chem. Soc.*, **1960**, 4693.
1797. LEADBETTER, A.J. and J.E. SPICE. *Can. J. Chem.*, **37**, 1923 (1959).
1798. LEHMANN, H. *Chem. Techn.*, **14**, 132 (1962).
1799. LEMAN and LEPOUTRE. *Compt. rend.*, **226**, 1976 (1948).
1800. LEITNAKER, J.M., M.G. BOWMAN, and P.W. GILLES. *J. Electrochem.*, **109**, 441 (1962).
1801. LEITNAKER, J.M. and W.G. WITTEMAN. *J. Chem. Phys.*, **36**, 1445 (1962).
1802. LEVERNE, P.F. and L.G. HEPLER. *J. Phys. Chem.*, **53**, 110 (1959).
1803. LEVITIN, N.E., E.F. WESTRUM, and J.C. CARTER. *J. Am. Chem. Soc.*, **81**, 3547 (1959).
1804. LI, J.C.M. *J. Am. Chem. Soc.*, **78**, 1081 (1956).
1805. LI, J.C.M. and N.M. GREGORY. *J. Am. Chem. Soc.*, **74**, 4670 (1952).
1806. LI, J.C.M. and K.S. PITZER. *J. Am. Chem. Soc.*, **78**, 1077 (1956).
1807. LIFSHITZ, C. and F.A. LONG. *J. Phys. Chem.*, **69**, 3731 (1965).
1808. LIPPINCOTT, E.R. and M.C. TOBIN. *J. Am. Chem. Soc.*, **75**, 4141 (1953).
1809. LOEHMAN, R.E., R.A. KENT, and J.L. MARGRAVE. *J. Chem. Eng. Data,* **10**, 296 (1965).

1810. LOHR, H.R. and B.B. CUNNINGHAM. *J. Am. Chem. Soc.*, **73**, 2025 (1951).
1811. LOHR, H.R., D.W. OSBORNE, and E.F. WESTRUM. *J. Am. Chem. Soc.*, **76**, 3837 (1954).
1812. LONG, L.H. *Quart. Rev.*, **7**, 134 (1953).
1813. LONG, L.H. and J.F. SACKMAN. *Trans. Faraday Soc.*, **53**, 1606 (1957).
1814. LONG, L.H. and J.F. SACKMAN. *Trans. Faraday Soc.*, **54**, 1797 (1958).
1815. LONG, L.H. and J.F. SACKMAN. *J. Inorg. Nucl. Chem.*, **25**, 93 (1963).
1816. LONSDALL, H.K. and J.N. GRAVES. *Thermodynamics of Nuclear Materials.* International Atomic Energy Agency, Vienna, 1962, p. 601.
1817. LORD, G. and A.A. WOOLF. *J. Chem. Soc.*, **1954**, 2546.
1817a. LORD, R.C. and C.M. STEESE. *J. Chem. Phys.*, **22**, 542 (1954).
1818. LORENZELLI, V. *Compt. rend.*, **253**, 2052 (1961).
1819. LOVEJOY, R.W., J.H. COLWELL, D.F. EGGERS, and G.D. HASLEY. *J. Chem. Phys.*, **36**, 612 (1962).
1820. LOW, D.J.R. and E.A. MOELWYN-HUGHES. *Proc. Roy. Soc.*, **A267**, 384 (1962).
1820a. LOWE, TOPLEY, ALBRIGHT, and WILSON (cited in [1482a]).
1821. LUDWIG, J.R. and W.J. COOPER. *J. Chem. Eng. Data*, **8**, 76 (1963).
1822. LUFT, N.W. *J. Chem. Phys.*, **21**, 1900 (1953).
1822a. LUFT, N.W. *J. Chem. Phys.*, **22**, 155 (1954).
1823. LUFT, N.W. *J. Phys. Chem.*, **58**, 928 (1954).
1823a. LUFT, N.W. *J. Chem. Phys.*, **23**, 973 (1955).
1824. LUFT, N.W. and O.P. KHARBANDA. *J. Chem. Phys.*, **22**, 956 (1954).
1825. LUNDIN, C.E. and J.P. BLACKLEDGE. *J. Electrochem. Soc.*, **109**, 838 (1962).
1826. LUNGU, S.N. *Studii şi cercetări fiz. Acad. RPR*, **13**, 29 (1962).
1827. LYNDS, L. and C.D. BASS. *Inorg. Chem.*, **3**, 1147 (1964).
1828. LYON, T.F. *Condensation and Evaporation of Solids.* New York, London, Goldstein and Irulson, 1964, p. 435.
1829. LYONS, V.J. and V.J. SILVESTRY. *J. Phys. Chem.*, **64**, 266 (1960).
1830. McBRIDE, J., S. HEIMEL, J.G. EHLERS, and S. GORDON. *Thermodynamic Properties to 6000°K for 210 Substances Involving the First 18 Elements.* NASASP-3001, Washington, 1963.
1831. McCARLEY, R.E. and J.W. RODDY. *Inorg. Chem.*, **3**, 60 (1964).
1832. McCLELLAN, A.G. and G.C. PIMENTEL. *J. Chem. Phys.*, **23**, 245 (1955).
1833. McCORMACK, J.M., J.R. MYERS, and R.K. SAXED. *J. Chem. Eng. Data*, **10**, 319 (1965).
1834. McCULLOUGH, J.P., D.R. DOUSLIN, J.F. MESSERLY, I.A. HOSSENLOPP, T.C. KINCHELOE, and G. WADDINGTON. *J. Am. Chem. Soc.*, **79**, 4289 (1957).
1835. McCULLOUGH, J.P., H.L. FINKE, M.E. GROSS, J.F. MESSERLY, and G. WADDINGTON. *J. Phys. Chem.*, **61**, 289 (1957).
1836. McCULLOUGH, J.P., H.L. FINKE, W.N. HUBBARD, W.D. GOOD, R.E. PENNINGTON, J.F. MESSERLY, and G. WADDINGTON. *J. Am. Chem. Soc.*, **76**, 2661 (1954).
1837. McCULLOUGH, J.P., H.L. FINKE, W.N. HUBBARD, S.S. TODD, J.F. MESSERLY, D.R. DOUSLIN, and G. WADDINGTON. *J. Phys. Chem.*, **65**, 784 (1961).
1838. McCULLOUGH, J.P., H.L. FINKE, J.F. MESSERLY, S.S. TODD, J.C. KINCHELEE, and G. WADDINGTON. *J. Phys. Chem.*, **61**, 1105 (1957).
1839. McCULLOUGH, J.P., H.L. FINKE, D.W. SCOTT, M.E. GROSS, J.F. MESSERLY, R.E. PENNINGTON, and G. WADDINGTON. *J. Am. Chem. Soc.*, **76**, 4796 (1954).
1840. McCULLOUGH, J.P., H.L. FINKE, et. al. *J. Am. Chem. Soc.*, **77**, 6119 (1955).
1841. McCULLOUGH, J.P., H.L. FINKE, et. al. *J. Am. Chem. Soc.*, **80**, 4786 (1958).
1842. McCULLOUGH, J.P. and W.P. GOOD. *J. Phys. Chem.*, **65**, 1430 (1961).
1843. McCULLOUGH, J.P., W.N. HUBBARD, F.R. FROW, I.A. HOSSENLOPP, and G. WADDINGTON. *J. Am. Chem. Soc.*, **79**, 561 (1957).
1844. McCULLOUGH, J.P., J.F. MESSERLY, R.T. MOORE, and S.S. TODD. *J. Phys. Chem.*, **67**, 677 (1963).
1845. McCULLOUGH, J.P. and D.W. SCOTT. *J. Am. Chem. Soc.*, **81**, 1331 (1959).
1846. McCULLOUGH, J.P., D.W. SCOTT, H.L. FINKE, M.E. GROSS, K.D. WILLIAMSON, R.E. PENNINGTON, G. WADDINGTON, and H.M. HUFFMAN. *J. Am. Chem. Soc.*, **74**, 2801 (1952).
1847. McCULLOUGH, J.P., D.W. SCOTT, H.L. FINKE, W.N. HUBBARD, M.E. GROSS, C. KATZ, R.E. PENNINGTON, J.F. MESSERLY, and G. WADDINGTON. *J. Am. Chem. Soc.*, **75**, 1818 (1953).
1848. McCULLOUGH, J.P., D.W. SCOTT, R.E. PENNINGTON, J.A. HOSSENLOPP, and G. WADDINGTON. *J. Am. Chem. Soc.*, **76**, 4791 (1954).
1849. McCULLOUGH, J.P., S. SUNNER, H.L. FINKE, W.N. HUBBARD, M.E. GROSS, R.E. PENNINGTON, J.F. MESSERLY, W.D. GOOD, and G. WADDINGTON. *J. Am. Chem. Soc.*, **75**, 5075 (1953).
1850. McDONALD, J.E. and J.W. COBBLE. *J. Phys. Chem.*, **65**, 2014 (1961).
1851. McDONALD, J.E. and J.W. COBBLE. *J. Phys. Chem.*, **66**, 791 (1962).
1852. McDONALD, J.E., J.P. KING, and J.W. COBBLE. *J. Phys. Chem.*, **64**, 1345 (1960).
1853. McDONALD, R.A. and F.L. OETTING. *J. Phys. Chem.*, **69**, 3839 (1965).
1854. McDONALD, R.A., G.C. SINKE, and D.R. STULL. *J. Chem. Eng. Data*, **7**, 83 (1962).
1855. McDONALD, R.A. and D.R. STULL. *J. Chem. Eng. Data*, **6**, 609 (1961).
1856. McDONALD, R.A. and D.R. STULL. *J. Phys. Chem.*, **65**, 1918 (1961).
1857. McDONALD, R.A. and D.R. STULL. *J. Chem. Eng. Data*, **7**, 84 (1962).

1858. McDOUGALL, L.A. and J.E. KILPATRICK. *J. Chem. Phys.*, **42**, 2307 (1965).
1859. McDOUGALL, L.A. and J.E. KILPATRICK. *J. Chem. Phys.*, **42**, 2311 (1965).
1860. McDOWELL, R.S. and L.B. ASPREY. *J. Chem. Phys.*, **37**, 165 (1962).
1861. McDOWELL, R.S. and F.H. KRUSE. *J. Chem. Eng. Data*, **8**, 547 (1963).
1862. McEWAN, W.C. and M.M. WILLIAMS. *J. Am. Chem. Soc.*, **76**, 2182 (1954).
1863. McGEE, P.R., F.E. CLEVELAND, A.G. MEISTER, and C.E. DECKER. *J. Chem. Phys.*, **21**, 242 (1953).
1864. MACHARÁŎEK, K., A.I. ZACHAROV, and L.A. ALJOŠINA. *Chem. Prům.*, **12**, 23 (1962).
1865. MACHLAN, G.R., C.T. STUBBLEFIELD, and L. EYRING. *J. Am. Chem. Soc.*, **77**, 2975 (1955).
1866. MACKLE, H. *Ann. Reports*, **54**, 71 (1957).
1867. MACKLE, H. *Tetrahedron*, **19**, 1159 (1963).
1868. MACKLE, H. and R.T.B. McCLEAN. *Trans. Faraday Soc.*, **58**, 895 (1962).
1869. MACKLE, H. and R.T.B. McCLEAN. *Trans. Faraday Soc.*, **60**, 609 (1964).
1870. MACKLE, H. and R.T.B. McCLEAN – cited in [1879].
1871. MACKLE, H. and R.G. MAYRICK. *Trans. Faraday Soc.*, **58**, 33 (1962).
1872. MACKLE, H. and R.G. MAYRICK. *Trans. Faraday Soc.*, **58**, 230 (1962).
1873. MACKLE, H. and R.G. MAYRICK. *Trans. Faraday Soc.*, **58**, 238 (1962).
1874. MACKLE, H. and P.A.G. O'HARE. *Trans. Faraday Soc.*, **57**, 1070 (1961).
1875. MACKLE, H. and P.A.G. O'HARE. *Trans. Faraday Soc.*, **57**, 1521 (1961).
1876. MACKLE, H. and P.A.G. O'HARE. *Trans. Faraday Soc.*, **57**, 1873 (1961).
1877. MACKLE, H. and P.A.G. O'HARE. *Trans. Faraday Soc.*, **57**, 2119 (1961).
1878. MACKLE, H. and P.A.G. O'HARE. *Trans. Faraday Soc.*, **58**, 1912 (1962).
1879. MACKLE, H. and P.A.G. O'HARE. *Tetrahedron*, **19**, 961 (1963).
1880. MACKLE, H. and P.A.G. O'HARE – cited in [1879].
1881. MACKLE, H. and P.A.G. O'HARE. *Trans. Faraday Soc.*, **59**, 309 (1963).
1882. MACKLE, H. and P.A.G. O'HARE. *Trans. Faraday Soc.*, **59**, 2693 (1963).
1883. MACKLE, H. and P.A.G. O'HARE. *Tetrahedron*, **20**, 611 (1964).
1884. MACKLE, H. and P.A.G. O'HARE. *Trans. Faraday Soc.*, **60**, 506 (1964).
1885. MACKLE, H. and P.A.G. O'HARE. *Trans. Faraday Soc.*, **60**, 666 (1964).
1886. McLAREN, R.O. and N.W. GREGORY. *J. Phys. Chem.*, **59**, 77, 184 (1955).
1887. McLELLAN, R.B. and R. SHUTTLEWORTH. *Z. Metallkunde*, **51**, 143 (1960).
1888. MADIGAN, J.R. and F.F. CLEVELAND. *J. Chem. Phys.*, **19**, 119 (1951).
1889. MAGEE, E.M. *J. Inorg. Nucl. Chem.*, **22**, 155 (1961).
1890. MAGNUS, A. *Z. phys. Chem.* (GFR), 9, 141 (1956).
1890a. MAGNUS, A., H. HARTMANN, and F. BECKER. *Z. phys. Chem.* (Leipzig), **197**, 75 (1951).
1891. MAH, A.D. *J. Am. Chem. Soc.*, **76**, 3363 (1954).
1892. MAH, A.D. *J. Phys. Chem.*, **61**, 1572 (1957).
1893. MAH, A.D. *J. Am. Chem. Soc.*, **80**, 2954 (1958).
1894. MAH, A.D. *J. Am. Chem. Soc.*, **80**, 3872 (1958).
1895. MAH, A.D. *J. Am. Chem. Soc.*, **81**, 1582 (1959).
1896. MAH, A.D. *Bur. Mines Report of Investig.*, 5600, U.S. Dept. of Interior, Wash., 1959.
1897. MAH, A.D. *Bur. Mines Report of Investig.*, 5965, U.S. Dept. of Interior, Wash., 1962.
1898. MAH, A.D. *Bur. Mines Report of Investig.*, 5972, U.S. Dept. of Interior, Wash., 1962.
1899. MAH, A.D. and L.H. ADAMI. *Bur. Mines Report of Investig.*, 6034, U.S. Dept. of Interior, Wash., 1962.
1900. MAH, A.D. *Bur. Mines Report of Investig.*, 6171, U.S. Dept. of Interior, Wash., 1963.
1901. MAH, A.D. *Bur. Mines. Report of Investig.*, 6177, U.S. Dept. of Interior, Wash., 1963.
1902. MAH, A.D. *Bur. Mines, Berkeley Thermodyn. Lab.*, Berkeley, Calif., 1963, 12 pp.
1903. MAH, A.D. *Bur. Mines Report of Investig.*, No. 6337, U.S. Dept. of Interior, Washington, 1963.
1904. MAH, A.D. *Bur. Mines Report of Investig.*, No. 6415, U.S. Dept. of Interior, Washington, 1964.
1905. MAH, A.D. *Bur. Mines Report of Investig.*, No. 6518, U.S. Dept. of Interior, Washington, 1964.
1906. MAH, A.D. and B.J. BOYLE. *J. Am. Chem. Soc.*, **77**, 6512 (1955).
1907. MAH, A.D. and N.L. GELLERT. *J. Am. Chem. Soc.*, **78**, 3261 (1956).
1908. MAIER, C.E., L.G. FASOLINO, and C.E. THALMEYER. *J. Am. Chem. Soc.*, **77**, 4524 (1955).
1909. MAJER, J.R. and C.R. PATRICK. *Nature*, **201**, 1022 (1964).
1910. MANN, D.E. *J. Chem. Phys.*, **22**, 762 (1954).
1911. MANN, D.E., N. ACQUSTA, and E.K. PLYLER. *J. Res. Nat. Bur. Stand.*, **52**, 67 (1954).
1912. MANN, D.E., J.H. MEAL, and E.K. PLYLER. *J. Chem. Phys.*, **24**, 1018 (1956).
1913. MANN, D.E. and E.K. PLYLER. *J. Chem. Phys.*, **23**, 1989 (1955).
1914. MANN, K.H. and A.W. TICKNER. *J. Phys. Chem.*, **64**, 251 (1960).
1915. MANNCHEN, W. and K. BORNKESSEL. *Z. Naturforsch.*, **14a**, 925 (1959).
1916. MANNCHEN, W. and G. JACOBI. *Z. Naturforsch.*, **206**, 178 (1965).
1917. MÅNSSON, M. and S. SUNNER. *Acta chem. scand.*, **16**, 1863 (1962).
1918. MÅNSSON, M. and S. SUNNER. *Acta chem. scand.*, **17**, 723 (1963).
1919. MANZONI-ANSIDEI, S. *Atti accad. nas. Lincei, Rend., Cl. Sci. fis. mat. nat.*, **1**, 465 (1940).
1920. MARGRAVE, J.L. *J. Phys. Chem.*, **66**, 1209 (1962).

1921. MARGRAVE, J.L. *Nature,* **197**, 376 (1963).
1922. MARGRAVE, J.L., M.A. FRISCH, R.G. BAUTISTA, R.L. CLARKE, and W.S. JOHNSON. *J. Am. Chem. Soc.,* **85**, 546 (1963).
1923. MARGRAVE, J.L. and A.S. KANAAN. *J. Phys. Chem.,* **66**, 1200 (1962).
1924. MARKIN, T.L. and D.E.J. ROBERTS. *Thermodynamics of Nuclear Materials,* International Atomic Energy Agency, Vienna, 1962, p. 693.
1925. MARKLEY. *Fatty Acids, International Publishers Inc.,* New York, 1947.
1926. MARKOWITZ, M.M., R.F. HARRIS, and H. STEWART. *J. Phys. Chem.,* **63**, 1325 (1959).
1927. MARONNY, G. *Electrochim. acta,* **1**, 58 (1959).
1928. MARONNY, G. and G. VALENSI. *Intern. Comm. Electrochem., Thermod. and Kinetics,* London, 1957, 1958.
1929. MARSHALL, J.G., L.A.K. STAVELEY, and K.R. HART. *Trans. Faraday Soc.,* **52**, 19 (1956).
1930. MARTIN, D.L. *Can. J. Phys.,* **38**, 25 (1960).
1931. MARTIN, D.L. *Proc. Roy. Soc.,* **A254**, 433 (1960).
1932. MARTIN, D.L. *Proc. Roy. Soc.,* **A254**, 443 (1960).
1933. MARTIN, J.J. *J. Chem. Eng. Data,* 7, 68 (1962).
1934. MARTIN, J.J., J.A. CAMPBELL, and E.M. SEIDEL. *J. Chem. Eng. Data,* 8, 560 (1963).
1935. MASHIKO YOICHIRO. *J. Chem. Soc. Japan, Pure Chem. Sec.,* 79, 963 (1958).
1936. MASHIKO YOICHIRO and K.S. PITZER. *J. Phys. Chem.,* **62**, 367 (1958).
1937. MASI, J.F. *J. Am. Chem. Soc.,* 74, 4738 (1952).
1938. MASSAZZA, F. *Ann. chimica,* **51**, 898 (1961).
1939. MASSAZZA, F. *Ann. chimica,* **52**, 51 (1962).
1940. MASSAZZA, F. and M. CANNAS. *Ann. chimica,* **51**, 904 (1961).
1941. MASSAZZA, F. and R. FADDA. *Ann. chimica,* **54**, 95 (1964).
1942. MATTHEWS, J.F. and J.J. McKETTA. *J. Phys. Chem.,* **65**, 758 (1961).
1943. MATTRAW, H.C., C.F. PACHUCKI, and N.J. HAWKINS. *J. Chem. Phys.,* **22**, 1117 (1954).
1944. MAYER, J.R., C.R. PATRICK, and J.C. ROBB. *Trans. Faraday Soc.,* **57**, 14 (1961).
1945. MAYER, S.W., B.B. OWENS, T.H. RUTHERFORD, and R.B. SERRINS. *J. Phys. Chem.,* **64**, 911 (1960).
1946. MAYO, D.W., H.E. OPITZ, and J.S. PEAKE. *J. Chem. Phys.,* **23**, 1344 (1955).
1947. MEADOWCROFT, T.R. and F.D. RICHARDSON. *Trans. Faraday Soc.,* **59**, 1564 (1963).
1948. MEARS, W. and R. STAHL. *Thermochem. Bull.,* **2**, 5 (1956) (cited in [679]).
1949. MEL, H.C., Z.Z. HUGUS, and W.M. LATIMER. *J. Am. Chem. Soc.,* 78, 1822 (1956).
1950. MEL, H.C., W.L. JOLLEY, and W.M. LATIMER. *J. Am. Chem. Soc.,* 75, 3827 (1953).
1951. MELIA, T.P. *Trans. Faraday Soc.,* **60**, 1286 (1964).
1952. MESCHI, D.J., W.A. CHUPKA, and J. BERKOWITZ. *J. Chem. Phys.,* **33**, 530 (1960).
1953. MESCHI, D.J. and A.W. SEARCY. *J. Phys. Chem.,* **63**, 1175 (1959).
1954. MESSER, C.E., L.G. FASOLINO, and C.E. THALMAYER. *J. Am. Chem. Soc.,* 77, 4524 (1955).
1955. MESSERLY, J.F., S.S. TODD, and H.L. FINKE. *J. Phys. Chem.* **69**, 353 (1965).
1955a. MESSERLY, J.F., S.S. TODD, and H.L. FINKE. *J. Phys. Chem.,* **69**, 4304 (1965).
1956. METLAY, M. and G.E. KIMBALL. *J. Chem. Phys.,* **16**, 774 (1948).
1957. MEZAKI, R. M. Sc. Thesis, Univ. of Wisconsin, 1961 (cited in [1958]).
1958. MEZAKI, R. and J.L. MARGRAVE. *J. Phys. Chem.,* **66**, 1713 (1962).
1959. MEZAKI, R., E.W. TILLEUX, D.W. BARNES, and J.L. MARGRAVE. *Thermodynamics of nuclear materials,* International Atomic Energy Agency, Vienna, 1962, p. 775.
1959a. MIKAWA YUKIO. *J. Chem. Soc. Japan,* Pure Chem. Sec., **81**, 1512 (1960).
1960. MIKUS, F.F. and S.J. CARLYON. *J. Am. Chem. Soc.,* 72, 2295 (1950).
1960a. MILES and HUNT. *J. Phys. Chem.,* **45**, 1346 (1941).
1961. MILLER, A.R. and A.W. SEARCY. *J. Phys. Chem.,* **67**, 2400 (1963).
1962. MILLER, A.R. and A.W. SEARCY. *J. Phys. Chem.,* **69**, 3826 (1965).
1963. MILLER, G.A. *J. Chem. Eng. Data,* 8, 69 (1963).
1964. MILLER, G.A. *J. Phys. Chem.,* **67**, 1363 (1963).
1965. MILLIGAN, D.E., E.D. BECKER, and K.S. PITZER. *J. Am. Chem. Soc.,* 78, 2707 (1956).
1966. MILLIGAN, D.E. and M.E. JACOX. *J. Chem. Phys.,* **39**, 712 (1963).
1967. MILLIKAN, R.C. and K.S. PITZER. *J. Chem. Phys.,* **27**, 1305 (1957).
1968. MILNE, T.A. and P.W. GILLES. *J. Am. Chem. Soc.,* **81**, 6115 (1959).
1969. MIRATA, H. and K. KAWAI. *J. Chem. Phys.,* **28**, 516 (1958).
1970. MITACEK, P. and J.G. ASTON. *J. Am. Chem. Soc.,* **85**, 137 (1963).
1971. MITSUTANY, A. *J. Chem. Soc. Japan,* **80**, 888 (1959).
1972. MIYAZAWA, T. and K.S. PITZER. *J. Am. Chem. Soc.,* **80**, 60 (1958).
1973. MOLE, M.F. and J.C. McCOUBREY. *Nature,* **202**, 450 (1964).
1974. MONCHAMP, R.R. and F.A. COTTON. *J. Chem. Soc.,* **1960**, 1438.
1975. MONTGOMERY, R.L. *Bur. Mines Report of Investig.,* **5445**, U.S. Dept. of Interior, Wash., 1959.
1976. MONTGOMERY, R.L. *Bur. Mines Report of Investig.,* **5468**, U.S. Dept. of Interior, Wash., 1959.
1977. MONTGOMERY, R.L. and T.D. HUBERT. *Bur. Mines Report of Investig.,* 5525, U.S. Dept. of Interior, Wash., 1959.
1978. MOORE, C.B. and G.C. PIMENTEL. *J. Chem. Phys.,* **38**, 2816 (1963).

1979. MOORE, G.E., M.L. RENQUIST, and G.S. PARKS. *J. Am. Chem. Soc.*, **62**, 1505 (1940).
1979a. MOREAU, H. and M. DODE. *Bull. Soc. chim. France*, **4**, 637 (1937).
1980. MORFEE, R.G.S., L.A.K. STAVELEY, S.T. WALTERS, and D.L. WIGLEY. *Phys. a. Chem. Solids*, **13**, 132 (1960).
1981. MORI, M. and R. TSUCHIYA. *Bull. Chem. Soc. Japan*, **32**, 467 (1959).
1982. MORI, M., R. TSUCHIYA, and Y. OKANO. *Bull. Chem. Soc. Japan*, **32**, 462 (1959).
1983. MORRIS, D.F.C. *Phys. a. Chem. Solids*, **5**, 264 (1958).
1984. MORRIS, D.F.C. *Rec. trav. chim.*, 78, 150 (1959).
1985. MORSY, T.E. *Bunsenges. phys. Chem.*, **68**, 277 (1964).
1986. MORTIMER, C.T. *"Thermodynamics", Proc. of the Symp. on Thermod., Aug. 1959*, London, Butterworth, 1961, p. 71.
1987. MORTIMER, C T. and P.W. SELLERS. *J. Chem. Soc.*, **1963**, 1978.
1988. MORTIMER, C.T. and P.W. SELLERS. *J. Chem. Soc.*, **1964**, 1965.
1989. MOUREU and DODE. *Bull. Soc. chim. France*, **4**, 637 (1937).
1990. MUJLHOFF, F.C. *Rec. Trav. chim.*, **82**, 822 (1963).
1991. MUKAIBO, T. and K. NAITO. *J. Atomic Energy Soc. Japan*, **5**, 601 (1963).
1992. MUKAIBO, T., K. NAITA, K. SATO, and T. UCHUIMA. *Thermodynamics of Nuclear Materials.* International Atomic Energy Agency, Vienna, 1962, p. 645.
1993. MUKAIBO, T., K. NAITO, K. SATO, and T. UCHUIMA. *Thermodynamics of Nuclear Materials.* International Atomic Energy Agency, Vienna, 1962, p. 723.
1994. MULDER, H.D. and F.C. SCHMIDT. *J. Am. Chem. Soc.*, 73, 5575 (1951).
1995. MULDROW, C.N. and L.G. HEPLER. *J. Am. Chem. Soc.*, 78, 5989 (1956).
1996. MULDROW, C.N. and L.G. HEPLER. *J. Am. Chem. Soc.*, 79, 4045 (1957).
1997. MULDROW, C.N. and L.G. HEPLER. *J. Phys. Chem.*. **62**, 982 (1958).
1998. MULFORD, R.N.R., J.O. FORD, and J.G. HOFFMAN. *Thermodynamics of Nuclear Materials.* International Atomic Energy Agency, Vienna, 1962, p. 517.
1999. MULFORD, R.N.R. and C.E. HOLLEY. *J. Phys. Chem.*, **59**, 1222 (1955).
2000. MULFORD, R.N.R. and G.E. STURDY. *J. Am. Chem. Soc.*, 77, 3449 (1955).
2001. MULFORD, R.N.R. and T.A. WIEWANDT. *J. Phys. Chem.*, **69**, 1641 (1965).
2002. MULLIKEN R.C. and K.S. PITZER. *J. Chem. Phys.*, 27, 1305 (1957).
2003. MUNIR, Z.A. and A.W. SEARCY. *J. Electrochem. Soc.*, **111**, 1170 (1964).
2004. MUNSON, M.S.B. and J.L. FRANKLIN. *J. Phys. Chem.*, **68**, 3191 (1964).
2005. MÜNSTER, A., G. RINCK, and W. RUPPERT. *Z. phys. Chem.* (GFR), **9**, 228 (1956).
2006. MURAD, E. and M.G. INGHRAM. *J. Chem. Phys.*, **41**, 404 (1964).
2007. MURGULESCU, I.G. and E. TOMUS. *Ann. Univ. "C.I. Parhon", Ser. stiint. natur.*, **9**, 913 (1960).
2008. MURPHY, G.M. and E. RUBIN. *J. Phys. Chem.*, **20**, 1179 (1952).
2009. MURPHY, G.M. and J.E. VANCE. *J. Chem. Phys.*, **18**, 1514 (1950).
2010. MURSH, L.E. and W.F. GIAUQUE. *J. Phys. Chem.*, **66**, 2052 (1962).
2011. MUSGRAVE, M.J.P. *Phys. Letters*, **5**, 97 (1963).
2012. MUSTAJOKI, A. *Suomalais. tiedeakat. toimituks. Sar.*, A VI, No. 9, 175.
2013. MYERS, C.E. *J. Phys. Chem.*, **65**, 2111 (1961).
2014. MYERS, C.E. and A.P. BRADY. *J. Phys. Chem.*, **64**, 591 (1960).
2015. NACHTRIEB, N.H. and N. CLEMENT. *J. Phys. Chem.*, **62**, 876 (1958).
2016. NAGARAJAN, G. *Current Sci.*, **30**, 377 (1961).
2017. NAGARAJAN, G. *Z. phys. Chem.* (GFR), **31**, 347 (1962).
2018. NAGARAJAN, G. *Bull. Soc. chim. belg.*, **71**, 65 (1962).
2019. NAGARAJAN, G. *Bull. Soc. chim. belg.*, **71**, 77 (1962).
2020. NAGARAJAN, G. *Bull. Soc. chim. belg.*, **71**, 240 (1962).
2021. NAGARAJAN, G. *Bull. Soc. chim. belg.*, **71**, 324 (1962).
2022. NAGARAJAN, G. *Bull. Soc. chim. belg.*, **71**, 337 (1962).
2023. NAGARAJAN, G. *Sci. a. Cult.*, **28**, 140 (1962).
2024. NAGARAJAN, G. *J. Sci. a. Ind. Res.*, **B21**, 356 (1962).
2025. NAGARAJAN, G. *J. Sci. a. Ind. Res.*, **B21**, 463 (1962).
2026. NAGARAJAN, G. *Z. Naturforsch.*, 17a, 702, 1962; *Bull. Soc. chim. belg.* 71, 73 (1962).
2027. NAGARAJAN, G. *Z. Naturforsch.*, 17a, 871 (1962).
2028. NAGARAJAN, G. *Austral. J. Chem.*, **15**, 566 (1962).
2029. NAGARAJAN, G. *Austral. J. Chem.*, **16**, 908 (1963).
2030. NAGARAJAN, G. *Bull. Soc. chim. belg.*, **72**, 5 (1963).
2031. NAGARAJAN G. *Bull. Soc. chim. belg.*, **72**, 346 (1963).
2032. NAGARAJAN, G. *Bull. Soc. chim. belg.*, **72**, 351 (1963).
2033. NAGARAJAN, G. *Bull. Soc. chim. belg.*, **72**, 524 (1963).
2034. NAGARAJAN, G. *Z. phys. Chem.* (GDR), **223**, 27 (1963).
2035. NAGARAJAN, G. *Z. phys. Chem.* (GDR), **224**, 256 (1963).
2036. NAGARAJAN, G. *Indian J. Pure Appl. Phys.*, **2**, 179 (1964).
2037. NAGARAJAN, G. *J. chim. phys. et phys.-chim. biol.*, **61**, 338 (1964).
2038. NAGARAJAN, G., E.R. LIPPINCOTT, and J.M. STUTMAN. *Z. Naturforsch.*, **20a**, 786 (1965).

2039. NEALE, E. and L.T.D. WILLIAMS. *J. Chem. Soc.*, **1954**, 2156.
2039a. NEALE, E. and L.T.D. WILLIAMS. *J. Chem. Soc.*, **1955**, 4535.
2039b. NEALE, E., L.T.D. WILLIAMS, and V.T. MOORES. *J. Chem. Soc.*, **1956**, 422.
2040. NELSON, R.A., W.H. JOHNSON, and E.J. PROSEN. *J. Res. Nat Bur. Stand.*, **62**, 67 (1959).
2041. NELSON, T., C. MOSS, and L.G. HEPLER. *J. Phys. Chem.*, **64**, 376 (1960).
2042. NEUGEBAUER, C.A. *Dissert. Abstr.*, **17**(7), 1478 (1957) (cited in [679]).
2043. NEUGEBAUER, C.A. and J.L. MARGRAVE. *J. Phys. Chem.*, **60**, 1318 (1956).
2044. NEUGEBAUER, C.A. and J.L. MARGRAVE. *J. Am. Chem. Soc.*, 79, 1338 (1957).
2045. NEUGEBAUER, C.A. and J.L. MARGRAVE. *J. Phys. Chem.*, **61**, 1429 (1957).
2046. NEUGEBAUER, C.A. and J.L. MARGRAVE. *Z. anorg. allg. Chem.*, **290**, 82 (1957).
2047. NEUGEBAUER, C.A. and J.L. MARGRAVE. *J. Phys. Chem.*, **62**, 1043 (1958).
2048. NEUMANN, B., C. KRÖGER, and H. KUNZ. *Z. anorg. allg. Chem.*, **218**, 379 (1934).
2049. NEUVONEN, K.J. *Am. J. Sci., Bowen Issue*, pt. II, 1952, p. 373.
2050. NEWMAN, E.S. *J. Res. Nat.Bur. Stand.*, **61**, 75 (1958).
2051. NEWMAN, E.S. *J. Res. Nat. Bur. Stand.*, **62**, 207 (1959).
2052. NEWMAN, E.S. *J. Res. Nat. Bur. Stand.*, **A68**, 645 (1964).
2053. NEWMAN, E.S. and R. HOFFMAN. *J. Res. Nat. Bur. Stand.* **56**, 313 (1956).
2054. NICHOLSON, G.R. *J. Chem. Soc.*, **1957**, 2431.
2055. NICHOLSON, G.R. *J. Chem. Soc.*, **1960**, 2377.
2056. NICHOLSON, G.R. *J. Chem.Soc.* , **1960**, 2378.
2057. NICHOLSON, G.R., M. SZWARC, and J.W. TAYLOR. *J. Chem. Soc.*, **1954**, 2767.
2058. NICKERSON, J.K., K.A. KOBE, and J.J. McKETTA. *J. Phys. Chem.*, **65**, 1037 (1961).
2059. NICKERSON, J.K. and J.J. McKETTA. *Bull. Chem. Thermodynamics, I.U.P.A.C.*, No. 3, 47 (1960); NICKERSON, J.K., Ph. D. Thesis, Univ. of Texas, 1960.
2060. NIELSEN, J.R., H.H. CLAASSEN, and D.C. SMITH. *J. Chem. Phys.*, **18**, 1471 (1950).
2061. NIELSEN, J.R., C.Y. LIANG, and L.W. DAASCH. *J. Optic. Soc. Am.*, **43**, 1071 (1953).
2062. NIELSEN, J.R. and R. THEIMER. *J. Chem. Phys.*, **30**, 103 (1959).
2063. NIWA, K. *J. Fac. Sci. Hokkaido Univ.*, **2**, 201 (9138); 3, 17, 75 (1940) (cited in [1773]).
2064. NOGAREDA, C. and W. RODRIGUEZ De La TORRE. *Ann. Real. Soc. espan fis. y. quim.*, **B60**, 145 (1964).
2065. NÖLLING, J. *Ber. Bunsenges. phys. Chem.*, **67**, 172 (1963).
2066. NOMURA, S. *J. Phys. Chem. Japan*, **16**, 1352 (1962).
2067. O BRIEN, C.J. and K.K. KELLEY. *J. Am. Chem. Soc.*, **79**, 5616 (1957).
2068. O DWYER, M.F. *J. Molec. Spectrosc.*, **2**, 144 (1958).
2068a. O HARE, P.A.G. and W.N. HUBBARD. *J. Phys. Chem.*, **69**, 4358 (1965).
2069. OETTING, F.L. *J. Phys. Chem.*, **67**, 2757 (1963).
2070. OETTING, F.L. *J. Chem. Phys.*, **41**, 149 (1964).
2071. OETTING, F.L. *J. Chem. Eng. Data*, **10**, 122 (1965).
2072. OETTING, E.L. and N.W. GREGORY. *J. Phys. Chem.*, **65**, 173 (1961).
2073. OETTING, F.L. and R.A. McDONALD. *J. Phys. Chem.*, **67**, 2737 (1963).
2074. OLIVER, G.D. and J.W. GRISARD. *J. Am. Chem. Soc.* **74**, 2705 (1952).
2075. OLIVER, G.D., J.W. GRISARD, and C.W. CUNNINGHAM. *J. Am. Chem. Soc.*, **73**, 5719 (1951).
2075a. OLOFSSON, G. *Acta chem. scand.*, **19**, 2155 (1965).
2076. OLSON, W.M. and R.N.R. MULFORD. *J. Phys. Chem.*, **68**, 1048 (1964).
2077. ORTNER, M.H. *J. Chem. Phys.*, **34**, 556 (1961).
2078. OSBORNE, D.W. and E.F. WESTRUM. *J. Chem. Phys.*, **21**, 1884 (1953).
2079. OSBORNE, D.W., E.F. WESTRUM, and H.R. LOHR. *J. Am. Chem. Soc.*, **77**, 2737 (1955).
2080. OSBORNE, D.W., E.F. WESTRUM, and H.R. LOHR. *J. Am.Chem. Soc.*, **79**, 529 (1957).
2081. OTT, J.B. and W.F. GIAUQUE. *J. Am. Chem. Soc.* **82**, 1308 (1960).
2082. OTTO, E.M. *J. Electrochem. Soc.*, **111**, 88 (1964).
2083. OVEREND, J. and J.C. EVANS. *Trans. Faraday Soc.*, **55**, 1817 (1959).
2084. OWENS, B.B. and S.W. MAYERS. *J. Inorg. Nucl. Chem.* **26**, 501 (1964).
2085. PACE, E.L. and R.J. BOBKA. *J. Chem. Phys.*, **35**, 454 (1961).
2086. PACE, E.L. and J.S. MOSSER. *J. Chem. Phys.*, **39**, 154 (1963).
2087. PACE, E.L. and B.F. TURNBULL. *J. Chem. Phys.*, **43**, 1953 (1965).
2088. PALM, A. and M. KILPATRIK. *J. Chem. Phys.*, **23**, 1562 (1955).
2089. PALMA, E.E., E.A. PIOTROWSKI, S. SUNDARAM, and F.F. CLEVELAND. *J. Molec. Spectrosc.*, **13**, 119 (1964).
2090. PANISH, M.B. *J. Chem. Eng. Data*, **6**, 592 (1961).
2091. PANISH, M.B., B. MORTON, and L. REIF. *J. Chem. Phys.*, **37**, 128 (1962).
2092. PANISH, M.B. and L. REIF. *J. Chem. Phys.*, 38, 253 (1963).
2093. PANISH, M.B. and L. REIF. *J. Chem. Phys.*, **34**, 1915 (1961).
2094. PANKRATZ, L.B. and K.K. KELLEY. *Bur. Mines Report Investig.*, 6241, U.S. Dept. of Interior, Washington, 1963.
2095. PANKRATZ, L.B. and E.G. KING. *Bur. Mines Report of Investig.*, 6175, U.S. Dept. of Interior, Washington, 1963.
2096. PANKRATZ, L.B., W.W. WELLER, and K.K. KELLEY. *Bur. Mines Report of Investig.*, 6287, U.S. Dept. of Interior, Wash., 1963.
2097. PANKRATZ, L.B., W.W. WELLER, and K.K. KELLEY. *Bur. Mines Report of Investig.* 6446, U.S. Dept. of Interior, Washington, 1964.

2098. PAPADOPOULOS, M.N. and W.F. GIAUQUE. *J. Am. Chem. Soc.*, 77, 2740 (1955).
2099. PAPADOPOULOS, M.N. and W.F. GIAUQUE. *J. Phys. Chem.* **66**, 2049 (1962).
2100. PAPE, R. De and J. RAVEZ. *Compt. rend.*, **254**, 4171 (1962).
2101. PAPE, R. De and J. RAVEZ. *Compt. rend.*, **259**, 3549 (1964).
2102. PAPESCU, I. *Stud. cercetări stiint. Acad. RPR, Fil. Jasi, Chim.*, **10**, 25 (1959).
2103. PAPOUŠEK, D. *Z. phys. Chem.*, **211**, 361 (1959).
2104. PAPOUŠEK, D. *Coll. Czech. Chem. Comm.*, **26**, 1909 (1961).
2105. PAPOUŠEK, D. *Trans. Faraday Soc.*, **57**, 884 (1961).
2106. PAPOUŠEK. D. *Coll. Czech. Chem. Comm.*, **27**, 1 (1962).
2107. PAPOUŠEK, D. and M. VALENTOVA. *Coll. Czech. Chem. Comm.*, **26**, 1458 (1961).
2108. PAPOUŠEK, D. and M. VALENTOVA. *Coll. Czech. Chem. Comm.*, **26**, 3157 (1961).
2109. PARKINSON, D.H., F.E. SIMON, and F.H. SPEDDING. *Proc. Roy Soc.*, **A207**, 137 (1951).
2110. PARKS, G.S. *Chem. Rev.*, **27**, 75 (1940).
2111. PARKS, G.S. and H.M. HUFFMAN. *J. Am. Chem. Soc.*, **52**, 4381 (1930).
2112. PARKS, G.S., H.M. HUFFMAN, and J. BARMORE. *J. Am. Chem. Soc.*, **55**, 2733 (1933).
2113. PARKS, G.S., K.K. KELLEY, and H.M. HUFFMAN. *J. Am. Chem. Soc.*, **51**, 1969 (1929).
2114. PARKS, G.S., W.D. KENNEDY, R.R. GATES, J.R. MOSLEY, G.E. MOORE, and M.L. RENQUIST. *J. Am. Chem. Soc.*, **78**, 56 (1956).
2115. PARKS, G.S. and D.W. LIGHT. *J. Am. Chem. Soc.*, **56**, 1511 (1934).
2116. PARKS, G.S. and K.E. MANCHESTER. *Thermochem. Bull., I.U.P.A.C.*, No. 2, 8 (1956).
2117. PARKS, G.S., K.E. MANCHESTER, and L.M. VAUGHAN. *J. Chem. Phys.*, **22**, 2089 (1954).
2117a. PARKS, G.S. and G.E. MOORE. *J. Chem. Phys.*, 7, 1066 (1939).
2118. PARKS, G.S. and H.P. MOSHER. *J. Chem. Phys.*, **37**, 919 (1962).
2119. PARKS, G.S. and J.R. MOSLEY. *J. Am. Chem. Soc.*, **72**, 1850 (1950).
2120. PARKS, G.S., J.R. MOSLEY, and P.V. PETERSON. *J. Chem. Phys.*, **18**, 152 (1950).
2121. PARKS, G.S., S.B. THOMAS, and D.W. LIGHT. *J. Chem. Phys.*, **4**, 64 (1936).
2122. PARKS, G.S., S.S. TODD, and W.A. MOORE. *J. Am. Chem. Soc.* **58**, 398 (1936).
2123. PARKS, G.S. and L.M. VAUGHAN. *J. Am. Chem. Soc.*, **73**, 2380 (1951).
2124. PARKS, G.S., T.J. WEST, B.F. NAYLOR, P.S. FUJII, and L.A. McCLAINE. *J. Am. Chem. Soc.*, **68**, 2524 (1946).
2125. PARRIS, M., P.S. RAYBIN, and L.C. LABOWITZ. *J. Chem. Eng. Data*, **9**, 221 (1964).
2126. PASAGLIA, E. and H.K. KEVORKIAN. *J. Appl. Phys.*, **34**, 90 (1963).
2127. PAULE, R.C. and J.L. MARGRAVE. *J. Phys. Chem.*, **67**, 1368 (1963).
2128. PAULE, R.C. and J.L. MARGRAVE. *J. Phys. Chem.*, **67**, 1896 (1963).
2129. PAYNE, D.H. and E.F. WESTRUM. *J. Phys. Chem.*, **66**, 748 (1962).
2130. PEARCE, M.L. and N.R. McCABE. *J. Inorg. Nucl. Chem.*, **27**, 1876 (1965).
2131. PEDLEY, J.B. and H.A. SKINNER. *Trans. Faraday Soc.*, **55**, 544 (1959).
2132. PEDLEY, J.B., H.A. SKINNER, and C.L. CHERNIK. *Trans. Faraday Soc.*, **53**, 1612 (1957).
2133. PEHLKE, R.D. and J.F. ELLIOTT. *Trans. Metallurg. Soc. AIME*, **215**, 781, 1959 (1960).
2134. PELL, A.S. and G. PILCHER. *Trans. Faraday Soc.*, **61**, 71 (1965).
2135. PEMBERTON, R.C. and N.G. PARSONAGE. *Trans. Faraday Soc.*. **61**, 2112 (1965).
2136. PENNINGTON, R.E., H.L. FINKE, W.N. HUBBARD, J.F. MESSERLY, F.R. FROW, I.A. HOSSENLOPP, and G. WADDINGTON. *J. Am. Chem. Soc.*, **78**, 2055 (1956).
2137. PENNINGTON, R.E. and R.A. COBE. *J. Am. Chem. Soc.*, **79**, 300 (1957).
2138. PENNINGTON, R.E., D.W. SCOTT, H.L. FINKE, J.P. McCULLOUGH, J.F. MESSERLY, J.A. HOSSENLOPP, and G. WADDINGTON. *J. Am. Chem. Soc.*, **78**, 3266 (1956).
2139. PEPPLER, R.B. and E.S. NEWMAN. *J. Res. Nat. Bur. Stand.*, **47**, 439 (1951).
2140. PERROS, T.P., T.R. MUNSON, and C.R. NAESER. *J. Chem. Educ.*, **30**, 402 (1953).
2141. PETERSON, W.B. and G.C. PIMENTEL. *J. Am. Chem. Soc.*, **75**, 532 (1953).
2142. PETERSON, D.T. and J. REXER. *J. Inorg. Nucl. Chem.*, **24**, 519 (1962).
2143. PETRAKIS, L. *J. Phys. Chem.*, **66**, 433 (1962).
2144. PFLUGMACHER, A., R. SCHWARZ, and H.J. RABBEN. *Z. anorg. allg. Chem.*, **264**, 204 (1953).
2145. PIERRE, G. St. and J. CHIPMAN. *J. Am. Chem. Soc.*, **76**, 4787 (1954).
2146. PIESBERGEN, U. *Z. Naturforsch.*, **18a**, 141 (1963).
2147. PIESBERGEN, U. *Z. Naturforsch.*, **19a**, 1075 (1964).
2148. PIGON, K. *Helv. chim. acta*, **44**, 30 (1961).
2149. PILCHER, G. – cited in [1360].
2150. PILCHER, G., A.S. PELL, and D.J. COLEMAN. *Trans. Faraday Soc.*, **60** 499 (1964).
2151. PILCHER, G., H.A. SKINNER, and A.S. PELL. *Trans. Faraday Soc.*, **59**, 316 (1963).
2152. PILCHER, G. *Phil. Trans.*, **258**, 23 (1955).
2153. PILCHER, G. and L.E. SUTTON. *J. Chem. Soc.*, **1956**, 2695.
2154. PILLAI, M.G.K. *Z. phys. Chem.* (GDR), **218**, 334 (1961).
2155. PILLAI, M.G.K. and F.F. CLEVELAND. *J. Molec. Spectrosc.*, **5**, 212 (1961).
2156. PITZER, K.S., R.E. GERKIN, L.V. GREGOR, and C.N.R. RAO – see [2313], p. 211.
2157. PITZER, K.S., L. GUTTMAN, and E.F. WESTRUM. *J. Am. Chem. Soc.*, **68**, 2209 (1946).
2158. PITZER, K.S. and J.L. HOLLENBERG. *J. Am. Chem. Soc.*, **75**, 2219 (1953).
2159. PITZER, K.S. and J.L. HOLLENBERG. *J. Am. Chem. Soc.*, **76**, 1493 (1954).

2160. PITZER, K.S. and J.E. KILPATRIK. *Chem. Rev.*, **39**, 435 (1946).
2161. PITZER, K.S. and W. WELTNER. *J. Am. Chem. Soc.*, **71**, 2842 (1949).
2162. PLATTEEUW, J.C. and G. MEYER. *Trans. Faraday Soc.*, **52**, 1066 (1956).
2163. POLLOCK, B.D. *J. Phys. Chem.*, **63**, 587 (1959).
2164. POLLOCK, B.D. *J. Phys. Chem.*, **65**, 731 (1961).
2165. POLO, S.R., A. PALM, F.L. VOELZ, F.F. CLEVELAND, A.G. MEISTER, R.B. BEANSTEIN, and R.H. SHERMAN. *J. Chem. Phys.*, **23**, 833 (1955).
2166. POLO, S.R. and M.K. WILSON. *J. Chem. Phys.*, **21**, 1129 (1953).
2167. PONTARELLI, D., A.G. MEISTER, F.F. CLEVELAND, and F.L. VOELZ. *J. Chem. Phys.*, **20**, 1949 (1952).
2168. POPE, A.E. and H.A. SKINNER. *J. Chem. Soc.*, **1963**, 3704.
2169. POPE, A.E. and H.A. SKINNER. *Trans. Faraday Soc.*, **60**, 1402 (1964).
2170. POPE, A.E. and H.A. SKINNER. *Trans. Faraday Soc.*, **60**, 1404 (1964).
2171. PORTE, H.A., E. GREENBERG, and W.N. HUBBARD. *J. Phys. Chem.*, **69**, 2308 (1965).
2172. PORTER, R.F. and S.R. GUPTA. *J. Phys. Chem.*, **68**, 280 (1964).
2173. PORTER, R.F. and S.R. GUPTA. *J. Phys. Chem.*, **68**, 2732 (1964).
2174. PORTER, R.F., P. SCHIESSEL, and M.G. INGHRAM. *J. Chem. Phys.*, **23**, 339 (1955).
2175. PORTER, R.F. and W.P. SHOLETTE. *J. Chem. Phys.*, **37**, 198 (1963).
2176. PORTER, R.F. and G.H. CADY. *J. Am. Chem. Soc.*, **79**, 5628 (1957).
2177. POTTER, R.L. *J. Chem. Phys.*, **17**, 957 (1949).
2178. POTTER, R.L. *J. Chem. Phys.*, **26**, 394 (1957).
2179. POTTER, R.L. *J. Chem. Phys.*, **31**, 1100 (1959).
2180. POTTIE, R.F. *J. Chem. Phys.*, **42**, 2607 (1965).
2181. PRESCHER, K.-E. and W. SCHRÖDTER. *Z. Erzbergbau Metallhüttenw.*, **16**, 352 (1963).
2182. PRITCHARD, H.O. *Chem. Rev.*, **52**, 529 (1953).
2183. PRITCHARD, H.O. and H.A. SKINNER. *J. Chem. Soc.*, **1950**, 272.
2184. PRITCHARD, H.O. and H.A. SKINNER. *J. Chem. Soc.*, **1950**, 1099.
2185. PROPHET, H. *J. Chem. Phys.*, **38**, 2345 (1963).
2186. PROPHET, H. and D.R. STULL. *J. Chem. Eng. Data*, **8**, 78 (1963).
2187. PROSEN, E.J., W.H. JOHNSON, and F.V. PERGIEL. *J. Res. Nat. Bur. Stand.*, **61**, 247 (1958).
2188. PROSEN, E.J., W.H. JOHNSON, and F.V. PERGIEL. *J. Res. Nat. Bur. Stand.*, **62**, 43 (1959).
2189. PROSEN, E.J., W.H. JOHNSON, and F.D. ROSSINI. *J. Res. Nat. Bur. Stand.*, **36**, 455 (1946).
2190. PROSEN, E.J., W.H. JOHNSON, and F.D. ROSSINI. *J. Am. Chem. Soc.*, **72**, 626 (1950).
2191. PROSEN, E.J., F.W. MARON, and F.D. ROSSINI. *J. Res. Nat. Bur. Stand.*, **46**, 106 (1951).
2192. PROSEN, E.J. and F.D. ROSSINI. *J. Res. Nat. Bur. Stand.*, **34**, 263 (1945).
2193. PURANIK, P.G. and E.V. RAO. *Indian J. Phys.*, **35**, 177 (1961).
2194. PURANIK, P.G. and E.V. RAO. *Proc. Indian Acad. Sci.*, **A56**, 233 (1962).
2195. PURNELL, J.H. and C.P. QUINN. *J. Chem. Soc.*, **1964**, 4049.
2196. PUTNAM, W.E. and J.E. KILPATRIK. *J. Chem. Phys.*, **27**, 1075 (1957).
2197. PUTNAM, W.E., D.M. McEACHERN, and J.E. KILPATRIK. *J. Chem. Phys.*, **42**, 749 (1965).
2198. RADHAKRISHNAN, M. *J. chim. phys. et phys.-chim. biol.*, **60**, 1084 (1963).
2199. RADHAKRISHNAN, M. *Z. Naturforsch.*, **18a**, 103 (1963).
2199a. RALEY, J.H., F.F. RUST, and W.E. VAUGHAN. *J. Am. Chem. Soc.*, **70**, 88 (1948).
2200. RAMAN, C.V. *Proc. Indian Acad. Sci.*, **A57**, 1 (1963).
2201. RAMASWAMY, K., K. SATHIANANDAN, and F.F. CLEVELAND. *Molec. Spectrosc.*, **11**, 14 (1962).
2202. RAMBUSCH, U.K., W. BARHO, G. ERNST, A. SCHABER, and D. STRAUB. *Atompraxis*, **8**, 339 (1962).
2203. RAMETTE, R.W. and R.F. BROMAN. *J. Phys. Chem.*, **67**, 942 (1963).
2204. RAMETTE, R.W. and E.A. DRATZ. *J. Phys. Chem.*, **67**, 940 (1963).
2205. RAMSEY, J.N., D. CAPLAN, and A.A. BURR. *J. Electrochem. Soc.*, **103**, 135 (1956).
2206. RAND, M.H. and O. KUBASCHEWSKI. *United Kingdom Atomic Energy Research Establishment Report AERE-R3487*, 1960 (cited in [1578]).
2207. RAND, M.H. and O. KUBASCHEWSKI. *The Thermochemical Properties of Uranium Compounds.* Oliver a. Boyd, Edinburgh a. London, 1963.
2208. RANDALL, S.P. and J.L. MARGRAVE. *J. Inorg. Nucl. Chem.*, **16**, 29 (1960).
2209. RAO, R.V.G. and W.F. GIAUQUE. *J. Phys. Chem.*, **69**, 1273 (1965).
2210. RATHJENS, G.W., J.N.R. FREEMAN, W.D. GWINN, and K.S. PITZER. *J. Am. Chem. Soc.*, **75**, 5634 (1953).
2211. RAUHER, H. *Chem. -Ing. -Techn.*, **2**, 331 (1950).
2212. RAY, J.D. and A.A. GERSHON. *J. Phys. Chem.*, **66**, 1750 (1962).
2213. RAY, J.D. and R.A. OGG. *J. Phys. Chem.*, **61**, 1087 (1957).
2214. RAY, J.D. and R.A. OGG. *J. Chem. Phys.*, **31**, 168 (1959).
2215. RAY, J.D. and R.A. OGG. *J. Phys. Chem.*, **63**, 1522 (1959).
2216. RALEY, J.E., F.E. RUST, and W.E. VAUGHAN. *J. Am. Chem. Soc.*, **70**, 88 (1948).
2217. RAZIUNAS, V., G.J. MACUR, and S. KATZ. *J. Chem. Phys.*, **39**, 1161 (1963).
2218. REBBERT, R.E. and K.J. LAIDLER. *J. Chem. Phys.*, **20**, 574 (1952).
2219. REDMOND, R.E. and J. LONES. *U.S. Atomic Energy Comm.*, Nat. Sci. Foundat., Washington, D.C., ORNL – 1342, 3–20, 1952.

2220. REIN, R.H. and V. CHIPMAN. *J. Phys. Chem.*, **67**, 839 (1963).
2221. RENNER, T. *Solid State Electronics,* **1**, 39 (1960).
2222. RENTZEPIS, P., D. WHITE, and P.N. WALSH. *J. Phys. Chem.*, **64**, 1784 (1960).
2223. RICHARDS, A.W. *Trans. Faraday Soc.*, **51**, 1193 (1955).
2224. RICHARDS, A.W. *J. Appl. Chem.*, **9**, 142 (1959).
2224a. RICHARDS, R.E. *J. Chem. Soc.*, **1948**, 1931.
2225. RICHARDS, R.R. and N.W. GREGORY. *J. Phys. Chem.*, **68**, 3089 (1964).
2226. RICHARDSON, F.D. *J. Iron Steel Inst.*, **175**, 33 (1953).
2227. RICHARDSON, F.D. and J.H.E. JEFFES. *J. Iron Steel Inst.*, **171**, 165 (1952).
2228. RICHARDSON, F.D., J.H.E. JEFFES, and G. WITHERS. *J. Iron Steel Inst.*, **166**, 213 (1950).
2229. RIDEAL. *Proc. Roy. Soc.*, **A99**, 153 (1921).
2230. ROBERTSON, A.J. *Trans. Faraday Soc.*, **48**, 228 (1952).
2231. ROBIE, R.A. and J.W. STOUT. *J. Phys. Chem.*, **67**, 2252 (1963).
2232. ROBINS, D.A. and J. JENKINS. *Acta metallurg.*, **3**, 598 (1935).
2233. ROBSON, H.E. and P.W. GILLES. *J. Phys. Chem.*, **68**, 983 (1964).
2234. ROCK, P.A. and R.E. POWELL. *Inorg. Chem.*, **3**, 1953 (1964).
2235. ROCKENFELLER, J.D. and F.D. ROSSINI. *J. Phys. Chem.*, **65**, 267 (1961).
2236. ROCQUET, P. and M.F. ANCEY-MORET. *Bull. Soc. chim. France,* **1954**, 1038.
2237. RODEWALD, H.J. *Helv. chim. acta,* **43**, 878 (1960).
2238. ROSENBLATT, G.M. and C.E. BIRCHENALL. *J. Chem. Phys.*, **35**, 788 (1961).
2239. ROSENQUIST, T. *J. Iron Steel Inst.*, **176**, 37 (1954).
2240. ROSS, L.W., F.H. HAYNIE, and R.F. HOCHMAN. *J. Chem. Eng. Data,* **9**, 339 (1964).
2241. ROSSINI, F.D. *J. Res. Nat. Bur. Stand.*, **3**, 189 (1934).
2242. ROSSINI, F.D. and P.A. COWIE – cited in [2243].
2243. ROSSINI, F.D., P.A. COWIE, F.O. ELLISON, and C.C. BROWN. *Properties of Titanium Compounds and Related Substances (with an Appendix by M.C. Arsem). ONR Report ACR-17.* Washington, Oct., 1956.
2244. ROSSINI, F.D., K.S. PITZER, R.L. ARNETT, R.M. BRAUN, and G.C. PIMENTAL. *Selected Values of Physical and Thermodynamic Properties of Hydrocarbons and Related Compounds.* Pittsburgh, Carnegie Press, 1953.
2245. ROSSINI, F.D., D.D. WAGMAN, W.H. EVANS, S. LEVINE, and I. JAFFE. *Selected Values of Chemical Thermodynamic Properties, Circ. Nat. Bur. Stand.*, 500, 1952.
2246. ROTH, J. *J. Chem. Phys.*, **30**, 596 (1959).
2247. ROTH, W.A. *FIAT Reports of German Sci. 1939–1946, Inorg. Chem.*, **4**, 214 (1948).
2248. ROTH, W.A. and MEYER. *Z. Elektrochem.*, **39**, 35 (1933).
2249. ROTH, W.A. and H. TROITZSCH. *Z. anorg. allg. Chem.*, **260**, 337 (1949).
2250. RUBIN, T.R. and W.F. GIAUQUE. *J. Am. Chem. Soc.*, **74**, 800 (1952).
2251. RUDZITIS, E., H.M. FEDER, and W.N. HUBBARD. *J. Phys. Chem.*, **67**, 2388 (1963).
2252. RUDZITIS, E., H.M. FEDER, and W.N. HUBBARD. *J. Phys. Chem.*, **68**, 2978 (1964).
2253. RUDZITIS, E., H.M. FEDER, and W.N. HUBBARD. *J. Phys. Chem.*, **69**, 2305 (1965).
2254. RUDZITIS, E., R. TERRY, H.M. FEDER, and W.N. HUBBARD. *J. Phys. Chem.*, **68**, 617 (1964).
2255. RUEHRWEIN, R.A. and T.M. POWELL. *J. Am. Chem. Soc.*, **68**, 1063 (1946).
2256. RULON, R.M. and L.S. MASON. *J. Am. Chem. Soc.*, **73**, 5491 (1951).
2257. RUSSEL, A.S., K.E. MARTIN, and C.N. COHRAN. *J. Am. Chem. Soc.*, **74**, 1466 (1951).
2257a. RUSSELL, H., D.R.V. GOLDING, and D.M. YOST. *J. Am. Chem. Soc.*, **66**, 16 (1944).
2258. RUTHER, F. *J. Chem. Eng. Data,* **7**, 398 (1962).
2259. SAALFELD, F.E. and H.J. SVEC. *Inorg. Chem.*, **2**, 46 (1963).
2260. SAALFELD, F.E. and H.J. SVEC. *Inorg. Chem.*, **2**, 50 (1963).
2261. SABA, W.G. and W.E. WALLAGE. *J. Chem. Phys.*, **35**, 689 (1961).
2262. SABA, W.J., W.E. WALLAGE, H. SANDMO, and R.S. CRAIG. *J. Chem. Phys.*, **35**, 2148 (1961).
2263. SAEGUSA, F. *Sci. Rep. Tohoku Univ.*, **34**, 55 (1950).
2264. SAEGUSA, F. *Sci. Rep. Tohoku Univ.*, Ser. 1, **34**, 104 (1950).
2265. SAHAMA, T.G. and D.R. TORGESON. *Bur. Mines Report of Investig.*, 4408, U.S. Dept. of Interior, Wash., 1949 (cited in [1681]).
2266. SAKAMOTO, Y. *J. Sci. Hiroshima Univ.*, **A18**, 95 (1954).
2267. SALKIND, A.J. and P.F. BRUINS. *J. Electrochem. Soc.*, **109**, 356 (1962).
2268. SANDENAW, Th.A. *J. Phys. Chem. Solids,* **16**, 329 (1960).
2269. SANDENAW, Th.A. *J. Nucl. Mater.*, **10**, 165 (1963).
2270. SANDENAW, Th.A. and R.B. GIBNEY. *Progress in Nuclear Energy,* **1** (V), 1956, p. 384 (cited in [63]).
2271. SANDERSON, B.S. and G.E. McWOOD. *J. Phys. Chem.*, **60**, 314, 316 (1956).
2272. SANDERSON, T.A. *J. Phys. Chem. Solids,* **26**, 1075 (1965).
2273. SATO SHUN-ICHI. *Bull. Inst. Phys. Chem. Res., Tokyo,* **21**, 127 (1942).
2274. SAVILLE and GUNDRY. *Trans. Faraday. Soc.*, **55**, 2063 (1959).
2275. SAWAGE, W.P., D.E. HUDSON, and F.H. SPEDDING. *J. Chem. Phys.*, **30**, 221 (1959).
2276. SCAIFE, D.E., A.G. TURNBULL, and A.W. WYLIE. *J. Chem. Soc.*, **1965**, 1432.
2277. SCARPIELLO, D.A. and W.J. COOPER. *J. Chem. Eng. Data,* **9**, 364 (1964).

2278. SCHÄFER, H., G. BREIL, and G. PFEFFER. *Z. anorg. allg. Chem.*, **276**, 325 (1954).
2279. SCHÄFER, H. and K.-D. DOHMANN. *Z. anorg. allg. Chem.*, **299**, 197 (1959).
2280. SCHÄFER, H. and H. HEINZ. *Z. anorg. allg. Chem.*, **332**, 25 (1964).
2281. SCHÄFER, H. and H-J. HEITLAND. *Z. anorg. allg. Chem.*, **304**, 249 (1960).
2282. SCHÄFER, H. and R. HORNLE. *Z. anorg. allg. Chem.*, **263**, 261 (1950).
2283. SCHÄFER, H. and F. KAHLENBERG. *Z. anorg. allg. Chem.*, **294**, 242 (1958).
2284. SCHÄFER, H. and F. KAHLENBERG. *Z. anorg. allg. Chem.*, **305**, 178 (1960).
2285. SCHÄFER, H. and F. KAHLENBERG. *Z. anorg. allg. Chem.*, **305**, 291 (1960).
2286. SCHÄFER, H. and F. KAHLENBERG. *Z. anorg. allg. Chem.*, **305**, 327 (1960).
2287. SCHÄFER, H. and F. LIEDMEIER. *Z. anorg. allg. Chem.*, **329**, 225 (1964).
2288. SCHÄFER, H. and J. NICKL. *Z. anorg. allg. Chem.*, **274**, 250 (1953).
2289. SCHÄFER, H., G. SCHNEIDEREIT, and W. GERHARDT. *Z. anorg. allg. Chem.*, **319**, 327 (1963).
2290. SCHÄFER, H. and E. SIBBING. *Z. anorg. allg. Chem.*, **305**, 341 (1960).
2291. SCHÄFER, H. and A. TEBBEN. *Z. anorg. allg. Chem.*, **305**, 317 (1960).
2292. SCHÄFER, H., A. TEBBEN, and W. GERHARDT. *Z. anorg. allg. Chem.*, **321**, 41 (1963).
2293. SCHÄFER, H. and F. WARTENPFUHL. *Z. anorg. allg. Chem.*, **308**, 282 (1961).
2294. SCHÄFER, H., F. WARTENPFUHL, and E. WEISE. *Z. anorg. allg. Chem.*, **295**, 268 (1958).
2295. SCHÄFER, H. and H. WIEDEMEIER. *Z. anorg. allg. Chem.*, **296**, 241 (1958).
2296. SCHÄFER, H., F.E. WITTIG, and M. JORI. *Z. anorg. allg. Chem.*, **287**, 61 (1956).
2297. SCHÄFER, H., F.E. WITTIG, and W. WILBORN. *Z. anorg. allg. Chem.*, **297**, 48 (1958).
2298. SCHÄFER, H. and F. ZEPPERNICK. *Z. anorg. allg. Chem.*, **272**, 274 (1953).
2299. SCHEER, M.D. *J. Chem. Phys.*, **20**, 924 (1952).
2300. SCHEER, M.D. and J. FINE. *J. Chem. Phys.*, **36**, 1647 (1962).
2301. SCHEIBE, H. and W. ERMISCHER. *Kernenergie*, **6**, 178 (1963).
2302. SCHICK, H.L. *Chem. Rev.*, **60**, 331 (1960).
2303. SCHINDLER, P. *Helv. chim. acta*, **42**, 577 (1959).
2304. SCHINDLER, P. *Helv. chim. acta*, **42**, 2736 (1959).
2305. SCHINDLER, P., H. ALTHAUS, and W. FEITKNECHT. *Gazz. chim. ital.*, **93**, 168 (1963).
2306. SCHISSEL, P.O. and O.C. TRULSON. *J. Phys. Chem.*, **66**, 1492 (1962).
2307. SCHISSEL, P. and W. WILLIAMS. *Bull. Am. Phys. Soc.*, **4**, 139 (1959).
2308. SCHJÅNBERG, E. *Z. phys. Chem.*, **A172**, 197 (1935).
2308a. SCHJÅNBERG, E. *Z. phys. Chem.*, **A175**, 342 (1936).
2308b. SCHJÅNBERG, E. *Z. phys. Chem.*, **A181**, 430 (1938).
2309. SCHLÄFER, H.L. and H.H. SCHMIDTKE. *Z. phys. Chem.* (GFR), **1**, 297 (1957).
2310. SCHNEIDER, A. *Z. anorg. allg. Chem.*, **277**, 37 (1954).
2311. SCHNEIDER, A. and G. GATTOW. *Z. anorg. allg. Chem.* **277**, 41 (1954).
2312. SCHNEIDER, A. and H. KLOTZ. *Z. Naturforsch.*, **46**, 141 (1959).
2313. SCHNEIDER, A. H. KLOTZ, J. STENDEL, and G. STRAUSS. *"Thermodenamics', Proc. of the Symp. on Thermod., Aug. 1959*, London, Butterworth, 1961, p. 13.
2314. SCHNEIDER, A. and G. ZINTL. *Z. anorg. allg. Chem.*, **308**, 290 (1961).
2315. SCHNEIDER, B. and J. ŠTORK. *Coll. Czech. Chem. Comm.*, **26**, 1221 (1961).
2316. SCHOONMAKER, R.C. *"Condensation and Evaporation of Solids"*, New York, Gordon and Breach, 1964, p. 379.
2317. SCHOTTKY, W.F. and M.B. BEVER. *Acta metallurg.* **6**, 320 (1958).
2318. SCHRÖDER, K. *Phys. Rev.*, **125**, 1209 (1962).
2319. SCHULTZ, D.A. and A.W. SEARCY. *J. Phys. Chem.*, **67**, 103 (1963).
2320. SCHUMAN, S.C. and J.G. ASTON. *J. Chem. Phys.*, **6**, 485 (1938).
2321. SCHÜTZA, H., M. EUCKEN, and W. NÄMSCH. *Z. anorg. allg. Chem.*, **293**, 293 (1957).
2322. SCHWABE, K. and W. WAGNER. *Chem. Ber.*, **91**, 686 (1958).
2323. SCHWABE, K. and W. WAGNER. *Z. Elektrochem.*, **65**, 812 (1961).
2324. SCHWIETE, H.E. and C. HUMMEL. *Forschungsber. Wirtsch. u. Verkehrsmin., Nordrhein-Westfalen*, No. 515, 1105 (1958); HUMMEL, C. and H.E. SCHWIETE. *Glastechn. Ber.*, **32**, 327, 413 (1959).
2325. SCHWIETE, H.E. and G. ZIEGLER. *Z. anorg. allg. Chem.*, **298**, 42 (1959).
2326. SCOTT, D.W., D.R. DOUSLIN, H.L. FINKE, W.N.HUBBARD, J.F.MESSERLY, I.A.HOSSENLOPP, and J.P.McCULLOUGH, *Phys. Chem.*, **66**, 1334 (1962).
2327. SCOTT, D.W., D.R. DOUSLIN, M.E. GROSS, G.D. OLIVER, and H.M. HUFFMAN. *J. Am. Chem. Soc.*, **74**, 883 (1952).
2327a. SCOTT, D.W., H.L. FINKE, M.E. GROSS, G.B. GUTHRIE, and H.M. HUFFMAN. *J. Am. Chem. Soc.*, **72**, 2424 (1950).
2328. SCOTT, D.W., H.L. FINKE, W.N. HUBBARD, J.P. McCULLOUGH, M.E. GROSS, K.D. WILLIAMSON, G. WADDINGTON, and H.M. HUFFMAN. *J. Am. Chem. Soc.*, **72**, 4664 (1950).
2329. SCOTT, D.W., H.L. FINKE, et al. *J. Am. Chem. Soc.*, **74**, 2804 (1952).
2330. SCOTT, D.W., H.L. FINKE, W.N. HUBBARD, J.P. McCULLOUGH, G.D. OLIVER, M.E. GROSS, C. KATZ, K.D. WILLIAMSON, G. WADDINGTON, and H.M. HUFFMAN. *J. Am. Chem. Soc.*, **74**, 4654 (1952).
2331. SCOTT, D.W., H.L. FINKE, W.N. HUBBARD, J.P. McCULLOUGH, C. KATZ, M.E. GROSS, J.F. MESSERLY. R.E. PENNINGTON, and G. WADDINGTON. *J. Am. Chem. Soc.*, **75**, 2795 (1953).
2332. SCOTT, D.W., H.L. FINKE, J.P. McCULLOUGH, M.E. GROSS, R.E. PENNINGTON, and G. WADDINGTON. *J. Am. Chem. Soc.*, **74**, 2474 (1952).

2332a. SCOTT, D.W., H.L. FINKE, J.P. McCULLOUGH, M.E. GROSS, J.F. MESSERLY, R.E. PENNINGTON, and G. WADDINGTON. *J. Am. Chem. Soc.*, 77, 4993 (1955).
2333. SCOTT, D.W., H.L. FINKE, J.P. McCULLOUGH, M.E. GROSS, K.D. WILLIAMSON, G. WADDINGTON, and H.M. HUFFMAN. *J. Am. Chem. Soc.*, 73, 261 (1951).
2334. SCOTT, D.W., H.L. FINKE, J.P. McCULLOUGH, J.F. MESSERLY, R.E. PENNINGTON, I.A. HOSSENLOPP, and G. WADDINGTON. *J. Am. Chem. Soc.*, 79, 1064 (1957).
2335. SCOTT, D.W., W.D. GOOD, G.B. GUTHRIE, S.S. TODD, I.A. HOSSENLOPP, A.G. OSBORN, and J.P. McCULLOUGH. *J. Phys. Chem.*, **67**, 685 (1963).
2336. SCOTT, D.W., W.D. GOOD, S.S. TODD, J.F. MESSERLY, W.T. BERG, I.A. HOSSENLOPP, J.L. LACINA, A.G. OSBORN, and J.P. McCULLOUGH. *J. Chem. Phys.*, **36**, 406 (1962).
2337. SCOTT, D.W., W.D. GOOD, and G. WADDINGTON. *J. Am. Chem. Soc.*, 77, 245 (1955).
2338. SCOTT, D.W., W.D. GOOD, and G. WADDINGTON. *J. Phys. Chem.*, **60**, 1090 (1956).
2339. SCOTT, D.W., M.E. GROSS, G.D. OLIVER, and H.M. HUFFMAN. *J. Am. Chem. Soc.*, 71, 1634 (1949).
2340. SCOTT, D.W., G.B. GUTHRIE, J.F. MESSERLY, S.S. TODD, W.T. BERG, I.A. HOSSENLOPP, and J.P. McCULLOUGH. *J. Phys. Chem.*, **66**, 911 (1962).
2341. SCOTT, D.W., W.N. HUBBARD, J.F. MESSERLY, S.S. TODD, I.A. HOSSENLOPP, W.D. GOOD, D.R. DOUSLIN, and J.P. McCULLOUGH. *J. Phys. Chem.*, **67**, 680 (1963).
2342. SCOTT, D.W. and J.P. McCULLOUGH. *The Chemical Thermodynamic Properties of Hydrocarbons and Related Substances. Properties of 100 Linear Alkane Thiols, Sulfides, and Symmetrical Disulfides in the Ideal Gas State from 0° to 1000°K. BULL. 595, BUR. MINES*, U.S. Dept. of Interior, Washington, 1961. See also: AIVAZOV, B.V., S.M. PETROV, V.R. KHAIRULLINA, and V.G. YAPRYNTSEVA. *Fiziko-khimicheskie konstanty seraorganicheskikh soedinenii (Physicochemical Constants of Sulfur-Organic Compounds).*– Izd. Khimiya. (1964).
2343. SCOTT, D.W., J.P. McCULLOUGH, W.D. GOOD, J.F. MESSERLY, R.E. PENNINGTON, T.C. KINCHELOE, I.A. HOSSENLOPP, D.R. DOUSLIN, and G. WADDINGTON. *J. Am. Chem. Soc.*, 78, 5457 (1956).
2344. SCOTT, D.W., J.P. McCULLOUGH, W.N. HUBBARD, J.F. MESSERLY, I.A. HOSSENLOPP, F.R. FROW, and G. WADDINGTON. *J. Am. Chem. Soc.*. 78, 5463 (1956).
2345. SCOTT, D.W., J.P. McCULLOUGH, J.F. MESSERLY, R.E. PENNINGTON, I.A. HOSSENLOPP, H.L. FINKE, and G. WADDINGTON. *J. Am. Chem. Soc.*, **80**, 55 (1958).
2345a. SCOTT, D.W., J.P. McCULLOUGH, K.D. WILLIAMSON, and G. WADDINGTON. *J. Am. Chem. Soc.*, 73, 1707 (1951).
2346. SCOTT, D.W., J.F. MESSERLY, S.S. TODD, G.B. GUTHRIE, I.A. HOSSENLOPP, R.T. MOORE, A. OSBORN, W.T. BERG, and J.P. McCULLOUGH. *J. Phys. Chem.*, **65**, 1320 (1961).
2347. SCOTT, D.W., G.F. MESSERLY, S.S. TODD, I.A. HOSSENLOPP, A. OSBORN, and J.P. McCULLOUGH. *J. Chem. Phys.*, **38**, 532 (1963).
2348. SCOTT, D.W., G.D. OLIVER, M.E. GROSS, W.N. HUBBARD, and H.M. HUFFMAN. *J. Am. Chem. Soc.*, **71**, 2293 (1949).
2348a. SCOTT, D.W., G. WADDINGTON, J.C. SMITH, and H.M. HUFFMAN. *J. Am. Chem. Soc.*, **71**, 2767 (1949).
2349. SEABORG, G.T. and J.J. KATZ. *Natl. Nuclear Energy Ser., Div. IV*, **14A**. *The Actinide Elements*, 1954.
2350. SEARCY, A.W. *J. Am. Ceram. Soc.*, **40**, 431 (1957).
2351. SEARCY, A.W. and A. McNEES. *J. Am. Chem. Soc* 75, 1578 (1953).
2352. SEARCY, A.W. and C.E. MYERS. *J. Phys. Chem.*, **61**, 957 (1957).
2353. SEARCY, A.W. and A.G. THARP. *J. Phys. Chem.*, **64**, 1539 (1960).
2354. SEEL, F. and D. GÖLITZ. *Z. anorg. allg. Chem.* 327, 28 (1964).
2355. ŠEHA, Z. *Chem. Listy*, **49**, 1569 (1955).
2356. ŠEHA, Z. *Coll. Czech. Chem. Comm.*, **26**, 2435 (1961).
2357. SEHON, A.H. *J. Am. Chem. Soc.*, **74**, 4722 (1952).
2358. *Selected Values of Chemical Thermodynamic Properties*, Pt. 1. *Tables for the First Twenty-Three Elements in the Standard Order of Arrangement.* WAGMAN, D.D., W.H. EVANS, J. HALOW, V.B. PARKER, S.M. BAILEY, and R.H. SCHUMM. Nat. Bur. Stand., Technical Note 270–1, issued October 1, 1965.
2359. SELIG. H. and J.G. MALM. *J. Inorg. Nucl. Chem.*, **24**, 641 (1962).
2360. SELLERS, P. and S. SUNNER. *Acta chem. scand.* **16**, 46 (1962).
2361. SENFTLEBEN, H. *Z. angew. Phys.*, **17**, 86 (1964).
2362. SETTLE, J.L., H.M. FEDER, and W.N. HUBBARD. *J. Phys. Chem.*, **65**, 1337 (1961).
2363. SETTLE, J.L., H.M. FEDER, and W.N. HUBBARD. *J. Phys. Chem.*. **67**, 1892 (1963).
2364. SHANON, T.W. and A.G. HARRISON. *Can. J. Chem.* **39**, 1392 (1961).
2365. SHENKEL, R.G., B.G. HOBROCK, and R.W. KISER. *J. Phys. Chem.*, **66**, 2074 (1962).
2366. SHERMAN, R.H. and W.F. GIAUQUE. *J. Am. Chem. Soc.*, **75**, 2007 (1953).
2367. SHERMAN, R.H. and W.F. GIAUQUE. *J. Am. Chem. Soc.*, 77, 2154 (1955).
2368. SHIMAZAKI, E., N. MATSUMOTO, and K. NIWA. *Bull. Chem. Soc., Japan*, **30**, 969 (1957).
2369. SHIMIZU, K. and H. MURATA. *Bull. Chem. Soc. Japan*, **32**, 1158 (1959).
2370. SHIMIZU, K. and H. MURATA. *J. Molec. Spectrosc.*, **4**, 214 (1960).
2371. SHIRLEY, D.A. *J. Am. Chem. Soc.*, **82**, 3841 (1960).
2372. SHIRLEY, D.A. and W.F. GIAUQUE. *J. Am. Chem. Soc.*, **81**, 4778 (1959).
2373. SHOLETTE, W.P. and R.F. PORTER. *J. Phys. Chem.*, **67**, 177 (1963).
2374. SHOMATE, H. *J. Am. Chem. Soc.*, **69**, 218 (1957).

2375. SIEMONSEN, H. *Z. Elektrochem.* **55**, 327 (1951).
2376. SIEMONSEN, H. and U. SIEMONSEN. *Z. Elektrochem.*, **56**, 643 (1952).
2377. SILBERT, L.S., B.F. DAUBERT, and L.S. MASON. *J. Phys. Chem.*, **69**, 2887 (1965).
2378. SIMON, A., H.G. SCHUERING, H. WÖHHRLE, and H. SCHÄFER. *Z. anorg. allg. Chem.* **339**, 155 (1965).
2379. SINGH, D. *J. Sci. Res. Banares Hindu Univ.*, **6**, 131 (1955–1956).
2380. SINKE, G.C. *J. Phys. Chem.*, **63**, 2063 (1959).
2381. SINKE, G.C. and Th. De VRIES. *J. Am. Chem. Soc.*, **75**, 1815 (1953).
2382. SINKE, G.C. and D.L. HILDEBRAND. *J. Chem. Eng. Data*, **7**, 74 (1962).
2383. SINKE, G.C. and F.L. OETTING. *J. Phys. Chem.* **68**, 1354 (1964).
2384. SINKE, G.C. and D.R. STULL. *J. Phys. Chem.*, **62**, 397 (1958).
2385. SKINNER, G.B. and H.L. JOHNSTON. *J. Am. Chem. Soc.*, **75**, 4549 (1951).
2386. SKINNER, G.B. and R.A. RUEHRWEIN. *J. Phys. Chem.*, **59**, 113 (1955).
2387. SKINNER, H.A. *Roy. Inst. Chem., Lectures Monogr. a. Reports*, No. 3, 1958, pp. 1–52.
2387a. SKINNER, H. *J. Am. Chem. Soc.*, **87**, 5554 (1965).
2388. SKINNER, H.A., J.E. BENNETT, and J.B. PEDLEY. *"Thermodynamics", Proc. of the Symp. on Thermod., Aug., 1959*, London, Butterworth, 1961, p. 17.
2389. SKINNER, H.A. and FAIRBROTHER – cited in [1353].
2390. SKINNER, H.A. and N.B. SMITH. *Trans. Faraday Soc.*, **49**, 601 (1953).
2391. SKINNER, H.A. and N.B. SMITH. *J. Chem. Soc.*, **1954**, 3930.
2392. SKINNER, H.A. and N.B. SMITH. *Trans. Faraday Soc.*, **51**, 19 (1955).
2393. SKINNER, H.A. and A. SNELSON. *Trans. Faraday Soc.*, **56**, 1776 (1960).
2394. SKITA and FAUST. *Ber.*, **B64**, 2878 (1931).
2395. SKITA and FAUST. *Ber.*, **B72**, 1127 (1939).
2396. SKOCHDOPOLE, R.E. *Iowa State Coll. J. Sci.*, **29**, 499 (1955).
2397. SKOCHDOPOLE, R.E., M. GRIFFEL, and F.H. SPEDDING. *J. Chem. Phys.*, **23**, 2258 (1955).
2398. SKURATOV, S.M., KOZINA, PREVALOVA, KAMKINA, and ZUKO. *Bull. Chem. Thermodynamics, I.U.P.A.C.*, No. 1, A21 (1958).
2399. SKURATOV, S.M. KOZINA, SHTECHER, and VARUSHYENKO. *Thermochem. Bull., I.U.P.A.C.*, No.3, 25 (1957).
2400. SMILTENS, J. *J. Phys. Chem.*, **64**, 368 (1940).
2401. SMISKO, J. and L.S. MASON. **72**, 3679 (1950).
2402. SMITH. *Trans. Am. Inst. Chem. Eng.*, **42**, 983 (1946).
2402a. SMITH, D.F., D. BROWN, A.S. DWORKIN, D.J. SASMOR, and E.R. VAN ARTSDALEN. *J. Am. Chem. Soc.*, **78**, 1533 (1956).
2403. SMITH, D.F., A.S. DWORKIN, and E.R. VAN ARTSDALEN. *J. Am. Chem. Soc.* 77, 2654 (1955).
2404. SMITH, F.J. and R.F. BARROW. *Trans. Faraday Soc.*, **51**, 1478 (1955).
2405. SMITH, J.F. *"Thermodynamics of Nuclear Materials"*, International Atomic Energy Agency, Vienna, 1962, p. 271.
2406. SMITH, J.F. and J.L. CHRISTIAN. *Acta metallurg.*, **8**, 249 (1960).
2407. SMITH, J.F. and R.L. SMITHE. *Acta metallurg.*, 7, 261 (1959).
2408. SMITH, I., L. BJELLERUP, S. KROOK, and H. WESTERMARK. *Acta chem. scand.*, 7, 65 (1953).
2409. SMITH, M.B. and G.E. BASS. *J. Chem. Eng. Data*, **8**, 342 (1963).
2410. SMITH, N.K., G. GORIN, W.D. GOOD, and J.P. McCULLOUGH. *J. Phys. Chem.*, **68**, 940 (1964).
2411. SMITH, N.K., D.W. SCOTT, and J.P. McCULLOUGH. *J. Phys. Chem.*, **68**, 934 (1964).
2412. SMITH, P. *J. Chem. Phys.*, **29**, 683 (1958).
2413. SMITH, W.T., J.W. COBBLE, and G.E. BOYD. *J. Am. Chem. Soc.*, **75**, 5777 (1953).
2414. SMITH, W.T., G.D. OLIVER, and J.W. COBBLE. *J. Am. Chem. Soc.*, **75**, 5785 (1953).
2415. SMITHELLS, C.J. *Metals Reference Book*, London, Butterworth, 1949.
2416. SMUTHY, E.J. and A. BONDI. *J. Phys. Chem.*, **65**, 546 (1961).
2417. SNELSON, A. and H.A. SKINNER. *Trans. Faraday Soc.*, **57**, 2125 (1961).
2418. SOULEN, J.R. and J.L. MARGRAVE. *J. Am. Chem. Soc.*, **78**, 2911 (1956).
2419. SOULEN, J.R., P. STHAPITANOUDA, and J.L. MARGRAVE. *J. Phys. Chem.*, **59**, 132 (1955).
2420. SPANGENBERG, H.J. and H. KRIEGSMANN. *Z. Chem.*, **3**, 270 (1963).
2421. SPANGENBERG, H.J. and H. KRIEGSMANN. *Z. phys. Chem.* (GDR), **224**, 273 (1963).
2422. SPEDDING, F.H. and J.P. FLYNN. *J. Am. Chem. Soc.*, **76**, 1474 (1954).
2423. SPEDDING, F.H., J.J. McKEOWN, and A.H. DAANE. *J. Phys. Chem.*, **64**, 289 (1960).
2424. SPEDDING, F.H. and C.F. MILLER. *J. Am. Chem. Soc.*, **74**, 4195 (1952).
2425. SPEISER, R., R. BLACHBURN, and H.L. JOHNSTON. *J. Electrochem. Soc.*, **106**, 52 (1959).
2426. SPENSER, J.G. and L.G. HEPLER. *J. Phys. Chem.*, **64**, 499 (1960).
2427. SPICE, J.E., L.A.K. STAVELEY, and G.A. HARROW. *J. Chem. Soc.*, **1955**, 100.
2428. SPRINGALL, H.D., C.T. MORTIMER, and FLETCHER. *Thermochem. Bull., I.U.P.A.C.*, No. 3, 12 (1957).
2428a. SPRINGALL, H.D. and T.R. WHITE. *Research (London)*, **2**, 296 (1949).
2429. SPRINGALL, H.D. and T.R. WHITE. *J. Chem. Soc.*, **1954**, 2764.
2430. STACK, W.F., G.A. NASH, and H.A. SKINNER. *Trans. Faraday Soc.*, **61**, 2122 (1965).
2431. STALINSKI, B. and Z. BIEGANSKI. *Bull. Acad. Polon. Sci. Ser. Sci. chim.*, **8**, 243 (1960).
2432. STALINSKI, B. and Z. BIEGANSKI. *Roczn. chem.*, **35**, 273 (1961).

2433. STALINSKI, B. and Z. BIEGANSKI. *Bull. Acad. Polon. Sci., Ser. sci. chim.*, **10**, 247 (1962).
2434. STALINSKI, B. and Z. BIEGANSKI. *Bull. Acad. Polon. sci., Ser. sci. chim.*, **12**, 331 (1964).
2435. STALINSKI, B., J. NIEMIEC, and Z. BIEGANSKI. *Bull. Acad. Polon. sci., Ser. sci. chim.*, **11**, 267 (1963).
2436. STAMENKOVIÉ, J. *B. Kidric Inst. Nucl. Sci.*, **15**, 293 (1964).
2437. STAMM, R.F., F. HALVERSON, and J.J. WHALEN. *J. Chem. Phys.*, 17, 104 (1949).
2438. STAMPER, J.G. and R.F. BARROW. *Trans. Faraday Soc.*, **54**, 1592 (1958).
2439. STAMPFLER, J.F., C.E. HOLLEY, and J.F. SUTTLE. *J. Am. Chem. Soc.*, **82**, 3504 (1960).
2440. STASKIEWITCZ, B.A., J.R. TUCKER, and P.E. SNYDER. *J. Am. Chem. Soc.*, 77, 2987 (1955).
2441. STATHIS and EGERTON. *Trans. Faraday Soc.*, **36**, 606 (1940).
2442. STAVELEY, L.A.K., N.R. GREY, and M.J. LAYZELL. *Z. Naturforsch.*, **18a**, 148 (1963).
2443. STEACIE, E.W.R. *Atomic and Free Radical Reactions*, New York, Reinhold Publ., 1954.
2444. STEELE, W.C. and F.G.A. STONE. *J. Am. Chem. Soc.*, **84**, 3599 (1962).
2445. STEIN, L. *J. Phys. Chem.*, **66**, 288 (1962).
2446. STEINKOPF, H. and W. HÜTTIG. *Kernenergie*, **6**, 178 (1963).
2447. STEPHENSON, C.C., D.R. BENTZ, and D.A. STEVENSON. *J. Am. Chem. Soc.*, 77 2161 (1955).
2448. STEPHENSON, C.C. and D.J. BERETS. *J. Am. Chem. Soc.*, **74**, 882 (1952).
2449. STEPHENSON, C.C., H.P. HOPKINS, and C.A. WULFF. *J. Phys. Chem.* **68**, 1427 (1964).
2450. STEPHENSON, C.C. and O.R. LUNDELL. *J. Phys. Chem.*, **66**, 787 (1962).
2451. STEPHENSON, C.C. and J.C. MORROW. *J. Am. Chem. Soc.*, **78**, 275 (1956).
2452. STEPHENSON, C.C., C.A. WULFF, and O.R. LUNDELL. *J. Chem. Phys.*, **40**, 967 (1964).
2453. STEPHENSON, C.V. and E.A. JONES. *J. Chem. Phys.*, **20**, 135 (1952).
2454. STEPHENSON, C.V. and E.A. JONES. *J. Chem. Phys.*, **20**, 1830 (1952).
2455. STERN, J.H. and F.H. DORER. *J. Phys. Chem.*, **66**, 97 (1962).
2456. STERN, J.H. and J.J. JASNOSZ. *J. Chem. Eng. Data*, **9**, 534 (1964).
2457. STERN, J.H., R. PARKER, L.S. PEAK, and W.V. VOLLAND. *J. Chem. Eng. Data*, **8**, 40 (1963).
2458. STERRETT, K.F., W.G. SABA, and R.S. CRAIG. *J. Am. Chem. Soc.*, **81**, 5278 (1959).
2459. STERRETT, K.F. and W.E. WALLACE. *J. Am. Chem. Soc.*, **80**, 3176 (1958).
2460. STEUDEL, R. and P.W. SCHENK. *Z. phys. Chem.* (GFR), **43**, 33 (1964).
2461. STEUNENBERG, R.K. and R.C. VOGEL. *J. Am. chem. Soc.*, **79**, 1320 (1957).
2462. STEVEN, J.H. and A.A. PASSCHIER. *J. Phys. Chem.*, **66**, 752 (1962).
2463. STEVENS, C.G. and E.T. TURKDOVAN. *Trans. Faraday Soc.*. **51**, 356 (1955).
2464. STEVENSON, D.P. and D.M. YOST. *J. Chem. Phys.*, **9**, 403 (1941).
2465. STOUT, J.W. and E. CATALANO. *J. Chem. Phys.*, **23**, 2013 (1955).
2466. STOUT, J.W. and R.C. CHRISHOLM. *J. Chem. Phys.*, **66**, 979 (1962).
2467. STOUT, J.W. and R.A. ROBIE. *J. Phys. Chem.*, **27**, 2248 (1963).
2468. STRÄTER, F. *Beiträge zur Kenntnis der Thermochemie der Chlorsulfane*, Köln, 1961.
1469. STRITTMATER, R.C., G.J. PEARSON, and G.C. DANIELSON. *Proc. Iowa Acad. Sci.*, **64**, 466 (1957).
2470. STROH, H.-H., and C.-R. FINKE. *Z. Chem.*, **3**, 265 (1963).
2471. STRUBELL, W. *J. prakt. Chem.*, **26**, 319 (1964).
2472. STUBBLEFIELD, C.T., H. EICK, and L. EYRING. *J. Am. Chem. Soc.*, 78, 3018 (1956).
2473. STUBBLEFIELD, C.T., H. EICK, and L. EYRING. *J. Am.Chem. Soc.*, 78, 3877 (1956).
2474. STUBBLEFIELD, C.T., J.L. RATLEDGE, and R. PHILLIPS. *J. Phys. Chem.*, **69**, 991 (1965).
2475. STUBBLES, J.R. and F.D. RICHARDSON. *Trans. Faraday Soc.* , **56**, 1460 (1960).
2476. STUBBS, M.F., J.A. SCHUFLE, and A.J. THOMSON. *J. Am. Chem. Soc.* **74**, 6201 (1952).
2477. STULL, D.K. *J. Am. Chem. Soc.*, **59**, 2726 (1937).
2478. STULL, D.R. *Bull. Chem. Thermodynamics, I.U.P.A.C.*, No. 2, 6 (1959).
2479. STULL, D.R. and G.C. SINKE. *Thermodynamic Properties of the Elements. Advances in Chemistry. Ser.*, No. 18. Washington, 1956.
2480. STULL, D.R., G.C. SINKE, R.A. McDONALD, W.E. HATTON, and D.L. HILDEBRAND. *"Thermodynamics", Proc. of the Symp. on Thermod., Aug., 1959*, London, Butterworth, 1961, p. 315.
2481. SUDO, K. *Sci. Repts. Res. Inst., Tohoku Univ.*, Ser., **A2**, 513 (1950).
2482. SUNDARAM, S. *Can. J. Phys.*, **39**, 370 (1961).
2483. SUNDARAM, S. *Z. phys. Chem.*, (GFR), **34**, 225 (1962).
2484. SUNDARAM, S. *Z. phys. Chem.*, (GFR), **34**, 233 (1962).
2485. SUNDARAM, S. *Z. phys. Chem.*, (GFR), **36**, 376 (1963).
2486. SUNDARAM, S. and F.F. CLEVELAND. *J. Chem. Phys.*, **32**, 166 (1960).
2487. SUNDARAM, S. and F.F. CLEVELAND. *J. Chem. Phys.*, **32**, 1554 (1960).
2488. SUNDARAM, S. and F.F. CLEVELAND. *J. Molec. Spectrosc.*, **5**, 61 (1961).
2489. SUNDARAM, S., F. SUSZEK, and F.F. CLEVELAND. *J. Chem. Phys.*, **32**, 251 (1960).
2490. SUNNER, S. Thesis, Lund Univ., 1949; *Svensk. Kem. Tidskr.* **58**, 71 (1946).
2491. SUNNER, S. *Acta chem. scand.*, **9**, 837 (1955).
2492. SUNNER, S. *Acta chem. scand.*, **9**, 847 (1955).
2493. SUNNER, S. *Acta chem. scand.*, **11**, 1766 (1957).

2494. SUNNER, S. *Acta chem. scand.*, **13**, 825 (1959).
2495. SUNNER, S. *Acta chem. scand.*, **17**, 728 (1963).
2496. SUNNER, S. – cited in [1879].
2497. SUNNER, S. and B. LUNDIN – cited in [1558].
2498. SUNNER, S. and S. THOREN. *Acta chem. scand.*, **18**, 1528 (1964).
2499. SUNNER, S. and I. WADSÖL. *Trans. Faraday Soc.*, **53**, 455 (1957).
2500. SUZUKI, S. *J. Chem. Soc. Japan*, **73**, 278 (1952).
2501. SUZUKI, S. *Sci. Repts. Res. Inst., Tohoku Univ.*, Ser. 1, **37**, 15 (1953).
2502. SUZUKI, S. *J. Chem. Soc. Japan*, **74**, 219 (1953); *Chem. Abstr.*, **47**, 10970b.
2503. SUZUKI, S. *J. Chem. Soc. Japan*, **74**, 269 (1953).
2504. SVEC, H.J. and G.D. FLESCH. *Science*, **142**, 954 (1963).
2505. SWAIN, H.A., L.S. SILBERT, and J.G. MILLER. *J. Am. Chem. Soc.*, **86**, 2562 (1964).
2506. SWANSON, M.L. *Can. J. Phys.*, **40**, 719 (1962).
2507. SWIFT, R.M. and D. WHITE. *J. Am. Chem. Soc.*, **79**, 3641 (1957).
2508. SYKES, K.S. *J. Chem. Soc.*, **1958**, 2053.
2509. SYKES, K.W. and S. TOWNSHEND. *J. Chem. Soc.*, **1955**, 2528.
2510. SZWARC, M. and A. SEHON. *Ann. Rev. Phys. Chem.*, **8**, 439 (1957).
2511. SZWARC, M. and J.W. TAYLOR. *J. Chem. Phys.*, **23**, 2310 (1955).
2512. SZWARC, R., E.R. PLANTE, and J.J. DIAMOND. *J. Res. Nat. Bur. Stand.*, **69A**, 417 (1956).
2512a. TAFT, R.W. and P. RIESZ. *J. Am. Chem. Soc.*, **77**, 902 (1955).
2513. TAKAHASHI, Y. and E.F. WESTRUM. *J. Chem. Eng. Data*, **10**, 244 (1965).
2514. TAKAHASHI, Y. and E.F. WESTRUM. *J. Phys. Chem.*, **69**, 3618 (1965).
2515. TANAKA, T. *Bull. Chem., Soc., Japan*, **32**, 1258 (1959).
2516. TAYLOR, A.R., E.T. GARDNER, and D.F. SMITH. *Bur. Mines Report of Investig.*, 6157, U.S. Dept. of Interior, Wash., 1963.
2517. TAYLOR, A.R., T.E. GARDNER, and D.F. SMITH. *Bur. Mines Report of Investig.*, 6240, U.S. Dept. of Interior, Wash., 1963.
2518. TAYLOR, A.R. and D.F. SMITH. *Bur. Mines Report of Investig.*, 5967, U.S. Dept. of Interior, Wash., 1962.
2519. TAYLOR, R.D. and J.E. KILPATRIK. *J. Chem. Phys.*, **23**, 1232 (1955).
2520. TAYLOR, R.C. and G.L. VIDALE. *J. Chem. Phys.*, **26**, 122 (1957).
2520a. TAYLOR, R.D., B.H. JOHNSON, and J.E. KILPATRIK. *J. Chem. Phys.*, **23**, 1225 (1955).
2521. TAYLOR, R.E. and R.A. FINCH. *J. Less-Common Metals*, **6**, 283 (1964).
2522. TAYLOR, W.J., D.D. WAGMAN, M.G. WILLIAMS, K.D. PITZER, and F.D. ROSSINI. *J. Res. Nat. Bur. Stand.*, **37**, 95 (1946).
2523. *Techn. Rept. Ser. Internat. Atomic Energy Agency*, No. 14, 44 (1963).
2524. TEN HU, and L.G. HEPLER. *J. Chem. Eng. Data*, **7**, 58 (1962).
2525. TERANISHI, H. and S.W. BENSON. *J. Am. Chem. Soc.*, **85**, 2887 (1963).
2526. TERPILOWSKI, J. and W. TRZEBIATOWSKI. *Acad. Polon. sci., Ser. sci. chim.*, **8**, 95 (1960).
2527. TERPILOWSKI, J., E. ZALESKA, and W. GAWEL. *Roczn. chem.*, **39**, 1367 (1965).
2527a. *The Uranium – Carbon and Plutonium – Carbon Systems, Technical Reports*, No. 14, IAEA, Vienna, 1963 (cited in [1131]).
2528. THEARD, L.P. and D.L. HILDEBRAND. *J. Chem. Phys.*, **41**, 3416 (1964).
2528a. *Thermodynamic and Transport Properties of Uranium Dioxide and Related Phases, Technical Reports*, Ser. N 39, International Atomic Energy Agency, Vienna, 1965.
2529. THEIMER, R. and J.R. NIELSEN. *J. Chem. Phys.*, **27**, 264 (1957).
2529a. THEIMER, R. and J.R. NIELSEN. *J. Chem. Phys.*, **26**, 1374 (1957).
2530. THEIMER, R. and J.R. NIELSEN. *J. Chem. Phys.*, **30**, 98 (1959).
2531. THOMPSON, A.J., M.F. STUBBS, and J.A. SCHUFLE. *J. Am. Chem. Soc.*, **76**, 341 (1954).
2532. THOMPSON, C.J., G.C. SINKE, and D.R. STALL. *J. Chem. Eng. Data*, **7**, 380 (1962).
2533. THORN, R.J. *Argonic Nat. Labor.*, 1957 (cited in [96]).
2534. THORN, R.J. and G.H. WINSLOW. *J. Phys. Chem.*, **65**, 1297 (1961).
2535. THYAGARAJAN, G. and F.F. CLEVELAND. *J. Molec. Spectrosc.*, **5**, 210 (1960).
2536. THYAGARAJAN, G. and F.F. CLEVELAND. *J. Molec. Spectrosc.*, **5**, 210 (1961).
2537. THYAGARAJAN, G., S. SUNDARAM, and F.F. CLEVELAND. *J. Molec. Spectrosc.*, **5**, 307 (1960).
2537a. TIENS, V.V. Thesis, Cornell Univ., 1962 (cited in [1219]).
2538. TJEBBES, J. *Acta chem. scand.*, **14**, 180 (1960).
2539. TJEBBES, J. *"Thermodynamics", Proc. of the Symp. on Thermod., Aug. 1959*, London, Butterworth, 1961, p. 129.
2540. TJEBBES, J. *Acta chem. scand.*, **16**, 253 (1962).
2541. TJEBBES, J. *Acta chem. scand.*, **16**, 916 (1962).
2542. TODD, S.S. *J. Am. Chem. Soc.*, **72**, 2914 (1950).
2543. TODD, S.S. *J. Am. Chem. Soc.*, **73**, 3277 (1951).
2544. TODD, S.S. *J. Am. Chem. Soc.*, **74**, 4669 (1952).
2545. TODD, S.S. *J. Am. Chem. Soc.*, **74**, 4742 (1952).
2546. TODD, S.S. *J. Am. Chem. Soc.*, **75**, 1229 (1953).
2547. TODD, S.S. *J. Am. Chem. Soc.*, **75**, 3035 (1953).

2548. TODD. S.S. – cited in [677].
2549. TODD, S.S. and R.R. BONNICKSON. *J. Am. Chem. Soc.*, **73**, 3894 (1951).
2550. TODD, S.S. and J.P. COUGHLIN. *J. Am. Chem. Soc.*, **73**, 4184 (1951).
2551. TODD, S.S. and J.P. COUGHLIN. *J. Am. Chem. Soc.*, **74**, 525 (1952).
2552. TODD, S.S. and K.K. KELLEY. *Bur. Mines Report of Investig.*, 5193, U.S. Dept. of Interior, Wash., 1956.
2553. TODD, S.S. and E.G. KING. *J. Am. Chem. Soc.*, **75**, 4547 (1953).
2554. TODD, S.S. and R.E. LORENSON. *J. Am. Chem. Soc.*, **74**, 2043 (1952).
2555. TODD, S.S. and R.E. LORENSON. *J. Am. Chem. Soc.*, **74**, 3764 (1952).
2556. TODD, S.S., G.D. OLIVER, and H.M. HUFFMAN. *J. Am. Chem. Soc.*, **69**, 1519 (1947).
2557. TOMASCH, W.J. *Phys. Rev.*, **123**, 510 (1961).
2558. TOMBS, N. and A. WELCH. *J. Iron Steel Inst.*, **172**, 69 (1952).
2559. TOMLINSON, J.R., L. DOMASH, R.G. HAY, and C.W. MONTGOMERY. *J. Am. Chem. Soc.*, **77**, 909 (1955).
2560. TOPOL, L.E. and L.D. RANSOM. *J. Phys. Chem.*, **64**, 1339 (1960).
2560a. TORKINGTON, P. *Trans. Faraday Soc.*, **46**, 894 (1950).
2561. TOSHIO YOKOKAWA, KOIZUMI MASUMISHI, SHIMOJI MITSUI, and NIWA KICHIRO. *J. Am. Chem. Soc.*, **79**, 3365 (1957).
2562. TROWBRIDGE, J.C. and E.F. WESTRUM. *J. Phys. Chem.*, **67**, 2381 (1963).
2563. TROWBRIDGE, J.C. and E.F. WESTRUM. *J. Phys. Chem.*, **68**, 42 (1964).
2564. TROWBRIDGE, J.C. and E.F. WESTRUM. *J. Phys. Chem.*, **68**, 255 (1964).
2565. TROWBRIDGE, J.C. and E.F. WESTRUM. *J. Phys. Chem.*, **68**, 2381 (1964).
2566. TRULSON, O.C. and H.W. GOLDSTEIN. *J. Phys. Chem.*, **69**, 2531 (1965).
2567. TSCHUIKOW-ROUX, E. *J. Phys. Chem.*, **66**, 1636 (1962).
2568. TSCHUIKOW-ROUX, E. *J. Phys. Chem.*, **69**, 1075 (1965).
2569. TURNBULL, A.G. *J. Phys. Chem.*, **65**, 1652 (1961).
2570. TURNBULL, A.G. *Austral. J. Chem.*, **17**, 1063 (1964).
2571. TURNBULL, A.G. and J.A. WATTS. *Austral. J. Chem.*, **16**, 947 (1963).
2572. UHLIŘ, A., J. UHLIŘOVÁ, J., J. KOLINSKÝ, V. RŮŽIČKA, and J. PAŠEK. *Chem. Prům.*, **14**, 470 (1964).
2573. UUSITALO, E. *Suomen Kem.*, **31**, B228 (1958).
2574. VALENTIN, F.H.H. *J. Chem. Soc.*, **1950**, 498.
2575. VALENTINE, R.H. and W.F. GIAUQUE. *J. Phys. Chem.*, **66**, 392 (1962).
2576. VALENTINE, R.H., T.F. JAMBOIS, and J.L. MARGRAVE. *J. Chem. Eng. Data*, **9**, 184 (1964).
2577. VAN ARTSDALEN, E.R. and A.S. DWORKIN. *J. Am. Chem. Soc.*, **74**, 3401 (1952).
2578. VANDERZEE, C.E. and R.A. MYERS. *J. Phys. Chem.*, **65**, 153 (1961).
2579. VANDERZEE, C.E. and J.A. SWANSON. *J. Phys. Chem.*, **67**, 285 (1963).
2580. VAUGHN, J.D. and E.L. MUETTERTIES. *J. Phys. Chem.*, **64**, 1787 (1960).
2581. VENKATESWARLU, K. and K.V. RAJALAKSHMI. *Acta phys. polon.*, **22**, 417 (1962).
2582. VENKATESWARLU, K. and K.V. RAJALAKSHMI. *Indian J. Pure Appl. Phys.*, **1**, 62 (1963).
2583. VENKATESWARLU, K. and K. SATHANANDAN. *Z. phys. Chem.* (GDR), **218**, 318 (1961).
2584. VENKATESWARLU, K., S. TAGATHEESAN, and K.V. RAJALAKSHMI. *Proc. Indian Acad. Sci.*, **A58**, 373 (1963).
2585. VENKATESWARLU, K. and R. THANALAKASHMI. *Acta phys. polon.*, **22**, 423 (1962).
2586. VERHAEGEN, J.L., G.O. ROBBRECHT, and W.N. BRUYNOSGHE. *Appl Sci. Res.*, Sect. B, 8, 128 (1960).
2587. VERHAEGEN, G. and J. DROWART. *J. Chem. Phys.*, **37**, 1367 (1962).
2588. VERKADE, P.E. and J. COOPS. *Rec. trav. chim.*, **47**, 608 (1928).
2589. VERKADE, P.E. and J. COOPS. *Rec. trav. chim.*, **52**, 747 (1933).
2590. VERKADE, P.E., J. COOPS, C.J. MAAN, and A. VERKADE-SANDBERGEN. *Ann.*, **467**, 217 (1928).
2591. VERKADE, P.E. and HARTMAN. *Rec. trav. chim.*, **52**, 945 (1933).
2592. VERKADE, P.E., HARTMANN, and J. COOPS. *Rec. trav. chim.*, **45**, 373 (1926).
2592a. VERSTEGEN, J.M.P.J. and J.A.A. KETELAAR. *Trans. Faraday Soc.*, **57**, 91 (1961).
2593. VICTOR, A.C. *J. Chem. Phys.*, **36**, 1902 (1962).
2594. VICTOR, A.C. and Th.B. DOUGLAS. *J. Res. Nat. Bur. Stand.*, **A65**, 105 (1961).
2595. VICTOR, A.C. and Th.B. DOUGLAS. *J. Res. Nat. Bur. Stand.*, **A67**, 325 (1963).
2596. VOELZ, F.L. *J. Chem. Phys.*, **20**, 1662 (1952).
2597. VOELZ, F.L., A.G. MEISTER, and F.F. CLEVELAND. *J. Chem. Phys.*, **19**, 1084 (1951).
2597a. VOELZ, F.L., A.G. MEISTER, and F.F. CLEVELAND. *J. Chem. Phys.*, **20**, 1498 (1952).
2598. VOLGER, J. *Philips Res. Repts.*, **7**, 21 (1952) (cited in [2243]).
2599. VOZZELLA, P.A., A.D. MILLER, and M.A. De CRESCENTE. *J. Chem. Phys.*, **41**, 589 (1964).
2600. WADDINGTON, G., J.W. KNOWLTON, D.W. SCOTT, G.D. OLIVER, S.S. TODD, W.N. HUBBARD, J.C. SMITH, and H.M. HUFFMAN. *J. Am. Chem. Soc.*, **71**, 797 (1949).
2600a. WADDINGTON, G., J.C. SMITH, D.W. SCOTT, and H.M. HUFFMAN. *J. Am. Chem. Soc.*, **71**, 3902 (1949).
2601. WADDINGTON, G., J.C. SMITH, K.D. WILLIAMSON, and D.W. SCOTT. *J. Phys. Chem.*, **66**, 1074 (1962).
2602. WADDINGTON, T.C. *Trans. Faraday Soc.*, **55**, 1531 (1959).
2602a. WADSÖ, I. *Acta chem. scand.*, **19**, 1079 (1965).
2603. WAGMAN, D.D. *J. Am. Chem. Soc.*, **73**, 5463 (1951).
2604. WAGMAN, D.D., J.E. KILPATRIK, K.S. PITZER, and F.D. ROSSINI. *J. Res. Nat. Bur. Stand.*, **35**, 467 (1945).

2605. WAGMAN, D.D., J.E. KILPATRIK, W.J. TAYLOR, K.S. PITZER, and F.D. ROSSINI. *J. Res. Nat. Bur. Stand.*, **34**, 143 (1945).
2606. WAGMAN, D.D., T.R. MUSON, W.H. EWANS, and E.J. OROSEN. *Nat. Bur. Stand., Report* 3456, Aug. 30, 1954.
2607. WAGNER, H. and K. NEUMANN. *Z. phys. Chem.* (GFR), **28**, 51 (1961).
2608. WAGNER, J.B. and C. WAGNER. *J. Electrochem. Soc.*, **104**, 509 (1957).
2609. WALLAGE, D.C. *Phys. Rev.*, **120**, 84 (1960).
2610. WALLAGE, D.C., P.H. SIDES, and G.C. DANIELSON. *J. Appl. Phys.*, **31**, 168 (1960).
2611. WALFAFEN, G.E. and D.M. DODD. *Trans. Faraday Soc.*, **57**, 1286 (1961).
2612. WALSH, P.N., E.W. ART, and D. WHITE. *J. Phys. Chem.*, **66**, 1546 (1962).
2613. WALSH, P.N., D.F. DEVER, and D. WHITE. *J. Phys. Chem.*, **65**, 1410 (1961).
2614. WARD, Ch.R. and C.H. WARD. *J. Molec. Spectrosc.*, **12**, 289 (1964).
2615. WARD, Ch.R. and SINGLETON. *J. Phys. Chem.*, **56**, 696 (1952).
2616. WARING, W. *Chem. Rev.*, **51**, 171 (1952).
2617. WARTENBERG, H. v. *Z. anorg. allg. Chem.*, **244**, 337 (1940); **249**, 100 (1942); **252**, 136 (1943).
2618. WARTENBERG, H. v. *Z. anorg. allg. Chem.*, **258**, 356 (1949).
2619. WARTENBERG, H. v. *Z. anorg. allg. Chem.*, **299**, 227 (1959).
2620. WARTENBERG, H. v. and J. SCHEIFER. *Z. anorg. allg. Chem.*, **278**, 326 (1955).
2621. WATANABE, M. and T. YOSHIDA. *Sci. Repts. Inst. Tohoku Univ.*, No. 1, 62 (1959).
2622. WEBER, L.A. and J.E. KILPATRIK. *J. Chem. Phys.*, **36**, 83 (1962).
2623. WEBER, L.A. and J.E. KILPATRIK. *J. Phys. Chem.*, **66**, 829 (1962).
2624. WEBER, A., A.G. MEISTER, and F.F. CLEVELAND. *J. Chem. Phys.*, **21**, 930 (1953).
2625. WEIBKE, F. and O. KUBASCHEWSKI. *Thermochemie der Legierungen*, Berlin, Springer, 1943.
2626. WEIGEL, F. and H. HANG. *Chem. Ber.*, **94**, 1548 (1961).
2627. WEINSTOCK, B., H.H. CLAASSEN, and J.G. MALM. *J. Chem. Phys.*, **32**, 181 (1960).
2628. WEINSTOCK, B., E.E. WEAVER, and J.G. MALM. *J. Inorg. Nucl. Chem.*, **11**, 104 (1959).
2628'. WEISER, K. *J. Phys. Chem.*, **61**, 513 (1957).
2628b. WEISSMAN, H.B., R.B. BERNSTEIN, S.E. ROSSER, and A.G. MEISTER. *J. Chem. Phys.*, **23**, 544 (1955).
2629. WEISSMAN, H.B., A.G. MEISTER, and F.F. CLEVELAND. *J. Chem. Phys.*, **29**, 72 (1958).
2630. WELLER, W.W. and K.K. KELLEY. *Bur. Mines Report of Investig.*, 6343, U.S. Dept. of Interior, Wash., 1963.
2631. WELLER, W.W. and K.K. KELLEY. *Bur. Mines Report of Investig.*, 6357, U.S. Dept. of Interior, Wash., 1964.
2632. WELLER, W.W. and K.K. KELLEY. *Bur. Mines Report of Investig.*, 6511, U.S. Dept. of Interior, Wash., 1964.
2633. WELLER, W.W. and E.G. KING. *Bur. Mines Report of Investig.*, 6147, U.S. Dept. of Interior, Wash., 1963.
2634. WELTNER, W. *J. Am. Chem. Soc.*, **77**, 3941 (1955).
2635. WELTNER, W. and K.S. PITZER. *J. Am. Chem. Soc.*, **73**, 2606 (1951).
2636. WELTY, J.R., C.E. WICKS, and H.O. BOREN. *Bur. Mines Report of Investig.*, 6155, U.S. Dept. of Interior, Wash., (1963).
2636a. WENDLANDT, W. *Science*, **122**, 831 (1955).
2637. WENDLANDT, W. and T.D. GEORGE. *J. Inorg. Nucl. Chem.*, **19**, 245 (1961).
2638. WEST, E.D. *J. Am. Chem. Soc.*, **81**, 29 (1959).
2639. WESTMORE, J.B., H.H. MANN, and A.W. TICKNER. *J. Phys. Chem.*, **68**, 606 (1964).
2640. WESTRUM, E.F. *Nat. Luclear Energy Ser., Div. IV*, **14B**, *The Transuranium Elements*, Research Papers. Ed. G.T. SEABORG, J.T. KATZ, and W.M. MANNING, Pt. II, New York, Toronto, London, 1949, p. 926.
2641. WESTRUM, E.F. – cited in [2689].
2642. WESTRUM, E.F. *Thermodynamic and Transport Properties of Gases, Liquids and Solids.* Am. Soc. Mechan. Eng., New York, 1959, p. 275.
2643. WESTRUM, E.F. *"Thermodynamics", Proc. of the Symp. on Thermod., Aug., 1959*, London, Butterworth, 1961, p. 241.
2644. WESTRUM, E.F. *J. Chem. Eng. Data*, **10**, 140 (1965).
2645. WESTRUM, E.F. – cited in [735].
2646. WESTRUM, E.F. – cited in [1959].
2647. WESTRUM, E.F. and A.F. BEALE. *J. Phys. Chem.*, **65**, 353 (1961).
2648. WESTRUM, E.F. and A.F. BEALE. *J. Chem. Phys.*, **34**, 1087 (1961).
2649. WESTRUM, E.F. and G.A. BURNEY. *J. Phys. Chem.*, **65**, 344 (1961).
2650. WESTRUM, E.F., H.G. CARLSON, F. GRÖNVOLD, and A. KJEKSHUS. *J. Chem. Phys.*, **18**, 1670 (1959).
2651. WESTRUM, E.F. and C. CHOU. *J. Chem. Phys.*, **30**, 761 (1959).
2652. WESTRUM, E.F., C. CHOU, R.E. MACHOL, and F. GRÖNVOLD. *J. Chem. Phys.*, **28**, 497 (1958).
2653. WESTRUM, E.F. and G.A. CLAY. *J. Phys. Chem.*, **67**, 2385 (1963).
2654. WESTRUM, E.F. and L. EYRING. *Nat. Nuclear Energy Ser., Div. IV*, **14B**, *The Transuranium Elements*, Research Papers, Ed. G.T. SEABORG, J.T. KATZ, and W.M. MANNING, Pt. II, New York, Toronto, London, 1949, p. 908.
2655. WESTRUM, E.F. and L.R. EYRING. *J. Am. Chem. Soc.*, **73**, 3396 (1951).
2656. WESTRUM, E.F. and L.R. EYRING. *J. Am. Chem. Soc.*, **74**, 2045 (1952).
2657. WESTRUM, E.F. and G. FEICK. *J. Chem. Eng. Data*, **8**, 176 (1963).
2658. WESTRUM, E.F. and G. FEICK. *J. Chem. Eng. Data*, **8**, 193 (1963).
2659. WESTRUM, E.F. and G. GRENIER. *J. Am. Chem. Soc.*, **79**, 1799 (1957).
2660. WESTRUM, E.F. and D.M. GRIMES. *Phys. a. Chem. Solids*, **3**, 44 (1957).

2661. WESTRUM, E.F. and F. GRÖNVOLD. *J. Am. Chem. Soc.*, **81**, 1777 (1959).
2662. WESTRUM, E.F. and F. GRÖNVOLD. *Thermodynamics of Nuclear Materials,* International Atomic Energy Agency, Vienna, 1962, p. 3.
2663. WESTRUM, E.F. and F. GRÖNVOLD. *Thermodynamics of Nuclear Materials,* International Atomic Energy Agency, Vienna, 1962, p.71.
2664. WESTRUM, E.F. and F. GRÖNVOLD. *J. Phys. a. Chem. Solids,* **23**, 39 (1962).
2665. WESTRUM, E.F., J.B. HATCHER, and D.W. OSBORNE. *J. Chem. Phys.*, **21**, 419 (1953).
2666. WESTRUM, E.F. and B.H. JUSTICE. *J. Phys. Chem.*, **67**, 659 (1963).
2667. WESTRUM, E.F. and N.E. LEVITIN. *J. Am. Chem. Soc.*, **81**, 3544 (1959).
2668. WESTRUM, E.F. and H.P. ROBINSON. *Natl. Nuclear Energy Ser., Div. IV,* **14B**, *The Transuranium Elements,* Research Papers. Ed. G.T. SEABORG, J.T. KATZ, and W.M. MANNING. Pt. II, New York, Toronto, London, 1949, p. 914.
2669. WESTRUM, E.F. and H.P. ROBINSON. *Natl. Nuclear Energy Ser., Div. IV,* **14B**, *The Transuranium Elements,* Research Papers. Ed. G.T. SEABORG, J.T. KATZ, and W.M. MANNING. Pt. II, New York, Toronto, London, 1949, p. 930.
2670. WESTRUM, E.F., SHU-SING CHANG, and N.E. LEVITIN. *J. Phys. Chem.* **64**, 1553 (1960).
2671. WESTRUM, E.F., Y. TAKAHASHI, and N.D. STOUT. *J. Phys. Chem.* **69**, 1520 (1965).
2672. WESTRUM, E.F., Y. TAKAHASHI, and F. GRÖNVOLD. *J. Phys. Chem.*, **69**, 3192 (1965).
2673. WESTRUM, E.F. and D.H. TERWILLIGER - cited in [1045].
2674. WHEELER, W.H., H. WHITTAKER, and H.H.M. PIKE. *J. Inst. Fuel,* **20**, 137 (1957).
2675. WHIFFEN, D.H. *J. Chem. Soc.*, **1956**, 1350.
2676. WHITE, D. - cited in [1930].
2677. WHITE, D., K.S. SESHADRI, D.F. DEVER, D.E. MANN, and M.J. LINEVSKY. *J. Chem. Phys.*, **39**, 2463 (1963).
2678. WHITE, D., P.N. WALSH, H.W. GOLDSTEIN, and D.F. DEVER. *J. Phys. Chem.*, **65**, 1404 (1961).
2679. WHITE, D., P.N. WALSH, L.L. AMES, and H.W. GOLDSTEIN. *Techn. Repts. Internat. Atomic Energy Agency,* No. 14, 1963, p. 417.
2680. WIBERG, K.B. and W.J. BARTLEY. *J. Am. Chem. Soc.*, **84**, 3981 (1962).
2681. WICKE, H. *Nachr. Akad. Wissensch. Göttingen, math.-phys. Klasse 89.* 1946.
2682. WIDEMEYER, H. *Z. anorg. allg. Chem.*, **326**, 225 (1964).
2683. WILCOX, D.E. and L.A. BROMLEY. *Ind. Eng. Chem.*, **55**, 32 (1963).
2684. WILHOIT, R.C. and I. LEI. *J. Chem. Eng. Data,* **10**, 166 (1965).
2685. WILHOIT, R.C. and D. SHIAO. *J. Chem. Eng. Data,* **9**, 595 (1964).
2686. WILKINS, L. and R.L. ALTMAN. *J. Chem. Phys.*, **31**, 337 (1959).
2687. WILLA, H. *J. Soc. Chem. Ind.*, **1950**, 59.
2688. WILLIAMS, W.S. *J. Phys. Chem.*, **65**, 2213 (1961).
2688a. WILLIAMSON, K.D. and R.H. HARRISON. *J. Chem. Phys.*, **26**, 1409 (1957).
2689. WILSON, L.E. and N.W. GREGORY. *J. Phys. Chem.*, **62**, 433 (1958).
2690. WILSON, M.K. and S.K. POLO. *J. Chem. Phys.*, **20**, 1716 (1952).
2691. WIRTH, H.E., J.W. DROEGE, and J.H. WOOD. *J. Phys. Chem.*, **63**, 152 (1959).
2692. WIRTH, H.E., J.H. WOOD, and J.W. DROEGE. *J. Phys. Chem.*, **63**, 149 (1959).
2693. WISE, S.S., J.L. MARGRAVE, and R.L. ALTMAN. *J. Phys. Chem.*, **64**, 915 (1960).
2694. WISE, S.S., J.L. MARGRAVE, and H.M. FEDER. *J. Phys. Chem.*, **66**, 381 (1962).
2695. WISE, S.S., J.L. MARGRAVE, H.M. FEDER, and W.N. HUBBARD. *J. Phys. Chem.*, **67**, 815 (1963).
2696. WISE, S.S., S. STEPHEN, J.L. MARGRAVE, H.M. FEDER, and W.N. HUBBARD. *J. Phys. Chem.*, **65**, 2157 (1961).
2697. WITT, W.P. and R.F. BARROW. *Trans. Faraday Soc.*, **55**, 730 (1959).
2698. WÖHLER, L. and N. JOCHUM. *Z. Phys. Chem.*, **A167**, 169 (1933).
2699. WOLF, E. *Z. anorg. allg. Chem.*, **313**, 228 (1961).
2700. WOLF, E., W. STAHN, and M. SCHÖNHERR. *Z. anorg. allg. Chem.*, **319**, 168 (1962).
2701. WOLLAM, J.S. and W.E. WALLAGE. *J. Phys. a. Chem. Solids,* **13**, 212 (1960).
2702. WOOD, R.H. *J. Am. Chem. Soc.*, **80**, 2038 (1958).
2703. WOOD, J.L. and M.M. JONES. *J. Phys. Chem.*, **67**, 1049 (1963).
2704. WOOD, R.H. and L.A. D'ORAZIO. *J. Phys. Chem.*, **69**, 2562 (1965).
2705. WOOLF, A.A. *J. Chem. Soc.*, **1951**, 231.
2706. WOOLF, A.A. *J. Chem. Soc.*, **1954**, 4694.
2707. WOOLF, A.A. *J. Inorg. Nucl. Chem.*, **14**, 21 (1960).
2708. WORRELL, W.L. *J. Phys. Chem.*, **68**, 952 (1964).
2709. WORRELL, W.L. *J. Phys. Chem.*, **68**, 954 (1964).
2710. WORRELL, W.L. and J. CHIPMAN. *J. Phys. Soc.*, **68**, 860 (1964).
2711. WÖSTEN, W.J. *J. Phys. Chem.*, **65**, 1949 (1961).
2712. WÖSTEN, W.J., and M.G. GEERS. *J. Phys. Chem.*, **66**, 1252 (1962).
2713. WU CHING-HSIEN, M.M. BIRKY, and L.G. HEPLER. *J. Phys. Chem.*, **67**, 1203 (1963).
2714. WULFF, C.A. and E.F. WESTRUM. *J. Phys. Chem.*, **67**, 2376 (1963).
2715. WULFF, C.A. and E.F. WESTRUM. *J. Phys. Chem.*, **68**, 430 (1964).
2716. WUNDERLICH, B. *J. Phys. Chem.*, **69**, 2078 (1965).
2717. WUYTS, J. and J.C. JUNGERS. *Bull. Soc. chim. belg.*, **58**, 80 (1949).

2718. WYDEVEN, Th. and N.W. GREGORY. *J. Phys. Chem.*, **68**, 3249 (1964).
2719. WYSS, H.-R. and H.H. GÜNTHARD. *Helv. chim. acta*, **44**, 625 (1961).
2720. YATES, R.E., M.A. GREENBAUM, and M. FARBER. *J. Phys. Chem.* **68**, 2682 (1964).
2721. YOKOKAWA, T. and O.J. KLEPPA. *Inorg. Chem.*, **3**, 954 (1964).
2722. YOKOKAWA, T., M. KOIZUMI, M. SHIMOJI, and K. NIWA. *J. Am. Chem. Soc.*, 79, 3365 (1957).
2723. ZAGIC, V. *Jaderna energie*, No. 6, 200 (1960).
2724. ZAVITSANOS, P.D. *J. Phys. Chem.*, **68**, 2899 (1964).
2725. ZEISE, H. *Elektrochem.*, **48**, 476 (1942).
2726. ZEISE, H. *Elektrochem.*, **48**, 693 (1942).
2727. ZIEGLER, W.T., and J.C. MULLINS. *Cryogenics*, **4**, 39 (1964).
2728. ZIHLMAN, F.A. – cited in [2218].
2729. ZIMMER, M.F., E.E. BAROODY, M. SCHWARTZ, and M.P. McALLISTER. *J. Chem. Eng. Data*, **9**, 527 (1964).
2730. ZIOMEK, J.S. and E.A. PIOTROWSKI. *J. Chem. Phys.*, **34**, 1087 (1961).
2731. ZOUBOV, N. De, and F. DELTOMBE. *Rapp. Techn.*, No. 26 (1955).
2732. ZÜRCHER, and H.H. GÜNTHARD. *Helv. chim. acta*, **38**, 849 (1955).
2733. ZÜRCHER and H.H. GÜNTHARD. *Helv. chim. acta*, **40**, 89 (1957).

INDEX

ELEMENTS

Promethium	Pm	209
Protactinium	Pa	202
Radium	Ra	215
Radon	Rn	222
Rhenium	Re	220
Rhodium	Rh	221
Rubidium	Rb	217
Ruthenium	Ru	222
Samarium	Sm	248
Scandium	Sc	238
Selenium	Se	239
Silicon	Si	242
Silver	Ag	3
Sodium	Na	172
Strontium	Sr	253
Sulfur	S	223
Tantalum	Ta	257
Technetium	Tc	260
Tellurium	Te	260
Terbium	Tb	259
Thallium	Tl	272
Thorium	Th	262
Thulium	Tm	275
Tin	Sn	250
Titanium	Ti	264
Tungsten	W	284
Uranium	U	275
Vanadium	V	281
Xenon	Xe	286
Ytterbium	Yb	290
Yttrium	Y	288
Zinc	Zn	291
Zirconium	Zr	294

ORGANIC COMPOUNDS

1, I	303
1, II	307
1, III	317
1, IV	323
1, V	324
2, I	324
2, II	326
2, III	335
2, IV	338
3, I	338
3, II	339
3, III	342
3, IV	343
4, I	343
4, II	344
4, III	350
4, IV	352
5, I	352
5, II	353
5, III	358
5, IV	359
6, I	359
6, II	360
6, III	365
6. IV	366
7, I	367
7, II	369
10, II	386
11, I	387
11, II	388
11, III	389
12, I	389
12, II	390
12, III	392
13, I	392
13, II	392
13, III	393
14, I	393
14, II	394
14, III	395
15, I	395
15, II	396
16, I	396
16, II	397
16, III	398
17, I	399
17, II	399
17, III	400
18, I	400
18, II	400
18, III	401
19, I	402
19, II	402
20, I	403

Printed in Israel
Manufactured at the Israel Program for Scientific Translations, Jerusalem

Made in the USA
San Bernardino, CA
08 August 2018

Amy Sumida

Copyright © 2013 Amy Sumida

All rights reserved.

ISBN-10: 1490311173
ISBN-13: 978-1490311173

DEDICATION

To Kaitlin and Daniel Cummings, my half-sister and half-brother who I love completely.

ACKNOWLEDGMENTS

Most of the people in this book are fictional, based on myths of gods and goddesses, but there are a few characters who exist and I'd like to acknowledge them here.

Sommer Castor is as strong as her character, the most loyal friend I've ever had. Tristan and Jackson are actually Richard Harrison and Cliff Green respectively. They are as witty and entertaining as Jax and Tryst are, making it impossible for me to resist adding them to my stories.

Tahnee Ross is as sweet as she is here and is now passing that sweetness on to her children. Her dogs are just as lovable as she, fierce defenders of their mistress and, on occasion, myself. Justin, her husband, is a smart man, not only in his scientific research but for marrying such a wonderful person. Also, Pamela Young really is a local news reporter and a lovely lady. Thank you all for enriching my world.

More Books by Amy Sumida

The Godhunter Series(in order)
Godhunter
(Of Gods and Wolves)
Oathbreaker
Marked by Death
Green Tea and Black Death
A Taste for Blood
The Tainted Web

Series Split:
These books can be read together or separately
Harvest of the Gods & A Fey Harvest
Into the Void & Out of the Darkness

Perchance to Die
Tracing Thunder
Light as a Feather
Rain or Monkeyshine
Blood Bound
Eye of Re
My Soul to Take
As the Crow Flies
Cry Werewolf
Pride Before a Fall

Beyond the Godhunter:
A Darker Element
Out of the Blue

The Twilight Court Series:
Fairy-Struck
Pixie-Led
Raven-Mocking
Here There be Dragons

Witchbane
Elf-Shot

The Spellsinger Series
The Last Lullaby
A Symphony of Sirens

Fairy Tales
Happily Harem After
The Four Clever Brothers

Other Books

The Magic of Fabric
Feeding the Lwas: A Vodou Cookbook
There's a Goddess Too
The Vampire-Werewolf Complex
Enchantress

Pronunciation Guide

Bilskinir: Bill-ska-neer

Estsanatlehi(Mrs E): Es-tan-AHT-lu-hee

Froekn: Fro-kin ("valiant" in Old Norse)

Huitzilopochtli: Weet-seal-oh-POACHED-lee

Intare: In-tar-ay ("lion" in Rwandan)

Járngreipr: Yarn- gri-per

Kirill: Key-reel

Megingjord: Mey-gen-yord

Mjollnir: Myul-neer

Nyavirezi: Nee-yah-veer-ez-ee

Rouva: Roo-vah

Tima: Tee-mah ("heart" in Rwandan)

TryggulfR: Truh-gul-fur

Tsohanoai(Mr. T): So-ha-noe-ayee

UnnúlfR: Un- nul-fur

Valaskjálf: Vah-lask-chalv

VèulfR: Vey-ul-fur

Chapter One

Was draining a god's power in self-defense still considered murder?

It's not like the police were going to come knocking on my door. "I swear, officer, it was a self-defense draining!" I groaned as I looked over my reflection in the mirror. Yes, I killed gods, but I did it to protect my race from their manipulations. I did it because gods aren't really gods, they're Atlanteans. Yep, from that Atlantis.

After destroying Atlantis with their quest for power and magic, they moved across the world in a diaspora of soon-to-be deities. They found us, humans lacking their skills but full of magical potential, and with their flashy magic, they convinced us that they were gods. Then they took the sacrifices we made and used them to make the fiction a reality.

Oh, but we got bored with them. We forgot most of them, moved on, decided to consolidate down to just a handful of gods. Unfortunately, they did not forget about us. They had grown accustomed to our energy, using it to prolong their lives and refresh their magic surplus. So, the forgotten ones banded together and found a new way to do things, a new way to steal our power. They manipulated mankind, infiltrated governments, plotted and schemed to bring us to war against each other, and then they took our dead as their sacrifice.

When I first discovered this conspiracy, I thought all gods were bad. I hunted them, tracing through the Aether; a place of thought and magic which binds our world to the God Realm. I didn't know there were gods who viewed relationships with humans as a symbiotic exchange of energy. I didn't know there were those among them who still loved us, guarded us, and guided

us. But that was before I met Thor.

Now, not only do I know about the division among the gods, I know that as a human witch, I have the ability to take back what they stole. I can drain a god of his magic until there's nothing left to sustain them. Till they die and go wherever the hell it is gods go to when they die. Thus, my current situation.

I killed Aphrodite, the Goddess of Love. Except, you see, she wasn't all that loving. She was in the middle of torturing me to death when I began to drain her, simply because I had nothing left to defend myself with. Now, I had her magic of Love, Lust, War, and Victory. Also, I had a healthy dose of pretty ladled on me. My hair was longer and shinier. My skin was perfect for like, the first time ever. My lips were fuller, my eyebrows would never need another plucking, and everything felt a little tighter; if you know what I mean.

So there I stood, perusing this new improved Vervain Lavine, and wondering why I felt so guilty about it. Maybe it was the way it made me feel less than human somehow. Of course, this new near-perfection was the least of my current concerns. You'd think hanging with gods would be cool, dating one even better, but so far, all it had meant for me was a lot of drama.

I was dating Thor, God of Thunder, the Sea, yadda yadda. He was fantastic. Gorgeous. Un-fucking-believable. But somewhere along the way, I'd saved the life of a werewolf. A prince, no less, and I had unknowingly bound him to me in some weirdo Froekn, aka werewolf, ritual. Now Trevor, the werewolf prince, had to touch me monthly or he'd die. I'm not exaggerating either; he'll waste away and die if we don't get skin to skin. Something about being separated from the part of his soul he gave me. No pressure.

Thor was handling this surprisingly well. I'd be going apeshit if some hot chick had to touch him once a month or die. But then Thor's a god, he's probably used to all this bullshit. I,

however, am only human (I think) and having a sinfully sweet werewolf come onto me all the time, giving me these big freakin' puppy-dog-eye stares, was driving me insane. Oh, and then there's Blue.

Blue, aka Huitzilopochtli, is the Aztec God of the Sun. His name drives me crazy, so I shortened the English version of it–Blue Hummingbird on the Left–down to Blue. It's appropriate in so many ways, but let's not digress. Blue is also the Father of all Vampires. He's beautiful and broken, charming and vicious, evil and brilliant . . . oh, and out of his fucking mind.

My new magic wants to save him, fix him, but I have no idea how to go about doing that. *He* wants me to be his Blood Bride or some shit. Queen of the Blood? Vampire Empress? I don't know, it's too twisted to think about. At the moment, it's kind of moot, since he hasn't shown his hot Aztec face in over a week. I'm not sure if that's a good or a bad thing. I *am* sure it's one more thing I have to worry about.

I needed a vacation. Or a massage. Or a massage on my vacation. Sighing, I went to lie down and find some peace in my dreams. I had maybe an hour of peace before Trevor came barreling into the room I shared with Thor in Bilskinir, Thor's Hall in the God Realm of Asgard.

"What, you don't knock?" I lost my smirk when I saw the frantic look on Trevor's face. "What is it?" I sat up and moved to the edge of the bed.

"We have a problem, Minn Elska," he curled around my feet and laid his head in my lap.

Oh boy, here we go. Trevor was bonded to me, but I wasn't bonded to him. That didn't stop the Binding from exerting a little influence on my hormones though. Just being around Trevor made it difficult to be faithful to Thor, but when Trevor touched me and called me "my love" in Old Norse, I turned into silly putty.

“Are we out of ice cream?” I tried to fend off the attraction with a shield of humor.

He shook his head a little and stared up at me with wide, honey-colored eyes. “I don’t know. Should I go check?”

“It's a joke, Trevor.” I sighed and stroked his hair. He immediately nuzzled his face into me and hugged my legs with a satisfied grin. “So what’s the problem?”

He looked up, as if suddenly remembering the reason he was there, and blushed, “My father.”

“Fenrir?”

“Yes, him,” Trevor rubbed against me again and sighed; warm breath tickling my bare legs where my silk slip had rode up.

“What about him?” I was trying to block out the lust that was spreading in delicious waves out from my lap. I dearly wished that I wasn't still sitting in bed, a very bad location to be having such a reaction to Trevor.

“He wants to meet you.”

“Well, that doesn’t sound so bad.”

A sweet feeling of contentment was weakening my limbs, fogging my mind. Trevor's hair was so soft in my hands, but I couldn’t even remember reaching out. He rubbed his face harder against me, and the muscles in my thighs relaxed, falling open so he could shift closer.

“It *is* bad,” Thor’s booming voice snapped my head up and my thighs back together. He fell onto the bed beside us and yanked Trevor out of my lap. Trevor started to growl, but Thor shoved him away from the bed. “You can’t think straight when you’re touching her. Believe me, I have the same problem. And you need to tell her about the trial.”

“Trial?” I looked back and forth between them. “I’m a witch, I don’t like the T word.”

Trevor shook his head and frowned. “You’re right, Thunderer, I apologize. The Binding is hitting me hard.”

“Tell her,” Thor gentled his tone a bit.

“Father doesn’t think that I’ve chosen wisely.” Trevor looked down, his jaw clenching and his eyes twitching. “He wants you to be tested for worth.”

“Tested? Does he know I didn’t ask for this?”

“He says that you bound me, knowingly or not, and you must prove yourself worthy of the honor or he’ll remove it.” Trevor looked up at me, clearly shaken.

“If your father is so unhappy, Trevor”–I had to handle this delicately, but I was ecstatic that there was a way to release him–“maybe we should just let him remove the Binding.”

“Vervain.” Thor took a deep breath and shook his head at Trevor, who looked so stricken, I thought he’d be in tears at any second. “She doesn’t get it, Trevor, relax. Vervain, there’s no way to undo the Binding in the sense that you mean. Fenrir is speaking of killing you to free his son, hoping Trevor will live through it. Fenrir thinks the bond is unconsummated, and so he believes there’s a chance for Trevor to break free of it upon your death.”

“Unconsummated?” I frowned and then blushed. “R-i-i-ight, I remember now. But since we *are* consummated or whatever, what would happen to Trevor if I died?”

“He’d die too.” Thor watched me carefully as it sank in.

“But you’re immortal.” I searched Trevor’s face for an ounce of hope that I’d misunderstood. “I mean, you can die if someone hurts you bad enough, but otherwise you’d live forever,

right?"

"Not anymore." Trevor didn't look the least bit disturbed by his death sentence. In fact, he looked calm and peaceful; damn happy even.

"You've traded immortality to be bound to me in a one-sided bond?" I was horrified.

"I'd be dead without you anyway." He shrugged casually, his hands deep in the pockets of his jeans. Very flippant, very James Dean. Werewolf without a cause.

"I was the one who nearly killed you in the first place."

"Because I was attacking you." Trevor grinned lopsidedly. "It was the best day of my life."

"This is not our problem right now." Thor stood up and glared at the both of us.

"What?" I blinked up at him. "Oh, right. So, just tell Fenrir that it's consummated and he needs to get over it."

"I have"–Trevor looked away–"he doesn't believe me."

"Why not?" I was so frustrated, I could spit.

"I don't carry your scent." Trevor started to blush a pretty shade of rose.

"What do you mean 'carry my scent'?" I stared at him and then at Thor. They both wore matching looks of embarrassment. "Cheese and rice! No way! He sniffed you to see if he could smell sex?"

Trevor nodded and Thor sighed.

"What it comes down to, Vervain"–Thor sat back down and took my hand–"is this. You can either consummate the bond in

front of Fenrir or accept the challenge."

"So I'm to either fuck or fight for his entertainment, is that it?"

Trevor's shoulders slumped, and he looked at the floor in misery.

"That's it." Thor, at least, met my eyes.

"What kind of trial are we talking about?" I asked.

"You'll have to face three warriors of my father's choosing." Trevor looked up, smiled, and shrugged. "I know you can win, you're my Lady Huntress. You've fought the wolves before and won. You've even beaten me, and I'm the best of our fighters, with exception only to my father."

"Are you sure it'll only be werewolves that I'll have to fight?" I looked at Thor and then back at Trevor.

Trevor nodded, but Thor was the one who answered. "Fenrir can only use his own power to test you. It's our law."

"Fine, set it up." I slumped back, then shot up again. "Do I have to kill them all or just win?"

"You just need to disable them. They can change and heal if you let them." Trevor smiled and shook his head. "Your compassion is such a treasure to me. It's humbling."

"Yeah, great. Let's just hope it has the same effect on your father." I smiled weakly. "Now, when is this test going to take place?"

"Two days hence." Trevor grimaced, and I groaned. "He wanted to test you tonight, but I begged him to let you prepare. So, he granted us two days."

"He's not too happy with you for giving up your

immortality, is he?" *I* wasn't too pleased about it, so I could only imagine what dear old Dad would think.

"He's furious." Trevor nodded.

"Let's just hope I can keep us alive till the end of the week, and then we'll take it from there."

Chapter Two

I had my butt-kicking, Matrix-chic on; the outfit I normally wore out to hunt gods. Usually, I wouldn't bother putting on make-up, but this time I was wearing lipstick. Nothing said "I'm worthy" like red lips. My hair was in a tight bun at the nape of my neck. I'd be able to take it down easily at the end . . . and I was also able to use it as an excuse to wear my new present from Thor: a pair of silver hair-sticks in the shape of lightning bolts. He'd assured me that not only were they balanced for throwing, but the edges of the bolts were softened so I could stab with them and not injure myself. Maybe I was being paranoid, but I had a feeling that I'd need all the weapons I could carry.

"You look amazing." Thor stood in the doorway smiling, even though his eyes were worried. "Are you ready?"

"As ready as I'll ever be." I smiled back. "You look damn fine yourself."

I eyed the leather pants Thor was wearing; the same pair he'd been wearing the first time we'd met. They were brown and cross-gartered all the way up to his thighs. Over them, he had on a white tunic with a T-shape opening which bared a nice amount of solid chest that I could spend all day admiring. He also wore an iron belt and matching gloves. I would've called them gauntlets, seeing as how they were made of metal, but he called them gloves . . . whatever. Off of his belt hung a T-shaped, thick hammer.

Not only did all of these accessories look spiffy, they all had names. The belt was Megingjord, the gloves Járngreipr, and the hammer was Mjöllnir. Thor told me that Mjöllnir made lightning when he struck it on stone and became a thunderbolt when it was thrown. Cool, huh? His hair hung loose except for two

small braids on either side of his face, tied with leather. Thor was going native.

"It's traditional." He gave me his arm and I took it, letting him lead me out.

In the hallway, Trevor was already waiting with the God Squad: the small group of gods who had teamed up with me to fight on behalf of humans. They were all going along to cheer me on. At least I'd have my friends there to cry if I died. That was something, right?

"Thank you." I looked at them all. "You guys are the best."

"I just want to see Fenrir's Hall." Horus sniffed.

The Egyptian Falcon God was a little uptight, but I was working on that. I leaned over and kissed him on the cheek and his eyes sparkled at me for a second before going blank again.

"Whatever the reason"–I took a deep breath and suppressed my morbid thoughts–"thank you."

They all nodded, giving me words of encouragement and little pieces advice before we traced to Fenrir's Hall. I actually liked Brahma's suggestion the best.

He had whispered in my ear, "Don't get dead."

We reformed in an elaborately decorated sitting room that was unlike anything I'd been expecting to find in the lair of the Wolf God. I peered around me at the hand-painted wallpaper, gilded chairs, and glass display cabinets filled with statues of wolves from every culture in the world. There were sculptures in glass, ceramic, and even gold. Each one looked priceless, like museum pieces. The Wolf God collected tchotchkes; how sweet.

Emerald eyes sparkled out of the gold wolf statue I was studying, and I could swear it winked at me. I looked away

quickly, and then noticed that the crown moldings were even carved with wolves. The whole effect was amazing, breathtaking, and a little frightening. I thought I knew who I was dealing with, but this room did not belong in the home of the god I'd envisioned. Mind . . . blown.

"VèulfR." A huge man entered from a door on our left. He had to bend to get through it because he was larger even than Thor. "You will introduce me to your potential mate now."

This was more like it. He was over seven feet tall with enough muscles to make Arnold beg for mercy, a long, lean face with a stubborn chin, long hair that ran wild and dark down his back, bright honey eyes like Trevor's, and scars everywhere. Including a long one that bisected his left brow, jumped the eye, and started again on the cheek, to go straight down his jaw. He looked mean and mad, even those sweet eyes couldn't soften him. Phew, it was good to know I wasn't slipping. He was exactly what I'd been picturing. I smiled in relief, and he stopped mid-stride to stare at my grin with rapid, eye-blinking shock.

"You smile at me, woman?" Fenrir recovered and stalked forward so he could loom over me.

Not like he even had to try with me, or anyone for that matter. I felt like I needed a stepladder just to speak to him. But even his height had been expected; Fenrir's mother was supposed to be a giantess.

I craned my neck back and then held up a finger. "Hold on a sec." I ran and grabbed a chair, then pulled it over to him. Fenrir's jaw dropped as I climbed up, spread my legs to give myself surer footing, and planted my hands on my hips. "That's better, and yes, I was smiling at you. Don't people ever smile at you?"

I heard a few coughs and choking sounds coming from behind me, but other than that, everyone was silent as they waited

for Fenrir's response.

"Not usually, no"–he planted his huge fists on his hips to mimic me–"and especially not women."

"Well, that just sucks, big guy. Maybe you should try smiling at them first." I crossed my arms and tilted my head to the side so I could properly consider his dilemma. "Some women are scared of scars, but I think they add character. Thor could use a couple."

"I've always thought that as well." Fenrir crossed his arms like me and nodded. "I could give him some if you'd like."

"That's mighty kind of you." I smiled as if he'd just offered me a cup of tea. "I think it would have to be up to him, though. It might fall under the umbrella of the getting-a-tattoo-of-your-girlfriend's-name curse."

"Girlfriend's name curse?" Fenrir frowned at me like I'd started speaking another language.

"You know; they get your name tattooed on their butt, and then bada-bing, bada-boom, they're telling you to kiss it and hit the road." I shrugged. "Besides, if he's going to get any scars, I think I'd like to be the one to give them to him."

Fenrir's jaw dropped again before his entire face lit up and he roared with laughter. "Who are you, little frami?"

"Father"–Trevor stepped forward proudly–"this is my mate, Vervain Lavine."

"This little woman with such a big mouth?" Fenrir smiled lopsidedly, just like Trevor, and it finally became apparent that Trevor did actually inherit his good looks from his father. Fenrir just hid them beneath his bluster.

Trevor nodded and took one of my hands. I let the other

one fall to the side since I could never manage the one-arm-crossing-the-waist thing. It always ended up making me look like I had a stomach ache. Fenrir came closer and leaned his face into my neck. He inhaled long and deep, then kept sniffing me down the line of my body. Boy was I glad I'd showered.

"You may not have made such a bad choice, after all, Son." Fenrir regarded me solemnly, staring straight into my eyes. "I still don't approve of a human, though. She'll drag you down to the grave with her."

"I totally agree." I nodded, and Fenrir's eyes got wide as his head reared back.

"You allowed the bonding." Fenrir narrowed his gaze then. "Why allow it, if you disapprove of it?"

"I'm an ignorant human. What can I say?" I shrugged. "I thought I was doing your son a favor by letting him out of any obligation to me. I had no idea I was accomplishing the exact opposite."

Fenrir looked at Trevor and Trevor held out his hand, palm up. "I told you she didn't understand."

"That's no excuse." Fenrir frowned and chewed his lip pensively.

"Yeah, yeah. Ignorance of the law is no excuse for breaking it. I've been pulled over before." I jumped down. "Well, let's get this party started then."

"You're going to consummate the match?" Fenrir's eyes started to glow and I backed up.

"Father"–Trevor stepped in front of me–"I told you it was consummated."

"Stop lying to me. Neither of you has scented the other

intimately. Do it now or we go to the arena."

"I'm not here to have sex with your son." I pushed the chair away. "We consummated it without getting undressed, but it was done. I felt it."

"That's not a proper mating." Fenrir frowned. "Either you're joined or you're not. Our magic would not have settled for less."

"This *isn't* a proper mating, but I can assure you, it was consummated. I don't think it'll make a difference to you, though." I patted the short sword at my hip. "So, just show me the damn arena."

Fenrir's eyes glowed brighter and he smiled in anticipation. "You really are the Hunter?"

"Yep, that's me." I sighed. "I know; you thought I'd be taller."

"No; I thought you'd be a man." Fenrir snorted. "But this shall be a pleasure. No matter what sex you are."

"Oh, gee"–I rolled my eyes–"an equal opportunity killer, thanks."

Fenrir laughed as he opened a door at his end of the room. I suddenly felt like Alice. Nobody ever thinks about how dangerous Wonderland was, about how many times Alice could've died horribly. Hell, one misplaced foot and she would've been stepped on while she was talking to those bitchy flowers. Not a way I'd like to go. Do not put me down for: squashed like a bug and then scraped off a giant shoe. But nobody thinks about those gory scenarios when they read that children's book. No one but me, that is. And there I was, walking through that tiny door which led into Wonderland's garden. I wouldn't be at all surprised to hear a few shouts of "Off with her head", when it closed behind me.

Fenrir ushered me into a long stone passage, echoing with shouts that filtered in from an impatient crowd. I knew no one else would follow me into that corridor. No one else could. My heart sped up a little. I admit that I'd already gotten used to having backup, and walking through the dark, to an unknown fight, all by myself, was bringing back memories of taking on the gods alone. How had I done it? How had I found the courage to trace into a god's territory and kill them, all by myself? Simply navigating the Aether had been ballsy. If I had done it wrong, mispronounced a tracing chant or misdirected my energy, I could have wound up stuck in the Aether, my body nothing more than a thought, floating among other thoughts, for all time.

In the dark tunnel, with the Wolf God at my back, and the sound of his bloodthirsty children before me, I couldn't imagine it. In fact, all I could think was that I'd been a complete idiot. Now, I was about to face three werewolves to win the honor of having a bond that I didn't want in the first place. Maybe I should have left the gods alone.

I heard Fenrir close the door behind me with a thud, and then came the unmistakable scrape of a bolt sliding home. My breathing seemed fast and harsh in the stone confines of the tunnel, so I took a second to slow it down. I may have been an idiot, but somehow I'd been good enough to survive, and now I had even more of an arsenal. With Aphrodite's magic, I had a much better chance at making it through this alive. I just had to keep my cool and remember that.

Darkness gave way to smoky torchlight as I stepped out into a pit. I'd like to say it was a gladiatorial arena or something equally dramatic, but it wasn't. It was a pit. A large pit, but a pit nonetheless. Carved from rock, it was rutted with claw marks and worn with age. The claw carvings were kind of a good thing because they gave the ground back the traction that time had worn away. There were dark stains here and there as well, just adding to the overall ambiance of despair. I stared up at the high walls

penning me in and the faces which peered down at me eagerly, then nodded as I crossed my arms. Yep, this was exactly what I expected a werewolf fighting pit to look like.

The wolves in the seats above me didn't taunt or jeer, they growled and howled. I kind of liked the atmosphere. Insults could get distracting, growling just kind of blended into the sounds of a fight. In fact, it was appealing to the more primitive part of me, the genetic memory of not only hiding in caves from the beasts, but of finally getting the nerve to go out into the dark and confront them. My blood was racing with the thrill of the hunt, not for food, but for survival. The wolves were at my door, and this time I wasn't going to hide.

At the opposite end of the pit was another tunnel and above it, in a balcony perched high on the wall, Fenrir appeared. I saw the God Squad gathered behind him. Trevor stood off to the side, looking tense but calm. Thor had a carefully neutral expression on his face, and most of the Squad was following his lead, but Persephone looked like she was on the verge of tears. I quickly focused back on Fenrir.

"Vervain Lavine," Fenrir shouted and the wolves quieted immediately. "You've claimed my son as your bonded mate, but you are not Froekn. Will you prove your worth by claw and tooth? Will you fight to become one of us?"

I almost shook my head. I just couldn't believe I was there, fighting for my life, because I had spared Trevor's. No good deed and all that. I heaved a sigh and rolled my eyes. Then I collected myself and took a deep breath. If I was going to do this, I might as well do it with style.

"I will!" I shouted and the wolves howled; in approval or rage, I had no idea. I didn't speak wolf yet.

"So be it!" Fenrir shouted back. "TryggulfR!"

I looked at Trevor, and he smiled at me, but I caught the

slight shakiness in it. That name was pretty similar to his given name of VéulfR. I hoped it wasn't his brother. I mean, they're all related to him in a way, but I hoped this wasn't one of his litter-mates or whatever werewolves called them. Oh well, nothing to do about it now. I threw my hands down, and the metal claws sprang out of the finger-less gloves I wore. They were my favorite weapon, once the property of a god, with a nice magic kick to them. I turned them out, and the four blades that protruded over the tops of my fingers caught the light. The wolves howled more, and I was pretty sure it was in approval this time. See, I'm a fast learner.

"Where can I get me some of those?" I looked up and saw one of the most beautiful men I'd ever seen in my life, and I've seen some heartbreakers recently. But this guy . . . whooee, he could make you faint with desire just by looking at you. I was half surprised he didn't have a bunch of groupies gathered around him, fanning him and feeding him grapes.

"Maybe if you're a real good boy, Santa will bring you a pair for Christmas," I yelled up at him.

The crowd, as they say, went wild. Everyone laughed and howled, including Mr. Drop Dead Gorgeous. He leaned on the edge of the wall with golden arms of steel and smiled luscious lips at me before he winked a deep amethyst eye. His dirty blond hair fell around him in sexy disarray, begging to be touched.

"But when I'm bad, I'm better," he called down.

"If you know what's good for you"–I saw Thor saunter closer–"you'll stay away from my woman, Loki."

Oh shit, that was Loki? The trickster god was hot! That probably worked out well for him. I had to tear my gaze away, though, because I heard the pounding of feet coming down the tunnel in front of me. From the sound of it, I'd be facing a full wolf. I was glad. Werewolves in the natural shape of a regular wolf seemed to be easier to deal with than when the Froekn took

complete werewolf form. I just had to get over the injuring an animal part. I started a mantra in my head: It's not a real wolf. It's not a real wolf.

Unfortunately, it wasn't just any wolf that came running out into the pit of despair. It was a really, really big wolf . . . two reallys. It was also really fast. Only one really though, so I was able to duck and roll out of the way before it hit me. I could've pulled my sword, but I knew the claws impressed the wolves. It was as if I was battling on their terms, and I didn't want to actually kill anyone. So I swung to my feet and fell into a fighting stance.

Some part of my magic rose with my adrenaline and started to thrum in delight. My body felt energized, my blood surged with power, and my eyes saw every nuance of muscles under the thick black coat of the wolf I fought. Aphrodite's war magic had awoken. Along with it came the small part of Trevor that he'd given me in the Binding, like the magic had woke up my sleeping dog. *Come out and play, little wolf.*

Without thought, I sunk lower to the ground and let out a vicious sounding growl that quieted the crowd to an unnatural stillness. Surprisingly, the sound hadn't come from the little part of Trevor inside of me, it had come from my Nahual, my animal twin who was basically the embodiment of my magic. I'd been meditating with her for awhile, developing our powers so we could fight Blue, but she'd never come out unbidden before.

I saw her clearly in my head; a gleaming white jaguar with golden-brown markings and dark eyes. She wasn't about to let me have all the fun, especially not with wolves. Another growl rose out of my throat, a very un-wolf-like sound; a sort of rumbling vibration that rose to a sharp snarling peak. It was a bit frightening, even to my ears. To the Froekn, who had no idea a human could hold animal magic, it must have been terrifying.

Sure enough, my jaguar sensed the fear in the air and delighted in it. Her joy was, of course, my own. It lifted me up and

I laughed low in my throat. A few whimpers crept through the otherwise silent crowd, wolves drawing back a little in trepidation. Suddenly, I had become an unknown threat. A quick glance at my friends showed me that they were a little shocked as well. I laughed again; I knew I had an interesting conversation to look forward to.

The wolf across from me twisted his head back and forth, peering at me uncertainly. I just waited and watched. I wanted an opportunity to disable this wolf with the least amount of bloodshed. Finally, TryggufR just decided to leap at me and give it the old college try. I flattened myself to the ground at the last second, and he flew right into the wall behind me.

I rolled up and swiped at the middle of his hind legs, in an effort to try and disable him. He howled and twisted around to face me again, this time with a heavy limp. My gaze zipped over him, noting all possible weaknesses and points of attack. The war magic was incredible, giving me a strategic edge I hadn't counted on. The victory magic was tingling through my veins too, making me feel a little lightheaded. I thought I heard the roar of the crowd, but it was just the rush of blood through my ears. The wolves were actually watching in complete silence. In fact, it began to get a little eerie.

I backed up a space and crouched again. TryggulfR took another leap at my neck, but his leg threw him off balance and he fell toward my shoulder instead. I punched his mouth away, hot blood spraying across my face. I swiped quickly at the blood with my palms to try and clear my vision, but TryggulfR was a seasoned killer and he knew an opportunity when he saw one. He came at me fast, and I had to rely on my hearing alone.

In the silence, it wasn't too difficult to hear the clicking of claws on the stone floor and the rapid breathing of my opponent. I flung out an arm and caught his leg, but it was a foreleg and he was able to twist down and latch onto my arm. When I screamed, there was an answering boom of thunder above me. Thor was about to lose it, which wouldn't be at all helpful. I needed to end this fast

before the fighting spread from the pit to the seats above.

I punched TrygguIfR in the face again, my blades sinking in deep, and he let go with a shrill whimper. It gave me enough time to wipe the blood away, so I was able to watch him as he limped back and circled the end of the pit as if he wanted out. His face was a torn mess and his hind leg buckled every other step. He was beaten. I just had to wait for him to admit it.

"TrygguIfR," I called to him. "I don't want your death. It was an honor to fight you. Heal yourself; I'll stand down."

TrygguIfR gave a sharp yip, then lay down and changed into a dark-haired man, very similar in looks to Trevor, except his face was a little wider and his eyes were blue. He stood up and walked proudly forward with a total disregard for his impressive nudity. I enjoyed the show, of course. I'm only human.

He stopped in front of me and smiled as he met my eyes. "Welcome, Sister," his voice rang out, and the wolves howled in response to it. Then he took my arms and leaned forward to lightly rub cheeks with me. "Good luck," he whispered, then turned and left to loud applause.

I used the time to catch my breath and adjust my glove to cover part of my wound. It hurt, a deep aching pain, but I was able to ignore it with the help of my magic. It was a good thing too because I didn't have long before Fenrir appeared again. His face looked a little tense, and his voice was definitely louder when he spoke to me.

"Huntress, you've just bested my third-born son." Fenrir snarled at the clapping wolves and they quieted. "Now, you meet my second. UnnúlfR!"

Oh, we were starting with the easy and working our way up. Well, I guess that was normal. I shook out my shoulders and concentrated on the tunnel. I couldn't look up and see Thor. If he gave me "scared eyes", I'd get distracted.

“Beautiful job, Godhunter,” Loki called. “Well done indeed. You’re not just winning the fight, you’re winning the Froekn.”

I ignored him. Mainly because I didn't have a witty comeback, but also because there was shuffling and scratching noises coming from the tunnel, and I was betting the new guy wasn’t taking me on in full wolf form.

Sure enough, a huge werewolf came striding out of the dark. He was actually graceful for such a big guy. The werewolf had a pale yellow pelt and his eyes were oddly human; an icy blue, so light he almost looked blind. I was reminded of a husky I once saw, so strangely beautiful. This werewolf was just as striking as the husky, except I had no desire to pet him.

I stilled as he approached. My arm had stopped bleeding and had begun to throb, but I tried to concentrate instead on the sleek wolfman stalking me. He got within five feet of me and began to circle. Instead of following him, I closed my eyes and waited. I heard a few murmurs but, just as I expected, the crowd went silent again. They were probably wondering what the hell I was up to.

It's actually quite simple. There are two routes to go when your opponent circles you. You can either try to keep him within your sights, running the risk of losing your footing when you shuffle about, or you can close your eyes, and you’ll be able to hear his feet moving, giving away his location. Also, you’ll be prepared for him to attack you from behind because where else is he going to attack you from, given the opportunity?

So I listened, waited, and sure enough, when he reached my back, he sprung. I twisted and spun downward, doing a spiraling slice while I leaned a leg out to steady myself. Catching him across the thighs, I cut him deep and had to fling blood and bits of gore off the blades while he landed in a heap. There were a few gasps and even some howls, but it quieted again quickly. This was not

the entertainment they'd been expecting.

UnnúlfR sprang up, but gave me a wary look. “Nice move, human.”

I bowed, and he leapt at me, just as I figured he would. Turning the bow into a tumble, I kicked my legs out as soon as I was beneath him. His high pitched whine indicated that I’d hit something tender. When I got to my feet, I looked back and saw that I’d actually torn stripes up his stomach with my boot hooks. He was a bit mad about that. Snarling, frothing mad.

I settled down into my crouch and snarled back at him. The war magic within me itched to pull my kodachi, but the jaguar rejected the weapon, feeling more at home with my bladed gloves. The claws were my favorite weapon anyway, and they seemed to be a crowd pleaser. I decided I'd go with them for as long as I could.

“Maybe I’ll lay you down and fuck you after I beat you, since my brother hasn’t had the balls to do it yet.”

“After this is through, you'll answer to me for that, UnnúlfR,” Trevor shouted above the boom of rolling thunder which suddenly shook the hall.

“Come and pull me off her, if you dare,” the pale wolf taunted back. He trailed a hand over his groin, and there were a few howls of encouragement from the watching wolves.

Thor stood with his arms crossed, staring at the wolf like he was memorizing his face for future reference. He didn’t say anything, but the thunder still shaking the walls and the lightning flashing in his eyes spoke volumes. There wasn't much more he could take.

“As soon as you can find your equipment within all that fur, let me know and I’ll think about being afraid. At the moment, however, I’m still waiting to be impressed.” I settled further into

my stance, watching him closely.

UnnúlfR launched himself at me; boy this wolf was predictable. He was an old wolf, an assassin, so he should have learned restraint by now. It said a lot about his personality that he hadn't. I dropped down and gave him a roundhouse kick to the head. Bam, he went down, and I would have leapt up immediately, if he hadn't lashed out with an arm and slashed my brand new leather pants.

"Son of a bitch," I swore, and the crowd gasped. That probably wasn't the best choice of curses for this particular bunch. "These were brand new pants!" I shouted at the downed wolf, and then my Nahual let out another long growl for good measure.

UnnúlfR started to get up, and I kicked him in the head. He went slack. I didn't break his neck, but he wouldn't be getting up anytime soon. I was a little peeved at the "fuck" comment, but it was the torn pants that really threw me over the edge. Don't mess with my fashion.

All of a sudden, everyone started clapping, howling, and stamping. Two men came through the tunnel and carried the pale wolf away, eyeing me warily as they went. I got to my feet and realized the cuts on my lower leg were pretty deep. I was going to be at a distinct disadvantage in the next fight. My new power was keeping me going, but with a wound like that, I'd be limping soon. At the very least, I'd be slow. Not good at all.

"Enough," Fenrir stood at the ledge again, and everyone settled into silence. "VèulfR has already admitted that he lost his battle with you. This means that you've bested my first three sons: my honor guard. So now, there's only one wolf left for you to fight."

He vaulted over the wall, and the wolves howled and clapped. Fenrir landed with a loud thump that vibrated through the stone floor, barely even bending to break his fall.

“Father,” Trevor was at the wall, along with Thor and the whole God Squad. “You cannot fight her. She’s my mate. If you kill her, you’ll kill me!”

“She’s no mate of yours, my boy,” Fenrir stared at me with glowing eyes. “You’ll find another better suited.”

“Yes, she *is*!” Trevor shouted as he too jumped over the railing. He placed himself between me and Fenrir, and snarled as he began to shift.

“You have no right to interfere,” Fenrir growled. “Get out of my way, cub.”

“All you seem to understand is blood and death,” Trevor's clothes ripped away as his body completed the change, leaving him in his hulking werewolf form. He was still only just as tall as his father. And Fenrir had yet to shift. “So, I'm going to make this very clear to you. You'll have to kill me to get to her.”

A shocked silence fell as they faced off. I don't know who was more amazed by Trevor's declaration: me or Fenrir, but I did know that Fenrir didn't have to kill Trevor to get to me. He could easily incapacitate his son, and then I'd have to face an even angrier Fenrir. All Trevor was doing was buying me more time.

So I used it to think.

I couldn’t beat Fenrir when I was wounded. Fear was already seeping through my weakened limbs just from looking at him, and my Nahual was even pulling away. I wasn’t too sure I could beat him even in my most optimum shape and my Nahual seemed to agree.

So what did that leave? I could try and drain him like I had Aphrodite, or maybe one of my new powers could help. War and Victory were doing all they could just to keep me standing, so that left Love and Sex.

“I admire your pluck, boy”–Fenrir laughed–“but you forget yourself. I can beat you in my sleep.”

I reached up and pulled my hair sticks free, then undid my bun. My long hair tumbled down, magic sparking along its length, and Fenrir stopped mid-conversation to stare at me. Hope filled my chest; this just might work.

I gently nudged Trevor aside and tossed the hair sticks to the ground casually. They made pretty tinkling noises as they settled, and then I let the love magic have free rein. The butterflies started to fill me, fluttering delicately in my chest. Sex might have worked faster, but I had a feeling it would have been dangerous to tease Fenrir, especially with Trevor so close. So, love butterflies it was.

“Fenrir,” I purred, and even I didn't recognize the sweet voice that flowed over my lips. “You rule with strength, Wolf God, but what do you know of tenderness? What do you know about love?”

I heard Trevor's sharp intake of breath, but I ignored him as I walked forward, rolling my hips smoothly so I could mask my limp. I held Fenrir's gaze firmly. The power filled me, and I let it rush out to him. I felt it when it hit, heard his startled gasp, and a contented sigh left my lips. Between us ran an invisible line, and I poured Love down it. I set the butterflies free into that cord, until it flapped wildly with life. Fenrir's eyes widened and his hands began to shake.

“Stop,” Fenrir breathed the word out like a prayer as I approached.

I connected to his heart then, and it opened to me like sunken treasure; heavy with the weight of time and with fathoms of anguish. There was gold there, but it was covered in silt, caked with an ocean's worth of cynicism, and sunk deep beneath the shipwreck of his soul.

I saw his life clearly, felt his loneliness. The rejection of his mother upon seeing that she'd birthed a monster. The long search for a home and family of his own. Hunted by the other gods until he grew too powerful to kill, he'd been the first to leave Atlantis, years before its downfall, and he'd wandered for years alone.

Fenrir had found comfort in women occasionally, women who were drawn to his power, but most of them had left after birthing his children. Showing the same distaste for their babies that Fenrir's mother had for him. They had driven deeper the ugly word that had been branded on his soul from birth: Monster.

By the time I stood before him, tears were pouring down my face and my gloves were lying on the ground behind me. Fenrir had dropped to his knees and still, he towered over me, but I felt no fear of him. Only tenderness, empathy, and overwhelming love. I knew what it felt like to be alone, but his loneliness had been so much worse; peppered with the sting of rejection from those he had loved the most. From those who should have loved *him* the most. Love had failed him horribly, over and over, and I felt responsible for it, now that Love belonged to me. I needed to right this wrong.

My power whispered to me seductively: *Heal him. Free the wolf. Show him what love really is.*

"I see no monster," I whispered so that only he could hear me. His pain was private and I refused to share it. "Only a god."

I slid my hands up the sides of his face, pushing back his wild hair and revealing the striking features he'd been hiding. I let my love and admiration shine through my eyes. I let it bathe him in healing radiance and concentrated all my will on filling him with my magic. I felt him take a shuddering breath as it poured through him and chased away the shadows of all of those lies.

"The blessing of Love be upon you," the words spilled from my lips unbidden. My magic was talking, not I. "Freely

given, richly deserved, and long overdue. We failed you once, Wolf King, but never again. You shall have your Queen."

I kissed him chastely on the mouth, and something passed through me and into him with that light touch. When I pulled back, I knew that I'd taken his pain and replaced it with hope. There had been the flash of a face, a beautiful woman with patient hazel eyes. My magic had found her, and shown Fenrir that he would find her too.

"She loved me for the dangers I had passed," he whispered, his voice shaking, his eyes overflowing, "and I loved her that she did pity them."

Fenrir gave a great shuddering sigh and sank his face into my hair. Beneath my hands, his shoulders shook, and I felt his tears soak into me, but he cried silently, safely hidden within my arms. I pulled the remnants of his pain from him, drew it out bit by bit with those butterflies, and then sent them flying away so he could never draw it back. I stroked his hair, combing the heavy locks with my fingers and soothing his back until his cries subsided. It felt strangely sacred, like an ancient rite or Communion.

Fenrir dried his tears in my hair and sat back to look at me. "You've given me a great gift, little frami." He held my face as I had held his. "I had never thought I'd feel hope again."

"There's always hope"–I smiled gently, my face still streaked with my own tears–"and, for one like you, there will always be love. Just open your arms and it will find you."

I kissed him again, this time it was purely me doing the kissing, and the wolves murmured and exclaimed. I'd almost forgotten about them.

Fenrir kissed me back as gently as I did him, and it was all the more precious for the strength I felt behind it. When he pulled away, he lifted me off my feet and up into the air above him. The

wolves went crazy; howling, stamping, and cheering as their god turned me in a slow circle like a war prize he wanted to show off. Fenrir finally settled me in his arms and faced Trevor.

"You've found not only a worthy mate, but a worthy adversary." Fenrir didn't have to shout for his voice to ring out over the cheering. "I give my blessing to my heir's chosen mate and welcome her to the Froekn as our Rouva!"

Rouva? Oh crap, what had I done now? I looked up at Thor with wide eyes, and he shook his head with a small smile. I guess it couldn't be all that bad if Thor was smiling. When I looked over at Trevor, he beamed at me like a boy who'd just been given a pony. He stood gloriously naked before us; he must have shifted back to human when I was healing Fenrir, but it was Trevor's eyes that held my attention, not his nudity. His eyes were so beautiful; shining with pride and love.

Then Fenrir handed me carefully to Trevor, and Trevor held my gaze as he lowered his mouth to mine. I kissed him back (what else was I supposed to do?) and the wolves cheered louder. Trevor lowered me to my feet and wiped the remnants of my tears away. Then he shook his head, wonder filling his eyes and a soft smile stretching his lips.

"The best day of my life was the day it became yours," he whispered. "Thank you for whatever you did for my father. He looks happy. I don't think I've ever seen him happy."

Before I could say anything, the man in question stole me away from his son. Fenrir's hair hung down his back, shining from the magic I'd combed through it. His face had even changed. Unhampered by his bitterness, he was breathtaking, and I heard the women murmur in appreciation. They were leaning over the sides of the walls to stare only at him now. He smiled, and it was a cocky male grin that shouted confidence in his own appeal.

"I've created a monster." I laughed and ran a hand down

his face. For some reason, I needed to touch him. I felt drawn to the trace of my magic.

His smile turned mischievous as he took my hand and kissed it. "That's not what you said earlier."

I shook my head as I felt my love for him rise up. I knew then, the price of my power. I could bring men to their knees, hell, probably women too, but I'd be tied to them forever. I'd love the Wolf God, not in the way that I loved Thor, not in a sexual way, but in the way children love. A pure, simple way. Eternally.

"This is a different beast entirely." I felt the love pour out of my eyes and his face softened. "But yes, you've every right to be arrogant."

Fenrir threw back his head and howled with laughter. "Come along, Trevor," he put an arm around his son as he carried me out, through the tunnel on his side of the pit. "Let's present our new Rouva."

We exited the tunnel and came out into a wide antechamber filled with people. The wolves pressed in around us, sniffing the air, marveling at the change in their god. Fenrir lowered me down to my feet, and I felt Trevor pressing his warmth against my back, rubbing a comforting hand over my shoulder.

"Little frami," Fenrir took my hand again and pulled me forward. "Come and meet the Froekn. Come and meet your new family."

They closed in around me, but Fenrir and Trevor had both taken positions at my sides so I didn't feel nervous. They didn't push and jostle like humans would, they simply flowed around me like the tide. A warm welcoming tide. Bodies rubbed along mine, circling the three of us and making soft contented sounds. Eyes flashing up and away. Hands darting out to flick over me. I held my hands out to them, the love power rising to meet their own animal affection like a sibling, and they trembled around me in

delight.

I was tied to them all and completely unable to stop it. I didn't even know if I wanted to stop it. I felt like I was home, safe and loved. You know the feeling you get when your pet curls up to you and bathes you in their love and loyalty? Well, multiply that by ten and imagine that unconditional loyalty and unbreakable love being given to you by people. Humans just don't love like that, with the freedom of an animal, but the Froekn do.

When they finally withdrew a bit, it was only to draw us along with them into a huge feasting hall where long tables were already piled with food. I guess it didn't matter if I'd won or lost, they'd have celebrated either way. I smiled, finding no offense in it, only more love for the wolves who lived life to the fullest. Every day should be celebrated, every moment explored for all it had to offer. They understood that.

I turned and looked for Thor. He caught my eye and smiled his assurance before waving me along. The rest of the gods were with him, and they were all looking a little shell-shocked. Horus especially peered about him in morbid fascination. Persephone was the only one avidly enjoying every second. She had Hades on her arm, and he wasn't looking pleased by the way she was looking at the Froekn.

Fenrir had one of my arms and Trevor had the other. They led me to a table on a dais at the end of the hall. It was heavy wood, but covered with white linen and china. The wolves may have barbaric tendencies, but they liked to coat it in luxury.

Fenrir seated me on his left in a massive, padded chair, and Trevor sat on his right. On my left, I was pleasantly surprised to find TryggulfR. He rubbed his cheek against mine and kissed me lightly on the lips after he got seated.

"I've never been so jealous of my brother," he whispered with laughing eyes.

"Thank you." I smiled shakily. I was still coming down off my high of endorphins and magic. "But I'm sure you have no trouble finding women. Good looks seem to run in the family."

"You're flirting with me? Now I'm really mad he found you first." TrygguIfR leaned in closer and waggled his eyebrows. "You want to trade up? I'm younger, full of more stamina, and very eager to please."

"I think I've got enough trouble on my plate without adding a second helping, but thanks anyway."

"Well, let me know if you change your mind, Vervain." He gave me a quick wink. "Pretty name that, I've always liked human names."

"What does TrygguIfR mean?"

"It means *faithful wolf.*" He twisted his lips into a smile. "Once I give my loyalty, it's eternal."

"Are your names always accurate descriptions of your personalities?"

"They're chosen by magic, so they usually are, but you may have to dig deep to see it sometimes." TrygguIfR chuckled and leaned in again. "UnnúlfR means *to love a wolf.*"

"What?" I laughed, and as I looked up, I met Thor's worried gaze. He was seated as an honored guest at a table on my left. The other gods were around him, having a great time, but he was looking at me as if I was slipping away.

"Yes," TrygguIfR continued. "But then it says nothing about him *giving* love in return, so you see, it *is* accurate. It can be dangerous to love a wolf."

"Yes"–I kept my gaze locked with Thor–"I see that it can be."

I wanted to get up and run over to Thor, to kiss him and tell him that I loved him, but I was pretty sure it would be bad form to go snuggle with my boyfriend when I had just been accepted as Trevor's mate. So instead, I tried to reassure Thor with my eyes, and after a moment, I felt him pushing at the shields in my mind. I dropped them instantly and let him in.

It wasn't really him speaking to me. There was no voice in my head, but it was like I suddenly felt him there and knew he could feel what I was thinking. I let him invade me, knowing he needed the reassurance, but feeling a little upset that he did. He needed to trust me, and as soon as I thought it, I saw him smile and lift an eyebrow. I felt his amusement run lightly over me, and then he showed me an image of Trevor, covering my body with his and shuddering through an orgasm.

I closed my eyes tight and sighed deeply. Yeah, he may have had a point there. When I opened my eyes, Thor was staring at me with a smirk. He shifted his gaze to TryggulfR, then back to me again, and I smiled ruefully. I sent him waves of apology, imagining myself showering kisses all over his face. He laughed, loud and booming, every head in the hall turning toward the sound. Thor didn't even notice the attention, he just lifted his glass up in a salute before he drank it down.

"And what was that about, little sister?" TryggulfR had evidently been watching the whole exchange.

"Your brother bound himself to me because I spared his life." I looked at TryggulfR to see if he'd known. He nodded. I leaned in closer and dropped my voice to the tiniest whisper. "I didn't bind myself to him. I didn't even know the Binding had occurred until Trevor told me." He raised both brows and I hoped he'd understand. "Trevor knew I was with Thor when he bound himself to me. He knows I can't truly be his mate and he's accepted that. I just don't know if your father will."

"He knows that you two aren't having sex." TryggulfR

looked around me to Fenrir, who was speaking with Trevor excitedly. “Trevor has been honest with him. Father just has this tendency to hear only what he wishes to.”

“I can see that about him.” I looked over at Fenrir, and I knew my heart was in my eyes. I'd need to really work on controlling that, or every time I used the magic, I'd be making moon eyes at someone else.

“Are you in love with my father?” TryggulfR’s whisper was low and horrified.

“Not like you mean.” I looked back at him and laughed at his relieved expression. “I’ve recently come into a new power, and in using it on your father, I’ve formed an affection for him. It's more of an admiration than a sexual attraction.”

“A new power.” TryggulfR looked at me as he chewed at his lower lip. “You’re a witch, I can smell it on you now, but before I was confused. You smelled like a goddess.”

I inhaled sharply. “There’s a goddess smell?”

Someone should bottle that.

“Of course.,” He frowned thoughtfully. “I can smell it still, but the witch is there now too. It was like the goddess scent masked the witch earlier.”

Well didn’t that just make perfect sense?

“The power I came into belonged to a goddess originally.”

“You stole a goddess’ power?” If TryggulfR's eyes got any bigger, they’d pop out and go rolling across the table.

“She was trying to whip me to death at the time.” I gave him my innocent-eyes and lifted my hands, making a *give me a break* gesture. “It called for desperate measures, okay?”

"Okay, okay." TrygguIfR laughed and looked up, over my head.

"What are you two whispering about?" I turned and found Fenrir looking at us with a small smile.

"Vervain was telling me about stealing a goddess' power–umph."

I cut off TrygguIfR's honesty with a swift elbow in his ribs, but he just laughed.

Fenrir's face went serious, and then his jaw went slack. "Aphrodite," he whispered.

"Yes," I stared at him intently, waiting for any further reaction.

"Once"–Fenrir's eyes looked distant for a second–"she wielded it like you do, but her nature corrupted it and the magic was poisoned. You've cleansed it and made it pure again."

"I did?" That was *so* not what I was expecting to hear.

Fenrir smiled warmly and shook his head. "You've saved many from heartache. Did you kill her?"

"Yes." I looked away. "I had no choice."

"You don't need to defend yourself here, little frami." Fenrir brushed my hair back over my shoulder. "At least not anymore. We've accepted you and that's forever. *We* will defend *you*."

"What does 'frami' mean?" I asked after I'd taken a moment to process.

"Courage." Fenrir chucked me under the chin. "It means courage."

"Vervain." Teharon, the Mohawk God of Healing, who didn't actually have a mohawk, was suddenly behind me. "Let me see to your wounds before you eat."

"What would I do without you, Teharon?"

"Bleed a lot," he actually said it with a straight face, "and die horribly."

"Most likely." I chuckled as Teharon helped me up. "I'd definitely have a lot more scars to show off."

I couldn't believe I'd forgotten that I was hurt. The warm welcome of the wolves had drowned out the pain, but when Teharon had drawn my attention back to it, my body began to ache and throb. I let him lead me to a corridor and then into an unoccupied room. Before I left the hall, I saw Thor get up to follow us. So, I wasn't surprised when, shortly after Teharon closed the bedroom door, Thor came in and closed it again.

"Are you hurt badly?" Thor asked as he strode over to the bed Teharon had sat me on.

"Nah," I put on my best British accent, "it's only a flesh wound." Both of them stared at me blankly. "Monty Python? Come on people." I sighed and laid back. "I'm dying here."

"What?" Thor took my hand. "Is it that bad?"

"No," I groaned. "I mean you that guys are killing me. It's an expression, Thor." He frowned again and I looked at Teharon. "Just shoot me."

"Vervain," Thor spoke sternly. "I don't like this joking about death. You'll stop it now . . . please."

"I suppose since you asked so nicely." I smiled and played with Thor's shiny braid as he bent over me, but I ruined the magic moment with a loud hiss of pain when Teharon prodded my

wound. I tried to recover it with, "I love you."

I was happy I could say it aloud to him finally.

Thor's smile was radiant. "I know. You showed me in some pretty graphic ways. Thank you for that."

I blushed as I wondered exactly what he'd seen in my head. Thor laughed and kissed me sweetly.

"I enjoyed every detail, darling," he whispered.

Teharon cleared his throat, pushing his braid over his shoulder; it was a thin braid like Thor's, but Teharon's was adorned with a blood-tipped feather.

"You're all healed up, *darling*," Teharon smiled at me, then at Thor.

I groaned and threw a pillow at Teharon.

"Damn gods and their super senses." I sat up and looked myself over. The wound was closed up and shiny pink. "Nice job."

"Of course." Teharon spread his hands as if I shouldn't have expected anything less. "I'll see you two back in the hall."

Teharon left with a secret grin.

"What have I got myself into?" I asked Thor as Teharon closed the door.

"Haven't they explained everything to you yet?"

"I understand that I'm like family now, but I'm kinda getting the impression that I've gained status as well."

"You think?" Thor lifted a brow and gave me a sarcastic smile.

"What's a Rouva?" I recalled the title Fenrir had given me.

“The word means Queen, but I think it’s got a lot to do with politics. You’ll have to ask Trevor for clarification.”

“It’s a title for the highest ranking royal female of the Froekn. It will be yours until Father chooses a mate.” Trevor had come in silently, so both Thor and I jumped a little. He shrugged and smiled. “Sorry; Dad’s asking for you.”

“I’m the highest ranking royal woman?” I shook my head. “I’m not even a werewolf. Won’t I be stepping on a few toes?”

“You may not have been born a wolf, but you have a part of me inside you now.” Trevor stroked my arm, and I felt that piece of him shift and rise to greet him.

“Werewolf by injection, eh?” I waggled my brows at him.

“Vervain,” Thor groaned.

“You *are* Froekn, and no one resents your position,” Trevor continued after giving me a secret smile that made my heart speed up just a little. “Well, I don’t know about UnnúlfR yet. He came in right after you left, and let’s just say; I’m glad he’s sitting next to me and not you.”

“Great,” I lamented. “I don’t suppose we could just kiss and make up?”

“He’s a little grumpy right now,” Trevor laughed. “The teasing he's getting isn't helping either, but he’ll get over it.”

I just made enemies wherever I went.

“Alright, we better go back,” I huffed.

I kissed Thor quickly before I took Trevor’s arm and let him escort me out.

Chapter Three

I didn't remember my gloves and hair sticks until the meal was over.

"Oh shit." I grimaced and Fenrir looked over with a raised brow. "I left my gloves in the pit."

"The pit?" He looked at me like I was a walking comedy routine.

"Sorry"–I gave him my *oops* face–"I mean, the arena."

"Your pretty claws?" Fenrir stood up and lifted me to my feet. "Let's go get them."

Fenrir led me back through the tunnel and into the pit. I found my hair sticks and wrapped my hair back up, tucking the sticks in as I continued to look around. The gloves, however, were gone.

"What the hell?"

"What's wrong?" Thor had followed us down.

"My gloves are gone." I looked at Fenrir.

"None of our wolves would take your weapons, little frami." His expression was reproving.

"I know, Dad." I blinked, wide-eyed in the aftermath of those words, but he just beamed at me. I cleared my throat and tried not to notice Thor's shocked expression. What the hell had made me say that? "But who would want my gloves?" As I asked the question I remembered a comment made early on in the trial. "Loki!" I screamed.

A round of curses flew out of Thor's mouth and he ran off down the tunnel. I looked back at Fenrir. He had a rueful smile on his face and was shaking his head.

"My father has a thieving nature." Fenrir laughed softly. "Don't worry, we'll get your gloves back."

"That's right." I snorted. "I forgot that he's your father. Does that mean he's like my grandpa now?"

Fenrir howled in laughter. "Don't say that to him, I think he likes you for the time being. It would be best to keep it that way." He took my arm and started leading me back to the hall.

"He likes me, so he steals my gloves?" I squished my lips up in distaste. "What is this, the fifth grade?"

"He stole Thor's iron belt and gloves before too." Fenrir gestured toward Thor, who was approaching us with a grim expression.

"He's gone," Thor reported. "That thieving trickster is gone."

"We'll return her gloves, Thunderer." Fenrir patted Thor's shoulder. "Don't get so upset. Come on, it's time for the dancing."

The rest of the night was spent in music and laughter. I didn't know wolves were such good dancers. They all wanted to dance with their new Rouva, and man after man asked to accompany me. They were so exuberant. I was lifted and swung about more than a few times. When Trevor finally got a chance to dance with me, I was flushed and a little sweaty.

"You look like you're having fun, Minn Elska." Trevor swung me around, higher than the others had. Men always had to outdo each other.

"I am." I felt shiny with happiness. Pure happiness is rare

for me, so when it comes along, I try to fully enjoy it.

"You also look beautiful." His eyes started to warm, then glow.

"You don't look so bad yourself." And sweet, furry, wolf god it was true; he looked magnificent.

Trevor had on black leather pants which molded to his perfect ass and a saffron sleeveless tunic with gold embroidery down the sides that brought out the gold in his eyes. It wasn't half bad at showing off his biceps either.

"Thank you, Rouva." He gave me a little bow. "It's nice to know my appearance doesn't disappoint you."

"Disappoint?" I snorted. "Not possible. Especially after you so gallantly defended me earlier."

"I couldn't exactly sit back and watch as my father killed you."

"You sat back and watched me fight your brothers." I lifted an eyebrow.

"I knew you could handle my brothers." Trevor shook his head like it was a given, and I have to admit that it felt pretty good to know he was confident in my fighting skills. Why couldn't Thor have that kind of faith in me?

"Your father is pretty intimidating." I laughed.

"Intimidating?" Trevor's laughter joined mine. "He probably would have killed us both if you hadn't done whatever it was you did. I think you actually saved my life again."

"I never saved it the first time." I shook my head.

Trevor had just done one of the most romantic things anyone had ever done for me, he'd risked his life to save mine, and

he was blowing it off like it was nothing.

“You stood up to your father for me, risking death and disgrace in the eyes of your family . . . and after meeting your family, I'm not sure which would have been worse for you.”

He wavered his head like it was a toss up.

“Don't make light of it.” I touched the tip of his nose with my finger. “Thank you; you gave me enough time to use my magic.”

“You're welcome,” he said seriously, then he got a mischievous look, and I narrowed my eyes on him.

He swung me out, and when he pulled me back, he did it hard enough that I smacked against his chest. I could feel his heart pounding through his shirt, and when I looked up at him, I felt mine start to beat faster too. Spicy musk surrounded me as if scent could have substance. I wanted to roll around in it, wrap myself in his smell like I would with a warm blanket. A Trevor scented blanket that I could take home with me. Or maybe I could just coat myself in it till it was in my skin, till his scent became mine.

“I . . .” Trevor looked a little lost. He swallowed with some difficulty and wet his lips. “I wish . . .” He shook his head and smiled ruefully.

“What?” The scent thickened, fogging my thoughts, but one thing was clear; I needed him to finish the sentence.“You wish what?”

The skin around his eyes tightened, his jaw clenched, and he looked away.

“I wish I could dance with you all night.” Trevor's smile seemed brittle. If I brushed my hand across his lips, they might break. “But the dance is over.” He bowed over my hand, and before I could protest, Thor swept me up and danced me as far

away from Trevor as he could get me.

I smiled up at Thor, instantly horrified that I'd felt such a strong attraction to Trevor. I looked over my shoulder and saw him talking to a group of men. Trevor glanced up as if he'd known the exact moment my attention had turned to him. His eyes looked shiny, feverish, and a little sad. I looked away quickly. I couldn't afford to contemplate the meaning of Trevor's stare. So, when my eyes began to prickle, I hid my face in Thor's chest and blinked rapidly while simultaneously trying to still the shaking deep in my belly. What was wrong with me?

"You're quite a hit." Thor rubbed my back, pulling me in closer.

"They do seem to like me ." I snuggled into his arms and tried to concentrate on how much I loved him and only him.

"Yes," he spoke into my hair quietly, "some more than others."

Chapter Four

"But that doesn't mean you have to go home," Thor was still arguing with me when we arrived in the living room of my little house in Kaneohe, Hawaii.

"I'm perfectly safe now, babe." I sighed and dropped my suitcase on the floor before letting Nick, my gray tabby, out of his cat carrier. "With the Froekn as my allies now, and Aphrodite dead, I'm probably safer than I've ever been."

"So, you're saying they can protect you better than I." He glowered at me.

"No, I . . ." I'd finally taken a good look around my living room and noticed Jackson standing in the middle of it with a shocked expression on his face. "Ah, hi, Jackson."

"Hey," he whispered.

"Who the hell is this?" Thor roared.

I guess he'd reached his limit, what with Trevor bonding me, Fenrir fighting me, and now me moving back home. A gorgeous man standing in my living room, like he belonged there, was just too much for the Viking to take.

"This is Jackson." I jumped in front of my friend, who knew nothing of my secret god-hunting life. "Remember how I told you about having a friend who came over to check on Nick occasionally? This is him. Jackson, this is Thor."

"You guys just"–Jackson waved distractedly at the place we'd traced in–"you just . . ."

"Yeah, um." I looked at Thor for help, but he was still

staring furiously at Jackson. “Thor! Jackson is one of my best friends. He's also in a committed relationship . . . with my friend *Tristan*.”

“Tristan?” Thor blinked as if he was coming out of a daze.

“Yeah, Tristan.” I sighed. Sheesh, with the jealousy already. “Um, Jackson, yeah, you know how I'm a witch?”

“Uh-huh.” Jackson was staring at Thor now, taking in the wild hair, muscles, and Nordic features.

“So, I, uh, oh hell.” I looked at Thor again. He was starting to relax, as it finally occurred to him that Jackson had absolutely no sexual interest in me. “Help me out here, baby.”

“What?” Thor frowned, and then realized he'd just traced in front of a human. “Oh, I'm a god. Thor. Nice to meet you.” He extended his hand, and Jackson stared at it as if he'd never seen one before.

“Great, Thor, very subtle.” I smacked his hand away.

“What I say?”

“Jackson, have a seat.” I settled us on one sofa while Thor took the other one, and I started explaining what I'd really been doing with most of my time.

Jackson sat quietly through it all, and when I was finished, he blinked and seemed to surface from his shock. He looked over at Thor again, this time with utter fascination. A wrinkle marred his forehead as things started to really click, and I just waited, Nick curling around my feet, purring. Nick was so happy to be home.

“What about the lwa?” Jackson burst out.

Jackson was a practitioner of Voodoo, being introduced to it at a young age by his grandmother. In Voodoo they believed that God was too busy to interact with humans so he had created the

lwa. The lwa were supposed to have been living people once; people who had accomplished great works in life and so, upon death, were elevated to an almost angelic status. They helped humanity, and their devotees served them with offerings and deeds that were supposed to feed the lwa and keep them strong. Practitioners devoted themselves to one lwa in particular and served them for life. Jackson's was Erzulei-Freda, the lwa of love, beauty, and wealth.

"They're ours as well," Thor answered for me. "Atlanteans."

"Have you met her?" Jackson looked to me eagerly.

I smiled, I should have known he'd take it so well. He probably suspected a lot of what I'd told him already. I also should have known that his first thought would be for Erzulie. I mean, who wouldn't immediately wonder what their version of Deity was really like? I guess it was a perfectly normal response for an incredibly unusual situation.

"I haven't met her yet." I patted his hand when his face fell. "But I've met Yemanja. Thor dated her."

"You what?"

I could see all of Jackson's preconceived ideas about the lwas start to crumble.

"Have *you* met Erzulie-Freda?" Jackson asked Thor.

"I have," Thor said simply, and I turned sharply to face him. "She's lovely."

"Is she?" I felt my brow rising. "Did you date her too?"

"No, she cries too much for my taste." Thor shrugged. "She's very sensitive, and I'm uncomfortable around weepy women."

"What else is she like?" Jackson was absorbing every word.

"She's,"–Thor sighed and spread his hands–"dramatic and very particular about things. Oh, and she has a thing for birds."

"Birds?" Jackson asked. "You mean doves? That's the animal associated with her."

"No, just birds," Thor snorted. "It's another reason we never dated. I hated having to constantly be on the look out for falling bird shit. I hate birds."

"Can you introduce me?" Jackson sat on the edge of the sofa, leaning toward Thor.

"Sure," Thor shrugged. "If I see her again. We don't cross paths often. The lwa don't have the same problems a lot of the other gods have. Their followers still believe in them, and they give the lwas energy aplenty. But if I do see her, I'll try and work out an introduction."

"That would amazing."

"Yes, amazing." I stood. "But I'm kinda beat guys, and I still have to unpack. Can we catch up more later?"

"Of course." Jackson jumped up.

"You know," Thor mused, "you could ask her to come speak with you. Let her know that you know the truth, and she won't have a reason to hide. She may be pleased to have a follower she could show herself to without having to go through that whole possession thing."

"Really?" Jackson walked to the door in a daze.

"Sure."

We said our goodbyes and I was finally able to get not only Jackson, but Thor, out of my house. Then I was alone. No gods in

the next room, no werewolves waiting outside in the bushes. No complicated attractions to men I shouldn't be attracted to. I didn't have to prove anything or kill anyone there. I breathed deeply and smiled. It was good to be home.

I went to bed contemplating the possibility of becoming a shut-in.

Chapter Five

I grimaced at the sorry state of my herb garden as I pulled out the weeds. I'd neglected my home for way too long. It was a good thing Kaneohe rained so often or they'd all be dead. I already had about three bags of rotten fruit to throw away from the fruit trees in the back yard. I would have been crushed if my herbs had kicked the bucket too.

A shadow fell over me, and I turned around, startled. There stood Blue with determination spread across his face. I inhaled sharply, dropping the weeds as I jumped up. Before I could react any further, he grabbed me by both of my upper arms and traced us out of Hawaii. We ended up standing before the pyramid he'd brought me to the first time he invaded my dreams.

“How the hell did you find me, Blue?” I sucked in deep breaths as I backed away from him. Tracing without preparation was not healthy. Like going underwater without taking a breath first.

“I've always known where you live, little witch.” Blue smirked. “I could have taken you at any time, but I meant what I said to you before. I wanted to win you. I wanted you to see me, to come to love me back. So I gave you time and space. That's what all your modern literature advises.”

“Are you talking about self-help books?” I gaped at him. I had a vision of Blue, relaxed in a chair, reading *Men are from Mars, Women are from Venus*.

“I brought you here because I wanted you to see my old home in person.” He gestured around him, totally ignoring my comment.

I followed his hand and looked out around me. The pyramid was as big as the one in my dream, but the stones were worn and much of the complex had been obliterated by time. Even in its diminished state, though, the Pyramid of the Sun loomed menacingly above me as I marveled up at it. The street we stood on was called the Avenue of the Dead and was lined with low, stone-faced structures (No, I didn't ask how it had got its name; I didn't want to know). The vibrant colors had faded and the city that had once surrounded the complex was gone, buried partly under Mexico City.

"So, this is where you lived?" I turned away from the rising hulk of the pyramid to stare at Blue.

I had to keep calm. If I kept the conversation polite and calm, maybe Blue wouldn't murder me. Or maybe I could stall long enough for Thor to get there. *Thor!* I screamed in my head, waiting impatiently for some kind of answer. None came.

"For many years, yes," Blue was looking at the pyramid like an ex-lover he still pined for; he wanted to hold her and reclaim her, but knew it was impossible. "The Pyramid of the Sun was mine. It's 700 feet square at its base. Isn't it magnificent?"

"Yes, it's something alright." I stared up the wide steps to the temple at the top where Blue had brought me in the dream. *Thor, where the hell are you?* I screamed silently again.

"Your lover can't hear you. I've blocked him out," Blue said casually, and then continued on like it wasn't a big deal. "My sister's pyramid is the Pyramid of the Moon, over there." He pointed down the lane to the second largest structure.

"What?" I almost hadn't caught what he said about Thor. "Did you say you blocked Thor from my mind?"

"Yes. And my Father's pyramid was in a great enclosure there." Blue pointed in the other direction, and I saw the small pyramid I'd glimpsed in his memories. "We lived in the palaces

surrounding it."

"How the hell did you do that?" I watched as he tore his attention away from the pyramid to look at me.

"Quite easily, the palaces were very large and beautiful."

"No, damn you, I meant the blocking out Thor bit."

"Never mind that leather-wearing lout, you need to pay attention, Vervain. I'm telling you about my family." He took my hand. "I wanted you to see my birthplace. I thought that maybe if you could see it, if you could feel what was once here, then maybe you could understand why I am what I am."

He looked so sincere, I almost believed him, but how could I let anything he said sway me after learning the truth about his actions from Aphrodite? Maybe he did love me, but it was a twisted, self-serving love, and that wasn't the kind of love I wanted.

I wasn't wise enough in the ways of the heart to know for certain that my idea of love was the only true way to love someone. In fact, the only thing about love I did know for certain was that I'd never know all the forms it could take. Just because I held the love magic now, didn't make me an expert.

So I couldn't denounce Blue's love for me as being so different from the ideal that it wasn't love at all. Who was I to say how he felt? I could, however, say with absolute conviction that it wasn't the version I wanted in my life. Not to mention the fact that he was acting like a complete psycho.

"I do understand you." I stared up into the blood pools of his eyes. They were almost beautiful, those crimson irises surrounded by thick lashes and framed by sleek, black hair. "It doesn't mean I can accept you. I hate what happened to you, and I believe you were justified in killing your brothers, but what it's made you is monstrous. I truly want to heal your hurt, take away

the pain, and reveal the man you were, but I can't do that now."

"Why?" He took me by the arms and pulled me against him. "Why won't you love me?"

"You make it impossible."

Blue's face fell into cold, hard lines. He dropped one of my arms, but kept his hold on the other, to pull me behind him as he walked down the Avenue of the Dead. I could feel his anger start to heat his skin, and I knew if he got too hot, he'd burn me. The thought of death reminded me that it wasn't just myself I had to worry about anymore. If I went down, I was taking Trevor with me.

Trevor! What had he said about calling him? Just say his name into the wind or something like that. Did he mean it literally or was that just pretty werewolf poetry?

"Trevor," I whispered over my shoulder as I hoped for a miracle. "I need you!"

Blue pulled me along towards his father's temple, and as he did, his memory flared through me with a sudden, shocking burst. I saw the bodies of his brothers piled at the pyramid's base. I saw the blood everywhere, malicious strokes of scarlet over the walls and floors. He had drenched the temple in blood as he consumed them, and it had poured in rivers down the steps. The human body held a lot of blood, I knew that, I just hadn't been confronted with such graphic evidence of it before.

I closed my eyes and swallowed the scream that threatened to rise. Never let them see you sweat. Just breathe; calm breaths, in and out. While I continued to do my breathing exercises, Blue continued to drag me up the steps to his father's temple. We reached the top, but the temple itself had long ago crumbled away to dust. The stones were clean, the bloodstains gone. Nothing was left to testify to the horrendous massacre that had occurred there.

Blue dropped my arm and paced the open space, lost in his despair for a moment. I fell to the floor and wrapped my arms around my knees, in an effort to try and stop my trembling. I'd faced down the Wolf God, you'd think a little ol' vampire god wouldn't scare me. But Blue wasn't just any god or any vampire. He was a god other gods feared. He could take my mind, turn it against me, and make me do exactly what he wanted without ever lifting a finger. I didn't stand a chance and I knew it. In this instance, knowledge was not power.

The stone beneath me was shockingly cold; the kind of cold you get when the bath water's too hot and the air conditioning's too high, so that the merging of the two extremes makes you feel like your exposed flesh will never be warm again. You keep adding more hot water until you're pink and sweating. You keep turning up the heat until the chill is gone. I looked at Blue and I could feel the waves of heat rolling off him. For the first time in my life, I preferred the cold.

"Can you see them?" Blue covered his face with his hands and screamed. "You did this! You made me feel again! You gave me back my heart, and now you rend it to pieces. You've taken away the only thing that's kept me from going insane: my apathy." He dropped to his knees and started to weep; great giant sobs racking his body. Then he looked up at me with tears still pouring from his eyes. "You take away my control, and then you call me a monster. Well look upon your creation; am I not everything you hoped I'd be?"

"No" I covered my face. "I didn't do this. I didn't make you a monster."

"No, you didn't." Blue pulled me to my feet and yanked my hands away from my face. "You made me *feel* like one!"

His hands seared my skin, pulling a scream from me as the smell of burnt flesh filled my nose, but he seemed distracted. Blue turned his head to the side as if he were listening to something.

Then I heard it too, a slight ringing. A rushing sound of movement. An almost hypnotic, pulsing sound.

"Your wolf is here." Blue pulled me in tighter as I screamed again, and in moments we were in the stone entry room of his home in the God Realm.

He pushed me to the floor with disgust and poured the waiting pitcher of blood over his head. He took a deep breath as the blood sank in, quenching his heat, then looked at me steadily before he started forward.

"You said you loved me." I slid backward on the floor away from him, the pain of my burns taking a backseat to my panic.

"I do," he smiled and his fangs were startling white against his dark skin.

"Love is wanting what's best for someone." I stumbled to my feet. "Love doesn't seek revenge or punishment."

"No, little witch"–his smile grew even more wicked–"love is a madness and you have driven me to it."

I blanched and nearly fell again. "So, now you kill me to regain your sanity?"

"No, sweet flower." Blue's face softened, but I knew it was a lie. "I won't kill you. I'm going to make you as I am. Then we can be monstrous together."

"No." I shook my head and backed up. "Hell, no!"

I turned and ran. I knew the only way out was behind me, but I ran anyway. It was instinctual, pure and simple. Danger was behind me, so I'd go in the opposite direction. I ran through the hallway, through Blue's bedroom, and then out into the jungle. His laughter followed me, and I tripped and fell into the thick

undergrowth, scraping my hands and breaking open the blisters on my arms. My heart raced as I jumped to my feet and pushed further into the dense wilderness.

Hide. Run. Hide. The words pounded through me. I couldn’t let him catch me. I couldn't become a vampire. I thought about the centuries passing as I was bound to him. Forced to take blood to live. My mind not my own. A servant as much as his priests were, but worse, I’d be serving him in bed. I’d share eternity with him, bound in blood and sex, and he’d make me love every moment of it . . . love him. My mind and body would not be my own anymore.

I shoved aside vines reaching out to strangle me and felt my breath coming harshly. I couldn’t outrun him. Where would I go? I didn’t even know where I was really. I stopped and bent over, trying to catch my breath, and that's when I heard them.

Thrashing sounds echoed around me. They weren't even trying to be quiet, they were making as much noise as possible. He’d sent his vampire priests out to herd me in. Panic filled me, and then the spark that was Trevor . . . no . . . VèulfR, came to life within me. It filled me with wild energy, and I leapt forward. My Nahual added her instincts to the mix, this being more her territory than the wolf's, and for the first time ever, they worked together.

I cleared fallen debris and wove through the jungle like it was home to me. The branches that reached for me passed harmlessly by as I instinctively swerved to miss them. My path appeared clear before me, my eyes instinctively going straight to the best course. For a second, I felt joyous, free among the wild things. My legs and lungs seemed more powerful. I could run for miles and nothing could stop me.

Then I heard his voice behind me, calling to me sweetly, as if I were already his lover, and I turned towards it automatically. The ground fell away in that one distracted moment, and I fell with it. I felt my body tumbling, and I reached out around me for

anything to break my fall. I felt earth fill my nails as I pulled grass free from the soil, but still, I found no purchase. My sides burned where roots and rocks ripped at me. The world spun as I rolled, until I felt a warm hand grip my arm and pull me to a stop.

I looked up and saw Blue's face above me. He smoothed my hair back gently and I began to cry. I couldn't help it; the adrenaline, the chase, the fear, and the need for escape, it all came crashing down on me. I had failed; it was all over.

"Shh." Blue eased me onto his lap, and I saw that we were halfway down a slope into a ravine. "It's going to be alright now," he whispered as he lowered his mouth to my neck.

I kept crying in futility and I hated myself for it. The adrenaline was leaving me, the wolf soul curling up within my belly in submission, and the jaguar growling softly as she backed herself into a corner. I sobbed as he drank from me, cried at the horror my life was about to become. Blue stroked my back and his mouth on my neck started to feel sensuous. I whimpered as my traitorous body responded to him.

Blue lifted his head and there was a drop of blood on his lips, his tongue flicked out and licked it. "Sleep now, little witch, sleep."

My nightmare had begun.

Chapter Six

I was so tired, my limbs heavy and aching, but I knew I had to get up. Something was wrong. My back felt cold and bruised, made worse by the smooth stone beneath it. My neck throbbed, my hands and arms burned, and my head was foggy. Then I opened my eyes and saw only darkness. Panic flooded me for a second before I realized it was just cloth. I was covered in black silk. The cool caress of it flowed over my nude body. I groaned. This didn't bode well.

"She awakens," I heard a soft voice say on my left, and then the cloth was slowly pulled down till my face and shoulders were exposed to the night air.

I was in the little clearing I'd breakfasted in with Blue once, all those months ago. Around me were Blue's priests, wearing white loin cloths, fastened with gold belts. Their bodies were painted with red geometric patterns that seemed to jump out at me in the firelight. Horror washed over me when I realized it wasn't paint at all but blood. I gasped and tried to get up, but a heavy weight around my wrists and ankles held me tight. Looking down my body, I saw thick chains binding me to the stone altar.

Blue came striding through the trees then, resplendent in his Aztec finery. A gold crown sat atop his head, tall colorful feathers sticking straight up from it, and a wide, beaded collar encircled his neck. A heavy belt of gold held a swath of red fabric around his hips, but his chest was bare. He wore no paint, no blood I mean. It was just beautiful bare skin shining in the light of the torches that encircled the clearing.

"This feels awfully familiar, Blue." I stared hard at him, willing the terror in my belly to fade away.

"This is the altar that used to stand atop my pyramid." He reached my side and grabbed a handful of the silk covering me. "I'm about to make our dream a reality."

Great, just great. The dream he referenced was one in which he had made love to me on top of an Aztec altar. There were fangs involved, fangs in very intimate places. Of course, he had stolen into my mind and clouded my thoughts in order to create the dream, so the sex was not entirely consensual. It wasn't a moment I wanted to repeat.

"Can't we at least have a little privacy?" I looked down at my body and then pointedly at the priests.

"Don't worry, little witch." Blue stroked my cheek, and I felt my teeth creak as my jaw clenched. "They'll be in the jungle, forming a living circle of protection around us." He gave the vampires a nod, and they disappeared into the trees. "I don't intend to ever share you again."

I saw his hand start to pull the silk from my body, and I began to shiver from the cool caress. It flowed over me like water, revealing bare skin as it went, then drifted away on a warm breeze. I closed my eyes, and tried to block out the sight of myself lying chained and naked before him. How ironic that the Godhunter was about to be a sacrifice . . . or maybe it was fitting, in a twisted way.

Blue's blood-filled eyes roved over me indolently, possessively, and my body tensed, unsure whether to be furious or terrified. When his hand followed his gaze, I automatically jerked at the chains, trying my best to pull away from him. His laugh was cruel; sandpaper against my abused pride, and I had to swallow my outraged scream. I closed my eyes, searching for calm, knowing that if there was any chance of me getting out of this without a new set of pointy teeth, I had to keep calm to find it.

In my desperation, I reached out to him through our link and felt it connect. Maybe I could change his mind if I changed his

point of view. I showed him how he looked to me the first time he abducted me. I showed him how disgusting it was for me to see him cover himself in blood and then gulp it down. I let my revulsion pour down that line between us.

He looked at me sharply and then shook his head.

"I can't help but be what I am"–the torchlight danced over his face, giving it a demonic twist–"or how unappealing you may find it. You will learn to live with it, as I have."

"You said you loved me." I begged him with my eyes. "Don't do this to me. Remember how much your lover hated you when you changed her."

"She was in shock." He waved dismissively. "I should've stopped her, and kept her with me until she had calmed enough for me to reason with her, but I was weak. I let her go because of my guilt. I'll not make the same mistake twice."

I sent him more images, and he stumbled a little, catching himself on the edge of the altar. I showed him how I'd look drinking blood from Thor, the passion I'd feel, the bloodlust. How he'd be the first man I ran to as soon as I was freed. Then I sent Blue an image of me covered in blood, my hair drenched, thick rivers of the stuff running everywhere, and my dark eyes staring out at him accusingly. I may have used the movie *Carrie* for inspiration on that one. Blue started to scream, and he yanked his feathered crown off to throw it into the jungle.

Thank you, Sissy Spacek and Stephen King.

"No." Blue rubbed his fists into his eyes before lowering them decisively. "You'll never return to Thor. Once I change you, you'll be bound to me completely. You'll be even more beautiful than you are now, and you'll live forever. Can't you see what a gift this is, Vervain?"

"You were the one who said it was both a blessing and a

curse." It was really hard to speak reasonably when you were naked and fearing for your human existence. "I'm only showing you what you want to make me. You want to keep me with you? Fine, but don't turn me into a monster. Please, Blue."

"You and I will share eternity together." He took a deep breath and stroked a hand down my stomach. "You're just frightened, but that's normal. I'll be strong for you. I can take care of you. You'll be my Queen, give life to my children, and no one will ever hurt you again."

"No!" I screamed and sent him a picture of me sitting serenely in bed, breastfeeding a baby. He started in surprise, and then smiled, his features going soft, his eyes tender. I showed him more; me stroking the infant's head, then crying out as blood seeped out around its mouth and over my breast. Blue screamed, but I continued playing the images; I pulled the child away to show a wicked set of fangs glinting from its gaping, bloody mouth. I offered the child up to him. Another sacrifice for his bloody altar.

"One happy little family." I stared accusingly at him. "Is it everything you expected it to be?"

"Enough!" He roared. "You'll not change my mind by showing me twisted lunacy. Our children will not be such as that. Do you think I bled my own mother?"

"Your powers were different then." I was shaking, but whether it was from rage or fear I couldn't tell. "You've no idea what a child of yours would be like."

"He would be a god," Blue growled.

"Or a monster." I made an exasperated sound. "Will I even be able to bear children after you turn me?"

"Of course you will. How many times do I have to tell you that the mortals got it wrong? I'm not offering you death. I'm offering you life eternal. You will be as you are now, only better.

Your body will be able to bear children with more ease and absolutely no danger to you." His jaw clenched, but he took another deep breath and calmed himself. "You'll feel differently once you've birthed them."

"So, you're telling me there are vampires out there making babies?" I had pictures of happy little vampire families dancing in my head.

"No." Blue sighed and made a dismissive gesture. "Only I have the ability to pass on life so purely. Only with me would you be able to have children. Without me, you'd be in stasis, unable to conceive."

"I guess that at least is a relief." I abandoned my dancing, vampire baby imagery á la Ally McBeal. Ooga chacka, ooga chaka.

"Enough of this." His eyes narrowed. "I suspect you're stalling."

I shivered and started shaking my head. There had to be some other way to stop him. The Nahual! I'd been meditating with my jaguar ever since I'd discovered her through studying Aztec magic, and I'd been getting stronger and stronger with each meeting. Would she be strong enough to fight Blue?

She had backed down earlier, but she'd done so reluctantly, almost as if she were biding her time. I wasn't sure if she could destroy Blue himself, but I *was* suddenly sure that I could send her down the link between me and Blue, and perhaps she could find his own Nahual. Maybe she'd make me strong enough to become Nahualli; a sorcerer who could control another person's animal twin.

According to Aztec myth, everyone was born with an animal twin, but I was pretty sure the "everyone" meant all the humans. There was a chance that Blue didn't actually have a Nahual, but I was betting that, as an Aztec god, he was influenced

by his people's beliefs, and did actually carry an animal twin inside him. If not, I was totally screwed.

I called my Nahual with my need and will, sending my fear into the depth of my soul. Projecting my magic inward instead of outward, as she had taught me. I saw her clearly; a white jaguar with golden spots and dark brown eyes. Her body was tensed to spring and her mouth hung open on a snarl; she'd been waiting for my call.

She seemed to jump through me, running down the line connecting me to Blue without any prompting from me. In her wake, the butterflies of my love magic stirred and then rushed to follow her. What the Hell?

My jaguar shown bright inside the darkness of Blue's mind, a star streaking across his night sky, and it was easy to follow her progress. It was easy to see her pounce and pull back with her prey in her mouth. It wasn't easy to see the prey itself, though.

Blue's Nahual was a hummingbird, go figure, but the bird was coated so thickly in a black viscous fluid that I could barely make out its form. The substance dripped from it, hissing and smoking when it touched my jaguar. She dropped the foul thing, spitting and growling at it while it flopped pathetically.

The butterflies swooped in and I cringed. They wouldn't stand a chance against that oil slick of hatred, and I knew instinctively that the black fluid *was* hatred. Distilled and condensed rage. Blue was weighed down under a layer of hate so thick that his animal twin couldn't fly anymore. How could my fragile butterflies hope to win against it?

As they landed on the poor hummingbird, one lone butterfly flew back to me. It came to rest inside my chest, and I was immediately at ease. These weren't normal insects, they were pure magic. Pure love. Every butterfly had once been a caterpillar. Fat and fuzzy, wriggling its way across the earth before it changed

itself into something beautiful and learned to fly. Love held the power to transform, to take a grounded thing and give it wings. A bridge between earth and air, a link between spirits and hearts. The shape it had chosen wasn't a silly, girly symbol, but a representation of its strength, its untouchable beauty, and its ability to soar.

I focused back on the hummingbird and wasn't at all shocked to see the darkness peeling away from its feathers. The butterflies buzzed with intensity, their little legs working at the black shell and scraping it away into dust. It took only moments for the bright colors of Blue's Nahual to start to show through.

"What are you doing?" Blue's whisper held a touch of fear.

"Teaching you to fly." I turned my face to his and kissed him.

His arms wrapped around me, and his kiss filled me with heat. I felt him pour his rage into me, press it against my magic like a shield. The blackness rose up in a wave, threatening to drown not only the hummingbird, but my butterflies and jaguar as well. It was too late, though. As the wave started to crest, Blue's hummingbird rose amid a flock of butterflies and shot up to meet it. My jaguar roared, calling my love magic home as she turned away. She knew they were no longer needed there, and sure enough, as she padded home with the butterflies flocking around her, the wave shattered and turned into a glittering cloud of light.

The explosion shot through us both as Blue convulsed above me. I thanked my Nahual, and sent her back into my depths to recover. She blinked dark eyes at me and huffed, her warm breath filling me with peace, before she turned and sank into my soul. Then I was pulled back into Blue's mind.

The hummingbird hovered, the rapid beating of his wings pulling traumatic memories in and merging them with happier ones; blending them into a bittersweet confection palatable enough

to be swallowed. The horror of Blue's dead mother was softened by the memory of her dark, laughing eyes and gentle smile. His sister's decapitated head was covered over with her laughter and a picture of her pointing to the Moon in delight. His father's last screams were banished by the sound of his rich voice telling Blue that he was the hope of his people; the first child born off Atlantean soil.

Each memory shot through Blue, shaking his body over and over like a seizure before they were laid to rest. When he finally lifted his head, I felt as battered as he must have, but also relieved. His hatred was gone. I had felt it wash away like filth in a mountain stream, replaced by the clear flow of pure life. My chest was wet with his tears, but his eyes were dry when he raised them to me . . . and green, a striking jade green.

"Oh wow," I said with wonder and felt my own eyes fill with tears.

"What is it, little witch?" Even his voice was different. Still soft as velvet, but warmer, richer.

I shook my head and reached to touch him, but the chains rattled and stopped me. Blue looked down as if he'd just noticed them. With a cry, he rolled off me and unlocked the chains. They fell away, clattering against the stone with the ring of freedom. I rubbed my wrists distractedly as he knelt beside the altar and retrieved the black silk.

"Forgive me, Vervain." He handed me the silk and stared up at me with those bright eyes.

I wrapped the material around me and tied it securely, holding his gaze the entire time. "Your mother was right."

"My mother?" Blue shook his head with a little frown, "About what?"

"Your eyes *are* beautiful." I stroked his face as it filled with

wary hope. “They’re not just jade, but Imperial jade; a vibrant, translucent green. I’ve never seen eyes this color before.”

He closed those intense eyes and touched his fingertips to them gently.

“It’s true, I see the world as it was.” Blue looked around himself in awe. “I’d forgotten how vivid the colors were without a veil of blood over them.”

I smiled as he got to his feet and spun around, taking everything in. His priests came through the trees slowly, warily watching his strange behavior. They looked at me, unbound and unmarked, and then back at him. Their eyes widened and they fell to their knees.

“Vervain.” Blue turned back to me and I felt it then, the connection my power had made through the healing.

I loved him, as I loved Fenrir before him, and I’d carry that love with me always. I'd carry *him* with me. Instead of scaring me, I found it comforting. I held my arms out to him, and he picked me up to twirl me around.

“I love you, little witch,” Blue whispered in my ear as he set me down.

“I love you too, Blue.” I smiled, but some of my hesitation must’ve shown through because he searched my face with concern.

“There’s more.” He sighed. “You don’t love me as you do Thor.”

“No,” I said as gently as I could.

He nodded and took a deep breath. “I think I can accept that now. Do you need to leave immediately?”

“He’ll be very worried.” I bit my lip. “I'm sure Trevor's told him by now.”

“Then you must return.” Blue took my arm and escorted me inside his palace. “I think I need some time to process all of these changes anyway.”

Chapter Seven

I traced into my living room wearing only black silk and a smile. The entire God Squad was there, along with Trevor, filling the space to its capacity. Thor's face filled with relief and then happiness as he rushed over to me, but it was Trevor's face that would haunt my dreams.

I stared at the wolf over Thor's shoulder while Thor hugged me, and from Trevor's eyes to mine, something was exchanged that I have no name for. Relief was too mild a word for what I saw in Trevor. His were the eyes of a drowning man in the moment he clasped hands with his rescuer.

"What happened?" Thor finally choked out, loosening his hold marginally and forcing my eyes away from Trevor. "Trevor found after you called for him. He said he caught traces of both you and Blue, but was unable to follow you. I reached for you down our link, but it was worse than blocked, it was like you were lost behind a void."

"Blue's known about my house in Hawaii this entire time. He was just playing with me, and he finally decided to end the game. He wasn't prepared for Aphrodite's magic in my hands though, and I won." I pulled back and smiled at everyone. "Thank you guys for being here for Thor."

"We're here for *you*, Vervain." Trevor pulled me away from Thor and hugged me, burying his face in my neck and breathing deeply. A shudder wracked his body before he finally let go and let the others get their hugs in.

I even got hugged by Horus.

"Did you kill Huitzilopochtli?" Teharon asked what I'm

sure they were all wondering.

"Yes"–I smiled–"in a way."

Chapter Eight

"Are you ready yet, darling?" Thor called from the living room. "The party's already started. We have to go."

It was December 22, and we were going to the Yule celebration at Valhalla. It was a sacred holiday for the Atlanteans and the only time Thor saw his father anymore. His behavior was a cross between that of an excited child and a nervous groom. No matter that they were on opposing sides of the God War, Thor loved his father deeply, and he missed him. This was a big night for Thor, and I didn't want to spoil it.

I was just a tad concerned about going into Bad Guy Inc. as a guest, though.

"I'm almost ready," I called out as I applied my powder and then stuffed it into my little red bag.

I looked my reflection over, checking that the red lipstick was perfect, the black eyeliner smudged properly, my cheeks blushed just slightly, then I nodded. I'd curled my hair and pinned little pieces of it around my face with red, crystal pins, but I left the rest loose to hang about my hips. I still couldn't get over the changes in my appearance. It was like staring at a stranger sometimes. After all the changes that my life had been through in such a short time, I kinda *felt* like a stranger too.

I stepped back and smoothed the deep ruby gown Thor had bought me. It had a tight, corset bodice which showed off my cleavage to its best advantage. I always said it wasn't what you had, it's how you display it, and this dress did some serious displaying. Made of heavy silk taffeta, it belled out a little from my hips, falling all the way to the floor. I loved the swishing sound it made when I walked and the sparkle of the Swarovski crystal

encrusted bodice. The ruby colored gems spread down and spaced out over the skirt till they were just a sprinkling at the hem, but around my decollete, they formed a solid front. My purse and shoes were covered in the crystals as well. I sparkled and swished with every step, and I adored it. Isn't it funny how a wonderful dress that swishes can turn you into a little girl?

I found Thor in the living room with Nick on his lap. He looked up when I entered, and his mouth fell open. He stood, Nick pouncing from his lap with an annoyed cry, and as he walked toward me his eyes roved over me from head to toe. By the time Thor reached me, he was smiling so wide, I thought his face was in danger of cracking.

"You like?" I twirled so I could sparkle and swish for him.

"I like," he growled low in his throat, "I like a lot."

He pulled me against him, and I pushed back laughing. "You said we had to go."

"Fuck the party, fuck Odin"–he dove into my neck–"and fuck me… please."

"Well, as long as you say please." I laughed deeper and felt him shudder. "Later, baby, if you're a really naughty god."

"Oh, I can be naughty." Thor pulled me in tight again.

"I know, but right now we have to be good little children and attend your father's party." I pulled my face back to eye him. "You know you want to see him; it's been a year."

He groaned louder and pulled away. "Alright! Let's go before I lose all familial loyalty."

Thor held me, and I held a large bag filled with Yule gifts, as he chanted the spell to take us to Valhalla. When I opened my eyes, we were in the tracing room. I took a deep breath and looked

around. The last time I'd been there had been the first time I'd met Thor. He'd been trying to steal the same battle plans that I had. Then he'd invited me to join him and his little band of merry gods.

The tracing room was just a plain, empty space now; nothing to fear. The walls were carved wood, runes snaking down them, the ceiling beams carved in the same manner. The floor was polished stone, completely unadorned. Very simple, as I'd found most tracing rooms to be.

A short, dark-haired man with a buff build came running up to us and bowed to Thor. "My Lord, please follow me and I shall announce you." He took my bag for me and walked down a stone corridor.

Thor squared his shoulders and held his arm out to me. He had a black suit on with a red shirt to match my dress. It made his shoulders look even broader and his chest massive. His bright hair was slicked back into a braid and looked very debonair. The severe hairstyle made his jaw seem more rugged, the angles of his face sharper, and his eyes gleamed from their bright lining of lashes. He was breathtaking, and I was proud to be walking in on his arm.

"His Highness, Thor Odinson," the man announced as we crossed the threshold, and his voice rang out into the crowded dining hall, "Prince and Defender of the Realm of Asgard. Master of Thunder, Storms, and Sky. God of the Sea and Justice. Accompanied by Rouva Vervain Lavine. Mistress of Love, Lust, War, and Victory. The Godhunter."

I hesitated when I heard the last bit, but Thor's grip on my arm was steady and he propelled me forward without a hitch.

"It's a title of respect," he whispered to me. "They're trying to honor you as a great adversary."

I smiled and spoke through clenched teeth, "You promised I wouldn't need my weapons tonight." I scanned the room. "I've only got my bodice dagger."

“You brought a dagger even though I told you it wasn’t necessary?” His voice was filled with humor.

“I didn’t want to go into the lion’s den unarmed.” I smiled at Ull, Thor's stepson by his ex-wife Sif, as we passed him and the gorgeous blonde woman with him. Then we continued on to the head table. The table was on a raised dais and we had to climb a couple of steps to get up to it.

“You can be very silly, darling,” he whispered to me and I laughed low.

“Only you would call me silly when I’m armed with enchanted steel.”

“You’re never defenseless, Godhunter.” Thor kissed my neck, right where his lightning scar snaked down my skin. He'd given it to me to cover a bite mark Blue had left.

“Welcome to my hall, Godhunter.” A large Viking with long, dark-brown hair and a leather patch over one eye, stood to greet us.

He had harsh but handsome features, and his one eye was a piercing, peacock blue. I don’t mean it was a bright blue. I mean it was blue but shimmered purple and green depending on how the light hit it, like a peacock feather. It was framed with sin-black lashes and was so beautiful, it made me mourn the loss of the other eye. His mouth was framed by a neatly trimmed beard, at odds with his lumberjack physique which was clad in rich blue velvet. But it was the eye that held me; it was set on me intensely, as if it could convey a whole conversation in one look.

Odin: Thor's father and King of the Norse Gods.

I felt a trickle of anxiety go through me. This was one of the bad ones, known to be untrustworthy even by his friends. They called him Oathbreaker, and I was instantly wary of him. It was said that Odin had undergone strange rituals to gain magical

abilities. Oh, and the eye he was missing, he reputedly gave it up willingly, so he could drink from a well of knowledge. He was said to be very cunning and very lethal. It's why I'd never attempted to assassinate him. Even stealing from him had scared the hell out of me.

"Thank you for allowing me to attend."

I knew the celebration was a truce among the Viking gods, but I was hoping for some confirmation that I was included in that truce as well. I slipped my hand into the one he extended and Odin kissed it gallantly.

"You've caused quite a stir, but allay your fears. You're welcome here, Rouva"–Odin's smile grew–"for tonight."

I laughed low and long, and saw heads turn to stare. Right; tone down the hilarity. "Thank you for that. I always appreciate honesty."

"As do I, Vervain." I had a feeling that his use of my given name was meant as a compliment, but it put me on edge. "I don't know if you've heard, but I hold a great fascination for the occult, and I've been told you read the cards. Maybe we could talk later?"

"I'd be honored, of course." What the hell else could I say; I'd rather chew bricks?

"Great." Odin smiled at me but it didn't reach his eye.

His beautiful eye was haunted, focused constantly on a ghost instead of the living. Thor told me about Odin's ex-wife, and how he still mourned her. I hadn't before, but now I understood why it was hard for Thor to be around his father.

"Father." Thor clasped arms with his father, and I saw a sliver of warmth creep into Odin's face before it was replaced by ice once more.

"It's good to see you, Thor." Odin sighed. "I wish you would visit more often."

"You know why I don't."

"We all have our roles to play." Odin looked out at his guests. "And now I have to play mine. If you would excuse me?" He smiled wanly at me again and I nodded. "I have to greet my guests. The Froekn are arriving; perhaps you should play your role as well, Rouva. Fenrir will want his Queen at his side." For a second, the peacock eye twinkled, but then it was doused by pain once again.

"I'm here with Thor tonight." I lifted my chin. "But I'll see to my family. I know where I belong, Odin."

The one-eyed god flinched, though I have no idea why. Then he seemed to recover. Odin smirked and turned away, descending the steps and melding into the throng.

"Well, he's a delight." I took my bag of gifts from Thor. "You wanna come with me to see the Froekn?"

"Like I'd let you face the wolves alone?" Thor smiled, but his smile was lacking, an imitation of his father's.

"Don't carry his pain." I laid a hand on Thor's lapel and he looked down at me. "It's bad enough that Odin must bear it. There's no reason for you to shoulder it with him."

"I would carry it for him if I could." Thor frowned. "You know, it's funny that you say that. I've always had this strange feeling that his pain would be mine one day. I think it's part of the reason I don't come around much."

"Heartache isn't a disease, nor is it meant to be carried." I reached up and rubbed at his frown lines. "It's meant to be tossed about like a hot roll until it's cooled enough to eat. Then you consume it and use it to make you stronger. You don't sit with it in

your hands, staring at it till it turns moldy and gross."

"A hot roll, eh?" Thor's lips were quirking up. "Are you perhaps getting hungry, darling?"

"Oh, holy hand-grenades, yes!" I laughed and achieved sweet success when he laughed back.

"Maybe we should feed you before we go greet the Froekn." Thor looked over his shoulder at the long table the wolves were settling down at.

"No, I can wait." I saw Trevor look over at us expectantly. "Besides, there are only appetizers out now." I reached over and grabbed a stuffed mushroom before heading down the dais.

I surreptitiously admired the grandeur of the hall as I munched on my snack. It was huge. The hall, not the snack. The myths I'd read had described Valhalla as being wide enough for eight hundred warriors to walk through it abreast. I tried to imagine that, and I was pretty sure it was possible. Wooden trestle tables ran down the center of the room, three rows to either side, placed before the high table. Open space stretched between the tables and the walls of the hall, filled with islands of lush carpets, on which comfortable, but apparently ancient, seating waited in an assortment of styles.

Gods milled around, holding cocktails served by the largest, meanest looking waiters I'd ever seen. I took a glass from one warily, eyeing his missing ear, as we passed through the crowd. The guests wore an interesting mix of varied ethnic dress and modern wear. They were beautiful and fascinating, but it was the walls of Valhalla that held the greatest fascination for me.

They were solid gold, with curving Viking designs carved into them, and hung with gold shields. They glowed intensely in the bright lights; I could even make out a glimmer of the walls to either side in the far distance. God technology, not electricity, lit the hall with no discernible source, and it made the shields glow

even brighter. In fact, it almost looked as if the light came from the gold.

I wasn't so fascinated by my surroundings that I missed all the attention I was getting, though. By the time we reached the Froekn, I was a little irritated by the stares and heated whispers that followed us. Most of these gods were my enemies. They tolerated my presence merely because it was a holy day and I was accompanied by Thor. I had a distinct impression that had it been otherwise, they'd happily tear me to pieces.

"Fenrir"–Thor held out a hand to my new, adopted father–"it's good to see you."

"Thor." Fenrir looked incredible in a black on black suit, his dark hair hanging in silky waves down his back. There was a gold torque with wolf heads on either end, gleaming at his throat. He shook Thor's hand. "I'm happy to see you as well."

"Fenrir." I smiled and reached both arms out to him.

"Little frami," he chided as he scooped me up and kissed my cheek, "call me 'Dad'."

"Okay"–I laughed–"just put me down first."

"You outshine them all tonight," Fenrir whispered as he lowered me to the floor.

"Thanks, Dad." I winked at him, and then turned toward Trevor. "Happy Yule, VèulfR."

"Happy Yule, Rouva" Trevor enveloped me in a hug.

I closed my eyes and let the scent of him wash over me. Inside me, I felt the wolf shake off slumber and come running forward to greet its other half. I shivered as it rubbed against Trevor through my skin, nuzzling and nudging. I felt Trevor sigh deeply, his own wolf rubbing against me as well. It was the oddest,

most sensual feeling I'd ever experienced, being stroked beneath and above my skin all at once. It was as if my nerve endings were trapped between two animals in heat, so that every sensation I felt was magnified by their fur and lust. It was then that I knew that although Trevor had given me a part of himself, it had changed when it rooted within me. It was my wolf now and it was all bitch. Go ahead and giggle.

Thor cleared his throat and reminded me of where I was. I pulled away from Trevor, certain that my face was as red as my dress, and bit my lip as the Froekn laughed knowingly. Trevor's eyes were all honey heat, and I felt caught in them. I shivered like a fly struggling in that sweet death. Then my embarrassment flowed away with the honey and I smiled at my wolf.

"I have something for you, little frami." Fenrir saved me from making an even bigger fool of myself. "TryggulfR." He turned as TryggulfR came forward with a large, blue velvet box.

Fenrir opened it to reveal a heavy torque of gold with a wolf head on each end. He took it out reverently and slipped it on my neck. The weight of it felt comforting, but there was also a tingle of something more. Something that felt a lot like magic, wild magic.

"It's beautiful." I touched it, then looked at the matching one Fenrir was wearing.

"This is the symbol of your status." Fenrir held me by the shoulders. "The Rouva torque is yours until I find my own mate." He smiled like he didn't think I'd be wearing it long.

"I'm honored to wear it until you find your Rouva." I kissed his cheek. "I've something for you as well." I reached towards Thor, and he pulled a painting out of the bag of gifts. I handed it to Fenrir. It was a portrait of him, smiling his *I'm too sexy* smile and looking magnificent. Wolves surrounded him; sprawling, sitting, and howling. "This is the first piece I've painted

in a very long time. I've lacked inspiration, I guess. I want you to have it so you can see what I see when I look at you. In case you ever doubt how incredible you are."

Fenrir took the painting from me and his jaw clenched. He swallowed roughly, his throat convulsing. There was a sudden sheen to his eyes, and he took a deep breath before he leaned down and gave me a kiss on the cheek.

"You make me envy my own son, little Rouva," he whispered into my ear. I shivered as I met his eyes and saw a hint of what might have been between us. Whoever snagged him was going to be one lucky woman.

"I have a gift for you as well." Trevor reclaimed my attention. He reached behind him and pulled out a small, gold box with a big red bow on it. "Happy Yule."

I unwrapped the box with shaking fingers. Inside was a heavy gold bracelet in the shape of a wolf. The body of the wolf formed a circle, like he'd be forever chasing his tail around my wrist. In his mouth was a large diamond. I inhaled and forgot to exhale for a second.

"Breathe, darling." Thor patted my back and I exhaled sharply.

"Thank you," I said softly to Trevor as I put the bracelet on and admired the way the diamond sparkled. "It's amazing, I love it."

"I'm glad." Trevor flashed a look behind me, and I felt Thor's hand tense on my back.

"I have something for you as well." I had to hit Thor to get his attention, he was focused so strongly on Trevor. "Thor, the gift for Trevor please."

Thor finally fished a box out of the bag and handed it to

me. I handed it to Trevor, who smiled grandly and tore through the wrapping like a kid. Paper went flying, shreds of ribbon drifted to the ground. Did I say kid? I meant animal. Finally, the gift was revealed and Trevor made an exuberant whoop.

"*Vibes* and the complete season of *Firefly*." Trevor held up the DVDs. "How did you get Vibes? I've been looking for it forever."

"I have my ways." I smiled delightedly.

"Have you handled a machine gun before?" Trevor asked me with mock seriousness.

"Sure, lots of times in high school." I smirked as I gave him the correct quote. "I was captain of the machine gun team."

"Yes!" Trevor laughed and punched the air. "And you can just call me Captain Tight Pants."

"Now you're switching to *Firefly*, give a girl some warning." I laughed. "He's my favorite you know. I love Mal. So sexy."

"I'm more a fan of Inara myself." Trevor waggled his brows at me. "I love me a hot brunette."

"If you don't lay off *my* hot brunette, you're gonna regret it." Thor glowered.

"Oh, but we can't die. You know why?" Trevor barely spared Thor a glance, just continued with the quotes.

"Because we are so . . ." I began, and Trevor joined me; together we sang out, "very . . . pretty!"

Thor groaned as I laughed. I finally had a partner in my annoying movie quoting habit.

"These are the best gifts ever!" Trevor exclaimed. "I've

never met anyone who's even heard of *Vibes*, much less could quote it."

"Are you kidding me? I'd give you the finger, but I'm too refined," I said in my best Cyndi Lauper imitation.

"Oh, man, I love you." Trevor grabbed my face in both hands and planted a quick kiss on me.

We pulled apart to find everyone staring at us in horrified fascination. Thor took my waist and pulled me into his side as I laughed nervously.

"It's a movie from the 80s and an old TV series by Joss Whedon." I shrugged. "I knew Trevor wanted them, and they also happen to be favorites of mine, so . . ."

"How exactly did you know he wanted them?" Thor scowled down at me.

"I . . ." I started to frown as well. How *had* I known? Trevor had never actually mentioned it.

"It's a Froekn thing," Fenrir said smugly. "An aspect of the bond. Trevor has become a part of her. Vervain knows him as well as she knows herself."

Thor's entire body tensed.

"The only way this can work," I spoke softly, but still had everyone's attention immediately, "is if all of you help me to make it work. I can't do it if I have to constantly mediate between you both. Now, Thor has been very understanding, considering the circumstances, and I'd appreciate a little respect and consideration back. I didn't ask to be bonded with Trevor, but it happened, and I'm not sorry it did. You've all made me feel loved and accepted, and I want the Froekn to be a part of my life, but not at the expense of Thor's feelings. So, please, no more passive aggressive attacks on my boyfriend . . . not by you, Fenrir." I stared hard at him. "Or

any of you." I looked over at Trevor and his two brothers.

"Okay, little frami." Fenrir sighed. "I concede your point. My apologies, Thunderer."

"Accepted." Thor nodded. He'd begun to relax during my speech, his chest expanding, and a smile playing over his lips. "We all love her, Fenrir."

"Yes"–Fenrir smiled resignedly–"we certainly do."

Chapter Nine

When the music began, thc wolves stood and immediately went to the dance floor. The Froekn loved to dance, and as it turns out, I was no exception. I started with Thor, but Trevor claimed the next round. I laughed in delight as he swung me around and passed me from wolf to wolf till I ended up with Fenrir. The Wolf God smiled at me, then something over my shoulder caught his attention and he raised a brow. I followed his gaze and saw Odin approaching the dance floor with a bevy of beautiful women. Fenrir laughed at my expression.

"They're his Valkyries," Fenrir whispered and then nodded to some of his male wolves.

The wolves flowed through the dancers, stalking the women. The Valkyries laughed and twirled away from the wolves, who continued to chase them around the dance floor. It looked as if they'd played that game before. I raised a brow and looked up at Fenrir.

"My boys are very popular with the fighting ladies." He waggled his brows at me and I laughed.

"May I steal your Rouva for a dance, Fenrir?" Odin was standing next to us, reaching a hand out to me.

Fenrir did this sort of tilted nod and released me to Odin. In the next moment, I was being held in two beefy, Viking arms as I stared at a wide chest. Odin was so much like Thor, except in coloring, that it was surreal. I felt like I was dancing with Thor's evil twin.

This man had caused so much damage to my world. Odin was a physical representation of what I was fighting against. He

was my enemy. The enemy of the entire human race.

He was also my boyfriend's Daddy.

“Do I make you uncomfortable?” Odin peered down at me strangely.

“I don't generally dance with my enemies”–I shrugged–“just a policy I have.”

“You name me enemy *here*, Godhunter?” He spoke in a tired, almost disinterested way. “This is a holy day for us. A day to lay aside grievances.”

“Hey, you asked.” I sighed. “But you're right, I shouldn't have said that. You welcomed me here and I got lippy with you. I apologize. I'm always saying things I shouldn't. I'm in desperate need of an Off switch.”

Odin’s one eye crinkled at the corner. “You have a strange appeal.”

“Do I?” I smiled reassuringly. “But don’t worry, you’ll get over it. I’m sure the Powerpuff Girls over there can help you with that.” I waved a hand at his Valkyries, who’d finally allowed themselves to be caught and were dancing with the wolves. “They give new meaning to the Puff motto: Saving the world before bedtime.”

Odin burst into shocked laughter, so exuberant that he had to stop dancing and pull away from me, so he could lean on his leg to catch his breath. The gods stared at us in horror and amazement. The wolves just smiled and kept dancing. I guess they were already used to their little comedian.

“Uh, you okay there, buddy?” I patted Odin’s shoulder and smiled at the staring gods. “He’s very ticklish,” I called out to the gods as I wiggled my new manicure at them. “Who would’ve thought?”

Odin looked up at me with wide eyes for a second, and then started a new round of laughter. Finally, I gave up and crossed my arms as I waited for him to settle down. I was almost to the point of missing Mr. Gloomy.

He calmed down after a bit, but instead of going back to the dance, Odin took my arm and led me off the floor and over to a private table in the cavernous space to the right of the high table. There was actually a massive fireplace over there, freestanding, with the hall continuing on behind it. It goes to show how big the hall was that I hadn't even noticed it.

There were pillars out there too. Placed intermittently, to hold up the roof, I presumed. The only thing that kept it from looking like the Mines of Moria from *Lord of the Rings*, was the décor. Odin had gone to a lot of trouble to create some luxurious spaces for people to congregate in. The one he'd brought me to was particularly comfortable, with a thick Persian carpet on the floor, wide cushioned chairs, and an inlaid table carrying refreshments.

"Um . . . ah." I looked back at the dance floor and saw Thor frowning over at us, but he was soon whisked away by a long-legged goddess.

"I wanted to have a little chat with you." Odin settled me into a chair and then took a seat across from me.

I looked around a little nervously and caught Thor's stare again; he was looking even more concerned. That couldn't be a good sign.

"Alright." I focused on Odin, dropping my polite face. "So, talk."

"Relax, Godhunter." Odin waved, and a man was immediately there to pour him a mug of something frothy and set a glass of wine in front of me. "I told you; I'm an avid student of the occult and I was wondering if you'd do me the honor of reading my cards?"

I sighed. I swear, once your friends know you can read the tarot, you became a source of ready entertainment at every party. I felt like a traveling gypsy attraction sometimes. Now, it appeared that even gods weren't above the draw of an oracle.

"I don't have a deck with me." I shrugged.

"You may use mine," his voice dropped low as he studied my face and pushed an old wooden box towards me.

I felt the magic before I even touched the box. "What have you done to them?"

Odin smiled and nodded in approval. "I'd hoped you'd feel it too." He flipped the lid open. Within the faded blue lining nestled a beautiful deck of tarot cards. Worn, but beautiful. They were hand painted, thick like the antique decks always were, and gilded with real gold.

I reached for them, but then pulled my hand back suddenly. "So, what *have* you done to them?"

"I've done nothing to them." Odin looked at them with reverence. "I found them on one of my quests. They were buried in a cave."

"Buried in a cave?" I narrowed my eyes. "Was there anything else in this cave? Say . . . a corpse?"

"There may have been." He smiled secretly.

I hissed and withdrew my hand. "You stole cards from the dead? They're full of a dead person's magic?"

"A dead witch actually." Odin nodded. "I happen to be God of the Dead." He waved his hand to encompass his servants, and I took a closer look at the waiters.

They were all thickly muscled and had the look of battle about them. I'd never contemplated the truth in the religions

created by the Atlanteans. The stories; yes, the religions; not so much. Was Valhalla really the home of fallen warriors? How was that even possible? I didn't think they were really gods in that respect. I didn't think the Atlanteans could actually provide an afterlife.

"Are you trying to tell me that we're being served tonight by dead Vikings?"

"Yes." Odin frowned. "Do you not know of Valhalla's purpose?"

"I do, but I didn't know you Atlanteans could actually provide for the dead. I know the stories are half truth/half myth. I just assumed that the afterlife was the myth part."

"I bound these warriors to me in life." Odin's eye glittered. "When they died, I owned their souls, so they came to me."

"You own their souls," I whispered and shook my head, "that's not possible."

"They believed it, and the strength of their belief kept them bound to me," his voice had dropped low. "Belief is everything. Right, witch?"

It was. Belief gave magic power. Without it, the magic failed. I nodded and stared back at the cards.

"The witch who these cards belonged to . . ."

"She was a lover of mine." Odin leaned forward and touched my hand where it lay on the table. "You may use them without fear. We have a truce tonight; I wouldn't break it."

I picked up the cards and felt the tingle of old magic. It rushed into me like a pair of watchdogs set loose, and I felt my stomach clench in preparation for the bite. The bite never came, though. Instead, they pulled up short and seemed to scent the air. I

stared into those canine eyes and saw only my own reflection shining back at me; no curse, no magical backlash. I sighed as the magical warding seemed to rub up against me in welcome. My eyes closed, and I found myself stroking the cards lovingly.

I heard Odin draw in a sharp breath and whisper something that ended in *ine* or *ene*.

My breath caught and my eyes flew open. "What did you say?"

"Nothing." Odin stared at me with a wide, horrified eye.

"Nothing, my ass." I glared at him. "What did you say?"

"Please." He closed his eye, and that horrible, haunted look I'd first seen on his face was back, only worse. Like ten times worse. "Just read the cards . . . Vervain."

I frowned, but the cards felt so good in my hands; I couldn't help myself. They wanted to be read. They needed me to use them. So I shuffled them, slipping into the trance-like state that always came over me when I read. Then I handed them to Odin.

"Go ahead, sweet raven, ask the cards for guidance."

"What did you call me?" The cards sat in Odin's hands, forgotten, as his face went slack.

"Raven, I think."

Interesting, I'd just spoken automatically. I tried to remember the stories I'd read about Odin. Yes, he could shapeshift into a raven, into anything actually, just like Loki, but Odin preferred the form of a raven or eagle. It must be why I'd called him that. Strange, but that was about par for the course when I was reading. I'd been known to spill out secrets before laying down even a single card. I had very little control of the talent, which was one of the reasons I didn't read the cards often.

"One of your powers is the ability to shift into a raven, right?" I asked Odin.

He stared hard at me again, and then finally nodded. I nudged his hands and Odin flinched from the contact before dropping his gaze to the cards. He began to shuffle. Odin closed his eye as he focused, and the cards flew expertly through his fingers. Then he handed them back to me, and looked away as he took a deep breath.

I took the cards and began to turn them over onto the table one by one. "The Emperor." I smiled, go figure. "Obviously you, the man and his empire. You rule your world completely." I flipped another card and inhaled sharply. "You're covered by The Moon; deception and lies, lunacy driven by obsession." Another four cards went in a circle around the main card. "The knights. All four of them," I said with wonder. The odds of that happening were slim. I looked into the faces of the normally valiant men painted on the cards, and instead, saw cruel twists to their lips and traitorous thoughts filling their eyes. "You're surrounded by warriors, but instead of guarding you, they plot against you." I laid more cards out as the people painted on them seemed to come alive, miming out some elaborate play.

"This wide and universal theater presents more woeful pageants than the scene in which we play," I murmured.

"What?" Odin looked from the cards, to me, and back again.

"Nothing, sorry." I motioned *never mind* with a hand while I tried to keep my concentration. "I randomly spout lyrics and poetry when reading the cards. Usually Shakespeare. I have no idea why."

"Ah," he grunted. "The fool doth think he is wise, but the wise man knows he is a fool."

"Did you just call me foolish?" I lost the trance completely

and looked up at him.

"No." Odin blinked rapidly. "I just meant that I was a fool not to get the reference."

"Oh." I frowned. "I never got that line anyway. I mean if the fool thinks he's wise, but he's still a fool, and the wise man knows he's a fool, than that would mean that everyone's a fool."

"I never thought about it like that." Odin's brows lifted. "Huh."

"Anyway"–I looked back down at the cards and let myself sink into the trance again–"you feel trapped, like you can't move without being cut. See how the woman is surrounded by swords?" Odin nodded and stared at the cards intently. "She's blindfolded by her fear and tied up by her doubts. If only she could believe in herself, she would see that she's not completely surrounded. She can walk right out of there. You need to let go of your fears and trust in yourself. The path to set you free is right in front of you."

"Right in front of me," Odin murmured as he stared at me.

"Here is the Seven of Swords," I continued. "See the thief running away? There's one in your midst."

Odin looked over at the gathering and frowned at someone. I followed his gaze and saw Loki staring at us with interest.

"Son of a bitch, there is a thief here." I made to stand up, but Odin spoke first.

"Not tonight, Godhunter. This is currently sacred land. Any quarrel you have with Loki is going to have to wait."

Odin touched my hand lightly but it was like my finger had been a fuse and his the match. Something zinged up my arm and detonated in my chest. I fell back into the chair with the impact.

I swallowed hard and cleared my throat. My hands were

shaking and, for a second, they didn't look like my own. They were paler, thinner, the fingers more elegant. I shook the vision away determinedly, and went on with the reading. Damn cards, they always messed with me.

"The . . . uh, the Seven of Swords can also mean failed plans. Your plots may not go the way you think," I said.

Odin frowned at me.

"Here's the Devil." I pointed to the card. "You're enslaved by your ambitions and have a tendency towards violence if you don't get your way. It can also signify addictions; things you are bound to."

He smiled ruefully and nodded. "Please, continue."

"There are swords everywhere." I watched the painted characters lift their weapons and swing them at each other across the boundaries of the cards. "You live in the heart of battle. It's invaded your home and you don't know who to trust, but there's a new beginning coming." I laid the Death card, the Six of Cups, and then The Star. The fighting stopped, all those little faces peering at the final three like they held the most significance. "Death and rebirth, life and reincarnation; a card of transformation." My stomach filled with the Love butterflies, as if I'd summoned them with the word. Was it talking about me? Was I supposed to transform Odin? I looked at the Six of Cups and sighed in relief. It wasn't me he needed. "Someone from your past will return and bring new hope. This person will give you the answers you need and help you transform your life. When you are lost, they will be your guiding star."

When I looked up, Odin was staring at me with a funny look. "Thank you," he whispered.

I nodded and took a deep breath, coming out of my semi-trance. "My pleasure. You have a fine deck here; take good care of it."

I gathered the cards and placed them gently in their box before I started to stand.

"Vervain." Odin caught me by the wrist, and I shivered like someone had walked over my grave. "Take them." He handed me the cards.

"No." I started to reach for them automatically, despite my protest, but I quickly closed my hand into a fist. "I can't; they were your lover's."

"I know whose cards they are." He kept staring at me intently, and for a one-eyed man, he could manage some serious stare. "She'd want you to have them. Please take them as my Yule gift to you."

I searched his face for some sort of trick, but found nothing to betray the honesty in his voice. The raw, emotional honesty. Part of me wanted those cards badly and part of me was screaming to just run away. Run away from Odin, from the party, from everything connected to the gods.

In the end, pride won out. I couldn't let all of those gods see me running away from Odin, and it would be rude to refuse such a generous gift. Plus, I just plain wanted them.

"Thank you." I took the cards and held them to my chest. Before I knew what I was doing, I laid a soft kiss on Odin's cheek. I pulled back suddenly to stare at him in shock. Swallowing hard, I stood abruptly. "Thank you, Odin, and Happy Yule." It took all of my willpower not to run.

"Happy Yule . . . Vervain," his whisper followed me, feeling more intimate than it had the right to.

"Oh, what fresh hell is this?" I groaned as I walked away on shaky legs.

I stopped short of the dining tables and looked around me

at all of the shiny faces, all the deceitful gods who Odin called friends. They toasted each other and laughed, never knowing that their leader knew of their duplicity. Odin saw more with his one eye than any of them did with two. They plotted behind his back and their arrogance blinded them to his wisdom.

"In the land of the blind," I said as I stared at the room with a little smile.

"The one-eyed man is King," Thor's voice came from behind me, and I jerked around, still clutching the box of cards. "Vervain, what did Odin say to you?"

"Nothing really." I swallowed past the sudden lump in my throat. "I read his cards, and then he gave them to me as a Yule gift."

Thor frowned and reached for the cards, but I clutched them tighter.

"Are those Sabine's cards?"

"He said they belonged to an old lover; a witch," I said. They felt good, even through the wood box.

"Sabine." Thor nodded. "She was Odin's only human wife, and his only weakness."

"That was his third wife, right? The woman he still mourns?"

I felt cold and sad suddenly. Sabine. Was that what he had whispered? Had I unknowingly made his pain worse? Reminded him of her? Maybe he'd given me the cards in an attempt to finally let her go.

"Yeah, one and the same." Thor shook his head. "Odin buried those cards with Sabine, but then he went back later for them. He said he could still feel her in the paint. I can't believe

he'd give them to you so easily. What did my father make you promise in exchange for them?"

"Nothing."

Thor stared so hard at me, I cringed.

"I swear. I even refused them at first, but he insisted that I take them. Odin said she'd have wanted me to have them."

Thor looked shaken. He turned toward the table where Odin still sat. Odin was staring back at us and he smiled at Thor, but there was no happiness to his smile. It was a smile full of regret and irony. Thor narrowed his eyes and started to walk over to Odin, but I stopped him with a hand on his arm.

"Are you sure there's nothing wrong with those cards?" Thor looked at the box like it might suddenly turn into a snake and bite him.

"There's magic in them, but it's gentle with me." I rubbed the worn wood. "It holds no threat. Don't worry about it; I'm fine." I smiled and pulled Thor toward the high table. "And I'm hungry. Can we eat already?"

"Of course, darling." Thor laughed and followed me to our seats.

Chapter Ten

It had been a long night, but the party was still going strong when we left. I gazed upon Valhalla from Thor's balcony at Bilskinir and smiled as the sound of revelry drifted across the lake to us. The golden hall looked huge, even from so far away, but it still didn't appear to be as massive as it truly was.

"I have a gift for you," Thor whispered from behind me, and a silver chain dropped in front of my face.

There was a hand-blown glass dolphin hanging from it. It was deep blue with hints of green and reminded me of Thor's eyes. Even with the vibrant coloring, it was so life-like, it looked as if it would leap off the chain at any second. Thor put it around my neck as I wiped at my suddenly wet eyes. His body enveloped mine, one arm around my waist, the other lightly touching the dolphin where it lay on my chest.

"To remind you that courage sometimes means leaping into the unknown." He kissed my cheek. "And that sometimes the unknown is wonderful."

"*You're* wonderful." I turned in his arms and studied his gorgeous face. "I may know Trevor like I know myself now, but half the fun in a relationship is discovering the other person. You're absolutely right, the unknown is sometimes wonderful."

"Happy Yule, darling." He gave me a bright smile.

"Thank you, baby." I pulled away from him and headed back inside. "I have a little something for you too."

"You do?" He followed me, his face lighting up like a child's.

“You thought that I forgot about you?” I raised a brow as I handed him a tiny box.

Thor lifted a brow back at me and held the minuscule present between his thumb and pointer finger.

“Great things come in small packages,” I chided.

“Yes, I can see that.” He leered at me, and I smacked him.

“Open it, will you?”

Thor pulled at the tiny bow, but only managed to get it knotted tighter. I would have helped him, if watching his big fingers fumbling with the wrapping hadn't been so damn amusing. Finally, he cursed, pulled out a dagger, and cut the ribbon away. He grinned at me smugly as he tore the paper. The lid fell off, and he pulled out a thick, gold ring. Thor's face fell into serious lines as he studied it, and my stomach dropped. He had totally misunderstood the gift and gotten the wrong impression. It wouldn't have been so bad if he wasn't so obviously opposed to the idea.

“Don't worry.” I tried to make light of it, but I have to admit it stung. I'd thought he was open to the idea of a long-term relationship, pushing for it even. I guess I'd been wrong. Again. “It's not that type of ring; just a ring.”

“Why would I be worried?” He transferred his frown to me.

“If you thought I was proposing or something.” I shrugged. “I'm not; it's just a ring.”

“I didn't think that.” Thor's head cocked to the side and his lips tilted up. “You're a very blunt woman, darling. If you decided to propose to me, I doubt you'd do it like this. Besides, I'm sure I'll propose before the thought even enters your head.”

“Uh.” My Love butterflies were going crazy in my belly.

"What do you think of the ring?"

"I was staring at it because the gold seems to be encasing something dark." He looked up at me sharply. "Is that your hair?"

"Yes." I smiled as he finally got it. "I had it made from some of my old jewelry, so even the gold has been close to me. I thought that since I had your oath, you should have something of mine."

"Vervain," Thor breathed as he touched the ring reverently. "You're a witch, so I know you're aware of the ramifications of giving me your hair and items you've worn."

"Yeah; I want not only you, but everyone who sees this, to know how much I trust you." I took the ring and held it out to him. "Will you wear it?"

"Of course I will." Thor held out his hand and let me slip it on his pointer.

"The pointer finger, for success," I murmured.

"I already feel like I've won." He pulled me against him and lowered his face to mine for a scorching kiss. "Thank you, darling."

"You're welcome, baby thunder."

Chapter Eleven

Grand Opening New Year's Eve Party

Gods and Goddesses, Wolves and Witches

All are welcome at

Moonshine

Please go though our special VIP entrance for oathing.

Moonshine is a magic-free club for the safety and enjoyment of all.

I looked over the flier that had been passed around the God Realm, as our limo pulled up in front of Moonshine, Trevor's new club. I was more than a little shocked to see the line of people waiting to get inside, not to mention the local media. I smoothed the brown leather of my dress nervously and checked to make sure it was still in place. My curves had a tendency to fall out of dresses when they were cut too low, and this one had a deep V neckline. Its hem was ragged like it had been pieced together from unfinished hides, giving it a savage look, which seemed appropriate for both the occasion and the way I was feeling.

I threw my long, dark ponytail over my shoulder and checked out my date. Black slacks clung to Trevor's thick legs and a bit of muscled chest flashed through the open collar of his matching silk shirt.

Trevor was a prime piece of wolf flesh. At six-foot-six and built like a pro-wrestler, the Froekn Prince was the most impressive of all Fenrir's children. It was no wonder why Fenrir had wanted better for Trevor; perhaps a goddess, anything other

than a human witch who would pull Trevor down into death with her. Sigh. It was not the night for morbid thoughts, better to focus back on the Prince.

He'd been growing his black hair out since we'd first been bonded, so it hung a little past his wide shoulders in loose, bad-boy waves, framing features a romance novelist would call chiseled. I called them perfect. He had that manly look I preferred. I don't like pretty men, beautiful–yes, but not pretty. Yes, there's a difference. I like men to look like men, and Trevor, though not technically a man, looked all male.

His honey colored eyes could deepen to amber and they were striking, lined with thick black lashes. They were his one delicate attribute. Why was it the men who always got lashes like that? Although I suppose I couldn't complain anymore. I got some nice long ones when I'd absorbed Aphrodite's magic.

Trevor got out of the limo first, then reached back and helped me out with a smooth movement. Immediately, people pressed in close and cameras flashed. I blinked rapidly, trying to clear my vision and frowning in confusion. A new club opening in Hawaii shouldn't cause so much of a stir. Why were all the cameras there?

Then I looked a little closer.

Some of the "news reporters" were a little too slick looking, even for television. There was a sheen about them that seemed off, and their cameras flashed a strange blue. What the hell? The gods had their own reporters?

And soon they would all have a picture of the Godhunter. I almost groaned aloud.

"Mr. Fenrirson." Pamela Young, one of our local news reporters and one of the actual human reporters there, pointed a microphone at Trevor. "What makes your club so different from the swarms of others we already have here in the islands?"

“This isn’t a place to come to if you like the music loud enough to burst your eardrums.” Trevor put an arm around my waist as he talked. “We’re keeping it at a nice level so you can still have a conversation with someone. We’ve also tried to keep the interior unique and safe. If you get tired of dancing, have a seat on the grass and our surveillance system, as well as our security team, will see to it that no one bothers you unless you want them to.”

“The grass?” Pamela was wide-eyed with surprise.

“Moonshine has an outdoor theme; there are trees and grass inside the club.” Trevor grinned his endearing, lopsided grin. “We even have a waterfall.”

“Fascinating. It sounds like a place an older crowd might appreciate.” Pamela smiled and I smiled back. She had no idea how much older he was intending the crowd to be.

“We hope so.” Trevor steered me past her. “This is definitely not a place for the kiddies.”

“Thank you, Mr. Fenrirson.” Pamela turned back to the camera to finish her report.

“Prince VèulfR,” one of the god reporters called, in a low tone. “How about a picture with your new Rouva?”

“Of course.” Trevor angled me toward the man who I was now absolutely positive was a god, and a blue flash went off.

Yep, that picture was going to be passed around to all of my enemies. I smiled big.

“How do you respond to rumors that this club was created to appease the Godhunter, who it's said has demanded the Froekn change their ways?” A young man with golden-blond curls held out a shiny microphone. He had a casual suit jacket on over his jeans and looked like he belonged on a college campus.

"What did you say?" I was about to go Godhunter on his ass, but Trevor caught my arm.

"I'd say your information, as always, is only partly correct, Hermes." Trevor smirked. "I did open this club because I knew how my Rouva felt about the Froekn's . . . previous occupation, but it was not at her behest. I was influenced by a new perspective and decided to give my family the opportunity to try something different if they so wished. I was happily surprised to find that quite a few of my people wanted the change. So, you see"–he pulled me against his side–"Vervain has already become a good Rouva, without even lifting a finger."

"You did this for me?" I whispered in amazement.

Trevor's response was a quick wink.

"And what about reports that she has bewitched not only you but your father as well?" Hermes continued. Boy, he was an annoying bastard. No wonder his daddy had made him a messenger. "That you are both in love with her?"

"Well, they're half right." Trevor was so cool under pressure. I wanted to shove that mic down Hermes' throat. "I'm in love with her, but Dad just thinks of her as a daughter."

"But isn't Thor involved with this woman?" Hermes pushed the mic even closer, and I saw a gold emblem of outspread wings on the handle of it.

"Yes," Trevor said simply. "You can love someone and not make love to them. You, above all people, should know that."

"I do." Hermes nodded as his eyes narrowed, and he lowered the microphone. "I know all about love and loss. Your new Rouva took one of those loves away from me. I can smell Aphrodite's power on her," he hissed.

"What; you too?" My mouth fell open. "How many men

was that woman with?"

"We have a son together." Hermes ignored the insult. "She was a true goddess; beautiful, magnificent, beautiful . . ."

"Yeah, we got that she was a looker." I rolled my eyes.

"And now you wear her magic like a trophy, you murderess!"

I looked over my shoulder to see the human reporters starting to take an interest in what was happening, but then some Froekn bouncers slid between us, effectively blocking the view.

"*She* was trying to kill *me*," I hissed back at Hermes.

"Because you're the Godhunter," he snarled. "She was defending her people."

"She was defending her claim on another god." I stepped away from Trevor. "She didn't care about the rest of you; she was just mad that Huitzilopochtli wanted me instead of her."

"You're a filthy human," Hermes scoffed, "a pale comparison to a goddess like her. There is no way Huitzilopochtli would prefer you over the magnificent Aphrodite."

"Enough." Trevor had finally gotten mad. "Insult my Rouva once more, messenger boy, and you'll find out firsthand that this wolf is far from tamed."

"You're a fool." Hermes pointed his finger at Trevor, and blue flashes went off from all the other god reporter's cameras. "She'll destroy you too."

"Oh"–Trevor grinned evilly–"but what a way to go."

Before Hermes could say another word, Trevor turned me around and a bouncer slid in smoothly behind us. We were ushered into the club amid more flashing lights.

"Well, that was unsettling." I sighed.

"Don't concern yourself with it." Trevor guided me through the entry room. "Heralds aren't allowed into the club."

"Excuse me?" I stopped him. "Heralds? What's a herald?"

"Heralds"–he waved behind us–"news announcers. In the God Realm, we refer to them as heralds."

"So wait." I shook my head. "Are you telling me that you guys have your own news network? Your own broadcast stations? TVs?"

"Not as you do," Trevor said. "I wish we did. I bet we could make some amazing movies, but no, we only communicate things of great importance. There are only a few chosen gods deemed neutral enough to relay notable events to the rest of us. They record things they believe other gods need to know about, and then send their messages to us magically."

"So, you do have TVs." I had an image of Hermes sitting behind a news desk with a big photo of me and Trevor pasted on a screen behind his head. Neutral, my ass.

"No." Trevor laughed. "Every god is different, we each have our own receptacle to collect the messages in and play them back later for us."

"Receptacle?"

"Yeah, like father has a mirror."

"A mirror?" My eyes got wide. "Does he have to say something to activate the magic?"

"Of course." Trevor frowned a little.

"Is it; Mirror, Mirror on the wall?" I giggled, thinking of Fenrir flipping back his hair and asking who the fairest of them all

was. “Oh, please say it is.”

“Did you just compare my father to the wicked queen in *Snow White*?”

“Uh, yeah.” I gave Trevor my *of course I did* look.

“You are unbelievable.” He chuckled. “Don't ever say that to his face.”

“I'm not suicidal.” I grimaced, thinking about all the other things I'd said to Fenrir. Maybe I was suicidal. “Hey, back to those Harold people.”

“Heralds”–Trevor laughed harder–“with an E.”

“Yeah, those guys.” I rolled my eyes. “So, you think Hermes is gonna influence popular god opinion about me?”

“Seriously?” Trevor raised his brows. “The Godhunter is worried about what gods think of her?”

“Not worried about what they think exactly.” I shrugged. “I just don't want a whole bunch of angry gods gunning for me.”

“Vervain, you hunt gods.” He shook his head. “Hermes could swear you're a saint, and it wouldn't matter one bit. They'd still hate you. We can't all fall for your charm and beauty.”

“Har har,” I huffed, and finally took a good look around the sparkling white entryway.

There was a line of gods waiting for passage through the special VIP room Trevor had set up. The entire club was warded, so anyone with strong magical abilities had to be sworn in with an employee in the VIP room before being allowed inside. There was an additional door next to the public entrance which let the gods into the club. Normal people just saw a line of VIPs, but actually, they were gods waiting to make an oath that they wouldn't harm anyone while on the premises.

The club would be an area of truce. Good, bad, and in between; they could all come and party together without killing each other . . . hopefully.

Above the doorway to the VIP room was a sign which read: For all our Divinely Special Patrons. Trevor had made sure that the god world knew his policy, but if some other magic wielder showed up and tried to get in without being oathed, they'd be caught at the door where the bouncer on guard would immediately "recognize" our VIP and direct them to the oathing room.

"Oh my god." I stopped short when we got inside the club.

It really was amazing, what he'd done with an old warehouse off of Nimitz.

"Not exactly"–Trevor grinned–"but my dad's one."

"Trevor, it's beautiful."

It was an indoor forest. Ahead of me was a dance floor made of tough but soft vinyl in dark green. It was mostly an open space, but there were also a few trees rising out of it majestically, their branches brushing the steel ceiling. People were already dancing around the trees. You'd think they would have been obstacles, but they actually added an intriguing touch of privacy. I'm sure no one felt like they were being watched, which was a good thing since everyone was.

There was a full moon hanging from a ceiling painted to look like the night sky, dusted with little sparkling star lights. The moon housed some Atlantean security cameras. Top of the line and donated to Moonshine by Fenrir, I'd been told. Those cameras could spot not only hidden weapons but hidden intentions. When someone used magic or experienced strong emotions, their aura changed and the cameras could detect that shift. They were actually able to see if someone was about to start a fight . . . or get lucky. Security by moonlight.

“Thank you, you don't know how happy it makes me to see that look on your face.” Trevor steered me around a pond fed by an impressive waterfall which fell from the upper floor.

The gentle sound of rushing water melded with the music spilling out of ingeniously hidden speakers. Real plants grew from sunken moats around the walls, the bases of the fake trees, around boulders, and in other assorted nooks, lending their fragrance to the illusion. Even the AC blew gently around us, ebbing and flowing like a natural breeze.

“Did you really do all of this for me?” I swallowed past the sudden lump in my throat. “Tell me you didn't.”

“I can't.” Trevor had subtly led me to a private nook beside the waterfall. “I hate lying to you.”

“Trevor.” I shook my head.

The wolf inside me jumped and danced at my accelerated heartbeat. I tried to tamp it down by thinking of Thor. He would never have agreed to me accompanying Trevor on his big night, if he'd known Trevor was going to use it as a chance to romance me. I like to think that I wouldn't have agreed to come either, but, just like Trevor, I hated lying to me.

“Don't look at me like that, Minn Elska.” The endearment made something ache in my chest. Salt in the open wound of my heart. “I did this to make you happy, to make you proud of me. You hate how the Froekn are paid assassins for the gods. This way, you can be proud of, and fully embrace, your new family.”

“Yes, I hate it”–I bit my lip–“but I don't want you, or them, to feel like you have to change for me. I would never ask that of any of you.”

“I know.” Trevor grinned and took my face in his hands to lay a quick kiss on my lips. “It just makes me love you more.”

I nearly groaned. Trevor had taken to announcing his love for me openly, ever since the Yule party. No matter who was present and whenever he got the chance. Now, it was going to be on GNN, the Gods News Network.

His cavalier behavior was pushing Thor to the edge. I'd had to get creative in bed, to coerce my lover to even let me escort Trevor tonight. Thor had put up with a lot, and I didn't blame him for his frustration. I would have been a raving lunatic by now.

"It *is* preferable to their previous vocation." I smiled because it was hard not to when Trevor looked at me with his heart in his eyes. I smiled even more when I saw TryggulfR making his way over to us. I'd recently discovered that he went by the name Ty when he was among us humans.

"Greetings Rouva." TryggulfR rubbed his face along the side of mine.

"I can't wait till Fenrir finds a mate, so you all can stop calling me your Queen." I looked around and relaxed even more when I didn't see UnnúlfR. "You're alone?"

"UnnúlfR's around here somewhere." TryggulfR grinned. "Don't worry, big brother's in a good mood tonight."

"The only one I'd be worried about, would be him." I smiled back. "Cause I'd have to kick his ass all over again, if he ruined Trevor's big night."

"No ass-kicking tonight, Minn Elska." Trevor nuzzled my ear and shivers raced down my spine.

"Stop working the Binding." I pushed him back. "Thor will be here any minute."

"I'd never use the Binding against you," he said softly. "What you feel for me is all you, Vervain."

"Then it's even more important that you stop touching me so much." I looked away from his steady gaze. "It's hard enough to make this situation work without adding fuel to the fire."

"I'd never pressure you into anything you didn't want." Trevor backed away. "Do you feel threatened by me? Unsafe?"

"No," I groaned. "Not threatened, but you *are* dangerous for me. I feel like an alcoholic who has to constantly cozy up to a bottle of Jack Daniels. Maybe I should start calling you JD." I laughed to try and alleviate the tension.

Ty was looking away while he waited for us to finish our conversation, valiantly trying to give us some privacy, but I knew his werewolf hearing was picking up every word.

"Call me whatever you want, Lady Hunter." Trevor kissed my hand before leading me to a set of stairs beside the waterfall. "As long as you keep calling."

The upper level of Moonshine was reserved for VIPs, so there was another Froekn guarding the bottom of the stairs. He let us by with a half bow and I nodded to him. I think his name was Joseph, but I wasn't sure. I'd met so many werewolves lately.

"Now, do you think you could leave the ass-kicking to the bouncers tonight?" Trevor escorted me to a couch, cleverly disguised as a little hill.

"I guess so." I sat down and was happy to find the "grass" to be comfortable. It was washable too, according to Trevor.

"Thank you." I saw him shoot a pained look over his shoulder at Ty. So I elbowed him, and let him feel some genuine pain. I'm nothing if not accommodating.

On our right, a stream poured out of an opening set into the bottom of a wall and over some rocks before flowing down to the waterfall, gurgling happily as it went. A railing covered in ivy

partitioned it off, discreetly telling people to stay away from the water without taking away from its beauty. Small trees and flowering plants were strewn about, making the open balcony into a hanging garden. I reached over to gently stroke the delicate petals of an orchid affixed to a tree just behind our seat.

"Behind there"–Trevor pointed to the wall across the stream from us–"is the upper level of a running track I built inside the walls. It follows the perimeter of the warehouse along the ground floor, but we had to take it up over the entryway so it could remain continuous."

"A track?" My eyes widened. "For the Froekn to run?"

"Yeah." Trevor was shiny with happiness, and I couldn't help but think it was a good look for him. "The entrance to the track is in the Wild Room, reserved for VIPs of course." He winked at me. "The room looks even more like a forest than out here. Froekn can change to wolf and be totally free in there, and when they feel the need to run, they can use the track. I lined the track with plants so it would feel like we were running through the woods. Except, in there we don't have to worry about gods attacking us or humans spotting us. I've used it a bunch of times already. I'm very happy with the way it turned out."

"It sounds wonderful." I squeezed his hand, an odd sense of pride filling me.

Trevor had known nothing but killing his entire life. For him to make a turn around like this was mind boggling to me. Of course, being an assassin had paid extremely well, and opening the club was no financial hardship for him, but to handle the business end of it and to do it successfully . . . I was impressed.

I got up and walked to the edge of the balcony so I could check out the downstairs from a bird's-eye view. Trees "grew" thicker around the walls, but people were wandering through them, lounging on the flat-topped boulders and grassy patches found

there. Werewolf waitresses flowed through the crowd, expertly taking orders and delivering drinks. Sharp reflexes and enhanced hearing were going to come in handy for them.

On the opposite side of the club was the bar. The counter was an amazingly long piece of slate left in its natural form with weathered grooves and all. Tree stumps carved into seats and coated with varnish, swiveled on hidden pivots as patrons spoke animatedly to each other, the air around them thrumming with excitement. People were already three-deep behind the seats, waiting for the eight, hardworking, Froekn bartenders to get to them.

A fine mist hung in the air to my right, rising from the waterfall; little rainbows from the subtle lighting flashed through it. My gaze followed the water down to where it pooled in a surprisingly natural looking basin of plant adorned rocks. Tucked in among the plants were also little two-seater niches for people to take a breather or steal a kiss. Past that was the entrance, and past the entrance was a long wall enclosing the Wild Room Trevor had spoken of. Around the corner, a large Froekn bouncer guarded the doorway to it.

Music was playing at a comfortable level and there were werewolves dancing among the people on the dance floor already. The Froekn looked like they were in Wolfie Heaven and I was sure their delight would go up another notch as soon as they checked out their special retreat.

“So, how do you like our little paradise, Minn Elska?” Trevor’s arms slid around my waist, and I felt his chin come to rest on my head.

His scent enveloped me; exotic spices and wolf musk. It resounded inside of me the way some smells do, as if it were connected to a memory. It wasn't a memory though, just a feeling. Calm perfection; the scent meant safety, home, and love. I tried to push it away and remind myself of the fact that those were the

things I felt when Thor held me as well.

"It's beautiful, amazing; I've never seen anything like it." I rubbed his arms, the corded muscles tightening in response. I could only be strong for so long, okay? "Is Fenrir coming?"

"I'm here, little frami," Fenrir's deep voice came from behind us, urging me around to face him.

"Where did you come from?" I asked.

"The Family Room." Fenrir pointed back over his shoulder at a door marked: Employees Only. It was hidden partially behind a tree.

"The Family Room?" I edged away from Trevor so I could give him an inquisitive look. "How many special rooms are in this place?"

"The tracing wall is back there." Trevor shrugged.

"Tell her about the vamp rooms." Fenrir smiled proudly at his son.

"There are light-tight rooms with single cots and steel doors back there as well." Trevor leaned against the railing and crossed his ankles. "If any of our guests happen to be vampires who party too long and get caught by the dawn, they can pay a small fee to spend the night. The rooms can also be used as holding cells if anyone gets out of hand."

"That's brilliant, Trevor." I was overwhelmed by his thoroughness. "You've thought of everything."

"Yes"–Fenrir looked out over the club–"this is quite an accomplishment."

Fenrir greeted us both with a face rub before turning to greet TrygguIfR. Trevor beamed at me. There was nothing like a father's praise.

"Would you like a drink, Father?" Trevor waved at a waitress who was working the upper floor.

"Yes, I'll have some mead." Fenrir looked at the waitress and paused. "Samantha?"

"Yes, Valdyr," the girl greeted him formally with a slight bow.

"Have you taken *all* of my wolves?" Fenrir turned back to Trevor as Samantha went to get his drink.

"He's trying to make honest wolves of you." I left Trevor to wrap an arm around Fenrir and felt my love magic reach out to him.

"Assassination has been an honest living for centuries." Fenrir stared down at me from his impressive height, with those honey-eyes that were so like Trevor's.

"It's not anymore." I reached up to tuck a long strand of glossy black hair behind his ear, which I could only do because I was wearing stilettos. "You don't need to kill for anyone anymore. You have more than enough wealth, and now your Froekn can learn other ways to make a living."

"How can you be so fierce and yet so soft, little frami." Fenrir set me back next to Trevor a little reluctantly.

"You can only be truly fierce if you have great passion"–I resisted sliding an arm around Trevor's waist–"and passion is the root of compassion. All great fighters should have something to fight for, something they love."

"Sometimes your words make me laugh"–Fenrir walked over to the railing beside me with a secret smile–"and sometimes they make me think, but they always make me grateful to have you as our Rouva."

For once, I didn't ruin a grand compliment with a joke. I just took Fenrir's huge hand and gave it a quick squeeze. "Thank you."

He nodded curtly and stared out over the club. "VèulfR, you've done well . . . in so many ways." Fenrir glanced down at me.

"Thank you." Trevor pulled me in against him, and I looked up at him abruptly. Was that jealousy? I remembered what Hermes had said and frowned. No, those were just stupid rumors, Trevor wouldn't believe them.

Still worrying over the possibility of a jealous wolf, I looked down into the club and saw a thickly muscled man making his way swiftly to the stairs. He was way over six feet tall, with long dark hair in a thick braid hanging past his shoulders, and a neatly trimmed beard. I looked over his jeans, blue T-shirt, and black leather jacket with interest. It was kind of surprising to see Odin dressed so mundanely.

The black leather eye patch he wore was familiar, though, and no one could mistake the swagger of a powerful god. The bouncer let him by with a respectful nod, and Odin came bounding up the stairs, taking them two at a time. I was finally able to read the writing on his shirt: Berserkers do it like crazy. I choked back a laugh.

"Fenrir," Odin said, and they nodded to each other politely before he looked my way and smiled. "Vervain, it's a great pleasure to see you again."

"Nice to see you too, Odin." I reached out to shake his hand, and he smoothly turned mine over to kiss it instead.

Tingles spread out from the skin where his lips were pressed and raced down to my toes. I quickly withdrew my hand in an attempt to stop the sensuous marathon. I really didn't need my love magic to start whispering to me that he was worthy, that I

should share my magic with him. That happened way too often these days.

Sometimes it felt like I had a little hippie girl living inside me. Free love and all that. She just wanted to share herself with everyone–at least everyone she thought was hot.

"VèulfR." Odin finally broke his pensive eye contact with me and greeted Trevor. "You've created a masterpiece. I wish you success with it."

"Thank you, Odin." Trevor shook Odin's hand respectfully.

We all sat down on the couches together, the men talking about the club while I held back, taking the opportunity to sort through my thoughts. Why was it that Odin made me so nervous?

Ever since I'd met him at Yule, he'd had this effect on me. He'd look at me and it would just creep me out. Sometimes it creeped me out because I enjoyed him looking. How weird was that? Even sitting close to him was bothering me. I needed to figure this shit out so I could get over it. I had bigger fish to fry than Odin the Oathbreaker.

While the men were talking and I was pondering, the God Squad arrived.

Pan came springing up the stairs first and I ran over to give him a big hug. Pan was an average looking guy; he was about six feet tall with brown curly hair (that hid a couple of horns), hazel eyes, and a pointed chin. The thing was, the more you looked at Mr. Average, the more you listened to his happy little voice, the less average he became, and the more charming he seemed.

"The others are right behind me," he said, and then dropped his voice to a whisper, "Thor's here too."

"Thanks, Pan," I kissed him on the cheek for the warning. I knew my man was coming, but it was nice to be prepared for his

arrival.

Sure enough, there was Thor, the very next person up the stairs. Even the discreet lighting couldn't stop his fiery hair from shining, framing a strong face and even stronger shoulders. He came over and kissed me thoroughly, hands sliding around my waist and pulling me in tight. I was a little unsteady when he finally released me.

"Hey, you." Thor winked at me and then walked over to greet the others.

"Hey," I whispered to his back.

I caught Trevor's annoyed look and shrugged. If that was the extent of Thor's public displays for the evening, I was going to count myself lucky. Not that I minded being public with Thor, but I really didn't want to rain on Trevor's parade, and Thor was the God of Thunder. He just couldn't help it.

Then Persephone came up the stairs.

"Hey, girl." She gave me a hug, and I was instantly refreshed.

Persephone could be a little childish, but she had a wonderful magic that not only made things grow, but also made you feel the growth, the potential for new life, the hope. Hope was a good thing, especially when you were faced with a jealous boyfriend you needed to find a way to appease without rubbing his status in your admirer's face.

"Hey, Sephy." I looked around her lithe figure, and sure enough, there he was. "Hi Hades, how ya doin'?"

"I'm very excited to be here." Hades kissed my hand, á la Casanova. "Thank you so much for the invitation."

For some reason, Hades didn't get invited to a lot of

parties. He hadn't even met any of Persephone's friends until he'd shown up at my house one night when she was running late. In order to stop a lover's spat of dynamic proportions, I'd performed some kamikaze counseling. I was pleased with the results, but some of the other gods were a little concerned about the consequences.

Due to our talk, Hades had become more appreciative and romantic with Persephone. In return for his efforts, Persephone had stood up to her controlling mother and moved in with Hades. The previous arrangement had them living together for only three months out of the year, even though they were married. I'd only found this out recently; the marriage part that is. I'd thought they were only dating. Gods can be so vague, but then Sephy told me she had married Hades centuries ago.

"You're always welcome, Hades." I smiled at him and he pushed up the shades he'd been wearing.

I tried not to let his eyes disturb me. Hades was Mr. GQ; average build and height, with dark brown hair, and clean-cut good looks. He had a smile that was boyish when it appeared, which matched Sephy's girlish one perfectly, but his eyes . . . they were truly windows into his soul.

The irises were translucent brown, like colored glass, and behind them, a fire raged. It was like staring through a peephole into a furnace. It was also a little unsettling. Maybe that was why he didn't get many invites.

"Vervain." Finn saved me from having to make small talk with the Lord of the Underworld.

"Finn." I gave him a quick hug.

"You haven't seen my father have you?"

"No." I glanced out behind him at Brahma and Horus, who were coming up the stairs. "Trevor told the bouncers not to let Lir

in. You're priority, honey."

"Thanks, Vervain." Finn's gorgeous, green eyes softened, and he gave me a gentle kiss before he went to sit down with the others.

"Hey, guys." I hugged Brahma and then Horus quickly. Brahma was a horrible flirt and Horus was only just starting to tolerate me, so I didn't want to linger over either greeting.

"Vervain, you look lovely." Brahma ran his hand down my arm as he slid by with his Bollywood good looks and Hollywood good suit. Horus just nodded curtly, sticking his sharp nose in the air as he pretended to hate the fact that I'd hugged him.

"Thank you." I turned back to the group. "What time is it, Brahma?"

The Hindu god was Mr. Punctuality.

"It's 11:06." Brahma peered at his Rolex importantly. "Exactly fifty-four minutes till midnight."

"Yes, we can count, Brahma." Ull came up behind me, and I yelped in surprise.

"Ull." I flung my arms around his neck. His long, blond hair tickled my nose, and I let him go to rub at it.

"Vervain." Ull smiled down at me. "You look amazing."

"Thanks." I flushed and looked away.

I still couldn't see what some of the gods saw in me, even with the make-over from Aphrodite's magic. I looked better than I had before, but I was still nowhere near as beautiful as most of the goddesses I'd met.

Thor had told me once that they were attracted to my magic. Since gods fed on the energy of humans, which was

essentially our magic, they could feel it when they got close to a human with natural abilities. The magic wanted to return to the source. Like a magnet, it pulled them to me. So, they weren't necessarily attracted to my outer form, it was more an internal thing.

I'd been kind of insulted back then, but Thor had pointed out that it was no different than liking someone for the color of their hair or shape of their body. In fact, it was kind of what most women wanted; a man who was attracted to them because of what they were inside. Once I got past the human concept of physical attraction, I was okay with it, but honestly, I'm still a bit confused.

"Vervain." Teharon set his calming hand on my shoulder, and I turned to give him a hug. His long, straight, black hair swung down around us like a heavy curtain when he bent down.

"I'm so glad you're here." I smiled up into his turquoise eyes, so shockingly bright in his dark face. "I feel safer already."

"Let's hope you don't need any healing tonight," he teased, and then backed away so I could greet the couple behind him.

"What is this; a war party?" I hugged Estsanatlehi and then her husband Tsohanoai, who I called Mrs. E and Mr. T respectively.

The nicknames were simply because I embarrassed myself whenever I tried to pronounce their full names. I could pronounce Hawaiian words just fine, but Native American ones threw me for a loop. The Navajo couple was dressed up, a first in my memory, and I was suddenly glad that they usually dressed down. I'd probably be struck speechless if they looked that good every day.

"We Indians"–Mr. T winked at me, his usually glowing skin, mercifully toned down–"like to travel in packs like your Froekn."

"You look lovely tonight." Mrs. E reined in her husband

with a gentle hand. Her voice was deep and strong like a rushing river, and a warm wind seemed to flow around her constantly.

"Thank you. Would any of you like something to eat?" I gestured to a long banquet table that had been set up along the railing, where the upper floor turned to line the wall. The upper level nearly encircled the building, broken only where the track dipped up The side portions were wide enough for several slate tables as well as some grass covered couches.

"Just a small plate maybe."

Ull came up and took my arm as Mrs. E let her husband guide her to the banquet table.

"You didn't offer me anything to eat." Finn pretended to pout, but I caught a hint of something more serious in his tone.

"Finn, the first thing you do whenever you come over to my house, is rummage through the fridge." I took a seat next to Trevor since I was supposed to be his date. "I figured that you'd have no problem finding the food on your own."

"Point taken." Finn held up his hands in surrender.

"How cozy," a new voice intruded, and we all turned toward the stairs.

A voluptuous woman with hair the color of corn posed there. Can you say: Vogue? She was wearing a gold gown that hugged her curves all the way to the floor where it shimmered in a pool around her feet. Her face was a little wide, but beautiful, with a strong chin and a generous, almost greedy, mouth.

"Mommy." Persephone jumped up and went to hug the woman.

"That's Demeter?" I whispered to Trevor.

"Yes, I'm Demeter." She patted her daughter on the

shoulder and then strode forward like a movie star.

I almost groaned. I kept forgetting that gods had super senses, everything was heightened on them, including hearing.

"Welcome to Moonshine," Trevor said as we both stood to greet her. Trevor shook Demeter's hand, but when I reached out, she stood back pointedly.

"I have a quarrel with you, Godhunter." Demeter stared down her nose at me.

"Yeah?" I kind of figured this was coming. "Get in line."

"How dare you." She moved her hands like she was about to use her magic, which no doubt was intended to put me in my place before she remembered that she couldn't cast inside the club.

"How dare I?" I was pissed. To bring this issue to me on that particular night was rude. "How dare *you* come here to harass me on New Year's Eve? What did you do; just sit at home waiting for the perfect opportunity to ruin my evening?"

Trevor groaned behind me, and there were a few horrified gasps, but Persephone got between us before I could say anything more to her mother. I was a little shocked, and impressed, by Persephone's interference.

"Mother." Persephone grabbed Demeter's arm. "Stop blaming Vervain; it was my decision, and I've never been happier."

"You're a silly child who doesn't know what she wants," Demeter sniffed. "That scoundrel can't possibly make you happy. He's a kidnapper, a pervert, and your father's brother." Demeter stroked Persephone's hair.

"Hades is her uncle?" I whispered to Trevor, who just nodded distractedly, his eyes fixed on the show. "That's kind of

sick."

"Brother in his pantheon; they don't actually share the same parents, now shh." Thor was suddenly standing beside me, holding my arm protectively.

"For one thing, I'm not a child anymore, Mother." Persephone took Demeter's hand from her hair gently. "You need to stop coddling me. For another, Hades didn't exactly drag me away kicking and screaming . . . not genuinely at least." She looked a little sheepish, her eyes skittering away before finding the courage to look back at her mother.

"What do you mean, 'not genuinely'?" Demeter scowled at Hades, who'd come up behind Persephone and laid a hand on her shoulder.

"I'd been courting your daughter for awhile before I took her home with me." Hades met Demeter's hard gaze levelly. "Even though you refused my suit."

"I knew you wouldn't allow us to get married." Persephone took a deep breath before she continued. "So we met secretly. Then one day Hades just threw me over his shoulder and said he'd had enough, he was abducting me."

"Your dramatic shriek was very convincing, Bunny-Nose." Hades kissed Persephone's cheek.

"Yeah, until I ruined it by giggling." Persephone slid her arm around Hades's waist.

Demeter looked as if she'd swallowed a corn cob whole. And unhusked.

"You"–Demeter turned back to me and pointed a sharp, gold fingernail in my face–"this is all your fault."

"How is this my fault?" I was kind of surprised to be

included in the drama again.

"If you hadn't told her to grow up, she'd still be my little girl."

"You want her to be a child forever?" I couldn't keep the note of disdain from entering my voice.

The whole situation was ridiculous. The woman shouldn't have had a child, she should have got herself a dog. A lap dog, to be precise.

"She's my little girl." Demeter reached for Persephone, but the little girl in question backed up, holding up a defensive hand. "Do you see what you've done? You've turned my child against me."

"No." I crossed my arms. This goddess had tried to keep my friend from becoming a woman, and I couldn't feel much sympathy for her. No wonder Persephone was so annoyingly infantile sometimes. "*You* did that all on your own. How many years have you had her? It must have been centuries, and that's a hell of a lot more than a human mother gets. Be thankful Persephone stayed with you this long."

"It matters not what a human mother is allowed." Demeter put her hands on her full hips. "I'm a goddess. I created her; she belongs to me."

"Selfish much?" I snorted. "You're supposed to want what's best for her. You're her mother; it's in the rules."

"I don't follow rules."

"Obviously." I looked back at Trevor, who'd put his hand on my other arm. He looked a little worried.

"Fix this, Godhunter, or you will not like the consequences." Demeter had completely dismissed her daughter

and had focused completely on me.

“There’s nothing to fix, Demented . . . oops sorry, I mean Demeter.”

“You make jokes?” Demeter’s cornflower-blue eyes flashed. “About *me*?”

“What else can I do?” I shrugged. “You’re being ridiculous. I have no control over your daughter, and neither should you. She is *of* you, but doesn’t belong *to* you. Get some therapy, read a couple self-help books, and get a life.”

“She’s right, Mother.” Persephone stepped between us again. “Don’t threaten my friends.”

“I’m not threatening your friends.” Demeter tried to push her daughter aside, but the new kick-ass version of Persephone stood firm. “I’m threatening the Godhunter. Do you honestly believe that someone who kills gods is your friend?”

“If you start a war with the Godhunter”–Fenrir came up to stand behind us, his massive form looming protectively over me–“you start a war with the Froekn, but more importantly, you start a war with me.”

“I have no quarrel with you, Wolf God.” Demeter finally showed a hint of unease.

“You will if you upset my Rouva.”

It was all I could do to keep from smiling. Inside, I was doing cartwheels and yelling things like; Take that, you stupid corn husker! Outside, I was cool, calm and collected. For the most part.

“I’m starting to get a little upset.” I fanned my hand in front of my face and batted my eyes at Fenrir.

“You do look a little put-out, Daughter.” Fenrir's lips twitched.

“Fine,” snarled Demeter, “circle your wagons. I’ll get you yet.” She slashed at the air with her talons, then turned and stalked away.

“And your little dog too,” I cackled after her. Fenrir’s face clouded with confusion. I asked him, “Don’t you *ever* watch movies?”

“Have you seen a TV in my hall?” Fenrir tossed me up into the air, effectively dislodging both Thor and Trevor. I giggled like a little girl.

“Then you’ll have to come over to my house for movie night.” I put my arm around Fenrir's shoulder as he held me against his side, one-handed.

“Movie night?” He thought it over, and then nodded. “Yes, we will watch these movies you and VèulfR love so much.”

“Not all of the Froekn, Dad; only you,” Trevor said as he came up and pulled me out of Fenrir’s arms. He set me diplomatically between himself and Thor.

“How big is your home, little frami?”

“Big enough for you, but not for our entire pack. If you would come for a visit sometime, you’d know that,” I chided him and then shook my head. “I’m sorry, I think I just morphed into my grandmother for a second.”

“I can’t believe you just took my mom on like that.” Persephone had been trying to wait patiently for us to finish our conversation, but she wasn’t big on patience. I did mention that she's a little childish.

“I can’t believe *you* stood up to her.” I chucked her on the shoulder. “Impressive, very impressive . . . and very mature.”

“I agree.” Hades wrapped his arms around his wife's waist

and pulled her back against him.

"Thanks." She smiled shyly. "It felt pretty good. I just hope Mom doesn't keep giving you a hard time over it."

"There's nothing to be done about it now," I said.

"Except be on our guard." Thor frowned at me. He'd been worried for months about this exact thing happening.

"What did I miss?" Blue came up the stairs with Kuan-Ti at his side and everyone went silent. "Vervain invited us, are we not welcome?"

"Of course, you're welcome." I turned and glared at the others before I went over to greet the new arrivals. Technically, they were still on the wrong side in the god war, but then so was Odin, and everyone was cool with him. So, it must've been our history that upset people. However, our history was just that . . . ours and history, so my friends needed to back off.

"Thank you for inviting me." Blue gave me a hug, and I smiled up into his jade green eyes.

"Happy New Year, Blue, and to you, Kuan-Ti," I said to the Chinese general, and he gave me a sharp bow.

Kuan-Ti had been close friends with Blue for a very long time, and I was glad that he was there with Blue since my friends were being such asses. I linked my arm with Blue's and felt the warm connection my magic had established between us.

"I just had a run in with Demeter," I said casually.

"The Harvest Goddess?" Blue frowned, creasing his perfect, Aztec face, and then pushed thick, straight, black hair out of his eyes.

"That's her." I smirked. "Apparently, Persephone and Hades's relationship is all my fault."

“I can’t believe you called her Demented.” Persephone giggled.

“It seemed appropriate at the time.” I shrugged.

“I’ve missed you.” Blue laughed, flashing a bit of fang, and kissed my forehead. Trevor growled a low warning, and Blue looked at him in surprise. So did I. “Be easy, Wolf Prince. I’ve no romantic intentions toward your Rouva. At least not tonight.”

“And if anyone should be upset,” Thor interjected, “it is I.”

Trevor shot to his feet, and I wasn't sure who he was about to confront; Thor or Blue. Either would be bad, so I walked over to take Trevor's hand before he could do anything stupid.

“Isn’t it time for us to go down and address the crowd?” I pulled on Trevor's hand until he stopped staring down Blue. Guess that answered the question on who he wanted to confront. “We have to do the countdown, remember?”

“It is 11:48,” Brahma intoned.

“You’re right.” Trevor sighed, rubbing at his neck. “Enjoy the food everyone. We’ll see you next year.”

“And behave yourselves while I’m gone.” I kissed Thor, then looked hard at all the men. “Ull, could you try and keep the peace for me?”

“No prob, Vervain.” He gave me a wink.

“Why Ull?” Fenrir frowned, looking regal even though he was reclining on a couch that was masquerading as a hill. “I think I’m more capable of keeping the peace.”

“You’d be the first one into the fray, Valdyr.” I gave him my *duh* look.

Fenrir snorted, managing to look proud at the same time,

"Perhaps you're right."

I shook my head and followed Trevor downstairs to the bar. The crowd was thick, and from the tingles going down my arm, I knew there were a lot of VIPs in the mix.

It took a little while to maneuver through the packed bodies, and my claustrophobia started to set in, so I was seriously grateful when we made it to the bar. Trevor took a mic from one of the bartenders, lifted me up onto the bar top, and then climbed up himself. There wasn't a stage. Trevor said that if he ever decided to have a live band, they could play along the side, in the trees.

Trevor signaled the DJ, in his hidden booth behind the bar, and the music faded away.

"Thank you all for joining us tonight," Trevor's sexy voice carried over the crowd, and when I looked out, I saw quite a few women staring at him with interest. I smiled; the Werewolf Prince was definitely hot. "I'm Trevor Fenrirson and this is the love of my life, Vervain Lavine."

I watched those interested faces twist with envy as Trevor put his arm around me. My jaw went slack and I searched out Thor anxiously. He was glowering at Trevor from the railing of the VIP balcony. Shit.

"Oh yeah, she's also my business partner," Trevor went on. There were the appropriate chuckles, but I just stared at Trevor with even deeper shock. Business partners? When had that happened? "We just wanted to welcome you to Moonshine, and tell you to grab that special someone because it's countdown time." He looked down at his watch and pulled me closer. "10, 9, 8, 7," the crowd chanted with us, "6, 5, 4, 3, 2, 1 . . . Happy New Year!"

The air was filled with cheers and applause as large sparklers went off all over the club and lights that simulated fireworks burst across the fake sky. Trevor threw the mic to one of

the bartenders and kissed me till everyone faded away and it was only me and him.

I felt Trevor's magic roll around me, invade me, and push everything else aside. I couldn't think of anything but the feel of his lips on mine, the taste of him, and the sound of his heart pounding in unison with mine. And I could hear his heartbeat as clearly as if I had my ear pressed to his chest.

There was only Trevor, and the person I became when I was with him like this. When he pulled away, I was shaking so much that he had to steady me, and I had no idea who I was anymore. Was I the woman in love with Thor or the woman falling for the Werewolf Prince?

Then my Nahual raised her angry head and roared that I was neither; I was the Godhunter. Oh, this *so* was not good.

"I love you, Vervain." Trevor laid his forehead against mine.

"Happy New Year, Trevor." I put a hand against his chest to try and give myself some distance, but all it accomplished was putting me in contact with the beat of his heart. It thudded beneath my fingers, strong and determined, matching the glint in his glowing eyes.

I took a steadying breath and tried again to back away. Glowing eyes on a werewolf meant extreme emotion, and I wasn't about to deal with it in front of a crowd of gods, humans, and Froekn. Oh yeah, and my boyfriend.

I looked over at Thor, and even across the room, I could see the lightning flashing in his eyes. It was Thor's version of glowing werewolf eyes, and as much as I cared for Trevor, Thor was more important to me. Thor's eyes had to be my priority, as did his heart.

Trevor must have realized that he'd pushed his luck enough for one evening because he helped me down, and then just stood

beside me, looking out at the celebrating crowd. The Froekn were jumping and hugging each other, even the employees. The gods were more reserved and merely smiled, lifting their glasses to one another in acknowledgment of another year bested. The humans were hanging on each other and kissing everyone who would let them near.

I looked back up to the second-floor railing, lined with my friends. I waved and they all waved back as Trevor and I made our way through the throng. Thor was starting to simmer down, and I sent him a grateful smile for his understanding. My smile lasted right up until I looked over at Odin.

Odin was staring again; in the strange way he did that made me feel even stranger. Then he smiled slowly, like he knew something I didn't, and I almost bumped into a couple kissing in front of me.

Trevor pulled me aside at the last second, and looked at me with amused concern. I could be a little klutzy sometimes, but I usually paid attention to my surroundings. He directed me into a corner next to the waterfall instead of taking the stairs back up to the VIP level. The vines and other assorted foliage hanging from the second story railing gave the nook a good amount of privacy.

"Are you alright?" Trevor had me in the corner, shielding me from everyone with his body.

"Business partner?" I neatly sidestepped his question.

"Surprise!" He grinned lopsidedly as he threw his arms out to the sides.

"Uh-huh"–I grimaced–"definitely, but what did you mean by that?"

"I've made you the co-owner of our club." Trevor held up a hand when I began to protest. "You don't have any responsibilities. I just want you taken care of. You're my mate, no matter what our

relationship is beyond that. It's my right to provide for you, and by our laws, half of what I own is yours anyway."

"I can't take half your club, Trevor." I rubbed at my suddenly throbbing temple. "Thor's been trying to give me money for months, but I won't let him. If I take it from you, he'll blow a gasket and probably level half of Asgard."

"Then don't tell him." Trevor shrugged. Why was everything so simple for him?

"Don't tell him– I can't keep that from him!"

"Why not?"

"Because . . ." I frowned. Why couldn't I? "Because it would be wrong."

"Wrong, why?" Trevor leaned a shoulder on the wall beside me. "This is between you and I. It's Froekn law, something you can't avoid, and if you think it will upset your lover, I see no reason for you to tell him. It's called courtesy."

"It's called *lying*."

"Not if he doesn't ask you about it."

"So, if you and I really were fully mated and some guy had to give me money because of some weird law"–I lifted an eyebrow at him–"you'd think it would be considerate of me if I just kept it from you?"

"If it was something you could do nothing about and I would be happier not knowing?" Trevor cocked his head like he was really thinking about it. "Yes."

"Yes?" I narrowed my eyes at him.

"Yes." He nodded resolutely

"Okay, fine." I sighed. "This just better not come back to bite me in the ass."

"It won't, but I might." Trevor pushed away from the wall grinning and held a hand out to me. "Now, I think we'd better get back upstairs before Thor comes looking for you."

"Vervain, Vervain!"

I turned away from Trevor and saw my friends; Jackson, Tristan, and Sommer push their way through the crowd.

"Hey." I hugged them all. "Thank you for coming."

"Are you kidding?" Tristan shook out his spiky maroon hair. "Thanks for getting us into the hottest New Year's Eve party ever! This place is amazing."

"Thank you." Trevor put an arm around my waist.

"Uh, guys." I fumbled for a title to give Trevor. Mate was out of the question. "This is Trevor. Trevor, this is Sommer, Tristan, and Tristan's boyfriend, Jackson."

"We're her best friends in the whole world." Tristan looked Trevor over. "But I don't know you. So, who are you?"

"Tristan." Sommer rolled her bright blue eyes at Tryst. "Be nice, we haven't even met him yet."

"I'm just wondering what our friend here is doing kissing another man." Tristan shrugged. "When she's already in love with a hottie."

"We saw that kiss, shug," Jackson's accent shortened the word; sugar, but lengthened the sound, with a touch of New Orleans. "I also saw Thor walking through here earlier, so I know you aren't cheating. Spill."

"Trevor is." I looked to Trevor for some help, but he just

smirked.

"Just about to get his paws off my girlfriend." Thor came up behind my friends and laid a hand on Jackson's shoulder. "How you doing, Jackson?"

"Fantastic." Jackson turned to shake Thor's hand, then introduced him to Tristan and Sommer.

Tristan gawked as he tried to keep his hand from being swallowed by Thor's. Sommer just nodded; she'd been in the Navy for awhile. I think being in close quarters with all those guys had made it difficult for a man to impress her. Either that, or she had a real good poker face.

"Why don't you guys come up and join us on the VIP balcony?" Thor waved them up the stairs, and Trevor took the lead. I took Thor's hand, squeezing it in gratitude. "You're gonna have to tell them the rest of the story someday," Thor whispered to me.

"I know"–I shook my head–"I'm just hoping it's not tonight."

Sommer looked back at me with a lifted brow, then smiled as she shifted her stare back to Trevor's ass, which was preceding her up the stairs. I guess she wasn't as immune as I'd thought. Then I had a weird moment of picturing her and Trevor together. I had to do some slow breathing to calm my inner wolf down.

Crazy, I know. It's not like I didn't have a boyfriend already. I should be thrilled if Trevor was ever able to have a relationship with someone else, and I certainly didn't begrudge my friend a good man . . . which she already had! That's right. Sommer was married; happily married with children. I had nothing to worry about. Wait; why the hell had I been worried?

I needed to find a way to stop this insane infatuation with my mate, er my wolf who was mated to me, uh bonded I mean. Oh,

whatever. It just needed it to stop.

Chapter Twelve

Asgard was beautiful at night.

I leaned against the stone railing and inhaled the sweet, clean, salt-laced air as I pondered why the stars looked different on this side of the Aether. Thor was pressed against my back, his warm body surrounding me, one hand in mine and one at my hip. We had just traced in from Moonshine, and we both needed a few minutes of peace. It was easy to find with Thor.

You'd think that being with a god of storms would be, well, stormy, but wasn't the heart of the storm always peaceful? Thor's heart was my refuge now. Everything could be blowing about me in turmoil, but as long as he held me, I was at peace.

Part of me hated that, hated being so emotionally invested in someone that they could wreck my world by simply not being a part of it. I wanted to be strong on my own, without a man standing beside me. Then I realized how it took much more strength and courage to allow him to stand there, knowing it may not be forever, than it did to stand alone.

I'd lost Thor once, to my own stupidity, which is usually how my relationships end. I'd thought I'd never recover. I did, of course. I dusted myself off and got back on my feet, but there had been an ache in my chest that I wasn't sure I'd ever be free of.

We made up, and I thankfully didn't have to find out how long that ache would have lasted, but the memory of it haunts me. Like a ghost without a voice, it screams silently, and I'm left to imagine what it's trying to tell me. I have a very fertile imagination.

I took Thor's hand from my hip and pulled it across my

chest as if he were my security blanket and could protect me against the memory of losing him. I felt his breath catch and his scent enveloped me as he leaned down to kiss my cheek.

"Is there something you wish to talk about?"

"Why do the stars here look strange?"

Thor angled his head up to look where I was. "They are reversed, of course."

"Of course?"

"Our worlds are like the faces of a coin," he tried to explain. "A flip, and you're on the other side."

"Or a mirror." I thought of my favorite story; *Alice in Wonderland.* "A reversed image like in *Through the Looking Glass.*"

"Yes, exactly." I could feel him smiling against my cheek. "But isn't there something else you'd like to talk about?"

"No." I snuggled back into him and returned my attention to Asgard. "I just want to forget about everyone else but you for awhile."

"That's the most intelligent thing you've said all night," Thor said snidely.

"I guess I deserve that." I sighed. "I'm sorry you have so much to put up with."

"It's not like you sought this situation." One of his hands was stroking my hair, and I could feel the little sparks that were already building between us. They raced along my hair like blue fire, lifting a few strands out to the side.

"No." I smoothed the strands back into place. "I didn't pursue it, but I haven't established enough boundaries either. This

is so unfair to you. If you had done this to me, I would have left you by now."

"I don't believe that." He turned me around to face him, and I was blinded for a second by the light pouring out onto the balcony from his bedroom. I blinked up at him. "You'd never leave me for something beyond my control. I know you have more honor than that, and I know you know that I have more honor than that as well."

"That's a lot of honor." I gave him a half-grin. "Unfortunately, honor doesn't equal happiness. In fact, if you're having to be honorable, it usually means you're not at all happy about it. I want you to be happy, Thor. At the very least, I don't want to be the cause of your unhappiness."

"I'm happier being in this mess with you than I would be without you and your chaos." His face went serious. "I love you, Vervain. I love you no matter what comes along to try to hinder that love. I'm yours and you're mine; end of story."

"Yes"–I smirked–"but is it a *happy* ending?"

"It's about to be." Thor grinned and lifted me off my feet. He carried me swiftly to his massive, four-poster bed.

I didn't have the time or the inclination to admire the carvings in the bed posters as I usually did. I was too busy admiring the thick muscles being revealed to me as Thor divested himself of both shirt and pants. Somewhere in the middle of my lust haze, my clothes were removed as well and we were soon pressed skin to skin.

Thor kissed me, and the electricity of his magic shot along my nerves and raced through my body. I held on as best I could, wrapping my legs around him. His hair fell around us, glinting in the flashes of lightning that were suddenly striking Asgard. I groaned against Thor's lips; every time we made love, his power would flare and it would begin to storm. It was exhilarating and

flattering, but at the same time, it was a little embarrassing. It was like announcing to all of Asgard that we were getting busy.

He pulled my thighs wider apart and was inside me with one swift stroke. Thor knew his sparking magic had already prepared me, and he wasn't wrong. I was more than ready, needing out union as desperately as he did. What I wasn't prepared for was the violence of his need. The intensity of his passion. It rushed over me; a tidal wave of lust, love, and magic pouring from Thor and into me, without a moment for me to adjust. He went straight from lightning to thunder without the pause in-between. Pure, raw, elemental sex.

I felt like I was drowning in it, drowning in Thor, and I clung to him as if he could save me. There was no safety, though. That was the point, wasn't it? To be completely lost in each other without a net to catch you if you fell.

So, I let go. I let Thor carry me exactly where he wanted me to go, and when I finally screamed my release, I knew that falling was the very best part.

Chapter Thirteen

“That would be beautiful on you.” A pair of vivid blue eyes peered over my shoulder and met mine in the tabletop mirror.

“Thanks.” I smiled nervously and edged away from the stranger as I put the necklace I'd been admiring back on its display.

“You're not going to get it?” He was just your average tourist; pale skin, light eyes, and a horrible Aloha shirt printed in obnoxious colors, but there was something familiar about him.

“No.” I shrugged. “Still looking. I think I'll keep my options open.”

I tried to wander away towards a rack of belts.

“I've heard that about you, Godhunter.” He smiled when I turned abruptly back to him.

“Who are you?” I whispered harshly as I narrowed my eyes on him.

“Has it been so long?” He grinned wickedly. “The last time we spoke, you were in the Froekn arena showing off your pretty claws . . . right before I stole them.”

“Loki.” I rolled my eyes and relaxed. “I was wondering when you'd make an appearance. Fenrir said you always give your victims a chance to regain what you've stolen.”

“You make me sound so naughty.” He pursed his lips and some of his extraordinary good looks peeped through.

“Give me back my gloves,” I said calmly.

"Why don't we grab a coffee?" He gestured to the door.

"Then I can have my gloves?"

"Then we can talk about your gloves"–he smirked–"over coffee, like civilized people."

"A civilized person wouldn't have stolen my gloves."

"True," he agreed. "But I do enjoy some role playing, don't you?"

I made a face at him and he left the store.

I sighed and followed him out, knowing that he had me by those painful little hairs. I wasn't looking forward to the hoops Loki was going to make me jump through, but I wasn't too worried. I didn't think he'd actually try to hurt me since I was kinda related to him now. Besides, hurting me could have serious repercussions on his grandson . . . like death.

You never know, though. I mean, look at the way Loki had treated his son. He was definitely a self-centered bastard.

Loki left me seated at a wrought iron table outside Starbucks while he went in and got us coffee. I pondered him as he sauntered back, wondering why he'd donned a disguise. Maybe he just got tired of being stared at. No, no way. I was almost positive that Loki loved attention. So, why the subterfuge?

As he sat down, I felt my magic rise and whisper a warning. I caught my breath at the disturbing sensation. The butterflies of my love magic actually fluttered away and hid. I could feel them trembling low in my belly. They'd never done that before. Usually, if they didn't like someone, they just kept quiet.

Evidently, Loki wasn't worthy, in like, a really big way. I almost dropped my coffee with this new revelation. He didn't strike me as an evil guy. Self-centered, yes, but evil?

"How did you find me?" I sipped my coffee as I tried to figure out what was setting off the alarm bells with my butterflies.

"I see that you have your priorities straight." Loki grinned, and it was a practiced grin. I suddenly had a vision of that big snake, Kaa, singing "Trust in me" to Mowgli in *The Jungle Book.* "Gloves first, then tracking techniques."

"So spill." I waved a pointedly glove-less hand at him.

"I have your gloves in a safe place." He leaned on an arm, coming in closer. "I tracked you through VèulfR; he told me where you'd be."

"Trevor betrayed me to you?" I felt like I'd just been slapped in the face. Repeatedly. By a bat. Baseball, not vampire.

"Your wolf"–Loki took a sip of his steaming coffee–"is my son's firstborn, and he'll do as I ask."

Ask, not say. A good distinction, but still worrisome. Did I like being tied to a wolf that did the bidding of the Trickster God? Not so much. I suddenly felt the need to get a little jab in.

"You mean he's your grandson." I kept my expression blank, like I had no idea that he'd be insulted.

"He is my son's firstborn. I don't like the title of grandson." Loki made a moue of distaste. "Do I look like a grandfather to you?"

I decided that discretion was the better part of valor, especially since I really wanted my gloves back. "Perhaps not, but I'm sure there are a few girls who'd like to be bounced on your knee."

Loki laughed and held his cup up to me in salute. "I like your weapons, but the gloves don't fit me." He sent me a look that suggested it was all my fault.

"I apologize for not anticipating your thievery and having them sized for you." I gave him as much sarcasm as I could stuff into words.

"You have a sharp tongue, Rouva." Loki patted my hand. "I like that, but you should be careful lest you cut yourself with it."

"I've got a friend that's a great healer." I shrugged off his warning.

"Yes, I saw the Mohawk's handiwork. My congratulations on taming not only VèulfR, but Fenrir as well. I thoroughly enjoyed watching your victories."

"Thank you." I withdrew my hand. "Now, what's the deal? How do I get my gloves back?"

"A friend of mine wishes to test your skills too." Loki crossed his arms as he looked at me with glittering eyes. *Tru-u-ust in me*. I almost started humming along. "Come to my Hall for a little challenge, and not only can you have them back, you can use them in the fight."

Another fight already, I nearly groaned. "Fine, who am I fighting?"

"Sif."

I gaped at him, and into the silence came, "Zalacadoo la mettricaboo la bibbity bobbity boo." I blanched as my *Cinderella* ring tone filtered out of my purse. I tore into the bag and answered the phone.

"What?" I ground out as Loki chuckled.

"Where are you?" Thor growled back.

"I'm having coffee with Loki." Go figure, Thor *would* call, right after Loki told me he wanted me to fight Thor's ex-wife. Were gods psychic or what? I'd known a few that were psychotic,

but psychic? I really hoped not.

“You're *what*?” Thor's voice rumbled through the phone. “I just woke up and you were gone. No note, no nothing, and now I find out you went to meet Loki. When were you going to tell me?”

“I didn't sneak out to meet Loki.” I rolled my eyes, and Loki chuckled more. He was enjoying himself immensely. At least that made one of us. “I went shopping because you sleep like a damn bear, and I *ran into* Loki. He just told me that the price for getting my gloves back is fighting Sif.”

“What?” Thor roared.

“I know.”

“You will not.”

“I know.”

“The thieving bastard.”

“I *know*.”

“I'm going to kill him.”

“Me first.” I narrowed my eyes on Loki. “Gotta go now, babe. I'll see you in a little bit.”

“No, Vervain, don't you hang–” I clicked off the phone and stuffed it back into my purse.

“Sif doesn’t want to test my skills,” I ground out. “She wants to kill me.”

“So did the wolves,” he said, “and you handled them just fine.”

“They weren’t the scorned ex-wife of my boyfriend.”

“Yes.” Loki smirked at me. “I heard something about you

enchanting Thor away from Sif's vast charms."

Sif had vast charms? Great.

"Look, they've been divorced for years. I didn't steal him away, but it doesn't matter. Pick someone else and I'll fight them, but I can't fight Sif."

"But it's perfect." He spread his hands. "You both get to work out your pent up hatred for each other, and I get to watch two hot babes duke it out."

"Very funny, but I don't hate Sif, and I can't fight her. I'm dating her ex-husband, and I'm friends with her son. If I kill Sif, they might be a tad upset, and frankly, I don't think I can go up against her without one of us dying."

"What a quandary." Loki shook his head like he actually sympathized with me. "So, what are you going to do?"

"Get used to life without my gloves." I got up and started towards the parking lot.

My gloves weren't worth destroying my relationship with Thor over, and I was pretty sure that killing Sif would be the last straw on my Viking's back.

"She'll just come after you." Loki grabbed my arm, and even though I stared at his hand pointedly, he kept it firmly planted. "She's really mad now that you've killed Aphrodite. You know how close they were."

"Let her come." I shrugged. "If she attacks me, and I defend myself, that's one thing, but if I agree to a fight with her, then it becomes my choice. Well, my choice is to leave it up to her. I won't make the first move. Keep the gloves, may the fact that they're useless to you, frustrate you forever." I tried to pull away, but he kept me trapped.

"No one ruins my plans," he ground out, and his face hardened. "You *will* fight her."

"Shove it where the sun don't shine, Grandpa." I tried once more to yank my arm away, but he tightened his grip and reinforced it with a hand on my other arm.

"You *will* fight, Vervain," Loki's eyes melted back to their original purple.

I was so distracted by the change that I didn't realize he was chanting a spell to trace, until it was too late. Not that I could've done anything about it anyway, he had my arms in a vise grip.

One minute we were in front of Starbucks in Kailua, the next we were hurtling through the Aether. Solid mass became thought-forms, pure waves of energy riding the realm of magical possibilities, before reforming into our bodies again. The whole process took seconds, and normally, I handled it pretty well, what with all the practice I've had at it in the years since I'd first learned to manage tracing. But Loki had taken me by surprise. Without preparation, tracing is a terrible strain, not only on your body, but on your mind, which can find it difficult to process.

I was left bent over double, dry-heaving, when we reformed in a large room done in cold-bastard chic.

Black leather couches loomed together on cinder-gray carpeting, and a whole wall of entertainment equipment sparkled and pulsed with green lights. The walls were empty expanses of dark metal, and there wasn't a single window to be found. When I finally adjusted, Loki took one of my arms and pulled me through the room toward an open door.

"You can't do this to me, Loki." I tried to sound calm, but my heart was racing. "I'm bound to VèulfR. Don't you have any loyalty to your family?"

"No," he snapped over his shoulder. "Haven't you heard? Loki is loyal only to Loki." He continued to pull me along into a stone passageway, and then down a flight of stairs.

"Where are we going?" I thought about dropping to the floor to become dead weight, but I was pretty sure he'd just drag me, and that would be painful in my sundress.

"To the pens." He kept heading down while a horrible feeling crept up from my stomach.

"Pens? You wouldn't happen to mean writing implements, would you?" I stumbled, and Loki turned around, lifted me over his shoulder, and just kept going like it was a choreographed move.

That was it. I'd had just about enough of all that. I wasn't going to be carted down like a sack of potatoes to be thrown in storage. I pulled the lightning bolt hair-sticks out of my hair, and stabbed them both into the base of Loki's back, pulling them out quickly before he dropped me.

Loki screamed and clutched his back as the blood poured out of it. I ran back up the way we had come, chanting a tracing spell and clutching my purse like a silly girl. Before I could get very far, he shifted into a sabertooth tiger and leapt in front of me.

Now, I knew Loki was a shapeshifter, that he could be anything from a flea to Godzilla, but a freakin' sabertooth? Really? Conceited much? It was like an episode of *The Flintstones*. Except, not funny, or animated, or entertaining at all.

He faced me with a low growl; long, sharp teeth glinting at me. I felt my blood go cold, even the war and victory magics cowered inside me. My Nahual and Trevor's wolf? Nowhere to be found. They knew when a bigger predator was in the room.

How do you fight eight-hundred pounds of prehistoric muscle topped with knife-like teeth and claws? I backed away, and he shifted into gorgeous Loki form again.

"All I want is a little entertainment." He spread his hands wide, showing me that he wasn't holding any concealed weapons. Since he was naked from shifting, it was a moot point. He didn't really need any weapons anyway, did he? "Is it so much to ask; a little sport to entertain your new *grandpa*?" He ground out the last word as he closed the distance between us.

I was more scared than I'd ever been. So, of course, I was as polite as possible. "Fuck you, freak."

"That might be entertaining as well, Rouva." His hand moved with a speed I couldn't track and buried itself in the hair at the base of my neck. Loki jerked back on it painfully and lowered his face to mine. "You'll find me a perfect gentleman once my needs are met. Fight Sif, and you can take your toys and go home. Refuse me again, and I tear this dress off you, and take you in my previous form. Ever been raped by a sabertooth? Their cocks are barbed."

I blanched, and couldn't stop the trembling that immediately started in my legs. Loki smiled cruelly as he sensed my defeat. Amethyst eyes raked over me slowly, and I was so disgusted, I almost threw up all over him. Wouldn't that have been a great comeback? I couldn't even appreciate his beauty anymore, which really sucked since the full monty was on display.

Loki tossed me over his shoulder again. I clutched the lightning bolts and my purse tightly as I watched the stone floor pass beneath us, and I had to fight even harder to not toss my cookies.

We went down into what I instantly thought of as a dungeon, but was actually the aforementioned pens. They were rooms of stone with a small bed and a toilet in each of them. That's it, and frankly, I was grateful for the toilet when I got a look around at the rest of the accommodations. I was lucky it wasn't just a bucket.

Loki tossed me on a wooden bed and stalked from the room. The door slammed, and I heard a bolt slide home. I instantly pulled out my cell phone, but of course, there was no reception in the God Realm. Thor had probably been calling me from my house earlier, or from some god phone, he hadn't told me about. I never knew what new machine he'd pull out of his pocket, but my puny human phone was not going to work there. If I ever met that Can-you-hear-me-now guy, I was going to smack the shit out of him.

I sat down heavily, drew my legs up to my chest, and laid my chin on my knees. I needed to think. How did I get myself out of this one? If only I could stop the horrible churning in my gut, I might actually be able to come up with a plan. But I just kept thinking about how my magic had been right on the money, and how foolish I was to not immediately start running in the opposite direction of Loki.

What would Thor do when I didn't come home? What would he do to Trevor when he found out it was Trevor who'd given up my location to his grandpa? I groaned and thought seriously about giving in to tears. Hell, it was a moot point if Sif killed me. Trevor would probably die right alongside me.

Five minutes later, I was glad that I hadn't started with the waterworks because Loki came tromping back into the pen. He threw my gloves at my feet with a pile of leather that I had the sneaking suspicion was supposed to be clothing. I looked up and tried to keep my expression blank.

"For your fight." He gestured to the pile. "I'll come back for you tomorrow."

"Tomorrow?" I stood up. "Why not now? Let's get this over with."

"I have to invite a few friends"–he grinned viciously–"including your God of Thunder and all of your wolves. I'm sure they'll want to be here for the show."

"Wow." I shook my head. "You're *so* not what I expected."

"Which was what?" Loki smiled, and for a second it brought his face back to its former glory.

"I don't know." I shrugged. "I guess I thought you'd be fun. I thought the Trickster God would be mischievous, not cruel, but I should've known better after what I saw in Fenrir's heart."

"What's that supposed to mean?" He narrowed his eyes.

"I saw how Fenrir's mother cast him out."

"She was not pleased when he first shifted." Loki's eyes went distant for a moment before returning to me.

"She wasn't pleased?" I sneered. "Wasn't she a giant?"

"I like big women"–he shrugged–"so what?"

"I mean, she wasn't exactly normal either," I huffed. "How could she turn her back on her child for being different?"

"I haven't the foggiest." He leaned against the door frame and frowned at me.

"What about his scars?"

"What about them?"

"How did he get them?" It was like pulling teeth with this idiot.

"What do you mean?" Loki looked at me like I was the idiot. "He got into fights."

"But he's a werewolf god." I wanted to slap the bastard. Did he know nothing about his own son? "He could just shift and heal. Why didn't he heal before the scars formed?"

"Oh, that." He made an irritated face and picked at his

nails. "Fenrir wasn't very good at the whole shifting thing at first, he got into quite a few scraps before he learned to heal himself. So, what does all of this have to do with me?"

"Where were you?"

"What do you mean?" Loki finally looked up from his manicure.

"When your son was thrown away like garbage by his own mother when he was beaten and tormented for being a monster, when he had to flee his only home to avoid being hunted like an animal, *where were you*?"

I felt the strength of my anger tighten my muscles as I stood to glare at Loki. I loved Fenrir, and he'd gone through hell all by himself because of this man. So, this was personal for me.

"I was busy. I don't know how to rear children."

"You were busy?" I gaped at him. "You're his father! Your child grew up alone and hunted because you were *busy*?"

"It made him strong." Loki looked down his nose at me. "Fenrir welcomes me to his hall. He knows I did him a service, and he respects me for it."

"Fenrir still has a child's desire for his father's love." I was shaking from holding back the tears I refused to shed in front of this asshole. "He wants you to see how strong he is, how much he's accomplished. He wants your approval because you're his father, even though you're a heartless bastard."

Loki slapped me hard enough to send me to the floor, and as I spat blood, I laughed. He dragged me to my feet and shook me.

"You find me funny now, witch?"

"Yeah, I do." I licked the blood from my lips and grinned at

him. “You sent the one person who could’ve brought real happiness into your life away, and now you have to find thrills in blood and death. You didn’t ruin his life with your selfishness, you ruined your own.” I laughed again, and it was the best witch cackle I could manage.

He threw me onto the bed so hard, it wobbled and groaned. “You’re right, your blood does thrill me, Godhunter. Maybe if you survive Sif, I’ll keep you. I think that might make me *happy*.”

“Well, since it makes you so happy, here you go.”I spat a mouthful of blood on him. “Enjoy it while you can because after I fight Sif, I'm coming for you.”

Loki glanced down at the blood on his white shirt and smiled a twisted, horrifying version of happiness before he stomped out of the room.

Chapter Fourteen

I dressed in the outfit Loki had given me, only because I couldn't fight in my cotton dress. The leather was black, but that's the only resemblance it had to my usual fighting gear. It was more holes than leather, and wouldn't offer me any protection. I was wearing a sadist's wet dream, but at least it wouldn't hinder my movements.

I frowned as I looked down at the amount of flesh the bustier bared. It would've fallen, if not for the tightness of the fit and the lines of boning running through it. It had spaghetti straps and three, long, ragged stripes going across my belly to right below my breasts, like some huge cat had got a hold of it. One probably had, knowing Loki.

The pants were attached, making it some kind of S&M jumpsuit. There were long stripes cut out of the legs as well, front and back, and there were unnecessary buckles everywhere. I really hate unnecessary buckles.

I had curves hanging out of the leather, and not the normal ones that I don't mind showing. The underside of my breast peeped through in one spot. I don't know why the underside seems more intimate than the top, but it does to me, and I wasn't comfortable with it showing. I also was uncomfortable with parts of my ass showing through the stripes on the back. To top it all off, there were matching heels to go with the ensemble. Yeah, like I was going to fight in heels. Right. Only a man would think that was a good idea.

I put them on with every intention of kicking them off, once the fight began. I tightened my ponytail, then twisted my hair up into a bun and fastened it with my hair sticks. It wasn't as secure

as the braid I usually wore wrapped around my head, but at least it was out of the way and wasn't going to provide an easy handhold for Sif. If I had to use my sticks, the pony would still keep my hair out of the way. It would have to do.

When everything was in place as best as it could be, I strapped on my gloves and immediately felt better. I hadn't realized how much I'd missed them. They had been with me from the beginning of this whole god-hunting fiasco, and they'd saved my life more than a few times.

As a witch, I knew enough to enchant my weapons to give them some added juice, but what I didn't know was how much power could really be put into leather and steel. God weapons were far superior to anything I could have created, and I needed that extra boost since gods needed to be decapitated to be killed. It's not easy to cut someone's head off, but those gloves made it seem that way. They made me feel powerful, confident, and like I had a chance against the Atlanteans. It was good to have them back, but what price was I about to pay for them?

“They’re all anxious to see you, Rouva.” Loki stood in the open door, and I seriously contemplated attacking him right there.

Then I remembered the comment about the sabertooth's cock. I needed to be better prepared before I fought Loki. I sure as hell wasn't going to battle him in a dominatrix costume.

“Let’s not keep them waiting.” I grabbed my dress and purse, then walked toward him.

I wasn’t about to leave anything of mine behind again. Loki backed up, indicating the direction I should take with a little hand flourish. As I walked down the cold corridor, I felt the stones vibrating beneath me. A thin tremor, like laying your ear on the train-tracks when a train is nearby. You know immediately that if you don't move, death will come for you.

This wasn't a train. The roar came from the throats of gods,

not the steel belly of a man-made beast. Nonetheless, the danger was the same, and so was the instinct. If I wanted to live, I'd best move my ass.

I looked over my shoulder at Loki and he smiled viciously.

"It turns out that a lot of my friends are interested in seeing you fight." He pointed to a door at the end of the hall. "Right through there, Hunter. Sif is waiting."

I turned sharply on my heels and strutted through the door. If I was going to be entertainment, I'd give them a hell of a show. Thor said the gods were afraid of me because it's easier for a human witch to kill them. Something about them taking our energy made them vulnerable to those of us with the power to take it back. But even with that kind of PR, I'd never run into a god too scared to fight me. Maybe this fight would help my image. If I did it right, they'd all think twice before coming after me.

When I opened the door, I was hit with the noise. It was almost palpable. The pulse of contained magic and the cheering of powerful voices were enough to stop me for a second. I looked around, surprised to find a large, open, stone space with terraced seats circling it. It was nothing like the Froekn pit. This was an actual fighting arena. Sheesh, Loki really was a bloodthirsty bastard.

The seats were filled with stomping, screaming gods, and growling, barely-restrained wolves. I saw Thor at the far end with Fenrir. The God Squad had to hold him back when he spotted me. Trevor and some of the Froekn were with Thor as well, but it was just a handful of them. I guess Loki hadn't allowed the whole pack to invade. Wise of him. There probably would have been a war.

I gave them all a reassuring smile before I took another look at the cheering throng. My friends were outnumbered; there were more gods there who wanted to see me fight than who didn't.

I strode forward, showing off my outfit as I worked the sex

magic. The shouting settled into murmurs and then into silence. Across from me on the fighting ground stood a tall, blonde woman dressed in brown fighting leathers and carrying a short sword. Why she got a real outfit while I had to wear something from Sluts-R-Us, I had no idea.

I automatically reached for the short sword I usually wore hunting, before I remembered I didn't have my kodachi. I'd have to fight Sif with claws and daggers alone. Shit. Oh well. I tossed my stuff to the side and faced her.

Sif walked forward, swinging her sword in a couple testing arcs as her long braid swung out behind her. I smiled. Stupid woman; I was going to use that braid against her if I got the chance. Hell, I'd use every trick I had, no matter how dirty. I didn't bother with honor when I fought gods.

I walked forward, swishing my hips with the help of those high heels and smiling coldly. When I walked past Loki, who was sitting in a bottom row in the middle of the arena, I bared my teeth and said, "Pay close attention, Loki. You'll be next."

"You're going to die slowly, bitch," Sif yelled at me before Loki could say anything. "I'll grind that pretty face under my boot when I tire of your screams."

"Blah, blah, blah." I flung my hands down so the claws popped out with a loud snick, and the gods inhaled sharply.

The Froekn were calm, they'd already seen that trick, but I silently reveled in the effect my weapons had on the rest of the audience. My claws were always a crowd-pleaser.

"Aphrodite said something like that too, and we both know what happened to her. Oh, and by the way, she had me chained to a wall at the time."

The entire crowd gasped, and my pleasure went up a notch. This might be kinda fun after all. I kicked off the heels and planted

my feet firmly on solid stone, stretching my toes and my arches by doing a little bouncing. There weren't any grooves carved out of this floor, so going barefoot wasn't a big deal. I lowered my face, eyeing Sif patiently, looking her over for any possible weakness I could exploit, and letting everything else fade into the background.

She ran at me and I reached for the war magic, feeling strength and agility flow through my muscles. I watched her blade as she swung, concentrated on the angle of it, and then dropped lightly to my knees. It passed harmlessly over my head. While I was down there, I punched Sif in the gut, tearing at her as I twisted my wrist and stood. She doubled over and I kicked her in the butt to send her tumbling.

There were a few laughs and howls, but mostly the throng held their breath as Sif got to her feet. She looked down at the blood pouring from her belly, and narrowed her eyes on me. The blade swung up onto her shoulder in a graceful arc as she came at me more carefully.

Her anger brushed against me like a living thing. Snake scales, dry and smooth, with that reptile stench and the threat of poisoned fangs. I used it to keep me focused. This was kill or be killed, if I had to get all cliché about it. I had just gutted her, and Sif had got up like it was a freaking flesh wound. That meant only one way would do. I had to take her head. Thor was watching, and I knew Ull was beside him, but I couldn't let their possible reactions sway me. I had no choice. I wasn't ready to die. Not even for love. Hell, especially not for love, that was just plain dumb.

Sif's stomach was healing as she approached me, and I frowned as I tried to remember what Ull had told me about her. She was a grain goddess. A goddess of the crops. Harvest and renewal. I groaned. This bitch could regenerate like the wheat in the field; cut her down and she'd grow back. A rare talent for a god, but just my luck, Sif had it.

Here's to hoping she couldn't regrow her head.

“Let’s see what else you got, witch,” she sneered.

Why did they always use the *W* word like it was an insult?

“Well, today I've only got lollipops or ass-whoopings,” I called out loudly, “and I’m all out of lollipops.”

The gods cheered and the wolves howled in laughter, but I heard a few groans as well. Sif wasn’t too impressed with my comedy routine. She went back to cursing me and calling me all kinds of uninventive names. I mean come on; if you’re going to put on a show, put on a show. Sif knew about this fight way in advance; she should’ve had some material prepared.

I studied her face as she approached. I felt like I should really know what Sif looked like before I killed her. The better to haunt my nightmares. Maybe it was some kind of twisted form of respect or penance. Maybe I just didn't want to be a psychopathic killer, and this was my way of preventing it. Either way, I believed that humans wouldn’t kill so indiscriminately if they still had to look their opponent in the eye. With the invention of far-reaching weapons, came the birth of casual killers. Push a button, pull a trigger, and close your eyes. A child could do it . . . and has.

I had a terrible thought occur to me. How many gods sitting there, watching me, had helped create those weapons of mass destruction? Would bombs have even been invented if gods hadn't decided they needed more sacrifice? Was there a beautiful muse out there, screaming for Sif to kick my ass, so she could go back to inspiring greater weapons?

My rage rose up like a tide; salty-sweet and cold with the waters of the deep. Was Sif a part of it? How many deaths had she orchestrated so that she could regrow her flesh like that? So she could live as a goddess and not have to worry about death or old age. The wave rushed through me, and I knew it would stop today. Today I'd cut down the harvest goddess and salt her earth. Nothing was going to grow back after I was finished.

I went back to memorizing Sif. I took in her white skin, her icy gaze and pale blonde lashes. I memorized her straight nose, her straight brows, and her straight lips. The woman was all pale and rigid. She even stood perfectly, her small breasts barely touching the line of her stiff body. It was like looking at a female icicle.

If this was what Thor found beautiful, I had no idea what he was doing with me. I was pretty much her physical opposite; curvy, short, dark-haired, and dark-eyed. I was a multiracial mix, and she was the poster child for the Aryan race. We were very yin and yang in a horrifying, murderous kind of way.

When Sif got within striking distance, she lifted her sword expertly and twisted it about so it looked like she could be striking from anywhere. I watched it twirl, taking in her body movement with my peripheral vision, but keeping my attention firmly on the sword.

People will tell you to watch the eyes, or watch your opponent's body, but I've never had luck with either of those. I watch the weapon, especially if it's a sword. If you keep your eyes on the hilt, you know which way they're going to strike, just from the angle of it. So I watched the hilt, and when Sif lunged, I twisted my body to the side. She missed me, but I wasn't able to get a strike in either. My gloves were cool, but her sword gave her a longer reach.

We turned back to each other, and the crowd found its voice. There were cheers for Sif, but surprisingly, there were a few for me too, and they didn't all originate in the corner my friends occupied. Humph, fickle friends Sif had there, but then again they probably weren't her friends at all. They'd just come to see the Godhunter get her comeuppance.

"You can't hurt me, human," Sif sneered. "You're like a fly buzzing in my ear. A simple annoyance."

I smiled brightly. "The Egyptians used to give medallions

of flies to their best warriors. It was considered the greatest honor to be compared to a fly. A fly is very hard to catch."

She brought her sword down, and again, I stepped aside.

"See? Told you so."

"You cannot run forever, little fly." Sif stalked back around. "I will swat you."

"Are you gonna do something, or just stand there and bleed?" I smirked at her offended face and then dove at her, taking us both to the floor in a writhing heap.

I heard Ull's shocked bark of laughter at my *Tombstone* quote, but I blocked it out and concentrated on Sif. I was in close enough that she couldn't use her sword, but she blocked her neck well. I decided to take a tip from the wolves and try clawing open her stomach again. I knew it wouldn't kill her, but maybe it'd make her lower her arms.

Sif screamed in agony as I dug into her like a dog digging up a bone, and she dropped the sword to try and dislodge me. A punch in the head sent me rolling to the side with a painful ringing in my ears. Before I could get up, I saw her sword descending, and I rolled again. The sword slashed into my thigh, cutting deep.

I stumbled to my feet through a haze of pain and backed away. Blood started to gush down my leg. That was bad; I had to end this soon or I could bleed out. Great, no pressure or anything. Pressure! One of those damn useless buckles was actually going to come in handy. There happened to be one just above my wound and I quickly tightened it, hoping it would be enough of a tourniquet to keep me alive.

It hurt like hell, but the pain had to be pushed aside, fought through, or I'd die even sooner. So, I grit my teeth and continued to move. The victory magic helped, but my leg still throbbed with every step. I ignored it and concentrated on Sif. I knew I had to get

in close, even though my speed had just gone down a couple notches, and I wasn't sure I could manage it without taking more damage.

Sif had already healed by the time I went for her again. Come on! I mean seriously? I just couldn't catch a break. I needed to step things up or I'd be dead before I landed another blow. So, I ran straight for her, then twisted to the left and clawed her wrist hard.

The snap of broken bone preceded the clang of her sword falling to the floor. Then all noise was swallowed by the cheering throng. Sif looked around her with open hatred before she bent to gather the sword and swing it at me left handed. I kicked downward, on top of her knee, but my bare foot lacked the force I needed to break her kneecap. All it did was make her stumble.

Sif fell over me, trapping my hands between our chests. A wicked smile spread across her face as she leaned back slightly and turned her sword down so she could place the tip against my throat. I dug my claws into her chest, but she just kept smiling. She was about to plunge her blade home when I heard Thor yell.

"Sif, please!"

Sif's body jerked at the sound of Thor's voice, and the tip of her sword swung far enough left that it only cut the side of my throat instead of skewering me. I used her surprise to roll out from under her. She was on her knees by the time I'd angled myself around her, and I leaped onto her back, shoving her right back down.

I wound her braid around my hand and used it to pull her head up, exposing her throat. Before she could get her hands out from beneath her, I slit her throat with my claws, leaving four gushing, gaping wounds. I heard horrified gasps, but I couldn't stop. One of us was going to die soon, and I didn't care who . . . as long as it wasn't me.

I cut Sif again with my claws, and blood spurted out of her lips, but as I watched, the flesh began to fill in and heal. I cursed, and got to my feet, using her hair to yank her over onto her back. I stomped on her hand till she released her sword, and then planted my feet in a firm shoulder-width stance as I lifted the sword above my head.

"Vervain!" Thor cried, and I looked up to see him staring at me in horror.

As I hesitated, Sif recovered enough to reach up and dig her fingers into my wounded thigh. I screamed and brought the blade down, falling onto my knees with it. The full force of my weight sliced Sif's head cleanly away. It was done in an instant, part gut reaction and part gravity. There was no second guessing, no slow motion of self-doubt. She hurt me, and I lashed out as I fell. I couldn't have stopped the motion if I'd wanted to.

Her head didn't roll away with the force of the blow, just slid a couple of inches. Enough to know there was no recuperating for Sif. She wasn't getting up, and as I fell to my side, I wasn't sure if I'd be getting up either. The gods went wild and the wolves howled with delight. Then the pain rushed back in full force, and I had a horrible feeling it was just the beginning of my agony. I may have just killed a lot more than Sif.

I lay there, inches from Sif's corpse, and watched as blood poured out of her neck, flowing around her head and soaking into her hair. Those cold eyes stared at me indifferently, warmer without the force of Sif's hatred to chill them.

I rolled onto my back, taking the pressure off my wound as I also took away the sight of her dead face. But I carried Sif with me now, and even when I closed my eyes, I still saw her severed head. Part of me gloried in the victory, but another part of me mourned. Sif's face wouldn't be the only one to haunt me. Thor's expression would be etched into my memory as well. The deep lines drawn beside his mouth as he shouted a denial. The pain

flashing in his eyes. He had turned away from me and reached for Ull, clasping his stepson to him in their shared grief. I had just killed a woman Thor once loved, and Ull's mother, all in one fell swoop.

I didn’t think I'd had a choice, but I wasn’t sure. Things get a bit hazy when you’re fighting for your life. Could I have backed out when I had her down? Would she have let me walk away? I’d never know, and I’d always pay for that ignorance. I’d also revel in it. I’d won. A cruel part of me wrapped the conquest around myself like a cloak and whispered; There can be only one. I covered my face with my hands before my hysterical laughter poured out.

It was always jokes with me. Need to avoid confrontation? Make a joke. Need to block out pain? Make a joke. Need to deny the fact that you’re a cold-blooded killer? Three men walk into a bar: a priest, a rabbi, and a terrorist . . .

“Vervain.” Teharon's concerned face floated above me.

Although I was thankful for his desperately needed attention, Thor's absence beside him confirmed my fears. It also hurt, much more than the wound in my thigh.

Teharon pulled my leg out straight, and tore my makeshift tourniquet open to get at the gaping cut. My vision swam as he chanted over me and drew his hands across the bloody flesh. The dark ceiling blurred, and I blinked rapidly to clear away my tears. The pain in my leg was easing, but a new hurt was rapidly moving in a little higher up.

Can a Mohawk healer fix a broken heart? No, wait, that was my job now. I held the love magic. By the power of Grayskull, I have the power! Kind of a redundant line, but I think both She-Ra and He-Man had used it, so someone must have thought it worked. I swallowed another demented giggle. I bet She-Ra never had these kind of man problems. Wait, did she have a man or was she a lesbian? No, I think that was Xena.

Don't judge me. I was in shock from blood loss.

By the time Teharon was done with my thigh and neck, I was surrounded by Froekn. They rubbed against me soothingly while they helped me to my feet. Their pride and relief surrounded me, a palpable energy coursing through the air like shivery static. I wrapped it around me, desperately needing some acceptance, some comfort. Fenrir came over as I was thanking Teharon for saving my life, yet *again*.

"Daughter," Fenrir boomed proudly. "You defended yourself with courage and brought honor to your pack. Tonight we feast to celebrate your victory!"

He lifted me into the air and planted a kiss on my forehead before putting me down on my still shaky legs.

"Thank you, Valdyr," I was surprised to hear my voice ring out clearly. "May I always bring glory to the Froekn."

The wolves clapped and howled as they reached out to stroke me with approval. Fenrir's eyes shone, and he kept a hand planted firmly on my shoulder. Trevor eased up to my other side and rubbed his cheek against my face before taking my waist in both hands and kissing me lightly. His forehead touched mine.

"I'm so sorry, Vervain," Trevor whispered. "I had no idea that Loki planned this."

"It's not your fault." I touched the side of his face gently. "Just be a little more wary of him in the future."

"Yes, Minn Elska." He smiled sadly and rubbed his nose along my cheek.

"Vervain." Persephone eased me away from Trevor to look over me quickly and then pull me into a hug. "I'm so glad you're okay!"

“Thanks, Sephy.” A little of my anxiety eased. At least she hadn't deserted me.

“I'm glad you killed that bitch,” she whispered harshly. “I'm sorry for Ull, but Thor shouldn't have tried to stop you. I mean, pick a side already.”

“He left, didn't he?” I pulled away to look her in the face.

Surprisingly, it was Hades who answered gently, “He needs some time, that's all.”

My body became a steel shell, my heart flash-frozen like a ripe berry. It was free falling through my emptiness, rapidly approaching the bottom. When it hit, would it shatter into shards, ripping me to shreds like a landmine? Or would it simply crack and ooze, lying there to rot and poison me from the inside out?

“He took Ull home with Sif's body. They'll burn her, as is their way.” Brahma met my gaze with sympathy before reaching out to pull me into a quick hug. “Horus and the Natives went with them, but they're all glad you're alive. As I am. Thor will come around.”

“We love you, V.” Pan took my hand and kissed my cheek. “Just let Thor go for now. You know he loves you too.”

“He doesn't deserve you,” Finn added, touching my cheek.

I took a shaking breath, and Trevor pulled me away from my friends, easing me against his chest and rubbing my back.

“I will always be here,” Trevor whispered. “No matter what happens, I'll stand with you. I'll love you till you take your last breath, and then I'll follow you into the light.”

It was exactly what I needed to hear . . . from Thor. I clenched my teeth against the pain as my heart crashed and shattered, shooting out shrapnel into my vulnerable soul. Well, at

least it wouldn't rot. I hated smelling bad.

"It's time to go home, Rouva." Fenrir's big hand enveloped my shoulder as his deep voice vibrated through me. There was a tone to his voice, not just sympathy, but understanding.

Fenrir knew rejection better than anyone. Every woman he'd ever loved had left him. Beginning with his mother. One of the reasons I admired Fenrir so much was that he hadn't continued the cycle. When his women had born his children and then abandoned the "monsters" upon their first shift, he cared for the babies. He gave them the love he never had, and kept them as safe as he could. He built a life for them, clawing his way out of the dark hole he'd been thrown into, and fought for them as I knew he would now fight for me.

Having him standing beside me made Thor's rejection a lot easier to bear.

"You're leaving so soon?" Loki's voice made me clench Trevor's shirt in my fists.

I dearly wished it was Loki's throat within my hands, but I was still too weak to fight him. I might have to pay him a special surprise visit, say in the middle of the night when he was sleeping. It's not like I hadn't done it before.

"We're taking Vervain home with us." Fenrir glared down at his father.

"Yes, I heard." Loki smiled at me like I'd just finished a perfectly performed piano sonata. "Well done, Godhunter. I shall come by shortly to join the festivities after my guests leave."

"No." Fenrir continued to glare and Loki continued to smile.

"What do you mean 'no'?"

"You're no longer welcome in my hall." Fenrir's voice echoed a little, and people stopped to stare.

"Why would I be unwelcome?" Loki finally started to lose his grin.

"You've betrayed me for the last time, Loki." The impersonal use of his father's name triggered a round of startled gasps. "Your games are evil, and you almost killed not only my new daughter but my first born as well."

"She was going to win," Loki scoffed. "I merely helped her get a chance at Sif before the bitch could come upon her and take her by surprise. I gave Vervain a better chance of survival."

"You've lied to me enough. I'm done listening to your bullshit." Fenrir motioned with his hand, and the Froekn gathered around us to form an honor guard and escort us from the hall. "My wards will no longer let you pass, and if you try to approach Vervain again, I'll kill you myself."

I picked up my things, clutching my white dress and purse as I walked, huddled in Trevor's embrace, and let my Froekn family take me home with a few of my god friends tagging along.

Chapter Fifteen

I celebrated with the wolves, and I loved every minute of it. At least every minute I wasn't thinking about Thor. So, out of six hours, I guess I enjoyed about three minutes total.

Fenrir was even happier than the night of my trial. Standing up to his father had lifted a huge weight from his shoulders, and I had a sneaking suspicion that he thought Thor's departure was kismet, and we'd now be one big, happy, furry, family.

Trevor stuck beside me all night, and the little part of him inside me even tried to rise up and comfort me from within. My Nahual didn't try to comfort me. Since she technically *was* me I guess it made sense that she wouldn't, but her continued wariness pricked at me beneath the skin, and I could see her eyes every time I closed my own. They were resigned and sad.

I smiled and let the wolves take care of me, but I knew that at the end of the evening, I'd have to go back to Bilskinir. Thor had left, fine, but he hadn't told me that we were through, and I wouldn't go slinking away before he did. I hadn't done anything wrong. Besides, he had my cat.

So, at the end of the night, I kissed Trevor on the cheek and returned to Bilskinir. Fenrir had frowned at me until I promised to return soon. He just couldn't see why I wouldn't spend the night there with Trevor "where I belonged", but I told him I had my own home, and I had things to consider before I moved in with Trevor. Trevor snickered, knowing I was full of crap, but it seemed to satisfy Fenrir a little.

What remained of the God Squad was opposed to me confronting Thor so soon, but I told them that if Thor wasn't fully on Team Vervain by the time I got to Bilskinir, then I didn't want

him anymore. I needed a man who was gonna stand beside me no matter what happened. I had thought that man was Thor, he'd told me so himself, but if it wasn't him, I wanted to know right away. I deserved to know right away.

In fact, the more I thought about it, the angrier I became at Thor. He should never have left me like that. I could understand him being upset, but you don't just walk out on someone you love when they're mortally wounded. Even if you know they're about to be healed.

I hadn't expected him to be happy. Thor could have stuck around and yelled at me, and it still would have been better than his leaving. Walking out was a pussy move, and I wasn't going to stand for that crap.

By the time I got to Fenrir's tracing room, I was a lot more pissed off than I was hurt.

Chapter Sixteen

I arrived in the tracing room of Bilskinir and as soon as I walked into the hallway, Nicky was weaving around my feet, purring.

"Hey, baby." I picked up my gray tabby and let his musky scent comfort me. "I missed you too."

I stroked him a bit, gathering my courage before I put him down and went in search of Thor. I found Ull first. He was walking through the hallway that led to Thor's bedroom. He stopped in his tracks and stared at me, mouth hanging open.

"What?" I felt cold shivers run down my spine. "You didn't expect me to ever show my face again?"

"No, Vervain." Ull looked away, frowned, then looked back at me. "I know you had no choice. I'm sorry we left you there, but the Froekn were with you, and I needed to take care of my mother's remains."

Remains. I had done that, turned his mother into a euphemism.

"I know, Ull. I'm sorry too. Thank you for understanding." He nodded, but he held himself back from me and I understood that as well. "Is Thor in his room?"

"Yes." He sighed. "I don't know what kind of reception you'll get right now."

"I have to see him." I rubbed my hands along my bare arms. I'd changed back into my white sundress at the party. There was no way I was going to stay in that ridiculous slut suit. "I need to know where we stand."

“Good luck then.” Ull started to turn away and then stopped. “I’m your friend no matter what happens with my father, Vervain.”

“Thank you, Ull.” I wanted to hug him, to cry and beg him to forgive me for killing his mother, but I knew those things were for my benefit, not his, and I had no right to take any more from him that night. So, I just let him go and contented myself with the knowledge that it wasn't forever.

I knocked on Thor’s door and heard a gruff command to enter. I hadn’t realized I was shaking until I put my hand on the doorknob and twisted. Whether it was from fury or trepidation, I couldn't tell you. My emotions were rapidly zinging from one end of the spectrum to the other.

Inside, I found Thor sitting in a big wingback chair, staring into the fireplace. The fire bathed him in a warm glow, but his face was cold when he turned to look at me. His eyes widened for a second before he turned back to the flames.

Why did they both think I’d run? I’d never run. Well, at least I wouldn’t if it meant leaving Nick behind.

“Honey, I’m home,” I called.

Thor stood with a sigh, slowly–like an old man, and came around the chair to face me.

“Why did you do it?”

Wow, right to the accusations.

“Thor, she was trying to kill me.” I gaped at the stranger in front of me. “I had no choice.”

“I stopped her from killing you, and you turned around and executed her.”

Oh, so that was it, he felt guilty, and so he was going to

punish me for it.

"This isn't your fault," I whispered.

"I didn't say it was," his voice turned to ice, and I took an involuntary step back. "I said it was *your* fault. You used my love for you to kill her."

"What?" I stared at him dumbfounded.

"I called to her to stop her from killing you, and when I asked you for the same mercy, you took her head."

"I would have shown mercy." I held my hand out to him. "I would have done it for you, even though I knew she'd come back and try to kill me again. I'd have spared her *for you,* but when I drew away, she used the distraction. She tore into my thigh wound. You must have seen that. I tried to show mercy, and she tried to kill me."

"Her tearing into your leg would not have killed you." He shook his head like he was disappointed that I'd try to lie to him.

"Damn you, Thor!" I screamed, and he narrowed his eyes on me. They flashed with lightning, and it hurt me to see that it was in anger instead of passion. "I'd been losing blood from that wound for awhile by the time she tore into it. If I'd gone without healing any longer, I'd have bled out. I'm not a goddess. I can't heal myself like the rest of you."

"No, you're not a goddess," he said it coldly, like my DNA explained all my traitorous shortcomings. It felt like a punch to the gut, low and breath-stealing.

I knew then that he needed someone to blame, someone to lay his guilt on because it was too much for him to carry. He'd chosen me for two reasons. First, I was the most obvious scapegoat, and second, by punishing me, he punished himself. Two birds, one stone. Two broken hearts, one shattered love.

Sif had won after all.

I felt my face go cold. The chill spread down through me and over my skin like a fever in reverse. My throat constricted around the screams of denial that tried to rise up as my exhausted body began to shake.

Deep inside, I heard the echoes of my doubts. I told myself I'd been right all along. How could I have expected this to work? Even after all we'd been through, I wasn't good enough for him. I was so stupid to trust him, to believe he could love me completely. No one ever loved you more than they loved themselves. That's just the way it is. I told myself all those horrible, hateful things I always tell myself when things don't work out, and then, when I felt cold enough, strong enough, angry enough, I looked Thor in the eye.

"I want to be very clear with you, Thor. This is one of those moments you'll never be able to take back." I swallowed hard and steeled myself even further. I already knew how this would end, knew the answer to my question, but I still had to ask. "If we end this here, we're over for good. You told me just days ago that you'd love me no matter what tried to hinder our love. If you turn that into a lie, I will *never* forgive you. No second chances this time, no dream visits. I will block my connection to you like I did with Blue. You and I will never be together again. So, I'm only going to ask you this once. Are we done?"

"Yes," he whispered. A bare breath of sound over the thin slash of his lips, but it sounded loud and clear in my ears.

I nodded curtly and walked out. When I closed the door quietly, I closed my mind tightly against him along with it. For a second I thought I heard him crying, but I closed my ears to him as well and went to find Nick. My chest felt cold, like the ice from my expression had spread down to my heart, and I rubbed at it distractedly. One tiny word had changed my life. How odd.

I found Nick sleeping in one of the spare rooms. He opened one eye when I picked him up, giving a soft mew of discontent when I laid him in his carrier. I headed for the door, but my reflection in the dresser mirror caught my attention.

I walked over and looked the hard-faced stranger over. Even in my feminine white dress, my hair held up with my lightning hair-sticks, I looked like a stone-cold killer. What should have been frightening, was how much I liked it.

I reached up and pulled out the lightning bolts. My hair tumbled down around me like my life had become; brisk and heavy. I ran my hand over the sharp point of a hair-stick and wondered if it would have been any worse if I'd killed Sif with Thor's gift instead of her own sword. No, I decided, things couldn't get much worse between us.

I’ve never been one to chuck things out just because I didn’t like the guy who gave them to me. By the same token, I wasn’t one to give things back out of spite either, but when I looked in the mirror and saw the scar running down my neck, the lightning bolt Thor had given me to cover Blue's bite, I knew the matching thunderbolt sticks would hurt me more than any enemy I used them against. I couldn’t take them with me. It was bad enough I had to bear his mark. I left them sitting on the dresser.

If only I could have left the remains of my heart with them.

Chapter Seventeen

I woke up, and for a few blessed moments, I was in a confused half-state where I didn't know that my life had taken a terrible turn off the strange path I'd been stumbling down. Then I remembered.

I braced myself for the pain, but there wasn't any. I'd started this road knowing it would be a lonely journey. It was hard to get close to a man when most of your time was taken up killing things he didn't believe existed. Then along came Thor, and although he was perfect for my lifestyle, he was immortal, and I had no delusions of our relationship being permanent. I couldn't grow old with a man while he stayed young. It was just too depressing.

Thor always insisted that things could change. That even though you were one thing today, it didn't mean you'd be the same tomorrow. It implied too many things for me to consider, so I hadn't allowed myself to consider them. I wasn't sure I wanted to live forever, even if it was possible. There's a reason life is short.

And sometimes there's a reason relationships are short. Sometimes the best relationships aren't the longest ones. I needed to appreciate the time I had with Thor and treasure the good memories while I moved on to make some new ones with someone else.

So, I pushed back the covers and got out of bed with a surprising lack of heartache. Partly because I'd been expecting my relationship with Thor to end, and partly because I was just plain numb from the cold that had settled over my heart.

I pondered the cold as I wandered into my kitchen and started the coffee. I loved Thor, didn't I? The last time we broke up, I'd wallowed in my heartache until I finally became sick of it.

Where was that heartache now? Why wasn't I wallowing? Maybe once was enough for me to wallow over a man. Or maybe it was because this time it wasn't my fault. It made things so much easier when you could blame someone else.

The only problem was, it made my view on relationships even worse than it had already been. Trevor had been saying all the right things to me the night before, but under my current wave of cynicism, his words looked contrived. He was saying what I needed to hear so he could swoop in and snatch me up when I was vulnerable.

My inner wolf began a whining protest at these thoughts, but I blocked her out, my Nahual snarling her into submission. The wolf was biased, coming as she did from Trevor. Everything male was suspect from this point on as far as I was concerned. Well, everything male except for Nick.

My cat crawled into my lap when I curled up on the sofa with my coffee. He was the only safe boy in my world, and I think that largely had to do with the fact that he couldn't talk. Who knows what kind of mischief he could get into with a vocabulary. I stroked him as I sipped my coffee, but a knock at my front door disrupted his peace, and Nick went scrambling away.

I leaned over and pulled back the white gauze lining my living room walls (my Moroccan themed living room was draped like a tent) and then peered out the crack between the panels of the black-out curtain which covered my picture window. It was Trevor. I let the gauze fall back into place and continued to serenely sip my coffee.

The knock came again, louder. I got up and went into the kitchen. I just couldn't deal with Trevor. His earnest eyes and pretty words would be too much for me to take. I'd probably hurt his feelings within five minutes flat and then end up feeling bad about it.

Another knock.

"Vervain," he called, "I know you're home, so just open the door."

I shook my head as I rooted through my fridge for breakfast.

"Minn Elska, I can feel your pain. Let me comfort you."

I was nearly mad enough to open the door for that one. It was an obvious lie since I wasn't experiencing any pain. Here was solid proof that Trevor was just playing a part to get into my bed. What did he think, that I'd be so impressed by our link that I'd go running into his arms? Too bad he hadn't counted on me being completely frigid.

"I'm not leaving till you let me in," Trevor persisted.

"Then you can rot there, for all I care," I muttered as I headed back into my bedroom with a carton of spumoni ice cream and a spoon. Spoon and Spumoni, it was all that I needed.

The last thing that was going to endear Trevor to me was stubbornness. I needed to be alone. I needed to figure out what I was going to do next. I needed to decide if I still cared enough about *man*kind to keep fighting the fight against *god*kind. But most importantly, I needed to find out what the bottom of the ice cream carton looked like.

Chapter Eighteen

I was lying in my bed, staring at the intricate carvings of its ceiling. Yes, my bed had its very own ceiling. The walls of my Chinese wedding bed were carved with dancing images of dragons and phoenixes, the carvings going straight through the wood panels, so the walls were more like lattice, allowing for air flow. It was like a tiny room unto itself, and being in that lush space, smelling lightly of the sandalwood oil I used to polish it, made me feel safe. Normally. At the moment, I felt nothing. I didn't feel safe. I didn't feel unsafe either. I didn't feel anything.

How odd.

I stared at a particularly complex carving as I tried to work out my lack of emotions. Was this something I'd done consciously or had it happened all on its own; a response to overwhelming emotional stimulus? I didn't know, and frankly, Scarlet, I didn't give a damn. I huffed and got myself out of bed.

I hadn't painted anything in weeks, and I still had to make a living. God-hunting was a full-time business, but it didn't pay the bills and I had a kitty mouth to feed. So, I trudged into my art studio and put a canvas on the easel. Then I sat down and stared at it.

I scratched my nose.

I picked up a paintbrush.

I put it down.

I riffled through my tray of paint tubes.

I poured some turpentine.

Some linseed oil.

Even the familiar smell of the paint, turpentine, and oil didn't spark my creativity. I just continued to sit there like a useless shell of an artist. I would have panicked if I hadn't been so devoid of feeling. As it was, I just continued to sit there, wondering why I couldn't seem to get the paint onto my palette, much less the canvas. I was an uninspired artist, and I was going to be homeless and starving if I didn't get my act together, but I still didn't care.

I don't know how long I sat there staring at the white rectangle of limitless possibility without a single possibility entering my head, but the light had changed in the room, the shadows had grown darker and longer, when a soft sound invaded the quiet. Why was "Bibbity Bobbity Boo" playing in my house?

Oh right, my ringtone. My cell was ringing. Maybe I should get it. Hmm, that would mean I'd have to stand up. I really didn't care who was calling me, so I just sat there and let it ring. After awhile, my butt started to get sore from the wood stool so I went back to bed. My bed may not hold the same secure sense of safety it had before, but it was still more comfortable than the stool.

I closed my eyes and drifted back to sleep.

Chapter Nineteen

"Vervain?"

"Hmm?"

"Vervain."

"What?" I groaned and rolled over in bed to squint at the crack of light shining in from the doorway.

"Miss V, we've been calling you for days and you haven't picked up the phone," a disembodied voice said.

"I'm busy, go away." I burrowed back into the warm blankets.

"Uh-uh, shu-ug," it persisted. "You're getting up."

Something tore my blankets away from me, so I opened my eyes and blinked till I was able to make out Jackson's face, framed by the bed's opening. Tristan was standing behind him, peering over his shoulder with a frown. Part of me thought I should be angry at the rude awakening, but I couldn't muster up the feeling. I just huffed and closed my eyes. I could make do without the blankets.

"Vervain Lavine!" Jackson shouted, and I sat upright in shock. "Get out of this bed, this instant!"

"Alright, alright," I grumbled as I crawled out the opening at the foot of the bed. "You don't have to get so snappy about it."

"What's wrong with her?" I heard Tristan whisper.

"I don't know." Jackson looked me up and down critically.

“I think I might,” a gruff voice came from behind Tristan. The boys parted to let Trevor through. “I never thought of the consequences. I'm so sorry, Minn Elska,” he whispered as he touched my face with his fingertips. “I was only trying to save you the pain.”

“What did you do?” I wasn't even curious, it just seemed to be my line in the script.

“I used our connection to take away your pain,” Trevor's perfect forehead was creased with thick lines. I poked at them distractedly and he took my hand. “But you're still human, and I didn't realize it would have a different effect on you. Instead of me feeling your pain for you, I've been taking all of your emotions. You don't feel anything, do you?”

“Nope.” I shrugged.

“Well, you can just put them back then.” Tristan had a hand on his hip. “And how the hell did you do that anyway? Is this one of those god things?”

“Yes, and I will put them back, but I'd like to try to prepare her first.” Trevor pushed me gently down on the edge of the bed. “Minn Elska, you've had three days of total emotional silence. When I give you back your feelings, it's going to be a shock. I want you to just focus on my face and hold onto me if you need to. Okay?”

“Okay.” I didn't see what the big deal was.

Then they hit.

It was like coming out of a coma in the middle of an amusement park. The world was suddenly a whirling, screaming, sticky-sweet, musky, kaleidoscope of colors, sounds, scents, and tastes. Without my feelings, my senses had been dulled, so it was the physical things I noticed first. Everything was sharper, brighter. I could see flecks of green in Trevor's honey-eyes. I could hear his

uneven breathing like a rushing wind. My nose filled with his spicy musk and my tongue curled in distaste over three days worth of bad breath. I really needed to brush my teeth.

Before I could get up to go to the bathroom, the emotions hit. The baddest of the bad hit first. I screamed and fell against Trevor. His arms were strong around me, his hands stroking my hair, and he was muttering soft things into my ear.

I could barely breathe, the pain was so intense. Could a heart explode from sorrow? Mine felt like it had, but I knew it was still there, still beating, because I could hear the pounding in my ears. No, wait, that was Trevor's heartbeat. Maybe my heart really was just a pile of mush.

Another bout hit, and I screamed again. There were more hands on me, more soothing voices, and slowly they seeped through. I let out a shaky breath as the pain receded, and I was able to think again. But, like the ocean against the shore, my emotions kept hitting me in waves.

Next came anger, and my Nahual responded to it; if the snarl that came from my lips was any indication. Trevor went still against me, but it wasn't him that I was angry at. My anger wasn't for anyone really, it was just mine. Pent up in Trevor for so long, it had finally come home, and my fury was reveling in its freedom. My muscles tensed, my teeth clenched, and my nails dug into my palms.

Thankfully, control came in right on its heels, and I was able to wrestle my anger down. You didn't know that control was an emotion? Think about how you feel when some idiot driver nearly hits you on the freeway, and then speeds off without even realizing it. You control the urge to chase them down and run them off the road, but it costs you. That rolling, sour, clenching is the feeling of control.

I welcomed it, though. I needed it to get through the rest of

the onslaught of emotions pouring from Trevor into me. Fear was next, and I went from near murderous rage to cowering in a corner of the bed. Trevor held the boys back when they would have chased me. He knew, on an instinctual level, to never approach the cornered victim, the wounded animal. He let me have my space and just continued to coach me gently.

"Keep breathing, Minn Elska," he urged. "It will pass. There's nothing to be afraid of. Your friends are here, your mate is here. We love you and we won't let anything bad happen to you."

My breath was coming in fast pants, and my attention shot from one man to the next rapidly as I tried to keep them each in my sight. Then my pulse started to slow, and a faint glimmer of hope started to sparkle through. My heart still hurt, but I knew it was mending. I knew I'd make it through this pain. There would be much more life for me to live, and maybe someone wonderful to live it with. I looked at Trevor with new eyes.

I would have reached for him, crawled over to him, but the next emotion to come home was doubt, and if there was one thing doubt was good at, it was smashing hope to bits. I shrank back into the corner, but Trevor sensed the difference and pursued me this time. He took my face in his hands and met my suspicious gaze.

"Stay with me, Minn Elska." His eyes were spilling tears. "I've lived with these emotions for three days now. I know how rough they are, but you're stronger, you're tougher than they are. You're going to be just fine."

"You'll leave just like the rest," I whispered the accusation, but it cut the silence to the quick. "You might as well do it now. I don't need you, and I don't want to."

"No." Trevor smiled patiently. "I will never leave you. I'm your mate. You have a part of my soul inside you." He held his hand over my chest, and I felt the wolf rise inside me to greet him. "I will be your solace, your foundation, your safety net, anything

you need me to be, and I will always be here for you. That's what it means to be a mate."

Doubt fled under the light of conviction in Trevor's eyes, and relief poured in. I crumpled into his arms, and he caught me; my self-proclaimed safety net. I cried, and he held me as the softer emotions returned and I became whole again. At some point, I heard the boys say goodbye, and I mumbled a response back to them, but the emotional journey didn't let up till the witching hour. By the time I could fully feel again, I was completely exhausted. Trevor and I slept, curled around each other, like the true mates he wanted us to be.

Chapter Twenty

I woke up starving. The bed was warm, the pillow beside me had a head-shaped dent in it, but Trevor was gone. I was unsure whether I was relieved or not by his absence. I settled on relieved as I made my way to the kitchen and began rooting through my fridge.

I jerked back, startled by the realization that I hadn't eaten in three days. The last thing I'd had was that ice cream. When Trevor had taken my feelings away, he'd truly made me apathetic about everything, including food. It was amazing I'd managed to stay hydrated. Then again, hunger pains go away, but when you're dehydrated, you feel the thirst constantly.

Why had Trevor done it? I took out the eggs and started heating a pan as I considered things. Did he truly think he was protecting me by taking my pain? Anyone with any sense in their head would know that you have to work through your issues, not hide from them. Hiding from things only winds up causing more trouble in the end.

I threw some bacon into the pan, and soon the smell was filling the kitchen. A meow alerted me to Nick's presence, and I remembered what else I'd been neglecting for the past three days. At least he had an automatic feeder and water dish from when I used to go hunting alone. He also had a cat door, so he wasn't stuck inside, but still, I had forgotten about Nick, and that just doesn't happen. I broke off a piece of bacon and held it out as a peace offering to the cat.

"Sorry, baby," I scratched his ears as he gobbled the crispy meat while purring loudly. "I swear it wasn't my fault this time."

He seemed satisfied, beginning a thorough cleaning of

himself after he was done, so I went back to finishing my meal preparations.

My emotions were my own again, and in normal proportions, but normal at the moment was heartbroken. So, as much as I appreciated getting back to myself, I resented the burning ache in my chest that said clearly; I wasn't over Thor. I guess it was too much to hope for, that within the mess of losing my emotions and then getting them back with interest, I'd somehow manage to dull the Thor heartache.

Thor. What a stupid name. What was Odin thinking? It rhymed with bore, and snore, and gore. Thor, Thor, Thor. I repeated it, hoping it would stop making sense and just become a meaningless sound, but it didn't work. Each repetition only brought a thump of pain with it. Stupid pain. Stupid man. Stupid heart.

I saw his face again, harsh in anger. I'd never thought I'd see Thor look at me like that. Even knowing the why of it all didn't help. It almost made it worse to know that he valued his guilt more than our love. The way we had loved had been thunderous, literally. Sparks would fly, again literally. It was the most fantastic sex I'd ever had, and he was the most fantastic man I'd ever met.

He'd been so patient and understanding through the mess with Trevor, sticking by me when most men would have bailed. Thor was the one who'd shown me that there were still good gods who cared about humanity and who would fight for us instead of making us fight each other. I loved him, and I thought he'd felt the same. Thor had told me that he waited two years to be with me. He said he loved me. No matter what. Men are all fucking liars. At least I wasn't bitter, though.

I was sitting at the dining table, staring down at my food, and I had no idea how I'd gotten there. I shook my head free of thoughts of Thor and decided not to pine. I had no choice in the ending of our relationship, so it was only fair that if anyone should pine, it should be him. I refused to pay the price for his actions.

Yes, he had ended us, but that didn't mean it was the end of me. Vervain Lavine was still here, and I was still the Godhunter. A hungry Godhunter who still hadn't had her breakfast. I started to eat with gusto.

I tried to focus on all the things I didn't like about Thor as I ate. He was overbearing, domineering, and could just plain be an ass. I should be grateful that I wouldn't have to deal with his crap anymore. I'd never have to explain where I'd gone off to while he was sleeping in. I'd never have to fight with him over my life being too dangerous for his tastes. I'd never get to see the lightning flashing in his eyes when he made love to me.

Tears were sliding down my cheeks, and I swiped at them vigorously. No, this wouldn't do. If he could harden his heart against me, I could pay him back in kind. I'd become that cold-hearted woman I'd glimpsed in the mirror the day I left Bilskinir. It would probably make killing gods easier. Yeah, I could do this. I was the Godhunter; a ruthless, killing machine, and if that didn't work, I could go drink him away for free at Moonshine.

Chapter Twenty-One

Moonshine was packed, if you'll excuse the pun. At least I didn't have to wait in line. The Froekn at the door spotted me right away and ushered me past the long line of gussied up patrons. He started to escort me to the VIP lounge upstairs, but I stopped him with a hand on his shoulder.

“I'm just gonna grab a drink at the bar.” I smiled my gratitude.

“Of course, Rouva.” He did a quick head bow and went back to door duty.

I slid through the crowd and made my way to the bar. The Froekn bartender nearly dropped the Jack he was pouring when he spotted me. Actually, I think his name *was* Jack, no Jason, that's right. I smiled and waved, and he smiled back, finishing the drink without mishap. He laid it on the bar, took the cash, and quickly came over, ignoring the shouts of the other patrons.

“Rouva, what are you doing down here, fighting your way to a drink, when you could be up there?” He waved toward the VIP area.

“I wanted to get lost in the crowd tonight,” I shrugged. “How are you liking your new job, Jason?”

“I love it actually.” He beamed. “I get to interact with people without them screaming in terror. It's kinda nice.”

“Good for you.” I laughed.

“Now, what can I get you?”

“A Long Island please.”

"Coming right up." He worked his magic and a tall glass appeared in front of me, brimming with alcoholic goodness.

"Thanks." I saluted him with the drink and turned to face the club.

Trevor had hung paper lanterns in the trees. They made soft islands of light for people to congregate within while making the unlit areas seem darker by comparison, more intimate. There were also fantastical statues in the trees. Little imps, elves, and mini dragons clung to branches next to more mundane creatures, as they peered down at the club goers. It was Wonderland, and the reference to my favorite book reminded me of the conversation I'd had with Thor about the stars in Asgard. I shook my head free of thoughts of him and went back to perusing the scenery.

The dance floor was full, but it was hard to tell where it ended, what with the trees breaking it up and the way people just danced wherever they felt like it. Overall, the atmosphere was sensual but classy. The women were dressed to the nines, the men polished. Word must have gotten out that you had to make an impression to get in. Trevor was doing well.

"Hello, Vervain," came from beside me.

Great gorgeous vampire god, I knew that velvet voice. Sure enough, I turned to see Blue standing next to me. I smiled and shook my head as I leaned in to give him a hug.

"What are you doing here?" I just couldn't see Blue deciding to go hang at Moonshine for an evening.

"I felt something amiss through our link." Blue shrugged. "What's happened to cause such strange fluctuations in your feelings? First, it was almost as if you were gone completely, I felt so little from you, then your emotions seemed to go into overdrive. I nearly fell out of my chair."

"I'm so sorry, Blue." I pretended to be calm as I inwardly

freaked out. “I thought I'd blocked our link.”

“You did”–he frowned–“but when you established a new link with your magic, things began to trickle through . . . mainly emotions.”

“Oh crap.” I took a long swallow of my drink.

“Why don't we sit down?” Blue gestured to a grassy couch off to the side, and I followed him over to it. “Now, tell me what happened.”

I told him, and he stared at me with his mouth hanging open. I was still getting used to his green eyes, so I ended up staring too. We just sat there looking at each other, each wrapped up in our own thoughts, until Trevor walked up.

“Vervain?” Trevor looked back and forth between me and Blue. “Jason just told me you were here. Wouldn't you be more comfortable upstairs?”

“No thanks.” I felt the pull on my wolf immediately.

Yes, I'd made that little part of Trevor mine, but even combined with me, she still knew her source and constantly longed for her other half. It was kind of irritating. I just wanted to get good and drunk, forget about things for awhile, and there was Trevor, literally under my skin and in my face. So maybe I shouldn't have come to Moonshine if I didn't want to see Trevor, but I hadn't really known I didn't want to see him until I saw him. Great, now I wasn't even making sense to myself.

“Uh, okay.” Trevor frowned like he could hear my internal insanity. “Well, I'll be in my office if you need me. I can drive you home later if you get too tipsy.”

“Thanks, I'll be fine.”

“Alright.” He walked away stiffly.

"I think you hurt the Wolf Prince's feelings." Blue raised an amused eyebrow.

"I just want a little breathing room, you know?" I sighed. "I just broke up with Thor, and people are all in my face about picking someone new. I need to be alone for a little while. It's totally normal to not jump into a new relationship."

"Yes"–Blue stroked the tip of his Aztec nose–"but I'm told that nothing gets you over the last, like getting under the next."

"Holy shit"–I choked–"you *so* did not just say that to me."

"I did." He grinned, very proud of his modern joke.

Blue was one of those older gods who were still assimilating into the new times. I found the odd mix of old world manners and modern style to be charming, but I was still trying to get Blue up to speed. If for no other reason than having him understand my jokes. A joke is ruined if you have to explain it.

"You're learning"–I patted his knee–"good for you."

"Vervain,"–Blue looked over to where Trevor was lingering at the bar–"what are you going to do about that one?"

"Nothing." I followed his gaze, and Trevor looked up as soon as I did. I looked back to Blue. "I'm five days out of the most traumatic relationship of my life. I can't make any decisions right now. Maybe I should have stayed home."

"I don't know about that," Blue grimaced, "but you might have at least picked a different social outlet."

"I know, but it's safe here for me. I can get wasted without worrying and I my drinks are free."

"Free?" Blue laughed. "Being Trevor's mate has its perks. Maybe I should date a werewolf."

“Being co-owner has its perks.” I waggled my brows. “And as far as dating a werewolf goes, I can tell you that they're some of the most vibrant, loving people you'll ever meet. You could do much worse than falling for a wolf girl.”

“Hmm.” Blue looked around at the Froekn waitresses with new interest. “Before I embark into the wonderful world of the Froekn, maybe you'd consent to a dance? All we've done together, and I've never danced with you. At least, not in the flesh.”

“How could I say no to that?” I smiled and stood.

Blue took my hand, and I expected him to lead me to the dance floor. He didn't. He pulled me gently to him right there, one hand slipping around my waist and the other holding my hand properly. I smiled at his old-fashioned style, but my smile didn't last. It slipped slowly away as Blue started to move with grace and more sensuality than I was prepared for.

The small space between us was a deception. It made me think: safe, polite, when it was anything but. The space between us wasn't empty; it was filled with tension. It was a tease. Blue's hand at my waist controlled my movement, holding me back as he rocked his hips forward, pulling me in as he swayed back. A slight brush against my leg left me gasping, wanting more.

I was suddenly glad he'd kept us in the relative privacy of the treeline. If I was with him amid the crowd, I would have been horrified. Then again, the shadows made our dance even more intimate. I felt like a married woman out meeting her lover in a secret garden. Our dancing was a type of foreplay that would start a scandal in public.

“Little witch,” Blue whispered as he closed the distance with a lean, “you look flushed.”

Blue swung me out, and when he pulled me in, my back was pressed to his front. His lips were against my neck, silencing anything more he might say. I knew what he was thinking about,

though. Not Thor's lightning mark, but the scar below it. The bite he'd given me on an altar, once upon a dream, when he was a different man.

I shivered beneath his mouth, and felt him shake in response. His arms were around my waist, his head lowered so that his hair fell in a shining curtain to hide his face. Not like I could have seen his expression anyway, since my eyes were closed tight.

I felt Blue breathe deep, then lift his face, and swing me away. My heart was pounding fast when we returned to the teasing, face to face stance. The space between us was smaller, both of us having difficulty keeping even that tiny amount empty. His eyes were muted in the dark, the green of damp moss, calling me to just lay down and give in to oblivion. But it was a fairy bed that he offered, and I knew I'd be lost as soon as I touched its softness.

"Blue," I whispered, "it's too soon."

"I know." Blue sighed. "And our dance is over." He brought my hand up for a kiss before he led me the few steps back to our seats. Then something caught his attention and he chuckled, breaking the spell. "I guess you're not the only one who thinks so highly of the Froekn."

I followed his gaze to the dance floor, where Odin's Valkyries were paired up with Froekn men. I wasn't surprised. The Froekn loved to dance, and the warrior women rarely had such exuberant partners. Wait, Valkyries. Where there were Viking fighting babes, there was sure to be an Odin. I looked around cautiously.

"The fighter babes dig werewolves," I said distractedly as I searched the crowds. I really didn't want to see Thor's Daddy tonight. I couldn't handle the one-eyed-wonder in my fragile state.

"Oh, there's Odin." Blue spotted him first. "I think he's coming over. You know, this club is a good idea for your side.

Keep all the gods partying, and they won't have any time to plot against humans."

"Uh, I have to use the restroom." I stood up and downed my drink. "Will you excuse me?"

"Of course." Blue stood as well and took my empty glass before I hurried away.

Downing a Long Island iced tea is never a good idea. My vision swam for a second before it righted itself, and my legs were wobbly as I pushed against the swinging door to the ladies room. I squinted in the bright light, a total shocker after the dim club. Then I frowned as the sound of a woman crying carried out of a stall. Oh well, none of my business. It's not like I haven't been there myself recently.

I went into a stall on the end, and the crying stopped, toilet tissue spinning off the roll. I tried to mind my business as I took care of it in my own stall, then went to wash up. Samantha, one of the Froekn waitresses, came out of her stall with puffy eyes and a red nose. Crap, this *was* my business.

Her eyes widened as she saw me. "Oh. Greetings, Rouva. I didn't know you were here tonight."

"Hey, Sam." I wet a paper napkin and held it out to her. "Here, cold water helps."

"Thanks." She started to pat her face, transferring her attention to the mirror. "I'm sorry you had to see this."

"Honey, never apologize when you're feeling bad," I advised. "It's the one time when you can do whatever you want, and people have to give you a break about it."

She looked over at my reflection and smiled back. "You're right, fuck em all. I think I'll just go home."

"Oh no, you're not. I'm assuming this has to do with a man?"

She nodded, so I turned her to face me and took the towel away. I carefully wiped away her running makeup, then pulled out my powder and lipstick.

"You're going to fix your make-up, and then we're going to Nashville."

"Nashville?" She was supremely confused. "You want to trace over to Tennessee?"

"No." I laughed. "I meant Nashville, Waikiki, the country bar. Looks like we both need to get the hell out of Dodge and find us some sweet talkin' cowboys."

"Okay," she grinned and went to work on her make-up.

Chapter Twenty-Two

Within half an hour, we were knee deep in slow-talkin', dimpled, hat-tippin', tight jeans-wearin' men. So, basically cowgirl heaven.

Too bad I kept thinking about a pair of honey-colored eyes and the spicy musk of a wolf. And I wasn't the only one. Samantha was having a great time, hadn't paid for a single drink, but every once in awhile she got that look on her face.

"So, you don't like anyone here?" I whispered over to her.

"Oh, they're nice enough, but I couldn't be with any of these guys." She shrugged.

"Why not?" I looked over the buffet of men and thought there was pretty much something there for any taste.

"They're not Froekn" Samantha looked at me like she thought I might be messing with her. Or testing her.

"So?"

"So I can't mate with them."

"Says who?" I rose a brow. "I'm your Rouva and I'm human. Why would you think you'd have to choose a Froekn?"

"I . . ." Her mouth dropped open. "I don't know. I was raised to believe that I had to mate a wolf and make little Froekn babies."

"Sounds kinda sexist to me." I grimaced. "Why don't you pick one of these, and have a trial run of it." I waved my hand toward the men surrounding her.

"I couldn't do that," she gasped.

"Yeah, I'm not much for one night stands either." I shrugged. "But desperate times and all that. You need to prove to yourself that you can have anyone you want, not just a Froekn."

"I do?" She looked over the men with new eyes as a smile spread across her lips. "I can really have one?"

"Hell, baby"–I giggled–"take 'em all."

"Oh, UnnúlfR will be so pissed," she whispered.

"Please tell me that's not who you were crying over." I grabbed her shoulder.

"He broke up with me." Sam bit her lip. "Said he didn't think I was the one."

"Well, you dodged that bullet." I sniffed. "You can do so much better than that asshole."

"You think?"

"Hello? Look around you." I waved at the waiting men. "Hey, who wants to get my friend another drink?"

Hands shot up everywhere.

"I rest my case."

"But UnnúlfR is the second born." She looked like she was trying to understand quantum physics. That shit always gave me a headache. "He's the best a Froekn girl could get, next to Trevor that is, and he's already taken."

"He's the best according to who?" I thought about how he had threatened to rape me at my trial. Not someone I would put high on any "best of" list.

"According to us." Sam shrugged. "It's all rank in the pack, and he's two steps away from being in charge. It's sexy, you know; power and all that."

"So, why not go after Ty?" If I hadn't been in my unusual situation with Trevor already, I might have been interested in his baby brother. Ty was smokin' hot. "He's the next in line and has a much better personality."

"Ty doesn't want me, UnnúlfR does."

"Actually"–I smiled gently to soften the blow–"you just told me that he doesn't."

"Right." Her face fell.

"But he's a dick." I pushed her shoulder to get her to look at me. "Wouldn't you rather have a regular guy who treats you like a Princess than someone who could actually make you a Princess, but treats you like shit?"

"Huh." She tilted her head, looking for a second like a hound who'd just caught a new scent. "I'd never thought of it like that before."

"Well, get on your thinking cap, girl." I waved at the eager men and told them, "She's drinking amaretto sours. Why doesn't she have a fresh one yet?"

The men scurried off and we giggled like little girls.

Chapter Twenty-Three

I rolled over gingerly, expecting a splitting headache and a good dose of nausea after the previous night's activities.

No headache. I sat up. No nausea. Not to complain, but what the hell? I must've had four Long Islands, and then there were all those amaretto sours that Sam couldn't drink. The last round of men had brought her five. Two Long Islands put me in a bad way, three and a hangover was guaranteed. I felt great and I'd had four plus those extras.

"Must be magic," I said to Nick, who was curled up at the foot of the bed.

Then I stopped and really thought about it. *Was* it magic? I'd taken Aphrodite's power, every last drop of it till she dropped dead. I had changed a little physically. Maybe it had improved my health as well as my looks. Maybe I could do more than I'd realized. Like trace the Aether worldwide. I gave a little gasp as the possibilities opened up.

I scooted out of bed with a hopeful bounce. Ever since I'd met Thor and the God Squad, I'd lamented the fact that I couldn't trace from location to location in the Human Realm like they do, but instead had to be given a piggyback ride.

I could trace from here to the God Realm and back with no problem, but that was only because I had the spells for it. I'd found them in the book I took from Ku's house. They were very specific though, only allowing me entrance to certain god homes, and then back again. I assume they were meant to enable Ku to visit his friends, as no god can enter another god's home without the proper entrance chant. They had come in handy back when I was hunting gods alone, but I'd used most of them, and none of them are for a

location in the Human Realm.

I asked Thor about it once, and he'd said it was something they learned by experience. As children, they would trace with their parents until they got the hang of it. It was something inexplicable, like telling someone how to walk. You could describe how to lift one leg and then the other, but would you be able to explain how to use the leg muscles? Not only how each fiber flexes and pulls together, but how to make them flex? Thor said that tracing for him was simply asking the Aether to take him to his destination. When I commented that he made the Aether sound like it was sentient, he said that in a way, it was.

Every time someone worked with it, they left some of their energy behind. So, the Aether wasn't a single consciousness, but a collection of little parts from many minds. I admit that kind of creeped me out. Traveling through bits and pieces of other people's minds just sounded icky to me, but Thor insisted that it was an untapped resource. If someone could find a way to not only trace through it, or use it to manifest spells, but to simply sort through the knowledge stored there, they would have access to amazing amounts of information. Unfortunately, or maybe fortunately, no one's been able to master that ability yet.

Either way, I was still left unable to figure out how to trace to anywhere on the globe without limitations.

I looked at it as the difference between jumping up in a straight line and pole vaulting. The Aether was sandwiched between our worlds, so leaping through it and out the other side was more or less a straight shot. Tracing without exiting, but instead, turning around and coming back, was a curve. A completely different equation. The question was; could I make the curve now?

It was food for thought. An even bigger question was; did I have the nerve to test it? If something went wrong, I could be stuck in the Aether. Basically floating around in magic till I died of

starvation. Or worse, living on forever. I swallowed hard and sat back down. Trapped in the Aether forever. That threat alone would keep me from trying. Add to that, the fact that I'd been tracing with Thor and company for over a year, and still hadn't caught on. Attempting it on my own would be plain stupid. It wasn't worth the money I'd save on plane tickets and gas.

Mind made up on not tracing alone, I went in search of coffee and food. My stomach was rumbling hard. I found my purse abandoned in the hallway and picked it up with a smile. I must have been seriously plastered to drop my purse on the floor. Not that I was a huge neat freak; the purse was a Chloe, and I had spent way too much money on it for it to be dumped on the floor. Hell, for that kind of money, it should have its' own niche in the wall, with a spotlight to display it. I placed it carefully on the sofa, and nearly tripped over Nick, who'd been following me, chastising me in meows for my base behavior.

“Hey,” I defended myself, “at least I didn't bring anyone home.”

Then I noticed a handful of paper scraps spilling out the top of my purse. What in the world? I went over to investigate, with Nick following closely on my heels. They turned out to be phone numbers. Lots of phone numbers with names written above them. I groaned as it all came back to me. Drinks thrust into my hand followed by phone numbers, drunken moves on the dance floor, ending in more papers being tucked into my bra. The worse part was, I'd encouraged it all. I had enjoyed every minute of it.

“Oh, wow.” I gathered them all up and took them to the kitchen garbage can. “I'm not calling them,” I said to Nick's accusing glare.

Nick stuck his tail in the air, obviously unsatisfied with my answer until I filled his dish with food. Then happy purring ensued, and I was once again in his good graces. I laughed over the fickleness of felines as I made coffee and pondered my breakfast

options while simultaneously trying to block out the rest of the night. It didn't work. Along with my new powers of recuperation, came a great memory.

What really stuck out though, wasn't all those sweet country boys. It was my dance with Blue. I guess I'd known we'd eventually come to this. The attraction between us had been enough to tempt me, even when he was my enemy and a fucking psychopath. Now that he was a changed man, and I was a free woman, it was nearly impossible to resist. What really confused me, though, was how I *wanted* to resist, and it had nothing to do with timing. It wasn't because I was fresh out of a break-up. I just knew that Blue wasn't for me.

I knew we'd be hot together. Literally hot, since heat was part of Blue's magic, him being an Aztec god of the sun and all. We'd be amazing in bed. I'd already had a hell of an experience with him in a shared dream, back when he was still my arch nemesis. It made me shiver every time I thought about it–now that I could think about it without being furious. Blue was incredibly sexy, intelligent, refined, and occasionally quite funny. Why then, did I not want to leap into his bed?

I had no freaking idea.

A knock on my door interrupted my confused thoughts. I answered it after peeking out the window and confirming it wasn't someone who wanted to kill me. No, not paranoia, just common sense.

"Ms. Vivian Lavine?" A disembodied voice wafted through a huge floral arrangement, along with the scent of narcissus.

"It's Vervain." I nearly groaned at the common mistake.

"Huh?" The vase lowered so I could see a pimply-faced blond boy.

"My name is Vervain, like the herb."

"An herb?" That seemed to peak his interest.

"No, you can't smoke it." I grimaced and his face fell.

"Oh, like a spice then?"

"No." I sighed. "Just a plant."

Why my Mom had to name me after a magical plant which very few normal people even knew existed, was a puzzle I'd been pondering for most of my life. I mean, yeah, vervain was a powerful herb, but the only people who knew that were fellow witches. Oh, and gods. That was a plus to joining the god world. No one ever screwed up my name.

"Uh, okay." The boy was obviously too young to process the workings of a female mind. "These are for you." He thrust the flowers at me, and I took them, nearly staggering under the weight. "I need a signature."

"Okay, hold on," I huffed as I deposited the arrangement on the low Moroccan table in my living room. It looked pretty good there.

I grabbed some cash as I went back over to the kid, and his face brightened out of his confusion when I handed him the tip.

"Thanks!" He took back his clipboard and nodded to me. "Have a good day Ms. Vervain."

"Thank you." I almost tipped him more just for remembering the correct name. "You too."

I closed the door and eyed the blooming monstrosity. I was almost positive there would be a name on its card to match one of the scraps of paper I'd just thrown away.

"I need coffee for this."

I grabbed a mug of steaming salvation and sat down in

front of the flowers. There was a little white card tucked in among the dark purple irises and narcissus. What an unusual selection. I liked that, it showed a certain amount of creativity. Maybe I'd have to give the country boy a chance after all. I plucked the card from its little pitchfork holder, and prepared myself for what it probably said.

"What the . . . ?" I plopped back against the multitude of cushions on my low sofa and re-read the card.

I know it's barely been a week.

But you know it's your heart that I seek.

As soon as you're ready, I'll be here.

As long as it takes, a day or a year.

Give us a chance and you will see.

Just how amazing we can be.

Finn

"Wow." I blinked. "That was *so* not what I was expecting. Who knew Finn could be so cheesy?" I looked over at Nick, who stopped his almost OCD fur-cleaning to look back at me. His tongue was stuck halfway out of his mouth due to the interruption, and I laughed. "My sentiments exactly."

Chapter Twenty-Four

“So, what are you gonna do?” Samantha peered in morbid fascination at Finn's ridiculously large floral arrangement, sitting on the table between us.

“I have no idea.” I let my chin fall into my cupped palm.

“What did he say when you told him you didn't think you'd make a good match?”

“He said it was the heartache talking”–I sighed–“and that I'd change my mind after I had time to heal.”

“Crap.” She frowned.

“Exactly.” I shrugged. “What can I say to that? Or rather, what can I say that won't crush him like a bug?”

“Why worry about it?” Sam narrowed her eyes on the blooms. “Men never give us that kind of consideration.”

“Baby girl.” I snapped my fingers in front of her distracted gaze. “You've been around the wrong kind of man. There's a whole world of good guys out there, you just have to wade through the bastards to reach them. They're like little islands of goodness amid a sea of stupidity.”

It occurred to me that her opinion had been very close to my recent views on men. I guess it was standard operating procedure for us women to go through the *I hate men* phase after a break-up. Must be part of the healing process, but I think seeing her so bitter was helping me to heal even more than being bitter myself. It showed me how silly I was being and forced me to be rational once more. I could feel my cynicism easing back a bit.

"Maybe you're right." She sighed. "So why am I drowning in the sea?"

"Because he's really good in bed?" I shrugged. "It's called oxytocin; a hormone that's released during orgasm. It makes you bond with your partner, think about them, obsess about them. Basically, it makes us insane."

"Oxytocin? Are you telling me this is all chemical?"

"Partly, not all." I winked. "Don't worry, it'll fade in about a week. That's why they say nothing gets you over the last like getting under the next. The jerk just knows how to make you feel good, and unfortunately, women forgive a lot for that."

"Yeah." She laughed. "That's probably it. Though Kurt was pretty damn good too."

"Kurt, eh?" I waggled my brows. "Is that the blond you left with the other night?"

"That's him," she confirmed. "He's a jeweler."

"Oh, I like him already." I grinned. "You're practically guaranteed good presents."

"Who cares about diamonds, when he can kiss like that." She grinned back.

"So what's the problem?"

"The problem is"–the grin disappeared–"I keep seeing UnnúlfR's face when Kurt stops the kissing."

"Ah."

"Yeah." She sank back into the sofa. "What do I do, Rouva?"

"Well, first you stop calling me Rouva." I took a sip of my

soda. “We could always rearrange UnnúlfR's face.”

She grimaced.

“No? Fine,” I huffed as if I were extremely disappointed. “Then there's only one thing you need”–I smiled wickedly–“revenge.”

“Revenge?”

“He broke your heart, right?”

“Right.”

“So, let's see what we can break,” I suggested. “Starting with that precious ego of his. Do you think Kurt could come out tonight?”

“Oh, yeah.” Sam was beginning to understand.

Chapter Twenty-Five

Samantha was right on time, walking in looking gorgeous, with her long, dark hair in a pin straight curtain down her back. Kurt had ditched his cowboy duds for slacks and a dress shirt, open at the collar. The white shirt showed off his tan and his shoulder-length, blond locks made him look more professional surfer than professional jeweler. He was eye candy, top of the line–we're talking Godiva.

I smiled gleefully as I watched UnnúlfR glance over and then do a double take. He looked like a cartoon, his jaw practically scraping the floor, when Sam walked by without even a single look in his direction. Her eyes were all for her date, and then for me when she located me up in the VIP section. I smiled and waved her up, the Froekn bouncer at the bottom of the stairs gave her wide-eyes as they passed him.

"You're stunning," I said as they approached, and then I stood to give her a hug. I whispered quickly, "He's dying, you're absolutely killing him."

"Thanks." Her smile went up ten notches. "You remember Kurt?"

"Of course, how are you, Kurt?"

"Great, thank you." He looked over at Sam, like his state of well-being should have been obvious to me, given the gorgeousness of his date. "This place is amazing, thanks for the invite."

"Anytime." I sat back down on my little "hill". "Want something to drink? To eat?"

“I'd love a Jack and Coke.” he took a seat on the hill across from mine. A flat-topped boulder/table crouched between us.

I waved at one of the waitresses hovering around the VIP level.

“Hey, Jess.” I smiled at her shocked expression when she took in Sam's human date. “Could you bring us a Jack and Coke, a Long Island, and . . .” I waved to Sam.

“Oh, uh, could I get a Long Island too, please, Jess.”

“No prob.” Jess's face started to clear and then brighten.

Jess looked the way I imagine I had, the first time I walked into a Sephora; as if a whole new world had just opened up to me. I think dating humans was about to catch on with the Froekn.

Jess rushed off with a new bounce in her step. I felt like jumping up on the railing and shouting; Fortune favors the brave! or Failure is impossible! *S*ome type of suffragette slogan. I settled for winking at Sam.

“Vervain.” Ull approached our group warily.

That uncertainty hurt my heart a little. He was my friend, and there was so much I wanted to erase between us. So much I wanted to say.

“Ull.” I got up and tried to sum up my feelings in case he was here to say goodbye. “It's so good to see you. I've missed you.”

Sam and her date were staring, but I didn't care. Pride was a non-issue for me when it came to friendships. He meant more to me than that. I held an arm out to him, and miracle of miracles, he took my hand and pulled me into a warm hug.

“I've missed you too, V.”

I settled into his arms, burying my face in his chest as I fought back tears. I didn't realize how much I might have lost when Thor told me we were through. To have Thor's step-son holding me, forgiving me for my part in his mother's death, was more than I'd thought I'd get. Was more than I thought I deserved, on some level.

"It's going to be alright, V," Ull whispered into my hair. "You're doing just fine."

"I know." I pulled back and smiled at him. "I just didn't consider that I might lose all of you when I lost him."

"You didn't." Ull squeezed my hand. "We're all still your friends. Nothing's changed there. We just thought we'd give you a little time to work things through."

"Thank you." I took a deep breath. "So, how about having a drink with your old friend?"

"Love to." Ull grinned and looked over at the couple. "Hey, Samantha, who's this?"

"This is Kurt." Sam waved at her man. "Kurt, this is Ull."

I could tell she was pleased that Ull had remembered her name, and inwardly I praised Ull for being the gentleman he was. They really didn't make 'em like that anymore. Ull shook Kurt's hand, and then he took the seat next to mine. Poor Jess returned just then, and we had to send her back down for Ull's drink, but I think Ull's appreciative smile made it all worthwhile to the newly liberated she-wolf.

"I'll be right back with that," she purred, and Ull grinned wider.

"I *really* like your club, V." Ull stared after the departing waitress.

“Easy, Tiger.” I pushed at his arm, and it was at that exact moment that UnnúlfR decided to join us.

Kurt had his arm around Sam, his eyes filled with adoration as he stared at her. Sam was staring back with sparkling confidence, her hand on his leg. I was so happy about Ull's presence that I didn't even notice Trevor's younger brother until he was right upon us, practically snarling.

“Rouva,” UnnúlfR gritted out the greeting.

“UnnúlfR.” I nodded. “How are you?”

“Well, thank you.” His tense stance made a mockery of his words. “Samantha, can I talk to you for a minute?”

Sam looked at me with wide eyes, and I tried to subtly reassure her with a tightening of my own and a slight nod. She firmed her lips and looked over at her date. Kurt was eyeing the newcomer carefully while feigning a nonchalance that I wanted to applaud. It was obvious there was something going on between Sam and UnnúlfR, but Kurt decided to play it cool. Smart man.

“I'm sorry, honey,” Sam imitated Jess's earlier purr to a T. “This is probably just business. I'll be right back.”

“No problem.” Kurt smiled and settled further back into his chair.

I could practically hear UnnúlfR's teeth grinding. He gestured stiffly to a more private nook behind a tree nearby. Sam swung her hair over her shoulder and preceded him to the spot. Once they were there, I wasn't able to pick up their conversation, but judging from Ull's expression, he could hear just fine with his super god senses.

“What?” I leaned over and whispered to Ull, giving the impression we were together, so Kurt wouldn't feel like we were talking about Sam.

“He's pissed,” Ull smiled sensuously at me, working with my ruse.

Ull and I had shared a light flirtation from the day we'd met, but it had never been serious, and I was certain it never would. Ull just loved women, all women, and he made no bones about it. Then his face went hard and he glanced back at the now-openly-arguing couple.

“You better get over there, Rouva.” Ull gave me a little push for good measure.

“Okay, okay.” I looked over to Kurt. “He's probably trying to get her to work extra shifts again. I better go regulate.”

Kurt nodded politely, but I could tell that he wasn't buying it. I hurried over to the escalating argument.

UnnúlfR raised a hand back and up.

“Whoa.” I held out a hand and stepped between them smoothly. “I know you weren't just about to hit her, right?” I glared at UnnúlfR until he backed down.

“No, I wouldn't.” He swallowed hard and looked away. “She's acting like a human whore.” He gestured angrily at Sam as he turned a fierce look on me.

“Excuse me?” I pointed a finger into his face. “You wanna re-word that statement?”

“She's Froekn,” UnnúlfR growled. “She belongs with another Froekn.”

“You sound like a white supremacist.” I looked him up and down with distaste. “Do you forget that your Rouva is human?”

“No, I don't forget.” He lowered his face to mine. “I *never* forget.”

"What you should never forget, is that this human kicked your ass." I got up in his face as much as was possible with our height difference. At least I was wearing heels. "And I have no problem with doing it again. I passed Fenrir's test; your king and your prince have both accepted me."

"My *Prince,*" he spat the word, "is allowing you to ridicule our culture by flagrantly abusing the First-Born. Drinking and dancing with other men right in front of him. You're a disgrace to the title of Rouva, a humiliation to the Froekn, and you make a mockery of the mate bond. Now, you have the nerve to wonder *why* I have a problem with you?"

I felt my jaw fall open, and UnnúlfR's face went smug when it became clear that his verbal barbs had hit their mark. I shook my head, completely baffled and at a loss for words. Was he right? Was I humiliating Trevor by doing what most women did after a break-up? All I did was have a few drinks, dance a little. Where was the harm?

I looked down to the lower level, where I could see Trevor talking to a bartender. He looked up immediately, as if I'd called his name out loud, and my heart clenched at the misery I saw in his face. It didn't matter how harmless my intentions had been. I *had* abused him. I should never have brought my post break-up blues here, where Trevor was trying to build a new life for the Froekn . . . for me.

I was being cruel in my total disregard for his feelings. How would I feel if our places were reversed? If I had to put on a brave face to my family as the man I was married to paraded other women before me? And to add salt on the wound, I had to admit that UnnúlfR was right. Boy, did that leave a sour taste in my mouth.

Trevor's expression changed as the full weight of what I'd done hit me. I don't know if he could feel it through our link, or if he was just reading my face, but he suddenly looked over at

UnnúlfR and scowled. Then he was at a dead run across the club, taking the stairs two at a time in his rush to reach me. Before I knew it, Trevor was there, gripping my upper arms and peering into my face.

UnnúlfR backed away, finally realizing that winning an argument doesn't always get you what you want.

"What is it?" Trevor followed my gaze to UnnúlfR. "What did you say to her?" He roared at his brother. "What have you done?"

"I told her the truth!" UnnúlfR yelled back. "I told her what we've all been thinking. What no one else had the balls to say."

"Curse you, UnnúlfR!" Trevor let go of me to face off with his brother. "This isn't your concern. She's my mate, not yours!"

"Is she?" UnnúlfR sneered. "She's sitting here with the Thunderer's son, not you, and she's teaching *my* woman to behave like a whore too."

Before either I or Sam could protest his harsh assessment, Trevor hit him. One minute UnnúlfR was standing, the next he was sliding down a wall with blood dripping from his mouth. UnnúlfR shook his head a little as his eyes began to glow, and then pushed himself to his feet to face off with Trevor.

"Enough!" I snarled, my wolf bitch raging to the surface and exploding from my throat on a wave of echoing sound.

The fighting wolves cringed, whimpering a little as they looked at me with sudden respect. I blinked, having no idea what had just happened or where that powerful voice had come from. I took a calming breath and felt my wolf simmer down enough that I could think straight.

"You deserved that. I will not tolerate disrespect to me or to any other Froekn. I am your Rouva. I won the title by claw and by

blood, so you would do well to remember that," I growled to UnnúlfR, and then held up a hand to stop him from saying anything. "But you also have some valid points."

I turned to Trevor and reached a hand out to his face. He went instantly into happy-puppy mode and smiled brightly as he held a hand over mine. I pulled his face down and kissed him gently on the lips. I felt his wolf right beneath the surface, nuzzling me back through Trevor's mouth. It was an odd sensation, but one I could get used to, and my wolf returned the gesture with surprised joy. I pulled away, surprised myself, when I realized I had tears in my eyes.

"I've been cruel," I whispered. "I may not know if I can be with you, but you don't deserve to have your face rubbed in it. I'm sorry, honey-eyes."

"You have nothing to apologize for." Trevor's hand was in my hair and his eyes were intensely earnest. "I built Moonshine for you. If a few drinks and some dancing are what you need to get over Thor, I'm okay with that. Do whatever you need to do. I'd rather have you do it here, where I know you'll be safe. The Froekn can't judge you, this situation is new to all of us. I, at least, have the certainty of the bond to guide me. You've been stumbling through it blind and half-bound. UnnúlfR forgets that. He speaks as a Froekn, unused to the way a human woman thinks. The only reason I even understand is because of what I feel through our bond, but I *do* understand, Vervain. This hasn't been easy on you either. You saved my life, and I've made you pay for it. It was unfair to drag you into my world like I did, but you walked in and faced down the Great Wolf himself for me. No matter what UnnúlfR may think, no matter what may or may not happen between us, I am *proud* to call you my mate. You're an amazing Rouva. Look at how you care for my people already. I can't ask for anything more."

I didn't know what to say. I was crying full out by the time he finished, and I was afraid I'd say something horrible to mess up

the moment. So, I just went into Trevor's arms and held him like he was the only solid thing left in my world.

I'd felt like no one understood me for so long; like I kept trying to do the right thing, but just ended up fucking things up worse every time. What he said changed everything. It's funny how far a little understanding can take you.

Our wolves met in between us with an almost audible sigh of relief. When they touched, I got a glimpse of what it would be like to truly be with Trevor, and I have to admit; if the movie was anything like the trailer, it would be a blockbuster.

"Forgive me, Rouva," UnnúlfR spoke stiffly as he stared at the ground near my feet. "I spoke out of anger and love for my brother."

"Forgiven," I said from the warm confines of Trevor's arms. "I understand your anger, and I'll do my best to remedy my part in it, but as far as Samantha goes; you don't get to speak to her like that. If Trevor can mate a human woman, there's no reason Samantha can't date a man. In all honesty, UnnúlfR, I don't think that's what has truly upset you. Maybe you should sit down and contemplate why the thought of Samantha with someone else bothers you so much."

"It's not . . . I don't . . . oh, whatever," UnnúlfR growled and turned away, trudging downstairs while he continued to mutter to himself.

"You okay, Samantha?" Trevor reached out a hand to her, and she flowed forward, rubbing her cheek against his hand.

I was suddenly glad for the cover the tree provided. I don't think we'd have been able to explain all of that to Kurt.

"I'm fine, First-Born," Sam said, "but I better get back to my date before he runs off."

“Enjoy your human.” Trevor stroked her silky hair as she walked by.

“Oh, I have every intention of doing just that.” She winked at Trevor and he laughed.

“What are you doing to my wolves, Minn Elska?” Trevor whispered down to me.

“Opening their eyes”–I tapped his nose–“and it seems they're returning the favor.”

Trevor gave in to one last snuggle before he escorted me back to our seats. Kurt was looking back and forth between Ull and Trevor, totally confused. Sam and Ull were both smiling.

“Hey, Trevor, what's up?” Ull lifted his drink in salute.

“Oh, just settling a family disagreement.” Trevor helped me into my seat and then sat next to me.

“Trevor's the other owner of Moonshine,” Sam said to her date. “Trevor, this is Kurt.”

“Hey there.” Trevor shook Kurt's hand.

“Nice to meet you.” Kurt finally gave up on being confused and just grinned through it.

“Do you think the others would come over to my place for movies and dinner tomorrow?” I asked Ull. “I'd love to see them.”

“That can probably be arranged.” Ull laughed. “I think Horus misses you the most. He's been even more annoying than usual.”

“He loves me.” I shrugged and smiled like it was a given.

Ull laughed louder.

"Loves me, loves me, loves me," I went on in a sing-song tone.

"Well, who wouldn't?" Trevor whispered down to me.

"I'd like for you to come as well." I peered up at Trevor.

His smile was radiant and a little mischievous.

"I'd like that too."

Chapter Twenty-Six

"Okay, the name of the game is Seven Card Stud." I dealt the cards, two down and one up in front of everyone.

"You are so hot when you talk like a Vegas dealer." Ull wagged his brows at me from across my dining table.

"I agree," Pan added.

"Are we flirting or playing poker?" I looked around the table.

"I vote for flirting." Trevor raised his hand.

"Very funny," I growled and then eyed Finn. "Put your hand down, Finn."

"What?" He grinned innocently. "I was just going to ask what the ante is?"

"It's a quarter." I sat back, happier than I'd been in days. I had all of my god friends around me again. Well, all but one.

"A quarter," Hades scoffed as he looked over at Persephone. "I got this, Bunny-Nose." He threw two quarters into the pot.

"I don't want you to 'get this'," she grabbed back one of the quarters, returned it to his pile, and threw out her own. "I want to play with my own money."

"Women are insane." Hades rolled his eyes, and the other men at the table nodded in commiseration.

"You just feel like that because you all think with your

penises." Persephone sniffed, and I choked on my root beer.

Trevor's hand pounded my back and then stayed there to rub lazy circles over my skin. I allowed it because it just felt so good, but after awhile I leaned forward and he took the hint. It wasn't that I didn't want Trevor. It was that I wanted him too much.

I was all mixed up about Thor and Trevor. I guess Blue and Finn should have factored into my thoughts as well, but I knew deep down that they weren't for me. It was Trevor. It felt like it had always been Trevor. The only problem was, I still loved Thor.

Even after all he'd done, I couldn't just flip a switch and hate him. I was seriously pissed off at him. I fantasized about him groveling to me, and then I would just laugh at him as I walked away. I wanted him to suffer like I was. But I didn't hate Thor. I couldn't. I just wasn't built like that.

I never understood it when people talked about great love turning into great hate. Real love doesn't turn into something else. It can be killed, but it can't be altered like that. At least, not for me.

If you hate someone you once loved, it's because they did something horrible to you. And if someone you thought loved you, does something horrible to you, then they really didn't love you in the first place, did they? That kind of realization can kill love. You cease to love them because you realize your love was one-sided, and it's difficult to continue to love someone who doesn't love you back. It has nothing to do with change, it's not a transformation. It's a death.

Maybe one of the reasons the love magic felt so at home with me was because I didn't kill love. I wouldn't murder my love for Thor just because he did something awful. When I love, it's for good. It's forever. I will always love Thor, and I will always miss him because even though I still loved him, I could never be *in* love with him again.

Thor had ruined our chance, and I had to accept that. I had

to accept that he hadn't loved me like I loved him. I think the hardest part of loving, is realizing that the only love you have control over is your own. You can't make the other person love you truly. All you can do is hope and believe in them, but then real love doesn't need to be reciprocated. Real love just is.

I glanced over at Trevor and had an epiphany. I wasn't scared that Trevor would do what Thor did. I wasn't worried about giving him my heart and having him not truly love me in return. I was scared that for the first time ever, I might have found someone who loved just as completely as I did. I was afraid because I knew that if I ever gave Trevor my heart, his would be mine just as entirely, and I wasn't sure if I was ready for that. Even in the midst of loving Thor, I knew our relationship would end eventually. There were too many complications for it to last.

When I looked at Trevor, though, all I saw was forever.

"Minn Elska?" Trevor was smiling at me with just a hint of concern.

"What?"

"Are you going to ante up?" Trevor lifted his brows and looked from me to the pile of coins in the center of the table.

"Oh, yeah." I threw a quarter in. "Sorry, I was a million miles away."

"Were you?" My Wolf Prince whispered with a knowing grin. "You felt a lot closer than that."

"Could you two stop playing footsie for ten seconds so we can play some poker?" Horus glared at us.

"Go ahead." I nodded to his cards. "You have the highest, you bet first."

I put on my poker face, and it wasn't to hide my hand.

Realizing why I was being careful with Trevor didn't change anything. In fact, it made me even more paranoid. It was just too soon after my break-up with Thor for me to be thinking straight concerning matters of the heart.

What if Trevor was just a rebound? What did I do if I was totally wrong and I didn't end up loving him? He'd still be bound to me, but he'd have memories of being with me to go along with it. Would memories be better than nothing, or worse? Like I said, I couldn't think straight when my heart was still healing. So, the decision would have to be put off for a little longer.

Most people prayed for reprieves, but not I. I liked action. A reprieve meant no action, which in turn meant I'd be sitting around stewing about what needed to be done. Over and over. I hated stewing; it was definitely something that should only be done by food. Besides, I didn't have anyone to pray to.

Chapter Twenty-Seven

Shopping was just what I needed. I was with Sephy and Samantha at Ala Moana, supposedly the largest outdoor mall in the world. They kept adding to it, so they must be constantly fighting for the distinction. We were in one of the newest additions, Nordstrom, which the mall had actually built an overpass to accommodate.

"I love this soup," I groaned over my tomato soup. We'd taken a break and were having lunch at the Nordstrom Café.

"This has been such a fun day." Sam grinned over her duck pizza. "Thanks for inviting me."

"We all needed this." I dunked my cheese toast happily.

I had stayed away from Moonshine ever since my fight with UnnúlfR. Not because of any bad feelings, but because I'd gone past the partying stage in my heart healing. I'd cried my eyes out–check. Toughened up and accepted things–check. Partied up and reaffirmed my attractiveness–check. Now, I was just trying to relax and get used to being alone again.

Sometimes the phantom pains of a relationship were the hardest to get rid of. Waking up in the middle of the night because something just didn't feel right, and realizing it's because no one's lying next to you. Turning to laugh with someone who wasn't there anymore. Buying more groceries than you need or buying something you'd never eat. All the little things you don't realize you do when you're part of a couple. People don't know how much they change to fit someone else into their life, until that person is gone.

So, now I was trying to readjust, and I was finally

beginning to feel like I was walking on solid ground again. As much as I tried to be this tough-as-nails Godhunter, I was a girl at heart, and I loved to go shopping. Being out with Sephy and Sam was therapy for me. For all of us, I realized as I looked at their shining faces.

"You look like you're having fun," Demeter's voice called the therapy session to a halt. We might be needing some professional therapy after this.

My stomach dropped to the floor. I was completely unarmed, thinking I'd be safe in the company of a werewolf and a goddess. Shit, I knew better than that. "Always be prepared" is a good motto, those boy scouts know what they're talking about. I looked over the table and discreetly palmed Sephy's steak knife.

"Mother." Persephone didn't look concerned, but then Demeter wouldn't hurt *her*. "What are you doing here?"

"You never return my calls." Demeter slid into the seat next to Persephone. "You've forced me to trail you like a miscreant."

"What do you want, Mom?"

Sam and I held our breaths as we watched mother and daughter face off. This could go bad quickly, and we were in a very public place. Was it wrong that I was more concerned about the possibility of being black-listed from Nordstrom than I was about the fight itself? I looked at my bowl of soup sadly. Was this the last bowl of tomato bisque that I'd be able to enjoy? Sigh.

"I want my daughter back."

"Well, I'm not coming back." Sephy lifted her chin. "This subject is closed. I'm done talking about it, and that's why I won't answer your calls. Now go away."

I gaped at Persephone. Visions of sending in covert

operatives, aka werewolves, to smuggle me out tomato soup, started to form in my head. Oh, but the shoes. I have to try on shoes. I couldn't just send someone else in to get them for me. Shit. Goodbye, Nordstrom. I will miss you, my friend.

“I understand that,” Demeter said reasonably. “I'm willing to accept your living arrangements. I'm willing to compromise. I miss you.”

I gaped more. I had to move my soup, so my chin wouldn't land in it. At least it wasn't going to be my last bowl. I distractedly ladled another spoonful into my mouth, since it was already open. Plus, drama like this was so much better with food.

“What?” Persephone was just as surprised.

“I miss you.” Demeter smiled, and it looked like she was really making an effort to appear genuine.

Did that mean she really was genuine and just hadn't had a lot of practice at it, or did that mean she was faking? Damn, I was utterly confused.

“Will you spare some time for your mother?”

“I have to think about it.” Persephone didn't seem too convinced either.

Demeter's eyes flashed for a second before she controlled herself.

“Okay.” Demeter patted Persephone's hand. “Call me when you're ready.” She got up gracefully, her cornflower blue suit still crisp even though she'd been sitting. She didn't even look at, or acknowledge, me and Sam as she left. It didn't matter. I couldn't have spoken anyway, my mouth was full of soup.

“Wow,” Sam said it for all of us. “Do you think she meant it?”

“Not for one second.” Sephy frowned and sighed. “Which means she's up to something.”

“Not to sound conceited”–I grinned–“but it's probably some horrifying plot to cause me more pain.” I laughed mirthlessly.

“What's so funny?” Sephy looked concerned for my sanity.

“It's just that I used to think that all of those people were so egotistical when they'd say 'Why is God punishing me?' I mean, how could one person be so important that a god would sit around trying to come up with ways to torture them?” I snorted. “Now here I am, faced with the reality of a goddess, who probably spends quite a bit of time sitting around, thinking of ways to torture me. Should I be flattered?”

“I won't let her hurt you.” Persephone took my hand.

“Thanks, Sephy.” I reached over and took Sam's hand too. “Look at us, we're the power of three.” I giggled. “Either that, or we're a bad joke.”

“Excuse me?” Sam pulled her hand back and acted affronted.

“You know,” I huffed, “a witch, a werewolf, and a goddess walk into a restaurant.”

We got our good mood back instantly, laughter chasing away the dread that Demeter's presence had brought. I was so relieved; I really didn't want my day spoiled. We hadn't even made it to Sephora yet.

Chapter Twenty-Eight

"So, I have to ask." Sam eyed me over her cappuccino.

We'd made it through Sephora, Dior, Juicy, and Victoria's Secret–where I'd bought a brand new bra and panty set, in the hopes that I'd soon be able to decide on who got to see it. I'd also bought some new lipstick because a new lipstick always seems to make things better, and a new perfume because a life change always required a new signature scent. I went with Clean's Provence, a nice fresh-start of a fragrance.

"Go ahead." I sipped my own coffee and seriously considered another Madeleine cookie.

"Why, by all that is good and holy, are you hesitating on jumping Trevor's bones?"

I sputtered and nearly spilled hot coffee everywhere.

"Yeah," Persephone agreed. "What she said."

"He's so hot." Sam sighed. "If he'd even once showed some interest in me, I wouldn't have looked twice at UnnúlfR. I would have done that boy anywhere and anytime he wanted."

"Here, here." Sephy nodded with a sultry smile.

"You're both sluts," I whispered in my *horrified schoolteacher* voice before I chuckled. "I know he's amazing, but so was Thor. I'd been alone for quite awhile before I got together with Thor, and it took me a long time to let him in. Once I did, I was gone. I loved him, and once I love someone, that's it, I love them for life."

There was a sudden clenching in my stomach, followed by

a shiver that had nothing to do with Thor. It was almost a premonition, a feeling that there was more for me. That my love for Thor was nothing compared to what I was soon going to feel for someone else. If I didn't know better, I'd say it wasn't a premonition at all, but a memory. I frowned. Not possible, I'd never loved anyone like I loved Thor. Maybe it was some strange side effect of housing the love magic. It could be the magic's memory or the magic's potential.

"Vervain?" Samantha tilted her head to look up into my face. "You okay?"

"Ah, yeah." I shook my head free of the temporary weirdness and smiled. "Sorry, fazed out for a second there."

"Yeah, that happens when I think about UnnúlfR sometimes." Sam grimaced. "Uh, Vervain, we have something to tell you."

"What is it?" I looked back and forth between her and Persephone's worried expressions.

"We weren't sure if we should tell you at all." Sephy bit her lip. "But I'd want to know, if it were me."

"Thor's been whoring around the God Realm," Sam blurted out and then hunched over a little with a horrified expression on her face.

"Excuse me?" My coffee had turned to lead inside my belly.

"She's right." Persephone sighed. "Thor's been dating lots of goddesses lately. I think he's actually settled on one, though; Epona. That's why I thought you should know. He's moved on, so it's okay for you to as well."

"Thanks." I smiled, even though it felt like my face was cracking. It's never fun to discover that you're easily replaced.

“You were right to tell me. I really appreciate it, guys.”

“I knew you'd want to know.” Sam nodded. “Oh, and I broke up with Kurt.”

“What? Why?” I tried to let go of my awkward feelings in light of her distress.

“It was fun, but it's really hard to be with a human.” Sam shrugged. “I guess there's a reason we all mate Froekn. We don't have to hide what we are or explain things to each other. I bit Kurt during sex, and he kinda freaked out on me.”

“Over a little love nip?” I looked at Sephy and she shrugged.

“It was more than a nip.” Sam blushed. “I just got a little carried away. Anyway, it made me realize that I didn't want to be with a human. On top of everything else, one day he's going to die, and I won't.”

My body went cold. There it was, my main issue with Thor. It wasn't an issue with Trevor, but only because he was bound to me and would die when I did. That in itself was an issue for me. Not only would all of my new friends outlive me, but I'd take Trevor down to the grave with me. Sam seemed to realize her mistake and put her coffee down to take my hand.

“I'm so sorry, Rouva.” She paled. “I didn't think. Forgive me.”

“Hey, don't go all 'Rouva' on me.” I squeezed her hand before letting it go. “You've just brought up a valid point, and I think it's good that you realized this before you got in too deep with Kurt. He served his purpose anyway; he made UnnúlfR jealous.”

“Yeah, I think he did.” Sam grinned. “ UnnúlfR's been calling me.”

“Really?” I brightened up. “What did he say and why haven't you mentioned this already?”

“I haven't answered.” She giggled. “Avoiding him has been so much fun, and I'm not really sure I want him anymore. After being with Kurt, I know how I want to be treated, and I don't think UnnúlfR is capable of treating me that way.”

“Wow.” I sat back. “Good for you. I wish I could figure out what I want so quickly.”

“You know what you want, Vervain.” Sephy put her hand on my shoulder. “You're just scared that you might get it.”

“I just have this feeling that as soon as I decide on Trevor, something earthshaking is going to happen in my life.” I frowned, trying to recapture the premonition.

“Yeah”–Sam grinned–“*sex* with Trevor.”

Chapter Twenty-Nine

"This show is ridiculous." Trevor glared at the TV.

We were watching *Glee* in my living room, the cabinet doors of my antique, Moroccan armoire were pulled back so the TV was visible. Trevor sat beside me, an arm thrown over the back of the couch behind me, as I snuggled into his side. We were trying a night alone together, and so far it had gone well. I sank right into a feeling of comfort with him. There was a Vervain shaped dip in his side, almost as if he'd been made to cuddle me.

Thor had always been a little too large. Too large to snuggle with well. Too large for my bed. Too large for my life. Trevor fit just right. I smiled as I rubbed my cheek against his crisp cotton shirt. Nick was curled up against Trevor's other side; my cat taking to my wolf like they were litter mates. It was so perfect, it was scary.

"I love the ridiculousness of it." I laughed as Puck was thrown into a dumpster by the jocks who used to be his friends, just as he'd done previously to the geeky members of the glee club.

"I guess it's amusing." He chuckled a little.

"You don't understand because you've never had to go through high school." I popped some Pirate Booty cheese puffs in my mouth. "And if you had, you'd probably be one of the popular jocks."

"I resent that assessment." Trevor moved his chest so that it jostled my face. "I could have been a theater geek."

"Are you seriously arguing with me over being popular, *Wolf Prince*?" I sat up and raised an eyebrow at him.

“Things weren't always as they are now.” He turned a little serious and a little sad.

I frowned. I didn't like sad Trevor.

“I know about how your father lived.” I thought about what I'd seen in Fenrir. “Are you saying you lived it with him?”

“They didn't stop hunting Fenrir until we established a power base.” Trevor nodded. “It wasn't until the second generation of Froekn was born that we were strong enough to stay in one place. For many years, life consisted of constant hiding and fighting. I remember being afraid for most of my childhood. Then one day, we were an army, and the fear was gone. It was incredible. All of us from the first generation swore that we'd never live in fear again.”

“You are *so* not the man I thought you were,” I whispered in awe.

“Who did you think I was?” He smiled his lopsided grin and tucked some hair behind my ear.

“I don't know.” I felt like I'd been so wrapped up in myself, I hadn't noticed anything beneath Trevor's surface. I had a part of his soul bonded to mine. I should have known. I should have seen that he was more than the frivolous prince who just bought a club to please his mate. “I guess I just didn't think about it. I didn't see beyond the now, didn't consider that you had a past that had shaped you.”

“Everyone has a past, Vervain.” Trevor so rarely used my given name, and it seemed even more intimate when paired with the intense look in his eyes.

“Not like yours.” I was amazed.

To practically come out of the womb fighting for your life. To never have the security of home. To never have a mother's love.

That he had taken such obstacles and used them to become this healthy, happy man was mind-blowing. The strength of spirit it would take, the perseverance and determination. The Froekn's love of life and luxury all made sense now. I'd revel in it too if I'd been denied it for so long.

"Or yours," he whispered, and it finally occurred to me what he was talking about, what past he was urging me to let go of.

"Wait." I was stalling, but something was bugging me. "How did you get a second generation of Froekn without mating outside the family?"

"We mated *inside* the family." He smiled at my horrified look. "They were all from different mothers, raised together on the run. It's not as disturbing as you may think. When you share such a traumatic life with someone, you can't help but bond with them."

"So, the first Bindings were made between brothers and sisters?" I still couldn't get past it. I thought of my half-brother, TJ, and almost threw up a little in my mouth.

"It was a long time ago, between savage wolves on the run." Trevor looked disappointed that I couldn't understand. "We found comfort where we could, and magic happened. The Binding was created and our pairings became pure."

"I'm sorry." I took the hand that he'd let fall to his leg. "I have no right to judge. I'm looking at it from a modern perspective."

"I never found my mate." He smiled a little at our joined hands. "Father just accepted that it wasn't for me, but you're right. Some part of me couldn't accept a sister for a lover, even a half-sister. Then the years passed by, and more generations were born, but I still couldn't find a wolf who was right for me. I suppose I always knew my mate would be different; special."

"I'm glad you waited." And I was. The wolf inside me was

rejoicing, and I was surprised to realize that the rest of me agreed with her. Even my Nahual.

I had every chance to turn away as Trevor slowly lowered his face to mine, but I didn't. I didn't want to, and with the first touch of his lips, I knew I'd never turn away from his kisses. My whole body reacted to the slight pressure on my mouth. A delicious shiver rolled through me, sending my hands jolting to his shoulders. Trevor groaned and deepened the kiss.

He tasted like the ginger ale he'd been drinking, sweet and sharp, but beneath it, he tasted rich. Trevor tasted like full moon magic; bright and tempting with its secret knowledge. A whisper of satisfaction within grasp; of the fulfillment reached at the end of a ritual. As a witch, the call of magic wasn't new to me, but it was impossible to resist in Trevor. It bowed my back, my body curving into his automatically, and pulled sounds from my throat that I'd never heard before.

Trevor's hands roamed over me, pulling me further into his lap, but he kept them in respectable places. There was no push from him, no feeling of anxiety that I might have to pull away to slow him down. He just kissed me thoroughly, slowly, as if he savored every second, and then he gently pulled away and put his forehead to mine. We were both breathing heavily, so it took a moment for him to speak.

"I know you need time, Minn Elska," he whispered, "but I can't hold back much longer if you keep kissing me like that."

"Sorry." I leaned away, but I was pretty sure the smile on my face belied my words.

Sure enough, Trevor laughed and pulled me back to snuggle against him again. Poor Nick must have run off during the make out session because he was nowhere to be found.

"Don't ever apologize to me again for something so incredible." Trevor's hand was stroking my hair and it felt like

something we'd done together all of our lives. I'd never felt so comfortable, so quickly, with anyone.

"Deal," I said into his chest.

"Now, where were we?" He waved at the screen that had turned to blue after the DVD had run to its end. "You wanna watch another episode?"

"I wouldn't dream of torturing you like that." I angled my head up so I could see him. "How about you pick a movie?"

"Okay." Trevor reached over and picked up my movie list folder. "I have to admit, I've never seen anyone with so many movies that they had to make a list just so they'd know where they all were."

"It also makes it easier for guests." I stuck my tongue out at him.

"Don't point that thing at me unless you intend to use it, Godhunter," he growled playfully and nipped at my lips.

I laughed, free and happy, completely unburdened of the pain I'd been shouldering since Thor left me. It was the turning point, the moment when everything changed again for the better. The moment I'd been idiotically dreading. What was wrong with me?

The girls were right, I should have leapt into Trevor's arms, or at least not protested so much. Maybe I'd been one of those females who was only happy when I was miserable. Who knows? It didn't matter because I was a changed woman. One kiss and my Wolf Prince had woke his Sleeping Godhunter.

"How about *Underworld*?"

"Seriously?" I laughed. "You want to watch a werewolf movie?"

"Hello? I love werewolf movies. They're hilarious." Trevor got up to find the folder *Underworld* was in. It was somewhere among the numbered assortment next to the TV. "Besides, it's got vampires in it too."

"And a hot babe." I smirked as he put the DVD in.

"What would I do with another hot babe?" Trevor tucked me in beside him as he sat back down.

"Oh, you're good," I huffed.

"You have no idea," he quipped back.

"I think I might," I whispered as the movie began.

Chapter Thirty

“I for one, think it's about time you gave into that hottie.” Tristan took a sip of his obnoxiously blue drink.

We were having a late night breakfast at Denny's, one of the few places you could get biscuits and gravy in Hawaii, and the only place you could get it at 1 AM. I smiled at Tryst over my own dish of pancake puppy sundae, imagining places on Trevor I'd like to lick hot fudge off of.

It was getting bad. Trevor was taking things slow for me, and I was mostly in agreement, but it was also driving me crazy. Part of me acknowledged it had only been a month since Thor and I had broken up, but the rest of me didn't care. I wanted Trevor so bad, I was having to substitute with ice cream and fantasies.

“I agree.” Jackson nodded. “Who cares about how long it's been since Thor. That boy loves you, go for it.”

“I didn't realize you guys were on Team Trevor.” I laughed. “You barely know him. How could you possibly know he loves me?”

“Is she kidding?” Tristan made a face at Jackson.

“How much of those horrible post-break-up days do you remember?” Jackson asked carefully.

“Very little.” I thought back to it and got some flashes, but most of the time I just remembered lying in bed.

“Do you remember us waking you up?” Tristan lifted an impeccably dyed, red eyebrow.

“Of course.” I snorted. “It was shortly after that, that I had

to take back all of my emotions from Trevor."

"Right." Jackson looked thoughtful for a minute. "So, you know that he took the pain from you. You realize that he'd been feeling that pain for you, so you wouldn't have to?"

"Oh." I'd known that Trevor had taken my pain, and had mistakenly taken every other emotion as well, but I hadn't realized what that really meant. I hadn't realized that the pain had gone to him instead, almost as if he'd been siphoning it away from me.

"Yeah," Jackson said. "Do you know how long you were out?"

"Three days, right?" I had a hazy memory of waking up and talking to Trevor the first day. "Did Trevor come by the first morning? Is that when he took my pain?"

"Honey, he didn't just come by." Tristan looked astounded over my ignorance. "He *stayed*. We found him camped out on your doorstep when we got there. Something about telling you that he wouldn't leave until you let him in."

"Holy shit," I breathed the word out as it all sank in. "I remember now. I didn't care. I was so mad at everything. He sat out there for three days? How is that even possible? What about food? Water?"

"I'm assuming he drank from your hose." Jackson shrugged. "I don't know, maybe he left for short spans to eat, but I don't think so, Miss V. He looked bad when we got there."

"Between the pain he was taking from you, and the lack of sustenance, he looked real bad." Tristan grimaced, " Kinda smelled bad too."

"Tristan!" Jackson snapped.

"Well, he did." Tryst made a snarky face.

“He sat there for three days,” I whispered again.

I'd had some suspicions over Trevor taking my emotions. I'd even been a little angry about it. I'd had no idea, yet again, what kind of man Trevor really was.

“Yeah,” Jackson said gently. “Now, can you see why we're so sure? I don't even need to touch you to know that this one's a keeper. No premonition required.”

“I gotta go.” I stood up and pulled some money out of my wallet.

The boys just shushed me away.

“Just go, honey.” Tristan laughed. “Go put a big grin on that boy's face.”

“I'll do my best.” I ran for my car.

I drove home filled with thoughts of Trevor. What kind of man camped out on your porch for three days because he knew you were in pain over *another* man? What kind of love was that? The love magic rose inside me, twirling around the wolf.

“True love,” whispered the rushing flock of butterflies, and I knew.

This wasn't the simpering true love of Hallmark cards and chick flicks. This was the pure, unrefined source. Love unbound, unlimited by circumstance or conditions. It existed whether you wanted it or not. An unfailing, never ending, rush of raw emotion with a single thought, a single focus: to make the object of its affection happy.

All Trevor had wanted, from the day we were bound together, was to see me happy. He was content when Thor was good to me. Yes, there had been an attraction between us, an underlining craving that I saw sometimes in his eyes, but Trevor

accepted my relationship with Thor. He accepted whatever I needed him to accept because he loved me.

I pulled into my driveway finally and nearly broke my ankle in my rush to get out of the car. Inside, the lights were already on, and I smiled, knowing that Trevor was there. We'd had dinner and watched a movie earlier. He had been passed out on the couch when the boys called. So, I had left him a note telling him he was welcome to stay and that I'd be back soon.

I opened the front door carefully.

Sure enough, Trevor was curled up with Nick, asleep on the long sofa. The TV was still talking softly to him. I locked the door and turned off the TV before turning to study my wolf.

He loved Nick, and I thought that was hilarious. You know, the whole dog and cat thing. I just assumed werewolves wouldn't get along well with kitties. I was wrong again. That seemed to be a constant theme, me being wrong about Trevor.

Trevor's hair curled down around his neck as he slept, clinging to the pillow and shining like a pelt. I had tried to deny my attraction to Trevor for so long that ignoring his good looks had become a habit. I had finally admitted that I wanted him, but I still hadn't really seen him. His beauty had become a part of the scenery, as his love had become a part of my home. Just another thing to take for granted.

As I looked at Trevor lying there, I felt the part of me I'd given to Thor come rushing back, its violent return shaking the cobwebs from my eyes. My breath caught as I saw Trevor's striking face clearly for the first time. I followed the strong line of his jaw, admiring the dramatic angles. It was clean shaven, and I knew he'd freshened up for me. His thick lashes swept down over sculpted cheeks, tangling in a curl that had fallen over his forehead. The half-light bathed his skin, turning it into antique gold. Liquid metal stretched over a wealth of muscles, earned not

from a gym, but from living life to the fullest.

Everything Trevor did was filled with joy, and it shone throughout his body. It showed in the thick arms he used to hold me, the wide shoulders he shrugged off sorrow with, the corded legs he danced on, and the faint lines of laughter around his eyes. He was love, and light, and everything that made life meaningful. Why had I fought this?

I knelt beside him as his love washed over me. Even asleep, it flowed from him to me. It was partly the Binding, but I knew then that it wasn't entirely magic. It was Trevor, VèulfR, my Sacred Wolf, and I loved him. I wasn't afraid anymore, and I was done waiting. I was done fighting. I was done taking things slow.

I brushed the curl off Trevor's face and ran my fingers back through his thick hair. It was so silky, more the texture of fur than hair, and I let myself take the time to fully enjoy it. I wouldn't let him stop me this time. I needed to warm myself with the fire inside him, the magic. I wanted to let it rage. I wanted to feel it spread and consume. I opened myself to him and felt it burn away my reservations, turn my past regrets into smoke and ashes. His eyes opened slowly, and he blinked at me, then smiled a sleepy, lopsided grin.

“Vervain.”

I loved the way he rolled my name over his tongue, almost growling it.

“Hey, baby.” I stared at him and let the wolf rise within me. She was already excited, her heart racing along with mine.

His lips parted, and he frowned a little. “There's something different about you.” He frowned deeper. “No, about *us*.”

“Yes.” I smiled gently and stood up.

Trevor's mouth dropped open a little further and his eyes

searched mine with guarded hope. Gently, he moved Nick to the sofa and stood up. He towered over me, but then he hunched down, so he could peer into my face.

"Please don't do this unless you're sure, Vervain." He swallowed hard, and the look in his eyes was so vulnerable, it tore at my heart. "If you use me to get over him, and then just move on, it will break me."

I hated myself a little then, for denying what was right in front of me.

"I'm sure, VèulfR."

Trevor groaned as his name left my lips, and then pulled me to his chest. His kiss was gentle strength, savagery softened by love. His lips were worshiping mine while his tongue conquered. It was such a wild mix of urgency and adoration, I was almost dizzy by the time he'd carried me to bed.

The dragons and phoenixes on my bed's walls waited anxiously for us. They seemed to dance back and forth, twining about each other in anticipation. The bed sheets were high-count cotton sateen in a brilliant sapphire. The comforter was matching blue velvet and the pillows were goose-down. From the back corners, two lights peered out, shining gently, illuminating the sensual stage for our performance.

There was only one way into the bed: from the opening at its foot, and Trevor sat me there before returning to our kiss. I felt him pull up the dress I was wearing, and I lifted my hips so he could get it over my head. He withdrew so that he could kick off his pants, and then he pulled his shirt off impatiently. When Trevor stood in his boxers, he stopped like he was suddenly aware of my lack of clothing.

He knelt before me. "You've no idea how badly I've wanted this." Trevor ran his palm lightly over me, from collar to belly, and I shivered. "How many nights I've dreamed of you just

this way." He looked up at me as he slid his hands up my back and then pulled my chest against his. "I love you, Lady Hunter. I love you more than the moon and the call of the night. I love you more than all of the Froekn, and may they forgive me, but I'd deny them for you. I'd turn my back on everything I am, if you asked it."

"I'll never ask that of you." I laid my lips on his gently and then pulled back. "I wouldn't want you to change, not ever. I love the Froekn as my own family, I love your father as my own father, and I love you, just as you are."

Trevor groaned and tightened his arms around me, teasing me with his tongue as he filled me with his love. I lay back into the softness of the bed and took him with me. He rolled to the side, pulling me up further onto the mattress. His hands were at my bra and then my panties. Soon, I lay nude beside him and felt no hesitation, only eagerness. I reached for him, but he stopped me.

"I need to see all of you, Vervain," he whispered. "I need to touch all of you."

He pulled me into the curve of his arm, rolling me onto my back as he remained on his side next to me. His hand hovered over my face, then gently traced the line of my cheek, down my neck, across my shoulder, and over my chest. He skimmed the tops of my breasts and I shivered, reaching for his hand and pressing it lower.

"Please, Minn Elska"–he kissed my forehead–"let me love you slowly this first time."

I whimpered, but he didn't laugh at my frustration, he kissed me, long and deep. His hands trailed over the tips of my breasts as we kissed; first one, then the other, and I writhed beneath him. He was barely touching me, and I was so wet with wanting, I thought I'd melt away.

He drew back and held my gaze with his honey-eyes. They started to glow with a fire I felt burn into me, sparking low and

then raging higher. A rumble of excitement vibrated through his chest and into mine, spreading along my nerves until they reached my core. The tingling built and my legs shook as I came a little. I looked at him with wide eyes.

"How did you do that?" I was half afraid and half enthralled.

"Our pleasure comes from every touch, not just the intimate ones." He smiled as he lowered his face to my breast.

Trevor stroked me, not with his tongue, but with his face. He rubbed his entire face over me, inhaling deeply, and then sighing hot breath over my skin. When he had touched every inch of my breasts, rubbing his lips across the overly sensitized nipples, he gave each peak a long lick of his tongue before breathing warm air over them. I weakly tried to sit up, to pull him to me, but he slid his body over mine and pushed both his hands up to press me down by the shoulders. I heard him growl low in his throat, and the wolf in me responded, going limp.

Trevor had always sweetly given in to my wishes. Not in a submissive way, but in an indulgent, caring way. To have him take control was surprising and surprisingly exciting. I couldn't stop shaking, just a continuous light tremble that seemed more of a vibration. Almost like my body reached for him on every level, including sound. My body was singing to his.

He slid down me, rubbing his face back and forth, everywhere he went. Trevor left no part untouched, no skin unscented or unexplored. He stroked my arms, holding them to his chest as he splayed my fingers over his face and tasted the tips of each. He took each of my legs, lifting them up to stroke his face along them, drawing up to my toes and pressing his whole body against me as he went. Trevor even rubbed his cheek into the arch of my foot. I'd never felt more beautiful or more loved.

When he finished with my legs, Trevor turned me over and

started all over again at my shoulders, pressing his body against mine as he slid down my back, so I could feel him hard and ready. When he got down to the curves of my ass, he lifted my hips as he rubbed against me, and I got to my knees eagerly. Reaching up my sides, he drew his hands down my waist, then my hips, before he slid them between my legs and gently nudged me apart. He scooped my thighs up from beneath, lifting them so they rested on his shoulders. I moaned, the odd position making me feel vulnerable and unsure whether I liked the fact that I liked it so much.

Trevor rubbed his face against me and I came, screaming and shaking. He held me, with his face pressed against me tenderly, until I subsided, then he gave me a long, thorough lick, and I came again. By the time he'd lapped and bit, licked and swirled, thrust and rubbed me to his satisfaction, I was on an endless roller coaster of pleasure. I barely realized that he'd lowered me down until he thrust himself deep, and my head flew back in ecstasy.

Trevor was done being slow and gentle. He gripped my hips and bucked into me wildly. I reached out and grabbed the wall of the bed to brace myself. I felt him wrap the length of my hair around his fist and pull hard enough to get me to lift my head. He curled his other arm around my waist and pulled me up, claiming a breast to rub and knead. I cried out over and over as he drove deep. Then he let me go, pushing me back down as he followed me. He flung my hair to the side, and I felt his teeth close over my neck, right where Thor's mark was.

Trevor bit me hard, not enough to break the skin, but enough that I knew there would be teeth marks left behind, and I screamed with the combined pain and pleasure. He didn't let go, didn't even lessen the pressure, but I didn't want him to. I felt his tongue lick me as he bit, then he pressed down with his face and pushed me into the bed. I lay trapped beneath him as he covered and consumed me, his breath panting fast in my ear. With one last

hard thrust, he came, finally releasing my neck, to howl savagely before dropping languidly over me.

I couldn't move. My body was racked with aftershocks on the level of full orgasms. I just kept riding each wave of pleasure until they finally drifted away like the tide, and left me sated on the shore. Trevor's body was shaking as well when he rolled over and pulled me with him. He curved me into his side, and I felt my heartbeat slow to match his, my chest rise and fall as his did. He stroked my back gently as we recovered. My breathing regulated, and I found enough energy to look up at Trevor and smile.

"Baby," I breathed the word, it was all I could manage.

He opened his eyes, and they were back to his normal honey-amber. "Yes, Minn Elska?"

"What the hell was that?" I smiled broadly, and he chuckled. The vibration of it rolled through his chest t jostled my face.

"That was the mating of a bonded couple." He stroked my hair back and stared at me. In his eyes, I saw the same wonder I knew was in mine.

"You haven't done that before?" I gasped.

"Of course not." He frowned, but it was more in surprise than dismay. "You can only experience such pleasure with your mate. You haven't felt it before either, have you?" His eyes held a hint of concern.

I laughed and kissed him. "You brat, you know I haven't. Stop fishing for compliments."

Trevor pulled me completely on top of him and ran his fingers through the hair on both sides of my face. "I'm male," he purred, "I'll never tire of listening to you praise my prowess, but I'll also never tire of telling you how much pleasure you give me

back."

"Well, since it's such a fair trade." I rested my chin on his chest, and he lowered his eyes down to my face. "I guess I can manage a few compliments."

"I'll start." He slid his palm up my cheek and used it to press my face to his chest. "When you tremble, you send shivers through my body, and when you moan, it tingles along my skin. I love the way your flesh flushes pink, and the way you smell both sweet and spicy. The way you throw your hips against mine when I thrust into you, makes me want to howl and rage to the moon that you're mine at last, completely mine."

The trembling started in my chest with his first words. By the time he'd finished, I was shaking through another orgasm that left me breathless and weak. Trevor moaned and pulled me against him tighter.

"That's all the compliment I'll ever need, my Lady Hunter."

Chapter Thirty-One

"Where are the chips?" Finn's voice filtered out to the living room, muffled, as he rooted around in my cupboards.

"Above the fridge," Trevor said as he walked out of my bedroom, pulling on his shirt. His hair was sleep-tousled and he was rubbing his eyes. Cats weren't the only ones who liked to nap.

Everyone turned to stare at him. Brahma with a little smile and a lifted brow, Teharon with a tiny frown, Persephone with glee, Hades with calm acceptance, Mrs. E & Mr. T with concern, Pan with a *go figure* shake of his head, Horus with distaste (I was kinda glad to see it wasn't just me he gave that look to), and Ull just looked at Trevor in shock.

Finn came out of the kitchen to silence.

"What I miss?" Finn looked from the Squad, back to Trevor, and then over to me.

I was sitting on the floor, in front of the low Moroccan table, we occasionally used for card games.

"Uh," I cleared my throat, "I was about to tell you guys."

"You and Trevor?" Persephone reached over and hugged me. "How wonderful, I hope you'll be happy together."

Trevor sat down next to me and wrapped his arm around my shoulder. "Thanks, Sephy," he smiled at her.

"So, you're even using her nicknames now?" Finn threw the bag of chips on the kitchen table and crossed his arms.

"What of it, Swan Boy?" Trevor's voice had gone into its

werewolf rumble.

“It’s okay with me.” Persephone eyed the two men with confusion. “I like the name.”

“Swan Boy? You think that I'm a child, little puppy?” Finn stalked further into the living room, and Trevor stood to meet him.

“Enough.” I stood up as well and pushed Trevor back down. Okay, he let me push him back down. “Finn. Outside. Now.” I pointed at the backdoor and Finn's eyes widened, but he went. “Anyone else got a problem with me and Trevor?” I looked around the room and everyone shook their heads except for Ull. “Ull?” I went and stood before him. “Do I need to take you outside too?”

“No.” Ull looked at me with resignation in his eyes. “I’m just worried about Dad.”

“Your father has been dating every goddess who’ll have him,” I ground out.

Ull looked shocked, but he looked guilty as well.

“And you evidently knew about it,” I noted.

“I didn’t want to hurt you.” Ull sighed.

“How many of you knew?” I asked the lot of them.

Everyone except Persephone, Hades, and Trevor suddenly had somewhere else to look.

“And none of you thought that I might like to know? It didn’t occur to any of you that knowing my ex-boyfriend has moved on, might help me to move on as well?”

“He hasn’t moved on,” Teharon spoke softly, as he always did, but somehow it was even softer right then, gentler.

“What do you mean?” I narrowed my eyes on him. “I think dating half the female deities in existence constitutes as moving on.”

“Thor has never been a playboy,” Brahma took over for Teharon, who was looking a little lost. “It makes one wonder; why the sudden change?”

“Ugh.” I threw up my hands in the air. “Fine, you guys had your reasons, whatever. I can’t deal with this right now. I have to go find out what Finn’s problem is.”

As I walked out the backdoor I heard Horus mutter, “*I* know what Finn’s problem is . . . he’s an idiot.”

I shut the door behind me and sighed. Finn was at the small iron bench set beside the koi pond. I went over and sat next to him. He was staring at the shiny koi fish as they hovered on the bottom, sleeping and dreaming fishy dreams.

“So, what gives?” I leaned back and crossed my legs.

“What gives?” Finn shook his head as he eyed me with disgust. “Are you really that cruel or are you just oblivious?”

Shit. I was hoping this wasn’t going to be personal. I mean, I knew that Finn was interested in me, but I really didn’t think he’d been expecting anything to happen. I thought I'd made that clear when I talked with him about the flowers he sent. He’d made a few comments and some casual touching to test the waters, and during the whole of it, he never made my butterflies rise. My love magic just wasn't interested in Finn, which in turn, translated into me not being interested.

Besides, Finn was smokin’ hot. Any woman would have loved a chance at him. They had to be practically throwing themselves at his feet. I really didn’t think Finn would sit around waiting for me. He also knew Trevor was bound to me, and I couldn’t help being attracted to him back.

The thought made me frown and wonder how real the attraction was between us. How much of it was werewolf magic? No, I wasn't going to start questioning my relationship with Trevor. I wasn't going to fuck this one up.

"You don't have anything to say to that?" Finn brought me out of my musings.

"I don't know what to say, honestly." I closed my eyes for a second and sighed. "I think you're great, Finn. It just hasn't been the right timing for us."

"The right *timing*?" He turned on the bench to face me better. "You saved my life before you saved the wolf. Hell, he was trying to kill you!"

"Is that hell with one L or two?"

"What?" Finn looked like he was about to throttle me.

"Hel, the Viking goddess, or Hell, the place? Okay, not the time for jokes." I took his hand. "Trevor shared his magic with me. He bound himself to me forever, knowing at the time that he might never share my bed, and yet would never want to share anyone else's."

"So, he gets you because he played dirty?" Finn's beautiful face twisted in jealousy.

It made me uncomfortable, to say the least.

"He didn't play dirty." I counted to ten. "He played honorable, or whatever the opposite of playing dirty is. That's Trevor. Bonding to me wasn't some underhanded ruse of getting into my pants. He'll never be with another woman. He's sacrificed a lot, including his immortality. He has literally given up his life to be with me. The way he loves me is humbling and mind-boggling."

"You're in love with him already?"

I don't know what was worse, the anger I felt from Finn or the disbelief.

"Already?" I dropped his hand. "You make it sound as if I jumped from one man's bed to the next, throwing my heart like a trophy to the winner."

"Isn't that how it is?"

I slapped him, and it was hard enough that his face twisted and the sound of it echoed in my ears. "Snap out of it!"

Finn stared at me furiously.

"Not much of a Cher fan, huh?" I rolled my eyes as confusion muted his fury. "Go watch *Moonstruck* and work out your issues, Finn. I've enough of my own. I have so many issues, they're full subscriptions. I don't need yours as well."

"Vervain, I watched you with Thor, and I contented myself with your friendship." Finn took both of my hands and dropped to the ground in front of me. "I stood by while Thor seduced you into loving him and then betrayed your love. I waited for you to heal. I've been trying hard to be the friend you need when I really want to be so much more."

I tried to pull him back up to the bench, but he resisted.

"Finn, I find you attractive, real attractive, but my heart wants Trevor."

"Your heart is following your body's lead." Finn pulled on my hands urgently. "You don't really love him. You're attracted to him through magic and pity. Your heart is so big, Vervain. You can't bear to have him bound to you while you're with someone else."

I frowned, Finn was playing on my doubts, and I didn't like

that. Doubts were like family; you could insult your brother all you wanted, but if someone else said a single bad word about him, you'd punch them in the nose. Finn was bad mouthing my brother-doubts, and he was about to get a bloody nose.

"I don't fuck men out of pity." I stood up and Finn fell back into the grass. "I love Trevor, and I'm sorry things never went anywhere with us, but they didn't, they just didn't, and if you can't handle that, you need to stop coming around."

"Vervain, I'm sorry." He grabbed my ankle as I walked by, and I had to stop myself from shaking him off like he was garbage.

Finn wasn't garbage, he was my friend, and he'd stuck it out with me. He didn't deserve to be treated like that. I sighed and helped him up.

"No, Finn, I'm sorry. I just don't know how to handle all this attention. Growing up, I felt fat and stupid. One side of my family was all about looks. I have a Pageant Queen for an Aunt, and that side constantly made me feel like I needed to improve my appearance. The other half couldn't care less how I looked, as long as I was smart. 'Study more Vervain.' 'Have you decided what you're going to do with your life yet?' I never felt good enough for either of them, so I created a third option; I became an artist. You don't need brains *or* beauty to paint."

"How could anyone make you feel ugly or stupid?"

"They're my family. I love them and I trust their opinion." I sat back down on the bench heavily. "If I'm not good enough for them, how can I be good enough for anyone else?"

"You don't have to be good enough for them." Finn sat down next to me. "You just need to be good enough for *you,* and I think you are. I think you're happy with yourself, deep down."

"Yeah." I smiled and flicked his nose. "You're right. I am, and part of me knows my family pushed me out of love. They only

wanted me to be the best I could be, but another part of me is constantly whispering, 'He can't want you. You're not pretty enough, or thin enough, or smart enough for him,' and I look at you all and wonder if it's just some big joke. If one day you'll jump up and say 'Hah, we got you good, you should've seen your face, Vervain.' I have a hard enough time with normal men, but here I sit with gods, and they tell me they want me; *me,* Vervain Lavine, who didn't lose her virginity till she was eighteen. I just don't know how to handle you all."

He stared at me for a minute while he digested everything I'd just blurted out at him. Then he took a deep breath, nodded, and stood up.

"Let's go back inside." Finn reached down to help me up.

"We okay?" I searched his face.

"Yes." Finn led me to the back porch. "You're right; you have enough issues of your own, you don't need mine. I mean, eighteen? How could you not have had sex until you were eighteen?"

I laughed and slapped his shoulder, but I was relieved, and so was everyone else when they saw us walk in, hand in hand.

Chapter Thirty-Two

Half an hour later, The God Squad had left, I had showered, and was climbing into bed next to Trevor.

"Sweet dreams, Fur Face." I kissed his chest.

"Vervain, that's what you call Nick sometimes."

"Well, if the shoe fits." I grinned, waiting for the explosion . . . three, two, one–lift off.

"Take it back or you'll be kissing my furry ass." He rolled me over and held my hands above my head.

"Kiss *my* big, white ass." I stuck out my tongue and suddenly felt like Persephone. It made me giggle, which *so* didn't help.

"I'll *bite* your ass." Trevor rolled me over again, and I yipped as his teeth sank through my panties. I never wore anything but panties to bed. I just didn't see the point.

Trevor bit the edge of the panties and pulled them away as I bucked him off me. Then I jumped off the bed and ran. Looking over my shoulder, I caught the glint of excitement in his eyes. I slammed the bedroom door as he was getting slowly off the bed, a wicked smile on his face.

I ran for the door, grabbing his long leather coat as I went. The bedroom door slammed open, and the sound of padding feet echoed down the hallway. My heart started to beat faster, adrenaline pumping through my veins with muscle-quivering heat. I yanked open the front door and ran out, closing it with a soft click.

Let the wolf sniff me out, it would be half the fun.

I heard Trevor move about the house, searching for me, then he stopped suddenly, and I knew he was scenting me. I felt a shiver run down my spine, and I wrapped the coat tighter before I crept along the house toward the backyard. I froze for a moment, remembering the last time I'd tangled with a werewolf there. Maybe I could erase the bad memory with a good one.

I heard Trevor leave the house, and I looked around me in a panic. I wanted him to find me, I wanted him to catch me, but on some deep instinctive level, I also wanted to run and hide from the wolf. The beast was on the hunt, and the prey had to run, it was the law of nature.

I searched desperately for a hiding place. The high, thick mock orange bushes that fenced in my yard offered no options, but they did fill the air with the heady scent of orange blossoms. It added to the exotic smell of the night blooming jasmine which grew alongside my house. Maybe they could mask my own scent. Oh, who was I kidding? Trevor could find me in a sewer.

My backyard was wide, spacious, and open, with only a few fruit trees granting very little cover. I looked at the pond with its gurgling waterfall in the corner, and then the mango tree opposite it. Maybe I could hide behind the trunk.

I had just made it to my pathetic attempt at cover, when I heard a twig snap nearby. My heart was pounding so fast, it was taking extreme effort to keep my breathing quiet. I closed my eyes tight and tried to make myself as small as possible, but it really was pointless. Trevor knew exactly where I was.

I yelped when a large paw grabbed my arm and pulled me out into the moonlight. Trevor was magnificent in half-form, his sable fur shining and soft, his eyes glowing from the hunt. Instinctively, I pulled away, twisting my arm out of his grasp and attempting to run again. He growled low and stopped me with

ease, scooping me up around the waist. I had to swallow back a scream as I lashed out, kicking and pummeling him until he fell on me to hold me down.

I writhed, horrified that he was going to make love to me in his werewolf form, but also strangely aroused. He was Trevor, no matter what shape he took, and I loved him. The emotion overcame the physical reservations I had, and as he pressed against me, his fur stroked me seductively. It was so different from skin on skin. Instead of a slick slide, it was thousands of points of silk flowing over me, heightening every movement he made. I ran my leg up his side, delighting in the feel of him, and let out a small moan. His growl turned into a rumbling, desire-filled plea, and I met his eyes with my answer.

Trevor knocked the coat open as he took both of my wrists in one large paw and held them high over my head. The scent of spicy musk thickened, blocking out everything else. The world narrowed down to my wolf, hard yet silken above me, one hand holding me down as the other roamed roughly over my bared body. I looked down between us, my skin seeming to glow under the moonlight; a bright contrast to his darkness. A wild, rushing excitement ran through my veins when I saw him rising up hard and slick between my legs, still very much a man where it counted.

I tossed my head to the side, cool blades of grass cushioning my cheeks as Trevor's face lowered, his muzzle rubbing against my neck, scenting me, before his rough tongue stroked me up to the ear. His paw-like hand squeezed my breast, surprisingly gentle despite its claws, the pads of his fingers soft against my sensitive skin.

"We can stop," the gravel of Trevor's voice tickled my ear, lower and thicker from that lupine throat. His face was pressed so close to mine. "Just tell me to stop, Vervain, and I will."

"Stop," I whispered, and his body froze over me, "talking. Stop talking and fuck me, you beautiful wolf."

Trevor's control broke immediately. He was suddenly wild and wonderfully intense. My legs fell to the sides as he slid into me, grasping me tightly at the hip to keep me still. He was bigger in every way in this half form, and my body stretched around him with a slight twinge of pain that was soon lost to the onslaught of pleasure. He released my hands, and I immediately brought them to his shoulders, pulling him closer with fists full of fur.

He was so large. I gave up on trying to wrap my legs around him and planted them on the ground, giving me enough leverage to push back. Low, savage sounds were coming from his throat, quickening my pulse and the flow of heat between us. The feeling of his hard body slamming against me, cushioned by thick fur, was wickedly sensual and somehow perfectly natural. The pleasure surged up, slamming me into heaven, and I buried my face in his shoulder to muffle my screams.

With a small desperate sound, Trevor pulled out and flipped me over. He yanked the coat off me, and his paws cradled my hips as he drove into me savagely from behind. I could barely keep myself up on hands and knees, but I clenched my fists into the earth and held on. He went so deep, I cried out, and he growled once before latching onto my neck in his favorite spot. A bolt of fear shot through me as his teeth closed over my vulnerable neck, but then I was lost again to the pleasure that rode me as hard as he did.

I barely noticed his fangs lightly piercing my skin as his jaw tightened possessively; I was so overwhelmed by his dominance and the animal urges it was bringing out of me. I wanted nothing more than to be joined with Trevor forever, to feel him in me again and again, to know that life would be erotic and dangerous, but I'd always be safe with him. I'd always be loved.

With a hoarse cry, Trevor came, one last thrust driving me flat into the grass. I felt myself crest a second time, coming with him, and it was brilliantly wild; like a caged beast suddenly released. The first flight of joyous freedom that lets the soul shine

brightly. When the pleasure finally released us, he lay gently over me, shivering and twitching until he reached around me and turned me into him, taking us sideways so I could curl into the warmth of his chest.

Trevor wrapped himself around me as we shared delicious little aftershocks and gazed contentedly at the moon together. The geckos were singing in the trees, and I heard Nick stalking an insect through the bushes. I was happy as I'd never been before; the happy you get when everything is perfect and you know that no matter what happens, the perfection of that moment will last forever.

Chapter Thirty-Three

"They're called: The Dark Horses." Trevor had his arm casually slung over my shoulders as we watched the band play in a clearing between the trees, on the bottom floor of Moonshine. "What do you think?"

"I think they're great." I watched as the lead singer sauntered over to an enthralled woman who was leaning against a tree. She was probably having a hard time standing in front of such a buffet of beautiful men. "The Dark Horses, eh? Are they really horses?" I turned my attention back to Trevor suspiciously.

"I didn't think it would take you too long to figure it out." He chuckled. "Yes, they're Epona's boys."

"Epona?"

"The Goddess of Horses," Trevor explained. "The drummer is from her personal stable, if you know what I mean."

"Oh, that's nice, Trev." I grimaced. "Hey, isn't that the one Thor's dating?"

"The drummer?" He raised a brow over a twinkling eye. "I didn't think Thor swung that way."

"Stop it." I laughed. "You know I meant Epona."

"Yeah, they're dating, but don't hold it against her." He kissed my cheek. "I've known Pony a long time, and she's good people."

"Pony?"

"Well it fits, doesn't it?" He gave me his *Big Bad Wolf* grin.

“Goddess of Horses. Pony.” I shook my head. “I only wish I'd been the one to come up with it. You know how I love inventing nicknames.”

“I'm particularly fond of 'honey-eyes'.”

“So am I.” I waggled my brows at him, and he chuckled.

“I think they'll be a big draw.”

“I think you're right.” I looked the band over again, more carefully this time.

They had a rugged grace. Not lean exactly, but not as thickly muscled as most of the Froekn men were. They were sleek, like every edge had been softened just a bit to make them more aerodynamic. They were all brunettes, which fit their name, but the lead singer's hair was as black as Teharon's; that slick, Native American black that looked more like polished stone than hair. They were all gorgeous, I could see that even from the VIP balcony, but the most important thing was: they could play.

The music filling the club was dynamically powerful. A raging, thumping, call of the wild. It made you want to lift your arms, close your eyes, and just move. It didn't matter how you moved. It didn't matter who was watching or dancing with you. You just wanted to move. I was swaying a little in my seat.

“Okay, enough ogling.” Trevor turned my face to his. “You don't want to make a bonded werewolf jealous.”

“Thor!” I gasped.

“Then again, maybe you do.” Trevor frowned.

“No.” I turned his head toward the top of the stairs. “Thor's here.”

“Oh.” He frowned harder and stood up to greet my ex. “Thunderer.”

"Wolf Prince." Thor nodded as he strode forward.

My heart was pounding, my stomach churning. In my head, I'd run through scenes of finally seeing Thor again, over and over, but I really wasn't prepared for the sight of him. He looked amazing. Long red hair hanging wild around his shoulders, stern face set in chiseled lines, wide shoulders, thick legs, eyes that didn't know if they wanted to be green or blue. Oh, and he was the size of a small mountain. I had to look up an impossible distance when he finally stood before me. Thor ended up taking pity on me and sitting down on the hill-shaped couch across from us. Trevor sat as well, looking casual, but I could feel the tension zinging through the leg he pressed against mine.

"Would you like something to drink?" Trevor played the role of host automatically.

"No, thank you." Thor grimaced. "I'm sure I'm the last person either of you wants to see right now."

"Nah"–I shrugged–"you're a step above Demeter."

"Thanks," Thor made a surprised huff. "I . . ." He took a deep breath and hung his head for a moment. "I'd forgotten how your humor never fails you. Even in the worst circumstance, you can make a joke."

"I try." I smiled grimly. "What do you want, Thor?" Yay, my voice sounded hardcore, even to me.

"We need you with us, Vervain." Thor sighed. "I know there's bad blood between you and me, but it doesn't change the fact that we're both on the same side of this war. The rest of the team said that the only way you'd come back was if I asked you to. They said you wouldn't believe we could work together again unless you spoke to me first. So, I'm here to ask you to come back . . . to the Squad."

"Huh." I looked over at Trevor and he shrugged. "Well,

they were right. I wouldn't have thought we could work together again. I told you the day I left that I'd never forgive you, and I meant it."

"I don't expect your forgiveness." Thor's jaw clenched. "I'm not even asking for it, Vervain. I'm asking for you to put aside our differences so we can work together again. This is bigger than both of us. The war isn't going to end because our relationship did."

"I know that," I ground out.

"Look, I didn't come here to fight with you." He wiped a hand over his face, and for the first time, I noticed the dark circles beneath his eyes. "I want to fight *beside* you. You're an integral part of the team, and we need you. Especially now that we believe Blue is back in action."

"Wait, what?" I held out a hand as if I could physically stop the bad news. "Did you just say Blue?"

Trevor's hand was on my leg, and Thor was staring at it. Thor shook himself and looked up at me.

"The illegal aliens in Arizona are gathering in the Phoenix area." Thor looked grim.

It was a shame, Thor used to smile so much that I took pleasure in vexing him just so I could see his face change. It cut deep to know that I'd help put that seriousness there.

"That's not exactly watertight evidence of his guilt." I leaned back as Trevor put his arm around my shoulders. "They've been having problems with illegal immigrants for a while now. Why would you think that this is being instigated by a god, much less Blue in particular?"

"It's become more violent than the usual protests." Thor shook his head. "There have already been attacks from the Mexican population on non-Mexicans, and the Caucasian

population of Arizona is starting to retaliate. If we don't do something, it'll be a full-out race war. You know half the men in Arizona carry firearms."

"And the other half prefer knives. Then there are the women." I sighed. "So, it probably is a god. Why do you suspect Blue?"

"He's their god, Vervain." Thor looked at me like I was being deliberately obtuse. "Who else could lead them so effectively?"

"Okay, you've got a point, but he's not the only Aztec god." I thought about the dance we'd shared not so long ago. "I just don't think this is Blue's style."

"You mean, unlike trying to murder an innocent woman so he can bring down an oil company?" Thor's eyes started flashing with lightning, and Trevor leaned forward, growling in response to it.

"It's okay, Trevor." I touched his hand, and he calmed a little. "That was before I changed him, Thor, and you know it."

"So, you work your love juju on him and everything's all better?"

Wow, Thor was really bitter.

"It healed him." I sighed. "He's not the same man without all that rage. I never knew that his change bothered you."

"It doesn't," Thor huffed. "It just really looks like it's him, Vervain, and we need you with us on this."

"Alright."

"Alright?" Thor looked at me with shocked, wide eyes.

"Alright." I leaned forward and held out a hand. "Truce?"

“Truce.” Thor took my hand as he watched me carefully. “We leave in an hour.”

“Well, at least you gave me advanced notice.” I jerked my hand away.

“It's not exactly a situation that can wait.” Thor shrugged.

“Point taken.” I sighed as I watched the band wrap up their last number.

The women screamed for more.

I had a bad feeling that I'd be hearing a different type of screaming soon. I just hoped it wouldn't be mine.

Chapter Thirty-Four

Phoenix, Arizona is Hell.

I apologize to any die-hard Arizona fans, but anywhere that's so dry that I can actually feel the moisture being sucked out of my face as soon as I arrive, is not my idea of paradise. I felt like I'd aged ten years. I almost had a heart attack when I looked in the mirror and saw some fine lines that hadn't been there the day before.

It was April, so we had just missed the chilly nights in Phoenix. No snow mind you, just cold without the fun stuff. I was told it would soon be hot enough that the trees would become fire hazards. Anywhere that they cut the tops off the palm trees, just in case it got hot enough for them to spontaneously combust, was a place that I didn't want to be.

Yet the residents of Phoenix loved their city, and I'm sure most of them would be offended by my harsh criticism of their home. All I can say in my defense is; when you live in Heaven, Hell looks all the hotter. What I can say in *Phoenix's* defense is that it's full of wonderful cuisine, culture, and people. The people of Phoenix are a warm, welcoming bunch. At least they are when the resident illegal alien population isn't trying to start a riot.

We walked the streets as I silently wished that we'd rented a car. Everyone looked on edge. People eyed us warily, and I was thankful for the first time in my life that I didn't have dark skin to go with my hair and eyes. It wasn't a good time to look ethnic in Phoenix. Or maybe it was, it just depended on what side you looked at it from . . . or were on.

"How do we stop this?" I looked around as we entered an IHOP.

The place was, well . . . hopping. The smell of bacon and biscuits permeated the air with an invader's will to conquer, and it packed one hell of a wallop. I was salivating in less than twenty seconds. The patrons were predominately white, but I was betting there were more than a few Mexicans working illegally in the kitchen. I just hoped they weren't going to pull a *Ghost Ship* and poison the soup.

Note to self: Don't order soup.

All of the God Squad was there, including Hades, who I'm sure felt right at home in Arizona. We piled into a booth, and I almost started giggling at all the looks we were getting. With so many beautiful gods and goddesses at one table, people must've thought they were filming a movie nearby. I always felt so plain among the gods, but hey, Trevor made me feel beautiful, and that was all that mattered.

Trevor, in fact, was pressed up against me like someone might snatch me away from him at any second. I couldn't blame him for being nervous. Bad things had a way of happening to me. C'est Lavine. Such is *my* life. Hell, I was getting a little paranoid about it myself.

"Well, we could go around spreading love, good cheer, and peace on earth, but I've forgotten my Santa hat." Horus peered disdainfully into his stained coffee mug, then down at the cracked vinyl cushion behind him. "Why must we always mingle with . . ."

"Normal people?" I smiled at his discomfort, my smile widening as a waitress walked up with a thermos of coffee.

I nodded at her unspoken question, and she left it in the middle of the table for us. My favorite thing about IHOP was how you got your own pot of coffee.

"Oh, please tell me this isn't normal." Horus waved a hand around, giving a tiny shudder when his gaze passed over a table full of large, dirty, workmen.

"Horus, these are hardworking Americans you're insulting." I gave him my *mad mama* glare. "They deserve to have a nice breakfast without your scorn poisoning it."

"If they wanted a nice breakfast, why did they come here?" Horus's lips were twitching at the corners. I was convinced that he enjoyed our little exchanges almost as much as I did. "For that matter, what are *we* doing here?"

"This is a great breakfast place." I opened his menu and pointed out my favorites. "Try the steak tips or maybe some crepes. They just might sweeten your temperament."

"Those would have to be some magical crepes to sweeten Horus." Ull chuckled.

Horus's eyes glowed for a second as Ull lifted his coffee cup. The cup shook violently and Ull spilled coffee on his lap.

"Damn you, Horus." Ull put the cup back down and wiped at his jeans frantically.

Horus smiled smugly.

"I did nothing" Horus sipped his own coffee, and I saw Ull start to retaliate.

"What are you; five?" I reached across Trevor and smacked Ull. "No food fights, at least not in public." I glared at Horus for good measure.

"I'm innocent." Horus spread his hands wide

"As a viper," Ull growled.

"A viper does only what's in his nature to do." Horus tilted his head pensively. "Does that make him evil?"

"Enough," Thor rumbled and then smiled suddenly as the waitress approached us again.

Everyone was on their best behavior for the girl, but as soon as she left, the hot looks returned. I swear, it was like working with toddlers.

"Could we get back to the issue at hand please?" I asked.

Trevor put his arm around me so that I could lean into him. I snuggled closer, but when I looked up, Thor was giving me his grumpy face. I sat up straight with an apologetic glance at Trevor. Thor and I may not have been on the best of terms, but shoving a new relationship in the face of your ex is just bad form.

"We need to find the source." Thor's gaze softened on me. "A few calming spells wouldn't hurt either, but they'll have only a band-aid effect. We need to fight the god in charge, or we'll just be right back where we started in twenty-four hours."

"I agree, but how do we find him?" Teharon looked comfortable, perfectly at home. I loved that about him; he could fit in anywhere.

"Do you still have the stone I gave you in Washington?" Mrs. E had her hair in two long braids, looking so ethnically appropriate that all she was missing was a buckskin dress.

"Sure." I fished the white stone out of my purse. "I just need to reactivate it, and it can alert us to any god magic in the vicinity."

I murmured a spell over the stone, and it glowed for a second as the magic opened up within it.

"It didn't work so great the first time," Pan pointed out gently.

"It worked fine," Mr. T defended my magic. "We were just too slow."

"Is there any kind of organization to their protest . . .

riot . . . whatever?" I looked around the table as the waitress dropped off our orders.

Horus warily eyed the stuffed french toast sitting in front of him.

"There's talk of some kind of demonstration, but no location yet." Brahma cut into his crepes with gusto.

"Okay." I took a bite of my biscuits and gravy. I love gravy. I'd probably eat cardboard if you smothered it in gravy. I even liked the word *smothered.* Yum. "So, we wander around, calming people where we can, and waiting for my rock to go off, while keeping an ear peeled for protest locations."

"Waiting for your rock to go off." Pan gleefully repeated the line with a naughtier tone.

"Pan." Mrs. E shook her head.

"I think that's pretty much it." Thor didn't look too happy, but that was how fighting gods usually went. You blundered through and hoped for the best. Even when you had actual gods on your side.

"This is amazing." Horus took another bite of french toast. "The bread is crisp on the outside, but almost like cake inside, and this filling with berries and cream cheese is superb."

The whole table stared at Horus in shocked silence, but Horus was so fascinated by his food that he was oblivious to everything else. I started to giggle, then it caught on until everyone was laughing.

Horus looked up and around him with a smear of cream cheese on his lips. "What?"

Chapter Thirty-Five

We walked aimlessly for awhile; Mrs. E spread calm, Persephone doled out hope, and I filled people with a general feeling of love. Yes, we were like the Hare Krishnas without the flowers and bad hairdos. Oh yeah, and the funny clothes.

Horus had taken to the skies in his falcon shape, to see if he could spot anything from above, but the rest of us had to scan the area from the ground. It was working, people instantly became calmer and happier as we passed by, but I seriously doubted we could walk the entire Phoenix area in time to stop an uprising. Although we were making progress, it felt hopeless to me, and more than a little silly.

Then my stone vibrated and I grabbed it, instantly seeing where the god magic was being used.

Unfortunately, the user was completely hooded. He did look to be about the same size as Blue, but I wasn't going to let size alone convince me. The hooded god was standing in a clean, but sparsely decorated room, filled with Mexicans whom I presumed were illegally in the country.

The magic-using figure was huddled in a corner, invisible to them, but keeping out of the way so that no one would accidentally bump into him. He put out a hand, and it was covered in a golden gauntlet. I inhaled sharply, the last time I'd seen armor like that, Blue had been wearing it.

I didn't want to believe it was Blue. He'd come so far from the malicious mastermind he was before; I didn't want to believe he could fall back into evil so easily, and I didn't want to have to fight my friend. But when it came down to it, I'd do whatever needed to be done to prevent a war.

I scanned the room, trying to discover the exact location. It was just an average living room, no clue as to where it was, except that the furnishings were old and worn. So, it was most likely in a poor neighborhood. I bit my lip in frustration and continued to look. Finally, I noticed a piece of mail lying on the coffee table.

I had an address.

I let go of the stone and opened my eyes to find Trevor holding me, and everyone else circled around me expectantly. I quickly gave them the address. Ull pulled out his cell phone and called a cab. I raised a brow at that, but Thor explained how it'd be easier to let someone else drive us, someone who knew the area. Plus, we didn't have a car.

So, we signaled to Horus, who decided to follow us from the sky, and we piled into a cab. A minivan cab actually. It took us about half an hour to get to the location, and when we did, we could hear a commotion coming from inside the house.

We piled out of the minivan while Thor paid the driver. I had one of my surreal god moments. Every now and then, I'll be watching my god friends doing something so mundane, it seems ridiculous, and the moment takes on a surreal quality for me. I usually end up having a good laugh, but I held it in this time. Even though Thor made the minivan look like a clown car when he squeezed himself out of it.

I couldn't go in since I didn't have the ability to cloak myself. Cloaking was one of those advanced god magics I couldn't do yet. So, I stood outside, trying to look inconspicuous as the cab drove away, and the gods cloaked themselves in invisibility so they could enter the house.

I sent my love magic flowing inside to help the others diffuse the situation, and after a few moments, I felt an easing in the air, like the neighborhood had taken a deep, calming breath. I was watching the house closely for any sign of what might be

happening inside, so I caught the flash of gold and black easily when the instigator tried to sneak out the back.

I ran through the yard after the billowing cloak and caught more flashes of the golden armor beneath. There was a good chance it was Blue's armor. He was the only one I'd ever seen wearing anything like it before, but I still wasn't completely sure.

I had to be sure.

"Blue!" I called out and he stopped, flinching in shock.

The hood turned slightly towards me before he started running again. I chased after him, through yards and over fences, until he finally had enough distance to be able to pause and chant a tracing spell. Blue traced away before I could reach him. I came to a skidding halt in the spot he'd just been occupying

Now I was sure.

"Son of a bitch!" I panted and turned around to start the long trek back. It was Blue, and the chicken shit wouldn't even face me. "If you think you're getting away that easy, you're not half as bright as I thought, little boy blue."

I muttered the whole way back to the house, only stopping when I saw the others waiting for me on the sidewalk. They looked grim, and I didn't feel much better. How could he do this? We'd just shared that dance at Moonshine, and he had seemed so sweet. Then again, Blue was always charming. Even back when he'd been a psychopath, threatening to kill me when he got bored, he'd still been charming about it.

"What happened?" I looked from one anxious face to another.

"We got this group under control, but from what we were able to hear of their conversations, this is only one of many." Ull smiled grimly. "We've got an address on the next bunch, though.

It’s going to be a long day, but we should be able to make the rounds.”

“It was Blue,” I delivered my own news concisely.

“I knew it,” Thor said, and then cursed in a language I didn't recognize.

“I’m going to go have a talk with him,” I tried to keep my voice neutral, but I think the anger poked through. “Can you guys handle things without me?”

“Sure, we’ll be okay. Right, guys?” Pan glanced around for confirmation.

“Just be careful, Vervain.” Thor grabbed my shoulder tightly. “Remember, Huitzilopochtli never joined our side, and he’s not going to. Don’t kid yourself about his loyalties.”

“I’m going with you.” Trevor took my hand.

“Okay.” I squeezed Trevor's hand. “Backup is probably smart.”

“Meet us back at Bilskinir when you’re done,” Thor said as Trevor and I stepped into the Aether.

Chapter Thirty-Six

Blue's only tracing point was a room made completely of stone. The furniture, the floor, and the walls were all a cream-colored stone. The windows were glass, but devoid of curtains. Nothing flammable was allowed. It was necessary since Blue often returned home fresh from a battle, and battle heated him to the burning point . . . literally. The only way to cool him down was to cover him in blood. No big surprise, he's the father of vampires.

There was no pitcher of blood on the table waiting for him, and the room was empty. I was a little surprised that Blue wasn't standing there, waiting for me. Surely he knew that I'd come to confront him. Maybe he thought I wouldn't venture into the lion's den.

He should've known better.

"Blue," I called his name as I walked out of the room, and Trevor trailed after me.

"Vervain?" Blue came out of his bedroom with a smile on his face; he'd always been a good actor. "What a pleasant surprise. How are you?" He frowned. "You don't look well. Is there anything I can do?"

"You can stop trying to incite the illegal aliens to riot in Phoenix," I said it so casually, Blue didn't catch it at first.

Then his face changed.

"Maybe we should all have a seat." He gestured to the dining room.

Trevor and I followed Blue into his dining room and took seats at the massive table. Nothing had changed there either; the

room was still all white and gold, and it still felt like sitting in a giant, gilded marshmallow. Trevor sat on my right and Blue sat across from us.

“Would either of you like something to drink?” Blue waved a hand and one of his vampire-priest servants appeared. They really creeped me out. “Some coffee or tea perhaps?”

“No, thank you.” I gestured impatiently.

Blue was always polite. He’d been a complete gentleman right up until the point where he tried to turn me into his vampire love slave. Well, at least mostly, off and on. It was a good indication of how well he played a gentleman that half the time I hadn't been sure whether he was being a scoundrel or not.

“As you wish.” Blue spread his hands and then settled back. “Now, what are you accusing me of?”

“Do we really have to go through the song and dance?” I sighed and tried to send all of my disappointment to him through my eyes. “You saw me chasing you. We both know what this is about.”

“I honestly have no idea, little witch.” Blue’s eyes held only confusion, and just for a second, I wondered if I was wrong.

Then I remembered how the hooded figure had turned slightly to me; there had been an unmistakable pause of recognition. I gritted my teeth.

“Alright, fine,” I was speaking through my clenched teeth. “I’ll play your stupid game. I’ve just come from Phoenix, where we’ve been trying to prevent an uprising of the Mexican illegal aliens residing there. We tracked some god magic to a little house filled with people preparing to riot . . . your people. Your beloved Aztecs were talking about war again. Then out of the house comes this cloaked figure, the instigator making a run for it, and I chased him. Do you know what happened when I called out your name?”

"I'm sure you'll tell me." Blue's beautiful jade eyes started to go cool.

"He stopped and looked back at me a second before he started to really run for it."

"And you saw my face?" Blue looked smug, he already knew the answer to that.

"You know I didn't, you were hooded"–I waved dismissively–"but I caught a glimpse of your armor as well. Not too many gods out there wearing gold armor."

"There were quite a lot of golden suits of armor that came out of Atlantis." Blue frowned. "You're right though, I haven't heard of too many gods who don them anymore."

"I just want to know for certain that we're going to be fighting each other again." I rubbed at my temples. "I thought you were my friend. I know how you feel about taking power from humans, but somehow I believed in you anyway, or at least I had *hoped* for you. I hoped we wouldn't have to reach this point."

"We still haven't reached that point." Blue gestured impatiently. "Why won't you believe me, Vervain?"

"Are you really saying that you had nothing to do with this?"

For some stupid reason, I felt hope spring up in my chest. I tried to squash it back down, but it kept jumping up again like a damn jack in the box. I could almost see that horrible grinning head of hope, springing back and forth inside me. The cheeky little bastard.

"I swear it." Blue stood up and came around to my chair.

"Will you open your mind to me?" I had to have some proof or the God Squad would just think I had gone soft.

“I don’t know if I like that idea,” Trevor had finally said something.

“*I* don’t like the idea that you don’t trust me.” Blue’s face twisted into an expression I hadn’t seen in awhile.

“I *want* to trust you.” I leaned forward, but Blue leaned back. “Blue, come on.”

“Come on?” He lifted an eyebrow. “No, I would like for you to leave now.”

“Blue, if I leave without proof that this isn’t your work, the others will proceed as if it is.” I gave him my best pleading look, but evidently, it wasn’t good enough.

“So be it.” Blue's face went even more distant. “If you want to start a war with me over something I didn’t do, then there’s nothing I can do to stop you, but you will regret waking this sleeping giant, Godhunter.” He stood up abruptly. “Now, I think it’s best that you leave before I decide to start the war early.”

“Fine, Blue.” I sighed and got up. “If you’re telling the truth, I’m deeply sorry, but I can’t return to the others with only my trust in you as an answer.”

Blue's face started to clear, but then the coldness seeped back in. “Get out, Vervain. I won’t tell you again.”

Chapter Thirty-Seven

"So, it's him then." Horus was perched on the end of a chair like a bird. He did that a lot.

"I'm not too sure." I sat on a couch with Trevor.

We were all gathered in the library of Bilskinir. The library was one of my favorite places in Thor's home. It was the kind of library I'd always wanted, but I didn't have the palace to put it in. The room was two stories tall with books crowding the shelves all the way up. The only parts of the walls that didn't have shelves were where the door and the fireplace were, everywhere else was covered. There was very little room for new additions, which was probably why there were piles of books on the floor of Thor's bedroom . . . okay, *so* not going there.

An elegant brass ladder with rolling feet was attached to the shelves on a rail, just waiting for some hot librarian to climb up it and stretch seductively as she replaced books. I sure as hell had never seen Thor on it, so that had to be what it was for. Or maybe two story tall libraries just automatically came with ladders. Either way, it looked right at home against the rows of silken, leather-clad volumes.

One overstuffed couch and six wing-backed leather chairs invited guests to sit and enjoy some light reading. Light normally flooded the room from the inset fixtures on the ceiling, but Thor had decided to leave them off so that the room was lit only by the soft glow of small reading lamps and the dancing light of the fire. The low lighting turned all the hunter green textiles and maroon leather into midnight versions of themselves, darkened and mysterious beneath the shadows.

"He wouldn't let you verify it." Thor's brow creased

deeply. “That doesn’t speak well for him.”

“He wanted me to trust him.” I rubbed at my temples. “I can’t say that I blame him. If one of you came to me and accused me of something like this, and then asked to see into my mind to make sure it wasn’t me, I’d tell you where to shove it.” I sighed. “I guess I could try to spirit-walk.”

Teharon had taught me to use the blood-link I had with Blue to slip into his mind and rifle through his thoughts. It was called spirit-walking.

“I'm not sure that whatever you found would even be the truth,” Thor growled. “He'd expect you to try something like that. He could easily fill his head with thoughts of innocence in preparation. Even if it wasn't him, we wouldn't be able to trust what you saw.”

“Huitzilopochtli is a very proud god,” Teharon’s calm voice came from the other side of Trevor. “He would find insult in Vervain’s lack of trust. Yet we must treat him as the enemy for now, or we may find ourselves made fools of.”

“What do you want to do; pull a *Godfather* and put a horse head in his bed?” Something in my gut twisted at the thought of Blue gone bad again. Then I caught the look in Thor's eyes, remembered who he was dating, and I grimaced. “I didn't really mean that we should go out and kill a horse; it's a movie reference.”

Thor's face tightened.

“I like horses,” I swore.

“We can’t get to Blue until he leaves the God Realm. His home is warded,” Thor waved aside my ill-timed humor as he spoke. “We’ll just have to wait for his next move.”

“We’ve quieted the illegal immigrants for now,” Teharon

said. “That doesn’t mean that they can’t be incited again.”

“Do you really think he’ll try the same game twice?” Trevor had his arm around my shoulder; he used it to pull me a little closer.

“Why not?” Ull shrugged. “I would. I mean, after all the effort Blue's already put into it, why back off now? And it's exactly what he did with Maria Putina. It was like once he got the thought of killing her into his head, he couldn't stand to let her live.”

“We’ll have to keep a close eye on Arizona,” Thor’s voice rumbled and I shivered.

I experienced a brief moment of missing Thor, but then I snuggled into Trevor and felt his wolf comfort me. I guess it was naive to think I was over Thor completely, but I had really thought I was. I would always love Thor, but I'd moved on with Trevor, and I didn't regret my decision one bit. I had thought that meant that I could be around Thor without my feelings getting in the way. My heart hadn't got the memo, though, and being in Bilskinir was giving me flashbacks of being with Thor. I had to leave.

“I’m sorry, everyone.” I stood and Trevor followed suit. “We have some personal business to attend to before tomorrow, so we’re going to take off. Call us if anything else happens.”

“Personal business”–Pan chuckled–“I’ve never heard it called that before.”

Everyone laughed except Thor.

“I’ll come by if anything changes,” he said grimly.

“Thank you.” I sent him a look that said clearly how much more I was thanking him for. It really was nice to be back with the God Squad, and it wouldn't have been possible if Thor hadn't asked me back. As much as I was still angry over the way he'd ended things, I could appreciate the way he'd tried to make a new

beginning.

Thor nodded. “Vervain . . .”

“I have to go.” I turned and pulled Trevor with me out of the room.

I wasn't ready for a full on forgiveness session yet, and even if that wasn't where Thor was heading, I didn't want to hear what he had to say. There was only so much maturity that I could pretend to have for one night. Call me bitter, it's fine, I can own that.

Chapter Thirty-Eight

"So what's this personal business?" Trevor grinned.

"Exactly what you think it is." I led him down the hallway to our bedroom.

Funny how I already thought of it as ours. We'd been together for only a little over a month, but Trevor fit into my life as if he'd been made for it. He'd moved in with me kinda by default. He was simply there all the time.

"Oh, I like personal business." He scooped me up and carried me the rest of the way.

"I love you," I told him as he laid me down.

"I love you too." He searched my face. "What is it? Why the rush to come home and make love to me?"

"Can't I just want to be with you?"

"Of course." He kicked off his shoes and pulled off his shirt.

"I still love Thor," I confessed quietly.

My shoes had already been discarded on my way down the hall, so I just pulled my feet up beneath me.

"I know." Trevor scooted to the edge of the bed to take off his jeans.

He wasn't wearing underwear, and I lost my train of thought for a moment. Derailed by derriere.

"You know?"

“You forget; there's a part of me inside of you.” He gave me his lopsided grin as he crawled up to me.

“And I'd like another part of you inside me.” I smirked as I admired the part I was referring to.

“Soon.” Trevor smiled and pulled back the covers.

He tugged on my dress until I pulled it off, and then he undid my bra for me. I slid my panties off my legs, threw them through the opening of the bed, and crawled under the covers with him. The sheets were cool, but he was hot, giving off enough heat to make the AC a requirement, not a luxury. I snuggled up against Trevor, enjoying the slide of his flesh against mine.

“You knew how I still felt because my wolf tattled on me?” I wasn't really upset, just curious.

“No.” He kissed my forehead. “My wolf is yours now. I still need the connection, but I feel the difference. She's changed, the biggest change being that she's a *she* now.” He laughed. “But when we first bonded, we had a moment of total communion. Didn't you feel it?”

“I remember feeling like there were no boundaries to our bodies.” I thought back to the day we had consummated our bond. “Like we were one entity, turned to mist and pushed together.”

“But you don't remember getting an influx of knowledge about me?”

“No.” I frowned. “Should I have?”

“In a normal Binding, yes.” Trevor smiled a little sadly. “I guess ours was different. You got a piece of me, and I got to see you, know you in totality. I know everything about you, Minn Elska. From the way you take your coffee to the side of the bed you prefer to sleep on.”

"Everything?" I squeaked.

"Yes." Trevor stared at me like I was still beautiful. He knew it all and he still loved me.

"Wait." I had a thought. "I knew what to get you for Yule, remember? I bought you those DVDs, and they were exactly what you wanted. I couldn't figure out how I knew, but Fenrir said it was part of the Binding."

"Yes, that you'd always know what would make me happy." Trevor's hand wandered over my hip. "And you do. So maybe you know more about me than you think."

"I'm sorry about Thor." I sighed.

"I'm not." Trevor kissed my forehead. "Without Thor, I'd never have met you, and if you didn't love like you do, you'd never love me so completely. I knew you still loved Thor because I know the way you love. Once you start, you don't stop. Thor betrayed your love, and I don't think you could ever completely forgive him for that. You'll never be able to trust any words of love from him after what he's done. Yet it doesn't change the way you feel, and I'm okay with that. Because, like I said, you're mine now, and that's all that matters to me."

Trevor kissed me and pulled me on top of him so that I could show him the other way I loved.

Chapter Thirty-Nine

I woke up to a loud pounding and opened my eyes cautiously, scanning my surroundings. I was safe in my own bed. Trevor, however, was not.

A moment later, I heard him open the front door, and a muted conversation drifted back to me. His footsteps were soft thumps down the hallway, and I groaned, knowing it was something I'd have to deal with.

It was too early for this crap.

"Rouva?" Trevor poked his head in, and he was using my title so I knew it was bad.

"Wha-a-a-at?" I whined and slammed my fists down on the bed repeatedly.

"Thor's here." Trevor stifled a laugh. "We need to go."

"But I'm still *tired*," I grumbled and threw the covers over my head.

"They're rioting in Arizona," Trevor persisted.

"What?" I sat up in bed and the sheet fell, exposing me.

Trevor's eyes went from concerned to appreciative.

"Vervain, we need to . . ." Thor froze in the doorway behind Trevor, his mouth going slack as he stared.

I dove back under the covers with a yelp, and Trevor growled as he pushed Thor back down the hall.

"I'm sorry, I'm going, I'll wait in the living room," Thor

stammered.

Trevor's eyes were glowing with anger when he finally turned back at me. He came into the room and shut the door behind him with a thud. I dropped the covers again as he approached, and his anger simmered down beneath his rising lust.

"That was an accident," I whispered. "He didn't exactly come back here expecting to get an eyeful."

"It doesn't change the fact that he did." Trevor crawled across the bed and straddled me. There was a growl to his voice. "You're my mate; your body should be for me alone."

He slid his hands over the tops of my breasts and around them to cup and lift them gently. I sighed in delight as he rubbed his face against me, his early morning stubble pleasantly abrasive. Then liquid heat enveloped me as his mouth did, and I almost came off the bed. Trevor's tongue swirled in lazy circles as his thick hair tickled my skin. I gushed with immediate desire, and he groaned, scenting my excitement most likely, as his arms circled my back.

When Trevor transferred his attention to my other breast, I had a clear-headed moment to remember Thor. I let Trevor keep going a little more anyway, it just felt too damn good. I ran my fingers through his hair, and even pulled his face against me tighter, but then I sighed and pushed him away.

"We can't finish this right now." I kissed him to take the sting out of my words. "Thor's waiting outside."

"Forget Thor." Trevor's eyes gleamed. "Fuck me."

"Honey-eyes, I love you, you can have me anytime you want"–I stroked his face–"even now, but do you really want to be that cruel to Thor just because he caught a peek?" Of something he's already seen before, I added in my head.

"You're right," he groaned and laid his head in my lap for a second. Then he got up and quickly moved off the bed. "Let's get dressed."

Trevor slid down the bed and headed to the closet while I crawled after him. I ran into the bathroom to perform some quick morning necessities before I slid into my fighting gear. Trevor put on an old pair of sweat pants and a T-shirt, fighting gear for werewolves. They needed something that could either be removed quickly or could be shredded easily. I, however, needed a lot more coverage, and my gear consisted of black leather pants and a high-necked, long-sleeved shirt, reinforced with sheets of metal that were sewn into pockets of material.

I'd sewn in the plates myself after having to defend myself against werewolves last year. I'd left them out of the pants because I thought it would make it too difficult to run, and sometimes being able to escape was more important than being claw-resistant.

To this ensemble, I added my heavy boots that had a small metal hook poking out of the heels, my kodachi short sword, and my bladed gloves. I braided my hair around my head like a crown to complete the look. I never leave my hair hanging loose when I fight. All it does is gives my opponent a handhold.

When we stepped into the living room, we found Thor waiting anxiously by the door.

"Let's go," Thor said as he held a hand out to us.

Chapter Forty

The riot was two blocks away, but we could hear the cacophony as if we were standing smack dab in the middle of it.

We were all there, dressed to kill . . . literally. Thor wore his Viking gear, as did Ull, which consisted of leather, cross-gartered pants, a long-sleeved tunic, and assorted archaic weapons. Brahma had a long maroon tunic on with some kind of tooled leather armor over it. Horus looked like an Egyptian warrior, in white cloth and boiled leather. Finn wore leather armor enhanced with pieces of strategically placed metal plates.

Hades matched me, in black leather pants and a black dress shirt, minus the metal plates. I guess Sizzle-Butt didn't need armor. Pan and Mr. T seemed to share his thinking and were dressed casually, but Mr. T was wearing an Indian breastplate over his white, long sleeved shirt. It didn't look like it could stop much, but you never know with gods. The knives in my gloves shouldn't be able to cleave a god's head from his body, but they could. Easily.

Persephone, Teharon and Mrs. E were going to stay out of the battle, so they had forgone armor as well, but Teharon and Mrs. E both had a bow slung on their backs just in case. It kind of bothered me that Sephy didn't have a weapon. Her magic was of growth, making things blossom and bringing feelings of renewal. How was she going to defend herself with that?

We were just about to move out when a roar rose above the sound of fighting. It rolled over to us like distant thunder, bringing with it the promise of a storm. We all froze, looking over at each other in confusion. The street we were on was deserted, the locals either hiding or joining in the riot, so it wasn't hard to spot the lions heading straight for us. Not that lions on a Phoenix street at

mid-day would be hard to spot anyway.

They glided forward, savagely beautiful and confident in their fur. Most were shades of gold, but here and there I spotted a few shining white. Thick manes swished, sculpted muscles flowed gracefully, and padded feet moved silently over the pavement as they surged forward in a widening half circle.

"I'm sorry," I said with wonder as I walked forward a step, staring in morbid fascination. "Are those lions?"

"Werelions," Trevor's nose was doing double time. He shifted with a shimmering surge, and fur flowed over his body as he grew about two feet in height. The sweatpants tore apart, but clung to him determinedly. His voice dropped to a low growl, "That means Nyavirezi is here."

"Very good, Wolf Prince." A statuesque, chocolate-skinned goddess appeared behind the Pride. She had a head full of thin, long braids and a lush figure. The lions stopped and looked back at the sound of her voice, waiting for her signal.

The funny thing was, I wasn't as shocked to see a pride of lions as I was to see Blue standing beside their goddess. At least I thought it was Blue. He was dressed in that gold armor again, with a black tunic over it and a cloak over that. I couldn't even make out his eyes through the slits in his helm. It had to be him, though. Why else would someone go to so much trouble to disguise themselves?

"Oh, hell no." I threw my hands down and released the blades from my gloves. "We're ending this right now. I'm going to tear that helmet off his head, and be certain it's Blue, once and for all."

I was about to go racing toward Blue when Thor grabbed me.

"Remember the last time you went charging in towards the

Aztec without thought?" Thor reminded me.

I was about to give Thor a piece of my mind when I realized that he was right. I get carried away in a fight, the last time it was literally carried away . . . by Blue. Wasn't the definition of insanity doing the same thing over and over, while expecting a different result? Maybe it was best to stop giving people pieces of my mind, I evidently needed them all. So, instead, I waved my hand as I bowed in an *after you* motion to Thor.

Thor pulled his Viking hammer, Mjöllnir, from his belt and threw it. It changed mid-air into a lightning bolt which struck the Lion Goddess smack dab in the middle of her chest. She stumbled back, screeching as her eyebrows sizzled and a significant amount of her hair burned away.

"How dare you?" Nyavirezi screamed as the bolt disappeared, and the hammer reappeared in Thor's hand.

"That thing is amazing." I gaped at Mjöllnir, and Thor smirked. "You're going first from now on!"

The wind started getting colder, and I looked up as the sky turned black. Oh, this couldn't be good.

Blue pulled a sword from the sheath at his belt, and I started to shake with fury. The sword had sealed it for me. It looked exactly like the sword Blue had inherited from his father. You can't expect me to believe that all Atlanteans had matching swords too.

Mr. T strode forward and started to glow; heat flowed off his body as the power of the sun shot out of him in a blurring wave that pushed the cold back. It sparked and popped, dropping sizzling rain between us and the lions. The animals retreated a few steps.

Then Blue's gauntlet-clad fist shot out, sending a dazzling-white jolt of energy toward us. The cold disappeared entirely as it went by, impacting with Mr. T's magic in a subtle but stunning

display. Heat swirled with heat above our heads and the dry Arizona air grew even drier and hotter.

They always said fight fire with fire, but as I watched the magical battle above me drip sparks down around us, I realized that was a stupid idea. Fight fire with fire and all you got was napalm.

Nyavirezi growled low in her throat, and it was all the lions needed. They leaped forward, and I crouched in anticipation. There must have been thirty of them filling the street already, but even more were stalking out of alleys behind the goddess. Just lions and more lions, not a single lioness. Where were all the females? I thought it was the girls that did all the hunting.

Nyavirezi started to shimmer, her body going hazy, and then she reformed into a lioness. So, they had at least one female. She was beautiful . . . and huge. Nyavirezi roared; a long, rumbling warning, and I had a momentary frightening thought that we were fucked. Then my Nahual answered Nyavirezi's challenge with a snarling growl that echoed off the buildings until it faded away eerily.

The lioness lifted her head and scented the air warily. It made me smile, and when I looked around at my friends, I smiled wider. I used to have to fight the gods alone. Now, I had gods backing me. That had to be an improvement, right?

Trevor launched himself forward, and I followed my mate, my wolf rising up to join my jaguar in excitement. Along with it came my war magic and I felt Victory fill me as well. My body felt amazing, able to fight forever, power running through my veins like a drug. I pulled my kodachi and struck at the first lion to attack me. The sword was light in my hands, but as I struck, War and Victory surged, and I nearly cleaved the poor lion in two.

Part of me shrank back from the carnage, I hated hurting animals, but another part of me gloried in the kill and knew that

this was no ordinary beast. This was an enemy who'd come to bring death to me and my friends. I swept past the carcass to attack another predator.

Over and over I swung, my arm never tiring. The war magic preferred sword to claws, and it was delighted that I'd finally chosen the kodachi. I could feel it zipping through me, dancing in my veins happily.

Behind me, I heard Thor's thunder and his lightning lit the sky, adding to the drama between Blue and Mr. T. Most of the other gods were in hand-to-hand combat around me, flashes of their magic lighting my peripheral vision, but Pan stood on the side with Teharon. I caught a quick hand movement from Pan, and then the lions around me were going wild, leaping at each other and backing away. I smiled and gave chase.

Panic was a useful magic in battle.

Then I had an epiphany. Thor had told me how human magic empowered gods, and how difficult it was for one god to kill another. It was almost as if one magic canceled the other out. He'd said it was the reason they feared me. As a human witch, the magic craved me. When I was around, it wanted to return to me. It was one of the reasons some gods found me attractive, but more importantly, it was the reason I could kill them. And I was the only human witch there. No wonder Thor wanted me back in the gang. I tipped the scales.

Unfortunately, the lions recovered fast, scales tipped or not. They rallied behind Nyavirezi, who had joined the battle. She ran straight for me, and I suddenly found myself in the middle of the pride. Claws tore into my side, glancing off metal plates, and I swung my blade out blindly. Nyavirezi crept forward as the rest of her honor guard backed off into a loose circle. I set myself down into a battle stance, waiting for her make the first move.

Then I heard Trevor cry out from my left.

"Vervain." Trevor's wolfman body leapt over the lions in his haste to get to me, and I couldn't help my gasp of dismay.

The lioness jerked her head at my reaction, then turned and ran in Trevor's direction.

"Trevor!" I started to follow her, but the lions Nyavirezi left behind had formed a solid wall between us. "Trevor!"

I saw him rise over the bodies again, nearly to me, but then the lioness caught him from the side, her massive jaws seeming to close on Trevor's stomach in slow motion as I screamed. My heart caught in a brutal fist of terror, paralyzing me, and the distraction was enough for one of the lions to pounce and grab me by the neck.

I swung my blade, but another lion bit down into my arm, crushing my upper arm between the metal plates hidden there. I felt the sword slide from my grasp. Warm fur pressed down against me, the pleasurable sensation in direct contrast to the pain of teeth sinking into the back of my neck.

Mauled by lions . . . not exactly one of my top ten ways to die.

"No!" I heard Thor's voice and saw a flash of light, but it was too late.

The lion had gentled his bite, but he still had me firmly by the neck and was dragging me backward like a mother cat with her kitten. I was actually kind of relieved for the mauling respite.

"Damn that Thor," I heard Nyavirezi curse, once again in her human form. "He's thrown the hammer and leveled my lions. Retreat!" Then she growled and the lions swarmed around us.

Where was Trevor? Was he alive?

Blue gave an angry snarl as he lowered his sword and

turned to stare Nyavirezi down.

“Retreat to fight again,” Nyavirezi snarled back.

I struggled to claw at the lion who held me, but he was moving too fast, jarring me too much, for me to do much damage. So instead, I put most of my energy into protecting my body from the asphalt he was dragging me over. I kicked my legs and pushed down on my forearms to try to save my torso, but the injury to my right arm prevented me from using it, and I had to give up.

The leather of my pants was getting scraped all to hell, and my shirt caught on stones until it finally tore open to reveal the metal plates beneath. They screeched something awful, but I was thankful to have them. Better that the metal's damaged than my flesh.

Finally, the lion stopped and released me, but by the time I struggled to my feet, he’d shifted to human form. I had about a second to gape at the expanse of muscled, naked, golden male before he punched me hard and I went down.

Chapter Forty-One

I moaned and rolled over, surprised to find myself unchained for once. I was in an empty room. Wow, unchained and no one around to torture me, things were looking up. I took a more relaxed look around.

Wood paneled walls and hardwood floors, even the ceiling was made of wooden beams. I stood up and tried the door. Why not? You never know.

It was locked, so I slammed my weight against it. It didn't budge. I gave a big harrumph and folded my arms while I tried to think. My gloves were gone, along with all the other knives I'd hidden on myself, and my sword had been lost on the battlefield. I could only hope that someone had picked it up. I was most likely Nyavirezi's prisoner since it was her lion who punched me, and I didn't recognize the room as one in Blue's palace.

"Hey!" I kicked the door. "Lion lady! Blue Balls! Open up, you chicken shits!"

I heard some movement beyond the door, and then rapid footsteps. After awhile, footsteps approached, and then the door was flung in, leaving me faced with the lion goddess and Blue. He was still wearing that stupid get-up. Like it even mattered at this point.

"Well, it's about frickin' time." I crossed my arms. "Where are my gloves?"

"She *is* arrogant." Nyavirezi looked at Blue like she was shocked to find that some vicious rumor was actually true.

"Blah, blah, blah." I sighed, making a talking motion with

my hand. "Can we get this over with? My neck and arm both hurt like a bitch."

"You want to get this over with?" Nyavirezi sneered. "Fine, it's your death."

Nyavirezi started forward, but Blue stopped her with a hand on her arm. The lion goddess looked back at him in shock, and he shook his head. Humph, guess he wanted to kill me himself. Or maybe there was some little piece of the good Blue left. I'd seen inside his heart when I healed him. I knew he had the capacity for good.

"Blue, don't do this," I tried to get through to him. "I know you don't want me dead."

They both looked over at me, paused, and then went back to glaring at each other.

"How can you even think about doing this to me?" I asked.

"She's mine," Nyavirezi growled at Blue, who hadn't even acknowledged that I spoke again. "She killed my lions."

My gut clenched. I just couldn't believe that Blue could be so cruel to me after all we'd been through. Was my ability to judge a man's character so broken that I could be so wrong about Blue? I had actually believed him when he denied being a part of this. Yet there he was, arguing with a lion goddess over me.

As they fought over who got to kill me–I was so touched by that–I weighed my options. I knew I didn't stand a chance against both of them together. I could drain Nyavirezi, but Thor had warned me that draining another goddess may be too much power for me to hold, and I was pretty sure that Blue was simply too powerful. It didn't look like I had a choice, though, the love magic would be useless against these two. Even though it had previously liked Blue, now I felt it curl up and hide inside me–another damning mark against him–and the idea of using sex magic against

them was just plain gross.

I was about to center myself and reach out for Nyavirezi's magic, when their fight ended. The lion goddess grabbed me and yanked me out the door. I elbowed her in the face, and she went down hard. Blue reached for me, and I knocked his hand away before I booked it down the hallway.

“Darius!” Nyavirezi screamed, “Grab her!”

I hazarded a glance over my shoulder, but the two of them were alone. Where was this Darius person? When I turned my head back to the front, I had my answer.

A gorgeous, dirty-blond stepped out in front of me from a side room. He was your average hot blond except for his bright turquoise eyes. Those eyes pushed him right over the edge into Josh Holloway territory. They leaped out of his face like they were trying to make contact, and they made you feel like they wanted that contact with you alone.

Or maybe that was just because he’d been *ordered* to make contact with me. I stopped short and looked over his wide chest. He was only wearing a pair of jeans, and suddenly I remembered where I’d seen it before; the chest, not the jeans.

“You again.” I pointed at him accusingly. He was the jerk who punched me. “It’s not polite to hit ladies.”

“It was either that or rip your throat out,” he said softly, and then he raised his voice, “I don’t see any ladies here.”

I blinked a couple of times and cocked my head to the side. Following his gaze over my shoulder, I saw Nyavirezi getting to her feet as she wiped blood off her face. Holy shit, he didn’t like her. Maybe I had some kind of a chance.

“Alright then”–I smiled–“hitting a bitch may be okay, but hitting this one isn’t too smart.”

He chuckled a little before he dove for me. I sidestepped and knocked him with my joined fists in the back of his head. He grunted and fell, but with a rolling maneuver, he was on his feet again, grinning.

"Not bad, Godhunter."

"I get better when I'm bad, Darius is it?"

He bowed quickly before resuming a fighting stance. I watched his muscles bunch and flex under all that golden skin. He wasn't as big as Trevor or Thor, maybe six-foot-three, but that still made him a foot taller than me, and I wasn't sure if I could take him down quickly without my claws. I lowered myself into a crouch and shifted to watch him better. That's when the second guy grabbed me from behind.

"Fuck," I cursed under my breath.

I'd made a beginner's mistake. Never lose sight of your surroundings and always be on guard for someone coming up behind you.

I felt hot breath on my neck and looked over my shoulder to see a man who looked remarkably like LL Cool J. He was smiling at me. The resemblance was so uncanny, I actually looked down to see if one of his pants' legs was rolled up (yes, LL used to do that, Google it if you don't believe me). No luck there, just tight jeans all the way down and bare chest behind me. It must've been the uniform.

"Boy, you guys don't come in *ugly* do you?" I eyed his toned chest.

The man holding me raised an eyebrow over a hazel eye. Okay, he was hotter than LL. There's nothing quite like a dark-skinned man with light eyes. Darius laughed loudly, drawing my attention away from Mr. Rap-Star-Good-Looks.

“Thank you, Godhunter.” Darius winked at me. “It's nice of you to notice.”

“Call me Vervain.” I lifted my leg and brought my foot down on LL’s knee.

He cried out and let go of me as he went down.

“I’m sure we’re going to be the *best* of friends,” I said.

I saw a flare of admiration light Darius’ eyes before I ran past him and down a corridor to the left. His boots hit the floor hard behind me, and then another set joined in. I guess LL was a fast healer or had a high pain tolerance. Then came the worst sound ever. Rising above the pounding footsteps, and my pounding heart, was insane feminine laughter. Nyavirezi. I was really starting to dislike that bitch.

The pounding was coming closer, damn lions were fast, faster than wolves I’d wager. As I thought that, the little wolf in me rose up. I found myself skidding and turning into a curve that left me crouched and facing off with my pursuers. I snarled and growled a low warning that stopped the boys in their tracks. They gave each other a quick, shocked glance before looking back at me.

“Surprise, surprise,” I continued to growl, “Red Riding Hood has a little wolf in her.”

“We don’t want to hurt you, Vervain,” Darius whispered. “Please don’t make this difficult.”

“There’s no way out except through the tracing point.” LL was crouched low, but held his hands up pleadingly.

“And why would you care about hurting me?” I stared hard at Darius.

“I’ve no quarrel with you.” Darius looked back over his

shoulder. “We're only carrying out her orders.”

“Yeah? Well if you don’t like her so much, why don’t you just leave or revolt or something?” I wasn’t about to buy this crap. “Viva la Revolucion!”

“She made us”–he looked cautiously at LL–“she can destroy us.”

“*Made* you?” I frowned. “Like she’s your mother. ‘I brought you into this world and I can take you out of it’ kind of thing?”

“No,” LL rumbled, “like she’s our goddess and can kill or torture us with a thought.”

“The Intare are made through magic, not birthed like Froekn.” Darius shook his head. “We don’t have time for this, she’s coming.”

I heard the click-clack of heels on the wood floor before Nyavirezi rounded the corner. “What’s taking so damn long? Grab her–now!”

The men shot me an apologetic glance, then leapt forward. I was suddenly off my feet, dangling by the arms, which each man held one of. I fought and kicked, but it was useless; they both had a hell of a grip. My wolf rose up, along with my Nahual, and I felt my body tense in response. All sorts of growling sounds were coming out of my throat. I sounded like a cornered animal, which I guess I kinda was. Well, more like caged.

“Take her into the common room.” Nyavirezi waved her hand down the opposite corridor, and then followed after us.

We turned and walked through a doorway. Well, some of us walked, one of us was carried. The door opened onto a huge room. It was heaven. Maybe they’d already killed me, and I just hadn’t realized I was dead yet.

Gorgeous men were everywhere; the room was filled with them. I could have sworn that I heard the Weather Girls singing about ripping the roof off and staying in bed. Then suddenly, it made sense. If Nyavirezi turned men into lions, she'd pick the best she could find, of course. And wouldn't you know it, there wasn't a single female in the lot.

"Hallelujah." I shook my head. I could still hear the chorus to "It's Raining Men", when what I needed to be singing was "I Will Survive". Come on, Gloria, do your thing. But Gloria Gaynor wasn't in the mood to sing. I looked over the man buffet and all I could think was; I'm gonna go out and let myself get, absolutely soaking wet. I would've started tapping my toes, except for the whole dangling in mid-air thing.

"Intare," Nyavirezi called out as she came up beside us. "You fought well today, and although we lost the battle, we took their Queen. The game can still be ours!"

"Oh good, a chess reference." I sighed. "How original."

Nyavirezi shot me a heated look. "Maybe you should have studied the game yourself, Godhunter," she snapped. "Then you'd know more about strategy."

"Oh, here we go again," I groaned. "Can you just do what you're going to do, without all the stupid babble?" I got a vicious slap for my comment and felt Darius's hand twitch a little on my arm.

"Fine." She smiled big. "You don't want to hear my babble? I'll be short and sweet." Nyavirezi turned back to the men, who eyed her warily. "Just this once, my babies, you can have another woman. As your reward, the Godhunter is yours. Just try not to kill her. We have other plans for her."

Blue had his arms crossed over his chest. I still couldn't see his damn eyes, and for some reason, that really bothered me. I should have been able to look him in the eye while he betrayed me.

I think I at least deserved that. He wouldn't even raise his head, though, just stared at the floor, and then turned away, walking from the room stiffly.

“Nyavirezi,” I called out as I felt myself go cold.

She turned back to me with an arrogant glare, and I met it steadily.

“Ever notice how every once in awhile, you come across someone you shouldn't fuck with? That's me. You really shouldn't have fucked with me.”

“Toss her in!” Nyavirezi shouted.

The men looked at each other, and Darius gave me a gentle squeeze before they threw me to the others. I had a brief sensation of weightlessness, and a moment to wonder how bad the sudden stop was going to hurt, and then nothing. I never hit the ground. Big hands grabbed me everywhere and lifted me up. There were so many faces, I couldn’t focus on any single one, but I felt the heat of them closing in. None of them said a word, they just moved me carefully back into the room until I felt myself lowered to the ground.

“Goodbye, Godhunter.” Nyavirezi laughed. “Turns out, I'm not going to be the one fucking with you after all. Have fun. Some of my men haven’t had sex in years. I’m sure they’ll show you a good time. I’ll be back to check on you tomorrow.”

I wouldn’t scream. I wouldn’t scream. I wouldn’t scream.

Darius was gone and so was LL, though I wasn’t sure if either of them would help me anyway. Hell, they might just be getting in line. I almost started laughing hysterically. Instead, it came out more like a hiccup. The hands pulled away at that small sound, and I was able to sit up and look around me.

They were all crouched in a circle, all those hotties that

were about to rape me . . . probably repeatedly. One or two of them, and I might have stood a chance, but even if they were gentle, I wouldn't live through sex with what must've been close to eighty men. One woman can only take so much. I jumped up in a crouch and they leaned back, wariness fighting with eagerness in their expressions.

"Okay, boys." I smiled humorlessly as I settled into a fighting stance. "Who wants to go first?"

They watched me hungrily like, well, like lions hunting antelope. Or men watching strippers. Either way, it didn't bode well. Fucked to death. I looked around at the wide chests and gorgeous faces. What a way to go. I chuckled a little at the horrifying ridiculousness of my life, which seemed to make the men even more cautious.

"Don't be afraid," a dark haired one said gently. "We'll be careful with you. We won't hurt you."

"My body won't be able to handle all of you"–my smile twisted–"no matter how careful you are."

I couldn't believe I was having a pre-rape, polite conversation. My hands started to shake.

"We won't all take you today." He reached out a hand, and I promptly slapped it away. "It could be enjoyable if you let it."

"Sure, honey." I laughed. "One on one with you would be great, no doubt, but being gang-banged is not on my top ten list of things to do before I die . . . or *how* to die."

There was a shuffling among them, and they pressed in a little closer.

"Look, I appreciate that it's been awhile for some of you, but come on, I went five years once and I wasn't even remotely thinking about raping anyone."

"I'm sorry, Godhunter." The black-haired one lowered his face, shame heating his cheeks. "We never get to be with any woman but her. Even then, it's only when the mood strikes her, and her idea of making love is not always pleasant. It's been so long since I've even touched a woman and, well . . . we're all really just animals at heart."

The men around him rumbled in agreement.

"That sucks"–I nodded–"and believe me, I'd love to help you out, but I've got a really jealous boyfriend, and I don't think he'd go for it."

"The Wolf Prince isn't here." Mr. black-hair moved forward so fast, I barely saw it. I was on the floor in a second, legs spread with the lion between them. "Please," he whispered as he kissed my neck.

It might have felt pretty good if I hadn't been rigid with rage. Fear mixed with adrenaline was one hell of a mood breaker, even with a hard appendage placed strategically against me.

"Get off her, Aidan," Darius' voice flowed over us like cold water, shocking to Aidan, but a cool relief to me.

"Wait your turn," Aidan growled over his shoulder before returning his attentions to my cleavage. A moment later he was hanging mid-air, in Darius' grip. "What the fuck, D? The Goddess told us to, even if I didn't want to fuck her, I still have to."

"Don't use that as an excuse to become a rapist." Darius put Aidan down gently. "We don't have to behave like animals just because she made us into them. We're still men."

"Maybe *you* are"–a large man with a shaved head pushed his way forward–"but I'm past acting human. I'm Intare, and I just got an order from my Tima. An order I fully intend to make use of since it's rare that her demands give *me* any pleasure."

The other men pressed in closer, nodding and muttering encouragement to Baldie. I saw LL standing off to the side, arms crossed and face filled with disapproval. I felt awful about kicking his knee when I saw that. Sure, he was standing on the side, not helping defend me in the least, but he wasn't actively plotting my rape either.

I stood up and set my back against the wall, scanning the men and looking for any possible escape routes. I was just about to make a break for it when the crowd lurched forward, and Darius shimmered out of focus. His form blurred and was replaced by a lion. A really big lion. He roared, and I was tempted to cover my ears, the strength of it left my head a little numb.

The men backed up, eyeing Darius warily, and eyeing each other in confusion. They outnumbered him, like eighty to one, but they were afraid to go up against him. I was impressed.

He stalked back and forth in front of me, low sounds of menace coming from his snarling mouth. Then he turned toward me, and it was all I could do to not drop into a battle stance.

Darius padded over and rubbed his body along mine as he circled me once. The sexy sensation of warm fur stroking my arm was actually soothing. It was almost as soothing as the sight of him dropping to the ground in front of me to lie there casually, as if it was something he did every day. Good kitty.

Another shimmer heralded the change of a possible adversary, but Darius barely twitched. It wasn't till the lion got within range that he finally reacted, swiping at the other beast almost playfully. The challenger yelped and backed away, melting into the wall of men.

I sat down behind my defender and watched the man-tide recede. Darius's big, lion head turned slowly to look at me, and I felt my heart speed up under his glowing gaze. Thick muscles moved beneath golden fur, reminding me of the way they had

moved beneath his skin earlier, just as striking, but in a completely different way. He was magnificent and terrifying.

"Thanks," I said, feeling like it was completely inadequate.

I would swear he smiled, but I wouldn't know a lion's smile from a bear's grimace, so I couldn't be sure. He did, however, nudge his head into my stomach in a distinctly friendly manner. I stroked the thick mane of hair around his face, and was shocked at how silky it was. Not like I'd had a lot of experience touching lions before, but I always thought that their manes would be coarse. I was even more shocked when he laid his head in my lap, coiling his body around me protectively.

"Um, okay," I said.

Darius had just saved me from certain rape. If he wanted a little scratch behind the ears and a cuddle, it was a small enough price to pay. I continued to stroke his mane, and his claws began to knead the thick, tan carpeting while a rumbling sound vibrated out of his chest. Strange, lions weren't supposed to be able to purr. Silky manes and purring; I guess magic lions were different than their normal cousins.

"Nicely done." LL strode through the men, who had drawn back and were amusing themselves with the pool table and video games sprinkled around the room. I'd failed to notice all the other sources of entertainment in my preoccupation with potential rape scenarios.

Darius lifted his head, sniffed, and nodded before dropping it back into my lap. I grunted from the weight, a lion's head is heavy. LL sat down next to us and surveyed the room like a weathered soldier. The lions, or Intare as they evidently called themselves, were all trying to look at ease and completely unaware that I was still there.

They sucked at it.

"You gonna guard her all night?" LL leaned back on one arm and Darius huffed. I assumed that was a yes because LL nodded. Oh, hell, I'd had enough with calling him that.

"What's your name?" I glanced at him before going back to watching the others.

He hesitated a second too long, so I looked back at him again. Flashing, sharp eyes met mine with confused surprise.

"Fallon," he said finally. "Sorry, it's just been a long time since someone asked me that."

"Don't get out a lot, huh?" I went back to my guard duty.

"The only time we leave is when the Goddess takes us out." He shrugged. "Usually it involves hurting someone. We don't get to socialize much, and when she does bring someone here, they couldn't care less about us. We're scenery, bodyguards, or even worse . . . toys."

"Well, at least you're not bitter." I smiled sympathetically, and he laughed.

"I've forgotten how wonderful women can be." Fallon's eyes crinkled at the corners as he looked at me.

"Naw, it's not women, just me." I flipped my hair over my shoulder dramatically. "I'm fabulous . . . and modest too."

Fallon laughed hard enough to lose his balance and fall back. The rest of the men looked over, shock evident on their faces. I saw Aidan lose interest in his pool game as he stared at us. He threw his cue on the table and wandered over cautiously. Fallon and I only watched, but Darius rumbled out a low warning before the black-haired eye-candy got too close.

"I just want to talk to her." Aidan got down on the floor and crept forward on his hands and knees. "You're lying in her lap, but

I can't talk to her?"

Darius lifted his head off my lap to give me a look that clearly said it was up to me.

"Have a seat." I waved to a spot on my left, opposite Fallon.

Darius immediately lowered his head back to my lap.

Surprisingly, I didn't hold a grudge against Aidan. In fact, the love and sex magics were swirling together in excitement now that mass rape had been avoided. My magic wanted to reach out and touch those boys, help them, save them. I frowned at that thought, but it was true, they needed saving. Too bad I couldn't save them without their help. All Nyavirezi had to do was order them to attack me, and I was done for, they couldn't refuse her. What had Darius said about that?

"Fallon." I turned back to him. "What did Darius mean when he said Nyavirezi could destroy you?"

"It's one of her powers," Fallon said. "You know nothing of us then?"

"I didn't even know you guys existed until today." I shrugged. "Sorry."

"It doesn't matter." LL, I mean Fallon, waved it away. "The Goddess changed us into lion shifters through her magic, but it's still her magic and we're tied to her by it. Through that link, she can kill us without so much as lifting a finger. We'd rise up against her if not for that. She cares nothing for us, only for what protection we can give her . . . or pleasure. We're no better than slaves."

"So, let's take her down," I whispered.

"By 'take her down', you mean?" Aidan cocked his head

and crept in closer.

“I mean, let's kill her.”

Chapter Forty-Two

"Why didn't you just gang up on Darius?"

It had been two hours since we'd decided to kill Nyavirezi, and Fallon was still out talking to the others; recruiting, for lack of a better term. Aidan had done his fair share of recruitment as well, and there were a good number of men in our circle.

"It's a lion thing," Jared, one of the new recruits, answered. I heard a lilt of an Irish accent beneath his words. It went perfectly with his shaggy red hair and green eyes. "Darius established dominance, so we let him win the argument. That's how it works. Otherwise, we'd be killing each other all the time over petty squabbles."

"That sounds pretty humane for being a lion thing." I smiled at the redhead.

In my opinion, redheads are either ugly or exceptionally good looking, no in between. Example A. Carrot Top or Eric Stoltz. Guess which one Jared was.

"Humane," Jared scoffed, "when have you ever heard of animals polluting their environments or torturing each other for fun? I'd rather be compared to an animal than a human any day."

"Ah, a philosopher." I shifted so I could lean back against Darius. A lion makes a very comfortable back rest. Warm, fuzzy, and a nice vibration when they purr. Well, at least magic lions. If you can find one, I highly recommend it. "I think I have to agree with you there. Isn't it wonderful to have a door into both worlds?"

"You don't think we're monsters?" A dark-haired man with a thick British accent pushed through the growing crowd. He

stared at me intensely, and when I looked around, I realized everyone had stopped to listen to my answer.

"No," I said firmly. "How could this be monstrous?" I waved my hand at Darius. "It would be like saying the ocean is monstrous or the fish that swim in it."

"Those things are natural"–Fallon came back and took a seat beside me–"we are not."

The rest of them sat as well, and I was able to see that the whole room of men had been brought over. My heart raced; step one complete. This was my chance to win over the Intare. I had to be careful about what I said in the next few hours, and that frightened me to no end. I had no filter. Things went straight from my brain and out of my mouth. For once in my life, I was going to have to think before I spoke. I opened my mouth, then closed it, and rethought my words.

"Oh fuck it," I exclaimed, and I got a few chuckles for that one. "I'm not very good at the whole profound speaking thing, so I'm just going to tell it like I see it."

"And how do you see us, Godhunter?" It was the bald guy who had tried to get a piece of me earlier. He had his arms crossed over his chest and a frown on his face. So, no pressure there.

"I see a brotherhood"–I looked around at the men standing side by side–"a family. I see respect and love."

"We do try to be a family," the thick silence was finally broken by Aidan, "but it's hard when there are only men. We're not a real pride. We're reversed."

"Excuse me?" Reversed? They all looked pretty straight to me, but you never know, sometimes my gaydar goes on the fritz.

"Do you know anything about lions?" Fallon spoke softly from my right.

"A little." I shrugged.

"Do you know how many lions are in a pride?"

"Is that a trick question?"

"No." Fallon gave a quick laugh. "Lions as opposed to lionesses. Do you know how many males there are in a pride?"

"Oh." I thought about it. "One, unless there are babies. The rest are females right?"

"Bravo," Aidan said. "Now, look around you."

"I see." I nodded, what else could I say? "So, do the lions in you rebel at this reversal?"

"No, quite the opposite," Fallon answered for everyone. "That's why this is so monstrous. The lions inside us are drawn to their Goddess, ecstatic when she shows us favor, but the part of us that is human, rebels. We're humiliated by her treatment of us, and horrified by what she's made us into. We *are* monsters, Vervain."

I blinked rapidly. There was this ridiculous stinging in my eyes. These guys were going to rape me and now I what? Pitied them? Admired them? Wanted to comfort them? Yep, I guess I did. I guess sometimes life isn't about living, it's about surviving, and that's all these men had been doing for a long time. They'd been doing so much surviving that they'd forgotten what it was like to live.

"No." I took a deep breath. "I've seen monsters, and you're not that. You're men born of magic, and magic is of the earth, of nature. So you *are* natural. Does the bird worry that flight is magical and therefore monstrous? No, it simply flies. You're like a flock of birds, staring at the sky, knowing it's where you belong, but hating yourselves for it. That's what I find unnatural. You say you're monsters who once were men. I say you're men, enslaved by a monster. You're melded with a beast, and not just any, but the

king of them all. Inside, you have all the instincts of a lion tempered with all the knowledge of a man. A perfect blending that is miraculous, not monstrous. It's just that no one's ever taught you how to fly."

"You're wrong, Vervain." Fallon's jaws clenched and he swallowed roughly. "You're very good at speaking profoundly."

Everywhere I looked, eyes stared at me intensely, haunted with horrors I couldn't even begin to guess at. The Intare were like abused children, turning hopeful stares to kindness, but not knowing quite yet what to do with it . . . and afraid it wouldn't last. The love magic fluttered its butterfly wings inside me and whispered to me about how great those men could be with the proper support, with the right woman to heal them and give them back their wings.

And I wanted to be that woman. I looked out at all those faces and felt Aphrodite's old magic expand, filling every part of me with purpose. It didn't matter how I'd come to be there, I was glad for it. If I died in the morning, it would be worth the chance of helping these men escape their chains. Though I had no plans on dying. I fully intended to kill that horrid bitch and make her pay for every hurt I saw in their eyes.

Those eyes were focused on me, and it seemed that I could feel their hearts beating in unison. A primitive drumbeat, urging me on. The butterflies were flapping wildly within me, desperately wanting to be unleashed, and I finally set them free, not knowing how my magic could possibly handle so many hearts at once, but hoping it could. With a jolt, I felt it connect to every heart within the room, and I was immediately assailed by terrifying images of torture and abuse.

I started to shake, and then, when it got to be too much, I began to scream. I felt the men reaching out to me, but I held out my hands to stop them, and then covered my head with my arms. I couldn't witness this much trauma, it was going to tear my mind to

pieces. I began to breathe deeply and slowly, trying to sink into the meditative state that Teharon had taught me.

Finally, I felt calm enough to construct a barrier against the images that were assaulting me from all of those haunted hearts. When it fell into place, I was able to take a deep breath and push the magic further, encourage it to take those horrible memories and destroy the power they had over those men.

My mind filled with white as the magic fulfilled my wishes in one sudden rush, amazing me with its power. The Intare let out startled sounds and then, like puppets cut from their strings, they all dropped to the ground as one.

I let the barrier down as the love magic flew home to me, and I caught glimpses of freshly healed hearts. The memories were still there, but they held no sway over the Intare, not after I'd shown them how magnificent they truly were. Now, their hearts beat with confidence, courage, and determination. They would never be made to feel that way again.

I thanked my magic for its hard work and felt a light, giggling response. I got the impression that it was happiest when it was being employed; the more hearts I could give it, the stronger it would get. My own heart felt lighter too, having given the lions some measure of comfort, but my mind was quickly remembering the awful things I'd seen in their memories, and that calm was turning to rage.

I got to my feet and met their stares boldly.

"Nyavirezi was given a gift; the ability to meld man with beast, to bring together the best of both and create a supernatural being of power and instinct, tempered by logic and honor. Yet all of you were filled with self-loathing and fear of your creator. I saw the things she did to you, the things she made you do. They were horrifying and truly evil, but these things are not you. I know you can see that now, you know what kind of men you really are. You

no longer need me to tell you how I see you, as if my perception is more important than the truth that lies inside yourself. You feel this truth now, but despite that, I will tell you what I see. I see beautiful, fierce, honorable men who should never have to question their humanity again. Be the man! Be the beast! Take them both and glory in them, for you are Intare!"

A roar of liberation thundered through the room, mixed with cheering, shouting, and applause. Darius had jumped to his feet and was roaring the loudest, one forepaw clawing the air as if Nyavirezi was standing before him, ready to be gutted. There were handshakes and back slaps, shouts of joy and tears flowing freely. I had never seen anything so powerfully emotional in all my life. My own cheeks were wet from the tears I hadn't realized I was crying. I felt the love magic rise up again in response, glimmering down the silken threads that bound us together, making us stronger.

"Forget profound"–Fallon came over and took my hands in his–"you're fucking amazing. What the hell was that? I feel like a new man, like every horrible thing that had been weighing me down is now suddenly gone."

"It's magic, baby." I winked at him and then suddenly yawned.

Fallon laughed and then turned to address the Intare.

"Alright everyone, come on, we've got some planning to do." He gestured them towards the other side of the room before turning back and saying to me, "Get some sleep. Darius will stay with you."

Darius huffed and nudged his head into my back before settling down on the floor. Looked like I'd be sleeping on lion fur. Fine by me, Darius looked more comfortable than the carpet.

"You sure you don't need me to help with the planning?" I eyed the wild gestures and eager faces across the room.

“You've done more than enough.” Fallon smiled and pushed me gently down. “I feel like I can take on the world; that bitch doesn't stand a chance. We'll brief you in the morning. Now, sleep well, Vervain. You're safe tonight.”

Soon, I was surrounded by a sleeping lion. I'm not really sure why Darius remained in his lion form, even after all the men had joined us. Maybe it took a lot out of him to change. Maybe he just liked being a lion. Or maybe he thought that I'd be more comfortable with him to sleep on. Whatever the reason, I was grateful for it.

I laid my head down on Darius’s paw and his body curled around me, warming me better than a blanket. The last thing I heard before I drifted off to sleep was the steady beating of Darius’ heart. His lion heart.

Chapter Forty-Three

"Vervain." someone was kissing the side of my face, running a hand down my stomach, and whispering into my ear. "Wake up."

My eyelids fluttered as I pushed sleep away, and I was surprised to find an angel leaning over me. I smiled up at the angel; Gabriel or maybe Michael. He looked a little tough, and he smiled back at me, but his smile wasn't angelic. Quite the opposite. In fact, I'd classify it more as a leer than a smile. As I puzzled that out, I realized that the body he was pressing against me was completely naked.

"Darius." The knowledge hit me like an angry werewolf, and that's exactly what I'd have on my hands if Trevor ever found out about this.

"There you are." Darius's leer softened into a more appropriate smile. "Do you need to use the bathroom before we get started?"

"Uh, sure." I got to my feet and followed him to a side door, keeping my eyes firmly on the back of his head. Then I went past him, into the bathroom. "Thanks." I shut the door on Darius and went about my morning business.

After I splashed water on my face and told myself over and over that this really was happening, I went out to face the Intare. Thankfully, they were all dressed, so they were relatively easy to face.

They went over the plan quickly with me. It was very simple, as the best plans usually are. Nyavirezi could use the boys against me, they were her biggest weapon, so they were simply

going to grab Blue and get out of the way. Out of the room, out of the palace, hopefully. They'd go tear Blue a new one while I'd attempted to kick Nyavirezi's ass . . . permanently. Fallon had found a sword for me sometime within the night. I had a weapon, and therefore, a chance.

"Are you all sure about this?" I walked among them, looking at each of them, and giving them all an opportunity to back out. "I don't want you to be upset after the fact. If I kill her, it's pretty permanent. We're not even sure what will happen to all of you if she dies. What if you die with her?"

"It will be better than living like this." Fallon walked through the men and handed me the sword. "Does anyone disagree with me?"

Fallon looked around the room, and every man shook his head. It said a lot about Nyavirezi's treatment of them that death was preferable, or at least worth the risk, for freedom. Having seen just a sampling of her work, I didn't blame them.

"So mote it be." I took the sword with calm determination, and maybe just a little bit of righteousness. "If it's possible to not kill Blue, I'd appreciate it. We need to talk."

The thought of Blue dying kind of hurt my heart, but he had literally thrown me to the lions, so it was hard to justify that hurt. If they killed him, I would accept it.

"Blue?" Darius was in jeans again.

I wasn't sure if I was grateful for that or not.

"Blue." Right, we hadn't talked much about Nyavirezi's companion. "It's a nickname. Don't ask. I'm talking about Nyavirezi's friend in the gold armor. The one you're going to take care of."

"Oh, sure." Darius frowned a little in confusion.

I'm sure he thought the nickname was an odd choice for the Aztec God of War, but I really didn't have time to explain it to him.

"Consider it taken care of," he said.

"Great, thank you." I went to hide next to the door, so I could surprise Nyavirezi when she came in. I wasn't above using every advantage I could get against a goddess, against anyone really, when my life was at stake. Play dirty and live to feel bad about it. I think I might make that my new motto. If I lived through this.

Chapter Forty-Four

An hour later found me sitting beside the door, still waiting on Nyavirezi. I had almost given up on her when I heard footsteps approaching. I guess they'd both slept in, snug as bugs in a rug, knowing I was being raped by lions just a few yards away. It must've been better than a hot toddy or a glass of milk. Torture your enemy. It's the perfect cure for insomnia.

I shook off my dark thoughts as I stood and prepared myself. I was so scatter-brained half the time that a little pre-battle meditation was always a good thing. I took a few breaths and reviewed my grievances. Let's see; she tried to torture me to death, she mistreated some of the hottest men on earth–taking them off the market and therefore mistreating all single women as well, she was in league with Blue, and she hurt Trevor (I was not going to even consider the possibility that he was dead). Yep, that's enough for me. The bitch was going down. I centered myself just as the door opened.

For a moment, things were calm, even when I'd placed the tip of my blade to the back of Nyavirezi's neck. Then the lions rushed the door, flowing gracefully around me and Nyavirezi while taking Blue out with them. It only took a few seconds before I was alone with the Lion Goddess.

I shoved the blade forward, hoping to end it before it had barely begun, but of course, that was only wishful thinking. Nyavirezi slipped deftly aside, shifting as she went. She kicked out with a back leg and caught me in the thigh, making me stumble. I waved my arms out and recovered just in time to see her tail swish arrogantly. That really pissed me off. She thought that this was going to be fun. Well, I was about to ruin her play time.

I reached for my war magic and heard, for a second, the sound of steel clashing on steel. There was a roar in my head, and in my veins, of shouted battle cries. I smelled the tang of death and felt the thunder of hooves vibrating the earth. On my lips was the salt of blood and sweat. New strength flowed through me, all of my pain receding, and my arm lifted the sword as if it were just an extension of myself.

I stalked toward the lioness, and she roared out her rage. She must have sensed the change in me, or maybe she scented the magic. Either way, she wasn't happy anymore. I barely paid any attention to her tantrum, though. My focus was on two things only: her neck and her chest. Either spot could gain me a kill, or get me killed. The sound of fighting came through the open door, and the big cat head swung toward the distraction. I, however, stayed focused and used the opportunity to my advantage.

The turning of Nyavirezi's head had bared her neck to me. I lunged in, but once more, her reflexes were too fast. She twisted and the blow cut through her shoulder instead. She cried out again, but this time it was in pain. Huge yellow eyes narrowed on me in a very human way, and all of my animal sympathies, that were usually a hindrance to me when I fought shapeshifters, went out the window.

"Thanks for last night," I taunted her. "The boys are very hospitable."

I watched her lean into her haunches, gathering her muscles, and I tensed in anticipation. I didn't have long to wait, she was air-bound in moments. I had the pleasure of being the nimble one that time. I rolled expertly out of the way and ended up in a fighting stance behind her. Nyavirezi twisted quickly, then leaped again, and again she barely missed me.

"Is that all you got?" I sneered, but then frowned when I realized there could be no banter. "Damn it! Why'd you have to shift? It's just not as fun if you don't taunt me back. Didn't you get

the memo? Missed your weekly arch nemesis meeting? You're supposed to rant and rage, telling me your plans to rule the world, in great detail, before you leave me to certain death at the hands of one of your minions. Oh wait, you don't have any minions. They're all mine now."

Nyavirezi lunged out with her humongous paw and actually landed a light scratch. I edged back and gave up the taunting in favor of concentrating on not getting killed. Fair trade I think.

She went on the offensive again, roaring and flailing powerfully. I ended up on my back, and I wasn't sure how I got there until I felt the burning in my side. My left side again, right over the bruises I was already sporting. She was so strong, she'd actually torn through the metal plates. I'd have to rethink those. Torn up as it was, the metal ended up hurting more than it was worth. Sharp edged metal pressing into a fresh cut is not the most enjoyable sensation. Maybe I'd have to switch to high impact plastic.

"Fuck," I hissed and stumbled to my feet.

I wasn't there for long. Nyavirezi took me down again, not with a swipe, but with both paws on my shoulder. My sword went flying and I heard my collarbone crack from the pressure. Such a small sound really, but it heralded some immense pain, and I screamed like a little girl. I was really embarrassed, and I hoped the guys couldn't hear me, wherever they'd taken Blue. How funny was that? I was about to be savagely killed by a lion goddess, and all I could think about was how embarrassingly I screamed.

The good thing was, my embarrassment took my mind off the pain and refocused it on the subject at hand. Mainly *not* getting savagely killed. Long, glistening teeth were inches away from my face, and Nyavirezi's lion eyes were filled with triumph. My sword glinted at me from beneath a pool table, mockingly out of reach. There was only one thing left for me to do, only one trick left up my sleeve, and it didn't matter if it killed me because, at that point,

it was just a question of how, not when. I'd rather be in charge of the how than let psycho kitty have the honor.

So, I reached out for her magic, imagining the power being drawn into my body like I did when I gathered energy for a spell. The triumph shining in Nyavirezi's eyes became confusion, but I knew better than to hesitate. I almost screwed things up the last time by hesitating; I wasn't about to do that again. Instead, I pulled strongly on the spark I found inside her, mentally gripping it with both hands and tearing it from her soul.

Nyavirezi jerked back and opened her mouth to roar, but what came out was a very human, very feminine scream. If it hadn't been so horrifying, I would've been relieved to hear her scream worse than I had. But it *was* horrifying, as well as deeply and psychologically wounding; watching a lioness writhe and scream with a woman's voice. I knew I had fodder for years worth of nightmares.

I stood to face her. I closed my eyes and focused on the power, on the bright rivers of energy flowing into me, the strength of the magic melding with my bones. I felt my wolf rise up, almost in challenge to the new power. They faced off for a moment, pausing the transfer, before my Nahual inserted herself between lioness and wolf, and forced them to get along for the greater good. The lioness padded through me, finding a space all her own and then stretching out in it until I thought my skin would burst.

Then the power hit me, and I fell to my knees. It was warm, thick fur, quiet strength, musky sex, and the calm confidence of a predator. I heard a thundering sound, like hundreds of lions roaring at once, and smelled the comforting scent of clean cat, thick in my nose. It was like burying my face into Nick . . . times ten . . . thousand. Heat zipped along my skin, tingling over my body in waves until finally receding to a pulsing thrum of energy.

I tried to open my eyes, but images flashed before me, replacing the carpet with rocky soil, the room with open grassland,

and I shut them again quickly. They continued even brighter against my eyelids; the ground was flying beneath my feet, no . . . my paws. A herd of some sort of long-legged, deer-like animal ran before me. I leapt and felt my teeth sink into a furry neck. Warm blood flowed into my mouth, and it tasted good, so good. Sweet-salty heaven flowing down my throat, giving its life for mine. I shook my head free of the image, but when I opened my eyes, I was closer to the floor than I should've been. I blinked slowly in confusion and opened my mouth to say, "What the hell?", but all that came out was a growl.

Oh, shit. Oh, fuck. Oh, shit!

I looked down and saw paws. There, beneath me, were thick limbs covered in golden fur. I swung my head, looked over my shoulder, and saw my tail swish quickly in agitation.

I guess I shouldn't have been so shocked. I mean, what else would Nyavirezi's power have been? But you try shifting into a four-hundred pound lioness. You would have needed some recovery time too. Unfortunately, I didn't get it.

A small whimper drew my attention. Nyavirezi was dying. I was a little surprised that she wasn't dead already. I padded over to her, and she stared at me in terror. I'd never seen such stark horror before, and I would never have imagined it could thrill me like it did.

On top of her delicious fear, I felt great. All of my cuts, scrapes, and broken bones had healed in the change. I roared triumphantly, the sound echoing back to me from the walls, and then pressed into her shoulders like she'd done to me. She had changed back to human, and it was human fear I smelled on her, human fear that excited the animal I'd become.

Without thought, I closed my mouth over her neck and ended what would have been a slow death, quickly. Maybe I should have let her slip away, maybe she deserved every second of

pain I could give her, and I'd most likely regret it later, but the lioness was too strong in me at that moment, and animals didn't engage in torture. It's just another sign of their moral superiority to humans, I guess.

With Nyavirezi's blood, came the last of her magic, rushing over my tongue in metallic vibrancy. It whizzed through my veins like it was looking for the finish line, while her life blinked out softly. Dying was probably the most gentle thing she'd ever done. Just a whisper of breath as I crunched through her neck like a Ritz cracker. I knew I should be horrified, but it just felt so amazing, tasted so luscious; warm, silky and thick. That's what life tastes like, and I wanted more, I wanted it all. No wonder Trevor loved the hunt.

Trevor.

I saw his face clearly, his honey-eyes boring into mine with disapproval. "We never eat human flesh," I could hear his voice inside my head. "We may hunt them, we may kill, but we do not eat of their flesh. We are not mere animals, we are the children of gods."

I shook my head, droplets of blood flying everywhere. I wasn't an animal, and I wasn't a god, but I *was* human. I hoped. I'd cling stubbornly to that until someone proved otherwise.

The body beneath me suddenly sickened me, and I backed away until I was huddled near the door, naked and shivering in my human body. I don't know how or when I'd changed back, but as I rubbed my arms frantically, I realized it was skin beneath my fingers, and I was grateful to be back in my own, as it were.

"Shouldn't have fucked with me," I whispered to Nyavirezi's corpse, but the final taunt lacked the bravado it required.

I'm not sure how long I sat there looking at Nyavirezi, watching the blood puddle grow, rubbing my limbs, and trying to

be as human as possible. It could have been a few minutes, it could have been a few hours, but I didn't focus on anything else until a pair of jean-clad legs blocked my view. I looked up them slowly and was instantly soothed by the sight of Darius.

His eyes widened as he took me in. It probably had something to do with me being naked and covered in blood. He dropped to his knees and inhaled sharply before he brushed the hair back from my face tenderly. I saw his body shiver, muscles quivering, triggering an instant and violent response in me.

I wanted him. I could smell the desire on him, richer and sweeter than cheesecake. I licked my lips as a purr vibrated my chest. My purr! He leaned his head in and laid it gently on my shoulder, silky hair falling over my hot skin like rain on summer asphalt, cooling and steaming at the same time. His breath caressed my chest as intimately as I wanted him to kiss me, and with no other thoughts in my head, I started to reach for him.

A wolf howl resounded inside my head, countered by the roar of a lioness. Claws to claws, teeth to teeth, my allegiances were being ripped apart from within. The ludicrous battle of my inner beasts effectively woke me out of my lust-induced stupor. I pushed Darius away gently, but firmly, and the cacophony quieted. I took a deep breath, looked around, and finally noticed that all of the Intare were there . . . and I was still naked.

"Can someone please get me something to wear?" I pulled my wild hair around me and stared up at them.

More than a few of them took in deep breaths and drew closer, but I heard one pair of footsteps break away, and hoped he was fetching some clothing.

"So, the good news is; I won." I tried my best to smile at them, and act as if almost snogging Darius while I was naked and covered in blood was a normal occurrence. "But there's a bit of a side effect. I had to take Nyavirezi's powers. It looks like I'm one

of you now."

They all dropped to their knees beside Darius, just as Fallon came in with a cotton robe. I thanked him and pulled it around me as I stood up. I was a little dismayed to see how I instantly stained the pure white fabric, blood is such a bitch to get out, but I was even more discomfited when Fallon fell to his knees with the others.

"What are you guys doing?" I sighed as I belted the robe. "A simple thank you would have been fine . . . and maybe some pointers on this lion magic."

"It's not lion magic," whispered Darius who still hadn't moved from the spot I'd pushed him back into. "It's lion*ess* magic, and you are the new lioness. You're our new Tima, and I, for one, am glad of it."

There was a strong murmur of agreement, and then a lust haze so thick, I almost fell to the floor when it hit me. My whole body trembled in response, my eyes closing and my head lolling back. They were all mine, and I wanted them, needed to feel their bodies against mine, inside of mine. I cried out as the wolf clawed my insides again, howling in rage. This time it actually hurt. I would have been pissed off, but the pain really helped clear the fog-o-lust.

"What's going on, boys?" I tried to sound casual, but my whole body was trembling like a crack addict going through withdrawals. "Why do I feel like jumping all of you?"

"Do you know what happens when a new male takes over a pride?" Fallon was creeping toward me on hands and knees, sniffing the air.

I didn't like the look in his eyes, or maybe I liked it too much.

"No." I backed up slowly. I knew better than to run.

"The females go instantly into heat," his voice lowered, and his eyes started looking a little weird.

"So, this is the same thing, just with the sexes reversed?" I looked at all the hungry faces and wondered if I'd jumped out of the rape pot only to land in the fires of lust. Out of the gang-bang and into the orgy.

"Yes," Aidan sounded a little out of breath, maybe it had something to do with him panting like a porn star.

"Oh, fuck," I whispered.

"Exactly," said Darius who had somehow managed to sneak up behind me.

I jumped back and he caught my sleeve, pulling my robe open. The room took a breath, and I almost fainted from the sudden lack of oxygen. Instead, I stumbled, and Fallon caught me, laying me back tenderly as Darius crawled up my body. I had a sudden flash of Trevor, crawling up me with a playful smile, and I started to cry. I didn't want to betray him, but it looked like I wouldn't have a choice.

My tears stopped the Intare in their tracks. They sniffed at me and backed up, making soft mewling sounds. Lions turned into kittens. Fallon wiped the wet tracks off my cheeks, then rubbed his face against mine, and Darius pulled my robe gently shut. The lust thinned out of the air, leaving a tremulous peace in its wake.

"Forgive us, Tima." Darius helped me sit up. "Sometimes it's hard to fight the animal inside, but our first instinct, above all others, is to protect you. Your tears are our tears. Please don't cry."

It took me awhile to catch my breath and concentrate on what he'd said. It was like my life was changing every few minutes, and I was trying desperately to keep up. My body shook, my eyes still wide, and I was swallowing convulsively.

“Tima?” I frowned as a horrible suspicion crept up behind me on tippy toes. Any minute now it would yell *Boo!* and scare the crap out of me. “That doesn’t happen to mean Queen, or Princess, or any other royal bullshit does it?”

“No.” Fallon pulled up a knee to rest one arm on casually.

It was amazing how fast they'd gone from passion-crazed to calm. From sixty to zero in sixty seconds.

“Phew.” Maybe my instincts were off. I started to relax.

“It means *heart.*” Darius sprawled out on the floor and stared up at me, in what I was fervently hoping was not an adoring manner, no matter how much it appeared to be. “You’re the heart of the Intare now. The source of our magic and our life.”

“Oh.” I waved dismissively. “You don’t have to live in fear anymore, guys. I promise not to kill any of you unless you try to kill me first.”

“That’s very reassuring, Tima.” Aidan chuckled, though I saw quite a few relieved expressions. “But that’s not what Darius meant. You’re our goddess now, and you’ve just inherited not only Nyavirezi’s powers, but all her belongings . . . which include us.”

Boo! Screamed that damn suspicion, and I nearly screamed right back, just once I’d like to be wrong. Well, at least when what I’m expecting is unwanted.

“You’re no one's belongings.” I felt my jaw clench in anger. What gave Nyavirezi the right to treat them that way? “You’re all free now. Free to fu . . . make love to whomever you like and go wherever you want.”

“Really?” The bald one with the bad attitude was changing his tune. “You’ll allow us freedom?”

“I’m not *allowing* anything.” I sighed. “You’re free. Period.

That was the point of all this, remember? Go off and do . . . well, whatever you want to do. Spread your wings, little birdies."

"You're not understanding." Darius finally sat up. "If we run off to be free, you're allowing it. Whether you like the idea or not, you're the Tima of the Intare. You're our goddess and our heart. We can't survive without you, and we can never be truly free. We'll always belong here . . . with you."

"Please tell me this isn't a case where you'll all die if I don't touch you every month." What; did every shapeshifting club have that rule?

"No, it's not about touching. It's about control, and without it, we won't die"–Fallon's eyes were glittering dangerously–"we'll just go wild."

"What?" I laughed a little hopefully. "Like *Girls Gone Wild* or something? Should I get a camera crew to follow you around?"

"No." Darius touched me gently on the arm, and I felt my new power shift to stroke against him through my skin. He looked startled for a moment, but quickly recovered and splayed his hand against my skin to feel it better. "More like *men gone crazy.* You hold not only the magic of the Intare, but our sanity as well. Without you, we will literally lose ourselves to our beasts. We *need* you to lead us, Tima. To keep us sane. To remind us that we're men as well as lions."

"Lead you?" My laughter was slowly turning into hysterics. "I can barely lead myself away from the salad bar. I get into trouble every time I leave the house . . . Exhibit A." I waved my hands wide to encompass them all. "And I live with a werewolf who's not going to be pleased about me bringing home another eighty stray cats."

"We'll continue to live here, Tima." Darius patted me lightly. I don't think he was used to a woman getting hysterical on

him. "We'll just need you to check in with us. Often."

"How often is often?" I narrowed my eyes on him. "Often as in the way Trevor looks in on his club, or often as in how much you need to stir risotto?"

"I honestly don't know how to answer that." Darius' eyes had gone wide and his voice astonished.

"The first," Fallon answered calmly.

"When did you learn how to speak *Crazy Woman*?" Darius whispered dramatically to Fallon.

"Hey!" I pushed at Darius, and he smiled at me affectionately.

"When I started watching the Food Network," Fallon said, completely straight-faced. "Risotto has to be stirred constantly."

"Wait a second." I looked around.

Nyavirezi's body was gone, and I wanted to hug whoever took care of her remains, but we were still one body short.

"What happened to Blue?"

"Gone." Fallon shrugged. "Traced out before we could deliver the killing cut."

"Okay." I was kind of relieved that he was still alive. I can't help it, I'm only human. Wait a second . . . "Am I still human?"

"As much as we are, I expect." Aidan shrugged.

"Not so much then." I grimaced as my stomach clenched against the awful truth. What did it mean? "Are you all immortal?"

"As long as you're alive"–Darius shrugged–"so are we."

"That's what I'm trying to find out." I felt my face wrinkle

in thought. I really needed to watch that, the fine lines were creeping in already. Or maybe I didn't have to worry about that anymore. I just didn't know for sure. "Do Nyavirezi's powers make me immortal? I don't think Aphrodite's did, so I guess it stands to reason that Nyavirezi's won't either."

"I suppose we'll just have to wait and see," Fallon said, looking as unconcerned about his possible mortality as Trevor had when he'd gained his.

"Can I still go out and sleep with whomever I want?" Baldie had been waiting as patiently as possible for the conversation to head back to where he wanted it, but evidently, it wasn't getting there fast enough for his libido.

"Yes, er, what's your name again?" I smiled my lopsided *sorry, I've just met eighty werelions in one evening* grin.

"Alfred," he actually said it without laughing.

"Your name's Alfred?" I vaguely recalled hearing it as something different. "Oh, but I can call you Al, right?" I laughed as Paul Simon sang in my head. Alfred, aka Al, didn't get it.

"Yes," he said; still blank, still lifeless, until he returned to the subject closest to his heart. "So, can I go get laid or what?"

"Yes, Al"–I waved imperiously, like I was the bloody Queen of England granting her knight a favor–"have at it."

Al didn't wait a second longer. He ran out of the room with a few men trailing after him. I was kind of surprised I didn't hear any *Yippees* to go along with their excited exodus. They all but skipped from the room. I laughed at how much they resembled a college fraternity set loose. Frat boys with the strength of lions. Sigh. No good could come of it.

"They'll be okay right?" I watched them leave with a little concern. "They have spending money and, er . . . protection?"

Aidan laughed, but beneath the laughter, I caught a hint of growing affection. "She's already a better Tima than Nyavirezi."

I looked at Darius in question, but he wasn't laughing when he answered me. He actually seemed very serious. "Nyavirezi never concerned herself with our needs. That you would think of such trifling things as money and condoms for Al, shows what kind of leader you'll be. I'm thankful you came to us, Tima."

"I don't know how long that will last." I rubbed at my head, and instantly, hands were on my shoulders, kneading away my tension. "Oh, uh, thank you." I sighed and relaxed a second before I remembered that I couldn't sit there dawdling when my friends and my lover were probably wondering if I was even alive. "I really need to go home, guys. I'm sure everyone is concerned about me, and Trevor must be climbing the walls. Maybe literally. Damn, I hope my walls are okay."

"Of course." Darius stood and pulled me up with him. "Fallon and I will accompany you."

"Ah, I don't know if that's such a good idea."

"They will have questions," Fallon said matter-of-factly, "some of which you'll not know the answers to. I think Darius is right, we should escort you."

"Alright, but no fighting." I started out the door and then stopped abruptly. "Do either of you know where my gloves are?"

Chapter Forty-Five

When I got home, it was to find my living room full of gods.

"I think this room has exceeded its divine capacity," I announced.

They all stood with different degrees of shock on their faces. Trevor was the only one who recovered enough to rush forward and swing me up into his arms.

"By all that's holy!" Trevor buried his face in my neck so the rest of his words were muffled. "I knew you lived, but we couldn't trace in. Nyavirezi had her home warded well. I was going crazy, Minn Elska, knowing she was going to kill you, and not being able to do a damn thing about it."

"That seems to happen to me a lot, huh?" I stroked his thick hair as he let me slide down his body till I felt my feet touch the floor.

Trevor rubbed his face along mine tenderly before pulling back. My wolf was finally happy.

"How many times do I have to tell you, not to do that to me?" Trevor said.

There were signs of strain all over his beautiful face, and I smoothed them away gently with my fingers. Trevor sighed as he closed his eyes.

"I told you all that she'd be fine," I heard Horus say flippantly, but there was a note of relief in his voice.

"Shut up, Horus," Thor thundered, and came forward to

kiss me on the cheek. “We’ve all been here trying to come up with a plan to get you back.”

“My heroes,” I sighed dramatically.

Then the rest of them were hugging me and welcoming me home. What a change from the days I hunted the gods alone, coming home to a cold house and a warm cat. I'd be lucky if the cat didn't yell at me.

When we all gushed in relief enough, we sat down, and Trevor went to make a pot of tea for me. Persephone sat beside me and eyed the bloodstains on the robe I still wore.

“I had a bit of an altercation,” I said grimly and then told them what happened with Nyavirezi, Blue, and the Intare.

“Vervain.” Trevor groaned. “Why can’t you stay out of trouble for five minutes?”

“Oh, I’m sorry, is my life inconveniencing you?” I couldn’t help it, saying it once was excusable, but twice was making me mad.

“Rouva”–Trevor's jaw clenched as he inclined his head slightly–“you know I meant no disrespect.”

“Oh, stop with the Rouva thing.” I threw my hands up and fell back against the couch. “All I’m trying to say is; it’s not like I intentionally go out shouting; ‘Someone try and kill me please’! I’m trying my best here, Trevor, and I could use a little support.”

“So, you think I’m not supportive enough?” His tone went low and his eyes were starting to glow.

“Fuck.” I rubbed at my face. “Where the hell did this conversation take a turn into Splitsville?”

“We’re not breaking up,” Trevor growled.

"Well, that's the end of the line for the track we're currently on." I sat up and sighed. "I'm not saying that you don't support me, I'm just saying that blaming me when shit happens is not conducive to a loving relationship. I need your help here, and I don't particularly like fighting with you in front of everyone. So, what's it gonna to be?"

"Shit, Vervain." Trevor shook his head. "Having a fight doesn't automatically lead to ending a relationship. Who taught you that?"

"Huh, really?" I frowned as I rethought my idea of relationships.

Usually, I got involved with someone, did something to mess it up, we yelled at each other, and then it was over. Isn't that how it works?

"Yes, really." Trevor took my hand and squeezed it. "The healthiest relationships aren't with couples who never fight. They're with couples who know *how* to fight and how to compromise. I can accept the fact that you're a walking magnet for supernatural trouble, if you can accept the fact that I have trouble dealing with you being in trouble."

"Okay, deal." I grinned in relief. "Now, what do I do about the Intare?"

"You're lucky that you're alive," Thor's deep voice rumbled through my chest. "I told you not to try taking another god's power. How are you feeling? Are you dizzy at all, breathless?"

"I'm fine, Thor." I slumped over my tea. "I'm a little tired, a little sick of shapeshifters telling me that they need me to survive, but other than that, I'm great. A lot better than I'd be if I *hadn't* killed Nyavirezi."

"Okay"–Thor held up his hands–"point taken. I don't want

to fight with you either."

"I'm not trying to start fights." I clawed my hands through my hair and roared in frustration. Yes, roared.

Everyone sort of sat back a little and stared at me in fascinated horror. The funny thing was, I didn't even realize what I'd done at first. Occasionally, when I fought, I'd growl like a wolf or snarl like a jaguar. That little piece of Trevor's soul or my Nahual would surface and help me out. This roar was all lion, though, and everyone knew it. When it finally sank in for *me*, I raised my pale, horrified face to my friends.

"What the hell was that?" I looked at Trevor, who was looking a little pale himself.

Were wolves afraid of lions? I guess if they had any brains, they would be. Lions seriously outweighed them.

"I think your new power is having some side effects," Thor answered for Trevor, and I looked toward him for more help, more answers. "It may be what's shortened your temper as well. Try to breathe deeply and acknowledge the lion inside, let it know who's in charge, but make it feel welcome. Like a child, you must discipline it, rein it in."

The steady sound of his voice calmed me, cleared my head, and I was instantly able to use the technique Teharon taught me to take look inside and see every part of my powers clearly. The butterflies of my love magic played around the sleeping wolf. The lioness sat proud and defiant in her corner, eyeing the shining Victory with interest. War sort of sat back in the shadows, a churning mass waiting to be called, and Lust swirled deep red in my center, watching everything with lazy curiosity.

I took a deep breath and called to the lioness. She cocked her head to the side, looking at me suspiciously. Then, from the dark below, I felt something stirring, and the lioness felt it too. She sank into her haunches, wiggling in anticipation of an attack, as I

sifted through the shadows blindly. There was another presence, another magic that was so much a part of me, I'd forgotten to bring it into the mix.

My Nahual.

As soon as I remembered her, my Nahual came forward and seemed to light every dark recess with her presence. She was a white jaguar with golden spots and rich, brown eyes. My soul given shape, a light that could connect me with myself, if I ever lost my way. She was more me than I was, if that makes any sense. The magic I was born with, my spark, and I'd forgotten her.

I accepted the feelings of guilt over the slight, but she only glowed brighter, those dark eyes twinkling with humor. Guilt was unnecessary, silly even, when you were dealing with yourself. My Nahual was there for me no matter what, she *was* me, and there was no forgetting her, only remembering. Now, I was remembering.

Even though she'd made an appearance when I'd gained the lioness magic, I hadn't consulted her for guidance. I'd just figured they'd all learn to get along, but now I realized that I needed more than a truce inside me. I needed unity. That kind of cooperation didn't come from just leaving warring factions alone. It came from mediation.

As I sent a wave of warmth to the lioness, the jaguar looked on with approval, but underlying the welcome was my determination to remain in control; of my life and my magic. I opened my soul to her, so she would know the type of woman she now inhabited, and I felt her reach through me, sniffing out the secrets of my heart. When she was done, she lay down and rolled onto her back, offering me her belly like a trusting cat. I mentally stroked her and gave her the love that was needed to bind us together. A vibration rumbled through me, bringing an amazing peace. She was purring.

A rushing wave of energy flowed out from my Nahual and enveloped the other magics, connecting them together in a circle of light. It pulsed brighter and brighter, but within the light, I could still make out the forms of the individual magics. They glided to my jaguar slowly. The darkness of War was absorbed instantly, then Victory followed quickly with the flash of steel. Lust was an orange heat, swirling low around the jaguar and curling into her belly, but Love was a flock of butterflies diving straight to my Nahual's heart, leaving a pulsing blush on her coat. Finally, my wolf and lion approached together.

The three animals bowed their heads together, and where they met, the light flared with a burst of colors. A true union had been forged. My jaguar formed a bridge between my wolf and lioness. Jungle, mountain, and plain. Soul, heart, and body. Each represented something different and special to me. I saw the pattern clearly in the light of their joining. The light that grew brighter and brighter.

My eyes popped open with a sharp inhale.

"How long was I out?" I asked the intent faces around me.

"Just a few seconds." Trevor's brow was wrinkled deeply, and I reached up automatically to smooth it again. His smile was full of relief. "It worked."

"I think so." I reached a hand out to Thor, and he took it with a half smile. "Thanks for the advice. It's getting a little crowded in there, but I think I can handle it now."

"I know a little about shifting from my father. It's different than being born a Were." Thor nodded to Trevor. "If you'd like, I'll have Odin come and speak with you about it. He could give you more pointers than I."

"I'd appreciate that." I smiled gratefully at Thor, but part of me was nervous about seeing Odin again.

Then I remembered the lions.

"So, any suggestions about my Thundercats?" I looked over at the others hopefully.

"Nyavirezi's shapeshifting ability was created through magic," Teharon said thoughtfully. "So, you should now be able to create more lions with the magic."

"Yeah, Darius told me about all that. Evidently, I can also use it to kill them." I grimaced. "But what about all his talk on how I need to lead them, and how her home is mine now?"

"Well, it is," Pan piped up. "All her stuff is yours. To the victor go the spoils. How cool is that?"

"Who's Darius?" Trevor's voice had an undercurrent of a growl, and I turned to him sheepishly.

Not the best way to approach a wolf.

"One of the werelions." I smiled hesitantly.

"Which werelion, was he at the battle?"

"Well, of course, he was at the battle." I sighed. "They all were. Nyavirezi commanded it, and they had to follow her or die, basically. Well, not anymore."

"Now they follow you?" Trevor's growl was becoming more pronounced.

"That's what I'm trying to figure out, Trevor." I nudged him playfully. "You wanna give me some suggestions?"

"Tell them all to take a flying leap?" He grinned maliciously.

"Trevor, please." I poured myself another cup of tea. "I need to know what's going to happen to the Intare if I walk away.

Darius says they'll resort to their animal natures without me, so they can't rule themselves. Does anyone know if that's true?"

"I'm afraid it is," Brahma said. I was a little surprised that he was the one to answer. "You need to lead them, Vervain. If you don't, we'll have a bunch of wild werelions on the loose."

"Wow, wild werelions." I scrunched up my face. "Try saying that three times fast."

"This is serious, Vervain." Thor ground his teeth.

"You think I don't know that?" I took a deep breath and pushed the lioness back down. Boy, she sure had a temper. "It's either laugh or cry, and I don't like crying."

"Fine, laugh it up"–Trevor had evidently been stewing about the damn lions–"but you're not moving in with them."

"Sweet werewolf lovin'," I swore. "Will you listen to yourself? I don't want to live with them. I've got enough crazy shifters in my house as it is."

"Okay, Minn Elska." Finally, his Trevor smile was back and so was his hand on my neck. "You're right, I'm sorry. I don't know why I'm getting upset over some man I've never met. What happened to that lion who drug you off, by the way? I'd like to get my hands on him for hurting you."

"Actually, you should be thanking that lion." I grimaced again. I couldn't blame Trevor, hadn't I wanted to do the same thing? "His orders were to kill me. He knocked me out instead."

"And you know this how?" Trevor's eyes narrowed.

"Because he told me." I counted to ten before I continued. "It's Darius, he was the one who helped me and urged the others to back me in our plan."

"So, Darius was the blond midget?"

I raised my eyes at Trevor's tone.

"Um . . . first of all, they prefer the term *little people.*"

What the hell was up with him? Trevor had always been the calm one, what was with the about face?

"Secondly, he's at least a foot taller than me, so what does that make me, a member of the Lollipop Gang?" I asked.

"Actually, I think you'd be in the Lullaby League, since you're a girl," Pan added in an overly serious tone that immediately drew laughter from the God Squad, even Trevor grinned.

"Okay, maybe he wasn't *exactly* a little person," Trevor relented.

"But you're bigger than him." I sipped my tea calmly. "Yes, I get it. You're a big bad wolf, and he's a fraidy cat. You're a manly man, and he's a pussy. You're a sexual powerhouse, and he probably can't even get it up. Did I miss anything, O Seventh Wonder of the World?"

"I'm the Wolf Prince, and he's a royal pain in the ass," Trevor asked solemnly.

"So, what do I do about the ass pain?"

"I believe they make an ointment for that." Horus delivered the joke so dryly, everyone just sat blinking and gaping at him.

"Holy crap!" I laughed and broke the stunned silence. "An ointment." I laughed more.

"I guess you'd know about those kinds of things, Horus." Pan recovered a heartbeat after I did.

"Yes, I do"–Horus grimaced–"but you won't sit still long enough for me to rub it on you."

“And he just keeps going and going.” I laughed again. I had to put my tea down, I was afraid I’d spill it.

“Yeah, he’s the god-damned Energizer Bunny.” Pan didn’t take too kindly to having his joke turned back on him.

“Speaking of bunnies,” I interrupted. “I shifted into a lioness . . . and I kinda liked it.”

“What’s that got to do with bunnies?” Pan was the only one who wasn’t staring at me in rapt fascination.

“Absolutely nothing, but it got you to stop fighting, didn’t it?” I smiled serenely and Pan smiled back.

“Did you want to chase bunnies when you were a lioness?” Pan continued helpfully, oblivious to everyone else’s reaction. “Maybe that’s where the bunnies come in.”

“No.” I frowned. “At least I hope not. I don’t particularly want to kill Thumper. Although I did enjoy snapping Nyavirezi’s neck when I shifted. You were the only thing that kept me from eating her actually,” I said to Trevor and saw his face turn as serious as the sudden silence felt. “I heard you in my head, telling me how you never ate human flesh, that you’re not just animals, but gods as well. Remembering you, helped me to remember me. I changed back instantly.”

“You controlled the beast on your first shift?” Thor leaned forward in his seat. “That’s amazing, Vervain. Animal forms can be very overwhelming, all of your senses going into overdrive. Dad had to study and meditate long hours before he even attempted his first shift.”

“Father helped me back from my first change.” Trevor was staring at me with something that looked a lot like awe. “It took me hours to conquer the wolf and return to human form. A first timer, with no training, no guide? You should have been lost for days. There would have been a good chance that you’d never come

back."

"Never?" I think my voice actually squeaked. "As in, I'd be a lioness forever?"

"Yes, Minn Elska"–I felt Trevor's arms slide around me, shaking a little, but I was still staring off into space–"that's what I mean by 'never'. But you're okay, and plainly one hell of a bad ass."

"Holy cannoli," I whispered. "I could have been a liongirl forever. Hey, can I be a lionwoman? Can I half-shift like you?" I looked hopefully at Trevor.

"I don't think so," he said. "Nyavirezi's power was to change into a lioness, not a lionwoman."

"Bummer." I shrugged. "Oh well, I probably wouldn't be as hot as you are in half-form."

"You think I'm hot as a wolfman?" Trevor's grin turned into a leer.

"Uh, yeah." I gave him my *duh* face. "Don't you remember that night in the backyar . . ." I trailed off as I realized I had everyone's rapt attention.

"I told you they're sexy," Persephone whispered to me, but the gods' super senses insured that everyone heard her anyway.

"What's this?" Hades turned Persephone's face back to his. "Since when did you find fur sexy?"

"Since that time you bought that rabbit fur glove, and you rubbed it mmmrrhh . . ."

Hades' hand stifled the rest of Persephone's sentence; to my, and everyone else's, great disappointment. At least I wasn't the only one blabbing.

"That's enough, darling." Hades removed his hand slowly, as if afraid Persephone might suddenly blurt out more details of their sex life.

"So, back to you finding me sexy." Trevor nuzzled my ear.

"Why don't we get back to her being able to turn fuzzy," Thor interrupted.

"I've only done it the once"–I swallowed past the nervous lump in my throat–"so far. When I took the power, it changed me. I'm not even sure how I'd do it again."

"Dad can help you," Thor offered gently.

"*I* will help her." Trevor slid his arm more firmly around me.

"Trevor." I pushed at him and moved to the edge of my seat. "That's enough."

"She inherited her power." Thor put his hands up in a placating gesture. "I just thought that his insight might be more helpful in her situation."

"I will take care of my mate, thank you," Trevor growled.

"Enough, I said." I pushed at Trevor's puffed up chest. "Could we maybe focus on my issues for now? We can get back to your male insecurities later."

"My what?" Trevor looked like he'd just swallowed a lemon . . . whole.

"Focus, Trevor." I patted his hand a second before I turned back to everyone else. "What happened with the riot? Are all those people okay?"

"The police showed up and handled it with minimum bloodshed." Horus twisted his mouth in the imitation of a smile.

“Once in awhile you humans actually do something right.”

“Thanks for the overwhelming vote of confidence.” I sighed and leaned back, suddenly exhausted.

“Tima?”

A knock sounded on the front door, and I jumped up. I had completely forgotten that the boys were giving me a few minutes to break the news to everyone, and then were tracing into Hawaii. I'd given them the address.

“*Who* is that?” Trevor growled and got to his feet.

“It’s Darius and Fallon.” I pushed him back down. “Two men who you should be grateful to for literally saving my ass. In all sorts of ways.”

“What does that mean?” Trevor's eyes narrowed.

“Just trust me,” I said. “They’re good guys, and I owe them, so be nice. They thought you might have some questions, so they gave me a head start and then followed me home.”

“Tima, are you alright?” Fallon’s deep voice came through the door.

“I’m fine.” I hurried over and said the ritual words to unward the house for them before I let them in.

Thankfully, they’d found some T-shirts to put on. I didn’t think Trevor could have handled their previous uniform.

“Have you told them?” Darius eyed the large gathering with hesitation. “Have you explained?”

“Yep.” I motioned them further in. “The beans are everywhere, the bag is completely empty of cats, the fan has been hit, the–”

"Okay, Tima, we understand." Fallon smiled gently.

Pan and Brahma both got up so the boys could have a seat right in the middle of things. I think the ulterior motive was to have the werelions surrounded, but I decided to pretend it was just plain consideration. The lions took the offered seats, but kept a wary eye on the gods.

"So, Vervain tells me that I have you two to thank for her safe return," Trevor's words sounded skeptical

I sat down beside him hard enough to jostle him.

"Nyavirezi was a tyrant," Darius said casually. "In helping Vervain, we helped ourselves. You owe me no thanks. I, however, owe you some answers. Is there anything she hasn't covered? Anything you want to know?"

"Yes." Trevor leaned forward. "Do you want to fuck my mate?"

"Trevor!" I pushed at him as my face turned bright red.

"It's an honest question, Vervain." Trevor wasn't the least bit fazed by my smack. In fact, he hadn't taken his eyes off Darius. "If you're to lead these lions, I want to know everything; starting with this guy's interest in you."

"Yes," Darius interrupted, and everyone stared at him in shock. "I want her. She's my Tima and the bond has sexual aspects. It can't be helped." He shrugged and looked at Fallon, who gave me a cocky half-grin and nodded. "I'm not going to lie to you Wolf Prince, you know she's attractive, but when Nyavirezi gave her to us to use physically, it was I who stopped the others from taking their pleasure with her. If I wanted her bad enough to accomplish the deed dishonorably, I would've taken her when I had the chance."

"Nyavirezi gave you to the lions?" Trevor turned back to

me with a horrified, bug-eyed look.

"Yeah, but nothing happened." I sighed. I was so hoping this wouldn't come out. "Darius stood up for me and talked the others out of it. We made nice, made plans, freed them from the evil kitty's nasty clutches, and now they can have sex with whoever they want. Except me. The end."

"Why didn't you tell me about it?" Trevor was growling at me as if we were fighting alone in our bedroom. He knew I hated to fight in public. We'd just gone through this a few minutes ago.

"Maybe I wanted to wait until we were alone," I growled back. "Maybe it's a sore subject for me, asshole."

"I'm sorry, Tima." Darius leaned forward. "Don't fight with your mate over this. I shouldn't have brought it up in my defense. You're right; it's a private matter and an embarrassment to the Intare."

"It's alright, Darius." I watched Trevor's eyes stray back to the lion and soften imperceptibly.

"Is there anything else you'd like to know?" Fallon spoke up, he seemed to be pretty close to Darius, and I was assuming he was trying to alleviate some of the pressure on his friend.

"I have a question," I spoke before Trevor could add more fuel to my shapeshifter fire.

"Yes, Tima?" Fallon looked at me with a quick smile.

"What does leading the Intare entail exactly?" I wanted everything laid out in specific terms in front of me so there would be no confusion. Mainly on my part. I was easily confused.

"Honestly, Tima"–Darius shrugged–"besides being around and giving us commands, Nyavirezi didn't do much. Anything you'd like to add to that would be icing."

"What Dare is trying to say"–Fallon nudged his friend in the arm–"is that we're in dire need of a Tima who actually cares about us, who actually is our heart. I think you can do it, Vervain. I think you can help us, but basically, we just need you to visit with us once every few weeks, or more often if you'd like, and give us some guidance where needed. Maybe sort out any squabbles, make pertinent decisions. You know; rule."

"I *don't* know about ruling"–I squished my face up at him–"but I'll try my best. How about I come over tomorrow and we have an official meet and greet? I'll address any issues you guys have and we can go from there."

"That sounds perfect." Darius looked around. "Did anyone else want to ask anything or should we go?"

"Yes. I'd like to know"–Persephone leaned forward and Darius turned politely to her–"did Nyavirezi scout the globe for the hottest guys she could find or what? I mean, were looks her prime requirement for joining the lion club? Cause you two are smokin' hot."

"We're *so* having a talk when we get home." Hades stood up, lifting Persephone into his arms in one fluid motion.

She squealed in delight and waved at everyone.

"Goodnight"–Persephone winked at Darius and Fallon–"thanks for a fabulous evening."

My lions had stood when Hades had, and they both bowed gallantly to the departing couple. I couldn't help feeling a little proud of their courtly manners. *"That's my boys,"* I said in my head. They sat down, and I smiled my approval at them. If this was how they all behaved, ruling would be a piece of cake.

Oh cake. I hadn't eaten in like, forever.

"How many Intare are there?" Thor moved into the seat

Persephone vacated, distracting me from my hunger.

“There are seventy-eight of us,” Fallon answered after looking to me for permission. Okay, so I was off by two in my estimation, still pretty close.

“And you all live in Nyavirezi’s home?” Thor's eyes had a calculating gleam.

“It’s now Vervain’s home, but yes,” Darius took over the answering. “It’s more than large enough to house all of us.”

“Do you all sleep in that room?” I asked.

I didn’t think one giant room with everyone crashing on the floor would be very comfortable.

“No, Tima.” Darius’ eyes went soft when he looked at me. “Don’t worry, we each have our own room. It’s a very luxurious home actually. The room Nyavirezi put you in with all of us was the common room, where we gather for leisure. You have the master suite now, of course, but all in all, there are over one-hundred-twenty rooms in the palace. That doesn’t include the common room, the numerous bathrooms, the kitchen, the dining room, the fitness room, the laundry, the inner courtyard, the music room, the armory, the wine cellar, the theater, the library, the larder, and the ballroom. Outside the palace, the grasslands are ringed by mountains, nourished by a central lake, and well stocked with wild game for our hunting needs. We are very self-sufficient. I hope you will lead us on a hunt soon, Tima.”

Whoa, that was a lot to process.

“I don’t like the idea of hunting, but I have a feeling that the lioness inside me will need it.” I sighed, “So, I guess I’ll take you up on that sometime.”

I couldn’t stifle my yawn; what a day. Did I eat first or go straight to bed?

“Okay, I think that’s enough for tonight,” Trevor declared. Have I mentioned how much I love that wolf? “We’ve gone over everything we need to, and we’ll notify you all if anything changes. As for you two”–he turned to Darius and Fallon–“Vervain will see you tomorrow. Thank you for coming.”

I nearly choked when I heard Trevor's acceptance. The boys seemed a little shocked by it too, but they just nodded and came over to kiss my hand before leaving. Of course, it was more of a face rub combination kiss, but Trevor didn’t say anything, so neither did I. The rest of the God Squad all got up, and we made our goodbyes before I raced Trevor down the hallway to our bed.

Sleeping on a lion was nice, but I was looking forward to an actual mattress.

Chapter Forty-Six

"I really don't think it's a good idea for you to go alone." Trevor watched me from the doorway as I finished applying my lipstick.

"And I don't think it's a good idea to bring my werewolf boyfriend to the first meeting of Vervain's Werelions Anonymous." I walked past him, into the bedroom, and slung my purse over my shoulder.

"You're literally walking into the lion's den without me." Trevor followed me out to the living room.

"I'm safer than Daniel," I said. "I have more than God on my side, I am God, or rather *their* God, er . . . Goddess."

"Great." Trevor sighed. "Good job; you see what happens when a witch tries to reference the Bible?"

"Hey." I pointed my finger at him. "You got the point, and there's nothing wrong with a witch referencing to the Bible. You, of all people, should know that, wolf."

"Fine," he grumbled, "but if you're not home in time for supper, I'm coming after you, and the fur is going to fly. Do you understand me, young lady?"

"Yes, papa wolf." I kissed him on the cheek and waved as I traced out.

It didn't take me too long to find my lions. They were roaming the halls freely now that the evil lioness was dead. The lioness is dead! Long live the lioness! I approached the first guy I came across, a buff babe with short, dark hair and dark eyes. I had to hand it to Nyavirezi; she had good taste in men.

"Hey you," I called in my most friendly, *I'm the new boss but I'm totally cool* voice. "Do you know where Darius is?"

His eyes widened a second before he dropped to his knees and lowered his forehead to the floor. I guess my cool voice needed some work.

"Stop that." I bent over and tapped him on the head. "Get up, it's a new regime in the lion kingdom . . . er, queendom . . . lionessdom. Now, I'm sounding dumb."

Before I could go on, the love magic took over, flowing down the link it had already established between us, and calming his anxieties.

"Tima?" His voice was low and just as sexy as his body. He raised his eyes and met mine with a hesitant smile as he got to his feet.

Holy hot lions, Batman, didn't I have enough temptation as it was?

"You can call me: Vervain," I patted him reassuringly. "And you are?"

I know, you'd think having a magical connection would at least supply me with all of their names, but it didn't seem to work like that.

"Lucian." He tilted his head and regarded me intently. Waiting for my next trick perhaps.

"Do you know where Darius is, Lucian?"

What the hell, did they all have names straight out of a bodice-ripper novel? I guess it matched their hot physiques. Then I remembered Alfred.

"Sure." He fully smiled. "I'll escort you to him if it pleases you."

"It would do much pleasing of the me." I laughed, but he just smiled politely and held out his arm. "Whoa, you really meant 'escort', huh? Okay, why not?"

I took his arm, and the boy puffed his chest out so far that I was afraid he might float away. My lion balloon led me through the hallways, and I was promptly lost. I hoped they didn't turn into scary possessive lions because I wasn't sure I could make it back to the tracing point on my own.

As we walked, we passed other lions, who dropped to the ground upon seeing me. I spent a great deal of time picking them up and telling them to lay off on the scary cult-worship crap. From now on, Kool-Aid was off the menu for these boys.

By the time we found Darius, my back was starting to ache from bending over so much, and I was hating Nyavirezi all over again. Thankfully, Darius didn't try to bow to me, he just waved an arm toward the patiently waiting Intare. I found myself standing on a raised dais, about to address a room full of werelions.

"Okay." I cleared my throat and looked out over the crowd.

They were all there, and they were all straight out of a Chippendale review. At least they were wearing shirts with their jeans this time; some of what I'd said before must've sunk in. The shirts did nothing to hide their hotness, though. In fact, I think it actually added to it. They looked less like love slaves and more like real men. It was a little intimidating. It was also a little exciting. I wanted to jump up and down and shout, "Mine, mine, mine", but that was probably highly inappropriate. And wrong, of course, very wrong.

"Well, I guess I'm your new Tima." I swallowed with some difficulty. They were all watching me expectantly. "I'll try to lead you to the best of my abilities, and I hope it will be good enough, but I want you all to know that if for any reason, you're not happy, or there's something I'm doing wrong, then you can come to me,

and we'll work it out together. We're supposed to be a pride right? That means we're a family now. So, I want you all to think of yourselves as my brothers." Insert inward-sigh here at the mass amounts of maleness that will never be mine.

There was a restless shifting as the men looked at each other in concern. The murmuring reached Darius, who finally approached me.

"Tima." He bowed at the waist, but before he could say anything else, I interrupted.

"That's another thing, actually," I added. "No more bowing, okay? Family doesn't bow to each other." There were a couple of gasps at my announcement. "Okay, sorry Darius, go on."

"Tima." Darius shook his head a little, but he was also smiling. "If we are to consider you family, does that mean you won't be mating with us? I'm asking on behalf of the others." He gave me a conspiratorial wink.

I sputtered, coughed, and cleared my throat.

"Yes, I thought I was pretty clear when I said that I had a boyfriend, Darius. There will be no . . . mating going on. At least not with me."

"So, what you said the other day stands? We may take our own mates?" Darius had a half-hidden smile, but the rest of the men stared at me like . . . well, like lions.

"Of course," I said firmly. "I try not to go back on my word. You may all sleep with whoever you please. As long as they're willing." I waved my finger at them, and the murmuring turned into shouted questions. I felt like a new celebrity at my first press conference. "Whoa, whoa"–I held up my hands–"one at a time, guys."

"Tima, there are no lionesses in our pride." Darius was

obviously the spokesperson. "Are you saying that we may mate with humans?"

"As long as those humans want to mate with you, then yeah. Mate with whoever you like, humans, goddesses, gods; I don't judge. Do your thing."

What the hell was the big deal?

A loud cheering filled the room, and I didn't know whether to be pleased or insulted. Were they happy because they didn't have to sleep with me? Okay, admittedly, that was a stupid thought. Damn those insecurities. How many hot gods did I need to hit on me before I acquired some self-confidence? I blamed it on Barbie dolls and fashion magazines. Then I did my best to smile at the Intare.

"You like that, huh?" I laughed a little when the cheering got louder.

Then they fell to the ground all at once. Let me tell you, standing on a dais while a room full of gorgeous men fall to their knees to worship you, is not half bad. I highly recommend it.

"Okay now, what did I say about that?" I waved at them futilely. "Come on you guys, get up, please."

They slowly got to their feet, and they all wore similar looks of disbelief. Shit, they *were* abused children, and they were expecting me to pull the rug out from under them at any second. Get abused long enough, and everyone starts looking like a rug-pulling Bogeyman. Even my connection to them through the love magic couldn't erase the ingrained behavior that all those years of abuse had instilled in them.

"I'm not Nyavirezi," I said clearly, addressing them without a hint of uncertainty for the first time.

The love magic may not be able to burn away their

memories, but it *was* able to guide me. It knew exactly what they needed, exactly what needed to be said and done for their well-being. I didn't have to know how to lead them, the magic would show me the way.

"I'm Vervain Lavine," I continued, and I saw the whole assemblage grow still. "There will be no fear between us, no humiliation, and no abuse. Instead, I will do my best to protect you from those who would harm you. I promise to guide you, and help you, if you promise to guide and help me as well. Together, we can become a true pride, a real family. We can make this bond into something great, something powerful. What do you say?"

They cheered again, and I found myself blinking back the tears. For the first time, I felt a sense of fate, of destiny. I wasn't struggling in the shadows anymore. I was exactly where I needed to be. No confusion, no fear, no indecision. This was something that was all mine. I would lead the Intare on my own, and I wouldn't have to worry about werewolf father-in-laws or hurting the feelings of an old boyfriend who happened to be the God of Thunder. If I made mistakes, my lions would help me through them. We would be stronger together. We would be a family. No matter what else came or went, we would stand side by side through it.

We were Intare.

I stepped down from the dais, and they stalked forward to surround me. They didn't flow like the Froekn, but they had their own form of grace, or beauty, rather. They moved like confident hunters, muscles bunching and limbs moving in motions you only see in cats. A rolling in the shoulders. Hips lifting at strange but sexy angles. It was graceful in the way that martial arts can be graceful. Beautiful, but with a deadly undercurrent.

Lucian came forward. He took my hands in his and lifted them to his lips as he lowered his forehead to mine. It felt very formal, almost like a ritual, and a part of me recognized it

instantly. Then his scent washed over me, through me really, as if it melded into my cells from where our foreheads touched. The smell of him was unique, like nothing I'd ever smelled before, and I knew I could recognize him anywhere by smell alone. I could pick Lucian out of a crowded room, blindfolded.

I realized that Lucian hadn't been truly mine until that moment This last step was integral. This was our true bonding. The love magic didn't hold a candle to the magic of the Intare. This was truly knowing someone on a depth that even love couldn't go. Love is a risk, an action of faith in what you believe someone to be, this was the actual knowing. I didn't need faith. From the top of his head to the soles of his feet, I knew Lucian like I knew myself, and I wondered if this was what Trevor had felt, how he knew me.

As soon as I had the thought, I knew this was a different connection than what I had with Trevor, a different kind of knowing. Trevor may know me intimately, but he didn't know the way my blood flowed, my heart pumped, or my muscles clenched. He couldn't see the layers of skin, tissues, bones, and organs, or stop them with a thought. I gave a small gasp, and Lucian backed away so that another lion could take his place.

I swallowed hard, my mind racing. I'd been told that I could kill them, but to have it displayed so clearly to me, right after I committed myself to protecting them, was distressing. I pushed the thought away in exchange of a better one. If I could hurt them, maybe I could help them instead. It was worth looking into. Later. Right now, I had to focus on the rest of my lions.

By the time I got to Aidan, I was riding high on a cloud of kitty pheromones. I smiled at him brightly and placed my hands in his. Our foreheads met and my scent index made a new entry labeled: Aidan. Instead of pulling away, though, he angled his face so that we connected one more time.

I heard the lions make a low warning growl and knew that Aidan was pushing things. Like his lips to mine. I felt his hands

slide up my back as his tongue slid against my mouth. I reacted automatically; I pulled away and slapped him.

Aidan barely moved, he even continued to hold me, but his eyes heated. Not with anger, but with lust. I guess it's true, you never forget the first woman who slaps you. I raised an eyebrow, and he smiled seductively. When I tried to pull away, he held my hands tight and dropped to his knees.

"My apologies, Tima." Aidan bowed his head, but quickly looked back up at me. The lions settled a little as power was reestablished, and part of me wondered if it had been a test. "I just wanted a taste."

"No tasting the Tima." I wagged my finger at Aidan as I finally extricated myself from his grip. "You're a free lion now." I motioned with my hand. "Go find yourself another woman to taste."

"I have a feeling," Aidan said as he stood, "that none will be quite as sweet."

"I'm sure you can find plenty of sweet women," Darius growled from my left, and Fallon took a place on my right. Aidan moved away as the pair took my hands, and I was immediately comforted by their gallantry.

I knew I could trust them all, that every single one of these men would die for me in a heartbeat. I knew what kind of men they were, who was honorable and who was playful, but there is a difference between getting to know someone and instantly knowing them through magic.

I knew the type of men they were, but I didn't know what their pasts were, the things that had made them into these men. I didn't have the history with them that would make us friends. That would take time. For now, though, it was enough to know them by blood and by magic. It was enough to be able to feel their hearts connected to mine, beating in time with mine.

I knew then why I was called the heart of the Intare.

I pulled back my awareness before it started traveling down those threads between us, and took a deep breath. The ramifications of it all were a little too much for me to process. I needed a distraction.

"Alright gentlemen, time for a tour. Show me the place."

Chapter Forty-Seven

The men led me around the palace (that's pretty much what it was), and I tried my best to remember my way. Aidan stayed at my side the entire time, occasionally inserting some comment about the building or décor, but mostly staring at me in an obsessive stalker kind of way. Darius and Fallon kept inserting themselves between us, but Aidan kept finding a way back. He was an Intare boomerang.

Finally, we made it through the many, and I mean many, bedrooms which were located on both the ground level and the underground basement level. The palace was two stories, but instead of going up, it had been built downward. There were two sets of stairs; one grand stairway in front of the library and a narrow spiral set of stairs inside the kitchen that led down into the huge larder and connecting wine cellar.

On the top floor, the ground level, was the massive dining hall with huge, curving windows overlooking the grasslands in front of the palace. Next to it was an industrial size kitchen with a massive fireplace. It was very impressive and I could imagine spending late nights baking in it. Directly across from the dining room was the armory.

The armory was filled with every weapon a girl could want, and even some for the boys. The firepower was massive, but the guns adorned the walls like forgotten relics. The lions were like me, they preferred the sharp stuff. There were all sorts of swords, a few were even Japanese like my kodachi. I thanked my lucky stars that Trevor had found it after the battle. I love that sword, and working the spell to empower it against gods had taken me over a month. Learning to master it had taken years. Suffice it to say; it had sentimental value.

There were also throwing knives and stars, wrist blades, boot knives, chest straps which held blades all the way down, switchblades, hunting knives, butterfly knives, scimitars, gurkha kukris, and even maces. I just stood awhile and sighed, basking in the shiny glory of it all. I think I might've said something like, "Oooooohh... pretty," but I'm not sure, it's all a shiny metallic haze in my mind.

Down the corridor from there, was the ballroom. Can you believe that the armory was near the ballroom? Darius said it was tactical. I don't know what kind of dancing they'd been doing, but it was going to stop.

The ballroom was beautiful, though. It was twice the size of the dining room and had mirrors running down one wall which seemed to double the space. The room itself jutted out from the main building and had its own separate veranda, with two sets of French doors leading out to it. It was a half-moon shaped veranda as opposed to the rectangular one at the front of the palace.

Speaking of the front of the palace, the safari-esque main veranda led to a double door entry, which then led into the grand foyer. Basically, it's a large empty space in which to greet guests and show them some of your expensive stuff right away. It didn't make any sense to me since most of the guests would be coming in through the tracing point which was at the back left corner on the ground floor; the opposite side of the house. So, no one was really going to see the stuffed giraffe . . . and who the hell stuffs a giraffe anyway? Okay, I thought it was kinda cool.

To the right of the foyer (if you were facing the front doors) was the kitchen, but to the left of it was the library; a place I instantly fell in love with. It wasn't quite as big as Thor's library, but came in a close second. The first thing I noticed was the enormous curved windows looking out over the grasslands, mirroring the dining room at the opposite, front corner of the house. The view was fantastic and the light would be great for reading.

Next, I discovered the large collection of occult and spell books that I'd never seen before, and I was looking forward to months of reading. There was mahogany furniture everywhere; tables, chairs, and display cases, but it must not have been enough because there was an attached sitting room to entertain in. Humph, very hoity-toity. I loved it.

The common room was just around the corner from the library, but right in front of the library was a large wooden staircase that went to the lower level. Down there, there was a larder–a huge chilly room where racks of food filled the space. Inside it, was the wine cellar with its very impressive collection of properly stored wine.

Right next to the larder, was the fitness room. What the architect was trying to say by placing the fitness room next to the larder was not appreciated by me. I don't like to work out. I do it because I have to, not because I enjoy it in any way. So, the rows of shiny equipment merely made me groan.

The music room, right next door, would have been phenomenal if I had any musical talent, which I don't. So, it was merely impressive, with its baby grand piano sitting beside towers of stereo equipment, a drum set, and numerous guitars.

What I did find amazing was the humongous theater at the back right corner. You had to pass the laundry room to get to it, but the surround sound system in it was cinema quality and would have no problem drowning out the sound of the dryers. It was done in a vintage style; with red velvet curtains covering the walls and lots of gold fretwork. There were rows of overstuffed, red velvet recliners; enough seating for all of the Intare and anyone we might want to invite. There were even balcony seats. For a movie buff like me, it was paradise.

The tour ended back on the ground level where they showed me to the master suite which was now mine. It was in the center of the palace, the best place to defend me, I was told. It was

beautiful and spacious, done in the same Ralph Lauren safari theme as most of the palace was. It had a luxurious bathroom and a four poster bed made of bamboo, but the most amazing part of it was my private inner courtyard.

The wall directly across from the bedroom door was one large window broken up only by a set of French doors, which opened onto a tranquil inner garden as large as the bedroom and the private bath combined. It was home to some of the most exotic looking blooms I'd ever seen, and I've seen exotic, being raised in Hawaii and all. It was a little shocking to see the tropical flowers in the midst of the safari style palace, but it somehow made the courtyard all the more precious. I wasn't much into African-themed décor, so I knew the courtyard would be a sanctuary of sorts for me, a place where I could find peace.

It was as if it had been built just for me. The foliage was thick, but in an English garden sort of way, not jungle. It was harnessed chaos, with riotous swaths of color. Swarms of butterflies flew everywhere, and I was told that they hung from the trees in massive colonies at night, looking likc monstrous, multicolored wisteria. I was enthralled.

I sat down on a stone bench, beside a little pond which sparkled with bright fishes, and stared about me contentedly. Around me, the lions dropped to the ground, content as well to bask in the afternoon sun shining down through the screen-covered opening above us. The air was sweet with the scent of all the flowers and thick with the lazy flapping of butterfly wings. It was spectacular.

"Tima"–Darius sat on the ground beside me–"We've planned a picnic outdoors, but if you prefer, we can move it in here."

"A picnic?" I was thrilled.

I'd expected the day to be about responsibilities; work

without fun. But it seemed that the lions had the potential to live like Froekn, filling every day with as much joy as possible, and I wanted to encourage that.

"No, let's stick with your plan. I'd like to see the outside as well."

We wandered out the front doors, down the veranda steps, past a swimming pool complete with massive waterfalls flowing into it (one of them a disguised slide– whoopee!), and a grilling area.

A few of the men were already cooking steaks. They nodded to me as we strolled by, and I waved gaily. The smell of the meat made my stomach rumble, and one of the cooks laughed and gestured to the growing piles of meat on platters by his side.

"I'll bring you the choicest piece, Tima," he called to me.

"Thank you"–I scented the air instinctively, and his scent separated from the rest, sparking in my mind and forming a name–"Ryan."

The chef smiled wider and began fixing me a plate. Darius guided me to a tree-shaded spot, covered with large blankets, and sat me in the middle of the Intare. They settled around me, some of them heading off to help with the cooking and food distribution, but most lounging contentedly.

"Thank you," Darius was looking at the others as he spoke to me, but he turned back to look me in the eyes. "Thank you for giving us our lives back."

"I would kill a hundred of her to keep the Intare safe," I swore softly.

"I know, Tima." A tear slid down his cheek and he quickly swiped it away. "We are finally free. We're finally a pride, thanks to you."

“Not just me.” I looked out over the grassy landscape, spotted with flat-topped trees, then back to his open face. “You got them to rally behind me, you and Fallon.” I looked over at the regal man on my left. “The Intare made a choice to free themselves. I was merely the tool.”

“No, not the tool”–Fallon took my hand–“a weapon. You were the blade which, once flung into the unknown, unerringly finds its target. We backed you, propelled you, but never wielded you.”

“So”–I squeezed his hand quickly–“we were a pride from the beginning.”

“Yes,” they both spoke at once.

“We may have taken the role of females in a pride,” Fallon said with a thoughtful frown. “But that role is not completely without choice. In the wild, the males will fight for ownership of the pride, but the females will drive off any male they deem unworthy before he can even get close enough to challenge their lion.”

“We may have spoken to the others,” Darius continued for Fallon, “brought them to you, but it was you who won them over. They looked on you and saw a true champion. Someone they could allow to challenge their lioness. The Intare chose you.”

“I'll try my best to honor that choice.”

I stared at the open grasslands again. The delicate trees gave shade, but very little cover for the herds of animals that roamed the plains. It was a hunter’s paradise; lots of game and no place to hide. I was shocked to feel a twinge of excitement at the thought of changing into a lioness and chasing my prey. I could almost feel the grass being crushed beneath my paws, the scent of prey on the wind, and my heart racing with the rhythm of the hunt. I had to focus to tear my thoughts away.

The scenery was beautiful, but it was barren compared to Hawaii. I'd grown up with tropical lushness, and part of me cringed away from the stark landscape. Another part of me exalted in the change, though, and it was only a place I'd visit anyway. I wasn't moving in or anything. It would be fine. Fine? What was I talking about? I'd just inherited a palace in the middle of a Safari paradise. That's a little beyond fine.

"Does our land end at the mountains?" I pondered the way we seemed to be surrounded by the tall peaks.

"In a way, yes." Fallon turned slightly and took the plate from Ryan, who'd come up behind me. He placed it before me before taking his own.

"Thanks," I smiled up at Ryan, and he winked at me before heading back to the grills.

"And in a way no?" I steered the conversation back.

"Our territory ends at the mountains," Darius took the helm. "Beyond, there are other god territories, but we can't pass into them without permission."

"Of course, all the god lands are connected." Sometimes it was hard for me to remember that the God Realm lay over ours, with the Aether sandwiched in between and holding them together like mystical glue.

"Yes." Fallon nodded. "It's very similar to Earth, but it functions on a magical level. You know this already, though, you're a witch."

"That's how I know about the Aether." I started to cut up the beautiful piece of steak before me. "But I didn't know about the God Realm until I killed Ku."

"I've heard stories about you." Aidan plopped down with his plate. "You were one of the many things Nyavirezi used to

scare us with. 'Don't try to leave the palace without me, or the Godhunter will get you', she'd say."

"Shut up." I laughed around the huge piece of steak in my mouth.

"It's true." Darius smiled grimly. "Instead of frightening me, it made me want to meet you."

"I have to admit"–Fallon's mouth twisted into his secret smile–"I was intrigued as well."

"Oh, I see how it is." I looked around, surprised to notice that the Pride had all found spots close to us. Avid eyes watched me, and I'm sure their ears were tuned in as well. "You needed a goddess dead, so who better than the Godhunter, right? Was this a setup?" I teased.

"Hardly," Darius scoffed. "I just quickly realized, that day in Arizona, that keeping you alive might benefit us more than killing you."

"Well here's–" I looked around suddenly. "Does anyone have something to drink? I'm parched; this is some dry country."

Fabio walked up and handed me a glass of ice water. Okay, so it wasn't Fabio, but damn the boy looked like him. Well, better than him actually; younger and a bit softer around the mouth. He smiled at my staring and flipped his thick mane of blond hair over his shoulder. Yep, I was definitely calling him Fabio . . . in my head. His name was actually–sniff, sniff, sniff,–Aaron.

"Thanks, Fa–ah . . . Aaron," I smiled, and he nodded before taking a seat behind me.

"Tima," Darius practically growled the word.

"What?" I looked guiltily over at him.

"You were saying?"

“I was?” I glanced back at Fabio/Aaron distractedly. “Oh, right.” I held up my glass. “Here’s to hasty decisions.”

Darius shook his head with a smile, his hair slipping in silken waves over his shoulders as he raised his glass to mine. I watched him settle his body into a more alluring pose and glanced back at Fabio/Aaron to test a theory. Yep, when I looked back at Darius, he was frowning and puffing out his chest. This couldn’t be good.

“So, who wants to go to my club tonight?” I asked my pride, and they all cheered. “I guess that’s everyone then.”

“Are you sure your mate will approve?” Fallon whispered to me.

“Nope.” I shrugged and tried a bite of the potato salad. It was good, real good. “Yum. Ryan, did you make the salad as well?”

“Yes, Tima,” I heard his voice carry over from the grill. “I'm glad you like it.”

“Tima.” Fallon sighed. “Do you really think that shoving us in the Wolf Prince’s face is a good idea?”

“He has to get used to you.” I took a swig of water. Boy, it was hot, and the water was almost a necessity. “I want him to meet the Pride, and this way it will be on his turf, where he’ll feel more at ease. I think it’s about as good a situation as I can hope for. I’ll call and let him know. Trevor will probably want the Froekn there as too.”

“Maybe you’re right.” Fallon’s face cleared as he looked at me with renewed confidence.

“I’ve lasted awhile among the gods.” I smirked. “I’m not a complete idiot. Although there are times I wonder.”

"There is something else we need to discuss." Fallon's face grew serious.

"We don't need to burden her yet." Darius shot him a glare.

"Don't you think she'll be upset that she wasn't informed immediately?" Fallon glared back.

"Alright, children." I waved my napkin between their faces. "You have to tell me now, so there's no sense in arguing. Out with it."

"There is one of the Pride who is ill." Fallon's eyes held a wary pain that made me want to resurrect Nyavirezi and kill her all over again.

"What the hell?" I stood up, my food suddenly forgotten. "Why didn't you tell me? I could have brought Teharon with me today. Someone escort me back to the tracing point so I can go get him."

Before I could wander off, Darius took my hand and pulled me back down.

"It's not that kind of an illness, Tima." Darius placed the food back into my lap.

Like I could really eat after they dropped that bomb.

"I'm *waiting*," my voice rose an octave in my concern. "What's wrong with him? Tell me now. In great detail."

"He's bonkers," Aidan spoke up, but was quickly silenced with a look from Darius.

"One second you guys are praising my strength, and the next you're treating me like I'm a useless, fragile idiot. Don't beat about the bush. Tell me what the fuck is wrong with my lion!"

The men around me stared with wide eyes before soft

smiles started to spread like butter in the sun. It wasn't until I noticed Fallon's satisfied gaze, that I realized what I'd said and how I was acting. I smiled back at them for a second before turning to Darius for my answers.

"Nyavirezi had her favorites," Darius' voice had dropped, like speaking it any louder would give power to words he'd rather bury. "Kirill was her first consort, the one she summoned the most, and he suffered for it. As much as we craved her attentions, actually receiving them was often unpleasant."

"Why does that not surprise me?" I stared down at my half eaten plate before putting it aside to give Darius my full attention.

"Kirill not only took the brunt of her passions, but was forced to aid her in her pleasures." Darius looked at me with haunted eyes that begged for understanding, so he wouldn't have to spell it out.

"She tortured all of you, tortured him, and when she was tired, she made him torture you," my words fell into a thick silence.

I remembered the glimpses I'd had of their memories. Darius nodded.

"How long has she been abusing Kirill?" I asked.

"My guess would be; a couple of centuries"–Darius shrugged, looking anything but casual–"give or take a few years."

"And now he's insane?"

I couldn't imagine being tortured, then forced to torture men who were like brothers to me, all the while being expected to sexually service the horrid bitch who commanded me, for centuries. I barely made it out of one night in Aphrodite's dungeon. Years with a sexual sadist was probably akin to a lobotomy.

“We keep him as comfortable as possible, but he must be constantly chained.” Darius looked away and his throat worked convulsively before he continued. “I believe that a swift death would be merciful at this point, Tima. Nyavirezi has always refused to kill Kirill, but I know you will not fail him.”

“What?” I looked around at the suddenly sober faces and felt my heart sink. Why did it always come down to murder? And why was I always the one who had to do the killing? Did I have a neon sign flashing above my head? “No, not without trying to save him first.”

“Tima, it’s not a pretty sight.” Fallon took my hand gently. “He’s violent, often shifting from man to beast till he’s exhausted himself enough to find some peace in sleep. He would ask you for this, if he could.”

“I'll judge that for myself.” I stood and dropped Fallon’s hand. “Take me to him. Now.”

Chapter Forty-Eight

At least the room was clean, that was about all I could say for it. The walls, floors, and even the ceiling were scarred with deep gouges, and the only touch of comfort was a mattress that had seen better days. There was a doorway leading to a bathroom, which looked close enough for his chain to reach, but the door was nowhere to be seen. Light poured in from a high window, but there were no light fixtures on the ceiling and no lamps, so the room would be completely black by nightfall. I guess it wasn't such an issue for lions, but it made me sad to think of Kirill alone in the dark.

In the center of the floor was a massive metal plate with a chain attached to it. On the end of the chain was a man. When I first entered, he was lying serenely on the mattress; naked, and even more beautiful than the men behind me. It was clear to see why Nyavirezi had chosen him as her favorite.

Perfect, lightly tanned skin stretched over taunt muscles that stopped just short of being too massive. He was tall, but even that was not extreme; I guessed him to be around six-foot-four. His long hair streamed in gentle waves of ebony down his chest to pool around his hips. His strong features weren't relaxed, even in sleep, but strained together as if his battle was constant and fierce.

"How does he keep his hair so beautiful?" I whispered.

At the sound of my voice, his eyes shot open, fixing me with an indigo stare so dark blue, it was almost black.

"Shifting makes everything brand new again," Darius' voice came from behind me, laced with a choking despair.

"Kirill," I spoke softly. "I'm Vervain, and I'd like to help

you."

The man on the bed shifted his head a bit, but continued to stare at me so blankly that I wasn't sure he'd even heard me. I was beginning to doubt their claims of violence when he suddenly sprang, shifting as he went, at my face. The chain stopped him short, and he fell with a crash and a horrible whimpering sound. My eyes shot to his ankle where what I'd thought had been a manacle, revealed itself to be a bar inserted between his bones and welded on each side to the heavy chain.

"Why is he chained like that?" I turned my sickened eyes to Darius.

"He shifts, Tima," Darius said quietly, his eyes never leaving his fellow lion, "it's the only way to keep him restrained."

I took a shuddering breath and sank to the floor, weighed down by misery as I stared at the horror my predecessor had created. Darius placed a hand on my shoulder, but I shook it off. I couldn't be touched. If someone touched me, I'd lose it.

"Get out," my voice trembled, but I wasn't sure what emotion it was filled with, there were so many vying for attention. Horror, anger, sadness, and a creeping despair.

"Tima." Fallon started forward, but I cut him off.

"All of you." I looked back at the Intare, at their scared, confused faces, and I tried to soften my tone. "Please shut the door when you leave."

The lion paced in front of me as the door shut behind me, roaring and lashing out at the air between us. Even in his animal form, he was exceptional; an impossible black with blue highlights that matched the slightly human eyes staring out at me. I searched those eyes for some sign of humanity, for some glimmer of sanity, so I wouldn't have to destroy something so beautiful.

There was nothing, only anger and hopelessness swirled in the glassy orbs. He couldn't be saved, the boys were right, the kind thing to do would be to put him out of his misery. But it was so atrocious, such a devastating waste, to have to kill this man. The weight of it hung on me, drooping my shoulders and making my heart clench. My lioness roared inside me, desperate to reach her lion, desperate to protect him from what I had to do.

I tried to reach out to him down a thread of magic, a thread like the others were connected to me with, but there was nothing there; we hadn't established a connection yet. I had no way to reach him. I wouldn't even be able to kill him gently without that thread in place. I'd have to behead this magnificent creature with my sword. The mere thought of it tore me in two, and the pain poured out of me, overflowing my eyes and streaking down my cheeks in hot rivers.

I pulled my legs in, hugging them to me as I mourned. Mourned the small piece of my heart that would be killed along with Kirill. Mourned the humanity that was slipping away from me bit by bit, and most of all, I mourned Kirill himself.

The lion before me was lost, even though I'd won the fight and freed his brothers. Kirill was still lost to me, and maybe it was hubris to think that I could save them all, but I had. I wanted to. I needed to, and the knowledge that I couldn't, that one of my first acts as their leader would be to destroy one of them, one of *us*, the very first werelion created, was acid on my soul.

I cried so violently, so freely, cried as I hadn't allowed myself to in such a long time, that it took me awhile to realize the lion had quieted. Sniffling and wiping at my eyes, I looked up and found him lying before me, head on his paws, studying me with a new expression: curiosity. My heart leapt with sudden, and most likely useless, hope.

"Kirill?"

The big head turned to the side, regarding me seriously before sniffing the air between us and letting out a small whimper. My mouth fell open as I tried to remember how to breathe again. There *was* something left of the man within the beast. I lay down face to face with him and gave him a long, slow blink. He blinked back, and I caught my breath. I was using techniques you use to calm cats. Would it work with a lion?

I needed something with my scent on it, something I could reach out to him with, so he wouldn't feel threatened. That left out the kodachi. Hmm. Oh, screw it, I took off my tank top and held it out to him. Kirill snagged it with a claw and dragged it closer. His head dropped and he inhaled deep without removing his gaze from me. He blinked again and rubbed his face into the material, snuffling and making little lion sounds. Okay, next step. This was the scariest of all because if it didn't work, I wouldn't just get scratched, I might lose my hand.

I slowly stretched out my hand to him. Kirill watched it closely as it crept forward, completely still until I reached his paw. Cautiously, I stroked one finger down the silky fur over the deadly paw, and he eyed it just as cautiously until I tried to pull it back. Then his head shot out and he bit me.

I inhaled sharply, but forced myself to go limp and not scream. Cats often bite you lightly when they don't want you to stop petting them. Granted, his was not the lightest bite, but I still had my hand attached to my body, which I considered to be a good sign. So, I relaxed, trying not to show any fear, and waited.

My blood dripped down my wrist and made a soft tap as it hit the floor. It was barely a noise at all, but it was enough to bring Kirill back to some sort of reason. He dropped my hand and started to lick it, carefully cleaning the wound before nuzzling against it. I was so relieved, I almost started to cry again. I braved a quick stroke of his face. The lion leaned into my hand, rumbling satisfaction through his chest. He was purring.

Then the door opened and all hell broke loose.

"Tima," Darius' voice was soft and awed, but the sudden sound startled Kirill.

I found myself dragged back under the shaggy body as Kirill roared and lashed out at the others. They backed off, frantic but wary, and I was left to view the world from beneath thick black fur while I pondered my sanity. Even lying beneath the massive beast, I still couldn't find regret for my actions. Instead, I was filled with hope. Kirill was showing signs of protectiveness, which made me believe that somewhere beneath all his pain, there was still a kind heart.

"Get out," I told them again. "If you care anything for me and your brother you will leave. Come back in an hour."

They stared at me like I was crazy.

"Tima." Darius dropped to his knees. "You must kill him, please. You can do it painlessly, just concentrate on him going to sleep and dying without pain."

Kirill tensed around me, and I automatically reached out to stroke him. How demented was it that I'd never felt safer in my life? Somehow, I knew that he wouldn't hurt me. His magic had finally recognized mine, and even though my lioness had been used to hurt him, I knew she had the power to heal him as well. I knew she *wanted* to heal him, wanted to repair the damage she'd been forced to do.

Then he lay his head to mine, and his scent rolled through me. I inhaled deep, metaphysically grabbing his thread with both hands and tying him to me. I could feel his heart now, feel the strength of it, and I knew I could stop it painlessly if I wanted to. I also knew that I'd fight to my last breath to prevent that because this thread was special. Our connection glowed and pulsed, thrumming with a unique magic. There was something inside him that was important to the Intare, important to me, and I knew he

needed to live.

“I’m not Nyavirezi,” I kept my voice low and calm. “I won’t keep him alive for spite, but I will keep him alive for hope. I’m not giving up on him yet. Look at him; look at how he’s protecting me. He’s not completely lost to us. Give me some time and a little faith. Oh, and someone go let Trevor know I’m not going to make it home for dinner.”

Chapter Forty-Nine

Night found me reading fairy tales to my very own Beast. The boys had brought me books, a portable stereo with CDs, bedding, and a lamp. Kirill wouldn't let me retrieve the items until they left, so they had to place them by the door and lock us in. By the time Darius brought our dinner, I had made me a little nest on Kirill's mattress in the corner.

Kirill had calmed shortly after the others left us the first time, and had remained so; content to simply watch me, listen to the music I played or the sound of my voice as I read to him, until they returned. Every time someone else stepped foot into the room, he'd go wild, pulling at his chains, roaring, swiping at them, and moving his body to block any path to me.

Instead of worrying me, his behavior reassured me. He had obviously sunk into his beast to escape whatever had been done to him, and now he was so deeply entrenched that his understanding was only an animal's. I could work with that. Didn't I live with a werewolf? Didn't I think of myself as mother to a cat? And most importantly, didn't I hold three beasts within me already? I could do this.

I was just finishing the story of *The Ugly Duckling* when the sound of a commotion warned me of imminent visitors. Kirill jumped out from behind me, unbalancing me since I'd been laying on him, and stalked to the end of his chain.

"Kirill," I called, just as the door opened and Trevor strode in. "Stop, Trevor!"

My werewolf was in a tizzy, but he automatically halted at the sound of fear in my voice. He took in the scene quickly and was left in obvious confusion. Kirill made a low sound of warning

as he immediately determined Trevor to be his greatest threat and faced off with him.

“What the fuck is going on here?” Trevor’s fearless gaze went from me in the rumpled bed to the angry black lion.

“I’m trying to save one of my lions,” I said calmly, keeping my voice in the soothing tone I’d been using all day. “He’s been tortured, honey-eyes, and I don’t want to put him down like a dog just because Nyavirezi was a sadist.”

Trevor eyed the bar chaining Kirill to the floor, took a deep breath, and rubbed a hand over his face.

“Loving you has been my greatest joy, Godhunter,” he sighed, “and my greatest frustration. I concede your point, but playing him music and reading him bedtime stories aren’t going to be enough.”

“I’m open to suggestions, baby.” I smiled at him, overwhelmed by my love for this amazing man and my luck at having him in my life.

Trevor smiled back at me, hopefully seeing some of what I was feeling, and shut the door on the anxious Intare who were waiting in the hall. He wandered over to a far corner and sat down with his back to the wall.

“How dedicated are you–no, don’t answer that,” he shook his head. “This could take weeks, Minn Elska, and I’m not pleased with the prospect of you shacking up with some deranged cat, but I’ll tell you what I think needs to be done.”

“I love you,” I said simply.

Kirill looked back at me, and then over to Trevor. Perhaps he sensed the weight of my words or maybe there was enough man left in him to understand. Either way, he didn’t like it. A low growl began in the back of his throat.

“Stop it,” I looked at Kirill and shook a finger in his face. “This is my mate. You’ll find your own after you’re better.”

The massive head turned to the side, his dark eyes starting to fill with a more human intelligence. Finally, he gave a great *humph* and sat back on his haunches.

Trevor chuckled in his corner. “That’s my girl. If she can’t tame the wild beast, she’ll just confuse it.”

“Yes, very funny.” I smirked at him. “Now, tell me your plan, O wise werewolf.”

“Well, I’m going to have to leave, which I don't like too much, but I think it’s necessary. Then I’d recommend taking that thing out of his ankle.” He pointed to the offending bar. “You’ll never win him back if he’s in constant pain. Animals lash out when they're hurt.”

“I agree.” I thought about it for a second. “We’ll just have to cut an opening in the door so the boys can bring us food.”

“Sounds good,” he agreed. “Then you need to tell him exactly what’s happened here; over and over until it sinks in. He needs to know the bitch is dead and he’s safe. Tell him every day, and if possible, get him to change into his human form. In between that, just do what you’ve been doing. You’ve got good instincts, Rouva.”

“Why thank you, sweet Prince,” I said only half mockingly.

“I’ll come and check on you in a couple of days.” Trevor got to his feet and gave me a sarcastic bow. “I’ll also go speak with Fenrir and see if he has any ideas.”

“Thank you.”

“I love you.” He winked at me.

“I love you too.”

As soon as the door shut, Kirill returned to his spot on the bed, settling into the thick blankets and nudging me until I lay back against him. I looked down at the book in my lap and sighed.

"I think it's time for a different story."

Chapter Fifty

"You can't release him, Tima." Darius eyed Kirill, who was sitting calmly, but resolutely, between us.

"It was Trevor's idea." I lifted my chin. "If my boyfriend thinks it's okay, then you should have no problem with it. Now, lay the tool down and get out."

"Fine, but I'm cutting a window out of this door right now."

"Great, now go." I watched him lay down the wrench and open the door. "Darius."

"Yes, Tima." His back was stiff and he didn't turn to face me.

"It's going to be alright."

Darius nodded curtly, but some of the tension seemed to flow out of his shoulders. When the door was firmly shut and the sounds of a Dremel started coming through it, I went and picked up the wrench. Kirill eyed the door and then the wrench in my hand. I approached him slowly and casually sat at his feet.

"Okay, I'm going to take this out," I reached for the bar and his head shot down to sniff at me. "It might hurt a little but then you can shift and heal. Do you understand me? I don't want you to be chained anymore."

He blew a hot breath over my hand and nodded before looking up at me. His eyes held even more humanity this morning, and I hoped that boded well for what I was about to do. I set the wrench to one of the bolts, tightened it down and, holding firm to the other end, began to loosen it. Kirill inhaled sharply and

growled, but his attention was fixed on the offending piece of metal, not me, so I continued.

Blood had seeped into the groves, rusting the metal and making my work much more difficult, but I was finally able to remove the nut and then the bolt. I tried to pull the bar free, but his skin had healed to it. No wonder he didn't shift often, his flesh must tear and heal each time. I bowed my head to hide the tears I felt rising and hoped I had the courage to tear the metal away from him.

"It's bonded to you." I looked up into Kirill's eyes. "This is going to hurt, honey, real bad, but I'm here with you."

The thread connecting us twitched, and I could suddenly feel his heartbeats in the palm of my hand. The desire to comfort him, to take some of his pain away, rose in me until I felt a jolt in my palm. Then a slow ache grew in my left ankle and a heavy weight settled in my chest. His pain, both physical and emotional, was mine now too. Kirill's body shook, but when I looked up, his eyes were steady.

"Can you feel me with you?"

A low rumble vibrated through him, a soft purr, and he nudged my cheek with his own.

"Okay, we'll do this together. Are you ready?"

Those deep blue eyes regarded me solemnly, blinked once, and peered down at the metal. He nudged my hand, and when I continued to just sit and stare at my task, he licked the tears roughly from my cheek.

"Okay, I'm going to loosen it slowly, so I don't take too much flesh with me," I moved to the other side and took a firm grip. "Here we go."

I held his foot and started to twist the bar gently side to

side. Pain bloomed up my leg, but I gritted my teeth and breathed through it. Kirill's breathing grew heavy too, but he didn't move. I felt the bar loosen a bit as a trickle of blood seeped out, so I twisted a little harder–and screamed. I could feel the flesh breaking away and the metal scraping against bone. My hand began to shake and I knew I needed to finish it soon or I'd pass out.

Then I felt a warm breath on my neck, a rough tongue against my skin, and a feeling of acceptance filtered down the link from him to me. There was an almost audible click, and then Kirill's scent became stronger, his presence in my mind more real. It was like Darius had said; I could try to wrestle the Intare away from Nyavirezi, but without their approval, I wouldn't have gotten very far. Kirill had just given me his approval and made our connection complete.

I didn't even realize how much I'd been straining to hold onto his thread until then. It wasn't like the others who had accepted me and given me their connection willingly. Kirill had been holding back, unsure of me. It was like I'd been playing a game of tug-o-war, and had suddenly won. Instead of my opponent falling on his face, though, he fell into me, and I caught him easily.

Kirill's falling empowered me, helped me to think past the pain, and I was finally able to continue. I worked at the bar until I was able to turn it completely, and then I eased it out of his leg. The pain was piercing, but Kirill shut me off from it as he flung himself into a corner, pulling in his injured limb and whimpering as he licked at it.

"Change, baby." I crept toward him and he fixed me with a stare gone suddenly feral. "Shit, Kirill, don't go back now."

I tried to reach down the thread for him again, but it ended in a wall. I knew I could have torn down that wall, but that was something Nyavirezi would have done, and I wanted to show Kirill that I was nothing like her. So, I allowed him his choice and pulled away.

"Shift; you'll heal as soon as you shift. Go on."

The air glimmered and his shape blurred, changing into a huddled man, arms wrapped around his knees and bright eyes staring steadily at me over them. His hair fell around him like a cloak, and I suddenly wanted to paint him. Fragile beauty and vulnerability, housed in an unmistakably powerful body, and framed by all that hair. Those thick waves belonged on a woman, but he was so aggressively male, it didn't make him look feminine. It somehow made him look even more masculine. Like how a jeweler will lay a diamond on black velvet to make it sparkle brighter; the contrast of his hair's softness showed off the facets of his diamond-hard looks.

"Kirill." I sat down carefully in front of him.

"Vhat." He swallowed roughly and cleared his throat. "Vhat is your name?" His accent was thick. Russian maybe. Ukrainian? Czechoslovakian? I don't know, one of those cold places.

"Vervain." I waited, hoping there would be more, but he just sat there looking at me.

After a few minutes, I lay down on my side and closed my eyes, giving him my company while still affording him some privacy, as well as showing him that I wasn't afraid of him.

Two hours later, I woke up in the bed, surrounded by warm, naked male. I tried not to jolt up in shock, focusing on my breathing as I looked over my shoulder at him. Kirill was wide awake, staring at me in open fascination. His hand reached up and gently touched my cheek, stroking the outline of my face with a fingertip.

He leaned forward, his hair falling around us, making me feel like I'd fallen into a separate reality where nothing existed but us. Kirill's scent wrapped around me; warm, musky cat, and the lioness in me rose up and stretched out, reaching for him. His face

came to a stop next to mine, cheek to cheek. He buried his face in my hair, his breath hot, but comfortable, on my neck.

Inside of me, my lioness lifted her head until it felt like her face was just beneath the surface of mine, her eyes looking out of my eyes. The wild magic tingled on my skin, igniting everywhere Kirill's body touched mine. He pressed in tighter, and, for a second, it was as if we were completely engulfed in magic; two little boats caught in a whirlpool, rapidly plunging down into the unknown.

I turned in his arms and clung to him blindly, letting the cat in me take over, and she rubbed wholeheartedly against Kirill. Surprisingly, it didn't feel sexual. It was fiercely sweet, a gentle ache rushing from me to him. I flowed with it, plummeting down our link and into him.

Inside him, I felt the terrible breaks of his mind and heart. I was able to touch them, to push my energy into them, and repair them with bits of myself. Weaving back and forth, healing with the rough lick of a cat's tongue and the intricacy of a focused witch, I found every scar, every pain, every broken piece of him, and I welded them back together with my will and pieces of my soul.

"Tima, dinner!" Darius called from the little window, just big enough to push a tray of food through.

Kirill roared, dislodging me in a flurry of limbs and blankets as he launched himself at the door. He reached through the hole, forcing Darius to back up quickly.

"Kirill!" The sharp sound of my voice made him wince and turn back to me guiltily. Then I had a new thought. "Look at your brother." I stood up and slowly approached Kirill. "Darius. His name is Darius and he loves you. All of your brothers want you back. They want you to heal and remember them. Nyavirezi is dead. You have nothing to fear anymore."

"Brother." Kirill stared hard at Darius through the door. He

sniffed the air between them and frowned. “Darius.”

“Kirill?” Darius started to come closer.

“No, Darius, wait!” I shouted and he stopped just before Kirill reached out to grab him again. “He needs time. Let him adjust to his memories. Kirill, come and sit down so I can get our dinner.”

Kirill eyed Darius and then the bed where I patted my hand. He stalked back and folded himself down beside me. I reached out and took his hand to give it a reassuring squeeze, and he looked down at our joined fingers. Lifting them up, he held them in front of his face and tilted his head. Then with a swift movement, he pulled me sharply against him, wrapping me in a hug.

“Vervain,” Kirill whispered. “Zank you.”

I hugged him back, and started to cry, sensing his return, but hardly believing I'd accomplished it in less than two days. I don't think I could have done it without that healing session. Kirill clung to me tighter, his shoulders shaking from his own relieved tears, before he let me go to lean back and take my hands in his.

“Tima?” He searched my face.

“Yes.”

“Nyavirezi?”

“She’s dead.” I took a deep breath and let the stress of the past few days flow out with the exhale. “I killed her and took her magic. She’ll never hurt you again. No one will, if I can help it.”

Kirill scowled at the chain in the floor.

“You’re free now, Kirill,” I said.

His eyes shot back to my face.

"They only chained you to prevent you from hurting others, but you're better now."

"Zey vanted you to kill me." Kirill's voice was steady, without any hint of blame, and that was definitely a Russian accent.

"They thought it would be a mercy." I smiled gently. "I disagreed."

"So, you saved my life as vell as my mind." He made an effort to smile back at me, but it looked strained, as if he'd forgotten how to be happy.

"I'm your Tima, it's part of my job." There, I knew my sass would make a come back eventually.

"I wish someone had told Nyavirezi that." Darius had come quietly into the room and Kirill stood up to face him.

"Dare?" Kirill searched Darius' face.

Darius swallowed hard, then took another step forward, and another. On the third step, Kirill launched forward, and Darius braced himself, but Kirill only caught him up in a fierce hug, dragging the smaller man off his feet. The two started laughing, crying, and pounding on each other's backs in an exuberant show of relief and joy. After a few minutes of mumbled exchanges, the boys wandered out of the room to find the other Intare, without so much as a backward glance at me.

"Huh, I guess that's why they say it's lonely at the top." I laughed to myself and headed out to find my room, and hopefully some clothes that would fit me.

I needed a shower before I headed home, and then I needed to sleep for about a week, snuggled up with my favorite werewolf. I was glad that the boys had Kirill back, ecstatic that I'd been able to save him, but I had no problem leaving them to their celebration

and heading home. There was only so much excitement a girl could take.

I finally found my way through the endless corridors to Nyavirezi's old room. It was amazing that I remembered where it was in the maze of hallways. Even though I knew it was at the center of the palace, finding that center wasn't so simple.

It was a beautiful, airy room, dominated by a massive bamboo, four-poster bed in the center of it, with white netting draping the whole thing. I had no idea that bamboo grew so large; the posts were each a single piece, and they were at least thirty inches around. It was so tall, I practically needed a step ladder to get into it. The height appealed to me, but the idea that it had belonged to Nyavirezi didn't. Who knows if I'd ever be able to actually sleep in it.

The floor was covered with cushion-thick straw mats, which I intended on replacing with carpet as soon as I had the chance, and the walls were painted off-white. Light poured through the large window that made up the wall opposite the door, making the room even brighter, and softening the faces of the numerous tribal masks that filled an entire wall to the right. Oh yeah, those were gonna go too.

On the left wall, there was a bamboo vanity and a matching rack of light, cotton clothes; another thing I had to do something about. How could a woman only have one small rack for her clothes? It was preposterous, especially with all the space she had. I fully intended on building a closet.

Closer to the right-hand wall was a sitting area with a loveseat, two chairs, and a table, all done in the same bamboo and upholstered in white. The table held a beautiful chess set, reminding me of Nyavirezi's taunt about studying the game more. Humph; I actually played chess quite well, but it was never a good idea to brag to your enemies. Better to let them underestimate you.

“Checkmate, biatch,” I snapped at the poor innocent chess set.

I headed past it with a smug grin, sparing a quick glance for the butterflies fluttering around the window-wall, and then went through the door on the right wall, and into the bathroom. I had yet to see a bathroom as beautiful as Blue’s jungle-themed triumph, but Nyavirezi’s was a winner as well.

The tub was sunken into the floor and looked like it could easily hold five. It was white marble and round, with seats along the rim and stairs leading down into it. There was one of those extra large, rain shower heads hanging from the ceiling over the middle of the tub. Shower curtains were unnecessary since the tub was so wide; the water would never spray out far enough.

The floor around it was marble as well, but had strategically placed woven reed mats that I actually thought were a good choice. The counters and storage chests were all made out of bamboo, the sinks were the same white marble as the tub, and the screened off toilet was marble too. There was a large mirror over the sinks, trimmed in bamboo, and flanked by wall sconces. The bulbs shone brightly with god magic instead of electricity, and were shaded by reed panels. Nyavirezi seriously lacked creativity, but evidently had unlimited resources.

I threw off my clothes, walked down into the tub, and turned the water on with the knobs set into the floor along the rim. Water poured down from the shower head, and I stepped into it eagerly, longing for the relief that the heat would give my aching muscles.

As I soaked, I thought about the tangle my life had become. All in all, my days with Kirill had been the best days I’d had in awhile. While I was focused on him, his pain and healing, I was able to forget about my own issues. I had a feeling that my new palace was going to be a sanctuary for me in many ways. I could sure get used to the shower.

When I finished, I grabbed a towel from the cabinet and dried off as I went back into the bedroom. Towel at my head, I was vigorously rubbing my long hair when I noticed that I wasn't alone in the room. I shrieked and quickly covered up, gaping at Kirill. He was sitting on the loveseat, patiently waiting for me. At least he was dressed this time. So, that made one of us.

"My apologies, Tima." Kirill studied his hands until I was covered.

"Kirill." I eyed the rack of clothes across the room from me, wondering if it would be possible to squeeze into one of Nyavirezi's dresses, and whether or not I wanted to attempt such a feat in front of a witness. I decided to stay in the towel for the moment. "I thought you'd be catching up with your brothers."

"I've caught up." He was eyeing me in a strange way, making me suddenly doubt whether I'd successfully healed him."I'd like to speak vith you before you leave."

"Alright." I carefully sat next to him on the loveseat, only because I didn't want to have to worry about the towel exposing too much if I sat across from him.

"Take me vith you."

"I'm sorry, what?" I rubbed surreptitiously at my ears, maybe they were waterlogged.

"Don't leave me here." Kirill swallowed roughly, and I realized how difficult it was for him to ask me, like a child, to not leave him behind. "I don't know if I can handle being apart from you yet."

"Oh, shit." I closed my eyes, willing the situation to change, but when I opened them, he was still there. Still looking at me with sad kitty eyes. "Did I bind you or something? Because I can assure you that all I set out to do was heal you."

“Not bound.” Kirill looked down at his hands again and then back up at me with firmer resolve. “You pulled me avay from insanity, zat is our bond. You are first female to touch me vith kindness in over two-hundred years, and part of me needs you now. I need to see you, know zat you’re real, and not just some drug hallucination.”

“She drugged you?”

Boy, this bitch just kept getting worse and worse.

“Ven I couldn’t perform, vich vas pretty much all time at end.” He waved a hand and chased away the evil memories. “It doesn’t matter, vat’s important is you, me, Intare. I need to know you’re safe and I vant to provide zat safety.”

“Trevor’s not going to like it.” I wondered if Kirill even remembered meeting Trevor.

“I know of your mate, and he has nothing to fear from me,” Kirill met my eyes with clear honesty. “I vould never touch you in inappropriate vay. I just vant you to make me your Ganza, hand zat holds dagger, dagger zat protects heart. I vant to be able to protect you, Heart of Intare.”

“You can protect me when we’re together, but at home I have Trevor.” I touched his shoulder gently and he twitched.

“Just for now, Tima.” His eyes were full of fear again, and I hated that. “Just for little vile, let me stay vith you. I’ll sleep outside your door. Surely your mate vill not begrudge you extra protection.”

“I’ll tell you what”–Trevor was so going to kill me–“you can come with me, and if Trevor is okay with it, you can stay until you’re more comfortable.”

“Zank you.” Kirill squared his shoulders, and I noticed how much bigger he looked now, without the weight of anger and

insanity weighing him down. He had pulled all of his hair back in a tight ponytail, and the severity of it highlighted the sharp lines of his face. He looked more like a bodyguard than a romeo. Maybe that would help.

"Don't *zank* me yet," I sighed.

Chapter Fifty-One

"Hey, baby, I know that you really like cats, so I thought; why not bring home one more? No, no." I turned to pace in the other direction. "So, how about a new alarm system? No, that's stupid. Trevor, you remember Kirill, he wants to crash outside our bedroom for a few days. Oh, fuck, that won't work."

"Tima?" Kirill entered the bedroom carrying a small backpack. "Are you ready to leave yet?"

"Ah." I looked down at the obscenely tight dress I'd taken from Nyavirezi's wardrobe and hoped that it would help Trevor be a little more sympathetic, or at least distracted enough to agree. "I guess so."

We walked to the tracing point (which by the way, was a wall at the end of a corridor) together in silence. We'd already said our goodbyes to the others, and although Darius had pouted awhile, everything had gone smoothly so far. Which was mainly because we hadn't left yet. I had a feeling the smoothness would end as soon as I stepped through the Aether.

Once in the tracing room, we traced out easily and arrived on my front doorstep. I said the ritual words to allow Kirill entrance, then unlocked the front door and peeked my head in. The house was quiet for about ten seconds before I heard a loud thump, and then two pairs of feet running down the hallway; one werewolf-sized and one kitty-sized.

"Minn Elska." Trevor pulled me through the door and into a wild embrace involving much kissing and heavy petting.

"Baby," I gasped between rounds, "honey-eyes, hold on."

"I'm trying to, but you keep wriggling." Trevor leered as he headed toward the bedroom with me in tow. "I could tie you up, though, that might work."

"Sweetness, we have a guest."

That stopped him cold.

"What?" Trevor looked back over his shoulder and finally noticed Kirill standing patiently inside the doorway, determinedly studying a framed Kuchi headdress. "Who's this?"

"This is Kirill." I watched Trevor carefully, but he seemed to remain calm.

"Hello, Kirill."

"Prince." Kirill nodded his head curtly. "Please don't stop on my account. I vill make my bed here if zat's acceptable."

"What he means to say"–I turned Trevor's face back to mine–"is that ever since he recovered from insanity, he feels an urgent need to guard me, and hopes that you will allow him to stay with us for awhile until he is completely recovered and feels more secure with allowing me out of his vicinity. Just a little while, baby, what do ya say?"

"You're home a lot sooner than I expected you." Trevor sighed. "I guess this means you worked some lion juju on him and now he's a little antsy?"

"Something like that." I smiled in relief. "So, it's okay?"

"Coupled with the fact that you're asking, not telling, I suppose so."

"Thanks, honey-eyes." I rubbed my nose against his. "Kirill, there's blankets and pillows in the hall closet. Make yourself at home and feel free to raid the fridge."

"Yes, Tima."

A demanding yowl brought my attention to Nick. I bent down and picked up the tabby, giving him a good rub.

"This is Nick." I brought him over to Kirill.

Kirill smiled gently and held out a hand for Nick to sniff. Nick sniffed and then nudged the proffered hand in silent demand. After a few head rubs, I handed Nick off to Kirill.

"Here, get to know each other while I get reacquainted with my wolf."

Chapter Fifty-Two

It was Three AM and I was up. Why was I up? There it was, the sound that must have woken me. It was a soft shushing, like hair along fabric. My body tensed and I slowly opened my eyes a slit. There seemed to be a large shadow at the opening of my bed. My heart lurched and started to race before I realized who it must be.

"Kirill?" I whispered.

The only other sounds were the low hum of the AC and Trevor's steady breathing.

"Tima," Kirill sounded frightened.

I carefully edged down the bed and off the mattress without waking the sleeping wolf. It's always best to let sleeping wolves lie. Just as carefully, I raised a hand and touched Kirill's forearm. He was strung so tense, it felt like any sudden movement would snap him. His hair was as wild as his eyes, tangled around his hips, and the top button of his jeans was undone. I slid my hand down into his and gently tugged on it until he followed me out of the room.

Three AM. Why did the worst things seem to happen around three AM? I remember hearing someplace that it's the time when the human will to live is at its weakest, the time when most people commit suicide or give up the fight in their hospital beds. I've also heard urban myths saying it's when paranormal activity reaches its height. I don't know if any of that is true, but it does seem to be a magnet for general badness. Whenever I was having a bad run and found myself up and thinking terrible things at three AM, I always told myself that all I had to do was make it a few hours, and when the sun rose, things would seem better. And they

did, every time.

I led Kirill to the sofa he'd been sleeping on and left him there while I heated up some water for tea. I got the whole service together on a tray, knowing that comfort was sometimes found in the mindless action of things. I took the tray over to the sofa, placing it on the low table in front of us.

Kirill watched me anxiously as I calmly poured two cups of tea, stirring in sugar and cream till the chai turned soft beige. I handed him the delicate teacup; it was Royal Copenhagen and my favorite. It looked odd in his big hands, but those strong fingers closed gently over the thin porcelain and his body started to relax.

"I'm sorry, Tima," his voice was thick and rough. "I needed to see zat you are okay. I didn't mean to vake you."

"Better me than Trevor." I smiled to let him know I was teasing, but he still wrinkled his face with worry. "It's alright, Kirill, drink your tea."

He nodded and took a sip, then another, his face and body relaxing little by little. I put my own cup down and went to retrieve a hairbrush and an elastic band from the bathroom. He continued to sip, watching me as I came over and slipped up onto the back of the couch behind him, giving me some height for my task. Kirill gave me a curious look, but remained quiet. I pulled over a thick blanket, laid it on his shoulders, pulled his hair out, and began the long process of brushing it.

I heard him sigh before he spoke. "Tima, zis is unnecessary; I can brush my own hair."

"Shush." I kept up the gentle brushing. "It's not about the can, it's about the caring. Relax and let me do this for you. Sip your tea, close your eyes, and know that you're somewhere safe; somewhere where you're loved."

"Loved." He shook a little and took an even shakier breath.

"Your love is so much different zan hers."

"That wasn't love," I said.

The sound of the brush slipping through his amazing hair was a sweet calming sound, like waves on the shore.

"That was the opposite of love. Love doesn't seek to harm, it does hurt sometimes, but not in the way that she hurt you. I don't profess to know all the forms it can take, but I'm certain that what she did to you was *not* one of them."

"She made me . . ." he hesitated.

"You can tell me." I began to braid the shiny waves. "I'll never judge you by what she made you do. Whatever happened, whatever she forced upon you, it's not you. You are the sum total of *your* choices, not the choices of others."

Kirill's head hung down a moment before his shoulders straightened and his chin came up defiantly. I had a flash of the man he must've been before Nyavirezi changed him, and it was impressive. Maybe someday that man would return.

I smiled and finished fastening the band around the end of Kirill's braid, then I pulled him back against me, my legs spreading around his waist to bring him even closer. He relaxed back against me, and I held him as he spoke, confessing Nyavirezi's sins as if they were his own.

"She vas so nice to me first." Kirill swallowed and looked back at me. "Not like you, but still an affectionate woman. She made me love her, zen tormented me for it. Ven I first confess my love, she laughed. Zen next time she sent for me, another voman vas vaiting in bed. She told me, if I love her, I vould do anything for her, or anyone. She stood at foot of bed and vatched vile zat voman used me like I vas noting but tool."

I held him tighter, rubbing my cheek against his as the cat

within me rose up in commiseration. Kirill turned his face into the comfort, and I kissed his cheek gently, letting him gather his strength before he continued. I knew he would, he had to get it all out, purge the poison, before he could be whole again.

"I cried ven it vas over, and she laugh at zat too. I never felt so unvanted or unmanned." His eyes were staring far away and he was beginning to speak as if the story had happened to someone else. "Ven I accepted our new relationship and knew my love for her had been lie, she changed game. She started to chain me, beat me, force me to do humiliating acts or service her vhile she tortured me. Ven I vas unable to perform, she'd use magic or drugs."

"She could do that?" I was horrified and morbidly fascinated.

"She controlled our bodies"–he leaned his forehead to my cheek–"and now you do, Tima. Zough I don't zink you'd have to resort to such means."

I felt a delicious shudder course through me before I concentrated on Trevor, sleeping trustingly in the next room.

"We're going to have to find you boys some girlfriends fast." I gave a shaky laugh. "You're far too tempting for a mere mortal."

"You are not *mere* anything." Kirill turned to face me, wrapping his arms around my waist and pulling me down into his lap. I stiffened a little, but he stroked my cheek gently. "You are as safe vith me as I am vith you. I vould never do anything you didn't vant, Tima. I just vanted to hold you."

"I know, Kirill." *It's not you I distrust*, I added in my head. "Tell me the rest."

His eyes looked away and then back into mine, resolved. "I tried to kill her once vile she slept, but she cast me off easily,

deflecting my claws as if zey nothing but irritation. Zat vas ven she began making me kill for her entertainment. She said I obviously had it in me to be amusing as both sex partner and murderer, so I vould be both for her from zen on. If anyone displeased her, zey vere brought to an empty room vere only she and I vaited. I vould tear at zem until she vas satisfied or zey vere dead."

"The blade is not to blame for the kill; it's the hand which holds it that murders." I stroked his face.

"I suppose you're right." Kirill opened the blanket and wrapped me inside it with him. I ended up resting my head against his shoulder. "It's still difficult to exonerate myself of all I've done to my brothers. I can't believe zey still care for me after everything she made me do."

"That's why you're here, isn't it?" I kept my voice neutral. The last thing I wanted was for him to feel accused. "You're hesitant to live among them."

"Partially," he admitted, "but not because I fear zem. I just don't know how to be one of zem anymore. I also have need to protect you, to be your Ganza."

"You didn't really explain that to me." I might as well get some knowledge while I was at it. "What exactly is a Ganza?"

"I guess closest definition vould be head of security." Kirill smiled an endearing half-grin, a little like Trevor's, and I was totally lost to it. "Ganza is your hand, to defend you, to mete out your justice . . . or vengeance."

"My right-hand man, huh?" I snuck another peek up, and found him still smiling.

"Somezing like zat."

"Are you sure you want me to use you in that capacity after she did the same thing?"

“It’s not same.” Kirill pushed me back from his chest so he could look at me. “You vill never be same.”

“Okay, okay.” I patted his arm. “No need to get all moody about it. You’re hired.”

“Zank you.” He looked down. “I vasn't sure you'd vant me after vhat she did.”

“She raped you, Kirill.” I pulled his chin back up. “Body and mind.”

“It vasn’t rape exactly.” His eyes went still before he looked away from me.

“Yes, it was.” I turned him back to me once more. “It was rape, believe me, I’ve been there.”

I was completely unprepared for his anger; and so was the rest of the neighborhood. Kirill roared furiously, lifting me up as he stood. I shushed him as I heard the telltale sounds of unsettled humans.

“Who?” Kirill snarled, holding me by both arms. “Who violated you? Tell me and I vill tear him apart slowly.”

“Someone want to tell me why our guest is vowing murder before the sun is even up?” Trevor stood leaning in the passage to the hall, arms crossed and trying hard to look nonchalant. But I could see the pulse pounding in his throat. He’d probably been terrified when he woke to a roar and an empty bed.

“Calm down, Kirill.” First things first, I had to talk the werelion down before I dealt with werewolf questions. “He was a different man then. I forgave him.” I just wouldn't mention Blue's latest role in the potential Intare rape scenario.

“Him?” Kirill let me go to start over to Trevor. “Your mate did zis to you?”

“No, no, no, no.” I shot between them. “Trevor would cut a limb off before hurting me. Don’t ever question his loyalty to me again.”

I felt the tension ease out of both of them and knew we’d just been on the verge of the biggest dog and cat fight ever.

“Zen who, Tima?” The fight had mellowed, but hadn’t completely left him.

“Someone you don’t know.” I pushed Kirill back towards the sofa. “And I’ll be damned if I tell you now.”

“Tima, as your Ganza I must know of any possible threats.” Kirill sat obediently, but continued to stare at me with steady determination.

“Someone better tell me right now what’s going on.” Trevor had lost his casual pose and had taken up a new post attached to my arm.

I swiftly and briefly explained the situation, but even then, it took another two hours of talking to first one and then the other of them before I could get back to bed. By the time I was curled up snug and safe in werewolf arms, I was exhausted, but my mind wouldn’t relax. I kept thinking about Kirill and the Intare, and Trevor and the Froekn. What was I going to do about my men?

All seventy-eight of them. I mean; seventy-nine.

Chapter Fifty-Three

The smell of vanilla mixed with a light undercurrent of citrus. I breathed it in deeply, loving the feel of the grass beneath my feet as well as Nick snaking happily around my legs while emitting heavy purrs. I smiled and reached down to give him a quick scratch before moving back to finish watering my vanilla orchids. They grew off chunks of tree fern which I'd hung in the orange tree in my front yard, and their smell alone made them valuable to me, but when you added to that their fragile beauty, it was clear that they were nothing short of works of art.

The sound of an expensive engine cut into my peace, and I looked over my shoulder to see Trevor pulling into the garage behind the wheel of my Jag. I dusted my hands off as I watched him and Fenrir get out of the car. A big smile spread across my face.

"Zis is Wolf God?" Kirill jumped down from his perch in the orange tree, where he'd been keeping guard, and watched the men approach carefully.

Kirill's stance was casual, relaxed even, but I could tell that he was missing nothing. He'd probably already gauged the best ten ways to bring Fenrir down, in case it became necessary.

Fenrir, for his part, had also been sizing up my new bodyguard with unconcealed interest. By the time he and Trevor stood in front of us, Fenrir had a small smile playing about his lips. Before he could say anything, though, a violent barking assaulted us from the yard beside mine.

I looked over in shock to see my neighbor's two German shepherds snarling at us over the wooden fence. I'd seen them bark at strangers before, but I'd never been the focus of their fierce

attention. I was stunned. Nick, however, was severely annoyed and let the girls know it in no uncertain terms. The dogs stopped a second to stare at my hissing feline before once again renewing their vigorous disapproval of my guests.

"Vasse! Roxy!" My neighbor Tahnee came running out of her house and pulled the girls down from the fence. They immediately quieted and circled her happily, although they continued to cast suspicious looks toward Fenrir. "I'm so sorry, they get spooked sometimes."

"No problem." I reached down to calm my own upset animal, but Nick just flicked his tail at me and took off. "My Dad's kinda big. He's probably what got them so excited."

"This is your Dad?" Tahnee looked over at Fenrir with open curiosity.

I could almost feel Fenrir stiffening under her gaze, taking offense to what he assumed she was thinking. I, however, knew those thoughts weren't anywhere near what Fenrir was expecting. Tahnee's one of those genuinely sweet people who you just keep thinking will someday let her façade fall, and then you'll discover that she's a serial killer or something. But it never does, because she actually *is* that sweet.

She moved in last year with her husband, Justin, who'd taken a job doing research at the University of Hawaii, and we'd become fast friends. Something that didn't happen very often with me. So, I knew the next words out of her mouth would be something that would endear Fenrir to her forever. Tahnee didn't disappoint.

"So, you must take after your Mom in the height department, huh? Does he play basketball?"

I laughed, more at Fenrir's pleasantly shocked expression than at Tahnee's innocent observation. "He's actually Trevor's father, but I call him 'Dad' too, and I don't think he'd know a

basketball if it bopped him on the head."

"Oh." Tahnee smiled. "I should've recognized the handsome face."

Fenrir's smile turned into a leer. "Thank you." He started sauntering over to her, drawn like a moth to the flame of her fiery curls and genuine smile.

I grabbed Fenrir's arm before he could get too close. "How's your *husband* doing, Tahn?"

"Oh, fine, fine, you know Justin," Tahnee looked over her shoulder at the little two-bedroom they were renting. "He's watching the football match and eating pretzels. He'll realize I'm gone when the pretzels run out, and he starts to get hungry." She gave a cute little laugh.

"He obviously doesn't appreciate you enough," Fenrir slipped out of my grasp to lean against the fence beside Tahnee.

I swore under my breath, but before I could do anything more, the dogs once again shot up and resumed their barking, this time directly in Fenrir's face. Fenrir leaned back a little in surprise, and Tahnee let out an expletive that still sounded sweet because she said it. She pushed the dogs back down with an exasperated huff.

"I'm sorry, I better take them inside." She shook her head.

"We're heading in too." I waved at her. "I'll catch you later."

"Alright, take it easy, mate." She shooed the girls into the house as I turned to do the same with my boys. "It was nice to meet you, Trevor's Daddy," Tahnee called out as she closed the door.

"Did she just call you her mate?" Trevor looked like he

didn't know whether to be upset or intrigued.

"She's Australian, you moron." I pushed at him until he started into the house. "It's their term for friend."

"Huh." Trevor frowned. "Oh, so when she said Justin was watching football . . ."

"She probably meant soccer." I sighed and rolled my eyes.

"Ah, I thought so." He nodded sagely.

"Yes, you're brilliant, everyone says so," I let the sarcasm drip from my words, but Trevor didn't seem to notice.

I formally invited Fenrir into my home so my wards would recognize him and let him pass. Fenrir spoke the proper acceptance and then ducked to come into my suddenly tiny house. I was a little nervous, but he smiled widely.

"This is a good den, little frami."

"Thanks, Dad." I gestured to the low sofa, wondering how his knees would fare. "You ready for movie night?"

"Most definitely." Fenrir surprised me by easily lowering himself into the seat, and then relaxing back with a contented sigh. "What are we watching?"

"Well, since we have all day and night." I grinned as I held up three DVDs. "I thought we'd go for a classic trilogy; Star Wars, The Empire Strikes Back, and Return of the Jedi."

"Star Wars," Fenrir seemed to consider it, "sounds like appropriate entertainment for gods. I accept your proposal."

Chapter Fifty-Four

"There are many good lessons in these stories," Fenrir mused, hours later, surrounded by empty beer cans and scraps of pizza. "I especially like the little toad creature with the speech impediment. It shows how power can come in even the most repulsive of forms."

"Little toad?" I squished up my face at him. "Do you mean Yoda?"

"Yes, yes." Fenrir waved dismissively. "I enjoyed the humor of the cowboy captain as well, but I think the main character, this Walker of the Skies, I think he's a lover of men."

"What?" I choked, but Trevor and Kirill started to literally howl in laughter.

"He's a total pufta," Trevor agreed.

"Luke Skywalker is not gay." I looked from one man to another. "He was just young. He grows and matures through the sequels."

"Grows and matures into gay man," Kirill said quietly, sending Trevor and Fenrir into fresh bouts of laughter.

Kirill smiled wider at the shared camaraderie, and I found myself easing off because of that one look. I badly wanted him to feel accepted and at ease around my Froekn family.

"OK, maybe he's gay, but Han Solo is totally straight."

"A little bit of a weasel, but with enough honor to make him likable," Fenrir agreed.

"Did you just call Han Solo a weasel?" I blinked as my mouth fell open.

"He reminds me of my father." Fenrir's face got pensive.

"Whoa, hold it right there, Wolf King." I waved my arms about wildly. "Calling him a weasel is one thing, but I will not stand for you comparing Han Solo to Loki; it's just not right."

"Okay." Fenrir reached over and tousled my already tangled hair. "I'll stop ridiculing your hero."

"Thank you." I nodded curtly.

"Hero?" Trevor snuggled closer. "I thought I was your hero."

"Well, technically, I saved your life first." I grinned unabashedly at him. "So I'm *your* hero."

"What I'm confused about," Fenrir interrupted a potential debate, "are those little fluffy things living in trees. Nature would not create such as they. The short legs alone are not conducive to survival in a forest setting, and how would they be able to build their homes in the trees like that? It's impossible."

"Take it up with Spielberg, Dad." I yawned.

"Ah, the great huntress is tired." Fenrir leaned over and kissed me on the forehead. "I'm glad you're home safe, Godhunter. Get some sleep, and I'll come visit again."

"Okay." I snuggled up to Trevor, enjoying the feeling of him lifting me and carrying me to our bedroom. "Goodnight, Dad."

I drifted off to the voices of my lion and my adopted werewolf father.

"He is a weasel though."

"Zat is true."

"And why was that woman wearing her hair in the shape of

breakfast pastries?"

"I zink she vants to look delicious."

Chapter Fifty-Five

"I like him."

It was the last thing I expected to hear from Fenrir, and judging by the way Trevor was staring at his father with huge horrified eyes, he shared my surprise. The focus of our discussion was standing ten feet away, surveying the interior of Moonshine from the second-floor railing. He most likely knew we were talking about him, what with the super hearing of the shifters and all, but he showed no signs of his attention wavering from the task of guarding me. He was better than Kevin Costner.

"You *like* him?" Trevor's voice had that careful edge to it, the one he got right before he exploded.

"You needed some backup protection for our Rouva,"–Fenrir looked from me to Trevor–"since you insist on living outside of the God Realm where you'd be truly safe. You're too easily distracted by her to make a good guard."

"Quite a few of my worst moments have been in the God Realm." I grimaced.

"I meant in my Hall"–Fenrir's lips twisted–"where I can guarantee that nothing will cause you the slightest distress."

"Uh-huh." I smirked. "One of the aforementioned worst moments was in your fighting pit, *Dad*."

"Girl, you're trying my patience," he rumbled.

"Could we get back to the conversation we were having about us having a new cat in the house"–Trevor glared at us both–"a tomcat."

“Did you forget that I’m the Queen Cat?” I lifted a brow. “I don’t think we need to resort to name calling, puppy.”

“Minn Elska”–Trevor sighed–“stop trying to pick a fight. I’d just like to get some sympathy from my father, but there doesn’t seem to be any forthcoming.”

“I do sympathize with you, Son.” Fenrir patted Trevor’s knee. “I wouldn’t want male sex kittens rubbing all over my mate either, but the fact of the matter is, the boy seems pretty honorable, and although he’s half in love with our girl here, I think it’s the more courtly version of pining without pursuit.”

“Lancelot pined like that for Guinevere.” Trevor sat back in his seat hard, taking me with him since his arm was tight around my shoulders. “And you saw how that ended.”

“I think you just threatened to burn me at the stake.” I blinked melodramatically. “You know how much I don’t like that kind of anti-witch talk.”

“Guinevere took sanctuary in a convent.” Trevor looked over at me in exasperation.

“Yeah, after Lancelot rescued her from the huge pile of highly combustible sticks that her husband had tied her to.” I rolled my eyes. “Men and their jealousies.”

“*Men* and their jealousies?” Trevor sputtered. “So, you think it was okay for Gwen to sleep around on her husband, who also happened to be the king?”

“No, I don’t think that was okay.” I shook my head. “God, babe, irrational much? I’m just saying that burning her at the stake was a little harsh.”

“That was a just punishment for royal adultery back then.” Trevor looked a little smug.

"Oh, I get it now, *Prince* VèulfR." I gave him my *you just lost big points, buddy* look. Yes, I have a lot of looks, with a lot of names. "Are you longing for the good ol' days when you could burn your wife for cheating on you? Not exactly a great argument for marriage, baby. And here's another thing; why did the women get burned for finding love outside of marriage, but the men got to cheat with every courtesan who caught their eye? Hell, if he was the king, they practically couldn't say no to him. Didn't those kings constantly recognize bastard children? That's absolute proof of adultery, but no one started a little fire under their royal asses, did they?"

"Are you enjoying being a little taller?" Fenrir was reclining back, delighting in our exchange immensely, if I was reading his expression accurately.

"Excuse me?"

"The soapbox you're standing on sure is a big one." Fenrir took a casual swig from his mug, and then choked when I gave him a little magical nudge, making him spill beer down his front–a trick I'd learned from Horus. "Hey, you're not supposed to use magic in here."

"It's good to be the boss." I grinned. I'd been studying god spells out of Ku's book, and I was thrilled that I'd gotten that one down, even if it was just a small push of energy.

"Trevor's right"–Fenrir looked a little concerned–"you're awful touchy tonight. You know damn well he'd never harm a hair on your head, much less burn you at the stake. What's your problem, Rouva?"

I sighed. "I'm sorry, it's the cat in me. She likes to fight, especially with the doggies."

"We can fight later, Minn Elska," Trevor whispered into my ear, sending chills down my spine. "I'll chase you around the garden again."

I laughed and settled back into him. Our garden chases were the best, especially when they turned into catches. Which was every time.

I looked around at the mingling Intare and Froekn, and hoped they weren't having the same urge to fight that I was. Then I spotted Fallon talking to Samantha and changed my mind. They could give new meaning to the term "interracial couple". What would the children be like? I had to veer away from that thought, the possibilities were a little too unsettling.

"I don't like your cats, Rouva." UnnúlfR plopped down onto the faux hill next to us and began to sulk.

"Just discovered that there are no female kitties, huh?" I laughed.

"That has nothing to do with it." He glared at Fallon's back.

"Oh, so then it's a particular lion that you're angry with. Perhaps for talking to Samantha?" I laughed harder at UnnúlfR's narrowed gaze. "They are some lookers, my boys, that's why they were chosen, after all. Don't hate them because they're beautiful."

"I can hate whoever I choose," he grumbled.

"Whomever, and no you can't." I pushed at him. "They're good boys for the most part, and they've been abused by a terrible woman who denied them sex for years. And when they did get it, it was only with her. Have a heart, little brother. Imagine having to go without sex for that long."

"Years huh?" He swallowed hard. His name didn't mean "to love a wolf" for nothing, UnnúlfR had a reputation with the ladies. "That would suck."

"Yes"–I winked at him–"besides, imagine all the tail you could get with back up like that."

"Hmm." UnnúlfR started to see the light.

"Girls will flock," I murmured.

"Like pigeons to that crazy bird lady," he muttered.

"I'm sorry." I sat up straight and looked at UnnúlfR with huge, shocked eyes. "Did you just make a *Mary Poppins* reference?"

"What?" UnnúlfR had a panicked moment where he forgot to be cool, before he realized that bluffing was always the best way to go. Deny, deny, deny; it was the American way. "I have no idea what you're talking about."

He got up quickly and stalked off to the nearest grouping of Intare and gorgeous women.

My Intare were having the time of their lives, and I was thrilled to see it. All except for Kirill that is, who stood at alert attention and barely looked at the women who gathered the courage to go talk to him. I sighed, this wouldn't do at all. I patted Trevor's knee.

"I need to go do a little kitty counseling." I leaned in to kiss Trevor, but he twisted his face away.

"With Kirill? Just leave him be, Vervain."

"I want him to mingle." I frowned at Trevor. "I thought it might be nice for him to find a girlfriend."

"Oh." Trevor's face changed instantly. "By all means then"–he waved to Kirill–"go get the cat laid."

"You are so horribly transparent." I grimaced as I got up. "Could you give your son some perspective while I'm gone?" I gave Fenrir an exasperated look. "Like how life with an unhappy mate can be. Or maybe how the dance floor looks when you're hanging by your feet over it."

"I'll see what I can do." Fenrir tried hard for a serious tone, but failed miserably.

"Take your time," Trevor called after me.

"Tima," Kirill's soft voice washed over me as I approached. He continued to patrol the whole club with his eyes.

"The security here is top of the line, you know." I waved at the moon. "Those sensors can pick up any form of magic or ill intent. I'm perfectly safe here."

"Yes, you are"–his gaze flickered over me quickly and then went back to scanning–"as long as I'm here."

"Oh-ho." I laughed. "Conceited much?"

"No, Tima"–he made a small snort of amusement–"dedicated."

"That's one word for it." I leaned on the railing and nudged my shoulder into his. "Another would be obsessive, or there's morose, or even just plain ignorant."

"Ignorant?" Kirill finally turned away from his incessant patrolling to look at me.

"I've been fighting gods for years now." I gave him a hard look because I was pretty sure that's what it would take to get him to ease up. "I resent the implication that I'm no longer capable of defending myself, especially when I'm so obviously secure."

"Tima, I meant no offense," he stammered, visibly shaken.

"I appreciate the back-up, Kirill"–I patted his shoulder–"but tonight I want you to enjoy yourself."

Kirill looked over at some of the Intare, flirting heavily with young women, and grimaced. "If you insist, Tima."

"You don't have to do anything you don't want to." I pulled him back when he started to leave. "All I said was; enjoy yourself. If you're not interested in anyone here, then come and sit with me and the Froekn. Just stop with the patrol."

His face cleared and he swallowed hard. "I vant you safe. I *enjoy* making sure of your safety."

"Well, come enjoy it over here then." I pulled him over to the grouping of little "hills" we were all lounging on, and pushed him over to one near Fenrir.

"You're doing a fine job, lion." Fenrir leaned over and pounded Kirill's shoulder, leaving my poor lion a little shaken . . . literally.

"Zank you." Kirill nodded curtly. "I vould prefer to be on guard, but my lady insists."

"*Your* lady?" Trevor growled.

"Trevor shut up." I whacked him and his growl turned into a whimper. "Ignore him, Kirill. Tell me, are you originally from Russia?"

"Yes, Tima." His mouth always softened into a smile when he looked at me. I thought it was a good sign that he was beginning to loosen up and trust a little.

Trevor didn't share my opinion.

"Commi bastard," Trevor muttered.

"One more comment out of you, young man," I began to growl myself, "and you can go to bed without your *dinner*."

"Aw, Minn Elska," he whined and did the puppy dog eyes.

"Don't even try it." I shook a finger at him. "Enough. How long has it been since you've seen Russia, Kirill?"

"Eighty-four years," Kirill sounded a little wistful.

"Do you want to go for a visit?" It made my heart ache, the way his eyes filled with guarded hope. "I went to Russia last year when we were chasing Blue, but I didn't get to sight-see. I could wear all the coats I never get to wear."

"Yeah, all of them at the same time," Trevor snorted. "It's really fuckin' cold there."

I slapped him in the back of his head.

Hey." Trevor held a hand to the spot.

"Stop being a prick." I turned back to Kirill. "Do you want to go?"

"I do." Leave it to Kirill to keep it simple.

"Okay, great." I looked at Trevor expectantly.

"What?"

"When can we go?"

"Oh, *now* you need me." Trevor smirked.

"I always need you, you jackass." I smiled softly. "Unless you'd rather me and Kirill go alone. He could trace us there."

"Fine, I'll take you to the wasteland," Trevor said immediately.

"Zank you," Kirill's voice was regal, but filled with a wealth of feeling. It even stopped Trevor's sarcasm.

"You're welcome." My wolf grimaced when he caught me smiling at him.

"It warms my heart to see how broken up you are over misjudging me," Blue's voice jerked my head up and silenced the

whole top floor. "Couldn't wait to come apologize to me, could you?"

"Blue." I stood in horror. How dare he come here after all he'd done? "You have some god-damned nerve."

"You *still* believe it was me?" His face fell into shocked lines.

"You thought that I wouldn't know it was you, just because you kept your shiny helmet on?" I growled. "I begged you to help me, and you just walked away."

"I don't know who walked away from you, but it wasn't me, Vervain!"

"No, it was some other guy wearing gold armor, who happens to have a connection to the Mexicans, and can also use the heat of the sun in battle." I stared at Blue hard, part of me wishing it was all just a big misunderstanding.

"The heat of the sun?" Blue frowned.

"Yeah." I shook my head. "Maybe you should have hung back from the fight. That bit of magic was pretty damning."

"I am not the only god of the sun." Blue lifted his Aztec nose into the air.

"No, you're not." I smiled viciously. "Maybe it was Apollo."

"Apollo's neutral," Trevor said from beside me. "He rather sunbathe than do anything else."

"Hmm, not him then." I frowned thoughtfully. "Who else could it have been?

"You accuse me unjustly, and then joke about it?"

“Not unjustly.” I narrowed my eyes on him. “I didn't believe it was you. Not truly. Not until you stepped out beside Nyavirezi and called down the sun. Then I couldn't dispute it any longer. That hurt, Blue.”

“Nyavirezi?” Blue looked me over more closely. “You killed the Lion Goddess? Is that the difference I sense?”

“Oh, cut the shit.” I took a deep breath. “Get out before I violate the rules of Moonshine.”

“The truth will be revealed one day, Vervain.” Blue looked suddenly sad, and my heart twinged once in automatic sympathy. “You will be sorry then, but it will be too late.” He turned and left.

“I want to go home.” I shook my head, sick to my stomach. Something didn't feel right about this whole mess. Could I be wrong about Blue?

“Alright,” Trevor agreed. “I need to stay here and finish up a few things. I want you to trace home with Kirill and strengthen the wards when you get there.”

“Okay,” I said.

“I'll see you soon.” Trevor kissed my forehead and then pulled Kirill aside. They started speaking urgently and quietly.

I made the rounds to say goodbye to everyone, making sure that all my lions were safe and able to get home on their own. There were a few drunk ones, but the others promised to take care of them. They were a good bunch, my big cats. They’d learned to rely on each other, much the same as soldiers do in battle. You become closer than brothers when you save each other's lives on a regular basis.

When I finally made it back to Trevor and Kirill, they both had serious looks on their faces that didn’t bode well for my peace of mind. Trevor tried to give me a half-smile, but I could feel the

tension in his muscles when he folded me into a tight hug.

"I won't be too long." His lips brushed my temple. "Wait up for me?"

"Of course." I gave him a saucy wink, but I had a feeling that this wasn't going to be a night for lovemaking.

Trevor handed me over to Kirill with a look a General would envy, and for his part, Kirill did all but salute Trevor back. I almost groaned. It felt like I was about to place myself under house arrest.

"Come on then." I pulled Kirill into the Family Room so we could trace home.

As the door closed behind me, I glanced back and saw an anxious expression on my wolf that sent tremors racing through my stomach.

Chapter Fifty-Six

"Trevor!" I woke up screaming.

Kirill was instantly beside me in the otherwise empty bed, but I couldn't see him. My vision was focused somewhere far away.

Trevor was in pain, and my wolf was raging through the confines of my body, trying to get to him. I jumped out of bed, stumbling because my sight was laid over with Trevor's. I dropped to my knees with him, seeing the back of the club laid over the walls of my bedroom, asphalt under his wolfman hands, and those paws were laid over my own hands on the carpet. Trevor's arms were shaking, about to give out, but something pulled him up and back. He howled in rage and so did I.

"Tima." Kirill was shaking me. "Vat is it?"

"It's Trevor," I gasped as I stood, pulled on a dress, and grabbed my kodachi. "Get me to Moonshine."

I ran to the front door with Kirill close behind. He pulled me close and traced us over to the club. I shot out of the Family Room and down the dark stairs, taking them two at a time. Kirill didn't ask anything more, just followed, and I loved him for it.

I fumbled with the door lock in the dark until Kirill reached around me and opened it. We went spilling out into the street, and Kirill immediately lifted his head and scented the air.

"Blood," he said simply, and started running to the parking lot behind the club.

I ran after him, pulling my kodachi as I went. We both came skidding to a halt when we got around the corner. A form in

gold armor was holding Trevor down, a gold gauntlet clamped tight in his wolfman pelt, golden greaves digging into Trevor's thighs, and golden hair hanging over a dark cape. All that hair shifted as Trevor's assailant turned to regard us smugly.

"Demeter," I whispered in shock.

She laughed cruelly. "If the Prince here hadn't knocked my helm off, you'd probably still be calling me Blue. Not too bright, are you?"

"Get away from him!" I launched myself at her, casting a quick glance at Trevor, whose face had turned a frightening shade of blue.

She leapt backward, laughing again. "You were so pathetic. 'Blue, stop. Blue, no, don't do this.' Who is this Blue person anyway?"

"Someone I was very wrong about." I clenched my teeth as I faced off with Demeter. Talk about bad timing. Why couldn't this have all come out a few hours earlier? "Give me a few minutes, though. I'm about to make things right."

I swung at her, feeling War rise up to meet the challenge, but she blocked with an armor-clad forearm, and punched me in the gut. I flew back, hitting the brick wall behind me and falling into an ungraceful heap. I got to my feet, gasping for breath.

"You took someone I loved from me, Godhunter," Demeter sneered. "So, instead of killing you, and believe me this was a hard decision, I've killed your wolf. You will have to learn to live with the pain of loss, just as I have."

"I didn't kill Persephone, you crazy bitch," I growled as I stalked closer. I swung my sword up, but a whimper from my left distracted me.

Kirill was backed against the wall, staring at Demeter like a

toddler stares at the darkness in their open closet. His whole body was shaking, his skin pale. I followed his gaze back to a smug Demeter, eyes shining with fresh glee. Monster and victim faced off, and wouldn't you know it, the monster wasn't the werelion.

"Kirill?" I called to him and broke the spell.

"It's her." Kirill cleared his throat and spoke louder, "The voman I told you of."

"It's been a long time, Kirill," Demeter smiled with a pedophile's sweetness. "How have you been?"

"You disgusting, sadistic, pervert," I spat when I realized Demeter was the woman who had helped Nyavirezi rape Kirill. "Don't you even fucking look at him." I threw my sword at her face. It flew in a graceful arch, making her cringe away and break her evil stare with Kirill. "I don't care anymore that you're Sephy's mother. You're dead. I'm going to fucking drain you dry until you die screaming."

I held out a hand and reached for her magic. It was hot, like a summer's day, and I realized then that she could fight with the seasons themselves. I pulled on that heat, and watched her start to tremble. I smiled viciously when she dropped to her knees. I even bared my teeth at her when she fell forward.

"Scared yet," I growled. "You should be. You should be screaming. Why aren't you fucking screaming?"

"Tima." Kirill was beside Trevor. "Your mate needs you."

I snarled, looking between Demeter's desperate eyes and Kirill's. My lioness was enraged. She wanted blood and magic. She roared for Demeter's death. But my wolf was crying, pawing at my chest in an effort to reach her mate. Trevor wasn't dead yet, but he would be soon.

"Decide!" Kirill shouted. "Revenge or love. Decide now!"

“Fuck!” I screamed and released Demeter.

Kirill had said exactly what I needed to hear. There was no way I'd choose revenge over Trevor. I ran to my wolf.

I heard Demeter mumble something, and felt the tingle of her entering the Aether. She was gone, but I'd find her again. I'd have another chance for revenge, but love couldn't wait. Trevor was cold, his lips blue with little sparkling ice crystals on them. I pulled him into my lap and started briskly rubbing his skin. What the hell had she done to him?

“Trevor.” I placed my lips to his, willing him to respond, but all there was to give me hope was a faint breath.

“Tima.” Kirill squatted beside us. “Reach for him vith link. Give him energy. Heal him like you healed me.”

“That was different.” I watched a tear fall on Trevor's cold face and realized that I was crying. “That was emotional. This is physical, and I'm not a healer. Teharon!” I looked up at Kirill. “We have to get him to Teharon.”

“Tima.” Kirill took my shoulder gently. “Trevor vill not make it. You must heal him now. Give him enough to make it to healer.”

“I don't know how!” I wailed.

“Stop.” Kirill slashed the air with a hand. “You are Rouva of Froekn and Tima of Intare. You know how. Now heal!”

I looked down at Trevor, and just like that, the link opened between us. I held nothing back. It was like I'd blown a dam. I just went rushing into Trevor, filling him and finding his faltering heart. I sent my will into it and forced it to continue to beat. I informed it calmly that it was mine and would continue to beat for me until I told it otherwise.

Trevor's heartbeat grew stronger, and I felt his body take a shuddering breath. I pulled back enough to look up at Kirill and tell him to take us to Fenrir. As I felt Kirill's arms close around us both, I went back in. Trevor's blood was sluggish, his tissues too cold, but I filled them with magic. Even as we traveled the Aether, becoming only thoughts, I was still inside him. In fact, the Aether helped me meld further with Trevor, giving me added strength until I felt us leave.

We become physical once more, and I doubled my efforts. I watched the glow of my magic go gushing through the tiny veins under Trevor's skin, watched it warm his flesh, watched it like it was on a screen before me. It surged from head to toe till he shone under my hands like he'd swallowed the sun. Trevor warmed, the magic pulsing in time with his heart, but he still didn't revive.

I heard shouting all around me, but I couldn't lose focus. If I let go for just one second, I knew I'd lose Trevor. So, I concentrated on him, on keeping his heart beating, until I felt another power join with mine. Cells multiplied, damaged blood and tissues repairing under the guidance of this new magic. Soon, his heart pumped all on its own, and Trevor took a few gasping breaths. I pulled away, exhausted, and opened my eyes. He was already looking up at me.

"Minn Elska," he whispered. "Did you save my life again?"

"No." I kissed him gently and turned to where I knew I'd find Teharon. "Teharon did. I just kept you going till he could get to you."

"And he would have died without your quick thinking," Teharon acknowledged.

"Not mine." I looked around for Kirill and found him standing next to Fenrir at the forefront of a circle of Froekn. Fenrir had tears running down his face, but his expression was relieved. "Kirill told me I could do it, pretty much bullied me into it."

Fenrir looked sharply at the lion, and Kirill glanced at him and then away.

"I'm Ganza." Kirill shrugged. "Teharon did healing, I only say vords."

"And traced us both here," I added, my own relieved tears started streaking down my face.

"Thank you." Fenrir took the hand hanging at Kirill's side and shook it. "You're welcome at my hearth and table always, as a friend and brother."

"You're velcome, Volf God"–Kirill nodded–"but I did it for Tima. She loves your son."

"Whatever your reason," Trevor added. "Thank you. I wasn't ready to die. And thank you, Teharon. I never expected to need your magic."

"My pleasure, Wolf Prince." Teharon smiled kindly and then stood.

"I can't believe Demeter would try to kill you." I looked bleakly at my nearly-dead mate and quenched the spark of hatred that flared up for the goddess. This was not the time; better to focus on life for the moment. I looked over at Teharon. "Thank you for coming so quickly."

"Of course." Teharon sighed. "I'm sorry about Demeter."

"She will die," Fenrir growled, and all of the Froekn added to it until the growl was a rumbling, living thing, circulating through the tracing room of Fenrir's Hall.

The Froekn had stayed neutral in the God Wars, but it looked like things were about to change. You couldn't attempt to murder their Prince and get away with it. Demeter was going to pay for this, and my heart hurt to think of how it would affect

Persephone. I would never have thought I'd have to kill the mother of yet another friend of mine, much less want to, but this could not go unavenged. Demeter had gone too far.

She had helped kidnap me, had me literally thrown to the lions, raped one of said lions, and then tried to murder my lover. I was beyond allowing Sephy's feelings to be a deterrent. Even if I didn't kill Demeter–and believe me, I wanted to do the deed personally–her fate was sealed. She was dead the moment she decided to kill the First-Born of the Froekn.

"Oh, no," I whispered.

"What is it?" Trevor peered anxiously up at me.

"It wasn't Blue." I closed my eyes and shook my head. "All this time, it's been Demeter. Blue is innocent."

"No wonder he was so pissed." Trevor grimaced.

"I failed him." My heart clenched with the hurt I'd caused a friend. "I'm his friend. I should have trusted him."

"All the evidence was against him," Fenrir growled.

"All the evidence except what I'd felt inside him." I took Trevor's hand and kissed it tenderly. "I touched his soul. I knew he was innocent, and yet I didn't stand up for him. I need to try and make this right."

"How?" Kirill asked the ultimate question.

"I wish I knew."

Chapter Fifty-Seven

"Blue?" I called out into the empty, cold, stone room. I was kind of shocked I'd been able to trace in. I would have thought Blue would have warded his home against me. "Blue?"

I stepped out into the hallway and headed toward his bedroom. I barely made it five paces before the door was thrown open and Blue stalked out to stare at me with a mixture of shock and grim satisfaction. He lost the shock as he strode forward, gaining aloofness and disdain.

"So, you've finally learned the truth."

"Blue." I swallowed and started again. "Blue, I'm so sorry. I failed you as a friend."

"Yes." The ice cracked for a second before it reformed. "Yes, you did. You turned against me because of what others said. Even though you knew, in your heart, the kind of man I am. I was honest with you. You knew I wouldn't lie to you, yet you humiliated me by asking me to show you my thoughts. You scorned me in front of others and hurt me, Vervain. How could you have opened me up to emotions and then used that weakness to exploit me? And you called me a monster?"

"I know." I hung my head. "I've said everything you've just said, to myself over and over, since I've learned it was really Demeter." There was a small twinge of satisfaction in his eyes. "You knew it was her."

"As soon as you mentioned the sun magic," he confirmed.

"Why didn't you tell me?"

"Tell you?" He scoffed. "As if you would have believed

me? As if I wanted to help you? You deserved to find out the hard way."

"Point taken." I felt my teeth clench. "She almost killed Trevor."

"Is the Wolf Prince alright?" Blue surprised me by asking.

"Yes, he's fine." I reached out to Blue, but he just stared at my hand like it was a poisonous snake. "I understand. I would hate me too. I just had to try. I had to at least apologize to you, and tell you that you were right. I should never have doubted you. I hope that someday you might forgive me, but if you can't, please at least know that I feel the most bitter regret for what I did to you."

"Regret." He sneered as his hand shot out to grip my upper arm in a vise. "You'll be feeling more than that."

I screamed as he pulled me into his bedroom. It was automatic, and just one more thing for me to be ashamed of, but the look on Blue's face was all about death. He threw me on his bed, following me quickly to cover my body with his own. My pulse beat frantically as he pinned my arms to my sides and took a handful of my hair. He pulled violently, twisting my neck back, and then stared down at me with narrowed eyes.

"I am not a toy to be jerked around on a string," he snarled. "I am a god, and you will now truly understand what sacrifice is about."

He bit viciously into my neck, right over Thor's lightning scar, tearing at the wound and causing as much pain as possible. I couldn't even scream, I was too terrified, all I could do was gasp. It seemed to be enough of a reaction for him; he made a happy little growling noise around the flow of my blood.

Then my head cleared and peace washed over me. If he needed this, I would let him have it. Somewhere inside myself, I knew that he wouldn't kill me, and I knew that I needed to finally

show Blue the trust I'd denied him. I inhaled slowly and let my body relax beneath his.

I felt it the moment Blue realized that I wasn't going to fight him. He stilled, his mouth still locked on my throat, but drinking very little. Blue eased up on my arms, and when I didn't make any sudden movements, he lifted his head and looked down at me. There was blood at the corner of his mouth and he idly licked at it as he pondered my face.

"What is this?" He finally asked. "A new trick?"

"No trick." I lifted a hand and touched his cheek. "I owe you an act of trust, so drink. I'll believe in you now, Blue, as I should have done before."

"And what if I kill you?"

"You won't." I felt a tear drip down my cheek. "I've seen your soul, remember? You're capable of violence, but you are not cruel or unjust. You're hurt and I am the cause. I accept your anger, but I will not fail you again. So, go ahead." I pulled his face back to my neck and felt his teeth slide into my skin.

Blue's arms went around me and he drank. I wrapped my arms around him as well and rubbed his back as I would soothe a child. The tense muscles beneath my hands started to loosen. His arms around me tightened and a small tremor shook through his body. I felt the hot, wet, fall of his tears start to soak my hair as he continued to drink my blood.

A few more sips was all Blue lasted before rolling to the side to stare at the ceiling in misery. He dropped a hand over his eyes to cover his crying, and I quietly got up and headed into the bathroom to find a cloth to press against my neck. I came out and stood at the end of the bed, waiting for him to recover.

"Get out," he said quietly.

"Blue, I *am* sorry."

"Yes, Vervain," he snapped and sat up. "You're sorry, you're so very sorry for all you've done to me." He waved his hand at his tear-streaked face. "I am the Aztec God of War! Yet I sit here, crying because a woman has hurt my feelings. This is your fault!"

"Blue–"

"Get out!" He flung a hand toward his bedroom door and it crashed open. "Get the fuck out of my domain, and don't ever come back, Godhunter."

"Blue, please." I backed to the door.

"Now! Before I forget the man you've made of me."

I turned and ran.

Chapter Fifty-Eight

"Do you want me to stay?" Thor leaned down to look me in the eye.

"No, it's fine." I glanced at him and gave him a wan smile. I was still upset about my run-in with Blue; I could barely rustle up my usual awkward feelings for Odin.

"She's perfectly safe with me, Thor." Odin held out his hand. "Come along, Godhunter. We can't be shifting inside."

I looked down at Odin's hand and, just for a second, it looked different; darker, tanned from long days in the sun. I saw it in the sunlight, reaching for me while a child's laughter rang through my ears and through my heart. Tears blurred my vision and I blinked them back rapidly. What the hell? Had Blue fucked with my head?

"Thank you, Thor." I nodded to him as I took his father's hand. "I appreciate you arranging this."

"I'll be right across the water if you need anything." Thor turned away and headed toward Valhalla's tracing room. Before he took the corner, he glanced back over his shoulder. I couldn't read the look he gave me, but I felt the weight it carried.

"So, how much do you know about shifting?" Odin led me through Valhalla's main room and out a side door.

"Nothing really." I surveyed the open yard we'd stepped into.

It was bordered by the Asgard forest. Off to the right was a large vegetable garden. To the left, a path wound around the hall. I could hear the sounds of warriors practicing their skills, coming

from that direction. Above us, the sun was bright, but its heat was tempered by the chill air. I looked down at Odin's hand, still in mine, and shivered. What was that vision all about?

"Are you alright?" Odin finally let go of me.

"Yes." I took a deep breath of the crisp air. It helped. "I'm just a little out of sorts today."

"Of course." Odin's one, beautiful eye looked down and then back up at me. "I'm glad to hear that the Wolf Prince is doing well."

"Thank you." I tried not to notice how good Odin looked in his white, drawstring pants, but it was hard. As hard as the thick muscles snaking over his bare upper body. There was a long scar down his right side that fascinated me. It didn't detract at all from his appeal. In fact, I had the sudden urge to run my tongue up it. My face flushed and I looked away. What the hell was wrong with me?

"So, Thor tells me that you've only shifted the once," Odin's voice brought me back to reality, and I focused on his face determinedly.

"Yes." I swallowed past my dry throat.

Focusing on his face was just as bad. Odin surpassed his son in his hotness level. I always said you had to know your own hotness level. A lot of men don't. You see them all the time, hitting on women way younger and way hotter than themselves. Some women even do it, then have the nerve to sit around afterward and weep over the rejection. Know your own level, and that won't happen. Sometimes people luck out when the higher levels don't know they're so hot. It was how I'd got Thor. Thor just didn't know his hotness level, but I knew mine, and I knew Odin was way above it. For that matter, so were most of the men in my life.

"Okay." Odin was giving me a funny look. "So, let's run

over that first experience. What were you feeling at the time?"

"Scared shitless."

"Okay." Odin laughed. "Maybe it was fear that triggered it. The shift reacts to extreme emotion. Thor says that you shifted back because you thought of Trevor. So, I'm assuming love brought you back."

"I don't know." I frowned. "I guess so. I shifted because I took Nyavirezi's power, and the draw works better if I don't fight the incoming magic. I let it in, and it turned me into a lioness. I don't think it had anything to do with fear. I shifted back when the lioness wanted me to eat Nyavirezi's body. I remembered Trevor telling me that the Froekn never ate people."

"Trevor was your conscience." Odin frowned thoughtfully. "It's probably the only thing that would have worked for you in that situation. You needed something to shock you out of the change. The animal's instinct clashed with your human morality, and it cleared your head enough for you to remember who you are."

"You're saying that it wasn't really Trevor?"

"No, I'm saying that Trevor was only a part of it. You used Trevor's words as a catalyst, but it was your own horror that let you remember them."

"Am I going to have to shock myself every time I want to change back?" I wasn't comfortable with that.

"No." Odin stretched his shoulders like he was getting ready for a round of boxing. "You just need to hold onto that feeling of humanity. When you shift, you think of the lion. You let yourself feel like her, her muscles bunching, paws on the earth, intricate scents in her nose. Then you'll become her. When you want to be a woman again, you let yourself feel like a woman, the breeze in your hair, the sun on your skin." His hand reached out

and trailed over my arm, leaving gooseflesh in its wake.

"I . . ." I trailed off. "I think I get it."

"Good." Odin took a step back. "I'll shift into a lion so you can get a feel for it. Then you try. If we manage to get you shifted, we can go for a run and see how you do in the wild. Then I'll help you shift back."

"Okay." I chewed at my lip and fingered the linen robe he'd had me change into earlier.

Odin turned his back to me and undid his pants. I blushed and looked away as they fell, but I couldn't resist a quick peek. Odin had a great ass, and that's all I'm going to say about it. I did feel a little dirty, admiring the father after sleeping with the son, but I didn't think it was quite the same when you were dealing with gods. Thor and Odin looked more like brothers than parent and child. Besides, I was just looking. Where's the harm?

I felt the magic before I saw the change. It was light, a happy feeling. The brush of feathers, no, fur. I closed my eyes and inhaled deeply as the feeling of fur sharpened and began to prickle, like all those little hairs had become plastic. It poked at me, but not hard enough to draw blood, more like someone was rubbing some AstroTurf gently over my skin. Weird, but kinda nice.

I opened my eyes to find a massive lion sitting on his haunches in front of me. I sucked in a startled breath as I looked into its single eye. The other eye was simply closed. No disturbing scarring, just a slight indentation to betray the fact that there was nothing behind the lid. I'd never seen Odin without the patch before, and I wasn't sure this even counted. I remembered then how Odin had supposedly willingly given up his eye. It made sense that the removal was probably done with careful precision. He probably didn't have scars in his human form either.

The lion let out a low grunt, and I nodded. It was my turn.

I thought about the feeling Odin's magic had given me. The way the fur had flowed against my arms, and then the sharp turn it had taken. My lioness perked up inside me, lifting her head and scenting the air. She didn't move, though, just sat there looking thoughtful. I tried to reach for her, call out to her and get her to come forward, but she just continued to sit there. Then she started to clean herself. Typical cat.

I growled in frustration, and Odin's lion laughed at me. It was a strange sound; a sort of rumbling wheeze. It took me awhile to recognize it for what it was. When I did, I crossed my arms and glared at him. That only made the wheezing stronger.

"Laugh it up, One-Eye," I ground out. "When I do get in lioness form, I'm gonna kick your furry butt."

He roared, and I shrank back, instantly horrified that I'd made the mistake of provoking an enemy god in lion form. But my lioness recognized the nuances in the sound and came striding forward. The roar wasn't anger, it was a healthy challenge. Odin was telling me to come and get him if I could, and my lioness's interest was piqued.

I let myself fall into that feeling and realized what I'd been doing wrong. I shouldn't have used the way Odin's magic made me feel to try and change. His magic was different than mine. I needed to know how mine felt and concentrate on that feeling to change. So, I focused on the feelings I'd had the first time I'd shifted. I recalled the way the ground had felt beneath the pads of my toes, the strength in my limbs, and the joy of being an animal. No concerns, but the breeze, the sun, and the hunt.

This time I felt the change. I felt the fur flow over me like a favorite blanket. I felt my limbs stretch like they were coming out of a deep slumber and reshape themselves into something better suited for running; for chasing things that I could tear into. I could smell them in the air; the little creatures who would perish beneath my claws and drip their life down my throat. I took in a deep

breath filled with forest and fresh air, then let it out in a thunderous sound of triumph. I was Intare.

Odin's lion was rubbing along my side, circling me, and huffing into my fur with his wet nose. Just saying hello. I nipped at him, scenting him back and storing the scent in my lion memory for future use. This was an ally, a partner to hunt with, a potential mate.

I almost lost my lioness at the shocking thought of Odin being mate potential. I stumbled a little before I let her take over again. She growled a warning at me before scenting something warm and tasty, and jumping off into the forest. Well, she was used to having her pick of males. I guess it was natural for her to be interested.

Then we were one again, and her thoughts were indiscernible from mine. I felt free as I leapt over high roots, forgoing the beaten path for the thick woods. I was fascinated by the heavy trees, the thick underbrush, the rich loam smell; all the things I didn't have at Pride Palace. There were so many new scents, it was hard to keep my goal in sight, and I lost the trail of the animal I was hunting.

Odin pushed in front of me and made an encouraging sound before taking off at a run. I chased him happily, the huntress inside of me finding new prey. Trees sped by, colors lost to me, but textures and shapes sharper. The scents made up for the lack of color somehow, and everything seemed more vibrant. I could close my eyes and still see.

The lion I was chasing turned sharply, and I swung left after him. Branches caught at me, but found no purchase in my fur. I slid through the foliage like water off a rock. I was running full speed now, leaping things and dodging instinctively. My blood rushed through me, my breath quickening. The tail before me twitched, and I nipped at it, but missed. A tawny head turned to me briefly before continuing on. I delighted in the fun.

Suddenly, we stopped, and I registered the appearance of an arrow in the tree above Odin's shoulder. My human brain supplied the knowledge of the weapon when my cat floundered. I lifted my muzzle and caught the new scent: man. *We* were being hunted now. I growled low and long, my muscles bunching in preparation.

Odin shot forward, stopping right before the archer with a wide stance and an angry roar. The archer pulled back, visibly paling beneath his deep tan. His dark hair was in a tight braid, his stance just as wide as Odin's. He had on a pair of jeans, moccasins, and a faded green T-shirt. He lowered his bow, looking chastised.

"Father, I'm sorry. I had no idea you were roaming as a lion today." The hunter looked over at me, and I snarled. "Or that you had a guest shifter. Who is this?"

Odin's form blurred, and I fought the urge to shift back with him. My body just wanted to follow Odin's lead, but my lioness felt that we'd be safer in her form. I trusted her instincts and stayed put. Odin stood up in his full nude glory and went to hug the other man. He pulled back, smacking the archer on the shoulder as he did.

"No harm done." Odin smiled. "Vali, this is Vervain, the new Goddess of the Intare. Vervain, this is my son, Vali."

"New Goddess?" Vali eyed me. "What happened to the old one?"

"Vervain killed her," Odin's voice was matter-of-fact. "The lions are better off."

"Well," Vali grunted, "I'll take your word on it. Never met the Lion Goddess. It was good to see you, Father. I'll let you get back to your hunt."

"Wait." Odin grabbed his son's arm. "I've missed you, Vali. Come by sometime, maybe share a fire with me at night?"

Vali stared at Odin for a long time, eyes wide. Finally, he swallowed hard and answered. “Maybe.”

“Okay.” Odin nodded and released him. “May your journey be easy and may others sing your praises for you.”

As the man slipped soundlessly back into the forest, Odin shifted back to lion. He tossed his head and let out a long bellow. I twisted my head down, away from the pain in it. I could smell his despair, his loneliness leaching from him, and it hit me like a kick in the chest. I fell back with a soft whimper. Odin stopped immediately and twisted around to face me. A quick lick from his rough tongue and then he was on the run again.

I let go of the human emotions he'd made me feel and returned to my beast. The lion knew nothing about heartache, she couldn't cope with it, but freedom and fleetness she understood. We ran until our limbs burned and we dropped into a pile on an open space of grass. Odin stretched and curled around me, and my chest began to vibrate happily. I was completely content. I was sleepy and warm. I was purring.

Chapter Fifty-Nine

I struggled against the heavy fog of sleep weighing me down, and in that half-aware state, a thick arm encircled my waist. A feeling of complete satiety flowed over me, making the fog thicken. I hummed a little in appreciation of how good it felt to snuggle back into that warm body, to breathe in a fresh male scent. I'd never felt more safe, more at home, or more happy.

I sighed and snuggled deeper. Hot breath tickled my neck and a hand started drifting in lazy circles over my belly. Heat rose under those careless fingertips, and I went liquid with wanting. Thickly muscled thighs pressed tight against mine, lips opening on my neck, the tip of a tongue tasting the salt on my skin. I rolled my head on the cradle of a massive bicep and looked up into a face I recognized, but somehow knew shouldn't be exactly where it was.

"What the fuck?" I jumped up and away from Odin, too shocked to even worry about my nudity.

He sat up more slowly and looked me over even slower. There was a strange look on his face, but other than that, he seemed completely at ease. Odin pulled a knee up and swung a hand over it as he braced himself on his other elbow.

"Sorry bout that," he said with a little smile. "I couldn't resist. You were all warm and rubbing against me."

"I think I can do this on my own now." I glared at him, "Thanks for the lesson. I'll show myself out."

"Vervain." Odin stood up and held out a hand in supplication. "It was just a little taste; I didn't mean any harm. I apologize for offending you."

"Fine," I grumbled. "Let's go."

I changed back into a lioness before he could say anything else. Mainly because I was way too naked, and so was he. I needed to get away from naked Odin and back to the real world of clothes and werewolf boyfriends.

I was happy with how easily the shift had come to me this time, but I had a feeling that my supreme embarrassment had something to do with it. The lioness, however, didn't know about embarrassment and frankly didn't see the problem with a few good licks between friends. I tried to tell her to take her slutty kitty ways and shove them where the sun don't shine, but really, that doesn't make much sense when the creature you're telling to shove it only exists inside of you. Can you tell someone to shove it up their metaphorical ass? I decided that you could.

So, I once more told her to shove it as we ran away from Odin in what she was feeling was a very *come and get me, big boy* manner. For me, it was the opposite of that. At least I hoped it was the opposite. Was my tail twitching too suggestively? Oh shit, was he staring at my furry ass? I picked up speed and thankfully made it back to Valhalla in no time.

I found my discarded robe, picked it up with my teeth, and ran behind a trellis of grapes to change. It was just as easy to change into a woman, and I was relieved that I was able to do it and get my robe on before Odin even made it out of the tree line.

Odin sniffed the air and then changed immediately back to himself, making it look as easy as breathing. I stepped out from behind my fruit shield warily as he pulled on his pants. He looked over at me with a sheepish grin. He hadn't made it as far as putting on his eye patch yet, and I got to see that his lid was indeed in perfect condition, just a little concave. He affixed the leather about his face and lost his smile.

"Does it bother you?" He waved a hand at his missing eye

casually, but the question seemed to have some weight.

"Not at all." I frowned. "I was just wondering why you never got a glass eye."

"I don't like the feel of them," he said with some relief. "Besides, I think I kind of look like a pirate with the patch."

"You *are* a pirate." I laughed. "You're a Viking, one of the original pirates."

"Ah yes." He grinned. "I never took part in raiding, but my people did enjoy it a bit."

"A bit?" I huffed. "Thank you, Mr. Understatement, for reducing the years of plundering, raping, and pillaging your people made a living by, down to four letters."

"Well, at least it wasn't a four-letter word."

"A four letter word would probably be more apt." I grimaced at him.

"Yes, yes." Odin chuckled and indicated with a wave that I should precede him into the hall. "They were a feisty lot, but they were also excellent traders. Would you like some refreshment before you leave?"

"No." I sobered. "I think I should be going.

"I assure you, the food was all procured in a non-violent manner." He tried a little boy grin on me.

"I'm sure it was." I stopped my mad dash for the tracing room and turned back to him. "I appreciate the lesson, Odin. You've been a big help, and I owe you one."

"The Godhunter owes me one." He grinned wider and raised a brow.

“Within reason.” I narrowed my eyes on him.

“Rest assured”–Odin had a horrible twinkle in his eye–“I shall endeavor to find a reason soon.”

Chapter Sixty

"How was the training?" Trevor's voice made me jump guiltily.

"Fine." I was grateful it was so dark in our bedroom. I was sure that I was flushed.

"Good." He rolled over and went back to sleep.

I huffed happily. Now that I was home, the incident with Odin was fading fast. I hadn't done anything wrong, after all. I'd just woken up a little confused. I was blaming Odin entirely. He had even apologized, and I had kind of accepted. So, why did I have this weird feeling like I'd wanted it?

Probably cause I did.

But that didn't matter. Wanting and doing were two different things. I was not an animal, I only turned into one occasionally. I wasn't a slave to my baser instincts. In fact, there were a lot of men I was attracted to who I wouldn't be having sex with. It's called being in a relationship. I was a grownup and I was in a grownup relationship. I'd chosen to be faithful and I would. There was no doubt in my mind over that. I loved Trevor; completely and devotedly, and he loved me.

So what if I'd now have fantasies about my ex-boyfriend's father? Eww, that sounded awful. I have to be honest with myself, though. White trash or not, I knew I'd have a naughty little spot in my mind reserved for Odin now. I know it was just one little kiss on the neck, but the neck was my yum spot and Odin worked it well. Sigh.

I climbed into bed with my wolf, recalling that Kirill was

sleeping down the hall in my art room. It made me happy that I was able to give Kirill a place that made him happy. Calm spread over me as Trevor wrapped me in tightly against his side, and I let everything that happened in the last twenty-four hours slip away. My fantasies instantly focused back on Trevor.

And they were good.

Epilogue

Life went pretty much back to normal, as normal as it can get for the Godhunter/Rouva/Tima. Balancing my life as Rouva to the Froekn and Tima to the Intare has become second nature, although I secretly longed for the day Fenrir found his mate and I could hand over the Rouva title to her. I barely had time to paint, what with trying to keep my boys in line and keep the wolves legally employed.

Kirill took up residence in my art room, so painting isn't the solitary release it used to be, but when it was all said and done, I didn't mind. I enjoy Kirill's company, and I think that Trevor does too. He definitely appreciated the extra manpower in case of an attack, and I could tell that he's relieved to be able to leave me with a bodyguard when I don't go to work with him.

I worry about Kirill though. He's making me the center of his life, and as much as I appreciated that, I want him to live for more than just guarding my back. Baby steps, though. I suppose he's making great progress for a guy who was been chained and horribly tortured for years. Maybe someday Kirill will remember how to live for himself again.

The rest of the Intare are embracing their new found freedom wholeheartedly, sometimes a little too wholeheartedly. I have discovered why they so desperately needed a Tima. It seems like every other day I'm mediating fights and counseling them. But along with all the headaches comes immense rewards as well.

We were becoming a Pride. Every dispute I settled, every grief I assuaged, or problem I helped solve, bonds me closer to my lions. I'm beginning to see more than appreciation in their eyes, now there's also respect and affection. I'm hoping that one day

there might be love there as well because I sure do love them, my wild boys, my cubs.

Trevor is becoming more and more supportive of my cats. The more time he spends with them and realizes that they're not out to steal his girlfriend, the more relaxed he becomes around them, and the more he enjoys their company. I think Kirill has been the most helpful in that regard.

There have been a couple of little scraps between the wolves and the lions, about women of course, but we've stumbled through them mostly unscathed and I thank Fenrir for that as much as my fast talking. Anything I can't handle with words, he can handle with fists.

I haven't spoken to Odin since our episode in the woods. It's all so messed up, waking up naked with my ex-boyfriend's father, and then snuggling with him as if I was supposed to be there. I know it's not my fault, that it was just a brief moment of half-awake pleasure which Odin took advantage of, but whenever my mind wanders back to the forest of Asgard, I don't feel regret. I don't feel embarrassment or anger over his behavior. All I feel is . . . need. A horrible, aching, need.

Odin's pull is strong, but the desire I feel for Trevor isn't exactly minor, and Trevor's lovemaking is never lacking. He is, and probably will always be, the most amazing lover I've ever known. He does get help from the bonding, but I've never been one to complain about sexual aids. Who could possibly complain after being loved so thoroughly by Trevor? Not I.

So, I'm trying to let go of my strange need for Odin, my still bruised love for Thor, my heartache over Blue–who still hasn't forgiven me, and my hatred of Demeter–who is on the loose and plotting my downfall, no doubt. It's not too difficult when I snuggle in to sleep at night with my Werewolf Prince holding me. I just wish a certain one-eyed, Viking god would stay out of my dreams.

Did you enjoy the book? If you did, please take the time to let the author know by leaving her a review.

And... keep reading for a sneak peek at the next book in The Godhunter Series:

Oathbreaker

Chapter One

Ever dance with a werewolf in the pale moonlight?

A gentle breeze brushed against my cheek, and the scent of vanilla orchids embraced me. I sighed as I nestled closer into the thick arms that held me as we swayed to primal music. The sound of drums became more of a feeling, a percussion in my blood that was drowned out when I laid my head against his chest. His heartbeat was a precious melody, and his scent, that spicy wolf musk I thought of as home, was sweeter to me than the orchids. His heat warmed me and enriched his scent all at once. I looked up and smiled at the way the moonlight turned his face into a half-mask of dramatic shadows.

Those shadows suited Trevor's mood lately, he'd been so up and down since we'd made our relationship official, it seemed like he was two different people. I couldn't blame him, though. Between the one-sided Froekn Binding which shackled him to me for life (but not me to him), the Thunder God ex-boyfriend I couldn't avoid, and my new collection of werelions, it was understandable. I'd be a little insecure too.

We were dancing on the VIP level of Moonshine, our club Trevor had built to give the Froekn more morally (my morals not theirs) acceptable jobs than assassin work. The werewolves had killed people for the gods and had made a good living out of it for several more years than I'd been alive. The gods had difficulty killing other gods (a magic thing) and since the Froekn technically weren't gods, more of a subspecies like the vampires, they didn't have a problem with it. Plus, the wolves enjoyed to hunt, so things had worked out well for them all around.

Until I came along.

The Godhunter. A mid-level witch turned vigilante in the name of humanity. When I think back to the early days of my godhunting escapades, I'm shocked to be alive. I really knew nothing, just the basic facts; that gods were the survivors of Atlantis, using their advanced technology and magic to control and manipulate humans.

The Atlanteans had set themselves up all over the world as deities, and when worship started to wane, they developed other ways to suck energy from us. They claimed the dead from wars as sacrifice, but in order to have war casualties, you must first have a war. So they continued their manipulating ways and began to instigate war among us. That's where I dropped in. The witch crusader, executing gods with righteous indignation.

Only, like I said, I knew very little. I had no idea, for instance, that some of the gods were opposed to the way humans were being treated. Some gods actually took pride in forming symbiotic relationships with their followers. Keeping to the original plan; they gave guidance, protection, and good fortune in exchange for the worship they received.

After years of hunting gods who I thought were evil, discovering good gods was a bit of a shock. Kind of like following a Neo-Nazi home to find out that his oldest son was in love with a African-American girl and was running away from home to be with her. Shocking, but in a good, fist-pumping, happily ironic, kind of way.

I got over my shock and joined a group of rebel gods led by Thor, the Viking God of Thunder. I'd fought beside them and occasionally with them. Thor and I had dated, but things didn't work out. A couple of times actually. I have a talent for fucking things up in my love life. Okay, in my life period. But the last break-up I take no responsibility for. It was all Thor. I'm still a little bitter and, maybe, a lot in love with him.

Then, in the midst of the Thor debacle, my very own Werewolf Prince Charming came in and swept me off my feet. It's always darkest before the dawn, and all that crap. I thought I'd never get over Thor. I mean how do you get over loving a god? I'll tell you how: move on with a werewolf. They're faithful, sexy, built like gladiators, have great stamina, and are great to snuggle with when they turn furry. Hell, even when they're not furry.

Trevor's real name is VéulfR, it means "Sacred Wolf", as in the first born son of Fenrir, the Wolf God. So, I'm not kidding when I call him a Prince. We bonded while Thor and I were still together . . . and I don't mean normal couple bonding, so don't judge. I didn't even have a choice about it. It's a long story, but basically I have a little piece of Trevor's soul inside me now. When I die, that connection will pull him into death with me. A fact his father was a little upset over at first, since Trevor was previously immortal.

I'm not bound to Trevor, however, making ours the first one-sided mating bond in the history of Froekn society. Since it's a werewolf thing and I'm a human, that makes us another first. Two firsts; I was throwing the werewolf world into a tizzy.

I tried to resist Trevor after I'd broken it off with Thor, but in the end, I gave in. Call me weak, but take one look at the tall muscled frame, amber eyes, movie star good looks, and thick dark hair, then see if you could walk away. I dare you. Double dog–er double werewolf dare you.

So, it was me and Trevor now, and even though the Binding has had some drawbacks, it's had a lot of perks too. The simple act of touching Trevor can be an erotic experience. For example, dancing with him in this replica forest, the fake moonlight from the "moon" surveillance system shining down on us, his hot hands skimming over the thin silk of my dress, was turning into torture. Fabulous, sizzling-hot, werewolf torture.

I broke away from Trevor, just a tad out of breath, and he

smiled down at me knowingly. I was used to this since at five-three (and a half), most people look down on me, but I still took umbrage over his expression. I slapped him on one thick bicep.

"Take pity on the poor human," I sauntered over to the railing, so I could watch the rest of the Dark Horses' performance. Trevor had hired the band pretty recently, but we could already see an improvement in business. Since business was great to begin with, that was saying a lot. Maybe it had to do with the fact that all four members of the band were gorgeous horse-shifters. It made me wonder about the saying: hung like a . . . oh, never mind.

"You're a goddess now, remember?" My wolf came up behind me, grabbing the rail to either side of me and effectively trapping me, but I didn't mind. I mean, are you really trapped if you want to be there?

"How could I forget?" My gaze wandered over to Kirill, my Ganza.

Kirill was staring at me, of course. It was kinda his job as my right hand man . . . er, lion. It was also just Kirill. My Russian black lion had been horribly abused by his last Tima, and I had saved him from both insanity and death. It made him a little clingy.

So how did I get to be the heart of the Intare, Tima to a pride of werelions? Well, I have this unique ability for stealing back the energy gods took from humans. I could drain their power completely, effectively taking their magic and killing the god. Previously, I'd been the boogeyman of the god world, simply for hunting them, but this new power was turning me into Dracula, Jason, and Freddy Krueger combined into one. I'd killed not one, but two, goddesses already, collecting numerous powers and an entire pride of werelions along the way. Oh, and a cool new palace.

I was now the Goddess of Love, Sex, Victory, War, and Lions, but I usually simplified it to Love and Lions, as Sex, Victory, and War were all a part of one goddess' power. Inside me

curled a lioness just waiting for the chance to come out and play. Yes, I could turn into a huge cat. Then there was that little piece of Trevor inside me. The wolf soul had changed me a little, and I had changed it as well. It had gone from male to female, now viewing Trevor's wolf as her mate. I know, it's a little strange but if you think that's odd, wait till you hear about my Nahual.

My Aztec spirit animal is essentially the animal me. We all have them, but most of us don't know about them. Through some deep meditation and a healthy dose of necessity, I connected with her. She's a white jaguar with beautiful golden spots, and she was definitely in charge of my little menagerie. She regulated, like when the wolf and lion went at it, and settled disputes quickly. I know, talk about your internal battles.

At least War, Sex, and Victory weren't animals, and my Love magic took the less aggressive form of a flock of butterflies. Funny since, out of all of my magics, Love was the most powerful. Love could empower people to do great things or inspire them to evil. It could manipulate or guide, be a muse or a sadist. Love could start wars *and* finish them.

When Aphrodite held the magic, she took it to a darker place. I liked to think that I saved it from her, and that I would never abuse the power of love. It's a tricky magic, though. Sometimes using it for what you believed to be good, could have unsettling repercussions. I was still new to it, still learning, but there were moments when I worried about turning into ol' Afro.

We were watching *Lord of the Rings* the other day, my friend Tristan is a junkie and has to get an occasional *LOTR* fix, and we got to that part where Galadriel refuses to take the ring. For those *two* people out there who have never seen *LOTR,* Galadriel is an elf and the ring has enough power to level kingdoms. She goes through this whole enactment of what were to happen if she took the ring. She likes to think she'd do good with it, but she knows in the end, she would become this dark goddess, using the power to dominate. It's a very striking image, and it made me squirm a little.

Would Love do that to me eventually? Or even one of the other magics? Or the combination of all of them? What would happen if I lost control or, even worse, lost my mind?

Thor had warned me once about taking too much magic. He wasn't sure how much my human body could hold or handle. He said that even though I was full of magic, it didn't make me an immortal, and I needed to be careful or the magic could kill me. Pan had added his own comment to that; "Yeah, look at Horus, he's full of shit, but that doesn't make him a toilet." So, if the threat of turning into an evil, murderous bitch wasn't bad enough, I had the whole dying thing to add to it. Good times.

Dark Horses finished their set, much to the disappointment of the Monday night crowd, and dispersed into different directions. I watched the bassist, Ilario, head toward the bar, but he got waylaid by a gaggle of women. I smiled as he smoothly wound his way through them and set a fresh course toward refreshment. I was watching his progress so intently, I didn't notice the lead singer coming up the steps behind me. Trevor did, though.

"Hey, Rain," Trevor's greeting turned my head towards the stairs.

Rain. Short for Rainieri. All of the Dark Horses were Italian, but Rain was Roman, as in Roman Legionnaire. He smiled at me as he approached, but the smile didn't reach his eyes. Maybe it was just me, but Rain never seemed happy, never really at ease. I'm sure his female fans would disagree with me, but every time I looked at him, the only thing I wanted was a stiff drink. He was the first man I'd ever met who my War magic responded to like a long lost friend. It leaped to attention when Rain was near, the sounds of battle filling my head briefly. The screams of horses were the worst; innocent tools of battle struck down mercilessly. For the first time ever, I wondered how many battles Rain had fought in equine form.

"Hey, Boss," Rain answered in his quiet, low voice. It was

like he saved all the volume for the stage. I'd never heard Rain speak to someone in a voice louder than mid-range. "Vervain," his eyes were deep, chocolate brown, a color I wished my own muddy brown ones could be, and when he said my name, his voice matched them, becoming a purr worthy of any Intare.

I felt Trevor tense beside me and shot a frantic look at my mate. There was the shadow-side again, like Trevor's evil twin, jumping to the surface to cause havoc. He'd always been so easy going before, it was odd to see him behave this way. Not that I blamed him in the least. I would have left him if I had to put up with a pack of hot women hanging all over him, but then I tended to bail on relationships for the smallest little thing. It was a flaw I was trying to work on; even more so since Trevor had become my guy.

"You sounded great tonight," I said lightly as I shot Rain my *what the fuck* look.

"Thanks," he leaned casually against the rail a little down from me and gave me a lazy grin. "I'm glad you enjoyed it."

Trevor began to growl.

"Relax"–Rain laughed–"I was just teasing. Keeping you on your toes. Just because you got some werewolf bond going on, doesn't mean you should go lax with protecting your relationship."

"Our relationship is fine, thanks." I frowned at him, wondering what his game was.

I'd known Rain for two months, and I'd already come to realize that the one thing he took from his Legionnaire days was an aptitude for strategy. Rain always had a plan.

"Good." Rain looked out over the crowd as if uninterested in the conversation. "If I were your man though, I'd do everything in my power to make sure you *remained* mine." He straightened, winked at me and walked away.

I stared after him, frowning as I saw him reach the bottom of the stairs, and then I watched the throng wrap around him, the women making eager passes and the men wanting to shake his hand. What was he doing now? Why in the world would he want to mess with my love life? I was 99.9% sure Rain had no interest in me sexually, so I didn't think he was trying to break me and Trevor up. If I didn't know better, I'd think Rain was Loki in disguise.

The Trickster God happened to be Trevor's Grandpa, but that didn't stop him from messing with me. Loki had forced me to fight Sif (Thor's ex-wife) to the death, thereby ensuring the death of either myself or my relationship with Thor. Obviously, it was the later. Hmm, maybe Loki had been on Trevor's side after all. I never would have left Thor for Trevor otherwise. Damn, I hadn't thought about it like that before.

When I looked back at Trevor, it was with a new suspicion. Did he have anything to do with it? Trevor had been the one who had told Loki where to find me. I shook my head. No, that was crazy. Trevor would never have knowingly put me into harm's way, if for no other reason than it would be risking his own life as well. Then again, maybe he viewed the risk worthwhile, and he did have an over abundance of confidence in my fighting skills. I'd bested him and his two brothers in a fight. It gave me a certain amount of prestige with the Froekn, I guess. But no, Trevor wouldn't have done that to me. He loved me.

"I love you," Trevor said suddenly, almost as if he had read my mind. He pulled me over to a hill-shaped couch, nestled back in some trees.

"I love you too, honey-eyes." I laughed, trying to let go of my dark thoughts, and snuggled into his side, pretending for just a moment that we were a normal couple. There were no werewolves, no werelions, no vampires, and no gods. Just us, in love for real.

The thought made my teeth clench. For real? What did that mean? What we had *was* real wasn't it? Why couldn't I just leave

things alone and be happy? I always had to pick at my happiness and worry about it. Like there was only so much happiness allowed one person, and if you got too much, the Happy Police would knock down your door and take you away. “Sorry Ma’am, you’ve violated section 28.3 of the Happiness Code: Excessive happiness with a werewolf. I’m going to have to take you in.”

“Hey, you okay?” Trevor tucked his face down to look at me.

“I'm great.” I ran my fingers through the hair at his temple and he sighed, his eyes closing automatically. His body swayed forward, pushing me into the faux-grass covered back of our couch. I felt his arms wrap around me, and then his mouth was on mine, ferocious and demanding. I finally pulled back, holding his face in my hands. “Are *you* okay?”

“I just have this horrible feeling that you’re pulling away from me.” He shook his head and sighed.

I didn’t know what else to do, so I lowered my hands to his shoulders and began to massage them.

“I love you.” I sighed as the music faded into the background. “It’s just, sometimes I wonder how much of it’s magic.”

“Excuse me?”

“You love me because of the Binding, baby,” I tried my hardest to be gentle. “Is it really love if you don’t have a choice?”

“The Binding isn’t about love, it's about commitment.” Trevor looked like he was about to throttle me. “It builds desire, but only to solidify the commitment, the bond. When werewolves perform a Binding, it's assumed that love is already there. We wouldn't bind ourselves if it wasn't.”

“So, it doesn't make you love me?” Boy had I

misunderstood.

"No, I love you because you're amazing. I love you because you have the spirit of a witch and the heart of a Froekn. The Binding isn't what makes me love you. It's just an excuse to stay with you, even if you stop loving me."

His words had the immediate effect of unleashing the waterworks, and his expression softened as he wiped my tears away gently. My big bad wolf could be such a softie and it made me wimp out too. All my anxiety flowed away and the tears were half from relief–half from affection. I pulled Trevor against me, holding on tight, hoping that this new security would last.

"How could I ever stop loving you?" I whispered into his shirt.

Trevor pushed me away gently and dropped to his knees while he took my hands in his.

"Then marry me." He stared up at me intently, wolf eyes all aglow.

"What?" I barely got the word out.

"If you love me, then marry me." He kissed my hands. "You don't have to bond with me, just marry me like humans do."

Like humans do. The words swirled in my brain, coming to their obvious conclusion. A conclusion that I'd already known, but hadn't felt so profoundly until that moment. Trevor wasn't human . . . he'd never *been* human. What kind of future did we have? I'd begun to think Trevor was perfect for me. He wasn't immortal since he'd bonded to me, so we could grow old together like regular people, and he seemed to love like I did: completely. With Trevor came some semblance of normalcy, but what would marriage mean? Was I ready to marry a werewolf? Have little wolf babies? Pups? I just didn't know.

“Vervain,” Trevor started to look wounded.

Damn it, Trevor didn’t play this game; acting the victim was a Thor thing. Why was he being like this?

“Trevor.” I knelt with him and took his face in my hands. “I don’t know if I’m ready to take that step. It's so soon.”

“So, you love me, you say you’ll never stop”–the hurt look was turning into a furious one–“but you won’t commit to me?”

Commit. Sweet baby Jesus, wasn’t that a woman’s word? I sighed, but before I could say anything more, Trevor stood up and dropped my hands. I stared up at him in shock, feeling lost, there on my knees alone. Trevor was furious. The little piece of him raced around inside me, like he was tearing at me from the inside as well as the outside. It was almost unbearable.

“Trevor.” I stood on shaky legs and reached for him, but he pulled away.

“Enjoy your evening, Rouva.” Trevor's face fell into the cold angles of a stranger as he turned and walked down the stairs.

I just stood there like an idiot, gawking after him. I didn’t call him back. I couldn’t get my voice to work. I just kept thinking; *He can’t leave me, he can’t*. Trevor was the one who was supposed to stay. Forever. No matter what. This was the one relationship I shouldn't have been able to fuck up. But it looked as if I could find a way to screw up the un-screw-up-able.

Then the voices came. The same voices that taunted me when Thor ended our relationship. Telling me men are all the same. They all leave in the end. They all hurt you no matter what they say in the beginning. The worst part is knowing that those voices are all mine. It's just me. Why do I do this to myself?

I sank to the ground, up against the couch, and hugged my knees to my chest. The bastard had just stormed off like a child. I

was getting mad and I welcomed it. I pulled that anger around me like a shield because if I didn't, I was going to fall apart. Is this what I'd been missing all those years I'd been single? Well, who needed it? I was better off alone; just me, my cat, and a lot of batteries. There's a reason why some women turn into little old cat ladies. Cats are easy; you feed them, you love them, and they love you back.

"Vervain."

I looked up, hoping it wasn't Ty. I didn't want to have to explain things to Trevor's little brother. It wasn't Ty, though, it was Odin. Much, much worse.

I'd gone to Odin for training with my shifting magic. During the course of the training, we'd fallen asleep and I woke up to him kissing my shoulder. I know, not exactly cataclysmic, but Odin had unnerved me *before* the incident. After that little kiss, I couldn't get him out of my head for weeks.

There were so many reasons why forming an attachment to Odin would be a bad thing. Not the least of which would be the werewolf who'd just stormed off, but also, the fact that Odin was Thor's father, kind of squidged me out. Then there's him being one of the "bad" gods who I was technically at war with. Oh, the list goes on. So basically, I'd avoided Odin ever since. He was the last person I wanted to see after fighting with Trevor.

"Are you alright?" Odin had his one eye focused intently on me.

Why do people always ask you if you're alright when you're obviously not? And why do those words always send you over the edge and make you lose what little control you may have gathered? I started to cry; big, ugly, body-wracking sobs, like my world was falling apart. The poor guy looked appalled for a second before he dropped to his knees and pulled me into a tentative hug.

He rocked me gently and, amazingly, I felt calmed by him.

It felt good to be there. It felt right, like I'd been held by him a thousand times before. I snuggled closer, desperately needing to feel something steady. Then the crisp scent of clean mountain air filled my nose. Smelling Odin was like standing on a cliff, you could almost feel the wind blow through your hair. It cooled and invigorated me. It filled my lungs and refreshed me. My tears dried and I looked up at him, startled.

Odin had wrapped his leather jacket around us, and I hadn't even noticed. I could feel the warmth of his body, but still, I was pleasantly cool. His face was close to mine, and I pulled back to get him into focus.

Dark brown hair falling to his shoulders, close-cropped beard along his angled jawline, a long nose, and sharp brows. Odin's one, beautiful eye gazed down on me. Suddenly, there was a bright flash. I blinked and saw him with both eyes. The image was fleeting, like a memory superimposed over reality, but it was vibrantly clear, and it made me gasp.

"What is it?" Odin stroked my cheek gently, wiping away the remnants of my heartache.

I just stared at him awhile. Most men would have gotten nervous or repeated their question, but Odin just waited patiently. He was the God of the Dead as well as the Sky, so it made sense that he'd have patience. I appreciated the quiet; my vision had been disturbing.

I took a few breaths, listening to the stream behind me make its way to the edge of the second floor where it flowed over the side, becoming a waterfall and crashing into the pool on the first level. From serene to violent, it felt like an appropriate soundtrack for my emotions.

I'd never been one to have visions before, and now I'd had two. Both connected to Odin. The last had been during our training session. He had reached out a hand to me, and I had a glimpse of

that same hand looking darker, more tan. I thought I heard something too, but for the life of me, I couldn't recall it anymore.

It just made no sense. Why would I see images of Odin looking differently? What did it mean? It's not like seeing him whole was some great revelation. I already knew he hadn't been born with only one eye. Weren't visions supposed to tell you something important? Weren't they supposed to foretell the future? I was so screwed up, I couldn't even have a proper prophecy.

"When did you lose your eye?" I finally asked.

He blinked rapidly. "A very long time ago. I gave it to Mimir as payment for a drink from his well. The well is an old relic of ours and can grant great knowledge, if the sacrifice is just as great. Mimir always said my eyes were too beautiful for me to have two of. So, now one of them belongs to him." Odin shrugged as if losing an eye were like losing a tooth. "Why do you ask?"

"I just saw you with both of them." I frowned, his information hadn't helped at all. I'd never even met Mimir. Would this person have a part to play in my future? Or maybe the knowledge Odin had collected was important to me? "I don't know why, it makes no sense."

Odin's face went still, and I pulled further away, studying that stillness. Then he took a deep breath and bowed his head. I forgot about my own pain as I watched his flicker across his face. It must have been hard for him to remember being whole. I wondered if he regretted giving up his eye. Maybe the nonchalance was just a mask for his sorrow. I felt bad for judging him so quickly. My hand moved up through his hair, brushing back some hanging strands as I leaned down to look into his face.

"I didn't mean to bring back painful memories," I said.

I thought I heard him whisper, but it was too low to make out. I could've sworn Odin had said something about *me* being the painful memory, but that's just ridiculous. I hardly think one

shoulder-kiss could cause heartache. I may have Aphrodite's Love magic, but I hadn't used it on him.

"What was that?"

"Nothing." Odin looked up and changed the subject. "Are you going to tell me what happened with Trevor?"

Trevor! I felt the crushing hurt return and inhaled sharply. "He asked me to marry him."

"And this upsets you?" Odin sat back on his heels with a shocked thump, and pondered me like I was a new species.

"No." I sighed. "We just started living together, it's too soon to get married. So, I upset *him* when I pointed that out, which in turn upsets me. Trevor thinks I should commit to him if I love him."

"No pressure then," Odin smirked, and I laughed.

I couldn't believe he cracked a joke in the midst of my misery. That was kind of my specialty.

"Exactly." I shook my head. "That's the thing with Trevor. There's always been pressure on me, even before we were a couple. He bonded himself to me without my knowledge or permission, and then suddenly I've got the responsibility of this man's life on my hands. I have to touch him at least once a month or he'll get sick and die. Die! How's that for pressure?"

"Binding is very serious." Odin frowned. "He shouldn't have entered into it with you without your consent."

"He says that since I saved his life, it belonged to me anyway." I leaned back as I explained. "I started the Binding without even realizing it, when I refused his offer to defend me."

"Right"–Odin nodded–"I'm familiar with the process. It's supposed to show that they're steadfast, and you're deserving, or

some shit like that."

"Yeah, but usually it's between two wolves, and they both make the bond." I rubbed my aching temple. "Trevor was bonded to me before I knew what was going on. I didn't want him to be tied to me, wasting his life being faithful to me while I loved another man, but Thor said I'd become his happiness and Trevor would be content just to touch me occasionally."

"Then you and Thor had a falling out," Odin prompted.

"Yes, and Trevor took care of me." I shook my head. "I'm making it sound like Trevor wheedled his way into my life and took advantage of my vulnerable state."

"And he didn't?"

"No, he was just there to help me. At one point, Trevor used the bond to transfer my pain to himself. He literally carried the weight of my heartache for me. He camped on my porch for three days, waiting for me to let him in. Trevor has been amazing. Then we got together, and Fenrir started pushing for babies. Can you believe that? He's like an annoying mother-in-law." I pounded my head back against the couch. "Trevor gave me half of this club, and we're living together, but he still says I'm pulling away. Now, he wants marriage. He told me before, that he'd be around no matter what, even if I were to leave him for someone else. So, why has it all suddenly changed?"

"The Froekn can be very psychic." Odin shifted to lean against the couch beside me. "Something about their ties to the moon. Maybe he senses something coming."

"Nothing's coming." I looked around at the beautiful club Trevor had created; all the work he'd put into giving the Froekn legitimate jobs so that I'd be happy. "I love him. Maybe I should just marry him."

"No!" Odin sat up straight. I looked at him sharply, and he

relaxed back. "I mean; don't give in to Trevor just because he's insecure. You should marry him only if you want to, not because you feel like you have to."

"Maybe you're right. I don't know, maybe it's a moot point and I've already lost him."

"He'll never be lost to you," Odin's voice wavered. "He's a bonded Froekn, nothing you do will ever keep him away."

"Yeah, but you forget that I'm part lion now." I grimaced. "The cat has changed things. There are times when I feel like my lioness wants me to be with a lion. I get strange urges, I focus on things I shouldn't. I can feel her pushing at me like an instinct, like an animal consciousness telling me that I'm going against the laws of Nature by mating a wolf. It's like she doesn't care about my feelings, there's no compassion to it, just right and wrong. Simple."

"You don't give her enough credit." Odin cocked his head and looked at me over the top of one leather-clad bicep, perched on his knee.

"My lioness?"

"Aren't you a cat lover?" He frowned at me.

"Yes." I thought about Nick, my gray tabby. I'd never accuse him of being heartless. "But a house cat is vastly different from the wildcat it's descended from."

"The cat was born when the lion sneezed," Odin said with a smile. "They are very alike."

"Yeah, they hunt and kill things for fun." I smirked.

"Saved by the Lioness."

"What?" I frowned at him. "Are you speaking in code?"

"It was a show on Animal Planet the other day." Odin

grinned, and I had the oddest image of him sitting in front of a TV, in a EZ chair, watching a television show about animals.

"You have a TV in Valhalla? How exactly does that work?"

"I have something even better"–Odin grinned like a two-year-old with a puppy–"a device called Hlidskjalf which allows me to see into any realm. It also catches cable."

"It catches . . ." I blinked several times. "Holy shit, you're Santa Claus!"

"Hardly." He made a face and looked pointedly over his excellent physique.

"You can see anywhere? Everywhere?"

"Yes."

"And you have a beard."

"Yes."

"Asgard does get pretty cold."

"Yes, but it's not the North Pole."

"Do you own any reindeer?"

"No."

"Elves, red suits, a sleigh? Do you ever have the urge to make toys or fill socks with candy? Is your favorite color red?"

"No, Vervain." Odin chuckled (rather like Ol' St. Nick). "You're getting me off track."

"Oh, right." I thought back. "Back to your Santa-esque ability to see all over the world and also catch cable. I'd like to point out that I don't even catch all the cable channels, and I

actually live in this realm."

"If you're finished griping about your lack of channel choices?" He looked at me with a raised brow. It was raised over the missing eye, so it was a little disturbing.

"Of course"–I waved my permission–"please proceed, Santa. Or would you prefer that I called you Nick? Like my cat."

"Keep it up, and I'll start calling you Vivian," he threatened.

"Damn you, how do you know about that? You *are* Santa!"

My biggest pet peeve was when people insisted on calling me Vivian instead of Vervain. The friendly and helpful (by that, I mean; rude and unaccommodating) people of the DMV were constantly trying to correct the typos in my name. *Yes, my name is actually Vervain Alexandrite Lavine. No, not Vivian Alexandra. Yes, I know it's strange, it's my name, I'm quite familiar with it. No, I don't want to change it to make your life easier. Could you please just print up my driver's license now?*

"I told you"–Odin smirked at me and tapped his one, remaining eye–"I have an eye for it. Just the one, but it sees all."

"You perv."

"I beg your pardon?"

"You should, you big, perverted Santa Claus." I glared at him. "You better not have ever watched me in the shower."

"Vervain!"

"Okay, okay." I sighed, but inside, I was giggling. Odin could actually be fun. Who knew? "Tell me about the Disney Channel."

"Animal Planet." He sighed right back. "There was this

show where they follow some poor creature around, filming its life, but not interfering."

"They call that reality TV." I patted his head like he was slow. "Was it the cooking one or the sewing one? There's lots more, but those are the really good ones. Oh, I do like the ghost hunting ones too. There's one with this really buff host who always ends up screaming like a little girl in pigtails. Oh, yeah, and there's a new Southern version of it with guys who look like they're in ZZ Top, going around saying things like; 'My ghost radar is goin' off like a buck in ruttin' season.'"

"How does anyone manage to finish a conversation with you?" Odin looked truly baffled. "It's an animal show. On Animal Planet. I told you it was called *Saved by the Lioness.* Are you doing this to torture me, or do you find this subject completely boring?"

"I'm sorry." I let one little giggle out, and he shook his head at me. "Go ahead. I just have to say first that I hate those shows. They follow an animal around, and when it gets into trouble, they're all like 'Oh this poor zebra is gonna drown, but we can't help it because that would be interfering.' How messed up is that? You know that zebra is like; 'Hey, a little help here? You've been filming me all day, but you can't even toss me a damn rope?'"

"I quite agree." Odin patted *my* head. "Now, shut up. This particular show was following a baby wildebeest around, and it got lost from its mother."

"See, I'm already depressed."

"If you would allow me to continue for possibly five minutes without interrupting?"

"Sorry."

"In the process of trying to make its way back to its mother, the baby was surrounded by a pack of hyenas." Odin narrowed his

eye on me when I made a face at him, so I kept quiet. "It looked as if the show was going to be quite a short one, but along comes this lioness, and she saves the little wildebeest from the hyenas."

"Not," I said, dumbstruck.

"Yes, indeed." Odin looked thrilled to be finally impressing me. "She ran off the hyenas, and the baby, who was too young to know that it should fear this predator, followed her and cuddled with her a bit before he went on his way."

"That's amazing."

"Yes, but what does it say to you, Lion Queen?"

"That a lioness can show compassion."

"Exactly." He nodded like he was a professor and I, his worst, but somehow finally cogitating, student. "It isn't simply compassion, though. She shows mercy to an animal she would normally hunt. She has compassion for her prey. Just because your lioness has personal views on who she believes you should be with, it doesn't mean she has no understanding of love, or sympathy for your views. Give her some respect, and maybe she will help you with your hyenas. Metaphorically speaking."

"Wow." I frowned, fighting the urge to make yet another Santa joke. "That's kind of beautiful and really insightful. Thank you."

"Of course." Odin reached over and took my hand.

"Well, isn't this sweet?" Thor was suddenly standing over us, glaring at our joined hands.

What the hell was he doing here?

"Is this why I saw Trevor stomping off?" Thor asked.

Odin started to get up, and I could feel his anger like a drop

in barometric pressure. I squeezed his hand, and when he looked at me, I shook my head. This was my battle. Odin leaned back and inclined his head to me.

"Odin's just offering some comfort because Trevor kind of abandoned me."

I was used to Thor's rudeness, so I could keep calm. Some part of me actually welcomed it after the strange way Trevor had been acting. This was some much needed normalcy.

"So why did Trevor abandon you?" Thor sat down on the end of the couch.

"We had a disagreement."

"About what?"

"About none of your business, that's what." I raised a challenging brow at him.

"Yet it seems to be Odin's." Thor's eyes were starting to fill with lightning.

"Ah, fuck, Thor."

Both men stared at me with wide eyes.

"Trevor proposed, okay? I said I wasn't ready, and he got pissed. You happy now?"

"Why aren't you ready?" The lightning immediately started to fizzle down to little sparks.

"It's only been a year." I dropped my head to my knees.

"More than that since you bonded," Thor corrected me, and I looked up at him in surprise.

"I'm just not ready."

"You'll never be ready," Thor's voice was too sad to be concerned over Trevor.

"What's that supposed to mean?"

"You pick things apart, Vervain." Thor glanced at Odin with unease, but continued. "You need to find things to blame, in case something does go wrong. Then you can say 'I told you so', and be done with it."

"I didn't pick *us* apart." I felt my teeth clench.

"Vervain"–Thor rubbed his forehead–"I came here tonight to apologize to you. I love you. I miss you, but I want you to be happy. Why don't you let yourself be happy?"

"So, you think I should marry Trevor?"

"No." Thor sighed. "Yes. Whichever makes you happy. Stop worrying about ifs and whens. Just do what feels right."

What made me happy. What did make me happy? I frowned as I considered the question. Trevor made me happy when he wasn't acting like a jealous idiot, but would marriage to him make me happy? Maybe. Did I want little werewolf babies? Maybe not, but then I wasn't sure if I wanted *any* babies, werewolf or otherwise. Would waking up next to Trevor every morning for the rest of my life make me happy? I suddenly thought it might.

"Alright." I got to my feet.

"What are you going to do?" Thor's face twisted into concerned lines.

"I'm going home." I leaned over and hugged him tightly, letting myself remember us in a good way for moment. It had been so long since I held him. I inhaled Thor's wonderful scent, felt the massive muscles under my cheek tense, and then I let him go. In every way that I could. "Thank you, Thor, and thank you too,

Odin."

I turned and looked down at the one-eyed god who was still lounging against the couch.

"Before you go." Odin got up, brushing off his jeans. "I was wondering if I could speak with you later."

"Tonight?" I squeaked a little in surprise.

"No." He smiled. "I was thinking more like later this week. I have something I need to discuss with you. It's actually why I came down here in the first place."

"Sure." I nodded. "Why don't you come by Moonshine on Thursday?"

"Around seven in the evening?"

"That works for me." I handed Odin a business card. "In case you get lost and have to call me." I kissed him on the cheek and whispered, "Thank you again," before I turned and kissed Thor's cheek too. "I told you when I left that I'd never forgive you." Thor's face fell. "But I think I'd like to make peace with you anyway."

"Peace, then," Thor pulled me into another hug before I could escape. "I'm always here if you need me, darling."

"Thanks, Baby Thunder," I whispered and pulled away before I embarrassed myself even more.

I made my way downstairs and through the "trees" that grew right out of the floor, passing the waterfall and the Froekn bouncers, to walk out the main exit. I walked around back, to the employee parking lot, but as I was making my way to my car, I felt a strange tingle between my shoulder blades. I turned slowly, preparing to flick my hands down and release the blades housed within my gloves. One quick movement, and I'd have four stilettos

sticking out above my fingers, each imbued with god magic.

In the shadows across the lot from me, a dark figure stood. He came forward a little when he saw my regard, and the light hit his face. His skin was pale, his eyes dark, and his smile was feral, but it was his elongated canines that gave him away.

“What do you want, vampire?”

Kirill growled, and it startled me even more; I hadn't realized he'd been following me. It showed just how badly Trevor had shaken me. Kirill followed me everywhere, I should have known he'd be there.

“Nothing.” The vampire chuckled. “Just browsing.”

With that, he turned and was gone.

“Great,” I growled. “Cause I just didn't have enough weird shit going on right now.”

Chapter Two

Trevor wasn't at home as I'd expected him to be.

I curled up with Nick and fell asleep on the low sofa in my Moroccan living room as Kirill watched me intently from the dining room table. I hadn't said anything about Trevor, and he didn't ask. He already seemed to know that something was wrong. So, he just went into guard mode while I went to sleep.

Before I knew it, it was morning, and I was achy from camping out on the sofa all night. I rubbed my face and pushed the blanket away. Blanket? When had I grabbed a blanket? Kirill. Must have been. He was like a mother hen sometimes. I got up and went into the bedroom.

No Trevor.

I had a horrible sinking feeling as I approached the closet, but his clothes were still there. I let myself feel a small measure of relief before I grabbed the phone and called his cell. No answer; it went straight to voice mail. I texted him "Where are you?", and still no response. Then I called TrygguIfR. He hadn't seen Trevor, and Fenrir was at his Hall in the God Realm.

I didn't want Fenrir to know about our fight, so I said no to Ty's offer to fetch him. I couldn't face the inevitable questions and the distinct possibility that it was all my fault. My hands began to shake, so I went into the kitchen to make a pot of PG Tips tea while I waited. There really wasn't anything else to do.

I took my tea out to the backyard and sat on the iron bench next to my koi pond, hoping that the scenery might calm me. After a little while, Kirill joined me, sitting beside me quietly and

holding my hand. I tried to contemplate the beautiful fish, but every time their scales flashed gold, I'd think of Trevor's eyes. I ended up just staring at Nick as he lazed in the sun, feeling my eyes lose focus on his soft fur, imagining another, darker pelt beneath my hands. I shook it off and tried to look somewhere else, somewhere safe.

It didn't matter; everywhere I looked there was a Trevor memory. The whole damn house was infused with him. I'd made love to him in a spot not too far from my feet. It had been a perfect moment, a perfect love, even though he'd been in werewolf form at the time. It hadn't mattered to me; it was Trevor. So why had it mattered when he proposed? Maybe Thor was right.

Yet even sitting there, feeling my heart constrict with a horrible aching pain, a part of me held back. I loved Trevor, more even than I'd loved Thor, but a part of me whispered "No, not yet". A part of me held its breath, waiting for something big, or maybe just waiting for something to fuck it all up–like I probably just had.

I started to imagine a future without Trevor. No warm arms around me, no fierce kisses, and no laughter. An empty shell of a life. He'd come to visit, of course; he'd have to, but they'd be cold visits, cold touches, just long enough to keep him alive, and wouldn't that be worse? Instead of being able to move on, I'd have to break open the wound every month. When I died, he'd die with me, but it would also be alone, each of us in our own beds, separate, till death did us part for good.

Great, now I was crying again.

Chapter Three

Nick was chasing chameleons in the mock-orange bushes bordering my property when Trevor finally came home. He came bursting through the back door, stopping suddenly when he saw me, and the panic eased out of his face as we stared at each other across the yard. My tears had finally stopped, and I'd been sitting in a red-eyed stupor with Kirill's arm around me. Hope sprang to life in my chest, and I had to stop myself from getting up and running over to Trevor. I couldn't handle the rejection if this was merely goodbye.

Trevor walked over to us, eyeing me warily the whole way. I saw his nose twitch as he scented the air, his forehead crease as my swollen eyes registered. He never truly lost his animal instincts, even in human form, and I realized that I didn't want him to. I didn't want Trevor to be anyone but Trevor. I didn't want a human anymore, I wanted him.

I set my cup down carefully on the wrought iron bench and stood up. Kirill had faded into the shadows and silently left us. He always knew what was needed of him. So like a cat.

"Minn Elska," Trevor whispered shakily, and the tears started falling as I launched myself at him. "I'm sorry," he buried his face into my hair, and I felt his body start to shake. "I love you so much, it makes me crazy sometimes."

"Why are you so jealous all of a sudden?" I squeezed him hard before leaning back enough to look at him. "What's changed? What have I done to make you so insecure?"

"It's not you." Trevor sat down on the bench and pulled me

into his lap. His face was strained; dark circles under his eyes, and a tight, self-reproaching look around his mouth. “I keep having these nightmares about you being in love with someone else.”

“Nightmares?” I remembered what Odin had said about the Froekn being psychic, and a shiver went down my spine.

“The dream is always the same; this man comes up to me and tells me that you loved him first. He says I can’t stand between you. He says *nothing* will stand between you.”

“What man?” I stroked his cheek. “There’s no one from my past who could take me away from you.”

“Not even Thor?” Trevor searched my face. “In the dreams, I can’t see his face, but something about him reminds me of Thor.”

“No, Honey-Eyes, not even Thor.” I kissed him gently.

Trevor picked me up to carry me inside. I found myself clinging to him, burying my face in his neck. He smelled like musk and warm, spicy wolf. He smelled like home. My whole body reacted, shaking in relief and desire.

My dress disappeared, along with Trevor's clothing, before he laid me on the Chinese wedding bed that dominated our bedroom. The walls of the bed, which was like a little room all on its own, were carved with dragons and phoenixes. Light filtered in through them, patterning me with their strange shadows, and the smell of sandalwood seeped into the air. Trevor crawled over me, and I felt the magic rise up to tease me; the magic which bound him to me and made every slight touch rapturous. Trevor growled low in his throat, and tremors shook through me.

Trevor rubbed his face along mine, then down my neck and over the cleavage pushed high by my red bra. The part of his soul I owned was swirling inside me, filling me with delight as he stroked pleasure over my skin. I raked my fingers through his thick, black hair as he continued to draw his face down my body.

He hadn't scented me like that since the first night we were together, and I was glorying in the gentle attention.

"I'm still yours." I stroked his cheek, and he looked up at me with eyes that were glowing with passion.

He was beautiful, with those bright, wolf eyes, and all that black hair falling in loose waves around him, making his eyes stand out even more. Trevor's arms were bunched with the effort of holding himself above me, creating sexy angles and curves. His wide chest was devoid of hair, odd when you thought of how furry he could get, but I liked the smooth planes of it. He lowered himself, pressing his chest to mine.

"I know, Minn Elska." He kissed my stomach, and a sweet fluttering started beneath his lips. "I just need my body to accept it. The wolf in me needs to reclaim his mate."

"Claim away." I laughed, spreading my arms wide.

Trevor smiled wickedly before yanking off my underwear and then flipping me over to repeat the marking process on my back. When he had covered every inch of my skin, he turned me over again and spread my legs, sliding his hands up my inner thighs and around my hips. The glow of his eyes captured and held my own as he lowered his face to me, and I was shaking even before he licked me slowly, in one long, sensuous, lapping motion.

Hot breath blew over me as he focused on the perfect spot, and began to flick his tongue quickly. I nearly came off the bed, but Trevor held me down with arms around my hips. Then he bit me, not hard, just a love nip, and growled as he worried at me gently. The growl vibrated through me, pushing me over the edge. I screamed as I came, my legs shaking so much, I was afraid they'd fall off and roll away. Bye, legs, nice knowing you.

My eyes were closed in ecstasy, so I didn't see Trevor crawl up me, but I definitely felt him through the entire way-too-short journey. Then his warm, wet mouth was working my skin

again. I found a reservoir of strength and wrapped my legs around him, so that I could arch up and rub against him. Trevor's tongue was magic, just slightly rougher than a human's. It was the perfect texture for licking skin–mainly mine. I came again; my breasts have always been sensitive, but with the addition of a little Froekn magic, it was eye-rolling. I was losing track of the number of orgasms already; was that two or three?

"I want you on top." Trevor rolled onto his back and pulled me with him. "I want to see you above me, claiming me as well."

I widened my eyes at him. This was new. I was used to getting marked. Blue had left bite marks on my neck, and then Thor had covered them with a lightning bolt shaped scar that went from just below my right ear to my collarbone. When I'd finally ended up with Trevor, he'd covered the lightning with his bite, but his teeth marks eventually faded. Even though Trevor renewed his bite every once in awhile, Thor's lightning still curved down my neck. The idea that I'd finally get to do some claiming of my own for once, excited me. Maybe I'd even leave my own mark.

I smiled slowly.

Before I climbed on top of Trevor, I slid down between his legs. He lifted his head as well as an eyebrow. I gave him my secret, libidinous look as I took him in hand and began to work my own magic on him. His legs tensed around me, lifting a little and pulling in to hold me. The scent of his arousal filled my head, and his body flinched deliciously. When I lifted back up, Trevor's eyes were glowing brighter, casting shadows under his cheekbones. The cheekbones themselves seemed sharper, more defined. I continued on until his breath was coming fast and he was gripping my shoulders desperately.

"No more," he groaned, "get up here now, or I won't last."

I slunk up him and straddled his body, guiding him inside me. He fit so perfectly, it made us both sigh, and I once more

appreciated the fact that he wasn't overly endowed. Women always rave about a “large” man, but frankly, they scare me. I like a normal size that fits as it should, without pain or stretching. I don't want to have to work at making love to someone. Trevor was my normal, perfect sized man, at least when he wasn't in werewolf form.

I reached up and took a hold of the bed’s carved ceiling. I was able to weave my hands through the wood slats and use it to steady myself. It was a good thing that the bed was an original antique and not a new reproduction, or it might not have been able to withstand our treatment of it.

Trevor moaned, and I looked down to find him sliding his hands up my waist to cup my breasts, which were lifted high from my raised arms. Heat and pleasure swirled around us, tingling against my skin. The magic grew in strength until it permeated us and sank deeper, to join our souls along with our bodies. In my mind, I saw the wolf inside me slinking around another wolf. Even though my wolf was his originally, she'd been influenced by me and changed had her sex from male to female. Trevor's wolf nipped at her playfully before they twisted together, blending until I couldn't tell which was which. I cried out with the intense pleasure, the perfect completion, then let go of the bed to fall over him.

My face landed perfectly in his neck and I bit him gently. Trevor’s arms tightened around me, pulling me closer while he made gruff sounds of pleasure. Encouraged by his ardor, I bit harder, and he bucked his hips up into me. His flesh filled both my mouth and my body while his arms surrounded me. I felt lost completely in Trevor, ceasing to be just Vervain; I was becoming something new.

I sucked as I bit in, feeling wild and powerful with his body thrusting inside me, and my teeth in his neck. My Nahual and lioness even raised their heads, letting out rumbled sounds of pleasure. The orgasm shook through me, and into Trevor, then

back to me in a circle of sensation that left us both screaming.

When there were only aftershocks trembling through us, I sank to the bed beside Trevor, and he pulled me into his side, his arm cradling me while he stroked my hair. I looked over and saw a set of dainty teeth marks in his neck, enclosing a dark red stain. A smile spread across my face. It felt good to have proof of my possession. Horrible, but true; I finally understood why my men loved to mark me.

"You took the claiming to heart, Rouva." Trevor had a huge smile plastered on his face.

"Look at you." I laughed and pulled back a little so I could see him better. "You're actually pleased that I bit you."

"Of course." His brows twitched in a quick, confused motion. "It's a sign of your desire for me. I've wondered why you haven't done it before."

"Bite marks are badges of honor?"

"Among the Froekn, yes." He smiled. "Now, I don't have to listen to TryggulfR tease me about not pleasing you in bed."

"You've been getting teased because I haven't bit you?" I sat up and gave him my *why do you have to be so difficult* face. "Why didn't you tell me?"

"Would you tell me if I didn't express my pleasure with you in a way you expected? Or would you just hope that someday we'd be close enough for me to understand all of your needs?"

"Point taken." I shook my head. "But there are things that I can't possibly know about, and I'd rather you tell me than leave me to be surprised by them."

"In the future, I'll tell you," he agreed, then pulled me back down. "Right now, I'd rather *show* you how much I desire you."

I smiled as he rolled over me. All that time, and I'd believed Trevor's bites were a primitive way of him marking his territory. I had let it go because I'd assumed it was part of his wolf nature, and Nature was a demanding mistress. Knowing that it was a display of desire put a whole new spin on it. It was a hell of a lot more sexy than just being branded like a cow. It also explained why the female wolves had all smiled knowingly at me when they saw the bites he'd left. I guess I was destined to be a chew toy . . . a love chew toy.

I could live with that.

And if you enjoyed The Godhunter Series, you may like The Twilight Court Series, the new fantasy series by Amy Sumida.

Keep reading for a sneak peek at the first book: Fairy-Struck

Fairy-Struck: Several types of conditions such as paralysis, wasting away, pining, and unnatural behavior resulting from an enchantment laid by an offended fairy.

Chapter One

Once upon a time, isn't that how all fairy tales begin? Except this isn't your average fairy tale. There are no charming princes or wicked witches within these pages and the fair maidens are more deadly than any big bad wolf. This is a fairy tale in the truest sense of the words; a story about fairies... the real story.

My name is Seren Sloane and I'm an Extinguisher. That will mean nothing to you, I'm sure, so let me go back a little further. No one knows the true origins of the fey, I don't think even the fey themselves remember, but theories abound. One theory has them evolving alongside us but where we advanced in groups, banding together to become stronger, the fey morphed out of those outcast predators who were too wild for a pack. Those who don't believe in evolution, think instead that the fey stem from divine creations, angels fallen from God's grace. Yet another tale insists they were gods themselves, or demi-gods, led by a mother goddess named Danu.

A final theory suggests they were not gods or angels or outcasts, merely nomads from an advanced civilization. The Scythians or Sidheans, from which the word *sidhe* originates. Myths tell of these talented Sidhe coming to Ireland where they flung about their magic and generally wrecked havoc until the aggrieved locals fought back and forced the fey to retreat into their raths, holy shrines now known as fairy mounds. History has disguised the raths as burial mounds even though originally, they were thought to be royal palaces for portal guardians. Although I cannot validate the rest of the tale, I do know this; the fey don't live under mounds of dirt. The original descriptions strike closer to the truth. The raths shrouded portals not corpses. Hidden paths to the fairy world, a realm laid parallel to ours and not at all underground.

Anyway, we did just fine living side by side with them until

humans started destroying the environment around those entrances to Fairy. Fairies don't like it when you mess with nature and when they stroll from their magical abodes to find that mess strewn all over their backyard, they get even more pissy. So they began to fling the mess back. All those old stories about fairies stealing babies and striking people with wasting diseases, stem from this time period. Things got real bad, so bad that those of us who had the gift of clairvoyance and could actually see fairies, joined together to defend the human race.

The first Human-Fey war erupted across Eire, now known as Ireland, and the losses on both sides were staggering. After the third war, a grudging truce was finally attained and councils were created to mediate between the races and support the truce with laws approved by both sides. A good start to be sure but laws flounder and fail if they can't be enforced. Both councils conceded jurisdiction over their people to the other, agreeing upon the penalties to be meted out should someone be found guilty of a crime. Rules for determining guilt and administering justice were set into place and military units were sanctioned to carry out the verdicts of the councils.

The fairies created the Wild Hunt. They gathered the fiercest, most terrifying of their people and trained them to stalk the shadows of our world, watching us like guardian angels until one of us breaks the law. Then the angels become devils who do much more than watch. Trust me when I say you don't want to ever meet a member of the Hunt.

To police the fey, we created the Extinguishers. Formed of the five great psychic families who originally defended humanity, the Extinguishers inspire a fair amount of fear as well. Armed with clairvoyance among other talents which varies by person but can include; telekinesis, pyrokinesis, telepathy, and psychometry, we also have some serious combat skills. Most humans don't have the ability to see a fairy unless that fairy wants to be seen, so both council members and Extinguishers must at least possess

clairvoyance. The Council keeps an eye out for humans with exceptional psychic abilities so they can recruit more into their fold but Extinguishers are born into the job. I'm one of those lucky few.

Kavanaugh, Teagan, Sullivan, Murdock, and Sloane. The first five psychic families of Ireland. Over the centuries we've become a secret society so big it spans the globe, gaining strength by breeding only within the five. This has virtually guaranteed powerful psychic gifts in our children. I'm the product of a Sloane and a Kavanaugh. Over thirty generations of contrived breeding(not inbreeding, thank you very much) has given me abilities which rank me as one of the top ten Extinguishers of all time.

I was trained from childhood to become what I am; an Extinguisher, a hunter of fairies, remover of the light of the Shining Ones. Childhood wasn't horrible for me but it was definitely not what most would consider to be normal. Bedtime stories were non-fiction accounts of Extinguisher heroism and instead of receiving platitudes that monsters weren't real, I was told most emphatically that they were and that when checking beneath my bed at night, I should always have an iron blade in hand. My only friends were children from other Extinguisher families and every game or toy had an ulterior motive behind it. Like the dolls my mother made me which showed what each type of fairy looked like... and had their weaknesses written on their backs in red ink.

Still, I was a child and I knew nothing else. Life seemed magical to me, not just in the way that life is magical to all children but in a literally magic way. I was taught to move objects with my mind, create fire in the palm of my hand, and make things materialize anywhere I wanted them to(that's called apportation in case you're curious, not teleportation which is a thing of science fiction). When I got older, I was taught to fight and finally, to kill.

Despite all of that, I wasn't raised to hate fairies. Quite the contrary, I was taught to care for them and protect them if need be. The job of an Extinguisher exists first and foremost to protect the

peace. We kill fairies only when they disrupt that peace and then we do it in the most efficient and merciful way possible... after we receive a warrant of execution approved by the Council. We are, essentially, peace keepers.

That changed for my family when my mother was torn to pieces by a pack of pukas. I know, it sounds funny, doesn't it? A pack of pukas. In reality a bunch of fairy dogs the size of ponies, with teeth sharper than a shark's, shredded the flesh from my mother, gobbled down every last bit of it, and then gnawed on her bones till they could suck out the marrow. That reality killed all the mercy in my father and a lot of the compassion in me as well.

We immersed ourselves in the job, taking every warrant issued for criminal fey we could get our hands on until the Head Extinguisher himself finally noticed and called us to heel. We were sent to a small territory where very little fey crime occurred and where we were supposed to get our shit together. Most humans would love to live where we do now and when I tell you where we were put, I'm sure you'll roll your eyes but let me assure you that this place becomes a slow death for an Extinguisher. Peace keepers need a certain amount of action to keep us sane and Hawaii has very little of that on the fey front.

Yes, I've been exiled to paradise and for someone with my fair Irish skin, Hawaii imitates Hell in so many ways. Sure beauty abounds and the people here embody that tropical temperament of almost Gaelic hospitality but when you're itching for a fight, you don't want to be scratching at your peeling, sunburned skin too. Plus, the only fey to be found, the little local variety called menehune, frolic about causing mischief but never mayhem. Yep, Hawaiian fairies exist. Does that shock you? It shouldn't, I've already mentioned how the Fairy Realm lies parallel to ours. Mounds connect more than merely Ireland to Fairyland, they form bridges between Fairy and places all over the world. The fairies who frequent these paths seem to be influenced by the culture they cross over into.

And the fairies don't just visit. Ever since the creation of the Councils, a lot of fey have moved into our world in an effort to support the peace. There was also the issue of the numerous entrances to Fairy which needed to be guarded. So several fey council members have very human jobs with very powerful positions. I think you'd be pretty damn surprised if I told you which companies secretly belong to the fey.

We don't have any of those powerful companies here in Hawaii because, as I mentioned before, this place isn't all that important in the whole fey-human interrelations department. So my life has become a constant preparation for a battle it doesn't look like I'll ever be allowed to join, in a place whose beauty only feels like salt in my wounded heart. I will admit that my anger has lessened over my time here, as the memory of who my mother was slowly overshadows the memory of how she died, but for my father, this exile has only served to make him even more bitter, more vicious, and more intent on killing the entire fairy race.

Chapter Two

"No way," I looked down at the fax in my hand with amazement. "This can't be right."

"What is it?" My dad walked into our office, his sea blue eyes narrowing on the piece of paper in my hand like a hawk who's spied a mouse.

It was a small office with just a cheap particle board desk littered with all the necessary items; a computer, a phone, a fax machine, and a copier. There was an old desk chair in front of it, a cracking plastic mat beneath that to protect the boring beige carpet, and a beat up filing cabinet to the right. That was it and with us in the room, the tiny space was almost full. Still, it fit our needs. The office was purely for communication with the Council and for record keeping. The bulk of our work was done outside these bare walls.

"A warrant of execution," I handed the fax to him. "From the Fairy Council."

"The *Fairy* Council?" His narrowed gaze transformed into surprise which returned some vigor to his sorrow-lined face.

"When's the last time you saw one of those?" I asked.

"Never. To get one here is..." he looked up at me, a lock of his black hair falling into one eye. He brushed it away distractedly. He hadn't bothered with a haircut in awhile. Things like that tend to get neglected when you're on a quest for vengeance.

"Suspicious?" I lifted a brow.

"Fortunate," he began to grin.

"Dad, doesn't this make you at all wary?"

"I get to kill a fairy," he shrugged, "that it's a request of the fey themselves is simply a bonus."

"Maybe we should contact our council first," I glanced at the picture included with the warrant.

A willowy woman with huge mossy eyes and long, hair the color of young pea pods, smiled back at me. Her skin was a deep tawny umber and in combination with that hair, I knew her to be a dryad. So she was probably a member of the Seelie Court. Not that it made any difference, Seelie or Unseelie, Light or Dark, all of the fey were dangerous and her sweet looks could be hiding the heart of a monster. Still...

"It says she murdered a sidhe male," I held out my hand for the warrant and he handed it back to me so I could read it again. "Dylan Thorn. Aren't the Thorns one of the stronger fey families? The Unseelie King is a Thorn, isn't he?"

"Which is probably why they want this bitch killed," Dad grinned. "She murdered a royal, they take that very seriously."

"But *how* did a dryad kill a fey royal?" I stared at the picture again. "Dryads are generally timid and their magic is low class compared to that of a sidhe, much less a royal sidhe."

"You should know better than anyone that the amount of magic a person holds has nothing to do with their capability for murder," my father was already pulling out his Extinguisher gear from the little closet in the left wall.

He laid a mini crossbow on the desk and followed it up with a quiver of iron-tipped arrows and an iron knife. Guns were dangerous around fairies, even when filled with iron bullets. A lot of fey magic was born of the elements and fire used in a particular way, such as igniting all of the bullets in a gun at once, could make the weapon explode, harming the wielder more than the intended

victim.

Non-combustible iron weapons were the way to go with fairies. Something about the chemical composition of the metal reacted to their blood and if they were actually struck with a piece of the stuff, it would burn their skin. If they were shot with an iron arrow or cut with an iron knife, the iron would poison their blood and without purification, they'd die. So iron was the metal of choice for Extinguisher weapons and when we used it in combination with our psychic abilities, we did pretty well against the fey.

"Why aren't you getting ready?" Dad asked pointedly.

"So we aren't calling the Human Council?" I tried one more time.

"Not necessary," he strapped a specially made flat quiver to his back with practiced movements and then layered his coat over the top as I tried to push my unease away.

It wasn't that I didn't want to kill the fairy. I would have no problem extinguishing any fey I had a warrant for. The problem was, this warrant came from the fey themselves and if our Human Council didn't approve of it, we shouldn't be executing. It could get us into a lot of trouble and frankly, if this was just some high up fairy wanting someone else to do his dirty work, I'd rather not help him out.

My Dad began to hum an old Irish tune as we headed out the door. Yeah, getting in trouble with the Human Council hadn't been an issue with him for a long time.

Chapter Three

You'd think hunting fairies would be difficult. Beings with magic at their disposal and the ability to become invisible should be hard to track but when you're an Extinguisher, you're trained to use their magic against them. All magic leaves traces of energy and when combined with the powerful aura of a fairy, the resulting glow reaches up and around its host like the Northern Lights.

Still, you had to find the right sky to search in order to see those lights and tracking the murderess took most of the day. We finally found her hiding amid the crowds of Ala Moana, a massive, outdoor shopping mall on the outskirts of Waikiki. I thought it a strange place for her to be hiding, she would have fared much better up in the mountains, but maybe she'd thought she'd be safer in a crowd.

"I'll circle around behind her," my dad whispered to me. "You grab her and we'll get her out of here so we can kill her without witnesses."

"Alright," I agreed.

Even though most humans couldn't see fairies, when one was killed, they lost their magic, starting with their invisibility. That wouldn't be the issue with this particular fairy, though. She was completely visible, her oddly colored hair tucked up into a baseball cap and her large eyes covered with a pair of celebrity sunglasses. That wasn't too surprising. Using invisibility magic ironically made a fairy even more visible to those of us with the sight. Magic was energy and energy burned brightly to clairvoyants. So if she wanted to hide from Extinguishers, using the least amount of magic was her best option. She hadn't seen me

yet but I had no doubt she would soon. Fairies could see Extinguishers almost as well as we did them. All those psychic gifts made our auras stronger than most humans.

She was sitting on the edge of a long, oval shaped, cement planter set in the center of one of the open pathways between the shops. Plants rose up behind her and one of her hands was laid against the slim trunk of a palm tree. The fey liked to be close to nature but that touch was a clear sign that she was scared or at least nervous. Her slim body was hunched in on itself, as if she were pulling away from the humans sitting around her, and her lips were pressed into a thin line. A baby cried and she flinched.

It made sense that she would be scared but usually, a murderer has some kind of plan. They don't just sit in the middle of a group of humans and touch plants. Was she waiting for someone? Maybe she had an accomplice. This could be a lot more complicated than we'd thought. My steps slowed as I searched the area for signs of another fey but there weren't any to be found.

I was about five feet away when her head lifted and she looked unerringly in my direction. Her hand released the plant with a blur of movement and she stood, looking as if she didn't know which direction to run in. I tensed for the chase as her gaze flitted over her shoulder, where I knew my father was coming up behind her. Then she took a deep breath and started walking calmly in my direction.

I was so startled, I froze for a second and a Japanese tourist bumped into me from behind. It jolted me back into action. I pulled the fey handcuffs from my pocket and opened them with automatic ease. They were iron but lined in silicone so they wouldn't burn her, just prevent her from using her magic. When I reached her, she gave me a nod and held her hands out submissively. I put the cuffs on her with complete bafflement.

"Aideen Evergreen, I have a warrant of execution for you from the Fairy Council," I took her arm and started walking her

through the crowds. She was taller than me, as most fey are, probably around six feet. I was five-five and although I was leanly muscled from all the training I did, I'd inherited my mother's curves and next to Aideen's willowy, fragile form, I must have looked like an Oompa Loompa.

"Asylum," she whispered and I jerked to a halt.

"What did you say?" My eyes slid over to her with the slow slide of incredulity.

"I ask for asylum with the Human Council," she stated more firmly. "I have information that could lead to the destruction of the entire human race."

"What?!" I turned to the side so I was facing her. The flow of foot traffic split around us with irritated murmurs. "Did you say...?"

"I'm talking about the extermination of your whole race, Extinguisher," she hissed. "Now get me to your Council."

"Yes, Ma'am," I swallowed hard and started ushering her more quickly through the shoppers, using a combination of telepathy and telekinesis to nudge them out of our way. Possible extermination called for excessive measures.

Here's a sneak peek into Amy's Reverse Harem fairy tale collection, entitled:

Happily Harem After

Here are the first couple chapters of the first story in the collection:

Wild Wonderland

Chapter One

The house seemed hollow without Uncle Ted in it. I looked around the rambling Victorian mansion and wondered how he had made it feel so warm, so homey. Now, it felt like a mausoleum; a place haunted by the past.

I was entirely alone.

My parents had died when I was a child; some awful car accident that I don't remember. Uncle Ted was all the family I had–was the only company I had–period. He had looked after me, raised me, and saw to it that I had a good education. Most importantly, he had loved me.

Yeah, he was a little strange; a fact that I hadn't realized until I had begun to attend school. Then I discovered that not all little girls learned self-defense at age three, or swordplay at five, or jujitsu at seven. Well, maybe the last one, but I'm not certain of that. Most parents didn't have a laboratory in their basements either, nor did they warn their children about touching mirrors or the dangers of unknown holes in the ground.

My childhood may have been a bit lonely, but it had also been magical. Uncle Ted told me stories about imaginary worlds where men could turn into animals and where kingdoms were divided by the suits of playing cards. In Uncle Ted's world, caterpillars smoked hookahs, mice drank tea, and rabbits wore waistcoats (whatever that was).

Uncle Ted would have tea parties with me when I was a little girl, warning me that drinking too much would shrink me down to the size of a pea, but eating the cake would restore me. He admonished me to always tread lightly through flowerbeds because

you never know when the flowers might be napping, and how would I like it if someone tromped through my bed and woke me up? He taught me the value of time and instilled a deep respect for it in me. I knew never to waste it or take it for granted because that was very rude as well. Ted had been the best man I'd ever known, and now, he was dead.

I dropped to my knees and sobbed, covering my face with my hands. I'd never made any friends, mostly because Uncle Ted discouraged it. As much as he was a kind and generous man, he was also extremely paranoid. Ted didn't trust anyone and had hammered that same sense of distrust into me. I was angry at him for that because now that he was gone, I had no one. I had buried him without a service since there had been no one there to mourn him except for myself, and then I had come home to this empty house. We were wealthy people, which was probably why Uncle Ted was so paranoid, but money is nothing if you have no one to share it with.

“Well, it's about damn time!”

My head jerked up at the sound of the masculine voice. There, on the stairs before me, stood a man. He was about my age, with pure white hair and pale skin. He wore an old fashioned suit without a jacket, but with a lovely tapestry vest, from which he pulled a gold pocket watch. He peered at the watch, then at me.

“I was expecting you thirty-three minutes ago,” he chided me.

“Who are you?” I asked him as I stood. “And what are you doing in my house?”

“This isn't simply a house, my dear.” He grimaced. “It's a gateway.”

“A gateway to what?”

“To where,” he corrected me. “And I suppose that was

inaccurate as well. The gate lies *beneath* the house. The building itself is merely a disguise. Subterfuge for the subterranean entrance to Wonderland."

"I know jujitsu," I warned him.

"Yes," he drew out the word as he narrowed his eyes on me. "I assume that's some kind of warrior training that Theodore taught you."

"You knew my uncle?" I gaped at him.

"Alice, dear," he huffed. "I knew your whole family. I was present at your birth."

"Well, how was I supposed to know that?" I nearly shrieked.

"Didn't Theodore tell you?" The man scowled. "That was remiss of him. Perhaps he left you a letter somewhere?"

"A letter? Telling me that a man was going to meet me after his funeral?" I rolled my eyes. "Sure, it must be here somewhere."

"A letter telling you who you really are, Alice Wild," the man said sternly.

"Wild?" I asked. "My last name is Turner."

"By all that's bloody, it is not!" The man appeared deeply offended. "What an awful name. I suppose Theodore thought it was amusing–turning away from Wonderland or something silly like that. Turner is an action, not a name, and it is *not* yours. It belongs to an earther, one of *those* people." He waved his hand toward my front door. "You are a Wild, the last Wild in all existence, and heir to the throne of Wonderland."

"Oh, wow." I blinked at him. "You're bonkers, completely mad. There's a crazy person in my house."

“As if that has any bearing whatsoever,” he huffed. “Now, I assume that Theodore would have left something for you in his laboratory. Shall we?”

“How do you know about the laboratory?”

“Alice, do keep up,” he snapped. “I know you and your uncle. I've been here several times to check on you and receive progress reports for Their Majesties. The Card Kings of Wonderland are very concerned for your safety.”

“The Card Kings?” I asked as I followed him downstairs to the basement. “You just said that I was the heir. Maybe you should rethink your delusions.”

“Ugh.” He rolled his eyes. “I don't have the patience to explain all of this to you, just hurry up!”

“Where are we going?”

“To Wonderland!” He stopped and turned to stare at me in bafflement. “Are you a bit slow? Theodore never told me you were stupid.”

“I am not stupid!”

“All right then,” he growled, “let's go.”

“I'm not going anywhere with you! I don't even know your name.” I stopped midway down the stairs.

“I am Warren White.” He bowed. “At your service, Queen Alice.”

“Oh, now I'm a queen.” I chuckled. “I can't believe this day.”

“You must!” Warren declared. “If you do not believe, we are all lost, Your Majesty.”

"All right, easy now, Warren." I held up my hands. "It was an exclamation. Although, I'm not too sure what you want me to believe in."

"Why, in yourself, of course! And it would be foolish not to since so many others already believe in you. Truly; how much belief does one woman require?"

"Who believes in me?"

"Nearly all of Wonderland," Warren growled. "Enough of this! Let's go, Alice! We're already late!"

"Okay, Warren." I rolled my eyes and followed him down to the basement.

I know it sounds crazy, but I was just happy not to be alone. I didn't care if the man was a lunatic, at least I didn't have to think about Theodore lying dead in the ground while I laid in an empty house. Anything was better than that.

"Aha!" Warren was in my uncle's laboratory, at his desk, and had found an envelope in the drawer. "Here it is. I knew he'd leave word for you."

Warren handed me the envelope, and I saw that it had my name scrawled across the front of it in my uncle's handwriting. I scowled at it a moment before I tore open the sealed envelope and read it aloud.

"Alice, my sweet girl, there is so much that I haven't told you, but I'm sure that Warren will explain; either him or Nicholas. You can trust them completely, as well as the Card Kings. They all have your best interests at heart because your best interests are also theirs. Things are about to get topsy-turvy for you, Alice. I wish that I could be there to help you, but if you're reading this, it means that time has come to an end for me. It runs here, not like over there, and I have lost track of it, it seems. But your time is now, Alice. I have done the best I could for you. I have given you the

tools you'll need in the days to come. Fight, my sweet girl; fight for Wonderland and her people because both belong to you. You are the last of the Wilds, and Wonderland needs you. Remember what I've taught you; all the stories are true. Keep your heart and mind open; love is not always what we expect it to be. All my love, Uncle Ted. PS Follow the white rabbit."

"Okay, are you ready now?" Warren asked impatiently.

"No, I'm not ready now," I huffed. "What does this mean? Wonderland needs me? I'm the last of the Wilds? Follow a damn rabbit?"

"That last bit would be me," Warren said. "But first, we need to make you small enough to follow me."

"Will this start making sense soon?"

"Absolutely not," he declared primly. "Sense is for earthers; wonderlanders know that the best sense is non. Ah, yes, here it is!" He took a crystal bottle down from a bookshelf and handed it to me. "Just one sip. Too much and you'll be the size of–"

"A pea," I finished as I took the bottle.

"He did tell you! Excellent. Drink up."

"This is absurd," I said as I took the bottle. Then I noticed the label tied to it. Again, my uncle's handwriting. I read, "Drink me, Alice." I grimaced at the bottle. "Well, that's to the point. Oh, why not?"

I uncorked the bottle and took a sip.

"Hurry; hand it over before you drop it," Warren said as he snatched the bottle away from me and tucked it into his vest.

His voice seemed to echo around me as my world grew, or I shrunk, rather. I jolted in shock as I stared up at Warren's massive

body. His legs were like redwoods.

"All right, in you go." He waved his hand behind the same bookshelf that he had taken the bottle from. "Don't worry; I have the cake." He patted his vest pocket.

I went to the edge of the bookshelf and peered around it. It was pulled out just enough for a small animal to crawl behind it, or a very small Alice. And there was a hole in the stone wall.

"Come on, Alice. I don't have all day," Warren huffed.

Then Warren's body shimmered and shrank. I leapt back as he became a fluffy, white rabbit. All of his clothing disappeared except for his tapestry vest, which shrank along with him. Warren the White Rabbit hopped past me and into the hole.

"Follow the white rabbit," I whispered to myself. "What the fuck is happening to me?"

"Hurry up, Alice!" The White Rabbit called.

So, I followed him into his hole. At the point, I really had no choice.

Chapter Two

A few feet into the hole, the ground dropped out from under me, and I started to fall. I screamed for awhile, and then I realized that I was floating more than I was falling. I opened my eyes warily and saw the root-veined earth slowly shift into raw stone, and then into polished marble. I ran my hand along the side of the tube I fell through and found myself slowly approaching it as my point of gravity altered. Everything turned around on me, and the walls of the tube became the bottom of a shaft until I was sliding down the slick stone and out into a circular room. My butt skidded across the marble floor, losing momentum, and then I came to a squeaking stop.

Warren was still in his rabbit form, waiting for me near a curved wall, tapping his foot impatiently.

"Hurry up, Alice!" He hopped over to one of five doors that were spaced around the room and kicked it open.

The door Warren chose was the only rabbit-sized door in the place. The other doors were of a size more appropriate for the average human. Since I was still a miniature version of myself, I didn't concern myself with the other doors, but I did note that they each bore a symbol from a deck of playing cards; the heart and diamond were both red, and the spade and club were black. I hadn't caught the symbol on the back of the tiny door, or if there had been one at all, and I didn't think about looking for it until after I was through.

Then I had other things to concern myself with.

At first, I thought we were in a forest; then I realized that the monstrous trunks, slick and green, were actually flower stalks.

I had stopped to stare up through the cover of their enormous leaves, at the vibrant petals above me, and Warren hadn't noticed. He just kept hopping ahead, all Little Bunny Foo Foo–until the flowers attacked me.

With a trumpeting sound, a daffodil knocked me off my feet. Then a tiger lily growled and undulated its stalk down to . . . well, stalk me. I shrieked and rolled into a fighting stance, ready to punch out some petunias, when Warren doubled back and placed himself before me protectively.

"This is the Wild Heir, you foolish flowers!" Warren shouted as he thumped his back leg. "Do you not know your queen?"

The flowers froze, then lowered their heads to brush me with inquisitive petals. I straightened out of my crouch, looking at the monstrous blooms warily. By the time they were done inspecting me, I was covered in pollen, but they seemed satisfied. The blossoms bent double as if they were bowing.

"Now, if you don't mind," Warren said primly, "we're expected at tea. I swear, the hurrier I go, the behinder I get!"

The flowers eased back, properly chastised, and Warren and I continued up the path.

"Do not tarry, Your Majesty," Warren snapped. "Tulgey Wood is full of many dangers, and we've only just entered it. We still need to pass by the Bandersnatch burrow before we reach our rendezvous point."

"Who are we meeting?" I asked.

"The others," he said. "You'll know them when you meet them."

"Obviously," I huffed and trudged after him. "Can't we get big now? Then we wouldn't have to worry about joining the War

of the Roses. Also, I can't believe I just said that."

"What have I said about belief, Alice?"

"To have some?" I was baffled.

"Absolutely," he said approvingly. "We cannot grow right now. It's easier to get by the bandersnatch when you're small."

"What's a bandersnatch?"

"A frumious creature with a long neck and snapping jaws," Warren said gravely.

"What the hell does frumious mean?" I gave him my bewildered face.

"It is the concise word for the bandersnatch's fuming and furious character," Warren instructed me. "Don't you have words that combine other words into one, much more simpler word?"

"Uh-huh sure."

"The bandersnatch is very quick, but pays no mind to small creatures such as we are currently."

"Why not?"

"Well, what sort of meal would we make?" Warren huffed. "We aren't worth the effort. If he paid us mind, he'd have nothing left to give the larger creatures."

"Oh, I see." I veered around a pebble the size of a boulder and scowled at my black dress. "Maybe I should have changed before we left. You might have warned me about the terrain."

"You did change"–he glanced at me with a frown–"you're much smaller than you were."

"I meant my clothes," I snapped.

"Oh." Warren stopped and looked me over. "Yes, I see. Nothing to be done for it now. Perhaps we can find you something more colorful at the tea party. Come on; we're late."

"Yes, so you've said." I rolled my eyes. "Colorful, indeed. Yes, that's the problem with my outfit; it's not colorful enough."

Creepy cries echoed through the woods around us, and the underbrush we journeyed through shivered as if it were afraid. I was tense, searching this strange place as we walked through it, uncertain which direction trouble would come from, but sure that it would come. Through the swaying blades of grass, I could glimpse massive tree trunks looming above us. They seemed too large to exist and made horrendous creaking noises that hurt my ears. Beetles the size of a VW bug scampered up to us, startling me, but Warren just huffed at them, and they hurried away.

"How much farther?" I asked. "You realize that I'm wearing heels?"

"Heels?" Warren narrowed his beady rabbit eyes on my feet. "Now, why would you do that?"

"I just got home from my uncle's funeral!"

"Keep your voice down," Warren hissed. "We've only just passed the bandersnatch."

"You said that he wouldn't bother with us."

"You don't seem like you'd be a bother," a voice purred from above us. "No bother at all."

"Cat!" Warren cried. "Well met."

"Yes, well, indeed," the voice intensified as a feline face parted the grass to peer at me. It was a dark gray tabby with green eyes that glowed. "You two are late."

"I keep telling her that, but she doesn't seem to hear me."

Warren gave me an annoyed look.

"I can hear you just fine." I rolled my eyes. "I just can't walk very well in these shoes."

"Why did you put them on if you can't walk in them?" The cat asked.

"I didn't think I'd be walking through the woods today."

"Hmm, not much of a planner, are you?" The cat sniffed me. "But you are a Wild, that much is certain."

"Of course she's a Wild," Warren snapped. "I fetched her myself. This is Alice."

"Then I am at your service, Your Majesty," the cat said.

"Who are you?" I asked it.

"Interesting question," the cat murmured. "I knew who I was when I got up this morning, but I think I must have changed several times by then."

"I don't need you to give me some esoteric bullshit on your inner you," I huffed. "Just tell me who you are."

"Do you want my name, rank, or affiliation?" The cat asked as its head turned in a complete circle.

I gaped at it until I realized that the cat was floating and his whole body had turned along with his head. Oh yes, a floating feline is so much easier to accept than a fully rotating head.

"This is insane," I whispered. "Utter madness."

"Don't worry about that," the hovering cat said. "We're all mad here. I'm mad, you're mad, he's mad."

"How do you that I'm mad?" I huffed. "We've only just

met.

"You must be, or you wouldn't have come here."

"Oh, fantastic," I said dryly. "And to answer your earlier question; just a name will suffice."

"That's no fun," the cat pouted. "How can I show off my prowess to my new queen if she doesn't allow me to give her my rank and affiliation?"

"Then why did you even ask me?"

"I was being polite."

"Would you just tell her who you are already so that we can get on with it?" Warren grumbled.

"I am Nicholas of the Order of Cheshire, Knight of Wilds," the cat bowed. "And I shall see you safely to tea, Queen Alice."

"I am seeing her safely to–oh, never mind." Warren started hopping away. "We're late enough as it is. I can't find my damn gloves either," he kept muttering as he went.

"My uncle told me to trust Nicholas," I said. "Is that you?"

"Yes, I knew your mother's brother well. I knew all of your family. If you will climb onto my shoulders, Your Majesty?" Nicholas said as he lowered himself before me. "I shall carry you to the rendezvous point faster than you can walk."

"Thank you, Sir Nicholas." I climbed onto his shoulders and took huge handfuls of fur.

"Call me Nick," he said and shot through the air.

"Do not start the meeting without me!" Warren shouted after us."

I clung to the flying cat as Tulgey Wood whizzed by, but soon, he was slowing down to circle a clearing. In the center of this clearing there was a little house, and in front of the house, there was a long table set haphazardly with all manner of porcelain plates, teacups, saucers, and eating implements. An enormous cake sat in the middle of the table, with smaller cakes surrounding it, and several teapots ranged down each end. Three individuals sat at around the table: a man, a brown rabbit, and a mouse.

"A mouse drinking tea," I whispered, thinking of my uncle's stories. "The stories really are true."

"I'm sure they are," Nick said. "whatever you're speaking of. There's usually a grain of truth in every word uttered. It's just that sometimes you have to search harder to find it. Once you do, however, you can make some lovely bread."

"You cannot make bread from grains of truth," I said.

"Of course you can." Nick smoothed his whiskers sagely. "Truth bread is the tastiest, but it can be hard to swallow."

"Then you should eat cake!" The man at the table declared. "Where's the cake?"

"It's right in front of you, Hatter." Nick rolled his eyes and himself, taking me along for the ride. "I prefer bread and butter."

"Is that she?" The man asked as he stood so violently that his chair crashed back onto the Persian carpet that had been laid over the grass.

Hatter; well, he did have a large hat on, so his name seemed appropriate. It was a garish green hat, with a paisley band about it and a flat brim. A card tucked into the band read: In this style 10/6. Whatever the hell that meant.

"Yes, this is Queen Alice," Nick said as he floated down to the table.

"You're awfully small for a wild queen," Hatter noted. "I seem to remember the Wilds as being much more magnificent in stature. Much more muchier. Have you lost your muchness?"

"She took some of Theodore's potion so that she could come through the gate," Warren panted as he hopped into the clearing. Then he shifted into his human form, regaining his lost clothing, and smoothed out the wrinkled fabric. "I will rectify her size immediately."

Warren strode over to me as I slid off of Nick's neck. He took a petite four out of his pocket and placed it on the table beside me. I stared at it in consternation.

"I don't think–" I started to say, but was cut off by Hatter.

"Then you shouldn't speak!"

I rolled my eyes and began again, "Please tell me that you don't expect me to eat all of this."

"Of course not," Warren cried. "You're not a pig, are you?"

"Pig!" The brown rabbit exclaimed, spilling his tea as he jerked in fright. "I hate pigs! They have a disturbing tendency of turning into babies."

"Shut up, March Hare!" The mouse squeaked as it jolted out of its teacup. It had fallen asleep over the rim. "There aren't any pigs or babies here."

"Oh, yes, quite right, Dormouse." Hare settled down.

"Just take a little nibble, dear," Dormouse said to me. "The more you eat, the bigger you get, and we don't want you squishing us."

I followed her instruction and took a bite. Tingling spread through my body, and I fell over the edge of the table as my form grew. My feet touched the ground before my butt could hit, and I

stood to my normal height.

“That's better.” I sighed. “I've imagined being little before, but that was so much worse than I'd thought it would be.”

“Never imagine yourself not to be otherwise than what it might appear to others that what you were, or might have been, was not otherwise than what you had been, would have appeared to them to be otherwise,” Hatter said sagely.

I gaped at him.

“Ah, yes, I see the resemblance now.” Hatter peered at me with dark eyes as he settled his jacket more firmly about him. “You look like your mother.”

“She does, actually,” Nick said with some surprise. “Striking resemblance.”

“Why is that shocking?” I asked the floating cat, who was paddling through the air currents on his back.

“It's not.” Nick smirked. “What's surprising is that the Mad Hatter noticed it.”

Then Nick's form shimmered like a heatwave on a highway, and the blur of his body grew. When he came into focus again, he was a sleekly muscled young man with short, dark hair stripped horizontally with gray. He wore a soldier's uniform; leather boots, cotton pants, a sword belted at his waist, and a tunic emblazoned with a small gold jester's cap on its breast.

“Your Majesty.” Nick gave me a more formal bow.

“A wild card,” I said as I noted the emblem, which was positioned inside the outline of a playing card, like a coat of arms.

“Your family's heraldic device.” Nick waved a hand to the emblem.

"A Jester?" I chuckled. "How fitting. This feels like a joke."

"Do you mean that it feels like a laugh?" Hatter asked. "Because a joke has no feeling."

"Yes, I suppose I did." I shrugged.

"Then you should say what you mean," the Hare chided me.

"I do." I scowled at the rabbit. "At least, I mean what I say–that's the same thing."

Dear God, now they had me talking like them.

"Not the same thing a bit!" Said the Hatter. "You might as well say that 'I see what I eat' is the same thing as 'I eat what I see!'"

"You might just as well say that 'I like what I get' is the same thing as 'I get what I like,'" added the March Hare.

"You might as well say," Dormouse added as she drifted back to sleep, "that 'I breathe when I sleep' is the same thing as 'I sleep when I breathe!'"

"Yes," I agreed. "The jester is fitting because I'm surrounded by fools."

"The fool can do anything," Hatter said sagely, "because he doesn't know that he can't."

"Okay, zen master," I muttered.

"I am absolutely a master of then," Hatter declared. "Or is it now?" His face fell.

"*Then;* it's definitely then," Hare helped.

“No, you simpleton, it's now,” the mouse argued.

“Do you know what they're talking about?” I asked Nick as I eased away from the table.

“It's the curse,” Nick said soberly. “Hatter once tried to sing for the Queen of Hearts, and she accused him of murdering time.”

“She sentenced him to death,” Warren said as he joined us.

“Off with his head!” Hatter shouted.

“But Hatter escaped,” Nick added. “He's almost cat-like in his ability to slip away.”

“He escaped?” I lifted a brow, pointedly looking at the man who was currently trying to fit an entire slice of cake into his mouth.

“He may be insane, but it's a mad genius,” Nick said. “It's why we chose to include him in our alliance.”

“All right,” I gave in. “But what is the 'then and now' all about?”

“Time got angry that Hatter was not punished for his murder,” Warren explained.

“Excuse me?” I blinked at the serious men.

“Well, to be fair, Hatter *was* convicted,” Nick said.

“Of murdering time,” I added.

“Yes, *Father Time*,” Warren said.

“Time is a person?” I asked.

“He is a being,” Nick clarified. “But that's neither here nor there.”

“How can it not be here or there?” Hatter asked. “If it can be anywhere, it must be in one of those two places.”

“Just so,” Nick agreed and then returned to his explanation. “Time was angry that Hatter escaped, and when he confronted Hatter about it, Hatter, being Hatter, made a few jokes and recited some poetry.”

“Oh,” I murmured.

“How Doth the Little Crocodile,” Warren said.

“How doth he what?” I asked.

“No, that was the name of the poem Hatter recited.”

“I prefer Twinkle, Twinkle, Little Bat,” Hare said.

“Or The Mouse's Tale,” Dormouse added.

“Yes, both are lovely.” Warren grimaced. “But Father Time does not like poetry.”

“Time halted himself in respect to the Hatter and his favorite companions, cursing them to forever live in the hour of 6 PM.”

“Tea time,” Warren said grimly.

“Forever stuck having tea,” I said. “I would grow tired of cake.”

“Cake? I love cake!” Hatter said, splattering cake crumbs everywhere. “You can never have too much cake or tea. Though I do enjoy little sandwiches now and then.”

“What is it; now or then?” Hare asked.

“Dear me! I don't know!” Hatter declared. “I think it's forever now, but it could be forever then. How long is forever?”

"Sometimes, just a second," Hare said.

"A second! Yes, I'll second that second," Hatter cried as his eyes started to get larger–crazier.

"George," a deep voice came from behind me, "easy now, old friend. You are both now and then. All the seconds are yours."

I turned to see a hooded man walk into the clearing. He had a warrior's build, and a sword buckled to his hips that cemented my initial impression. His hands were thick and calloused, but a gold signet ring adorned one of them. He walked quietly, and so did the men who accompanied him. I barely noticed that they were there until they surrounded us.

"Relax," Nick said as I tensed. "It's the King of Spades; he's on our side."

The King of Spades laid a hand on Hatter's shoulder. Hatter–George–went still and stared up into the shadows of the hood. His eyes softened, and he calmed.

"Thank you, Jaxon," Hatter whispered.

"Of course," Jaxon, the King of Spades, turned to face me as he pushed back his hood.

I swallowed convulsively and prayed that I wouldn't make a fool of myself, despite it being my family crest. King Jaxon was the most gorgeous man I'd ever laid eyes on. And that includes in movies. No celebrity could hold a candle to this Card King. He had features that looked as if a love goddess had personally sculpted them to be the most perfect example of mankind. His lips were lush but not too soft, his nose was regal but not too slim, and his brow was noble but not too high. And in the middle of all of that was a pair of eyes bluer than the Pacific on a hot day.

I felt a little dizzy. Was I going to faint? Oh, please don't let me faint. That would just be the cherry on top of my sundae of

insanity.

"Queen Alice?" His voice was like honey over hot stones; sweet and steamy.

"Yes," I squeaked, and then cleared my throat. "Yeah, that's me, I guess."

"You guess?" His brows lifted. "You should never guess about something so important."

"I just found out about all this today, Spade," I growled. "Give me a fucking break."

I nearly smacked my hand over my mouth. I had a tendency of being a bitch to attractive men. Maybe it was bitter grapes over knowing that I could never have them. Whatever it was, it was subconscious, and I had no control over it.

"Did you just call me 'Spade?'" His lips twitched.

"Yep. You want me to call you Jax instead?" I asked. "I don't know the etiquette between monarchs, and frankly, J-Spade, I don't give a damn. I've been shrunk, fell through a hole, assaulted by flowers, and forced to tromp through the woods in high heels today–my patience is wearing thin."

King Jaxon burst out laughing, and the soldiers standing around us, dressed all in black and very menacing in appearance, stared at their king in shock. I stared at him in open longing. Laughter made him ten times hotter. Ugh, I was going to get really mean, I just knew it.

"Charming," King Jaxon whispered. "Just like your mother."

My face fell. I had very few memories of my mother, and they were all hazy. First Hatter had said that I resembled her, and now this guy made another reference. On top of his untouchable

hotness, it was too much. I'd just buried my last family member that very day, and I had reached my breaking point.

I turned around and walked out of the clearing.

"Alice?" Nick called after me.

"I need a minute," I called back, waving my hand over my shoulder absently. "Don't worry, I know about the bandersnatch burrow."

I wandered just a few feet away and found a convenient tree to lay my forehead against. The rough bark felt real, more real than this place had a right to be, and I placed my palms against it for good measure. Then a pair of strong hands folded over my shoulders. I was so startled that I swung about and flat-palmed a punch into my attacker's solar plexus.

Except he wasn't attacking me. The King of Spades had been trying to comfort me and had not been expecting me to attack him. Nonetheless, he responded with impressive speed; deflecting my punch with his wrist, and using my momentum to pull me off balance.

I teetered, he caught me, and I wound up in his embrace, staring up into his stunning eyes. I was so close that I could see striations of indigo and amethyst in them. Jaxon stared back at me, his eyes going liquid and his arms tightening. His smell hit me then: cedar and musk. I breathed in deep.

"Duke Theodore taught you well," he whispered, his stare falling to my lips. "But I'm your ally, Alice. I swear to you; you're safe with me."

"I know," my voice had dropped to a low purr. "You just startled me."

"My apologies, Your Majesty." He smiled. "I only wanted to offer you some comfort."

“I'm good.” I pushed out of his arms, even though it was the last thing I wanted to do, and his eyes betrayed his disappointment for just a second. “It's been a rough day. I simply needed a few seconds to process.”

“I understand,” he said crisply. “Are you ready to return now? We have much to discuss.”

“Sure.”

I took King Jaxon's arm and let him escort me back to the Mad Tea Party

And here's a final look into the first book in the Spellsinger Series:

The Last Lullaby

Chapter One

I hunched my shoulders in an attempt to lift my coat collar a little higher around my ears. The weather in Seattle was dismal in December. Hell, in my opinion it was dismal during most times of the year. I longed for the kinder climate of my home, where even the rain was warm. But I couldn't go back to Hawaii yet, I still hadn't met with my client, and the payday for this job promised to be worth a little discomfort.

I finally made it to the top of the ridiculously long driveway, my eyes scanning the area surreptitiously from within the cashmere confines of my coat. I'd had the taxi drop me off a little ways down the street so I could do a bit of surveillance on my approach. Even in the gray, grim weather, there were at least eight guards spaced around the front of the house. One of them moved to intercept me, and I acted as if I hadn't seen him.

"Hold on, Miss. This is private property." The overly muscled man in combat pants held a gloved palm out to me in the traditional "stop" gesture. I saw the gun on his hip, but he hadn't drawn it. That was mistake number one. I was in the driveway already, which made me a threat.

Bad guard, no biscuit.

"I'm expected." I could have announced myself right then, but I wanted to test Adam MacLaine's security team.

That was my client, MacLaine–or he would be soon. If this guy was an accurate representation of MacLaine's security, it was a wonder the man wasn't dead already.

"Do we have a guest arriving today?" Mr. Combat Pants

asked a little microphone clipped to his shirt.

He had to open his leather jacket to access the mic, giving me a flash of the knife he had secured to an inner pocket. Damn this guy was dumb. He even turned away from me to talk into his comm. Like he couldn't conceive of a woman being a threat. I could have killed him three times already. I suppose I should have berated him for his bad habits, but I hated doing other people's jobs. And it was definitely someone else's job to whip this guy into shape. The mere thought exhausted me. I do not suffer fools.

“Name?”

“What?” I asked, completely distracted by his ineptitude.

And the spaghetti stain on his shirt. It was nearly invisible from a distance, but now that I was up close and personal, I could clearly see the crusty red mark on the black fabric. So, a fool and a slob. Definitely not the type of man I'd have chosen to protect me.

“What's your name, Miss?” the slob asked.

“Tanager,” I said, whispering to see if he would make the mistake of coming in closer to hear me.

“What was that?” He sure did. He leaned in close enough for me to stab him in the throat.

Of course I would never deign to dirty my hands in such a manner. My mother raised me better than that. I killed like a lady.

“The name is Tanager,” I said more clearly. “And I'm cold.”

Whoever was on the other side of the microphone heard me, and must have barked something into the muscle-head's ear. He flinched, then straightened.

“Sorry, Ms. Tanager,” he stammered and gestured to the looming house. “My team wasn't notified. Go on in. Someone will meet you at the door.”

“Thank you, Mr. . . ?” I drew it out into a question.

“Uh, you can call me Jake, Ms. Tanager,” he stammered.

“Thank you, Jake.” I walked off, striding quickly to the beckoning warmth of the open front door.

A woman stood within the golden light of the doorway, her features as stern as her severe bun, and her eyes razor sharp. She nodded to me, and shut the door behind me after I entered.

“May I take your coat, Ms Tanager?”

“Yes, thank you.” I slid out of it and sighed.

I had worn my usual getup to greet clients–pencil skirt and modest blouse. But instead of heels, I'd chosen knee-high boots. It was just too cold outside to go without something covering my calves. The woman looked over my prim outfit, and nodded in approval. With my long, dark curls pinned up, I looked very professional.

“I am Mrs. Chadwick,” the woman introduced herself as she hung up my coat. “Mr. MacLaine is waiting for you in his office. I'll take you there now.”

I followed Mrs. Chadwick down a corridor much too wide to be called a hallway. It was lined with expensive artwork, and the sounds of our footsteps were muffled by a silk carpet runner that looked as if it had taken years to weave. It was nice, but I'd seen all of this before. Done better, to tell the truth. My clients were the wealthiest people in the world. They had to be in order to afford me.

“Mr. MacLaine, she's here,” Mrs. Chadwick said as she walked through an open door.

“Thank God,” a man's voice groaned.

It was a pleasant voice, and it matched the office I entered.

Not nearly as pretentious as the rest of the house, this room was more personal. It held framed family photos, an old chair that must have come from a time when MacLaine wasn't so wealthy, a wide desk made for function instead of form, and several sitting areas; one before the desk, one before a picture window to the right of the desk, and one in front of a modest fireplace. That's where MacLaine had been, at the fireplace enjoying its comfort instead of working at his desk. In the crowd I normally contracted with, that said a lot.

Adam MacLaine was around forty, with a trim build that suggested he didn't spend all of his time making money. His oak-brown hair was lightly sprinkled with white at the temples, and his skin had a healthy tan, but not the sunbed tan so prevalent in Seattle. His skin had seen real sun. Blue eyes crinkled as he smiled in relief, and came to meet me halfway across the room, hand extended.

"Thank you for coming, Ms Tanager." He shook my hand firmly. "Could you close the door on your way out, Mrs. Chadwick?"

"Of course, sir." She smiled a little, showing a hint of affection for her employer. That said a lot too.

"Would you like something to drink?" MacLaine offered as his hand swept to a sideboard where several bottles waited. Not decanters, mind you, he had straight up liquor bottles out on display. The social elite would be shocked.

"No, thank you."

"All right then." He looked unnerved by my refusal. "Would you care to have a seat?"

"Yes." I slid into the chair across from his, and he relaxed a little, coming over to join me.

"I don't know how–" he started to stammer, but I held up a

hand.

"Mr. MacLaine, who wants you dead?" I cut through the pussyfooting.

"I believe it's a man named Jonah Malone." He sighed, and sank back into his chair. "His company was failing, and I bought it at a . . . well, for a song, really."

"Uh-huh." I chuckled at the song reference.

With the exception of his ironic wording, my clients's stories were always so similar. Someone got the better end of a business deal. Or they were cheating on their spouse. Or cheating on their mistress. Or cheating on their taxes. No, that last one doesn't require my intervention. Not usually. But the issue was often about someone screwing someone else in some form or another.

"I assume you've compiled a dossier on him?"

"Oh, yes," MacLaine fumbled with something on the floor beside him, and then handed me a manila folder.

"What exactly do you want me to do to Mr. Malone?" This was the line I asked all of my clients. I needed to be very clear with them. A lot of them assumed I was purely an assassin, but that wasn't the case. I thought of myself more as a fixer. I could kill when necessary, but death was the most extreme result I offered.

"I . . ." He gaped at me. "What are my options?"

Just as I'd thought. Cer hadn't told him. My old friend was having a laugh at my expense right about now. MacLaine had doubtless been referred to me by one of his friends, but he'd had to go through *my* friend, Cerberus Skylos, before he could arrange a meeting with me. Cerberus made sure the client was someone I'd want to work with before he passed on the info. And he usually did me the courtesy of explaining who I was, or at least, what I could

do, to my potential customers.

"Do you know what I am, Mr. MacLaine?" I asked gently.

"An assassin," he whispered, as if he might be overheard.

"No," I shook my head. "I have killed people, but that's not who I am. Or *what* I am."

"Uh." He started to look confused. "Are you a vampire?"

"Good guess," I chuckled, "but no."

The mere fact that I was sitting there, facing him, meant that Adam MacLaine knew about the supernatural world that existed in the shadows of the human one. "The Beneath."– or just plain "Beneath." is what we, the denizens of said community, called it. So, MacLaine knew of it, but it was very doubtful that he knew the scope of the situation. He hadn't even known the correct term for a vampire–blooder. The wrong titles give away ignorance in a heartbeat.

Humans who were aware of the Beneath usually knew about the forerunners of paranormal society, the obvious races; loups (don't call them werewolves, they hate that), other shapeshifters, and blooders. Sometimes they knew about fairies, but the Shining Ones were really good at covering their tracks, so that was rare. What was even more rare was when humans were acquainted with the other races; gods, witches, demons, dragons, angels, and so forth. Things that went bump in the night, and did a fair amount of rabble rousing during the day as well. We just knew how to hide our supernatural gifts better than the shifters and blooders.

"A friend of mine told me about you. He said you were the best. That you never failed," MacLaine's face started to fall into the sharp lines that always preceded my revelation of the Beneath. It was like they could sense I was about to tell them something that would change their entire life. Or at least their ability to sleep

through the night.

"That's true," I agreed. "So you know about vampires. What else do you know?"

"What else?" He scowled. "The shapeshifters, of course."

"And that's it?"

"There's *more*?" MacLaine's eyes widened.

"Oh yes," I smirked. "There's quite a bit more. But that's not for me to reveal. I only have the right to tell you about my own kind. Now, do you know what a siren is, Mr. MacLaine?"

"Like in the *Odyssey*?"

"Yes, exactly," I smiled, relieved that I wouldn't have to explain everything. "My mother's people are considered to be a class of god. They were minor deities, more like an entourage to the more powerful gods, but still considered a divine race."

"Are you seriously telling me you're descended from gods?" He started to stand.

I quickly sang the lyrics from Hollow Point Heroes' "Sit Down Shut Up."

I had a whole arsenal of quick-draw lyrics just like this one, ready to be shot out like a bullet when necessary. I didn't even need the song to say exactly what I wanted to accomplish. All that I needed was one word to work with–sit, dance, die. You know, the usual. And then I could visualize, and direct the magic from there. This particular lyric just happened to work really well. And you'd be surprised how often I employed it.

MacLaine froze, his eyes going wide with horror as his body disobeyed him, and plopped back into the chair. He leaned forward onto his forearms, and regarded me intently. Giving me his full attention, just as I'd commanded.

“Good.” I pushed down the power that rose whenever I began to sing. “Now, don't look at me like that. You're perfectly safe. I simply needed to demonstrate what I could do before you wrote me off as insane. I put no permanence into the spell so the effects will wear off momentarily.”

“What did you just do to me?” Adam strained to push his words past the weakening magic.

“I'm getting to that,” I smiled. It wasn't often that I got a chance to talk about my heritage. “As I was saying, my ancestors were minor deities, companions of the goddess, Persephone. You do know who Persephone is?”

“Yes.” He sighed deeply as the effects of my spell wore off. “I didn't think she was real, but yeah, I'm familiar with her myths.”

“Oh, she's very real.” I laughed to think of what Persephone's reaction to his disbelief would have been.

She just couldn't accept that people didn't believe in the gods anymore. I told her she was in denial, and she told me there were several rivers in the Underworld, but the Nile was not one of them. The Greek goddess has a silly sense of humor.

“When Hades did his little abduction routine, Persephone's mother, Demeter, enlisted the aid of my family to find her daughter,” I said. “She gave them wings, and bade them to search the world for Persephone.”

“I've never heard that part of the story.” He was relaxing more and more now that it was apparent that I wasn't going to attack him. “They never found her, I imagine.”

“No, Persephone wasn't in the world. She was with Hades, in his domain. So my ancestors failed,” I confirmed, “and Demeter cursed them for it. They were turned into sirens–women who sing eternally to their missing mistress, begging for her to return home.”

“I thought the sirens were mermaids who lured men to their deaths.”

“They're closer to birds than mermaids, but they do lure men to their deaths,” I said. “Their song is so beautiful, few can resist its pull, but it's also tragic. And tragedy can only create more tragedy.”

“Are you saying that you're a siren?” MacLaine cocked his head at me, fascinated, when really, he should have been afraid.

“No, only part,” I shook my head. “The other part of me is witch.”

“What? Like a Wiccan?”

I burst into laughter, and he scowled at me.

“No, Mr. MacLaine,” I got my humor under control. “Real witches are nothing like those tree-hugging, circle dancers. They're a separate race entirely, grisly and powerful. People you should hope to never encounter. My mother lured one of them to her, but he was strong enough to withstand the pull of death in her voice. In fact, he decided he quite liked her, and her music. He married her.”

“You're the child of a warlock and a siren?” MacLaine's voice rose in shock.

“The word 'warlock' means liar. Oathbreaker, from the Saxon waerloga. Male witches are still called witches.”

“Oh.”

“Yes.”

“So you're the daughter of a siren and a witch?”

“Yes.”

“Oh. Um.” He chewed at his lower lip a bit. “What does

that mean exactly? What does that make you?"

"It makes me rare, Mr. MacLaine," I smiled slowly. "Very rare."

"And you can sing people to death?"

"I can do much more than that," I decided to put him out of his misery. "My kind, though rare, have been born before. We are called spellsingers. We can transform songs into enchantment, bring lyrics to life."

"Like how you made me sit down," he whispered.

"And shut up, yes," I laughed. "There are a lot of races living among humans. Spellsingers are only one variety, though we are, admittedly, one of the most dangerous."

"Other races?" MacLaine looked as if he couldn't take much more, so I took pity on him once more.

"Don't worry about that right now," I waved a hand. "They aren't the ones who want you dead."

"Jonah," MacLaine growled. "I can't believe he's taken it this far."

"Mr. MacLaine," I said carefully, "my kind have toppled kingdoms, burned cities, changed the history of the world. I can do anything to Jonah Malone that you wish... for the right price."

"So, from conqueror to mercenary, eh?" MacLaine chuckled.

"I have no desire to destroy monarchies or watch Rome burn–that was my Grand Aunt Adelaide's thing," I rolled my eyes.

"Wait– the burning of Rome, where Nero supposedly fiddled . . ." He exhaled roughly. "A relative of yours did that?"

“Nero didn't own a fiddle,” I grimaced. “That instrument wasn't invented till much later. He played a cithara.”

“A what?”

“It looks kind of like a lute . . . never mind that.” I was terrible with tangents once I got talking. “Nero wasn't in Rome at the time of the burning. He hired Adelaide, just as you're hiring me. Someone else played music for her while she set Rome ablaze.”

“Someone else . . . you can start fires with your song?”

“I told you,” I huffed. “I can do anything the words permit me to do. If I sing about fire, stuff burns. If I sing about water, someone drowns. Sometimes, a whole continent,” I shook my head. I wouldn't tell him about Uncle Eilener and Atlantis. He still got flack over that fiasco.

“So you're . . . wait. Nero hired someone to burn Rome?”

“Sure.” I shrugged. “Everyone hated him. After Rome burned, Nero came in with food and supplies, opening his own gardens to house people. He polished up his image while secretly deciding on a spot to build his new golden palace. It was good PR, and smart property management.”

“What a bastard,” MacLaine winced.

“Yeah, Aunt Adelaide regretted working with Nero. That's why I'm a bit more choosy with my clients,” I smirked. “But what do *you* want, Mr. MacLaine? What result would you like, concerning Jonah Malone?”

“I'd like for him to just back off,” he huffed. “But I don't see how . . .” He trailed off as he saw me smiling. “You can do that? Just make him change his mind? Permanently?”

“Absolutely,” I inclined my head. “And it's even cheaper

than killing him. Only two and a half million."

"Two and a half *million*?" MacLaine huffed. "That's more than I paid for the company."

"Your acquaintances did warn you about my price, correct?"

"Yes, but," he frowned, "that's when my life was in danger."

"Your life is *still* in danger," I stood. "I haven't agreed to take your case yet."

He gaped at me for two seconds before standing, and offering me his hand again. "Two point five million is just fine, Ms. Tanager."

"Wonderful, then we have an agreement." I shook his hand, then started heading for the door. "And just a suggestion." I stopped–halfway there–and looked back at him. "Fire your security team and get some professionals. Even without my magic, I could have killed them all within ten minutes. Especially the one called Jake."

"You . . . what . . ." He blinked, and then recovered. "Alright. I'll do that today."

"Smart man." I smiled. Maybe he would live long enough to pay me. After all, he hadn't hired me to do his–

"How much for you to head my security?"

"No." I shook my head. "I don't have time for that, and you don't have enough money to pay me." His face fell. "However"–I pulled a card from the pocket of my skirt and handed it to him–"this man will help you."

"Cerberus Security," MacLaine read, and then looked up at me. "This is the guy I called to arrange our meeting."

I nodded.

His eyes went wide, "Please tell me this isn't the same Cerberus who . . ."

"Guarded the Greek Underworld?" I laughed. "That was a giant dog, Mr. MacLaine. With three heads, I believe."

"Oh." He laughed, but it sounded strained. "Just a reference to the protection skills then?"

"Yes, exactly." I smiled. Nope, I wouldn't tell him that he had guessed correctly.

Cerberus was actually a shapeshifting god with a fondness for practical jokes and dangerous women. I'm unsure which had cost him his job. I've known him for centuries, and he still hasn't told me. I know that Hades personally kicked his old, guard dog out of the Greek Underworld. Gave him the fiery boot. So now, Cerberus watched over humans. Humans who could pay him enough to soothe his wounded, puppy pride. Cer was damn good at what he did, but he was better at defense. He lacked the subtlety for a proper offense. If you told Cer to kill someone, he would probably just punch them in the face, really hard. I doubt he'd even stop to ask if the guy needed killing to begin with. So he kept to the security side of the business, and he called me for anything beyond that. Conversely, when my clients had a bunch of buffoons guarding them, I sent them to Cerberus.

"Ms. Tanager?" MacLaine stopped me again.

"Call me Elaria." I smiled at him.

"That's lovely." He grinned. "You must call me Adam then. I was just wondering . . . isn't a tanager a type of bird?"

"Why, yes, it is, Adam." I was still smiling as I left. It was always nice when someone appreciated the subtleties.

Chapter Two

Jonah Malone was a gangster. Or a mobster. Probably a whole lot of words that ended in “er.” He had clawed his way to the top, and then discovered that he didn't actually have a head for business. All of his enterprises were failing, not just the one MacLaine had purchased, and Jonah was reverting to his old thug ways to handle the frustration.

It had been a simple thing to schedule an appointment to see him. I simply sang to the receptionist over the phone, and she found a spot for me that very day. Then I walked into Jonah Malone's office, closed the door, and sang to him. In five minutes, he had completely forgotten why he wanted to kill MacLaine. He also decided to sell off his remaining businesses, and get out while he could. Perhaps meditate more. I figured why not help improve the guy while I'm messing with his head?

I walked out feeling relaxed, and satisfied with a job well done. I had video taped Jonah's “change of heart”, and sent it to Cer, who would pass it along to MacLaine as confirmation. Within ten minutes, MacLaine had transferred my payment into my account. I could finally go home. Maybe I'd have a Mai Tai on the plane as a special treat. Hell, maybe I'd have two.

I was on the way to the airport, when Cerberus called.

“Got another one for you, El.” Cerberus didn't bother with a greeting.

“I'm tired and cold, Cer.” I sighed. “Give it to someone else. I'm going home.”

“No one else can handle this. It's bad.”

"How bad?"

"Blooder army bad."

"That's pretty fucking bad." I made a face at the phone.

"Yes."

"Fuck."

"Yes."

"Whose army?" I asked.

"Some guy named Lincoln." Cerberus's voice had a shrug in it.

"Like the president?"

"Yep." He didn't offer anymore info.

"Where is this army going? What do they want? Who's the client?" I huffed. "You wanna give me anything without me pulling your fucking canines to get it?"

"Whoa, easy now," Cer chuckled. "You're turning me on, Elaria, sweetheart. You wanna stop in Denver and make good on some of your promises? We can fly to Kansas together after your failed attempts at pulling my pearly whites."

"Kansas!" I nearly screeched, causing my driver to look back at me in concern. "It's fine. I'm fine," I told the driver. To Cer, I said, "I'm not going to Kansas. Who do you think I am? Dorothy?"

"You'd look cute in a little gingham dress," he offered.

"The only way you'd get me in gingham is if you put on a collar and let me call you Toto," I shot back.

"For you, baby? Anytime."

“Great.” I rolled my eyes. “Now we have our next couple's costume planned.”

“No, really.” I could hear Cerberus smirk. “I look good in a collar.”

Cerberus and I had been playing this mating game since we met, back when I was sixteen, and we'd never concluded it. Part of me wanted to see if he was as good as he implied, but the other part of me knew our friendship was worth too much to risk it. Plus, we did business together, and everyone knows that saying about mixing business with Percocet. Or something like that.

“Look.” Cerberus got serious. “The guy is an old friend of mine. He's a blooder, a gheara, but he keeps his people in line, and they don't cause any trouble. He's one of the good ones.”

“I don't know about a blooder being good, but I'll believe the bit about him keeping his people in line.” I chuckled. “It's not like you hear a lot of vampire stories originating in Kansas. I didn't even know that Kansas had a Beneath. I thought they'd all flown away to Oz.”

“Banning's a tough one. He fought his way out of Europe, and now the fuckers are coming for him.” Cerberus didn't even acknowledge my jokes on the Beneath, aka the paranormal community. Which he knew irritated me. I put effort into my comedy; the least he could do was acknowledge it.

“Lincoln doesn't sound European,” I noted dryly.

“He's not.” Cer finally laughed. “He's a local hire. Mercenary.”

“Ah,” now that I could relate to. “So the guy is just doing a job. I can't hold that against him.”

“Yeah, but he contracts with the Falca all the time. Those elitist bastards wouldn't even bother to come to America, and kill

Banning themselves," Cer huffed. "Lincoln, what kind of stupid merc name is that?"

"So what do you want me to do?" I rolled my eyes, something I did a lot when I talked to Cer. He had a thing about names, especially professional ones, and was always going on about them. And the fact that I didn't have one.

"Ma'am? We're here," the cabby called back to me.

"Hold on, Cer." I stuffed my phone into my purse and pulled out some cash for the driver. I hurried out of the cab and over to a semi-secluded bench, then pulled out the phone again. "You there?"

"Why do you always shove your phone in your purse when you put me on hold?" Cerberus grumbled. "Just press the fucking hold button. You think I like listening to all your lady loot knocking against the mic?"

"I'm going to hang up," I threatened.

"Fine," he growled. "I can get you ten million for the job."

I nearly dropped the phone. Ten million was twice my assassination fee. But then I thought about it. An assassination was one person, and Cerberus was asking me to kill . . . Wait, how many blooders *was* he asking me to kill?

"How big is this army?" I asked.

"I'm not sure," he muttered.

"How big, Cer?"

"Big enough that a gheara blooder can't handle it with his entire gura backing him," Cerberus snapped.

Blooder, as I mentioned before, is the correct appellation for a vampire. Kind of obvious, I know, but that's how those names

usually came about. I mean look at my race, the spellsingers. Well– duh. But the word gheara was a little more interesting. It was Romanian for "fang," and it indicated that this particular blooder was a big deal, akin to a king, maybe even bigger than that. There were usually hundreds of blooders in a single gura– that's the group of vampires who kiss the gheara's pale patootie. In fact, most people call them a kiss, but the blooders don't like that. Probably because of the ass-kissing thing. The polite term is gura, which is yet another Romanian word, meaning "mouth". Then there was the Falca, which were the elite blooders who controlled everything in the blooder world. Falca meant "jaw" in Romanian. Yeah, I guess all the names were obvious; they just sounded less so in another language.

Anyway, if this guy had an entire gura looking after him, and Cerberus still couldn't help him without me, then there must be a whole lot of mercenary blooders coming after Cer's friend. Crowds were tough; it was much easier to weave a spell around a single mind. To alter the free will of thousands of people at once was nearly impossible. So I would probably have to go another route. I could sing a spell to affect the environment, and attack them physically, leaving them their free wills. Or I could enchant a few of them at a time, and force those to attack the others. Possibly even a combination of both. It would be exhausting, and probably take me multiple songs to complete. I wasn't even sure I could do it.

"Ten million per song," I said to Cerberus.

"What?" Cer shouted into the phone.

"An assassination usually takes a few lines, half a song at most." I explained my reasoning. I never arbitrarily picked a price. "And I charge five mil for a kill. So ten million for an entire song is a bargain, especially when you'll be wanting me to kill hundreds, possibly even thousands, of blooders. You know I'll need to sing more than one song to take out an army, so your friend can pay per song. If it gets too expensive, he can tell me to stop singing, and

handle the survivors with his gura."

"Gods damn you, Elaria," Cerberus snarled. "You have the mind of Archimedes and the cold calculation of Hades himself."

"Thank you," I said primly. "But you know as well as I that you were trying to dick me over on this one, Cerberus, and I'm not happy about that."

"He's a friend, El," he sighed.

"Yeah, that's why I'm letting you slide," I acknowledged.

You'd think immortals would end up having tons of friends, what with our extensive lifetimes. But it's actually the opposite. When you live as long as we do, you end up breaking most bonds. Family is usually the exception, but even they can drive you crazy enough to make you avoid them for a few decades. When you form a friendship that lasts, like mine and Cer's, it means something.

"So, are you meeting me in Kansas?" I finally asked him.

"You'll do it?" Cerberus asked with a measure of surprise.

"Of course I'll do it." I rolled my eyes. Again. "Any friend of yours, and all that heroine bullshit."

"Thanks, El," he said sincerely.

"Of course," I said just as sincerely. "Now, where in Kansas am I going?"

"Head to Lawrence," Cer said. "Check into the Springhill Suites–it's one of the nicer hotels there. A Marriott."

"Well, as long as I can stay at a Marriott," I teased.

"I'll book a room for you," he promised. "Under your usual alias."

“Florence Nightingale,” I agreed. “Perfect.”

“And I'll come and get you after I arrive.”

“Alright,” I agreed. “See you in Kansas, Toto.”

“Bring your sexy red heels, Dorothy. I'll pack my collar.” Cer laughed as he hung up.

Chapter Three

Ah, Kansas. It was actually kind of pretty. Lawrence was a bustling town, but not quite as busy as Seattle, and not nearly as cold. It was November, so there was a nip in the air, but something about that breeze coming off the water in Seattle, made things so much colder there. Lawrence was more mellow with its chill, like Seattle's hippie sibling. Autumn had painted the city in its vibrant colors, and there was the smell of the season on the breeze–dry leaves and cooling earth. I breathed deeply of it as my cabby drove me out to the Springhill Suites.

As promised, I found a room already booked, and paid for, under my alias. I showed the surprised clerk my Florence Nightingale ID, and he handed me the keys with a twitching smile. I gave him the standard line: my folks had thought it was a great joke to name me Florence, what with our last name being Nightingale and all. The clerk let his lip twitching take the shape of a proper smile.

I went up to my room, threw my bag on the bed, and started digging around for a change of clothes. I needed a hot shower, and something more comfortable than my secretary get-up. I found a pair of jeans and a cotton blouse with bell sleeves. Perfect to relax in, and maybe go grab some dinner. Then I headed to the bathroom. When I came out, dressed but still rubbing at my damp hair, my phone was ringing. I snatched it up and answered.

“There's no time for me to meet you,” Cerberus said urgently. “Get over to the Crouching Lion Country Club now.” He rattled off an address.

“What?” I glanced out of my picture window at the night

sky. It was still early; the stars hadn't even brightened yet.

“Now, Elaria!” Cerberus roared. “They're here!”

“Fine,” I snapped and disconnected him, muttering to myself, “Crouching Lion. What is it, a kung fu country club?”

I grabbed the essentials and rushed out of the room. When I got to the street, I paused, not really knowing what I was going to do. I didn't have time to call a cab, and I couldn't exactly show up at a blooder battle with an innocent human in tow. So I needed to grab some wheels of my own. I scanned the road, where a steady stream of cars drove by. I was considering running out to flag one down, when a red sports car pulled away from the pack and screeched up to the hotel. A smarmy guy got out of the car, and I smiled at him.

“Excuse me.” I ran over before the valet could reach him, and then leaned in close.

“Hello, pretty lady.” He leaned closer.

I began to sing, and his face went blank.

“Here.” He handed me his keys. “I think you need to borrow my car. I'll be at the bar when you get back.” Then he walked past the stunned valet, and into the hotel.

“Some people are so nice,” I gave the valet a sweet smile before I climbed in the . . . what the hell was it? Oh damn! A Ferrari. Talk about luck.

I squealed away from the hotel and hit the convenient GPS on the dash. Within minutes, I was pulling up the tree-lined, private road of the Crouching Lion Country Club. As I approached, the night brightened until finally, florescent flood-lights illuminated the outskirts of a blooder horde. They considerately stayed off the road, too intent on crossing the massive golf course to bother getting in my way. It was the straightest path to their

goal.

A line of blooders stood before the main building of the country club. They posed in the aggressive manner employed by determined defenders throughout history. There were quite a lot of them, all armed despite the fact that they were blooders, and could have been considered weapons themselves. But I suppose when you faced an army of your own kind, your talents, no matter how impressive, negated themselves.

At the head of this fierce flock stood Cerberus, towering over Banning's gura. His massive muscles looked a little too He-Man next to the more mundane physiques of the previously human blooders. Cer's long, dark hair was pulled back in a no-nonsense ponytail, and his even darker eyes were narrowed on the oncoming army. Until he saw me.

Cerberus smiled, an altogether chilling thing to see since it showcased a set of prominent canines that were a little thicker than your average blooder's. He let out a triumphant howl, and the line of mercenaries paused to look around at what had excited the shifter god. When they saw only me, a woman in a sports car, they went back into attack mode. Obviously I wasn't a threat.

A guy at the center of the horde paused a little longer than the others, watching me carefully as I sped past him. I had my chosen playlist on pause, my iPod hooked up to the car's stereo, and I hit the button as I raced alongside the golf course. Music blared: Fall Out Boy's "My Songs Know What You Did in the Dark" going into its long intro. I shot up the drive before the club, and pulled the car to a screeching stop right in front of Cerberus.

The door slammed open with my violent shove, and I leapt out. Music blasted out of the vehicle as I jumped on the hood. I could feel the beat of it in my bones, vibrating through the metal beneath my feet. I glanced back at Cerberus and winked, my eyes briefly catching the shocked expression of the man beside him. He was blond and a blooder. Had to be Cer's friend, Banning. Not that

it mattered. I turned back around just as the lyrics began pelting my ears.

I started singing absently as I thought out my battle strategy. I knew I'd have to rein in these mercenaries as fast as possible so that they didn't make a run for it before I could get to them all. I couldn't leave any alive to make a second attempt. That's just sloppy work.

Fire would be perfect for forming a blooder-proof barrier. But I had to work up to it, wait for the words in the lyrics that would magnify my intent. So I started with the poor sods in front. My hand lifted to them as words shot from my mouth like bullets. Aggression blaring in my ears. Tension coiling in my thighs. The stuttering strength of the song cut through the cold air. Every blooder I pointed to exploded as if I'd blown their heads off with a missile launcher.

The crowd behind me started muttering as Cerberus chortled.

"Isn't she wonderful?" Cerberus sauntered up to lean over the top of the car and watch me work. "An artist. A true artist." He laid his chin in his palm.

I continued to slam out the vicious verses, ignoring Cer. The song was filling me, becoming a part of my being, and the strength of the spell was rushing around me. A tornado of charged molecules clambering for motivation. Waiting for me to give them a direction. An objective. I felt glorious, powerful enough to make all those mercenaries mine. And I did, I snatched up their minds. Their will. Then I used the next line to vent the brewing musical malice. The blooders before me turned on their companions, and started tearing them to pieces.

"Holy fucking hellfire." The blonde man moved up beside Cer.

I sensed him there, felt his intense stare on me, but didn't

have the time to look at him. Still, his face flashed in my mind–a picture of aloof male beauty. Strong jaw, regal nose, eyes glowing green in the shadows. Nice.

"I told you!" Cerberus laughed harder as I continued to pour my lyrical rage over the mercenaries. "She's worth every penny."

The chorus came, giving me what I needed to manifest fire. I angled my hand flat, bringing it down like a blade with every sharp word. Each slice brought a line of flames surging up around the faltering army, causing many of them to shriek in terror and stumble back into their companions. The hand motions were more for me than the magic, like a conductor directing his symphony. This symphony didn't need me to conduct it. All the magic required was for me to picture the result I desired, and sing. That was it. So I let my arms fall limply to my sides as I screamed the cataclysmic conclusion to the chorus, and my fiery prison penned the blooders in. The ring closed, and the magic surged through me, responding to the triumph I felt.

"Oh my god, I think I'm in love," I heard one of the blooders behind me groan.

"Of course you are," Cerberus called back to him. "For fuck's sake, I'm rock hard right now."

The blooder who had watched my approach more carefully than the others rushed forward. He snaked through the terrified mass, but he wasn't trying to calm them; he was simply trying to reach me. I was obviously his biggest threat, and he was obviously a take-action sort of guy. It had to be Lincoln, coming to kill me before I could slaughter his entire army. It was a smart move, probably the best option available to him. Cut the head off and all that.

Too bad it was useless.

The song turned truly tragic, as if sensing my need. I

looked right at Lincoln, directing the destruction at him alone. The merc leader flared up like a torch, blooders pulling back from him in horror. But the bonfire didn't last long. It burned so hot, so intensely, that it turned Lincoln into cinders within seconds. He exploded into sooty snowflakes, swirling down over his army. Blooders cringed away from the remains, hardened soldiers turning into bawling babies.

The song surged on, and I spread my arms out in welcome to it. It was a confession now. A baring of what I had been born. A show of the hand that life had dealt me, and what I had done with it. What I had become. A creature of nightmares. A sorceress of songs. The villain no one could escape. The lyrics couldn't be more perfect for me. It was a declaration of pride in my own monstrosity, and a deep, secret fear of it. I let them see me.

And that's when the real screaming started.

It went on for another two songs, during which I killed every mercenary there in various lyrical ways. The blooders behind me were cheering, some of them singing along with me, and some even mimicked the motions I made. I had blooder backup dancers. Maybe we could take this act to Vegas. A song, a dance, and some magic. We were perfect for Sin City.

By the time I ended the third song, I was trembling, on the verge of passing out. But it was okay; the threat had been eliminated. My fire-oriented playlist had kept the heat up, ensuring that no one escaped, and those within the ring were dead or dying. I let the flames die down as well, until the only illumination originated from the building behind me and the scattered lampposts. The soft glow gently lit a field of corpses, slowly turning into the ash of the undead. One good thing about killing blooders; there was very little clean up involved.

The next song started to play. My shoulders fell in exhaustion. I turned to Cerberus and held my arms out to him like a little girl. Even with me standing on the hood of the car, he was

still nearly as tall as I was, and he easily picked up my five-foot-four frame. Cer set me down on the road, but held onto me long enough to make sure I could stand on my own. He gave me a concerned look, blocking my shaking body from the cheering crowd. We never let others see our weaknesses. I nodded that I was all right.

Cerberus gave me a kiss on the cheek, and backed away. "Thanks for coming, El."

"No problem, honey." I smirked, then looked at the blond.

"I'm Banning Dalca." The blooder held his hand out to me.

"Nice to meet you." I went to shake his hand, but he did that suave, old-school vamp thing and kissed my hand in a way that was so much more sensual than a human could make it.

"Thank you for your assistance, Ms. Tanager." Banning smiled slowly at me, his eyes lingering over my face.

"Just make sure my payment goes through by tonight," I said abruptly as I pulled away.

Banning's eyes widened, and he looked as if he was going to say something more. But I was too tired to deal with him. I needed to get out of there before I passed out.

"I gotta run." I looked back at Cerberus. "I'll wait for you at the place, babe." I spoke vaguely on purpose. The last thing I needed was for an entire gura to know where I was crashing for the night.

"Of course," Cer said with a smirk, as if we were an item.

I smiled back; it was our routine when some client flirted with me. Cer acted like I was his, and the guy usually backed off. This guy didn't buy it, nor did he back off. As I slid into the front seat, and turned down the music, Banning Dalca followed me. He

leaned in, his eyes fading to mint under the car's interior light, and gave me a very unsettling look.

"Please don't leave, Ms. Tanager," he whispered. "I'd dearly like to speak with you."

This seemed way past some mere flirtation. It was weird, and it sent chills racing down my spine. The guy was hot, but I didn't sleep with clients, and I especially didn't sleep with blooders. Blooders were bad news.

"Maybe another time." I tried to reach past him for the door handle, but he didn't budge.

"Please," he said again.

"Get away from the car, Mr. Dalca," I said in a dangerous tone.

"Ban," Cerberus growled. "What the fuck, man?"

"Five minutes of your time." Banning tried once more.

"No," I snapped. "Now are you going to back away or do I have to make you?"

"All right, Ms. Tanager," he sighed, but produced a business card, and stuffed it into my hand. "Please call me after you've rested. I promise you, I have the most honorable of intentions."

"Uh-huh." I slid the card into my bra. "Thanks; I got it."

Banning sighed again, then eased away, shutting the door for me. I gunned the engine and yanked the car about, but I couldn't help looking back at Banning as I drove off. He stared after me like I was breaking his little, undead heart. But the strangeness didn't stop there.

Just as I hit the border of golf course turning into forest, I

saw a movement in the shadows. A flash of skin. I was instantly alert, despite my exhaustion, and angled the car enough to shine the headlights into the area. There he was, a gods-damned fairy. One of the fucking Shining Ones was standing in the trees of Lawrence, Kansas, watching me like some otherworldly peeping tom. Instead of hiding when my lights hit him, he held up a hand in greeting.

I nearly drove off the road.

I didn't though. I veered back onto the asphalt and kept going. If a fairy waves at you from the forest, you don't stop for him. Heading over for a little chat is a great way to get yourself abducted. The Fey were generally considered to be the perverts of the paranormal world. They'd fuck anything, anywhere, anytime. A fairy's interest wasn't flattering; it simply meant you had a heartbeat and were within reach.

Okay, so maybe that was a bit of an exaggeration. The lesser fey–pixies, leprechauns, trolls, goblins, those sorts–would mount you in a heartbeat if you let them. Most would try even if you didn't let them. However, the elite sidhe, those who were known as the Shining Ones, were a bit more discriminating in their choices of bed partner. That didn't make them any less terrifying. In fact, the Shining Ones had all sorts of seductive spells on their side. They might not technically be rapists, but with that kind of magic, the technicalities blurred. And once they got you, they tended to keep you until you were completely used up. I've heard stories of all manner of debaucheries going on in Tír na nÓg. So it didn't really matter, lesser or greater, fairies were freaks.

It was that whole hedonism thing. No one did it better than the Shining Ones. They lived every moment of their immortality to the fullest, believing that they shouldn't do anything they didn't want to, and conversely, they should do everything, and every*one*, that they did want to do. They ate the best food, drank the finest wine, and wore the most luxurious clothes. They loved to mix it up too. They didn't care who created an item; if it was the best, they

wanted it. Several of them lived this side of the Veil for that very reason, the luxury.

The Veil is what we call the border between worlds. Planes of Existence. Realms. Again, take your pick. These places were laid on top of each other, separated by an invisible sheet of magic. If you were sensitive enough, you could feel the magic, and in some places the Veil was thick enough that even people who weren't so sensitive could feel it. But to cross it, you had to either be magically powerful or know someone powerful enough to take you through. Which meant that the fairy dude standing in the forest, waving at me like it was just another casual night in Kansas, was powerful. And very pale.

I have good eyesight, okay? I caught a lot in that glimpse of flashing headlights. Though I didn't really need my advanced perception. The guy was really white. His hair was white. His skin was white. I couldn't see the color of his eyes, besides them being pale, so maybe they were white too. His delicate features and slim figure nearly hid the fact that he was a guy, but that he was definitely masculine.

Not that his looks mattered. What mattered was what he was doing in those woods. Had he been watching me? Listening to me sing? Or had he been there for Banning? Maybe he'd been the blooders's backup, something more subtle to go in afterward on the off chance that the army of blooders didn't succeed. I almost turned around, but I knew I was too exhausted to be of any help. So I kept driving, and left the Shining One to Cerberus. If the dog-god couldn't handle one fairy, he might as well give up protecting people for good.

About the Author

Amy Sumida is the Internationally Acclaimed author of the Award-Winning Godhunter Series, the fantasy paranormal Twilight Court Series, the Beyond the Godhunter Series, the music-oriented paranormal Spellsinger Series, and several short stories. Her books have been translated into several languages, have made it to the top seller's list on Amazon numerous times, and the first book in her Spellsinger Series won a publishing contract with Kindle Press.

She was born and raised in Hawaii and brings her unique island perspective to all of her books. She doesn't believe in using pen names, saving the fiction for her stories. She's known for her kick-ass heroines who always have a witty comeback ready, and her strong, supporting male characters who manage to be sensitive and alpha all at once.

All she's ever wanted to do since she was a little girl, was to write novels. To be able to do so for a living is a blessing which she wakes up thankful for every day. Beyond her books, she enjoys collecting toys, to keep herself young, and cats, to keep herself loved.

Author Information

If you enjoyed this book, please let the author know by leaving a review. Reviews help her sell more books and keep her writing.

For information on new releases, detailed character descriptions, and an in-depth look into the worlds of Godhunter and the Twilight Court, check out Amy's website;

http://www.amysumida.com/

Sign up for her newsletter and receive a free gift:
http://google.us11.list-manage.com/subscribe?
u=398603e0fc6b3876340e37356&id=3abd32edce

You can also find her on facebook at:

https://www.facebook.com/AmySumidaAuthor/

or

https://www.facebook.com/groups/1536008099761461/

On Twitter under @Ashstarte

On Goodreads:

https://www.goodreads.com/author/show/7200339.Amy_Sumida

On Instagram:https://www.instagram.com/ashstarte/

On Tumblr: http://vervainlavine.tumblr.com/

And you can find her entire collection of books in her Amazon store:

http://astore.amazon.com/amysum-20